# JONATHAN BARRETT, GENTLEMAN VAMPIRE

*Also by P.N. Elrod*

*The Vampire Files*

BLOODLIST
LIFEBLOOD
BLOODCIRCLE
ART IN THE BLOOD
FIRE IN THE BLOOD
BLOOD ON THE WATER

RED DEATH
DEATH AND THE MAIDEN
DEATH MASQUE
DANCE OF DEATH

# JONATHAN BARRETT, GENTLEMAN VAMPIRE

RED DEATH
DEATH AND THE MAIDEN
DEATH MASQUE
DANCE OF DEATH

P.N. ELROD

Printing History: Ace edition/November 1993


Printing History: Ace edition/July 1994


Printing History: Ace edition/February 1995


Printing History: Ace edition/March 1996



Published by arrangement with:
Ace Books
a division of
The Berkley Publishing Group
200 Madison Avenue
New York, NY 10016

ISBN 1-56865-188-0

Printed in the United States of America.

# CONTENTS

As this story was written to give entertainment, not instruction, I have made no attempt to re-create the language spoken over two hundred years ago. There have been so many shifts in usage, meaning, and nuance that I expect a typical conversation of the time would be largely unintelligible to a present-day reader. As I have had to "shift" myself as well to avoid becoming too anachronistic in a swiftly changing world, modern usage, words, and terms have doubtless found their way into this story. Annoying, perhaps, to the historian, but my goal is to clarify, not confound, things for the twentieth-century reader.

Though some fragments of the following narrative have been elsewhere recorded, Mr. Fleming, an otherwise worthy raconteur, misquoted me on several points, which have now been corrected. I hereby state that the following events are entirely true. Only certain names and locations have been changed to protect the guilty and their hapless—and usually innocent—relations and descendants.

—JONATHAN BARRETT

# RED DEATH

*For Mark,*
*thanks for the push!*
*Literally!*

*And for Ursa,*
*we miss you, sweetie-girl,*
*and for The Mite,*
*'cause we love you, too, fuzzball,*
*and Big Mack,*
*welcome to the hearth.*

*And a special thanks to*
*special people:*
*Joy Marie Ledet,*
*Roxanne Longstreet,*
*Louann Qualls,*
*and the REAL Barretts,*
*Paul, Julie, and Christopher.*

# CHAPTER 1

*Long Island, April 1773*

"You are a prideful, willful, ungrateful wretch!"

This was my mother speaking—or rather screeching—to me, her only son.

To be fair, it was not one of her better days, but then she had so few of those that none of us were accustomed to noting any difference in her temper. Good or bad, it was best to treat her with the caution and deference that she demanded, if not openly, then by implication. Today, or at least at this moment, I had failed to observe that unspoken rule of behavior, and for the next five minutes was treated to a sneering, acid-filled lecture detailing the negative aspects of my character. Considering that until recently she'd spent fifteen of my seventeen years removed from my company, she had a surprisingly large store of knowledge to draw upon for her invective.

By the time she'd paused for air I'd flushed red from head to foot and sweat tickled and stung under my arms and along my flanks. I was breathing hard as well from the effort required to hold in my own hot emotions.

"And don't you dare glower at your mother like that, Jonathan Fonteyn," she ordered.

*What, then, am I to do?* I snarled back to her in my mind. And she'd used my middle name, which I hated, which was why she'd used it. It was her maiden name and yet one more tie to her. With a massive effort, I swallowed and tried to compose my face to more neutral lines. It helped to look down.

"I am sorry, Mother. Please forgive me." The words were patently forced and wooden, fooling no one. A show of submission was required at this point, if only to prevent her from launching into another tirade.

Unhampered by the obligation of filial respect, the woman was free to glare at me for as long as she pleased. She had it down to a fine art. She also made no acknowledgment of what I'd just said, meaning that she had not accepted my apology. Such gracious gestures of forgiveness were reserved only for those times when a third party was present as a witness to her loving patience with a wayward son. We were alone in Father's library now; not even a servant was within earshot of her honey-on-broken-glass voice.

I continued to study the floor until she moved herself to speak again.

"I will hear no more of your nonsense, Jonathan. There's many another young man who would gladly trade places with you."

Find one, I thought, and I would just as cheerfully cut a bargain with him on this very spot.

"The arrangements have been made and cannot be unmade. You've no reason to find complaint with any of it."

True, I had to admit to myself. The opportunity was fabulous, something I would have eagerly jumped for had it been presented to me in any other manner, preferably as one adult to another. What was so objectionable was having everything arranged without my knowledge and sprung on me without warning and with no room for discussion.

I took a deep breath in the hope that it would steady me and tried to push the anger away. The breath had to be let out slowly and silently, lest she interpret it as some sort of impertinence.

Finally raising my eyes, I said, "I am quite overwhelmed, Mother. But this is rather unexpected."

"I hardly think so," she replied. "Your father and I had long ago determined that you would go into law."

*Liar. I* had decided that in the years she had been living away from us in Philadelphia. If only she had stayed there.

"It is our fondest hope that you not only follow in his footsteps, but surpass him in your success."

My mouth clamped tight at the unmistakable sarcasm in her emphasis of certain words. This time the anger was on Father's behalf, not for myself. How could she think him a failure?

"To do that, you must have the best education possible. Don't think that this is a mere whim of ours. I—we have studied the choices carefully over the years and determined that Harvard is simply not capable of delivering to you the best that is available. . . ."

Just after breakfast, she'd sent for me to come see her in the library. I was mildly apprehensive, wondering what the trouble was this time. It was yet too early in the day for me to have done anything to offend her, unless she'd found something to criticize in the way I chewed my food. I was not discounting it as a possibility.

We'd eaten in uncomfortable silence, Mother at her long-empty spot at one end, and my sister, Elizabeth, across from me as usual in the middle. Father's place at the head of the table was empty, as he was away on business.

Such silence at the morning meal was new to this household. It had settled upon us like some heavy scavenger bird with Mother's return home. Elizabeth and I had learned that it was better to remain quiet indefinitely than to speak before spoken to lest we draw some disapproving remark from her.

The servants were not as lucky. Today one of the girls chanced to drop a spoon, and though no harm was done, she received a lengthy rebuke for her clumsiness that left her in tears. Elizabeth exchanged glances with me while Mother's attention was distracted from us. It was going to be a bad day for everyone, then.

Somehow we got through one more meal under this threatening cloud. Weeks earlier, my sister and I had agreed to always finish eating and leave at the same time so that neither had to face such adversity alone. We did so again, asking permission to be excused and getting it, and had just made good our escape when one of the servants caught up to us and delivered the summons. I was to come to the library in five minutes.

"Why couldn't she have said something when we'd been right there in the room with her?" I whispered to Elizabeth after the servant was gone. "Is speaking to me directly so difficult?"

"It's her way of doing things, Jonathan," she replied, but not in a manner to indicate any approval. "Just agree with whatever she says and we'll sort it out with Father later."

"Do you know what she wants?"

"Heavens, it could be anything. You know how she is."

"Unfortunately, yes. May I come see you afterward? I shall need you to bind up my wounds."

She burst into that radiant smile reserved only for me. "Yes, little brother. I'll go look for some bandages immediately."

Mother had seated herself in the chair next to Father's desk; it would have been overdoing things to actually take over *his* chair. She was canny enough to avoid that. The idea was to suggest his invisible presence approving her every action and word. I was sharply aware of this and not at all fooled, but not about to inform her of it. In the month since her return, I'd had to face her here alone on a dozen minor offenses; this was starting out no more differently than the others. I'd guessed that she'd noticed the new buckles on my shoes and was about to deliver a scorching opinion of their style and cost. The other lectures had been on a similar level of importance. I was glad to know that Elizabeth was standing by ready to soothe my burns when it was over.

Mother had assumed the demeanor of royalty granting an anxiously awaited audience, studying some letter or other as I walked in, her wide skirts carefully arranged, the tilt of her head just right. She could not have been an actress, though, for she was much too obvious in her method and would have been hooted from the stage in a serious drama. Farce, perhaps. Yes, she might have been perfect at farce, playing the role of the domineering dowager.

Marie Fonteyn Barrett had been very beautiful once, slender, graceful, with eyes as blue as an autumn sky, her skin milk white and milk soft. So she appeared in her portrait above the library fireplace. In the twenty years since it had been painted the milk had curdled, the grace turned to stiff arrogance. The eyes were the same color, but had gone hard, so that they seemed less real than the ones in the painting. Her hair was different as well. No more were the flowing black curls of a young bride; now it was piled high over her creased brow and thickly powdered. In the last month it had grown out a bit and needed rearranging. Perhaps she would even wash it out and begin afresh. I could but hope for it. Her constant stabbings and jabbings at that awful pile of lard and flour with her ivory scratching stick got on my nerves.

The curtains were open and cold April sunshine, still too immature for warmth, seeped through the windows. The wood in the fireplace had not been lighted, so the room was chilly. Mother was a great believer in conserving household supplies unless it concerned her own comfort. The lack of fire gave me hope that our interview would be mercifully short.

"Jonathan," she said, putting aside the paper in her hand. I recognized it as part of the normal litter on Father's desk, something she'd merely grabbed up to use as a prop. Why was the woman so artificial?

"Mother." The word was still awkward for me to say.

She smiled with a benevolent satisfaction that raised my apprehensions somewhat. "Your father and I have some wonderful news for you."

If the news was so wonderful, why was Father not here to deliver it with her? "Indeed, Mother? Then I am anxious to hear it."

"You will be very pleased to learn that you will be going up to Cambridge for your university education."

That was hardly news to me, but I put on something resembling good cheer for her sake. "Yes, I am very pleased. I have been looking forward to it all year."

Her brows lowered and eyes narrowed with irritation. Perhaps I was not as pleased as had been expected.

"I shall do my absolute best at Harvard to make you and Father proud of me," I added hopefully.

Now her mouth thinned. "You will be going to *Cambridge,* Jonathan."

"Yes, Mother, I know. Harvard University is located in Cambridge."

Somehow, I had said the wrong thing. Fury, red-faced and frightening to look upon, suddenly distorted her features so she hardly seemed human. I almost stepped backward. Almost. Her rages were not uncommon. We'd all seen this side of her many times and learned by trial and error how to avoid them, but this one mystified me. What had I done? Why was she—?

"You dare to mock me, Jonathan? You dare?"

I raised one hand in a calming gesture. "No, Mother, never."

"You *dare*?" Her voice rose enough to break my ears, enough to reach the servants' hall. Hopefully, they would know better than to come investigate the din.

"No, Mother. I swear to you, I am not mocking you. I sincerely apologize that I have given offense." Such words came easily; she'd given me ample opportunity for practice over the weeks. I finished off with a bow to emphasize my complete sincerity. Yet another opportunity to study the floor.

Thank God that this time it worked. Straightening, I saw her color slowly return to normal and the lines in her face abruptly smooth out. This swift recovery was more disturbing to me than her instant rage. Since her return, I'd quickly adjusted to the fact that she was not at all like other people, but that was hardly a solace during those times when her differences were so acutely demonstrated.

Dominance established, she resumed where she'd left off, almost as though nothing had happened. "You are going to Cambridge, Jonathan. Cambridge in *England,* Jonathan," she repeated, putting a razor edge on each syllable as though to underscore my abysmal ignorance.

It took me some moments to understand, to sort out the mistake. I suppose that she'd been anticipating a torrent of enthusiasm from me. Instead, my face fell and from my lips popped the first words that came to mind. "But I *want* to go to Harvard."

That's when the explosion truly came and she started calling me names.

You know the rest.

What was she saying now? Something about the virtues of Cambridge. I did not interrupt; it would have been pointless. She wasn't interested in my opinions or plans I might have made. Any and all objections had been drowned in the hot tidal wave of her temper. To resurrect them again would only aggravate her more. As Elizabeth had reminded me, I could sort it all out with Father later.

Did Father know about this? I couldn't believe that he would not have spoken to me about it before leaving yesterday. Surely he would have said something, for he, too, had planned that I should go to Harvard. That she had carefully waited until he was absent before breaking her news took on a fresh and ominous meaning, but I couldn't quite see the reason behind it yet. It was difficult to think while she talked on and on, pausing only to get the occasional nodding agreement from me at appropriate times.

Why was she so concerned about my education after fifteen years of blithe neglect? Marie Fonteyn Barrett had been singularly uninterested in either of her children since we were very small. It was a mixed blessing for us, for growing up without a mother had left something of a blank spot in our lives. On the other hand, what sort of broken monsters might we have been had she stayed with Father instead of moving to Philadelphia?

She'd only made the long journey from there to our home on Long Island because of all the turmoil in that city. With the rebels stirring things up at every opportunity, it had become too dangerous to remain, so she had written Father, and he, being a good and decent man, had said her house was there for her, the doors open. Her swift arrival caused us to speculate that she had not actually waited for his reply.

She'd just as swiftly assumed the running of the household in her own manner, subtly and not so subtly disrupting every level of life and work. Surprisingly, few servants left. Most were very loyal to Father and had the understanding that this was to be only a brief visit. When things had settled back to normal in Philadelphia, Mother would soon depart from us.

A likely chance, I thought cynically. Surely she was enjoying herself too much to leave.

She paused in her speech; apparently I'd been delinquent in my latest response.

"This is . . . is marvelous to hear, Mother. I hardly know what to say."

"A 'thank you' would be appropriate."

Yes, of course it would. "Thank you, Mother."

She nodded, comically regal, but not a bit amusing. My stomach was starting to roil in reaction to the tempest between my ears. I had to get out of here before exploding myself.

"May I be excused, Mother?"

"Excused? I should think you'd want to hear all the rest of the details we have planned."

"Truly I do, but must confess that my brain is whirling so much now I am hardly able to breathe. I beg but a little time to recover so that I may give you my best attention later."

"Very well. I suppose you'll run off to tell Elizabeth everything."

To this, a correct assumption that was really none of her business, I made another courtly bow upon which she could apply her own interpretation.

"You are excused. But remember: no arguments and no more foolishness. Going to Cambridge is the greatest opportunity you're ever going to receive to make something of yourself."

"Yes, Mother." I bowed again, inching anxiously toward the door.

"This is, after all, for your own good," she concluded serenely.

Anger flushed through me again as I turned and stalked from the room. How fond she was of *that* idea. God save me from all the hideous people hell-bent on doing things for my own good. So far there'd been only one in my life, my mother, and she was more than enough.

Quietly shutting the door behind me, I slipped down the hall until there was enough distance between us for noise not to matter, then began to run as though the house were on fire. Not bothering with a coat or hat, I threw myself outside into the cold April air. The woman was suffocating. I needed to be free of her and all thought of her. My feet carried me straight to the stables. With its mud, muck, and the irreverent company of the lads, this was one place I would be safe.

"Over here, Mr. Jonathan!"

My black servant, Jericho, waved at me. He was just emerging from the darkness of one of the buildings. Though he was primarily my valet and therefore supposed to keep to the house, neither of us paid much attention to such things. He was fairly high up in the household hierarchy and able to bend a rule here and there as long as nobody minded. If he chose to play the part of a groom, he suffered no loss in status, because working with horses was a source of pleasure for him. Right now, he was a godsend, for he had saddled up Rolly, my favorite, and was leading him out to me.

I couldn't help but laugh at his foresight. "How did you guess? Magic?"

"No magic," he said, smiling at the old joke between us. He used to tease the servant girls about being able to read their deepest thoughts and being a sharp observer of human nature made him right more often than not. The younger ones were awed, the older ones amused, and one rather guilty-hearted wench accused him of witchcraft. "I'd heard that Mrs. Barrett wanted to speak to you. Every other time you've come here to ride it off."

"And here I am once more. Thank you, Jericho. Will you come with me?"

"I rather assumed you would prefer the solitude."

Right again. Perhaps he did have hidden powers of divination.

He held Rolly's head as I swung up to the saddle and helped with the stirrups. "I'll tell Miss Elizabeth where you are," he said before I could ask him to do exactly that.

I laughed again, not at him but at the wonderful normality he represented, and took up the reins. Knowing what was to come next and how eager I was to get started, Rolly danced away and sprang forward with hardly a signal from me. Doing something that Mother would disapprove of was what I needed most, and leaving the stable yard at a full gallop to jump over a wall into the fields beyond was a most satisfying form of revenge.

Rolly was almost as perceptive as Jericho and seemed to sense that I wanted to fly as fast and as far as possible. The cold wind roaring past us deafened me to the strident echoes of her voice and blinded me to the memory of her distorted face. She shrank away to less than nothing and was lost amid the joy I now felt clinging to the back of the best horse in the world as he carried me to the edge of that world . . . or at least to the cliffs overlooking the Sound.

We slowed at last, though for a moment I thought that if Rolly decided to leap out toward the sea instead of turning to trot parallel to it he would easily sprout the necessary wings to send us soaring into the sky like some latter-day Pegasus and Bellerophon. What a ride that might be, and I would certainly know better than to try flying him to Mount Olympus to seek out the gods. They could wait for their own turn . . . if I ever let them have one.

The air cutting over us was clean with the sea smell and starting to warm up as the sun climbed higher. I drank it in like a true-born hedonist until my lungs ached and my throat burned. Rolly picked his own path and I let him, content enough with the privilege of being on his back. We went east, into the wind, him stretching his neck, his ears up with interest, me busy holding my balance over the uneven ground. The trot sped up to a canter and he shook his head once as though to free himself of the bridle as we approached another fence.

The property it marked belonged to a farmer named Finch who kept a few horses of his own. His lands were smaller than Father's and he could not afford to have riding animals, but the rough look of the mares on that side made no difference to Rolly, aristocrat though he was. In his eyes a female was a female and to hell with her looks and age as long as she was ready for a good mounting. I barely had time to turn him and keep him from sailing over the fence right into the middle of them all.

Rolly snorted and neighed out a protest. One of the other horses answered and I had to work hard at getting him out of there.

"Sorry, old man," I told him. "You may have an excellent bloodline, but I don't think Mr. Finch would thank you for passing it on through his mares."

He stamped and tried to rear, but I pulled him in, not letting him get away with it.

"If it's any consolation, I know just how you feel," I confided.

I was seventeen and still a virgin . . . of sorts. I'd long since worked out ways around certain inevitable frustrations that come from being a healthy young man, but instinctively knew they could hardly be as gratifying as actual experience with an equally healthy young woman. Damn. Now, *why* did I have to start thinking along those paths again? An idiotic question; better to frame it as a syllogism of logic. Premise one: I was, indeed, healthy; premise two: I was, indeed, young. Combine those and I rarely failed to come to a pleasurable conclusion. However, I was not prepared to come to any such conclusions here in the open while on horseback. Talk about doing something to garner maternal disapproval . . . and I'd probably fall out of the saddle.

The true loss of my virginity was another goal in my personal education I'd planned to achieve at Harvard—if I ever got there, since Mother had said that everything was settled about Cambridge. I wondered if they had girls at Cambridge. Oh, God, this wasn't helping at all. I kicked Rolly into a jarring trot, hoping that it would distract me. The last thing I needed was to return home with any telltale stain on my light-colored breeches. Perhaps if I found a quiet spot in the woods . . .

I knew just the one.

As children, Elizabeth, Jericho, and I had gone adventuring, or what we called adventuring, for we really knew the area quite well. Usually our games involved a treasure hunt, for everyone on the island knew that Captain Kidd had come here to bury his booty. It didn't matter to us that such riches were more likely to be fifty miles east of us on the south end of the island; the hunting was more important than the finding. But instead of treasure that day, I'd found a kettle, or a sharpish depression gouged into the earth by some ancient glacier, according to my schoolmaster. Trees and other vegetation concealed its edge. My foot slipped on some wet leaves and down I tumbled into a typical specimen of Long Island's geography.

Jericho came pelting after me, fearful that I had broken my neck. Elizabeth, though hampered by her skirts, followed almost as quickly, shouting tear-choked questions after him. I was almost trampled by their combined concern and inability to stop fast enough.

The wind had certainly been knocked from me, but I'd suffered nothing worse than some scrapes and bruises. After that initial fright passed we took stock of our surroundings and claimed it for our own. It became our pirate's cave (albeit open to the sky and to any cattle that wandered in to graze), banditti's lair, and general sanctuary from tiresome adults wanting us to do something more constructive with our time.

Now it seemed that it was still a sanctuary, not from adults, but for adults. Just as I'd guided Rolly down to the easy way into the kettle, I noticed two people far ahead near the line of trees marking the entry. A man and woman walked arm in arm there, obviously on the friendliest of terms. Even at that distance I abruptly recognized my father. The woman with him was Mrs. Montagu. She was a sweet-faced, sweet-tempered widow who had always been kind to me and Elizabeth, everything that Mother was not. Mother, thank God, knew nothing about her, or life for all of us would truly become a living hell.

It was a quietly acknowledged fact in our household that most of Father's business trips took him no more than three miles away so that he might visit Matilda Montagu. Their relationship was hardly a secret, but not something to bring up in open conversation. They had not asked for this privacy, but got it, anyway, for both were liked and respected hereabouts.

I'd pulled Rolly to a stop and now almost urged him in their direction. No. Not fair. Father had little enough happiness of his own since Mother's return; I would not intrude upon him with my present troubles. We could talk later. Besides, I had no wish to embarrass him by bringing up the disagreeable details of his wife's latest offenses before his mistress.

Father and Mrs. Montagu continued their leisurely walk, unaware of me, which was just as well. It was interesting to watch them together, for this was a side of Father that I'd never really seen. I was somewhat ashamed of my curiosity, but not so much that I was willing to move on. Not that I expected them to suddenly seize each other and start rolling on the cold damp ground in a frenzy of passion. Nor would I have stayed to watch, my curiosity being limited by the discretions of good taste. But between the demands of my preparatory education and all the other distractions of life, I'd had few opportunities to observe the rules of courtship in the upper classes. So far it hardly looked different from the servants', for I'd occasionally seen them strolling about with one another making similar displays of affection.

He had one arm around her waist, one hand, rather. Her wide skirts kept him from getting much closer. He also leaned his head down toward her so as to miss nothing of whatever she was saying. And he was laughing. That was good to see. He had not done much of that in the last month. What about his other hand? Occupied with carrying a bundle or basket. Full of food, probably. It was hardly the best weather for eating comfortably out of doors, but they seemed content to ignore it as long as they were together.

Interesting. Now they paused to face each other. Father stooped slightly and kissed her on the lips for a very long time. My own mouth went dry. Perhaps it was time to leave. As I dithered with indecision their kiss ended and they turned to walk into the shadow of the trees. They did not come out again.

Rolly snorted impatiently and dropped his head to snatch a mouthful of new grass just peeping through last year's dead layer. At some point my fleshly cravings had also altered so that carnality had been supplanted with extreme hunger. The sun was high and far over; I'd been out for hours and had long since digested my breakfast. And there was Elizabeth, who would be wondering whether I'd been thrown. She loved horses too, but didn't trust Rolly to behave himself.

I turned him back up the rise leading around the kettle, heading home.

The horse being more valuable than its rider, I took care of Rolly myself when we reached the stables. As a menial job, I could have easily left it for one of the lads to do and no one would have thought twice about it. Especially Mother. I was raised to be a gentleman and could clearly imagine her disapproval while going about my caretaking tasks. But where horses were concerned, such work was no work at all for me. Defiance doubled, I thought, humming with pleasure. Jericho wasn't there or he might have willingly helped out—if I'd invited him. I made a fast job of it, though, and before long was marching up to the kitchen to wheedle a meal from the cook.

Then someone hissed from the corner of the house. Elizabeth stood there, eyes comically wide and lips compressed, urgently waving at me to come over. Curiosity won out over hunger.

"What is it?" I asked, trotting up.

"Not so loud," she insisted, grabbing my arm and dragging me around the corner. She visibly relaxed once we were out of sight from the kitchen.

"What is it?" I repeated, now mimicking her hoarse whisper.

"Mother was furious that you missed lunch."

I gave vent to an exasperated sigh and raised my voice back to normal. "Damnation, but I'm an adult and my time is my own. She's never minded before."

"Yes, but she wanted to talk to you about Cambridge."

"She told you all that nonsense?"

"In extraordinary detail. She seems to have decided how you're to spend your next few years down to the last minute."

"How very kind of her."

"She's in the kitchen with Mrs. Nooth planning out meals, and I didn't think you'd want to run into her."

I took one of Elizabeth's hands and solemnly bowed over it. "For that, dear sister, you have my undying gratitude, but I am famished and must eat. A fellow can hardly spend his life going about in fear of his own mother."

"Ha! It's not fear, it's only avoiding unnecessary unpleasantness."

She was quite right. I really didn't want to face the woman on an empty stomach; some alternative needed to be thought up, but not out here. The day had warmed a little, but Elizabeth's hand was icy. "Let's go inside, you're freezing. Where's your shawl?"

She shrugged indifferently. "Upstairs someplace. You should be the one to talk; look at yourself, riding all morning without hat or even gloves. It will serve you right if you get the rheumatics, God forbid."

I chuckled. The ailments of age were still very far away for me. My morning's ride was worth a spot of stiffness in the joints. We went in by the same side door I'd used to escape, and Elizabeth led me to the library. A good fire was blazing there now, and forgetting her lack of concern about the cool day, we rushed toward it like moths.

"So you think your going to Cambridge is nonsense?" she asked, stretching out her hands and spreading her long fingers against the flames.

"Mmm. The woman's mad. When I see Father I'll sort it out with him as you said.

"She's very sure of herself. What if he's on her side?"

"Why should he be?"

"Because he usually does whatever she wants. It's not as noisy as arguing, you know."

"I don't think he will for something as important as this. Besides, look at the impracticality of it all. Why send me all the way to England to read law? It may garner me some status, but what else?"

"An education?" she suggested.

"There's that, but everyone knows you really go to a university to make the kind of friends and acquaintances who can become useful later in life.

I can do that in England, but they'll all be left behind when I return home."

"You've become cynical already, little brother?" She was hardly a year older than me, but had always taken enjoyment from her position as the eldest.

"Realistic. I've spent a lot of time in this room listening to Father and his cronies while they're sharing a bottle. I can practice law well enough, but I'll be better at it for having a few friends 'round me as he does. Which reminds me . . ." I quit the fireplace to open a nearby cupboard and poured out a bit of wine to keep my strength up. My stomach snarled with ingratitude at the thoughtful gesture.

Elizabeth giggled at the noise. She looked remarkably like the portrait above her. Prettier, I thought. Livelier. Certainly saner.

"What is it?" she asked, taking note of my distraction.

"I was just thinking that you could have almost posed for that." I indicated the painting.

She stood away for a better look. "Perhaps, but my face is longer. If it's all the same to you, I would prefer not to be compared to her at all."

"She may have been different back then," I pointed out. "If not, then why did Father ever marry her and have us?"

"That's hardly our business, Jonathan."

"It certainly is since we're the living results of their . . . affection? . . . for one another."

"Now you're being crude."

"No I'm not. When I get crude, you'll know it, dear sister. Who do I look like?"

She tilted her head, unknowingly copying Mother's affected mannerism, but in an unaffected way. "Father, of course, but younger and not as heavy."

"Father's not fat," I protested.

"You know what I mean. When men get older they either go to fat or put on another layer of muscle."

"Or both."

"Ugh. But not you. In a few years you'll get the muscle and look just like him."

"That's reassuring." We had always regarded Father as being a very handsome man.

"Peacock," said Elizabeth, reading my face and thus my thoughts. I grinned and saluted her with my glass. It was empty, but I soon corrected that. The wine tasted wonderful but with no food in my stomach it was shooting straight to my head.

"Mother will burst a blood vessel if you turn up drunk in the kitchen," she observed without rancor.

"If I really get drunk, then I shan't care. Would you like some?"

"Yes," she said decisively, and got a glass. "She'll make drunkards of us all before she's finished. I'm surprised Father isn't. . . ."

"Father has other occupations," I said, pouring generously and thinking fondly of Mrs. Montagu.

"I wish I did," she muttered, and drained off half her portion. "Father goes out, you have your riding and studies, but I'm expected to sit here all day and find contentment with needlework, household duties, and numbering out my prospects."

"Prospects?"

Elizabeth's mouth twisted in disgust. "After she finished going on about Cambridge, she started asking me about the unmarried men in the area."

"Uh-oh."

"*All* of them, including old Mr. Cadwallader. He must be seventy if he's a day."

"But very rich."

"Now who's taking sides?"

"Not I. I was just thinking the way she would think."

Elizabeth groaned and finished off her wine. I made to pour her another and she did not refuse it. "I hope things settle down quickly in Philadelphia so she can go back. I know that it's wicked, wishing one's mother away, but . . ."

"She's only our mother by reason of birth," I said. "If it comes to it, Mrs. Nooth's been more of a mother to us than that other woman." I nodded at the portrait. "Or even Mrs. Montagu. I wish Father had married her instead."

"Then neither of us would have been ourselves and we wouldn't be sitting here getting drunk."

"It's something to think about, isn't it?"

"Wicked," she concluded with an unrepentant grimace.

"Yes, I'm born to be hanged for that one."

"God forbid," she added.

As one, we lifted our glasses in a silent toast to a lot of different things. I was feeling very muzzy now, with all my limbs heavy and glowing with inner warmth. It was too nice a feeling to clutter up with the inevitable scolding that awaited me the moment I stepped into the kitchen.

"P'haps," I speculated, "I should leave Mother and Mrs. Nooth to their work."

Elizabeth instantly noted my change of mind and smiled, shaking her head in mock sadness for my lost bravado.

"P'haps," I continued thoughtfully, "I could just borrow a loaf of bread from one of the lads, then pick up a small cheese from the buttery. That would fill me 'til supper. Father should be home by then and Mother will have something else to worry about besides me."

"And have one of the servants blamed for the theft of the cheese?"

"I'll leave a note, confessing all," I promised gravely. "Mrs. Nooth will surely forgive . . ." Then something soured inside and the game lost its charm. "Damnation, this is my own house. Why should I creep around like a thief?"

Someone's shoe heels clacked and clattered hollowly against the wood floor of the hall. Elizabeth and I instantly recognized her step and hastily replaced the glasses and wine bottle in the cupboard. The answer to my plaintive question swung into the doorway just as we shut everything away and turned our innocent faces toward her in polite regard.

Mother.

She wasn't fooled by our pose. "What are you two doing?" she demanded.

"Only talking, Mother," said Elizabeth.

Mother sniffed, either in disbelief or disdain. Fortunately she was too far away to pick up any fumes from the wine. She turned an unfriendly eye upon me. "And where were you all day? Mrs. Nooth placed a perfectly good meal on the table and your portion went to waste."

With as many servants as we had, I doubted that. "I'm sorry, Mother."

"You'll tender your apologies to Mrs. Nooth. She was very offended."

And very forgiving. And in the kitchen. "Indeed, Mother? I shall go to her immediately and make amends."

She'd heard me but had not listened. "Where were you, Jonathan?"

"Inspecting the fields," I answered easily. It was mostly true, but I resented the fact that this woman was turning me into a liar.

"Never mind that. You've far more important duties before you than farming. From now on you will leave such menial work to those men who have been hired for it."

"Yes, Mother." My head was spinning with that peculiar disorientation that I associated with intoxication. With each passing minute the wine soaked more deeply into me, increasing its effect, but I was careful not to let it show.

"As long as you're here I want to continue our talk about your education. You may be excused, Elizabeth."

From where I was standing, I could clearly see the flash of anger in my sister's eyes at being dismissed as though she were one of the servants.

Her mouth tightened and her chin lifted, but she said nothing, nothing at all, quite loudly, all the way out the door.

Mother did not ignore her so much as she simply did not notice. Her attention was fixed entirely upon me. She crossed the room to the chair she'd claimed next to Father's desk and arranged herself. I was not invited to sit, nor did I ask to do so. It might unnecessarily prolong our interview. My stomach, presently awash with wine, would provide me with a valid reason to depart soon enough. I was still hungry, but that was outweighed by the need to hear her out, the need to gain information in order to present a logical argument against it later. With Father. I knew better than to contend with his wife, who was familiar with only her own unique logic and no one else's.

She produced her ivory scratching stick from somewhere and tapped it lightly against the palm of one hand. "And now, Jonathan," she announced importantly, "we will talk about what you are going to do once you get to Cambridge." She paused to poke vigorously at a spot above the nape of her neck with the stick. My teeth instantly went on edge.

Never, never in all my life was I so glad to be drunk.

# CHAPTER 2

Some twenty minutes later Mother generously excused me, by which time I'd developed a pressing need to rid myself of all that wine. A good deal of it still remained behind in my head, though, for it was aching badly. The pain so interfered with my thinking that afterward I couldn't decide whether to visit the kitchen or retreat in misery to my room to sleep it away.

Jericho resolved things when he emerged from the hall leading to the kitchen carrying a covered tray.

"Is that for me?" I asked hopefully in response to his smile of greeting.

"Miss Elizabeth suggested it," he said. "Something to see you through until supper."

"Then God bless her for being the dearest, sweetest sister anyone ever had. Where is she?"

"Out taking a ride of her own."

"Yes. Since Mother came back the horses are getting more than their share of exercise. Come, put that down somewhere."

"I would myself suggest that you take it in your sitting room. To avoid interruptions," he added significantly.

I glanced uneasily back at the library and indicated that he should lead the way upstairs. Somehow I was able to follow, leaning heavily on the rail and gulping frequently. Hot in the face and dizzy, I staggered the last few feet into my room and collapsed at the big study table. Jericho smoothly moved some books around to make space for my meal. He had the enviable skill of being able to balance the tray with one hand while his other quickly and quite independently made order out of chaos. Between the blink of one eye and the next he put down his burden and whipped off the cloth revealing a plump loaf of bread, some cheese, and a squat jug. From the latter he poured out something to drink and gave me the cup.

"More wine?" I asked dubiously.

"Barley water. It will thin the wine in your blood."

"Good idea." I drank deeply and felt better for it and looked at the food with more interest than before, falling upon the cheese. "There's too much here for me, have some."

Jericho hesitated, looking uncomfortable.

"Is something wrong?"

"No, sir, but I do not think it would be quite—"

"Of course it wouldn't, so . . ." I kicked out a chair for him. "Those fools in Philadelphia are rebelling against the king without a second thought, so I shall rebel against our local queen. It's been a hard day, Jericho, and I need your company. Eat or not as you choose, but do sit with me."

He closed the door to the hall and only then allowed himself the ease of the chair and the comfort of good food.

He was slightly older than I and his father was my father's valet. After I was born, they decided that he should assume that duty for me once I had outgrown the nursery. Though a servant, Jericho and I had been friends long before the establishment of his place in the household and this new deference in him troubled me.

"Is it Mother?" I asked, reaching to tear off a piece of bread. I made a mess of it, scattering crumbs everywhere.

"In an indirect way," he admitted. "We've all heard that you're to go off to England soon."

"I most certainly am not. She's got this idea lodged in her head, but Father will shake it loose and that will be the end of it."

"My *bomba* isn't too sure of that," he said. Jericho spoke perfect English, but sometimes used a few words his father had brought with him from Africa, the only baggage he'd been allowed by the slavers.

Knowing that Archimedes might be privy to information I didn't, I said, "Why does he think so?"

"Because your father does what your mother says."

"Now you're sounding like Elizabeth," I complained. "But Father is the head of this house. Mother will have to do what he says and she knows that. She waited and told me only after he was gone. She wanted me on her side so he would say yes to please me. I've gone along with it, but only until he comes home." I took a few more vicious bites from the cheese. Damnation. The woman was treating me like a petulant child and now I was beginning to sound like one.

"But until then nothing is settled," he said.

"Why are you worried?"

"I heard some things in the kitchen. She was talking to Mrs. Nooth and I wasn't supposed to be listening."

"Never mind that. What was said?"

"She wanted Mrs. Nooth to be asking around to find a proper English servant to look after you."

For several moments I lost the power of speech. "To . . . to . . . ?"

"To take my place," he said calmly.

"Impossible. She can't mean it."

"But she does. And she plans to sell me."

The blood hit the top of my head so hard that blue and purple smoke clouded my vision. Without knowing how I got there, I found myself up and pacing the length of the room. Nothing intelligible came out of me for quite some time and Jericho knew me well enough not to interrupt.

"It's *not* going to happen," I told him finally. "It's absolutely not going to happen. It's ridiculous . . . utterly . . . stupid." Then a cold thought rushed past. "Unless you want to . . . ?"

Now it was his turn to be upset, though he was so self-disciplined that in no wise was it comparable to my own display. "No. A man must work and if I must work then I would rather work here. I do not wish to be sold. But your father might still do it for the sake of peace in the family."

I shook my head. "Mother can throw whatever sort of fit she pleases, but you are *not* going to be sold."

He looked reassured. "I have hope then. This is a good place to be and I know of no better. When other servants visit with their masters I hear of the most terrible things. Here we are treated well and given good care. No beatings, no starvations."

"That's something the whole world can do without," I added. He seemed to feel better, but I continued to pace. "Suppose Father arranged for your freedom? Then I could hire you. Mother wouldn't have anything to do with it."

"Except dismiss me, then hire a replacement. You have no rights of your own until your twenty-first birthday."

"Blast. Well, no matter what, I won't let it happen. I'll run away to sea first and you can come with me."

A smile crossed his dark features. "But then you would be guilty of theft."

"Jericho, you've been hanging about with lawyers too long."

The smile broadened for a moment, then gradually fell in upon itself. I stopped my restless pacing and leaned against a wall and wished Father home immediately. "Why on earth does she want to hire another valet for me? You're the best there ever was."

He nodded regally at the compliment. "It is not a question of finding someone better. It is because Mrs. Barrett is extremely fond of all things English. She wants an English servant."

"No, thank you. He'd only put on airs, correct my speech, and rearrange my clothes so that I couldn't find anything for myself. And who would I have for company? Except for you and old Rapelji, there's no one intelligent to talk to."

His brows pinched together. "But your sister and father—"

"Are my sister and father. You know what I mean. Some of those long conversations we've had with Rapelji would have bored them to death."

He nodded agreement and his brows dropped back into place. "Speaking of him, did he not give you some more Greek to interpret?" He looked at the pile of books on the table before him.

"Doesn't he always?" Greek was not my favorite study and my tutor well knew it and thus emphasized it more than any other. "I'll see to it later tonight. My head hurts too much for that kind of work right now."

"I'll go get you some moss snuff," he said, rising.

"Ugh, no. Mrs. Nooth can take it herself. It's never helped any headache I've had and never will. I'll just lie down until the pain's out of me."

Pushing away from the wall, I wandered over to the bed and almost dropped into its welcome comfort. Almost, because Jericho was instantly at my side to remove my coat. Since a lazy refusal would only inspire silent, long-suffering reproach from him, I gave in and gave up. Once started, off came the waistcoat and shoes as well, all to be taken away for brushing or polishing. I managed to retain my breeches and outer shirt; both would be changed before going down to supper so it didn't matter if I napped in them or not.

"When Father comes home . . ."

"I shall inform you," he promised, as he started for the door.

Then peevishly, I asked, "What the devil is that row?"

Jericho listened with me. "A coach, I think."

My heart jumped, but only once. Father had left on horseback, not in the coach. Jericho and I looked at one another in mutual puzzlement, then he gave back my shoes. Curiosity triumphed over my headache. I reached for an especially florid, Oriental-looking dressing gown that Elizabeth had painstakingly made for me, and shrugged it on.

"Let's go see," I sighed.

No one was in the upper hall, but as we came downstairs we glimpsed one of the maids haring off to the kitchen, no doubt with fresh news for Mrs. Nooth. Mother emerged from the library like some ship under full sail and stopped the girl with a curt order. The little wench came to heel and hastened to open wide the big front door. Outside stood a battered-looking coach and four, and there was much activity about the baggage and two alighting passengers. With a great smile, Mother went out to greet them.

I shifted uneasily and glanced at Jericho. He shrugged slightly. Having endured an extremely long month of Mother's quirky temperament I was hard-pressed to imagine that anyone or anything could give her joy. Apparently the possibility existed; we'd just never seen it before.

"They must be friends of hers from Philadelphia," I speculated.

Outside, Mother exchanged a kiss on the cheek with a woman and extended her hand to a man, who bowed deeply over it. Rather too deeply, I thought. What sort of people would find Mother's company so agreeable that they would come for a visit?

Through the broad door the wind blew in a few stray leaves and other . . . rubbish. That's the word that occurred to me when I got a good look at them. They swept into the house, surveying it with bright eyes as if they owned the place. They noticed me at the same time and the woman gave a little exclamation of pleased surprise.

"Dearest Marie, is this your good son, Jonathan Fonteyn?" she demanded in a loud, flat, and childishly thin voice.

I winced.

Mother was capable of swift thought and judgment and her conclusion was that now was not the time for introductions; I was not properly dressed to greet guests. "A moment, Deborah, a moment to catch my breath and then I shall ask him to come and meet you."

Deborah, correctly deducing that she'd been importune, turned a beaming face to Mother and ignored me entirely. The man copied her.

Mother issued a sharp order to the maid for tea and biscuits and then invited her guests into the parlor with a graceful gesture. As they proceeded ahead, she swung a livid face in my direction and pointed upstairs meaningfully.

"Good God," I muttered sourly, masking it with a cordial smile and a nod of understanding. Jericho followed as I fled to my room.

"You know who they are?" he asked, putting down my clothes and smoothly moving toward the wardrobe.

"Friends of hers from Philadelphia. Deborah Hardinbrook and her brother, Theophilous Beldon. I've heard her talk about them. At length. She's the widow of some captain who drowned at sea and he's supposed to be a doctor, God help us. Whatever you do, don't mention my headache to anyone lest it get back to him and he offers to cure it."

Jericho removed a claret-colored coat from the wardrobe and shook it out.

"Why this one?" I asked, as he helped me into it. "It's not my best."

"Exactly. To wear anything really nice might tell these two you wish to impress them. This coat will tell them that you could care less about their favor, but at the same time inform them that you are the head of this house in your father's absence and it is their job to impress you."

"It will?"

"It does. Trust me on this, Mr. Jonathan."

I would, for he was always right on such details. "Elizabeth. She'll have to be warned."

"And so she shall be," he promised, pulling out a pair of shoes and inspecting the buckles for tarnish. There was none, of course.

"I have these," I protested, pointing at the ones on my feet.

"New buckles on old shoes," he chided. "It doesn't look right, not for a first meeting."

"We can switch them to another pair."

He firmly held the shoes out for me. "Wear these. They will demand respect. Save the others for Sunday."

I grunted and did as I was told.

He was finished in a very few minutes. "There. Sometimes you cannot avoid going into the lion's den, but when you must, it is better to be well-dressed."

"What makes you think this is a lion's den?"

"What makes you think it is not?"

"Excellent point. Go see to Elizabeth, will you?"

"Certainly."

In deference to my sober garb and still-buzzing brain, I did not rush downstairs, though it was tempting. Head high and with a serious face, I paced slowly across the hall to the parlor and paused in the doorway, waiting to be noticed.

Mother had her back to me, so it was Deborah Hardinbrook who looked up and stopped her conversation. Her brother, seated next to her, politely stood. Mother turned and assumed an unfamiliar smile.

"Ah, Jonathan. At last. Do come in and meet my very dear friends." She conducted us all through formal introductions.

On my best behavior, I bowed low over Mrs. Hardinbrook's hand and expressed my pleasure at meeting her in French. She was about Mother's age, with a hard eye and lines around her mouth that may have been placed there by laughter but not joy. She assessed me quickly, efficiently, and was fulsome with complements to Mother about me. I felt like a statue on display, not noticed for myself, but for the enlargement of its owner.

Dr. Beldon was in his thirties, which also made him seem quite old to me. He was wiry and dark, his brown eyes so large and rounded that they seemed to swell from their sockets. They fastened upon me with an assessment similar to his sister's but with a different kind of intensity, though what it was, I could not have said. We bowed and exchanged the necessary social pleasantries toward one another.

Mrs. Hardinbrook resumed her talk with Mother, giving her a full account of the harrowing journey from Philadelphia. At first I listened with resentful politeness, then with interest, for despite her exaggerations of manner, she was amusing. Mother actually seemed to be enjoying herself. Beldon smiled at appropriate moments and occasionally added comments. Unlike his sister, he made an effort to include me in the conversation. Smiling. Smiling. Smiling.

*Toad-eaters,* I thought behind my own twisted lips. Father had taught me to recognize their sort and to be 'ware of them.

"They're full of flattery and little else, laddie," he'd told me. "Having no merit of their own, they try to put themselves ahead by using others. Useless bloodsuckers, the lot of them, always looking out for their own good, but no one else's, and with bottomless stomachs. Don't let them fool you with fair words or use you in any way. No need to waste your time with any of them."

Perhaps Mother had not heard his opinion, or chose to ignore it.

"Where will your journey finally take you, Mrs. Hardinbrook?" I asked when an opening presented itself.

Her face was bright with a purposeful shortage of understanding. "I beg your pardon, Master Barrett?"

I ignored the little jibe of her address, meant to place me on a level with beardless children. "Your destination, madam. I was inquiring—"

"*This* is their destination, Jonathan," Mother said firmly, indicating the house with the curve of one hand. "Deborah and her brother are my guests."

This was not unexpected, but certainly unpleasant. Mother's guests, not Father's, and absolutely no mention was made of when they would leave.

"How delightful," I told them, my smile entirely genuine for there'd be the devil to pay when Father came home, and I was looking forward to that confrontation.

* * *

Supper was less of a disaster than I'd anticipated.

When Elizabeth returned from her ride, Jericho had headed her off at the stables and passed on the news. She charged up to the house immediately.

"What are they like?" she demanded after a quick thump on my door to announce herself.

"You'll have to draw your own conclusions."

"Jonathan, you're not a lawyer yet, so tell me."

"Toad-eaters, without a doubt. They seem clever about it, though, so be careful around them. You know what Father says."

She did, and hurried on to her room to change for supper. I waited in mine until it was time, then escorted her downstairs. She looked perfect in a dress of such a pale gray as to be nearly white with touches of dark pink throughout. The latter, I abruptly noticed, complemented my claret-colored coat in some subtle way. We would present a united front against these invaders, if they bothered to notice.

Mrs. Hardinbrook was again effusive in her praise when she and Elizabeth were introduced. Elizabeth returned one of the complements in French. Our guest was astonished that she was able to speak a foreign language so easily.

"It's nothing," Elizabeth demurred. "I understand that all the children in France do so."

This went right over Mrs. Hardinbrook's uncomprehending head; Mother glowered ineffectively, but Beldon smothered a knowing smile. When his turn came he bowed gravely over Elizabeth's hand and expressed his enchantment with her. She was politely cool and made no reply beyond a civil nod. Even Mother could find no fault with her for that.

We went in to supper, which, oddly enough, was made bearable by the presence of the guests. They distracted Mother and for the first time in a month the usual heavy silence was lifted from the table. The relief lasted for the whole meal. Elizabeth and I said next to nothing throughout, our ears instinctively open for information on these strangers.

Mrs. Hardinbrook managed to eat and talk at the same time, rolling along at a quick pace and cleaning her plate down to the last crumb. She spoke of this happening or that person, familiar to Mother, but not to us. Now and then she would touch on a general topic for a time and then our listening became less tedious.

Beldon was taciturn compared to his sister, who made enough speech for both of them. We already knew he was a doctor and learned that his practice had been unfairly disrupted by the unpleasantness in Philadelphia. One of the last people he'd been called to treat had been a victim of a mob of rebel ruffians.

"Poor fellow was dragged right from his home and beaten. They said he'd narrowly escaped being tarred and feathered except for the arrival of some of his friends. Then it was canes and clubs, gentlemen against the rowdies, who were soundly beaten themselves and sent away howling."

"Being beasts, they only got what they deserved," added Mrs. Hardinbrook with a giggle for her own joke.

"Beasts, indeed," sniffed Mother. "Why was he beaten?"

"He's Tory, which is reason enough for them," answered Beldon. "These rebel louts have nothing better to do with themselves than stay drunk most of the time, and that heats up the brain. Then it only takes the wrong word in the right ear to set them off like a bit of tinder. Some of these rebels are men of education, but most seem to be louts of the lowest class with more wind than brains and better able to blame the king for their woes than apply themselves to wholesome work. If there had been any proper enforcement of the law, they'd be in jail for sedition instead of hailed as heroes by the ignorant. No good will come of it, mark me."

"What about the injured man?" asked Elizabeth.

"Oh, he'll be all right, by and by, but went to live with his daughter on her farm. After tending to the poor fellow I came to realize that dear Deborah and I would no longer be safe ourselves, so we closed up the house and came here to accept the kind invitation your mother once extended to us."

"And glad I am that you did," said Mother. "Beatings, tar, and feathers. Why, the two of you might have been murdered in your beds."

Mrs. Hardinbrook shivered appreciatively at her narrow escape.

"The lot of them should be in jail, down to the last cowardly dog and the instigators hanged on the common. What do you think, Mr. Barrett?" Beldon turned toward me.

"I agree," I said heartily. Anyone who had the least responsibility for shifting Beldon and his sister from Philadelphia to my home certainly deserved some sort of severe punishment.

After supper, Mother suggested—or rather ordered—us to remove to the music room so Elizabeth could entertain us with something on her spinet. This was greeted with enthusiasm from Mrs. Hardinbrook and resignation from Elizabeth.

"Do you play an instrument, Mr. Barrett?" asked Beldon.

"Not a note," I said. "I enjoy music, but haven't the ear or hand to reproduce it for myself."

"What a pity," said Mrs. Hardinbrook. "Theophilous is quite good with a fiddle. Perhaps he could play a duet with Miss Barrett." She had a crafty look in her eye, the idea behind it so painfully transparent that Mother's head jerked warningly. If his sister did not notice it, Beldon certainly did.

"Another time, Deborah, I beg you. I am quite worn out from the journey, and any sounds I might draw from my fiddle would not be worth the hearing." He spread his hands in mock deprecation and a hard look swiftly passed between them that said more than his words. She burned for the briefest instant and abruptly subsided into a smile of sympathy for him.

"Yes, of course," she said, not quite able to smooth the edge from her voice.

Elizabeth looked relieved and assumed her seat before the spinet. She played well enough but with little enthusiasm. I drifted toward the door and lifted my eyebrows at Jericho, who had made it his business to keep close and listen in on things. It was partly to sate his own curiosity and partly at my encouragement.

"No sign of Father?" I whispered from the side of my mouth.

"None," he answered morosely.

"Have one of the lads sit out by the road with a lantern, then. We wouldn't want him to miss the gate."

He knew as well as I that there was little chance of Father losing himself. If nothing else, his horse knew the way home. I suspected that Mrs. Montagu was proving to be more charming than ever and Father had elected to take supper with her followed by Lord knows what else. He might even spend another night with her.

Jericho promised to see to things and disappeared just as Elizabeth finished her piece. I joined in the applause.

Mrs. Hardinbrook gushed forth with more praise. This time it seemed directed less at Mother and more toward Beldon, in an attempt to draw his attention to Elizabeth. His praise was more subdued and disappointingly neutral, at least from his sister's point of view. Then he stood and bowed to all of us.

"You will think me terribly rude, Mrs. Barrett, but I must beg leave to go to my room. I don't know where Deborah gets all her energy, but I am absolutely exhausted."

"I quite understand, Dr. Beldon. Pray do not let us keep you. Jonathan, show Dr. Beldon up to the yellow room, if you please."

It hardly pleased me, but I offered my own bow and waited for Beldon to join me in the hall.

"Your mother is a very kind woman to take us in," he said as we trudged up the stairs.

"Yes."

"I fully realize that this must be an imposition to you all, but Deborah and I are very grateful and glad to be here."

What a surprise, I thought.

"I would like to take this opportunity to let you know that I am entirely at the service of you and your house should you require it."

"As a doctor?" I asked, somewhat insolently, now that he was away from Mother's protection.

A perceptive man, he decided to take the light insult as a joke. "I'm afraid so. Doubtless I could make myself useful working in the fields, but I have more talent for doctoring than animal husbandry or farming."

I paused on the landing and looked at him squarely. "You consider yourself a good doctor, then?"

"As good as most. I studied with Dr. Richard Shippen of Philadelphia," he added with some pride.

"Did you really? The smallpox man?"

Beldon was surprised that I'd heard of him and said as much.

"I should think so. Years ago Mother had instructed Father by letter to pack Elizabeth and me off to the man for an inoculation against the pox. I still have the scar. Couldn't have been more than nine, but I remember it vividly, worst six weeks of my life. What a horrible thing to do to children."

"Less horrible than dying of the pox," he pointed out.

I was unwilling to relinquish my hostile opinion of the man. "I'd read that they had him up for body snatching three years back."

But Beldon was not to be drawn and only shook his head with amusement. "Something that every teaching physician seems to go through. He was accused of taking a woman's body for his dissecting class, but those subjects only ever came from the Potter's Field, never from Christian burial grounds. The whole business was utterly absurd. They said he'd dissected a woman in the winter who had died that summer of a putrid fever. Absurd," he repeated.

"Oh, yes, very."

Letting that one pass as well, he gestured at one of the doors. "Is this my room?"

"This one," I said, taking him farther down the hall.

"I understand that you have a good library here."

"Yes. Downstairs. Any of the servants can show you the way."

"I'll look forward to it. I was unable to bring many books. Perhaps you would like to inspect my own small collection?"

"Another time, Dr. Beldon. I must return to the ladies, you know."

Again the incessant smile, this one tinged with regret and goodwill.

"Yes. The ladies can be quite demanding. Good night, then, Mr. Barrett. Thank you once more for your kindness."

The man sounded utterly sincere. A bit nonplussed, I left before he could try drawing me into another conversation.

Tempting as it was to retreat to my room, I felt bound to go back to the parlor and look after Elizabeth. She was still grimly playing, missing a note now and then as her thoughts wandered. Mother was employing her scratching stick. Mrs. Hardinbrook looked bored.

At the end of the piece I applauded louder than the others and walked up to the spinet. "Excellent, Elizabeth. You get better every day."

She knew what I was up to and seized upon it smoothly and with both hands. "You are so kind, Jonathan." She stood up and away from the instrument and curtsied to her audience. "Ah, but I am weary myself. In another minute I'm sure I shall fall asleep on my feet."

"You have had a very long day," I agreed. "Mother, may we be excused? I want to see that Elizabeth makes it upstairs without stumbling."

"Poor thing," said Mrs. Hardinbrook, all sympathy. She started to launch into a no doubt pretty speech, but Mother interrupted her, granting us permission to leave. We took it.

Once outside, Elizabeth and I dropped our formal pretenses and marched toward the stairs as equals.

"Thank you for the rescue," she said.

"Always at your service."

"It looks like we're going to be lumbered with them for as long as Mother is here."

"Sadly, yes."

"Or at least until Father throws them out. Did you see how that harpy was trying to push her brother on me?"

"I noticed that he refused."

"Is that supposed to—"

"No slight intended, dear sister. I only meant to say that Beldon was aware that such a liaison would incur Mother's extreme displeasure. You have nothing to fear from him regarding unwanted attentions."

"Thank goodness for that," she sighed. "Do you think it would help to write to the king? We could ask him to send soldiers to Philadelphia to restore order there, then Mother and her friends could leave us in peace."

"I'm sure he would find it of great interest in forming his policies."

Her good humor and mine both in place, I saw Elizabeth to her room and gratefully returned to my own. Jericho had my things set out for the night, and a good fire was going as usual. The tray from our small meal had been cleared away, but he'd left a cup of wine and a plate of biscuits on the mantel for later. He'd also lighted the lamp on the table where my studies waited. Well, even Greek was preferable to the company in the parlor. I readied myself for bed, wrapped up warmly in the dressing gown, and opened the first book.

Rapelji had picked out an especially tricky passage for translation, but it took my mind away from present-day conundrums. The only time I looked up was when Mother and Mrs. Hardinbrook passed by my closed door on the way to their rooms. Their voices increased and faded along with their footsteps. I took the moment to stretch and look out the window.

High clouds obscured the stars and moon, making it very dark. Jericho would have called in the boy and his lantern by now. If he hadn't turned up at this late an hour, it could only mean that Father would be staying another night. Damnation.

The intricacies of an ancient battle and the warriors that fought it held my attention for another hour, then someone lightly knocked on my door. I knew who it was and, with a sigh of slight annoyance, answered.

Elizabeth stood waiting with a wan look and a drooping eye. "I couldn't sleep," she explained apologetically. My annoyance faded. It had been our habit in the past to visit one another for a late-night talk when wakeful. I'd missed those talks without knowing it until now.

I invited her in and shut the door quietly. "I could give you some of this Greek. It does the job for me."

She threw herself facedown on the bed and propped her chin on her fists. "Mother has that woman in her room and they're still yammering away. I had no idea that two people with so little to say could do so for so long."

"Why don't you listen in? It could be entertaining."

"I tried, but they don't talk about anything interesting. It's always about clothes, food, or people I've never heard of and wouldn't care to meet. Rubbish, the lot of it. What did you say you were doing?"

"Greek. Care to try some?" I wandered back to my chair and offered her the book I was working from.

She considered the offer, but turned it down. "Will you be seeing Mr. Rapelji tomorrow?"

"Yes, if I can get this finished. He'll probably put me over the coals as usual."

"Oh, may I come along and watch?"

"Yes, you may and very welcome. With you there it won't be so horrible."

"What exaggeration. You know he never even raises his voice."

"It's the way he doesn't raise it that bothers me."

She laughed a little, which was good to hear. "Perhaps he will find something interesting for me to do as well. I absolutely do not want to be here tomorrow. One thing I did hear through the wall was Mother making plans to visit some of the neighbors to introduce that woman. She said I'd be coming along. Nice of her to let me know about it, don't you think?"

"We can be gone before breakfast," I assured her. "Rapelji won't mind feeding us."

"Thank goodness. I'll wager that Mother wants to look the men over hereabouts in hopes of matching me up with one. Ugh!"

"Don't you want to get married?"

"Someday, but not to any man that she would pick."

"She picked Father, didn't she?"

"Huh. If Beldon is anything to go by then her tastes have changed."

"He's not so bad," I teased. She made a face at me. "He has pretty manners."

"So does my cat."

"The funny thing is that I did get the impression that he would like to be friends."

"Fine. You can be his friend. I'd sooner marry Mr. Rapelji."

"Or your cat?"

She laughed right out loud at that one and I joined her, joking about what her cat would be likely to wear when they went to church.

"Of course, you'll have to have a lot of cream for the wedding breakfast," I went on. "For the cat's side of the family."

She added a comment of her own, but I couldn't make it out for her giggling and asked her to repeat it. She struggled to take in the breath to do so, but in that moment my door burst open with such force that it cracked against the inside wall. Elizabeth choked with surprise and rolled upright to see better.

Mother stood on the threshold. Her eyes were wide with incredulity, her mouth torn downward with shock. She looked from one to the other of us, unable to decide which deserved her immediate attention. Elizabeth and I stared back at her with shared confusion.

"Is there something wrong, Mother?" I asked, rising.

Her mouth flapped several times. It might have been comical but for the raw fury contained in her. It did not remain there for long.

"You two . . . ," she finally gasped out.

"What is it?" I stepped forward, thinking she was ill. She looked feverish enough.

"You . . . filthy . . . filthy . . . unnatural wretches."

"What's the matter with her?" Elizabeth asked. "Mother?"

I put my hand out. "Come and sit down, Mother."

She slapped me away. "You miserable, depraved creature. How could you even think of such a horror?"

Elizabeth shook her head at me, a sign to keep my distance, and to communicate her own puzzlement.

"Mother . . . ," I began. But she came at me, her hand opened wide, and slapped me right across the mouth with all her strength. My head snapped to one side, my whole face ablaze from the stinging blow. I fell back, looking at her without comprehension, too startled to react yet.

She struck me again with her other hand, fairly rattling my head. Tears started from my eyes from the pain. Another strike. I backed away, suddenly aware of the invective flowing from her. None of it was too coherent, broken as it was by her hitting me and the intensity of emotion within. Her temper tantrum this morning was but a shower compared to this gale.

Elizabeth was off the bed by now and shouting at her. I put my hands up to guard myself and tried to back around toward the door and escape. Elizabeth got between us and took solid hold of Mother's arm. Now they were both shouting.

Then Mother hit Elizabeth. Not with an open hand, but a closed fist.

Elizabeth cried out and spun away, her hair flying. She fell against the bed, then dropped to the floor. Her next breath was a bewildered, angry sob. Mother loomed over her, shifting her weight to one foot. Before she could deliver what would have been a vicious kick to my sister's stomach I was reaching for her. I caught both her arms from behind and dragged her away. She screamed and squirmed and her heels flailed against my shins.

"What is it? Oh, dear, what is it? Marie, what is happening?" Mrs. Hardinbrook dithered in the hall, adding her foolishness to the din. Mother paid her no mind as she thrashed about. She'd used up her words and much of her breath. Hideous little animal grunts escaped from her clenched teeth.

I hoarsely shouted Elizabeth's name, breathless myself. She shook herself and found her feet, moving slowly, and holding her face. She was dazed, but had sense enough to keep clear. Stumbling toward the door, she ran into Mrs. Hardinbrook, who didn't quite know what to do with her.

"Get some help, you fool!" my sister bellowed, pushing her away. The woman squeaked fearfully and fled.

"Elizabeth?"

"I'm all right," she stated shakily.

"*Harlot!*" Mother shouted at her. "Filthy, unnatural *harlot*!"

Elizabeth gaped at her, then her eyes darted to my bed, where she had been giggling hardly a minute past. "Oh, my God. She can't mean *that.*"

Busy as I was, the realization of what she was talking about took longer to dawn upon me. When it did, Mother took advantage of my total shock to twist from my grasp and round upon us. Her carefully made-up hair had shredded into a tangled mess framing a beet red face. Her eyes were fairly popping with rage. She looked absolutely and utterly demented.

"You shameless creatures! It was a cursed day that either of you were born that you should come to this. You dirty, disgusting . . ."

"Mother, you are *wrong!* You don't know what you're saying."

She could have scorched me with those eyes. "I know what I saw, you unnatural thing."

Elizabeth came in to stand next to me. "She's incensed, Jonathan, don't try to argue with her."

"That was ever and always the excuse," Mother snarled. "*I* don't know what I'm talking about! Is that it? Is that what you'll say? This disgrace is upon you both. You'll be the ones locked away. Dear God, I should have seen this coming and been here to prevent it." She looked past us. "It's your fault, Samuel. You raised them as you would and *see* what has become of them. I swear, if any filthy bastard come of this unholy union I'll drown it myself. Do you hear me? I said, *do you hear me*?"

As one, Elizabeth and I followed her gaze, looking toward the doorway of my room. Standing there, still wrapped in his traveling cloak, was our tardy father.

# CHAPTER 3

He regarded his wife in a calm manner and nodded soberly. "I hear you, Marie," he said in a gentle, well-controlled voice.

Elizabeth and I began to rush toward him, but he swiftly brought up one hand, a sign to remain in place. He did not look at us but at Mother.

She glared back. "And where have you been while this wickedness has been going on? Or have you been a part of it? *Have you?*"

He declined to answer that one, his eyes shifting briefly over to me and back again. "Library. Both of you."

We gratefully fled. In the hall we met Beldon hurrying along with a black case in hand and his sister in tow. He was dressed for bed, but had thrown on a coat and shoved his bare feet into some shoes. Neither spared a word for us, though Mrs. Hardinbrook paused as though sorely tempted. But she went on to be with Beldon and thus watch whatever might come next. She was welcome to do so.

Partway down the stairs we encountered the first of the servants roused by the row, a sleep-drugged maid. I ordered her to the kitchen to brew up some strong tea. She tottered out of our path, her face coming awake with questions. I ruthlessly confiscated her candle.

The library was cold, but the fireplace had been swept and readied for tomorrow. I knelt and busied myself with the tinder, bringing it to fiery life with the candle flame while Elizabeth sank onto a settee.

"Are you hurt?" I asked.

Silence, and then an eloquent sniff. She rubbed her swelling and now wet cheek with an impatient hand. "Are you? Your face . . ."

"Stings." I began to shake all over. A piece of kindling dropped on the stone hearth. "My God, Elizabeth."

"I know. It's impossible. She's impossible. We can't live like this." Elizabeth hated crying and I hated watching her fight it. I left the fire and sat next to her, an arm around her slumped shoulders. It was as much for my solace as hers.

With only the one candle and the embyronic fire, the library was filled with shadows. I'd seen it like this many times, foraging down here for a book when the house was asleep, but never with such a heaviness in my heart. I was afraid. I was in my own house and afraid. It was not a child's fear of the dark, or even of that time when I'd fallen down into the kettle, or of a hundred other times and incidents. Those fears pass quickly and may eventually be laughed at; this was of an altogether different kind. It would not go away so easily, if at all.

"Why did she ever have to come home?" I muttered.

Elizabeth had recovered somewhat when the maid turned up with the tea. I had the girl pour; neither of us were steady enough to do it without dropping the pot.

"What's going on up there?" I asked her. I'd heard a lot of rushing about and voices.

"They're all taking care of Mrs. Barrett, sir. Mrs. Nooth is with her and so's that Dr. Beldon. Mrs. Nooth said she'd had some kind of a fit." The girl waited, perhaps hoping to glean more information from me. I disappointed her with a nod of thanks and a clear dismissal.

" 'Some kind of a fit'?" Elizabeth echoed sarcastically when we were alone.

"That seems to describe it well enough."

She pulled herself straight and reached for one of the cups. "I can see us describing it like that from now on. What are we going to *do* with her? Lock her in the attic? Or will we build her a little block house and hire someone to feed her through a slot in the door?"

"It won't come to that," I said.

"Better that than to go through this night again. I didn't hate her before, Jonathan, but I do now. What she said . . . what she thought . . . is unforgivable. It's twisted and horrible. I won't put up with it."

"But—"

"This is more our house than hers when you think of it. She had no right to come here and do this to us. We were happy until she came."

True. All true.

Elizabeth put down the cup, her tea finished. It must have been scalding, but she was too upset to notice. "Father will have to do something. After all this, he will have to do something."

We fell silent for a while. I went back to building up the fire. The chill of the room—and of other things—was seeping past my skin and into the bones.

Father came in just as one of the logs began to properly blaze. As one, Elizabeth and I ran to him for the embrace we'd been denied earlier. It was something we'd done as children and now we gladly returned to that simple and much-needed comfort. He smiled and his arms opened wide.

"Is that tea I spy?" he asked after a moment.

We loosened our grip and Elizabeth glided over to pour. He made a side trip to a cabinet and brought out a bottle of brandy, adding some to each cup.

"I think we all need this," he observed.

He'd shed the cloak at some point, but still carried some of the outdoors with him in his manner. His riding boots were stained with old mud. He'd been wearing them, I remembered, when he'd taken his morning walk with Mrs. Montagu. Such previous pleasures driven aside by tonight's pains, he looked tired. Older, I realized with another chill. But instead of being burdened by age, he was a man aged by a burden. His wife.

"Well?" he asked. "Which of you wants to talk first?"

Elizabeth stepped in. "Where's Mother?"

"In her room. That fellow with the popping eyes gave her a dose of laudanum to calm her down. He and that silly woman are sitting in with her. Said he was a doctor. Would he be Beldon, then?"

"Yes. The woman is his sister, Deborah Hardinbrook."

Father had heard enough about them from Mother to need no further introduction. "Proper little pair of toadies, but they seem to be making themselves useful for the moment. Now, please, tell me what happened."

Between us we managed to garble up the narrative enough for him to raise his hand in protest.

"Jonathan, your turn," he said firmly. "Pretend you're in court."

It was his way of reminding me to present all the facts, but as simply as possible and in good order. I did my best. Elizabeth added nothing, but nodded agreement as I spoke. When I'd finished, our brandy-laced tea was all gone.

Father sighed and ran a hand through his graying hair. It was his own, tied back with a now-wilted ribbon. He wore a wig only when engaged in court business or seeing a client. "A pretty mess," he concluded. "Are you badly hurt? Elizabeth?"

She shook her head. I did the same. The sting had faded, though my cheeks still felt tender to touch.

"But it might have been worse," I said. "If Mother had kicked her as she'd intended . . ."

Elizabeth dropped her eyes. "We must do something, Father."

"Indeed," he said, neither agreeing nor disputing. He stood and paced the room a few times. On the last round he checked the hallway for any listeners and closed the door before coming to stand before the fireplace. It was unlike him to behave so. I saw it as more evidence of how Mother's presence had changed life for us all.

"There is other news, too," I said.

"Tell me."

"She wants me to go to England to study law."

Father only nodded, which was a bit disappointing to me. "What else?"

"She wants to sell Jericho and hire on an English servant to take his place."

This was news to Elizabeth. "That's horrid."

"I told him I'd sooner run away to sea and take him with me."

Father gave out with a chuckle just then, but quickly smothered it. I'd sounded foolish, but just then we needed some foolishness. Some of the shadows looming over us seemed to drop back.

"But Jericho said that I'd be arrested for stealing him," I added.

"I see. Then Jericho is a most level-headed young fellow. Well, you need not worry about him being sold. Since I bought Archimedes with my own money, both he and his son are my property. Your mother can't sell either of them without my permission, and that is something I shall happily withhold. If she wants an English servant for you, she may hire one, but he will have to take his orders from Jericho."

I blinked with surprise, but Father was serious. We knew enough about the household hierarchies to know that no man of the type Mother would be looking for would accept work under such conditions. Elizabeth smiled at me, new hope and cheer blooming on her face.

Father's own smile came and went more quickly. "England," he sighed.

"I don't want to go, but she said that it's all been arranged."

"Then I've no doubt that it has. Cambridge, I suppose. Yes, she's mentioned it before and no, I did not know that she'd pursued it this far."

"Why?" I asked. "What is it she wants? Is Harvard not good enough for her?"

"That and many other reasons, laddie. Tell me everything you know."

I summarized this morning's conversation, leaving in Mother's tantrum, then went on to her lecture in the afternoon. The latter was little more than a sketch because of my condition at the time.

"She seems to have everything well in hand," was his comment when I'd finished. "It looks like she's been cooking this up with that bloody sister of hers for some goodly time."

"Aunt Theresa?" The name was not unknown to me, but unfamiliar on the tongue.

"Hmm." Father went to his desk and shuffled at the papers on top, plucking one from the pile and bringing it back to the better light. It was the same one Mother had been studying this morning. "This is it. You've been accepted at Cambridge; according to this, your studies are to begin at the Michaelmas term. How like her to leave it there for me to just 'find.' "

"She also waited until you were away before telling me. She did it on purpose, I think—"

"She does 'most everything with a purpose," he growled, putting the paper aside.

"But I don't have to go . . . do I?"

Father did not answer right away. Elizabeth's hand, resting on mine, tightened.

"Father?"

Always decisive and in control, he hesitated, frowning at the floor. "I'll talk to her," he said.

"Talk to . . . ? What does that mean?"

His chin snapped up and I shrank inside. But his face softened and the rebuke for my insolence went unspoken. "It means that both of you need to know what's really beneath all this so you can understand and make the best of things."

That didn't sound too terribly hopeful.

He poured out another swallow of brandy and drained it away, then looked up at his wife's portrait. "First of all, I did marry your mother because I loved her. If her father had realized that, then our lives might have been quite different. Whether for good or for ill, I could not say, but different, perhaps.

"All this took place in England. You know that I went to Cambridge myself. I was out and working with old Roylston when I met Judge Fonteyn and his family. He was wealthy but always looking to either increase it or raise his status in society. I did not fit his idea of an ideal son-in-law and he saw me not as I was, but as he perceived me to be. He put himself in my place and assumed that I was paying court to his daughter for his money.

"Admittedly, the money made your mother that much more attractive to me, but it was never my real goal. We might have even eloped, but Marie persuaded him to consent to our marriage. He did so with ill grace but provided her with an allowance. He also drew up a paper for me to sign, stipulating that this allowance was hers and hers alone and I was not to touch it. I signed it readily enough. He was surprised that I did, and at the same time contemptuous. There was no pleasing the old devil."

That sounded familiar, I thought.

"The marriage took place and we were happy for a time, at least we were when there was sufficient distance between your mother and her family. Her father was a terrible tyrant, couldn't and wouldn't abide me, and it was because of him that I decided to leave England altogether. Marie went along with it, because in those days she still loved me. You both know how we came to settle here, but it was your mother's money that bought this place and it still pays for the servants and the taxes."

"The paper you signed . . . ," said Elizabeth, beginning to see. It was like crystal to me.

"Means that I own none of this." He gestured, indicating the house and all the lands around it. "I have Archimedes, Jericho, and whatever I've gleaned from my practice. Now, I have made something of a living for myself, but as a rule, lawyers enjoy far more social status than they do money. When Fonteyn died, he divided his fortune between his daughters. There was quite a sum involved, but I'd promised to touch none of it and have kept to that promise. It . . . has never bothered me before."

"So Mother is paying for my education," I said.

"She always has. It was she who hired Rapelji, for example."

"And mine, too?" asked Elizabeth.

Father smiled with affection and satisfaction. "No, that was my idea. It is a sad and stupid thing, but the truth is your mother didn't think it worth trying. She's always had the mistaken idea that an educated woman is socially disadvantaged."

"And yet she herself—?" Elizabeth was swiftly sputtering her way toward outrage.

Father waved a cautioning hand. "I must clarify. She thinks a woman has gained sufficient knowledge if she reads and writes enough to maintain her household and be agreeable in polite company."

Elizabeth snorted.

"I never saw it that way, though, so I made sure that Rapelji was well compensated for the time he spent on you. Your mother was under the impression that you were learning no more than the limits she'd set: your numbers, letters, and some French."

"And my music from Mrs. Hornby?"

"Yes."

"Because every girl in polite society must know how to sing and play?" It was not a question so much as a statement of contempt.

"Yes."

"On the other hand, being able to reason and think would place me at a severe disadvantage?"

"In her view, yes."

Elizabeth rose and threw her arms around him. "Then, thank you, Father!"

He laughed at the embrace. "There now. I may not have done you any favors, girl."

"I don't care." She loosened her grip. "But what about Jonathan going away to England?"

His laugh settled into a sigh. "It is her money that runs this place, puts clothes on your backs, and food in your mouths, and because of that she feels entitled to choose where you are to be educated. She appears to have entirely made up her mind, but I will talk with her. There are other reasons for you to go to Harvard than the fact that it is closer than England."

"And if she doesn't listen?" I asked glumly.

"That possibility exists. You may have to face it."

"But after tonight . . . Mother isn't . . . well."

"You need not mince your words, Jonathan. We all know she wasn't in her right mind then. Her father was the same. He'd work himself into a ferocious temper until you'd think his brain would burst, then the fit would pass and like as not he'd have forgotten what angered him, even deny he'd been angry. Whatever poisons lurked in his blood are in your mother as well."

"And us?" Elizabeth's eyebrows were climbing.

Father shrugged. "It's in God's hands, girl, but I've tried to raise you two with the love old Fonteyn was incapable of giving. I think it has made all the difference."

"We're nothing like her," she said thankfully.

He touched her chin lightly with one finger and glanced at me. "Perhaps a little, on the outside. I wish you could have known her in those days." He indicated the portrait. "Everything was so different then, but over the years the poisons began to leech out. She changed, bit by bit. She began to expect things of me that I would not provide. She wanted me to advance on to the bench, but I never had the inclination to become a judge. She became fixed on that as hard and fast as her father was fixed upon his money. I could have done as she wanted, but it would not have been what I wanted. Eventually, I could see myself turning into her own little dancing puppet. I would not have been my own man, but rather something tied to her and, in turn, tied to her dead father. In her lucid moments, she knew this, but could never hold on to it for long."

"Is that why she moved away?" I asked.

"In part. After you were born, she got worse. Nothing to do with you, laddie. You were as sweet a child as anyone could ask for, but her nerves were bad. She no longer loved me by then and I . . . well, there are few things in life so miserable as a marriage gone wrong. I hope you two will make a better job of it than I did. She had some distant cousins in Philadelphia, so off she went. I think she found some happiness there with such friends as she's gathered 'round. I know I have been happy here."

One of the logs popped noisily. Happiness. I'd taken it for granted until now. Looking at Father, I began to see the heaviness of the burden he'd carried without complaint all these years. He hadn't told us everything, I could sense that, but I wasn't going to presume on him for more. What we'd learned tonight was sufficient. Because of it I suddenly knew I was not yet a man myself, but only a boy of seventeen and frightened.

I slept poorly for what remained of the night and was up to watch the dawn long before it happened. The house was quiet and I imagined it to be waiting, wondering what was to happen once Mother woke from her own slumber. I dressed warmly and crept outside to the stables to saddle up two horses. Elizabeth and I had not changed our plan to spend time with Rapelji. Father knew and encouraged it. He would have his hands full dealing with Mother and her guests and preferred us out of the way.

Rolly poked his head from his box hopefully, but I passed him by for Belle and Beauty, two mares out of the same dam who shared a calm temperament as well as a smooth gait. Rolly vocalized his displeasure, waking the lads who slept over the stable. One of them came down to investigate and sleepily stayed on to help with the saddling before wandering off to the kitchen in hope of an early meal.

I led the horses out to wait by one of the side doors, then went to fetch Elizabeth. She was just inside, pulling on her gloves. There was a sodden look about her indicating that she hadn't slept well, either. On her face, where Mother's fist had landed, was a large, evil-looking bruise. She'd made no effort to cover or disguise it.

"We don't have to go," I said. "It's not likely that you'll be called upon to go visiting the neighbors."

"No, but I can't bear to be in this house right now. Besides, *this* was not my fault." She tilted her head to indicate the damage done. "I've nothing at all to be ashamed of; people may think what they like."

"You don't care if they know about Mother?"

Elizabeth's face grew hard in a way that I did not like. "Not one whit."

"But why?"

"Why not? Sooner or later they'll start their speculations, their gossip about her. They may as well get the truth from us as make it up for themselves."

"But it's none of their bloody business!"

"As you say." She shrugged. "But mark me, they shall make it so, whether we like it or not. We have only to be calm and truthful and let Mother rave on as her fancy takes her. Then we shall see how many friends she has about her."

I was quite confused by this harsh attitude, for it was an alien one in Elizabeth, then I began to see the point of it all. "You're doing this hoping that Mother will . . . ?"

"A word here and there and she will be shunned by what passes for polite company in these parts. That's what she craves and lives for, the puerile attention and approval of her so-called peers. She's welcome to it, if she can find any willing to endure her company after this."

"What if they believe her and not you? What if she repeats her—that awful accusation against us? You know adults are more likely to believe other adults."

"But they know us here. They do not know her. And we are Father's children, raised to be honest and truthful. I think that favors us, Jonathan, so you needn't worry."

"Damnation, I will if I want to."

"Please yourself, then, but support me on this and there's a chance that Mother may move out, bag, baggage, and toad-eaters, and leave us all in peace."

That silenced me.

She handed me a leather bundle. "Here, you'd forgotten your books and papers."

"Thank you," I said faintly, my mind busy with all sorts of things. I couldn't choose whether to approve of her plan or not, but knew that she would go through with it, regardless of my objections.

She led the way into the yard and I helped her onto Beauty, her favorite. I swung up on Belle and we set off down the lane leading to the main road, turning into the rising sun. It gave no warmth save within the mind, but it was still a cheering sight.

Rapelji lived in a fine, solid farmhouse at the eastern edge of our property. The farm was not his—that had been annexed onto our own lands—but he had a good garden plot for himself and found additional support from several other students in the area. Some of them boarded with him for part of the year and helped with the chores to pay for their tutoring.

As early as we were, Rapelji was already up and about, a short figure in the middle of his troop of students as he led them through a peculiar series of hops and skips for their morning exercise. At a distance, you could only tell him from the boys by his flashing spectacles, which somehow stayed on no matter how vigorous his actions became. As we drew near, he had them all jumping and clapping their hands over their heads in time to shouting the multiplication table at the top of their lungs. It was great fun, and I'd done it myself at their age. He had the idea that if boys were going to make noise anyway, it might as well be for a constructive purpose.

They got as far as four times twelve when he called a breathless halt. Some of the boys had noticed our approach and had lost the count.

"Concentration, gentlemen," he admonished. "Concentration, discipline, and courtesy. What is required when you see a lady?"

As one, but with grins and playful shoving, the boys pretended to sweep hats from their bare heads and bowed deeply to Elizabeth. She returned their salute gracefully. My turn was next and I doffed my own hat to them. Rapelji said they'd done well and clapped his hands twice. It was time to start the chores. The boys scattered like stirred-up ants. Chores first, then breakfast, then studies.

"Good morning, Miss Elizabeth, Mr. Jonathan. Come in, come in. It's the girls' baking day and the first loaves are just out of the oven." He gestured us inside the house. We left the horses to the care of the boys and joined him. Along with a varying number of students, he shared the big house with his two housekeepers, Rachel and Sarah, two elderly siblings that he couldn't tell apart, so he called them "the girls." They weren't much for intellectual conversation, but kindly toward the students and doted on the teacher. Their cooking and herb lore were legendary.

The front room was where he taught. A long table lined with many chairs took up most of the floor. The walls boasted all kinds of books, papers, some stuffed animals, and his prize, a mounted skeleton of some type of small ape. He used it to explain anatomy to us. On another shelf he kept his geological finds, including a rather large specimen of a spiral-shaped sea creature, so old that it had turned to stone. He'd dug it up himself miles inland and delighted in speculating about its origins. The thing had always fascinated me and had sparked many a talk and good-natured argument.

Elizabeth took off her cloak and hat, hanging them on the pegs next to the door. This was a second home to us, Rapelji our eccentric uncle, but we hadn't been over together for some time, a point he commented upon.

"Things are a bit hectic at the house," said Elizabeth. "Two of Mother's friends have come to stay with us for a while."

"Ah, that's good. Company always helps pass the time away." Rapelji, as evident by his huge household, liked having people about him.

"Have you ever met Mother?" I asked. He'd never before mentioned her and I was curious to have his side of the story.

He pursed his plump lips to think. "Oh, yes, but it was years ago and only the one time when I answered her advertisement for a tutor. She interviewed me and sent me on to here. I was the only one willing to make the journey, it seemed. Your good father made the rest of the arrangements and that was that. Perhaps since she is here I should stop over and pay my respects."

"No!" we said in unison.

"No?" he questioned, interested by our reluctance. Then he noticed Elizabeth's face for the first time. Until now, she'd been keeping to the background. "Good heavens, child, what has happened to you?"

Though his shock must have been in accordance with Elizabeth's hopes and plans, it was still difficult for her. She bit her lip and dropped her gaze. "We've had some problems at home," she mumbled.

"Indeed?" Rapelji could see there was more to be learned. "Well, come sit here and rest yourself." He solicitously held a chair out for her. He peered closely at me, now, and noted the swollen skin that I'd seen in my shaving mirror earlier. I felt myself going red and not knowing why. As with Elizabeth, I had nothing of which to be ashamed.

One of the girls came in to set the table—I think it was Rachel—and her sharp eyes suddenly froze onto our faces in that way old women have.

"Goodness, children, have you been quarreling?" she asked.

Elizabeth's hand went to her cheek and she began to blush. I kept my hands down, but nodded to the concerned woman. "Yes, ma'am, but not with each other."

"I'll make you a nice poultice of sugar and yellow soap," Rachel promised.

Sarah appeared next to her, squinted at us, and shook her head. "No, dear, that's for boils. What you want is some cotton dipped in molasses."

"That's for earache," said Rachel.

"Really? I could have sworn . . ."

"Please, ladies," Elizabeth interrupted. "It's nothing to trouble over. I am in no distress. We must get back to our studies."

Dissatisfied as they obviously were and wanting to stay, Rapelji came to her support and the two ladies eventually removed themselves and their good intentions. He waited until the door to the kitchen was shut, then gently asked for an explanation.

"Mother . . . felt the need to discipline us, sir," I said stiffly.

"And your father agreed?" he asked with surprise. "To this?"

"No, sir. He persuaded her to cease."

Elizabeth heaved an impatient sigh, told me not to be such a diplomat, and gave Rapelji the bald truth. She did not, however, mention Mother's obscene accusation, only that she'd thrown an unreasonable fit. She went on to relate that Father had interrupted things in time and mentioned that Beldon's services as a doctor had been employed. I found myself listening with surprising interest. It seemed that Elizabeth had a talent for storytelling.

Rapelji, the poor man, was out of his depth, as I'd expected. He had no heart for violent domestic disputes, preferring his battles to remain in the history books; the more ancient, the better.

"I know I've embarrassed you, sir," she said. "And I do apologize, but I felt that of all people, you needed to know what has happened."

"Yes, yes. Oh, you poor girl."

"Anyway, you know the truth. I did not think it fair that you should be unaware of our situation. Mother has a horrible temper and it is liable to get away from her at the least provocation. Father said she'd inherited it. The doctor visiting us seems to have things in hand, though."

Rapelji heaved a sigh of his own. "Well, then, I can promise that your confidence will stay here"—he tapped one of his ears—"and shall go no farther. I am so sorry that you have this problem. If you are ever in need, I am at your service."

Past him, the ostensibly closed kitchen door moved slightly. Rachel and Sarah had heard everything, of course, and Elizabeth knew it. She'd made a point of speaking clearly and without moderating her tone to a lower level as others might have done while relating a confidence.

"Mr. Rapelji, you have already helped, just by being here," she said, patting his hand.

Our tutor smiled broadly. "Why, then, you are very welcome!"

This made Elizabeth laugh and he inquired if we had any other problems requiring assistance. That's when I stepped in and told him about the Cambridge business.

"And you don't want to go?" he cried. "Why ever not?"

"It's so far away," I answered. "And it was how she presented it." That sounded feeble even to me and Rapelji pounced on it.

"So it is the wrappings you object to, but not the gift."

"Gift?" This was not the sort of support I'd been expecting.

"Try looking at it as a gift, not a punishment, Mr. Jonathan. What difference if you had a rough introduction to the idea? The idea itself is what matters: the chance to attend one of the great and ancient centers of higher learning in the world."

"I had thought of it a bit, sir," I said with very wan enthusiasm, but the subtlety was lost on my tutor.

"Good! Think on it some more. If your father cannot turn Mrs. Barrett's mind from the idea, then you won't feel so badly about going."

"I should not like to wager upon that, sir," I muttered.

Rapelji thumped my shoulder, still beaming.

The front door swung wide just then as two of his other students arrived for the day's lessons. They were the Finch boys, Roddy and Nathan.

We stood and greeted them and Rapelji put them through the ritual of giving respects to my sister. Roddy, my age and awkward, blushed his way through his bow. Elizabeth was no doubt very beautiful to him despite her bruise. He gawked with curiosity, but said nothing except for a general inquiry about her health. For that he received a polite, but general reply that she was well enough today, thank you.

Nathan, a sullen-faced boy of fourteen who knew that manners were a waste of his time, barely got through his bow. It was just enough to accomplish the job, but not so little as to draw a reprimand.

"I killed a rabbit today," he announced proudly, eager to introduce a subject more to his liking.

"Did you now?" said Rapelji.

"A good fat one for the pot." From the cloth bag that carried all his things he hauled out a long, limp bundle of brown-and-gray fur. "Caught 'im in a snare and snapped 'is neck m'self."

"That's '*I* caught *him* in a snare,' Nathan," began Rapelji, always the teacher.

The boy scowled. "You did not, *I* did. If'n you did, an' it were on *our* land, then Da will shoot you dead for a-poachin'."

Roddy gave Nathan a cuff. "Mr. Rapelji didn't say *he* was a-poachin', he was telling you how to talk right."

Nathan glowered and grunted with disapproval. He was one of the more difficult students and would have been happier working the fields or hunting. Rapelji had often recommended it, but their father was determined that they learn their letters and grimly paid for the effort. Roddy had a better head and might have progressed more if he didn't have Nathan to constantly look after and keep in line.

Morning chores finished, the other boys began to wander in for their breakfast along with half a dozen others from neighboring houses. Nathan's rabbit was the subject of much interest and conversation and he was compelled to repeat his story of how he'd snapped the animal's neck.

He was happy enough to demonstrate this to everyone's satisfaction, but his method sparked off a debate on the various ways of snapping animal necks of all kinds. Elizabeth was not in the least fainthearted, but after several minutes of gleeful discussion she began to visibly pale. Rapelji noticed and dispatched Nathan off to the kitchen with his prize, as it was part of Finch's payment for his boys' tutoring.

Later, over tea, fresh bread, and hot porridge, we talked about all sorts of things that had nothing to do with Mother. Rapelji used these times to teach the boys how to conduct themselves in a civilized conversation as he called it. He was popular, but often their natural high spirits got away with them and pandemonium would reign as each boy contributed a comment more loudly than his neighbor, and at the same time. When this happened, Rapelji usually restored order with a gavel kept handy for this purpose.

When lessons began in earnest, Elizabeth lent a hand supervising some of the younger lads while Rapelji took a moment to check my Greek. He pronounced himself satisfied, which surprised me, considering the interruptions my work had suffered.

"Next, we shall try some original composition," he announced jovially, as though it were an event to celebrate. "Something with a rhyme to it. They often hold competitions at the universities on this and you'll want to have the practice."

"Yes, sir," I said, looking toward Elizabeth for sympathy and only getting a smirk for my pains.

Rapelji sketched out my exercise in Greek for the day, then I was privileged to help the others with their work. Our tutor was of the opinion that nothing drove a lesson home so squarely as one that you must teach to another. He was also careful to be sure that the information we used was correct. On one memorable occasion a boy had given his "students" the impression that Columbus had made landfall in 1493, which was cause for much confusion and at least one fistfight when Rapelji's back was turned.

All the company around us did, indeed, help pass the time away as Rapelji maintained. The girls emerged from the kitchen to announce that it was time for the midday meal, which was received with extreme enthusiasm by one and all. Papers and books were cleared away, hands were washed of chalk and charcoal, and the plates were set out once more. Elizabeth and I stayed on until well into the afternoon, enjoying every minute. There was a bit of unease when one of the younger ones unabashedly asked Elizabeth why she had a black eye and cheek. She gently pointed out that it was rude to ask such questions. She also told him a simple version of the truth, that her mother had struck her.

This did not cause much alarm, as most of the lads had no small experience with corporal punishment. They'd been curious and, once their need was satisfied, went on to other concerns.

"Why didn't you say you'd run into a door?" I asked her afterward, when we were riding home.

"That would have been a lie."

"I know, but if any of them mentions it to their families, it might start up a lot of gossip with no fact behind it. I thought you wanted to make sure people knew the facts."

"I do. But keep in mind what you said about adults believing more readily in other adults. I doubt if it will come up in conversation when they return home, anyway. Nathan's rabbit drew far more attention than I."

"Hah! Roddy Finch couldn't keep his eyes off you. This will get around, dear sister, don't you worry."

"You're doing enough for both of us, and what objections do you have to Roddy Finch?"

"None, really, just to his beastly little brother. That boy's going to be trouble one day."

Too soon and we were on the lane to our house. Never before had we been reluctant to return home. Neither of us knew what might be waiting there nor did we especially care to find out. After the cheerful noise and activity of Rapelji's everything seemed ominously silent and sinister.

"I hope Father's straightened things out," I said thinly.

Elizabeth agreed. We rode around to the stables and dismounted. The lads there went about their business with the horses quietly. Apparently they knew something of the happenings of last night and Elizabeth endured their staring curiosity. It would have been unseemly for her to answer their unasked questions, though, so she ignored them entirely.

"It's probably all over the place by now," I said as we trudged toward the house.

She nodded. "Today is Saturday. I shall have to decide what to wear to church."

I gulped at the implications. The whole village would see her tomorrow.

"And if anyone asks, I shall answer them truthfully," she added, looking serene.

Jericho must have been on the watch for us. He opened the side door and saw to our cloaks and my bag of books.

"What's happened today?" I asked.

"It's been perfectly quiet. Your mother kept to her room until the early afternoon, when she came down to eat. Mrs. Hardinbrook sat with her and the doctor went up several times. They're all up there in her sitting room now, having tea and playing cards."

"What about Father?" That morning I had asked Jericho to especially keep his eyes and ears open on my behalf. I had also told him what Father had said in regard to his being sold. At least one of us had been spared from suffering the tortures of an unknown future for the day.

"He had a very long talk with her—" He broke off, for Father emerged from his library and was striding toward us. He looked quite grim but his greeting was warm. Jericho, sensing that he was redundant, vanished.

By now I couldn't contain myself. "Father, tell me—"

"Yes, Jonathan, I did speak with her." He looked very tired and my spirits fell, for I knew what he was going to say. "She would not be moved, laddie."

"Oh, Father." I felt a knot tightening at my throat as surely as if I'd been standing on a scaffold with a hangman.

"She was like stone. You are to go off to England and Cambridge," he said, his voice as thick as my own.

Elizabeth groaned and put an arm around me.

"Then God have mercy on my soul," I said mournfully, and stopped trying to hold back the tears that wanted to spill out.

# CHAPTER 4

***London, August 1773***

"Ho, sir! Would yer likes ter get married?"

The nearly toothless young man who accosted me as I left the coach was sodden with gin.

"I've a pretty wife for yer, sir! Sweet 'n' willing."

That's not how I would have described the woman lurking just behind him. Well used and avid came to mind. She was also drunk.

"A good 'ousekeeper and seamstress. She knows a' there is ter know 'bout threadin' a needle, haw-haw!" He jabbed an elbow into my side.

It was an even chance that if his ribald joviality didn't knock me over his breath would. I pushed him off and checked to make sure my money was still in place. It was, thank goodness, so I bulled past him, seeking the sanctuary of the inn.

"A pretty wife, sir. A good wife ter carries a' the family name!" he cried after me hopefully.

Now that was an idea. Bringing home such a wench for a daughter-in-law would certainly set Mother on her ear, or even flying over a cliff.

I smiled at the image. Suitable reparation for all that I'd been put through.

My thoughts were as sour as the sea smell clinging to my clothes. Instead of the clear air washed by miles of ocean waves, they stank of filthy bodies, damp wood, and, disgustingly, rat droppings. Such was what I'd discovered upon opening a trunk in search of new linen. I'd grimly shook out the cleanest-looking shirt and neckcloth and donned them. Bad as they were, the stuff was still better than what I'd been wearing. I was to meet my English cousin at this inn today and futilely hoped to give a good impression of myself.

"A pretty wife for yer!" said the pander to the next man off the coach, who cursed and shoved him out of the way much as one would an annoying dog.

The door of The Three Brewers beckoned. I ducked through, bumping into another man before me. The entrance hall was dark compared to the outside and he'd paused to let his dazzled eyes adjust. We begged one another's pardon and I pretended not to notice as he surreptitiously touched a pocket where he must have his own money secreted. Perhaps I was not as well dressed as I thought, that or pickpockets had so great an income in London that they could afford such clothes that would allow them to pass for gentlemen.

The porter intruded at this point, giving a cheerful welcome and ringing his bell for a waiter to come see to us. We were shown into the stranger's room with others from the coach and there made our needs known. I was famished and settled that part of my business promptly, even before taking a chair. Used to dealing with an endless number of similar starving guests, the man wasted no time in seeing to everyone's comfort. This inn had a favorable reputation and I was thankful and pleased that it was living up to the praise.

A noisy family with an infant shrieking in its nurse's arms rolled in. They disdained the stranger's room and were shown to some more private place away from the other guests. Well and good, for my brain was feverish from the journey and lack of food, and I might have been tempted into slaughtering an innocent had they remained.

Only when a hot plate of fatty, boiled beef was placed before me along with a deep cup of wine did my temper improve. I hurriedly handed over a shilling and fell upon my meal with ravenous abandon. When the plate was clean, I followed it up with a pigeon pie and an excellent boiled pudding. Nearly replete, the dessert of apples and walnuts filled the last empty corners. It was the first fresh food that I'd had since we'd run out of eggs on the ship. If I ever chewed salt beef and weevil-infested bread again it would be too soon.

Well, perhaps not. Given the chance to turn 'round and sail straight back to Long Island today, I'd have taken it. I was homesick and likely to remain so. Rapelji had said to regard this as an adventure. If adventures meant bad food, coarse company, weeks of staring at miles of bottomless gray water, bumpy coach rides, and encounters with a gin-soaked pimp, then he was welcome to mine. To be fair, London promised many interests, excitements, and horrors, and the victuals of The Three Brewers were tasty, but not as good as Mrs. Nooth's table at home.

I cracked two walnuts against each other and wished for a speedy return. Regardless of Mother's presence, it was familiar. I smashed the shells into smaller shards and picked out the meat.

Mother. Other men regarded the word with love and sentiment; all it inspired in me was anger and frustration.

Father's reasoning had not moved her to change her mind, neither had my tears—not that I wept before Mother. To do so would have only invited her contempt. Instead, I arranged for a private interview, hoping that a direct plea might work. This took place the evening after the long visit with Rapelji, but was an absolute failure before I ever opened my mouth to speak. The naked disgust on her face as she looked upon me shriveled my liver down to nothing. I had no experience dealing with the mad, nor did I wish to gain any. My only desire was to leave the room and never see her again. Since my effort at persuasion had died stillborn, I had to supply another reason to justify my visit. Red-faced and with the sweat tickling under my arms I blathered out a stuttering apology to her and concluded with a little speech of gratitude for her kindness toward me despite my offenses.

I did not state what I was apologizing for; I would not give a name to those offences. I *did* feel like a complete fool, admitting guilt to something that only existed in her sick mind. If one wishes to count childish fibs, then it was not the first time I'd ever lied, but it was the first time I had ever lied at length and so convincingly. The further I went, the worse I felt. Even as the words bubbled up into elaborate constructions of remorse, I vowed never to place myself in such a position again. The experience left me feeling soiled and in no doubt that if I hadn't utterly besmirched my honor this day, then I'd very definitely thrown a shadow upon it.

It was an impossible situation, as Elizabeth maintained, but what else could be done? The woman was mad, but she was our mother and we were unhappily subject to her whims. The other problem, as Father had pointed out, was the money. For a good education I needed the sum that she'd set aside for me—which would be denied if I insisted on Harvard. Very well, then I'd go to Cambridge. If groveling to this demented creature for a few minutes would curry her favor, then I would grovel, and did so. Thoroughly.

It worked. A creaking, rattling ghost of a smile drifted across her face, smacking of smug triumph. I'd been forgiven. My future was assured. It was time for her evening tea. I had permission to be excused.

After that bitter humilation, I was less ready to judge Beldon and Mrs. Hardinbrook so harshly for their toad-eating.

After my shameful scene with Mother, I went to see Father. It took me a while to work up the courage, but I finally introduced an idea that had been stirring uneasily in my brain: the possibility of having her declared incapable. I had feared he would be angry with me, but came to realize that he'd already thought it over for himself.

"How do we prove it, laddie?" he asked. When I faltered over my answer, he continued. "It would be different if she wandered about raving at the top of her voice all the time, but you've seen how she is. She's been in a temper over that incident, but you need more than that to take to court. In public her behavior has always been above reproach."

"But we've plenty of witnesses here to the contrary."

"To what would be dismissed as an unpleasant altercation within a family. No court would judge in our favor with—"

"But surely as her husband, you are able to do something." I could not keep a whine from invading my tone.

Father's face darkened and with an effort, he swallowed back his anger. "Jonathan, there are some things that I will not do, even for your sake. One of those is compromising my honor. To go down the path you are suggesting would do just that."

My eyes dropped; my skin was aflame. For the second time I stammered out an apology, only now I meant what was said.

He accepted it instantly. "I do understand exactly how you feel, I've been there many times. Life is not fair, but that doesn't mean we can't make the best of what fate—or your mother—drops on us."

Cold comfort, I thought.

The morning after those talks marked the official opening of Elizabeth's quiet campaign against Mother. We rose early and left early for the church. She'd managed to keep out of Mother's sight since the fight for fear that Mother might stop her from showing herself in public once she saw the extent of the damage done. Elizabeth's dress had been carefully chosen for its color, which brutally accented her fully developed bruises. She made no effort to hide them. Being a favorite among the women of our village, she was surrounded by a group of the concerned and the curious almost as soon as she stepped from the carriage. While I sent the driver back to the house for the rest of the family, Elizabeth made excellent use of her time.

I still disapproved, but since she was telling the plain truth, I had no difficulty supporting her. When the carriage rolled up again to discharge Mother, Mrs. Hardinbrook, Beldon, and Father, the atmosphere of avid curiosity mixed with revulsion was nearly as thick as a morning fog. Distracted by her guests, Mother did not notice it. A few late-comers who hadn't yet heard the tale came over to greet her and meet her friends, but as soon as they detached themselves, others took them aside for a confidential whisper. If Mother had been oblivious to the subtle change in the people around her, Father was not. But what he guessed or knew, he kept to himself.

Somehow we got through the service and returned home, me to brood on my disappointment, Elizabeth to her first feeling of triumph. She was all but glowing with satisfaction when I found her in the library. This dampened somewhat when she looked up and successfully read my face. Not wishing to intrude upon her, I'd kept my news, or lack of it, to myself throughout the morning.

"She wouldn't listen, would she?" she asked, all sympathy.

I threw myself onto a chair. "I don't think she knows how. I talked with Father, but it's hopeless. He won't do anything."

"You're not angry with him?"

"No, of course not. If he could help, he would. I'm going to have to leave."

"I wish I could come with you, then."

"So do I, but you know what Mother would make of that."

"Something evil," she agreed. We fell silent for a time. "What will you do at Cambridge?"

"Be miserable, I'm sure."

"It will be a long, long time. When you come back, you'll be all grown up. We won't know you."

"You think I'll change so much?"

"Perhaps not, little brother. I'm only being selfish, though."

"Indeed?"

"Whatever shall I do with myself while you are gone?"

"You'll miss me?" I gently mocked.

"Certainly I'll miss you," she said, pretending to be insulted in turn.

"Nothing selfish in that."

Her pretense melted. "There is when all I can think of is day after day of facing that horrible woman and her toadies, instead of worrying about you being off by yourself."

"Oh."

"Don't think badly of me, Jonathan."

"I don't. Believe me, I do not. I've just never thought of how things might be for you while I'm gone."

"Then thank you for thinking of it now. But it mightn't last forever, you know. You saw how it went at church today. She and that precious pair plan to go calling tomorrow, but I believe many of the people they'll visit to be unavailable. Oh, dear, what's wrong?" Her forehead wrinkled at my expression.

"I just don't feel this action is worthy of you."

She started to either object or defend, then caught herself. Her face grew hard. "Indeed, it is not, but she hurt me terribly and I want to hurt her back. It may not be very Christian, but it does make me feel better."

"I know, I just don't want you to become so accustomed to it that it consumes you, otherwise when I return, I shall not recognize you, either."

The feeling behind the words got through to her. "You believe I might become like her?"

"Not at all, but I should not like to see you influenced by her into becoming someone you are not."

"God forbid," she murmured, staring at the floor. "Mirrors can be awful things, can't they? But they do give you the truth when you bother to look in them."

"I don't mean to hurt you . . ."

"No. I understand what you mean."

"What will you do?"

"Whether my actions demean me or not, I will see them through. If Mother leaves, well and good, if not, then perhaps I may adopt Father's example and leave the house myself. I have many friends I can visit, but give me some time, little brother, and trust in my own sense of honor."

There was a word to make me wince. After that, I stopped chiding her.

Hopes of a reprieve dashed, there was little else to do but follow Father's advice. I played the puppet in Mother's presence and it paid handsomely. The allowance Father was able to arrange for me was more than generous. Perhaps she was trying to buy my affection. Perhaps she just didn't care. Only later did I realize that her purpose was for me to make an impressive show to others. She gave many tedious lectures instructing me on how to behave myself once I was in England. I'd had lessons a few years before, but for a while feared that she'd hire another dancing master to refresh my memory about correct posturing in polite company.

The next month saw me through a round of farewell parties with our friends, fittings for new clothes, and careful decisions on what to take along. As Elizabeth had predicted, Mother's reception into our circle had turned decidedly cool, but there were some occasions that required the presence of our whole family, so the woman got her share of social engagements. These were enough to satisfy her, but Elizabeth was sure that once I was off to England a dramatic drop in invitations would take place. She promised to write me in full detail.

I used my penknife to work out more pieces from another broken walnut. Across the room an argument was going on between two drunken workmen that looked like it was going to develop into a full-blown battle. Their accents were so thick I couldn't make sense of what they were shouting, though the swearing was clear enough. A group of ladies huddled together and stopped up their ears, except for one who fell to praying. She started with a little scream when one of her friends accidentally brushed her ear with an upraised elbow.

My teeth crunched against some overlooked shell. I spat it out and continued munching more cautiously. One of the men took a wide swing at the other and missed, generating a lot of amusement in the crowd. Bets were made, but called off when the landlord and a couple of younger men intervened and escorted the drunks outside. A few others joined them, perhaps to see if the fight would continue. I had half a mind to follow, but was too full of food to be bothered.

I spat out another shard of walnut, smug with the knowledge that it would have offended Mother. Across the room the ladies had unstopped their ears and put their heads together for a good talk. One of the younger ones smiled at me. Carefully polite, I nodded back, lazily wondering who and what she was. By her dress, manner, and the company around her I decided that she was not a whore, or else I might have done more than nod. I hadn't forgotten the promise to myself that once on my own I would take the earliest opportunity to lose my virginity.

The pander and his woman came to mind again, only to be dismissed with disgust. I wasn't that desperate or drunk.

The young lady turned her attention back to her friends. My face grew warm as I deduced by their manner that they were talking about me. From the smothered smiles and bright looks thrown my way I concluded that their opinions were highly favorable. I smiled back. Perhaps that first opportunity was about to present itself.

Or perhaps not. The fight between the workmen had developed into what sounded like a proper war. Though I hadn't followed the two combatants outside, others had, and in a few scant moments sides were taken and blows were struck. Members of the inn's staff abruptly disappeared, though two of the maids clogged the room's one window trying to keep up with the course of the battle.

"Jem's got that 'un!"

"Arr, he's bitin' orf 'is ear! Get 'im, Jem!"

Then both girls squeaked and jumped back. A young tough with a bleeding ear sprawled half in and out of the opening. Before his admirers could rush to his aid, he raised up, threw us all a foolish grin of pure glee, and bobbed from sight. The girls returned to the window to cheer him on.

The more refined ladies of the neighboring table had produced screams of alarm, but crowded toward the door for the purpose of escape. They were hampered by others in the hall without, who were apparently trying to get out for a better view of the fight. The smiling girl was among them.

So much for that opportunity, however slim it had been. I stood, brushed stray crumbs from my clothes, and made for the window. Offering my apologies to the maids, I pushed past them and stepped through it into the courtyard to see what all the commotion was about.

A wild-eyed man who had lost his shirt, but retained his neck cloth, rushed past me waving a bucket and howling. The man he seemed to be pursuing was making an equal amount of noise but in a slightly different key. A dozen other men were having a sort of wrestling match with one another in the middle of the yard. On the edge of their muddy sprawl of arms and legs, I spotted the porter swinging a cudgel and bellowing in triumph each time he connected successfully with someone's head. He'd worked out a simple routine of knocking a man senseless, then moving on so the waiters could pull the body from the fray. They had the start of a fine stack of them by now, though it wasn't much of a discouragement to newcomers eager to join the riot.

"What's it all about?" I asked a young gentleman next to me, who was content to be only a witness rather than a participant. He wore dusty riding clothes and an eager expression.

"God knows, but isn't it grand? Five shillings that that big fellow with the scar will be the last to drop."

"Done," I said, and we shook on it. I kept my eye on the porter and was not disappointed. Before long, he worked his way 'round to the fellow in question and gave him a solid thump behind the ear. The result fell short of my expectations, for he only went down on one knee, shook his head, and was up and swinging as though nothing had happened. The waiters wisely passed him by.

"Bad for you," said the gentleman.

"There's time yet."

My faith in the porter's arm was given a second test. As he made another circle of the gradually diminishing fighters, he was able to use his cudgel on the man again. This time more force was applied and the fellow was knocked to both knees. He got up more slowly, but he did get up.

"What's his skull made of?" I asked. "Stone?"

"Cracked him a good one, though. He's drawn blood, see?"

That was a good sign. Stones don't bleed. I called encouragement to the porter for another try, but he was distracted when the man with the bucket blundered into him. Both fell over into the general melee and were momentarily lost. The porter emerged first, roaring with outrage. When he swung his cudgel back to deal with the newcomer, it caught the scarred man in the belly by mistake and he suddenly dropped from sight.

"Third time's the charm," I said. We waited, anxious for different reasons, but the man remained down. The waiters darted forward and dragged him out. Three more men waded in to help the porter and amid groans, curses, and with the breaking of a few more skulls, order was gradually restored to the courtyard.

The gentleman shook his head and paid up. "What a show. Pity it was so short." He was about my age or older, with a high forehead, long chin, and broad, childish mouth, the corners of which were turned down as he settled his debt. He had very wide-awake blue eyes that added to the somewhat foolish air of his overall expression.

"Pity indeed," I agreed. "Since there's no chance for you to win this back may I buy you something to ease the sting of your loss?"

He cheered up instantly. "That's very generous of you, my friend. Yes, you may. It's too damned hot out here, don't you think?"

We retired to the common room, but found it quite clear of waiters, maids, and guests.

"Probably still cleaning up the mess," he said, then proceeded to bellow for assistance. A boy cautiously appeared and I promptly sent him off to fetch us beer.

"Unless you'd prefer something else?" I asked.

He threw himself into a chair. "No, no. Beer's what's wanted on a day like this. I've been on the road all morning and have a great thirst."

"Traveling much farther?"

"Only to this roach trap. I'm supposed to meet some damned cousin of mine and take him home."

"Really?"

"Damned nuisance it is, but—" A new thought visibly invaded his brain. "Oh, dear, suppose he's out there among the wounded?" He launched from the chair toward the window and leaned out, shouting questions to the men in the yard. I sat back to watch the show. He excused himself to me and went over the sill to investigate something, but returned just as the beer arrived.

"Did you find your cousin?" I asked.

"Thought I had, but the man was too old."

"What does he look like?"

"Oh, about this tall, forty if he was a day, and bald as—"

"I mean, what does your *cousin* look like?"

"Oh . . . him. Damned if I know. He's fresh off the boat from one of the colonies. Probably gets himself up with feathers and paint like a red Indian."

"Really? What's he over here for?"

"Come to get an education. We're going to be at Cambridge together, but since he's supposed to be reading law and I'm doing medicine, we might be spared one another's company."

"What? You've never met the chap and you don't like him?"

"I daresay I won't if he has Fonteyn blood in him. Not that I'm against my own family, but some of the folk out of Grandfather Fonteyn's side of things would be better off in Bedlam, if you know what I mean."

"Bedlam?"

"That great asylum where they put the mad people. Damn, but that was good beer. Here, boy! Bring us another! That is, if you care to have one, sir."

"Yes, certainly. You intrigue me, sir. About this cousin of yours . . . would he be about my age, do you think?"

He squinted at me carefully. "I'd say so." His mobile face suddenly went blank, then his eyes sharpened with alarm. "Oh, good God."

"I'm not that awful, am I?"

His jaw flapped as he tried to put words to a situation that required none. As he floundered, the beer was brought in.

"Would you care for anything to eat, Cousin?" I asked while the boy put down his tray.

"A pox on you, sir, for misleading me," he cried.

"And my apologies, sir, for being unable to resist the temptation to do so."

"Well-a-day, I've never heard of such a thing."

"Perhaps it is the Fonteyn blood showing through. Jonathan Barrett, at your service, good cousin." I stood and bowed to him.

"A fine introduction this is, to be sure. Oh, pox on it!" He stood and gave a hasty bow, extending his hand and smiling broadly. "Oliver Marling, at yours."

"Oliver 'Fonteyn' Marling?"

He made a face. "For God's sake, just call me Oliver. I absolutely *detest* my middle name!"

Not that I'd had any misgivings about the man after the first few moments of speaking with him, but now I hailed him as a true kinsman in heart as well as by blood. We enjoyed more than a few beers that afternoon, ate like starving pigs that evening, drank an amazing amount of spirits, and talked and talked and talked. By the time we'd passed out and had been carried upstairs to our room by the staff, we were the best of friends.

The morning sunlight was mercifully subdued through the tiny window, but still enough to dangerously heat my brain to the bursting point. My eyes felt as though someone had hammered gravel into each socket. I groaned, but refrained from touching my head for fear that it might pop from my neck and go rolling around the floor. The noise alone would have killed me.

All I could see of cousin Oliver were his riding boots, which were on a pillow next to me. For all the movement on that side of the bed he might have been a corpse. Lucky for him if he were dead, for then he would be spared the abominable pain of recovery from a drinking bout that would have left Dionysus himself flat on his face for a week.

Around and below us came the sounds of the inn, which had apparently awakened some time ago. With no consideration whatsoever for our possibly mortal condition, business was proceeding as usual.

When I'd reached the point where walking around in agony would be no different from lying around in agony, I made an attempt to get out of bed. The thing was rather high, so the drop was an awful shock. The thud I made upon landing must have been heard throughout the rest of the house. It certainly echoed through my fragile head with alarming consequences. How fortunate for me that I was now within grasping distance of the chamber pot. I seized it and dragged it toward me just in time.

The next few minutes were really horrible, but when the last coughing convulsion had played itself out, I felt slightly improved. I wanted to crawl back to bed again, but hadn't the strength for it. Shoving the pot away, I flopped on my back and prayed for God to have mercy on one of his more foolish sheep.

Some idiot pounded on the door as though to break it down. Without pausing for an invitation, one of the waiters entered and looked things over.

"Thought I'd 'eard you stirrin', sir. Would yer be wantin' ter breaks yer fast now?"

I was wanting to break his neck for shouting so loudly, but couldn't move. All I could do was give him a glassy stare from where I lay at his feet and think ill thoughts.

"Well, p'haps not. Tell yer what, I'll 'ave some tea 'n' a bit of bread sent up. T'will do 'til you find yer legs, haw-haw." Booming with his own cleverness, he left, slamming the door so hard I thought the bones in my skull would split open from the sound.

There was a bowl and a pitcher on a table across the room. The idea occurred to me that splashing water on the back of my neck might be of restorative value. I managed to get to my knees and crawled over. The pitcher was empty. It seemed pointless to exert effort to return to bed, so I gave up and sat with my back to the wall, waiting for the man to reappear with the promised tea.

He must have been distracted by other duties. The whole long dizzy morning seemed to pass before he pounded on the door again and came in with his tray.

"Yer lucky, sir. Cook just had some fresh made up, 'ot 'n' strong." He put the tray on another table, poured out a cup, and brought it over. I held it tenderly in trembling fingers and sipped. "That'll set yer right as rain. Now what 'bout this 'un?" He indicated Oliver, who had not yet moved.

"Leave him," I whispered.

"Shouldn't leave 'is arm draggin' on the floor like that. 'E'll lose all feelin' in it." He helpfully pulled Oliver's arm up, but it only dropped down again. A second attempt got the same results, so he lightly flipped Oliver over on his back. Bidding us both a good morning, he left, thundering down the hall and stairs like a plowhorse with eight legs.

I drained the cup, waited a few minutes, and decided the stuff would stay down after all. Pushing against the wall, I stood, staggered to the table, and poured another, but drank it more slowly. Bit by bit, my brain began to cool and a few of the more alarming symptoms subsided. The chances that I would ultimately recover were increasing.

On his back, with his mouth sagging wide, Oliver began to snore. There was an almost soothing note to it, though it gradually increased in loudness. To take my mind from my own miseries, I listened with interest to see just how loud he could get.

Loud enough. My interest waned as the very blood under my hair began to throb in time to his rumblings. It was a wonder he did not wake himself from the noise. He snorted and snarled, gave out a gasp as though he'd inhaled an insect, and suddenly a prodigious sneeze exploded from his slack lips. It was enough to stir the cobwebs in the far corners. This did succeed in waking him, poor man. He stared at the ceiling with the same kind of glazed stupefaction as I had earlier.

Still whispering, out of respect to his heightened senses, I said, "It's just under the bed on this side."

He didn't take my meaning at first, but gradually his face turned a predictable green, and with the color came comprehension. He wallowed over on his stomach, clawed for the chamber pot, and made his own contribution to it.

"Oh, God," he moaned pitifully afterward, quite unable to move. With a cautious toe, I shoved the pot and its offensive contents back under the bed. Oliver put his hands over his ears and moaned again as it scraped over the bare wood of the floor.

I mercifully said nothing and poured him half a cup of tea. His hands were unsteady. Still lying on his stomach, partly off the bed, he drank it down, and I caught the cup before he could drop it.

"Well-a-day," he murmured, his head hanging down and his mouth muffled by the bedding. "We must have had a magnificent time last night."

"Indeed we did. So much so that we may never survive another. Was it you or that other chap who poured wine on the fiddler?"

"What other chap?"

"The little round fellow who lost his wig in the fire."

"He didn't lose it, you threw it there."

I took a moment to recollect the incident. "Oh, yes. The fool was bothering the serving maid and I thought he needed a lesson."

"Good thing for you he wasn't the sort to demand satisfaction or you'd have had to be up at dawn."

So terrible was the idea of getting up that early with such a pain in my head that it hardly bore thinking about. "Was it you or him?"

"What?"

"That poured the wine in the—"

"Oh. Him. Definitely him. Fellow had too much to drink, y'know. Disgraceful. What did you think you were doing defending that wench's honor, anyway?"

"I just can't abide a man forcing his attentions on a woman."

"Didn't know they raised knight errants in the colonies. Have to be cafrill . . . I mean, careful. The next man might force the issue, then you'd have to kill him and marry the girl."

"Why should I have to marry the girl?"

He paused in thought. "Damned if I know. What time is it? What *day* is it? Is there any more tea?"

There was and I gave it to him. Neither of us were ready for even the simplest of food, so we left the bread alone. When we each became more certain of our eventual recovery, I slowly opened the shutters to bring in some fresher air. The chamber pot was rapidly becoming a nuisance.

Oliver managed to leave the bed and join me at the table. He surveyed himself, peered closely at my face, and shook his head.

"This won't do. Can't go home looking like this. Mother would burst a blood vessel if she knew about this drunken debauch and we'd never hear the end of it."

In our rambling talk last night, he'd made frequent mention of his mother. His descriptions bore a remarkable similarity to my own parent.

"Won't she be just as angry if we're late?"

"Oh, I can say your ship was held up or something. We needn't worry about that. A day's rest will do us a world of good, but I don't fancy spending it cooped up here. What we want is a bit of activity to sweat all the wine out of us."

He lapsed into a silence so lengthy that I wondered if he was hoping I would take on the responsibility of finding a solution. Being an utter stranger to London, not to mention the rest of the country, the odds against my being of any help in the matter seemed very high.

"Got it!" he said, animation returning to his vacuous face. "We'll go over to Tony Warburton's. You'll want to meet him, so it may as well be now."

"Won't we be an intrusion upon him?"

"Hardly. Tony's used to it. He's part of our circle, you know, and since you're with me, that means you're in, too. He's studying medicine as well, but I'll see to it that he doesn't bore you."

Oliver assured me that his friend would not only welcome our visit, but insist that we stay the night. With this in mind I gladly settled things with the landlord and saw to it that my baggage was brought down. It took a surprising number of servants for this task, and several more turned up to receive their vails for services rendered during my overnight stay, including many that I'd never seen before. Perhaps they'd been on duty when I had not been in a condition to later remember them. It sufficed that some of the shillings I'd won from Oliver magically vanished in much less time than it had taken to win them.

In the courtyard, Oliver stood ready by his horse, a big bay mare with long, solid legs and clear, bright eyes. I couldn't help but express my admiration for the animal and in turn received a list of famous names in her pedigree. None of them meant anything to me, but they sounded impressive, nonetheless.

He had hired an open pony cart for our conveyance, meaning to lead the mare rather than ride her. The cart's inward-facing benches would allow us to enjoy conversation, yet there was enough space to stow my luggage. Another advantage was that the cart was narrow enough to navigate the crowded streets with reasonable efficiency.

I say reasonable, because once we left the inn and were well on our way, the noise and crowds of the city were all but overwhelming to my country-bred senses. Everywhere I looked were people of all shapes, classes, and colors, each of them busy as ants with as many occupations as could ever be imagined, plus a few beyond imagining. My long-ago visit to Philadelphia had not prepared me for such numbers or variety. Even the great and busy colonial city of New York, which I had glimpsed on my way to the ship that carried me here, was a bumpkin's backwater village compared to this.

The air hummed with a thousand different voices, each calling their wares, services, begging, or just shouting for no other purpose than to make noise. Soldiers and sailors, chimney sweeps and their boys, panders and prostitutes, well-dressed ladies and their maids, men of fashion and threadbare clerics all jostled, laughed, argued, screeched, or sang with no regard for anyone but themselves and their business. I forgot my aching head and fairly gaped at the show.

"Is it always like this?" I asked Oliver, raising my voice as well so he could hear me, though he was hardly an arm's length away.

"Oh, no," he bellowed back. "Sometimes it's *much* worse!"

I thought he was having a joke on me, but he'd taken the question quite seriously and expanded on his answer. "This is a normal working day in the city, y'know. You should be here on a holiday or when there's a hanging or two at Tyburn, then things really liven up!"

Oliver drew my attention to various places of interest whenever possible. The buildings loomed so high in spots that it was apparent that the sun even at its summer zenith was an infrequent visitor to the streets between. In one patch of open area, though, he was able to point out the masts of a ship standing improbably among the buildings and trees.

"That's Tower Hill, of course, and the ship itself is on perfectly dry land."

"What good is that, then?"

"Oh, it's done no end of good for the navy. If some unwary soul has the bad luck to stop for a look he has to pay dearly for his curiosity."

"What? You mean they offer a tour of the place? Is the fee so great?"

"Great enough for most. The fellow offering to show them around is part of a press gang. More than one hapless lad fresh in from the country has been trapped that way and may never set foot on land again. Foreigners are fairly safe, and so are gentlemen, and since you're both in one, you've nothing to fear from them. Still, I can't help but pity the poor men who wander into that pretty snare." He gave a sincere shudder and by some leap of thought I got the idea that he may have had some personal experience in the matter.

We jolted and wove our way through the many streets for more than an hour, though the distance we traveled could not have been more than a couple of miles. The sights and distractions were many and Oliver was pleased with my reactions to them, enjoying his role of playing the guide as much as I was at playing the tourist.

Presently, Oliver gave the cart man more specific directions and we stopped before a tall and broad house of white stone with black paint trimming the proportionately broad windows. Because Oliver had mentioned the tax upon windows, I could see that the owner of this place was in such a financial position as to be untroubled by the added expense. Already this looked to be a highly favorable exchange for the mean little room I'd had at the inn.

We left the cart, mounted the front steps, and Oliver gave the bell a vigorous pull. A servant soon opened the door and welcomed us inside. He was well acquainted with Oliver and, after sending a footman off to inform the master of the house about his guests, inquired how best to provide for our immediate comfort.

"Barley water, if you please," said Oliver, after a brief consultation with me. "And some biscuits if you have 'em and some ass's milk if it's fresh."

The butler appeared to be somewhat puzzled. "Nothing else, sir?"

"Crispin, if you'd drunk all that we had last night and woke up with all the agonies we had this morning . . ."

Abrupt understanding dawned upon Crispin's face and he vanished to see to things, including the cart waiting outside. He soon returned with a large tray and made us feel at home, explaining that his master would be delayed from joining us immediately. In the meantime, the barley water, though not as good as beer, quenched our thirst, and the biscuits settled the growlings in our stomachs.

"I took the liberty," said Crispin as he poured the milk from a silver pitcher, "of adding some eggs and honey to this. Mr. Warburton swears by its restorative powers."

"Lord, is he studying to be a physician or an apothecary? Never mind answering that. If old Tony has frequent occasion to turn to this for relief, then he's going to be a drunkard. Oh, it's all right, Jonathan, no need to look shocked. Tony knows it's all in jest. He's really a frightfully sharp student, but like the rest of us, he enjoys having a good time when he can."

The mixture in the ass's milk was more than palatable and after seeing to Crispin's vail and to the footmen for fetching my luggage in we were left on our own.

Our room was decorated well and in good taste, though a bit stuffy. I suggested opening a window, but Oliver pointed out that the close air within was preferable to the noisome odors without. Sensing my restlessness, he tossed me a copy of the *Gentleman's Magazine.* Father subscribed to it himself, but the issues we received were necessarily out of date by several months owing to the long ocean crossing. This one was only a month old and I welcomed the somewhat fresher news.

I flipped idly through the pages, taking note of an article about the comet that on my voyage had caused much excitement and interest in the middle of June. Owing to clouds, the writer was unable to add to what I had been able to see trailing across the southern sky. My chief memory was not so much of the comet, but the superstitious reaction the sailors had had to it. During the week or so that it was visible, there had been much muttering, praying, and wearing of charms against any evil it might bring. Though our captain was a man of very solid sense, he let them have their way in this, but saw to it that they were kept busy lest they brood upon their fears and get up to mischief.

I moved on to another article describing the bloody war raging between the Turks and Russians. There was an annex page that folded out into a very fine map of Greece, and from it I was able to pick out some of the famous cities that had been mentioned in my study of the language with Rapelji. The many details delighted me and I hoped that my father would share it with him when his issue arrived. I was about to comment to Oliver about it when the young master of the house chose that moment to make his entrance.

He was a bit haggard in his appearance, a match to our own, no doubt, and despite the amount of time he'd had to ready himself, he was clad informally in a sweeping mustard-colored dressing gown, plain cotton stockings, and bright red slippers. An elaborate turban covered much of his head, though it was very askew, showing the light, shaven scalp beneath. His eyes were a bit sunken and his flesh pale, but his manner was hearty as he came forward to greet us. Oliver introduced us and we made our bows to one another. Tony Warburton just managed to catch the turban in time to prevent it from dropping off at our feet.

"Oliver, my dear friend, I am delighted that you've come," he said, righting it and himself. He fell wearily into a chair. "The truth is something's happened and I if I don't tell anyone, I'm certain to burst."

Oliver threw me a glance to assure me that his friend's somewhat theatrical attitude was normal. "What has happened? You're looking a bit done in."

"Really? I feel wonderful."

"Not some calamity, I hope?"

"Hardly that. It's truly the best thing that's ever happened to me in my entire life."

My cousin now gave me a quick wink, which Tony missed, for he was staring wistfully at the ceiling. "If it is good news, then by all means, please share it."

"The greatest news possible for any man." He tugged absently at his indifferently knotted neck cloth. "Oliver, my best friend, the best of all my friends, I'm in love!"

Oliver clasped his hands around one knee, pursed his lips, and leaned forward with polite interest. "What? Again?"

# CHAPTER 5

Tony was oblivious to his friend's doubt.

"This is well and truly real love," he continued. "This is what I've awaited my whole life. Until last night all my existence has been a wasteland, a wilderness of nothing, a desert. . . ."

He went on like that for quite some time until Oliver managed to get in another question.

"Who is this girl?"

"She's not a girl; she's a fairy princess come from *A Midsummer Night's* what-you-call-it. No, she's more than that; she is a goddess. She makes all other women look like . . . like . . ."

"Mortals, I suppose. What's her name, Tony?"

"Nora. Isn't it beautiful? It's like some rare flower on a moonlit hillside. Oh, wait 'til you meet her and you'll see what I mean. My words fall utterly short of the reality."

Oliver doggedly went on. "Nora who?"

"Jones. Miss Nora Jones."

The name was still unfamiliar to Oliver. "She sounds wonderful. Where does she work?"

Tony snapped his head 'round, full of outrage. "Good God, man! She's a respectable lady. How dare you?"

Oliver made an about-face of his own toward true contrition. "I do beg your pardon, I'm sure. I had no idea. My most humble apologies, to you, to her, and to her family. Who are they, anyway?"

Tony settled back and after a moment's consideration, accepted the apology. "The Jones family, I suppose."

"From Wales, are they?"

"France, actually."

"France? How can someone named Jones be from France?"

"Obviously they're not, you great fool—she's just *come* from France! Been living abroad for her health and only recently returned to London."

"How did you meet her?"

"Robert—that's Robert Smollett—" he said as an aside to me, "had a musical evening on last night and she was one of the guests. She was there with his sister and Miss Glad and Miss Bolyn and all that crowd. She stood out like a rose in a field of weeds. She's the most beautiful, the brightest, the most graceful creature I ever had the fortune to clap eyes upon."

"She must be something if she can eclipse Charlotte Bolyn," said Oliver. "But we shall have to see her for ourselves to make sure your praises haven't been overly influenced by the strength of your feelings."

Tony smiled with patronizing confidence. "Of course, of course. Seeing is believing with you. But I can promise that you will not be disappointed. The Bolyns are giving a party of their own tonight and I've been invited, which means you can both come with me. It's in honor of some foreign composer who's gotten to be favorite in the more fashionable circles, but if we're lucky, we won't have to waste any time on him. Think you can come?"

"Given the chance to prepare. My cousin may need a bit of help. His clothes have been crammed into a sea chest for the last couple of months and—"

"Oh, that's nothing. I'll have Crispin look over the lot and dust everything off for you."

"Dust was hardly my concern, Mr. Warburton, considering that I was on board a ship the whole time," I put in.

Tony waved away my reservations. "Just leave it all to Crispin. You're in the hands of an expert. He never lets me out the door unless I look respectable. I only got away with this costume because he was busy with you two. You must both forgive me, I was up very late last night."

We protested that we were not in the least offended, then he lapsed into more praise about Nora Jones.

"I'm going to marry her, Oliver. I mean it. I'm quite serious this time, so stop laughing. Those other girls were a fool's whim, a passing fancy. This is the real and true thing. I know. I even dreamed about her last night. Thought she was right there in my room, so I shall have to marry her to save her reputation. For God's sake, don't you dare repeat that to anyone. The gossips in this town would turn a beautiful dream into a pit full of night soil given half a chance."

"And just how beautiful was this dream?" asked Oliver, unable to suppress a grin.

Tony's pale skin reddened. "None of your damned business, sir! I wish I'd never mentioned it. What are you here for, anyway, besides to distract me from joyful thoughts of my one true love?"

Oliver told him about our own party last night and the need to recover away from his mother's sharp and disapproving eye.

"Can't blame you for that," said Tony. "It's just as well my parents and the rest of the family are away at Bath taking the waters. Lord have mercy, I can hardly wait to take my examines this year. As soon as I set up a practice, I'm getting my own place. I might even be able to take Crispin along, if I can persuade him. He's a terribly superior sort, y'know. Might think it beneath himself to leave this household for another, even if it is mine. Servants!" He concluded with a shake of his head.

Oliver commiserated; I said nothing. Jericho could easily have come with me, but was convinced that if he left, his place in the house might be filled by another servant more suitable to my mother than myself, despite Father's promise to the contrary.

Jericho and I discussed the subject seriously and thoroughly and concluded that he would be happier left at home. Though I respected his wishes, I could not be accused of being content with the outcome. Now that I was off the ship and in surroundings similar in many ways to that home, I missed his company.

Perhaps it was for the best, for I'd realized he would look after Elizabeth in my absence and had left him a sufficient amount of money to post letters to me at regular intervals. I had charged him to send reports of all the other news that my sister might be unaware of or ignore from lack of interest. He knew how to read and write for I had taught him, having followed Rapelji's example that a lesson is more thoroughly learned when one must teach it to another. However, Jericho and I had long ago decided never to speak of it, for many people thought it dangerous to have educated slaves, and his busy life might be unpleasantly complicated by their disapproval. Father was in on the secret, though, and, of course, Elizabeth.

I wondered and hoped that they were all right and enjoying good health. That one hope and many, many nebulous worries about them returned sharply to mind, along with a familiar ache to my heart.

"Why such a long face, cousin?" Oliver asked.

"I feel like 'a stranger in a strange land,' " I replied mournfully.

"Eh?"

"He means he's a long way from home," explained Tony. "What we need is something to occupy the time until this evening. I was going to go someplace today, but I'm damned if I can remember where. Crispin!"

His shout brought the butler and a quick question got a quick response.

"You are to visit Bedlam today, sir," he said.

"Bedlam? Are you sure?"

"Your ticket for entry is on the hall table, sir."

Oliver was all interest. "Really? That would be a treat."

Tony was dubious. "You think so?"

"Oh, yes. You know how fascinated I am in such things." He turned to me. "You used to be able to get in whenever you pleased, but the governors of the hospital shut that down. It's a shame too, because they were bringing in a good six hundred a year from the admissions. Now one has to have special permission and a signed pass. Not everyone can get it, you know. This is a wonderful bit of luck."

"For you, perhaps," said Tony. "I don't feel I'm up to it, even if it is for the furtherance of my education. Why don't you go in my place, then tell me all about it later? I don't share your passion for studying lunatics."

"Surely you won't want to miss this opportunity?"

"Surely I do. I have other ways to entertain myself; I'm sure of it."

"This is hardly for base entertainment, Tony. I'll be going there to learn something."

His friend burst into laughter. "Oh, the things I could say to that."

Oliver scowled. "What things? What?"

"Nothing and everything. You're better than a thousand tonics, my dear fellow. You two go on to Bedlam and get all the education you want, but please, leave me to rest up here. After the excitement of meeting sweet, lovely Nora, I still feel quite drained and need to recover. I want to be at my best tonight."

Oliver's scowl instantly vanished and he gave up trying to fathom the cause of his friend's amusement. "If you're certain."

"Yes. I shall do nothing more strenuous today than compose some sonnet, an inadequate tribute to her beauty."

That ultimately decided things for Oliver. He pulled out a great gold watch. "Very well. We've plenty of time, perhaps we can even take in Vauxhall, too."

Tony held up a cautioning finger. "But I thought you wanted to remain sober?"

"Damn. Yes, you're right. We'd better stay away from there 'til later."

"Come back at six and I'll have my barber scrape your chins off."

* * *

We took our leave of Tony Warburton, redeemed our hats and walking sticks from a footman, then sent him off to secure a couple of sedan chairs for us.

"I think it's worked out for the best for him not to come," Oliver remarked as we waited outside. "When he's in this kind of a humor, he's likely to try out lines of his poem on us."

"He's such a bad poet?"

"Don't ask me to judge that. One and all, my friends assure me that I can't tell the difference between Shakespeare and popular doggerel."

"Then what's the problem?"

"It just occurred to me that it might be a bad idea to enter Bedlam followed by a lovesick fool who's sure to disrupt things by lapsing into verses about his wife-to-be whenever the fancy takes him. We might never get him out again."

The chairs arrived and I listened closely while Oliver haggled over the price with the men. The only way to cease being a stranger in this land was to learn how things were run and the minutiae of local customs. Since I would be living here for at least four years, it was to my best advantage to keep my eyes and ears open at all times.

This resolve, I was to find out, was somewhat restricted once I got into my sedan chair. Though it had two large windows on either side, the view was much more limited than the one I'd enjoyed on the pony cart. Owing to my natural height, my head nearly brushed the roof and frequently did so as the bearers bounced along their way. We passed by other chairs with more top room, something necessary to the ladies within who wished to preserve the state of their hair. I noticed that the leather ceiling of my own bore oily evidence that more than one woman had been here before, leaving behind a dark stain mingled with white flecks where the lard and rice flour had rubbed off.

"Have a care, sir!" one of the bearers warned when I leaned too far out a window to catch a glimpse of the myriad sights we passed. My enthusiasm was an endangerment to their balance. Having no wish to crash face first into the filthy cobbles, I forced myself to keep still and resolved to engage some other means of travel for the return trip. Anything, up to and including being pushed along in a barrow, would be considered. Confined like this and cut off from conversation with Oliver, the hundreds of questions popping into my head with each new sight had to go unanswered. There being so many, I regretfully knew I'd never remember them all later, for surely they would be replaced by others.

At least I was being spared the grime of the streets and shaded from the sun, but despite these advantages, the ride was long and wearisome. If not for the guiding presence of my cousin I should also be quite lost, for I had no idea where we were or where we had come from. Though the bearers might have little trouble navigating to and fro through the crowds boiling around us, I would not have been able to find my way back to Warburton's unaided.

I was very glad when we arrived.

Though our destination was a hospital for lunatics, it turned out to be a pleasant and restful sight; I had expected something much smaller and meaner than the building before us. Vast and long, three stories high, with tall towers marking the corner turning of each wing and the tallest of all in the center, Bedlam, once known as the hospital of Bethlehem, looked as fair as any edifice I had so far seen in this great city. We stood at the beginning of a wide lane leading directly to the central entrance from the street. On either side, a simple white fence enclosed sections of the front grounds, protecting the perfectly spaced trees within. If one grew tired of observing the inmates, this wholesome patch of greenery would serve to soothe the eye.

There were few people about, though the quiet air carried an odd note to it that I did not immediately identify. As we drew closer to the entry, it increased and became more varied until I finally identified it as the drone of human voices. Drone would serve for want of a better word, for it frequently broke off into high laughter or outright screaming. The hair on my head began to rise and for the first time I questioned my cousin's wisdom in bringing me with him.

Unaware of my misgivings, he presented his ticket to the proper authority and after a delay that only increased my unease, we were assigned a guide to take us around. Though Oliver was the medical student, I was not, but no question against my being here was ever raised. Oliver said the right things and asked intelligent questions, while I nodded and imitated his manner so as to not arouse suspicion. In truth, I need not have gone to such trouble. On the one hand, no one was too curious about us, on the other, after five minutes, I would not at all have minded being expelled.

Our guide led us into the men's wing only, the women's side being barred to us. Some of the more lucid inmates were allowed to take their exercise in the halls, all of them closely watched by their keepers. Only because they were somewhat better dressed than their charges, and armed with clubs and keys, was I able to tell them one from another.

Though assured by our guide that the straw in the cells was frequently changed, the stench of filthy bodies, night soil, and rotten food pervaded every breath in the place. My cousin and I found some relief by holding handkerchiefs to our noses, which amused the guide and the other keepers. They maintained that they were quite used to it and we should soon be, too. I prayed that we should not stay so long as to verify the truth of their statement.

Some of the more interesting cases were pointed out to us, and Oliver took time to study each with an absorption that surprised me. Flighty as he seemed most of the time, here he was a genuine student, apparently as serious in his pursuit of knowledge as I when the fit was upon him. It was contagious, for his comments to me quickened my own curiosity and sparked a lengthy conversation on the causes of madness.

"You and I both know that it can be passed along in the blood," he said. "There are whole families running loose that should be chained up in the basement. But some of these cases just seem to come out of nowhere as if the wretch had been struck by lightning. That fellow back there in the straw cap preaching so fervently to the wall is an excellent example. You missed hearing about him, but his keeper said that his was such an occurrence. He was once a curate and while doing his rounds one day, he just fell right over. They thought it was apoplexy or too much sun or the flying gout, but he fully recovered the next day, except for his wits, which were all gone. Now he thinks he's a bishop and spends all his time in theological argument with invisible colleagues. To add to the singularity of his circumstances, his arguments are quite sane and sound. I listened to him and he makes more sense than others I've heard of a Sunday."

The poor man was certainly in a minority, for all those around him either stared at nothing with frightened or blank faces or raved in their cells, rattling their chains and howling in a most pitiful way. If anyone became violent, then others might follow, so the keepers had to watch them constantly. I'm sorry to say that when drawn to one of the barred windows set in the stout door of a cell, the creature within began screeching in a most alarming way at the sight of me. I fell back at once, but that alone did not calm him and he continued until a keeper opened the door and threw a bucket of water on him. This inspired much merriment in those others who were able to appreciate it. The screams turned to sputtering, died away, and his door was again locked.

"That's the only bath 'e's like to get in a twelvemonth," the grinning keeper confided to me. "Lord knows 'e needs it." Considering the speaker's own utter lack of cleanliness, I thought he had no reason to judge another, especially one unable to care for himself. With my handkerchief firmly in place I caught up with Oliver, who was talking to a lad whose sullen expression reminded me of young Nathan Finch back home.

"I don't belong 'ere," he insisted. " 'm not like them others. I never 'urt no one nor meself, so they got no call to put me 'ere."

"Is this true?" Oliver asked our guide.

" 'Tis true enough the way 'e tells it. He never 'armed 'imself or others, but they put 'im 'ere anyways."

"Why? If he's not mad—"

"Oh, 'e's mad enough, sir, for they found 'im 'sponsible for slittin' open the bellies of a dozen cattle. Said 'e could 'ear the calves 'nside callin' ter get out 'n' 'e were just 'elpin' 'em along lest they smother. They'd a lynched 'im at Tyburn for 'is mischief, but 'e were judged to be too lunatical for it to do 'im any good, so he were brung 'ere. Leastwise 'e won't get no more chance to cut up no more cattle." Laughing heartily at this observation, the guide patted the lad on the head, and moved on. Looking back, I saw the boy make a murderous face at us, followed by an obscene gesture. Harmless or not, I was glad to see that he was solidly chained to a thick staple set in the floor.

The hideous stenches, the noise, the pervading sadness, anguish, and rage assaulting us from every direction were exhausting. After two hours, even Oliver's earnest quest for knowledge began to flag and he inquired if I was prepared to leave. Out of consideration for his feelings, I tried not to appear too eager, but indicated that a change of scene would not be unwelcome to me.

He consulted with the guide and he quickly led us to the entrance where we settled with him and were invited to return at our earliest convenience. Again, he laughed at this, giving the impression that he was not expressing hospitality, but something more sinister. We were outside and well down the lane before finally slowing to a more dignified pace.

"What did you think of it?" asked Oliver.

"While I can appreciate that seeing the sights within was a rare opportunity, I can't honestly say that they were entirely enjoyable."

"I'll be the first to agree with you on that point, but it was certainly of excellent value to a student of the medical arts. I hope I can remember everything for Tony later."

"If not, then please consult me. I'm sure I shan't forget a single detail for the rest of my life. I hope that man of his does as promised with my clothes, the stink of the place clings to me still. I shall want to change them, but what I'd most like is a decent bath."

"Well, if you think you need one," he said, but with some doubt in his tone. "I'm sure something can be arranged before the party tonight. There's the Turkish baths at Covent Garden, but we haven't the time or deep enough pockets, I should think."

"How much could it cost for a bit of soap and water?"

"Very little, but it's the extras like supper and the price of the whore you sleep with that add up, and that can go as high as six guineas."

I abruptly forgot all about Bedlam. "Really?"

Oliver misinterpreted my reaction. "Yes, it's disgusting, isn't it? Even if you forgo the bath and meal, the tarts there will still demand their guineas. And they're not much better looking than the ladies that trade at Vauxhall, who are considerably more reasonable in their prices, I might add."

My head began to reel with excited speculation. "Where is this place?"

He waved a hand. "Oh, you can find it easily enough. But another time, perhaps. We'll have to get back to Tony's before that barber he promised disappears."

It was just not fair. I'd spent a horrid afternoon in Bedlam when I could have been wallowing in a scented bathing pool like a turbaned potentate with any number of beauteous water nymphs seeing to my every need. Though Oliver and I had much in common, it seemed that our ideas on practical education were quite different. I wanted to ask him more about his experiences at Covent Garden and Vauxhall, but we'd reached the end of the lane and had to consider our mode of transport.

After expressing my preference of a cart over a sedan chair, we managed to find one going in the desired direction. This one had outward facing seats and was crowded with other passengers, two of whom were ladies of the respectable sort. Their inhibiting presence kept me from obtaining more details from Oliver, so I had to content myself with conversation on less exciting topics than the tarts of London.

Our trip seemed shorter, whether by speed of the horse, or the amusing nature of my cousin's comments as we traveled. The streets were just as busy as ever as people hurried to finish their errands before nightfall. Oliver said that the city could be a deadly trap to the unwary or the unarmed and if the footpads were bold enough during the day, they were positively bloodthirsty at night. Since we would be going over by carriage, with footmen running before and behind with torches, we would probably be safe enough.

"Can you defend yourself?" he asked.

"Oh, yes." With an easy twist, I opened my walking stick to reveal part of the Spanish steel blade within. Oliver whistled with admiration. "It was a present from Father," I added. "He'd ordered it nearly a year ago, intending it for my last birthday, but delivery was delayed. As it was, it made a fine parting gift for my trip here."

"Or anywhere," he added, his eyes lighting up with a touch of envy. "I shall have to take you along to the fencing gallery we have at Cambridge so you can show us your skill. Tell me, before you left, did you have any opportunity at all to put it to use against the Indians?"

* * *

My lengthy explanation about the lack of hostile natives on Long Island disappointed him, but served to fill the time until we reached Tony Warburton's front steps. Though ostensibly a guest in the house and therefore not subject to paying for lodging and board, I might have spent much less money had I remained at The Three Brewers. The many vails were adding up, and my supply of pennies dwindled before I came to an understanding with the butler that all things would be settled at the end of my visit. This promise, rather than putting the servants off, caused them to be more attentive than before, so my request for a bath was greeted as an easily met challenge rather than an impassable obstacle.

Because Mrs. Warburton was a great believer in maintaining a clean body (hence the family holiday at Bath), facilities were at hand, even if they weren't exactly ready. Two stout boys carried her bathing tub to my room and then lugged bucket after bucket up the stairs to fill it, while another man lighted a fire to warm the room. Though it was August, the weather was cool today, and they weren't going to risk my catching a chill while under their care. Their concern might also have been that if I died from that chill I should be unable to pay them for their trouble. Even so, the water they brought was barely lukewarm.

Ah, but it was water and I sank gratefully into the cramped tub for a much-desired soak. With a fat bar of soap and a flesh brush I was a happy man. Oliver and Tony came in for a short visit to view "the antics of this rustic colonial" as they joked to me. In turn, I shocked them by briefly recounting the many times on the crossing voyage that I had voluntarily stripped and had myself doused with seawater from the deck pump.

"Well-a-day, man, 'tis a wonder you're not dead," Oliver exclaimed with hollow-eyed horror.

"On the contrary, I found it to be refreshing and greatly improving to the appetite." I left off telling them about the awful food.

"He *is* still alive," Tony pointed out.

My cousin conceded that I was, indeed, still alive, by the grace of God and no thanks to my foolish habits.

"You made mention of Turkish bathing, Oliver. How is it so different from this that it is better for the health?" I asked.

"For one thing you're not slopping about in a drafty room, but working up a proper sweat wrapped in a hot blanket."

This didn't sound much like the marble-lined pool surrounded by the graceful seraglio I'd envisioned. He apparently didn't hear my invitation to continue his description, suddenly recalling a task he'd left undone in his room. Tony chuckled at his departure.

"Oliver is a bit bashful when it comes to talking about his wenching," he said. "It seems he'd rather do it than waste time in discussion, which is quite sensible, after all. Perhaps later I can persuade him to take you 'round to meet some of our fair English roses after the party."

*Well-a-day,* I thought, a deep shiver coursing through me at the prospect. I applied the soap to the brush, and the brush to my flesh with happy diligence.

As the boys carried the buckets of dirty water back downstairs, I worked to get my hair combed and dried before the fire. Mother had insisted on fitting me out with a wig, which I suffered to accept in order to keep the peace. However, the one she chose was a monstrous horseshoe toupet nearly a foot high with a sweep of Cadogan puffs hanging from the nape. No doubt another man would look quite handsome in it, but my first glimpse was enough to convince me that my own appearance would be extremely grotesque. I would sooner sport a chamber pot in public than to be seen wearing that thing. Brightly oblivious to my pained expression at the buffoon in my mirror, Mother pronounced that it would be perfect for any and all social functions I should be fortunate enough to attend and gave me lengthy instructions for its proper care. This upcoming musical evening would have met with her rare approval.

But she was thousands of leagues away and unable to command my obedience; I blithely cast the wig aside. This was no light decision for me, though.

During today's travels, I had ample opportunity to observe that no matter how mean their station in life, every Englishman I'd clapped eyes on that day (except for only the worst of the wretches in Bedlam) had worn a wig. Foreigners like myself who chose to eschew the custom were either laughed at for their lack of fashion sense or admired for their eccentricity. Since I had a full head of thick black hair, I would take a bit of sinful pride in what God had given me and wear it as is, tied back with a black ribbon. In this I was almost copying Benjamin Franklin, at least in general principle.

He'd made himself quite popular in polite society by choosing to dress simply and make an affectation out of his lack of affectation. He'd made a sober, but good-humored contrast to all the court peacocks, and had enjoyed no lack of female companionship. Though I utterly disagreed with his politics and those of his fanatical friends, I could admire his wit.

Tony Warburton's barber came and went, leaving my face expertly scraped and powdered dry. He grumbled unhappily over my attitude about the wig, which he had expected to dress. If all gentlemen made such a calamitous decision to go without, he would lose more than half his income. Before sending him on, I compensated him with a generous vail, having made it a practice to always be on good terms with any man who plays around my throat with a razor.

Crispin had lived up to his reputation; all my clothes had been cleaned, aired, and laid out as though new. After careful thought, I picked my somber Sunday clothes, but offset the severe black with an elaborately knotted neck cloth, and highly polished shoes with the new silver buckles. One of the younger footmen had been detailed as my temporary valet and I was pleased with his attention to detail, though I said little lest he develop an exaggerated idea about the size of his vail when I left.

"Heavens!" exclaimed Tony when he and Oliver came to collect me. "They'll think you're some kind of Quaker who came by mistake."

"That or a serious student of the law," I returned with dignity.

Oliver agreed with me. "I think he's made a wise choice. Everyone will expect him to be either an uncivilized savage or an insurrectionist lout. Dressed this way he looks neither; they may trouble themselves to stop and make his acquaintance first out of sheer curiosity at the lack of spectacle."

"Thank you, Cousin. I think."

"Don't mention it," he said cheerfully, and led the way downstairs.

With footmen running before and behind our coach, their torches making a wonderful light in the darkness, we suffered no interference from criminal interlopers on our coach ride to the Bolyn house. It was a big place, and though it probably presented a pleasant face to the world, I hardly noticed for all the people. There seemed to be hundreds of them milling about, reminding me of the crowds I'd seen in the streets earlier, but infinitely better dressed, with less purpose and more posturing. Oliver wanted to stop and talk whenever he saw a familiar face, but Tony kept us moving, as he was anxious to see his Miss Jones again and introduce her.

We did pause long enough to pay our respects to our host and hostess, and Oliver's prediction that my garb would inspire a favorable impression proved true, at least with them. I was asked many questions about the colonies, which I rather inadequately answered, hampered as I was by having lived in only one small part of them. Most of the interesting news had happened elsewhere, though I was able to provide some information regarding Philadelphia. For that I could thank Dr. Theophilous Beldon, who had quite exhausted the novelty of the subject in his efforts to cultivate my friendship before my departure.

He would have loved it here, for I saw many dandies of his type roaming the house and grounds, bowing and toad-eating to their betters to their heart's content. Several in particular stood out so much from the rest that I had to stop and gape. Elizabeth often accused me of being a peacock, but then she'd never seen these beauties.

Their wigs were so white as to blind an observer and so tall as to brush the door lintels. Instead of shoes, they appeared to be wearing slippers; a silver circle served in place of a buckle. They were painted and powdered and so richly dressed that for a moment I thought some members of the court had wandered in by mistake.

I had certainly given thought to augmenting my own wardrobe while in London, but if this was an example of fashion, I would sooner go naked and said as much to Oliver.

"Oh, those are members of the Macaroni Club," he informed me.

"A theatrical troupe, are they?"

"No, scions of wealthy houses. They've done their grand tour of Europe and brought the name back from Italy."

"Name?"

"Macaroni."

What Italian I had learned did not include that particular word, so I asked for a definition.

"It's a kind of dish made of flour and eggs. They boil it."

"Then what?"

"Then they eat it."

I tried to work out how boiled flour and eggs could be made edible and gave up with a shudder.

"Everything these days is done *a la macaroni,* you know. You could do worse than follow their example." He looked upon them with childish envy.

"Truly," I said, as though agreeing with him while thinking, *if worse existed.* "If you admire them so much, why don't you?"

"Mother won't let me," he rumbled, and for a few seconds a singularly nasty expression occupied his normally good-natured face. I'd seen it briefly last night when we'd talked about ourselves and our families while getting so terrifically drunk. It worked across the lean muscles of his cheeks and brow like a thunderstorm. Even without any knowledge of our family ties, I would have recognized the Fonteyn blood in him at that moment. He seemed aware that he was revealing something better left hidden and glanced away as though seeking any kind of a distraction to help him mask the thoughts within.

"Awful, isn't it?" I said aloud, without meaning to.

Though surprised, he instantly understood my meaning and looked hard at me, his eyes oddly clear and sharp with sudden weariness, as though waiting for an expected blow to fall now that I'd gotten his attention. None did.

The odd silence between us lengthened. "I just know it really is awful," I murmured, trying to fill it, but unable to think of anything better to say.

Some of the tightness of his posture, which I hadn't noticed until he shifted restlessly on his feet, eased. The anger and hatred against his mother that had battered against me like the backwash of a wave began to gradually recede.

"Yes," he said, the word emerging from him slowly, as though he were afraid to let it go. He sucked in his lower lip like a sulky child.

There was more that could have been voiced, months and years of it, perhaps. But nothing more came from him. Vacuous good humor reasserted itself on his face, first as a struggle, then as a genuine feeling. He dropped a hand on my near shoulder with a reminder that we should not lose sight of Tony, then carefully steered me through the crowd of Macaronis like a pilot taking a ship through dangerous waters.

Despite the people pressed close around, each talking louder than his neighbor to be heard, I discerned the clear tones of a harpsichord nearby. This was supposed to be a musical evening. Being unable to play myself, I had cultivated an appreciation for the art and expressed the hope that I might be allowed the time to enjoy the artist at hand.

"You'll have buckets of time, I'm sure," said Oliver. "The fellow here is frightfully good, but new here and his name escapes me. Knowing Bolyn's ambitions, he's probably German."

"What's his ambition to do with his taste for music?"

"It's well known that the king prefers German music, and Bolyn must be hoping that an evening like this will somehow get him royal attention."

"To what end?"

"Who knows? He's probably angling for at least a knighthood; they usually are. I never saw much point to playing such games. There was one fellow I knew whose father was knighted and the only advantage he noticed was for the tradesmen, who doubled all their bills."

We moved out of range of the music, through some wide doors, and into a graceful garden surrounding the house. Lanterns hung from flower-festooned poles, taking the place of the sun, which had departed on our drive over. Here we caught up with Tony, who had grown fretful.

"She's supposed to be here," he told us. "Mrs. Bolyn assured me that she acknowledged her invitation." Nervously, he tugged at his neck cloth. The afternoon's rest had restored his color and now it all seemed gathered in two dense spots high on his cheeks.

Love must be a frightening thing indeed to put a man into such a state, I thought, and wondered if I would turn into a similar wreck if the conclusion of this evening lived up to my expectations. I was in pursuit of physical gratification, though, and aware that other young men achieved it without exhibiting Tony's alarming symptoms. Perhaps if I were careful,

I would not fall in love with my hired mistress, and thus be spared such agonies. I was more than willing to take the chance.

A table with cold meats and other things had been set up in the garden and though Tony claimed to have no appetite, Oliver and I did, and took full advantage of the offerings. We each promised the other not to over-indulge in the matter of wine and with that understanding made up for it in the matter of food. In between bites, he would point out this person or that to me, always with some amusing note about them, which helped to fix their names in my memory.

"Over there is Brinsley Bolyn—that's Charlotte's brother, you know. She's the raving beauty this year, but no one's been able to marry her yet. They say their father is holding out for someone wealthy enough to do his family some good."

"Are they descended from Anne Boleyn? Or rather from her family?"

"No, but they like to think it and have put the story about so long and so often that people are beginning to believe them. I'd put as much stock in that claim as I would the footman who takes on his master's name and title and insists on being called 'my lord.' "

"Are there any real titles here?"

"I'm certain of it. Bolyn's spent enough on this to try to impress them. They wouldn't dare not be here." He nodded in the direction of a slight fellow conversing with a fat man. "There's Lord Harvey, for one. His title outlived the family fortune and he's looking around for an heiress to help him recover their lost dignity. I wonder why he's talking with old Ruben Smollett? That's Robert's father. Robert's part of our group, y'know. Unfortunately for Lord Harvey, Smollett's oldest daughter only just turned twelve. I doubt if his creditors will wait until she's old enough to be married off."

Tony rushed up just then, his eyes alight and hands twitching. "Wipe the grease from your faces and look lively, you two. She's here!"

"I should never have guessed," said Oliver. He passed his plate to a convenient footman and obediently dabbed the corners of his mouth. I reluctantly left my own tasty burden on a table where someone's lap dog jumped up to finish it for me. "Lead us to this paragon of beauty, my friend."

Oliver meant only to mock Tony's enthusiasm, but once we'd turned a corner formed of hedges we could see that his praises had been well placed.

"By God, Tony!" he gasped.

"Just as I said. What say you, Mr. Barrett?"

My words seemed to have deserted me. The young woman conversing with her friends on the path before us was beyond them, anyway. She had dark eyes, a pleasing nose, a mouth perhaps too wide for convention, and a chin too sharp, but the totality of all was such as to strike even a blind man speechless. I felt as though I'd taken a step and found the stairway mysteriously shortened, leaving me jolted from head to toe and ready to fall over.

"Just as I said!" Tony repeated gleefully.

Indeed, *yes,* I thought, and my heart began pounding so loud I could hardly hear anything else.

# CHAPTER 6

"I'll introduce you to her in a minute," Tony promised.

"Why not now?" my cousin demanded.

"Because you look like a dying fish. When you can properly breathe again, I'll invite you over. In the meantime, I must have a word or two with her."

He excused himself and joined the group of women. They received him kindly and with some giggling as he solemnly bowed to each. He reserved his lowest and most courtly bow for Miss Jones, who accepted it with no more than a nod and a polite smile. Evidently she was still unaware of his true feelings for her, though they were painfully obvious to anybody who happened to be glancing their way.

"His parents may not approve of this," Oliver remarked.

"Of what?"

"Him wanting to marry her. Old Warburton is a dreadfully practical man with a horror of penniless girls with no name. Unless she has money, property, family, or all three, they'll have to elope."

"So you're taking Tony seriously?"

"I think so this time. I've chided him on his susceptibility to beauty and for falling in love with a new girl every other week, but there's something different about this one."

That was an understatement. She was no less than astonishing. I couldn't pry my eyes from her. I also felt a familiar stirring that made looking away imperative lest something embarrassing develop within the snug confines of my black velvet breeches. But I continued to stare at the unearthly beauty not a dozen feet away, shifted and dithered uncomfortably, and had a passing thought about being caught on cleft sticks.

Then she looked right at me.

Oh, those *eyes* . . .

I gulped—unsuccessfully, for my mouth was dry—and my heart gave a lurching thump that everyone must have heard. She certainly seemed to, for she smiled, looked me up and down, and smiled again. By then I was certain the world had paused in its spin only to start over faster than before to make up for the time lost. In contrast to the one she'd bestowed upon Warburton, this smile was warm with interest. I had to turn and see if anyone was behind me, hardly able to believe that I was the focus of her attention.

She tilted her head to say something to Warburton, who instantly broke away and came back to us.

"Would you like to meet her now?" he asked.

Would the incoming tide like to meet the land? That's how I surged forward. Warburton made introductions that included the other ladies, but hers was the only name that I heard; hers was the only face that I saw.

She inquired about my health and I mumbled and muttered something back. With my blood running all hot and cold through my loins, I was too distracted to make intelligible speeches. It was wonderful, but agonizing, for I truly wanted to make a good impression upon her, yet found myself unable to think of anything to say or do except act like a stunned sheep.

Hardly a minute had passed and she was drifting off with Warburton. No doubt he would find some secluded spot in the garden, make his proposal, and that would be the end of any chance I might have to improve my own acquaintance with her. All the color suddenly drained out of my world.

"Something wrong?" asked Oliver. "Good heavens. Perhaps you'd better sit down. You're ill."

"I'm fine," I lied.

"You are not and nearly being a doctor, I should know. Come over here and I'll find you some brandy."

He led me to a bench and made me sit. Hopeless, I watched Warburton and Miss Jones disappear in the crowd. I had had my chance and now it was lost. When Oliver returned with the promised drink, I heartily wished it to be loaded with hemlock. I obediently drank without tasting a drop and either owing to the heavy meal or the force of my mangled emotions, it had absolutely no restorative effect.

"What has happened?" Oliver demanded, his face puckered with concern. "Oh, don't tell me. I can see it now. Good heavens and well-a-day, but this is turning into an interesting evening. Just promise me you won't get into a duel with Tony and murder each other over her."

"What?"

"That's how these things usually end up, and Tony's been my friend for years and I've gotten fond of you even if you are half Fonteyn and I'd rather not have you running each other through . . ."

I held up a hand. "Peace, Oliver. I'm not the sort of fellow to come between a man and his potential bride."

"That's a relief to hear. I mean to say, I wouldn't have known which of you to second."

For his sake and the sake of his jest, I grinned, but it faded the moment someone else claimed his attention and took him away. I remained on the bench thinking of everything and nothing and hoping to catch a glimpse of Miss Nora Jones again. A few of the young ladies that had been in her company descended upon me and tried to open a conversation, but I doubt that my replies to their remarks made much sense. When they drifted on it occurred to me that I was being a fool about the whole business. Yes, I had met an extremely beautiful girl, but it was an idiot's dream to think that I'd fallen in love with her at first sight.

Now *that* was a frightening word: love. The very fact that it had so swiftly cropped up in my mind had an immediate sobering influence upon me. It was utterly impossible, I concluded. Impossible because I knew nothing about love, about this kind of love, anyway. I did love my sister and father, my home and the people there, even my horse, but what did any of that have to do with what I was now feeling? Nothing. Perhaps some of the food I'd eaten had gone bad and the symptoms had manifested themselves at the same time I'd clapped eyes on Miss Jones.

Life would be so much simpler if that were true.

"Mr. Barrett?"

I gave a start. "Yes?"

A middle-aged woman with a pleasant smile and kindly eyes looked down at me. "I'm Mrs. Poole, Miss Jones's aunt."

A knot formed in my throat. "Yes? I mean, I am very pleased to meet you." Belatedly, I found my feet and made my bow to her.

"As am I," she said. "Would you mind very much coming with me? My niece—"

I didn't hear the rest. It was blotted out by a strange roaring in my ears. I did not think it had anything to do with the digestibility of my dinner. She led the way into the garden and I followed. We turned corner after corner until I thought we should run out of space to walk. We did not seem to be very far from the house, though. The hedges must have been laid out as a kind of maze. I liked that.

Then my knees went jellylike as we turned one last corner and came upon Miss Jones standing in the faint nimbus of light from one of the lanterns scattered throughout the place. Her eyes brightened and she extended her hand to me once more.

"Good evening again, Mr. Barrett," she said in her angel's voice.

I stammered out something polite, but before I could follow it up with anything better, a dark thought intruded upon me. "Where is Tony, that is, Mr. Warburton?"

"Gone back to visit with his other friends, I expect."

"I thought that he . . . that he was going to—" I broke off and found some difficulty in breathing.

"Yes," she said serenely. "He did propose to me, but I turned him down."

My eyes must have popped just then.

"We had a nice talk and got everything sorted out," she continued. "I am happy to say that once Mr. Warburton realized that I have no wish to marry, he pledged himself to remain my very good friend, instead."

Now what did she mean by that? I decided I didn't care. "Perhaps we may also become friends, Miss Jones." My words were light, but difficult to bring forth. Not knowing quite what to say or do, I babbled on. "I should like that very much."

"Of course, Mr. Barrett. That's why I asked my aunt to bring you here. I wanted to get to know you better, too. I hope you do not think ill of me for doing so."

"Not at all."

"Good. I do tire of all the rules that society has invented to prevent men and women from holding intelligent converse with one another. Sometimes it is tediously impossible. If it weren't for my dear aunt . . ."

At this second mention of Mrs. Poole I glanced around, thinking that she might take this opportunity to put in a word, but she was nowhere in sight. Leaving us alone didn't seem quite proper, or at least it would not be so back home. Here in England, though, things might be different.

"She's a little way up the path," said Miss Jones, correctly reading my thoughts.

"Indeed?" I was feeling all hot and cold again.

Her mouth twisted into a wry smile. "Oh, dear, this is difficult for you, isn't it?"

"I . . . uh . . . that is . . ."

Now she took my hand and came so close that all I could see were her wonderful eyes. They were darker than a hundred midnights, but somehow caught the wan light and threw it back like sparks from a diamond. I found myself blinking against them.

"It's all right, Mr. Barrett," she whispered soothingly.

And so it was. A great calmness and comfort overtook me as she spoke; a cheering peace seemed to fill me in the silence that followed. My worries and self-doubts over this new situation vanished as though they'd never been, and I came to realize that my inexperience, rather than trying her patience, was entirely charming to her.

Not quite knowing how we got there, I found myself sitting on a bench in the shadows chatting with her as though we'd known each other for years. She had me tell her all about myself. It didn't take long; I hadn't done very much yet with my life and thought any lengthy reminiscences of it might bore her. I need not have worried, for she seemed to find everything I said of interest. It was highly flattering and most encouraging to my own esteem, but eventually I ran out of subject matter. I burned to know more about her and thought that if I could put the right combination of words together I would learn everything.

While I paused to think, she took advantage of it to shift the subject slightly.

"You really are so very beautiful," she told me, her fingers brushing my cheek.

"Shouldn't I be the one to say that to you?" I asked. I was acting surprisingly calm, but inside I wanted to leap up and turn handsprings.

"If you wish."

"Perhaps you hear it too often."

"Often enough," she admitted. "And there are other subjects one may talk about with equal enthusiasm."

"If you asked me to name one, I don't think I could possibly meet the challenge."

"I judge that you underestimate yourself, Mr. Barrett. What about love? Have you ever loved a woman?"

Some of my earlier awkwardness returned.

"Oh, it's all right to talk with me about such things. Other girls might not be so minded, but I have always had a great curiosity. With some men, one may tell right away, but with others . . ." She shrugged. "So tell me, have you . . . ?"

"I have never loved a woman," I admitted. "I have never been in love . . . at least not until I saw you."

She was pleased, which pleased me, but I had hoped for a warmer response. No doubt other men had confided similar sentiments to her and repetition had dulled the meaning for her. I wanted to be different from them, but did not know what to say or how to say it.

As it turned out, I said nothing, for we were suddenly pressing close and kissing.

While growing up, I had seen others so engaged and had surmised that observation had little to do with active participation. My surmise proved to be more than correct. Until this moment I had had no real inkling of the incredible pleasure such a simple act could produce between a man and a woman. No wonder so many people took any given opportunity to indulge themselves. This was far more addictive than drink, at least for me.

My first efforts were less polished than enthusiastic, but she had me slow down to a pace more suitable for savoring and each minute that passed taught me something new. I was a very willing student.

She pulled away first, but not very far. "You've never before loved a woman?"

"No."

"Would you like to?"

I was not so far gone as to be confused by what she meant. "More than anything in my life."

"And I should very much like to be that woman. Will you trust me to arrange things?"

"Arrange?"

She drew back a little more. "I think it's best if we are both very discreet about this."

I understood and immediately agreed, but wasn't prepared to give her up just yet. Neither was she and we pursued our initial explorations until I was faint for want of air. Nora—for she had become Nora to me by now—did not seem to need any, but allowed me time to recover.

She knew that I was there with Oliver and Warburton and my disappearance for the evening would raise questions requiring an answer.

"Tell them that you met one of the servant girls and came to an arrangement with her," she suggested. "It's a common enough practice, so you need not provide more details than that. I shall excuse myself to the Bolyns and leave. You'll find my carriage waiting at the west gate of the grounds."

"I'll be there," I promised.

She had me go first. The maze wasn't difficult; I found my way out and was nearly knocked over by the light and noise upon emerging. The contrast between the activity by the house and the intense interlude in the garden made me wonder if I'd dreamed the whole thing. But a few moments later Nora glided out, graced me with a subtle and fleeting smile, and moved on. My heart began to hammer in a way that no mere dream could inspire.

I grew nearly feverish while searching the crowd for some sign of my cousin. My patience was nearly at an end when I spied Tony Warburton standing off by himself holding a half-full tankard by its rim. Distracted as I was, I noticed that he looked a bit disturbed, like a man trying to remember something important.

"Hallo, Barrett," he said, coming out of it as I approached. "Oliver told me you weren't feeling well."

"I'm better. Fully recovered, in fact." Almost word for word, I passed on the excuse Nora had provided for me. In the back of my mind, I thought that I really should feel some sort of remorse for what I was intending to do with the love of this man's life, but there was not a single twinge against my conscience. Nora had made her choice and who was I to argue with a lady?

"Yes, well, you have recovered, haven't you? Which one is she? Oh, never mind."

In spite of myself I couldn't just run off. "Are you all right?" He looked damnably white around the eyes.

"Yes, I think so. Little dizzy, but that'll be the drink, I expect." He raised the tankard and drained off a good portion of it. "Go off and enjoy yourself with your English rose. We'll see you in the morning? Good, good, but not too early, mind you."

Walking away, I glanced back. He had returned to his preoccupied state. It was so different from the excitement that he'd shown earlier. As a jilted suitor, surely he should have been morose or angry, anything but this calm puzzlement. I wondered what in the world Nora had said to him.

*Nora.*

Concerns for Warburton mercilessly cast aside, I asked directions and made my way to the west gate.

Oliver had wondered about Nora's finances. If one could judge anything by the well-appointed coach and matched horses drawing it, then she had no worldly worries at all. The only reason that I had the mind to notice it was the dismal fact that Mrs. Poole was unexpectedly with us. I had completely forgotten about her and got a bad shock when I entered the coach to find her sitting next to Nora. Both of them were amused, but not in a derisive manner.

"How nice to see you again, Mr. Barrett," she said. "I'm so glad that you and Nora have become friends."

"Er . . . yes," I responded idiotically. I dropped into the seat opposite them, confusion and doubt invading my mind and cooling my initial ardor. Was Nora setting things up to play some kind of cruel trick on me? It did not seem likely. What might she have told her aunt about us? I could hardly assume that Mrs. Poole knew of our plans for the rest of the evening. It wasn't the sort of thing one confided to one's guardian.

"How do you like England?" she asked with bland and benevolent interest.

Nora gave me a slight nod, a sign that I should answer. Perhaps her aunt was totally ignorant; that, or she knew all and had no objections, which struck me as odd.

"It's very different from home in ways that I had never imagined," I said truthfully.

The coach lurched forward. The noise of the wheels made quiet talk impossible so Mrs. Poole found it necessary to raise her voice to continue her conversation with me. Nora contributed little herself, content to simply watch me with her bright eyes. This, of course, made it difficult for me to hold up my end, as my thoughts were constantly wandering back to her. By the time the coach rocked to a final stop, my mind was in a particularly ruffled state.

A footman opened the door and assisted the ladies out. He was a young, handsome fellow with a cool demeanor, a trait he shared with the driver and the other footmen. All were in matched livery and carried themselves with quiet pride. For the first time since the practice was forced upon me, my offered vail was politely refused.

At a word from Nora, I followed her up the steps to the wide doors of her house. Within, all was clean and orderly and in careful good taste. I glimpsed a dozen paintings and sculptures decorating the front hall, booty from her tour of the continent, perhaps. I had no time to ask, for Mrs. Poole took my hand.

"The party has quite worn me out. You'll please excuse me, Mr. Barrett, if I retire now?"

I did so with mild surprise, but the lady favored me with another sweet smile and went upstairs accompanied by a maid. All the footmen had magically disappeared. Nora and I were happily alone.

"I'm sorry about the interruption," she said. "I could hardly leave my aunt behind at the Bolyns'."

"It's all right, but I confess that I am puzzled by her attitude. All of this puzzles me."

"What, that a lady like myself should bring a man home as I've done with you?"

"Well, yes."

"And yet if a man brings home a lady, no one thinks much on it."

She certainly had a point there.

"Now, if a lady is so inclined, should she not be allowed the same freedom as a man?"

"I suppose . . ."

"Put your mind at rest, dear Jonathan. My aunt and I have a perfect understanding of one another on this, as do my servants. My only demand of you is your discretion. May I rely on it?"

I could hardly blurt my answer to that one out fast enough.

"Very well, then. Now . . . would you like to see my bedroom?"

It was on the ground floor, but I was out of breath, as though we'd run up several flights of stairs. The air seemed very scarce once more. My chest was tight and my hands trembled with an intriguing mixture of fear, anticipation, and lust. Nora was aware of and enjoyed her effect on me, but in a sympathetic manner. She took my hand, kissed it, and gave it a reassuring squeeze before pushing open her door.

She ushered me into a room decorated for delight. Candles were everywhere, burning away with a supreme lack of thrift to turn night into day for us. Each added its small warmth to what was being produced by the fireplace, comfortably dispelling any chill that might have lingered from our drive over.

The walls were papered halfway up with Oriental-looking flowers on a dark pink background. The ample bed was draped with embroidered tapestries to match, and the sheets—when I got close enough to touch them—were of ivory-colored silk. A special recess in one wall held a lovely and striking portrait of Nora, wearing antique clothes.

"It is very like you," I said. "What was the purpose of the costume?"

"A whim of the artist. He was very talented, but eccentric."

"Did he love you?"

"How did you guess?"

"Anyone seeing this work would know."

Her wide lips curled in a smile that any man might die for and I found my arms going around her, drawing her tightly to me. We resumed the kisses begun an age ago in the maze.

"Slowly, Jonathan, slowly," she cautioned. "This is a special time for you. Don't let it go by so fast that you'll not remember what was done."

I laughed at that impossibility. With her help and encouragement—for I won't deny that I was nervous and shy—we began the lengthy and fascinating necessity of removing one another's clothes. As things progressed, I discovered a hundred places other than her mouth where a kiss might be joyfully applied. As for my first sight of a naked woman, I admitted some surprise at the silky fluff between her legs. I suppose I had been misled by what I'd read in the Song of Solomon when the bride's own charms were compared to jewels. The reality was hardly a disappointment, though, and certainly worthy of careful exploration.

"Heavens," she said in turn when the last of my things dropped away.

"I have chosen an eager stallion. Gently now, we'll find a place to stable him in good time."

This did not take long, fortunately, for I was almost to the point where I had to have release or go mad from the waiting. But Nora had grown warm enough under my hands and mouth to be in a similar state of near bliss. She gave a soft, happy cry as I went in and held the small of my back so hard as to nearly break it as we traveled from near bliss to its totality in a few swift moments.

When I finally caught my breath, when the sweat on my temples cooled and dried, when my heart stopped thundering between my ears, when my eyes rolled down to their proper place and I could see Nora beneath me, her head thrown back on the pillows, I knew that I was helplessly and hopelessly and forever in love with her.

Unable and unwilling to stop, I began kissing her again.

"You are so *very* beautiful," she said, repeating her earlier judgment. Her fingers teased at my hair.

I pulled them down to my lips and nibbled at them.

"And vigorous, too. Midnight's just gone by, are you not yet tired?"

"Never," I mumbled. "I shall always be ready and waiting for you."

Something like a shadow flowed over her face, but vanished before it could take hold. "Of course you will, but wouldn't you like something to strengthen you first?"

Since she'd awakened the idea, I realized I had worked up a tremendous appetite in the last few hours of activity. Disengaging from my grasp, she slid from the bed and crossed to a table holding several covered plates.

"Some cold meats and cheese?" she asked. "Some wine?"

Trailing after her, I wouldn't have cared if it were stale water and weevil-infested ship's biscuits. She saw to it that everything was within easy reach and watched while I ate.

"You must have something for yourself," I said.

She shook her head. "No, thank you."

As the food took the edge off the worst of my hunger and the wine made its way to my head, a dark thought began to curl unpleasantly through my mind.

"You've done this so often before," I pronounced.

"What do you mean?"

"The servants so well rehearsed, your aunt's cooperation, this all ready and waiting . . ." I gestured at the table.

"Yes. That is true, Jonathan."

"Who were they?"

"It doesn't matter, does it? You're the one here now. I only rarely ask anyone to come home with me as I've done with you."

"And who will be here the next time?"

"Please listen and understand, Jonathan." Her mouth hardened slightly and her eyes snapped.

I felt myself instantly sinking into their darkness.

"Please listen to me . . ."

And I did. And I tried to understand.

She loved me, but she had loved others, too, and would continue to seek them out. That was her nature and she wasn't going to change for my sake or for anyone else's. However, she could not abide jealousy in any form, and told me that I should not give in to it. Above all, I should not be jealous of her other lovers; otherwise I would never see her again. I knew she meant it and, nearly choking, I swore to do as she asked. The impossibility of her request knotted my throat with tears. How could I *not* resent those unnamed interlopers?

She talked to me, sweetly, soothingly.

Her voice filled my whole world.

Her voice *became* my world.

Then, like the sun breaking through a black cloud, it became entirely possible.

The best and easiest task I could ever take upon myself was to please her. And what she wanted of me was certainly within my abilities. I would love her and willingly share her and enjoy the privilege and honor of it with others. We would be like courtiers of old, gladly waiting upon the pleasure of our lady.

I had listened. I now understood.

My head and heart were at peace.

I finished my meal, content to simply look at her and marvel at the perfection of her face and figure. Nora was not as quiescently minded, though, and came around the table to sit on my lap. Since neither of us had bothered to dress, I found this to be very inspiring and began to express my feelings to her in a such a way as to leave no doubt over how I intended to conclude things.

I started to rise up to carry her back to bed, but she told me to remain in the chair. With a quick shift, she straddled my lap. I gulped, a little shocked at this new presentation of her boldness. I would never look at horseback riding in the same way again.

The chair creaked under our combined weight and exertions, but even if the damned thing had collapsed, we wouldn't have noticed or paused. She wrapped her legs around my waist and its back and pressed close upon me. Her lips dipped down along the column of my neck, her teeth and tongue dragging against the damp skin. With a sigh, she fastened her mouth on the pulse point of my throat and began sucking there.

At first it felt no different from the other kisses she'd given that I'd received with such joy, but it continued much longer and with no sign that she planned to stop. Not that I wanted her to; it was utterly wonderful. And the wonder of it only increased when she opened her mouth wide and her teeth dug deep and hard into my skin, finally breaking it. A full-blown cry of ecstasy burst from me then, along with the climax that overtook us both.

My loins were spent soon enough, but instead of the all-too-brief moment of glory I'd known before, the sensation there continued to increase. It spread to flow throughout the rest of me and went on and on and on, building upon itself like a great storm cloud seeking to touch the moon. Each breath I took was a long gasp of gratification; each exhalation a pleading sigh for more.

My brain was on fire; my body shuddered as though from fever as she held to my throat and drank the blood flowing from the wound she'd made. The triumphant couplings we'd shared before were *nothing* compared to this. I moaned and writhed and could have wept from the ecstasy that blazed like lightning over and throughout my flesh. One of my hands snaked up, the fingers pressing upon the back of her head, a silent invitation to dig deeper, to take more, to take as much as she liked, to empty me completely. . . .

But she had more control of herself than I. An hour might have passed for us locked together like this . . . or a week. I was too overwhelmed to know or care until she began a gradual and slow drawing away from me; something I sensed at once and tried to stop. She licked and kissed me in a most tender way, but remained firm, and eventually and most reluctantly I came back to myself again.

I don't remember getting there, but we'd returned to her bed, for it was only then that I really woke up, weary to the bone. She'd donned a dressing gown and was kneeling on the floor to put her face at a level with mine. She'd put out many of the candles, and those that remained seemed to have a strange effect on her eyes. The whites were gone, darkened . . . flushed with crimson through and through.

"How do you feel?" she asked, her brows drawn together with light worry.

"Cold," I croaked.

She tucked the coverlet around me and crossed to the fireplace to add more wood. Despite my listlessness, I noticed that the firelight shone right through the thin fabric of her gown, revealing every graceful line of her figure. In my head, I wanted to take action about it, but my body was inarguably insisting upon rest.

"Better?" She leaned over me, stroking my forehead with one finger.

"Tired." And dizzy. Warburton had been dizzy. . . .

"Have some of this." She held a cup of wine to my lips, but I could only manage a small swallow. "It will pass. I feared that I asked too much of you tonight."

Warburton . . . white around the eyes . . . and dizzy.

"What did you say?"

I dredged more air into my lungs. "Warburton. You did this to him earlier." I touched my neck where she had kissed . . . bitten . . . ?

"It's all right, Jonathan. Please trust me. Everything will be all right."

"What have you done?" Limited as my experience had been before this night, not once had I ever heard of women biting and taking blood from their men. My once-solid feeling of well-being was slipping away like a ragged dream.

"Exactly what you know I have done," she replied calmly. "There's no need to be alarmed over it."

"What do you mean? Of course I should be alarmed."

"*Shh.* You're not hurt, are you? Did it hurt then? Does it hurt now?"

*No* . . . I thought.

"Only the idea of it is strange to you but, my darling, let me assure you that it is entirely natural and necessary to me."

"Necessary?"

"For how I live, how I love."

"But the way we did it earlier . . ."

"Was the way of most men and women, yes. Mine was a variation that gives me the greatest form of pleasure, not just for myself, but for my lover. Did you not find it so? You didn't want me to stop."

"I must have been mad. Damnation, Nora, you were drinking my blood!"

Her features dissolved from concern to amused chagrin. "Yes, I was. But be honest, was it so terrible?"

That took all the wind out of me.

Amusement surpassed chagrin. "Oh, my dear, if you could only see your face."

"But . . . well, I mean . . . well, it's damnably strange."

"Only because it's new to you."

"This isn't, well, harmful, is it?" I asked.

"Hardly. You may wobble a bit tomorrow, but some sleep and good food will restore you."

"You're sure?"

She kissed my fingers. "Yes, my darling. I would never, ever harm you. If it were within my power I would protect you from all the world's harms as well."

I settled back, overtaken by another bout of dizziness and the oddity of dealing with her . . . preferences. It was hardly a struggle, for I found myself curiously able to accept them. The sincerity of feeling behind her last words was so sharp that it was almost painful to listen to them, but at the same time a thrill went through me. I'd hardly dared to hope that she would love me as I was loving her.

She was absolutely right about her needs not being so terrible, quite the contrary, in fact. And if she'd started kissing me again in the same spot and in the same way I would not have stopped her. Merely the thought of the light touch of her lips revived me greatly in mind and in spirit. My body, sad to say, was not yet sufficiently recovered for me to extend the invitation just now, but soon.

Gingerly, I explored the place on my throat with my fingers. It felt slightly bruised, nothing more, and the only evidence of her bite were two small, raised blemishes.

"They're not very noticeable," she said. "Your neck cloth will cover everything."

"Have you a mirror?"

"Not handy, and I don't like to trouble the servants this late."

"Good God, what time is it?"

"Close on to three, I should think. Time to sleep. My people will see that you get home in the morning."

"Not too early," I said, echoing Warburton's instruction. Instead of resentment toward him, I now felt an almost brotherly compassion and camaraderie. "Poor Tony. He's so terribly in love with you."

"Yes." She rose and lay down next to me, but on top of the coverlet. "Perhaps too much in love."

"Don't you love him?"

"Not in the way he wants. He wants marriage and children, and that is not my chosen path."

"Why not?"

"It's too long a story and I don't wish to tell it."

"But I know nothing about you." Her eyes were not so red now. The darker pupils were slowly emerging from their scarlet background.

"You know enough, I think." She stroked the hair away from my brow and kissed me. "You'll learn more in the nights ahead."

The dreamlike comfort that had begun to envelop my thoughts abruptly whipped away once more. "No I won't. I'm going up to Cambridge tomorrow, God help me. I'll never see you again!"

"Yes, you will. Do you think I'd let anyone as dear to me as you get away?"

"You mean you'd come with me?"

"Not with you, but I can take a house in Cambridge as easily as in London. The place is a dull and windy fen, but if you're there . . ." Her mouth closed over mine, warm and soft and tasting of salt.

Not salt. Tasting of blood. My own blood.

But I didn't care now. She could do what she liked as long as I had a place in her heart. She wholly filled mine.

We talked and planned for a little while, but I was exhausted and soon fell asleep in her arms.

I awoke slowly, lazily, my eyelids reluctant to lift and start the day. I had no idea of the time. The room's one window, though large, was heavily curtained. I was alone in the bed. Nora must have risen earlier and gone down to breakfast.

Rolling on my side, I noticed a fold of paper on the table by the bed. Written on it was the simple message, "Ring when you are awake." Next to the paper was a silver bell. I did as instructed and presently a large and terrifyingly dignified butler appeared and asked how he could be of service to me.

"Where is Miss Jones?"

"Gone for the day, sir, but she left a message for you."

I sat up with interest. "Yes?"

"She will try to meet with you again tonight, but if she is unable to, she will certainly see you in Cambridge within the week."

My disappointment fell on me like a great stone. I'd hoped for more than a mere verbal communication. A lengthy love letter would have been nice. A week? That was an eternity. "Where has she gone?"

"She did not confide that information to me, sir."

"What about Mrs. Poole? Would she know?"

"Mrs. Poole left early to go visiting, sir. I do not think she will be able to help you, either."

"Damn."

"Would you care for a bath and shave, sir?"

"Really?" Considering all the trouble Warburton's servants had been to yesterday, this was an unexpected boon. I accepted the offered luxury and while things were being prepared for me in another room, sat at the table and composed a note to Nora.

Like my first kisses, it was chiefly more enthusiastic than polished, but sincere. Some parts of it were doubtless overdone, but love can forgive anything, including bad writing. When I came to a point where I could either go on for several more pages or stop, I chose to stop. It struck me that the whole thing was highly indiscreet, and Nora had specifically asked for my discretion. Virtuously, I recopied it, but changed the salutation to read "My Dearest Darling," rather than "My Dearest Nora." I signed it with a simple "J" and threw the first draft into the fire. That was as discreet as I wanted to be for the moment.

Her servants saw to my every comfort, and made sure I was groomed, fed, and dressed in clothes that had been magically aired and brushed anew. I was—as Nora predicted—a little wobbly, but that was hardly to be compared with the stiffness in those muscles and joints unaccustomed to certain horizontal activities. I also found it necessary to tread carefully in order to spare myself from another kind of unexpected discomfort, for there was a decided tenderness between my legs due to last night's many endeavors. Perhaps a few days of rest would not be so bad for me, after all.

A coach was engaged to take me to Warburton's. It was early afternoon by now, but I had no great concern about my tardy return—not until the coach stopped at the front steps and Oliver burst out the door.

"My God! Where on earth have you been?"

"I told Warburton—"

"Yes, yes, and so you went off for the night. Well-a-day, man, you could have at least given him a hint on where you'd be so I could find you."

"Is there some trouble?"

"Only that we're supposed to be on our way to meet Mother by now."

Oh dear. With that pronouncement of doom hanging in the air like a curse, he hustled me inside.

Warburton greeted me with a grin and a wink and I had the decency to blush to his face. Courtiers to Nora we might be, but I wasn't yet ready to talk about it with him now. If ever.

"You're white as a ghost, but seem well enough," he said. "Poor Oliver thought you'd fallen into a ditch or worse."

I regarded his own pale skin with new eyes. "Yes. I do beg everyone's pardon. It was wrong of me to go off so suddenly. I didn't think that I would be so long."

"One never does," he purred. "Come in and sit and tell us all about her."

"Absolutely not!" Oliver howled from the stairs he was taking two at a time. "As soon as they bring down your baggage, we are leaving."

Warburton shrugged expressively. "Another day, then. She must have been extraordinary, though, eh?"

I had to remember that he was still under the impression I'd been with some servant girl. "She was, indeed. That is the only word that could possibly describe her."

His eyed widened with inner laughter. "Heavens, you've fallen in love, and after but one night. Do you plan to see her again?"

"Yes, I'm sure I will. At least I hope so."

"Then you'll have to lay in a supply of eel-skins. No offense against your lady, but you don't want to pick up a case of the clap or pox while you're with her. They'll also keep you from fathering a brat, y'know."

"Uh . . ."

"No arguments. There's not a doctor in the land who won't agree with me. Oliver would tell you the same, only I'm sure he's too shy, but once you're up at Cambridge, ask him straight out and he'll tell you where you can get some. Or me, if you can wait that long. I won't be leaving for another week or so."

He was different from the preoccupied man I'd left last night, and very different from the high-spirited suitor I'd first met: genial and interested in things outside of himself. I again wondered what Nora had said to him. I knew just how persuasive she could be but this taxed all understanding.

Oliver returned, followed by some footmen wrestling with my trunk and other things. He had asked the coach that brought me to wait and now supervised its loading. Finished, he rushed back and wrung Warburton's hand.

"Sorry to have to hare off, but you know how Mother is."

"It's all right, my dear fellow. I'll see you at the same rooms later this month?"

"Certainly! Come on, Jonathan. I'm not Joshua, I can't make the sun stand still, though God knows it would be damned convenient right now." He seized my arm and pulled me out. I waved once at Warburton, who grinned again, then tumbled down the steps and into the coach. Oliver's fine horse was tethered behind, its saddle and tack littering the floor and tripping me as I charged inside. By a lucky twist, I managed to correctly land my backside on a seat.

Oliver collapsed opposite me with a weary sigh. "Damn good fortune you picked this instead of a chair or wagon. When we're clear of the town traffic, we should make good time."

Once more I apologized to him.

"You needn't worry about my feelings, it's Mother who may take things badly. Some of her friends were at that party last night and it could get back to her that we were out having a good time instead of hurrying home to introduce you to her. She has to have things her way or it's the devil to pay otherwise."

That sounded uncomfortably familiar. Ah, well, if his mother and mine were so alike, I would only have to endure her for a short while. Cambridge had suddenly become appealing to me and if I was anxious to get there and take up my studies, then she could hardly object to such an attitude.

"Has Warburton spoken much about Miss Jones?" I asked.

"Eh? No, I don't think so. He got a bit drunk last night, but that's all I can recall. I suppose his proposal was a failure, but usually when a girl turns him down he sulks in bed for a week. He seemed in good spirits today."

"Why do you think it was a failure?"

"Had he succeeded, he would have told us."

"You seem incurious about it."

"It's hardly my business." His expression changed from indifference to interest. "Oh-oh, are you thinking of—"

"Of what?"

"If the beauteous Miss Jones has said no to him, it would smooth the path for you, wouldn't it? Only I'm not sure what Tony would make of that. He has the devil's own temper at times."

"The jealous sort, is he?"

Oliver shrugged.

That could be another reason why Nora refused his offer. "Jealous or not, it is the lady who should have the last word on who she chooses to spend her time with."

"Yes, I've always thought that way myself. So much the better if she chooses to spend it with you."

I lost my power of speech for a few moments.

"Don't look so surprised, I saw you following the girl's aunt into the maze. From the look on your face I knew it wasn't to have a quiet talk with *her.* You needn't worry; I'm not one to tell tales. I've found that it's healthier to stay well removed from any romantic intrigues that are of no direct concern to me. All I ask is that if you have a question, come on out with it. This hedging around for information is bad for my liver."

So. Dear Cousin Oliver wasn't as simple as he pretended. Perhaps it was the Fonteyn blood. I began to chuckle.

"All right. You've my word on it. I'll even drop the subject. It's bad manners to talk about a man when he's not present, anyway."

"Heavens," he said, returning to his normal careless manner. "Then what *shall* we talk about?"

"There's one thing that comes to mind. It's what Warburton was saying to me in the hall before we left."

"What's that?"

"He said you'd help."

"If I can. Help about what?"

"I'm not exactly sure. Could you please tell me . . . what's an eel skin?"

# CHAPTER

# ◄7►

My initial meeting with the family's reigning grand matriarch, Elizabeth Therese Fonteyn Marling, left me with the kind of lingering impression that months afterward could still raise a shiver between my shoulders. She had lived up—or perhaps down—to my worst expectations and more. She and my mother were eerily alike, physically and mentally, though my aunt was of a more thought-filled and colder nature, which, considering Mother, was really saying something in her favor. After that, it was about all I *could* say in her favor.

Her husband had died years ago—Oliver had only a faint memory of him—and since then she was the uncontested head of both the Fonteyn and Marling clans. She held her place over all the others, including the men, by the force of her personality and the wealth she'd inherited from her father. As my father had done, her husband had signed an agreement forswearing all rights to her money before he was granted permission to marry her. Whether it had been a match based on love or property I was never to find out.

As I entered her drawing room with a creeping feeling that I had not left home after all, she'd looked me over with her hard little eyes, her thin mouth growing thinner as it pulled back into an easy sneer. The surrounding lines in the heavily painted skin had been incised there by many years of repetition. I could expect no mercy or understanding from this woman, nor even the pretense of familial affection.

"Marie said that you were a devil and you've the looks for it, boy, but if you've any ideas of devilry while you're under my watch you can put 'em out of your head this instant."

Such were her first words to me, hardly before I'd completed my bow to her during introductions. "Yes, Aunt Therese," I mumbled meekly.

"You will address me as 'Aunt Fonteyn,' " she snapped.

"Yes, Aunt Fonteyn," I immediately responded.

"It's a good name and better than you deserve. If you didn't have a half share of my father's blood I wouldn't waste my time on you, but for his sake and the sake of my dear Marie, I'll do what I can to civilize you."

"Yes, ma'am. Thank you, ma'am." What did she think I would do, use the soup tureen for a chamber pot in the middle of a meal with the local curate?

Tempting thought.

"Something amusing you, Jonathan Fonteyn?"

"No, ma'am." I managed to hide the inevitable wince my middle name inspired.

"You, boy," she said, addressing Oliver as though he were a servant of the lowest order. He seemed to be staring hard at some invisible object just off her left ear. "Get out of here. Have Meg bring the tea. Mind that she has it hot this time if she knows what's good for her."

He fled.

She turned her gaze back upon me and I strove to find whatever it was that Oliver had seen. There was nothing, of course, but it was better than trying to face down her basilisk gaze.

"Nought to say for yourself, boy?" she demanded of me.

"I deemed it more fitting to wait upon your pleasure, Aunt Fonteyn."

"Ha! Talk like your father, do you? He could make a pretty speech twenty-odd years ago. Does he still have that sly and easy tongue?"

"He enjoys a good, intelligent conversation, ma'am," I said, trying to be neutral.

That stopped her for a moment. Perhaps she was considering whether or not I was making an impertinence about our own converse. My voice and face were all innocence, though. Mother might have pounced upon it with all fours, but Aunt Fonteyn let it pass.

"What about that sister of yours? How is Elizabeth Antoinette?"

Elizabeth, God bless her, hated her middle name as much as I did mine. I was glad she wasn't present for she might not have been able to hold on to a bland face. "She was well when I last saw her."

"She look much like your mother?"

"Many have remarked on the resemblance, ma'am, and say that they are very alike."

"In looks only, I'm sure," she sniffed, as though it were a crime rather than a blessing not to share the same temperament. "The Barrett blood, no doubt. Anyone to marry her, yet?"

"No, ma'am. Not before I left."

"She's past twenty, isn't she?"

"Nineteen, ma'am."

"She'll be a spinster for life if she doesn't hurry along, but I suppose there's nothing suitable on that miserable island of yours." She made my beautiful home sound like a barren rock barely able to stand clear of a high tide.

The tea arrived and I endured two hours and thirty-two more minutes of close questioning about my life and future and given summary judgments, all harsh, of my answers. I recall the time very well because of the presence of a clock on the mantel. It was clearly ticking, but I'd maintained an inner debate about whether or not the mechanism of the minute hand was defective, for the damned thing hardly seemed to move. I could have otherwise sworn that days had passed rather than hours before she finally dismissed me.

I nearly reeled out the door, horribly stirred up inside and sweating like a blacksmith. It was a nasty, familiar feeling; one I'd thought I'd left behind with Mother. Here it seemed doubled, for it was doubly undeserved. Mother was all bitterness and reprisal for imagined slights; Aunt Fonteyn had no such delusions, yet enjoyed inflicting pain for its own sake. She was worse than Mother, for Mother's graceless treatment of people might possibly be excused by her unstable mind; Aunt Fonteyn had no such excuse for her behavior. Mother could not help herself, but my aunt was very much her own woman.

Oliver met me in the hall with a cup of something considerably stronger than tea. Almost too strong, for the first sip left me choking.

"Steady, now, Cousin. Give it a chance to work," he cautioned.

His somber concern made me smile in spite of my red-faced anger. "You've done this before, have you?" I joked.

"Far too often."

"How do you stand it?" I asked, meaning to make it light, but it did not come out that way.

In echo to my tone, his eyes flashed at the solidly shut door to his mother's lair. "By knowing that if God has any mercy, I'll live to dance on her grave," he whispered with a raw vehemence that made me blink. He suddenly realized it and made an effort to cover with a careless gesture at my cup. "Come, finish that off and I'll show you around the old ruin, introduce you to some of the ancestors we've got framed on the walls. They're a dull and dusty lot, but quiet company. Your duty's done until supper."

I groaned slightly at the thought of actually sharing a meal with my aunt.

"It won't be too bad," he said with a sympathetic assurance that suddenly reminded me of Elizabeth. "Just agree with everything she says and afterward we can go out and get properly drunk. We'll leave for Cambridge at first light. My word of honor on it."

Oliver kept his word and we departed the next morning. Though still sickly from too much wine and another dose of Aunt Fonteyn, it was preferable to recover in a lurching coach than under that woman's roof. I don't remember much of this last part of my journey from Long Island: just being sick a few times, moping for Nora, and gaping with unhappy shock at the dreary monotony of the countryside as we got closer to our goal.

The thoughts of Nora were the best and worst part of the ride. I had no word from her, of course, but hoped for some. Several times I entertained the happy fantasy that she might overtake us in her own coach as if in some popular ballad or perhaps she was well ahead of us and already waiting for my arrival.

I was in love, a state that does not lend itself to logical thought. Eventually I stopped looking out the window and filled the time by speculating how long it would really take her to catch up to me.

Too long, I concluded, shifting restlessly in my seat.

We arrived in Cambridge the next day, choosing to spend the night at an inn to give ourselves and the horses a rest rather than pushing on into exhaustion. Had we known how black the sheets were we'd have made other, cleaner sleeping arrangements, such as the stables. Certainly they would have had fewer fleas than the ones we endured.

Nora had expressed a low opinion of the place that was to be my home for the next few years. True, there was little enough in the countryside to draw my interest, but the many buildings comprising the university were no less than magnificent. Oliver was very familiar with the area and I was happy to have him as guide, else I would have soon lost myself amongst the various colleges. He knew his business and with a surprising lack of confusion led me through the intricacies of where to go, which tutor to see, and finding a place to live.

The last was the easiest, for I was to share rooms in a house with Oliver and Tony Warburton, taking over one previously occupied by a friend who had passed his examines at the last term and left. With hope pulsing through my brain, I immediately wrote a loving note to Nora with my new address and posted it off to London. Cambridge wasn't very large, but I wanted to take no chance on our missing one another.

One day succeeded the next and I was kept extremely busy, for there were a thousand new things to learn before the start of the term. Between them, Oliver and Warburton had a number of friends who drifted in and out of the rooms to talk, share a drink, or even take a nap. Not surprisingly, many of them were also studying medicine, though there were a few reading law like myself. A sharp contrast to the placid pace I'd known on Long Island, I embraced the variety of this new life fully and strove to enjoy every moment.

But Nora was always in my head, and though fully occupied, the hours were far too long. I worried, fretted, and kept a lookout for her all the time that I was awake and dreamed about her when I was not. Each time I saw a coach and four—and there weren't that many in Cambridge—my heart jumped into my mouth, only to drop back into place with disappointment when it turned out not to be hers.

One drizzling evening almost a week later Oliver and I were returning from a dinner with some other scholars. A coach was waiting on the street outside our house. I recognized it instantly, swiftly discounted the recognition, for I'd grown used to having my expectations dashed, then threw aside my doubts once I saw the driver's livery. I rushed forward, leaving Oliver flat-footed in the thin mist and calling an annoyed question after me. I never did answer him.

The coachman knew me—fortunate, since I had forgotten his face—and had a folded bit of paper ready to hand over as I approached. It was an invitation. I gave it only a quick glance, enough to pick out the key words, before hauling myself into the coach, too impatient to wait for the footman's assistance.

Oliver trotted up, his mouth wide and eyes popping. I waved the paper at him. "She's here!" I cried from the window as we pulled away. He did not find it necessary to ask who and waved back with his walking stick to wish me luck. Just before I withdrew inside, I caught a glimpse of a man emerging from our house. Warburton. He paused to stare for a moment, then turned to Oliver for information. It looked like my poor cousin would be caught in the middle of things, after all.

Heartlessly, I left him to it. Any guilt I might have felt in assuming the place Warburton desired for himself simply did not exist. I was going to see Nora and that's all that mattered.

She lived surprisingly close and I speculated that she'd arranged it so on purpose, for surely she could have afforded something more fashionable elsewhere. Not that the house we stopped at was a hovel. It proved comfortable enough once I was ushered inside, but it was decidedly smaller than her London residence, and still bore signs that the unpacking was still in progress.

"Why, Mr. Barrett! How nice to see you again!" Mrs. Poole rustled down a steep stairway. "You're looking very well. Does the academic life suit you?"

Though I wanted to see Nora more than anyone or anything else, I was moved to patience by the sincere goodness of the woman's manner. "I believe so, ma'am, but I have not yet taken up my studies."

"I am sure that you will do well once you start. Nora tells me that you have a fine mind."

In the short time we'd spent together, Nora and I had hardly concerned ourselves with intellectual pursuits. I searched Mrs. Poole's face for the least hint of a false note or derisive humor and found none. She was about the same age as my mother and aunt, but there was a universe of difference between their temperaments. She guided me to a room just off the entry and saw that I was comfortable. A fire blazed away against the damp, and hot tea, cakes, and brandy were at hand. Candles burned in every sconce and in the many holders scattered throughout the room. I could not help but be reminded of that first night. My heart began to pound.

Mrs. Poole excused herself with a fond smile. She was hardly out of the room before Nora swept in.

My memory had played tricks with me in her absence. The face and form I'd carried in my head differed slightly from the reality. I'd made her taller and set her eyes closer together, forgotten the fine texture of her skin, the graceful shape of her arms. Seeing her now was like meeting her for the first time all over again and feeling anew the enchanting shock as time stopped for me. My heart strained against the pause as though it alone could start everything up once more. It needed help, though, and that could come only from Nora.

Her eyes alight, she rushed toward me. All the clocks in the world resumed their ticking even as the blood began to swiftly pulse within my whirling brain.

The next few minutes were a blur of light, of joy, of holding her fast while trying to whisper out my love in broken words. Broken, for I was constantly interrupted as she pressed her mouth upon mine. I finally gave up talking altogether for a while, which really was the best course of action to take, considering.

"I was afraid you'd forgotten me," I said, finally breaking away to breathe.

"Never. It took more time than I'd expected to ready everything for the journey."

"Can you stay?"

"For as long as I like." She smoothed my hair back with her fingers. "It shall be a very long time, I think."

My heart began to soar.

Further talk was postponed. We were too hungry for one another to wait and climbed the stairs to go straight to her room. As before, Mrs. Poole and the servants were nowhere to be seen.

The bed was different, but the silk sheets and feather pillows were there, along with her portrait and dozens of candles. I helped her from her clothes, my hands clumsy as I tried to recall how I'd done it before. Nora chuckled at my puzzlement, but encouraged me as well. My turn to laugh came when she tried to undo the buttons of my breeches. I had grown decidedly inspired while undressing her, and they'd become rather a tight fit. She was having trouble finding enough slack to accomplish her task.

"There!" she crowed finally. "Isn't that much better?"

My back to the bed, I teetered unsteadily on one leg as she worked to pull my breeches down. "Indeed, but I think that things might be improved if we . . ." Giving in to a second's loss of balance, I toppled onto the mattress, dragging her laughing with me. The bedclothes and pillows seemed to billow around us like clouds.

My heart was flying.

And thus began my real education at Cambridge.

Nora taught me much about love and she was ever interested in helping me explore and develop my own talents. While others might revile her experience, I reveled in it. She filled my life, my thoughts, the food I ate, and the air I breathed, but once the term started I did have to face the necessity of more mundane learning. But for her gentle urging to begin the work, then finish what I'd started, I might have abandoned the university completely to spend all my time with her.

My activities were—to my mind—unevenly divided between study, socializing with my friends, and Nora. I wanted to be with her constantly, but yielded to her sweet insistence that she had to have some hours apart for herself and her own friends. Soon we settled into a pattern that suited us both. I visited her several evenings a week as my studies permitted. Unless I had to get up early the next day, I would stay quite late, and occasionally the whole night. Her only irritating custom was to always wake first and leave me to sleep in. Irritating to me, for I would have liked to have the opportunity to make love to her once more before departing. I chided her on it, for at the very least she could stay to breakfast with me.

"I am not at my best in the morning, Jonathan," she replied. "So do not ask me to remain with you."

"The afternoons, then," I said.

"No." She was firm, but kind about it. "Your days are your own as are mine. This has always been my way. I love you dearly, but please do not ask me to change myself. That is the one thing I will not do for you."

Put in that context, I could hardly refuse her, though it troubled me at the time.

Of her other friends I saw little. If I arrived too early, I either waited in the street or Mrs. Poole would chat with me until they left. I could not help but notice that many of them were fellow students, Tony Warburton being in their number. They were young, of course, invariably handsome, fit, and moneyed. None ever stayed very long, hardly more than ten minutes as if they had only dropped in to pay their respects before moving on to some other errand. They paid scant attention to me or even to one another, which struck me as odd until I decided they were only complying with Nora's request for discretion. Certainly whenever we met elsewhere her name did not come up in conversation.

I had no jealousy for them and though they were aware of me, sensed none directed at myself. Tony Warburton was the exception to this, though much of what I observed may have been in my own imaginings. Now and then I would feel a pinch of guilt in the vitals, and doubtless the feeling would spill over onto my face in his presence. In turn, I was prone to interpret any odd look or comment from him as part of the resentment he should have felt for my taking the special place in Nora's heart he'd ardently hoped to achieve for himself. As the weeks passed I wondered whether I should talk to him about her, but when I raised the subject with Nora, she resolutely discouraged it, telling me not to worry.

Warburton's manner toward me was otherwise open and friendly as when we were introduced, but some points of his personality had altered enough so that even Oliver had to comment.

"He's not as preoccupied over women these days, have you noticed? Used to fall in love at regular intervals, y'know."

"He has been studying hard," I said.

"And drinking, too."

That I had not noticed. "We all drink, Oliver."

"Yes, but he's been doing more than the rest of us."

"He never seems the worse for it."

"He holds it well enough, but I know him better than you. I think his mind is yet fixed on Miss Jones. He didn't make much of a row when she refused him, which he's never failed to do before."

"Perhaps because he's still friends with her," I murmured.

"I've known that to hurt more than help. Sometimes it's best to make a clean break or else one or the other party ends up pining away for things that cannot be."

"If he loves her I can agree with you, but he's said and done nothing to indicate that."

"Not while you're around, anyway."

"He's spoken to you?"

"Not exactly, but he puts on a damnably grim face when he knows you're going over for a visit. He sulks awhile, then gets drunk."

"He hides it well."

"Doesn't he just? You don't notice because he's always passed out by the time you get back. He's always all right in the morning—except for a bad head."

"Should I do anything about him, you think?"

"Don't know, old lad. Just thought I'd mention it, is all."

*This is a warning,* I thought.

After that he refrained from further talk on the subject. More than once he'd stated that what went on between me and Nora and Nora and his friend was none of his business and seemed content to let it remain so. I respected this and did not attempt to draw him farther out, but now that I'd been made aware of them, I did note the small changes in Warburton, and thought about them frequently afterward. Again, when I spoke of him to Nora, she told me not to be troubled.

The social drawbacks of an institution like Cambridge became apparent from the start, as I realized that the majority of my activities precluded the presence of women. There were dinners and parties of all kinds, but for tutors and students only. Not once, but many times Nora and I discussed the utter unfairness of such ridiculous social segregation.

Yes, we did find time to talk. One can occupy oneself with lovemaking for only so long before requiring rest. During these pauses I discovered that Nora had a mind that was more than equal to her beauty. We found much common ground between us regarding people and politics, history and literature. Nora was very well read and, though officially barred from the many volumes in the university library, she somehow managed to gain access to them in pursuit of her own literary amusements. I assumed that one of her other courtiers assisted her in this.

"If it weren't for books I think I would become quite mad," she confessed once while paging through a rare copy I'd gleaned from a bookseller and presented to her as a gift for her little library. She had a passion for history, and a particular interest in biographies. This one was about the lives of various European monarchs.

"You are the sanest person I've ever met," I said. "Why ever should you go mad?"

"Why should any of us?" she countered, which was hardly an answer. Perhaps I was expected to supply one.

"My father thinks it's in the blood."

"He's probably correct," she said absently. She knew all about Mother's side of the family by now.

"Are you worried you might be risking yourself with me?" I asked this in light of her sensual preferences. "Courting the possibility of taking on madness whenever you drink from me?"

She looked surprised, then laughed. "Oh, my dear, hardly that. I was only agreeing with your father's opinion regarding one's natural inheritances such as hair or eye color. In regard to myself, I only meant if I did not have such friends as these"—she gestured at her shelf of books—"my life would become unbearably tedious. You have no idea how heavy an empy hour can be. I do. I once endured years of them, years of grinding ignorance and boredom muddled together with contempt and jealousy for that which I could not understand." There was no pain in her tone, though, only gloomy regret.

"How old were you?"

Her smile returned. "I was not old, Jonathan. I was young; very, very young."

I'd never asked her age, but by even the most generous estimate, she could not have been more than four and twenty, if that much. "I see. And now you are very, very old."

"Yes," she said lightly. "I'm positively ancient."

I fell in with her humor. "But you magically preserve yourself by drinking my blood."

"Of course."

"And that of others like Tony Warburton?"

Her eyes came up, on guard against any suggestion of jealousy from me. There was none, only curiosity. "Yes. I have to, you see. There's not enough in you alone to sustain me."

"You talk as though you live upon it," I said seriously.

"I do."

There followed a long silence from me as I sought to understand her meaning. "You're not joking, are you?"

She rested her chin on her hand, watching me carefully. "No."

"You must be." My voice had gone up a little. A small breath of unease curled against my spine like a draft.

"Believe what you will."

She was *not* joking. I knew it then. "How can you? I mean, how is it possible?"

Nora shrugged. "It's how it is with me. Accept it."

"Surely you know. Were you born like this? Did your mother nurse you on milk . . . or blood?" My unease was roughly swept aside by something else, something more solid than the air but just as invisible. Darker. Colder. It crept beneath my skin, oozed along my muscles, squeezed my lungs, chilled my racing heart.

Her secret, like a curtain hanging between us that I had previously—purposely—ignored, was torn away in that rush. I caught my first glimpse of what lay beyond. The understanding I thought I wanted burst upon my brain.

I suddenly knew, *knew* why there were so many handsome, healthy young men around her, why they came, why she required their silence . . .

And I was one of them.

Her favorite.

*Oh, dear God . . .*

She fixed her eyes on me. "Jonathan, it really doesn't matter."

My mind swooped like a bird struck by an unexpected rush of wind. I found myself struggling to fight it.

"It really doesn't matter," she repeated. Her voice was firm and clear and more forceful than normal. It coursed through my ears, my thoughts, my body. Nothing else was important. Not my new knowledge. Not my fear. Not even myself.

I abruptly gave up the struggle with a shrug of indifference. "No. I suppose it doesn't." My voice was normal once more, but at the same time it sounded as though someone else were using it.

"There's no need to be afraid. You'll feel better if you don't think about it."

A faint smile came up like smoke across my face.

She watched me for some minutes. Only gradually did the concern leave her expression and posture.

"Good. Now there's something that I would very much like to show you. . . ." She eased my arms around her body, placing them there as one might pose the limbs of a puppet. I had no resistance. None was needed.

I loved her. Trusted her. *Wanted* her.

My arms soon found their strength again and pulled her close on their own.

* * *

Packets of letters from home soon found their way to me. They were months out of date, but eagerly welcomed. I always read the last one first to be certain that all was well before putting them in proper order.

Elizabeth's were the longest, with page after page covered with news and the kind of observations she knew would amuse me. She lightly recounted the most mundane events of home, making them interesting; her writing was so clear that I could almost hear her voice in my ear again. I missed her dreadfully.

Father's letters were shorter, but full of affection and pride, which in turn gave me pride in myself as well as a certain humility that I should have such a man's high regard. He'd left many friends behind in England and encouraged me to seek them out to give them his greetings. In this task I was more than a little remiss, for some had died, others lived too far away, and by now I had friends of my own to occupy the days. I did manage to look up one or two old fellows who remembered him, but having little else in common with them, the visits were awkward. As quickly as common courtesy allowed, I would excuse myself to return to my own haunts.

Jericho had the least to say, curtailed by his own lack of free time and anything to write. This was a comfort, for it meant that the household was still running smoothly. He did state that Elizabeth's silent feud against Mother had eased somewhat. She'd made her point with the more alert members of the congregation that Sunday, but the less sensitive had ignored her bruises or simply disbelieved how she'd gotten them. This small group became part of Mother's new circle of friends. Though Elizabeth held them in contempt, they did divert much of Mother's attention from her.

Mother did not write at all. This was a relief, for it released me from the duty of writing back, and God knows I had nothing to say to the woman. I suppose it was the same for her.

Other notes were enclosed, from friends, from Rapelji, and surprisingly, from Dr. Beldon. He was cordial and warm and polite to the point of fawning. His letters I regarded with distaste, but felt obligated to answer. My replies were brief, and by their brevity, hopefully discouraging to further correspondence. It never worked. I would have felt ashamed, for he was an interesting and intelligent man, but those qualities were underminded by his toad-eating ways, else I might have welcomed his friendship.

My letters home were about my life at Cambridge and the direction of my studies. I wrote of my new friends and of Cousin Oliver, but left out quite a lot on the rest of the family. Doubtless Mother would be reading them and my true opinions of her dearest relatives would have turned her apoplectic. These views I confided to a private journal I kept that she would never see. Of Nora, at least in my letters home, I said nothing.

The last months of that year fairly galloped past. Though I did well enough in my studies, they did not hold my interest. Compared to Rapelji's style of tutoring what I worked on now seemed childishly easy. His most valuable lesson to me had been the cultivation of a good memory; this, combined with his frequent drilling of Latin and Greek, stood me through the most difficult of my reading. While other lads often despaired of pounding anything into their heads, I seemed to soak it up like a cleaning rag. This pleased me, for it left more time to devote to Nora. As the days grew shorter with the approach of winter, so did my nights with her lengthen and grow richer.

"This is my birthday," she said one evening in November in the same tone she'd used to comment on the weather.

We were comfortable in her drawing room, idly pushing around a deck of cards. Sea coal snapped in the fireplace; I was warm and pleased to sit back and digest the excellent supper I'd recently shared with Mrs. Poole. Nora had been at the table, but had not eaten, as was her custom. When her aunt had left us, she'd grown quiet. Perhaps this announcement explained her preoccupation.

I expressed my congratulations and regret that I had no present to offer to mark the event. "I wish you had told me."

"I hardly ever tell anyone. People make such a fuss over it and there's little enough that I want."

"There must be something."

"Yes, or else I wouldn't have mentioned it. It's not anything one may buy from a shop. It's something only you are able to give me."

This sounded most promising. "What, then?"

She wore a curious look as though appraising me as she had at the Bolyns' party. There was a change in her manner, though. This time her usual cheerful confidence seemed dampened. The quiet affecting her all evening was surely connected with her birthday. Some people take no pleasure from the event and I was surprised to learn that Nora might be one of that number.

I took her hand and leaned close. "What is it you want?"

A shadow, not really visible on her face, but as a subtle shifting throughout her whole body, came and went.

"Nora?"

"Do you trust me?" she abruptly asked.

"Yes, of course I do."

"Are you afraid of me?"

"Nora, really! What an absurd question."

"Is it, I wonder."

"Tell me what is troubling you."

The shadow vanished and she offered me a smile in its place. She caressed my neck with her fingertips, a familiar gesture by now and one that never failed to excite me. "Nothing, darling Jonathan."

I was inclined to be doubtful. "Are you sure?"

She gave no direct answer. "Come upstairs."

Well . . . I'd never yet refused *that* invitation, and notwithstanding her odd mood, I was not going to begin tonight.

As always with this type of activity, we fed upon one another's enthusiasm, seeking and gaining arousal with each touch and kiss until both of us were ultimately seized with that fever unique to lovemaking. We gave in to it, gladly surrendering our thoughts, our bodies to its heat. Nora laughed as she rode me, until she dropped forward and suddenly smothered the sound against my throat. I felt the light, sharp prick of her teeth, then I could have laughed, cried, or shouted as though from delirium when she finally pierced the vein and began to drain off the life welling from it.

She'd timed herself to match my own readiness. Somehow, she always seemed to know that exact instant.

A perverse speculation drifted through my mind that this present coupling could not possibly surpass the previous one.

Once more Nora proved me wrong.

Before my body had quite exhausted itself, she hooked a leg around one of mine and we rolled until I was on top. This was a change, for usually she would hold to my throat for a much longer period. A drop of blood from the tiny holes she'd made seeped down and splashed on her breast.

"My turn," she whispered, still rocking against me. Her hand came swiftly up and one of her long nails gouged deep into the white flesh of her own throat. She gasped out a brief plea to me, telling me what to do, but it was unnecessary. I closed my mouth over the wound and drank . . .

*Red fire.*

So it felt to me as it coursed into my belly and spread out from there to each limb. It seared my bones, ate outward toward the flesh, scorched my skin until Nora and I must both be consumed by the blaze. The totality of pleasure I'd known only seconds ago faded like a candle's flame against the sun. It was too much to bear, far too much—yet I could not stop.

Nora held fast to me as I had to her that first night, urging me to take more, to take everything from her. I had no will to do otherwise. I drew on her, partly conscious that the strength I'd freely given her was flowing back into me again. It was sweet and bitter, hot and cold, pleasure and pain, life and death, all tumbled together like autumn leaves caught up in a spinning windstorm. I fell, spiraling helplessly into its vortex, into myself, into everything and nothing, ultimately whirling down, down, down to seek sweet rest in a wonderful, bottomless silence that had no name.

I awoke first, sprawled on my back now, light-headed, but content with my lot. Nora lay next to me, one arm on my chest, her fingers spread wide as though her last act had been to stroke the hair there. I covered her hand with my own and slothfully considered whether or not it was worth the effort to rise and put out the candles. Some of them had begun to gutter and their flickering, uneven light was a mild annoyance to the satisfied state of my mind and body.

There was a clock on the table across the room. It was well past two. Nora and I had slept for hours. I was strangely wakeful. And hungry. This time the table, except for the clock, was bare. That was sufffícient to decide me. I'd take care of the candles on my way down to the kitchen.

Turning gently so as to disturb Nora as little as possible, I noticed that her eyes were slightly open.

I smiled into them. "You are truly astonishing," I said softly, bending to kiss her.

She did not respond. Her eyes remained open . . . and unblinking.

"Nora?"

I gently shook her. Her body was inert in my hands. *She's asleep,* I told myself, *she's only asleep.* I shook her until her head lolled from side to side.

*No . . .*

I reached across for the silver bell by the bedside and rang it, roaring for help. Eternities crawled by before the bedroom door opened and sleepy-eyed Mrs. Poole worriedly looked in. She accurately read from my agonized face that something was wrong and hurried over to Nora's side of the bed. She put a hand to her niece's forehead. My heart was ready to burst.

"Ah," she said. "Nothing to worry about, young man."

"Nothing to—"

She cut me off and pointed to the mark on Nora's throat, then to my own. "Taken from each other, haven't you?"

"I—"

"That's all it is. It just puts her into a deep sleep until she recovers."

The woman must have been blind. "She's not *breathing,* Mrs. Poole."

"No, she's not, but I told you there's nothing to worry about. It's like catalepsy. It'll wear off and she'll wake none the worse. Bless your soul, but she should have warned you this would happen."

I could not bring myself to believe her. Nora was so utterly, damnably *still.*

Mrs. Poole patted my shoulder in a kindly way. I suddenly realized I was quite naked with only the sheets to cover me; Nora was equally bare. However, Mrs. Poole was unperturbed by this, her concern centered solely upon my agitation. "There now, I can see you'll only listen to *her* word on it. Wait here and I'll fix things right up." She toddled away, her slippers scraping and scuffling as she went along the hall and down the stairs.

Nora remained as she was, eyes open and blind, lips parted, heart . . . as immobile as stone. I backed away from her, from my fear. Not able to look elsewhere, I clawed haphazardly for my clothes, pulling them on against the chill that had invaded me. I was nearly dressed when Mrs. Poole returned, carrying a cup of what I first took to be red wine.

"This will do it for certain," she promised, throwing a smile my way. She hovered over Nora, dipped a finger in the cup and wet the girl's lips. "Just a few drops of the life magic . . ."

"What is it?" I found myself asking.

"Beef blood," she replied. "We had a very fresh joint today and this is what drained off. Cook was saving it for something else, but—"

"Beef blood?" I echoed.

"Nora prefers—well, you and those other fine young gentlemen know what she prefers to have—but this does just as well for her." She let another few drops fall between Nora's lips. My own heart nearly stopped when those lips suddenly moved against one another. Her tongue appeared and retreated, tasting. "That's my girl. Come awake so Jonathan knows you're all right."

Her dead eyes closed slowly, then opened to look at me. "Jonathan?" She smiled drowsily.

Now it passed that I was the one unable to move. Her smile waned.

Mrs. Poole left the cup on the bedside table and excused herself, shutting the door softly.

"You were . . ." But I could not finish.

"I know. I should have explained to you before we started," she said. She raised up on one elbow. "It's . . . difficult for me to find the right words sometimes, especially with you. Other times it seems best to say nothing at all."

"Best for yourself?"

"Yes," she said candidly, after a moment's thought. "And now you're afraid of me again."

I could hardly deny that truth. "Perhaps you will simply talk me out of it as you have before," I murmured.

"Or perhaps you will do that for yourself."

I started to speak and ask her meaning and found it unnecessary. All I had to do was think of my father and remember his struggle to explain his estrangement from Mother. " 'I could see myself turning into her own little dancing puppet,' he'd said."

Her look sharpened. "Who said?"

"Father, talking about his wife." The room was deathly silent except for my heart. I was holding my breath, half expecting her to do something, but she made no move. "You don't want a puppet, do you?"

"No," she whispered.

After all, her life was filled with puppets: handsome young men who gave her blood to live on and gifted her with money to live with, each one happy with his lot, each one under her careful control. This night I had become the sole exception to her pattern. In asking myself why, I knew the answer as well as I knew every curve of her body. Whatever fear I'd felt melted as though it had never been. The fever I'd shared with her earlier returned, flooding me head to toe with a need more overwhelming than any other.

My blood began to quicken and grow hot, pulsing, teasing against the little wounds on my neck. "I'm very glad to know that," I said, my voice growing thick.

And then no more words were necessary.

# CHAPTER 8

***Cambridge, January 1776***

Celebrating the New Year with Oliver and several of our friends had once again proved to be a merry but depleting experience. It took a few days of rest before I was able to notice my surroundings again and so discover the packet of mail from home one of the more sober servants had left on my study desk. Breaking the seal, I found that it disappointingly contained but one letter, the singularity enough to cause me alarm before I even read it. After reading, I was in no better state of mind, and once the whole import of the news it contained had sunk in I was utterly horrified.

I had to see Nora.

It was fully dark out and raining, but she'd be receiving visitors despite the weather. I threw on some protection against it and bolted from the house.

The streets were slick with water and mud. Some of the houses had lighted their outside lamps, but these were little better than a will-o'-the-wisp against the murk. It hardly mattered. I could have found my way to Nora's blindfolded.

Mrs. Poole let me in, smiled, and said, "I'm sure she'll be out in just a few minutes."

Yes. True. A few minutes with each of them. That's all it took for her to get what she needed. I'd never begrudged her that, but this time the waiting was difficult. The letter rustled in my coat pocket as if reminding me of the calamity contained in its lines.

"Shall I take your things?"

Thus Mrs. Poole gently reminded me of my manners. I gave over my hat and slipped free of my cloak, dropping my stick in a tall jar holding similar items left behind by previous visitors. "Where are the servants?"

"Some are in bed, others are busy in the kitchen. I don't mind, Jonathan. Heavens, but it is a wet night out. If you'll excuse me I'll see that this is hung by the fire. That is, if you are staying awhile?"

"I don't—I mean—yes. I think so. Yes."

"Is there something wrong?"

My world was coming to an end, that's all. "I need to talk to Nora."

She chose not to press farther and left. Too nervous to sit, I paced up and down the hall, my boot heels thumping on the painted wood floor. I wanted Nora to hear and hurry herself. Unsuccessfully, I tried not to think about what she was doing beyond the closed door of her drawing room.

They were certainly quiet, but then it wasn't really a noise-making activity: perhaps a gasp or sigh, the slip of cloth on skin, a soft murmur of thanks from one to the other. My imagination was too ready to supply details, though in actuality I heard exactly nothing. The walls were solid and the door very thick and snugly fitted within its frame. Even a moderate amount of sound would not have escaped.

I paced and turned to keep warm. It had been a bad idea to relinquish the cloak to Mrs. Poole. I glared at the door. Damnation, how long did she need? It wasn't as if she had to take her clothes off, and all the man had to do was loosen his neck cloth for her to . . .

The door swung open. I belatedly thought that it might be better to step into a side room and give them the privacy to say goodbye, but it was too late now. And not overly important. To the departing young man I would doubtless be just another one of Nora's many courtiers stopping in to "pay my respects."

Damnation again. The man with Nora was Tony Warburton, still wearing his hat and cloak. They saw me at the same time. Nora's face, always beautiful whatever her mood, lightened with that special joy only I seemed to give her. Warburton's darkened briefly and didn't quite recover. He used to be better at hiding it and often as not hardly bothered anymore.

Nora saw, but let it pass and greeted me cordially. "What brings you here at this hour?" Her eyes were flushed scarlet from this, her latest feeding. Like many other things about her that had at first frightened me, I was now so used to it as to barely notice.

"I must talk to you. It's something important."

She could tell by my manner that I was greatly upset. "Of course. Tony, if you don't mind?"

Warburton seemed not to have heard her. He remained in one spot, looking hard at me. His neck cloth was back in place, but not as neatly as he was accustomed to wearing it. There was no mirror in the drawing room for him to do the job properly. There were few mirrors in the house at all, I knew. He was pale, not so much from blood loss as from high emotion.

"Tony?"

"Yes. I do mind," he said at last. His voice was too charged to raise above a whisper, but with all the pent-up choler behind it it was more effective than a bellow.

Nora's ruby eyes flashed on him, but he was looking at me. My own immediate troubles dimmed under his glare. That which had lain unspoken between us for so long was starting to surface.

But I had no desire to confront him. "Never mind," I said. "I'll go. I'm sorry for my intrusion."

Nora curtailed my effort to avoid a problem with a sharp lift of her chin. "Nonsense. You're here now and—"

"Of course you'll see him," said Warburton. "You'll always see *him.* No matter what it does to others."

"Tony . . . ," she began.

"No more. I can take no more of this." His voice had dropped even lower. I barely heard. Nora, standing next to him, had no such difficulty. She came around to stand directly before him.

"Tony, listen to me. Listen to me very carefully."

The air in my lungs settled there as though it had gone solid and could not be pushed out. I knew the tone in her voice, felt the power of it singing through my own brain, though it was not directed at me. I also knew what it was costing her.

Warburton was too upset to feel it. "No more. You want too much of me. Do you know what it's been like for me these years to be content with your crumbs while he—"

"Tony . . ."

*"No!"*

Nora dropped back a step, clearly surprised by him. This instantly transmuted into anger, but Warburton was too engulfed by his own to care.

"Always taking, taking, taking. First our blood, then our money. Did you know that that's how she makes her wage, Barrett? How she's able to afford her houses, servants, and all the rest? She collects a little from each of us every time she does it. Only a little, mind you, so it's not even missed. Gifts, she calls 'em. Well, no matter the name she chooses to put on the payment, a whore's still a whore whether she spreads her legs for it or not."

I started forward to knock him flat, but Nora was ahead of me. Her open hand lashed out faster than my eye could follow. Warburton grunted and staggered from what must have been a fearsome blow. The whites of his eyes flashed briefly before he shook it off. I made toward him, but Nora imperiously and inarguably signed for me to hold back.

"Mr. Warburton, I see no reason for you to remain any longer or to ever return once you've left," she said evenly.

Warburton blinked a few times as her words penetrated. His long face crumbled in on itself as he comprehended what he'd done. "Nora, forgive me. I didn't mean . . . it's just that I . . ."

"Get out of here." She glided past him to open the front door herself. Spatters of rain and a wave of cold air tore into the hall.

For a long time he made no move. I was hoping that Nora might ask me to force him out, though it would certainly end in a challenge and a duel. There was no reason to think that it might end otherwise, anyway. Nora coming between us had only postponed the formalities. I wanted to break his neck.

He finally stirred, started to speak, then aborted because of the venomous look she had for him. He winced as if from another blow and turned from her, eventually striding away and into the street. Only when he was lost from sight in the misery of the rain did Nora close the door.

"I'm sorry," I said.

"Was his jealousy your fault?" she demanded. She was visibly trembling.

"This was an ill-timed intrusion. I should have waited elsewhere, or first sent a note."

"You know you're welcome here anytime. So do they." She waved a hand to indicate her other courtiers. "So did he. I'm the one to apologize to you, Jonathan. I should have seen this coming. Prevented it."

"How? By talking to him?"

"In my way."

"I thought you'd already done so."

"I have. It just never seemed to work as well with him. I don't know why, perhaps it's his drinking." She shook off her speculations and came to me, her hands outstretched. "I'll try again, but later, when we've both cooled down."

"But, Nora . . ."

" 'A wholesome tongue is a tree of life, but perverseness is a breach in the spirit,' " she said, quoting from Proverbs. "There is something wrong in Tony's spirit."

"He mortally insulted you!"

"He told the truth and you know it. Granted, by the manner in which he told it, he meant to hurt me."

"For which I'll repay him handsomely when the chance comes."

Then she went still and distant and I felt the gentle wash of her anger flow over me like a icy wave. "This is not your concern, but mine, Jonathan."

I was suddenly unable look at her or say what I'd been about to say. My outraged objections died away, unspoken, not out of fear of offending her, but from the tardy admission to myself that she was right.

"Please leave it to me."

Had she ordered or demanded I just might have ignored it, but she gave this as a request, and that steadied me down. Much as I wanted to play the knight-errant and avenge the insults thrown at her it was for her to resolve things her own way. Interfere, and I would be no better than Warburton.

"Very well," I conceded.

Her face softened. I'd said nothing specific, but it was as good as a promise to her. She knew I would keep it. "Thank you." The tension that had unhappily pushed between us vanished. "Come in by the fire. Would you like some tea?"

I declined, but let her guide me into the drawing room to the divan by the fireplace. "What will you do about him?"

"Whatever I can, if I can. I think it was a mistake for me to have continued with him after I'd met you."

Cousin Oliver had also expressed a similar opinion. Often.

Nora's face suddenly twisted. With a shock, I realized she was crying. She was not a woman to easily give in to tears and disliked doing so. I quickly stood and gathered her in my arms, giving her the comfort of soaking my shoulder.

"I'm sorry," she mumbled.

"It's all right to cry when you're hurt."

"It's just . . . oh, God, but I *hate* losing a friend."

Whatever his faults, Warburton did have looks and no small portion of charm. Beyond the necessities of nourishment, she had enjoyed his company and counted upon him as a friend as I had. No more, alas.

The storm gradually passed and she pulled herself in to once more resume her usual air of self-possession. I started to offer her a handkerchief, but she'd brought her own out. It was spotted with a small amount of blood. Warburton's. I looked away as she dabbed at her eyes and blew her nose.

"Please don't tell me there are others to take his place. I'm not like that, Jonathan. I can't just take on any young man for what I do. It's not a matter of having to take whoever comes my way because they're handy. If it were for the blood alone it would be different. But there's more to it for me than mere feeding. I have to at least like the man and I do like Tony. Or I did."

"You need their love as well," I whispered.

"Yes. And more. It's so easy for men to love me, but for them to accept what I am . . . Even after I've talked to them, influenced them . . . it's not always there. Those are the ones I have to let go, and it's not always easy."

"Like Oliver?"

That startled her. "You knew?"

"I suspected. He's never said anything, of course, only acted a bit reserved about you."

She nodded. "He's a very sweet young man and I liked to listen to his prattle, but it became obvious that he was uncomfortable about my needs. I made him forget all that happened, but some ghost of that memory may still remain, though. He is reserved, he just doesn't know why."

"I can see that such power of influence that you have is a great help in avoiding unwanted complications."

"A help or a bad habit. I'm glad there are no such things between us anymore."

"Mmm." We sat close together on her divan and stared into the fire. Concerns over Warburton faded as I remembered what had brought me here. My heart began to ache.

Though she could not see, she was quick to sense the change in my mood. "What is it, Jonathan?"

"I have some bad news." God, was that *all* I could say about it?

But she heard the pain in my voice and turned around to face me.

I fumbled out the letter with some idea that she could read it for herself, but changed my mind. A summation was enough. More than enough. "My family. They want me to come home."

Now she did take it from me and read it through. She said nothing. Words were unnecessary. Inadequate.

"It's Father's writing, but I know it must be my mother's idea. Only she would be fool enough to tear me out of here before my studies were complete. It's so utterly witless! How could she do this to me?"

"Are you unhappy only about your studies?"

"Of course not! I hope you don't think—"

"No, Jonathan," she said gravely. "I know you better than that, but I agree with you. From what you've told me of your father he would be most reluctant to have you break off your education here . . . unless they really need you as he says."

"Our home is hardly in the thick of things. As far as anyone's concerned all the turmoil is in Boston, Philadelphia, and Virginia. We're miles and miles from those places, why should they need me?"

"It might be a case of want, rather than need," she gently pointed out. "I think that your father is afraid."

A bitter retort to this almost burst from me, but died when I saw her sad look. I took back the letter and read it again. The truth, as seen from this view, seemed to jump out and strike me right in the heart. I hadn't wanted to see it before; to do so would mean . . .

"But I can't leave you, Nora," I said, tears creeping into my own voice now. "I couldn't bear it."

"Hush," was all she said. She pulled me close, until my head rested on her breast, and wrapped her arms around me. Part of me wanted to weep, but I did not. What would be the use?

I all but crawled back to my room some hours later, dejected and hopeless and with no idea of how to avoid my duty to my father. I'd cautiously asked Nora if she would be willing to come home with me, but she was unable to give an answer. That had hurt, for I'd wanted her to immediately say yes. She was honest, though. She really did not know what to tell me.

"There is so much to think about," she said. "Give me the time to think it."

Pushing her to a decision would be importune. All I could do was accept and await. At least she'd not given a flat-out refusal.

The last person I wanted to see was Tony Warburton, but he was sprawled in his chair in the sitting room we all shared, waiting for me. Two empty wine bottles stood on the table next to him and he was in the process of draining away a third as I walked in. Nora's intervention had only postponed the inevitable as far as we were concerned. Somehow, I would have to resolve things with him in a way that would not result in a duel.

"Barrett," he said. He looked embarrassed and shy and his eyes did not quite meet mine. All his anger was gone.

I hadn't known what to expect: a challenge, censure, insults—anything but remorse. My own anger magically evaporated. I was sorry for him, but did not feel up to more talk, especially since he was drunk. I made to go past to my own room, but he lurched from his chair to head me off.

"Please . . . Barrett, please hear me out. I just wanted to apologize to you." His words were slurred, but sincere. A drunkard's sincerity, I thought. Oh, well, forgiveness was easy enough to find in my present mood. I had other things on my mind now.

"It's all right. I shouldn't worry about it anymore if I were you."

His slack jaw waggled a bit. "Oh, I say, you are such a decent man. I'm . . . I've been so wretched since . . . I said a lot that I don't mean, and I'm truly sorry."

"Yes, well, don't worry about it."

"But I—"

"Get some sleep, Warburton."

"No, I need . . . must apologize to Nora as well. I was too horrible to her. I won't ask her to forgive me, but I will apologize. I only want to do that and then I shan't bother her again. On my honor." He spread his hand over his heart.

"Tomorrow, then."

"Tonight! It must be tonight."

"No, you're much too . . . tired." I nearly said "drunk."

"Tonight," he obstinately insisted and pushed away from me. He found his cloak and dragged it over his shoulders. "You must come. She won't see me unless you're there."

I thought of trying again to persuade him to sleep, but knew it wouldn't work. He'd had just enough to be unreasonable and need watching, but not so much as to be incapable. He would go, with or without me, and in his condition he'd probably fall and drown in a gutter. Perhaps the cold air would help clear his head and I could talk him out of it for the moment. I hoped Nora would understand if I could not.

The weather hadn't improved, we were soaked when we reached her house. Warburton had forgotten his stick, so I'd lent him mine to steady his steps. He leaned on it now and complained about what a thoughtless oaf he was. I shivered and silently agreed with him as we tottered over the last few yards.

"At least knock first," I admonished, but he opened the door himself and walked right in.

"*Shh,*" he said, finger to his lips. "Don't want to wake anyone. Only Nora, but she'll be awake. Keeps late hours, y'know. Very, very late hours." He broke off into a sodden grin.

"What is this?" Nora emerged from the drawing room where I'd left her. "Jonathan, what is going on?"

I felt supremely foolish standing there holding Warburton up. "He wanted to apologize. I couldn't stop him and thought it better to come along."

Her exasperation never quite developed. She saw Warburton's condition and how things stood. Or wobbled. "Very well."

Oblivious to us, Warburton broke away from me to plow into the drawing room, muttering about the brandy there.

"One more drink and he'll have to be carried home," I said. "I'm sorry, Nora."

She dismissed my contrition with a smile and a shake of her head. "Go take care of him. I'll see if there's any hot tea or coffee left in the kitchen."

As expected, Warburton was pouring some brandy for himself. He looked up as I came in. "Where's the beauteous Miss Jones?"

"She'll be back."

"No. I want her here. She must be here." His sentimental repentance was rapidly vanishing, threatening to turn into belligerence.

I sighed. The tea would have to wait. "I'll fetch her."

He brightened. "You're a true friend, Barrett."

*A patient one,* I thought, turning away. Calling for Nora at the door, I only just caught her murmured acknowledgment from down the hall. Behind me, I heard two quick steps, but there was no time to look back to see what he was doing.

Something went *crack.* The room was engulfed in a dull white sheet and my legs dropped out from under me. I didn't see so much as feel the floor coming up.

When the white leached away I became acutely aware of a hideous knot of agony on the back of my head and my inability to move. I could breathe and suffer pain. That was all.

And see. Yes. That was Tony Warburton standing over me. Holding my stick. His movements were in control and quite steady. His face was no longer slack from drink. His face . . .

*Dear God.*

"A true friend, Barrett," he whispered.

I tried to speak. Nothing happened. Too much pain was in the way.

Holding the cane in both hands, he gave it a twist. I'd shown him and others the trick of it during practice at the fencing gallery. The handle came free and out slid a yard of Spanish steel, sharp as a razor.

*No . . .*

I must have made some sound; he raised one foot over my stomach and shoved down hard with all his weight. Air vomited from my lungs. No breath, no movement, no way to warn Nora—

Who was just coming in the door but he was ready for that and whipped around in time with the blade level and his arm went straight and all she could do was give a little wondering gasp as the steel vanished into her chest.

She seemed to hang in the air, held up by the thin blade alone. Her quivering hands hovered around it as though seeking a way to take hold and pull it out. Her eyes flashed first shock, pain, and more pain as she realized his betrayal. They flickered down at me, fearful. I was able to open my hand toward her. Nothing more.

Blood appeared on the ivory satin of her bodice. Over her heart.

Warburton made a soft exhalation, like a laugh.

Nora swayed to one side and fell heavily against the wall, flinging her arms out for balance. Warburton, still holding the sword-stick, followed her movement as though they were dancers.

Within my mind, I was screaming.

Without, silence.

Silence . . . until Nora began to slip to the floor with a whisper of fabric and her lips forming a sound halfway between a sob and a moan. Her wide skirts floated around her like flower petals. She stared at him the whole time, eyes brimming with anguish and anger and sorrow and loathing; stared until her eyes became fixed and empty and all motion and feeling drained away to nothing, leaving nothing.

Only then did Warburton draw the blade from her body.

Turned. Looked from her to me. He loomed over me like a giant and swung the sword so that the point lightly tapped, tapped, tapped just below my chin. He smiled at me. Cheerful, bright, interested in everything, and utterly normal—the same smile I'd seen the day I first met him. The smile of a sane man who is not sane.

He reached down to tear open my neck cloth, the easier to draw the sword across, from ear to ear. Better to remove the impediment than to cut through it. It flashed through my mind that things might look as though I'd killed Nora and then myself.

He placed its edge against my throat. I felt its cold pressure. Part of me would welcome what was to come for I would be with Nora, another part raged against it, denied it, fought it—

And could do nothing, *nothing,* to stop him. He batted my feeble hands away with no effort.

Useless. Useless.

If heaven were not my destination, then hell could offer no worse than the utter helplessness I felt in these last seconds.

The blade pressed upon my naked skin. It was stained with her blood.

He made that soft laughing sound again.

All I could manage was a groan as his arm flexed to drive—

Something seized his wrist like a striking snake. The sword jerked up and away from my throat.

Astonishment froze Warburton for an instant. He stared, all incredulous, before reason returned and told him that what he saw simply could not be possible. She had to be—must be—dead. The blood was yet there on her dress . . . dear God, I could *smell* it. No one could survive such an awful wound . . . no one human, I wailed.

Almost as though my thought had leaped into his head, Warburton flinched and backed from her, but she held fast to his arm, using his impetus to regain her feet. He tried to shake off her grip. Failed. Desperately clouted her head with his free hand. She didn't seem to feel it. Their natural difference in size and strength should have worked in his favor but it was as though none existed and he was suddenly aware of it.

There was a dull snap, Warburton cried out, and the sword-stick dropped from his nerveless fingers. Gasping, I was just able to crawl toward it, take it up.

But Nora did not need my help.

Her eyes burned with something beyond fury. She was still beautiful, but the hellfire blazing in those eyes had transformed her from goddess to Gorgon; to look upon her now was to see your own death . . . or worse.

And Warburton looked.

His jaw sagged as though for a scream. No sound came forth. I glimpsed in his face only a reflection of the horror he saw and that was enough. No shriek or howl or cry flung up from the depths of hell could have possibly expressed it.

Silence, dark and heavy and alive and hungry. Silence, like an eternity of midnights compressed into a single moment, ready to burst forth and engulf the universe forever. Silence, except for my own pained breath and the hard laboring of my heart.

No one moved. Warburton was like a man of stone, frozen in place by terror like a sparrow before a serpent: aware of what was to come, but unable to fly from it. Only his face changed, the sane insanity melted away, exposing the pitiful, raw despair within.

Then Nora whispered, "*No,*" and released him, soul and body. There was a thump and thud as he folded to the floor.

She stood over him, hands loose at her sides. He cowered away, his legs curling up to his chest, arms wrapping tightly around his head. He choked convulsively once, twice, then began to weep like a child.

I wanted to weep as well, but for another reason. Dragging myself up, I stumbled toward her.

* * *

It was an hour before I stopped trembling. The churning in my belly had settled, but the back of my head still put forth lances of pain whenever I moved. Nora had wrapped a piece of ice from the buttery in a cloth for me to hold over the spot. She said the skin was broken, but would not need to be stitched together.

Her manner was as smooth and cool as the ice. Her eyes roved everywhere, never quite meeting mine. She'd withdrawn into herself without having to leave the room. When I put my hand out to her, she would only touch it briefly and then find some other task to distract her away. At first I thought it had to do with me, until I perceived that her mind was turned inward, and what ran through it was not pleasant.

The sad drone of Warburton's crying had finally ceased and after a bout of prosaic sniffing and snuffling, he'd fallen asleep. We left him on the floor where he'd dropped and kept our distance as though he carried some kind of plague.

"Shall I take him home?" I asked.

"What?" She stirred sluggishly, having lingered over the lighting of a candle. Dozens of them burned throughout the room except for a dim patch around Warburton.

"It will cause less notice if I'm the one to take him home."

"What will you tell Oliver?"

"I'll think of something."

"Lies, Jonathan?"

"Better than the truth. More discreet."

I'd meant this to bring her comfort. Her lips thinned as she chose a more ironic interpretation.

"Everything will be all right," I told her, hoping she would believe it.

She shook her head once, then looked past me toward Warburton. "He tried to murder us, Jonathan. I can forgive him for myself, but not for what he nearly did to you. I was the indirect cause of that."

"He was mad, it's past now."

"He is mad . . . and will probably remain so."

"How can you—"

"I've seen it before. I may have stopped myself in time, but who's to say how it will be for him when he wakes up?"

"Stopped yourself?"

"From totally destroying him."

There was no need to press for further explanation; what I'd seen had given me more understanding than I wanted. I shifted, made uncomfortable by the memory.

Nora opened a drawer and produced yet more candles and lighted them all.

"What darkness are you trying to dispel?" I asked.

"None but that which lies within me. These little flames help drive away the shadows . . . for a time."

"Nora—"

Her hand brushed over the front of her ruined dress. "I live in the shadows and make shadows of my own in the minds of others. Shadows and illusions of life and love that fill my nights until something like this happens and shows them up for what they are."

Though I but dimly perceived her meaning, her words and how she said them frightened me. Instinct told me she was working her way up to something, but I didn't know what, and in my ignorance I was unable to gainsay her.

"At least you're not a shadow, Jonathan. I can thank God for that comfort, whatever may come."

This sounded ominous. "What do you mean?" I asked, hardly able to speak.

Now she sat by me and looked at me fully. "I mean that I love you as I've loved very few others before you."

My eyes filled. "I love you, too. I would sooner cut my heart out than leave you."

"I know," she said with a twisted smile. "But others need you as well, and I am now needed here." She glanced at Warburton. "To correct my mistakes, if that's possible."

"What are you—" But I already knew what she was talking about and she gave me no chance to alter her decision. It was now my turn to learn of betrayal and in the learning, to forget it. To forget many things.

"Please forgive me," she whispered.

And I did.

Without struggle, I slipped into the sweet darkness of her eyes.

It had taken no small amount of time and trouble to arrange my passage home. I was not looking forward to the trip, though the captain had assured me the winter storms were over. *What about the spring ones?* I wondered. Ah, well, there was no turning back at this point. I'd have to pray that Providence would be kind and brave it out with the rest of the passengers. They looked to be an interesting lot: some clergymen and their wives, a bright-looking fellow who said he was an engineer, an artist, and inevitably, some army officers. In the next few months we would doubtless grow quite sick of one another, but things were all right for now.

As he had been the first to greet me, Oliver was now the last to say farewell. We were waiting for the ship's launch to come for me and the others in a tavern by the docks. We'd secured seats by the only window and would be the first to know of its arrival. We drank ale to pass the time. I didn't care for mine much. Ale was for celebrations, not for partings.

"I stopped by the Warburtons' on the way over," Oliver said, his expression falling.

"How is he?"

"About the same."

It was a great mystery, what had happened months back, to Tony Warburton. Oliver had been the first to notice something was wrong, but had mistaken it for drunkenness. Everyone was used to seeing Warburton drunk. This time, he simply hadn't sobered up. His clothes were sopping wet from the weather and—Oliver discovered—his right wrist had been badly broken. He could not tell anyone how he had come by his injury, nor did he seem much concerned about it.

He still smiled and joked, but more often than not what he said was incomprehensible to others, as if he'd been carrying on a wholly different conversation in his head. He made people uneasy, but was unaware of it. He'd turn up for his studies, but had no concentration for them. Sooner or later he would wander out of the lecture hall. His friends covered for him until his tutor had had enough and called him in for a reckoning. After that interview, his parents were quickly sent for and Warburton was taken back home to London.

Like Oliver, I'd also stopped in to see him and say good-bye. I was received with absentminded cordiality, but he favored me with his old smile, which for some reason imparted a bad feeling in me. I tried talking to him; he paid scant attention. The only time he showed any animation was when his eye fell upon my sword-stick. His face clouded and he began rubbing his crooked wrist where the bones still ached. He shook his head from side to side and the watchful footman whose job it was to keep track of his young master stepped forward and suggested that I should leave.

"It's awful, isn't it?" I said.

Oliver agreed with me. "I plan to look after him, though. Now and then he has a lucid moment, the trick is to get them to last. Wish I knew the cause of it. The doctors they've taken him to say anything from the falling sickness to the flying gout, which means they haven't any good idea. And the treatments! Everything from laudanum to bathing in earth." He looked both grim and sad. Warburton had been his best friend.

"That's probably the launch to take me out to the ship," I remarked, pointing.

"Not long now." He turned away from the view and craned his neck toward the crowds strolling up and down the quay.

"Looking for someone?"

He shrugged. "I just thought that . . . well, that your Miss Jones might have come by to . . . you know, see you off."

No, she wouldn't be coming. It was daylight and Nora never . . . never . . . something. I'd gone blank on whatever it was I'd been thinking. Annoying, but it was probably of little importance.

"She's been very busy lately," I told him. "Poor Warburton's condition deeply affected her, y'know." Soon after Warburton had left for London, Nora had also moved back. "His mother told me that she often comes to visit him. Seems to do him good, though it doesn't last for long."

Nora's sudden departure from Cambridge had puzzled Oliver. "You and she—you didn't have a quarrel or anything, did you? I mean when you got that letter to go back . . ."

"What an absurd idea." But he did not appear convinced. "Let me assure you that we parted the best of friends. She's a lovely girl, truly lovely. It's been a delight to have had her friendship, but all good things must come to an end."

"You're pretty cool about it, I must say. I thought you were in love with her."

My turn to shrug. "I loved her, of course. I shall certainly miss her, but there are other girls to meet in this wide world."

"Something wrong?"

"Nothing, really. Just a headache." I absently rubbed the back of my head and the small ridge of scar hidden by the hair. Acquired on some drunken debauch earlier in the year when I must have stumbled and fallen against something, it occasionally troubled me. "You'll look after her for me as well, won't you?"

"If you wish. Won't you be writing her yourself, though?"

"I . . . don't think so. Clean break, y'see. But I'd feel better if you could let me know how she's doing. It strikes me that though she has many friends, she's rather alone in the world. I mean, she does have that aunt of hers, but you know how it is."

"Yes," he said faintly. Oliver didn't much approve of Nora, but he was a decent man and would do as I asked. I looked at him anew and realized how much both of us had grown in the nearly three years of my stay. In many ways he'd become the brother I'd never had. The weight of the world fell upon my spirit as I faced the possibility that I might never see him again.

The launch glided up and ropes were thrown to hold it to the dock; the oars were secured. A smart-looking ship's officer jumped out and marched purposefully toward our tavern.

It was time.

"God," I said, choking on the sudden clot of tears that had formed in my throat.

Oliver turned from the window and smiled at me, but the corners of his mouth kept tugging downward with his own sorrow. He made no comment. We each knew how the other felt. That made things better and worse at once.

"Well, I'm damned sorry to see you go," he said, his own throat constricting and making the words come out unevenly. "You're the only relative I've got who's worth a groat and I'm not ashamed to say it."

"But not in front of the rest of the family," I reminded him.

"God forbid," he added sincerely, and the old and bitter joke made us both laugh one more time.

Ignoring the stinging water that blurred our vision, we went out to meet the officer.

# CHAPTER 9

*Long Island, September 1776*

"They was my hosses 'n' wagon, Mr. Barrett, 'n' still mine but for that bit of paper. I figger 'twill take another bit of paper to get 'em back 'n' want you to do it for me."

Thus spoke our neighbor, Mr. Finch, as he sat in Father's library. He was angry, but holding it in well enough; I would have been in an incoherent rage over the theft. His had become a familiar story on the Island as the commissaries of the occupying army diligently worked to fill their pockets as well as the bellies of the soldiers.

"What sort of paper?" asked Father, looking grave.

"It were a receipt for the produce I were sellin' to 'em. I had my Roddy read it, but they left out how much I were to be paid 'n' said it would be filled in later." He placed the document before Father.

"And you signed it?" He tapped a finger against a mark at the bottom of the sheet.

Finch's weather-reddened face darkened. "They give me no choice! Them bloody soldiers was standin' all 'round us with their guns 'n' grinnin' like devils. I had to sign it or they'd a' done God knows what 'n' more besides. Damned Hessians they was, 'cept for the officer 'n' 'is sergeant. Couldn't make out a word of their talk, but the way they was lookin' at my young daughters was enough to freeze your blood solid."

We'd all heard of the outrages. The army sent from England was making little distinction between the rebels and the king's loyal subjects, not that even a war was any excuse for their mistreatment of the common people. In addition to wholesale theft and the occasional riot, many of them had taken it into their heads to use any unprotected womenfolk as their own private harem whenever they pleased, whether the ladies were willing or not. There had been courts-martial held, but the attitudes of the officers more closely resembled amusement rather than intolerance for the brutish actions of their men. Thinking of how I would feel should Elizabeth face such a threat, I could well understand why Finch had readily cooperated.

"So I made my mark, then one of 'em hops up and makes to drive away 'n' when I asks the officer what he thinks he's doin', he says the receipt included what the goods come in as part of the sale. 'The king needs hosses,' he says as cool as you please. I was a-goin' to argue the point with 'im, but those men was licking their lips 'n' my girls was startin' to cry, so it seemed best to leave 'n' try another way. The poor things only come along to help 'n' in return git shamed 'n' have to see their da shamed as well. Roddy felt awful about it, but he read the paper over 'n' couldn't find a way around it. Said that the way it were written could be taken as havin' mor'n one meaning."

Fairly well off compared with other farmers, Finch still could not afford to lose a good pair of work animals and a wagon. Still less, though, could he afford harm to his family.

"Anyways, if you c'n see yer way through to gettin' my property back, you'll not find me ungrateful, Mr. Barrett," he concluded.

Father's desk was stacked with similar complaints. He was himself a victim of the rapacious commissaries and their clerks. With a signed receipt from a farmer selling his goods, they could fill in whatever amount they pleased on the sale. It was usually a more than fair sum of money, but none of it ever reached the farmer, for that went into the pockets of the commissaries. Any complaint could be legally ignored, for the victim had signed, hadn't he? He was only trying to squeeze additional money from the Crown, the cheat. Any who refused to sell their surplus could have the entire crop confiscated. That, too, had happened.

"Will we be able to help him, Father?" I asked after Finch had left.

His answer was a weary grimace. "We'll do what we can, laddie. There's some forgery at the bottom of this case, else they wouldn't have been able to take the horses and wagon. That might make a difference. At the very least we can raise a bit of noise over it. Because of the way these things work, one can't help but expect to see the corruption sweeping in, but this business is getting completely out of hand. I'll write to DeQuincey. He's busy playing pot-boy to General Howe, but perhaps he'll take a moment to remember his neighbors."

Nicholas DeQuincey was one of the most ardent supporters of the king's cause and had been among the Loyalist troops waiting to greet Howe's army when it landed on Staten Island two months ago. Apparently he was so loyal he was willing to turn a blind eye to the resulting depredations of Howe's army. That Father was planning to ask for help from such a man was a clear indication to me that he'd pretty much given up hope of using the civil courts to settle matters. Now it would fall to calling on friendships and favors to achieve justice.

I ran my thumb over a pile of papers outlining various complaints against the occupying army. There was little hope in me that anything would come of them, even with DeQuincey's intervention.

"It's not fair," I muttered.

He looked up from the letter he was composing. "No, by God, it isn't. It's bad now and will only get worse. If that Howe had played the wolf instead of the tortoise he'd have captured Washington before he and that rabble ever had the chance to leave this island. At least then we would have seen the beginning of the end to this tragic nonsense. I don't know how far Washington will retreat, but there's enough country north of here for him to drag this out for months."

*Months.* Good lord.

Father finished his letter and addressed it. While he worked, I was busy turning Finch's complaint into language suitable for a court presentation. The day after I'd arrived home, Father had taken me on as his apprentice and I was glad of the honor and the chance to use what I'd learned in Cambridge. Later I would be making a second copy, though that was really a clerk's job. We had no clerks; the two lads that had been with us had since departed to be with their families or to join up with Loyalist troops. I possessed no inclination to follow their example, though Father hadn't encouraged me in one way or another. I shared his opinion that the fighting was better left to the soldiers who knew how. He needed my help more than they and more than one incident had occurred to justify my remaining close to home.

Back in January while I'd been making arrangements to return, Father had had the bad luck to be in Hempstead when a rebel troop led by Colonel Heard had ridden in to force known and suspected Loyalists to sign an oath of obedience to the Continental and Provincial congresses. He signed rather than submit to arrest, but later found little reason to be bound by his agreement.

"A forced promise is no promise," he told me. "They'll make no new friends to their cause with such methods and only turn the undecided against them."

Had Father been undecided before, their actions had clarified things for him.

For a time. Now our British saviors seemed to be doing their best to alienate those that had shown them the greatest support. Father's vast patience was showing signs of erosion as each new case came in. We'd seen five people this morning. That officer, his sergeant, and the troop of Hessians had been very busy. Doubtless they were also benefiting from their "legal" thefts.

When I'd finished my draft, Father paused in his own work to look it over.

"Is it all right?" I asked after a moment.

He gave a pleased nod. "Wait 'til we get you in court. If you do as well there as you do on this . . ."

If we ever had another court. The exacting work of civil law was yet another aspect of life interrupted by the rebellion. At this rate I would be serving an unnaturally long time at my apprenticeship.

Someone knocked at the door. At our combined invitation it silently opened and Jericho announced that the midday meal was ready. Father shed his wig, we put away our writing tools, and marched out in his wake to assume our accustomed places at the table.

The library was in a corner room of the house and with both sets of windows open was subject to a pleasing cross breeze that made it comfortable in the hot months. The dining room was not so advantageously located and had but one window. It was opened wide in a futile hope of freshening the close air within, but the wind wasn't in the right direction to provide much relief. We sat and stewed in the heat, picked lightly at our food, and imbibed a goodly share of drink.

Little had changed in the years I was absent and this ritual the least of all. Mother would hold forth on the most tedious topics, or complain about whatever had offended her in the few hours since breakfast, usually quite a lot. She was well supported by Mrs. Hardinbrook and, to a lesser extent, by Dr. Beldon. Both had become fixtures in the household, though Beldon could be said to be a contributing member by reason of his doctoring skills. He'd proved to be an able enough physician, but was still liable to fits of toad-eating. Elizabeth ignored him, Father tolerated him, and I avoided him, which was sometimes difficult because the man was always trying to court my friendship.

Today Mother was full of rancor against yet another rise in prices.

". . . four times what they charged last year for the same thing. If we didn't have our own gardens we should starve to death this winter. As it is, Mrs. Nooth will have to work day and night to build up our stores once the crops really start to ripen. It's a disgrace, Samuel."

"Indeed it is, Marie," Father said, taking a larger than normal draft from his wineglass.

"Of course, *if* we have anything left to harvest," she added. This was a not too subtle reference to the crop sold to the first commissary to come through the area. Under circumstances very similar to Finch's, Father had had to sign a blank receipt for a load of grain. The grain was collected, but we were still waiting to be paid for it.

Father spared a glance for me and raised one eyebrow. I smoothed out the scowl that was preventing me from properly chewing my food.

"I got a letter from Hester Holland today," Elizabeth said to me. She wanted to change the subject. "She'd heard that all the DeQuincey boys were serving under General Howe."

"Then God keep them safe and see them through to a swift victory," Mother responded. She didn't like Miss Holland, but the DeQuincey clan held her wholehearted approval. Mother was not beyond doing some toad-eating of her own, and the DeQuinceys were a large and influential family. They had money as well and a match between one of its scions and Elizabeth was something to encourage.

"Amen," said Mrs. Hardinbrook, but it was rather faint. She also had hopes for arranging an advantageous marriage, but in three years she had yet to successfully interest Elizabeth in her brother or her brother in Elizabeth. It was very frustrating for her, but amusing to watch, in a way.

Beldon was entirely aware of her efforts and now and then would commiserate with me on the subject. He had polite and honorable admiration for my sister, but that was as far as it went, he assured me, perhaps hoping to gain some praise for his nobility of spirit. I'd met others of his temper at Cambridge, men with a decidedly indifferent attitude toward women. Soon after my homecoming I'd had to make clear to him that I was not of that number, a fact he graciously accepted, though the toad-eating continued as before.

"Hester wrote that some of the soldiers being quartered in the old church are very handsome," Elizabeth said. Unlike Hester, she wasn't the sort to idly gossip about such things and I wondered why she'd bothered to mention it, until I noticed that she'd directed the remark in Mrs. Hardinbrook's direction. The lady had once taken pains to be present when a company of commissary men had marched by our gate to their camp, wearing her best dress and most winning smile for the thieves. Elizabeth thought—not without reason—that she was a great fool.

I now perceived this innocuous statement to be an acid comment on Mrs. Hardinbrook's immodest behavior. It might also be taken as an indirect reminder of Beldon's preferences and the futility of altering them with a marriage. Mrs. Hardinbrook had an outstandingly thick skin, but a twitch of her brows betrayed that she had felt the blow. Beldon's lips curled briefly—with humor, I was relieved to note, not offense.

Mother, innocent of this byplay, took it as something to pounce upon. "She would, I'm sure. Elizabeth, you really must try to cultivate a better class of friend than that Holland girl. If she's keeping company with soldiers then she's no better than a common tavern slut."

Mrs. Hardinbrook smirked, entirely missing the implication that she could be included in Mother's judgment.

Elizabeth's face flushed and her mouth thinned into nonexistence. For a few awful seconds she looked astonishingly like Mother during one of her rages. Father's eye fell upon her, though, and he solemnly winked. Her anger subsided at this reminder not to take anything that Mother said seriously. They had had plenty of opportunity to practice such silent communication and once again it had spared us all from a lengthy row.

Beldon had noticed—for he was always alert to notice what was going on around him—and visibly relaxed. Whenever Mother became unduly upset it always fell to him to help calm her down. His bottle of laudanum had proved to be very handy in the past, but as a good doctor he was reluctant to rely on it for every ill happening in the house. I'd seen more than one opium eater ruining himself at Cambridge, so on that point he and I were in accord.

"I saw Mr. Finch's eldest earlier," he said. "While waiting for his father he acquainted me with the family's misfortunes."

"Hmm," grunted Father discouragingly, unwilling to speak of business at the table.

"His son mentioned some other things as well," he added. "Mostly just to pass the time, I fear. A decent young man, but dull." He'd picked up his cue and made his tone of voice lazy and bored, as though it were hardly worth the effort to speak. He'd struck just the right balance between getting his message across yet not arousing anyone's curiosity. Mother and Mrs. Hardinbrook duly ignored him, having no interest in farmers' gossip.

Father looked up at this. Beldon met his eyes briefly, then contemplated the wallpaper. I could almost hear Father say "damnation" in his head. He grunted again and nodded at Beldon, then at me. This meant we were to both come to the library after the meal.

Silence reigned after that. The heat was too much for even Mother to maintain a dialogue of her many grievances for long. She turned down a thick slab of hot pie and excused herself. She usually had a nap in her room at this time of day unless there was entertaining to be done. Nothing was planned for tonight and no one hindered her exit.

Mrs. Hardinbrook was a woman with an appetite that no amount of heat could impair. She had her pie with an ample slice of cheese on the side, and an extra glass of wine. Groaning under that load she would certainly follow Mother's example and snore away the rest of the afternoon. One by one, the rest of us excused ourselves and left.

Elizabeth had been the first out and waited for us in the library. She'd also caught Father's signal and was interested to hear Beldon's news. Such informal gatherings had been called before; Beldon questioned her presence only once, at the first one. He thought that the gentle nature of her sex justified her exclusion from "business" but the tart reply she gave to his suggestion swiftly altered his view of things.

Father settled himself in his chair, Elizabeth and I took over the settee, and Beldon perched on a windowsill to take advantage of the breeze. Something of a dandy, he sported his wig at all times and in all weathers no matter how uncomfortable it made him. He flicked a handkerchief from his sleeve and mopped at the shining beads drenching his forehead.

"Tell me what you heard," Father instructed without preamble.

Beldon did so. "This is rumor, mind you, but young Roddy trusted the source."

"What source?"

"Some sergeant working with the commissaries. He was at The Oak and boasting about his successful collections to one and all. Roddy and Nathan Finch were keeping quiet in a corner and heard him talk about how the commissaries were not going to content themselves with waiting for the farmers to come to them. He did not exactly mention what they were planning, but it seems obvious that they will start visiting individual households next and making collections."

Father snorted. "Wholesale thievery is what it will be."

Beldon smiled unpleasantly. "They've dug themselves in well enough. They're familiar with the country and people by now and will be sharp to see anything suspicious."

Elizabeth had kept up on events. "You mean if anyone is hiding livestock or grain from them?"

"Exactly, Miss Barrett. They'll rake over this island like a nor'easter and take what they please—all in the king's name, of course, and the devil for the people they take from, begging your pardon."

"How is it that you know how they work?"

He paused, held in place by Elizabeth's penetrating eyes. Nothing less than the truth would suffice for her and he knew it. "From '57 to '59 I served under General James Wolfe during the campaign against the French," he said matter-of-factly.

We glanced at one another, brows raised and questions blooming at this revelation.

"You served in the army?" asked Father after a moment.

"Yes," he said shortly. "Wasn't much older than your son here at the time."

He'd not intended to surprise us, otherwise the toady in him might have provided a greater buildup for such a story.

"Why have you not mentioned this before?" asked Father, when he'd recovered from giving Beldon a wondering reappraisal. Elizabeth and I had unabashedly mimicked him.

Beldon's mouth curled inward as though he regretted imparting his information. "It happened a long time ago, sir. It is not one of my happier memories and I beg that none of you mention it to my sister. Deborah, as you may have noticed, enjoys talking and I fear she may try everyone's patience with the subject."

It abruptly occurred to me that Mrs. Hardinbrook knew nothing about this chapter of Beldon's life, else she would have long ago spoken of it in the hope of making him more attractive to Elizabeth. Recounting the exploits of a war hero would have been irresistible to her—unless Beldon had not been particularly heroic. . . .

I pushed that unworthy and dishonorable speculation aside. Some of Father's friends had also been involved in that great conflict and were equally reticent about their experiences. Whatever reason Beldon had for keeping quiet would be respected.

Similar thoughts may have rushed through Father's mind, for he said, "You have our word that we shall say nothing to your sister or anyone else, Doctor." A quick look to each of us guaranteed our nodding agreement to this promise. "Now tell us what we should expect from these soldiers."

"More of the same, I shouldn't wonder," he answered. "No one would suffer overmuch from their collections if they were honest enough to pay good coin for what they take, but we've seen proof that that is unlikely to happen. My suggestion is that we send word to the citizenry hereabouts to start preparing new spots to conceal their excess. Have some portion set aside to be taken away, some portion placed in their usual storage places and hide all the rest."

"Deception against the king's soldiers?" Father mocked.

"Defense against the jackals professing to serve those soldiers," Beldon countered, referring to the commissaries. "They serve only themselves and will continue to do so. I've seen their like before and no amount of feeding will sate their appetite for money. General Howe can chase Washington and his rabble from one colony to another until winter comes to freeze the lot of them to perdition, but these fellows have no such distractions. They will continue their plunders until nothing remains."

No one of us could doubt that. In his many letters to me, Father had often mentioned what a prize Long Island would be should there be a full-blown rebellion. In July we had heard talk that Washington was planning to send men through the counties to either drive all the cattle and sheep they found into the eastern end of the island or shoot the herds to keep them out of British hands. Not surprisingly, this was met with strong opposition, and from his own men. They were not terribly anxious to confront the Loyalist owners of the stock. It seemed that earlier efforts to disarm these citizens had failed and they'd made it clear to the rebels that they were entirely prepared to defend themselves and their property.

Washington fumed, the New York convention stalled, and in the meantime General Howe's brother, Vice-Admiral Richard, Lord Howe, arrived with his 150 ships crammed full with soldiers. Washington's attention was happily engaged elsewhere. Later, General Howe made his landing at Gravesend Bay and saved the king's loyal subjects from the threat of ravaging rebels. Unfortunately, he had scant interest in saving them from his own men.

"We'll have to have a meeting," I said. "Perhaps at the church after services. It's the best way for everyone to hear it all."

"Aye, including the soldiers, I think," said Father, reminding me of the new additions to our congregation. Some of us still hadn't determined whether the men were there to worship God or to make sure sedition was not being preached. "This is the stuff that charges of treason are made of. They'll think we're conspiring with those rascals over in Suffolk County rather than looking out for our own."

Instantly, I jumped to an alternative. "Then we'll call upon only those we trust and inform them directly."

Father's eyes glinted. "Which means there's nothing in writing that may be held against us. I think you have a talent for this, laddie."

I couldn't help but grin. Having grown used to the physical and mental stimulus of Cambridge, I was missing it; this business promised to be rare entertainment. It might also prove to be much more interesting than those old amusements, which chiefly consisted of getting drunk whenever the chance presented itself. "I can start at first light tomorrow."

"But not alone. Dr. Beldon, do you not go on mercy calls?"

"You know I do, sir," he said, wiping his brow once more, then pausing as he pondered the reason for Father's query.

"I think you should go with Jonathan on his errands."

I started to ask why Beldon's company was necessary and bit it off as comprehension dawned. A doctor had an infinite number of reasons to be riding from house to house. Beldon's profession would provide us with excellent cover should we be questioned by suspicious folk, whether they be rebels or soldiers in the king's army.

"Very good, sir," said Beldon wryly, understanding and approving.

"And what shall I do?" Elizabeth gently demanded. She clearly wanted to go with us, but the unsettled state of things abrogated her unspoken wish. She, too, had heard of the many outrages and was not so foolish to think herself immune to such insults.

"With Jonathan gone I shall need you to help me with the work here," said Father. "You write faster and more clearly than he does, anyway." I took no umbrage at Father's opinion of my penmanship, for it was true.

Elizabeth's archness vanished. She enjoyed helping Father and had done so in the past. Mother disapproved, of course—for it was not ladylike to play the clerk—but not so much as to forbid it.

"Between us I want to plan out how to conceal the surplus to last through the winter. I'm keeping in mind that we may have more than our own to feed. Your mother"—here he paused as though trying to overcome an indigestible bite from his last meal—"has written to those cousins of hers offering them asylum until the rebellion is past. They have yet to reply, but we will have to be prepared. We'll need a second buttery, some place to store the smoked meats . . ."

"Flour, sugar, spirits, yes." Elizabeth's face lightened. "I shall talk with Mrs. Nooth and Jericho about all of it. We'll have more hidden treasure than Captain Kidd."

"If I might recommend one more suggestion," said Beldon. "That is, I'm sure dear Deborah would be mightily interested in offering her assistance to you, but she is, after all, a rather busy lady."

This was met with another awkward moment of silence, then Elizabeth nodded. "Yes, Dr. Beldon. I believe it would be better not to disturb her or Mother with such mundane chores as these will be."

Beldon looked relieved. And so he was able to politely pass on his lack of confidence that his sister could hold her tongue in the wrong company.

"He's not a bad fellow, is he?" Elizabeth said as we strolled slowly around the house in the somewhat cooler air of the early evening.

"Beldon? I suppose not. I think he'd be better off without her, though." There was no need to mention the lady's name.

"Wouldn't we all?"

A few steps to the side of us, Jericho stifled something that might be interpreted as a cough. Or a laugh. It was quite a display from a man who took so much pride in a lofty household station that often demanded great reticence. However, he was away from the house and treading the same grounds that we'd tumbled over as rowdy children; he could allow himself to be himself to some extent. We could not go back to those days, but the memory was with us and comforting company.

"I think that staying here has been a beneficial experience for him," she said.

"In what way?"

"He's allowed the chance to be with a less demanding company of people, for one thing."

"He was hardly in isolation in Philadelphia."

"Yes, but his social life was certainly limited, if Mother and that woman are anything to judge by. Like attracts like, y' know."

I had no trouble imagining Beldon surrounded by a large group made up of the sort of people Mother would approve of, and freely shuddered.

"Since you've returned I've looked at him as though through your eyes and noticed that he's not the toad-eater he was at first."

"I've noticed no change."

"That's because you avoid him."

True.

"When he's away from her he can be quite nice."

"Good God, you're not thinking of—"

Elizabeth laughed. "Hardly. I'm just saying that he has a gentle nature and more than a spoonful of wit, but marriage to him is the last thing on my mind. His as well, I will confidently add."

"More's the pity for Mrs. Hardinbrook, then. She does so want to be your sister-in-law."

Elizabeth shuddered in turn. "What about you, little brother? Did you not meet anyone in your wide travels? You mentioned going to parties with Cousin Oliver. Surely there were young ladies there . . ."

"Indeed there were, and the lot of them as interested in the Fonteyn money as Mrs. Hardinbrook."

Except for one. Heavens, I hadn't thought of Nora in months. Perhaps if I'd asked her, but no; she'd said she never wanted to marry. She really couldn't because . . . because . . . well, for some reason. I absently probed for the scar on the back of my head. It was mostly gone by now. Harder to find.

"Something wrong, Mr. Jonathan?" Jericho inquired.

"Touch of headache. Must be the day's heat catching me up." I dismissed it and turned my mind to other things. "Remember the Captain's Kettle?" I asked, using our childhood name for it. We'd spent hours there, playing treasure hunt.

"Where you nearly broke your neck? Of course I do," Elizabeth replied.

"I was thinking that it would be an excellent place to hide our cattle. It's away from the usual roads and has shelter and fodder a-plenty."

Elizabeth murmured her approval and added the idea to the growing list of things to be done that she kept in her head.

"I'll ride by there tomorrow and look it over to be sure."

"Do you wish me to come along, Mr. Jonathan?"

Jericho knew all about my errands. How he knew was a mystery. "I suppose you could, if you want to. But won't you be busy here?"

"Jericho is offering to play the chaperon for you," Elizabeth explained.

I chuckled and shook my head. "I've nothing to worry about. The good doctor and I understand one another."

"A pity his sister doesn't. The year you left she got so tiresome about him that I spent two months with the DeQuincey girls just to get away from her."

And from Mother. Elizabeth had given me every detail in her letters. Unable to stand the constant judgmental scolding any longer, she'd arranged an invitation to visit her friends, packed some trunks, and departed with her maid. Mother had been livid about it, for Elizabeth hadn't shared her plans with anyone except Father, who pretended a detached interest in the matter as if it were unworthy of his notice. Eventually Mother seemed to adopt the same attitude (with Mrs. Hardinbrook aping her, of course) and things settled down again. So Jericho assured me when he wrote. When Elizabeth finally returned, she found Mother's disinterest in her to be a welcome improvement over their previous relationship.

But even with such respites, three years of tension and temper had had a wearing effect on my sister. She was older and certainly wiser, but much of her natural lightness of spirit had vanished. There was a watchful weariness in her expression that was forgotten only when she was away from home or with me. The rest of the time she wore it or assumed a bland mask as hard as armor. It was a trait she'd picked up, unconsciously I thought, from our long-suffering servants.

Some of them had left after they'd decided Mother's "brief stay" was becoming permanent. We'd lost two cooks, several maids, and five stable lads to her ire. All had been replaced as needed, and we still had the slaves, but when Mother was around, none of them had an easy time of it. Mrs. Nooth had remained, thank God, or the whole household might have fallen apart.

"I think," said Elizabeth, "that this would be a good place for the second buttery."

"But this *is* the buttery," I pointed out.

"Yes, and what better place to hide it? Don't you see? We'll have some of the lads dig the present one that much deeper, make a false wall only we know about . . ."

"Like a priest's hole?"

"But much larger."

"We can do the same thing for our other stores as well."

"Be sure to suggest it to those you talk to tomorrow. And please do be very careful, Jonathan."

I was thinking of making a jest at Beldon's expense, but the somber look on Elizabeth's face stopped me. Should the commissaries, should anyone either on the rebels' side or simply up to mischief find out what was being planned, everything we had could be confiscated. With no notice whatsoever Father and I, Beldon too, could be arrested for treason and even hanged. And by our own countrymen. The only worse punishment could have come from the rebels. Had they been in charge of the Island, I doubt that things would be much different except they would not have left us out of their battles. Their rabble's maxim that anyone not for them was against them had caused much grief and suffering. More than one man had been tarred and feathered by mindless mobs and died from it.

"I shall be very careful," I promised her. "Anyway, this won't last long. Just for the season, I'm sure. Beldon thinks that once Washington's great Continental Army gets a taste of real winter, they'll scurry back to their hearths like rabbits to a burrow. Then Howe can round up the so-called Congress and put an end to the matter."

"I hope so. Do you think they'll be hanged?"

"Only if they're caught. They were foolish enough to sign that treasonous declaration. What presumptuous gall they had to pretend they represented everyone. . . ." I'd read a copy of the thing along with Father and like him had raged against the inflammatory language of the charges against the king. (Though under our present circumstances I thought that the point about the military being independent of and superior to the civil power was well made. Now, issues that should have been decided in courts were being contested in battle.) We both concluded the absurd document should be consigned to the flames and its perpetrators to the gallows.

But . . . that was General Howe's problem, not mine, I reminded myself. I had other matters to worry about.

Well before dawn Jericho woke me out of a lethargic dream state as he came in with my morning tray. A vivid picture of Nora Jones was before me, but faded rapidly as I tried to hold on to it. Then it was completely gone and I gave up in mild frustration to the inevitable. Everyone's mind is full of doors that open only during sleep, and mine were the sort to slam solidly shut at the slightest hint of waking.

The dreams troubled me, for their content—whenever I had the rare instance of recalling one—was disturbing. Now and then my drowsy mind would throw out a bit of memory that made no sense, yet during the dream itself I had no difficulty in understanding. The most familiar one concerned Nora. We were at the Bolyns' party again; I danced with her in the maze, kissed her, made love with her. Pleasant enough, and true enough, in the way of a dream, but both of us were splashed from head to toe with blood. It was warm and just turning sticky and the heavy smell of it clogged the air. I could almost taste it. Neither of us and no one else ever seemed to notice, though.

The other dream memory was more mundane, but for an unknown reason much more frightening. It was really nothing: only Tony Warburton smiling down at me from some high place. The first time I remembered having it I'd awakened in a cold, slimy sweat, lighted every candle in the room, and shivered under the coverlet like a child. This reaction eventually passed, but I was never quite comfortable with that one.

"It will be very hot today," said Jericho as he went to the wardrobe to choose clothes for me.

I sipped tea, holding the cup in both hands. "It was hot yesterday."

"More so today. Eat what you can now. You won't want to later."

He was always right about such things. I worked my way through the food he'd brought, slowly adjusting my thinking away from senseless dreams to the tasks awaiting me this day. Even with Beldon's company, I planned to enjoy myself.

"Do you wish a shave?" Jericho asked.

I brushed a finger along one stubbled cheek. He'd shaved me yesterday and had we been following our usual routine, I wouldn't need another until tomorrow. Should I have a clean chin while calling on our neighbors, or not? Not, I decided, and said as much to Jericho. Most of the farmers and other men shaved but once a week for their churchgoing and thought it good enough. I didn't want to put them off by playing the dandy. That was Beldon's specialty.

"Is Beldon awake yet?" I mumbled around some biscuit.

"Oh, yes. Sheba just got his tray for him."

No need to comment how inappropriate it was for a young girl to be taking up Beldon's breakfast rather than one of the house lads. Not that Beldon made himself offensive in any way with anyone. The girl was safe enough with him, as was any lad in the house, for he was really a decent sort.

Except for the toad-eating, I reflexively reminded myself.

Upon consideration, I found it odd that Mother was capable of throwing herself into a foaming rage at an erroneous assumption of impropriety between myself and Elizabeth and yet could entirely ignore the doctor. I'd once mentioned it to Father, who opined that Mother simply did not know or, if she did, contemptuously disbelieved the possibility. Whether her ignorance was willful or not, Beldon was aware of it, and like many other facets of life, it seemed to amuse him.

Jericho laid out my old claret-colored coat. I had put on some muscle since I'd last worn it and the seams had been let out, the work carefully covered by fancy braid. While nowhere near being threadbare, it was less than new, and thus the correct item to wear while making informal calls upon our neighbors during their working day. Next to it he unfolded a fresh linen shirt, breeches, and my second-best riding boots. When I expressed a preference for a straw hat to wear against the sun, he pursed his lips, shook his head, and brought forth the correct head covering for the coat.

"No wig?" I queried lightly.

He started to reach for a box, but I hastily called him off.

Since Beldon had no valet to help him he came down to the library ten minutes ahead of me. Father, still in his dressing gown and silk nightcap, was with him and once more going over the names of the people we were to see. Beldon thought it was too short a list, but Father pointed out that it was better to see a few at a time rather than rushing about in noticeable haste.

"You're a doctor making your usual calls on your patients and Jonathan is along to visit with their families."

And to act as guide. Beldon knew most of our neighbors by now, if only from seeing them every Sunday at church, but he was less sure of where they lived unless they were regular patients. Rapelji, for example, was not in that number. His housekeepers, Rachel and Sarah, were adept at keeping him in excellent health with their herb lore. Many of the local farmers were content to see them for their illnesses as well, sparing themselves from paying a doctor's fee.

I noted that Father's mistress, Mrs. Montagu, was not among those named, though her home was along the route we would take. Perhaps he would see to informing her himself later. I hoped so. With all our late troubles, I felt that he was in need of some pleasant, relaxing company for a change.

He let us out the side door facing the stables and wished us good luck. Our mounts were ready, the doctor on a hack he'd purchased some time ago, and a similar working horse for myself. Rolly would have been a better ride, but could draw unwelcome attention. I had no desire to lose him on the high road to some avaricious officer with a sheaf of blank receipts in his pocket.

Beldon spent a moment fussing with his box of medicines, making sure it was secure, then swung up. The horses may have sensed a long day was ahead and made no effort to use up their strength with unnecessary prancing or high spirits. We paced sedately down toward the gate.

"It's good to finally be off," said Beldon. "I hardly slept last night, thinking of this."

I made a noncommittal noise I'd learned from Father. It was useful for expressing almost any sentiment, the interpretation of it being left to the listener.

"You do realize that I shall be making real calls, don't you?"

I said that I did.

"One of the Coldrup daughters has her migraines, and the youngest at the McCuins broke his arm. . . ."

He chattered on, a man interested in his work. He reminded me of Oliver in that regard and because of it I was better able to tolerate his company. He was, as Elizabeth said, "not such a bad fellow."

We turned east into the waxing force of the rising sun. As Jericho had prophesied, it was going to be very hot. I squinted against the searing light and tilted my hat down. I couldn't see where I was going too well, but the horse knew his business and kept to the road.

We passed Mrs. Montagu's gate on the right and a mile farther down I indicated for Beldon to leave the road. The Captain's Kettle was in this area. Our property line crossed over at this point. The boundary had been a bone of contention between Mrs. Montagu and Father soon after her husband had died fourteen years ago. Two sets of surveyors had come up with very different interpretations of where the correct line lay and the matter had ended up in court. Father had argued his case and would have won it had Matilda Montagu remained at home during the proceedings. Upon meeting her, he became sympathetic to her claim and dropped the litigation. With his sympathy and her gratitude as a beginning, they proceeded to form a lasting, satisfying, and highly discreet friendship.

I led the way now, weaving my horse between the trees. I hadn't been up here since that April ride so long ago, but the landmarks were unchanged. Within, I had the unnerving feeling that I would once more see Father and Mrs. Montagu walking hand in hand in the distance. That was foolish, of course, but the feeling lingered and strengthened as we drew closer to the kettle.

Birds squawked and squabbled overhead. Insects hummed and dodged them. The air was thick with their noise, yet seemed muted, flattened by the growing heat. Or distance. There didn't seem to be much activity where we were.

"I don't think we're alone," said Beldon, barely moving his lips and speaking just loud enough for me to hear him over the movement of the horses.

One can usually sense when someone is watching; I just hadn't recognized it. "Where?"

"Ahead of us. On either side. I think we should go back."

I wholly agreed with him and the two of us turned in unison without another word. It could be children at play or a pair of lovers on a tryst, but it could also be any number of less innocent threats. Better to return after the prickling on the backs of our necks went away.

We did not get that chance, though. Before we'd gone fifty yards a hard-looking man in uniform stepped out from a dense thicket of bushes, aimed his musket at us, and in a rough and accented voice ordered us to halt.

I knew the uniform. Everyone on the Island did. He was a Hessian.

# CHAPTER 10

A second man joined him and barked out another order at us.
"Down!" the first one translated.
Beldon and I exchanged looks. Heroism was the last thing on our minds. Not that we had anything to be heroic about. Once we'd identified ourselves we'd be able to leave.
I hoped.
We cautiously dismounted and kept hold of the reins. We studied the soldiers and were studied in turn. They saw by our clothes that we were gentlemen, but there were plenty of so-called gentlemen opposing the king these days. The men were flushed and their sweat-stained uniforms showed evidence that they'd been hiking through the woods for some time. It was certain to me that they had some purpose to the exercise, perhaps an ominous one for myself and Beldon. Beldon's horse, supremely unconcerned with the situation, dropped his head and began tearing at the grass.
The second man barked a question, but before the first could translate it, I hesitantly answered in their own language.
"This is Dr. Theophilous Beldon and I am Jonathan Barrett. This is my land. Why are you here?"
Though I'd only previously used it in my academics, my German was apparently intelligible. It surprised them, and to my tremendous relief the grip on their rifles slackened. The second man came to attention and identified himself as Detricht Schmidt and gave his rank, but I did not

know that particular word. He could have been anything from a simple soldier to a colonel, though his manner and the lack of trimmings on his uniform made the latter very unlikely. I repeated my last question and finally got an answer.

"They're looking for a band of rebels," I explained to Beldon. "At least that's what I think he said. Something about stolen horses."

Beldon nodded, also impressed by my linguistic gifts. "Where is his commander?"

"*Close by,*" said Schmidt, after I'd asked.

"Here," repeated the other man agreeably, waving an arm at the surrounding woods. His accent was heavy, but probably no worse than mine must have sounded to his ears.

"We want to go," I said to him in slow English.

Both of them shrugged. I tried to say the same thing in German, but garbled it up. However, Schmidt understood enough of my meaning.

"*You must stay,*" I was told.

"Here halt," his friend emphasized, making a sitting gesture with his palm toward the ground. Both were nodding and smiling, though, so perhaps they'd decided we were not with the rebels.

"They must want their commander to look us over first," I said.

Beldon was amiable. "Then let's all be pleasant about it, since it can't be helped." He smiled in return and pulled a snuffbox from his pocket, offering a pinch of its contents to our captors. They accepted with many friendly thanks and another piece of our initial tension broke away.

Schmidt excused himself after a moment and disappeared into the trees. The other man gave his name as Hausmann and complimented my German. "Schmidt soon back," he promised.

"*Is your commander English?*"

"*Jawöhl,* Herr Barrett."

"*Where are the rebels?*"

He shrugged, but it caused him to recall that they might be nearby and he checked the surrounding open area uneasily. "Trees go," he suggested, wanting to get into their cover.

Beldon and I led our horses in, grateful for the shade, though it cut us off from the wind. Hausmann kept his distance so as to have room to bring his gun to bear if we made it necessary. He'd relaxed somewhat, but it was clear that he was ready to deal with any threat until ordered to stand down by his commander.

"How many men are here?" I asked.

He puzzled out my meaning right away, but would only smile and shake his head.

"Not a good idea to give away the strength of your troop," Beldon, the former soldier, explained.

And I thought I'd only been trying to make conversation. I had better luck asking Hausmann where he was from and if he had any family. For that I got the name of his village and a number of relatives and their history in that district. Much of it was too rapid for me to follow, but I made encouraging noises whenever he slowed down.

"Your family?" he asked politely. "Your land all?" He indicated the area.

"Our land," I said.

He looked both envious and admiring. "Land is good. Here land I want."

"Here?"

He waved to show he meant some other land than what we stood upon. "Farm. Woman. *Das Kleinkind.*"

"What?" asked Beldon.

"He wants to have a family."

"What about the one he left in Europe?"

"I think they're all dead. He said the wars killed them."

Before he could express any sympathy, the three of us turned at the sound of several men approaching. Schmidt had returned. With him were two more Hessians and two men wearing the uniform of the king's army.

"Lieutenant James Nash," said the one with the most braid, making a succinct introduction.

I recognized the name. He was behind the theft of Finch's wagon and horses. He seemed a bit old to be a lieutenant, in his late forties, I guessed. Perhaps he'd been unable to advance further for lack of funding, patronage, talent, or opportunity. This new war was probably his last chance to change his luck and acquire some security for his old age. Too bad for Finch.

I introduced myself and Beldon to him and informed him as politely as possible that he was trespassing. I did not employ that particular word, but he knew what I meant.

"My apologies, sir, but we're on the king's business and cannot make distinctions between public and private lands. Those damned rebels don't and we have to follow where they run."

"I believe your men mentioned they were horse thieves."

"Aye, they are," he added with some warmth. "Tried to take a wagon too, but we foiled that."

I refrained from looking at Beldon and kept a very straight face. "What a shame. That they took your horses, I mean."

"We'll find 'em," he assured me. "If you know the area, you can help us."

I smiled graciously and hoped that it looked sincere. "I should be delighted to lend you any assistance, Lieutenant. That is, if I may take your invitation to mean that we are no longer in detention?"

"You never were, but my men do have to be careful. Some of the louts are armed and not afraid to shoot. I think they're headed for Suffolk County with their booty."

Or to Finch's farm.

"You've gone over this acreage thoroughly, then?"

"Not quite. Know of any hiding places?"

"These woods," I said truthfully, but vaguely. "But horses would slow them down. If they're in a hurry, then they'll be likely to swing back toward the road."

"*Herr Oberleutnant!*" Another Hessian rushed away from us, shouting.

"He's spotted them," said the sergeant. He snapped out orders to the men and they spread into the trees. Nash was content to let them do the sweaty work and followed more slowly. He wanted us to come with him.

"I have my rounds to make," Beldon protested, hoping to end the business.

"Won't be long. Best if we all stay together. You don't care to catch a stray bullet if things go badly, do you?"

Beldon did not and we resigned ourselves to Nash's company. He led the way, his stocky, paunchy body moving easily and making his own path. We did the best we could leading the horses. Despite the shade, the heat was worse now. I was damp from face to shanks and a bramble scratch between my sleeve and riding glove was beginning to sting. Nuisance. It was all one foolish, bloody nuisance.

Nash's men had entirely vanished, but I could hear them crashing along. They were headed in the direction of the Captain's Kettle. If the rebels were local—and I was certain they were—then the kettle would be the first sanctuary they'd think to use.

"*Down here! Down here!*" one of the Hessians called in the distance. It could only mean that they'd found it. Nash speeded up a little.

Damnation. Not only had the rebels trespassed our land and possibly thrown unwelcome suspicion upon Father, but they'd promptly given away our own best secret. We'd have to think up some other place to hide our stock this year.

Since they knew about the kettle, I suspected the thieves had to be the Finch boys, Roddy and Nathan. I mentioned this in a whisper to Beldon, who reluctantly concurred.

"I hope they have the sense to run," he muttered, his mouth tight and the corners turned down. If caught with the horses they would be hanged. Rebel or no, it was not a fate I could wish upon anybody.

"Mind yourself," I muttered back. If Nash heard him . . .

Someone fired a gun.

Beldon dropped and I instinctively imitated him. The horrid crash was well ahead of us, though, and isolated. No other shots sounded. Nash urged us to hurry and plunged forward, which struck me as a ridiculously foolish course of action. No soldier, I. Neither of us were armed. I felt terribly vulnerable.

Hausmann appeared and relayed information to Nash, who understood him.

"Nothing to worry about," he told us. "Fellow tripped on a root. Accidental discharge."

"Thank God for that," Beldon breathed out. He produced his handkerchief and scraped futilely at his streaming forehead. I sighed as well, but my heart wasn't yet ready to retire from the place where it had lodged halfway up my throat. As though reading my thought, Beldon grinned at me. I found myself returning it. That seemed to help.

Nash caught up with some of his men now and questioned them. They were pointing and gesturing. From this I deduced that they'd discovered the kettle and were trying to explain its geography to him. My horse swung his ears forward and neighed. Ahead of us and down, another horse answered. The trees were very thick here. If you weren't careful you could fall right into it. Beldon tied his animal up and walked over to investigate with the others. I did the same and hoped Nash wouldn't ask me anything awkward.

"Did you know about this?" he demanded, pointing to a break in the trees. From here it was easy to see the drop off.

"Of course I did," I said blandly.

"Just the place for a horse thief to hide, so why didn't you tell me about it?"

"I'm hardly familiar with how a horse thief thinks, Lieutenant. It never occurred to me to mention it." True enough. "Had your man not given the alarm, I would have taken you here." Blatant falsehood, but hopefully God would forgive me that one.

Nash may have had further comment on the subject, but he was more concerned with retrieving his . . . king's property. "Well, things have worked out. We got the horses back."

"Won't the thieves be close by, though?"

"That shot seems to have frightened them away. We're safe enough. Come on."

Beldon looked dubious despite Nash's confidence. "As simple civilians, may we be excused from this exercise? I have no desire to inflict any more damage to my clothes than they've already suffered."

Nash gave him a half-amused, half-contemptuous look that professional soldiers reserve for the rest of the world and went off after his men.

"You think they're still around?" I asked.

"I do not know. One thing I am sure about is that I should be very reluctant to enter a place like this." He stepped closer to the edge of the kettle and nodded at the woods on the opposite side of the depression. "With all his men down there, any rebels up here would have no trouble pinning them and picking them off as they pleased."

"Shouldn't we warn them?"

"There's probably nothing in it. They're chasing farm lads, not soldiers. I think—"

But I didn't hear the rest of Beldon's opinion. Across the kettle, I caught a glimpse of a pimply face suddenly obscured by a cloud of thick smoke. Roddy Finch, I thought. Of course. He'd be the one to . . .

Something struck my chest. I was shocked. The only thing I could think of was that for some insane reason Beldon had picked up a stone and smashed it into me with all his strength. All the breath rushed out and I staggered back from the blow.

Not Beldon. His hands were empty. He wasn't even looking at me; then his head turned, his eyes meeting mine.

Slowly. Slowly.

His normally tranquil expression sluggishly altered to alarm. I saw my name form on his lips, flowing out little by little, one syllable at a time.

My heels caught on something. My legs wouldn't respond. My arms thrashed empty air.

Beldon thrust his hands forward, but was too slow to catch me. I completely lost my balance and dropped. My back struck the earth solidly, driving a last pocket of breath from my lungs.

It dazed me. I'd thumped my skull in the fall. My tongue clogged my throat. I tried to shake my head to one side to dislodge it.

I could not move.

Stunned. Only stunned, that's all. It would pass.

Patches of sky leached through the leaves high overhead. Beldon came into view. He was bellowing. I couldn't understand the words, only that they were too loud. I winced and tried to tell him to lower his voice, that I was all right.

A gurgling, wheezing sound. From me. From my chest. A great weight had settled upon it.

Beldon's face was twisted into an awful mixture of rage and grief and terror and helplessness. What was wrong? What had happened?

The weight on me was crushing. My God, I couldn't breathe.

He put his arms under my shoulders and lifted me a little. He was trying to help me get air. But nothing happened. I clawed at my throat. At my chest. He pushed my hands off, but they'd already found it. They came away smeared with blood. Far too much blood.

I choked, tried to speak. The stuff flooded up my throat like hot vomit and spilled from my nose and mouth. I was drowning in it. In my own blood.

Beldon was talking to me. Yelling, perhaps. Weeping? Why . . . ?

Good God, *no.* It can't be.

My body thrashed, out of control. The weight on my chest was spreading, crushing me into the earth. I had to fight it or be smashed into a pulp like a worm.

Beldon, damn him, was trying to hold me still. He didn't understand.

Air. Please, God. Just a little air . . .

I breathed in blood instead. Sputtered it out again. Beldon was covered with it. Like that dream of Nora . . .

The memory whipped from my mind. I twitched and struggled to clear my clogged throat.

Elizabeth. Father . . .

Just a little air. Just a little that I might see them once more.

*Fight* it.

But my efforts produced only a bubbling, gagging noise. I was already panicked; to hear and know that it was coming from me. . . .

*Fight it.*

The pain I hadn't realized I felt suddenly ebbed. The weight on me eased.

*Fight* . . .

Eyelids heavy. Couldn't blink, though. Couldn't focus on anything. The light and leaves above blurred and merged and danced together.

. . . *it.*

A fluttering convulsion took me. Beldon cried my name in a hopeless wail.

But I was unable to answer as a soft stillness settled upon me. I lingered just at the threshold of waking and sleep. He was shaking me, trying to rouse me. It should have worked, but all that was me was in retreat. It was like rolling over against cold morning air and pulling the blanket down more snugly to seize another few minutes of blissful, warm rest.

Beldon stopped the shaking. I pushed the sleep off briefly, wondering what troubled him. He was yet within view, but his head was bowed as for prayer.

The pain was all gone now. No air yet, but I didn't seem to need it. The weight was also absent. Good. Good.

Nothing left to do now but give in to the sleep. Which I did.

I woke up smoothly, quickly, with none of the usual attendant grogginess. The room was like ink. Must have been well past moon set. That, or Jericho had closed the shutters of my window and drawn the curtains. I should have been baking from the day's lingering summer heat, but was not. Neither warm nor cold, the only feeling intruding on my general awareness was that my bed was uncomfortably hard.

Damnation. I must have passed out drunk on the floor. It wouldn't be the first time.

But . . . I hadn't really gotten drunk since leaving Cambridge. I was home. Surely Jericho would have taken care of me.

The back of my head rolled from side to side on the wooden planks, each irregularity of the bone against an unyielding surface made apparent by my movement. Damn the man. Even if my drunkenness offended him, he could have at least spared a pillow for me.

My shoulders pressed down heavily as well. And my backside. And my heels. I'd grow numb and stiff if I stayed like this.

He'd thought to give me a blanket, but had drawn it completely up over my head. I was having trouble pulling it away from my face . . . I could *not* pull it away from my face. When I tried to move my arms, my elbows thumped into—

What? The sides of a box? Where in God's name was I?

My eyes had been open through this. Or so I thought. It was difficult to tell, it was so black. They were definitely open now. In the cramped space I inched one hand up and felt them to be sure. Cheek. Lashes. Lids. Outer corner. *Blink.*

Nothing. I saw nothing.

It was the damned blanket. I tugged and came to realize it was wrapped around me and somehow tied over the top of my head like a . . .

No. That was ridiculous.

Sweet God, but it was quiet. I could only hear my own stirrings in what I now accepted as a small, enclosed space—the rustle of cloth, the scrape of shoe heels, even the soft creak of my joints—but absolutely nothing else.

But there *had* to be some sound. It was always there, even when one did not listen, there were hundreds of things to be heard. Wind. Bird song. The whisper of leaf and grass blade. One's own pulse, for God's sake.

Silence. Perfect. Unremitting.

Even my heart?

No. That was impossible. It was there—had to be; I was just too alarmed now to hear it.

I pushed against the blanket or whatever it was that covered me and promptly encountered the lid of the box I was in. Oliver and some of his cronies were having a game with me. Waiting until I was drunk, they'd put me in here for a bad joke.

But I was *not* in Cambridge. My mind was seeking any answer but the truth. I already knew it, or thought I did, but to face it . . .

My shoulders strained and muscles popped as I pushed on the lid. The bastards had nailed it down. The thing wouldn't budge. I'd be damned before I gave them the satisfaction of hearing me call for help. Oliver, I decided, had had no part in this. It was too spiteful for him.

Warburton, perhaps.

Warburton, white around the eyes and looking drunk. But he hadn't been drunk.

Warburton, curled up on the floor, weeping.

Nora, looking down at him.

Nora, looking at me.

Nora, talking to me. Telling me all the things that I must forget.

I shook away that memory as if it were rain streaming in my face. Just as persistently, it continued to flood down.

Rain. Yes, that was right.

It had been raining. Cold. Icy. Tony Warburton striding away into the night. And when I saw him again he was drunk and repentant. But he hadn't really been drunk. He'd gotten me over to Nora's and when she'd walked in, he'd . . .

No. That was only in a bad dream.

To the devil with them. I could not bear the silence and darkness any longer. My voice roared out—

And went no farther than the confines of the box. The flat sound of it rolling back on itself told me as much.

Beldon had also called for help. He and I had been . . . I'd just seen the Finch boy raise his rifle. But he couldn't have—that simply could not have happened to me. I couldn't believe, didn't dare believe. To do so meant that I was . . . they wouldn't have done this to me.

I was *alive.* The dead aren't trapped in the ground like this; God would surely spare the worst of sinners that torment. I could still think, move, speak, even smell. The odor of musty cloth and new wood and damp earth were making me sick.

Earth. In the *ground. Trapped in the ground.*

I heaved against the lid, calling for help. I did this many times, keeping the unthinkable at bay a little longer.

Useless. My arms dropped to my chest, drained, shaking with weakness.

Now I knew without doubt, without any deceiving fancies, *exactly* where I was, and no yell, no scream, no plea, no sobbing prayer would free me from this, my grave.

No. *No. Nonononononono.*

My thrashing body suddenly broke free and rolled down a slight grading. Facedown. Faceup. Stop.

I was . . . on the ground. Open ground. Trees. Their leaves whispered to one another. What a sweet song for my starved ears. I could still smell earth, but it wasn't as cloying as before. It was diluted by the other scents carried on the wind. Clover, grass, and a skunk, by God. I never thought I'd welcome *that* pungency.

Able to use my arms again, I finally tore away the cloth shroud binding me.

Shroud. I sat up and forced myself to look at it. *My* shroud. Yellow with age, for it had been stored in the attic since my birth, as was the custom. We all had one, Father, Elizabeth, Mother, all the servants, all our friends. Death was always around us, from a summer fever to a bad fall from a horse. One prepared for death as soon as one was born. One had to accept it, for there was no other alternative.

*Nora,* my mind whispered uneasily.

I was . . . in a graveyard. The one I passed each Sunday going in to hear the sermon.

But I could *not* be.

I pushed the impossibility away. It kept returning.

I pushed away the burgeoning fear. It held back for the moment.

An unbidden image came to me of standing at the edge of the drop-off, of noting without alarm the puff of smoke across the way, of not knowing what it meant, of falling, of pain, of blood . . .

Without any thought behind the action, I began unbuttoning my waistcoat. My fingers moved on their own and it was with mild surprise that I looked down to see my clothes opened and my chest bared. The wound that some hidden part of my mind expected to find was there, right over my heart, but closed up and half-healed. The surrounding skin was bruised and red, but not from inflammation. There was no pain. Not now.

*Nora.*

I grew very cold. Not from the soft air flowing past me, but from the stark memory of her slumping down, run through with my sword-stick. It had caught her in the heart. The blood covered her dress. Warburton had laughed and turned upon me. My dream, my nightmare, had been true. Nora had . . . had made me forget everything.

Had she been cruel or kind? From the bits and pieces of memory floating back, I knew that she had truly loved me and would have done anything to protect me from harm. But she also had herself to protect and so I'd been made to forget not only all that made her different from others, but my feelings for her, made to wall away half of my very soul. The enormity of her gentle betrayal numbed my thoughts. I drew my arms around my legs and rocked back and forth, overcome by the misery.

My eyes stared without seeing at the bright night sky, at the humps and angled shapes of the gravestones surrounding me, at the church's great gray shadow creeping over the ground. As a child, I would have taken on any dare but this one, to spend a single moment in this place after dark. Was I condemned to remain here? Was this my punishment for falling in love?

Such questions as these broke through the barrier I'd built up. Suitable for a ghost story, or the high drama of a stage play, but not for me. I wasn't a spirit or the recipient of divine vengeance, though I had no doubt now that I had died. My heart was silent. My lungs only worked when I consciously used them.

Nora had been the same. I could almost laugh to remember how alarmed I'd been when I'd noticed that. It had been on the night when we'd first exchanged blood. I was . . . I was like Nora now. By giving my blood to her and taking hers into myself, she'd passed on—what? Her immunity to death?

*Why* hadn't she told me what to expect?

Perhaps she hadn't known herself, I logically answered.

Then I did laugh. I laughed until I wept. Couldn't stop. Didn't want to stop, wholly giving myself up to a malignant self-pity blacker than the confines of my grave. I moaned and howled and cried and finally shrieked, my voice striking off the side of the church to vent itself in the open air. I did not recognize it. I did not even recognize myself, for I'd been turned into a most miserable wretch by the overwhelming despair of losing her.

But it passed. Eventually. My temper was not such as to leave me in the depths for very long. Sooner or later we must all emerge and deal with mundane practicalities.

I wiped at my nose and swollen eyes with the lower edge of my shirt.

They'd dressed me in my best Sunday clothes. I'd even been given a proper shave. Poor Jericho would have had to do it. I swayed, nearly falling into the darkness again by simply thinking of how he must have felt.

Later. I would worry about it later.

Levering stiffly to my feet, I kicked away the shroud and brushed at the earth clinging to my breeches.

What next?

Go home, of course.

It seemed a good idea. Then it soured. What would they think? How could I possibly explain myself? How could I explain Nora?

How—I was looking at the undisturbed mound of my grave—in God's name had I escaped *that?* The flat marks where the spades had tamped the dirt down were still there, blurred a little where I'd rolled off. There were footprints all around as well, men's and women's. I had no difficulty imagining them standing by it, listening to the service being read and weeping through the words. They were the real ghosts of this place, the living, with their grief twining about the low stones like sea mist. The dead were at peace; it was the ones they'd left behind that suffered.

Where did that leave me, who was neither alive or dead?

*Later.*

My bones were leaden, I was worn out by sheer emotion yet questions continued to pop into my head. I ignored them and trudged out of the churchyard. One foot before the other for a time, then I could rest. A little sleep in my own bed and I'd sort it all out for the others in the morning.

God, what would I tell them?

Later. Later. Later.

Forsaking all thought, I walked and let my senses drift. The road dust kicked up by my steps, the night insects at song, wind rustling the trees, these were most welcome distractions. Normal. Undemanding.

" 'Oo's there?"

The intrusion of a human voice jerked me back to myself.

"Speak up! I've a gun on ye." Despite his bold declaration, there was a decided quaver in his tone.

"Is that you, Mr. Nutting?" I called back. Something like relief flooded me as I recognized Mervin Nutting, the sexton. He was sheltered beneath the thick shadow of a tree, but I had no trouble spotting him. The puzzlement was that he could not see me standing not fifteen yards away in the middle of the road.

" 'Oo are ye?" he demanded, squinting right at me, then moving blindly on. He was holding a pistol. "Stand forth."

"I'm right—" Oh, dear. Perhaps this was not such a good idea after all: confronting the man who had most likely just buried me. My mouth snapped shut.

"Come on! Show yerself!"

I backed away a step. Quietly. Took another. My shoe crunched against a stone. Nutting swung in my direction with his gun. He looked terrified, but determined. His clothing—what he wore of it—suggested that he'd recently been roused from bed. His house was close to the church; he must have heard my rantings and come out to investigate. No wonder he was so fearful.

"Come on!"

Not this time, I thought, moving more carefully. Better to leave him with a mystery and to speculate at The Oak about hauntings than to come forward with the truth and frighten him to death.

"Vat is it, Herr Nutting?" A second man came up behind him, shrugging on a Hessian uniform coat while trying to keep hold of his lantern. He must have been quartered at Nutting's house.

"Thieves or worse," was the reply. "Hold it high, man, so we can see." He joggled the Hessian's arm.

"*Vorsicht! Das Feuer!*" he yelped, worried about dropping it.

The lantern may have helped them, but I perceived no real difference for myself. It was like a candle against full daylight to me. My eyes were used to the dark by now, but surely my vision should not be as clear as this.

Emboldened by having company, Nutting advanced them onto the road. I saw every detail of their faces, even the colors in their clothes; in turn, they were limited to the radius of their feeble lamplight. I kept backing away, but was unable to judge the right distance to avoid its most outside reach.

"*There!*" the Hessian cried. He pointed straight at me.

Whether Nutting understood German or not was debatable, but he got the general idea and brought his pistol to bear. He shouted an order. Or started to. I didn't wait for him to finish and pelted down the road faster than I'd ever run before.

Nutting was better at disposing of ale than foot racing and his companion was unwilling to proceed without arms. I soon gained distance. Far behind, but still visible to me, they gave up their pursuit.

Well, that had woken me right up. I slowed to a walk, albeit a quick one. I was not breathing hard. Good God in heaven, I wasn't breathing at all.

I groaned at that reminder.

What was to become of me?

All the questions returned, full force, and I had no answers. Time would take care of most of them, no doubt, but the encounter with Nutting made me realize what awaited when I got home. Not that I'd be facing another gun, but my return from the dead would certainly inspire the most dreadful fear at first. Was I ready to do that to them? Would it not be better to . . .

I didn't care. I needed them.

The last mile home is always the longest and I was growing very tired. My eyes hurt. I'd ask Beldon to look at them and hopefully prescribe some drops to help things. Heavens, but it would be good to see even Beldon the toad-eater again.

The sun would be up soon. My eyes were beginning to burn like coals. This sensitivity worried me. Common sense suggested that it would be better to avoid true daylight when it came, at least until I got used to it. *Nora* never *came out during the day.*

She'd slept—slept the day through however long the seasons made it. It had been one of her many unbreakable rules. We'd almost had an argument about it once. We'd gone to a party that had lasted all night. I wanted to watch the sunrise with her and she'd flatly refused, insisting on going home once she'd realized the time. I'd been stung by this, offended that she couldn't give up an hour of sleep for me, but she'd talked to me in that way of hers and then it hardly seemed to matter.

I'd forgotten that until now. She'd made me forget so much. Every memory that returned possessed both comfort and pain and no small measure of unease. I'd accepted—or had been made to accept—her differences from other people as eccentricities, but if a serious purpose lay behind each, then it was to my interest to imitate her.

I needed shelter from the sun, then, and very soon. Even now I had to shade my eyes against the glare stealing above the horizon. It was worse than during my morning ride with Beldon yesterday.

Had that only been yesterday? Or today? Had I been truly alive just this morning? How long had I been in the—

*Later,* I said firmly.

The house was too far away to reach in time; I'd have to settle for the most distant of our outbuildings, an old unused barn. It had once been the property's main barn and close by had stood the original house. That had burned down decades earlier and the remaining stone foundation and chimney had become a childhood playground. We'd been forbidden to go into the barn, but had explored it anyway. Children either have no concept of mortality, or honestly believe they will live forever. We'd come to no harm, though I later shuddered at the risks we blithely took then. The place had been filled with discards and old lumber, rats and snakes.

The doors were gone, but I'd expected that. Dodging a growth of ivy that had taken over the walls, I walked in, cautious of where I put my feet. The trash I remembered had long ago been hauled away and probably burned. Just as well. The stone floor was still in good condition, though clumps of grass and weeds grew in cracks near the entry as far as the sun reached in. They would serve as a guide for me to judge where the deepest shade might be found. It was noticeably darker inside despite the gaps in the high roof. Birds and other small animals had found refuge here. Hopefully, I would be safe as well until my eyes adjusted.

Outside the light grew unbearably bright. Perhaps I was being unrealistically optimistic about being able to leave. I fled to the most protected part of the place, a horse stall in a far corner. The brick walls were high; it must have been a dark and cheerless spot for the former occupant, but now offered a unique comfort to me.

"But I want to go home," I whispered, peering over the wall. I had to shield my eyes with my arm. The light was utterly blinding.

My limbs stiffened. No pain, but they were horribly difficult to move. So much had happened; the fatigue was inarguably catching me up. Rest. After a little rest I might feel better.

I was reluctant to sit. The floor was filthy with dust and other rubbish I preferred not to think about, but there was no choice. My legs folded on their own. My knees struck with a jarring double crack that deprived me of balance. I pitched over and landed on my side. My thoughts were as stiff and sluggish as my body. I felt no fear. I'd had a surfeit of it in the last few hours and could produce no more.

Dragged down by the natural pull of gravity, I rolled flat on my back.

My eyes slammed shut. The world may have spun on about its business, but I was no longer a part of it.

My eyes opened.

I lay as I'd fallen, but this awakening was far superior to the last one. My mind smoothly picked up its previous thread of thought as though I'd only blinked rather than dropped unconscious to the floor. I felt alert and aware and ready to deal with whatever the day brought. Fluidity had returned to my body; the wooden hardness of my joints was completely gone. I easily stood up to take note of my surroundings. Changes had taken place. Important ones.

Though the strength of the outside light was about the same it now fell from a different direction. By God, I'd slept the whole day away if I could believe that it was now sunset. It was yet painfully bright, but gradually dimming to a more comfortable level with each minute. Soon it would be fully dark—at least for other people. For me, there was only more of what I'd encountered last night. At least I should be able to avoid accidentally running into anyone out for a late walk on my way—

Home. I desperately wanted to be *home.*

Supper would be over by now. They'd probably be in the drawing room: Mother and her guests to play cards, Father to read, Elizabeth at her spinet. Perhaps not. The house was in mourning, after all. My heart ached for them and for myself. I would hurry.

Futilely, I brushed at my clothes. As if how I looked would matter to Father and Elizabeth when they saw me. I couldn't wait to see their faces, all of them; it would be better than Christmas. I'd ask Mrs. Nooth about leftovers first thing, because I was quite starved by now. I was really too hungry to know what I wanted to eat, though doubtless anything she had from the last meal would be gratefully consumed.

Swiftly, I marched from the barn and down the overgrown path leading to the road. I felt tired in body, but strangely sharp in mind. The strength of last night's terrors and doubts and worries had faded. I even found myself smiling about the encounter with Mr. Nutting. He'd only gotten a bad fright and a bit of exercise; I'd make it up to him at The Oak later, the Hessian, too, if he liked ale. I'd be the talk of the county, the Lazarus of Long Island.

My confidence faltered. How would the membership of the church receive this particular resurrection? Even the better educated might be reduced to a superstitious dread. The common folk I hardly dared consider. Would I be viewed as a heavenly miracle or an infernal mockery?

*Later*, I reminded myself once more and kept going.

Had they caught Roddy Finch yet? I'd been so occupied with my own immediate sorrows that I'd had no thought to spare for the man who had . . . killed me. No thought to spare and, until now, no anger. Murderers were hanged and rightly so, though in this case there was sufficient mitigation to prevent it. You can't hang a man for murder if the victim turns up to call things off, but the pimply-faced bastard would pay for this if I had to flog him myself. I was very definitely prepared to do it as my anger was not just for myself but for the awful grief he'd caused my poor family.

On the other hand, he might probably hang anyway, for the horses he'd stolen back from the Crown.

My mind started to spin a bit at the complications.

I'd have to talk with Father, sort it all out with him.

Later.

Less than half a mile from my gate, I became conscious of a wagon rattling up the road behind me. I saw it long before the driver could see me and debated whether or not to take cover until it passed. Sooner or later the news would spread of my return so I supposed it would make no difference to wait for him. Besides, he might be obliging enough to give me a ride. My feet were beginning to drag as my empty belly started to snarl to life. I consoled myself that soon Mrs. Nooth would put it to rest with her excellent cooking.

The driver was a stranger to me, though he was obviously a farmer or worked for one. I waited until certain the lighted lamps hanging from his wagon had picked me up from the general darkness, then gave him a friendly hail. He was startled, for the times were unsettled and a man out after sundown could rightly be viewed with suspicion.

"Who be ye?" he demanded, pulling on the reins. There was a long musket at his feet and he was ready to reach for it.

"I'm Mr. Barrett, at your service, sir. I live near here."

"Good e'en to ye," he replied cautiously, looking me over. "Have a spot of trouble?"

I fought down the urge to laugh. "Yes, quite a lot of it. I suffered a fall and am trying to get home." Close enough to the truth.

"Musta been a prodigious fall, young sir," he said agreeably. "I can give ye a ride if ye c'n tell me if 'm on the right road to Glenbriar."

"That you are, sir. And less than a mile from my own gate."

He took the hint. "Good, commun up, then." He made room for me on the seat and I readily joined him. "Name's Hulton. 'M on my way to sell goods to the soldiers." He got the horses going again. "Sun go down, but thought I'd push through."

"You're welcome to spend the night at my home. Or, if you stay on this road you'll pass The Oak. They'll put you up there right enough. I'd be careful about dealing with the commissaries, though."

"They not payin' good coin?"

"Even worse." I explained in detail about the blank receipts and the theft of Finch's property. Hulton took it all in with a stone face, then shook his head.

" 'F that be how things stand, then I may as well go home ag'in as go on. Least 'f the rebels steal from me I c'n get the soldiers to hang 'em, but who'll hang the soldiers?"

"The rebels, if they win," I said.

His eye sharpened. "You one of 'em?"

"Good God, no. My family are all loyal to His Majesty, God bless him."

"Amen," he said, amused by my wholehearted sincerity. "Still, can't 'ford to lose m' goods to anyone, be they soldiers or rebels. This'll take a bit of figgerin'. Can't figger like this. Need grease for the wheels to turn, y'see." He reached under the bench and pulled out a jug. Though one hand was busy with the reins, he expertly removed the cork and treated himself to a hearty swallow without dropping anything. "Care for a bit? Best applejack on the Island. Make it m'self."

I balanced my thirst against the ill effects drink would have on my empty stomach. The latter growled threateningly against the restraints of good sense. "Perhaps just a little . . ."

The stuff felt both warm and cold going down. I expected it to be unsettling and wasn't disappointed. I also expected it to go straight to my head; instead, it just seemed to roil in my guts like too many fish crammed into a small bucket.

Hulton grinned, taking my expression as a compliment to his skill as a distiller.

I hiccuped. Rather badly. The applejack wanted to come back up again. Hand over my mouth, I apologized and explained that I hadn't eaten all day.

"Shoulda said somethin'," Hulton gently scolded and produced a basket from under our seat. "Go through that. My missus cooked me a chicken to eat on the way. Take what ye please."

I unwrapped the greasy cloth covering. The applejack rumbling inside was most certainly affecting my senses. The chicken, which might otherwise have set me to drooling like a starved mongrel, smelled repulsive. There was a fat loaf of bread squashed in next to it. I tore off a piece and bit into that. It was crusty, tender, and obviously still fresh, but tasted all wrong. I forced it down my throat. It immediately went to war with the drink.

Hulton took another swig from his jug and offered it to me again. This time I politely refused. As I worked to chew through another piece of bread, he asked for more details about the commissaries. I offered them, but the flow of talk was interrupted by my frequent swallowing in order to keep the food down. Hulton noticed.

"Not settin' with ye?"

I shook my head.

"Then don't eat it."

What a practical suggestion. I'd been cramming the bread in because I thought I needed it, not because I wanted it. Hulton wrapped the basket up and put it away. "Not sick, are ye?"

I wished he hadn't mentioned that. The aftertaste of the applejack in my mouth was absolutely vile. As for the bread, I concluded that Mrs. Hulton must have been a perfectly awful baker. "Perhaps I've been without food too long," I said aloud.

"Aye. Go without 'n' 'tis best to start up ag'in easy. Maybe soup."

Soup. Ugh. I nodded to keep my lips sealed tight. Hulton thankfully did not produce any. I gulped and pressed a hand hard against my belly. It was beginning to cramp.

"Gate here. This be your place?"

Thank God. "Yes. Thank you, Mr. Hulton. You've been very kind."

" 'M well paid 'f you saved me from losin' m' stuff. Thank'e for the offer to stay, but I'll be on to The Oak. I want to hear all the talk 'n' figger that's the place for it. God speed to ye, Mr. Barrett."

When the wagon had fully stopped, I dropped down. The hard landing stirred my guts up to new rebellion. Pausing only long enough for a final wave of farewell, I stalked straight to the gate, but at the last moment veered to one side. The cramp was worse, doubling me right over. Arms clutching my middle, I retched up the bread and applejack onto the grass. There wasn't much, but I kept spitting and coughing as though my body wanted to rid itself of even their memory. Finally done, I weakly straightened and staggered over to rest against a tree.

I was still hungry.

But not for bread or soup or fowl or anything else that came to mind. Not milk or fruit or cheese or wine or . . .

She always and only drank blood.

The despair I thought I'd left behind in the graveyard seized me once more. I sank to the ground, unable to move.

*Sweet God, Nora, what have you done to me?*

# CHAPTER 11

*Life-magic,* Mrs. Poole had called it as she'd let a few drops of beef blood fall upon Nora's lips.

I could at least infer from that example that there was thankfully no need to seduce or assault any innocent lady for my own nourishment. After all the time spent with Nora, I knew better. The taking of blood from another human had an entirely different significance for her than just to keep her body fed, though that was there as well. I wasn't remotely ready to consider the complications of that aspect of my changed nature yet, though. Like a thousand other things, it could wait until later.

With a sigh of either resignation or acceptance, I got to my feet and opened the gates just enough to slip through. The weariness I'd noted before was much more pronounced. Manifested first in my bones, it had spread to the muscles and outward to drag at my very skin. I could lie down and rest, but knew that wouldn't help. Every moment streaming past stole away a little more strength. The time would eventually come when none remained. I trudged along the drive, shoulders slumping and head down to watch where my steps fell.

But my mind was wide awake and in need of distraction from the body. Unable to supply any answers about my immediate future, I fell to speculation over my past. Without a doubt I had become like Nora, but what—and I used the word in the most literal sense—was Nora? What had I become?

Most definitely not a ghost, I wryly concluded, not unless ghosts got hungry. I also had doubts that they expended much worry on whether road dust would permanently ruin the polish of their best shoes. (Yes, it was a foolish bit of diversion, but in my unsettled state of mind I needed it.) Anyway, I'd never really believed in ghosts since I was a child. Even then, such lapses of reason had been limited to foggy nights when the normal atmosphere thickened by sea mist lent itself to imaginings of a supernatural nature.

A demon, then? Since I believed in God, I knew there was also a devil. Had some fiend from hell taken possession of my mind and body, sending me forth from the grave to trouble the world? That did not seem too terribly likely, either. Besides, I'd had no difficulty calling upon God for help earlier when I'd panicked while trapped in—

*How* had I escaped that . . . that damned box?

For every other change within me I had some memory of Nora to serve as a pattern to follow, but this was the singular exception. My recollection of what had happened just wasn't there. The moment had been blotted out forever by a solid and sour-tasting terror that was yet powerful enough to raise a groan and set me to shuddering. . . .

*If I continued to give in to the fear I'd never learn anything.*

By force of will I straightened my shoulders and made myself stop trembling. Decisively, I shoved the fear away; an unwieldly thing, but controllable if I put my mind to it. Tempting as it was to sink to my haunches and wail like an infant, I would not surrender to it this time. There was too much to think about.

One last shake of the head to clear out the remnants, a deep breath, and I was in command of myself again and not a slave to outside forces or inner alarms. Measured against the rest of the wide world it wasn't much, just a small victory, but it was mine and I held it close and tight.

That was better. I resumed my walk toward the house.

Now I would have to try to assume a detachment from the experience. A doctor must do much the same thing in order to allow him to proceed with the practice of his art. If Beldon could do it, then I would, too.

In my mind's eye, I placed myself back in the ground once more. Without fear to obscure things, I was able to form a clear picture of that awful time—if one may make a picture from absolute darkness. Between the onset of panic and my sudden roll off the heaped earth, I found it. There had been a blank instant when I felt as though I were falling.

No . . . that wasn't quite it. Close. It was more like floating in water; except that didn't really describe it, either. A bit of both, perhaps? The result was that I had ceased to be trapped in my coffin and somehow came to rest on the ground some six feet above it. The line from Revelation about the sea giving up its dead came to mind and I toyed with the thought that that great and terrible prophecy had come to pass in some way for me. Only toyed, mind you. To assume that I alone had been singled out in such a manner struck me as being the height of folly-filled pride.

My recollection of other passages of the Bible and how they related to my situation was not very encouraging. There were some very firm laws against the drinking of blood, at least in the Old Testament, and some mention made of it in the New. Well, I could let myself starve in an effort to deny the necessities of my changed nature, or I could yield to its demands and, like many another poor sinner, ask God to forgive me.

Moral questions at rest for the moment, I returned to my original puzzle of how I'd escaped the grave. Reason dictated that answers lay in some other direction than divine intervention, most likely within myself.

If Nora had been able to survive a sword thrust into her heart, what other seeming miracles might she have been capable of accomplishing? In this light, my physical rising from the grave could be . . .

I paused in my tracks, feeling a hot burst of excitement within. Would I be able to repeat that escape?

I did not know.

And I was too apprehensive to even consider an attempt to find out.

Also, too hungry.

Intuition and appetite, having taken temporary precedence over reason, told me that I had no time to spare for experimentation, fascinating as it might prove to be.

*Get moving and keep moving.*

It was a great relief to me when the high white walls of my home loomed into sight amid the trees. It was a great hardship not to rush straight up and start hammering on the front door. Before undergoing any happy reunion, I would most definitely have to feed myself first. I couldn't possibly face the many questions and tide of emotions to come in my present state. Nor did I wish to suddenly acquaint them with the peculiar dietary needs my change required. One shock at a time.

How I was to satisfy those needs was gradually becoming apparent to me as I walked around to the back of the grounds. The two points on my upper jaw where my canine teeth emerged were feeling decidedly odd. Exploring the area with my tongue and finally my fingers, I learned that these teeth were longer than before and starting to jut outward at a slight angle from the rest. Nothing strange there; I'd seen Nora in the same condition often enough. Experiencing it for myself induced a mixture of anticipation and dread, not unlike losing one's virginity. I couldn't help but compare it to that first night with Nora, for though I was certain of having an extraordinary time, I had misgivings about botching things.

But whatever might lie ahead, this involuntary alteration of my teeth was—in its unique way—indisputably pleasurable.

I skirted the house and minor outbuildings and headed right for the stables. Chores done and their own stomachs filled, the lads had long since retired to their quarters above. Some were well asleep, others still settling in for the night. I felt both wonderment and charm that I could hear them, for like my eyes, my ears had likewise undergone a tremendous improvement over their original condition.

The two speakers were also the youngest; the only ones to have enough energy left at the end of a long day to put off their rest a little longer. Their talk was filled with speculation on how long the rebellion could last and whether or not they'd have a chance to join up with Howe's men before it ended. They certainly stretched my patience before exhausting the subject to begin drifting off to their dreams of soldiering.

My belly ached painfully over the delay, but the pauses between comments began to lengthen, and finally went unbroken. I gave them another quarter hour, then eased through a door for a cautious look around.

The first members of the household to greet me were our dogs. We had an even half dozen hunting hounds that slept where they pleased on the grounds. Two of them favored the stables year round, probably because of the vermin there. The smallest was a very talented rat catcher. He now bounced to his feet and joyfully rushed me. His brother roused and followed and the two of them knocked me right over and halfway out the door again. I was buried under wet tongues, stubbed-clawed feet, and small whines of eager welcome. They totally ignored my hushed pleas for silence. I gave up and let them have their way. Though terribly distracted by hunger, I still found this to be a gratifying homecoming.

The dogs eventually calmed down to go sniffing about the yard and I reentered the stable on tiptoes, listening for signs of disturbance from the lads above. Nothing but the occasional snore. Good.

The first stall I came to was Rolly's. God, but it was good to see him again. He seemed to think the same as I moved inside and patted him down. He bobbed his head and exhaled a warm blast of breath into my face. I ran a hand along the sleek line of his neck, taking in his scent as well, then stopped. Through the great curved wall of his chest I could hear the very beating of his heart.

Oh, but that was a tantalizing sound. And the smell. More than the ordinary, comforting fetor of stable and horses was here for me. One scent alone caught my full attention, drew me toward it, quelled any feeble protests. Dark and heavy and irresistible, it leached right through his skin and crashed against my spinning brain with the force of a nor'easter. I made hushing, soothing noises to Rolly, telling him to be quiet, then sank to my knees. And he did remain quiet, even as I felt out one of the big surface veins in his foreleg. He didn't once flinch as I brought my lips to the best spot, then used my teeth to cut through his thick flesh.

It welled up fast and though I swallowed as quickly as possible, some overflowed and dribbled past my chin. I ignored it.

The warmth of Rolly's living blood washed easily into me, spreading from my belly to saturate all my limbs. It was though I were drinking summer sunlight. My flagging strength returned to me, increased, doubled, tripled.

As the aroma was more enticing than any solid food I'd ever had, the taste was a thousand times better—not at all what I'd expected. During our exchanges, Nora's blood had certainly possessed a unique and erotic quality that enabled me to drink it without any hint of revulsion, but for all the sensual pleasure imparted, it still tasted like blood. That which I now consumed was wholly different, as was its effect on me. Instead of being engulfed in a blaze of red fire whose heat invariably took me to a supreme climax, I was inundated with the kind of sweet contentment that a starving man must feel when, after years of privation, he at last eats his fill.

I don't know how much I drank; it must have been quite a lot, perhaps as much as a tall beer flagon, perhaps more, but some inner signal told me when no more was needed. A little blood continued to seep from the wounds I'd made, but I pressed them with my hand until they clotted over. This was very messy, of course, but I'd take care of that soon enough.

Sitting back in the clean straw of the stall, I considered what I'd just done and decided that this sort of feeding was something I could not only put up with, but actively enjoy. I also considered what it might be like should the time come for me to take some lady to bed. The intuition I'd given free rein to tonight told me that that experience promised to be no less than incredible. As wonderful as it had been to be on the receiving end of Nora's kisses, how much better might it be to be the one giving the kiss?

*Well-a-day,* as my good Cousin Oliver would have said.

Quitting the stable, I started for the well, but changed my mind. Drawing water would perhaps be too noisy and I didn't want to rouse anyone until I was presentable again. There was a clear, running stream not a hundred yards from the house, better to use it, instead. As though spoiling for a footrace, I trotted lightly toward it, my previous exhaustion completely forgotten.

I startled two rabbits and a bush full of dozing birds along the way. The birds squawked and fell into guarded silence, but the rabbits dodged swiftly away into cover. I followed them for the sheer joy of movement. Had it been open ground, I thought that I'd have had a chance of catching them, too. I'd never been so fresh and alive before; had Nora also felt this? She'd been so serene and sedate; I wanted to turn Catherine wheels, to leap, to fly to the moon.

I had to settle for kneeling by the stream and cupping up water to wash away the stains of drying blood. Though comfortable enough splashed against my face and neck, it was extremely cold on my hands as I dipped in, biting cruelly as though it were mid-winter. They'd gone blue and were starting to shrivel before I'd finished. On the walk back I had to rub and work at them to revive feeling in my fingers. Very odd, it seemed, but having suffered an inundation of odd experience in so brief a time, the matter was hardly worth my notice.

There were too many other things to consider, the most important being how best to approach my family. Having seen me unquestionably dead and the corpse buried, I had no illusion that their first reaction would be that of utter terror. There was no way around that one. Hopefully, the joy to follow once I'd explained things would more than compensate their initial distress.

I would have to begin with Father and rely on his courage and wisdom to help me deal with the others. But inert as my heart had become, I could yet feel it shrink a bit at the idea of approaching him. The simple fact was that I was highly embarrassed about the whole business, for it would involve a lengthy confession on my intimacy with Nora, something I had only dared to confide to my private journal.

Heavens, I hoped that no one had found it and was lightly turning over those pages. Such thoughts as I'd recorded there were for my eyes alone . . .

*Later?* I questioned.

Later, an inner voice wearily confirmed.

As for any difficulties I might encounter with my family . . . in every possible way I had taken on Nora's abilities, so I had no doubt that if it came to it I could enforce my will upon them. I could ease their fears, even alter their very thoughts, if necessary.

But this was an abhorrence to me, for it meant that I might momentarily be forced to adopt my mother's hated precept of "doing it for their own good."

If it must be, then so be it. I needed them. Surely they would forgive me even as I'd forgiven Nora. If that happened, well and good, but if not, then I'd learn to live with it somehow. I would gladly ease any fear, but that's as far as it would go.

They would *not* be my dancing puppets.

Approaching the side door closest to the stables, I slowed and pondered a new problem: how to get inside my own home. With the times being so terribly uncertain, Father had had heavy bolts fixed to all the doors and ground-floor windows. Despite the warmth of the season these were always firmly locked by one of the servants after we'd all gone to bed. The heat was no real hardship, since everyone slept on the next floor or in the attic and those windows had no need to be locked. Standing back, I saw that all the ones on this face of the upper story were wide open, even the one to my room. Convenient, but only if I were a bird and able to fly in.

*Or float?*

I started to dismiss that one, but reconsidered as the idea had a lunatic attractiveness to it. If I could induce myself to that floating state, even learn to control it . . .

No. I shook my head. That was far too fanciful. Frightening, too. I was absolutely not going to explore that possibility. Besides, there had to be a much easier way in. I had only to look for it. A ladder would be just the thing. I seemed to recall there being one lying on its side against the house somewhere in the back, or perhaps in the stable. . . .

Going around to the rear of the house, I spied the cellar doors and gave them a hopeful try. Bolted. The hinges on the right half were rather free, though. There was enough play between the metal and the wood for me to force my fingers in and give an experimental tug.

For the second time that night I found myself bowled over on my backside. The right half flew up with a sharp crack as the hinge nails slipped from the wood. I'd gotten the balance all wrong or miscalculated my own strength. The door slammed down into place and would have made the devil's own row if I hadn't caught it at the last second. My hand was sorely bruised, but nothing worse. Righting myself and cursing with quiet intensity at the pain, I lifted it just enough to get inside.

The place was dank and dark, the latter coming as a surprise to me. I'd grown so used to being able to see impossibly well at night that I was momentarily nonplussed. Without a candle, I was doomed to blundering my way around any number of hazards like an ordinary man. Not having the means to make a light, I backed up and loosened the bolt on the doors and pushed on the half with the broken hinges. It slid to one side with an unhappy scrape that had me wincing at the noise, but the opening provided more than sufficient light. Now I'd be able to make my way up to the kitchen without stumbling over anything and breaking my neck.

As it was the custom to keep the fire banked and ready for the next day's cooking, the kitchen was very warm. I fled through it, for despite my lack of regular breathing, the lingering food smells still managed to penetrate my nose and set my stomach to writhing. I briefly thought about returning for a candle, but decided it was unnecessary. From here I could easily find the way to my room.

I took my shoes off before going upstairs and was careful to avoid the spots in the floor that creaked. The silence filling the place seemed to be a listening one. I hated playing the fugitive, but nothing else would have been right. I wasn't sure what would be, though, having consigned that problem to the nebulous and now fast-approaching future. Doubtless something would work itself out. After all my exertions my clothes were, as Mrs. Nooth might have said, "in a state." Confronting my family while so disheveled was not at all desirable, but that had become less important than changing for the sake of my own comfort. Once out of them and free of their attendant reminders of the grave, I'd feel much better and more of a mind to think.

An easy push on the door and I was standing in the familiar security of my own room.

The first impression I got was that it had been given a better than average cleaning by Jericho. The table I used for study was no longer stacked with its clutter of papers and open books. The former were gone and the latter all firmly closed and lined up in their case. This angered me. I hadn't finished with those yet and he knew it. . . .

But he also knew I'd never return to them again. I had died. Oh, my poor friend.

Other details impressed themselves upon me. On a table by the bed someone had placed a burning candle in a small holder within a wide bowl of water. I hadn't seen this sort of thing since Elizabeth and I had been very young children and wanted a light to chase away the night terrors.

The bed itself had been turned down as if waiting for my return. Laid out at its foot was the elaborate dressing gown Elizabeth had made me; on the floor were my slippers.

I recoiled from this otherwise innocuous sight. It was perfectly innocent, until you remembered that the missing occupant was dead and supposedly gone forever. Had they turned my room into some kind of horrid shrine to my memory? It was repellent, but then I might not have felt differently had I come in to find the place stripped of belongings and bare of all evidence of my existence.

It would change. Before the night was out, everything would be changed back. Perhaps not the same as before, but better than this ghastly, grief-filled present.

First things first. I had to get these things off.

Hastily, I stripped from my coat, peeled away shirt and breeches, and scraped free of stockings and underclothes. The air gently flowing in from the window was sweet upon my naked skin. I stretched to let it touch every part of me and combed back my tangled hair with my fingers. Marveling, I saw that the scar on my chest marking where the musket ball had gone in was much fainter and smaller than before.

My Sunday clothes I left in a pile on the floor, though I did remove the silver buckles from the shoes to place in their usual case in the wardrobe.

The wardrobe, unfortunately, unexpectedly, unhappily, and unreasonably, was quite, quite empty.

I stared at it like a brainless buffoon, jaw hanging and eyes popping for a ludicrous amount of time until white-hot outrage flooded through me. Couldn't they have waited just a little while before disbursing my things among themselves and the servants? I could understand the basic need to put me into the ground the same day I'd died, for the weather was far too hot for any delays, but it wouldn't have hurt to let a decent interval pass by before performing this other ritual of death.

Slamming the door, careless of the noise, I grabbed up the dressing gown and pulled it on, my movements made stiff by anger. I tried the top drawer of the chest at the foot of the bed. Empty. Not even a dusting of lint remained in the corners. Disgusted, I slammed it shut as well. I had nothing else to wear other than the dressing gown or my grave clothes and I'd be damned before I put them on again. Fuming, I returned to the wardrobe and checked its drawers. I didn't really think I'd find anything, but then I wasn't really thinking at all at this point.

Empty, empty, and empty. The little treasures left over from boyhood, too worthless for a sensible man to keep, too priceless to throw away, were gone.

Even my private journal, my diary, keeper of all my thoughts . . . gone.

This was the last straw.

The door to my room slowly opened. Elizabeth stood there, a shawl draped over her night dress and gripping a candle in one unsteady hand. She managed to look both uncertain and alarmed.

I was yet too insensate to be rational. All thought, all consideration of what had happened had been driven from my mind. With what I felt was justified exasperation, I turned on her. "Damnation, Elizabeth, where are my things?"

My sister had paused to look in upon me, doubtless drawn by the noise I'd been making. It was a normal sight for me to see her there. In the past had she not come in countless other times for a late conversation before retiring?

In the past. The past before I had *died.*

She froze, stock still, held in place by the unimaginable, paralyzed by the inconceivable. Her great eyes were stricken and hollow. No sound came from her open mouth. She didn't seem to be breathing at all and despite the warm glow of her small light, her skin went dreadfully ashen.

I froze as well, first with surprise at her expression, then with shock at my own unbounded stupidity as I belatedly realized that I was surely God's greatest fool.

Contrite, I reached out to her. "I'm sorry. I—"

She dropped back a step, her lips parting for a scream that she was too frightened to release. Never had I seen such a look of blank terror on anyone's face, much less that of my own sister. Remorse welled within me, choking my voice.

"Please don't be afraid. I'm not a ghost. Oh, please, Elizabeth."

She dropped her candle. The tiny flame went out in the fall; the stick struck the floor with a thud. Melted wax sprayed over the painted wood. She backed away one more step, making a soft *oh* as she did so.

"For God's sake, Elizabeth, don't leave me. I need you."

"No," she finally whispered, her voice high and blurred with tears.

Oh, the impossibilities were legion. I'd had the time to confront them one by one, get used to them, accept them; poor Elizabeth was having to do it all at once.

"It's all right. I *am* real. I—"

"What do you want?" Her words were so thin that I barely heard them. She seemed just on the point of tearing away and running.

My heart was breaking for her, for myself. I could feel it cracking right in two. "I want to come home."

"It can't be."

It must—or I should be forever lost. I needed my family, my home, they were all I had, without them I was truly dead. I could not go on without them. The impossible *had* to become possible.

My hand still out, I moved slowly toward her, close enough to touch, but careful not to do so. "It's all right. I am here. I am real. There's no need to fear, I would never, ever hurt you. *Please* . . ."

Perhaps the agony of feeling rather than the inadequate words broke through, but something inside her seemed to awaken. I could see the change gradually come to her face. Her eyes now traveled to my trembling hand, and with painful caution, her own rose to take it. Our fingers gently touched. I remained still, waiting for her thoughts to catch up with her senses.

"Jonathan?"

"I'm right here. I'm not a dream." I encompassed her tentative fingers lightly, all the time fearing she might pull away, but unable to stop. She did not draw back, though, and after a long moment her own grasp strengthened. Hardly aware of the movement, I sank to my knees, awed and humbled by this raw proof of her courage and love. As if in mirror to my own, crystal-bright tears were streaming down her cheeks.

"Oh, little brother . . . ," she began, but could not finish. Instead, she opened her arms and drew me close and we clung to each other and wept as though we were children again, finding common comfort in the sharing.

When the worst of the storm had passed, she pulled a limp handkerchief from the pocket of her gown and swiped at her eyes and nose. "I've none for you,"she said apologetically.

I laughed a little, that she should worry over such a trifle. "Never mind."

We looked at one another and I felt awkward and abashed to have been the cause of any distress to her. Elizabeth seemed to vacillate between joy and terror. Both of us realized it at the same time and that this was not the place to settle our many questions.

"Come," she whispered. I found my feet and followed her. My legs were shaking with relief and trepidation.

She'd left the door to her room open, but shut it as soon as we were inside. Within was evidence of the restlessness that had kept her up at such a late hour. The rumpled bedclothes were turned back and several candles were burning themselves away to dispel the darkness of the night and of the soul. Her Bible and prayer book were open on her table along with a bottle of Father's good brandy. While she rummaged in a drawer for fresh handkerchiefs, I poured a sizable drink for her.

"You need it," I said.

"By God, I know I do," she agreed, exchanging a square foot of soft white linen for the glass. I blew my nose as she drained away the brandy. Much stronger than the wine she was accustomed to, the stuff had its usual immediate effect on her, for she dropped right into her chair as her legs gave out.

I stared as if seeing her for the first time. In truth, I was seeing her with new eyes. How must Lazarus have looked upon his own sisters after his return from the dead? The comparison now struck me as being downright blasphemous, but I had no other examples to draw from in my memory. Did he see how vulnerable they were? Did he feel as aged and wearied by his experience? Or perhaps they were better sustained by the strength of their faith than I. At least none of them had been so alone in their ordeal.

The listening silence of the house washed against me, so profound that

I could hear Elizabeth's heart beat. Once part of the background, now it seemed to fill the room with its swift drumming. I knelt again and took her hand, pressing the inside of her slender wrist to my ear. This was music, the greatest music I'd ever heard. And the music was but one of a thousand, thousand other precious, fleeting things that I might never have appreciated or even known, but for Nora's . . . gift.

Elizabeth spread her fingers to caress my hair. "Oh, Jonathan, how is this possible?"

"I have no easy answer for you."

A smile fled over her face. The color was returning. "I don't think I could expect one."

"Is everyone all right? Is Father all right?"

Her expression fell. "What happened absolutely shattered him."

"Good God, I must go to him—" I started for the door.

"He's not home," she said. "He went out late this afternoon. He went to Mrs. Montagu. I made him go," she added, as if she had to apologize for his absence. "She couldn't possibly come here and he needed to see her."

Then he would at least be with someone who loved him. "That's all right, I understand, but soon I must see him."

"Of course. We'll have to go over right away."

"Yes. It'll be better for him if you're there. But please, tell me where my clothes are."

I must have sounded very forlorn. She suddenly slapped a hand over her mouth to stifle laughter that threatened to go to tears again. She leaned forward and held me, her head resting on my shoulder. I wanted to let her stay, but there was so much to do yet. She may have sensed it and pulled away to blow her nose. It had grown rather red. I loved it. I loved her.

She made a vague gesture to indicate my room. "That was Mother's doing. After the . . . services she ordered Jericho to pack everything up. I think Dr. Beldon got some of your better shirts. Oh, God, oh, God." She struggled against another sweep of emotion, shuddering from the effort.

"I'll sort it out with Beldon," I said quickly. "Is he all right, too? He looked so awful when . . . when . . ."

She broke off her work with the handkerchief to stare at me as we both realized the time for explanations was upon us. Everyone, even Father, would have to wait. "You must tell me," she whispered. "Tell me everything."

I rocked back on my bare heels and stood, pacing the room once or twice to put my thoughts in order. She watched my smallest move, her eyes wide as if she were afraid to look away or even blink, lest I disappear. Her hands clutched the arms of her chair like talons. Tonight her world had lurched and tumbled and yet she was prepared to face the next twisting blow. Very brave, but not the best state of mind for listening.

Elizabeth's cat lay on her bed, a tawny tom of considerable size and phlegmatic temperament. I picked him up and stroked him into a rumbling purr, delighting in the sensation of his warmth and softness. As with so much else, that which had been commonplace was now a wonderment to me. I took him over to Elizabeth and put him in her lap. He adapted to the change with indifference and continued his low murmur of contentment. She responded to it and began petting him. Her posture relaxed somewhat, though her eyes never left me.

Where to begin? In the churchyard? In my coffin? The ride with Beldon? Or much further back, with Nora? That was a tale I thought I'd never share with anyone. Ah, well, Elizabeth wasn't the sort to blush easily; I wasn't as certain about myself.

I tried to keep my story short and simple, and as neither could remotely describe it, muddled on some things. Elizabeth didn't help when she interjected questions, but my own embarrassment was the worst hindrance.

Elizabeth impatiently interrupted. "Jonathan, please stop trying to protect my sensibilities and just tell me what you mean. Was she your mistress or not?"

And I'd hoped not to shock *her.* I gave up and spoke plainly, making it easier for a time, until I got to the part concerning the mutual blood drinking. Bereft of all erotic description, it lost all attraction as well and sounded absolutely disgusting. Elizabeth's color faded again, but she did refrain from interruption on this. She could see how extraordinarily difficult it was for me to talk about it.

She had another glass of brandy, taking half during the fight with Warburton and finishing it when I came to my waking up in the coffin. Then I did try to spare her by passing over it quickly enough, but she fastened upon that which had left me so thoroughly puzzled.

"How did you escape?" she demanded.

"I'm not sure I know how to tell you," I answered with equal parts of truth and apprehension.

"Is it so terrible?"

"One could say that. One could also say that it is entirely absurd as well."

She pressed me, but my explanation, when it came, was met with gentle skepticism. "I don't blame you," I said. "It's not something I can easily believe and I've been through it."

For several minutes she was quite unable to speak. When she did, she had all the questions I'd posed for myself and was just as dissatisfied with my inadequate answers.

"Can you just accept it?" I asked, my heart sinking as Nora's must have done on other, similar occasions with me.

"If we lived in a time when intelligent and reasonable people still believed in witchcraft all this would be so much easier to take," she replied.

"Can you?" It was almost a prayer.

"It's not a matter of 'can' but of have to, little brother. Here you are and here you stand. But, by God, if this night ends and I wake to find I've dreamed it all, I shall never, never forgive you."

I began to smile, but smothered it. The feeling behind the mocking threat was too tender for crude levity. She'd finally reached her limit and this was her way of letting me know. I went to her and took her hands in both of mine. They were very cold.

"This is not a dream. I have come back and I will not leave again."

"God willing," she added quietly.

"God willing," I echoed.

She bowed her head over our clasped hands, whether for prayer or out of sheer weariness, I could not tell. Then she looked up. "Jonathan . . . do you have to drink blood as she did?"

"I'm afraid I do."

"Will you do the same things she did?"

My God, she was wondering if I'd be seducing dozens of young women in order to feed myself. An interesting idea, but not an example I intended to follow. "No, I will not do that. There's no need." I explained about my business with Rolly. "It didn't hurt him and I was much revived," I added, hoping that the knowledge might make her feel better.

"Oh," was all she could say.

"Probably best if you don't think about it," I quickly suggested.

"It sounds so awful, though."

"It's not, really. Not to me."

"What will you tell everyone?"

I was surprised. "The same as I've told you."

"*All* of it?"

Oh, dear. Sharing the truth with Elizabeth and Father was one thing, but spelling out the details of my intimacies with Nora to every yokel in the county was quite another. And as for popular reaction to what I required for sustenance . . . "Yes, well, perhaps not."

Elizabeth took notice of my distress. "Never mind. We'll talk to Father and decide what to do later."

Later. My favorite word, it seemed, but becoming rather annoyingly overused.

"We must find you clothing," she continued. "I'll get your shirts from Dr. Beldon's room—"

"Will you now? And what do you plan to tell him?"

"Nothing. He's not at home tonight."

"Then where the devil is he? You shouldn't be here alone."

"I'm hardly alone with all the servants—"

"Where is he?"

"Hunting." She said this with a meaning that passed right over me.

"I don't understand."

"Right after the . . . services for you, he left with the soldiers to go looking for the men who shot you."

I backed away until I bumped into her bed, then abruptly sat. While I'd been stumbling about, wholly occupied with my own problems, the world had spun on regardless. My life thread had been cut, knotted together, and worked back into weave again, but no one other than Elizabeth knew about it. "You must tell me everything that's happened since I . . ."

*Might as well say it.*

". . . since I died."

"Oh, Jonathan."

"I know of no other way to put it, so let the words be plain and honest. It's only the truth, after all. Now tell me. I must know all that's happened."

It was Elizabeth's turn to gather her wits and decide where to start. She was usually so self-possessed that her present discomfort was painful to watch.

"Did Beldon see who shot me?" I asked, hoping it would prompt her to speech.

It did. "No. He heard the shot and saw the smoke, then turned in time to see you fall. Do you not know who it was?"

"Roddy Finch."

She stopped petting her cat and went white. "Then it's true. Beldon said he thought the Finches were behind the horse theft, but I just couldn't believe that they would have—"

"Well, one of them did," I stated with no small portion of bitterness. The Finches had been schoolmates, friends, part of the Island itself as it related to our lives. The betrayal was monstrous.

"But for Roddy Finch to do such a thing?" She looked ill and I could sympathize with her up to a point, but no farther.

"For *anyone* to do such a thing," I reminded her. "If they catch him, he'll be hanged."

"But you're alive," she protested.

"He was stealing horses at the time, you know. They'll get him and those with him for that, if nothing else."

She groaned. "I don't want to think about it."

"Neither do I." There was no need; it was out of my hands and someone else's concern. "What happened afterward? What about the soldiers?"

"They brought you back. Both of you. Beldon was in a horrible state and weeping so hard he couldn't see. I was working with Father in the library and we saw them from the window, leading the horses in from the fields like some ghastly parade. Father rushed past me and out to the yard. God, I can still hear the cry he gave when he saw you. I shan't ever forget it."

I went to her and put an arm around her wilted shoulders, giving what comfort I could. "You needn't go on about that part. I couldn't bear to hear it, anyway. Let's get ready and go to him. We'll have to walk. If we stir up the stable lads now I'll be here all night talking to them."

"I don't mind. The air will clear my head."

With much tiptoeing, whispered directions, and the occasional misstep in the dark, we found some clothes for me, then went to our rooms to dress. As promised, Elizabeth raided Beldon's room for a clean shirt and stockings and I borrowed the rest from Father. It felt odd, pulling on an old pair of his breeches, but we were of a size now, and I didn't think he'd mind. My other boots and shoes had vanished, requiring that I use the one pair that remained, the ones I'd been buried in.

Elizabeth was very informally garbed in a dress she favored for riding. It was hardly a step up from what some of the servants wore, but she found it comfortable and needed no help getting into it. Out of habit, custom, and regard that she'd be calling upon Mrs. Montagu, she covered her loose hair with a bonnet and drew on a decent pair of gloves.

We slipped out the side door, shutting it firmly, but unable to reset the bolt. It would only be for a few hours, though. Cutting around to the front, we set off down the drive to the road at a good pace, though I felt like running again. However badly our reunion had begun, Elizabeth and I were together at last and one large portion of my enormous burden was lifted. Soon Father would understand everything as well and with their help . . .

My mind took a sudden turn down a path I'd studiously ignored until now. "Elizabeth . . . how did Mother take it?"

She looked at me sharply. "I was wondering if you would ever get 'round to her."

"Is she all right?"

"She wouldn't dare not be."

"What do you mean?"

"You know how she is, all that she does is determined by how she wants others to think of her. I don't believe the woman has a feeling bone in her body."

I pressed her for details and got them. My mother had been shocked, of course, but while others around her were giving in to their grief, she was busy getting the funeral organized.

" 'Someone has to see to it,' she said, and the way she said it, as if we were all weak fools. My God, even Mrs. Hardinbrook had a tear to shed for you, but not Mother."

I shouldn't have really been surprised. I was also impatient with myself for feeling so deeply hurt. "She's a sick woman, Elizabeth."

"I'm sorry, I shouldn't be telling you this."

I waved it off. "In a little while it won't matter."

We reached the road soon enough. Elizabeth tripped on some old wheel ruts and I had her hang on to my arm for guidance.

"You must have eyes like a cat," she muttered.

"Or even better. I am not without some advantages."

And I would have enlarged on the subject but for an interruption that for an insane moment brought me right back to that hot morning by the kettle. I felt the sun's heat on my face and the air lying heavy in my lungs. Without any thought behind the gesture, my hand fell protectively upon my chest as a Hessian soldier emerged from behind a tree and ordered us to stop. A second, then a third joined him and jogged toward us, their pale faces grinning like fiends in the moonlight.

# CHAPTER

# ◄12►

Elizabeth gave no outward sign of alarm, but her grasp on my arm tightened.

The soldiers closed on us and one of them shouted something.

In my halting German I asked them what they wanted. An ugly brute on our left sniggered as he looked at Elizabeth, but his companions thankfully did not seem of a mind to pursue his idea. I repeated my question. It finally got through to them that I was speaking in their language. As with the other Hessians, it had a favorable effect; unfortunately, the answer I got was far too rapid and complicated for me to follow.

The same man shouted again and got a reply from someone coming up behind us. I saw him before the others did.

"Another bloody Hessian," I told Elizabeth. "I hope this one speaks English."

"What are they all doing here?"

"I got the impression they want to ask us the same question. Mind yourself against that villain on the end. He's not polite."

She made a brief nod and murmur of agreement.

The newcomer was the sergeant in charge of those who had stopped us and at first glance he seemed a sensible, solid type. He gave me a brief greeting in English that was far more tolerable than my German, then conferred with his men. I gathered from their talk that a number of others were scouting up and down this part of the road.

"What are you looking for?" I asked, when he was free to place his full attention upon me.

"Perhaps for you, young sir," he said. "There are rebels here all around. Why are you and this woman out so late?"

With all the haughtiness I'd learned at Cambridge, I drew myself up and made formal introductions. I was careful not to be too condescending, but made certain that he knew he'd gotten off on the wrong foot. His vulgar reference to my sister would have more than justified my calling him out if he'd been a gentleman, or caning him since he was not, but circumstances required that I be flexible in the matter of honor for now.

The sergeant, who gave his name as Lauder, was not impressed. "Have you any papers, sir?"

"Papers?"

"Some papers to say you're who you are."

"My brother's word is proof enough in these parts, Sergeant Lauder," said Elizabeth. "If you need more than that, then you are welcome to follow us and our father will be more than happy to provide it."

"Your father will have to come to see you, miss. My orders say to bring in anyone out after curfew."

"This is utterly ridiculous," I said. "What curfew?"

"The curfew that has been ordered," he answered smugly, as though no further explanation were required.

"I have never heard of such a—"

He raised a hand. "You will come along now."

"Who is your commanding officer?"

"Lieutenant Nash. He will see you in the morning."

"Nash? But he's—"

"But I know him," Elizabeth said at the same time.

I stopped to look at her.

"He came to the funeral," she said under her breath to me.

"Awfully decent of him," I muttered in return, thinking low thoughts about his judgment that the rebels had left the area of the kettle. If he hadn't been so damned optimistic . . .

"That is good, then," concluded Lauder, ignoring this aside. "He will be most pleased to welcome you."

I wrenched myself back to the present. "An army camp is no place for a respectable lady, Sergeant. I insist that you at least return my sister to our home—"

"I have my orders."

"You have no right—"

"I have my orders," he repeated, pointedly patient. The man had turned woodenly polite, but was implacable.

*Damnation.* The glum look on Elizabeth's face indicated an exact concordance of thought between us on the situation.

"I'm sure Nash will sort this mess out for us once we talk to him," she said.

I sighed and nodded. I expected that he would be cooperative enough—once he got over the shock.

Elizabeth maintained her grip on me, but kept her head high. The sergeant's moderately respectful attitude had been noticed by his men and their discipline was such that no more coarse remarks were to be heard from them. Now that the initial excitement of a successful capture had passed, they were looking more sleepy than lustful, thank God.

"What's brought you out at this hour?" I asked the sergeant. "Even the rebels you're chasing must retire sometime."

"A farmer came in to tell us of a young man who had some misfortune. Lieutenant Nash sent us to find him."

So farmer Hulton had been gossiping in the tavern. "He turned all of you out just for that?"

"It was a most strange thing to hear."

"And what was so strange?"

"The young man told the farmer his name was Barrett. Yesterday the only young Mr. Barrett in the area was shot down dead by rebels. You are here and say that you are Mr. Barrett." Now he broke his wooden facade down enough to bestow upon me a look of amused suspicion.

"Oh my God," said Elizabeth.

"Sorry, miss," added the sergeant, misinterpreting her reaction.

"There's been a terrible mistake," she told him.

He invited her to go on, but his continued amusement was plain.

"Don't you see? That was my *cousin* who was killed."

"Pardon, miss?"

Elizabeth brought us all to a halt, Lauder regarding her with polite interest, me with dawning dread. What in heaven's name was she up to?

"My poor cousin, whose name was also Barrett, was the one killed yesterday," she said.

"I am sorry, miss."

"It was my brother here that the farmer met on the road."

"I see, miss."

"So there's no need to detain us."

Lauder shrugged minimally. "You must still come along." He moved on and his men herded us forward.

I patted Elizabeth's hand. It had been a good try.

She wasn't ready to give up yet. "Sergeant Lauder, I fully appreciate that you must perform your duty, but you are interfering with the king's business."

"In truth? It must be very late business."

"My brother and I were taking a very important message to our father from Colonel DeQuincey, who is on General Howe's staff."

"What message?"

"We are not at liberty to say."

"May I see this message?"

"It was not committed to paper, Sergeant. Surely you know how dangerous it could be if—"

Lauder held up a restraining hand. "It is not for me to say, only to follow my orders."

After that there seemed to be no further purpose to argument. Elizabeth subsided for the moment into a state of smoldering indignation that no word of commiseration from me would dispel. It gave her a goodly energy, though, for she set a smart pace for the rest of us in our march toward Glenbriar and The Oak, where Nash and his men were quartered. Not half an hour more passed before the road made a last gentle curve and I saw the familiar sign.

It was an old building, one of the first large structures on the Island with upper and lower stories and a vast cellar below, famous for the choice and quality of drinks kept there. The windows on the ground floor were open and some lamps and a candle or two were burning, but no one was presently in the common room.

Lauder left us standing outside while he entered, in search of additional orders, no doubt. Elizabeth crossed her arms and jerked her chin up to indicate her displeasure. Even the brute who had not been particularly polite kept his distance from her.

The sergeant returned shortly and issued a brief command to his men.

"What is it? What's going on?" Elizabeth demanded.

"You will be placed in the cellar until morning," he said.

"The what?"

"The cellar of the inn."

I started to object, but Elizabeth was well ahead of me.

"Absolutely not! We're loyal subjects of the king and will not submit to such insulting treatment. Where is Lieutenant Nash?"

"Those are my orders, miss—"

"To the devil with your orders, sir!"

"It must be so, miss. I have summoned the landlord to—"

"*Lieutenant Nash!*" she bellowed up at the windows above us. She was quite loud enough to wake everyone in the surrounding houses much less those hapless souls trying to sleep at The Oak. Lauder attempted to suggest that she exercise control and quietly go along to the cellar, but found himself drowned out by her continuous shouting. Then he indicated for his soldiers to restrain her and carry her off.

The first man who reached out to her got a punch in the eye from me. He dropped like a stone. The others, seeing me as the greater threat now, closed in. I lost sight of Elizabeth in the confusion of arms and legs and fists that followed.

Having my kind of upbringing, I'd no experience at street brawling, but natural instinct and anger made up for it. I had a vague impression of hitting one in the stomach, connecting with another's chin, and kicking a third in a place where no gentleman would have presumed to strike. In what seemed like an instant, the lot of them, including Sergeant Lauder, were prostrate in the dust and moaning. Coming back to myself, I regarded the scene with no small astonishment as I could not make out how I'd been able to do it.

Elizabeth, from her vantage in the doorway of the tavern, stared at me with wide-eyed wonder. "My God, Jonathan."

"Get inside," I snapped.

She ducked through the door with me at her heels and as one, we shot the bolt into place.

"My God," she repeated. "Four to one and all of them soldiers. What else did they teach you at Cambridge?"

"Ha," was all I could reply, being still too surprised myself for coherent speech.

She thought to go to a window to fasten it shut, lest the sergeant and his men gain entry that way, but found it unnecessary. "They're not getting up," she reported.

Surely I hadn't hit them that hard. I joined her looking out on the yard and found it to be true. Though there was some movement in the ranks of the wounded, none of them were attempting to stand just yet.

"We'll have to talk to Nash soon or there will be the devil to pay for this," she said.

I almost objected to this sudden degrading of her language when it occurred to me that she was greatly enjoying herself and our circumstances. "Very well," I said, though the encounter to come with Nash was not something I looked forward to with any eagerness.

The row had been more than sufficient to stir the heaviest sleeper and the narrow stairs were becoming crowded with the curious in various states of dress and undress. The company, all men, upon seeing that a lady was present, either finished putting on the clothes they had, or quickly retired to acquire more for modesty's sake. Elizabeth had the presence of mind and the courtesy to turn around and allow them the privacy to retreat.

Stumping downstairs against the flow came Lieutenant Nash. He'd managed to throw on the necessaries, but lacked a coat or even waistcoat, and his feet, though in shoes, were without stockings.

"What the devil's going on here?" he demanded sleepily. He pointed an accusing finger at me. "You! What's happening here?"

I was standing in deep shadow at this point, thankful for it, and reluctant to come forth.

"I'll handle this," Elizabeth said, and moved into the light. "Lieutenant Nash?"

His truculent manner commendably altered. "Good heavens, is that you, Miss Barrett?"

"Yes, and I must beg you for your help."

Nonplussed, but attempting to be gallant, he reached the bottom of the stairs and gave a dignified bow. "No need to beg, Miss Barrett, I am entirely at your service."

"Thank you, sir. Your Sergeant Lauder and his men wrongfully arrested us and were going to lock us in the cellar for the night. I only ask that you call him off long enough to hear me out."

"Arrested *you,* Miss Barrett? Upon what charge?"

"He was not very clear on that point, sir. He is, however, very devoted to his duty and I fear he will continue with his arrest unless he receives instructions to desist."

Nash opened and shut his mouth a few times, but decided to take action on her behalf. He unbolted the door and spent some time outside surveying his men. As Lauder was not yet in a condition to offer detailed explanations the business was concluded more quickly than one might otherwise expect. Through the window, more citizens, prompted by curiosity to forget about the curfew, had gathered to investigate. Some other soldiers had also emerged and Nash ordered them to disperse the crowd before coming in again.

The landlord of The Oak now appeared and was demanding to know the cause of the uproar. Nash looked expectantly at Elizabeth.

"Would you please show us to a more private room, Mr. Farr?" she asked sweetly.

His instincts as host helped him to maintain some composure and he gestured toward a door at the back. Elizabeth swept up a candle and glided ahead, but turned just enough to make sure that Nash was following her. She was such an uncommon sight with her regal bearing, humble clothes, and mysterious manner that he'd forgotten all about me. In their wake, I passed the landlord.

"Would you please bring along some brandy, Mr. Farr? The lieutenant is going to need it."

Farr rocked back on his heels. "My God!" He whispered, going deathly white.

I made hushing motions with my hands. "It's all right. There's been a dreadful mistake, is all."

"But I 'eard as they buried you . . ."

I shook my head, assuming an air of exasperation. "Very obviously they did not, Mr. Farr. Now, please get that drink and have one for yourself as well." I left him goggling and shut the door in his face.

Elizabeth had placed her candle on a table and was facing me as I walked in. The flame settled and the shadows stopped dancing. Nash now turned around, his expression one of expectation. It sagged into open-mouthed shock as he recognized me.

Elizabeth closely echoed my words to the landlord. "It's all right. There's nothing to fear."

Nash appeared not to heed her. He fell away until his back was pressed to a wall. I could hear his heart thundering so hard that it seemed likely to burst from his chest. His eyes, with the whites showing in abundance, tore from me to Elizabeth and returned.

"Sweet Jesus," he whispered as though in agony from a mortal wound.

And then the fatigue swept over me as I realized this was yet another in what promised to be an exhausting series of difficult confrontations. I could go all through it, as I had with Elizabeth, or . . . I might try an alternative. It might serve to at least abrogate his fear.

I stepped closer and looked at him straight. "Nash, you must listen to me . . ."

In this, I was repeating as nearly as I could the tone and manner that Nora had used often enough on me. I was not at all sure that it would have the same soothing effect on this terrified man until I realized that I'd already had some small practice at it with Rolly. It had worked then, it would work now.

I focused upon his eyes and spoke softly, as one might to lull a child toward sleep. Elizabeth's close presence, the room around us, the voices of the men outside, all retreated from my mind. I was aware of myself and Nash and nothing else.

His breathing slowed, as well as the laboring of his heart.

"You must listen to me . . ."

His eyes ceased to be so large, then clouded over.

"There's no need to be afraid," I droned on.

His whole face and posture went slack.

"Do you understand?"

"Yes . . . ," he whispered back.

That was all I wanted to hear. I stepped away from him. My head cleared and piece by piece the rest of the world returned to its proper place in the universe.

Elizabeth stood rooted to her allotted portion. Even as I'd taken the fear out of Nash, she seemed to have embraced it once more herself. "Jonathan, what have you done?"

"It's just a way of calming him. Nothing to worry about."

"Did . . . she do this to you?"

"Yes."

"I'm not sure I like it."

I shrugged. What mattered to me was that it had been successful. Nash wasn't fainting with fear or screaming the house down. He was, in fact, looking quite normal under the circumstances. His eyes had cleared and he was regarding me with no little puzzlement.

"Mr. Barrett?"

"Please sit down, Lieutenant." I indicated to Elizabeth that she should take a place at the table. She did so and we joined her. I was feeling light-headed from all the activity. When Mr. Farr came in with a generous tray, I welcomed the interruption as a chance to order my thoughts.

Farr was very nervous and clumsy for he could not look away from me. I smiled reassuringly and told him to be of good cheer, that everything would soon be explained. He left the room in haste, shutting the door with more force than necessary. Beyond it, I'd glimpsed a dozen faces eaten up by curiosity trying to peer inside.

"An explanation, Mr. Barrett?" prompted Nash.

Elizabeth had recovered somewhat from her apprehension, and both her brow and lips were puckered as she waited to hear what I was going to tell him. I suddenly wished someone else, someone quicker and more knowledgeable about such matters, was with us to do it in my stead. But Nora was very much elsewhere. It was up to me, but I wasn't sure I was up to it.

*Absurd,* I suddenly thought. For the next hour or more I might be delayed here trying to explain the inexplicable to this man and was it really any of his business? It was not. There were more important things for me to do while the night lasted than revealing my whole life to this stranger.

I reached for Elizabeth's hand to give her a reassuring squeeze, then once more fastened my eyes upon Lieutenant Nash.

It was easier this time.

* * *

Picking up the brandy bottle, I poured some into a cup, then tilted it toward Elizabeth questioningly. She shook her head. I had sore need of its bracing effect myself, but knew better than to try. The once appealing smell drifting in the air around us was now making my stomach churn. I passed the cup to Nash, who seemed willing enough to drain it.

Elizabeth looked more than a little dubious over what I had just done to him. She still did not approve, but saw that necessity outweighed any moral objections. Nash was different from the landlord in that he'd witnessed my death and burial, but under my influence he'd been able to accept an unlikely but more convenient story about my return from the dead. The truth, being so implausible, simply would not do this time. Besides, I knew that if a lie is repeated often enough it will become truth and the best person to begin the repetition was Nash.

"I hope everything is clear, Lieutenant," I said, sitting back. My head pained me a little.

He sounded absolutely normal. "Yes, Mr. Barrett."

"Now I suggest that you take yourself out there and offer some assurances to your men about this situation. Then I would very much appreciate it if you could arrange for a safe escort for my sister and myself."

"It will be a pleasure, Mr. Barrett," he said with a courteous and sincere smile. So saying, he rose, bowed to each of us, and went into the common room. The rumbling conversation there ceased upon his appearance, then started up as he was bombarded with eager questions. Pale faces once more peered in at us, eyes wide, wearing the same foolish expressions usually found on sheep.

I smiled and waved back at them until the door shut, then lowered my head into my arms with a weary sigh.

"I hope it works," said Elizabeth.

"It will have to. I'm too tired to think up anything else."

"You didn't anyway," she pointed out.

Very, very true. I'd taken her improbable story about a cousin having the same name and influenced Nash into thinking that that was the man who had been killed. It was hardly perfect, but would do, at least for those few in the army who were concerned with what had happened. Our immediate family and circle of friends would have to hear the facts, or something close to them, but that could wait until later.

"Are you up to the journey back?" she asked.

"Yes, of course I am." I straightened and put some starch into my spine. "I was just resting my eyes."

"It was . . . most strange to watch."

"What did it look like?"

"Like two men talking, but there was something more going on beneath the talk. As though you both understood one another but everyone else would miss the meaning."

"You didn't, though."

"No. I knew, but that poor man . . ."

"Is now going to do his best to help us," I told her gently.

"Well and good, but please don't mind if I choose to worry."

"What is there to worry about?"

She dropped her eyes, then raised them. "I last felt this way when you went off to England. I was afraid that you'd change so much that none of us would know you anymore. As it was, you did change, but you were still the same. I don't know if that has any sense for you."

"I think so."

"You were all grown up, of course, more polished, but still yourself. Now this night I've seen and heard things that would drive anyone to madness. I know that you are here, but some part of me cannot believe it. Are you my brother come back from the grave or have I gone mad after all and just don't know it yet?"

"You're the sanest person in the world, Elizabeth. Don't ever doubt yourself."

"It's just . . . I'm frightened. And I'm not used to being frightened. The worst part is that I've been frightened of *you*."

Oh, but it hurt to hear her say that. First shock, then joy, and shock again once she'd had time to think things over. All the unnatural aspects of my return were probably battering at her like hailstones. That's how I was feeling.

"You wonder if I'm a miracle or a monstrosity?"

Her eyes dropped once more.

"I've no answer to that. It could be both, for all I know. There have been tremendous changes within me. I'm able to do things that I can scarce comprehend, but I am yet the same brother you had before. Though I could dispel your fears as I did with Nash . . ."

She did not look up, but gave a small start.

". . . I will do no such thing. Not to you and not to Father. I swear upon my honor."

She raised her head now and the taut lines altering her expression eased as bit by bit she shed her fear. "And what about others?" She indicated the door. Nash's authoritative voice came through it as he repeated my own words to the men there.

"It's rather out of my hands now. If they wish to be afraid, they will be, so I suppose I can't help that. As for myself, I wish with all my heart that someone could take away *my* fears."

"Oh, Jonathan."

"As for the rest . . ." I shrugged.

The rest included Jericho, Mrs. Nooth, all the servants, Mrs. Hardinbrook, Beldon, Mother. So many . . . so many . . . so many . . .

"I want to see Father," I whispered, dropping my head down on my arms again.

Elizabeth's hand rested lightly on my shoulder a moment, then she rose and opened the door. "Lieutenant Nash? My brother would like to leave as quickly as possible."

Whether because of my influence or his desire to oblige my sister, Nash swiftly completed arrangements for our escort. We privately informed him of our destination and the need for discretion. Though Father's friendship with Mrs. Montagu was close to common knowledge in the area, they were each so well respected in their circles that everyone was content to overlook it. Nash had been in the world long enough to understand and do likewise.

He also extended himself and placed two horses at our disposal. He stated his willingness to conduct the escort himself and took one, I the other, and Elizabeth was boosted up behind me. It could hardly have been comfortable for her, but she held tightly onto my waist and made no complaint.

Nash had a man march before us with a lantern, which seemed foolish to me since I could see so well and might have led the way. I held my peace on the subject, though. Any display of my new abilities would needlessly stir them up.

The stars provided me with more than sufficient illumination and now that I had a moment of leisure to consider them, I felt a fresh awakening of awe at their beauty. They were like tiny suns, but unlike the sun itself, could be looked at directly. There also seemed to be many more than I was accustomed to seeing. Thousands of them crowded the sky like clouds of glowing dust motes. The light they shed upon the land was quite even and diffuse so that there was a singular lack of deep shadows in the surrounding countryside. Only beneath the thickest clusters of trees did I spy anything approaching real darkness.

Nash spoke up. "Miss Barrett?"

"Yes?"

"On the road you told my sergeant that you were on the king's business in regard to a message."

"What? Oh. Yes. Our father is a friend of Colonel DeQuincey, who was the one sending it. I fear that I cannot divulge the contents to you, for we are both under oath."

Nash was disappointed, but willing to persist. "I do find it odd that such duties must require a lady to be out so late."

"You are not alone in that opinion, Lieutenant," she said agreeably.

"Also that none of my men reported any messengers upon the road."

Then she took a chance, stepping out on the framework of lies she had formed and that I had placed in his mind. "My brother was the messenger. He is well acquainted with the geography hereabouts, so it is not surprising that he was able to avoid any encounters."

He turned his attention upon me. "You must have prodigious knowledge, indeed, sir. One can scarce throw a stone into the woods without it striking one of my men."

"True enough. I did not have an easy time keeping out of their way."

"But if you were on the king's business, then surely you would have had no need to avoid them."

"Being delayed was what I wished to avoid, Lieutenant Nash," I said stiffly. "My limited knowledge of German combined with the misfortune of falling from and losing my horse and papers all served to turn me into a most suspicious character in the eyes of Sergeant Lauder. After hearing Hulton's story, I can see why you sent your men out, but I keenly regret the loss of time." He started to reply, but I continued. "However, your speedy assistance in correcting the matter will not go unmarked or unrewarded."

He clearly understood my meaning and managed a slight bow from his saddle."Your servant, Mr. Barrett." He was an officer in the king's army, which made him a nominal gentleman, but the pay was meager enough to keep him open to compromise on some points. With the prospect of a bribe coming in the near future we could count on him to contain his curiosity for the moment—longer, should it become necessary for me to influence him again.

The night was getting on and despite—or perhaps because of—all the excitements, Elizabeth was growing sleepy. Her head nodded against my shoulder, matching the rhythm of our plodding horse. But for my change, I should have been in the same state. Though I'd experienced a certain mental lethargy after dealing with Nash and was suffering a great heaviness of spirit from the consequences of my change, I was yet energetic in body. Perversely, I found it to be annoying. I *should* have felt sleepy as well. I missed it. Our country custom of rising and retiring with the sun was, I thought, ingrained in my very bones. No more. That whole part of my life was now completely reversed. The nights that lay ahead did not bear thinking about, for they looked to be rather lonely. I could not expect anyone else to reverse themselves just to keep me company.

Noticing that her hands were coming loose, I roused Elizabeth. She jerked awake with a gasp.

"Just a little farther," I promised her. "We've already passed the turning to our home."

She murmured an inarticulate acknowledgment and endeavored to stretch a little. "I hope Mrs. Montagu has some tea. I should very much like a cup or two."

"I'm sure she will, but I suggest you go first and make the request before they see me. There's bound to be an uproar once I walk through the door."

Now she did come alert. "Heavens, yes. How are we going to do this? If I burst in on them in the dead of night with this news they'll think I'm as mad as Mother. And if you come in with me it could be worse."

"Actually, I did have the idea that you should precede me. Of course you don't want to burst in. Just knock on the door and take Father off for a quiet chat to get him prepared. Tell him whatever you need to about Nora and—"

"Jonathan, my dear little brother, there is no way in the world that I could possibly provide him adequate preparation for this."

"I'm under no illusions on that point, but I hope you will try."

"I shall, but no matter what I say, he's going to have a terrible shock when he sees you."

Alas, yes.

The man walking ahead with the lantern had paused, waiting for the rest of our parade to catch him up. Nash leaned down to confer with him, then straightened to squint ineffectually into what for him was true darkness.

"What's the matter?" I asked. I'd also looked around and saw nothing.

"Lauder's other men aren't at their stations," he rumbled.

Several reasons for that came to mind: they'd fallen asleep or were detained out of sight while attending to bodily needs or they'd somehow lost their way from the road. I did not give voice to them, for they sounded foolish enough as thoughts.

"Stay here a moment while we scout ahead," he told us and kicked his horse forward. The half dozen Hessians that had been marching at our heels followed on his barked order. I reined my animal to keep it in place and watched them go. Elizabeth and I were silent the whole time until one man finally trotted back for us.

Nash and the rest were gathered about the narrow road that broke off from the main one to lead to Mrs. Montagu's house. They were watchful, but not nervous.

"Where are they?" I demanded.

"Hereabouts," he replied with false conviction. Considering the fiasco yesterday that had cost me a normal life, I was irritated at once again seeing evidence of Nash's incompetence.

I stood in my stirrups for another look. Nothing but trees, fields, and empty, dusty road before and behind. Not quite empty. There was something lying across the ruts a little ahead, close enough to notice, but too far to identify.

"They must be very good at woodcraft," I commented. "I see no sign of them at all."

"It's a thick night," he said. "No moon. None of us can see much."

The damned idiot. Men gone missing and him thinking I wouldn't mind. We could be surrounded by rebels and he'd prefer to get shot than admit something was wrong. "I think we should go on to our destination, Lieutenant."

"Certainly."

"*Herr Oberleutnant!*" The man with the lantern had pushed ahead and stumbled over whatever it was on the road. His strident tone brought us all to attention. Nash moved toward him. I trailed along with them, having the idea of there being safety in numbers. Elizabeth tightened her hold around my waist.

They were all bending over it and the alteration of their manner was such as to make me stop short. I signed to Elizabeth that I was getting down and swung a leg over the horse's neck and slipped off. She dropped next to me.

I pushed into the middle of them and recoiled at once. At our feet lay the body of a young Hessian. His head was thrown back so his mouth was wide open as though for a scream. In contrast, his eyes were calm and quite dull. Limbs flung every which way, his chest was cracked open like an eggshell. The bloodsmell struck at my senses like a harsh slap. The stuff covered him and had soaked into the earth.

"Oh, my God," whispered Elizabeth.

My first instinct was to turn and drag her away from the awful sight. She made no protest. Her feet tangled one against the other; I lifted her up by the elbows until we were well distanced and set her down with a jolt. She swayed against me, gasping for air.

"My God, it was just how *you* looked," she said, freely shuddering.

Her words cut right through me, gouged into my vitals, and tore out again leaving behind chaos and a kind of blank agony.

Too much had happened. The rest and retreat I so desperately needed had forced themselves upon me. For a few minutes I simply could not think. It's a truly terrible thing to go through, when nothing—absolutely *nothing*—fills the mind. You don't really forget anything, not names or facts or memories, you just can't get to them. I was a sudden simpleton, unable to move or speak, unaware of time or events until Elizabeth's voice, insistently calling my name, finally brought me back.

"I'm all right," I replied to whatever question she'd asked.

"Are you?"

I breathed in a great draft of fresh night air and decided my legs would hold me after all. "Yes. What of yourself?"

She was unwell, but not the sort to faint, and told me as much.

"Stay here," I said. An unnecessary request. She wasn't about to budge from her spot. I returned for another view of the calamity. It was bad enough, but worsened for me when I recognized him.

It was Hausmann, the young man who had wanted land, a family, a new life. His life taken, his dreams dead, the children to come never born, he was so horrible and yet so pathetic. The two balanced each other to promote equal amounts of revulsion and pity. Was *this* what had happened to me? Was that the sight that had made my father cry out so?

Yes and yes.

Then inevitably, came the rage. It washed over me like a scarlet tide, fiery hot, frighteningly strong.

*Who had done this?*

Nash had dismounted and was regarding his man with a sad, hard face. During his life he had probably seen much of death, but he did not appear to be overly callous. He looked at me and something flinched in his face. I ignored it.

"Nash, I want to get the bastard that did this."

"We will, Mr. Barrett," he said, sounding nettled, perhaps, that I was presuming too much upon his goodwill.

To the devil with it. "Nash, listen to me . . ."

He flinched again, his eyelids fluttering as if against a strong wind.

"Tonight we are going to hunt down whoever did this and take him. Do you understand?"

He struggled for breath. Not all of the men knew my words, but they read my intent well enough. Those closest to us fell back.

"*Do you understand?*"

He was unable to speak and only just managed to nod. He'd gone very white and, when I released him, staggered a little. One of his men muttered and made a surreptitious gesture with his hand. I'd seen something similar while visiting one of the Dutch towns on the west end of the Island. It had been explained to me as being a sign to ward off the evil eye. I ignored that, too. Let them think what they liked as long as they obeyed Nash's orders and Nash obeyed mine.

I gave instructions, then grabbed up my horse's forgotten reins and stalked back to Elizabeth. "Nash has picked out two trustworthy men. They're to escort you safely to Father—"

"*What?*"

"I'm going to stay and help him settle things."

"You're what?" She had heard me, but wasn't ready to accept it.

"I have to do this."

"You have to see Father."

"Later."

"Jonathan—"

"No. *Listen* to me. The bastard that killed me may have killed that poor soul as well. I can't let another hour pass without doing something about it."

She looked over at the men standing by the corpse. "But Father—"

"Will understand."

"Are you so sure?"

I was and I wasn't and could form no answer for her, only frame another question. "Do *you* understand?"

Again she looked past me, then right at me. Her hand touched my chest where the musket ball had shattered every aspect of our lives, then fell away. "I'm afraid I do."

Relief, elation, love. "Thank you, sister."

"Thank me later, when I'm in a better mind to take it."

I lifted her up onto the saddle and gave her the reins. "If I'm not back before dawn don't worry. It only means that I had to find shelter for the day. Whatever happens, you'll be able to meet me at the old barn tomorrow after sunset. I'd come to the house, but . . ."

She leaned down and her fingers dug into my shoulder. Her voice was shaking. "As long as you *do* come back, because I couldn't possibly stand losing you twice."

# CHAPTER ◄13►

Nash and I made a thorough inspection of the area and drew a few conclusions. Hausmann had been shot at fairly close range and died where he'd fallen. His gun, powder horn, bayonet, and other gear were gone, along with whatever coin he might have possessed. Nash took the stripping of the body in stride and even seemed to approve.

"It'll make it that much easier to identify the rascals and hang 'em," he said.

There'd been at least two, perhaps more. The footprints were too muddled for us to make much sense of them. Our own tracks added to the confusion, but I was able to find where the rebels had crossed the road to head over the fields.

"They may be trying to get back to Suffolk County," I grumbled. "They'll find no lack of help there. The whole place stinks of sedition."

"Oh, yes, the 'Sons of Liberty,' " he added. "More like the sons of bitches. But if they're going to Suffolk, I should think it would be faster to stay on the road."

"Not if they know the land. The road curves farther along and would take them too much out of their way."

"We can't hope to follow them at night, not through all that with only a lantern." He motioned at the fields.

"Then have your man put out the light so our eyes can get used to the dark."

"Mr. Barrett, this is most impractical!"

"Or leave it by that poor boy's body. At least then no one will fall over him."

He had no objections to that suggestion. Someone had placed Hausmann in order, straightening his limbs and covering his face with a handkerchief. With the lantern sitting incongruously in the dust close by his head, he looked more macabre than when we'd first found him. My anger welled up again, for him, for me, for the grief that had happened, and that which was to come.

Nash sent one man back to Glenbriar on my horse to fetch more troops. He might have been content to wait for their arrival, but I was very conscious that the night was swiftly passing.

"If we tarry here the rebels will either bury themselves in Suffolk or have found a boat to take them across the Sound. We must set out now and let the others catch us up as they can."

"Their orders are to look for the men who were here to start with," Nash clarified.

"My guess is that if that lot are still alive, they'll be in pursuit of the rebels as well."

"My God, in this murk we could end up shooting each other."

"Lieutenant, I can see excellently in the dark and thus will be able to prevent such an occurrence, let us cease wasting time and proceed."

My voice had taken on an edge that he recognized and was not ready to contest. He gave some brief orders and indicated that I should lead the way. We left the road in single file, each man within sight of the one before him, the last one in line leading Nash's horse. Though it was obvious they were taking pains to be quiet, the whole parade seemed preposterously noisy to me. I winced with every careless footstep and snapped twig and fervently hoped that the darkness would provide us the same cover as it gave those we hunted.

Free of such limitations, I remained alert to the movement and place of each leaf and branch. It served. Some dozen yards along our rustic path I spied additional tracks heading away from the road. I did not point them out to Nash, as it was unlikely he'd be able to see well enough, but they did confirm my guess that our destination would be somewhere in Suffolk County.

Unless we hurried.

I urged Nash to greater speed and damn the noise—which was a decided error in judgment.

With Elizabeth gone a great portion of my mind that was unoccupied with more immediate concerns had been giving in to the temptation to think of the events of the last two nights as being a ghastly nightmare from which I might hopefully awaken. I did know in my heart that this was nonsense, but as if to confound the facts and confirm the wish came a near repetition of what had set everything off. Someone raised himself out of cover and fired his gun at us.

I saw the flash and smoke, heard the crashing report, and did nothing. As before, I simply could not take in the idea that anyone would want to hurt me. A very foolish assumption, considering what I'd been through, and very selfish, to stand there like a lout and not to consider the welfare of the other men with me. Veterans of battle, they sensibly dropped while I continued to stand and gape. Lieutenant Nash, with a foul curse, knocked a solid arm against the back of my knees and told me to do likewise.

Pitching forward, I threw out my hands and caught myself in time. Nash's blow seemed to jog my head back onto my shoulders, as it were, causing me to start thinking again. I whispered for him to stay put and lifted up just enough for a look around.

The man that had shot at us was quickly bearing himself away.

I shouted something about getting him and sprinted off. Nash yelled after, urging me to use caution, but I was deaf to any objections. The fellow had a good start, but there was no chance that he could match my speed. At best, he could go at a fast walk; unimpeded by the darkness, I was able to run. Dodging by trees and bushes, leaping over roots, I caught up with him like a hound after a crippled hare.

He heard me, glanced back once, and increased his pace. Too little, too late. I bowled into him and brought us both down with a satisfying thud that was more injurious to him than myself. The breath grunted out of him, leaving him too stunned to move. I got up, grabbed away his spent musket, and called for Nash and the others to come ahead. It took them some time to pick their path, but they followed my voice and eventually arrived.

"Who is he?" Nash demanded.

"A damned better man than you, you English bastard," the man snarled back.

Nash, an officer in what was surely the greatest army in the world, had no patience for insults from inferiors. He gave the man a hard kick in the side to encourage him into a more respectful attitude. The fellow had only just recovered his wind and this additional assault once more deprived him of air.

"Do you know him?" he asked of me.

"I've not seen him before," I said truthfully. Having been a regular churchgoer, I knew the faces, if not the names, of just about everyone in the area. "Where are you from?"

"Wouldn't you like to know?" he wheezed back.

Nash started to kick him again, but I persuaded him to hold off this time. Though a good beating might improve his manners it would also render him unable to speak.

"I think he's from Connecticut," I said, making an educated guess from his clothes and accent.

"I've heard the name," said Nash. "Where does it lie from here?"

"Across the Sound. Put a few stout fellows at the oars of a whale boat and you can row your way across quick as thought."

"Tory traitor," said the man in a poisonous tone.

"That, sir, is a contradiction of terms," I informed him. "Now unless you want these soldiers to hang you on the spot for a murdering spy, you'd better give us your name and business."

"I'm no spy, but a soldier myself, and deserve honorable treatment," he protested.

"Then act with honor, sir. Who are you?"

"Lieutenant Ezra Andrews and I have the privilege of serving under General Washington, God bless his soul."

"Can you prove that?"

"By God, what proof do I need beyond my own word?"

"Your commission as an officer?" suggested Nash. At a sign from him, two Hessians stepped in to drag Andrews to his feet and turn out his pockets. One of them found a substantial fold of paper, which he passed to Nash. He opened and tried unsuccessfully to read it in the starlight. Andrews cackled.

"Let me," I offered. So as not to startle them, I also made a show of squinting against the dark, then slowly read out enough words to confirm that Andrews spoke the truth about himself and his rank. Nash then informed the man that he was his prisoner.

Andrews spat on the ground. Luckily his aim, like his previous shot at us, was just as poor, and missed my shoe by several inches.

Nash took the commission and refolded the paper. "Where are the rest of your men?"

"You can find 'em yourself. I'll not help you."

*Yes, you will,* I thought. "Andrews . . . look at me. I want you to listen to me. . . ."

"I'll listen to no one," he snapped back.

"Listen to me, I say."

"The devil I will."

I stopped cold and blinked. What was the matter with the man? I was staring right at him and nothing I said was making any impression at all. As if he were . . .

Damnation.

I gave up in sudden chagrin. I could see him, but unless he could see me, my efforts were futile. It was just too dark for such work.

"Give him over and let's push on," I said to Nash. "His fellows can't be that far ahead of us."

"Mr. Barrett, you have done enough for one night by capturing this man."

"And there's more to be done, sir. Whoever killed Hausmann is still free." I made a point to emphasize Hausmann's name and gesture ahead of us. This was not lost on the Hessians, who looked expectantly at their commander.

Nash could not reasonably back down, not just yet. With ill grace, he ordered someone to bind Andrews's hands behind him and put him in the charge of the tallest and strongest-looking man in our small company. Andrews protested and the soldier told him to be quiet. Andrews did not understand German, but he did get the correct idea, subsiding when his captor graphically drew a finger across his own throat and made an appropriate hissing sound.

As we continued forward, I found signs on the ground that others had gone by earlier: trampled plants, broken branches. They'd been in much haste.

"I don't think they're very far ahead," I confided to Nash. Despite his reluctance at this job, he invited me to enlarge upon that opinion. "They must have heard us coming up, the wind's at our backs, you know. I believe Andrews stayed behind to fire a shot to discourage our progress."

"It worked," he admitted. "He bought them a quarter hour, at least, they could be anywhere by now."

*That* estimation of the time was a gross exaggeration. The man's reluctance was enough for me to accuse him of cowardice, but I held my tongue. "Not if they're waiting for Andrews."

His forward pace wavered. "What do you mean?"

"I believe there's an excellent chance that he was meant to fire his gun, then run after them. They may only be just ahead."

Now Nash completely stopped. "Meaning that those rascals are most certainly lying in ambush for us."

"Possibly, but I rather think they're more likely expecting Andrews, not us."

"I cannot take that chance with my men," he stated. "In the daylight, with sufficient reinforcements we can—"

"Lieutenant, I am not asking you to march them into any ambush, but to allow me to scout ahead."

It must have gone through his mind how bad he would look to his senior officers if a civilian was seen to be doing his job. On the other hand, he had no taste for the work to be done. "Very well, but no more than one hundred yards."

I intended to travel as far as was necessary, but decided that that information would only raise more objections. "Good. Now if you will instruct your man to give me Andrews's musket . . . and now I'll just trade hats with him."

Andrews had been listening to this exchange and instantly saw the danger it meant to his companions. He started to raise his voice to shout a warning, but I cut that off quickly enough by clapping a hand over his mouth. He began to vigorously struggle and his guard and two others found it necessary to wrestle the man to the ground. We made quite a clumsy mob before sorting ourselves out. Only after someone put a fist into Andrews's belly did I dare to remove my smothering hand. He groaned and puffed and by the time he was ready to use his voice again, was efficiently gagged.

I placed his hat on my head, crouched down to minimize my height (Andrews was half a foot shorter), and continued along the path the rebels seemed to have taken. The long barrel and weight of the musket slowed me down. I had to mind where it was pointing lest it catch on something above or to the side.

My much-improved night vision was a godsend; I covered my hundred-yard limit in very little time.

Other than the signs left on the earth of their late passage, I saw nothing of the rebels. It was safe for Nash and his men to follow to this point, but I didn't want to waste time going back for them. Nor did I want to spend too much time away, or Nash would become more nervous than ever. I could assume he would wait for a little while, then be able to honorably call a retreat. The problem was not knowing just how long he would wait.

I was trotting now, covering the distance much faster than an ordinary man, and marveling at my lack of physical fatigue. My steps were full of spring as though I were fresh and had bottomless reserves to draw upon. I'd felt this before when the chase was up for a hunt or riding Rolly. For a time the sheer joy of movement overcame the goal behind it, until the movement itself was the goal.

The feeling lasted until I saw a blur with a man's shape stirring under some trees just ahead.

"Andrews?"

The voice was pitched to a carrying whisper. Unrecognizable. I slowed, but kept coming.

"Mr. Andrews?"

I gave out with a grunt of affirmation and hoped it would be well received.

"Are you all right?"

Another grunt. I came closer. The shape clarified itself, separating out from the dense shadows where it had been crouching.

Roddy Finch.

I strode forward without thought. A kind of humming had seized my brain, or perhaps I was the one humming and was all unaware of it. I know that for several seconds I could hear nothing else.

Roddy asked another question. At least, I saw his mouth forming words and the expression on his face suggested that he was making an inquiry of me. I was unable to answer.

*Andrews?* I read the name from his lips.

My continued approach, continued silence alarmed him. He wavered between running and risking another question.

And while he hesitated I bore down upon him like a storm.

I threw away Andrews's musket. Roddy saw something of the motion and heard its landing, but could make no sense of it. He raised his own gun, but had left it too late. I grabbed it from his hands as one might take a stick from a very young child. He turned to run, but to my eyes he seemed to be moving unbearably slow. I caught him by the neck of his coat and plucked him from the ground.

My hearing returned. The screech he gave out went right through me. I did not stop, though. I jerked him right off his feet like a doll and twisted around and let go my grip. He went flying down the path to land in a stunned heap some yards away.

Behind me, someone yelled his name.

I was just turning to look, but instinct had the better part of me now and I dropped instead.

Once more I was deafened, but from without, not within, as a gun roared very close overhead. The sweet reek of its smoke engulfed me, stung my eyes. I was just able to see a young man emerging from the trees. Halfway to my feet, I sprang at him. He was fast. He swung the gun barrel at my head as hard as he could.

I got my arm up just in time or he'd have crushed my skull. It still felt like he'd broken something. The jolt of the heavy iron was enough to knock me right over. I roared from the pain and tried to get up. He struck again and I had no choice but to use the same arm as a shield. He caught me just below the elbow and the agony was so sudden and so awful that I knew the bone had definitely shattered under the blow.

As I fell away, he dashed past to Roddy and frantically urged him to get up. Roddy was too slow for him and needed help finding his feet.

"Come on, come on!" his rescuer cried desperately.

Like two drunks attempting to support one another, they staggered a little, then got aimed in the right direction.

No . . . he would *not* get away from me.

My right arm dangling loose and shooting white-hot darts straight into my brain, I lurched over just in time to catch him as they passed.

Roddy.

I used my weight and extra height and brought him down. His companion was bowled out of the way by my rush, but recovered and turned on me. Like Roddy before him, he seemed to be moving slowly—that or I was moving just that much faster. This time when he swung at my head with the musket barrel I was ready and caught it with my left hand. A snarl and a vicious wrench and it was mine.

He was surprised, but wasted no time staring. He doubled over and butted me in the stomach with his head. It pushed me backward a few paces and hurt, but was nothing compared to my arm. He followed up with two quick fists, but the results of his blows were disappointing to him. I felt them, but they hardly seemed to bother me. Next he tried to take back his gun and we played a very uneven tug-of-war for its possession.

His breathing was ragged, his poxy face gone red and dripping sweat. I could smell the stink from his bad teeth as his next charge brought us both down and rolling. Now he was biting and kicking like a fury, but I kept hold of the gun and, by God, I wasn't going to give it up. Had he been thinking, he might have used my bad arm against me by striking at it, but he'd lost his temper and his reason. I got the gun between us and tried to use it to ward off his fists. This bruised him and slowed him down, then Roddy's unsteady voice rang out.

"They're comin'! Run for your life!"

I heard a confusion of sounds, then the man beating at me was abruptly gone.

"Run for it!" yelled Roddy. He was on his feet now and the other man pelted past him. He shambled forward to follow.

*No . . .*

I discarded the gun as a useless weight and threw myself at him. We came down with a groan. When he attempted to crawl away, I put a knee into his side, stopping him.

"Mr. Barrett! Mr. Barrett!" called Nash. He and his men were blundering up, drawn by the shot, but uncertain of the right direction.

I started to speak. There was no air in my lungs. I replaced it, but as I did so the thought occurred to me that bringing Nash over would seal things forever for Roddy. This boy that I had known all my life would go straight to the gallows. My own death aside, they would certainly hang him for stealing back his father's horses. Though there was probably no direct evidence against him, men had died before for less.

I'd known him all my life.

And he'd known me.

"*Mr. Barrett?*"

We'd played at Rapelji's school, worked there, helped one another. We'd not been especial friends, but he *had* known me. And for all that, he'd still been able to coolly raise his gun and send me falling into this waking nightmare. He'd put my family through untold grief, put me through hell itself.

But they would *hang* him.

Oliver had once persuaded me to Tyburn to see some murderers pay for their crimes. It hadn't been pretty. The family of one man had hurriedly come forward to seize his legs and pull down as hard as they could to speed the progress of the strangling rope and end his sufferings. The sight had been sickening, but I'd been assured that the man more than deserved his punishment. Now I looked down at Roddy Finch and in my mind placed him at those gallows, his feet twitching and his neck stretching and his tongue thrusting out and his face turning black.

If I called now, it would be out of my hands and the law would run its course. Still, it would be the same as if I'd drawn the rope over Roddy's head myself.

"Mr. Barrett!"

I stood up. The humming had returned to my brain.

"Mr. Barrett!"

"We're over here, Lieutenant Nash. I have another prisoner for you."

The way we were seated on the ground, surrounded by Hessians, anyone would think that we were all prisoners. Andrews and Roddy both had their hands tied and I was in virtually the same immobile condition because of my injured arm. I felt weak and shaken. It hurt abominably. One of the soldiers had improvised a sling for me and another tried to tempt me with a flask of something that smelled terrible. I thanked him and politely refused. To them, I was the hero of the hour, but their admiration was rather lost on me because of the pain.

Nash made a show of going after the other rebel, but without my help, he had no chance of catching up. And I had no need or desire to help. We had Roddy Finch and that was the end of it for me.

The discarded muskets were recovered and one proved to be identical to those that the Hessians carried.

"A good night's work," said Nash, when he returned and was informed of this discovery. "You've done the Crown a great favor with your assistance, Mr. Barrett. I'm sure it will not go unrewarded."

Now our positions to aid one another had been reversed, though I had no doubt he would still expect some monetary token from my father later.

Father . . .

The urge to go home seized me, stronger than ever, now that the chase was past. Elizabeth had been disappointed, but understood; she would not be as charitable over additional delays.

"Thank you, Lieutenant. I would take it as a great kindness if I might be allowed to return to my sister."

He'd only been waiting half the night to hear those words and promptly volunteered his horse for my use. I declined. The effort of getting into the saddle would be too much for my arm. I was able to walk and said as much, preferring my own legs to being jostled around on a horse's back. After trading hats again with the surly Andrews, I set off, slowly leading the way for the rest. Since the object was to reach the road rather than go back on our own tracks, I struck off in a different direction to find it. Once there, they could make their own way back to Glenbriar.

Of the other men who had been at their post with Hausmann, we saw no sign. Andrews and Roddy refused to answer any questions on the subject. Nash was not optimistic.

"Probably murdered as well," he said. "If that's the case, then hanging will be too good for these two."

"Andrews is a soldier," I pointed out.

"More's the pity, he'll probably just be interned as a prisoner of war. The other fellow is no soldier, though, which makes him either a spy, a thief, a murderer, or all three. He'll hang."

Roddy heard him clearly—Nash was making no effort at discretion—went very white, and stumbled as his legs went weak. His guard held him up.

"Steady, lad," said Andrews, who had had his gag removed. "You're a soldier and I'll swear to it in any court they please to call. You'll live to fight another day."

"Ha!" said Nash.

Very likely I would never see Roddy again after this night. He would simply cease to be. I enjoyed no feeling of triumph for his capture. I wanted him punished, but the punishment itself had become distant and abstract. Someone else would handle all the details of prosecution and execution. My only concern now was to patch up the damage he had inflicted upon my life.

We might have done better to retrace our steps, for it took us an hour to reach the road again, and even longer to return to the point where we'd left it. I was growing weary. Those bottomless reserves were turning out to be finite, after all.

In the far distance, as we rounded a curve, we saw several lanterns bobbing about and many men moving around. The fellow Nash had dispatched for reinforcements had returned and they were gathered around the spot where Hausmann had fallen.

"That's Da's wagon and team," Roddy exclaimed when we got close enough for them to see details.

True enough, and rather ironic. It was being used to carry Hausmann's body back to Glenbriar. They'd already shrouded him in a blanket. The thing robbed him of face and form. God, I must have looked like *that* as well. I was glad Elizabeth was not here to see it.

Andrews and Roddy were turned over to others to guard and Nash busied himself with issuing orders and receiving news. The missing men had turned up on their own. They'd heard the shot that had killed Hausmann and given futile chase, but lost themselves in the dark. They'd wandered back sometime earlier, drawn by the lights and noise of the others.

"That's good," Nash concluded. "It seems that you and that lad are the only casualties. If you wish, I'll have them take you back to The Oak and find a doctor for you."

"Thank you, but I'm sure Dr. Beldon, who lives at my home, will see to things."

"Yes, of course. I'd forgotten about him. I imagine he's still out looking for your—ah . . ." Here he trailed off, in sudden doubt over what he should say next.

"For these two," I completed for him, indicating the prisoners. "I hope he hasn't come to harm. Please do tell your men to keep a lookout for him and send him home as quick as may be."

"Certainly." Nash recovered from his discomfiture, his altered memory secure once more. He insisted on providing an escort, so I found myself bracketed by two men who were instructed to take me to the door of the Montagu house. Each had a lantern, but our progress was slow. They understood that I was to be given every courtesy and interpreted that to mean setting a regal pace out of consideration for my arm. It pleased me well enough as I didn't feel like going any faster.

The thing had swollen rather badly. The sleeve of the coat I wore was snug around the injury. I was not looking forward to Beldon's ministrations for this. Not that I lacked confidence in his ability as a physician, but it would hurt damnably.

Though thankfully not suffering from fever, my mouth was very dry. I thirsted, and knew that water would not quench it. *I need blood,* I thought without abhorrence or any surprise.

Once the idea jumped into my head the thirst increased tenfold.

My throat constricted and my tongue thickened as it rubbed the dry roof of my mouth. My lips felt like salt and sand. The fingers of my good hand curled and twitched. My very bones seemed to burn with new pain around the break. Much as I wanted to see Father, it would have to wait. I could not tolerate this dreadful need for very long.

I walked faster. The soldiers made no comment and kept up. They'd become a sudden inconvenience and would have to go. I tried to recall the words I'd use to dismiss them, but the insistent thirst was too distracting. The phrases that kept coming up in my tumbled mind were either French or Italian or Latin.

As the Montagu house finally came into view, I paused and attempted to tell the men that I no longer required their assistance. My nervous state of mind, combined with my limited German, made it difficult to get the idea across. One of them knew a bit of English, though, so between us things were finally made clear. They looked somewhat worried for me, for I was fidgeting and the longer they lingered, the harder it was to conceal my anxiousness. With many a backward glance, they finally left, their pale lanterns swinging as they went. I managed to remain in one spot just long enough for them to walk a goodly distance, then whirled around to run toward the stables.

The building was unfamiliar to me and much smaller than our own, but the smells and routines were identical. I eased open the door and slipped inside, my eyes eagerly searching the dimness within.

Her carriage stood just inside, a lovely bit of work that she kept polished and new-looking for her rides to church and village. She had only the one coachman, who also served as groom, but he'd be asleep in the slave quarters now. The horses, a pair of matched bays out of the same bloodlines as my own Rolly, were quite unguarded.

The animals already sensed my approach, stirring in their boxes. I picked the quieter of the two and moved in next to him. His ears flicked back in doubt and he bobbed his head. I spoke to him soothingly and let him get my scent until he was used to me. It was not easy to stand there calming him while feeling so agitated. I was so close to relieving the ache in my throat and belly that the natural urge to hurry was hard to put off.

Finally, he stood very still and I was able to go on. My earlier experience with Rolly helped. This time my bite was more shallow, my control of the flow more certain. The effect of the blood, however, was the same and I gratefully drank my fill, relishing the warmth and rich taste. It was better than the sweetest water, better than the best wine, more sustaining than any food.

And healing. Some of the grinding agony in my broken arm receded. It was yet far from being whole—the swelling remained—but the promise of recovery was there. I could even move the fingers again, though nothing more than that.

The small wounds I'd made on the horse clotted over. The blood staining my mouth and chin was minimal; I could easily clean that off if I could just find . . .

The stable door, which I'd left open to give me light to work by, was no longer empty. The Hessians stood there, their lanterns raised high. I dropped down, but the movement made noise and they came inside.

*Damn* the men. Not put off by my dismissal, they'd doggedly returned, whether out of curiosity or a dedicated obedience to their commander to see that his orders were correctly carried out.

I swiped at my mouth. Blood on my hand now. The damned stuff was everywhere.There was no time to brush it away, they were already coming around to look in the box.

They stopped short as the lantern light fell upon me where I crouched in the straw. Each of us gave a start, they with surprise, me with sudden shame. I turned my face from them, but it was too late. They'd seen the blood, the eyes—which had flushed scarlet after my feeding. Nora's had always done so.

"*Blutsauger!*" one of them whispered with awe and horror.

The word had no meaning for me, but I knew the sound of fear. I raised myself and slowly faced them.

The older of the two backed away, making a recognizable witch sign against me with his hand. He invoked God's name in a hasty muttered prayer and kept going. His companion was too shocked yet to move.

"It's all right," I said, but it was hopeless to think I could calm them as I'd calmed the horse. I offered a placating hand, a wasted and foolish gesture. There was blood on it.

The older one recoiled, shouted a warning at his friend, and fled. He crashed against the edge of the doorway in his haste, but did not stop. The noise got through to the other fellow, who started after him.

I rushed up to the opening and watched them retreat across the yard and on to the beginnings of the lane. They'd probably run straight back to their company and pass along God knows what story. There was absolutely nothing I could do about it, either. I might possibly catch up with them, try to influence them, but what needed to be said to change their memories was beyond my limited German vocabulary.

A black cloud settled about me, sinking into my brain, deadening thought, but not feeling. The impossibility of my situation was too much to bear. While Elizabeth had been with me, I'd been able to take hope from her, but now even her support looked to be no more than an illusion . . . a dream . . . a shadow.

*I live in the shadows and make shadows of my own in the minds of others. Shadows and illusions of life and love that fill my nights until something like this happens and shows them up for what they are.*

Now as I leaned wearily against the wall of the stable and stared inward, I knew what Nora had meant. Its exact meaning had been driven into me by those two terrified men with almost the same force as that musket ball. My desire to go back to the life I'd known was never to be fulfilled. I might create an illusion of peace for myself but it would be only that and nothing more. Sooner or later the unnatural aspects of my condition would encroach upon and destroy that peace. This instance was surely the first of many others to come. The weight of such a future was enough to crush me back into the ground again, back into the grave that had rejected me.

Without thought or direction I left the stable and wandered out into a night that was my illusion of day. The only darkness for me now was from the heavy cloud that covered my heart and soul, weighed hard upon my spirit, and filled my mind. Even the careless glory of the stars filling the great sky with their light could not pierce or lift it.

I walked and walked, hugging my injured arm. My path took me through fields and across the road. I lost track of time and didn't care. I met no one and was vaguely thankful. I wanted no one to see me, not even Father. I was too ashamed of what had happened to me, of what I'd become.

Only when the sky turned unduly bright did I rouse somewhat from the self-pity that had such fast hold of me. I didn't wholly shake it off, merely thrust it aside out of mundane necessity.

My unmindful walk had been in the right general direction. I was on my own land and not too far from the old barn. Elizabeth might even be there. I'd told her about it. Yes. I could bear to see her again, but no one else.

The light flooding the sky increased, imparting clear vision to others even as it blinded me. My steps grew clumsy, uncertain. I staggered forward with greater speed, shielding my eyes and looking up only to stay on the path I stumbled over. The barn was only just ahead. I dived beneath the ivy hanging over the entrance and into the comforting shadows beyond with a sob of relief.

Apparently I was not so far gone in my mood as to forsake life just yet.

Had I stayed outside, I suspected the sun would burn me down to the bone. A musket ball was bad enough, but there were worse fates.

My steps dragging in the dust, I returned to the dark shelter of the stall. The only marks there were the ones I'd made earlier. I'd probably be secure enough for the day—at least until Elizabeth came the next evening. I was sorry she wasn't here, but it had only been a faint hope and I'd come to know the bitter difference between it and actuality. She was probably still talking to Father, poor girl.

I sat with my back to the wall, trying to ease my arm and groaning over the misery. This time I would welcome the sleep the day would bring . . .

. . . that whipped by without any knowledge that I *had* slept.

My eyes had closed and opened. That was all it took and the hot hours of another late summer's day were gone forever. All my future days would be spent like this one. I'd never again see the clouds against the sun, never see its rise and set except as a warning or as an inconvenience that must be endured. No illusions, shadows, or nightmares, but no dreams either, nothing but this unnatural oblivion and its inevitable reminder of death.

Whatever was to become of me?

Did I even care?

After a moment's sluggish thought, I decided the answer was yes. For my body, if not my spirit. Conscious or not, the enforced rest had done me much good. More movement had returned to my arm and the swelling was reduced. The pain was . . . noticeable, but not as bad as before.

Then I forgot all about it as I became aware I was not alone. Standing but a few yards away was Elizabeth. Her face bore signs of much fatigue and strain, but happiness as well as she looked at me. She held a lantern and standing next to her was Father.

A hundred years might have gone by since I'd last seen him in the library giving those final instructions to me and Beldon. He'd been so solid and concerned. And there'd been pride as well, pride for me, and for what I was doing. The kind of pride that always caught at my heart and made me pause and thank God that he was my father.

*Sweet heavens, but he's an old man,* I thought with dull shock, looking at this now near-stranger who was staring back with such painful astonishment. His face was so lined, so gray, the lips slack and pale, his eyes so hollow. Even his body seemed to have shrunk, the straight spine bent, the shoulders slumped and their strength gone.

*I've done this to him.*

My sight blurred and swam. I didn't want to look at him. Didn't want to see him like this.

"Forgive me," I pleaded, hardly knowing my voice, hardly knowing why I said it.

He slowly walked over, knelt by me. I could just see that much through the tears.

His hands tentatively touched my shoulders. They were steady and strong, making a lie of what I'd seen. Then his arms went around me and he pulled me toward him as he'd done often enough to give solace when I'd been very small.

"Oh, my boy," he whispered, rocking me gently. "My poor, lost child."

I said nothing, did nothing. My heart and mind began to clear as the realization dawned that he was yet my father and he loved me still, no matter what had happened or what was to come. All my sorrows, all my hurts were not so great that somehow he could not fail to help me bear them.

In a hot flare of shame I abruptly cast off my self-pity and gratefully surrendered to the comfort and love he wanted so much to give.

# CHAPTER 14

Elizabeth allowed us some moments for this precious communion, then came over and put down her lantern. Father looked at her.

"I am sorry I doubted you," he said.

She touched one of his hands and smiled wryly. "It's all right."

"What's this?" I asked, straightening a little. Father gave me a last reassuring hug, then stood. From my seat in the dust I once again saw him as the child in me had always perceived him, saw him as he would always ever be to me: a tall, handsome man, all strength and energy and honor with wisdom enough to know that he was not wise.

Elizabeth said to me, "I did mention that there was no way in the world . . . well, that it would not be easy."

"She told me everything . . . and I did not believe her." Father regarded me with quiet amazement. "I'm not certain that I even now believe."

I had some difficulty in swallowing. "Told you . . . *everything*?"

"Yes."

I felt my face go red.

He smiled kindly upon my disconcertion. "Dear child, whoever this woman was, I'm ready to fall on my knees and thank her for what she shared with you. You've come back to us. I don't care how or by what means. You've come back, that's all that's important."

I started to speak, found my voice had gone all thick, and tried swallowing again. This time it worked out a bit better. "It's just that this is still incredible to me, Father. I've doubts of my own, so many that I can hardly bear them. Sometimes I seem all right and then it overwhelms me and I don't know what to do."

"I think you've been alone too much with yourself. It's time to come home."

"But I'm afraid."

He looked at me and seemed to see right into my heart. "I know you are, Jonathan," he said gently.

That helped. With my eyes closed I could almost feel his love and understanding beating upon me. I welcomed it like the soft warmth of a fire against the bitterness of a winter night.

"You've been through all the worst things already," he said. "Don't you think it's time to give up your fear?"

He was right and I was being foolish. I opened my eyes, nodded shyly, then he reached down and helped me to my feet. A very bad twinge like the touch of a hot poker shot up through the top of my skull with the movement.

"What's the matter?" he demanded, steadying me.

"It's better than it was," I gasped. "But there's still some work here for Beldon." I cradled my injured arm in its sling. God, but that had hurt. It had been all right until I'd tried to unbend it.

Elizabeth took up her lantern to see better. "What has happened to you?"

"Didn't Lieutenant Nash send anyone over to give you the news?"

"He did not. What news?"

"I caught him. I caught Roddy Finch."

In the looks exchanged I marked an astonishing degree of family resemblance between them.

"That's how I was hurt," I added, which did not really explain anything.

This, of course, inspired many, many more questions from both of them about my most recent activities. Our slow walk back to the house fully occupied me with the effort to provide answers. It helped to keep my mind off the pain.

"They'll hang him, you know," Father said thoughtfully when I'd finished.

"Yes. I'm sure they will."

He said nothing more after that.

While Father and I waited near the stables, Elizabeth went ahead with the lantern to make sure that the way was clear. By that, her task was to get any servants out of the hall leading from the side door to the library. The other members of the household, Beldon, his sister, Mother, had forsworn social activities for the time being and could be counted upon to be in their rooms at this hour of the evening.

Beldon, I knew, had been especially hard struck with grief over what had happened to me. I asked after him and was told he was as well as could be expected.

"He loves you, you know," Father told me as we waited.

I nodded. "Yes, I'm aware of it, and I'm sorry for him that he does since I cannot return it as he would wish."

"He understands that, I'm sure."

"He's quite a decent fellow, though."

"He is. It was very bad for him being a doctor and yet unable to help you."

"He did what he could," I said. "I remember that much."

Father went all still. "Did it . . . was it . . . ?"

I instantly guessed what he was getting at and constructed a hasty lie, the only one I'd ever told him, but one he needed to hear. "I felt no pain, sir. It was very quick. Be at ease on that."

He relaxed. "Thank God."

"What about poor Beldon?" I coaxed, hoping to shift his mind down a different path.

He shook himself. "Perhaps Elizabeth can tell you more. My memory fails me. It was the worst day of my life and I never want to see its like again. I fear even now that this may be a dream."

"Elizabeth said something like that last night, but I am still here."

"Yes," he whispered. "It is a miracle, it must be. God has been merciful to all of us."

I shrugged uneasily, feeling myself to be the one person least able to offer an opinion on the subject. Once again I thought of Lazarus. Had he suffered this sort of confusion of heart? I was not inclined to think so. Doubtless his faith was greater than mine; besides, there had been people around to explain exactly what had happened to him. His resurrection *had* been a miracle. Mine, I wasn't so sure about.

Elizabeth's figure appeared in the side door and motioned for us to come inside.

The hall was dark—to them, merely dim for me. We hurried to the library and Elizabeth swept the door shut behind us. Father guided me to the settee near the dormant fireplace and made me lie upon it.

"Some brandy?" he offered.

I found myself stammering. "No . . . that is . . . I mean . . . I can't."

He swiftly and correctly interpreted the reason behind my distress and shrugged it off. Elizabeth had, indeed, told him everything. "Light some more candles," he told her. "I'm going to get Beldon." Before leaving, he paused by the cabinet that held his liquor and poured a good quantity of brandy into a glass and placed it ready on a table.

"The doctor will need it," Elizabeth explained when he'd gone.

I laughed a little, but with small humor. By God, he certainly would. I felt the need of it myself, but the scent of it, faint as it was, turned my stomach. "When did he finally come home?" I asked, to distract myself from the smell.

"Late this afternoon. He was in an awful state. He'd been out since the . . . services looking for the . . ."

"The rebels," I said, hoping that would help her.

Her mouth twitched with self-mockery. "For the rebels, then. He'd been with a group of soldiers led by Nash's sergeant for most of the time. They went right into Suffolk County, turning out every farm and hayloft along the way. They never found anyone, of course."

"That's hardly surprising. Those uniforms make people very nervous. I should think any rebels ran the moment they clapped eyes on 'em."

"So they did. Beldon came to realize it and decided to strike out on his own."

I was dumbfounded. "But that's terribly dangerous."

"He seemed not to care. It didn't do him much good, anyway, and in the end he came to no harm. When he gave up and dragged home at last, he was all done in. He must have slept the day through. Jericho took a tray up to him earlier, but Beldon sent him away."

"Have you talked to Jericho about me?"

"No."

It was to be expected. She would have been occupied enough talking to Father. "After I sort things out with Beldon, I must see him next."

"It'll be all right, Jonathan." She'd heard the weariness creeping back into my voice.

I managed a smile for her. "How were you received when you arrived at Mrs. Montagu's?"

Her manner stiffened. "I understood why you had to go off, but I'm not sure I'm ready to forgive you for leaving me like that."

I started to protest or apologize, whichever was required most, but she waved it away.

"Never mind, little brother." She'd been lighting candles all the while, and placing them throughout the room, filling it with their soft golden light. Though the curtains were drawn, cutting off any outside illumination I might have taken advantage of, this was a token return to normal sight for me and I relished it. No wonder Nora had been so fond of candles.

"How did it go for you?"

"It was not easy. Father was frightfully annoyed and the soldiers alarmed him. Under those circumstances I couldn't just blurt out my news to him. Thank God for Mrs. Montagu. She sort of tucked me under one wing and took me away while Father tried to talk with the soldiers. They didn't make much headway as I think his German isn't much better than yours. By the time he'd finished, I had some tea in me, which was a great help."

"What did you say?"

She sighed, remembering the exasperation. "I really couldn't say anything. Not about you. I just wasn't ready for it. I was still trying to take it all in myself."

"Elizabeth, I'm sorry. I should not have asked this of you."

Another wave. "It would have been the same whether you'd been there or not. Anyway, I told him that I couldn't stand to stay in our house alone and decided to walk over to be with them. He was very angry for a time."

Considering the reputation of the Hessians and their commanders with unprotected womenfolk I could see why.

"Then he asked me why I'd really come."

Father wouldn't have taken her story as given. He knew she was too intelligent to leave the house unescorted unless she had an excellent reason to do so.

"I asked Mrs. Montagu to give us some time alone and did my best." Finished with the candles, she took the chair next to the desk. "He tried not to show it, but I'm sure he thought I'd gone quite mad."

"No, I was the mad one, to leave you to do all that by yourself."

"Mad and selfish and inconsiderate," she added agreeably. "Perhaps someday I shall laugh about it. I'm much too tired to make the effort right now. It's all done, though. What really helped was when we got home and I took him up to your room to show him the clothes you'd left there. That was a shock, but I could see he was beginning to allow himself to believe me. It was then that he had us sit down and bade me tell him everything all over again."

"How did he take it?"

"He was very quiet. Told me to get some sleep, then he went out. He rode over to the churchyard."

"Dear God, he didn't."

"He most assuredly did. He looked so strange when he came back."

"What? Don't tell me he went to dig up the grave."

That idea horrified her as much as it did me. "No, he did not."

"Then what did he want there?"

"More proof."

"Proof? But what could be there that—"

"Your shroud."

That took all the wind out of me.

"He said it was all wadded up where you'd left it."

I dropped my head and groaned.

"So you should, little brother. You've been a blister and a boil for doing this to him, you should have stayed with me and not put him through it."

She was right, right, right. "I'm sorry."

"On the other hand . . ."

I looked up. "What?"

"He did understand why you had to go off last night. But please God, don't you ever put him through this kind of situation again."

To be honest, I didn't see how I possibly could, considering the uniqueness of the circumstances, but I made no sport of her feelings and gave her my solemn word to behave myself in the future.

"After showing me that thing he wanted to go straight out to the old barn, but Mother was being difficult about something and Beldon wasn't here to give her any laudanum so he had to stay with her."

Poor Father.

"But the moment he was free he got me and we left. I wasn't sure what to expect when we walked in. You'd told me what Nora had been like, but you were so *still.* It was hard not to think that . . ."

"That I was really dead?"

"Yes, that you were really dead. That some cruel mind was at play to give you back to us for a few hours only to take you away again. It was a very bad time for both of us, standing there, waiting and watching you. Father said that you had no heartbeat, that you were not breathing."

"How did you stand it, then?"

"He noticed that you were warm. He picked up your hand and held it, then made me take it to be sure. After that, the waiting was a little easier, but I don't think he fully believed until you stirred and opened your eyes."

"And your belief, sister?"

"Tested," she said archly. "I'm like you, still trying to make sense of it, to take it all in. I hope I shall get over it soon as I am damned tired of feeling this way."

We looked somberly at one another, then the dark mood vanished. She was the one to break first and I followed, the two of us suddenly seized by a fit of laughter. It was soft and firmly restrained by smothering hands. Necessary, for had we really let ourselves go, we'd have raised the whole house. It passed quickly, though. Elizabeth was half dropping from exhaustion and the movement aggravated the pain in my arm.

She drowsed now and I wondered what was taking Father so long. Perhaps he was trying to somehow prepare Beldon. Perhaps Beldon had taken a dose of his own laudanum. I hoped not. If drink had interfered with Nora's influence over Warburton, one could logically conclude that a drug might have the same effect. If I could not use my own power of influence to ease Beldon over those first few moments of terror, things might become very much more difficult, indeed.

Some lengthy minutes passed. Elizabeth's eyes were shut, though I could hear by her breathing that she was not quite asleep. I was very alert and filled the time listening to the normal sounds of the household. They were distant but strangely clear: the clatter of a pot in the far-off kitchen, the footfall of a passing servant. I found a secret delight in being able to identify each noise, picking it out or discarding it as I chose. I'd adapted rather quickly to this heightened ability; part of me enjoyed it, part shrank away out of the fear for the uncanny we all share.

Then I heard them descending the stairs together and the murmur of Father's voice. Beldon was silent as Father invited him to go on to the library.

"Elizabeth."

She jerked fully awake.

"They're coming. Stand ready with that brandy."

She rose and moved to the table.

"You know what I'll have to do?"

"Yes. What you did to calm Lieutenant Nash." Her tone indicated she still disapproved. "I told Father about it."

Good, for then he shouldn't be too surprised by what was to come. I nodded my gratitude and we waited. The back of the settee was toward the door. Beldon would not see me right away, which was just as well. I wasn't sure what to expect of him and found myself feeling the same dread and disquiet I'd come to associate with this experience. The reward was great, but the actual passage to that reward arduous.

Father played the servant and held the door for him, firmly closing it as soon as they were inside.

"Your patient's over there, Doctor. Just talk to him and all will be explained," he was saying.

Beldon put down his case of medicines and came around. He breathed out a quiet greeting to Elizabeth, then turned to confront his patient. His mouth open, he halted in mid-turn to stare, blink, and shake his head once, then stare again.

"I don't . . . oh, my God. Oh, my . . ."

"Beldon," I began, "there's nothing to be afraid of; please listen to me."

But Beldon was incapable of hearing anything. His already protuberant eyes bulged out that much more and his skin went so pasty as to make a ghastly match in color to his ever-present wig. Lamenting within that I should be the cause of this, I reached out to him with my good hand, offering words of comfort, while trying to fix upon his mind.

A vain effort. Overcome with the shock, Beldon turned drama into farce by pitching flat onto his face in a dead faint.

Elizabeth said "Oh," Father vented a ripe curse, and as one they dived for the boneless form heaped on the floor. Father turned him over and saw to it that there were no obvious injuries from the fall. Elizabeth gave Father a look of moderate disappointment and straightened Beldon's limbs.

Father was rather sheepish. "I suppose I might have found some better way to ready him for this, but for the life of me I couldn't think of one."

Elizabeth found a cushion and they put it under Beldon's head. When he began to show signs of reviving, the brandy was brought into play.

"Not too much," I cautioned. I lurched from the settee and knelt next to him. It seemed important that I be the first one he saw upon awakening.

"Yes," said Father, missing my real motive, which was to keep the man sober. "Don't want to choke the fellow."

Beldon's eyes fluttered. He was calm now, disoriented by his swoon. This was a great help to me, though. I took whole and heartless advantage of his confusion and fixed my gaze and mind full upon him. Taken so unawares, Beldon had no further chance to give in to his fear. His expression went slack and dull. The results—if disturbing to Elizabeth and a wonderment to Father—were gratifying to me. But the moment was brief, for yet again I was about to take on the task of giving lengthy and complicated explanations for my return from the grave.

And in the pause between taking away Beldon's conscious will and the drawing of my next breath, I realized I simply could *not* do it again.

In that instant I knew that if I imparted the least portion of the truth to him and the others who followed there would be absolutely no going back to even an illusion of the life I'd known before. The changes within me were staggering enough; I needed some kind of constancy for the sake of my mind's balance.

And the solution came hard on the heels of this realization: so neat and simple that I could condemn myself for a fool for not having considered it before.

Father and Elizabeth had the truth, for it mattered much to me that they know it. Nash had the lie, for he did not matter at all. As for the others in between . . .

Beldon's eyes cleared and his brow wrinkled in honest puzzlement. "Dear me, whatever has happened?"

"We're not sure, Doctor," I said. "You complained of dizziness and the next thing we knew, you went over like a felled tree. Are you all right? Nothing hurt?"

He took confused assessment of himself and pronounced that he seemed to be fit. "I remember nothing of this. I was in my room last . . . I'd had the most awful dream about you, Mr. Barrett."

"What sort of dream?" I asked innocently.

"It was the most . . ." He shook his head. "Oh, never mind. I should not care to talk of it, lest it come true."

I did not press him for more details, since I knew them already. If it worked with Beldon—and it had—it would work with everyone else. One by one I'd speak to them all and convince them that my death and burial had been nothing more than an unpleasant dream. Or nightmare. Either choice, they would be loath to mention it, even if I hadn't given instructions not to. With some unavoidable changes of routine for me, it looked like I might resume the semblance of a normal life again.

Elizabeth had initially opined that my idea was ludicrous, but hadn't any better one to replace it. She now gave me a grudging nod to acknowledge this evidence of my success and asked Beldon if he might not be more comfortable on the settee. He thought he would and she and Father helped him to move.

"I'm terribly sorry for this imposition, please excuse my weakness. I'm not normally given to fits of any kind," he told them.

"Of course you aren't," said Father, going along with the ruse as if he'd been born an actor. "But it has been exceedingly hot today. The sun's probably caught up with you."

Beldon offered no objection to that conclusion and accepted what remained of the brandy. He made short work of it and then took note of the rest of us, myself in particular.

"Why, Mr. Barrett, something *has* happened to you!"

I sighed and eased into the chair by the desk. "Yes, sir. Father brought you down to have a look at this. When you have sufficiently recovered, I should be most grateful if you would . . ."

"Great heavens, of course. I shall need my—oh, thank you, Miss Barrett." He accepted his case from Elizabeth and took charge of the situation. Except for my injury, as far as he was concerned absolutely nothing untoward had happened in this house. I felt a great surge of joy wash over me. To be looked upon as myself again and not as some ghostly horror come back to trouble the living, to simply be me, as if the last few days had never been . . . more and more my burden was becoming lighter. Over Beldon's shoulder, Father caught my eye and smiled, his expression of pleased relief like a mirror of my own feelings.

I was obliged to remove my coat, an exercise which I found most painful. Elizabeth offered to cut open a seam to facilitate things, but we managed to avoid that action. Beldon rolled up my shirtsleeve and clucked over the damage.

"How did this happen?"

"I already told you, Doctor. Don't you—oh, forgive me. It was just before your . . . ah . . . fall and you must have forgotten. I was helping Nash and got into a fight with one of those damned rebels. The fellow tried to crack my skull with his gun barrel and I found it necessary to thwart the attack with my arm."

"Definitely broken just here below the elbow," he stated. "It must have been a fearsome blow."

"It was," I wheezed. He was being very gentle, but to no avail. "Both of them."

"Yes, it would take more than one to account for this sort of damage. And you received them last night?"

I confirmed that fact with a short grunt.

"But why did you not call for me sooner?" He was accusatory.

"There were delays that could not be helped," I answered through gritted teeth in a tone that did not invite further comment.

He made none, distracted as he was by his examination. "*Very* odd."

"What is?" asked Father, leaning forward.

"The evidence I see is that this injury's several weeks old."

The blood had done it, I knew. Just as a man's body tells him to take in liquid to ease the pain of thirst, mine had compelled me to take in additional blood to quicken the process of repair. Father's face was eaten up with curiosity, but I quietly signaled to him that he should remain silent for the moment.

"The healing is remarkably progressed," Beldon marveled.

"Doesn't feel like it," I muttered.

"That's because the bone was not properly set. See, there's no swelling or bruising, but you can feel here—"

"Softly, Doctor, softly," I cautioned.

"I do beg your pardon, but if you run your finger along here you can feel under the skin where the bone has joined crookedly at the break. Combined with all the other fracturing, well, that explains why you're in such discomfort."

" 'Discomfort' is hardly the word that comes to mind," I snarled. "What can you do about it?"

"It will have to be rebroken, of course, then correctly set," he said matter-of-factly.

After all I'd been through, one would think that I could face anything, but the idea of breaking my arm once more in the endeavor to fix it again turned my guts to water. In the heat of battle an injury was one thing, but in the cool reason of the consulting room it's quite another.

"Might I have a little more time to recover and think this over?" I asked in a none-too-steady voice.

"Certainly, but I'd advise not delaying for very long or the healing will have gone too far, making the process of breaking more difficult to accomplish."

"It's all right, Jonathan," put in Elizabeth in response to the groan I could not suppress. "Perhaps it can be done during the day while you're unaware of things."

My qualms against this upcoming treatment swiftly vanished. "Heavens, sister, but that's a brilliant idea."

Beldon looked questioningly at her. We both suddenly realized her faux pas. She generously gestured for me to step in and mend it.

"I am an uncommonly sound sleeper, Doctor," I blandly explained. "I seriously doubt that anything, even having my arm broken again, could rouse me once I set head to pillow."

He made a noncommittal sound and looked highly dubious. Ah, well, if I had to influence him again, then it would just have to be done. Thinking it through, I could see its looming necessity, otherwise Beldon could not help but become alarmed while treating me during my daytime oblivion.

"In the meanwhile, is there some way in which you can make it more comfortable?"

The soldier's rough-and-ready field dressing was soon replaced by a proper splint and bandage. Beldon's work was practiced and thorough and Elizabeth helped by fashioning a better sling under his directions. I thanked them both and politely refused his offer of a solution of laudanum for the pain. Had I the remotest chance of keeping the stuff down, though, I would have taken it without hesitation.

Beldon announced that he was in need of some solid refreshment and begged leave to be excused so he could see to the inner man. We graciously gave it along with our united thanks for his help and he left.

Father gave a great sigh and dropped upon the settee in his turn. "That I have lived to see such wonders. You did it, laddie."

"The wonder is that I got through it, sir," I puffed.

"It's enough to persuade one into believing in the power of witchcraft," Elizabeth put in.

"Oh, now, that's hardly fair. You know I only did it because I felt I had to."

"Yes, but that doesn't make it any easier to watch." She hunched her shoulders as though to shiver. "And you're planning to give that same story about everything having been a bad dream to all the others?"

"It would seem to be the best compromise for my situation."

"Even your mother?" Father asked, leveling his gaze hard upon me.

I could not endure that look for long and let my own eyes drop. "I should like permission to do so, sir, as I seriously question whether she would be comfortable with the truth."

He snorted. "By God, laddie, I can respect that answer."

"You mean I—"

He held up one finger and echoed my earlier caution to Beldon. "Softly, now. We're all aware of what your mother is like; the danger I see is that you might use this—whatever it is—in such a way as to . . . well, sweeten her temper."

Genuine surprise flooded me. "Oh, sir, but it never occurred to me—"

"I'm very glad to hear it."

My face was burning. "Father, surely you don't think that I would do such an unworthy thing?"

"No, child. My purpose was to merely point out the temptations that lie ahead for you. This strange enforcing of your will and thoughts upon others can be a gift or a curse depending on how it's employed. I strongly suggest that in the future you rely upon it as little as possible."

I said nothing for some time, for his words gave me much to think about. I honestly hadn't considered this side of things. For all the use Nora made of it, she'd only done the bare minimum to ensure her own security. When it came to our relationship, she'd discarded it altogether, risking all in the hope that my love for her would overcome my fears. Sadly, though, at the end, she'd tried to make me forget that love.

Perhaps she'd thought it was for my own good.

My eyes stung at the thought. To do something for another's own good must surely be the greatest of all betrayals. It was Mother's favorite maxim and the one I hated the most, and yet I could not bring myself to hate Nora. In my heart, I felt she'd been sincere, and done it out of love for me rather than as a convenience or assertion of power for herself.

"Jonathan?"

I gave a start. "Yes, Father, of course you're right. To do otherwise would be most ungentlemanly and dishonorable."

"Good lad."

"But for what I'm to do tonight . . . ?"

"It is necessary. By this means, yes, make them all think it was but a dream. Beldon took hold of the idea fast enough."

"What about others like Mrs. Montagu and Mr. Rapelji?" asked Elizabeth.

"The same," he said heavily.

She turned on me. "Will you be able to convince the whole Island?"

"Elizabeth, think how hard it was for us both when you first saw me. Now multiply it by every person who knows what's happened. Would you put me through that with them all? Can you trust them to react as well as you have? I can't. I want to come home and this is the only way I can do it and not be marked out as some sort of grotesque thing fit only to be stared at or avoided. It spares them and it spares me."

She paced up the room and back while a number of ideas and emotions played over her face and made her stride uneven. "Yes," she murmured. "It's just that there are so many. I don't see how you can do it."

"I'll manage somehow," I said. "I must."

"Jericho, too?"

"Ah, well, perhaps not Jericho. It's impossible for a man to hide anything from his valet and in his case it would be pointless to try. I shall give him the truth, but there it must stop or the whole island will be privy to my personal concerns."

"Quite right," Father said. "Are you up to starting now? If you wait much longer they'll all be asleep."

As with many projects, the beginning was the most difficult part of the procedure, though there were some rough spots. Elizabeth, with her talent for organization, soon saw that speaking to each servant one after another would take us half the night. Eventually we worked out a faster way to deal with the problem. As each came into the room, I would influence them into a quiet state and ask them to wait. Once together, I could give up to half a dozen of them at a time the same story rather than tell the same story half a dozen times. From Mrs. Nooth to the humblest stable lad, I spoke to the lot of them, and released each back to their duties as they had come with lighter hearts and no worse for wear.

Mother and Mrs. Hardinbrook were the last ones I saw. Perhaps they should have been the most harrowing, but my poor brain was spinning by then from all my efforts; I was beyond further emotional upsets or excitements. Mother had fortunately slept off the effects of her latest dose of laudanum, making my expenditure of effort on her a success. I confess, though, that in watching her face going blank, I did experience an undeniable thrill. I was very glad to have had Father's advice already in mind, else the temptation to abuse this gift might certainly have proved to be too attractive in my future dealings with her.

Mrs. Hardinbrook was somewhat of a problem, in that she'd indulged herself in the matter of drink not so very long ago. She'd taken just enough to cause me worry, but not so much that I was unable to make an impression upon her. She was quiet when Elizabeth led her away, but I confided my doubts to Father.

" 'Tis to be relied upon that she won't be leaving us anytime soon," he said. "I expect that after she's fully sobered you may try again with more certainty on the outcome. How are you feeling?"

"Tired. Much more of this and my head shall split from the work."

But there was only one more left to see and that was Jericho. As with the others, I had to put him in a state where he could readily listen, but unlike the others, I gave him the truth. Still, before releasing him, I instructed—rather than requested—that he believe my story and accept it and myself without fear.

For this liberty upon his will, my only excuse was that I was too weary to do otherwise. Whether the soreness of my head was due to the excessive mental labor or the constant strain of imposing a raw falsehood upon so many didn't matter. What did was my reluctance to face another hour as harrowing as that first one I'd spent with Elizabeth upon my return. No more shocks like that for myself or anyone else, I resolved, and if Elizabeth or Father thought I was being selfish in my decision, neither made mention of it.

Coming back to himself, Jericho welcomed me with the same warmth and joy as if I'd only been away on a lengthy journey and nothing more. This return to normal was what I wanted, what I needed most. I accepted his welcome and submitted meekly to his disapproval at the state of my clothes. He begged permission to see to their improvement. Father and Elizabeth both made haste to agree that I very much needed some restoration and with their good nights floating behind us Jericho all but dragged me up to my room.

"But everything's been moved, Mr. Jonathan," he noted unhappily when he opened the wardrobe.

My shirts and coats and all other manner of clothing had been restored, perhaps not in the right order, but they were more or less back in place again. I came over to touch them and be reassured. With the return of my things it was as if my own self was made more substantial by their presence.

"Thank God. Elizabeth must have retrieved everything for me, bless her."

"Retrieved . . . ?"

"You know."

"Oh," he said, drawing it out with sober understanding. He instantly ceased to be outraged that someone had intruded upon his territory and plunged into straightening some of the more radically misplaced items to their proper areas.

"Is my journal in there?" I asked.

"I do not see it, sir."

"Damn. I wonder who's got it?"

"I shall endeavor to locate it for you as soon as may be."

"Thank you, though I can't write much in it with my arm all trussed up."

"It pains you?"

"A great deal, but I've been through worse."

He chose not to comment and concentrated on getting me in the same kind of order that he imposed upon the contents of the wardrobe. It was only when he was scraping away at my stubbled chin that he finally gave in to a reaction to the impossibility of my presence. He caught his breath and turned away suddenly.

"What is it? Jericho?"

His self-possession deserted him for a few moments and it was a struggle for him to wrest it back. The expression on his face kept shifting alarmingly back and forth between calmness and calamity.

"I'm sorry. It's just that the last time I shaved you was after they brought you . . . it was . . ."

*My poor friend.* "I know. It's all right. This is going to be strange for all of us for a time until we're used to things."

He nodded once or twice, rather forcefully. "I expect so, sir."

"But there's nothing to be afraid of; I'm still myself."

His nod was less abrupt and I looked elsewhere while he swiped impatiently at his eyes. When his hand was steady once more, he resumed and completed the job of shaving me.

As it was much too late and too much work to prepare a bath, we made do with a wet towel to refresh my grubby skin. A change of linen completed my toilet. Relaxing back on the bed with my dressing gown half on (out of deference to my arm), I felt more like my old self and better able to consider some of the grim practicalities of my changed condition.

"Something will have to be done about that window," I said. "I suggest that you close and lock the shutters and then find something to stop up the chinks."

"It will be like a sickroom, sir, with no air or light."

"In truth, that's the whole point. I don't seem to need air and I've found the latter to be highly inimical to my continued well-being. Please trust me on this, Jericho. I don't want a single ray of light coming in here tomorrow. And it will probably be best that my door remain locked. I shouldn't care for one of the maids to walk in while I'm . . . resting."

"Will it always be so for you?"

"I don't know. Perhaps later I can ask Dr. Beldon to suggest a way to help me improve the situation, but this is how it will be for now."

"And you say you are completely unconscious while the sun is up?"

"Yes, unfortunately. I can already see that it's going to be a deuced nuisance."

"More than a nuisance, sir."

"What do you mean?"

"Have you considered what could happen to you should the house—God forbid—catch fire?"

The horror of his idea went all over me in an instant and I sat with my mouth hanging wide as my imagination supplied such details as would have better been left unimagined. Out of necessity, we were all very careful in regard to fire and candles, but accidents happened and if one should occur during the day while I lay helpless . . .

"By God, I'll have to go back to that damned barn to get any rest!"

"I think you should remain here, Mr. Jonathan, where you can be watched and otherwise protected. It really is much more secure."

"But not as fireproof. I suppose I could sleep in the root cellar, though that might annoy Mrs. Nooth and alarm the rest of the kitchen."

"Actually, I was going to recommend some additional changes be made to the buttery," he said.

"The buttery?"

"There was some discussion before your . . . accident about enlarging it to accommodate hidden stores against the commissary men. It won't be too much extra work to make it larger than planned and fit it with such comforts as you might require."

"And live like a rabbit in a hole in the ground?"

"Rabbits have no fear of being burned alive while in their holes," he pointed out.

I laughed once and shook my head. "Yes, I suppose so. I'll talk to Elizabeth about it. Think she's still up?"

"Miss Elizabeth retired some time ago. Mr. Barrett as well."

Yes. They'd both been worn out and it was well past their normal bedtime, but I still felt a stab of loneliness for all that. It was as I'd anticipated and I would just have to get used to spending the greater bulk of the night on my own. Oh, but there were many, many worse things in the world and I felt to have been through a goodly number of them already.

"Very well. Hand me that volume of Gibbon from the shelf, would you?"

Jericho selected the correct book and placed a candle on my bedside table. With the shutters closed, I found I needed it. I cannot say that the conflicts of the late Roman empire held my whole attention while he worked to seal up the room from the sun's intrusion, but it helped. When Jericho had finished and I bade him to go off for some well-earned sleep, my study was even less successful. In the end, I left off with Gibbon in mid-word to search out and open my Bible.

I was seized with an uncommonly strong urge to read the eleventh chapter of John again.

# CHAPTER 15

Eyes wide, I frantically clawed up from my internal prison, drew in a shuddering breath, and rolled out of bed to slam against the floor. The impact jarred my maimed arm, sending me instantly awake and aware of its every insulted nerve.

"Mr. Jonathan?" Jericho's voice, alarmed.

I shook my head and would have waved him away if I hadn't been busy biting back the pain. He must have read something of it in my posture, and held off, only stepping forward when I was ready. It took some minutes before I extended my good arm and allowed him to help me to my feet.

"More bad dreams?" he asked.

I nodded and sought out the chair by my study table. I had no wish to return to that bed. Good elbow on the table and forehead resting on my hand, I breathed deeply of the stale air of my room and tried to collect myself. Jericho pulled down the quilts he'd draped over the window and opened the shutters. It was just past sunset, but my room faced east, so the natural glow flooding in was bearable to my sensitive eyes.

"Will you speak to Dr. Beldon?" he asked. His tone was not quite reproachful yet leaning in that direction. He'd made the suggestion yesterday evening and I'd summarily dismissed it.

Time to give in. "Yes, I'll see him, though God knows what good he'll be able to do me for this."

"Perhaps he can determine whether it is, at root, a physical or a spiritual problem."

*Or both,* I thought unhappily. In the three days since my return, I had gotten no rest to speak of while the sun was up. Cleaned and groomed and tucked away in the comfort of my own bed, my family life resumed with hardly a ripple, one would think that my troubles were abated, but not so. The utter oblivion that I'd known before, that had caused the day to flash by without notice, was gone. Now I was aware of every excruciating second of the passing time.

When the light came and my body froze inert where it lay, so came the dreams, sinuous things that wound through my mind like poisonous snakes. Striking at my most tender thoughts and feelings, I was helpless to escape from them by waking and yet could not fully sleep. All that was my life was drawn forth and twisted if pleasant, lived and relived without mercy if not. After three days of it I'd lost count of the times Tony Warburton had tried to kill me or the times I'd found myself back in that damned coffin screaming away my sanity.

After the first day of this private hell, I'd asked Jericho to stay and watch for signs of inner disturbances and to wake me should he see them. He saw nothing more than my still and unresponsive outer shell. The next time his instructions were to try waking me throughout the day, in hopes that that might help. Though I was aware of his presence and his efforts, it was ultimately useless. The dreams, worthy of the darkest fantasies of an opium eater, continued.

More weary now than when I'd retired that morning, I had to force myself to dress. Jericho managed to get me properly turned out except my coat. For that, I could only slip on the left sleeve and drape the rest over my shoulder. Previous attempts to straighten my arm had proved to be too agonizing to complete and the constant inconvenience was such that I would have to see Beldon, anyway. Loath as I was to have him rebreak it to put things right, it was rapidly coming to that point.

Leaving Jericho to continue his duties, I walked downstairs to the drawing room. Elizabeth was practicing something new on her spinet and having trouble with a particular phrase, but the sounds were a fresh delight to my ear. She stopped when I walked in, smiled, then went on.

Mother, Mrs. Hardinbrook, Beldon, and—I was surprised to see—Father were playing at cards. He usually had no patience for them, preferring his books, so I could guess that Mother had nagged him into joining their game. They also looked up and nodded at me.

Everything was so unutterably, wonderfully normal. I wanted to embrace them all for just being there. Until faced with its loss, I'd never truly valued all that I'd had.

"So you're finally up," said Mother.

"Yes, madam." Even she could not dampen my goodwill.

"You've missed the entire day, you know. How can you help your father with his work if you play the sluggard?"

If she had a talent for anything it was for asking impossible questions. It was also interesting to me that though possessed of an active contempt for Father's law practice she found it useful enough now to point out my apparent laziness.

I bowed toward Father. "My apologies, sir."

He restrained a smile. "Never mind. Just get that arm well, then I'll find work for you."

"You're too soft on the boy, Samuel," she sniffed.

"Perhaps, but he's the only one we have," he smoothly returned.

Beldon and his sister maintained a diplomatic silence during this exchange. Elizabeth paused again in her play to glance at me. My mouth twitched and I jerked my chin down once to let her know that everything was all right. It was becoming easier to find amusement, rather than resentment, in Mother's foibles. The three of us had passed through the fire and with that shared experience, we'd discovered that the irritations Mother had to offer were very minor, indeed.

I drifted over to the spinet to watch Elizabeth. "How you can read that is beyond me," I said, indicating her music.

"It's just like learning another language. One day it suddenly all makes sense."

"But to translate it with your eyes to your hands and thus to the ear . . ."

"Jonathan!" Mother's voice cut between us like an axe blade. Elizabeth missed her notes and stopped playing altogether. Mother glared at us with disturbing malevolence, recalling that awful night more than three years past and her obscene accusation. "Haven't you anything better to do with yourself than disrupting your sister's practice?"

Her lips quivering, Elizabeth was about to say something we might all regret. I quickly stepped in first. "Quite right, madam. I am being most inconsiderate. Please excuse me."

She said nothing, but some of the tension in her body eased back just a little. This was the only sign that I'd received her pardon. Her eyes flicked back to her cards. "Find something to do, then. Your wandering about the place is most annoying."

"Yes, madam. I only came down to ask when Dr. Beldon might have a free moment."

"Then you should have said so in the first place. The doctor is, as you can see, occupied."

Beldon raised his head. "Your arm?" he asked.

"Partly. But as you are busy, it can wait. I'll be in the library."

Beldon read enough from my manner to know that this medical call was not urgent, so he had no need to risk Mother's ire by immediately answering it. He resumed his play and I left the room.

My feet took me to the hall, past the library, and out the side door, leaving the flagged path to wander in the yard. It was better out here, the air more free, the scents it carried of earth and grass and flowers more pure. I wanted to roll in it like an animal. I settled for sitting beneath a tree and stretching out my legs. Here was peace and a kind of rest. I was so very, very tired. In days past, I napped here in the summer heat. No more. While the sun was down, sleep perversely eluded me, even when I tried to find it.

But I closed my eyes in another hopeful attempt. My other senses leaped in to take up the slack. I heard the rustle of every leaf and night creature, the sweet tones of the spinet, felt the cool ground and each tuft of grass under me, smelled the hundred messages on the wind, tasted the first dry swallow of thirst.

That would be tended to later, though, while everyone slept.

Mrs. Nooth's first instinct had been to provide food for me and thus she required further influencing on the subject. Now she and all the rest of the household simply ignored the fact that I did not eat with the family anymore, indeed, that I seemed not to eat, period. No one questioned it, no one remarked upon it. It was quite the best for all concerned.

Elizabeth's playing was interrupted again and I saw movement against the curtains of the drawing room. The card game may have ended. I heaved up and stalked back to the house, feeling considerably better for the respite outside. As much as I desired the company of my family, perhaps getting away from them now and then was what was needed.

Beldon was waiting in the library and I apologized for not being here as promised. He bowed slightly to dismiss the issue and I inquired if he would like some sherry, which he declined.

"I am still astonished at how quickly it healed after the injury," he remarked, nodding at my arm. "How is it for you?"

"The same. I still cannot straighten it."

"I fear we shall soon have to—"

"Yes, I know that, but I wanted to consult you about something else."

"Indeed?"

We seated ourselves and I explained my problem to him.

"You're getting no rest at all?" he asked.

"None. I seem to fall into a kind of waking doze, a halfway state, and can neither rouse from it or sink into true sleep. During this, I'm subject to endless dreaming, so even if my body rests, my mind does not, and that's what leaves me so fatigued all the time."

"And yet but a few days ago you assured me that you were a very sound sleeper."

"So I was—a few days ago."

"Has there been any change in your usual habits?"

*More than I could begin to number,* I thought.

"Any change in your room, bedding, or night clothes?"

"No, nothing like that."

"Does the pain from your arm keep you awake?"

"It only hurts when I try to move it and I take care not to do so."

"I can prescribe something to make you sleep," he said reluctantly.

Laudanum, or some other preparation, no doubt. I shook my head. "I should prefer some other treatment, Doctor."

He sat back and crossed his arms, studying me from top to toe. "There are always many reasons why a man cannot sleep. Has anything been troubling you lately? Any problem, no matter how minor, can prick at the mind like a thorn just at the moment when one most wants to forget it."

"Perhaps it's this business with Roddy Finch," I offered lightly, after a moment's consideration. "There's been some protest, but there's no doubt they'll soon be hanging him."

"And you were the one who turned him in. Yes, a burden like that can't be easy for a young mind like yours to bear. It's well out of your hands, though. Like it or not, justice will be served," he said grimly.

Justice or the law? I well knew there was often a wide difference between the two.

"The best thing for you is to try and forget about it."

My belly gave a sharp twist at these words. The knowledge flamed up in my mind that the one thing I could *not* do was to forget.

Knowing what his fate would be, I'd turned Roddy over to the soldiers without a qualm. Now the doubts were creeping in. I'd had dreams about him, about what his hanging would be like. I kept seeing his father rushing forward to drag on his son's heels to hurry the work of strangulation. After what my own family had experienced, would it do any good to put Roddy's through the same anguish and grief? How could that serve justice?

But it was the law that murderers and thieves and now spies should be executed, and Roddy was guilty of all three crimes as far as the courts-martial were concerned. It was out of my hands, but not my heart. Beldon thought I should forget it, but Father had always taught us to face our problems, not run from them.

"When you come to a fence either jump it or go through the gate, but don't let it hold you in," he'd said.

"Thank you, Doctor," I heard myself saying. "You've given me some ideas that want turning over." I excused myself and left before he could raise further questions. On the way up the stairs, I hailed Jericho and kept going.

"What is it, sir?" he asked, rushing into my room.

"Get my riding boots out. I want some exercise."

"At this hour, sir? The soldiers have been most discouraging to travelers out after curfew."

"To the devil with them."

He correctly read my mood, fell in with it, and found my boots. Before a quarter hour had passed, Belle was saddled and one of the stable lads gave me a leg up onto her back. I took the reins with my good hand and swung her around toward the front lane leading to the main road. Not sure how good her eyes were at night, I didn't ask for an impossible pace, especially along areas steeped in shadows, but once on the road, the way was fairly clear and I kicked her into a decent canter for as long as my abused arm could stand the motion.

Not very long.

She never really worked up a sweat, though if she had, the remaining walk would have cooled her down. Despite the curfew, we met no one along the way, not a single soldier until we reached Glenbriar and The Oak came into view. There I was challenged quickly enough, but after giving my name and a formal request for an audience with Lieutenant Nash, I was immediately escorted in to see him. Apparently the guards on duty hadn't heard any strange rumors about my blood drinking from their fellows.

"This makes a fine change from having to shout at you from the street," I said after greetings had been exchanged.

"Aye," said Nash. "You're still the hero with the men for all that you've done. That's a night I shall not soon forget myself. Your sister is in good health, I hope?"

"Very well, thank you."

"And I trust your arm is healing?"

"Middling fine, sir."

Nash took note of all the curious eyes trained on us and invited me to a more private room. It was the same one as we'd used before, but his manner indicated that it held no inconvenient memories. He inquired after the purpose of my visit.

"I wish to see the prisoner, Roddy Finch."

"May I ask why?"

There was more than sufficient candlelight to work with. "You may not," I said evenly, fixing my eye hard upon him.

He blinked only once and with no alteration of his expression, stood. "Very well, then, Mr. Barrett. I should be pleased to take you to him. You'll want that candle, as it's very dark."

"He's in the cellar?"

"There was no other place to put him. This village is too small to have a proper lockup."

Until the soldiers came we'd had no need of one, but I held my peace and picked up the candle. Nash led the way through the common room, where we were both—and I imagined myself in particular—subject to more staring. I caught a glimpse of the landlord, but he ducked from sight when I turned for a better look. Elizabeth's fear that I'd have to have a "talk" with the whole island had some substance to it. Well, Mr. Farr and the rest would just have to wait.

We reached a back passage near the kitchen, where a man with a sword and musket came to attention when he saw Nash. He moved from off the trapdoor where he'd been standing and slid back a bolt that looked to have been recently attached. Lifting the door, he took a ladder from the wall and lowered it into the darkness, then went down ahead of us. Nash took charge of the candle and I followed the guard as best I could, hindered as I was with my arm in its sling.

The place had a nauseating smell of food stores, damp, human sweat, and unemptied chamber pots. The roof was low; Nash and his man were all right, but I had to stoop quite a bit to keep from bumping my head.

"Over there," said Nash, pointing to a far corner.

I took the candle back and peered, needing every ray of its feeble light in this awful place. I could just make out two hunched shapes huddled close by a supporting pillar of wood. Drawing closer, they took on form and identity and became Roddy Finch and Ezra Andrews. Both stirred sluggishly and winced against the tiny flame. There were chains on their wrists, the links solidly fixed to the pillar with huge staples. Neither of them had much freedom of movement and they reeked from their confinement.

Turning toward Nash, I thanked him and made it very clear that he and the guard need not remain. As before, he gave no outer sign, but instantly obeyed my request. The two of them went up the ladder. The trap was left open, but I didn't mind.

"What do ye want?" Andrews demanded when I returned to them.

An excellent question and not one that could be answered while he was listening in. I knelt close so he could see me. "I want you to sit back and go to sleep."

I knew I'd reached him, but it was still a little startling to witness how quickly he complied. He gaped at me empty-eyed for a few seconds, then did just as I said, just like that. Oh, but I could see that Father was very wise in advising me to be sparing with this ability.

Roddy was also gaping, albeit for a different reason. "What—?"

"Never mind him, I came to talk to you."

He raised himself up, his chains clinking softly. There were raw patches on his wrists and his face was dirty and drawn. His own eyes were nearly as empty as Andrews's, but, again, from a different cause. Beneath the sweat and grime and the heavy miasma of night soil, I could smell the clear sour stench of his fear.

"Talk about what?" he asked. There was a lost and listless tone to his voice.

"About what happened to me."

He shook his head, not understanding. "I didn't do it, 'twere Nathan. An' I'm that sorry about it, though." He nodded at my arm.

"Not this, about what happened at the kettle when the soldiers were after you for the horses."

"They was our hosses. It weren't right as they should take 'em the way they did. I was only tryin' to get 'em back for Da."

"Yes, and you . . . killed a man doing it."

"What? I didn't kill nobody."

His protest was so genuine that it put me back a step, until I realized that under these circumstances he would certainly deny any accusation against him, especially one of murder.

"But you did, Roddy. I know. All I want to know now is why."

"You're daft," he stated, looking mulish enough to pass for his younger brother.

We could go around all night on this, but I saw no advantage to it, only wasted time. "Look at me, Roddy, and listen to me. . . . Do you remember the day you took back the horses from the soldiers?"

"Yes," he said in a voice as flat and lifeless as his expression.

"You were standing above the kettle and you looked across and you must have seen me."

"No."

"You saw me and raised your gun and shot me."

"No."

"You did, I saw you do it, Roddy."

"No."

*Damnation.* How could he *not* speak the truth while in this state? He was so far separated from his own will he couldn't possibly do otherwise. I was frustrated to the point of trying to shake it out of him, until a simple little thought dropped into my mind like a flash of summer lightning on the horizon. Since waking up in that damned box, I'd had a thousand distractions keeping me busy, keeping me exhausted, keeping me from seeing that which should have been obvious. In all the time since his capture I'd never once questioned why Roddy, of all people, had expressed no surprise at my miraculous return from the dead. I'd looked across the kettle and recognized him and his eye was sharp enough for him to know me in turn.

Or rather, I *thought* I'd recognized Roddy.

Nathan Finch. I hadn't seen him in three years. He'd have grown up in that time and at a distance . . . I'd taken him for his brother.

"Nathan shot that man, didn't he, Roddy?" I asked tiredly.

"Told 'im he shouldn'ta done it," he replied.

I lowered my head and groaned and wished myself someplace that didn't have soldiers or prisons or scaffolds.

"*Why?* Why did he do it?"

"They were comin' for us and Nathan said as that fellow in the coat must be their general, shootin' 'im would solve our problems. They'd leave off chasin' us and see to 'im, instead, and they did."

"Coat?"

"A fine red coat with braid, 'e said, which meant 'e were like to be General Howe. So Nathan got 'im."

Just as I'd mistaken him for another, Nathan had returned the favor. I found I could not speak for a very long time. It was absurd and awful and idiotic and unutterably sad.

It was the truth.

The whole night might have slipped past with me staring into nothing and trying not to think and failing if not for Roddy. He eventually woke up to regard me with both wariness and curiosity. He also seemed to have some vague memory of the questions I'd put to him.

"You goin' to turn Nathan in as well?" he asked.

"He killed that man, didn't he?" I returned. I still had enough wit to try maintaining the fiction of another's death.

"Well, it's war, ain't it? People get killed in wars."

There was no point in gainsaying him on that. "And what if it had been you? Would you care to have someone shoot you down just because there's a war?"

He shook his head, not for an answer, but in puzzlement. He'd never really considered himself as being a target before.

"Did Nathan kill that Hessian boy as well?"

Roddy's eyes dropped in reply.

"Then I suppose they'll hang you for that, too."

"But Ezra here said that—"

"They know you're no soldier. He can take any oath he likes on your behalf, but they won't believe him. They'll hang you for a horse thief or a murdering spy no matter what."

"But I'm no spy, an' how can I be a hoss thief when it was our own hosses we were takin' back?"

And how could I leave him to be hanged?

That was the only question spinning through my mind now and the unavoidable answer was that I couldn't.

"There's been enough death . . ."

"Eh?"

"Roddy, if I get you out of here, can you find a way off the island?"

"What d'you mean?"

"If you escape you'll have to get as far from here as you can. That means not going home or even to Suffolk County, as those will be the first places they'll look."

"I don't see as how it can be done, but Ezra here said as he knew where we could lay hands on a boat."

"Where is it?"

"Five miles, maybe less from here."

"Think you can make it there before light?"

"Easy. But how can—"

"Never mind how. I'll be back in a few minutes. Wake up your friend and tell him to keep his mouth shut when I come."

I left the candle with them and, bending low, made my way back to the ladder. Nash had gone but the guard was still at his station as I emerged.

"*All is well?*" he asked.

"*Ja.* Are you sleepy?" I added in English. I couldn't recall the right words in German.

"*Was?*"

"Sleepy?" I pantomimed a yawn, lay my head to one side with my eyes shut for a moment, then pointed questioningly at him.

He grinned and shook his head.

The idiot.

"*What is the German for . . . ?*" I repeated my pantomime.

Puzzled that I should want a language lesson, but flattered by my interest, he promptly supplied me with the weapon I sought.

"*Schlafen.*"

"Yes, *schlafen, mein Freund. Schlafen. Schlafen . . .*"

I caught him as he dropped forward, not an easy task with only one arm. A dead weight and unwieldy, I just managed to lay him out without making too much noise. His musket and sword caused a little clatter, but there were stout doors between us and the rest of the inn. I had to hurry, for Nash might return or someone else could blunder in and disturb me while I was clawing through the man's pockets. Snuffbox, a few coins—where did the fool keep it?

*There.* A ring heavy with keys. I grabbed it and dived down the ladder. Andrews was awake and looking belligerent.

"What d'ye plan for us? That we should be shot while escaping? Is that what yer up to?"

"Don't be such a fool, Mr. Andrews—"

"That's Lieutenant to you, ye lyin' Tory."

"Lieutenant, then." I sorted through the keys, trying to find the right one to fit the locks on their chains. "Think what you like, but keep your mouth shut. If you get caught again, then we're all for the gallows and I've no wish to die for the likes of you."

"He's tryin' to help us, Ezra," put in Roddy. As if to confirm his statement the next key worked and his hand was free. I gave him the ring and told him to finish the job while I kept watch.

The guard was as I'd left him, safe for us, but highly noticeable should anyone come in. My stomach turned over and over. If we were caught now—it still wasn't too late to put things back—it was too much to expect Roddy and Andrews to get away . . . there were too many soldiers about.

Turn and turn again.

Roddy's head appeared above the opening. He looked feverish with his sweat-smeared face and frightened and overly bright eyes. He goggled at the sleeping soldier, but sensibly nodded when I put a finger to my lips. He stepped out and made room for Andrews.

"Keys?" I whispered.

"I left 'em down there," he said unhappily.

Oh, well, I'd have to go back for the candle, anyway. "Through there," I said, pointing to a passage behind them. "It should take you outside and as you value your lives don't make a sound and don't be seen."

By now it had finally penetrated Andrews's hard skull that I'd had either a change of heart or of loyalties. He grabbed Roddy's arm and they were gone.

Stomach still spinning, I made one more trip down the ladder, painfully jarring my arm when my footing slipped on the last rung. I bit back a grunt and kept moving, retrieving the keys and candle from where they lay on the earthen floor. When discovered, the abandoned chains would be a considerable mystery to Nash.

A final clumsy climb up and I was stuffing the keys back in the guard's pocket with trembling hands. Looking at his stupidly peaceful face, I realized I couldn't leave him like this. Any hint of irregularity and the first course of action would be to check on the prisoners. They needed time to get away and I needed to put some distance between myself and my crime.

Good arm under his shoulders, I heaved the man to his feet, shaking him. The activity brought him awake and left him somewhat confused. Giving him what I hoped would seem a smile of friendly concern, I helped him pull himself together, dusting his clothes and hoping to confound him more with swift, incomprehensible speech.

"Dear me, but I thought you might have hurt yourself, everything all right now? Bumped our heads together, don't you know, when I'm came up, you went down, and bang! There you are, but accidents do happen. All's well now, eh, what?"

"*Was?*"

"Ah . . . *der Kopf* . . ." I tapped first my forehead, then his, and said "Ow!" while giving an indication that he'd fallen. For all my acting, I received a deservedly strange look from him, which I pretended not to notice. He picked up his musket, straightened his sword and scabbard, and tried to resume a dignified attitude. I indicated that he should close the trap and shoot the bolt.

"I'll just be off to see Lieutenant Nash. *Vielen Dank und gute Nacht.*"

The mention of Nash's name reminded him that I had some kind of special status. I gave him a couple of pennies for his trouble and left. Now, if he'd just leave his charges undisturbed for a while. A pity I didn't know much of the language or I could have arranged something more to my advantage. On the way back, I vowed to take some positive steps toward enlarging my German vocabulary before another week had passed.

Nash welcomed me and asked if my interview had gone well.

"Very well, indeed, sir. I am most grateful for your kindness. Just wanted to see the wretch one more time and to ask if you would be so good as to find a use for this." I produced a small purse and lay it on the table between us.

He pretended surprise. "But what is this, Mr. Barrett?"

"Let's just call it a contribution toward His Majesty's victory. I'm sure that you can find some way to make life a bit easier for your soldiers."

Peering into it, Nash looked quite gratified. He must have been worried that the bribe I'd promised would be unduly delayed. It was my own and not Father's money, though, part of what I'd managed to bring back from England. He'd written that good coin was becoming rare and the paper money in circulation hardly more than a grim joke. It seemed to me that a ready supply of silver and gold would be a very handy thing to have around and so it was now proved.

Nash gave warm thanks for my generosity and offered to stand me to the best the house could offer in the way of drink. He could well afford it, but I politely declined.

"I must head home before it gets too late . . ."

Someone began pounding on the door. "*Herr Oberleutnant!*"

Oh, good God.

But the man who rushed in was not the guard I'd left; however, his news was just as calamitous. Some eagle-eyed sentry had spotted two men haring out of town, recognized them as being the prisoners, and given the alarm.

"How the devil did they escape? You don't know? Then find out! Never a moment's peace," Nash complained. "I'd ask you to come, sir, as you might enjoy another hunt, but with your arm . . ."

Feeling that my face might crack under the strain of looking calm and brightly interested, I waved down his objections. "But I wouldn't miss this for the world, Lieutenant. I would be singularly honored if you allowed me to render such limited service as I might be capable of offering."

"Well, you do know the land and I was highly impressed with the sharpness of your vision the other night. One of the men said that you'd be like to find a black cat in a root cellar."

I laughed deprecatingly, wishing that he'd not mentioned cellars.

"Lauder reports that he believes they are only just ahead of us, sir," said the sergeant.

"He believes?" Nash sneered. "Go back and inform him that I am not interested in what he believes but what he knows."

The sergeant whipped off.

Nash had been optimistic when we'd started the expedition but as the night grew old and he and the men more tired, his high spirits had taken a sharp turn in the other direction. His faith in my ability to see well in the dark had also suffered a decided setback. At the first opportunity, I'd done what I could to lead them in the wrong direction, but it hadn't been very successful, largely due to the tracking efforts of one Hessian corporal. The man must have been part hunting hound, for each time I suggested a misleading course to take, he invariably brought us back on the right trail again. I was forced to hold myself back, lest Nash become suspicious.

We moved after the sergeant, Nash on his horse, I on Belle, and a dozen soldiers at our backs doing their best to stay in step over the uneven ground. Some carried lanterns like the two fellows trotting before us and the lot of them making enough noise to wake all this half of the island. Whenever we passed a house, the shutters would either open with curiosity or close in fear, depending on the boldness of its residents. If anyone deigned to call out a question, Nash's answer was that we were on the king's business and not to hinder us. No one did.

I stood up in the stirrups to get a look at things. Half a mile ahead was Lauder and his party, which included the corporal. The sergeant was almost to them, bearing Nash's impatient message. Another half-mile beyond, I made out two struggling figures against the clean background of an empty field. Had it been full daylight, Lauder would have been upon them in very short order.

Couldn't those fools move any faster? One of them seemed spry enough, but the other was having trouble of some sort, limping, perhaps. Damnation, at this rate they would be caught.

"See anything?" Nash asked hopefully.

I started to say no and changed it at the last second. "I'm not sure. I think I shall ride ahead with the advance party."

"It could be dangerous, Mr. Barrett."

"I doubt that; the prisoners are unarmed, after all." Before he could object, I put my heels into Belle's sides and she obediently shot forward at a fast canter. Oh, how that shook and tore at my arm. I clamped my teeth shut and concentrated on getting to my goal. We passed the sergeant without a word and I reined in Belle at the last second. A canter was bad enough, but the change in gait from it to a walk required some trotting in between and I wanted to keep that to a minimum and thus spare my arm.

"Any luck, Sergeant Lauder?" I asked. I brought Belle to a full stop, causing Lauder's party to halt as well. Anything to give Roddy and Andrews a little more of a lead.

"The tracks are very fresh," he replied. His manner was polite, but very cool as he hadn't forgotten our fight earlier. I was relieved to note that he was walking normally again, though. His corporal, who had a lantern, pointed at the ground where some grass had been crushed. "We will soon have them."

"You're sure? It doesn't look like much to me."

The corporal picked up on my disparaging tone and made a vigorous argument to the contrary.

"He says that they are here."

I obstinately continued with my pose of disbelief. "Perhaps, though I don't know how you can sort anything sensible out of that muddle."

Just as stubborn, Lauder repeated his previous statement and made indications that he would like to proceed. Just then, Nash's sergeant caught up and delivered his caustic message. Lauder maintained a phlegmatic face, but we could tell he was hardly amused at this questioning of his efficiency. He vented it upon the corporal and ordered him to proceed as speedily as possible.

I looked past them toward Roddy and Andrews. They seemed to be going slower than ever. Their three days of confinement in the cellar must have taken all the strength out of them. They'd never make it.

"Sergeant Lauder, I shall run ahead and see if I can't spot 'em. You go on with what you're doing."

I gave Belle another kick and—quite stupidly from their point of view—charged over the tracks the corporal was trying so diligently to follow. About fifty yards on, I veered off to the left so I was riding parallel to the trail.

Roddy was the one limping; Andrews supported him, but they hadn't a hope of breaking away at this pace. I drew up even with them, but some twenty yards to their left, and gave a soft hail.

"Roddy, it's me. I've come to help."

"More like to lead 'em to us," said Andrews.

"Please be so good as to keep your voice down, Lieutenant, or we'll all be chained in the cellar."

"What do ye want, then?" he demanded in a gruff, but somewhat softer tone.

"The Hessians are catching you up."

"Tell us something we don't know. Of course they're comin'."

"Good, then you know you'll need to go faster."

"Aren't we doin' the best we can? The lad all but busted his ankle gettin' away, though."

"I'm ready to loan you my horse, but we'll have to be careful—"

"Then bring 'im over here an' we'll get the lad—"

"Do that and a certain tracker back there will read the signs we leave like a book. There's a stony patch not far ahead. You'll have to make it that far first."

Andrews was for wasting time by asking more questions. I moved past and guided Belle down a slight slope to a wide place between the fields where the earth had been scraped away by some ancient and long-departed glacier. That's what Rapelji had taught us, anyway, when he'd once led our class out here to study geological oddities. I never thought then that his science lesson would have ever proved to be of any practical use to me in life. Blessings to the man for his thoroughness in pounding such diverse knowledge into our heads.

Roddy and Andrews finally caught up with me. I dismounted from

Belle and took her over to them. They'd both need to ride her, but Andrews insisted he could do well enough on foot.

"As long as the hoss is carryin' 'im an' not me, I'll be quick enough."

"Yes, and leaving your tracks as well. When we go I want that man to find only mine and Belle's, yours are to disappear completely."

The dawn finally broke for him. "Oh, I see what yer about. That's good brain work, young fella."

"If my brain were properly working, I wouldn't be out here. Get Roddy into the saddle and shift yourself up behind him. I'll lead the horse."

"Thank you, Jonathan," Roddy gasped.

"Later," I said. "When we know you're safe."

Both of them mounted. I took hold of the reins and led Belle away from the spot, resuming the path I'd been on earlier. Hopefully, the corporal would interpret things to mean that I was afoot for some reason other than the real one. If questioned later, I could always say that I'd wanted to give the horse a rest.

The boat that Andrews had been making for was still a mile ahead. Roddy's mere five-mile jaunt had been almost twice the distance because of the character of the land and their need to avoid the soldiers. They made better time now, but our speed was still limited to a walk. On the other hand, we knew where we were going and the Hessian trackers did not.

Before too long I heard the measured rush of sea waves carried on the fresh wind. Following Andrews's directions, we slipped quietly by some farmhouses, rousing only a barking dog or two along the way. I didn't care much for that row, but the animals were too distant to do us any real harm; there were other dangers waiting for us, instead.

Nash had boasted that you couldn't toss a rock into a field without striking one of His Majesty's soldiers, and now as we passed an old unused church I spied several of them walking over its grounds toward us. The church was occupied, after all, quartered with British troops. One of the men saw our figures moving against the general darkness, correctly assumed that we were up to no good, and gave a loud challenge.

I flipped the reins over Belle's head and pressed them into Roddy's hands. "Ride like the devil. I'll lead them off."

"But—"

Andrews sensibly gave Belle a kick and away they went, heading for the sea. I trotted after them, yelling to encourage the horse to go faster and to draw the soldiers' attention. It worked far better than I would have liked. Calling for help from their companions in the old church, they started for me with all speed. Without further delay, I took to my own heels, trusting that my improved vision would give me sufficient advantage over them to escape. On the other hand, I still had to keep them close enough to give Roddy his chance to get away.

"Over there!" someone shouted. Good king's English this time, and very understandable. So far they'd seen me only as a murky figure, I couldn't allow them a better look lest I end up taking Roddy's place at the gallows. I dodged under the shadows of a small orchard, went over a fence, and through a sheep pasture. As I trotted along, I laughed out loud to think what Jericho would have to say about this misuse of my riding boots.

I was still laughing when I made it to the top of a rise and stopped for a look back to see where my pursuers were. A foolish thing to do, for I'd underestimated their speed and overestimated my own. In that instant between pausing and turning, one of their sharp-eyed shooters found time to raise his gun and use it.

It was a skillful shot—that, or he had been uncommonly lucky. I felt the devastating impact and, as it had that morning by the kettle, time slowed and all the world was caught up in my illusion of everything coming to a halt.

Above, the glowing stars flowed and spun like water in a bright stream, swirling into glittering whirlpools and splashing up into self-made fountains of light. Below, the land twisted and changed places with them and by that motion I knew I was falling, tumbling helplessly down the other side of the rise.

My back was on fire . . . no, my chest . . . my whole body. The musket ball . . . oh, sweet God, not again.

But even as I cried out, my voice died away, breath gone, crushed out of me by the hideous weight of the pain. It completely closed over me, heavier and more horrible than the grave.

Then the sounds of the night, the soldiers, the rush of the sea, the unspeakable pain itself, abruptly faded, like the turning down of a lamp. One second I could see everything, the next all was gone, lost in a thick, dark gray fog.

The change was so great and so fast that I couldn't sort it out at first. I was beyond any thought for the longest time. I seemed to be drifting like a feather on the wind. No, not a feather. The lightest bit of down was yet too weighty compared to me. I was more like smoke, rising high and floating carelessly over the land, too faint to even have a shadow to mark my passage.

I was floating; I was falling. I was once again caught up by whatever force had seized and sent me flying from out of my coffin. Instinct and memory told me that much. Reason was fast asleep. Reason itself was an absurdity when measured against this. Instinct told me to be calm and not to fight what was happening, and I listened to it. I was beyond argument, beyond fear. I felt safe, like a tired swimmer who finally ceases to fight the water and gives in to its embrace only to discover his own buoyancy.

After what must have been a great while, my mind began to work again, forming questions and seeking answers. I could see nothing but fog, but felt no evidence of its damp presence. If I felt anything it always came from outside my body: the pressure of the wind, the rough kiss of grass below. Of my own body, I felt nothing. I knew I still had one, but I'd lost all form, if not the knowledge, of it. No arms or legs, no head to hold my thoughts, no mouth to express them. I could hear things, but only in a vague way as though my ears—if I'd had any—had been wrapped in a soft blanket.

Perhaps that musket ball had finished me off and the fog I drifted in was part of the process of dying. Perhaps . . .

Then it struck me how absolutely, utterly ridiculous it all was. Of course I was not dying. I was having one of those damned dreams again, or something very like them.

I gave myself a kind of internal shake, half in my mind and half in the body I knew *had* to exist.

And then I was sitting on the bare ground as if I'd always been there and with everything returned to its proper place in the universe: stars above, land below, and me in the middle. There was no sign of the soldiers and if I read things right, I was a good half mile from where I'd been before. Downwind. I'd traveled downwind. I'd traveled *on* the wind.

Falling and floating, or in this case, floating and drifting.

"Impossible." But giving voice to this first sign of reason was no help to my dazed brain, for my thoughts could only return to the question: how *else* could I have gotten here? How else could I have escaped the prison of my coffin that first night? The answer, however impossible, was undeniable.

No. I shook my head. It was far too fanciful. Frightening, too.

*But how else?*

The answer, the impossible answer, lay within me. Brought forth by panic or pain, the time had come to consciously grasp and hold on to it no matter what happened.

I shut my eyes to more easily remember what it had felt like. Slowly opening them again, I perceived that my vision was clouding over, as if a great gray shadow had fallen upon the world. The wide background hum of night noises began to fade. I raised my hand. It was gradually becoming as transparent as glass. The more ethereal it was, the less I could clearly see. Then the grayness consumed everything and I was totally blind, but *floating.*

The earth that once supported me was not really solid at all, but as porous as vapor. Then, as I began to sink in a little past its surface, came the thought that it was I, and not the ground, that was no longer substantial. I gave an instinctive "kick" and felt myself rising, until I sensed I hovered a foot or so above the grass and was even able to hold myself in place against the wind.

My concentration wavered. The night crashed back upon me. My arms jerked outward to regain lost balance and I landed hard on my feet. As before, I'd moved some distance from where I'd been.

Sweet God, what had I become?

Ghostlike, I had escaped the grave. I'd ceased to be solid and passed through the intervening ground to freedom. Just now I had virtually flown over the ground like a wraith on the wind to escape the soldiers.

And the pain.

It was gone. There was no sign of any wound on my flesh, though I was shocked to find a hole larger than my thumb torn through my clothes. The musket ball had gone in and out, leaving behind only this evidence of its passage, the same effect the sword blade had had on Nora's clothes.

My arm. My right arm, shattered and useless for nearly a week . . .

Restored. Completely healed. *Free* of pain.

I felt a small kind of sickness trying to ooze up from within. In the absence of a fast-beating heart, I could interpret this to be a symptom of the paralyzing fear that I'd pushed away so often before. As entitled as I must be to surrendering to it, I would not give in to the temptation. True, my situation was monumentally strange, but beyond the strangeness, beyond the changes, I was still the same man, still Jonathan Barrett, and I had no need to be afraid of myself.

*Accept it,* Nora had said whenever I'd witnessed anything supernormal about her. She had only to hold my eyes to make me do so, but always she'd given me the chance to abandon the confines of the mundane first. I usually failed her, requiring urging in the right direction. Whether because of her influence on me or my own temper, I did not begrudge her that liberty as it soothed away all unease between us. Could I do no less for myself now?

"Accept it," I said aloud, meaning *accept your new self . . . for the only other alternative must surely be madness.*

Accept without fear, without expectation, and with hope for the best. With God's grace and guidance I'd be able to manage whatever was to come.

Accept.

*Accept . . .*

# EPILOGUE

The sea sound roared in my ears; the sight of it seemed to bestow a kind of movement to my stilled heart. It was so beautiful, a living, glittering thing, restless and wild under the calm luminescence of thousands of minute suns. It stole their silver light, tossed it in the waves, and playfully threw it back again. I could have stood on the bluff and watched for hours more, but the night was beginning to turn and I had a long road ahead.

Below, in the shelter of a tiny cove, was Belle, her reins dragging on the ground. I was glad to see her, to finally find her. I'd been walking along the edge of the coast for a very long time, looking. She was no worse for wear and occasionally dropped her head to graze on a patch of grass.

There was no sign of Roddy Finch or Ezra Andrews. If their boat had been stored here, it was long gone. I wished them a safe journey.

I made my way down to Belle, took up the reins, and mounted her. Perhaps she sensed that we were going home; I didn't have to guide her in the right direction, she took it for herself and set a good pace. As we moved onto a clear and well-marked road, I gave her the signal to go faster and she readily obeyed. Trot, canter, and finally gallop. She would never match Rolly's speed, but she was smoother and more graceful. I crouched over her, one hand on the reins, the other stretched before me as though to taste the streaming wind.

*Accept* . . .

Accept the wind and the sky and the earth and the joy and the sorrow.

Accept this new chance at life.

Live and laugh again.

And I did laugh.

It grew distant and hollow as my solid hand began to fade and vanish along with the rest of the world.

I'd had much time to practice during that long walk, looking.

I stopped the fading at a point where I could just see through my flesh to the horse's bobbing neck below. The wind tugged at me, but not as hard as before, and I knew I could move against it or with it as I chose.

Now my hand was only just visible. The world was nearly lost in gray fog, but I was able to hold it like this if I concentrated. I could only just feel the horse's strong movement beneath me.

And then I was free of her. My booted feet drifted loose from the stirrups. I was above her now, arms thrown wide like wings, but carried along by my will alone. I pressed against the wind, matching Belle's speed for a moment until, with an unvoiced cry, I broke away.

Ten feet, twenty, thirty. Higher and higher.

I soared and turned and rolled like a nighthawk, flying ahead of Belle or falling behind, but always keeping her within safe sight.

I soared high over the rushing earth, caught up in my own soundless laughter as I embraced the dancing sky.

We were going home.

# DEATH AND THE MAIDEN

*For Mark,*
*here's to tracks five and six.*
*Woof!*

*Thanks also to*
*Gloria Shami*
*for the reality check,*
*my good friends in*
*"The Teeth-in-the-Neck Gang."*

*And a special thanks to*
*Roxanne Longstreet*
*for showing me that the*
*impossible* can *be done*
and *that tip about the creative*
*necessity of ice cream.*

# CHAPTER 1

***Long Island, September 1776***

"But this is miraculous," said Dr. Beldon, lifting my elbow closer to his large, somewhat bulging eyes. Next he ran his fingers over the point where the bone break had been. "It's not possible. There's not a single sign that you were ever injured."

Which was of great relief to me. For a time I'd feared I would never recover the full use of my right arm. Beldon had chanced to call on me this evening just after I'd awakened and had been surprised to see that the sling I'd worn for nearly a week was gone.

"And there is no more discomfort when you move it?"

"None," I said. Days earlier, Beldon had expressed to me the need to rebreak the bone so as to properly set it again, but I'd been putting it off. Now I was very glad of that procrastination.

His fingers dug a bit more deeply into the muscle. "Make a fist," he ordered. "Open. Close. Now stretch your arm straight. Twist your hand at the wrist." Eyes shut, he concentrated on the movement. "Amazing. Quite amazing," he muttered.

"Yes, well, God has been most generous to me of late," I said with true sincerity.

Eyes open, now his brows went up. "But, Mr. Barrett . . ."

"You said yourself that it was a miracle," I reminded him. Our eyes locked. "But I don't think you need take any notice of it. Should anyone be curious, you may certainly inform them that my arm has healed as you expected."

He didn't even blink. "Yes. I shall certainly do that." The only clue that anything was amiss was his slight flatness of tone and a brief slackening of expression.

"Nothing unusual about it at all," I emphasized.

"No . . . nothing un . . ."

I broke off my influence upon him and asked, "Are you finished, Doctor?"

*Blink*. "Yes, quite finished, Mr. Barrett, and may I express my delight that you are feeling better?"

We exchanged further pleasantries, then Beldon finally took his leave. My valet, Jericho, had silently watched everything from one corner of my room, his dark face sober and aloof yet somehow still managing to convey mild disapproval.

"It's only to spare us all unnecessary bother," I reminded him, shaking my shirtsleeve down.

"Of course, sir." He stepped forward to fasten the cuff.

"Very well, then. It's to spare *me* unnecessary bother."

"Is the truth so evil?" he asked, helping me put on my waistcoat.

"No, but it is unbelievable. And frightening. I've been frightened enough for myself; I've no wish to inflict that fear upon others."

"Yet it still exists."

"But I'm not afraid anymore. Bewildered, perhaps, but—"

"I was speaking of other members of the household."

"What other members? Who?"

He made a vague gesture rather akin to a shrug. "In the slave quarters. There are whisperings that a devil has jumped into you."

"Oh, really? For what purpose?"

"That has not yet been decided."

"Who is it that thinks so?"

His lips closed, and he busied himself at brushing lint from my shoulders.

"I hope you have discouraged such idle gossip," I said, adjusting my neckcloth. It had become rather tight in the last few moments.

"I have. There will be no problems from it. I only mentioned this because you were seen."

"Doing what?"

"Something . . . extraordinary. The person I spoke to said he saw you . . . flying."

"Oh."

"Of course, no one really believed him, but his story was disturbing to the more gullible."

"You hardly surprise me." One or two of our slaves, not as well educated as Jericho, would certainly be prey to all sorts of midnight imaginings, especially if they'd been listening to fanciful tales before bedtime.

"Can you fly, Mr. Jonathan?" Jericho's face was utterly expressionless.

I gulped, my belly suddenly churning. "What of it, if I could?"

There was a considerable pause before he replied. "Then I would suggest that you be more discreet about it."

My belly stopped churning and went stone still. "You . . . you've seen me?"

"Yes."

*Oh, dear.*

He stopped brushing at lint and turned his attention to the shelves in my already orderly wardrobe.

"You seem to have taken it rather calmly."

"I assure you, I was most troubled when I saw you floating over the treetops yesterday evening . . ."

"But . . . ?"

"But you looked very happy," he admitted. "I concluded that anything capable of giving you such wholesome joy must not be a bad thing. Besides, my *bomba* has told me tales of his childhood that talk of men turning themselves into animals. If a man can learn the magic to become an animal, then why can a man not learn the magic to fly?"

"This is not magic, Jericho."

"Are you so sure? Then what is it that turns a tiny seed into a tree? Is that not a kind of magic?"

"Now you're speaking of science or philosophy."

He shook his head. "I speak only of what's been said. If I choose to ascribe all that has happened to you to magic, then it *is* magic."

"Or superstition."

"That comes in only when one is afraid or ignorant. I am neither, but I have adopted an explanation that is tolerable to me."

"Maybe I should adopt it for myself, as well. Nothing else I've considered has come close to explaining things so handily. Especially things like this." I touched my miraculously healed arm.

"And this?" he asked, his hand hovering over a small mirror that lay facedown on one of the shelves.

"Yes, that, too. You can get rid of it, y'know." Since my change, I'd found that particular vanity item to be singularly useless, not to mention unsettling. I'd more or less known what to expect, but it had still given me a sharp turn to look into a mirror and not see a damned thing. I'd briefly and irrationally worried that that was what I'd become: "a damned thing." Father and I had discussed it thoroughly, for I was very upset at the time, but we'd been unable to explain the phenomenon. Perhaps Jericho was right and it was magic.

"As you wish," he said, tucking the offending glass into a pocket. "Does Mr.Barrett know about the flying? Or Miss Elizabeth?"

"Not yet. I'll tell them all about it later. The news won't grow stale for waiting. And I promise to take your advice and be more discreet."

"I'm relieved to hear that."

After a moment, I added, somewhat shyly, "It's . . . not really flying, y'know."

He waited for me to go on.

"I sort of float upon the air like a leaf. But I can move against the wind or with it as I choose."

He thought that over for a long time. "And what is it like?"

A grin and a soft laugh bubbled right out of me. "It's absolutely wonderful!"

And so it was. Last night I'd done the impossible and broken away from the grasp of the earth to soar in the sky freer than any bird. It was surely the most remarkable portion of the legacy I'd come into since my . . . death.

Or rather, my *change*.

The details of that particular story—of my death and escape from the grave—have been recounted elsewhere. Let it suffice for now that upon my return, I soon discovered I'd acquired the same characteristics that governed the waking life of a certain Miss Nora Jones, a lady with whom I had shared a very intimate liaison.

Like her, I was now able to influence the very minds and thoughts of anyone around me, thus allowing me to resume my former life with my family almost as though nothing had ever happened. I had learned the secret of how to heal swiftly and completely. And I was able to fly . . . so to speak. Though I'd never actually witnessed Nora indulging in such a display, I had no doubt that she was capable of doing it, since my own condition now so completely mirrored her own.

Mirrors. Yes, well, you've heard about them already.

Like her, I was also unable to bear sunlight, which might be considered a heavy burden, but for the fact that my eyes were so improved. The night had become my day; the stars and moon my welcome companions in the sky. When the sun was up, I slept—or tried to; I was having some difficulties there, but more on that later.

My strength was that of a young Hercules, and my other senses enjoyed similar improvements. Each evening I discovered a new delight to the ear, a fresh appreciation of touch, and, though I was not required to breathe regularly unless I chose to speak, I could pick out and identify a scent almost as well as one of our own hunting hounds. Taste had also undergone considerable alteration, though I never exercised it upon what might be considered a normal meal.

For, like Nora, I had come to subsist solely upon *blood* for my sustenance.

But again, more on that later.

"What are you writing, little brother?" asked Elizabeth, peering across the library as she walked in. Her nightly practice at her spinet had ended, but I'd been so absorbed in my work that I hadn't noticed when the music stopped.

"A letter to Cousin Oliver," I replied.

The early part of the evening had passed pleasantly enough amid familial congratulations on my recovery. Diverting attention from myself, I had given all the credit to Dr. Beldon, much to his great enjoyment. Father and Elizabeth, who, along with Jericho, knew the full truth about my changed nature, required a more detailed account from me, which I'd promised, but had yet to provide. By subtle gesture and with a wellplaced word or two, I gave them to understand that my healing was connected to my change, and thus not a topic for general discussion. We'd quietly arranged to talk later. As I had no interest in Mother's card game and was too restless to read, I'd taken sanctuary in the library to deal with some necessary correspondence.

"But you just sent one only . . ." Her voice trailed off.

"I know, but much has occurred since my last missive."

She thought about that awhile, then came over to stand next to Father's desk, where I happened to be working. "I have something for you," she said, pulling a flat packet from her skirt pocket.

I instantly recognized it. "My journal!"

She gave it over. "I kept it from your things when Mother was having your room cleaned out. I was afraid she'd either throw it away or read it herself, and I didn't think you'd have liked either of those choices."

"You're right, I wouldn't. Thank you."

"I didn't read it," she added.

This surprised me, not because Elizabeth was a prying sort of person, but because at the time she'd thought me dead. "Why not?"

"I couldn't bring myself to. These are your words and your thoughts, I just couldn't bear the idea of reading them so soon after . . . anyway, I wanted only to keep them safe. From her. I don't know what I hated most, her utter coldness over you or the way she ransacked your room like a bloody vulture."

Mother again. "It's all over now."

She put her hand on mine. "Yes, thank God."

"It would have been all right if you had read it. There's nothing in here that I wouldn't have minded sharing with you and Father."

She smiled at that. "But you're back and there's no need, is there?"

"May there never be another," I solemnly intoned, putting my hand over my heart.

That brought out another smile, which was most pleasing. Her good humor and mine restored, I picked up my pen and regarded the sheet of paper before me, wondering what to put down next.

"Mind if I keep you company?" From one of the desk drawers she pulled out a penknife and some goose quills.

"I should welcome it," I said absently.

Apparently Elizabeth was prepared to wait for Father to join us before calling for my promised explanation. Taking a chair next to the desk and close to my candle, she began carving a point on one of the quills. "Are you going to tell Oliver about what's happened to you?"

A brief laugh escaped me. "Hardly, or he'd think that the Fonteyn half of my blood had finally boiled my brain. Did I ever mention to you that tour we took of Bedlam?"

"In noxious detail." She steadily sliced away on a quill, pausing only to narrowly inspect the results of her work.

"I've no wish for Oliver to regard me as a potential inmate, so be assured that the details of my recent experience will find no place here."

"Then what—"

"Nora."

Her name temporarily halted Elizabeth's inquiries, and I took the opportunity to dip my pen into the inkpot. After reading again my few lines assuring Oliver of my continued good health and a wish for the same for him, I had to pause yet again and think how to proceed. Before leaving England for home some months ago, I'd asked him to keep an eye on Nora for me and in such a way as to leave no doubt that my relationship with her had quite ended. My lightness of attitude quite puzzled my poor cousin, considering his awareness that Nora and I had been passionate lovers for nearly three years.

But, of course, Nora had caused me to forget all that.

I wasn't sure if I should curse her or bless her for what she'd done to me. Some nights I did both. This was one of those nights, and they happened more and more frequently as my memories of her returned.

Though she had committed a great wrong against me, I yet loved her and missed her terribly.

"Ow!"

Elizabeth had had a mishap with the razorsharp penknife and nicked a finger. She ruefully held it close to the candle to inspect the damage, started to put her finger to her mouth, then stopped, her eyes suddenly shifting up to meet mine.

"Be more careful," I said, trying not to stare at the drop of blood welling from the tiny cut.

She lowered her hand slightly. "Does this trouble you?"

"Why should it?"

"Because you've an odd look on your face. Are you hungry?"

"No, I am not hungry." Not yet. Later, after everyone was asleep and the world was quiet, I'd slip out and . . .

"Then what?"

"I can smell it," I whispered, not without a feeling of awe.

She brought her finger close to her nose and sniffed, then shrugged at her failure to sense it. "A little speck like this?"

"Yes. It hangs in the air like perfume."

"That must be interesting for you," she observed. The bleeding had stopped, so she wiped away the blood on her handkerchief. Picking up the quill, she gingerly resumed her delicate work with the knife.

Disturbing, more like, I thought, unable to ignore the scent and the reactions it aroused within me. I raised one hand to cover my mouth and ran my tongue over my teeth. There, the two points on my upper jaw . . . a slight swelling, not painful . . . quite the opposite, in fact.

"Jonathan?"

"It's nothing," I said, a bit too quickly, letting my hand drop away.

But she seemed to know what I was hiding. "Sweet God, Jonathan, you've nothing to be ashamed of."

"I'm not," I said. "Really."

"Then why the glower?"

I made a fist and bumped it lightly against the desk, then opened it flat. "I'm not sure I . . . that I'm . . . comfortable with this part of what's happened to me."

"You do what you do because you have to."

"Yes, but I've . . . I worry about what people might think should they find out."

"But no one else knows but me, Father, and Jericho. We don't speak of it, and you're not likely to blurt it out in company."

"As if it's something shameful."

"Something private," she corrected. "Like your journal."

Unable to endure her steady, sensible gaze, I shoved my pen into a cup of lead shot and stood up to pace.

She continued to watch me. "Come now and listen to yourself. Worrying about what others may think is the sort of thing that bedevils Mother. There's no need for you to pay any mind to that same voice, or you could end up like her."

All too true. I *had* been haunted by a miserable chorus of dark voices muttering of nothing but doubt and doom. "It's just that most of the time everything is as it was for me before my . . . return. And yet"—I gestured vaguely—"everything is so different. *I'm* different."

She did not—thank God—gainsay me. The changes within that had literally brought me back from the grave were profound, and their full influence upon how I now lived were only just being realized. I slept, if one could call it that, the whole day through, unable to stir for as long as the sun was up. Since the household held to an exactly opposite habit, my enjoyment of its society was unhappily limited. The rest of the time I was alone. Very much alone.

And as for Elizabeth's little accident . . . well, it was yet another reminder of an appetite that the world would doubtless look upon as disgusting or at the very least react to with alarm and fear.

I paused by the bookcase and stared at the titles within without reading them. "Remember the night I . . . came back?"

She nodded. It was not likely that either of us would forget.

"After we'd captured the rebels, two of Nash's Hessians escorted me to Mrs. Montagu's. I thought I'd gotten rid of them, but they came back and saw me in her barn with her horses . . . feeding myself."

"Then what?"

"They ran like rabbits. They were terrified. One of them called me a name, '*blutsauger*.' "

She stumbled over my no doubt questionable pronunciation. "Bluetsaw"

I repeated the word for her. "It means 'bloodsucker.' Hardly flattering."

"Certainly not in the context that it was given."

"Not in any context."

"What of it? You're a 'bloodsucker,' I'm an eater of animal flesh."

"That's not the same."

"It would be if dining on a good hot joint was thought to be repugnant by most people. It's not like you to be feeling sorry for yourself, little brother. I hope you can get over it."

I idly poked at a crescent of dust gathered in a tight corner of the bookcase woodwork. One of the maids had been careless over her cleaning chores. Woe to her if Mother noticed. "Perhaps the Fonteyn blood is doing its work upon me after all, and I shall become mad."

"I think not, since you've been diluting it so regularly with that of our livestock."

My openmouthed stare was returned with a flash of her bright eyes as she cocked her head to one side. It was meant to convince me that I was taking myself far too seriously. "I do believe you have a fool for a brother," I said wearily.

"Better a fool than a corpse," she responded bluntly. "You're not going mad, you're just getting used to things. I still am, myself."

"And what do you do about it?"

"Ask God to sort it out for me, say 'amen,' and go to sleep." The point of one quill cut to perfection, she put it aside and picked up another. The feathering had not yet been trimmed away and she made a fine mess on her wide skirts as she worked to correct the oversight.

"Would that I could sleep," I muttered.

"More dreams?"

"Nothing but, and no waking to escape them is allowed."

"Dr. Beldon couldn't help?"

"He let me try some of his laudanum."

"And it didn't work?"

"Not really. He made up a draught and told me to take it when I was ready to retire, but I knew I'd never be able to keep it down. So I went out to the stables and drew off blood from one of the horses to mix it in and was able to drink that. It put me into quite a stupor, but the dreams were still there and more disturbing than usual. Never again." I dropped into Father's big chair by the dormant fireplace. "Damnation, but the only rest I've gotten since my return was when I was forced to shelter in the old barn."

"Perhaps you could go back and try it again."

"Why should my sleeping there be any different than here in my own bed?"

"I don't know. If you went back you might find an answer."

"It's hardly safe."

Her brows drew together as she glanced up from her fine carving. "No one goes out there anymore."

"The Hessians might. You know they wanted to take Rapelji's house away from him for their own lodging? He's lucky they changed their minds and took over the church instead."

"Not so lucky for the church."

"Better to have them there than at Rapelji's or even in our own house.

I've been down to The Oak to learn the news, and they're a pretty rough and savage lot. And they enjoy it."

"I've heard the stories, Jonathan," she said dryly. Because of the recent occupation, Elizabeth had hardly been able to stir a foot outside the door for fear of being insulted by the very army sent to protect us. "Anyway, you've wandered off the subject of the barn. Why don't you try spending the day there? Jericho can run out and check on you if you're that worried."

I grimaced. "It's so open and unprotected, without doors or shutters. I only used it because I had no other choice."

"But you were able to find rest then, with no dreaming."

That was inarguable. I was about to raise more objections anyway, just to keep up the flow of talk, when Father came in, shutting the library doors behind him. He was a tall man with a spare figure and a still handsome face, but lately more lines had begun to clutter his normally amiable expression. Imprinted there by the upheavals in our own lives and by the larger conflicts outside our home, they seemed to lift when he looked upon us, his children.

"Is the card game finished?" Elizabeth asked.

"No, they're still at it," he replied, meaning Mother, Dr. Beldon, and Mrs. Hardinbrook, who was Beldon's widowed sister. "They've changed to something that needs but three players to work well, so I made my escape."

"Why do you play if you don't enjoy it?"

"It soothes your mother's soul." He strode toward the cabinet that held a small supply of wine and spirits, then changed his mind with a sigh. "No. I'll be damned before I let that woman drive me to drink."

"That woman" referred to Mrs. Hardinbrook, not Mother.

"What did she do tonight?" I asked.

Father rolled his eyes, looking glum. "She opened her mouth, and that's more than enough. How she does clack on. I don't know as I've ever seen her pause for breath. At least when we're at cards she shuts up for the play."

"And when Mother is talking," Elizabeth put in.

Father grunted agreement to that, then turned all his attention upon me. "All right, laddie, what's the rest of your tale? Just how did your arm heal so quickly?"

Elizabeth left off her carving of pens and put her hands in her lap.

I gulped. It's one thing to promise an explanation, but quite another to actually deliver it, particularly when one doesn't know where to start.

"Well, it's connected with how I . . . escaped my grave." My last words came out in a rush, as I wanted to get past them as quickly as possible. I did not like to think about that time; it always made me feel ill. They could see how difficult it was for me to talk, and waited me out. Suddenly restless again, I launched out of Father's chair and stalked up and down the room.

"I . . . floated out," I finally said.

They exchanged looks. Father's brows went up. Somehow, this had been so much easier to talk about with Jericho, but then he'd already known something of the subject.

"That's how I got out without disturbing the earth. I can make my body . . ."

They leaned forward, silently encouraging me to continue.

". . . make it . . ."

"What?" demanded Elizabeth.

And the words just would not come. Their combined gaze left me entirely flummoxed over what to say next. I was being foolish again, worried they wouldn't believe me, or worse, that they'd be afraid of me. But they'd accepted so much already and now seemed willing to accept more, so such worries were certainly all in my own head.

"Jonathan," Father prompted, his expression kindly.

I nodded. "Yes. I'm trying. What it is . . . is that I have the ability to make myself insubstantial, allowing me to pass through solid objects. To float."

"Float?" he echoed.

"Yes, sir."

Neither said anything for a time, but they did exchange looks once more. They did not, thank God, laugh.

"Well," he finally said. "What has that to do with your arm healing?"

It was my turn to stare. The floating and the restoration were so linked in my mind that it had been natural for me to conclude that others would also see the connection.

"Uhh . . . that is . . . when I ceased to float around, I was all better."

Another lengthy silence.

"I know I'm not doing this very well—"

"No, not at all," agreed Elizabeth.

"It's like that business with mirrors. I've no explanation for it, it just *is*."

"Perhaps," said Father, "if you gave us a demonstration?"

I'd foreseen the need for one from the start. That knowledge did not make it any easier, though. I nodded, went to the windows and closed the shutters to prevent anyone from spying, then turned to face Father and Elizabeth. Holding my hands up before me that I might observe my progress, I willed myself to slip slowly into . . . whatever it was. The room seemed to fill with fog as I grew more and more transparent.

Elizabeth rose straight up from her chair to gape. Father staggered back, bumped against his desk, then suddenly sat down. On the floor.

Immediately becoming solid again, I started forward, but abruptly froze in place, held back by doubt, by their wide-eyed stares.

"Good God," Father whispered.

"I'm sorry," I said.

He gave himself a shake and inhaled deeply. Stood up. Stared some more. "Sorry for what, laddie?"

Then I seemed to see myself through his eyes. They were the only mirrors left to me. They showed an uncertain young man who might as well apologize for the color of his hair as for this new . . . ability. "Excellent question, sir."

He glanced at Elizabeth, who had gone very white, and touched her arm in a reassuring gesture. "You just surprised us, that's all. Nothing to apologize for." He put his hand out to me. I hesitantly came closer and took it. His grip was warm, encouraging. "You're solid enough, now."

Elizabeth took my other hand, but said nothing.

"Perhaps you could do that again," he suggested.

And so I did. Eyes shut so that I did not have to watch them fading into the fog, I repeated my action.

"He's so *cold*," said Elizabeth, her voice distant though I stood right next to her.

Then I let go of all ties to solidity. The pull of the earth, the feel of my clothes, the familiar constraints of my own body ceased to be. I held myself in place by thought alone.

"My God, he's vanished!" Father whispered.

*But I'm right here*, I protested, but of course, I had no mouth with which to speak. Opening my eyes now was something that could be exercised only in my mind, for in this state I was unable to see anything. Enough. I instantly resumed form again.

They yet held my hands and continued to do so. Father's grip increased somewhat, Elizabeth appeared too shocked yet to react.

"I vanished?" I asked. "Is it true? Father?"

He exhaled, turning it into a sort of laugh. "Clean away."

Oddly enough, after all the practicing I'd done, observing myself as I became more and more transparent until the gray fog engulfed everything, it had never occurred to me that I could become entirely invisible during the process.

"You're all right?" Elizabeth asked shakily.

"Yes."

"It doesn't hurt or anything?"

"Not at all."

"What does it feel like?"

"Sort of . . . like holding your breath, but not having to let it out for more air."

She thought that one over a bit. Father asked me to do it once more. I obliged, this time willing myself to travel some distance across the room before reappearing.

"Well-a-day," he said, borrowing one of my own expressions. "You said you floated, though?"

As the worst of the surprise was past, I was more willing to oblige their curiosity. This time I did not let the fog swallow me completely and held myself in a near-transparent state. Weightless, I drifted upward until I was right against the ceiling. I felt its restraining barrier, but knew I could seep through it to the floor above, if I wished. I did seriously consider it, but decided not to; tonight's performance was quite sufficient.

Growing gradually more solid, I sank to the floor.

They had a hundred questions for me, which I tried to answer, though some were unanswerable.

"I really don't know how it works," I said after nearly an hour of talk and a number of demonstrations that left me fatigued from the effort. "I don't know how it healed me. God knows, I wish I did."

"If it pleases God to keep the secret to Himself, then so be it," said Father. "You're whole again and that's what matters. We shall have to content ourselves with that and give thanks for it, for it seems a mighty gift."

"If not an alarming one," Elizabeth added.

"I'm very sorry for that."

Father laughed a little. "Don't see how it could possibly have been avoided, laddie. Have you any others we should know about?"

I shrugged. "I can't really say. That's why I was writing to Oliver tonight. I wanted him to pass a letter on to Nora for me. I've asked her a number of questions about what's happened to me, but it's going to be months before I hear from her . . . if she even answers."

"Why do you think she won't?"

"Because she made me forget so much."

"But from what you've told us of her, she strikes me as being a woman of honor."

"And overly secretive. She could have told me what to expect" I broke off and firmly smothered that tiresome lament. "I'm sorry. When it comes to Nora, I sometimes just don't know what to think. She's gifted me with a very fine double-edged sword, but failed to give instruction on how to safely wield it. If I'm not careful, I could injure myself or others."

"You're doing the best you can, laddie, no one can expect more than that. Anyway, there's no reason to think she won't answer. You might want to send more than one letter by different ships, though. Times are so unsettled that a single missive might not get through."

"Yes, I'd thought of that."

"Good. Get all your writing done tonight and I'll see that it's sent out for you tomorrow."

"Thank you, sir."

The words had hardly left my lips when the library doors were thrust open with a great deal of force. Mother stood on the threshold, glaring at the three of us turn on turn.

"What's going on here, Samuel?" she demanded.

"Nothing, as you see," he said, spreading his hands. "We were just talking."

"Talking? I'm sure you were." Despite the heavy powder coating her face, we could see that she was very flushed. "About what, may I ask?"

"Nothing important."

"Yet you still have to shut the doors?"

"We had no wish to disturb your card game."

"And the shutters?"

"There was a draft."

"You've an answer for everything except what's been asked, don't you?"

To that, Father made no reply. I wondered where Beldon had gotten to, as it looked to be one of those nights where his medical talents might be required.

"Jonathan Fonteyn."

I *hated* the contemptuous tone she always used when addressing me. "Yes, madam?" I whispered back.

"What were you talking about?"

"Nothing, really. I'm writing some letters, and Father promised to post them for me."

"And what are you doing here, Elizabeth? I'm sure that such conversation can't possibly be of any interest to you."

"I was just cutting some pens."

"No doubt, I can see the mess you've made all over the place. You can leave off with that. It's late and past time that you went upstairs."

Elizabeth pursed her lips and said nothing.

"Well, girl?"

"I shall be along shortly, Mother, as soon as I've cleaned up."

"You'll do as you're told and be along now."

"She's no longer a child, Marie," said Father.

"So you've noticed," Mother snarled back. "So you've *both* noticed! You think I'm blind to it? You think I don't see the three of you, the whispers, the looks you pass each other? It's disgusting."

"Marie, that's quite enough. You've made a mistake—"

"Yes, I'm always making mistakes. I'm always the one who's wrong, the one who imagines things. You'd like that, wouldn't you?"

Father said nothing. His face had become a hard, expressionless mask, as had my own, as had Elizabeth's. When Mother was in this kind of mood, no appeal to reason would work on her.

"The devoted father and his two *loving* children," she sneered. "God should strike the lot of you dead where you stand."

"Oh, Marie," sang out Mrs. Hardinbrook, coming up behind Mother. Her voice and manner were light and innocent of the situation she was walking into.

Mother's face underwent an immediate change. The Medusa abruptly transformed back to being a middle-aged matron, smooth of countenance and unblemished by vile thoughts.

"Yes, Deborah, what is it?" she cooed.

"We still have another hand to play out. I hope you will come back and finish it? Please say you will."

"Of course, of course. Do lead the way, my dear."

Mother shot us one last venomous glance before turning to follow Mrs. Hardinbrook. She pointedly left the doors open.

Father let out a pent-up breath and sat heavily in his chair. He didn't look well. "God," he said, putting his head in his hands. He rarely ever succumbed to the strain. Seeing him like this was enough to tear my heart in two. I went to him and knelt next to him, feeling dreadfully helpless and angry all at once.

Elizabeth crossed to the cabinet, poured out a portion of brandy into a cup, and took it to him. This time he had no objection to drink. When he'd finished, she poured one for herself and took it straight down as though it were water. I could have used one for myself, but knew better than to try.

"That Hardinbrook woman may be a clacking toad-eater, but she's a damned useful clacking toad-eater," Father finally said.

"I'll not say anything against her," I added.

Elizabeth looked past us to the open door, as if fearful that Mother might return. "What are we to do?" she asked Father.

"We needn't do anything. The fit will pass and she'll be all right. She won't remember any of this tomorrow."

She put down her cup and stood before him. "She's getting worse, Father. The things she said about me and Jonathan are bad enough, but to include you in with her filthy accusations is beyond endurance."

"What would you have me do?" he asked, all subdued.

She dropped her eyes.

"I could possibly send her away somewhere, but what good would come of it? She's all right here most of the time, and Beldon and his sister usually keep her in hand. I'm sorry for what she's doing to you two—"

"And to yourself, Father," I said.

He shrugged, as though his own pain was of no consequence. "I am sorry for that and if I could stop it, I would."

"Why can't you send her away?" Elizabeth murmured, again not looking at him.

"Because I made a promise when I married her. I promised to take care of her. Always."

"But she's getting more impossible every day. She's getting worse."

"And would become much worse if sent away. It's the same as if she were ill in bed with a fever. The fever she suffers from is in her mind rather than her body, but the principle is the same. She needs care, and it is my responsibility to see that she has it. For the sake of the promise I made those years ago and for the memory of the love we once had, it is my chosen duty. I will not dishonor myself by ignoring that duty just because it has become unpleasant."

"And what are we to do, then?"

"I have no answer for you, daughter. I'd rather hoped you'd give me one."

Elizabeth raised her head. She was blushing right to the roots of her hair. "I think I understand you, sir."

He lightly touched her hand. "I thought that you would. What about you, laddie?"

"We all have our duty, sir. I will not shirk mine."

"Good."

"But . . ."

"Yes?"

"If now and then, when we get filled up with it, would you mind very much if we complained a bit?"

He laughed. Some of the deeper lines lifted slightly. "Not at all. That is, if you don't mind my joining you."

It was late, and the house was very silent. I'd opened the shutters again to enjoy the air. It was damp and heavy with the sea smell, but clean. A draft stirred up the slivers of quill and feathers from Elizabeth's abandoned work. I put the finished pens in the cup of shot and used the edge of one packet of finished letters to sweep the leavings off the desk and into one hand. Some of the stuff dropped onto the floor, but the rest I threw out a window. My letters, sealed and addressed, I placed under the shot cup where Father might easily find them. There was a good four months' wait ahead of me—more likely six with winter coming on and slowing the passage of shipping—before I could even begin to look for a reply from either Nora or Oliver.

I had a hope, and no more than a hope, that once Nora knew of my situation she would answer by coming herself. Though to think that she'd cross all the way from England during the worst months of weather was rather a lot to expect of her. Not only was the risk of a winter crossing very bad, but there was also her special condition to consider. Confined to whatever sanctuary she could manage during the day was limiting enough, but the question of how she could feed herself during the voyage was not one I could readily answer, nor did I care to think on it much.

Mine was a fool's dream, though. She would not come; it was an impossible expectation. A letter. I would gladly settle for a letter.

But six months . . . damnation, that was an *eternity*.

My candle had burned low. With everyone asleep and the need to pretend its necessity removed, I blew it out. The gentle silver light of the night sky advanced into the room. It seemed to carry a world of scents to me: earth and plant, wood smoke and stable, sea and shoreline.

Time to sup.

# CHAPTER 2

Up in my room, I quietly changed into clothes more suitable for an outdoor excursion: dark coat, waistcoat, and breeches, my plainest shirt, simplest neckcloth, and the older of my two pairs of riding boots. Not that I was planning to give Rolly any exercise—I'd save that pleasure for tomorrow night—but boots were more practical for roaming the countryside than shoes.

Not that I planned to do much walking, either.

Leaving my other clothes on the bed for Jericho to see to in the morning, I also left him a note explaining my absence. He could talk to Elizabeth if he wanted more details.

I opened the window, intent on using it for my egress from the house, then had second thoughts, remembering my promise to Jericho to be more discreet. No one was in sight down in the yard, but that meant nothing. Though the prospect seemed unlikely, anyone wishing to spy on me could hide himself easily enough, even from my improved vision. I might be able to see as well in the dark as others could during the day, but I had yet to learn how to see through things. There were any number of trees, bushes, and buildings offering protection for a determined observer of demon-possessed mortals.

Good lord, but I hoped Jericho had successfully repressed *that* gossip. Not wishing to add to it, I stood well back from the window before relinquishing my hold on the physical and floating out. Briefly, I sensed the frame loom around me, then felt the tug of the wind drawing me forth into the open sky.

If not for my earlier practice before Father and Elizabeth, I might have found this experience of traveling blind to be extremely confusing. Indeed, to suddenly be without a body in the conventional definition, one might expect to maintain a certain level of confusion for some goodly length of time before finally mastering such an unusual sensation. I'd adapted remarkably quickly to it, though, and suspected that my casual assumption of this ability to be linked to the more obvious inner changes. While a caterpillar has no understanding of flight, after its metamorphosis into a butterfly it has no difficulty taking to the air. A similar gift of understanding must have somehow slipped into my being during my own metamorphosis in the grave.

Drifting high and far from the house, I very, very gradually assumed enough solidity to allow me to see exactly where I'd gone. As this action lent weight to my form, I lost some height, but not much. I held in place, arms spread wide like wings, and looked in wonder at the gray land below. It reminded me of the time Oliver and I had climbed to the roof of one of the buildings in Cambridge to take in the view. To ourselves, we seemed as aloof as gods from the small people and animals that crept about on the miserable ground beneath us, but in the end could not escape the fact that our means of rising above them, our lonely tower, tied us just as firmly to earth. Now I had no ties at all, except for those of memory, which could easily be set aside. For now, I was a bird or a cloud, with no concern for anything but to enjoy this strange freedom for its own sake.

I soared above the tallest trees, or dipped down to rush between their boughs like a hunting hawk, then down still more to coast just above the fields and pastures. Any wall or fence that presented itself I merely skipped over, smoother and faster than any jump I'd made while on Rolly's back.

Ah, but most pleasures have their price, and as with any exercise, I found myself growing weary for want of refreshment. A week ago, I might have satisfied my need with wine and a meat pie, but a week ago I was not able to fly. As my means of travel had changed, so had the demands and tastes of my appetite.

So far, the army had not completely stripped us of our stock. Some of our horses were pastured close to the house, and those were the ones I usually fed upon. We also had cattle, but I preferred horses, as they were groomed regularly and thus much cleaner.

I took on more substance to see better and found I'd traveled well to the south and had to circle back again. Just within sight of the house, I swooped low and solidified, my feet touching lightly down on the cropped grass of a small field. The horses dozing at the other end paid me no notice, but their ears flicked in my direction as I walked toward them. The interest became more marked when I reached into a pocket and pulled forth a small apple. Holding it high so they could see it, all I had to do was wait.

Eventually, Desdemona, who had a greedy temperament, decided that she deserved the bribe more than the others and ambled over to take it. While she crunched away on the apple, I got hold of her halter and soothed and stroked her until she went very still.

The smooth warmth of her silken coat proclaimed that she was well-cared for and in fine health. What little blood I needed to maintain my own strength she could easily spare with no ill effect. I knelt and felt out one of the surface veins in her near foreleg, brushing at it with eager fingers. My belly was twisting in a most pleasurable way, anticipating what was to come. My mouth and tongue were dry, but that would soon be amended.

The corner teeth in my upper jaw had grown longer than any of the others and tilted slightly outward. An odd sensation, that, but I quite liked it. I liked it even better when I bent over the vein and used them to gently and quickly cut through the intervening flesh.

God, but that rush of red heat was wonderful. It rolled right through me, sating, satisfying, comforting, sweeping away all the dark doubts I'd harbored. This was food in its purest form, as basic as a mother's milk. How like a suckling infant I felt, too, drinking in incredible, reviving nourishment such as I'd never known before. Consciously known, that is. Our memories of babyhood, of nursing, of that last physical link we have to our mother's is inevitably severed as we grow older, but the craving and need for fulfillment is ever with us. Others might strive their whole lives to recover that sweet estate in one form or another, but my own endeavors had apparently ended, if this serene gratification was anything to judge by.

The wounds I'd made were small, and the blood flow gradually ceased. I lapped up the last of it and drew away, giving Desdemona a reassuring pat and a second apple from another pocket. As though nothing at all had happened or was amiss, her velvet lips plucked up the fruit and she quickly disposed of it as I let myself grow lighter and drifted out of the pasture.

I went solid again on the other side of the fence, leaning on it and breathing in the early morning air. Dawn was not very far off, but I had more than enough time to get to the old barn before the rising sun became a problem.

I left the fence and struck out over the fields. Not that the novelty of flying had worn off, but I was finding the steady march enjoyable for its own sake. It also allowed me to exercise my improved senses, as they were always so muffled when I ceased to be corporeal. Eyes and ears open, I drank in sights and sounds as eagerly as I'd drunk in Desdemona's blood, for I craved nourishment for my mind as much as for my body.

Damp grass and leaves underfoot, night birds making their final calls to one another and day birds sleepily rousing themselves, the wind cool on my face, it was as though I were noticing it all afresh, like a newborn child. But unlike that imaginary babe, I could identify and appreciate it all. Science, philosophy or magic, whatever force had brought me back from the grave had taught me to value the beauties of the world anew. Things that I'd once dismissed as commonplace now caught my notice; the graceful shape of a branch or the soft pattern of moss on a rock. I wanted to see and touch everything, to know and understand all. I'd been given a second chance to do so; I would not waste it.

Though it was unlikely I'd run into an inconvenient sentry here on my own land, I took care not to make too much noise. I'd be able to deal with any trouble easily enough, but there was no point attracting it in the first place.

The worries I'd confided earlier to Elizabeth came back to me now, for they were not without foundation. The Hessian troops so recently thrust upon us by the rebellion were yet here and seeking shelter in every possible hovel. Some were lodged in private homes or had taken over the churches and inns and, along with the English soldiers, were stripping the Island of all stock and produce. We'd mostly been spared thus far, but were expecting the worst. Unless General Howe finally decided to take his men and pursue Washington's rabble across the water to Manhattan Island, there wouldn't be much left for the coming winter.

Of the battle that had taken place last month between those two commanders we'd heard many conflicting tales and hardly knew which to believe. The one common thread woven into them all had to do with the horrific brutality of the Hessians. Their own officers had been shocked by their vicious behavior. Stories came to us of surrendering rebels receiving no quarter, even sorely wounded men were heartlessly run through by bayonets, or shot, or clubbed to death by musket stocks.

My own contact with them had not been so violent. Indeed, I was treated with a degree of respect by some of the ones staying in Glenbriar for my assistance in capturing two rebels not long past. The fact that I'd later been instrumental in helping the rebels get away had happily escaped notice, so far. But this advantage was small and limited only to those who knew me. It was a wise man who stayed out of their way altogether.

The barn stood out from the shelter of some trees, though ivy had taken it over and blurred its lines. There had been a stormy night since I'd last been here, and my footprints in the dirt inside the doorway were gone, though the ones deeper within remained. I followed these in to a far corner where a shoulder-high partition had been built out from the wall to make a dim stable.The floor here also retained the marks of my previous occupancy. I now added to them, pacing slowly up and down, up and down, waiting for the sun to arrive.

If I hurried, I still had time to hurtle through the sky and make it back to my own room before it was too late. The safety of the house was certainly more attractive to me than spending the day sprawled in this filthy barn, but the comfort I should have drawn from my bed had eluded me since my return. Instead of rest and sleep, I endured endless hours of bad dreams and foul dreads which served only to remind me of things I'd rather forget. These bouts of darkness left me weary to the bone upon awakening; sometimes it was hours before I could fully shake it from my mind.

And with each passing day and emerging night, I was growing more and more *tired*. Though I could often dismiss it awhile—especially after feeding—I was never truly without it. In odd moments here and there, the weariness dragged at me, as though the earth were trying to draw me back into itself once more, to return me to the grave.

Nora, if I could trust my memory, had not suffered from such continual exhaustion. Occasionally she'd fall prey to a fit of melancholia, but it never lasted long, particularly when we were together. But these instances were hardly different than what I'd seen in others and in myself at the time, brief and transient. My present state was nearly constant.

Dear God, but I needed *rest*.

The events of the evening seemed to crowd one atop the other like bees in a hive. Buzzing and darting and often imparting a sting or two, I knew I was destined to have a raw time of it for the day. Before my change, such a state of mind had always deprived me of sleep; it would be no different now.

I sat in the darkest corner of the stall and grimly waited for the sun to roll above the horizon.

Soon. Just another moment or two. My limbs were already growing sluggish. No sense in letting myself freeze for the day in what would soon become an uncomfortable posture, I lay flat, eyes shut, waiting . . .

. . . waiting.

I sat up, certain that I'd heard something, then stopped, cold as a stone.

Utter confusion seized me. I could not move or think for some moments, not because of the approaching sunrise, but out of pure shock and disorientation.

*I was no longer in the barn.*

That bit of realization was the only fact to impress itself upon my mind. Like an unwelcome lodger, it remained there, crowding out all other thoughts. I wasted much time trying to understand what had happened to me. In one instant I'd been stretched out for the day on the hard floor, and the next I was suddenly on the grass under an open sky.

*Someone must have moved me*, I thought. Then I abruptly knew that I had slept the day through. It was happily anticipated sunset, not a dreaded sunrise to which I'd awakened.

After so many days without it, I'd finally achieved it. *Rest*. No bad dreams, no dreams at all, only sweet oblivion.

*Thank God*.

But how had I come to be outside the barn? Perhaps Jericho had come by to check on me and had taken it into his head to shift my location, though why he would do such a thing was beyond imagining. Where—?

Brain working again now that the surprise had passed, I stood and brushed myself off and looked around. I had heard something, and the noise was still with me. Human noise, human speech.

German speech, fast and for the most part unintelligible to me.

Hessians. Damnation. The Hessians had arrived.

Now it seemed obvious that they had been the ones who had moved me from the barn, and, irksome as it might be, I'd have to have words with them, or at least with their commander. Hopefully, he would know more of English than I did of German, and I could righteously demand an answer to why they were trespassing on my land.

Suffused with anger at their intrusion, I glared around and immediately spotted a sentry. I'd been taken to one side of the yard next to the barn, the outer wall of that structure being on my right. The man stood poised at the far corner, peering around it to what I concluded was some activity that did not directly affect him, but held his extreme interest. I stalked up and dropped a heavy hand on his shoulder.

"*Entschuldigen Sie. Your commander, where is he?*"

Alas, I discovered that what my tutor, Rapelji, had taught me was true: for every action, there is an equal and opposite reaction. My brusk though friendly greeting was violently met. The man whipped around, stared at me all wild-eyed, then let forth with as bloodcurdling a shriek as had ever been my misfortune to hear. Before I could do or say aught else, he backed away, his mouth hanging open. Though he'd lost breath for further screams, he was yet capable of an awful gasping and gagging. I thought he was having some sort of fit and stepped toward him, reaching out.

"*Nein! Nein!*" came his hoarse reaction as he backed off even farther.

He seemed to be perceiving me as some sort of threat. Before I could make any attempt to reassure him otherwise, he rushed around the corner of the barn, yelling incoherently.

Damnation again. I went after him, rounding the corner—and got my second shock of the evening as I was met by a phalanx of nervous-looking Hessians with their muskets all leveled and pointing at me. Instantly, I threw my hands high.

"*Freund!*" I squeaked. "*Ich bin ein Freund! Freund!*" The words for "Don't shoot" were unfortunately not a part of my limited German vocabulary.

My babbling gave them pause, though, for those first few critical seconds and they did *not* turn me into a sieve with their musket balls.

While they hesitated, I added, "*Where is your commander?*"

*That* struck a nerve. They were apparently disciplined enough to cleave to the military virtue of passing any difficult decision over to a higher authority. Some of them wavered, relaxing their tight hold on their weapons and looking to their left for guidance. Not turning my head from them, I let my eyes travel in that direction. There were several lighted lanterns about, making no difference to my vision, but helpful to their own. Standing in one such puddle of light in the doorway of the barn was a stocky man in an officer's florid uniform. I was not familiar with the trappings of Germanic rank—he could have been a lieutenant or a general for all I knew—but hopefully he would take charge now and persuade his men to calmness.

"*Good evening, sir,*" I said, trying to steady my voice.

He looked me up and down as though I were some sort of lunatic on display in a town marketplace and made no reply.

"*My name is Barrett. I live here.*"

His brows lowered and his full lips pushed out into a truly terrifying pout.

"*This is my land,*" I clarified.

The soldier that I'd first encountered hesitantly stepped forward and saluted. The smartness of the gesture was somewhat diluted by his twisting around to keep me in sight. The officer fixed his eyes on him and gave a brief, guttural acknowledgment, apparently permission to speak. There followed a quick burst of wordage, accompanied by gestures, as the fellow accounted for himself. He pointed at me quite a lot, and at the interior of the barn

*Oh, dear.* Like the sunrise I'd missed, the reason for all the uproar suddenly dawned in my brain. Oh, dear, oh, dear, and damnation again and again and . . .

"*You!*" The officer was addressing me. "*Come here.*"

Experimentally, I lowered my arms. His men did not fire. I walked over slowly, trusting that they feared him more than me. When close enough, I made a formal bow and reintroduced myself, this time with more dignity and less haste, and inquired after his own identity.

"Muller," he said, adding in something about his rank that was too quickly spoken for me to catch. He gave a curt sketch of a bow, then jerked ramrod straight, the better to look down his nose at me.

I asked him, as politely as I could, why he was here.

He countered with the same question.

I repeated that this was my land, that I lived here.

"*You live in a—*"

"*Pardon?*" I did not know the last word.

He pointed meaningfully at the barn.

I looked insulted and told him that my house was elsewhere on the property.

"*Why were you in the barn?*" he demanded.

My explanation that I'd had a long day of walking and had stopped for a rest did not sit well with him.

"*He was dead,*" put in my former guard, somewhat fearfully.

"*Asleep,*" I corrected firmly, keeping a bland face.

"*Dead,*" the man argued back.

I rolled my eyes and shrugged, trying to give the impression that the man had lost his senses. Few of the other men were willing to give up what must have been a vivid first impression of me, either. Several nodded agreement with the guard and made surreptitious gestures with one hand that supposedly protected them against the evil eye. These may have been the very ones who had first entered the barn and found my seemingly lifeless corpse, probably not the first they'd encountered in their military ventures, but very certainly the first that had ever revived.

"*Why are you here, sir?*" I asked the officer.

But he was not to be distracted into going on the defensive and demanded a further accounting to justify my own presence.

"*My German is poor, sir. Do you speak the English?*"

"*Nein,*" he said flatly, as though I'd insulted him.

"*The French?*"

"*Nein.*" This time it was a sneer.

Sighing, I decided to forgo asking after his skill at Italian or Latin, then an idea flashed up. *"Do you know Lieutenant Nash of the British? He is my friend."* Well, that was stretching things a bit, but perhaps a familiar name might improve this fellow's disposition.

"*Nein. What are you doing here?*"

I repeated myself.

"*He was dead*," insisted the guard.

The other men nodded.

The officer glared at him.

"*It's true! We found his—*"

Again, I had no understanding of this last word, but could guess that it meant "corpse" or "body." His gestures were eloquent as the man babbled on, anxious to prove his case that I was, indeed, deceased. His allies offered agreement whenever he paused for breath, then Muller had enough and cut him off with a sharp order. He was very good at glaring, and liberally demonstrated this talent to us all. The men came to attention for him, but it was uneasily held by the guard's allies. When things were quiet again, Muller growled at the guard, who saluted and went into the darkness of the barn.

When he emerged a moment later, he had another man with him, a civilian. The poor fellow's hands were bound and there was a rough sack over his head, but I instantly recognized him.

"Jericho! What in God's name have they done to you?"

Heedless now of their threat, I rushed over to him and tore away the sack. Jericho's face was covered with an uncharacteristic sheen of sweat, and he was very white around the pupils. His lip was split, and a bad bruise was swelling one eye shut. His clothes were covered with dust and torn, and his movements were slow, silent and plaintive indication of his ill treatment.

I rounded on Muller, so white-hot with outrage that I was unable to speak. Apparently my expression was eloquent enough, for this stone of a man actually flinched before recovering himself.

"Who did this?" I snarled, forgetting myself and using English, but Muller seemed to understand my meaning.

"Keiller," he said to the guard.

Keiller responded with another rapid explanation. I didn't bother to try following it, having no interest in excuses. Instead, I found my penknife and cut away Jericho's bonds.

"Are you badly hurt?"

"I shall be able to walk home," he said. "And if not that, then I shall certainly crawl."

"What happened?"

He rubbed his wrists. His hands were shaking. He was shaking all over.

"You came out to check on me, is that it?" I prompted.

He nodded. "It was getting on to dark. I was waiting for you to wake up when they came. They . . ." He gulped, clearing his throat. "Upon finding a Negro man with a dead white man, they concluded that I had killed you."

"Oh, my God."

"They were . . . their reaction was not gentlemanly. I . . . they were—" He was swaying on his feet.

"Sit down, man," I said taking his arm.

"*No*. Not before them, I won't." He straightened with a glare every bit as formidable as Muller's. "They were going to hang me, Mr. Jonathan. Kept waving a noose under my nose and laughing. Perhaps it might not have happened, but I am most pleased that you woke up when you did."

I stared at him, a great knot in my throat, once more at a loss for words. The situation was all but beyond speech, yet somehow I found it and turned it upon Muller.

"You barbaric son of a whore" I began. Muller may not have understood my words, but he could make sense of my tone well enough.

"Mr. Jonathan, now is not the time to antagonize the man," Jericho cautioned.

"He and his lot should be flogged for what they've done to you."

"Agreed, sir, but presently they have the numerical advantage."

I had more, much more, invective in me, but Jericho's reasoning had penetrated the anger fogging my thoughts. When I was once more my own master, I saw that the best course of action was for us both to get away as quickly as possible. Muller would doubtless object, but that was something that could be easily overcome.

*"Herr Muller, we are going home now."* I stated this as inarguably as possible, looking directly into his eyes. *"You will excuse us."* It was very polite, despite my hot feelings, but polite German was all I had. Fortunately, it served. I did not know Muller well enough to be able to read any subtle changes in his otherwise fierce expression, but my influence must have worked. He made no objection when I put a supportive arm around Jericho and led him away. His men, taking this as assent, parted before us. Some were very anxious to keep a goodly distance.

"By God, this is enough to turn me into a rebel myself," I growled as we left them behind.

"I would not recommend it, sir."

"Damnation to the bastards. Why not?"

"Because if this is how our friends treat us, how much worse might we receive from our enemies?"

"I'm so sorry, Jericho. This is my fault."

"Hardly, Mr. Jonathan." He paused in his walk, gasping a bit. "May I ask to simply lean on your arm, sir? I fear your well-intentioned assistance is somewhat painful to my ribs."

I let go of him and offered to run ahead and fetch the carriage and Dr.Beldon, but Jericho insisted that we could be home by the time I'd returned with help, and so it proved. With him holding onto me for balance, we hobbled up one of the graveled paths to the house. When we were close enough, my shouts brought forth one of the stable lads and all of the dogs. The noise attracted more people, more help, and finally Dr. Beldon arrived to assume his duties as a physician. I was very glad to turn the responsibilities of caretaking over to him.

"Jonathan?" My father came striding over even as Beldon supervised Jericho's removal into the house for treatment. "What in God's name is going on?"

After several unavoidable repetitions as more of the household came by to listen, I concluded my story to Father in the library. He understood from Elizabeth the purpose of my visit to the barn, and neither of them offered any objection to my slightly expurgated version of the facts. The important issue for us was that there were unwelcome Hessian soldiers squatting on our land.

"Beasts," said Elizabeth, in reference to Jericho's beating.

"You shouldn't have been out there to start with," said Mother, sniffing. "Perhaps next time you'll stay home."

Since her comment had added nothing of merit to the conversation, I readily ignored it, as did everyone else. Perhaps we'd gotten used to them after all this time, making the task easier.

"Samuel, tomorrow you will immediately go and seek recourse about having them removed from the property," she said. "This is intolerable. Next thing you know they'll be begging for food at our very door."

"It's more likely that they shall simply take it where it stands in the fields," he said.

"Then you will find a way to prevent that. They're here to fight the rebels, not steal from the King's loyal subjects. If they want food, they can take it from the seditionists but not from us."

"I'll do what I can, Marie."

"See to it." She jerked her chin up in a most insufferable manner, but my father suffered it. Argument with his wife was both aggravating and futile, so once more he refrained from doing so. She turned a cold eye on me. "And this time you will help him, Jonathan Fonteyn. You've no illness or injury to excuse you from an honest day's work anymore. This constant shirking is to end. I didn't spend all that money on your education for you to lie about the place doing nothing. What would people think?"

I considered that other people would hardly find my apparent inactivity to be in the least interesting, but kept that opinion to myself. "I'll do what I can, madam," I said, assuming Father's acquiescence. It seemed the wisest course.

Her expression was such as to indicate she found my response to be irritating, but not so much so as to upbraid me for it.

Dr. Beldon came in just then. "Your man is going to be all right, Mr. Barrett," he told me. "There's some extensive bruising and a couple of cracked ribs. He is in some discomfort and will be for some time, but he should eventually make a full recovery."

"Thank heaven for that. And thank you for your kind help, Doctor."

"To be sure, I am only too happy to—"

"That's another mistake that should be corrected," Mother interrupted.

Beldon cut himself short. He'd had much practice at it in her company.

The corners of her mouth turned down more deeply than usual as she looked at me. "If you'd sold that creature off and hired a proper English servant as I'd told you to do years ago, none of this would have happened."

I took in a sharp breath and glanced at Father. He shook his head ever so slightly. That particular conflict had long been put to rest; Mother was talking only to hear the sound of her own voice. She was overly fond of it, I judged.

"Well," said Father, standing up. "There's naught to be done about any of this tonight, so let's try to forget about it for a few hours. Marie, would you like to partner me at cards against the doctor and Mrs. Hardinbrook?"

Good God, but he *was* anxious to distract her to make such a proposal.

"Not yet, Samuel. I've some news of my own to impart."

He tried to put on a friendly, interested face, and almost succeeded. Mother's idea of news often turned out to be disappointingly trivial.

"I received a letter today from one of my cousins in Philadelphia. She says that conditions there are perfectly horrifying. The streets are awash with traitors, and their treatment of loyal subjects is a disgrace. She has wisely accepted my invitation to stay here until things are put right again."

"Really?" said Father, sounding a touch faint. "Which cousin might that be?"

"Cousin Anne Fonteyn, of course," she said impatiently, as though Father should have somehow divined her thoughts and known.

"Cousin Anne?"

"Yes, Father's youngest brother's daughter. You *know* her."

"Yes, I seem to recall . . ."

"Oh, for heaven's sake, Samuel, if you don't remember her, then say so, I can't abide it when you dither like that."

Father's expression grew harder, but he did not give in to his emotions.

Elizabeth's eyes met mine, silently communicating her anger and sympathy for his plight. I could almost hear her previous night's refrain: *she's getting worse*. To some extent I could agree with her, but could not help thinking that Mother was not worsening, only growing less inhibited in expressing her casual cruelties. It was when those expressions were questioned that she became worse.

"They'll be here any time, now, I'm sure."

"They?" asked Father.

"She said she was not traveling alone, as it's much too dangerous. I expect she'll have some servants with her. The other cousins are choosing to remain in the city."

*Thanks be to God for his mercy*, I thought.

"I don't want her to think that we're a tribe of uncivilized savages. All will have to be in readiness for her arrival, including getting rid of those soldiers." She made them sound no more threatening than an inconveniently placed wasp nest to be smoked out by one of the groundsmen. "I won't have them running about as though they owned the place. What would people think?"

"For a woman with such keen concern over the opinions of others, one would assume she'd have an equal regard for those of her own family," I later confided to Elizabeth when everyone had gone.

"Oh, bother it, Jonathan. The woman has no regard for anyone but herself." Elizabeth had taken her favorite chair near the settee. She'd found a piece of string somewhere and endlessly curled and uncurled it around her fingers.

"The woman?"

Elizabeth paused to wearily rub the back of her neck. "I'll call her 'Mother' to her face, but don't expect me to maintain any pretense of affection in private. She's no mother to me beyond the fact that I lived in her womb for some months before finally escaping."

"Good God!"

"No need to be so shocked, little brother, for have you not had the same thoughts yourself? I see that you have."

"Perhaps not so crudely put—"

"I know and I'm sorry, but that woman angers me so. Were a stranger on the lane to treat me as she does, I'd have nothing more to do with her, yet we have to put up with it day after day after day, and it's far more dreadful for poor Father." She twined the string around one finger tightly, turning the unadorned remainder of her flesh quite red from the constriction.

"At least he's able to find some solace with Mrs. Montagu. I think that's why he proposed an early card game."

"Yes, get the evening's torture out of the way so he's free to leave. I'm glad he has Mrs. Montagu; she must be of considerable comfort to him. I wish she could be our mother instead. In a way she was for all those years that that woman lived away from us. But she's Father's solace, not ours. I wish I could find some for myself." She unwrapped her finger and studied the ridges the string had impressed into her flesh.

"What do you mean? Take a lover?" I all but whispered the last word.

"Take a . . ." Her mouth sagged. "Oh heavens, Jonathan, of course not. What are you thinking?"

My face went hot. "That's the problem, I wasn't. Please forgive me."

She thought about it a while. "No need, I can see where you came up with that, and were I that sort of woman, I might consider it, but since I'm not, I shan't."

"But Mrs. Montagu is a perfectly respectable lady," I protested.

"Of independent means and with her own house, things which are denied me. What were you thinking this time?"

"If I answered that, I should be repeating myself," I said glumly.

She laughed again, as I'd hoped she would, but sobered after a bit. "It's just not fair. Men can follow all sorts of interesting pursuits, but women must be satisfied with babies and running the house and doing what other people tell them."

"Were you a man, what would you do?"

"Want to turn back into a woman, but as a woman, I might like to go to Cambridge as you did. I could study law or medicine, but perhaps not the clergy, as the work is much too hard: sermons every week, tea parties, and having to be nice to everyone, including people like *her*."

Mother. "What makes you think law or medicine is any less toilsome?"

"It's not, I'm sure, but I've a better head for it. I see how Father enjoys what he does; he plows through his law books like a farmer in a field and he's brilliant at it. I've also watched Dr. Beldon. He may play the toady for a place at table here, but he's a very good physician. I wonder why he doesn't set up his own household; he could easily support himself."

"It's too much to do. If he's busy running his own house, he might not have time for his practice."

"Then he should marry. There must be some woman out there who enjoys housework."

"I hardly think that wedlock is anything he'd want to try." I leaned back on the settee and put my feet up on the arm of Elizabeth's chair. "For a man of his nature, he's better off simply hiring a housekeeper."

"Has he been any problem to you lately?"

"Not at all. He's a gentleman."

"And extremely fond of you."

"I'm aware of that, dear sister. However, it is not within me to return his regard in a like manner. He understands that."

"It's all rather sad, isn't it?"

"I suppose it is."

"Your boots want a polish," she said after a moment's idle study, having apparently forgotten her length of string along with Dr. Beldon.

"Another time." Head cradled back in my clasped hands, I shut my eyes and sighed with vast contentment. "It worked, y'know."

"What worked?"

"Your idea about my sleeping in the barn."

"Really? With all the excitement about the Hessians, I forgot to ask. No bad dreams?"

"Not a one. I had no sense at all of the passage of the day—that's what left me so confused, else I might have handled things differently when I woke up."

"That's wonderful, but what will you do tonight? You can't go back to the barn."

"No, I can't, but the experiment was a success, and from that point perhaps I may determine why it was successful. What quality is there about the barn that allowed me to find true rest?"

"Darkness?" she suggested.

"I have that up in my room."

"Fresh air? I know there's none once Jericho closes the shutters and windows and puts up the blankets."

"That's something to consider. I could try sleeping in the basement today, plenty of air there every time the door opens. On the other hand, I do not breathe regularly, so why should I require fresh air, particularly when I am in a state that so perfectly imitates death?"

She tapped one of my ankles. I opened my eyes. Her own were sparkling with intense thought. "Consider this: where would you be had you not come back to us?"

"Out in the barn?"

"No! I mean where would you be if you hadn't come back? If you were still—"

Ugh. I hated to think about that.

She answered for me. "You'd be in your grave. In the *ground*."

"My body only, I should hope and pray that my soul might be more happily lodged in heaven."

"Exactly. But both your body and soul have returned to the earth. Might we consider that between your death and return that some sort of compromise is required?"

"What are you leading to?"

"Well, just look at it. The only time you obtained any rest has been in the barn, on the *bare earth* of the barn."

"Surely you're not asking me to return to my grave?" I found this idea to be not just repugnant, but enough to make my bones go all watery.

"Certainly not!"

"Then—oh, yes, I think I perceive it now. You're recommending that I simply sleep on the ground, preferably in some sheltered, sunless area."

"I—"

"But I've already proposed to sleep in the basement."

"With the scullery boy tripping over you and getting a fright like those Hessians? No, I'm thinking that you might take a quantity of earth with you when you go to bed this morning."

"Take the grave with me instead of me going to the grave? Oh, that makes lots of sense."

"It's worth a try. Why don't you like it?"

"Because the idea of pouring a bucketful of earth onto the fresh, clean sheets of my bed and then cheerfully wallowing in it for the day is hardly appealing."

"Jonathan, you ass, put it in a sack or something first."

"Oh. Well, I would have thought of that eventually."

Her mouth curled to one side, indicating that she didn't quite believe me.

"I'll think about it," I promised, which satisfied her, though her mouth remained twisted, albeit for a different reason.

"Move your boots, would you? You stepped in something awful and I'm tired of smelling it."

I shifted my feet from her chair arm and sat up. "So you don't think I should sleep in the basement?"

"Only if you insist. You'd have to have a little 'talk' with Mrs. Nooth, though, perhaps with the whole kitchen staff."

"No, thank you. The last time I did so much 'talking' I got a wretched headache for my trouble." Headache . . . that reminded me of something. "Do you know anything about this cousin who's about to inflict herself upon us?"It occurred to me that out of self-protection I might have to exert a little influence over her when she arrived.

Elizabeth chuckled. "I talked to Mrs. Hardinbrook about her—or rather she approached and talked to me. She hardly ever does that unless she wants to inform me of some glowing virtue about her dear brother that I may have overlooked in the last three years."

"What did she say about the cousin?"

"Only general pleasantries of how *nice* it will be to have fresh company, but might it not be just a *little* bit crowded? She does like to clack on, you know, but it was a touch forced this time. I can only conclude that she's worried her position as the household's chief toad-eater is about to be usurped."

"Yes, and if it does get too crowded, Mother will choose blood kin over her best friend."

"Otherwise, what *would* people think?" Elizabeth did a credible, if supremely unflattering imitation of Mother's favorite worry.

"Perhaps we may be sincere in our welcome of Cousin Anne, then. Unless she turns out to be as bad as Mrs. Hardinbrook . . . or worse."

"That would take a bit of effort. Anne may share our Fonteyn blood, but please God, perhaps she's been spared the Fonteyn temperament."

"Amen to that," I said fervently.

# CHAPTER
# 3

"Samuel, have you done anything about those soldiers on our land?" Mother demanded as she'd done every night at dinner for nearly two weeks.

"I have."

"And what of it?"

"The situation is under the most urgent scrutiny."

Not quite a lie, but hardly the truth, which Father had confided to me sometime ago. The Hessians currently sheltering in the old barn at the edge of our property would remain there until further notice. Without permission or even a hint of payment, they'd made themselves at home by felling trees and slaughtering some of our cattle that had strayed too close to their sentries. Father's protests to their commanders were politely accepted, and he expected them to be just as politely ignored. It looked to be a long winter ahead for us all.

"I want them out of there as soon as possible. We'll all be murdered in our beds and it shall be your fault."

Thus spoke Mother, and Father had the great good sense not to respond to her statement. Since I was in the next room (trying to read) and alone, I was allowed the luxury of privately making a face and shaking my head.

"Oh, but we are very safe, Marie," said Mrs. Hardinbrook. "I must confess that until Lord Howe landed I had my worries, but now that his brave men are all over the Island—"

"Like ants on a corpse," muttered her brother.

"Really, Theophilous! We *are* eating!"

"My apologies, sister, but in case you haven't noticed, it is those so-called brave men who are causing Mrs. Barrett so much distress."

"Well, of *course* there are bound to be *some* soldiers who may behave in a less than honorable manner, but I'm sure their officers keep them in line."

"I think you'll find the officers are quite as bad. And as for those Hessian troops" He broke off as though realizing that a detailed description of their atrocities might prove to be more offensive than instructive.

"They *are* foreigners, after all," said Mrs. Hardinbrook. "What do you expect?"

Like Father, Beldon chose not to provide an answer.

Mother was quick to step in where he had fallen back. "To be treated with the respect that is due to any loyal subject of the King."

"Amen to that," enthused Mrs. Hardinbrook. "Perhaps, Theophilous, you have not had the chance to meet some of the nicer officers, and therefore you've gotten a poor impression of our defenders."

"I've met enough to know that being an officer does not mean that the fellow is automatically a gentleman. My God, Deborah, if you'd seen what had happened to that poor Bradford girl this morning—even the beasts in the wild do not violate their young with such—"

"*Dr. Beldon.*" My mother's voice came down like a hammer. "I will not tolerate such talk at my table."

An awkward silence followed—a frequent occurrence in this house—then came the sound of a chair scraping over the floor as Beldon stood.

"Forgive me, Mrs. Barrett. I forgot myself and let my instincts as a physician overcome my manners. You are quite right to remind me."

It was humbly spoken and apparently enough to appease Mother. Beldon next excused himself, and I heard the dining room door open and close.

"As I was saying, Samuel . . ." she resumed.

But I stopped listening when Beldon walked into the library, his face flushed and hands twitching. He gave a slight jump when he saw me sprawled in my usual spot on the settee, mumbled something about not wishing to intrude, and turned to leave.

"No, it's all right, I should greatly appreciate some company, Doctor, if you don't mind. Perhaps you would like to have a glass of Madeira to help your digestion?"

I gave him no chance to refuse and was up and pouring the stuff myself, rather than call and wait for a servant to do it.

Nonplussed, for I had never really encouraged his company before, he accepted the drink and took another seat across from me. "You're very kind, Mr. Barrett," he said, cautiously.

I shrugged. "Mother is in one of her more acid tempers tonight."

"You heard?"

"It was impossible not to."

Now he had a turn at shrugging and downed a good portion from his glass.

"What's this about the Bradford girl?"

Beldon was a gossip, albeit a pleasant one, but this particular subject was not one he was willing to explore. "I've no wish to be indelicate, Mr. Barrett."

"Nor have I. My interest is anything but prurient, I assure you. Will the girl be all right?"

He made a face. "In body, if not in soul."

"What happened?"

"I . . ." He labored a bit, then finally sighed. "I was taking the air this morning when I saw one of the village midwives hurrying along the creek road. As I'd not heard any of the ladies on the farms in that direction were in an expectant state, I made bold to question the woman about her business. I got a short answer for my trouble, but she didn't protest when I came with her.

"We got to the Bradford house and found the girl still in a much agitated state, but able to tell her story. As soon as we got her calmed down, we both examined her injuries and made careful note of all she said about her outrage. Before another hour had passed I lodged a complaint with Lieutenant Nash about the incident. He said he'd look into it." Beldon's tone implied that he had little faith in Nash's investigative abilities.

"You've spoken to Father about this, I hope?"

"Yes, and he's also made a protest. I think it may count more with Nash than mine, but whether any of it will count for anything remains to be seen."

"I think that it was most generous of you to do so much and have no doubt that redress will soon follow."

"One can but hope. It's just the girl and her widowed mother, and they're all alone but for a few house servants and some field slaves. Their land's just enough to support them, but little else. When one has no money, one has no power. I just wish I could do more for them."

"But surely you've—"

"I mean that the girl has had more than her honor taken from her. There's such a thing as innocence as well. She's hardly more than fifteen and will likely carry this wretched burden with her all the rest of her life. It's enough to crack a heart of stone."

"But not, apparently, Lieutenant Nash's?"

"He's a self-important little coward hellbent on avoiding any problem that falls his way. I suppose he thinks that by not dealing with it, and telling his superiors that all is well, he'll finish out this campaign with a promotion."

"Coward?"

"To anyone in the army above the rank of lieutenant. I've seen his like before."

I did not question him on that point. He'd once served in the army years back during the war with the French, and loathed to speak of it. That he even made a reference to it now indicated to me the depth of his feelings.

"Is there no more to be done? Can we not speak to someone other than Nash?" I asked.

"I suppose so, but there's so much going on that I doubt anyone will listen. Poor Miss Bradford is but another report to those in charge. They've more pressing matters on their mind than to seek redress for some penniless, friendless farm girl. It's also sick-making to think her attacker is yet unpunished. He's probably boasting to others this very minute about what he's done and perhaps plans to repeat his crime."

"Did you get his name?"

He shook his head. "She described him well enough, though. It was definitely an officer, from the look of his uniform. Had a scar shaped like a backwards 'L' on his cheek. Shouldn't be hard to find him, but Nash put me off. Damn the man." He finished his Madeira.

"Another glass?"

"No, thank you. I appreciate your listening to all this. It's very kind of you to be concerned."

"At your service, sir."

He stood. "I think I'll just check on Jericho, then have a walk about the grounds."

I lifted my brows. "No card game with Mother?"

He shot me a guarded look. He was well aware of how things were in this family, with Father, Elizabeth, and myself drawn close to support one another against Mother's ill temperament. As a physician, he was often called upon to treat Mother's more severe attacks, but as a toad-eating dependant, he had to pretend, like his carefully blind sister, that nothing was wrong. It often left him adrift somewhere in the middle of the mess, and I felt sorry for him about it.

He perceived that I was not mocking him with my question. Such abuse came often enough from "dear Deborah," so I found no fault with his brief doubt against me. He shook his head and smiled shyly. "I don't think so. Haven't the stomach for it tonight. Good evening, Mr. Barrett." His step was slow as he left, his shoulders a little slumped. Sometimes sympathy can be as heavy a burden as contempt.

I put my book aside and ground my teeth for several minutes, which accomplished nothing. I'd been doing quite a lot of that lately: nothing.

It had been necessary for me to "talk" with the kitchen staff, after all, so that they would take no notice of me sleeping the day through in a remote corner of the cellar. It was very rough sanctuary compared with my excellent bed upstairs, but safe from fire and discreet. I rested better than a king lying on the tamped-down earth there. No longer prey to the distraction of constant fatigue, I now chafed for something to do.

My very early morning activities of exploring the sky above our lands had not yet palled, but there was a certain hollowness in such a solitary pursuit. To share the experience with a companion would have been a blessing, but that, I found, was an impossibility. My talent for vanishing was confined to myself alone. A few nights ago, Elizabeth had bravely agreed to participate in an experiment to see if she might be able to disappear with me. She'd been less than enthusiastic, but balanced it with cautious curiosity. Putting my arm around her, I gradually ceased to be, but she remained solid as ever and shivering with sudden chill.

"You seem to draw all the warmth out of the air when you do that," she observed upon my disappointed return.

"I wonder why that is? Perhaps I could ask Rapelji about it."

"You could try, but don't let Rachel or Sarah hear you or it will be all over the Island by noon."

"It was but jesting speculation, sister. What Rapelji and his housekeepers don't know won't hurt me. I'll keep my questions to myself."

Alone. I was tired of being alone. I was tired of being in the house. Any rides I took on Rolly were limited to the immediate grounds, as it was dangerous to go any farther after dark. I had no fear for my own security so much as that of my horse. Rolly was too dear to me to lose him to a stray musket ball or to a greedy soldier looking to confiscate some four-legged booty.

Well, if I couldn't distract myself with riding, then at least I could walk, and I had a mind to walk a goodly distance tonight. After a quick stop in my room to ready myself with hat, stick, and some spare coin, I made my escape out the side door. My only encounter was with Archimedes, Jericho's father and valet to mine. A naturally taciturn man, he merely raised an eyebrow at my leaving. I nodded back and told him I was going for a walk, should anyone ask after me. His brow twitched and his lips thinned. By that I understood that Father would shortly know of my nocturnal ramble. It hardly mattered. Father knew I would be safe enough.

It was much too early, and I was too close to the house, to try taking to the air; also, the wind was very gusty and strong with the promise of rain in it. I thought of going back for my cloak, but decided my plain blue wool coat would suffice. I was not at all cold.

*Yet another immunity, Nora?* I thought, trudging off into the dark that was not dark to me. To my best recollection, she'd never complained of the cold, not even during the worst of England's weather.

I left our long drive and turned onto the Glenbriar road. If I was careful and quiet, I would not need to worry about sentries until quite close to Glenbriar, and even then they were of little concern to me. The ones under Lieutenant Nash's immediate command all knew my face, though God knows what else they knew about me if those two Hessians I'd frightened a while back had been talking.

The walk was more invigorating than fatiguing despite the rough tug of the wind. I was not hungry, not yet, perhaps not even for the night, having learned that nightly feeding was not always necessary for my needs. Every other evening suited for me, that is, if I did not indulge in skyward antics, an exercise which naturally roused a good appetite.

I passed many familiar landmarks, marveling at them anew in the bright silver glow that seeped through the roiling clouds high above. Diffuse and shadowless, but occasionally uneven, it was like watching sea waves dance as the light fluttered over the ground and wove between the trees and hedges. I could have read a book by it, but for the distracting motion. On the other hand, why should I read when such fleeting natural entertainment offered itself? The book would be there when things calmed again.

The buildings gradually increased in number, and I caught the attention of a few dogs as I passed down the lane. Shutters opened or remained shut, depending on the courage of the occupants. I was challenged by two gruff sentries, but they recognized me and let me pass unquestioned. They were not the two who had called me "*blutsauger*."

The Oak was a venerable old inn that had started as a simple tavern back when the first settlers had come to take land from the local Indian tribes. It was said that many a grant and swindle had occurred over the tables there and little had changed since that time. It had grown quickly through the years and boasted several comfortable rooms now. Mr. Farr, the owner, brewed excellent beer and ale and had a good cook, but alas, I was no longer permitted to partake of those particular earthly pleasures again.

As Glenbriar was but a small village, the keeping of early hours had been the rule, but not anymore. The soldiers had turned the inn into a kind of headquarters, and they kept whatever hours their mood demanded. Perhaps Mr. Farr was making a healthy profit; he certainly deserved some compensation for all the inconvenience.

"Good evening, all," I said, crossing the threshold.

The common room held all varieties of soldiers, most of them divided into groups by subtle variations of their uniforms. There were a number of familiar village faces as well, also crowded together. I saw scant evidence of them mingling with one another. Because of the disruptions, outrages, and out-and-out theft by our saviors, there was little love between the civilians and the military.

"Mr. Farr." Smiling, I approached him where he sat smoking at his favorite spot near the fire.

He stood, looking all pale and awkward. Like many others in our community, he'd heard of my death and burial. And by now he'd also heard my sister's story that it had been a visiting cousin of mine of the same name who had died, not me. As with many other folk, he was in sore confusion over what to believe about the incident. He'd seen me more than once since the night of my return, but still suffered from a base and lingering fear of me. Without an overworking of my usual manner, I always tried to put the man at ease whenever possible.

I shook his hand and inquired after his health and got a halting reply about the ache in his bones, an unfortunate reminder for him. The last time I'd been by, my broken arm had been in a sling. His eyes traveled down to that particular limb, and he made a similar inquiry after my well-being.

"Feeling quite the best these days, Mr. Farr. Dr. Beldon is a miracle man. Patched me back together better than before. I'm sure he'd be more than happy to help if you wished to consult him yourself."

"Er—ah—yes, I s'pose I might do that some time, sir. Can I get you anything?"

"Not just now, thank you. I came by to talk with Lieutenant Nash. I hope that I may find him in?"

"He'll be in t'other room there. Quieter." He indicated a door off to one side. I excused myself to Farr, knocked twice to announce myself, and went in.

Nash was nearly finished with his supper. Quite a boneyard of chicken leavings was piled on his plate, and he was in the act of washing down a last crust of pie with his beer when I entered. He hastily swallowed, coughed, and stood up, wiping his mouth with the back of his hand.

"Good God, it's Mr. Barrett!" he exclaimed. His pleased surprise was highly gratifying. I hadn't known what sort of welcome to expect.

We shared a greasy handshake and he invited me to sit with him. I declined his offer of refreshment.

"How have you been, sir? Arm all better, I see?" he asked, settling himself once more.

"All better," I echoed and once again gave the credit to Beldon.

"That is good to hear. It was bothering you quite a lot the last time I saw you. Figured that's how we lost track of you that night."

I'd been "helping" Nash chase down some escaped rebels then, and he was right, my arm had caused me much discomfort at the time. "Yes, I'm sorry about that."

"Where did you get to, anyway?" he asked, his eye still sharp after what must have been a sizable flagon of beer.

*Oh, dear.* If I had one more mixed blessing to thank Nora for, it was being forced to learn how to lie quickly and well. I hated it, as any lie was a dishonor, but the alternative was even more dishonorable, depending on the circumstances. This time I judged them to be safe enough for me to bluff my way through.

"I'm not really sure, Mr. Nash. I recall trying to chase down those murdering thieves, and then I got all turned around in the dark. Very alarming, that. I've lived all my life here and know every stick and stone and then to get lost . . ." I gave out with a deprecating laugh. "When I got tired of blundering around, I gave my horse her head and she took me straight home, thank Providence. Beldon said I was a touch feverish, y'know. Went to bed and stayed there all the next day and the next, I was that worn."

"And in your wanderings, did you ever stray up toward the north road?"

"I've no recollection of going that far. If I had, then I might have found my way back without the horse's help."

"Very odd, sir, for some of the soldiers there reported seeing three suspicious-looking men that night. Two took off on a horse and went east on the road and the third ran away inland." Nash had left out one of the chief reasons for our hasty removal from the area, which was that the soldiers had fired upon us. We would have hared off anyway, but flying musket balls had lent additional speed to our exit.

"Three men? Sounds like your escaped prisoners found some help."

"My guess is that they ran into the fellow with the horse and persuaded him to treason."

"Persuaded?"

"That is, if he were a loyal subject. Though a mystery remains as to why he has not yet come forward about the incident. My other best guess is that the fellow was a traitor to begin with and, aware of their escape, took the first available opportunity to step in and help them get clean away."

"Have you taken steps to find him?"

"It did not seem necessary, as I thought that sooner or later he would come to me."

I put on a skeptical face. "Most obliging of him to do so, particularly if he's a traitor."

Nash looked me up and down. "Yes. Most obliging, Mr. Barrett."

"Any idea who he is?"

"A very good idea."

"Why, then, have you waited?"

He took his time before answering, perhaps hoping to make me sweat, but I kept a steady eye and an innocent manner. "Another thought occurred to me that the gentleman"—there was some emphasis on that word—"might find a disclosure of this incident to be not only bad for his health, but of supreme embarrassment to his family. I thought that the gentleman might appreciate an opportunity to avert such a catastrophic scandal."

"That's uncommonly kind of you, Mr. Nash, but might that not be compromising to your duty to the Crown?"

"Only if the gentleman decides to talk about the incident. It has been my experience that given the choice, most men would rather keep silent than put their necks in a noose."

"And silence has a price, does it not?"

"A reasonable one, compared to the alternative," he murmured.

"There's more than one alternative, y'know."

"Indeed?"

I leaned forward into the candlelight and fastened my eyes upon his. Circumstances had changed; I'd misjudged Nash's intelligence and greed. Time to end the bluff for both of us. "Yes, Mr. Nash, and that's for you to forget all about it."

He blinked several times. I worried that he'd had too much beer for my influence to have any effect on him. "Forget?"

"Forget about the gentleman and your suspicions about him. In fact, you have no mind for him at all. The rebels met a stranger on the road and they all escaped. They're someone else's problem now. There will be no bribes given, no further inquiries to other soldiers, to the gentleman, or to his family. It's quite for the best, now, isn't it?"

"Eh . . . yes, I suppose it is," he responded shakily. He seemed a little short of breath. I watched him carefully, worried that he'd been aware of what I'd done to him. After a moment, he appeared to be himself again, if not a touch distracted. I went to the door and called for another flagon of beer. When I came back to the table, Nash had assumed an air of puzzlement, as though trying hard to remember something important. I'd seen that look before on others as well as myself in the past—in the past with Nora. It told me that I'd have no more trouble with the man.

Drink delivered and pot boy gone, I resumed our talk, this time bringing it around to a subject of my choosing.

"I'm sure my father has been to see you more than once about those Hessians that have taken over our old barn," I said, pushing the beer toward him.

Nash eyed it as if undecided about having an additional drink, especially one I'd bought him. "He has, sir. Many others have as well, but I fear I can do nothing for any of them. The troops must be quartered, and better an unused barn than your own house. Everyone else has to put up with it; there can be no exceptions."

As he warmed to something familiar, his confidence returned and he ended with a polite, but uncompromising tone. There'd be no improvement for this situation. I'd expected as much. Besides, if I influenced Nash into ridding us of the men, it might look odd. There'd been enough oddness connected with our family already; I had no wish to augment it. Father and I had done our best. If Mother wanted the Hessians off our land, she could argue with them herself.

"We must all do our duty as the King's loyal subjects, Mr. Nash," I said. "I just hope that the Crown will be equally generous in recompensing us for all our hospitality."

"As do I, Mr. Barrett." Since Nash was into collections, not purchases, he was not responsible for paying people for their lost victuals. In any other time or place he'd be hanged as a thief.

"May I count on you to see that we are not ignored?"

"You may place your every confidence in me, sir," he said heartily. It was a vague enough promise. I trusted him to keep it so long as it did not cause him too great an inconvenience.

"I wanted to consult you about another problem that's come to my attention, sir," I continued.

He made an expansive gesture, certain that my complaint would be within his ability to correct, providing a suitable sum of money changed hands.

"As you've probably heard from both Dr. Beldon and my father, a young girl was outraged by one of the officers in this area"

"I think not, Mr. Barrett," he said, suddenly cool. "His Majesty's officers are honorable men and not likely to—"

"*Listen to me, Nash!*"

He left his sentence unfinished, mouth agape, and eyes gone wide and dull. I'd had enough of posturing and words with more than one meaning; some of my anger had broken out and threatened to escape entirely. Now that I had a vessel to pour it into, it was extremely difficult to keep it in check. There was a strong temptation boiling up within to let it free, but that, some instinct told me, would not be a good idea. Nora had once lost her temper while influencing someone, and the resulting shock to the other's mind had been most unfortunate.

The memory of that fearful encounter served to calm me. After a moment or so, I was my own master again and able to speak in a civil manner.

"Nash, I don't care about the honor of His Majesty's officers. All I want is redress for that poor girl. The bastard who violated her is to be punished in full, and you will see to it. You've heard his description, you must know who he is."

"Yesss . . ." he said faintly.

"Good. Then you won't waste another minute hunting him down and seeing that you make an example of him for his crime. You'll drum it into the heads of every one of your men, because if this happens again, I'm holding you responsible."

He was trembling. That made two of us, but for very different reasons.

"I want you to treat this business as though that girl were your own dear daughter, understand?"

Eyes blank, body shaking like a leaf in a gale, and brow streaming with sweat, he nodded.

"Then get started." I looked away, glancing back only when his sharp gasp announced that he'd recovered his senses.

He stood, deathly pale, and his eyes did not quite meet mine. "Y—you must excuse me, Mr. Barrett, but I've a most urgent errand to attend to just now." His hands nervously worked one against the other.

When I took a breath to make a reply, I picked up a sudden tang of scent from him and somehow knew what it was: fear.

*Well-a-day*.

I could have taken it away from him, but it pleased me that Nash should be afraid. Of me. In my Latin studies I'd read some Machiavelli and made note of his harsh but highly practical recommendation that "it is much safer to be feared than loved," so I left things as they were. The favorable regard of this one soldier was of little value to me; I could live without it as long as he did what was expected of him.

"Of course, Lieutenant. I wish you every success," I muttered to his back as he rushed out the door.

* * *

Nash collected all the uniformed men in the common room and left, much to the mystification of the remaining folk. I suppose I could have gone home then, but I was hungry for company. A change of company. He'd given me a sour belly, and unless I found some distraction, I'd likely carry the foul taste of his greedy game playing with me all the rest of what promised to be a long night.

When I emerged in his wake from the private room, questioning eyes focused upon me.

"What 'uz all that about, Mr. Barrett?" someone called.

I hesitated.

They ascribed an ominous meaning to that pause. "What is it, sir? Are there rebels about? They go off t' fight 'em?"

"Rebels? No, nothing like that." I abruptly saw things from their point of view. Having noted my lengthy talk with Nash and his subsequent hasty exit, they might well have thought I'd brought news of some unhappy incursion by members of the rebel forces. "Mr. Nash remembered a duty he'd left undone and went to see about it, that's all he would say to me."

Thus was I able to shrug off their additional questions. I was loath to mention the business about the Bradford girl. The story of her misfortune would carry through the village soon enough.

The coin I'd brought provided the distraction I craved. The price of a few drinks for the other customers guaranteed me all the companionship I could have wished for. Perhaps they weren't as clever or as sophisticated as the friends I'd left behind at Cambridge, but they were solid as the earth itself and honest enough when given the chance. I wondered if any of them had run up against Nash's genteel squeezing, then firmly put it from my mind. Few of them had any money to speak of, unlike me.

Though repeatedly invited to drink with them, I managed to dodge the honor by a solemn invocation of Beldon's name.

"He made my arm better, but tells me it's still mending itself inside. He's particularly strict about my eating and drinking, but never said I couldn't enjoy watching others do it for me."

This brought out an unexpected and extremely ribald comment from Mr. Thayer, an elderly farmer smoking his thin pipe in one corner. What he said and how he said it, combined with the man's age, doubled us over and inspired more talk along similar lines. Because business was so good, Mr. Farr—who usually did not tolerate much rough speech—ignored us and kept the drink flowing.

The ensuing hours passed quickly and pleasantly for us, perhaps more so for them than for me, as most of the jests were improved by the constant ingestion of beer and gin. I laughed along with most of the talk, though, and heard all the gossip and added my speculations to theirs about the progress of the war, such as it was. For us, it was as good as over now that Howe had chased Washington off the Island.

"He'll have to hurry to catch him up," said Mr. Curtis, who had a farm east of the village and was sometimes privy to more recent news than the rest of us. " 'Twill be over soon enough. I heard the whole rebel army was on the run and not planning to stop 'til they reached Connecticut."

"Good riddance to 'em," someone put in. "Connecticut deserves 'em, not us."

"Aye, they do," added another. "Connecticut, bah!" He spat on the floor.

"If you please, Mr. Davis!" protested Farr, preventing the rest of us from following suit.

Davis grinned and drunkenly apologized. "Think I'll take m'self 'ome, gen'lmn." He detached himself from his table and might have fallen flat if Curtis hadn't smoothly grabbed the back of his coat.

"You won't make it home walking on your nose, son," he observed.

"Reckon I won't," said Davis, bent hard over and talking to his shoes.

Since I'd been the direct cause of his drunken state, I thought it only right to see the man to his door. "Come along with you, Mr. Davis. Let's go look for some fresh air. Good night, all."

This time I got a hearty response; even Mr. Farr joined in the chorus of goodbyes as I collected Davis and steered him outside.

"No need t' be such trouble o'r me, Mr. Barrett," he said.

"It's no trouble, Mr. Davis."

Weaving, we made our way across the village common. His house wasn't very distant, and he wasn't much of a burden. Had I been in a hurry, I could have easily thrown him over one shoulder, but there was no need for haste or to remove what small dignity remained to him. Besides, the evening air that we sought was pleasant enough now that the wind had died off. It was still cool—as far as I could tell—and the sky yet had a promise of rain in it, but later, probably just before dawn.

Any sentries that were about left us alone. It had long since been determined that the rebel prisoners had made a clean escape, so Nash's unpopular curfew had been lifted. The presence of His Majesty's soldiers in Glenbriar had disrupted things mightily, but life was gradually getting back to normal. Much daily business went on as before and, as evidenced by the carousing at The Oak, the nightly business went on as well.

"Very kind of you, 'm sure," said Davis, mumbling to his shoes again. " 'M in your debt, sir."

"Think nothing of it, Mr. Davis. You and your friends have helped restore my faltering faith in the goodness of man's nature." He couldn't have understood one word in five, but it mattered little to me.

"What about the goodness of woman's nature?" a feminine voice inquired out of nowhere.

I stopped, nearly tripping Davis, who could ill afford a fall. "Who's there?"

She answered with a giggle, no doubt inspired by my startled tone.

Davis swayed in my arms and threatened to topple right over. I peered into the dark doorway of the house we were passing. The voice had come from the shadows within.

"It's Molly Audy, if you're that interested, Mr. Barrett," she said, stepping free of her shelter.

We'd had no formal introduction prior to this encounter, but as Glenbriar was such a small place it wasn't any surprise that she knew who I was, and I certainly had seen her before.

Molly earned her bread by sewing during the day, and the rest of life's necessities were earned on her back at night. She was shunned by the ladies of the village, but not to the point that they could oust her from the community altogether. Molly's behavior and dress were outwardly respectable and modest and she was famous for her discretion, a quality that the men could well appreciate. She'd been the object of much of my study before I'd been sent off to Cambridge, study made at a distance, mind you. She was five years older than I, which had seemed a great gulf of age at the time. I'd been much too nervous to approach her then.

Well, a university education and some spare money can do wonders for a young man's confidence, and, though surprised, I was not reduced to stammering out an awkward greeting as I might have done some three years ago. I wished her a good evening and she returned it to me.

"Looks like your friend's had too much, need some help?" She floated toward us, eyes bright and a smile hovering just behind them. As she came closer, the smile burst forth.

Davis had abruptly turned into a damned nuisance.

"No, uh—that is, yes! I certainly could use some assistance, Miss Audy. I'm not exactly sure which house he belongs to." Oh, dear, but lust does make easy liars of us all.

Molly's raised brows said that she was aware of the lie, but was willing to overlook it while letting me know she was doing just that. She had a remarkable range of expression, I noted.

"It's not far, just come along with me, sir."

At a faster pace than before, I all but dragged Davis along as Molly led the way. She unerringly found and pushed open a door to yet another darkened house. I had little desire to linger in my surroundings and stayed just long enough to drop Davis into a chair before following Molly out again.

"Will he be all right, you think?" she asked.

"I'm sure of it," I said as concern for Davis fairly galloped from my mind. "A good night's sleep is all he wants."

She giggled again. "Don't we all?"

I swept my hat off and bowed, which brought forth another giggle. "I'm deeply in debt for your help, Miss Audy. May I repay you in some small way by safely escorting you home?"

She slipped an arm into mine. "La, Mr. Barrett, but I do like the way you talk."

"I'll be more than happy to continue for as long as you find it entertaining."

"Then maybe you can tell me what you think about 'the goodness of women.' "

"On that subject, I'm sure to turn quite eloquent, given the proper inspiration."

We returned to her dark doorway, and she drew me first inside her house and then inside the reach of her arms. I bent down to give her a proper kiss and got a gratifying response.

"Such a big, strong fellow you are," she said, hands kneading away at my shoulders.

"And you are quite the beautiful lady."

"I try my best, though times are very hard, especially when one is all alone in the world . . ."

Instantly taking the hint, I groped for my money purse and we paused a moment to work out the mundane details of payment for services about to be rendered. Once business was out of the way, we resumed more intimate explorations. Molly, I discovered, very much enjoyed her work.

"Come back this way, Johnny boy," she cooed, slipping some fingers into the waist of my breeches and pulling me along.

To her bedroom, it turned out.

She threw the coverlet to one side and made me sit on the bed. A single candle burned in a holder set in a bowl of water on one table. The room was small but orderly, not that I cared much for her skills at housekeeping. She had other, much more interesting skills to hold my attention.

Like undressing herself.

One by one, she undid the hooks holding the front of her bodice together, playfully slapping my hand away when I offered to help. I gave up, lay back on my elbows, and watched. Free of the bodice, she put it on a chair and next attacked her wide skirts, petticoats, and other complications I couldn't begin to name. It took her some little time, but she finally worked her way down to her corset and shift. She retained her shoes and white silk stockings. I found her red garters to be particularly charming and said as much. For my benefit, she pulled a chair close and put one foot upon it, allowing me to make a closer examination not only of the garter, but the shapely leg it encircled. The lower part of the shift quite naturally fell back a bit owing to this change of position, gifting me with the chance to further my studies.

This time Molly made no objection when I offered assistance in the matter of undoing the lacings of her corset.

"You've done this before, my lad, haven't you?" she commented.

Oh, yes, but Nora was in England and Molly was very much *here*. I zealously plucked at the bow and loosened one loop after another.

"Ah, that does feel good," she said when I got the thing off. Understanding that she'd found its confines rather restricting, I did my best to help restore circulation to her upper body. Perhaps I was a bit too vigorous as she seemed to lose her balance and fell atop me onto the bed. But she was laughing, a laugh that I smothered as I pulled her mouth down to meet mine.

"Your turn," she softly announced a few very active minutes later. One-handed, she discovered the buttons on one side of my breeches and began to undo them.

"Not yet." I was too busy trying to get her shift off to worry about my own clothes. The garment finally flew up over her head and I dragged her close again and kept her fully occupied for awhile.

"Fair's fair, love," she protested. "I've a mind to see those muscles I been feeling." She teased open my neckcloth and began a fast assault on my waistcoat buttons, then my shirt. She was not, I was happy to see, disappointed with what lay beneath. "Now for the best part . . ." Her hand wandered down to my breeches again. I caught it and brought it up to my lips for a kiss, then returned to her mouth.

*It's different*, I thought. *Very decidedly different than before*.

Instead of a grand stirring of pleasure confined between my legs, I was stirred up, as it were, throughout all my body. It had never been this intense before. My God, if I felt like this now, what would our consummation be like?

*There's one way to find out, Johnny boy.*

We rolled and tossed around in a most energetic and pleasing way until Molly grew feverish and was impatient for me to finish things off. I kept her away from my breeches, though, for I understood now that their presence or absence would make little difference as to how this event ended for either of us.

She thrashed under me, breathless and calling for me to hurry. My answer was to seek out the pulse in her taut throat and firmly run my tongue over her smooth skin. Then she went utterly still.

"*Yes*," she whispered.

Teeth and tongue working together, I bit into her neck. Her nails, in turn, bit into my back and her whole body writhed upward against mine. I knew what Molly was going through, having received this kind of kiss myself. Nora had taught me to appreciate every second and to crave the next and that with care, the ecstasy could be drawn out indefinitely.

The red fire of Molly's blood drifted into my mouth a drop at a time, to be savored like the rarest of nectars. She shuddered and moaned and moved under me in such a way as to invite me to drink more deeply from her. The temptation was there; I'd *never* tasted anything so sweet, so perfect.

I drew in a bit more, a whole mouthful.

Swallowed.

It was almost too much to bear. For us both. She cried out and pressed hard on the back of my neck as though she wanted me to empty her to the dregs.

But that would be . . . not right. If I took too much from her, it would somehow be too much for me. For then I would lose myself; I'd be completely overwhelmed and lost.

Ah, but it was so sweet, so good.

*Very decidedly different* . . .

It was all that I desired and more wonderful than I could have ever imagined.

. . . *better. Much, much better.*

Except for Molly's heartbeat, all was silent within that room, but within myself I heard her blood roaring throughout my body, my soul. For a time I *was* overwhelmed and lost in the vast pleasure of that hot tide. I floated like a leaf and let it carry me along to . . . I don't know where. Perhaps it was a place where all my happiest dreams lived, safe from the harshness of normal existence, where body, mind, and soul could meld with one another, able to combine all their respective delights into one devastating sharing.

I didn't want to leave, but taking the life from Molly a mouthful, or even a drop, at a time could not last forever, and I would not hurt her for the world . . . or even to maintain this incredible joy. Eventually, after a very long while, I slowly made my way back.

My next clear memory was of kissing away the last traces of blood from her skin. There remained behind two small, angry-looking wounds, but I knew their alarming appearance would pass rapidly. By morning they would be much less noticeable and be completely gone in a day or two.

Unless I decided to return to her.

Molly lay quiet for some time as her breath returned to normal. The orange light from the candle gilded the sheen of sweat covering her. She seemed to glow like an angel in a painting. Propped on one elbow, I ran a hand over her body, taking enormous delight in simply touching all that lovely, lovely flesh.

She turned her face toward me. Her eyes swept me up and down, wide and not a little puzzled.

"What is it?" I asked.

Her mouth opened. She shook her head. "My God . . . is *that* what they teach you in England?"

"You liked it?"

"I didn't have much of a choice, Johnny boy. It sort of grabbed me up and I couldn't stop it—not that I wanted to try."

This wasn't the empty flattery of Molly the experienced prostitute wanting a steady customer; I sensed that right enough. I'd honestly impressed Molly the woman, which made me feel very good, indeed.

She squinted in the dim light. "Your eyes are funny. They've gone all red."

"It'll go away, nothing to worry about. You needn't mention it to anyone." I looked at her closely and ran my hand over the spot on her neck. "You needn't mention any of this to anyone."

But there wasn't enough light for my attempt to influence her to work. Her expression remained unchanged.

"Don't want people to know how you do it? Is that it?" she asked.

Perhaps another candle . . . or if we moved closer to the light . . .

She shrugged. "You've naught to worry about there, Mr. Barrett. Molly the Mum is what they call me, and with good reason. I start passing tales, and gentlemen'll think twice before they come for a visit. I'm like a doctor, I am, and I don't talk about those as come to see me."

"Oh," I said, temporarily nonplussed.

"Anyways, there's stranger things I've done with gentlemen and none of them nowhere as nice as this. God!" She pushed her head back into the pillow and stared at the shadowy ceiling, her eyes shining again.

Well, it looked as though my secret was safe enough without special prompting, though I did feel obligated to offer a caution to her on the subject. "It would not be a good idea for you to try this yourself on anyone, y'know. Or to have them do it to you."

Her voice had grown soft. "I think I figured that out for myself, sir. Besides, without you, it wouldn't be quite the same thing, now, would it?"

"You're uncommonly kind, Miss Audy."

"There you go again with that nice talk," she said, grinning.

"May I take that to mean I might be privileged to enjoy your delightful company in the future?" I asked, playing along with her.

She sat up a little to look right at me. "Lord have mercy, but if you promise to do *this* to me again"—she brushed her neck with her fingertips—"as God is my witness, Johnny boy, I'll be paying *you*!"

# CHAPTER 4

***December 1776***

"Then our mother said, 'Anne, we were *so* worried about you, thank heaven you've come at *last!*' and she threw her arms around her like she meant it."

"You think she didn't?"

"Knowing what she's really like?" Elizabeth snorted. "Maybe that's why she hates us so much, because we know the truth about her."

"I don't think she hates us so much as she has no regard for anyone but herself."

"No, little brother. She hates. It's covered up most of the time—that woman seems to have a bottomless supply of pretense—but it is there nonetheless. The fits that overcome her can't excuse it. There's a malignancy in her very soul."

"But not in yours," I said quietly, meaning to reassure.

Elizabeth gave me a sharp look.

"There is none of that in you."

Like a slow fever that refuses to rise high enough to burn itself out, more and more, Mother's dark presence intruded upon every subject, every activity for Elizabeth.

"I think you dwell on her too much."

She looked down, her face going red. "Am I trying your patience with my complaints?"

"No, but Mother is obviously trying yours."

What had begun as a light description of this morning's arrival of Cousin Anne had turned in on itself and soured. My sister, I was grieved to see, was not a happy woman, nor was her mood in danger of leaving.

"Is there no way that you can ignore her?" I asked.

"The way you and Father can? Hardly. It's different for me. Father has his work, and you're gone all the day. I can't leave the house because of those damned soldiers or the weather or some other thing comes up and prevents me from getting away from her. Even my room is no longer a sanctuary—you know how she always pushes in without knocking. You'd think she was trying to catch me out in some devilish crime when she does that. How disappointing it must be for her to find me reading, and when she does, she then criticizes me for wasting my time! *That's* how the Fonteyn madness will come upon me, Jonathan, Mother will drive me to it."

She pounded a fist against the side of her chair several times, then boosted to her feet to pace up and down the library. She wore one of her prettiest dresses, a light blue silk with touches of dark blue in the pattern. The colors were very flattering to her, bringing out her eyes especially, but she might as well have been in rags for all the effect it had on her spirits.

"Perhaps you could go stay with Miss Holland for a while," I suggested.

"I've been thinking of it. If no one else, Hester would welcome my company."

"What do you mean? You've lots of friends who would be delighted for you to visit."

"I know, but the way that woman hammers at me day after day, how I look or walk or questioning the very expression on my face, it makes me feel like no one would want to be seen with me. I'm not like that and I know it!"

"As do I, as does anyone with sense, which utterly excludes Mother."

She paused by the library doors. They were closed that we might enjoy a private talk before the party began, though it was something of a risk with Mother's uncertain temper. She had still not rid herself of her dreadful delusion about her children, and there was always a chance she might burst in and work herself into another fit if she found us alone together. Elizabeth was listening, perhaps, for her step.

"There's no one out there," I said.

"You're sure?"

"One of the maids went by a minute ago, that's all. Sheba, I think."

Her next look was brighter, more like herself. Interest in my improved senses never seemed to flag or lose its delight for her. "You can tell the difference?"

"It's not difficult after a little practice."

The delight faltered as her problems returned once more. "What am I to do? Oh, heavens, I *know* what to do, I just hate that *I* have to do it. She should be the one to leave, not I."

"You'll write Miss Holland, then?"

"After the tea party. I'd start now, but I don't want to risk spotting my fingers up with ink. *She* expects me to perform like some sort of trained monkey, and woe to me if I don't look just right for the show."

"Regardless of Mother's expectations of you, you do look perfect. Besides, the honor of serving the tea always goes to the daughter of the house."

"As I said, a trained monkey could—oh, never mind me, I'll get through it somehow. It's not as if I haven't had the practice." She swept up and down the room, her wide skirts threatening to overtopple a small table as she wasn't paying mind to where she was going.

"What's Cousin Anne like?" I asked, hoping to distract her.

"You can tell she's a Fonteyn with those blue eyes and black hair. She seems nice, but I've had no chance to talk with her or her companions. They've been resting from their journey most of the day."

"We'll get to know them better soon enough."

*Perhaps too well*, I silently added, having caught some of Elizabeth's pessimism. I was not looking forward to meeting any more relatives from Mother's side of the family. Though Cousin Oliver was a very decent fellow, his mother was a spiritual Gorgon. I worried that Cousin Anne might also carry a similar cruel streak, hopefully not, since it looked like she'd be staying with us awhile.

Sheba presently came and announced that we were wanted in the parlor. Elizabeth gave me a grim smile, set her chin high, and glided ahead like a ship sailing into battle. I followed in her wake, smoothing my own features as I prepared to meet our newly acquired house guests.

Despite Elizabeth's misgivings, she appeared to find enjoyment in her duties. It was a goodly sized party; several of our neighbors had turned up, and even Lieutenant Nash had gotten an invitation. I suspected Father had extended it, hoping to improve his relations with the commissaries.

Having smoothly taken her place at the tea table, Elizabeth saw to the measuring of tea from its chest and made sure the right amount of hot water was poured into the pot. Soon everyone filed past her accepting the first of many cupfuls for the evening.

Myself included, for I wanted to at least seem to participate with the rest. Father watched with amusement as I pretended to sip at my portion, knowing how difficult it was for me to even bring the cup to my lips. Once a favorite drink, it smelled awful to me now. As soon as he'd emptied his own cup, he took pity and exchanged it for mine at the first opportunity. We'd done this a number of times at other events and had acquired all the practiced ease of stage performers. No one noticed. Into the slop bowl went the dregs from his cup, which I then turned upside down on its saucer, placing the spoon across the bottom. Thus was I able to excuse myself from additional offers without causing offense. As hostess, Elizabeth was bound by courtesy to keep my cup filled, and with Mother watching, she did not dare to "overlook" me.

But tonight even Mother could not find fault with her, for most of her attention was upon her guests and Cousin Anne.

She was certainly worthy of notice.

She did indeed bear the striking Fonteyn features of blue eyes and black hair—though I had to take Elizabeth's word that it was black. It was powdered now and swept up high from her milk-white forehead and elaborately curled in the back. Her movements were polished and full of grace, no doubt part and parcel of the genteel manners practiced in Philadelphia. She wore a splendid dress of some striped stuff that rustled with her every movement and drew many enthusiastic compliments. She lapped them all up as readily as a cat takes to cream. Anne was young and beautiful and enjoyed being reminded of it.

"Yes, it was very fortunate that I was able to bring away most of my things," she said to the crowd of people gathered around her. "There were many, many others who had naught but the clothes on their backs, but then they'd not prepared themselves for an exodus, you see."

"And you've been ready since early in the fall?" asked Father, who seemed to be as taken with her as the other gentlemen.

"Since the summer, Cousin Samuel. We had a horrid time of it for all our readiness. Thank God you and Marie are here and so kind, or I should not have known what to do."

"You are very welcome in my house," said Mother, her face cracking a bit with one of her tight smiles. It did not touch her eyes, but then, none of them ever reached that far. "So you did get my reply to your letter?"

"Indeed, I did not, but then everything is in such a confusion these days."

Mother gave Cousin Anne her wholehearted agreement on that point.

"But with or without an answer from you I had to leave or suffer with the rest of the King's true subjects. I knew if I stayed I'd have no peace in that sad city, for the rebels are horrid in the extreme. Who knows what might have happened to me?"

"Well, you've arrived safely and can put all that behind you," said Mother.

"If I can. It was a horrid time. And so confusing."

Anne garnered much sympathy from her listeners, who begged her for more details about her flight. It took her some while to cover them all, but she eventually concluded that her whole experience was "horrid" and "confusing."

"Had I been on my own, I don't know what I should have done," she went on. "Cousin Roger thought that I should stay, but I just couldn't bear it anymore. Besides," she dropped her eyes and raised her brows, "I'm not all that certain of where he stands on . . . certain things. Political things."

"You mean his sympathies may lie with the rebels?"

"That's it, I just don't know. He won't say one way or another. He's so confusing. Never gives a proper answer, always laughing it off or changing the subject. It's horrid."

"Let's hope he makes up his mind before both sides take it into their heads to hang him," said the tall man standing next to Anne.

His easy remark shocked Mother, but any reproof she might have had for him was left unspoken. The man was no less than Lord James Norwood, younger brother of the Duke of Norbury, and Mother would have sooner cut her tongue out than say a word against such a jewel of the peerage. Instead, she joined with the others who had found what he said to be amusing. She put some effort into it, and the show looked to be quite convincing—at least to those unfamiliar with her true nature.

Norwood added to his comment, causing more merriment at Cousin Roger's expense. Mother laughed with the rest while I fairly stared, then bent low to whisper into Elizabeth's ear.

"My God, can you believe it? Mother's toad-eating."

"What did you say?"

"Mother's playing toady to Lord James."

But Elizabeth was paying but scant mind to me and none at all to Mother. I might have put it down to her occupation as busy hostess but for the fact that no one was near us.

"Just look at her."

"Yes, I see." Her head was pointed in the right direction, but her eyes were not on Mother. They were locked, instead, upon Lord James Norwood.

*Well-a-day*, I thought, the dawn figuratively breaking for me. Knowing that any further conversation would be futile, I backed away to watch my sister watching him. If I read the symptoms right, she was well and truly smitten, and no brotherly intervention would be able to penetrate to her just yet. Heavens, had I looked like that the first time I'd seen Nora? Probably, though no doubt I'd possessed considerably less composure and utterly lacked Elizabeth's innate winsomeness.

It struck me just then how vulnerable she had become, and so I also turned my concerned study upon Norwood.

He seemed a well-mannered, gracious sort, but I'd met many at Cambridge who showed one face to the world and revealed quite another in private. I worried that he might be of that number and vowed to get to know him better, although any shortcomings I might discover would make no difference with Elizabeth. Once one is caught up in that peculiar emotional state, one is deaf to all other things.

"Had Lord James and his dear sister not come to my aid when they did, I don't know what might have happened to me," Anne was saying.

The crowd around her turned toward that gentleman, who bowed deeply. "It was my pleasure, Miss Fonteyn, to be of service."

"You're the hero of the day, my lord," said Dr. Beldon, smiling broadly and taking his own turn at toad-eating.

"So brave and kind of you, I'm sure," put in Mrs. Hardinbrook, also smiling.

As he modestly accepted the general praise of the company, I drifted over to Jericho, who was supervising the punch bowl.

"What does his valet have to say about him?" I asked.

"His lordship's valet, Mr. Harridge, does not permit himself to associate with Negro servants," he said with icy dignity.

"Oh, really?"

"Mr. Harridge has informed the servants he does associate with that they may address him as 'my lord' should they need to speak with him."

"He must be jesting."

"Regrettably, he is not."

"I've heard of this happening in England, but not over here."

"It may be described as an importation of questionable value."

"It seems not to sit well with you."

"Mr. Harridge is a great stupid ass, sir."

I had a very hard time of it keeping my face composed. When the threat of laughter had subsided to the point where I could speak again, I asked, "Why should a man like Lord James keep such an insufferable fellow?" I knew Jericho well enough to consider his assessment of Harridge to be highly accurate and was not about to pass it off as anything petty.

"Like often attracts like when it comes to servants and masters," he said.

"Norwood strikes me as being an easy sort of man."

"Agreed, sir, but you've only seen him under these limited circumstances."

"Agreed, though time will remedy that, what with Mother insisting he stay with us."

"And his sister as well."

"I'd forgotten her. Where's she gotten to?"

"Lady Caroline is just over there by the hearth."

"Seems to be by herself, too. Think I'll play host for a bit, then."

Jericho filled a cup with punch and gave it to me. "For Lady Caroline," he explained.

"But this drink's usually for the men."

"A view not held in high esteem by her ladyship. She has had some already and expressed a great liking for it."

"All right. Let's hope she'll like a little more."

Weaving through the guests, I made my way toward Lady Caroline Norwood and put on my best smile when she looked up at me. She'd taken a chair close to the fire and had turned it so her back was to most of the room. It effectively cut her off from any but the most determined approach. I was determined, for she was very pretty.

"Feeling the cold?" I asked. We'd been introduced earlier.

She nodded. "The roads were very rough and the carriage drafty. I don't think I shall ever be warm again."

"Some punch?" I got a sweet thank you from her as she accepted the cup and drank from it. "Even in good weather the road from Philadelphia is not an easy one. It must have been an especially difficult journey now."

"Indeed it was, Mr. Barrett. I often thought it would never end. Your mother is very kind to invite us to stay here."

"It's our good fortune, Lady Caroline, and our way of thanking you for seeing to the safe arrival of our cousin."

"Poor thing. She was at her wit's end trying to get out of the city."

"How did you meet her?"

Lady Caroline smiled in a most charming way. "At a tea party very similar to this one. Philadelphia may be overrun with seditionists, but the rest of the population tried to maintain civilized habits for as long as they were allowed. Things were going from bad to worse, and several families resolved that they had to leave or be arrested by the rebels."

"I've heard of such foolishness. They've no legal authority to do so."

"Yet arrests have been made. People have been beaten, officials tarred and feathered . . . that was no city of brotherly love that we escaped from, sir."

"Certainly not. What prompted you to travel north, though? Surely a southward road would have been more appealing."

"We had to go with the others—we were with the Allen family and Mr. Galloway—and they were all headed for New York to speak with Lord Howe. They want to persuade him to march to Philadelphia and secure it for the Crown."

"That would be a fearful blow against the rebels."

"Mr. Galloway believes so. Nearly everyone in the city is yet a loyal subject, but the rebels have made them too afraid to do anything."

It had become an old story by now: a small group of knaves holding decent people in thrall with their threats and the frequent fulfillment of those threats.

"I suspect that this wretched trouble has provided you with a poor opinion of our colonies."

"Not at all. I think it is very grand over here. This will die down soon enough, I'm sure."

"How long have you and your brother been in America?"

"At least a year and a half now. James had some land holdings that were being adversely affected by the recent conflicts, and he had a mind to come over and sort things out for himself. I had a mind to see what the colonies were like, so I came with him."

"That's very brave of you."

"So everyone tells me. I did not feel very brave at times, especially when we got to New York. Such a sad place it has become."

"What's it like now?"

"It's terrible and, as I said, sad. There's wreckage everywhere, I don't see how they'll ever be able to clean it up. Wherever you turn are the ruins of buildings with their remains sticking up from the snow like charred bones. So many people were burned out of their homes, and I don't know where or how they keep themselves in this bitter weather. I was very glad when we left."

The burning of New York had been a wonderment and a horror to us all, though for months before the British army arrived there'd been rumors that it would happen. The rebels had threatened to set fires to deny the army sanctuary, and they finally made good their threats one windy night last September.

I'd been out then, testing myself against the strength of the sky. High over the tallest trees, I was doing my best to hover in one spot despite the gustiness of the weather. I chanced to spin toward the west, and it was then that I noticed a lurid glow in the distance so great that it pierced even my fog-clouded sight.

At first I had no understanding of what I'd glimpsed, nor could I gain any better view of it. Each time I grew solid enough to see clearly, I dropped like a stone and had to vanish again lest I come to a hard landing. The vanishing, in its turn, subjected me to the cruelties of the wind, and I had to fight to hold my place.

In spite of these frustrations I finally grasped that I was witnessing a fire of truly awful proportions and that it could only be the city of New York that was aflame. Like others afterward, when they learned the news, I was left stunned, not only by the wanton destruction of such an act, but by the depth of the evil that had inspired it. I was also afraid, for might not the rebels, emboldened by this, do the same for other cities? Worried for the security of my family, I rushed home as quickly as I could.

All was, of course, quiet, but I was so shaken that I had to see Father. I was reminded of those times as a child when I'd waken from a nightmare and rush to his room for comfort. Child no more, but still in need of comfort, it went right to my heart to see the shadow of anguish on his face when I told him the vile news. This was one dark fear that would not go away at a soft word from him.

"It's so much more peaceful here," said Lady Caroline. "Except for all the soldiers, one would never know that anything was amiss."

"But things are amiss, more's the pity. In fact, coming here puts you in more peril than if you'd remained in New York. We're not that far from Suffolk County, which is crawling with rebels, and just across the Sound is Connecticut, another of their lairs."

"You're not trying to frighten me away, are you, Mr. Barrett?"

"Hardly, but I do want you to be aware that though we are reasonably well protected, we are not entirely safe. No one is, these days."

"Now you are frightening me."

"I'm sorry, your ladyship. I mean only to instill caution. I hope that while you stay here you will take care not to wander alone from the house?"

"But surely the soldiers have abrogated any danger from the rebels."

"They have for the most part, but on the other hand, though they serve our King, they are yet men first and thus vulnerable to base temptations . . . if you take my meaning."

She did, and rather sensibly, though I was surprised at how coolly I'd been able to raise the subject to a woman, and a virtual stranger at that. This wasn't the sort of conversation one expects to have during a tea party, but I was finding that I liked her a lot, and with that liking came the desire to protect her.

"Thank you for your warning, Mr. Barrett. I shall certainly be careful in my comings and goings."

"What warning is that?" Lieutenant Nash had come up in time to hear just that much of our talk. He bowed to us both. "If I may be so bold as to intrude upon you?"

"You are most welcome, Mr. Nash," said Lady Caroline, beaming at him like the sun. "Mr. Barrett was explaining to me that there are more perils here than from the rebels alone."

"Really? What perils might they be?"

She went on in a most easy manner and gave Nash the gist of what I'd said.

Nash offered her a glad smile full of confidence. "That danger may have troubled us once, but no more, your ladyship. I can guarantee your safety, indeed, the safety of any woman on this part of the Island."

"That is very good news, then," I said. "Things are much improved, are they not?" There was enough of an edge to my voice to catch Nash's attention. Though he had no solid memory of our interview about the Bradford girl, he still possessed a lingering uneasiness toward me. Here in a comfortable, candle-filled room alive with many friendly faces, he'd forgotten that for the moment. My question served as an excellent reminder. His smile faltered.

"As improved as they can be, given the circumstances, sir. I do my best."

"That's only to be expected from an officer in the King's army," said Lady Caroline. If she noticed our byplay, she pretended not to.

Nash, his eyes tearing away from me and settling upon her, bowed again and thanked her. She gave him another bright smile, her face seeming much more alive than before.

I suddenly felt and consequently knew that I had become superfluous. Excusing myself, I went back toward the tea table. Elizabeth, however, was speaking with Norwood, and it would be as much as my life was worth if I imposed on *that* conversation.

"Never try to compete with a uniform or a title," Beldon advised me.

I gave a slight start at his sudden appearance at my side, and we shared a small laugh. His accurate appraisal was not lost on me. "You've been watching things."

"Only a little. Miss Elizabeth seems quite taken with his lordship, and Mr. Nash has apparently gained the favor of her ladyship."

"He hardly cuts a dashing figure," I said glumly, noting Nash's paunch and the overall stockiness of his body.

"Any man in a uniform is not only dashing but an instant hero in the eyes of a woman. If it's a comfort to you, I doubt if anything serious will come of it. Lady Caroline will hardly squander herself on an aging, penniless lieutenant. She'll enjoy the moment for its own sake, but that's the most of it."

"You sound as though you know Lady Caroline very well. Have you met her before?"

"Sooner or later you'll meet everyone you know a dozen times over, if you live long enough."

"I don't understand."

"It means that most people are the same everywhere. Have you not met someone who instantly reminded you of someone else?"

"Yes."

"And have you then noticed them behaving in a manner similar to that of another acquaintance?"

"I see where you are leading, Doctor. It is an interesting premise. So Lady Caroline reminds you of another lady you've met before?"

"She does. Untitled, but a very nice person, though feckless and fickle. I hope Mr. Nash will not be overly disappointed."

"He may not get that chance. I wonder what this means?"

A Hessian had entered the room, looking quite devilish with his boot-blacked mustaches and face reddened from the cold. He was familiar to me, having been one of the men who'd participated in Jericho's beating months back. I looked across to Jericho and saw that he'd gone quite immobile and his jaw was set and hard. Though he'd recovered completely as Beldon had promised, his spiritual wounds were yet raw.

The Hessian still wore his cloak and hat and seemed in a hurry. Silence fell upon our gathering as everyone stared at this intruder. He paid no heed to any of us, but strode right across to Lieutenant Nash.

Nash scowled and, though he kept his voice low that others might not hear, was obviously demanding an explanation from the man, who leaned close to provide it. Nash soon found his feet, his own expression grim. My father stepped toward him.

"What is amiss, Mr. Nash?"

"An unpleasant incident has occurred, sir, and I must go investigate."

"What sort of incident?" asked Norwood, having abandoned his conversation with Elizabeth.

Had anyone else made such an inquiry, Nash might have been able to ignore him, but he was not without a touch of the toad-eater, himself. "It appears that some rebels have rowed across from Connecticut and made a raid on a house north of here. I must go and see what has happened."

Father went bone-white. "What house?" he asked, in a faint voice.

"The Montagu place."

I caught my breath, my belly dropping to my toes. Father must have been experiencing a similar reaction, but was better at hiding it. Only Elizabeth, Jericho, and I knew what effort he was putting forth to conceal his feelings. Our guests were also shocked by the news and murmured their dismay to one another, for Mrs. Montagu was well liked and respected by all. She had been invited to the tea party, but declined to attend on account of a cough that had been plaguing her for the last week.

Norwood gave Nash a bland smile. "It sounds most interesting. I should wish very much to accompany you."

"This is army business, your lordship, and it could be dangerous."

"Sounds just the thing to do, then. I can't possibly miss this." Norwood did not wait for Nash to offer further objections, but left, presumably to ready himself for his outing.

"I shall come, too," put in Beldon. He'd an inkling about Father's relationship with Mrs. Montagu, but kept it to himself, for at heart he was a decent fellow. "I just need a moment to get my medicines." He bolted out on Norwood's heels.

"And I as well," added Father. "I want to know what's going on."

"As do I," I said, following him. I glanced back once. Nash's mouth was flapping but nothing intelligible spilled out, which was of considerable cost to his dignity. But the ordering of events had been deftly wrested from him, and he had no choice but to accept the help of so many willing volunteers.

Though it took but a moment to arm ourselves—I took my sword cane—and throw on some protection against the winter night, it was somewhat longer before our horses were saddled. The stable lads were by turns sleepy, alarmed, and excited at this excursion, and it took a sharp word from Father to put their minds to their business. I saw to the saddling of Rolly myself. He was restive for want of exercise, shaking his ears and dancing impatiently. I had no choice but to calm him in my special manner. The change from fiery nerve to abrupt docility was noticeable, and Norwood was the one who noticed.

"You've quite a way with horses," he remarked, quirking an eyebrow.

I stroked Rolly's nose and shrugged it off. Norwood continued to throw looks my way as I worked, but was soon distracted by the readying of his own mount.

Nash's man had not come alone; there were five others with him, all on foot. Father cursed under his breath.

"It's taking too long. I'm going ahead, laddie." His face was haggard with new worry. He'd been able to conceal it up to now, but his concern for the well-being of Mrs. Montagu had clawed its way past his self-control.

"Not alone, sir," I said, and we kicked our horses up at the same time.

Nash shouted as we dashed ahead, and the Hessians scattered before us. Norwood called something, and I heard him and Beldon gradually catching us up as we pounded down the lane to the main road.

"We can get there faster over the fields," I called to Father.

"Lead on, then!" He knew I'd be able to see clearly enough to do it.

I urged Rolly onto the road for a time, then cut away to the north, finding a narrow path that marked the informal boundary between our estate and the Montagu property. Sometimes we were at full gallop, but more often than not were reduced to a canter or even a trot depending how bad the footing was. Had I been alone, I might have left Rolly's back and soared ahead, for I could have covered the distance more swiftly, but with Beldon and Norwood along I was forced to limit myself to something less precipitant.

We came in sight of the house soon enough, approaching it from the side. There were no lights showing, not a single sign or sound came to us. Father cursed again and again, fearing the worst. He started to press ahead, but I pleaded with him to wait a moment more.

"Let me go in first and see what awaits. It'll be safer for all."

Torn between fear for Mrs. Montagu and the sense of my request, he hesitated in agony for a few seconds, then finally nodded. I slipped from Rolly and gave Father the reins.

"I'll be right back," I promised, hefting my sword cane.

"Go with God, laddie," he choked out.

"I'm coming, too," said Norwood.

Father told him to hold his place.

Norwood was insulted. "I beg your pardon, sir, but I only wish to help."

"You don't know the land, Lord James. My son does."

This terse statement caused his lordship to subside for now, for Father had all but snarled it. Perhaps it had gotten through to him that this was no adventurous lark, but something far more serious. I had no inclination to waste more time, and walked swiftly and softly over the snow toward the house.

Tracks were all over the yard, but some days had passed since the last fall, and the normal work of the household would account for them. Horses here, boot-shod feet there, I even picked up the faint trails left by small animals, their shallow shadows pressed upon the patches of white. If any of the other markings were caused by rebel raiders, I could not rightly tell. I would find out soon enough.

Reaching the wall of the house, I held hard against it and eased one eye around the corner. The yard on that side was also empty of life, which

I found ominous. The icy air was still, nearly windless; the least sound would have carried to me—had there been anyone about to make it.

Another corner, and I saw the barn. Its doors were open. There was no sign of movement within, which meant the horses were gone. I didn't know what to make of that. Moving closer, my eye fell upon a limp pile of brown feathers lying just on the threshold. It was one of the many laying hens that nested in the barn. Some hand had twisted its neck, then cast it away.

I quit the barn and went straight to the house. The doors were wide open there as well. Up the steps, into the entry hall and stop . . . the house had suffered a cruel invasion. Furniture was overturned, ornaments broken, it was a wretched mess. I called out, but received no answer. I listened to silence and felt chilled right through.

Where were they? Mrs. Montagu had several house servants, a coachman, some field laborers; there was no sign of them, not even of the noisy lap dog she doted on. I made my way toward the kitchen, hitting the catch on my cane and drawing the blade free.

It was dim there, but sufficient light from outside seeped in for me to see well enough. To anyone else, it would have been blacker than hell, and, indeed, the mess I found might have been a part of that dread pit.

The fire there had been banked for the night, an indication that the house had been in order as usual before whatever had happened had happened. Order was gone, now, for this place had also been thoroughly ransacked. The smoked hams that should have been hanging from the rafters were gone. They'd been cut down and taken away except for a very large one that might have been too heavy for the thief to carry. He'd dragged it a few feet, then abandoned it.

Other signs of looting presented themselves, but I let them pass, as they were far less important to me than finding out the fate of Mrs. Montagu and her household.

A sound . . . very soft.

It was not repeated and I couldn't really identify it, but it might have come from the cellar. With something like hope I strode toward the door and tried it.

Locked. Most promising. The lock on this side was broken, therefore someone must be on the other side. They'd probably taken shelter there when the thieves had come and didn't know that it was safe to emerge.

I called Mrs. Montagu's name and knocked several times. No answer. Well, they'd have to come out sometime. Perhaps they were too frightened to respond. I banged my fist a few more times, then decided to try forcing the door. Floating through it would have been less destructive, but much too difficult to explain. Besides, I was more than strong enough for the job.

Setting myself, I gripped the handle and slammed a shoulder against the door. It gave a bit, opening a long crack along the point where I'd struck. I put my mouth to it and called again and something staggeringly loud exploded right in front of me. Thrown back with a shout of surprise, I crashed against a large table. My legs abruptly stopped working. The floor came up, faster than lightning, striking hard all over when it hit me.

My ears rang from the blast, making me sick and dizzy; I could not hear anything subtle, but was aware of some sort of commotion going on nearby. People were yelling in fear and alarm, and somewhere a candle wavered and made the shadows dance.

"Oh, my God, it's Jonathan!" someone wailed. The voice was yet muffled by the ringing, but I thought it belonged to Mrs. Montagu.

"Shut yer mouth, ye damned Tory bitch!" a man ordered. The order was punctuated by something that sounded like a slap, and the woman cried out in reaction.

Groaning, I tried to sit up, and that's when a truly terrible pain lanced through my whole body. My groan turned into a gasp and I instantly gave up trying to move.

A large and unkempt man knelt over me. He had a smoking pistol in one hand and wore an expression in which fear and hatred had been fused into a single vile mask. I was already somewhat stunned from being shot; his face completed the work. All I could do was lie on the floor and gape as one of his rough hands probed my chest.

Behind him, Mrs. Montagu was staring at me, her usually pleasant features marred by a look of utter horror.

"This 'un's dead, Nat," said the man. "Or he's adyin'. Either way, 'e won't trouble us."

# CHAPTER 5

"You sure?" asked Nat, sounding peevish.

The big man's hand was momentarily heavy on my chest. He was pushing against me to get to his feet. " 'E's dead, I say. Let's git 'fore others follow 'im."

"Too late. I see 'em comin'. They heard yer shot."

"I'll give 'em 'nother, then." He drew a second pistol from his belt.

"Right, soon as one's through the door, you take 'im an' I get the next."

"For God's sake, just leave us!" Mrs. Montagu pleaded. I could see her huddled off to one side. Except for a red patch where the bastard had struck her, she seemed unharmed, though very frightened. Gathered around her were several of her servants; they also appeared to be well, but thoroughly cowed by the thieves. None of them were armed.

"Shut yer mouth or I'll cut yer throat," said Nat casually. He had a knife in one hand and a candle in the other. He blew the candle out and left it on the table, then stood with his partner on one side of the door leading to the scullery. Father and the others would most likely use it, as that was the fastest way into the kitchen. After hearing the shot, they'd not wait, but charge right in, and Father would be the first . . .

The pain was still with me, but so was the overwhelming need to get up and do something. Gritting my teeth seemed to help. I was very, very careful not to breathe in. With air in my lungs I might involuntarily vocalize what I felt.

Then Mrs. Montagu gasped when I moved, startled that I *could* move. I was terrified she'd draw the attention of the villains toward me.

"Shut yer face," hissed Nat, and I wholeheartedly agreed with him. He did not, fortunately, turn around, but continued to listen at the door.

Glaring at Mrs. Montagu, I raised one hand in a sharp gesture, hoping she would correctly take it as a sign to be silent. It cost me, for any motion on my right side doubled my pain. I wasn't even sure she could see well enough to know what I wanted until she bit her lips and nodded, her eyes wide and supremely unhappy.

"They're comin'!" whispered the big one gleefully.

Nat slipped back a little so as to be out of the line of fire.

I was on my feet, ready to take them on . . .

. . . weaponless.

The realization hammered home too late. I'd naught but my hands, not even a club. My swordstick . . . God knows where that had dropped when I'd been shot.

Father was almost here; I recognized his step.

Hands. Both of them. Edge of the table.

*Push.*

It was a very heavy piece of oak, sturdy enough to stand up to decades of abuse from various cooks over the years, but for me it might have been made from paper, as it all but flew across the room. The far end struck the larger of the two men in the back just below the waist with an ugly sounding thud. He may have made a noise himself, but it was lost in the general scrape, rattle, and bang of the table's swift passage.

His pistol went off toward the ceiling with a flash and a roar, and a cloud of smoke filled the air around him. I saw that much out of the corner of my eye as I lunged forward, reaching for Nat.

Surprised as he must have been, he was fast and whirled to meet me. He made a quick stab at my left side, but I just managed to knock his arm away before our collision. Balance lost, we crashed against a wall and fell. Kicking, beating, biting, and finally flailing at me with his knife, he did me some damage as we rolled over the floor. My fingers found his neck in the confusion and froze around it. He thrashed and gurgled. I squeezed harder and harder. His face went red, then purple, with his tongue bulging out as I squeezed harder and harder and . . .

"*Jonathan!*" Father's voice. Shouting.

I could barely hear him. Didn't want to hear him. Wanted to finish my work.

"Let go of him, laddie!"

He'd never raised his voice to me like that before, not even when he was angry. What was wrong? What had . . . ?

Hands on my arms. Pulling, tugging mine loose from their grip on Nat's throat.

What . . . ?

I let go, and they pulled me from him with a lurch. That's when my strength left me. I went limp, shaken and shaking, and the pain of the shot hit me all over again afresh. There was blood. The smell of it filled the room, mixed with the gunpowder . . . and the scent of death. For one awful moment I seemed to be spinning back in time to that hot August day in the woods, right to the very instant when I'd . . . died.

"*No*!" I said, forcing myself to sit up. I yelped and clutched at my wound.

"Lie back, Jonathan," said Father, kneeling over me.

I tried to push him off. I could bear the pain far easier than the memory. There was no way I could possibly lie still and let death steal up and seize me as it had before.

"Steady, now, it's all right." He stroked my hair as he used to do when I was little. "It's all right."

That calmed me as nothing else would. The panic faded, and I came to see the kitchen was suddenly a crowded, noisy, normal place again; the faces and voices were familiar, reassuring.

Beldon appeared. He was pale, but in control, and issued a few quiet commands. Someone lighted candles; another went to find brandy. Before I knew it the stuff had been poured into a cup and was being pressed to my lips. I sputtered and turned my head away.

"Don't force him, Doctor. Let him catch his breath," said Father. He turned to Mrs. Montagu. "Mattie? How is it with you?" She grasped his extended hand, her eyes all but lost for the tears. "I'll be fine, but for God's sake, see to Jonathan. The poor child was shot."

"Shot?" exclaimed Beldon, who was just starting a closer examination of my wound. "Come, gentlemen, help me with him. Quickly, please."

"I'm fine," I whispered.

They paid me no mind. Beldon, Father, and Norwood all lifted me onto the table. Orders were given to fetch water and bandaging.

"No, wait! Father . . . I'm—"

"Be still, laddie."

"But I'm—"

He bent over me. "Hush, laddie, let Beldon have a look at you."

"Remember my *arm*!"

"What?"

Beldon pulled open my bloodied coat and unbuttoned an equally stained waistcoat. This hurt like hell, as it pulled at something that seemed to be attached to my flesh. When I protested, he asked Norwood to hold my hands out of the way. He thoroughly ruined both waistcoat and shirt by cutting them to get to the source of all the bleeding.

"My arm!" I repeated, trying to fight off the well-intentioned Norwood.

Then Father remembered, but I could tell that he had no idea what to do next. To be fair, there wasn't much that he *could* do, but no matter; it was a relief that he finally understood me.

"What do you want?"

That was when I realized I had no idea, either. In the meanwhile, Beldon went on with his grim examination.

"That's odd," he said, sounding mightily puzzled.

*Damnation*. "Father? Get the others away, please?"

He instantly saw the wisdom in that and took steps to clear the kitchen. Mrs. Montagu was in a bad state, as might be expected of a woman whose home had been invaded and herself so ill-treated. Father took her hand and guided her out, murmuring that everything was going to be all right. He herded the other servants before them, then called for Norwood.

"Directly, sir. I want to make sure these rebels are no more threat to us." He was by the scullery door, checking the fallen men. His inspection did not take long, and he soon joined the others.

Distractions removed, I was better able to order my thoughts; however, I possessed far more questions than I had ready answers. Foremost in my mind was why I had not vanished. The last time I'd been shot, I had disappeared without any conscious effort, and upon my return had been fully healed of all wounds, old and new. What was different about now? I squirmed to try to see what had happened.

"Be still, Mr. Barrett," Beldon cautioned.

"Then tell me what's wrong."

His eyes rolled over to meet mine, but I exercised no influence on him. His puzzlement was firmly in place, and mixed with it was a touch of fear.

"Tell me!"

He jumped, for my voice was rapidly regaining its old strength. "You . . . there's . . . that is . . ."

Impatient, I nudged things the tiniest bit. "Tell me, Doctor."

His eyes wavered, then steadied. "The ball seems to have passed right through you, but the damage is . . . not as I expected. Perhaps I am mistaken. The bleeding makes it difficult to see very clearly."

I lay back and tried to vanish. No matter if Beldon saw, I'd deal with his memory later. I tried . . . and failed. The pain flared and flashed along my side.

"How bad?" I demanded through my teeth.

He was at a loss to answer. I pressed him again. More firmly. Face slack, he said, "There is no wound from the pistol ball. You've some wood splinters embedded in your flesh. They'll have to come out. That's where all the blood is coming from."

It occurred to me that I could ill afford to lose much of that precious substance.

"Then see to your work, if you please," I said through my teeth.

"I'll need help."

"Get my father."

Dear God, but the next quarter-hour was the longest I'd ever endured. Father was not an ideal doctor's assistant, either. He was more than willing to help, but it was difficult for him as a parent to bear the sight of his child's discomfort. Too late I thought of this as I watched him go from white to pale green as Beldon got on with the wretched business of drawing out the splinters.

"I'll be fine, sir," I promised him, then immediately followed this with a sharp grunt that could not have inspired him with any sort of confidence in my promise.

Beldon discarded a nasty-looking shard of wood and asked for Father to hold the candle closer and with more steadiness. He brought it close, but was unable to completely keep from trembling. As the splinters came out, though, my pain lessened, and with it, much of Father's anxiety melted away.

"The bleeding's stopped," Beldon announced, amazed.

"That's good, isn't it?" asked Father, though he was looking at me for an answer. For the moment, I was just too weary to provide one, not that I had any.

"But don't you see? The punctures have closed right up!"

Father could not help but share in his amazement, but he was more restrained in his reaction.

"It's *unnatural*, sir," Beldon went on, with emphasis. His voice rose a little.

Damnation. Tired as I was, something would have to be done. I glanced at Father, questioning. He frowned slightly, but nodded.

"Doctor . . ." I touched Beldon's hand and got his attention.

A few minutes later Beldon had finished winding a bandage around my middle. It was for show only, for with the splinters gone, my skin had knitted itself up again, leaving behind some red scars that were rapidly fading. Of the stabbings from Nat's knife, there were no signs, though there were plenty of holes in my clothes to mark where the blade had gone in. I dimly recalled those cuts, but had been too immersed in the madness of the fight to notice them at the time.

Finished, Beldon went out with Father to tell the others that I was not seriously hurt at all and that a full recovery was inevitable.

From the kitchen I heard Mrs. Montagu release a sob of relief and Father telling her to be of good cheer.

"Samuel, I am so sorry," she was saying.

"There's no need."

"But he might have been killed. I can hardly believe his escape even now."

"Tell us what happened, madam," suggested Norwood.

Manners and social customs will out under the most extraordinary circumstances. Father introduced Lord James Norwood to her, touching off a considerable reaction and flurry.

As they talked, their voices faded briefly for me. I found I could vanish again, for which I felt an absurd relief. Gone for a moment and then back, the lingering fire in my side completely abated. I offered heartfelt thanks to my Maker and decided that a little more rest would not be amiss.

Mrs. Montagu had some idea that she should play the hostess for Norwood, but he managed to steer her away from that and repeated his question.

The story gradually came out. One of the stablemen had been the first to give the alarm. He'd shouted a warning to the house and, after narrowly eluding capture, had run off in the direction of the old barn on our property where the Hessians were quartered.

"It's not far from here," she explained. "I'd told all the servants that if there was any trouble to either go there or to Mr. Barrett's house for help."

The rebels had not known about the closeness of the troops. They became so engrossed in their thievery that no one noticed the new arrivals until it was nearly too late. All but two fled, carrying what they could.

"We were hiding in the cellar and heard the row, and then it became quiet. I thought they were gone, but when I opened the door, those awful men pushed their way in. They were going to wait, thinking to let the soldiers get well ahead before making their own escape. They thought they could find help by going to Suffolk County."

"The only place they'll be going is a burying ground," said Norwood.

"What?"

Beldon murmured agreement. "Yes. One of them has a broken back and the other a broken neck. Young Mr. Barrett seems to have defended himself rather ably."

Young Mr. Barrett sat up on the table, all thoughts of rest vanquished. My mouth was like dust. Death. I had smelled death in this room.

Could still smell it. Could see it now.

The big fellow, the one I'd rammed with the table, was on his side, bent backward at the hips. Bent very sharply. Nat lay nearby, his head twisted over farther than what might have been considered comfortable to a living man. His face was suffused with blood; his black tongue thrust past his lips. The marks of my fingers were clear on his throat.

I stared at them and felt sick.

Beldon returned. "Mr. Barrett?" He saw the look on my face and came over, standing between me and the bodies.

"I killed them," I said. I'd lost much of my breath and not replaced it, so what came out was barely a sound at all.

He pursed his lips. "Yes."

"Oh, God."

"As a soldier in battle must kill," he added. "Think of it that way, and it may be easier to bear."

I swallowed with difficulty. Though there was nothing like food in my belly, it still wanted to turn itself inside out. "Was . . . was Father the first through the door?"

"Yes, and I was just behind him. Why?"

I motioned for him to stand away. Reluctantly, he did so. I looked at the dead men in their final, undignified poses; looked until the sickness in me passed.

"And you're both all right?" I asked.

"Perfectly."

Nodding, I managed a smile, though it must have been a ghastly one. "*That* makes it easier to bear, Doctor," I told him, as though it were a profound confidence.

He did not ask for any explanation.

Beldon decided that my removal from the kitchen would be of more benefit than risk to my health and helped guide my steps into the next room. I was well able to walk, but saw the need to maintain the pretense of still being hurt. Too quick a recovery would invite comment. Norwood found a chair and dragged it over, and Beldon made me sit.

"You're staying the night, Jonathan," said Mrs. Montagu. "You're dreadfully pale."

"It's but a scratch or two, madam, I've had worse falling from my horse," I responded in a stout tone. As for my lack of color . . . well, I had an easy enough remedy for that. "A little rest and I'll be able to travel, but I think that you should not be left alone here."

"Certainly not," said Father, smoothly stepping into the opening I'd given him. "I'd be honored to remain and make sure of your security, madam." He'd assumed a more formal manner of address to her, and she echoed it.

"If it would not be too much trouble, Mr. Barrett."

"None at all."

Such was the resumption of their gentle pretense that they were no more than good neighbors to one another, not mistress and lover. Only their eyes betrayed the real feelings beneath the innocent words, and for the thousandth time I regretted the circumstances that prevented them from freely uniting as man and wife.

While the servants tried to wrest some order from the wreckage, Lieutenant Nash and his troop of Hessians finally arrived. They charged into the house as though it were a battleground and halted, disappointed, perhaps, that there were no rebels to attack.

Nash stared at the lot of us in wonder, then his eye finally fell hard upon me. "What the devil's going on here?"

His greeting pushed home the fact that I was quite the terrifying spectacle with my bandaging and my torn and bloody shirt hanging from my shoulders.

"Things got a bit warm here, Lieutenant," said Norwood. "Some of your lads missed a couple of the rebels and it was left to Mr. Barrett to deal with 'em."

He'd said just the right thing at the right time, sparing us from any bullying Nash might have been prepared to deliver to us presumptuous civilians. The lieutenant was only too happy to listen to his lordship, and after inspecting the corpses commended me for my bravery and quick thinking.

"Thank you, sir, but had I been thinking quickly from the start I might have avoided this and somehow spared those men."

"They'd have hanged anyway, Mr. Barrett. I found no papers on them, which means they were mere looters, and part of no man's army. We've dropped more than a few from the gibbet over the months, and if this continues, we'll have others joining them, you mark me."

Cold comfort, I thought, but better than none at all.

Nash was of a mind to go track down the troops who had given chase to the other thieves. When Mrs. Montagu expressed concern for the servant who had run for help, he opined that the fellow was likely to be found with them. "Once a man gets the blood up for a hunt, there's no stopping him." He grimaced at Father, Beldon, Norwood, and finally at me. "If he's still in one piece, I'll see that he's escorted home again, madam."

With this reassurance, he left behind one of his clerks—an Englishman attached to the commissary office—to get a more detailed account of the raid and left with the rest. Norwood watched them go, unable to refrain from showing a resigned wistfulness. He turned away and looked at me and assumed a more neutral expression. It came to me that from his point of view I'd had all the "adventure" that evening. I looked him over anew and tried to understand why I'd come to that conclusion.

He was a solid, muscular man with a back like a ramrod, yet exuded a kind of restless energy. He had quick dark eyes and I hadn't noticed much expression in them, but put that down to the class he'd been born into. Such constant self-restraint must have been instilled into him from the cradle, if his raising proved to be similar to that of other duke's sons I'd met at Cambridge. His interest in the doings of Nash's men touched me, though, for his chances of participation in something more interesting than a tea party must have been rare to nonexistent for him.

"Why don't you go along?" I asked.

My question did not seem to startle him; he smoothly supplied the excuse I expected. "My duty lies here, Mr. Barrett, to lend what aid I may to the wounded son of my host."

"Not at all, Lord James," I said. "I am quite able to manage, and Dr. Beldon is here, after all. Go along with them, if you can talk Nash into it, then come back to the house and tell us all that happened."

His face lighted up, but he wavered, compelling me to urge him a bit more until he finally accepted the idea. He promised to provide a full account upon his return. So saying, he left, apparently seeing any objections Nash might have as being entirely surmountable.

"He maneuvered you into that, laddie," Father observed, speaking to me quietly from one side of his mouth.

"I know, sir. It doesn't matter."

"Doesn't it?"

"Not this time, anyway. Besides, I'm curious to know what's going on as well. Nash might be able to prevent you or Beldon from tagging along to see things, but he shan't turn down his lordship."

"By God, I wonder who's doing the maneuvering here?"

"I'm just taking advantage of what's been offered," I said modestly.

He smiled, a small one, with his lips tight together, and looked me over narrowly. "How are you?"

He was not asking after my wounds. "I don't know yet. I feel numb."

"When the numbness wears off, you come talk to me, y'hear?"

"Yes, sir."

Then he enfolded me in a brief, hard embrace.

Beldon and I got back well after midnight, but found the house still awake and ourselves the objects of excess worry. I kept my cloak tight about me at first, so as not to frighten Elizabeth, and told her and all the others that Father and Norwood were unharmed.

"And Mrs. Montagu?" my sister anxiously demanded, for like me, she also had a deep affection for the woman.

"Frightened and dismayed, but unhurt. Father and Lord James are staying there to reassure her and help better secure her home."

Without difficulty, Elizabeth took my real meaning.

"How is it with my brother?" asked Lady Caroline, also anxious. She was pale, except for two spots of color high on her cheeks, and I thought she looked very pretty, indeed.

Prompted by that and further questions, I shared all that I knew with them, with some exceptions. On the ride home I'd asked Beldon to say nothing of the men I'd killed, and so he'd remained silent as I skipped over the unpleasantness; with that omission, I was also able to leave out the business of my wounding. Beldon had taken my insistence on that point to be a combination of wanting to avoid excessive fuss and a desire to spare the ladies further worry, for which he was entirely correct. Later, I would tell Elizabeth the whole story, but I was exhausted now. It could wait until tomorrow.

Surrounded as I was by Elizabeth, Lady Caroline, Cousin Anne, Mrs. Hardinbrook, and—unfortunately—Mother, not to mention a dozen servants watching close by, I suddenly became aware of a desire to be alone that was as great as my weariness. I wanted time to myself, to touch and find assurance amongst the familiar treasures of my own room . . . to change from my wretchedly used clothes. With a deep bow, I begged leave to be excused and was able to escape for the most part. Elizabeth and Jericho went ahead of me, Jericho to prepare my room and Elizabeth because she saw there was more to things than had been said. Well, I wouldn't mind talking to them, but Mother . . .

"You could have been killed, Jonathan Fonteyn," she said, as we all took the stairs. She was just behind me; Beldon, box of medicines in one hand, hat in the other, came last. I glanced back at her, surprised by this show of concern, but came to a disheartening conclusion: Mother's words might have the show of worry, but their substance indicated that her worry was for herself. Had I been killed, how might she, herself, be inconvenienced? As that question had already been answered for me last August, I should not have felt such bitter disappointment now, but did, anyway.

Once at my room, Beldon invoked his authority as a doctor and requested everyone to leave, saying that I was in need of rest. For various reasons, no one was inclined to listen to him. Jericho busied himself pulling out my nightclothes, and Mother and Elizabeth stood just inside the doorway.

"There will be no more of this foolish running off with soldiers, Jonathan Fonteyn," Mother stated, arms crossed and head high. She didn't seem to be looking at me so much as at something just over my left shoulder. I knew nothing was there, it was just her way. It suited me, as I had little stomach for looking at her, either. "You're a gentleman, not some kind of idiotic camp hanger-on for those soldiers. They don't need your help to do their duty."

"No, Mother," I said meekly, hoping she'd finish soon and get out.

"And don't use that long-suffering tone with me, young man. You're far too impertinent."

"Forgive me, Mother. My fatigue troubles me and makes me short."

"Fatigue," she spat. "I wonder how long it will take you to recover from this? You tell me that. You're far too lazy as it is, sleeping all day and not lifting a finger to help your father even when you do manage to dislodge yourself from bed."

Each of her words beat against my head like some awful hammer. Bang, bang, bang. I'd been through enough disruption for one evening, but it appeared that more was waiting in store.

When Mother paused for breath to continue her tirade, Elizabeth stepped forward. "He's very tired, Mother, can you not see that? Please let him rest."

Mother, her mouth slightly open as she started to speak, stopped. She was still looking past me, but now seemed to see nothing. Her eyes . . . there was something dreadfully wrong there.

And without word, without warning, Mother raised her hand and swung her whole body around. Her palm struck Elizabeth's face with a resounding *crack* and my poor sister was knocked right off her feet. It was so swift that I was unable to take it in for the first few seconds, not until I heard Elizabeth's sobbing gasp of pain, and then I was moving toward her, arms out to help.

"I didn't send you to Cambridge for you to sleep your life away" Mother continued, as though nothing had happened.

"Mrs. Barrett!" cried Beldon from where he stood flat-footed in a corner, utterly shocked.

But before I could get to Elizabeth, she'd surged right back up again, swift as thought. She had the beginnings of a red mark on her face oddly similar to the one Mrs. Montagu had received; beyond that the resemblance ceased. Elizabeth's expression, indeed, her whole body, was suffused with it: blind fury. While Mother still babbled on, heaping more reproach upon me, Elizabeth launched herself at her.

Mother's speech abruptly stopped, replaced by a snarl of surprise and followed by thumps, howls, and thuds. They were on the floor, skirts flying and fabric ripping as they rolled on the floor and tore at each other like cats.

"You bitch!" bellowed my sister, landing one solid blow after another. "Bitch, bitch, *bitch*!"

Beldon joined me quickly enough, but it was hard going to find an opening. He and I finally managed to make a lucky grab each and pulled them apart. I had Mother, and he got Elizabeth out into the hall, perhaps with the idea of taking her to her room. He'd need help there, for Elizabeth was still cursing and crying and fighting him, her face contorted and looking uncomfortably like Mother's.

That lady was moaning in my arms, groggy, for she'd received the worst of it in the brief fight. Elizabeth had put all her rage-driven strength into it. Mother's face was bloodied, her hair all in disarray, and her gown in tatters. Any stranger seeing her in such a plight might have been moved to instant pity and an offer of immediate succor. But I was no stranger. I was her much disliked, if not despised, son, and hadn't the vaguest notion of what to do with her.

Jericho had frozen in place during all this and now looked torn between going after Elizabeth and remaining with me. He'd also noticed something.

"Mr. Jonathan . . . your clothes . . ."

My cloak had fallen open, revealing the—literally—bloody mess it had so handily concealed. "Oh, God." I pulled the edges together to cover it all again.

"But, sir—?"

"Jericho, I promise you that I am unhurt, but please, don't ask about it just now. Beldon can tell you"

Beldon returned before I could further confuse things. With him came our guests and servants, drawn by the commotion. My room and the hall grew noisy with all the questions, all called at the same time, making it impossible for them to hear any answers, had we been of a mind to give any. Then Beldon shouted for silence, shoved back those nearest, and slammed my door in their faces. It was the only impolite action I'd ever seen him take.

"Up there," he said briskly, returning to his patient and kneeling.

We lifted Mother to my bed. Beldon had his box of medicines open and was reaching for the laudanum bottle. He measured out and prepared a dose—quickly, as he'd had much practice—and got Mother to drink it. He then checked over her other injuries.

"She'll be all right," hc stated hollowly.

I accepted the news without a single flicker of emotion. I was dead inside. She was nothing to me. An irritant at the most, like a speck of dust in the eye that's washed away by a few tears and then forgotten. Except that I had no tears in me. Not for her, at least.

"I'm very sorry, Mr. Barrett," he murmured.

"Thank you." Other replies had come to me, but I'd ultimately settled upon the simplest as being the best.

"Do you wish your father to know what's happened?"

That one required thought. On one hand, Father would want to know; on the other, he had enough worries for the moment. "Yes . . . but there's no hurry. You can send a messenger to the Montagu house at first light tomorrow. Despite the presence of Mr. Nash's men, I don't think it wise for anyone to be traveling alone tonight."

"I agree. I shall see to your mother's needs, then write him a note. What about Miss Barrett? She was very shaken, if you want my help . . ."

"Thank you, but I'll talk to her myself."

I backed away, found the door, and let myself out. The people waiting there with their questions drew back from me and went silent, then obligingly parted as I stalked down the hall to see Elizabeth.

She was lying on her bed, turned away, hunched around a pillow, and sobbing into it. She hated to cry.

Young Sheba was with her, but the situation was beyond her ability. I wasn't so sure of myself, either, when I dismissed her to fetch hot tea and some brandy from downstairs.

I sat on the bed and put my arm around Elizabeth and told her it was over and that things were going to be all right. It was nonsense, but the object was to let her know she wasn't alone. By the time Sheba returned with her tray, the worst of the storm, I hoped, had passed, and Elizabeth was sitting up and making thorough use of a handkerchief.

Pouring the brandy myself, I signed to Sheba to close the door. Both Anne and Lady Caroline had hesitantly come forward to offer assistance, and I'd thought it best to politely refuse. They knew nothing of the situation; Elizabeth and I knew it all too well. The door bumped shut, affording us some much needed privacy.

I felt cold. And distant. From myself, strangely, but not from Elizabeth. And my feeling for her was sorrow that she was having to experience such pain in both body and soul. On her cheek was the red mark of Mother's hand; it would turn into a nasty bruise soon enough. I urged her to take some brandy. She offered no argument against it.

"Oh, Jonathan, how could I have done such a thing?"

I had no real answer for her. "You should ask yourself how could she have done such a thing."

But she wasn't listening. "Was it the Fonteyn blood showing through at last? Is that it?"

"It was *you*, not your blood. You, Elizabeth, who had been sorely provoked beyond all patience."

"Provoked or not, I shouldn't have done it. Something just came over me. It's as though I suddenly don't know myself."

"Oh, yes, you do. We all lose control now and then." My voice caught as I thought of Nat and his big companion. But a few hours earlier, these same hands holding Elizabeth's had squeezed and snapped the life from two of God's creatures. "It's not always good . . . but it is understandable. You've nothing to reproach yourself for."

"But I do. To have done such a thing . . ."

"Is understandable," I emphasized. "Even if you don't understand it, others will."

"I don't want others to know about this."

"Very well." It seemed pointless to mention that others did, already. Cousin Anne had been flighty and mystified in the glimpse I'd had of her, but Lady Caroline looked to have drawn some perceptive conclusions. It wouldn't take much for her to decide Mrs. Hardinbrook would be her best source of information on what was going on in this house. And that gossipy lady would certainly be more than happy to supply a few dramatic details to the sister of a duke. Not that any of it mattered.

"I feel awful," Elizabeth muttered.

"Sleep will cure that."

"And what about *her*?"

Mother. "Beldon's with her. I expect she'll recover. If it's like the other times, she won't remember a thing."

"How nice for her."

"I think it's a pity."

She sat up to stare. "What?"

"For her to not remember is a great pity."

"Why is that?"

"Because if she did, then she might think twice before losing control herself again. The sad part is, she probably won't, therefore you need to be careful around her. We all do."

"It's not fair."

"No."

Another idea sprang into her mind. "What about Father? Oh, God, what shall I tell him?"

"The truth, as always."

"How can I face him?"

"I think he will have the same concern for you as I do now. You needn't worry. Just remember how dearly he loves you. Nothing you've done will ever endanger that."

More protests, more assurances from me. In the end, though, she settled down, and I called Sheba in to help her get ready for bed. I left quietly and was surprised to find the hall clear. Beldon must have taken charge and sorted things out, God bless him.

Order had been restored to my room: Mother was gone, the bed's coverlet smoothed again and turned down that I might occupy it, which was all sham. As ever, I would sleep in the cellar.

I stripped out of my clothes. Perhaps Jericho could find someone in the servant's hall able to repair the cuts and tears, though I could take it all to Molly Audy some night. The thought of her warmed me up enough to draw out a faint smile. She and I had become very good friends over the last few months.

But the smile faded as other thoughts crowded Molly's pleasant company from my mind. Poor Elizabeth. Poor me. Poor Barrett family.

I washed my face and hands. Several times. What I really wanted was a scalding hot bath, but that was impractical at such a late hour. Pity.

It was all so absurd. There I'd been, trying to comfort her for having lost control when I was far more seriously guilty of it myself. Absurd.

And hypocritical, at least where my sister was concerned.

For in my heart of hearts, I was glad that Elizabeth had done it.

# CHAPTER
# ◄6►

***January 1777***

"A letter for you, Jonathan . . . I think it's from Cousin Oliver!"

I'd barely emerged from my cellar sanctuary when Elizabeth all but pounced on me, waving her packet. She usually reserved her greeting for later, after I'd had a chance to change clothes for the evening. Then we would sit in the library and she'd catch me up on the day's events. I was startled by this abrupt assault of news, but instantly recovered and eagerly accepted when she shoved it into my hands. The address was written in Oliver's sprawling scrawl and I wasted no more time before tearing it open.

"What does he say?"

I plowed through the first few lines. "All is well with him."

"What about Nora?"

"No mention of her yet. God, what writing the man has! I can barely make out . . . there's her name, let me see . . ."

I read on and my heart fell right into my shoes. It was readily apparent to Elizabeth, who insisted that I share my knowledge.

"Nora's no longer in England," I announced mournfully. "She's gone away and Oliver doesn't know exactly where."

"Gone? What's happened?"

I read a little more and shook my head. "Oliver thinks she may have followed the Warburton family to Italy sometime last November. He knows where they are staying, so he's written to them asking if they can find Nora for him. She was a regular visitor to Tony Warburton, y'know. Oliver thinks they might be able to get my letter to her."

"That's something, at least."

"Yes. More waiting for me. Probably months more."

"I'm sorry."

I shrugged. "It hardly matters now. Most of the questions I'd asked Nora have found their own answers after all this time."

"But some have not."

"True, but there's nothing I can really do about that. Thank you for bringing me this, though. What other news is there tonight?"

"Not much. It's just been one more dreary winter day."

"Did Lord James go with Father to Hempstead?" Last night he'd expressed a keen curiosity about Father's work and gotten an invitation to come and observe legal procedures.

"Just after breakfast."

"Lucky man." I should have been the one to go with Father, as I'd studied hard for just that purpose, but my condition utterly precluded it. Travel was no problem, so long as it was at night, but I'd never see the inside of a courtroom again, nor ever have the chance to practice law.

Elizabeth knew what I was thinking, for I'd made enough complaint about it over the months. "Father's left a huge stack of papers for you in the library."

*More copy work*, I thought. "Clerking, not real law. I'm like an artist who's forbidden to paint. The desire and talent are there, but the execution . . ." I flapped my hand in a throwing-away gesture.

"We're in like situations, so I understand what you mean."

"In what way are they like? You're able to stay awake while the sun's up."

"And do what? Housewifery? Needlework? Gossip?"

"Missing him, aren't you?" I asked, with sudden inspiration coupled to a desire to change the subject.

That delayed further speech from her as we left the kitchen and climbed the stairs. She made no inquiry about whom I was referring to, there being no need. Elizabeth blushed for a portion of the trip and opened her mouth several times to reply, then snapped it shut again every time she caught my grin. The topic of Lord James Norwood was a tender one with her.

"And he's been gone only a day?" I added.

She looked ready to explode for a moment, then abruptly gave it up. "Yes," came her rueful admission. "All bloody day and probably tomorrow as well."

"It will pass soon enough."

"It's forever," she grumbled.

"Does he know how you feel?" I paused at the door to my room.

"Sometimes I think he does. I wish I knew how *he* felt about me."

"You can't tell?"

She looked entirely helpless. "No."

"I could talk to him . . ."

"*No!* Don't you dare!"

"But if it will end your uncertainty"

"*No!* I absolutely forbid it, Jonathan! Don't! Please promise me you won't!"

"All right, all right. I just wanted to help."

"I'll do my own helping, thank you very much. You promise not to say anything to him?"

"I promise, though if you should change your mind . . . ?"

Brows high, eyes wide, and teeth bared, she shook her fists at me in mock rage. I pretended to cower away from her and, laughing, took shelter in my room.

Things had been easier in the house in the last few weeks as evidenced by our play and the shared laughter. Against all my expectations, it appeared that Mother had not conveniently "forgotten" the fight that had taken place between her and Elizabeth, after all. She never spoke of it, but since that time there was a marked change in her behavior toward us, particularly toward Elizabeth. So far there had been no more reproaches, no scoldings, no adverse attention or pointing out of our shortcomings. Instead, she utterly ignored us.

The first day or so of this was puzzling, as we anticipated her to return to her old pattern of behavior once she had recovered from her bruises. But as the days (or for me, the nights) followed one another we saw that she was either purposely or accidentally overlooking us in all things. She never addressed us directly and should we be in a room with her, her eyes simply skipped over us as though we were invisible.

The puzzlement was soon replaced by a grateful relief as we saw how things stood. We found it infinitely preferable to be ignored by her than to be subjected to her constant abuse. Even Father was benefiting from it as some of her more acidic commentary concerning him dropped off. She had become polite without the usual underlying tone of sarcasm.

Of course, he had not been pleased about what had happened, but his interview with Elizabeth on the incident had been a gentle one. He advised her to exercise more self-control, but so far she had been spared from testing herself further.

Another expectation of mine that had gone unfulfilled was the speedy exit of our guests. It had been a highly embarrassing episode and I'd thought that the Norwoods would soon invent an excuse and leave, but they stayed on. Lady Caroline was most gracious about the business and chose to regard Mother in the same way as Father did: that the woman suffered from bouts of illness over which she had no control. Norwood had missed it all, so any impression it might have made on him when he heard of it from others was negligible.

Cousin Anne was a bit less charitable, deciding that it was all "horrid" and "confusing," but she, too, stayed on, for she had nowhere else to go. As for Mrs. Hardinbrook, it was just another in a long series of unpleasantries that she found easy to dismiss after so much skillful practice.

I'd asked Dr. Beldon for his opinion about the change in Mother, but he was not as candid as he might have been. "It seems to be for the good," he said, "but I won't hazard to say how long it might go on. Mrs Barrett's condition has ever been an erratic one in the past."

"But she's always been consistent in her poor behavior," I pointed out.

"Ah, yes. One could say that. She has displayed a certain nervousness in her temperament." He was trying so hard to be tactful.

"Let's be honest, Doctor, her temper has been consistently bad, especially toward her family. Now she's become almost congenial. Without making comment on how it was brought about, I'd just like to know how it may be continued."

Beldon, so used to social pretense, floundered on that one. "I have no answer for you, Mr. Barrett. And as a physician I can hardly prescribe a reenactment of what happened between your mother and Miss Barrett as a course to take should the . . . nervousness return."

I winked at him. "Still, it's something to think about, isn't it?"

He covered his mouth with his fist and coughed trying to hide the smile there, but I'd seen it and thus did he confirm what Elizabeth and I had earlier determined: that a firm hand was needed with Mother. In other words, those few seconds of knocking about had done her (and the rest of us) more good than three years of constant placation and submission. Not that either of us planned to repeat the violence, but because of its occurrence it may have gotten through to Mother that she was immune to the consequences of her actions no longer.

I had come to like the winter, even as the worst of it settled upon us like a vast white bird with icy wings. With the nights so closely following the short days, my time and enjoyment of the society of our guests was happily increased. With Father's permission, I'd worked my influence upon them, ensuring that they found nothing unusual in my daytime sleep in the cellar or avoidance of the supper table. And so when I came down after changing into more suitable clothes for the evening, no one remarked upon it, or even thought to try.

I went straight to the library, planning to answer Oliver's letter right away and then get started on the work Father had left for me. However dull it might prove to be, I would do my best to help him in all things.

"Hallo, Cousin," said Anne, who was standing by the bookcase when I came in.

"Hallo," I returned. "Finished with my Gibbon already?"

"Hardly. He's very interesting, but I wanted something different tonight. Something a bit lighter than history."

"Hmm. Let's see, what about this one?" I plucked down a volume of Shakespeare.

"A play?"

"A comedy. It's about twins, a boy and a girl who are separated by misadventure, so to make her way in the world the girl disguises herself as a boy."

"You're jesting!" Anne found the idea to be a bit of a shock.

"Then she falls in love with a nobleman, but can't reveal it to him, and then a lady, also fooled into thinking she's a young man, falls in love with her and so on. Elizabeth found it all very amusing and so might you."

"But a girl dressing as a boy? It's so immodest!"

I shrugged. "There are even a couple engravings in there showing it."

Her jaw dropped, but curiosity won out over her objections. She seized the book and scurried off to explore its apparently vulgar pleasures, tossing a hurried "thank you" to me over her shoulder. I smiled after her and realized that I quite liked my cousin.

Anne had a sweetness in her nature at odds with her Fonteyn blood, so presumably she'd escaped its dire effects. However, she was not an especially clever woman, and much of her conversation was of a repetitious nature. She was pretty, though, and at her best when singing, for she had a lovely voice. As there was nothing to dislike about her, she was generally liked by others as well, so long as the conversation was not too intellectually taxing.

I thought that she might have a working mind hidden away somewhere; it just wanted a little encouragement to emerge. From what I gathered in listening to talk about what things were like in Philadelphia, a girl was not expected to have much of an intellect, nor was one needed. Pouring tea correctly, wearing a pleasant face no matter what, and keeping the servants in line was all that was expected of one; that, and being a good listener when a man was talking to you. I could see why Elizabeth had such a low opinion about what polite society thought desirable in women.

"You're very kind to her." A woman's voice. Lady Caroline.

I turned from the bookcase to find her at ease in Father's big chair by the fire. She had a book in one hand, her finger marking the place where she'd left off reading. I gave a little bow.

"It's nothing."

"Oh, but it is. I tried to interest her in Shakespeare ages ago and she wouldn't even touch it. Thought it might be too confusing. I admire the way you tempted her into it."

"Thank you," I said, with happy sincerity.

Where Anne was lacking was made up for by Lady Caroline, and I found myself rather strongly drawn to her. She was also very pretty and easy to talk to on many different subjects.

"What book have you found?" I asked.

"It's one I brought with me. It's music." She opened it to show the pages, which were indeed covered with bars and notes, all unintelligible to me. I left such art to Elizabeth, who had a natural talent for it.

"You're reading music? How can you do that without playing it?"

"I just can. It's no more difficult than reading words, I assure you."

"For you perhaps. Is there a story buried somewhere in your tune, then?"

She laughed very charmingly. "I think it would be easier for me to play it for you so you can work out your own story." Lady Caroline was accomplished at the spinet and attributed her skill from having taken lessons from Joseph Haydn during the years prior to his entering the service of the great and wealthy Esterhazy family where he was finding some fame these days. His name meant little enough here in the Colonies, but I'd heard it often while in England and was impressed.

"I should like that very much," I said.

"Your sister and I could take turns. She has an excellent ear and eye, I've noticed."

"She will be delighted to know you think so, Lady Caroline."

"I think quite a lot of your sister, you know . . . and so does my brother."

*Well-a-day*. "Indeed?" I nodded and raised my brows to indicate I was an interested listener.

"He's given me to understand that he has a very high and respectful regard in his heart for her."

Though Elizabeth had extracted my strict promise not to talk to Norwood about her, she'd made no mention about avoiding the subject with his sister. "Then his lordship will be pleased to hear—if he doesn't know already—that Elizabeth also has a very high and respectful regard for him."

"That is good news, as far as it goes, but what shall be done about it?"

"I believe that once the principals understand things, the situation will likely take care of itself."

"Ah, but there are other matters to consider, Mr. Barrett. Practical matters."

"What might those be?"

"Money, for instance, should it come to pass that my brother wishes to propose marriage to Miss Barrett. From the first when he began to confide his feelings to me about her, I could see that he would probably be too occupied with those feelings to even think about the dowry. I don't know if there are different customs over here, but in England, the bride is expected to bring a suitable sum into the marriage."

"There's naught to worry about there, Lady Caroline, for the custom holds here as well. In fact, upon marrying, Elizabeth comes into her full inheritance from her maternal grandfather's estate. It is a sizable sum with a very comfortable yearly income attached. Of course, any marriage she seeks must have the approval of her parents, or she forfeits everything." Such was Grandfather's hold from the grave on his female descendants. I had not been so restricted and had come into everything on my twenty-first birthday last summer.

"That requirement for approval must lessen the chance for any hasty elopements," she said.

"I believe that was the idea behind it." Though I knew Elizabeth was headstrong enough to ignore it if she felt she had to; in this case it was irrelevant and I said as much.

"Do you think your parents might bestow their approval on such a match?"

"That is something that Lord James will have to take up with them, though I can say that in my opinion I doubt they will have any objections." Father would not forbid Elizabeth any chance at happiness, and Mother would positively dote on the idea of having a duke's brother for a son-in-law. She would, of course, have to abandon her policy of ignoring Elizabeth. Or not. Well, we'd get 'round her somehow.

"That's good. Then I shall pass the good news on to James. It seems he gets all tongue-tied when in the presence of your dear sister and has been unable to speak to her of those things of the heart which most concern him."

We both took amusement from that picture, but it was somewhat at odds with my memory. Norwood had ever been smoothly articulate at all times. My guess was that he was genuinely interested in Elizabeth, but testing the waters via his sister. If he planned to press his suit, he'd want to be sure it was worth his while. This might be considered cynical, but it was the way things were done. Most marriages dealt with the issues of property and money before anything else, including love. But in this case, there seemed to be no problem over any of those concerns.

Lady Caroline, her questions answered, made leave to excuse herself. "I should like a chancc to practice," she replied against my objection. "Then I shall be able to give you a proper recital. Who knows, but I might even have the honor of playing for a wedding party soon."

I bowed deeply as she left and smiled after her. She was a lovely, graceful young woman and understandably, my thoughts of her drifted along some pleasantly carnal lines for many moments. I entertained also the thought of entering marriage with her. Though I had no title to offer, I did have money, and that counted for much in these troubled times. She would still retain her title, after all.

No, I told myself gently. It was not for me. Then that gentle negative grew in strength as it came to me that marriage to any woman was certainly a much more serious consideration for one such as I than it would be for an ordinary man. Firstly, any proposal would also have to entail a confession about my particular condition . . . and how I had come to acquire it. Very risky to the relationship, that, but the only honorablc course to take in order to be fair to the lady. It wasn't the sort of revelation one reserves for the wedding night.

My God, *why* had Nora always refused my many proposals? For all the intimacy of our relationship, we might as well have been married. And I had known all about her condition. Did she think I might reproach her for the other men she knew, the ones who willingly supplied her with money . . . and blood?

She would not have wanted for money with me, and I knew from experience that human blood was not her only source of food. Why, then, had she—?

The hurt washed over me like a cold sea wave, but dear God, how I missed her. Lady Caroline vanished from my thoughts, replaced by the shining image of Nora. How could I think of anyone else, think of marrying anyone else, even in play?

I'd write another letter to her, to follow the other and hope that they would reach her soon.

But first I would have to write to Oliver.

I settled in at Father's desk and put aside the work he'd left for me for the time being. There was a long night ahead, with little else to do; I'd get to it. For now I plucked up a pen, charged it with ink, and began a serious address of my cousin, thanking him for his efforts on my behalf and encouraging him to continue, if he wouldn't mind.

That business covered, I undertook to catch him up on the events of the last few months since my previous writing. Much was the same, yet much had changed, something of a mirror of my own condition. I included a guarded account of the incident at Mrs. Montagu's house, mentioning that I'd been wounded, but only slightly and was all better now. I said little about Nat and his large companion, only that they'd been killed, not a word on who had done the killing. I'd almost omitted the business altogether, but went ahead and put it down, anyway.

Father and I had had a long talk about it, or perhaps I should say he listened while I talked. It had not been easy to admit to that fatal loss of control, but to hold it tight within would have been worse. For several nights after I was bothered by the memory of Nat's red face and the feel of his flesh between my fingers as I squeezed the life from him. Like some latter-day Pilate, I found myself washing my hands every time the image turned up before my mind's eye. Thank God I was no longer troubled by bad dreams.

Perhaps because Nat's death was so vivid, I did not dwell as much on how I'd killed his friend. I thought this was because he'd been so eager to murder my father. It might be easier to bear such a burden when one is defending for another rather than attacking for oneself, but now and then, I could still imagine feeling the shock of the table edge as it slammed into the man's spine traveling up my arms. When that happened, I washed my hands.

Much to my disgust, Nash and others were hailing me as the hero of the hour, an honor I'd have been pleased to do without. I wearily maintained that my heroism was due to poor judgment and worse luck and asked that no more be said of the affair. It was then thought that I was being too modest. The story got out regardless and grew in the telling, much to my chagrin. Only Father and Beldon, both veterans of war, seemed to understand. At home the subject was hardly raised. I went on as usual, pretending to recover from my wounds, and gradually time worked its magic as present concerns supplanted past woes.

Most of them. That blooding often puzzled me. Why had I not disappeared for a swift healing when I'd taken the shot? Though the pistol ball had passed right through me as before, this time I'd been left with a bleeding wound. In discussions with Father and Elizabeth about it, we quickly concluded that the foreign matter of the wood splinters in my body had somehow prevented it, this theory confirmed by the fact that I'd been able to vanish again upon their removal. Why this should be escaped us, but I was not of a mind to further any researches and, much to their relief, had promised to do my best to avoid any situations of peril in the future.

The Montagu household had also come to settle down as the days passed by without further invasions, but they had lost quite a bit of property including two fine carriage horses, some cattle, and whatever food had been lying about, such as those missing hams. Their losses were not important when compared to the fact that no one had been hurt. Other houses similarly ransacked had not been so lucky, as the rebels had not hesitated to assault and even murder people in their quest for booty.

Norwood, upon his return from hunting the thieves with Nash, had reported the sad fact that everything had apparently been loaded into whaleboats and carried off to Connecticut.

"Don't know how they managed it with the horses and cattle, but their greed must have given them heart and ingenuity for the task," he said. "We found the spot on the beach where they loaded them in and pushed off. The water was like glass, so they must have made swift time getting home again. There was no other sign of them when we arrived, more's the pity."

"What about the other soldiers tracking them?" I asked.

He laughed. "Almost no sign of them, either. They'd gone about their duty with much enthusiasm, but little direction, and got lost in the dark. Poor fellows were so cold and tired from chasing after shadows all night they looked like a pack of stray dogs when we found 'em. Uniforms wet through and muddy, polish of sweat on their faces and the bootblacking smeared from their mustaches, I think they were more unhappy at not maintaining a smart turnout than in losing their quarry."

Nash had been just as disappointed as well as angry at the escape, for it reflected badly upon his ability to keep the peace in his allotted area. Not that his commissary duties called for him to do much soldiering, but the rebel actions did directly threaten his source of supply. In the end, despite Mrs. Montagu's objections (and Father's), a half dozen of his men were detailed to be quartered in the emptied stables.

Unhappy that his proposal was met with such a cool reception, Nash bulled ahead regardless, pointing out that the people and property would be safer for the presence of troops. He pledged his word on the integrity of their behavior, and so far there had been no trouble from them. Apparently my past visit concerning that poor Bradford girl had put the fear of God into him, and he'd passed that fear on to his men. Father had heard later that the guilty man had been punished, though privately, as the army was reluctant to show its dirty laundry to civilians. It was not a wise policy, as those outraged civilians could only conclude that nothing was being done on their behalf. But in this case, at least, we knew better and trusted that things would remain relatively peaceful.

Despite this settlement, Father began making a point of going over for a short visit nearly every day to see how things were for his lady, a courtesy that was much appreciated by her. He extended other favors, like the "loan" of two of our horses and a milk cow, that she might not be left stranded or without a source of butter and other necessities. Nash, for all his rapaciousness, made not the slightest move toward collecting the stock for his own people. I'd been there at the time, and though Nash's eyes had sharpened, they grew dull enough again when they chanced to meet mine. Since that last interview we seemed to have developed an unspoken understanding, so influencing the man into charity was unnecessary. He'd come to his own conclusion as to how I might view any requisitions made from her and decided to save himself the bother.

Not all of this was passed on to Oliver, of course, but I did fill up a page or two with news I hoped he might find of interest. On a lighter note, I told him all about our house guests at length, including the interview I'd just had with Lady Caroline. If things proceeded as I thought, we would soon have Lord James Norwood as a relative. I asked Oliver if he had any opinion on the Duke of Norbury and his family and closed with a wish for a speedy reply to my inquiry about Miss Nora Jones, no matter what the news might be.

This done, I took out more paper and began my salutation to Nora. What followed was brief, but from my heart as I poured it out to her. I had many new questions about myself and many more about her, and included my hopes and prayers for her well-being. It didn't seem enough, but it was all I had until I heard from her once more.

And a long wait that would be, unless she'd received my first letter by now. The reply might be on its way to me, or even arrive tomorrow. Hope was ever with me, but often a bitter companion for every day that it went unfulfilled.

Addressed, sealed, and ready to go out in the morning, or whenever the next post finally came, I placed my latest packet under the cup of lead shot as usual and, with a sigh, began examining the top paper on the stack Father had left.

Father and Norwood returned the next day, though I was unable to celebrate their arrival until my evening awakening. It was determined that another tea party should take place, though this one was on a smaller scale than that which had been interrupted by the rebel raid. As more and more supplies were being drained away by the British and Hessian armies, it was not considered wise to be too ostentatious in one's entertaining. If this limitation on our hospitality grated at Mother in any way, she did not show it.

There was only one other change besides the size of the party. This time Elizabeth was not pouring; that honor went to Cousin Anne. Elizabeth offered no objections. We'd discussed it and decided that it was one more way in which Mother maintained her new routine of ignoring her daughter. The usual custom was that if no daughter of the house were available, the task went to another unmarried lady. Lady Caroline might have taken it, but Anne was younger.

As it turned out, Elizabeth's not too convincing chagrin at losing the post was disguised delight, since it gave her a better opportunity to see Norwood. I'd repeated my conversation with Lady Caroline to her and apparently the lady had done the same with her brother. Norwood and Elizabeth had found a corner that afforded some slight privacy and the two of them were smiling at each other in a manner that could only be described as soppy.

"It looks as though the fever is sorely afflicting them," Beldon remarked to me, but with vast good humor.

" 'Tis a painless complaint, I hope."

"For now, certainly, and for evermore, God willing."

"You think they'll make a match for themselves, then?"

"I certainly hope so."

"Indeed?"

He pursed his lips. "Well, you are aware that my sister has ever entertained certain hopes. It will be of considerable relief to me if things arrange themselves so that she can gracefully abandon those hopes."

Perhaps not gracefully, but at least in silence, I thought. From the first day they'd descended upon our house Mrs. Hardinbrook had been badgering her brother to woo Elizabeth for his bride. As Beldon had no interest in women for matrimonial or any other purposes, the situation often became awkward for him. I could well understand that Elizabeth's marriage to another would provide him with a long desired ease from her nagging . . . until Mrs. Hardinbrook picked out a new prospect for him, anyway.

That lady was even now eyeing Elizabeth and Norwood and drawing some deadly accurate conclusions about the glowing, besotted looks passing between them. She glanced at her brother, scowled, then forced her eyes down into her teacup as though it might provide her with either inspiration or consolation.

My former tutor, Rapelji, came over. A short man with amazing energy, he had finished his tea but not yet turned the cup over.

"Would you like some more, sir?" I asked. "Or perhaps some punch instead?"

"Tea will do, but I'm enjoying this too much." He nodded at Elizabeth, his eyes shining with good-natured amusement. "Well, well, now I'm wondering if I should pass any of the news on to the girls."

"The girls" were his elderly housekeepers, Rachel and Sarah. They were known for their exhaustive herb lore, good cooking, and choice gossip.

"It might be a bit premature, yet," I said. "They've only just gotten to talking with one another."

"They seem to be talking remarkably well. I've never seen your sister looking prettier, and I daresay Lord James would agree with me."

"I think any man would agree with you on that point, Mr. Rapelji," said Beldon. Though indifferent to women, his nature was flexible enough to allow him to have an aesthetic appreciation of them.

"I shall not debate with you, sir. What do you think of it, Jonathan?"

"Think of what, exactly?"

"A match between those two, of course."

"I shall support whatever decision my sister is pleased to make."

"What? That almost smacks of disapproval."

"Or a trust in my sister's judgment."

"Hoho, sir, I wish I'd thought of that one."

Now Father came over to our group and some of our informality faded. "Good evening, gentlemen. Anything of interest?"

"We were just remarking on the beauty of the ladies, sir," I said, uncertain whether Elizabeth's occupation with Norwood was the right subject to bring up with him at this time.

"There is much to remark upon," he agreed. Then I saw his eyes light upon the couple in the corner and twinkle. They shifted to mine, and he winked. After passing some time with Beldon and Rapelji, he leaned in close to me. "I wondered when he'd work up the courage to finally approach her."

"For how long?" I asked.

"Since the morning we left for Hempstead. His mind was on Elizabeth for the whole trip, I think, as he was ever eager to talk about her. Can't say that I'm exactly pleased, though."

"Have you anything against Norwood?"

"No, he seems pleasant enough, but by God, I hate the thought of him taking away my little girl."

On that I could sincerely commiserate, for I hated the thought of losing my sister to . . . well, he was a lord, but still a virtual stranger to us. I'd have to try to get to know him better.

"Are you done with your tea, Father?"

"What? Oh, yes, sorry."

We quietly exchanged cups as usual and he drained away some of mine.

"Got it just right this time, laddie," he said with a grateful smile. Father enjoyed lots of sugar in his tea, a habit I'd learned to imitate for his sake.

"Did Cousin Anne make it strong enough for you as well?"

"Yes, but she's let it steep too long. It's been very bitter."

"She may be distracted tonight."

"Oh? She taken with you, then?"

"Ahh . . ."

"Or is it the other way around to cause such distraction?"

"Really, sir!" And then I saw that he was only playing.

"She's a pretty enough girl, long as she doesn't talk too much," he said. "I heard her mentioning Shakespeare with some enthusiasm, though, so maybe there's hope for her."

"Hope for what?"

"That she might get that mind of hers into some kind of activity. I also hate seeing waste, and a pretty girl not given the chance to think is a terrible waste, or so it seems to me. To other men, too, I've seen on occasion. Having a beautiful but empty-headed woman for a wife can be an altogether wretched existence."

He was looking at Anne in an absent sort of way, his words running on lightly as though there were not much thought behind them. Tea party conversation, nothing more.

Or was there? Then, with a bitter shock, I realized he was thinking of Mother. She had certainly been beautiful once, if that portrait in the library was anything to go by. What had he been like himself? Young, about my age now, good prospects ahead, and then he falls in love with the stunning Marie Fonteyn. Had he been so wrapped in its fever that he'd not noted the flaws amid the virtues? Possibly. It ran in the family, too, if my feelings for Nora were anything to go by. Perhaps it ran in the whole human race.

Mother had looks—once upon a time—but she was not especially clever. She got on well within the rules imposed by society and custom, but her intelligence was more of a kind of instinctual cunning than anything else. No wonder she worried so much over what people thought. They, all unknowing, essentially did her thinking for her, telling her what was right and proper to do and say. All that she did and said did not come from her own desires, but were a mirror of theirs.

I fairly gaped at my mother, feeling shock, horror, and pity swirling up through me in one uneasy swell. That was bad enough, but to look on Father and feel the same but more of it . . . God have pity on us all.

"Something wrong, Mr. Barrett?" inquired Beldon, who had returned to stand next to me. Father had gone off to the library with Rapelji. "You seem a little—"

*Haunted?*

"—pale."

"I think I should like some air, Doctor."

He stepped back to give me room to pass. "But it's very cold out."

"Good."

I left my upended cup and saucer on a table and quietly left, not wishing to draw any attention to myself. Going out the front door, I picked up my stride until I was safe from sight behind one of our larger trees. The snow was not so deep on this side of it, barely coming up over my shoes. Not that I was worried about that or much of anything for a time. I breathed in and out, as if to clear myself of the dusty taste of that suddenly stifling room.

"Mr. Jonathan?"

Bloody hell, I wanted to be *alone*.

Jericho came up, wearing a worried face.

"What is it?"

One of his eyebrows quirked. "I'm aware of what passed between you and Mr. Barrett."

Yes, he'd been standing right behind us, busy as usual with the punch bowl. Of course, he'd have heard everything. But could he have heard my very thoughts? He had a reputation for such in the servant's hall.

"Your father is a very great man," he stated.

More thought divination? No, but Jericho had correctly read my reactions. Having known me since birth, he'd instantly understood what had been set off by Father's most casual remark.

"He is a wise man, too."

"I'm glad you think it," I said roughly.

"But a wise man only becomes so after making mistakes."

"So Father marrying Mother was a mistake?"

"Your judgment of him is."

As soon as his words were out, I was flooded with shame and dropped my head. "I'm sorry."

"Your father is human, Mr. Jonathan. As is mine. As are all fathers, all parents."

"Yes, I know that. I've always known that, but tonight it just seemed to hit me all at once, all over."

"No children are ever happy to learn about the true vulnerability of their parents. It shakes their world up too much."

That's what had happened, I thought. "You're exactly right. I've been very stupid about the whole business."

This time Jericho remained diplomatically silent. For a while. "It is rather cold, sir."

"So Beldon said to me a moment ago. Very well." I let him lead the way back to the house. We stamped the snow from our feet.

"Will I look at him the same as before, though, I wonder."

He shook his head. "Never. But this time it will be with more understanding."

He returned to his duties as I eventually did to mine.

No one had missed us, apparently. The party was going well. Beldon was with Mother and Lady Caroline and saying something amusing. Both were smiling, though Mother's smile, as ever, was a brittle one. I don't think she had any kind of a sense of humor, but at least Beldon was trying. Elizabeth and Norwood were still in the corner, discussing all kinds of things, probably. Cousin Anne was alone at the tea table, so I went to her for a bit of company.

She reached for the teapot, but faltered, seeing that I had no cup.

"Had my fill ages ago," I told her, "but thank you very kindly."

"A single cup fills you?"

I shrugged amiably and changed the subject. "Enjoying that play, I hope?"

Her eyes glazed as she searched her memory, then brightened. "Oh, the one you gave me? Yes, very much. Some of the language was *very* antique, but it was quite interesting. I went back the next day and got another one to read. He's a bit confusing in language until one gets used to it, and then it abruptly makes sense. I seem to know exactly what he means, once I've worked things out. But people didn't *really* talk like that then, did they?"

I thought that Rapelji might provide her with a better answer and looked around for him before recalling that he was probably still in the library with Father. As I started to form my own opinion for her, the gentleman himself came into the room. The energy that constantly propelled him through months of rigorous labor pounding knowledge into stubborn skulls had suddenly deserted him. He seemed to have just enough strength to totter a few steps in and then had to grab the back of a chair to support himself. He was very white.

He'd been so quiet that no one had noticed but me as I just happened to be facing in the right direction. The dreadful expression on his face went straight to my heart. Something was wrong, wrong, *wrong*.

"The doctor," he whispered. "Where's Beldon?"

Now others stirred and looked over, but I paid them no mind as I was rushing out the door for the library. Had I been breathing regularly, I'd have been choked with terror. Instead, clawing and clutching, the stuff invaded my brain and body like a swift, icy fever.

# CHAPTER
# ◄ 7 ►

The fever did not abate, but increased its numbing effect on my mind, as I strode into the library and found Father stretched out on the settee. I called to him, but, disturbingly, he did not respond. He might have been taking a nap, but he was much too still and slack. His mouth was open, but his lips and skin had a blue cast to them that turned my cold fear into frosty panic. I was unable to move, and barely heard or felt Beldon pushing past me to get to him.

He loosened Father's neckcloth immediately, then pressed an ear to his chest to listen to his heart. I could hear its slow beat, noted his deep, slow breathing, but combined with his stillness, neither seemed . . . right.

Beldon shook Father's shoulders, trying to wake him, shouting his name as though the man were across an open field, not right in front of him. The others coming up behind me were greeted by this row, and worried questions began to be whispered in tight little voices. "What's going on? What has happened?"

"Jonathan?" Elizabeth's voice managed to penetrate to me. She put a hand on my arm.

I looked at her and saw a reflection of my own white and hollow-eyed face. I turned and hugged her close for a moment, and that seemed to help.

"Someone get my box," Beldon ordered.

From the corner of my eye I saw Jericho sprint off, taking the stairs three at a time.

Other orders were given and various servants rushed to obey him.

"Mr. Barrett."

This time he addressed me, not Father. I stepped forward.

"Help me get him to his feet."

"Is that wise, sir?"

"Just do it," he snapped. He was already trying to lift Father to a sitting position. I helped him complete the job, and between us we got him standing. Father mumbled a protest at this liberty and tried to push us away. "We must wake him up and keep him awake."

The three of us moved from the library into the larger hall like drunken sailors stumbling home from a debauch. The others parted out of our way, scuttling off and collecting in corners like dust. Jericho hastily came downstairs again with the box of medicines clutched in his arms. Beldon told him to put it in the library and then return. When he did, Beldon had him take his place helping me with Father.

"What is wrong with Mr. Barrett?" Jericho whispered.

"I don't know," I whispered back, unable to trust myself to speak with a full voice.

Back and forth we went, encouraging Father to walk and to wake up for us. He shook his head at this, whether in denial or in an effort to comply, I could not tell. His face was slack, but now and then a beatific smile spasmed over it and he mumbled unintelligibly. Most of the time he was unaware of us, virtually asleep on his feet.

Beldon, who had gone to the library, called Elizabeth in with him. She'd been watching our progress, in agony over the driving need to do something and the utter lack of anything to do, and now fairly jumped at this chance to help. They reappeared again, Beldon with a cup of something in his hand and Elizabeth carrying a cloth and a basin one of the maids had been ordered to bring. We stopped pacing a moment and Beldon managed to get Father to drink what was in the cup.

We resumed walking, with Elizabeth standing nearby. Not much time passed before Father's body gave a frightening, uncontrolled jerk and he doubled over. Biting her lips and with tears streaming unnoticed down her cheeks, Elizabeth held the basin for him as he vomited into it. When he was finished, Jericho and I had to support him completely. He groaned, head drooping. Elizabeth tenderly wiped his mouth with the cloth, then draped it over the noisome contents and took it back to the library.

Beldon lifted Father's head and pried open his eyes. They were like solid blue buttons, with hardly any pupil showing. A madman's eyes, I thought, a chill stabbing right through me to the bone.

"Doctor . . ." I couldn't bring myself to say more, but he heard the pleading tone and put a reassuring hand on my shoulder.

"He'll be all right, I'm sure. Just keep walking him up and down. I have Mrs. Nooth making some very strong cafe noir and he is to drink all of it."

"But what is it? What sort of attack has he had?"

"I'm still working that out, sir. For now, keep him moving. No rest, no matter how much he may protest."

At this point Father was incapable of protesting, period. His skin was dreadfully gray, but it looked marginally better than that unhealthy blue tint. When the coffee arrived, I held him steady while Jericho persuaded him to drink some. The first cup did not stay down, no doubt because of the purgative he'd taken earlier. Beldon had anticipated this, though, for another vessel had been brought in to catch it. The second cup stayed in him, and a third, and so on until the pot was empty. It took a while, but eventually Father was walking on his own, though he still needed help and looked far from well.

"There's something wrong, Jonathan," he murmured, over and over. "What's wrong? Please tell me, laddie."

"Would that I could, sir," I said, hardly able to hold back my tears.

"It will be all right, sir," said Jericho. I could not tell which of us he was trying to comfort.

After a brief word from Beldon, Norwood took charge of the others and urged them to all wait in the music room. Mother objected to this and demanded a proper explanation for Father's condition. There was no tremor in her voice, though it was respectfully lowered. I got the strong impression that she thought Father was himself responsible for his wretched state.

Beldon put on his best doctor's manner. "It's a bit early to tell, but I believe Mr. Barrett has had an attack of the flying gout."

"Gout? He's never had gout in his life."

"That's most fortunate, but this is the flying gout, with diverse symptoms and diverse manifestations . . ."

I felt a fist closing hard around my throat. Oliver had studied medicine and had shared many observations with me on the subject. Whenever a doctor mentioned flying gout, it almost always meant he did not know what was wrong. I glared at Beldon but did not question him or his medical judgment just then. That would come later, in private, and he'd damn well better be able to account for himself.

Mother was finally persuaded to retire with the others to wait and distract themselves with futile speculation. Elizabeth remained by the open door of the library, ready to rush forward if needed again. Archimedes had taken up a post at the parlor door and watched everything with a dour face. Only Beldon dared to pass him, and did, spending some time in that room before emerging to go to the library again.

More coffee was brought in and Beldon saw to it that Father had an ample sampling. The poor man was awash with it by now, and after Beldon called for a chamber pot we retired elsewhere to allow him a chance to relieve himself. Beldon took that pot away rather than turning it over to a servant, which I thought odd.

Up and down we walked, and Father ceased to ask me his heartbreaking and unanswerable questions. He was silent now, his eyes looking more normal but still dimmed and groggy despite the coffee and activity.

"Something's afoot," he said in a soft but clear voice. We'd just passed the library and seen Beldon within, though we couldn't make out what he was doing.

I said nothing, but silently agreed with him.

"And keep that lot away from me," he muttered.

We'd passed the music room and caught the combined stares of the others. I couldn't blame him for any shred of reluctance about talking to them. My heart lifted an inch or two. Father was sounding more like himself.

"God, I'm tired. I want to sit down."

I called Beldon, who came out and looked at Father's eyes again and listened to his heart. "Very well, but no brandy. Coffee only."

Father made a sound to indicate that he was sick of coffee, but he obediently drank more when it was offered.

"Can you tell me what happened, Mr. Barrett?" Beldon asked when Father was seated. Jericho had brought a chair out from the parlor.

"What d'you mean?"

"When did you start to feel sleepy?"

Father shook his head. "I'm not sure. I was at the gathering . . . talking . . . Mr. Rapelji and I came away to talk about his school . . . perhaps then."

"What did you eat and drink tonight?"

"Same as the others, I think. Ask them."

"No medicines?"

"No, I'm not ill, or at least I wasn't. What's this about, sir? Explain yourself."

Beldon looked to be in difficulties. He sucked in his lips.

"Yes, Doctor," I put in. "I know enough of medicine to understand about the 'flying gout.' What's really wrong with Father?"

He glanced around at us all. Elizabeth and Archimedes had both drifted closer; Jericho stood on one side of Father, I knelt on the other. The five of us looked back, each with the same intense need to know his mind.

"I really hope I am wrong," he began hesitantly. "If I am not, then we have a most unpleasant situation to deal with."

"Out with it, sir," said Elizabeth, her eyes fairly burning through him. "What is it?"

His expression was such as to make it clear he would have preferred to be very much elsewhere. "I've made a thorough examination of . . . things and—"

"What things?" I asked, sensing he was trying to be delicate.

"The—ah—contents of the basins and chamberpot."

I wrinkled my nose in reflex.

"I've also checked my medicine box and found . . . a notable discrepancy in the contents of the laudanum bottle."

No one spoke. The silence was that awful, brittle, waiting kind that happens when something terrible is about to crash into your life and it's impossible to leap out of the way.

Father was the first to break it. "You mean I've taken laudanum, Doctor?"

"Yes, sir. Quite a lot of it."

"Please clarify that," said Elizabeth.

"The dose was probably sufficient to have very serious consequences."

"How serious?"

Beldon's answer got stuck somewhere in his throat.

"*That* serious," stated Father in a very dry whisper. He rubbed his face and sighed heavily, unhappily. "How?"

"It would have to have been in your tea, the taste disguised by plenty of sugar."

At this, Father's weary eyes suddenly sharpened. His hand had been resting on my shoulder; its grip tightened.

"Tea? How might it have gotten into just one cup, then?"

"That is something that we shall have to ask Miss Fonteyn."

"You think that girl tried to—"

Beldon shrugged. "I don't know, sir. It hardly seems likely. People were milling about at one time or another during the party, especially when the first cups were being poured. Anyone could have made an opportunity for themselves. Questions must be asked . . . and answered, for there is a chance this could happen again."

"Again?"

"The amount of laudanum that was taken was more than enough to . . . well, not all of it may have been used tonight."

Elizabeth put a hand to her mouth and drew in a sharp breath. She looked as gray as Father, and for a moment I thought she might faint. I knew that because I felt the same way.

"Everyone must be questioned," Beldon insisted, pushing on, though he could see what it was doing to us, but the alternative was worse. The implications of what might happen should there be a yet unused portion of laudanum waiting in our future were frighteningly clear to us. "I said it would be unpleasant," he added forlornly.

Father made a soft, contemptuous snort at Beldon's understatement. "Yes . . . no . . . oh, how my head buzzes. I need rest. No questions tonight, Doctor. I'm not up to it."

"I can do that, sir."

"No."

"But, Mr. Barrett . . . ?"

Father gently waved him down. "No, sir. If any questions are to be asked, then I shall ask them. If someone in this house played a careless joke on me, then I shall face them myself. I'll not leave it to another to do my business for me."

His face went first pale, then red with outrage and fear; Beldon stared down at his patient. "Sir, you could have *died* tonight! This was not any kind of a joke, but a most serious and considered attempt on your life. I will not allow you to delude yourself into thinking otherwise."

"Nor have I. But I am asking you to be silent over it."

"But, *why*?"

"As you said, this promises to be a most unpleasant situation. Would you really care to question the entire household?"

"It's necessary in order to find out who's responsible."

"I believe I already know, sir."

That silenced Beldon. It silenced the whole room.

"Archimedes."

He straightened a little. "Sir?"

Father swallowed. With difficulty, as though ready to vomit again. "I want . . . want you to discreetly go through Mrs. Barrett's room. You'll be looking for . . . what? A twist of paper or a small bottle?"

Beldon murmured agreement.

"The doctor will show you what the stuff looks like. If you find nothing, then you'll look again tomorrow. Pay special attention to the pockets of the garments she's worn tonight. Jericho, I want you to check the parlor right now for the same thing, and the music room later after they're all out of there. Go through the drawers, check under the furniture, the whole room, every corner."

"Sir."

"And both of you . . . don't let yourselves be seen by anybody. What you've heard here, stays here."

Both nodded with grim faces and waited impatiently as Beldon went to the library for the bottle of laudanum to show them what they'd be hunting.

"What happens should they find it?" I asked.

Father let his head fall against the back of the chair and shut his eyes. "They give it to Beldon, who will lock it in his medicine box, once he has a lock put on the thing."

"What about Mother, though?"

"Nothing."

Elizabeth shot me an anguished look over him. "We can't do nothing."

Father was quiet. Thinking, or tired beyond thought.

"She tried to poison you!"

"It failed, by the grace of God. I have my warning and I shall be more alert now."

"No, Father! You can't live in a house with that woman, day after day knowing that the next bite of food you take could be your death. I won't have it!" Her voice had dropped to a shaken whisper, but was as forceful as a shriek.

Father made no response, but the lines on his forehead deepened as his brows came together.

"This has gone too far. You *must* do something about her."

"I will, but in my own way."

"But—"

He raised one hand slightly from the chair arm. "In my own way."

This did not sit well with Elizabeth, not at all well. Her eyes were burning red from tears shed and tears yet to come. "What is that, then?" she asked, her voice thin as she tried to maintain control.

"We'll take steps to see that the opportunity Dr. Beldon referred to has no chance to repeat itself."

"That hardly seems enough," she objected.

Father was still ill and greatly weakened or he might have chided her for that. All he could do was shake his head, reminding me that now was not the time for such discussions. Later, when he was well again, not now.

"We're worried for you, Father," I said unnecessarily, using it to cover a warning look thrown at Elizabeth. It got through and she shut her mouth, though her jaw worked dangerously.

"I'm worried for all of us. This was unexpected, but it can be dealt with. Actually, I'm not too terribly surprised that something's happened, I just didn't anticipate it would happen in quite this manner."

"What do you mean?"

"I've been careless, laddie. About . . . Mrs. Montagu. Your mother's finally found out and this"—he indicated himself—"is her reaction. I'd thought that should the day come, she'd fall into one of her fits, but she's changed lately. She's gotten more subtle."

"Suppose it wasn't Mother?" I asked uneasily.

His eyes opened. "Who else would want to?"

The names of all those people living with us tumbled through my mind. Longtime servants, guests old and new. None of them could possibly have any quarrel with Father. None. He was a well-loved, well-respected man. The only person in the house who did not love or respect him was Mother. She had had access to Beldon's medicines and was certainly familiar enough with the use of laudanum by now. The more I thought about it, the likelier it seemed.

She was a strong woman, but not stronger than Father, so a physical attack against him would ultimately be futile. But poison . . . now that would equalize things nicely. There was a horrid, repulsive coldness to poisoning, but also an ugly fascination in the process. To stand by and pretend concern while watching with secret interest as the stuff gradually carries away a life—that was of a kind of wickedness so alien that I could hardly credit its existence. But here it was, right in my own house.

"What will you do?" My voice was thin, ghostly.

"Take more care," came his simple reply.

You'll need more than that, I thought, my heart filled with leaden sickness.

Elizabeth made a choking sound and turned away to hide her tears.

*Much more than that.*

Archimedes and Jericho found no laudanum that night or in the days to follow. They had been uncommonly diligent in their searches, but we were left with the uncomfortable conclusion that either nothing was there to be found, or that Mother had been more clever at hiding it. Beldon offered the slim hope that the amount taken from his box had all been used that same night. No one was too eager to trust in that, though.

Beldon saw to it that a stout lock was attached to his medicine case and began to lock his room whenever he left it. He kept both keys on his person and soon developed a habit of now and then tapping the pocket they occupied to make sure they were there. Their soft clink was a source of great reassurance to him, it seemed.

He also continued—at Father's firm request—to perpetuate the fiction about the attack of flying gout. It was bad enough for us to know the truth behind his illness, but it would have been much worse for the others to know as well. For all to suffer with such knowledge . . . well, the strain and worry would have made the place impossible to live in.

The story also served well enough to cover the reason why Beldon demanded Mrs. Nooth's close supervision of Father's meals. As for drink, the cabinet in the library holding a small stock of wines and spirits also quietly acquired a lock. Father hinted to the locksmith about petty thievery of his stock and rather than confront the tippler, he preferred to confound him. The tale was so common that it would hardly be worth repeating, which was what Father hoped for and likely got.

Father was shaky the next day, his body still busy trying to recover from the aftereffects of too much laudanum and coffee, but he was more himself on the next, and out doing his usual business after that. He made one very brief visit to Mrs. Montagu, mentioning it to me later.

"I told her that things were becoming difficult here, requiring my presence, so she mightn't see me as often. I did not tell her what happened, nor do I wish her to know."

"Hasn't she the right?" I asked.

"Yes, but she's burdens of her own to bear at this time. Later, when I'm ready, she'll hear it all, but not just yet. In the meanwhile, I'd appreciate it if you'd look in on her now and then when you're . . . out and about. See that things are quiet. You know."

"I'll be happy to do so." He knew all about my flying adventures, such as they were. The winter nights were perfect for this activity, at least when the winds were not too fierce. The cold weather drove people indoors and kept them there, allowing me considerable freedom to enjoy the open sky without fear of being seen. More than once I'd let myself drift all the way into Glenbriar to socialize at The Oak or visit Molly Audy or both. Molly's fortune improved for all my extra business, and at the inn I was able to expand my knowledge of the German language by talking some of the night away with the Hessians there. Would that things were as amicable at home.

The evening following the tea party was a quiet one, though. Father was up in his room, the rest were downstairs pursuing cards or music. Beldon had gone so far as to tune up his fiddle and was attempting a duet with Lady Caroline. Norwood and Elizabeth managed to place themselves on the same settee, ostensibly to listen. Mother, Mrs. Hardinbrook, and Anne were attempting some sort of three-handed card game I couldn't readily identify. All appeared peaceful and normal. Perhaps it was, but my perceptions had been so altered that I was seeing things in a skewed manner.

Studying Mother's every movement and expression, I tried to read the truth within, if any could be discerned. I saw a middle-aged woman, her once beautiful face marred by years of unhappy passions and futile and frustrated goals. This was not a contented soul. Any peace in her life came from moments like this, where distraction from her own inner demons might be found in the company of her friends.

That was interesting. I'd always known it, but only now did the realization come to me: Mother was rarely ever alone. Mrs. Hardinbrook was with her most of the time, Beldon as well, then there were all those tea parties and making calls on others. For all the acid of her personality, she always managed to have some company around her. I wondered why. Was she so afraid of those demons she could not face them?

Having faced down a few myself, I couldn't blame her for that.

Elizabeth rose and excused herself during a break in the playing and walked unhurriedly out to the hall. As she passed me she raised her brows and gave a very small movement of her head to indicate she wanted to talk. Anything more open might draw unwelcome attention from Mother. After a moment or two, I unobtrusively followed.

She was not waiting in the hall as I'd expected, but there was a faint glow of candlelight coming from the open door of the library.

"This is hard, Jonathan," she said just as I came in.

"Tell me what it is first and I might agree with you."

She was blank for a moment, then waved her hand in a gesture of irritation. *"This*. Not being able to talk about last night or at least about the real truth of it. To pretend that nothing happened when all I want to do is scream about it to the heavens."

"I know you do."

"To sit in the same room as that woman . . . full of acting and pretense over something this serious. If we do much more of it I'll burst."

"You won't."

She snorted. "I shouldn't like to wager on that."

"Father will take care of everything."

"We can hope so, but . . . I don't trust that blind spot he has for her. Yes, he feels honor bound by an oath to care for her, but cannot that oath be broken or at least bent by this change of circumstances?"

"He'll think of something, I'm sure." My responses were easy and without much thought behind them. She mostly wanted someone to talk to, a chance to air her complaints and fears. As she was unable to speak to Father about it, I was now her only confidant, aside from Jericho and Archimedes. But they were servants and I was her brother. I accepted her fears and kept my own in check for the moment.

"You're wanting to tell Lord James?" I asked, prompted by an unexpected insight.

Her teeth were showing, but in a grimace, not a smile. "I don't know what I want. Yes, I do . . . oh, damnation!"

I couldn't help but laugh at her, but quietly. "You are in love, aren't you?"

Now she flushed red and paced up and down, wringing her hands together. "I think so. I don't know. I've never felt like this before. I can't see straight or think about anything but him or do anything for myself. Am I ill?"

"Definitely, and I hope you'll treasure that illness."

"But, it's frightening, too. Is that how you felt about Nora?"

"It depends on what sort of fear you mean." Nora had inspired several kinds in me during our relationship.

"I mean the sort of fear that comes when you stand on the edge of what you know to be a cliff. You have to step off, not knowing whether you'll fall into a stack of straw or dash to pieces on a pile of rocks."

"Yes," I said with a sigh of remembrance. "I've been through that."

"What did you do?"

"I stepped off, of course. I didn't have much choice. I just went, because any other choice would have hurt worse than landing on the rocks."

"That's what I want to do, but how can I do it without being truthful to him about things?"

"You really think it's necessary to tell him about last night?"

"It's . . . been preying on my mind. Coming between us. I want to tell him, but I'm not sure. He'll probably tell his sister and she might mention it to Anne or—"

"Just ask him to pledge on his honor to keep it to himself."

"Is it just that simple? I hate secrets unless they're happy ones, like a surprise present. Those are the only ones I'm comfortable keeping."

"A man like Lord James would probably be delighted to have your confidence and a pledge on his honor would be safe with him. It would make him feel quite the hero with you confiding such privileged knowledge to him."

"The point is not to impress him, but to be honest."

"He will be impressed, anyway."

"But the knowledge itself is so sordid. It might put him off me."

"I can't advise you on what to do in this, or how he might react, but if he really loves you, nothing will keep him from you."

"I suppose I'll have to think about it some more. It's just that sitting there with Mother behind us and playing cards as though nothing were wrong . . . my God, if Rapelji hadn't been with Father we might be weeping around a coffin right now."

Time to give her a hug. Past time. I put my arms around her and told her everything was all right. I'd been saying that a lot lately. I hoped with all my heart that it was true.

Footsteps. I recognized their purposeful clack and broke away from Elizabeth.

"What is it?" she asked.

I put a finger to my lips and faded away as fast as I could. And that was very fast. Elizabeth gave out with a little "oh" of surprise as she suddenly found herself alone in the room.

The steps, muffled for me by my present condition, halted, probably at the doorway.

"What are you doing here?" Mother demanded.

The reply was slow in coming. It might have been caused by my disappearance or by the fact this was the first time in ages that Mother had directly spoken to her, or by both.

"Nothing. I just wanted to find a book to show to Lord James."

"Where's your brother?"

"I last saw him in the music room."

"He's not there now." Mother stepped forward and around and circled the library. Assuring herself that Elizabeth was indeed alone and that I wasn't hiding behind a curtain or crouched under the desk.

Elizabeth remained silent. So did Mother. Eventually, she left. When I was sure she was far enough along not to hear, I returned.

My sister jumped when she saw me.

"Sorry. I thought it would avoid trouble if I—"

"My God." She put her hand to her heart and breathed out a laughing sigh of relief. "My God."

"I'm *sorry*."

"Don't be. I was just wishing that *I* could do that, too." She went to the door and looked out. "Gone back to her game, I think. You saved us from considerable unpleasantness just now."

"That was the idea."

"And a good one. Thank you, little brother."

I bowed good-naturedly. "She spoke to you."

She'd been smiling; now it faded. "Yes. I hope she won't make a habit of it. I . . . don't think so."

"Why is that?"

"Just a feeling. In the past she's never failed to find some fault with me and make some kind of disparaging comment over it. She had the opportunity now and did not use it."

"Perhaps she wants to maintain as much distance from you as you do from her and knows that talking to you would diminish it."

" 'Though this be madness' . . . ?"

"She knows 'a hawk from a handsaw.' "

We fell silent a moment and stared out the empty door. Distantly, Beldon drew a few notes from his fiddle, then sawed out a few others, but with more confidence. The spinet followed his lead, then passed him.

"Lord James will be missing you," I said.

"I'm missing him."

"What will you tell him?"

"I'm not sure. Talking to you about it . . . well . . . I have to think some more."

"Will you tell him about me?"

She was startled. "Why should I?"

"In the interest of honesty. Why not? It's a secret as well."

"But not an awful one. It's not the same."

"It's been pretty awful to me, at times."

"This must not have been one of them. You should have seen your face when you came back after she left."

"I wish I could."

Elizabeth knew all about my problem with mirrors. "Feeling sorry for yourself?"

I made myself smile and shook my head.

I wandered back into the music room some while later. Lady Caroline had relinquished the spinet to Elizabeth and was now sitting next to Norwood, but nothing else had changed. I listened as she and Beldon played through a few songs they both liked, nodded at anyone looking my way, and eventually wandered out again.

The mood was a familiar one: I was too restless to sit, or read, or do much of anything. I hated this kind of waiting, of not knowing exactly when it would end.

It was very cold when I finally thought to go outside. I had no cloak or hat, but the chill would not affect me for a goodly time, despite the high wind. The noise of it bothered me more than the low temperature. It hissed and snarled through the bare tree branches and sent loose crystals of snow skittering over the drifts. I plunged my bare hands into a thick white pile and dug out the makings of a sizable snowball. Packing it down solidly, I smoothed it, rounded it, slapped more snow in where it lacked.

There was ice mixed in and it cut me. I regarded the stinging slice in my finger for a moment, vanished, and returned. The cut was gone.

I liked that, and laughed at myself. Then I hefted my snowball and threw it as high and as far as I could over the trees. Couldn't tell where it landed. Couldn't hear. The wind carried the sound away.

Elizabeth had been right to question whether I was feeling sorry for myself, but my pity was for our family in general, not just for me.

Well . . . maybe *some* of it was for me . . . but I wasn't giving in to it, not for now.

I made more snowballs and threw them out into the pale winter night until my fingers grew stiff and blue, then went inside to thaw them by the library fire. Around me the house was gradually settling down for the evening. The last bit of cleaning was being seen to in the kitchen, along with preparations for tomorrow's cooking tasks. I heard Archimedes's stately tread going up the stairs to see if Father wanted anything more before retiring. Jericho made a last round to see that the doors and windows were locked, then went up to my room to set out my things as usual. He and his father came down together, their voices soft in the liquid sound of some African tongue. Jericho understood his father's language, but rarely spoke it where a white person might hear. He said it made them nervous.

The music had stopped and conversation had ceased. Norwood escorted his sister to her room. Beldon saw to the other ladies, then came to the library.

He did not see me as he cast about for a book for this evening's reading. I made sure of that. Only when he was gone did I return. I didn't usually vanish to avoid people, but tonight I didn't feel like having further conversation.

Beldon trudged up to his room, and one by one people upstairs and down retired to their beds. If I listened very carefully, I could just hear Mrs. Hardinbrook's first snores.

Other than that and the wind outside, all was quiet. When I was busy with clerking for Father or absorbed in a book, I hardly paid mind to any of it; now it all seemed to shout at me, "You're alone, alone, *alone*."

Indeed, I was. More so than most. Even Mother.

When the silence went on for an hour, I shifted myself from before the dying fire and quietly padded upstairs, carrying a candle. My shoes were on the hearth, still drying out from the snow, but I'd have left them off anyway.

On the landing I went left instead of right and paused outside Mother's door to listen. She was asleep. My hand dropped lightly on the handle and pushed, and I slipped inside.

In all her time here, I'd never been in her room. I'd never had an interest in seeing it since she'd moved back with us, nor had she ever invited her children to visit. Only Mrs. Hardinbrook had been welcomed here, and Beldon, when a doctor was needed. It had all the usual furnishings, including a very large mirror. I could ignore that for now.

She was buried under a thick layer of coverlets, the sheets made comfortable when one of the maids had passed a bed warmer between them earlier. Mother lay on her back, her carefully dressed hair wrapped up for protection against disarray in her sleep. Her face was thick with powder and paint, the feeble tools used to retain some ghost of her former beauty. She looked like a ghost, a very still one, with its mouth slightly open.

My throat was tinder dry and I knew I was afraid. I could back out even now and no one would be the wiser.

Mother grumbled uneasily and turned a little. The lines on her face that should have been smoothed by sleep deepened into a scowl. If she dreamed, then it was an uneasy one.

Elizabeth was right, there was hatred in this woman, but was it enough to inspire her to poison a husband she had ceased to love decades ago? The more I looked at her the more likely it seemed. And the more pressing my need to do something about it.

I glided to a bedside table and lighted the candle there from the one in my hand. The room had been too dark for what I needed to do. I found another candle and brought it over. Their three lights still seemed too feeble, that, or my fear was making them so. It was that skewed perception again.

Unhappily giving in to it, I turned up one more candle, just to be sure. Plenty of light now, no chance for failure . . . unless someone walking past in the hall noticed the golden gleam escaping under the door and . . .

No. None of that. I'd hear anyone walking past first. With my hearing, I'd know when they first set foot to floor from their beds.

*Get on with it.*

I had to work my mouth a bit to get enough spit in it to talk. Then I wavered and cursed myself for my hesitation.

Taking a deep breath, I leaned over Mother and gently shook her shoulder. It felt strange to touch her. She never encouraged it. The last time I'd touched her had been at my homecoming from England. It had been a very perfunctory embrace, no more than what was needed for show. After that, nothing.

I expected iron, or something equally hard and cold, but this shoulder was soft and flaccid under my fingers and I drew them back as soon as she stirred. She mumbled and shifted.

"Wake up," I whispered. I could barely hear myself.

*Have to do better than this.*

I shook her again, more firmly. "Wake up, now."

Her mumble turned into a whimper. I worried that she might have taken one of Beldon's sleeping draughts. Damnation if she had.

"*Wake up!*" A more fierce whisper.

"No," she moaned, drawing it out into a near whine. "No, Papa."

"Come on." I shook her again, trying to break her from her dream.

"Please, no, Papa. Don't."

"Mother . . . wake up!"

Her eyes flew wide and she gasped and shrank from me. I hadn't known what to expect when I woke her, but not this. Not this kind of shock, not this kind of naked fear. My God, what had she been dreaming about?

"What?" The last shreds of sleep tore away from her puffy eyes. They sharpened, cutting into me. "What are you doing here?"

Such was the force of her question and my ingrained habit of obedience that I nearly wasted time answering her. But I caught myself and said, "Quiet. You will be quiet, Mother."

Our eyes were locked together. That was what was important.

"You—"

"Quiet . . . and listen to me. You will *listen* to me . . ."

The fear, anger, hatred, outrage—whatever it was that drove her—eased instantly. It was frightening to see just how swiftly the change came over her, almost like one of her fits, but reversed.

No wonder Father had thought of this acquired talent of mine as both a gift and a curse and had asked me to use it sparingly, and so I had. For the most part. Nora had used it often enough to protect herself, letting her conscience guide her, and I'd taken that as a wise example to follow. Bullying Nash into a more compassionate behavior did not seem to be an abuse of power, after all, but what I was about to try now might be thought . . .

No. I would not start worrying about what people might think. Do that, and I'd end up like Mother.

I'd once agreed with Father that to enforce my will and thoughts upon others was not only ungentlemanly, but dishonorable. It had seemed so simple then to do so. The right thing. One of the first ideas to occur to him was that I might be tempted to influence Mother into better behavior, and I'd all but given him my word that I would take no such action. Now as I stood here and stared down at her empty eyes I felt shamed over having to betray his trust.

But what I was doing was right. It *had* to be right.

The agreement we'd made so easily last summer did not cover this threat, had never even considered it. I wasn't doing this for any other reason than to protect him, but then I wasn't planning to tell him about it, either. Out of considerations of honor, he might forbid me to do anything.

Damnation, again. I *was* becoming like Mother: for I was doing this for Father's own good, without his permission.

So be it, I thought wearily. For peace in the family and out of love for my father, so be it.

I straightened, resumed looking into Mother's eyes, and began to speak.

# CHAPTER 8

Days—and nights—passed and nothing happened, thank God. Responding unknowingly to my influence, Mother did what was asked of her, which was to do nothing.

I'd kept it to the absolute minimum, making the brief and simple request that she should not attempt to hurt or harm Father ever again. Once assured that she understood completely, I suggested that she forget my intrusion, but not her promise, and to go back to sleep. After a moment, when I stopped feeling so unsettled, I put out the candles, carefully returned them to where I'd found them, picked up the one I'd brought, and left.

Without, the hall, rooms, the whole house had been as silent after as before. A listening silence, said my guilty fancy, but I was safe enough from discovery.

Depending on one's conscience, guilt can be eased by the passage of time, and to my surprise, I found my conscience to be rather more flexible than I'd thought—at least in this matter. As one night succeeded another without further incident, I began to see that what I'd done had been the right action to take. The only drawback was not being able to speak of it to the others.

It would have helped them to know that their worries were over, but it seemed best to let things run on as usual. Not that I was indifferent to their concern; I offered reassurance when it was needed, but kept my mouth shut the rest of the time. After a while, life gradually relaxed back to normal. Or something close to it. Father resumed taking tea with us and ceased looking so dubious when presented with his evening meal. Elizabeth, distracted by Norwood, left off drifting along in Mother's wake whenever the woman left a room alone. Jericho and Archimedes stopped their searches for laudanum, though they continued to keep a sharp eye on Mother during any gatherings with food or drink.

Beldon remained watchful, though. Frustrated perhaps by Father forbidding him to ask questions, he'd continued to keep an eye on Mother as much as he could.

"I feel badly about this, Mr. Barrett," he confided to me one night not long after. "My carelessness was inexcusable. It shall not be repeated."

"Hardly your fault, sir. How could you have known? Or even anticipated?"

"But I should have." He touched the pocket where he kept the new keys to his medicine box and room. "Nevermore."

"Then surely there's no reason to feel bad."

He offered me a bleak look. "There is should your Mother decide to make another attempt, by another means."

I retained my serious face. "What is open to her, then?"

"There are a number of hunting arms in the house, some pistols, and you know that Lord James has quite a little collection of his own."

"You hardly need worry over that. Mother knows nothing about the loading or shooting of firearms. You have to know what you're doing to get them to work properly, and she doesn't."

That brought him a measure of solace, for it was entirely true. We had the arms and powder and shot at hand and ready to use because of the roughness of the times. With rebel raiders threatening to swoop upon us ready to commit common robbery under the thin guise of patriotism, Father had taken pains to augment his cache of guns over the months. However, it was impractical to leave them lying around loaded, as the powder might become too damp to fire. He did make certain that everyone in the house from Elizabeth to the scullery boy knew how to load and shoot, though. Everyone but Mother, who claimed to despise the noise and mess, and did her best to make a virtue of her willful ignorance. I think she may have regretted her attitude, for Lady Caroline turned out to be a most enthusiastic shootist, setting a good example for the rest of the ladies to follow.

"What other means of mayhem might she turn to?" I asked Beldon.

"A push down the stairs?" he hazarded, then shrugged sheepishly. "I know, I'm probably worried over nothing, but I am very fond of your family and should bitterly regret any harm that might come to them. Your father was uncommonly generous in taking my sister and me in and allowing us to stay."

That, of course, had been Mother's idea, for this was her house, not Father's, but in truth, Father had come to welcome their company, Mrs. Hardinbrook as a buffer against Mother, and Beldon as a physician . . . and friend. I was reluctant to admit that, unwilling to relinquish my first impression of the man: that of a self-serving toad-eater. But though he often fell into that habit, especially around people like Norwood, he'd ceased to do so with our family. Perhaps some of our own honesty with one another (with the exception of Mother) had made a favorable impression upon him.

"We're all grateful for your presence, Doctor, and for your concern, but things are well in hand now."

He looked skeptical.

"I don't mean that we should not be vigilant to potential trouble, but I think things are safe enough that we may be at ease most of the time." There, that was as much as I would tell anyone and much more than I'd wanted. Father and Elizabeth would certainly have been able to discern what was behind my words and to correctly guess what I'd done to be filled with such confidence. Beldon, though, did not. From his wan smile I got the impression he was putting it down to youthful optimism. I hoped he would choose not to quote me before others. That might prove to be rather awkward.

But this night, like the last few, was quiet. The usual game of cards went on; they might have had enough for a second table of play, but I had no desire to join them and Norwood was gone. Some business in Hempstead claimed his attention and he'd left at dawn that morning. Poor Elizabeth had had a dull time of it waiting for him, or so I gathered when she greeted me earlier. Now she poked glumly at the keys of the spinet, her eyes starting up every time she fancied hearing a noise that might be the announcement of his arrival home.

Lady Caroline was busy with some delicate needlework, and Anne was reading another of Shakespeare's works. They sat on either side of the table, close enough to share the candlelight. The flames lent a golden tone to their high-dressed and powdered hair that was soothing to behold. I had a book of my own, but my attention kept wandering from it to them, particularly Anne. Her brow was deeply furrowed in concentration, but it was not unattractive on her. I quite liked the effect, as it gave a more serious air to her pretty, but usually blank face.

Then she must have sensed me watching her. She looked up to meet my eyes. I smiled politely and got one in return. She tried to continue reading, but I'd spoiled it for her. After a few more efforts, she gave up and smiled at me again.

*Well-a-day*. I'd seen that expression more than once on others and recognized it, or thought I did. The question to face now was what to do about it. Possessing a healthy portion of curiosity, I decided to find out if I was mistaken. I nodded back to her with a friendly expression. Hers was also friendly . . . and maybe a bit more.

She quietly folded her book and left the room in such a way as to bring no notice to herself. That usually requires either talent or raw instinct to do well, and Anne apparently possessed both those qualities. As she passed me, I got another look from her. No, I had not been at all mistaken, so after an interval, I followed. I wasn't sure about my ability to be as quiet as she, but I tried.

She was in the parlor. The fire was out and the only light came from the single candle she'd taken with her. She put it on a table.

"Hallo," I said.

Anne briefly pulled her lips into a thin line, then said, "You seem to like me."

"Yes, I suppose I do."

"As a cousin, or as something more?"

"Ahh . . . well . . ."

"Is that why you were looking at me? Were you trying to decide?"

I laughed a little. "Maybe I was. I'm sorry if I've given you any offense."

She shook her head. "I'm not offended, but I am curious."

*What a coincidence*.

"I know we are blood cousins, but I . . . think you're very handsome . . . and kind."

"Thank you. I think you're very pretty and sweet."

She swallowed. "That's good."

I moved fractionally closer. "Perhaps it's just that we're both curious."

"Yes, I'm sure of it. But I . . ." Now she looked rather helpless and lost. Was she standing on the edge of that cliff Elizabeth had spoken about? What lay below, a soft landing or something painful?

"Do you think you might be in love?"

Her lips thinned again as she bit the lower one. "I don't know what answer to give you."

"What answer do you give yourself?"

"That I'm not."

"But you're still curious?"

"Yes."

"Then perhaps we should simply attempt to satisfy our mutual curiosity and leave it at that."

She thought it over and her face lightened. "What shall we do?"

"Yes, well, there are any number of things that may be tried."

"I'd like to kiss you."

"That's a good start."

"But I don't know how. You won't laugh at me, will you?"

"My word of honor," I said solemnly, which seemed to give her some comfort. And I was not playing with her, for I knew just how difficult and frightening total inexperience can be.

She straightened and composed herself. "Will you show me?"

Now I had a moment of difficulty, not from inexperience, but from the responsibility I was about to take on. I vividly recalled how Nora had been aware of it for herself. With her example in mind, I knew then that I wanted Anne's first kiss to be just as happy a memory as mine was.

"All right. Stand close."

She did so.

"Relax a bit." I placed my hands lightly on either side of her face, then bent a little and kissed her, just like that. Softly. Gently. "There now," I whispered. "It's very easy. Want to try another?"

"Mm-mmm."

I took that to mean that she did and so obliged her, taking more time. She seemed to enjoy it, but had a puzzled look when I pulled away.

"Is that all there is? Not that it wasn't nice, but I thought—"

"Actually, yes, there is more. Quite a lot."

"Oh, that's good. Will you show me that as well?"

"If you wish, but not everything. Don't want to overdo it the first time out, y'know."

I put my arms around her and she followed suit. She was on the small side, but we managed to put our lips together again. I slowly opened mine and after a pause she did the same, catching her breath as I tried a more intimate touch with my tongue. That woke her up.

"Oh, dear," she gasped when I paused.

I didn't ask whether she liked it or not; it was obvious that she did, but had only been surprised.

"Does everyone do it like this?"

"Perhaps not as well," I answered, eschewing modesty. I felt there was no need for such. Nora had, after all, been an excellent teacher.

"Again, please?"

Explorations proceeded on both sides. Her breath came faster and deeper and I could feel her heart pounding throughout her whole body. I was subject to some extremely pleasant reactions of my own, the most noticeable of which forced me to draw away before she discovered anything odd about my mouth. I began kissing her cheeks, forehead, temples, ears, and finally dropped as far as her throat.

And there . . . I had to reluctantly stop. My corner teeth were out and I was more than ready to put them to use, but that wouldn't have been right. Not for either of us.

"Are you—are you finished?" she asked shakily.

"I think it might be a good idea to leave off here," I murmured somewhat indistinctly.

"Do other people not continue . . . to other things?"

"Yes, but I'm not prepared to do so. That is for another person to do."

"Who?"

"The man you'll fall in love with someday."

"What if I changed my mind? What if I'm in love with you?"

"That would make me a most fortunate fellow, but you're not."

"How do you know?"

"I just do."

Her hands fluttered over her lips, paused at her breast an instant, and then clasped one another determinedly. She breathed in and out once. "Then what am I feeling?"

"The normal kind of lust that is often generated by bit of healthy kissing."

"Lust?"

"Yes."

"That's a bad thing, though. Isn't it?"

"You do have to be careful around it, but under the right circumstances it can be very good indeed."

"And these aren't the right circumstances?"

"And I'm not the right person."

"You're sure?"

"I'm afraid so."

Her eyes were sharp and guarded. "How do you know that?"

"Because if it were otherwise, you and I would be feeling far more than just curiosity for ourselves."

She thought that over for a time. "Or lust?"

"Exactly."

More thought. Her hands unclasped. She took one of mine and went on tiptoe. I leaned down once more and we kissed once more. Rather chastely. She was smiling afterward. "Well . . . Cousin, if and when I should fall in love with a man, thanks to you, I shall be better prepared to deal with him."

"I'm happy to have been of assistance."

"But he will have to be someone very exceptional, I think."

I bowed gravely. "You are most kind, Cousin."

Her eyes were playful again. "Do you still like me?"

"More than ever."

"But not enough to be that person?"

"No. You see, I've . . . been in love . . . still am in love."

"Who is she?"

"It doesn't matter."

"Why don't you marry her?"

"I really couldn't explain."

"And I am prying too much," she concluded.

"Not at all, I'd just rather not speak of it."

That should have put an end to things, but she made no move to leave. "I don't feel like going back to the others yet," she said shyly.

"Neither do I. Would you like to sit and talk awhile?"

For an answer she glided to one of the chairs, sat, and smiled up at me. "About what?"

For anyone else it might have been affectation, but Anne was blessedly free of such encumbrances. I laughed a little and decided that I liked her very much indeed. There was not any great depth to her yet, but she was quite charming in her own way. Innocence has its own strong appeal, either for corruption or for appreciation. I had a mind to be appreciative.

I took a chair opposite her. "Whatever comes to mind. How do you like living here, for instance?"

"Oh, it's very grand. Much better than Philadelphia. If Cousin Roger knew how nice it was here, he'd have forgotten his politics and come along with us. Your mother has been most generous to take us all in as she has."

That was almost what Beldon had said, although he'd ascribed the generosity to Father. The similarity was enough to start a line of thought for me. Questions that had hovered half-formed on the edges of my mind now bloomed forth.

"What do you think of Mother?"

Her brow creased once more. "She's a very great lady, but . . . nervous, I believe."

The memory of her first night here and the altercation between Mother and Elizabeth must have been before her. Like Beldon, she leaned on the side of diplomacy over honesty.

"Yes, she is very nervous," I agreed, hoping to make her comfortable. "I think you understand that I don't know her very well. She lived away from home for most of my life, y'see."

"That's very sad, I'm sure."

*A blessing, more like*, I thought. "And because of her nervous temperament, she's not very easy to get to know. I thought that you might be able to tell me more about her."

"I could try." She did not betray any great enthusiasm for that pursuit.

"Was Mother very nervous when she lived in Philadelphia?"

"Not that I noticed."

Probably not. Without her family there to bother her and—family—those odd things she'd mumbled when I'd awakened her . . . "What do you know about her as a girl?"

"Before she married, you mean? Oh, hardly anything. She often speaks proudly of her father, Judge Fonteyn, and shares news about her sister in England, but that's all. It's rather odd, to think on it. Most people like to tell stories about themselves now and then, things that happened when they were young, but . . ."

"Mother never does?" With her mention of it, I knew this to be true. In her time with us she'd been strangely reticent about her past.

"Yes. One would think that she never had been a young girl."

"I wonder why she is so silent. Did your father ever speak of his brother?" If I could get no information about my mother, then I'd settle for knowledge of my grandfather, though trying to find it out via my granduncle's daughter seemed a rather roundabout way of accomplishing it.

"He talked about his life at school, the little adventures he had there, but he never spoke about his home life—how odd."

"Perhaps life was very hard for them."

"Oh, but the Fonteyns are very rich."

"I meant that—"

"Oh, I see, that they might have had a strict upbringing? Yes . . . now that you call it to mind, I remember Father saying he was glad to leave home and go to school, which made him very different from the other little boys." She gave a sudden little shiver.

"So he never talked about his oldest brother?"

"No . . ."

"What, then?"

She shrugged, using her hands. "I'm not sure, but I got the impression that Father didn't like him much. His own brother. It's horrid, isn't it?"

"Very." But not too surprising. My father also didn't like the man, and from the scarce information he'd shared about him, I would have probably followed his suit. My grandfather had been a most disagreeable fellow, according to Father, a foul-tempered tyrant subject to fits of rage, which would certainly account for Mother's behavior toward us, since she seemed to have taken that as a proper example of how to treat one's family. That was what Elizabeth and I had come to call "the Fonteyn blood" and regard with dread lest we succumb to it ourselves.

But it did not explain why Mother had been afraid in her dream, the one I'd interrupted when I'd gone to see her that night. She'd been pleading like a frightened child. Her voice might well have been a child's voice, and I was forced to admit to myself that it had shaken me to hear it. At the time I'd been too preoccupied with what I'd been doing, but later that voice had come to haunt and worry me. And instead of looking upon Mother with my usual unhappy tolerance, I'd allowed a small piece of compassion to enter into my regard of her. It made her seem less of a barely controlled monster and more like . . . what? A lost and wounded child? Dear God, I could understand that, having been there myself. Perhaps Father was not the one in the family with thc blind spot.

"Was your father a strict man?" I asked almost absently, for the silence had stretched long between us. I needed fresh conversation between me and my thoughts.

Anne smiled. "Mother sometimes accused him of not being strict enough."

"He was a loving man, then."

The smile thinned and faded altogether. "No, not really. He cared for me, but I . . ."

"If this is painful for you—"

"No, really, I've just never thought of it before. I see it now. He never allowed himself to get close to anyone. How sad. I wonder why?"

"He may not have known how. Or been afraid to try."

"Father afraid?" She shook her head, then spread her hands, smoothly retreating into her most common defense against the harshness of life. "It's all too confusing for me."

*Or too close to the heart*. "Quite so. Besides, I was trying to learn about my mother."

"And I haven't been of much help."

"But you have . . . and I'm grateful for it."

Anne and I made an amicable parting and I trotted up to my room only to come down again soon after, garbed for the outdoors. I passed Jericho in the hall and told him I was going to take the air. He nodded, reminded me to put on some gloves, and resumed whatever errand I'd interrupted.

Gloves . . . yes, in the pocket of my cloak as usual. With my indifference to the cold weather, I sometimes forgot them. A spare handkerchief was therc as well, wrapped around two lumps of sugar. Good. Jericho was uncommonly efficient in anticipating my needs. I was hungry tonight and would find those items very useful.

I let myself out by the side door as usual and trudged over my own footprints toward the stables. The wind was high and the ground hard from the cold. My boots crunched and cracked against the frozen mud and snow. I paused outside the far end of the building away from the house and glanced around to be sure no one was watching, then vanished and pushed my way through the wall to get in. It was strange to feel the texture of the barrier, but not the solidity as I flowed through the minute cracks in the boards like so much water. Not exactly unpleasant, but not really enjoyable either. Using the door would have been better, but not as quiet. When on this business, I wanted to be very quiet indeed.

All was dim and dark within when I reassumed my form. Bereft of any outside light, my eyes were no better than anyone else's now, but I knew the way. Ahead on my right were the stalls, and one or two of their occupants sensed my presence and stirred slightly, dark shapes against a dark background. The familiar scents of horse, straw, and manure filled my head. I felt my way toward the first stall, then passed the second, and on to the third. Though the great animals could easily part with a sizable quantity of blood before feeling it—more than I could drink in one night—I took care not to feed from any single one more than once in a week. Since we had a number of horses and I needed to sup only every other night or so, their health remained blessedly robust.

My eyes had adjusted somewhat to the dark, and I found that Desdemona was in this stall. She turned her head 'round to get a better look at me. Like the others, she'd come to associate my late visits with some form of reward and may have already smelled out the sugar in my pocket. I decided to leave her alone, though, as she would be foaling in the spring. We'd mated her to Rolly and had high hopes for what was to come, and it seemed best not to require any more from her than to continue to quietly gestate, undisturbed by my hunger.

She gave a decidedly human-sounding snort of disgust when I moved to the next stall and began patting down Belle, who happily consumed the sugar and stood rock-still while I fed from her. As always, the taste was rich with life and entirely good to me. I had all but forgotten what other, more solid—more normal—food had been like. I did know that it had never imparted such a feeling of completion to me as the blood did now.

The second lump of sugar followed the first and I wiped my mouth clean with the handkerchief. Within my body I felt the red warmth flush throughout my vitals and spread to my limbs. It was like feeling summer sun soaking my soul from the inside out. No yearning existed in me to see that fiery orb again. There was no need to; I carried it in my veins.

I quit the stables by the same path and set out once more into the night.

The wind was a nuisance, but not unbearable, and the walking itself would keep me warm should the cold finally overcome my resistance to it. I pulled my cloak close and marched down the lane to the main road. Once I was out of sight from the house, though, I grew too impatient to stay on my feet and so took to the air.

It was hard going with the wind against me, but I relished the struggle. At least it was something simple and straightforward. I made most of the trip blind or half blind, being unable to retain much solidity as I moved low over the ground, but it was a familiar trip and did not take long. Just before reaching the first buildings of Glenbriar, I went solid again and walked the rest of the way.

As I'd expected, there were lights showing at The Oak. Freezing and windy or no, the soldiers here would not be kept from their drink, nor the locals, either. Some horses harnessed to a wagon were tethered outside, huddling miserably together and unable to put their backs to the wind. If the riders were too drunk and irresponsible to take care of their mounts, then I'd have to have a word with the landlord about them. No sense in letting the beasts suffer for their master's lack of concern.

I pushed through the door and called a general greeting to the company within. It was a mixed lot, uniforms, homespun, and fair to fine tailoring, each in their own groups, though there was some tentative mixing. One of the Hessian officers who had rather good English was holding forth about his war experiences to a spellbound crew. He could tell a good tale; I'd listened to enough of them myself on previous visits. His name was Eichelburger, and he'd been of great help to me in improving my knowledge of German. I waved over their heads to him and got a wave in return, all without interrupting his narration.

Mr. Farr had by now long adjusted himself to my return and came over to offer a glad greeting. His acceptance of me may have been tempered by my free-spending habits. I always bought an ale for myself and hardly ever failed to invite a few others to join me. Surrounded by a crowd, I could more easily get away with not drinking it, and if I wanted to empty my tankard, all I had to do was leave it unwatched for a moment by Noddy Milverton and he'd swiftly dispatch it for me. Not that we'd made any arrangements; Noddy just had an insatiable thirst and not much money. He was a bit simple, so few of his victims objected, least of all myself.

"There's some horses out front that are feeling the weather," I told Farr.

"I'll have someone see to 'em," he said, and signed to one of his pot boys. As it was so common an occurrence, no further instructions were needed; the lad nodded and went out. "They always come in for just a moment, then stay all night. Thankee for tellin'."

"Any news?" Again, there was no need to be detailed, as there was only one kind of news anyone was interested in.

He shook his head. "Soldiers all gone to ground for the winter. All's been quiet as far as I know, and I'm pleased for it to stay that way. The Suffolk County lads 'ave been restive, though. Stole some sheep t'other day."

"I s'pects we knows what they stole 'em *for*!" put in the ribald and unrepentant Mr. Thayer. He was in his usual corner, puffing on his pipe. I wondered if he had grown roots to that chair yet.

"Now, now, sir," cautioned Farr, but he was chuckling, too.

"Any more thieves from Connecticut?" I asked.

Farr shrugged. "Not in my hearing. There's plenty of tales if you want to hear 'em, but nothing I'd put my trust in. I've heard talk from the soldiers that the whaleboat boys sometimes shelter in Suffolk, but it don't seem too sensible. The rebels in Suffolk are more like to thieve for themselves, not be sharin' the pickin's with others. Same goes for Connecticut."

"And either way honest, loyal folk take the loss."

"Some of 'em, but not all. Gunsmiths 'ave been busy. Nothing like a few musket balls for helping a rebel to change his mind about taking your livestock."

I could appreciate that well enough. It was reassuring to know that things had been quiet elsewhere. The weather had been none too good lately, either full of wind or sleet or snow or a combination of the three. Hardly encouraging to an enterprising thief looking for booty. We'd all learned to dread quiet nights, especially when there was little or no moon.

We talked a bit more, and others joined in or moved off. Noddy took care of two other tankards besides my own, all without being noticed. I said good evening and made my way out. Mr. Thayer's seamed face cracked as he gave me a comically broad wink. He was used to seeing me leaving early, and his long experience told him why.

"Gi' my regards to Molly Audy, will ye?" he bellowed across the room. This raised a tidal rush of laughter that swept me right outside. I wasn't so sophisticated yet that I couldn't blush, but I may have escaped into the dark before anyone saw it.

Most of the villagers were indoors and either in bed or getting ready for it; of course, that meant something different to a woman like Molly. Going to bed and going to sleep were often mutually exclusive, depending on the success of her business. She was apparently doing well enough tonight. Lights were burning in her front room and bedroom. I quietly let myself in the door to wait until she was finished with this other customer. There were some interesting sounds issuing from beyond the closed door in the back, but I could not judge just how far along they were to concluding things.

Hat in hand, I paced a little. Friendly curiosity aside, my experience with Cousin Anne had provided me with sufficient inspiration to want to carry what she'd initiated forward to a more satisfactory conclusion. Further inspiration was this time provided by the noise Molly and her friend were making, and I was growing naturally impatient for my turn to come. After what seemed like an indecently lengthy interval, the bed and its occupants finally made their last groans together. The voices resumed normal speech, Molly murmuring admiration and the man making similar responses.

*Oh, dear*. Sudden recognition of the man's voice flooded me. My mouth went dry as sand. All the enthusiasm that had been building in me abruptly fled. Molly's customer . . . *damnation*.

Flat-footed as I was with surprise, I had enough time to recover and completely vanish before they emerged. I stayed that way until he was well and truly gone and even then waited long before returning.

Molly had gone back to the bedroom again and so I found myself alone in her "parlor" where she conducted her sewing business during the day. Bits of fabric, thread, and pins littered the place, adding a legitimacy to this half of her livelihood; as for the other half . . .

Well, she was the favorite of some of the more moneyed gentlemen of the village, so I needn't have been so startled by this latest visitor. The way things were, especially in the more civilized parts of the world, it was fairly common for a man to seek a degree of physical satisfaction with any lady who might take his fancy. Whether she was his mistress or a paid prostitute depended on his situation in life and the depth of his pockets.

But in this case I was so deeply disturbed because this particular fellow was paying suit to my dearly beloved sister.

Visions of rushing after Lord James Norwood and demanding an explanation or wrenching a promise from him to cease and desist clouded my eyes. Other visions also intruded, including a rather tempting one of caning him to within an inch of his life. Oh, but *that* would have brought such a lovely and wicked fulfillment to my baser nature: to thump him about the shoulders and finally smash his handsome face to a pulp for this insult to Elizabeth. How *dare* he pay honorable court to her one day and then—literally—pay out to Molly the next?

He'd be on the road back to the house for certain, easy enough for me to find him and then provide him a very solid lesson in polite behavior toward one's . . .

Damnation.

Elizabeth.

My anger leached from my heart as I thought of her. Certainly I could think of ways to deal with the man, but that would hardly change his status in her eyes. In fact, if he turned up in a less than perfect condition, it would certainly bring about a great flow of sympathy from Elizabeth. And if she demanded why I'd misused the fellow so, then I'd have to tell her the extremely painful truth and . . .

*Damnation*. Again.

Of course, Norwood was perfectly within his right to do what he liked. He and Elizabeth were not really engaged, after all, but this discovery was a singularly unpleasant one for me, made the more so because I didn't know what to do about it.

Several questions began to tumble through my mind as I wondered if he still planned to pursue his courtship of my sister. If so, and they were married, would he continue to improve the trade for women like Molly? That was enough to set my jaw to grinding and turn my hands into destructive fists.

If he caused Elizabeth the *least* unhappiness, by God, he *would* answer to me.

Molly emerged, saw me, gasped, and gave a jump. "Goodness, Johnny boy! I never heard you coming in. Why didn't you call out?"

I was almost as surprised as she, so involved was I in my speculations. Shoving them forcibly to one side, I pasted what I hoped to be a pleasing expression over my true feelings and went to kiss her hand. "I'm sorry, but I didn't want to disturb you if you had company."

"Oh, my company's been and gone. I was just starting to feel lonesome again. Glad I am that you happened by." She wriggled into my arms and made a good-natured inquiry on whether I planned to stay awhile.

"For as long as you'll have me," I replied.

"Then that depends on how long *you* plan to have *me*," she returned. "It's been much too long since I've seen you. Whatever have you been doing with yourself? Or is that it? Have you been doing it with yourself?" She ground her body against mine in a delightfully suggestive way.

"Never," I said with utter sincerity. Since my change, that was one form of carnal pleasure denied to me. But though my body's expression had altered, the appetite for it remained, and so Molly and I did share company fairly often. I had an idea that my maternal grandfather would have been rolling in his grave if he knew where a fraction of my inheritance from him had ended up over the last few months. That idea added a certain . . . piquant flavor to my frequent beddings with Molly.

The memory of Cousin Anne's curiosity reasserted itself and combined with the actuality of Molly; I found myself easily sweeping the latter up for a sound kissing. Her laughter—somewhat smothered by my lips—was genuine and I was once more pleased to realize that I was certainly her favorite customer. What matter to her if I kept my breeches up and drank her blood? She seemed not to mind those differences, but relished them as much as I, since it never failed to impress a lengthy and highly satisfying climax upon her. So when it came down to it, I was essentially paying her to have a good time. She'd once joked about paying me, but I never took her up on it. Thanks to Grandfather Fonteyn, I could afford to be generous.

She finally pushed me away, puffing for air. "This is lovely, Johnny boy, but it's drafty out here. Wouldn't you like to find a warmer place to finish things?"

"Indeed, yes."

It didn't take long for us to settle ourselves into her bed. She'd been wearing a thick wrapper of some kind and shed it quickly, throwing it atop the coverlet for extra warmth before diving into the sheets. She had good cause to complain of the cold, since the only thing she'd been wearing under the wrap were a number of goosebumps. I liked to think that some of them were due to my actions rather than the chill of the outer room. Perhaps so, as she was most eager and called for me to hurry myself.

I took off my cloak and spread it on the bed as well. My coat and boots went on a chair, but I kept the rest of my clothes on, as part of Molly's own pleasure included a great fondness for unbuttoning things. I slipped into the sheets with her. They smelled of her . . . and others. It had not bothered me before. Which of those musky scents had been left behind by Norwood?

"Was that Lord James I spied leaving here a bit ago?" I asked.

She'd just started to work on my waistcoat. "Mayhap it was, but then lots of gentlemen come here. You know that."

This, I remembered, was "Molly the Mum" talking. She never gave away names or told tales. Any other time I'd have applauded her discretion, but not now. "Decent fellow, I hope?"

"Very decent . . . but you're better."

"Tell me about him, Molly."

She finished the last button and paused. "Now, Johnny boy, that wouldn't be right. You know I don't gossip about any of my gentlemen. 'S not nice to gossip."

"I've a special reason, though."

"What's that?"

"He's courting my sister."

"Lucky girl, then."

"He's likely to marry her, too, so I'm curious—"

"What, you want to know what he's like with me so you can tell your sister?"

"Ahh, no! I mean, that's not—good God!"

Molly's giggles for my shock finally subsided. "Oh, I do like you, Mr. Barrett, and I understand why you want to look out for your sister, but I can't just tell tales whenever a gentleman gets curious."

"Perhaps I've not been as liberal with you as I should be . . ." I dug into a pocket with some spare coins in it.

She gave a firm shake with her head, eyes briefly shutting while she did so. "It's not that at all. I have my rules and I stick to 'em." She was being nice about it, but her manner indicated she would not be moved on the subject.

But there were ways around this. At least for me.

I looked right into her eyes. There was enough light for it this time. "That's very good of you, but I think you can make an exception this time."

And she did. Not that I gave her a choice in the matter. But now that she was willing to answer my questions, I wasn't sure what to ask her. Her thought that I might inquire about Norwood's habits in bed struck me as being far too personal, though I wouldn't deny the temptation was there. No . . . I'd let that one go. Better to find something else to talk about.

"Molly, tell me what you think of Lord James." That was the way to do it: ask her for an opinion she might have offered anyway if not for her damned rules.

"He's a nice enough sort," she intoned, a little flat, slurring her words.

"Do you like him?"

"Well enough."

"Anything bother you about him?"

She made a face. " 'E does like to haggle the price. Spends more effort trying to save a penny than 'e puts into 'is bedding. Must think I don't 'ave to work 'ard for it, but I do. 'E won't find no better than me for the price. Skinflint."

That was interesting. From this I might deduce that Elizabeth need not worry about him squandering her dowry, though too much thrift can be just as burdensome.

"How does he treat you, Molly?"

"Well enough," she repeated. " 'E's nice as it suits 'im. Not as nice as my Johnny boy, but all right."

"Thank you. Do you like him?"

" 'E's a nice sort . . ."

"Do you like him?"

Her answer was long in coming. "Not really," she said with some reluctance.

"Why not?"

She shrugged.

"Then why see him?"

"I need the money, love."

A foolish question, that. Like any person in trade, Molly would have to deal with all sorts of customers and be polite no matter what. I could certainly admire and respect her dedication to her work. "Think he'll be coming back to you?"

"S'pose 'e will when 'e's a mind for it."

"Think he'd have a mind for it were he married?"

Another shrug. "Won't be able to tell that 'til it 'appens. Wouldn't be the first time, nor the last."

I wasn't about to question her cxperience there.

Molly woke out of things gradually, unaware of what had happened, ready to pick up where we'd left off as if no time had passed. My influence on her had put her into an even more receptive mood than before, but my own was considerably dampened. I'd fed heavily and had a lot on my mind. It took a bit more effort on her part to drag me back to the business at hand, but we eventually made a consummation that suited us both. She'd had a long day, though, and the extended pleasure my nature provided for us only added to her exhaustion. She was asleep almost as soon as I pulled my lips away from her firm, sweet throat. I dressed quietly, made sure the covers were pulled up and tucked about her, put out the candles, and left.

Late. Or early, since it was well past midnight. High clouds obscured the stars, but I could sense the hour more or less. No need to hurry, but no need to tarry, either.

The wind was worse than before, very hard, very gusty. Better not to vanish and travel on the air in these conditions. I'd tried often enough before and found myself being carried along out of control, which is a very vile feeling. I got my flapping cloak wrapped tight around me, held my hat in place, and started down the road leading home.

Miserable stuff, wind. It roars in your ears, deafening you to all other sounds. If cold, it cuts through your clothes with more surety than the sharpest knife. It buffets the body, stealing your balance, and it makes harmless things like trees and grass seem more alive than they should be. When it's really strong it makes them whisper and laugh to one another, mocking and vindictive to all who pass them.

I felt their rancor, or fancied I did, while trudging along. The road was full of ruts and icy, but it was easier than facing the banks of snow on either side. There was no point in complaining to myself about any of it, but I did so, since it kept my mind off the larger problem of Norwood. I grumbled and mumbled, though my voice was a small and fragile distraction.

Then another sound intruded upon me, at first so faint and uneven that I wasn't sure I heard anything. It was behind me, that was for certain, the wind saw to that. I waited, listening, and finally caught the jingle of bits and the crunch of wheels going over the frozen ground. There was a slight bend in the road, and soon a wagon came around it into sight.

There were no lanterns showing, which was odd but understandable. As unsettled as things were in the area, it was a wise course not to draw attention to oneself. I would have—had my eyes been normal—preferred to take a chance and had some light with me in case of trouble.

Though going at a good pace, I thought it might stop long enough for me to get a ride to my gate. It would be a poor Christian indeed who would deny so small a favor to another soul on such a night. I walked a little more, but slowly, and let it catch me up.

The driver crouched over his reins, urging his horses forward. He was not much more than a shape to me even as he came closer. He wore a heavy coat and his hat was tied to his head by a rag of a scarf, the ends of which snapped in the wind like some tattered banner.

"Hallo!" I called, when he was near enough to see me.

He must have understood what I might ask of him, for he pulled on the reins.

"Commun over," he called back, when they'd stopped.

I wasted no more time and scrambled up next to him. "Very kind of you, sir."

"Aye. M'name's Ash. Who're you?"

"Jonathan Barrett."

"Y'sure o' that?"

I thought it a strange question to ask, but made no comment since he was being kind enough to give me a ride. However, we were not moving yet, as he seemed far more concerned with introductions than anything else. "Yes, I'm quite sure."

"Barrett as lives down the road? This road?"

"Yes—"

His face split in a big grin and he made a sudden move with one hand. Before I knew it the muzzle of a pistol was in it and the business end was shoved into my belly.

# CHAPTER
# 9

"My God, man, what are you about?" My outrage was genuine. I was too surprised to be afraid.

He ignored me. "Now, boys!" he shouted in my face.

When reason fails, instinct takes over, if you're lucky. I ducked blindly, but a fraction too late. Dark shapes, I don't know how many, erupted up from the back of the wagon, hands reaching for me. One of them caught me by the hair and strongly dragged me backward and down. My head cracked far too solidly against the wagon seat, and for the first time in months I saw the sun. It seared right through my skull and out the other side in an instant and was gone, leaving behind the most horrendous pain I'd ever felt in my life. It crowded out all thought, all motion, all sound. Nothing else was in my world but the hideous, explosive agony clamoring between my ears.

"Ye've killed 'im!" someone cried.

"Nay, 'e's but stunned. Git 'im in so we can go."

Helpless, I felt myself being hauled up into the back of the wagon; at least, that's what I worked out somewhat later. At the moment I was too stunned to know what was happening or to care anything about it.

"I got me a fine new 'at!" one of them sang out.

"Cloak too," added another. "See what's in 'is pockets."

Hands, prodding and rough, made a thorough search of me and grabbed away prizes, winners crowing in triumph. I didn't care, didn't have enough awareness to care. I wanted only to scream out from the pain, but was too paralyzed to do it.

Ash whipped up the horses. The wagon lurched forward.

If I could have moved, I'd have probably been sick, but nothing was moving, nothing at all. I might as well have been a corpse, but being drearily and inescapably shackled to my body, I knew I hadn't died.

Not yet.

We rattled quickly over the ruts. I lost track of time, drifting in and out of consciousness, perhaps. There was no way to tell. Some things were clear, others less so. The clear bits hurt.

"Easy now," said Ash. "Hessians quartered in a barn hereabouts, remember? Keep 'im quiet."

" 'E ain't movin'."

"Good."

Barn? Our barn. We'd passed my gate. I was being carried right away from my home . . . safety . . . help.

The wagon rumbled on, the men heedless of my silent objections.

*Why?* The question bobbed up in my mind like a piece of cork. *Why had they done this to me?*

The answer took a bit longer, for I'd faded out again, or so I assumed, since I was all too aware of waking up. The pain had dampened enough that I was better able to think, but only in a disjointed sort of way. I understood that I'd been attacked and had been robbed and was in the process of being kidnapped.

*Why?*

They'd been after *me*, not just any unlucky traveler on the road, but me.

*Wh—*

Then I didn't care why, couldn't think why. All I could do was . . .

. . . wake up again, some long time later. How long . . . ?

My eyes were open. They'd been shut before. I could blink.

But not much else. Fingers were cold. Couldn't move them. I'd forgotten to put on gloves again. Jericho would have something to say about that. No matter. The fellows here would have probably stripped them from me by now.

Now. *What* now? What was the time? I tried desperately to read the sky. It seemed lighter, but that might have been a normal reflection of the snowy fields on the low clouds. I didn't know the time, which was almost as hard to bear as my injury. Maybe they were linked. Whatever clock I had inside me had been thoroughly shattered when my head struck the wooden bench of the wagon.

Head. I could have done without the reminder. It ached abominably and I felt sick all over again, hot and cold at the same time. There was salty bile pooling at the back of my mouth, but I couldn't spit it out. Couldn't move yet.

Why . . . hadn't I vanished?

This hurt far worse than getting shot. I should have disappeared at the first shock. Were there splinters in my head where I'd . . . no, it didn't feel like that. This was different, duller, but no less forceful when it came to discomfort.

I tried to . . . vanish.

Nothing.

The effort left me shivering. And sicker than before. Overwhelmingly so. I lost track of time again, finding it I don't know how long later when the wagon gave an especially sharp jolt. This waking was a little better than the others. I knew what had happened, but still not why or . . .

Where were we?

Couldn't see anything but the sky and skeletal branches now and then when we passed under an occasional tree growing by the road. Couldn't tell if we were even on the same road. If we were, then I was being taken to Suffolk County. Despite the presence of all the troops, the place was crawling with rebels, absolutely the last spot on earth one of His Majesty's loyal subjects would want to be. I couldn't think of a worse place, unless it was in the middle of General Washington's camp.

Raving. Get hold of yourself.

Not raving. Righteously scared.

Get hold of yourself anyway.

Not being able to move my head yet, I couldn't see much of the others. The first heady feeling of victory had passed and now they were hunched against one another, probably feeling the cold. No one spoke or paid much notice to me. Only one face was visible, familiar, but still a stranger. I'd seen him . . . at The Oak . . . one of the other patrons.

Not that that was much help.

He continued to ignore me and remained silent.

Who were the others? Or did it matter? Perhaps not. They'd all be strangers to me, or else they wouldn't have had to be so sure of my name before attacking.

Why? What had I done? Why should these strangers . . .

Oh, God.

Now I did become sick. The pool in the back of my mouth filled and thickened into a foul mass. My guts were all watery as the realization seized me like a giant's hand. A nasty, bubbling sound issued from my throat like a death rattle. I shut my eyes tight and let the first wave of panic rush over and drown my thoughts. Fighting it wouldn't have done any good; better to let the body finish with its reactions, then let the mind take charge.

The wave passed. Slowly. It left me weak and worried, but not utterly frozen with terror. I swallowed and was surprised that the bile went down. And stayed there.

Better. I was feeling—very marginally—better. The pain was slightly less crippling than before. I could move my fingers; that was something.

I had also, with this small recovery, grown very angry. Instead of the burning heat or frosty chill running over my skin, it was simply warming. Comforting, like the taste of blood.

Blood . . . I could smell it. My own, of course. There was a cold patch on my head where the skin must have broken and bled when that fool had smashed my skull. The blood was cooling and drying in the harsh air. God, they might have killed me with that blow, though maybe it wasn't as bad as I . . . no. It was bad. Bad enough as I found when I tried to move more than my fingers.

" 'E's come 'round," said one of the men, having noticed my feeble attempts to master my body again.

"Just keep 'im quiet," said Ash.

"Drummond got 'im good. Thumped 'is 'ead like a summer melon. 'E ain't goin' to make no trouble."

The big fellow closest to me laughed at the compliment. Drummond. He would pay for this, I thought.

"When do we get there?" whined another man from the back.

"Soon, Tully," came the weary reply. From that brief intonation I got the impression that Tully whined rather a lot.

"It's been hours. I'm freezin' sittin' 'ere like this."

"Then get out and walk."

The suggestion was not received very well, but it shut Tully up for the time being.

Arms. I could shift my arms a little. Legs, too, after a moment of concentration. Didn't want to try vanishing just yet. Too weak. Better to wait.

As some of the pain receded, other discomforts cried out for attention, like the ride itself. I was on the unprotected wood bottom of the wagon and its hard, harsh surface bumped and jolted me with every uneven turn of all four wheels. No wonder I was so sick. My head was bad enough, but combine that with the motion of our travel . . . ugh.

I gulped again and tried to think of something else.

Like the cold. Apart with the other discomforts, I was finally beginning to feel its bite. Even the warmth derived from my anger wasn't up to fighting it off now. The damnable wind clawed at my exposed skin and seeped beneath all my clothes. I wanted my heavy cloak back. Which one of the bastards had taken it? Couldn't see him from this angle.

I silently cursed them and prayed to God for an ending to our journey. The answer came surprisingly soon when Ash turned the horses off to the left. The clouds spun over me and my stomach objected until I shut my eyes. The road became much worse than before and I had to hold my teeth hard together to keep from crying out at the change. Pity I couldn't have slept through it all; I wouldn't have minded missing this part.

We creaked to a halt and the men stiffly crawled from the back of the wagon. I had another instant of panic, thinking they'd leave me to die out in the cold until someone grabbed my ankles and pulled. All in all, I'd have preferred freezing to death. I was just able to lift my head to spare it from scraping over the worn boards, but that was the extent of my control. The same hands that had thrown me in now carried me out, this time with much grunting and complaint.

I briefly saw the walls of a poor-looking house, then we squeezed through a door and there was some general activity as they sorted and settled themselves. A big grumbling man was sent to take care of the horses and wagon. I was hauled over to a rough bed and dropped into it. The mattress was sparsely stuffed and so thin that I felt the supporting rope lattice beneath. My captors would get no objections from me; it was heavenly compared to the wagon. I was out of the wind and though the house was cold, it was not numbing.

A wretched place it was, to be sure. It seemed to have but one room and the fireplace could have been larger. Tully was busy there with a tinderbox, muttering to himself while another man offered unwanted suggestions. A table teetered in the middle of the dusty floor, surrounded by a long bench and some crude chairs. Those things and the bed were the only furnishings. The walls were stripped of any decoration or tools, indication that no one actually lived here. My guess was that these men had simply found the place and taken it over.

Ash had been more successful with his tinderbox and had lighted two lamps. He brought one over to have a better look at me. I took the opportunity to have a better look at him. I'd want to remember his face, all their faces. His was hardened by both the weather and a difficult life and possibly an even more difficult temperament. He grinned down at me with an evil satisfaction that might have been comical but for the grimness of my situation. I did not find him remotely amusing.

" 'E's a soft'un, I'll warrant. Ye din't 'ave to crack 'im so 'ard, Drummond. We coulda tied 'im up wi' a piece o' string 'n' led 'im 'ere like a lamb."

"Hah!" said Drummond.

"Pasty-faced Tory bastard," Ash went on. " 'E's soft as a slug from 'igh livin' on 'is pap's gold, that 'n' all 'is drinkin' 'n' whorin'."

"Where am I?" I asked, wishing to change the subject. My voice was thin, little more than a whisper. A stranger's voice. The fear that I'd managed to shove away for a time began to seep back at this lack of recognition for myself. I tried to pretend it wasn't there and concentrated on gaining useful knowledge.

"Yer with us, that's a' you needs t' know."

"Must still be in Nassau County," I remarked faintly.

"Hah!" said Drummond.

"We've got us a right stupid Tory bastard, don't we, boys?" said Ash, enlarging upon Drummond's short but informative comment. So I was in Suffolk County, miles from home. How many?

"I *have* to be there," I insisted. "We couldn't have traveled all that far."

"Fifteen mile, if it were an inch. Maybe more." He was proud of the accomplishment and contemptuous of my disbelief.

"Ridiculous." But I didn't press further, lest they catch on to what I was doing. "What do you want of me? Why did you bring me here?"

"What we want is fer ye to do what yer told, then Drummond won't be 'aving to cut yer heart out 'n' 'andin' it to ye."

"Hah!" said Drummond.

Not too reassuring, but at least they weren't planning to kill me right off. On the other hand, if I didn't get away from here before dawn, they wouldn't have to trouble themselves.

"I like them ridin' boots," said a thin fellow, talking through his hatchety nose.

"Be off with ye, Abel, I already claimed 'em 'n' everyone knows it," said another man who was homely enough to have been his brother.

"Yer feet is too big fer 'em!"

"Are not! You've got 'is cloak, I git 'is boots!" This declaration was followed by a noisy tussle. Ash watched the combatants with disgust.

"Those two should be Cain and Abel, not Abel and Seth," he growled to Drummond, who for once did not say "hah!" but did step in and roughly part the two. He lifted each by the collar, shook them soundly, then let them fall. The argument was over for the moment and I consciously relaxed my tightly curled toes. I had no desire to be hiking home in stocking feet.

The door opened and the other fellow who was almost as big as Drummond came in. I wondered if he was in charge of this lot, as none of them appeared to be impressively gifted with intelligence. He gruffly announced that the horses were bedded, then went to warm his hands by Tully's fledgling fire.

Six of them. Daunting even with my full strength, quite impossible now.

"What's the time?"

My question amused them. There was no clock in the hovel and probably never had been.

"Gittin' on to dawn in a couple hours, I should think," said Ash.

"I'm hungry," whined Tully.

"Then fix somethin'!"

Tully subsided and poked about in whatever supplies they had.

"Why am I here?"

Ash's grin, a singularly unpleasant one, returned. "Yer a prisoner o' war, that's why."

"I'm no soldier—"

"Aye, but yer mighty good at killin', ain't ye?" he sneered.

There it was, the confirmation of my worst fears. My heart sank and they could see it on my face. No need or point in pretense.

Ash leaned close. I could smell his rotten teeth. "Ye murdered two fine men, ye Tory bastard. Cut 'em down cold 'n' yer goin' t' pay fer it."

I snapped my mouth shut. There was also no need or point in arguing my side of it with them; I'd made that conclusion earlier when I'd guessed who they were. The panic threatened to return, but I couldn't afford it this time. I had to keep my mind free of it. Free . . . and thinking.

"You want something more, though, don't you? Or else you wouldn't have brought me here."

"Aye, we do. Yer rich pap's goin' to pay t' git you back, ain't he? We reckon 'e can spare the gold 'f he wants to see 'is brat again, right?"

I reluctantly nodded. For all the house and fine clothes, my father was not a wealthy man; Mother had all the money. I wondered if she would pay a ransom for me, then decided it didn't matter. These men were not going to let me live whatever happened. I kept those thoughts to myself and tried to look anxiously cooperative. "Yes. My father will do anything you say. Just name your price and he'll pay it."

It was exactly what they wanted to hear.

"Right!" Ash produced a dirty sheet of paper. One side was some kind of obsolete handbill, all patriotism and high emotion, and the other blank. "Put down what we tell ye."

"If I can." And I sincerely meant that, for I was going all weak again.

Drummond picked me up and dragged me to the table. I was dropped onto a chair, but he had to hold me up. Dizzy and suddenly shivering, I eased forward and tenderly cushioned my cruelly aching head on my folded arms.

"What wrong with 'im?" asked Tully.

"Got no belly fer man's work," said Ash, but he sounded worried.

I ground my teeth together to keep from sobbing from the pain. Very gently, I felt around the side of my skull where it was the worst. Dried blood matted my hair, but there seemed to be no fresh bleeding. There was a soft spot there . . . bruised and swollen skin, perhaps. I hoped that was all. Pain flared, threatening to blaze up into something truly unbearable if the tentative exploration continued. I moaned and shook involuntarily, hating my show of weakness, but unable to stop it.

My hosts were silent except for some hard breathing as they looked on. No one offered to help.

"Drummond hit 'im too hard," Tully stated mournfully. He was the youngest of the group, not much more than a boy, and an unhappy one at that. " 'E's gonna die on us. Did ye see 'is face?"

Ash snorted. "Not before 'e does us some good. Straighten up, you. Yer gonna write yer pap."

"Give me a minute," I pleaded, still gasping from it.

It came in waves, a relatively pain-free period followed by nausea, and I was going through a bad spot of the latter. Drummond's tossing me about like a rag toy hadn't helped. I wanted desperately to try vanishing again in the hope of healing, but my last attempt had knocked me out. It would have to be later, when I was stronger and not so hideously ill. As for these louts seeing it, I didn't care.

Ash snarled more frustrated threats, but did nothing. Someone found a bit of charcoal and pushed it into my slack right hand.

In a few minutes the worst of it passed and I found I could see once more. Not well. The lantern lights seemed unbearably bright to me. I could hardly open my eyes. Ash impatiently urged me to work. I felt for the sheet of paper. The charcoal slipped from my fingers and I had trouble trying to pick it up.

"I'm sorry," I whispered. "I can't. It's too much."

"You'll write it, I say." Ash again. God, what a miserable, scratching voice the man had.

"I can't. One of you will have to. I'm too badly hurt."

"But not so hurt ye can't talk? Write, damn ye, or Drummond'll start 'is cuttin'."

I groaned and managed to hold the charcoal. Despite all the discomfort, there was a warm and tight feeling of triumph in me. Ash's insistence that I do the writing meant that none of them could. Not one of them had made the least move to take over in response to my pitiful act.

Not that I was acting.

"What do you want to say?" I asked, barely audible.

"This is to yer pap. Tell 'im you've been captured."

Easy enough. *Dear Father, I've been kidnapped . . .*

I laboriously scraped the charcoal over the paper, trying to make clean, legible script and finding it difficult. The paper was cheap and rough; even if I'd had a proper quill and ink it would not have been any too easy. I took my time, the others staring at my every move as though I were performing some magical rite. Meaningless symbols to them, possible help for me.

"Yes . . . what else?"

"If 'e wants you back alive, 'e's to give six 'undred pounds in silver or gold to the man giving 'im this note."

I formed letters. *Being held about 15 miles from home in Suffolk by Montagu house thieves . . .*

Paused.

"Don't follow the man or we'll cut yer throat."

*. . . will try to escape. Hold and question this man.*

"Sign it."

*Jonathan.*

Ash took the paper up and looked it over with smug pleasure. "There it is, lads, a tidy 'undred fer each of us."

I buried my face in my arms lest I betray myself, though I really hurt too much to smile.

"Aye, but will we get it? What if Knox don't come back?"

"Y'sayin' I'm a thief, Abel?" Knox, the big fellow who'd tended the horses, had an ominous growl.

Abel backed down. "Not 'xactly, jus' what if somethin' should 'appen to ye?"

"Nothin' will. I'll be back with the money 'n' don't ye be thinkin' otherwise or I'll fold you in two the wrong way." His size made him more than capable of carrying out that threat.

"Abel, go saddle a horse for 'im," said Ash. "A fresh 'un, mind you."

Wrapped snuggly in my cloak, Abel went out.

" 'Ow long'll it take ye?" he asked Knox.

"Travelin', not long. Waitin' fer the money, I dunno. Ye'll 'ave to wait 'til I get back. Keep a sharp eye on the road. If you see soldiers, git to the boat 'n' git out. I'll catch up with ye later. With the money," he pointedly added for the benefit of any other doubters.

He left soon after. I kept my head down and rested.

The length of time between bouts of nausea was increasing and the sickness passed off a little faster, but I gave no sign of recovery, continuing to show them the worst possible side of it. A man in my poor condition would be seen as no threat, and I hoped they might get lax in their watch.

Indeed, it already seemed so. Food and drink were traded around and they did a fine job pretending I wasn't there while seeing to their own best comfort. None was offered to me. In fact, no one bothered to address me at all. That alone would have informed me of my eventual fate, had I not already figured it out. They weren't about to make friends with someone who was going to die.

An hour crept past, or more. It was hard to tell. I never moved, nor was invited to move. Tully took over the bed and began snoring. The others found spots to rest and talk amongst themselves before drowsing off. A natural topic was what they'd be doing with the money from this endeavor; they then warmed to other jobs, comparing them in terms of profit and effort. They'd stolen all manner of things, beaten and even killed people who attempted to resist them and one and all considered it work well done since—profit aside—they were doing it in a good cause. Any and all harm done to one of the King's loyal subjects was seen as a righteous blow for liberty, and the more harm inflicted the better.

I hadn't exactly hidden myself away from the war going on in the broader world beyond my own little piece of it, but it had not been very real to me for the most part. I had other concerns to keep me occupied, and the conflict was something that was happening to other people miles in the distance. These men were forcing me to see it as something much closer and consequently much more immediately threatening. Our big house with all its people, shuttered windows, and firmly locked doors was no safe fortress against such brutes. If they wanted what we had, they would simply take it. They weren't smart, but they did have a base, instinctual cunning that chilled me to the bone.

I raised my head, blinking, cautious of pain. It was there, drumming like thunder during a storm, but not as bad as it had been. I didn't want to push myself, but with the coming dawn I might not be left with any choice. Vanishing was first and foremost on my mind. If I was strong enough for that, then my greatest worries would be over. Then I could just float outside amid their confusion and get myself well away from here.

"Be light soon," said Ash. He and Drummond had shared the table with me, though neither of them had paid much notice of me once I'd finished writing the note.

"Aye." Drummond looked at me, cool and uncaring. I didn't like the possibilities that that implied, preferring Ash's raw hatred to this utter lack of regard. "Shouldn't we wait fer Knox?"

"That's been talked out. No matter if 'e gits the money 'r not, this 'un's got to go, we all agreed to it."

My belly turned over. Violently.

Drummond sighed. " 'Tis better to do it now, then, while the others are asleep."

I'd been expecting such talk, but that didn't make it any easier to hear.

"They need to git used to it," countered Ash. "This's a war on, not a damned tea party for fancy Tory bitches 'n their silks 'n' velvets."

*Not now, not yet*, I cried in my mind. I was still too weak and nearly frozen with alarm.

I looked back at them, trying to summon enough concentration to influence them. Which one? I couldn't do both. Too late I picked on Ash, but he was already up and moving. Drummond followed.

Too late . . .

"Up with ye," said Ash.

"Wait—I can pay you more money."

"Oh, aye?"

"I've money of my own, separate from my father's. You can make twice as much."

"An' run twice the risk. No thankee. What we'll be gittin' 'll more'n do fer us." He pulled out his pistol and prodded my ribs. "Commun. Up with ye."

"Maybe the others don't agree with you. Don't the rest of you want to double your money?"

Seth and Abel looked sullenly interested, but not enough to challenge Ash's authority. Tully continued to snore. Drummond had heard, but rejected the offer with a contemptuous snort of disbelief. There would be no sundering of loyalties in this group.

Ash grinned. "Commun, ye cowardly bastard. Move yerself or you'll get it right 'ere."

It was hardly a statement to inspire encouragement. Inside or out, I was to die. Where might not matter, but when . . . I wanted more time. They weren't giving me any. Not one more minute.

"You must help me. I can't stand. Dizzy." There was no point trying to plead for my life. They'd only find it amusing, especially Ash. I desperately wanted . . . needed time to think.

"Commun."

"I can't." It wasn't all an act; my legs were like water.

*Think* . . . but no miraculous idea popped into my head.

Expressing considerable disgust, Ash backed off so Drummond could assist me. With his now familiar lack of gentleness, he bent, hauled one of my arms around his neck, and stood, taking me with him. The sudden move to my feet was bad, but not as dreadful as I'd anticipated. I sagged, though, making him support me. He stank of ancient sweat and I could smell the remains of his last meal in the grease smearing his face.

I could also smell something else, something that woke me up more thoroughly than his rough handling or Ash's threats or even my own paralyzing fear.

Blood.

*His* blood, not mine. And the scent of it was good.

So very, very good.

Unaware, he pulled me along, my weight of no concern to him, paying no attention while I was stumbling in surprise at this inner realization. He had no mind for anything but to get the job at hand finished. I had no mind for anything but the fact that he was awash with what I needed to live. He carried satiation for my roused hunger, healing for my injury, strength for escape.

Red life, rushing, pulsing, *roaring* beneath his coarse skin.

Blood.

Dear God. I was *hungry*. Terribly so.

I stared without seeing anything as he took me through the door into the needle-sharp cold outside.

It was almost as though I were back in the wagon again, drifting in and out of consciousness, only now I was drifting between need and the shock of learning the true immensity of that need. Drummond marched me along over an empty field, the ground sloping slightly upward. I barely kept pace with him, distracted by trying to break free of the spell of my hunger, and succeeding to some degree.

Blood was blood to me, whether it was in a horse or a human. Even the miniscule amount I took from Molly Audy was food, when it came down to absolutes.

I looked sideways at Drummond. He continued to steadily and stolidly walk me on toward an ignominious death.

Dare I try it?

And more importantly, dare I *not*?

I could get on without. Perhaps.

Survival and escape were all that were important. It might be utterly revolting to have to drink from this man's filthy throat, but my instincts, those newly formed by my changed condition and those already innate to my being, told me that this was my best chance to get out alive, if not my only chance.

In the overall scheme of the world, I judged myself to be of considerably more value than Ash, Drummond, or any of the others in their miserable, brutal troop of killers.

So be it.

Now I had to find a way of arranging things to my advantage.

* * *

We crested the top of the slope, and the wind clawed at my inadequately protected body like a vengeful animal. I was shivering again and held on to Drummond for warmth as well as support. Snow clung to our boots, slowing us. Ash cursed as he struggled along in our footsteps.

The other side of the slope led down to the Sound. Had I known we were this close to it, I'd have made some mention in my note to Father. This part of the coast was vaguely known to me, and my heart rose a little. It was absurdly comforting to find I wasn't totally lost in an unknown land.

The water was gray and dangerous in the tormenting wind; I should not have cared to venture onto its restless surface in such weather, and I worried that that was what Drummond and Ash were planning.

Making myself more of an impediment than usual, I managed to get Drummond to halt by having my legs give out completely.

"A moment, for pity's sake," I cried in a thin, strained voice.

Ash caught us up. "Keep movin', let's get it over with."

"What . . . what will you do with me?"

"What do ye think?" He grinned down, mistaking my need to have details for more cowardice.

"Tell me! I've a right to know!"

My forceful insistence set him back a little, but he was too grudging to provide an answer.

I looked up at Drummond. "Please, sir. Tell me. If these are my last moments, let me not disgrace myself further."

Reluctantly, he said, "Yer to be shot."

Interesting way to put it, I thought, as though someone else were to do the dirty work.

"With honor, as for a soldier?" I asked, my manner pleading for him to say yes.

"Aye, with honor." There was amusement deep in his eyes. I pretended not to see it.

Ash spat, clearly having no use for what he must have perceived as a useless and trivial concept except when it suited him. He was dancing from one foot to the other from the cold. "Let's git to it."

We reached a level spot on the slope and turned into the wind, taking a path that eventually wound itself down to the shoreline. The wind seemed to grab the air from my lungs, so it was just as well I had no need to breathe.

"Will you bury me?" I gasped out.

Drummond gruffly said, "At sea."

I looked past him at the heartbreakingly bleak water. Truly it was to be a cold, deep grave for me in every sense of the word.

He correctly interpreted my expression. "Have to. Orders."

"Orders from whom?"

He made no answer. Ash, probably. Or Knox. It hardly mattered.

We came to the point on the path where it went down to the shore, but Drummond ignored it and continued to go straight ahead, breaking a way through virgin snow. It was much deeper here and the footing more treacherous, but his size helped. He had tremendous strength and bulled through the increasingly higher drifts as though they weren't there. The extra exertion was of no benefit to my head whatsoever. All I could do was hang onto him for balance and try not to fall.

We were rather far from the house.

Good.

Drummond paused, waiting for Ash, who was having a harder time of it. The wind was dying, I noticed, and the sky . . . growing lighter. Even with the thick clouds of winter between me and the sun, I'd be unable to hold myself conscious once it cleared the horizon.

"Right," said Ash. "Put 'im over there."

I was guided to what I first thought to be a taller than usual drift. It proved to be a slight rise that cut off sharply on the other side. It dropped straight down into water. All they had to do was shoot me and roll the body off and let the sea carry it away or drag it to the bottom. It might never, ever be found.

Ash watched as I worked it all out and enjoyed my reaction of horror. Drummond remained impassive and told me I'd have to stand on my own.

"I—I should like a blindfold, please."

Ash's face transformed into a study of indignant amazement. *"What?"*

"May I not have a blindfold? I should find it easier to take what is to come if I don't have to see."

He was practically speechless. "Of all the—"

"A last request, sir."

He worked himself into a spate of name-calling and I winced and clung to Drummond like a child seeking shelter.

"Let 'im," said Drummond, as I'd hoped he would. He was exasperated, but with Ash, not me. Ash was using more time venting his anger than it would have taken to grant my request.

"What?"

" 'Tis not much to ask. 'E can use yer scarf." Without waiting, Drummond let go his hold on me and backed away.

Damnation. I'd wanted one of them to go back to the house in order to fetch something suitable. Separating them would have made things so much easier for me.

"Might I also have some Bible verses?" I asked with rapidly increasing desperation.

"Got none, lad."

Well. I should have expected as much from a house where no one could read.

"The blindfold," I said. "Please . . . I—"

Drummond looked expectantly at Ash. With more cursing and complaint, he reluctantly untied the length of scarf that held his hat in place. He had to give his pistol to Drummond in order to do it properly. When he came forward to wrap it around my eyes, I lifted one hand in a begging gesture.

"Please . . ."

"What now?"

"A moment to pray. Just a moment for a prayer. Just a—"

I got another curse for an answer, but he made no other objection. I sank down to one knee. Drummond was now too far away to reach, but Ash stood right before me, clutching the scarf, impatient to finish the job and get out of the cold. I bowed my head.

"Heavenly Father, forgive me my sins . . . ." I began, and I meant it. To undertake such actions while in the middle of prayer must certainly be sinful, but I had no other choice left. Surely God would understand.

I smashed my fist into Ash's groin.

He made no scream; I think the agony was too great to be vocalized, but his face was eloquent as he doubled over and fell writhing into the snow. Then I forgot about him as Drummond came up.

He had the pistol ready and could not possibly miss at so short a distance. He was hardly two yards away, holding it centered upon my chest. The muzzle was as big as the door to hell, but I had to wrench my eyes from it to look at Drummond. Unlike the display I'd put on earlier, I would face my death, if that was what was to come. I'd survived other woundings, but was very weak now and unsure of what might happen next. I braced myself for the shot, glaring at him and trying to see if there was a soul behind his eyes.

He held off firing. Only stared. We stared at one another for what seemed like hours and I couldn't imagine why he was waiting. He paid no attention to Ash, who lay between us, curled around himself and grunting with agony; all he did was look right back into my eyes, unblinking, like a madman.

What was it? Was he hoping I'd beg? Why was he so still? Was it to break my nerve? What—?

Dawn. It was lighter now than . . .

Light. Enough light for him to see clearly. To see me. For me to . . .

With sudden comprehension, I staggered to my feet and told Drummond to throw his gun down. He did. I told him to get on his knees. He did. His impassive face remained the same, hard as stone . . . maybe just a little vacant about the eyes. That had been the delay for me; I didn't know him well enough to read any inner changes when my influence had taken him over.

My hunger, held in abeyance by so many distractions, now clawed its way back. Ravenous. Undeniable.

Unsteadily, I walked around Ash until I was quite close to Drummond. I told him to shut his eyes. He did. Then, with trembling fingers, I ripped away his rag of a neckcloth.

What came next didn't take long. Fortunate, since it was singularly unpleasant.

Except for the blood, of course.

I pushed his head away and to one side to draw the skin taut over his exposed throat. The scent coming through it—the bloodsmell—overmatched the stink of his unwashed skin and clothing. My teeth were out and my belly gave an inward twist, anticipating. Bending low, I cut hard into him, breaking through the tough skin and drinking in that first glorious swallow of life as it flooded forth.

He made a gagging sound once, and not long after sobbed once, but otherwise held himself as quietly as any of the other beasts I'd fed on in the past.

His blood was different. Tainted in some way I couldn't identify, but I liked the taint. It was comparable to the kind of difference one finds between beef and venison. Both fill you, but one has the tameness of the farm and the other yet holds to the wildness of the wood.

I drank deeply and well and felt the heat of it warming me from the inside out. Strength I thought lost returned and the pain . . . the dreadful pain from the disastrous blow he'd inflicted began to subtly fade. It had been so constant that it seemed strange not to have it anymore.

Pain gone, hunger abated . . . no . . . *fulfilled*. I'd never had better.

When I drew away and licked my lips clean, I found that I'd never taken such total satisfaction from any food in all my life. Perhaps it was because it had been human blood, perhaps it was because it had come from an enemy and was suffused with his fear of me, for Drummond was shuddering with it. Tears from his now wide-open eyes streamed down his cheeks. At some point he'd woken up from my influence and had been hideously aware of all that was happening to him.

I breathed in a great draught of air through my open mouth and released it as laughter. It soared up and was caught by the last of the wind and whipped away into the brightening sky.

It . . . was not a wholesome sound. And when it died away, I felt ashamed.

But why? I'd fed from a man as I'd have fed from any brute beast, and the wild predators of the world feel no shame for what they must do. They kill in order to live; that was their nature as given to them by God. I had been no different prior to my change, having eaten animal flesh, having killed in order to live. I'd felt the triumph of a successful hunt, but this . . . wasn't the same.

Then I understood. My sudden shame came not from my change, but rather from the fact that I'd used my new abilities to play the bully. I'd taken enjoyment from this man's terror. There's a vile streak of that kind of cruelty in all of us, and I'd given into it.

Bad. Very bad of me. I could imagine what Father might have to say about this; he'd been clear enough on the subject when I'd been growing up. Though I was no longer a boy tussling with others in Rapelji's schoolyard, the principle remained the same.

"Please . . . don't kill me," Drummond whispered, his voice broken and dry. He was deathly white, but nowhere near to dying. Yet.

Right. He was begging *me* for his utterly useless, damaging life. Begging for life from the man he'd been ready to kill without the least thought or regret.

"*Please* . . ."

A hundred caustic retorts to that sprang to my lips, but never came forth. What would be the point? He was what he was, a killer and a thief, and whatever I said would not change him.

Or would it?

I knew I'd have to protect myself from him anyway.

With another laugh, short and more bitter this time, I said, "Look at me. Look at me and *listen* . . ."

And he did.

I finished with him fast enough, leaving him with no memory of what he'd been through, only a deep desire to seek an honest path for himself in the world. It both soothed and galled me, for I knew I was at least trying to do the right thing, but my baser side wanted very much to throw him over the cliff as he had meant to do to me. So I might have done in a hot rage, but not now. There was no need. Besides, his death was not worth having on my conscience.

He was asleep, or in a state close to it, and would remain so until Ash woke him up. Ash himself had been too lost in his own trouble to be aware of what had occurred but a few yards from him. His back was to us, so I wasn't worried that he had seen any of it. I walked over and nudged him with a foot.

He burst out with a very creative string of curses, not the wisest thing to do, but then I'd already noticed his singular shortage of brain and could shrug off the abuse. It did stop, however, when he saw I had the pistol in my hand.

He gaped, then started to cry out something, a call to Drummond for help, I thought, but I slapped the other hand over his mouth and informed him that he'd get a second punch between the legs if he made another sound. That shut him up completely and he lay silent as I searched him for those items of mine he'd claimed for himself out of the robbery, namely a gold snuff box and my money purse. I also found another pocketful of coins, and a surprising quantity at that, which I thought might have come from other victims. This I put in with my own money. I had no need of it, but intended to turn it over to Father with the request that he donate it to our church. Doubtless that good place could put the funds to a better use than any Ash had ever planned.

It was growing lighter by the minute. If I was to try my influence with Ash, it would have to be—

" 'Old right there, you!"

I looked up to see Abel and Seth standing just this side of the kneeling Drummond. Abel had a pistol of his own, and it was pointed at me. I hadn't heard their approach. I wondered how long they'd been watching and how much they'd seen. Too much, from the stricken looks they wore. Abel kept trying to steal glances at the oblivious Drummond, which made it hard for him to hold his weapon level.

"*Devil*!" he shrieked when he saw the blood on Drummond's throat. "Ye filthy devil!" His hatchety face went red with outrage and disgust and fear. The gun went off. It may have been an accidental firing or not, but he was so upset that it spoiled his aim. The thing roared and the air was clouded with sudden smoke, but the ball completely missed me. He had one instant to regret it, less than a blink of an eye, and I was upon him.

A clout on the jaw was all that was needed. He was stunned, senseless and unresisting. I turned on Seth, but he'd backed away, jaw sagging and eyes popping, too frightened to move. As he watched, I dragged my cloak from his brother's body.

Ash was on his hands and knees and bellowing at Drummond, who looked to be waking up. Damnation to them. If I had more time I could have stayed, changed their memories to my advantage, but the dawn was against me. I had ten minutes, no more and very probably much less. It was hard to tell for the clouds.

I had to get out.

Slogging away from them over the open snow field was the best I could do. I threw the cloak around my shoulders and pulled it close, grateful for the brothers' greed. The only reason I could think why they'd followed out after us was for Seth to lay claim to my boots before his friends dropped them—along with my body—into the Sound. Abel may have come to try for them himself one more time, that, or to enjoy the execution.

I walked as quickly as possible, wanting distance between myself and the growing row behind me. Ash's voice rose high over the wind, suffused with anger. I looked back once and saw him on his feet, shaking a fist at me. Without a doubt, he was a dangerous man, but also stupid and incredibly foolish; I still had the pistol.

A perverse fancy took me. I stopped and turned, arm out in the best dueling style, my pose and posture unmistakable. He ceased moving, caught between horror and surprise. I pulled the trigger and felt the recoil jolt up my arm. The thing made a grand roar and I had the satisfaction of seeing Ash and the others duck in dismay. They weren't injured, I'd aimed just over their heads, but by the time they found enough courage to look again, they'd not be able to see me. I took that moment as the right time to vanish.

The thought belatedly came that they'd follow my trail. They'd find the discarded pistol and my tracks ending in the middle of the field as though I'd vanished into the air, which, indeed, I had. Well, it was too late now. Let them puzzle it out and be damned.

Glad I was that the wind had died. There was just enough of it now to give me a direction to push against, which I did with all my strength and will. I sped south and then west toward home, though I had not the faintest possibility of reaching it in time.

Panic?

Very likely.

There was also the hope that once I'd put enough distance between myself and that band of patriotic cutthroats, I could go solid, get my bearings and find some shelter for the day. All I needed was a shack or barn, someplace to hide from the approaching sun.

I hurtled forward for as long as I dared, then re-formed. The light was nearly blinding. The snow-blanketed fields reflected it, increased it. I shaded my eyes and searched all around for cover. Nothing, absolutely nothing, presented itself.

For want of anything better to do besides stand and gibber with fear, I vanished and continued forward. There were some trees in the distance, widely spaced and naked of leaves. Probably useless. Faster and faster I went until such senses as were left to me in this form gave me warning that I'd reached my goal.

This next re-forming was more difficult. The light much worse. My fear all but choked me. The trees were useless. Even in the high summer with their leaves, their shade would not have been sufficient. They were too far apart. There was no other choice, though. Perhaps my cloak would help . . .

Then I noticed that the trees farther on were strangely shortened. My sight was getting worse, but I was just able to discern that they were not really short, but were actually the top branches of other trees growing upon much lower ground.

The island was pocked here and there with depressions we called kettles because of their general shape. Rapelji said that they'd been carved out of the earth by ancient glaciers. Some were small, others much larger, with names to them. I had no name for this one, but immediately dubbed it "haven."

I charged forward, faded somewhat, and launched my partially visible body over the edge. It was quite different from the tumble I'd taken into one as a child. The landing was much less abrupt.

The high wall of earth on my left blocked the immediate threat of light; the other wall was not all that far away. The bottom would be exposed to sun for only a short time during the day. I could improve that if I—yes, there, where the wall bulged out, creating a little alcove, but to lie as one dead with only a cloak for covering . . . I was afraid Ash and his crew would come hunting and chance upon me while I lay helpless.

The snow. It had drifted in here all throughout the winter, deep and undisturbed.

It might not work.

Oh, but it *had* to.

I faded completely and sank beneath its unbroken surface, sank until I touched upon the more solid barrier of the frozen ground beneath and there stopped. Then gradually, ever so cautiously, I assumed form once more. Not at all easy, but the hard snow gave way to my frantic pushing and I made myself a kind of burrow. I twisted this way and that, but saw not the least hint of light. It would do. It would have to, for all my choices had been stolen away by the dawn.

It was a grave. No other word could describe this kind of darkness or silence. I was acutely conscious of the great weight of the snow above. Had I needed air, I'd have smothered in a very short time. As it was, my mind was in danger of smothering from the memory of my first wretched awakening into this changed life.

And then . . . all my worries ceased for the day.

# CHAPTER
# ◂10▸

I awoke to utter blackness, immobile from cold, and just disoriented enough to leap into a kind of groggy alarm. As my last thought had been about my hated churchyard coffin, I mentally kicked out in a—literally—blind panic, instinctively tried to vanish, and did.

By increments.

Bit by bit, I faded, feeling myself going at the extremities first as hands and feet, already numb, lost all further bonding with touch. It seeped past my skin and muscle, to the vitals, to the bones, until I was finally incorporeal and bumping gently against the sides of my tiny prison.

Nasty sensation, that.

During this agonizingly slow transformation I'd recovered some of my wits, recalling that I'd buried myself in a snowbank to escape the daylight. I also knew I no longer wanted to be here anymore. So thinking, I sieved slowly upward from the icy sanctuary until I seemed to be free of it, then tried to resume a solid body again.

It was a reverse of the vanishing, only slower, with me struggling to push it faster and not making very much difference at all. For a time, while but halfway formed, I was madly blinking to clear my fogged vision. My eyes were not themselves subject to any injury, but the lengthy return made it seem so. Once they were clear, I knew I was whole. I felt much better—until my legs gave out and I landed facedown in the snow like a felled tree.

After that, I became more cautious.

I was thoroughly chilled through and through, so much so that I had quite forgotten what it was like to ever be warm. My fingers were an unhealthy white and, though they moved, were far too stiff to be of much use. All my joints were stiff, for that matter. I felt as though I'd been hollowed out and filled from the toes up with slushy, half-frozen mud.

While trying to push the ground away, I reflected that if I didn't find some warmth soon, the mud inside would freeze the rest of the way. With that ominously in mind, success followed my next effort to stand; then I endeavored to walk . . . well, shamble. At least I was moving.

The kettle had high walls, but was mercifully open at the southern end, making for an uncomplicated escape. I didn't want to try vanishing again until my condition had improved. My pace was slow, but constant, and became more fluid the longer I stayed at it. When I started shivering, I knew I'd done the right thing, quite probably just in time.

I had to trudge uphill for a bit, then the kettle opened out into empty field. No fences were in sight, no signs of anything civilized, only snow and the stark black silhouette of a tree here and there. The road that Ash and his crew had used lay somewhere ahead. I was reluctant to find it, though. Since I'd determined I was in Suffolk County, the chances of encountering more of his rebel friends was great. It would not be terribly advantageous to my interests to escape one band of cutthroats only to be captured by another, but I supposed I could cope if it was unavoidable. For now I was too miserable to plan for anything more harrowing than the next few steps forward.

Lots of those. I didn't bother to count.

The going was very slow due to the uneven ground beneath the covering of snow. Thank God that Seth hadn't taken my boots away. Thank God I'd gotten my cloak back from Abel. It was heavy with damp, but more preferable to going without. All I needed now was something to cover my head. My ears were like chips of ice. And, as long as I was making wishes, some gloves would be—

Gloves . . . on impulse I checked the inside pocket of the cloak. They were still there. I'd have to give Jericho a special thanks for his foresight and another to Providence that Abel had overlooked these prizes. Though I was barely able to open and close my hands yet, I managed to pull the things on. Maybe they wouldn't give warmth, but they'd hold in what little I might produce and keep the cruelly cold air from stealing it away.

Each step became marginally easier than the last, and the line of footprints behind me grew longer and longer. A mile of it must have stretched back to the kettle when I saw the road. There was little to mark it from the rest of the countryside but the indentations of ruts and marks left by wheels and livestock. I chose the westward direction and walked and walked and walked.

After an hour of it, I decided my fears of meeting with more rebels were not to be realized. That comforting thought kept me in good spirits until the country silence was broken by the sound of hoofs.

Coming up behind. Rebels for sure. Hunting me down.

No place to hide, not a tree or a drainage ditch, no wall or even a bush.

Vanish? No. My insides were too unsettled yet.

Very well, hide in the open. Pretend to be what I must surely look like, a forlorn traveler on his way to shelter. I'd plod on and ignore them and hope they'd return the favor and pass by.

The sky was clear of clouds and there was a bright, nearly full moon out. The light was excellent. They'd probably have a sharp look at me before they went by. That's what I'd do.

How many? A glimpse over my shoulder showed only two riders. That was good. I could probably handle them if it came to it. I fervently prayed it would not.

They clip-clopped up, in no hurry, and came even with me. They stayed even with me. Damnation.

"You, sir! Who are you and where are you bound?"

An educated voice. A gentleman's voice. Familiar . . .

I looked up . . . right into the astonished face of Lord James Norwood.

My own expression must have matched his well enough, for we were both struck speechless. Then the second rider swung his leg over his mount's neck and slipped off.

"My God, Mr. Barrett, is it you?" Dr. Beldon, brimful of relief.

I was very glad to see him and deeply touched by this evidence of his concern for me, and raised a wan smile. It was meant to reassure, but had quite the opposite effect on the poor man.

"Sweet heavens, are you all right? What has happened to you?"

Norwood, prompted by the doctor's actions, also dismounted and echoed those questions and more. Both of them were obviously shocked by my doubtless wild appearance. They each took an arm to support me, though I'd been doing an adequate enough job before.

"You're freezing cold, man," said Beldon. "Here, I've a blanket in one of my bags . . ." He broke away to get it.

"Where have you been, sir?" asked Norwood.

"Some house near the shore," I answered. My voice was thick and strange in my throat. "Not sure. My family? Are they—?"

"They're very worried for you. Your father is out with another search party farther south."

"Search party?"

"Half the Island is out looking for you. As soon as that rascal turned up early this morning with your note, Mr. Barrett sent me off straight as a shot to fetch Lieutenant Nash and his men."

"Here," said Beldon, shaking out the promised blanket. "Get this up over your head. Your ears are quite blue."

I let him fuss, for it was incredibly good to be among friends again.

"Some brandy now . . ."

There was no way of refusing it gracefully, so I lifted the opaque bottle to my lips and pretended to swallow. A drop or two burned upon my tongue, but only for a moment.

"Are you fit enough to ride?" he asked.

"Yes."

"There's a farm not far ahead—"

"No. My own home. Take me right home."

"You're certain you can make it?"

"A dead run would be too slow for me."

Norwood laughed lightly at this. "And dangerous for the horses, but we'll see what we can do. Can you give him a leg up, Doctor?"

Having the larger and stronger of the two mounts, I was to ride behind him, hanging on as well as I could with my numb hands. He sprang into the saddle, held out a steadying arm, and Beldon gave me the boost I needed. I landed with a thud astride the horse's rump and might have fallen right off again if Norwood hadn't caught me. The exertion called back a ghost of dizzying pain from Drummond's initial assault. My balance was off, but I tried not to let it show, lest they hold to a slow pace.

The pace was slow anyway, at least to my mind, but Norwood kept the time filled by answering my questions on what had happened after Knox's arrival.

"The big brute was strutting around as though he owned the place, demanding to see Mr. Barrett. Ill-favored fellow, from what I saw of him. I only caught a glimpse at the time. Your father read the note he had, and you should have seen the look on the man's face when the servants were ordered to grab hold of him. Took a number of 'em, I must say, all the stable lads and those two black housemen as well were needed before they got him on the floor and tied him tight as a trussed bird. And the language. Your father had him gagged as well, to spare the ears of the ladies. Unpleasant business."

"No doubt."

"But that was a brilliant bit of business with the note, and the same for Mr. Barrett for catching onto it so fast. You took a risk over that, though."

"But it worked. That's what matters."

"Now, who were these fellows who captured you? How did you let it happen?"

"I didn't, they did."

"What? Oh, I see. Yes, certainly you didn't plan to let yourself be kidnapped. Well, then, did you get a good look at'em?"

"Much too good a look. I'll know them the next time I see them."

"Which will be soon, I hope. That is, if Nash and his men can find 'em before they get away."

"And Father's with them?"

"Looking in the wrong place, it seems."

"Sorry. I couldn't be more specific in the note as I didn't really know where I was until later."

"Tell me what happened."

I did so, briefly, leaving out certain details, and could see him swelling with anger.

"Bastards," he grumbled.

And that about summed it all up for me.

About three miles from home, Beldon said he wanted to run ahead to prepare things for me, kicked his hack to a canter, and disappeared. I approved, for it would mean any anxiety over me would be relieved that much sooner, and so it proved when Norwood and I finally arrived.

Jericho was there to help me from the horse, to help me inside, and to help me strip from my worse-for-wear clothes. Part of Beldon's preparations had included instructing Mrs. Nooth to boil large quantities of water. The bathtub was set up in the now steamy kitchen and my cold and highly abused body was soon ecstatically soaking in wonderful, reviving heat. A hot wet cloth was wrapped around my head to warm up my ears. I must have looked like some sort of down-at-the-heels sultan, but didn't care.

Mrs. Nooth had bathed me as a child and treated me little different now as an adult. Her one concession to the passage of years was to drape a blanket over the whole of the tub, but I thought that it was more for retaining the heat than to preserve my modesty. She added more hot water as it was ready until I felt like a hard-cooked egg, but got no complaints from me. Her instincts were to feed me something, anything. I managed to put her off on that. My past influence upon her helped there, for she didn't press.

The whole house, it seemed, was in the kitchen, eyes on me, full of questions. Even Mother was present, her mouth turned down in fearsome disapproval for the uproar and, possibly, my naked state, but with the blanket in place she had no cause for worry. Propriety, though somewhat strained, was intact.

Elizabeth had been in tears when Norwood and I had come in, and had thrown her arms about me in relief. I'd held her and told her I was fine and then came the first of the questions: What had happened? Where had I been? How did I get away? And so on. I repeated what I'd said to Norwood, with a few more details and a lot more interruptions. As before, I left out some things. No one noticed, or if they did, it was accepted without comment.

"You should have killed the fellow while you had the chance," said Norwood in regard to my bravado gesture of shooting over Ash's head.

I remained silent on that one and wallowed in the incredible glory of hot water. Beldon removed the soaking wet turban to check my ears and pronounced them to be normal again. He then made a careful examination of the spot where Drummond's near-deadly blow had connected.

"I see no sign of injury, sir," he said. His manner was reminiscent of the time he'd marveled over my miraculously healed arm.

I couldn't distract him out of it in front of all this crowd. "Perhaps it wasn't as bad as I thought."

"But your hair is—was quite matted with blood. It had to come from a cut in the scalp, and I can't find one."

"That suits me well enough, Doctor. Mrs. Nooth, might I trouble you for a bit of soap and a flesh brush?"

It was no trouble at all, and her bustling and cheerful chatter got between me and Beldon, as I'd wanted.

The two oldest stable lads had been dispatched on fresh mounts to find Father. Norwood thought of going, but didn't know the countryside as well as the lads. They weren't gone long; Father had been on his way home when they met him on the road. He'd galloped the rest of the way back and still smelled of winter night when he pushed his way into the kitchen to greet me. He knelt next to the tub, took my face in his hands and pulled me close, resting his chin on my head for a moment. Neither of us spoke. It didn't seem necessary.

He drew back and looked me over and combed a damp lock of hair from my face. "Oh, laddie, what have you done to yourself?"

"I'm really all right," I said. I'd said that a lot recently.

"Thank God." Then, with a wry curl of his lip, he added, "Are you tired of all the repetition?"

"Is it so obvious?"

"It's fine. You look all in, though. I'll ask my questions when you're up to them."

"Not long," I promised.

He told me I was a good lad, then turned to Beldon and Norwood for the story of how they'd found me. At the same time he unobtrusively herded the whole lot from the kitchen. Jericho remained behind. He'd already been upstairs to fetch me fresh clothes and was examining the old ones with a critical eye.

"There's blood on your coat," he said quietly, so Mrs. Nooth, busy on the other side of the kitchen, could not hear.

"Yes. That motherless—well, he gave me a bad knock. Near as I can make out he grabbed me by the queue and swung me right into the wagon seat like you'd break a chicken's neck. I'm lucky he didn't kill me."

"And one day later there is no injury to be seen."

I shrugged. "It's the way I've become."

His eyes briefly lighted. "Magic?"

I couldn't help but smile. "Why not?"

Bathed, shaved, and decently dressed: such are the things that mark us as civilized creatures. I was looking very civilized before Jericho gave me permission to leave.

They were all waiting in the parlor. Cousin Anne was serving tea. It might have been the same as any other evening at home except for the way they looked at me with the unease in their faces. It wasn't nice to see, and I was trying to think of a graceful way to excuse myself without seeming rude.

Father saved me the trouble by stepping forward. "Come, Jonathan, I've some things to tell you. No need to bore everyone. The rest of you carry on as you are."

A ripple went through them. Their faces all seemed strangely alike, blurred and blank, even Elizabeth's. Father took my arm and led me away to the library. He closed the door.

It was warm there. A fine big fire was blazing, merry as New Year. I was no longer cold, but the memory of it drove me to the hearth to hold my hands out to the flames. The heat baked my skin, soaked into the bones. Father moved up behind and came around, standing next to me. Watching.

"This feels very good," I said, uncomfortably conscious of his gaze.

He made no comment.

"You had some things to tell me, sir?" I prompted.

"When you can look me in the eye, laddie."

It was painful for some reason I didn't understand. Like looking into the sun. His face was as blurred as the others. I tried blinking to clear my sight and was shocked when tears spilled out.

"I'm sorry," I blurted.

"For what?"

"I . . . don't know."

"T'wasn't your fault, laddie."

I nodded and glumly swiped at my leaking eyes with both hands. It was stupid, so very *stupid* of me to be like this. I wheeled from the fire and threw myself on the settee. Snuffling. Father sat next to me. After a minute he put his arms around my stiff body and got me to relax enough to lean against his chest. Like a child. Thus had he comforted me as a child.

"You're all right, laddie," he told me, his voice husky with his own tears.

That's what broke it. That's when I gave out with a breathy hiccup and truly wept. He held me and rocked me and stroked my hair and never once told me to hush, just kept doing that until I was able to stop. I finally sat up, blindly fishing for the handkerchief Jericho always left in one of my pockets. Father had one ready and put it into my hands. I blew my nose, wiped my eyes, and suddenly yawned.

"Sorry."

"Don't be," he said genially.

"How did you know?"

"When you came into the parlor looking like a drawn rope about to snap, the possibility occurred to me. I've seen it before and it's no good trying to bury it. How do you feel?"

"Not so drawn."

He saw that for himself well enough, but was reassured to hear it confirmed. He went across to unlock his cabinet and poured out a bit of brandy, then locked up again. The habit had ingrained itself in him in such a very short time. He sat facing me in his favorite chair, the firelight playing warmly over his features.

"Well. Can you tell me all about it now?"

I could. And did.

It was easier than the previous tellings. I didn't have to pretend to be brave. I didn't have to lie. So very, very much easier it is to be able to tell the truth. I left out one thing only: the part about drinking Drummond's blood. At the time it had been my survival, but here in the light and peace of my favorite room, it seemed unreal, even monstrous. I was not comfortable about it—especially the fact I'd enjoyed the taste so very much—and was not prepared to offer such a burden of knowledge to my dearly loved father. He had more than enough troubles on his mind.

When I was done, he looked me over from top to toe and again I seemed to see myself through his eyes. There was worry there, of course, for my well-being, but I appeared to be strong enough to handle things now. There was also relief: that I was safely home and if not totally undamaged, then at least able to recover from it. "We've got the other fellow, Knox," he said. "Nash put him into that blockhouse he had built last fall."

"Will there be a hanging?"

"I don't know. The man keeps saying he's a soldier and thus a prisoner of war. Said he was doing his duty right and proper before his capture."

"Oh? And just how does he explain the ransom note he thought he was delivering?"

"Denies it ever was a demand for ransom. Claims he was given to understand it was a request from you to ask for help getting home. The other men had captured you by mistake and he'd come to fetch a horse to bring you back. He volunteered to risk capture himself in order to do you a good turn. Very aggrieved, he is."

"Has he convinced Lieutenant Nash of this tale?"

"What do you think?"

My answer lay in my return expression and we both had a short, grim laugh.

Father sipped his brandy, then sighed. "Tomorrow Nash will take him 'round to Mrs. Montagu's home for her and the servants to have a look at him. There are a few other places in the county to go to as well if she can't identify him. He had no commission papers—"

"A hanging, then."

"Quite likely."

Silence fell upon us, lengthened, and was so complete that I was able to hear to the distant kitchen where Mrs. Nooth was supervising the dumping out of my bathwater. Things were quiet in the parlor by comparison, just Norwood talking low, though I couldn't make out the words.

"Is Nash still out looking for me?"

I'd interrupted whatever gray thoughts had been floating between us. "What? Yes, I suppose he is. And in the wrong place. We were miles from where Beldon and Lord James said they'd found you. Oh, well, it'll do him good. He wants the exercise and if he shakes up a few rebels, all the better."

"What made you break off from him and come home?"

"You. I trusted what you said in your note about trying to escape. Worked out that you'd have to find shelter for the day, but you'd come home as quick as you could after dark. Thought I should be here to check, to see if I was right, and I was. Didn't expect that you'd hole yourself up like a badger in a burrow, though. Very ingenious, laddie."

"More like very desperate. Wish it'd been warmer, but if it had, then I'd have been without cover altogether."

"That had me worried, that you'd be out in some open area for anyone to stumble over. Knowing what you're like during the day, I'd feared you'd be taken for dead. There'd be misunderstandings, rumors—"

"Me having to influence everyone all over again." I shuddered. "No, thank you."

Father chuckled.

And I thought of something. "Do you think Nash would let me talk to Knox?"

"To what purpose?"

"I should like to get the truth from him."

He frowned for a time, knowing exactly what I meant. "A confession from him will mean his death for certain, Jonathan."

"At this point I think that's a foregone conclusion."

Another frown. More silence. Then, "Very well. A gift you have and a gift you should use. Let its use be for finding the truth. Besides . . ."

He trailed off; I urged him to continue.

" 'Tis only because I hate to admit it to myself, but I've a streak of vengeance in me. If he's one of the bastards who caused Mrs. Montagu so much distress, then I'll want to be there at dawn to put the rope 'round his neck myself."

Father finished his brandy and asked if I was up to facing the rest of the household.

"Only if there's no fuss. I've had enough to last me for months."

He could make no guarantee against that, but said I could leave whenever it became too much.

This second attempt to rejoin their company was more successful. The pale blurs were gone. Their faces were faces once more.

Thank God.

Elizabeth broke away from Norwood and came over to slip her arm around mine. "You had us so worried," she told me.

Apparently worried enough herself that in her relief she forgot all about Mother. I shot a glance in that lady's direction, but she wasn't reacting to us at all. She wore her usual joyless expression, nothing more. Well, I suppose it was preferable to one of her insane tirades. She hadn't had one of those for a while, certainly not since the night I'd "talked" to her. Perhaps she was building up to one. I hoped otherwise.

"Yes," said Cousin Anne. "Very worried. It must have been horrid for you."

This was about the fourth time tonight she'd expressed that sentiment. I'd heard the other three when I'd been soaking in the tub. I laughed now, more freely than I thought myself capable of, and assured her I was fine.

Her eyes lingered on me. There was a touch more depth to them than before. I wondered if that was from her own growth from this unpleasantness or because we'd shared a few kisses. Perhaps both. I smiled, took her hand and gave it a gentle squeeze to say *everything's all right*. She tossed her head slightly, smiling back.

Elizabeth made me sit in a comfortable chair and Anne asked if I wanted some tea. I accepted a cup with lots of sugar and pretended to sip, but it was easy to avoid drinking when all the questions started flowing freely once more.

Mrs. Hardinbrook had a strong interest in what the men had been like and what they had said.

"No words fit for a lady's ears, ma'am. Indeed, some of them made me blush." This raised a laugh.

Lady Caroline wanted to know why I hadn't come home right away if I'd made my escape so very early that morning.

"Truth be told, I wasn't in the best of condition. A tap on the head and all that rattling around in the back of a wagon for the worst part of fifteen miles—I was fair exhausted. I found a deserted shack and simply fell asleep for the day."

Norwood was curious as to whether the men had given away any clues about where they'd come from.

"Connecticut, for certain. Knox told them to take to a boat if they saw any trouble coming. I expect they're there now, probably sitting in some rebel hostel and telling a very different version of this story."

More laughter.

"But we'll find out the truth tomorrow," I added.

"How so, sir?"

"I'm going to have a little talk with Knox."

"To what purpose? The man's lied his head off from the moment he was taken."

I shrugged to show that that wasn't my fault. "I think he'll be truthful enough once he sees my face. Remember, he thinks I've been killed by his friends and no one the wiser. When I walk in on him the shock will turn him around, I'm sure."

"That should be interesting," said Beldon. "May I come along and observe this miracle?"

"I should welcome your company, Doctor, but would prefer a private interview with the fellow first."

He graciously accepted the sense in that.

"May I come as well?" asked Norwood.

This must have been how Nash felt when, like it or not, the lot of us had decided to go along with him to Mrs. Montagu's. There was no good reason to refuse, though. But Father was coming, and I trusted he would help if any difficulty arose.

"But tomorrow," put in Lady Caroline. "Mightn't it be rather soon for you? You really ought to rest a few days."

"I'd go tonight if I thought Lieutenant Nash would be there."

"You're in such a hurry?"

"There might be a chance to catch the other men once this one starts talking."

"But you just told us they'd be in Connecticut by now."

"True, but it doesn't mean they'll stay there. If they return, it would be very useful to know where and when and be ready for them."

"Good heavens, yes," said Mrs. Hardinbrook. "Why, they might even come here next, looking for revenge." She seemed to find that idea to be both alarming and fascinating.

I found it to be simply alarming.

Norwood bristled a bit. "They could certainly try, but they'd have the surprise of their lives if they did. Right, gentlemen?"

He got general assent for an answer. I went along with the others to be sociable. Norwood's interest in encountering excitement had bemused me before; now it had become something to bite my tongue over. I'd had my share and then some, and knew it for a fool's wish. A nice quiet life was all I desired. I wondered why, if he was so keen to find adventure, he did not join up with Howe's army. Certainly there must be a place for titled volunteers wishing to serve their king. I could only think that he was reluctant to leave his sister on her own. Then there was Elizabeth. If he loved her as I loved Nora, then running off to play soldier would be the last thing on his mind.

But I was fairly sure that he was a bit envious of me. He questioned me over and over about what had happened, eyes shining as he searched out every scrap of information from my memory. He was welcome to it, though I found no real charm in any of my talk. Perversely, the more I touched on the negative aspects of it, the more solid his admiration became.

It was flattering, in its way, but wearing. He had no idea of the true cost to me. To have strangers come in and attempt to destroy your life for their own gain is at best frightening, at worst, shattering. Father understood the hurt my soul had suffered, Norwood did not.

No, I thought, Lord James Norwood was better suited for something "safely" dangerous, more along the lines of riding to the hounds. There was always the chance of falling and breaking one's neck, but if skillful and fairly lucky, one could return invigorated, content that death had been bravely overcome. However, he could choose to ride or not. I hadn't asked to be kidnapped. That loss of control and choice was the single most important difference between the dangers.

I could *not* see him going through what I had gone through and still emerge filled with the same sense of naive enthusiasm. Though he was nearing thirty, I wondered which of us was the older and decided it was me. Experience can be very aging.

Elizabeth came over, put a hand on his arm and said, "Really, Lord James, you're positively exhausting my poor brother."

His attention went from me to her with (to my eyes) visible difficulty, but his face smoothly adjusted into a smile for her.

Elizabeth picked up on it, though. "I'm interrupting?"

"Not at all," he said. "And you're right. I'm being an imposition."

We made mock protests and other such talk, then they drifted away to their favorite corner for more private converse. I watched them and then with suddenly kindled heat remembered Molly Audy.

With all the other events filling my brain, my discovery of his visits to her had been altogether pushed aside. The incident and my questioning of Molly rolled to the front once more, leaving me flummoxed and fuming over what to do next.

No happy solution presented itself beyond a base desire to break every bone in his body. But, as satisfying as this might prove to be for me, I had to reluctantly admit that what went on between them was not really my business. If she found out, Elizabeth was more than capable of taking care of herself.

If she found out.

*I* could not be the the one to tell her. Any interference on my part would be a most unwise and importune course to take.

Still, if he upset Elizabeth with his actions, I'd be there for her. Fists at ready.

The next night, Father, Beldon, Norwood, and I sedately rode into Glenbriar. Father and Norwood had already been there early in the morning to sort things out with Nash. That worthy officer chose not to complain about their tardy report of my return home, for he was still in awe of Norwood's title and wished to present himself in a good light. He managed to do just that by swiftly dispatching himself with a troop of men to the road where I'd been found. They eventually located the hovel where I'd been taken, but the place was bare of rebels. There was a wagon in the barn, but no horses and no sign of a boat. Nash, with his ever acquisitive turn of mind, had confiscated the wagon, then ordered the burning of the house and barn.

"Why on earth did you do that, sir?" asked Norwood with some justifiable mystification. The four of us were with Nash at The Oak, listening to the account of his day.

"Because it's one less sanctuary for them to use," he replied.

"But the owner of the property—"

"Was not on the premises. A diligent search was made, I assure you."

"Seems to me," said Father, "that you could have quartered some of your men there."

"Possibly, but I considered it to be too far distant." From the long pause preceding Nash's statement, we could tell he hadn't before now considered the idea at all.

"Pity about that. If the rebels had decided to try returning, you'd have had them cold."

Nash reddened. "If they return, I'm sure the Suffolk Militia will be able to deal with them."

This was met with the kind of silence in which much is said. It was well known that the loyalty of Suffolk County was at the best, debatable, and that's what we were all thinking, including, belatedly, Nash.

"I'd like to see this Knox fellow," I said, before things got too embarrassing.

He'd already agreed that I could have my private talk, though he would have guards standing ready outside. The memory of the two escapees last fall was with him, and even if he'd been made to forget who had helped them, he was not inclined to take further chances. Now he fairly leaped at my offered distraction and issued orders for the man to be removed and brought in from the blockhouse.

"Where will you interview him?" asked Norwood.

I deferred to Nash, who said, "This room will suit, I think. The door is stout and the window too small for a fellow his size to squeeze through. Just remember that we'll be just out here if you want help with him."

I thanked him and then retired to a dark corner so Knox wouldn't see me until it was time. Not that it was necessary; I could make him talk no matter what. This was for the benefit of the others.

Soon four large soldiers marched Knox inside, their heavy steps thundering throughout the inn along with the clank and clink of chains. They shoved their charge in with me and came out again, slamming the door.

He was not in the best of condition. His tough face bore some truly colorful bruises, and one eye had swollen shut. He moved stiffly, evidence of more bruising along the rest of his body. His clothes were more ragged than before and much dirtier. He dragged over to the table in the center and dropped wearily into a chair. I had no pity for him. He and his cronies had been all too ready to kill me, and they'd certainly killed others. If I could prevent them from continuing, well and good; I was glad of the privilege.

I stepped from the shadows and slipped into a chair opposite him with the table in between. Folding my hands before me, I looked at him and waited.

Though there were plenty of candles lighting the place, recognition came slowly to him. The last time he'd seen me, I'd been in roughly the same plight he was in now, injured, and with other people deciding his fate. A change of clothing and posture had made a significant difference in my appearance.

" 'O're you?" he asked with a ghost of belligerence. There wasn't sufficient force in his voice for it to be a demand.

I studied him long, then said, "Jonathan Barrett."

The color draining out of his face made the bruises seem that much worse. His one good eye grew wide and his mouth sagged and the breath went right out of him as though I'd hit him hard in the belly.

"I—I didn't ever want t' 'urt you, mister—" he began.

"Never mind that, I'm not interested in your excuses. All I want is for you to listen to me."

"Listen?"

I leaned closer. "Yes . . . listen . . ." I went on, speaking steadily, calming him, putting him in a state that would make him very eager to answer any question at all.

His expression went slack, as they all did. It was a disturbing kind of vacuity, as though I'd stolen his soul, leaving behind a breathing but utterly empty vessel of a body.

Ignore it, I thought. "Now you're going to tell me all about your friends Ash, Tully, Abel, and Seth." I left out Drummond, confident that the fellow was applying himself to more constructive pursuits by now.

"Tell you . . ."

Now that I had him in such a helpless state, it was hard to keep my emotions in check. I sensed that if I allowed myself to let loose of any shard of my anger at this point, the results for Knox would be very distressing, indeed.

"Everything," I said, putting all my concentration into it until my head began to hurt and I had to ease off.

"Wha . . . ?"

He'd need guidance. I couldn't expect to get useful information from him unless I came up with specific questions. Well, I had no end of those; which one first?

Before I could draw breath for it I was interrupted by the abrupt sound of glass breaking, very close. My eyes shot to the small window. One of the panes was gone; bits of it lay on the floor below. The row had made me jump and after that I froze, staring. Nothing happened for what seemed like a long time, but could only have been a second or two. I started to move, though I had no idea exactly what I was going to do. Go to the window and look out, perhaps. I was too startled to call to the soldiers outside. There was no time, anyway. The brief two seconds passed and then came the hard, harsh *bang* of a pistol being fired.

Knox instantly slumped forward.

I must have yelled. The door flew open and men crowded in, but it was all over. They found me with my back pressed hard against the wall, as if trying to melt right through it. They wouldn't have been far wrong, either.

Knox was sprawled over the table with a terrible hole on one side of his skull and his brains and blood spilling out a much larger one on the other. Questions were shouted at me. All I could do was point at the window and one bright lad finally got the idea and bellowed something to Nash. A lot of confusion followed as some went to peer through the opening and others left to run outside.

The bloodsmell was everywhere, all but choking me the way it filled the room. One image impressed itself upon my overtaxed brain: the stream of blood flowing across the table and falling over its edge to the floor. I clearly heard the soft drip-drip-drip of it as it formed a ghastly puddle almost at my feet.

Then Father was suddenly there, looking as sick and horrified as I felt, but *there*, and dragged me out, thank God.

I was shaking, chilled through by sudden cold. Father got me to the common room and made me sit close before the big fireplace, somehow managing to wrest a sanctuary for us from the general tumult. I shut my eyes against it, held onto him, and shuddered once.

"It's all right, laddie," he murmured just loud enough so that only I could hear him. That pulled me away from the worst of it, and soon after, either warmed by the fire or by his soothing voice, my shivering stopped.

Beldon emerged from the death room, shaking his head to confirm what we all knew, that Knox was well beyond any earthly help.

He knelt before me to peer into my eyes and asked if I needed anything. I gulped and began to laugh in his face.

Father gripped my shoulder tightly. "Jonathan, behave yourself," he said in a severe voice.

That worked, helping to steady me. "I'm all right," I said after a minute, and was reasonably sure I meant it. Another gulp and I was able to haltingly tell them what little I knew.

"My God," said Beldon. Both men were clearly shocked.

"Where's Lord James?" I asked.

Father pointed toward the outside door of the inn where many of the soldiers had gone. "As soon as he understood the situation, he was off to the hunt."

Glory-seeker, I thought. "He's welcome to it, if he doesn't get his head blown . . ." My eyes were drawn back toward the room, but I couldn't see anything of Knox's body because of the many other people trying to get in for a look. Just as well.

"I'm going, too," Beldon announced and hurried away. Father and I followed him.

There wasn't much wind, but it slapped enough to sting. I shivered with a cold that was more imagined than actually felt and walked around the building until I reached the little window. It was small owing to the expense of glass at the time this part of the inn had been built. It had shutters, but they'd been pushed back to let in the meager winter light and no one had bothered to close them again; otherwise the assassin might have been stymied.

I thought I caught a whiff of acrid powder on the air, but discounted it as more imagination. The breeze would have swept that away by now. Several soldiers were gathered at this spot and I recognized a few, including my sometime tutor for German, Eichelburger. He and the others were making much ado over two prizes, one a pistol, the other a length of wood.

"What is it?" I asked in German.

He hefted the pistol, holding it so the light coming from the broken window fell upon it. I moved closer and realized I'd not been mistaken. The smell of powder lingered around the thing. "This he dropped, the killer. This"—he waved the piece of wood—"was used to break the glass."

I translated for Father and Beldon. "Where is Lieutenant Nash?"

He gestured at the empty yard around the inn and what lay beyond.

"Did anyone see who fired?"

Eichelburger shook his head. "We'll get him."

I did not suffer from his confidence and broke away to walk toward the limits of the yard. The wind carried vague sounds to me of men crashing about in the dark.

"It's hopeless," I said to Father when he caught up with me. "They can't see a thing in this. They need help."

"Good God, you're not thinking of—" But he saw that I was. "Jonathan, you've had enough for one night, you've had more than enough for a lifetime."

"Perhaps so, but I have to get out and do something."

His patience was thinning, but he was willing to stretch it a bit more. "Do you now?"

I took stock of myself. I'd been badly shaken, but was far from being a complete wreck over the unpleasantness and told him as much. "Those bastards plucked me up, carrying me off like I was just more stolen livestock, and just when I thought I might be able to do something about it, they took that away as well. Perhaps I'm being a fool wanting to find the killer of a killer, but if I have to stand idle, waiting for Nash to come back empty-handed, as doubtless he will, I shall go mad from it."

He frowned for a long time, then finally half-lifted his arms as if to give in. "You're no fool, laddie. I know how you feel. I'd like to come along, but 'twill be better if I stay. This lot around the inn are running around like headless chickens. They're wanting some one to argue 'em calm again. Just don't let yourself be seen. The soldiers out there are liable to be skittish. And for God's sake, be careful."

I gave him my most solemn word on that point.

There had not been any fresh snow in the last day or so; the ground had been well-churned by dozens of passing feet and I wasn't enough of a skilled woodsman to tell old tracks from new under these circumstances. But I wasn't planning to trail anyone if I could help it. I walked as quickly as I could, taking the general direction of the soldiers. They were out of sight and nearly beyond hearing; I deemed it safe to let myself fade away and rise on the wind like smoke.

Practice told me about how high I was: a little above the treetops. There I took on just enough solidity to see and hoped that none of the hunters below chanced to look up.

I spotted a few of them, gray shapes on gray ground, in a hurry, yet trying to be cautious. Willing myself ahead, I saw more and more and by their movements discerned they were all part of Nash's troop. None of them was purposefully rushing forward in that way a fugitive might.

An hour passed, they searching below, me circling high above and ranging far ahead of them. Neither of us saw anything. They headed north, toward the coast, and once there covered the shoreline, but I could have told them it was useless. No boats had been launched that I had seen. Though the killer had had a good head start and just might have escaped that way, I was not inclined to think so. He'd probably gone to ground in one of any number of places. Nassau County was loyal, but there were pockets of sedition here and there that a rebel might know about. Whoever had done for Knox was probably sheltering in any of a hundred innocuous buildings between the inn and the Sound.

Pale and tired from all my skyward exertions, I returned to Glenbriar and found Father and Beldon waiting for me at The Oak. Lieutenant Nash had come back a little earlier, just as weary and tremendously disgruntled.

"I'll hear your story of what happened, if you please, sir," he said to me.

I told him, unable to add any more details, though he very much wanted them.

"You saw nothing through the window?" he asked, just on the polite side of exasperation.

"Only a vague shape. The candles in the room made reflections on the remaining glass. I glimpsed the smoke, but that was all. At first, I couldn't believe what I'd seen or what had been done."

We were in the common room, surrounded by a few more soldiers and many more townspeople. Cold as it was, the front windows were open, and others outside had draped themselves over the sills to catch the news.

"And you found no sign of where he'd gone?" I asked in turn.

Nash frowned mightily. "My men are still looking. Lord James thought he saw something and took himself away after it."

"Not alone, I hope."

"No, certainly not."

Mr. Farr, supremely unhappy that such an awful murder had occurred in his house, pushed forward. "What I want to know is why anyone would do such a wretched thing. I run a very respectable place and this—" He clenched his hands, shaking them for want of words to express his outrage and fear.

"Revenge, possibly," said Dr. Beldon. "There are people aplenty hereabouts who would be happy to see someone like Knox in hell."

"He'd have been sent there soon as we were done with him," Nash grumbled. "First those two escapes and now this one shot before we could hang him. Mark me, I think his own rebel friends murdered him so he wouldn't betray them to us."

This inspired a rumbling murmur of agreement from the crowded room. Not one of us—least of all I—had any doubts over the viciousness of the so-called patriots who had troubled the whole county. That they should turn upon one of their own to save themselves was a dreadful and cowardly act, but not terribly surprising.

Nash was not only partial to his idea, but more than willing to act upon it. "Mr. Barrett, I'll want a complete description of the men who kidnapped you, as much as you can remember right down to the least scrap of clothing on their backs. Write it out. I want something I can pass along to my men. I'll be finding these traitors if I have to turn over every stone in the county."

# CHAPTER 11

*May 1777*

"You're more quiet than usual," observed Elizabeth.

"I didn't know it was usual for me to be quiet."

"It has been lately. What's been bothering you?"

"Long days and short nights." For me, such a complaint had quite a bit different meaning than it did for other people.

"And nothing else?"

"Waiting for Nora to reply, or at least for Oliver to send a letter. It's been ages." Plenty of time for a letter to find its way to the Warburton family in Italy and for them to pass it on to Nora. I worried that it had gone astray somehow, undelivered while I sat half a world away impatiently fuming for an answer that would never come.

"I thought it might be because of those men," she said.

That was how the household had come to refer to Ash and the other cutthroats. "Why should you think that?"

"Because that's when you started being so quiet."

And also when I discovered Norwood's liaison with Molly Audy. I didn't like having the knowledge, and keeping it a secret was affecting my behavior with Elizabeth. I was tempted to unburden myself about it, if not to her then to Father, or perhaps even Beldon, but since that time Norwood had not gone whoring. Of that I was sure since I'd made a habit of "questioning" Molly whenever I paid my respects. At least, a whispering voice in my head said, he hadn't been whoring with *her*. With all the soldiers around, there were any number of camp followers about, and if not as pretty or as skilled as Molly, they were cheap. I remembered her mention of his parsimony over the price.

A little "talk" between us would clear the air and either cancel my doubts or confirm them. If the latter, then Norwood and I would have a very serious talk, indeed. But I'd been putting it off, as one does any potentially unpleasant task.

"You haven't said much about it." Elizabeth brought me back to the present with her misplaced assumption about my reticence.

"Haven't really wanted to. Or needed to," I added, looking up at her with as much reassurance as I could muster.

She met my eyes over the mound of sewing piled before her on the dining table and hopefully saw that her gentle concern was appreciated, but not necessary.

"What about yourself?" I asked. "Getting nervous?"

"Only about whether I'll have this finished in time." She indicated the satin and silk she was sewing together.

"You will."

"So everyone tells me."

"The others would help if you'd let them."

She smiled and shook her head. "No, thank you. Sewing my own wedding dress has long been a fancy of mine, and I'll not ask others to share it with me."

The initial formalities had come and gone months ago. Lord James Norwood asked Elizabeth if he might petition Father for her hand in marriage and had been answered in a most positive manner. Father had granted permission in his turn, with the reluctance and pride all fathers experience when they must give up their daughters, and since then the house had been busy with preparations for the wedding. Much of it had to do with the making of many new clothes for the bride, and while Elizabeth had gratefully accepted help for her other dresses and things, she'd reserved the most important project for herself.

It was taking longer than expected. Amid the housecleaning, the hiring of new servants, the parties of congratulation and celebration and the thousand other details that seemed to arise when two people decide to join forces, Elizabeth hadn't had much time for her project. She rose early before the sun to work and was still at it long after dark. I kept her company, for the time was fast approaching when we would no longer be able to have these quiet talks. Soon Norwood would sweep her away and things would never be the same again. Well could I understand Father's mixed feelings in the matter. I was happy for Elizabeth's happiness, but sorry for myself at losing her.

I'd picked up a slight edge in her tone, or thought I had. "Has Mother been troublesome?"

"What do you mean?"

"I just wondered if anything had happened today."

"No. *She's* been quiet enough."

True, very true. Since that one talk I'd had with her, Mother had been behaving with remarkable restraint. She still ignored us as much as possible, but was otherwise almost civil. There was a marked lessening of her biting sarcasm, no shows of temper, no tantrums, no berserk fits, and far more important to me, no laudanum turning up in Father's tea. He commented now and then about the change in her, but thought it to be a result of Elizabeth's physical confrontation with her last December. I knew better, but still did not care to enlighten him about it, and if he'd guessed, he kept it to himself. As he cautiously (and more discreetly) resumed visiting with Mrs. Montagu, I found a great easing for any strain my conscience might have felt over the matter.

"What about her toady, then?" Things had been rather uneasy between Elizabeth and Mrs. Hardinbrook lately. The lady's disappointment at Elizabeth's marrying Norwood instead of Beldon had festered into bitterness.

"She's a fool and a wretch," Elizabeth said in a low voice. She flushed deep red and promptly pricked her finger on her next stitch.

I picked up the bloodsmell right away, but easily dismissed it. "What's she done?"

"It's what she says, and she says it in the nicest way possible. I'd managed to forget about it until now."

But not very well, since I'd noticed something wasn't quite right with her. "Tell me."

She stopped sewing and heaved a great sigh. "It was this afternoon when we were receiving some of Mother's cronies. Even if she doesn't look at me if she can help it, I had to be there. It's usually bearable, but Mrs. Hardinbrook had her head together with that awful cat, Mrs. Osburn. She was talking just loud enough for me to hear, but not enough so that I could really make a comment about it. You know how they—"

"Yes, I've seen it in practice. Go on."

"She was all pleasantries about me, but what she was saying was still full of spite."

"What did she say?"

"Well, it was about how *lucky* I was that Lord James had picked me. So very *lucky* that I hadn't ended up an old maid, after all. You'd think that James and I hadn't come to our determination together or that he'd taken pity on me or something."

"The bitch," I said evenly.

"Then she started going on about all the money he'd come into once we were married and as much as implied that *that* was why he'd pro posed. They laughed about it, because she'd make a joke of it, but it wasn't nice laughter. I looked at her to let her know I'd heard and all she did was smile back, pretending otherwise. How I hate her."

"She's a fool, definitely, and not worth your notice."

"I try to think that, but it's hard. I don't know how a person can go to church every Sunday, appear to listen so closely, and then act as she does toward me. It's wicked."

"The more so because she knows what's she's doing to you."

Her lips came together a moment and there was an excess of water in her eyes. "You don't know about this, but when you came home hurt from Mrs. Montagu's . . ."

"What?"

"Well, I overheard that beastly woman asking our mother who would get your share of Grandfather's estate should something happen to you."

That left me stunned at her bad manners, but not too terribly surprised.

"I—damnation—I'm finding myself cringing inside like a child whenever I see her, waiting for the next bit of poison to come spewing out. Sometimes I know what she's going to say next and then she says it, as though she's hearing my very thoughts. I don't know how Dr. Beldon puts up with her. Sometimes all I want to do is . . ." One of her hands formed into a fist, then she let it relax. "But if I did that then I'd feel awful afterward."

"Not nearly so bad as Mrs. Hardinbrook. She'd feel *much* worse."

She glanced up, her eyes slowly kindling with the beginnings of a smile. "You think so?"

"Oh, yes. She'd feel terrible. Can you imagine her consternation trying to cover the bruises with rice flour? There wouldn't be enough of that stuff on the Island to do a proper job of it."

Elizabeth fell into my humor, speculating, "I could black her eye . . ."

"Knock out a tooth or two in the front . . ."

"Cut her hair and throw her wigs down the well . . ."

"I wouldn't go that far, it'd foul the water."

By then she was laughing freely and when it had worn itself out, I saw that her usual good spirits had reasserted themselves.

"There," I said. "The next time you see her, try thinking of her as looking like that. She'll go mad trying to figure out what's amusing you so much."

"I don't know how I shall manage without you, little brother."

"You won't be living that far away. I shall visit so often, you and James will be sick of seeing my face."

"Never." She went back to her sewing again. "But I know that things will change. They always do when someone gets married. I've seen it happen to my friends, how they break away and move on like leaves dropping from a tree. The wind catches them up and off they go. I shouldn't like that."

"Then make sure James knows and perhaps you can avoid it."

"I can tell him, but there are some things that can't be avoided. You know he's talked about taking me to England. We'll probably even stay there. I might never see you or Father ever again." She looked in danger of tears.

"You can always call off the wedding."

The danger instantly passed. "I can't do that!"

"Well, then." I spread my hands.

She made a kind of growling sigh. "All right. Perhaps I *am* getting nervous."

"You've every right to be considering what you're taking on. It's not only getting married, but setting up your own household, getting the servants to work together . . ."

She nearly shuddered. "I can handle the ones I engage well enough, but that Harridge fellow makes me feel like I should curtsy every time he walks into the room."

In the front hall or the servants' hall, Norwood's valet was not a popular man.

"He's going to be a perfect ogre to the others, I know it," she said.

"Keep him busy enough with duties and maybe he won't have the time for it. That should be easy with all the work to be done in the new house."

She muttered a guarded agreement, but I could see the reminder of what was to come had been a cheering one. She was very much looking forward to setting up her own home.

By some miracle Norwood had found a suitable dwelling halfway between Glenbriar and Glenbriar Landing and had rented it, calling it their "nuptial cottage." The miracle had been finding anything at all. By now Long Island was not only flooded with soldiers, but with prisoners of war, and all of them in need of lodging. I suspected that Norwood had used his own kind of influence to secure it, trading on his title as much and as often as possible.

It was no vast hall, but certainly much more than a cottage, having belonged to a gentleman who had had the misfortune of being home when the zealous Colonel Heard and his troop of traitors had come calling over a year ago. Heard had already been to Hempstead hell-bent on extracting oaths of loyalty for his American "congress." Father had been caught up in that farce himself and had managed to shrug it off, but this other gentleman had not. Keenly feeling the humiliation of being forced to take an oath to support an illegal government he'd neither voted for or wanted, he'd put his place up for sale and packed his family off to Canada that summer—just before Lord Howe's arrival.

The house stood empty for only as long as it took for some officers to claim it and move in, and, being gentlemen, they hadn't the faintest idea how to organize anything of a domestic nature. It became very run-down, very quickly, enough so that any prospective buyer would turn away before passing the gate. The officers had long moved out, following Lord Howe to New York. With no owner present and the agent for the sale desperate for any kind of money, he'd been most eager to agree to the pittance Norwood had offered in the way of rent. His lordship had pointed out, quite correctly, that the house needed repairs and the only other likely occupants would be prisoners with little or no money at all. An agreement was made, and Norwood and his bride would soon be taking up residence.

Far too soon for me. I would miss my sister very much. Far more than when I'd been packed off to Cambridge. It didn't matter that she'd be living only a couple of miles away, things would change between us.

I supposed that it would be easier if I liked Norwood better, but that business about Molly had infused me with a difficult to overcome prejudice. For Elizabeth's sake I'd tried not to let it bother me and had been fairly successful. Time would inform me on whether I could maintain the attitude with any degree of sincerity.

"You're quiet again."

Time to make an effort, I thought, and assumed a sadly serious face. "Well, I . . . had a question for you."

She caught my tone and put aside the sewing once more, giving me all her attention, and bracing herself for whatever was to come.

"Tell me, when you write letters will you sign yourself as 'Elizabeth' or as 'Lady James Norwood'?"

She threw her thimble at me.

The spring lambing had been good, despite the best efforts by the army commissary, and it looked like we'd be having if not a profitable year, then at least a comfortable one. Nash kept himself very busy, ranging farther afield searching out the Island's bounty, but under my "tutelage" he'd turned into quite an honest fellow, paying the farmers for their goods. Mind you, it was a terrific wrench against his basic nature, so he was never too comfortable whenever he saw me coming. The lukewarm smile he wore when I walked into The Oak's common room tonight was the best that could be expected given the circumstances.

I hailed him like a long-lost friend and asked if I could have the pleasure of buying him a drink. Several of the regular customers, hoping to take a share of my generosity, soon crowded in to give me their greetings. Eternally parched Noddy Milverton moved in right next to me without my having to trouble myself to arrange it.

Nash accepted the offer and somehow all the others were included, and they drank to my health.

"Anything in the post, Mr. Farr?" I asked.

"A few things did chance to come in today," he said, fetching them. Chance indeed, for the post had not been a model of efficiency lately. He lay a string-tied packet before me and I made use of my penknife to cut it open. Had my heart been beating, it would have been audible from my surge of hope. But the hope was short-lived and the dashing of it was not unnoticed.

"Nothing from England?" sympathized Farr. He knew from my almost nightly visits to his place that I was expecting an important letter from there.

"No." Some stuff for Father from Hempstead, some things for Elizabeth, a note for Beldon. My disappointment was very acute. Noddy Milverton took the opportunity to swiftly drain my ale and continue his simpleminded innocence.

"Sorry."

"Another time, then." I asked for and got the latest gossip. There had been a raid at Sands Cove, with stock carried off in whaleboats. A valuable bull had been part of the haul, and the unhappy owner was both enraged and sickened that his breeding animal was probably already hanging from a hook in some distant butchery.

"What's to be done about it?" I asked Nash, rather unfairly putting him on the spot in front of everyone.

But he'd heard that question often enough and was ready for it. "All that can be done. The men up there watch the coast like hawks, but they can't be everywhere at once."

"There oughter be a way o' stoppin' 'um," someone put in.

"There is. The army is doing its best to track down the traitors across the Sound. Once order is restored you'll be free of trouble soon enough."

No one was encouraged by this pronouncement, but they'd not get anything different from him and knew better than to try. Most retired to other parts of the room, grumbling a little, but not to the point of rudeness. Nash was content to ignore them.

"This raid at Sands Cove," I said in a lower voice. "Any familiar faces there?"

He knew I meant Ash and his lot. "The descriptions were too vague to be sure. The fellows were definitely from Connecticut by their talk, according to the farmer. The rest of his family had been badly frightened, but he—well, I've rarely seen a man so spitting mad before. Thought he'd burst a blood vessel from it."

He must have been angry indeed for Nash to notice, having so blithely annoyed quite a lot of people with his collections. I made no comment on it. "Then there's been no fresh word on any of them?"

"None."

As there seemed little point in continuing the conversation, I bade him a polite good evening and retired to one of the chairs to listen to the other men's gossip. Nash, I thought, glimpsing at him from the corner of my eye, looked relieved. It must have been hard on him, always being vaguely uncomfortable about me and never knowing why.

The talk was more of the same, but leavened with a curse or two directed at the troublemakers. Occasionally the British army or the Hessians were the targets of their ire, but only in the lowest of tones. I fell under the eye of Mr. Curtis, who gestured for me to come closer, which I did. Room was made and I sat next to him.

"Well, Mr. Barrett, is that reward you're offering still good?"

Months ago I'd put up a sum of money for the arrest of my kidnappers. So far no one had been able to claim it. "It is."

"Real money?"

"In gold. What do you know?"

He didn't quite answer the question. "Just wanted to be sure of it in case we ran into 'em."

My brows went up. "You think there's a chance of that?"

He and the others were amused. "I reckon we might see a new face an' it wouldn't hurt to be wise about it."

"No, not at all."

More amusement and I joined them, albeit grimly now that I understood what they were about. Connecticut had its raiders, and so now did Long Island, and I was sitting with a few of them. It was a clear night, with a bright full moon, though, else they'd already be out trying to repay the many insults our neighbor across the Sound had made to us. I could imagine both sides passing each other in their whaleboats, all unknowing, the next time conditions for a stealthy crossing occurred.

"Mr. Curtis, I was wondering if you'd heard anything about raiders coming in from Suffolk County."

"I'm not as near there as you are. You'd know more'n me, wouldn't you?"

"Yes, but you have been blessed with a sharper ear than most. I thought some word might have come your way."

He shook his head. "What's your idea?"

"It's something Mr. Nash just said about the thieves he missed catching." I won a smile from them at Nash's expense.

"What 'uz that?"

"He said they must have been from Connecticut from their talk, and it seemed to me to have two meanings, that they either spoke of the place or the place itself was in their speech. An accent."

"What of it?"

"Well, I was recalling how those men spoke to me, and I don't think one of them had a Connecticut accent."

"It don't mean that they weren't from there, though. Lots of folk have had to move around with this war on."

"Perhaps so. But it was a very windy night back then and even after the wind had died, the sea would be no friend to anyone in a boat trying to make the crossing. I was thinking it might be easier for them to row along the shore for a few miles until they were deeper into Suffolk County."

"I'm no whaling man, but it makes sense to me. What'll you do about it?"

"There's not much I can do, except pass the word on to Mr. Nash and hope some good comes of it."

"Then good luck to you both, I'm sure."

Now the laugh was at my expense, I took it good-naturedly, knowing full well the seed had been planted. If any of them heard a whisper, I'd know about it. I wished them good luck in turn and took my leave.

Even after spending some time with (and money on) Molly Audy, I was home again just before midnight, and slightly startled to see lights still burning in the music room. I peered in the window. Mother, Mrs. Hardinbrook, Beldon, and Lady Caroline were at cards. Beldon and Lady Caroline were yawning their heads off. This was the latest I'd ever seen any of them stay up to play, but Mother was quite addicted to the games after all. If she insisted on another hand or two, she could count on Mrs. Hardinbrook to enthusiastically join in, dragging her brother along. Lady Caroline played, I thought, to be polite.

The rest of the house was dark and quiet, with everyone else presumably in bed. Father wasn't home, having left for an overnight trip to Hempstead, though I knew him to really be at Mrs. Montagu's. I wished him well. No doubt he'd left a stack of work for me in the library, but it wouldn't hurt to delay my start on it for a while. Molly had, as usual, put me into a mellow frame of mood and mind; I was content to stand outside and watch.

And wait.

The game went on, with Beldon and Lady Caroline growing more sleepy by the minute. Even Mrs. Hardinbrook was starting to droop. Mother was quite alert, though, her movements crisp. There was a certain nervousness in her manner, but that was familiar to us all. She had been staying up later and later over the months, asking for just one more hand, or continuing a conversation beyond its natural close. I don't think she slept very well, for I'd heard her pacing in her room at odd hours. Beldon gave her sleeping draughts when she asked for them, and though she drank them straight down, they must not have been doing her much good.

Now she looked to be trying the patience of her staunchest supporter, for when the hand was finished, Mrs. Hardinbrook made a great show of weariness and rose. Beldon lurched to his feet as well, then Lady Caroline. Mother remained seated and I felt an unexpected stab of pity for her as she looked up at them. She looked . . . lost. I hadn't forgotten how she never let herself be alone if she could help it.

It was probably awful for her, but there was little I could do about it. I had other things to concern me.

Beldon escorted Lady Caroline out of the room. They'd likely go straight up to their respective beds. Excellent. Mrs. Hardinbrook lingered, putting the cards away and offering one-word replies to anything Mother said. She put out all but two of the candles, taking one for herself and giving the other to Mother.

I pushed away from the window and, fading slightly, willed myself to silently drift around the house toward the back. It was still a clear night, but this side was in deep shadow, so I thought I could risk such behavior. The late hour was very much in my favor as well; all the servants would be asleep, even the lordly Mr. Harridge. I let myself rise up to a second-floor window, faded-away completely, and sieved through the shutters. There was a moment of brittle discomfort as I crossed the glass barrier of the window, then I was floating free in the hallway.

Waiting still, but not for long.

A door closed down the hall and around a corner. Mother's. Now Mrs. Hardinbrook would be coming along to her room. I went solid and saw that I was right. The glow of her candle announced her approach. She didn't half give a jump when she saw me standing by the window.

"Oh! Mr. Barrett, whatever are you doing there?"

"Just making sure the window is bolted. Can't be too careful these days."

"One certainly can't. Well, good night."

"A moment, please, I had a question for you."

That also surprised her, for I never spoke to her if I could avoid it.

"Yes, what is it?"

I stepped closer into the light so she could see me.

It didn't take long. And I'd had plenty of practice with people like Nash . . . and Drummond. I got her attention, saw her brightly empty face grow a little emptier, and that was that.

"I want you to cease being so cruel toward Elizabeth. Do you understand me?"

She whispered that she did. The candle began to tremble. I took it away before she dropped it.

"There's no room in this house for any of your spite. You can be civil or you needn't say anything at all. Understand?"

"Yes . . ."

Unpleasant woman, but perhaps less so now. "That's very kind of you, then." I released her from my influence. "I shall bid you a good night, Mrs. Hardinbrook."

She blinked several times and became suddenly puzzled at how her candle had jumped into my hand without her noticing. I didn't bother to explain, but gave it back to her with a little bow. Disturbed, she scuttled into her room and shut the door between us. I turned away, only just managing to keep my laughter silent. Though I'd not mention it to her, this was one of my wedding presents to Elizabeth. With all the other things claiming her attention, she could do without Mrs. Hardinbrook's little observations and innuendos. After the wedding it wouldn't matter, but at least until then there would be a bit more peace in the household.

I stopped dead cold. *Damnation*.

Beldon was standing at the corner, holding a candle high in one hand, with a book in the other. He'd probably been on his way to the library and had obviously seen and heard everything. I knew that what I'd said to Mrs. Hardinbrook had been innocent enough, if a trifle rude, but it might still be taken as a very odd exchange. From the look on his face, he'd correctly interpreted it in that manner. He stared and stared and stared, not moving, hardly even breathing.

I stared back, not knowing what to do or say until the long silence began to pile up between us, thick and dreadful, and I came to the reluctant conclusion I'd have to influence him as well. To make him forget what he'd seen.

But he never gave me that chance. He whipped around, heading for his room. Heart in my belly, I went after him.

"Dr. Beldon," I whispered, putting some urgency, not unmixed with exasperation, into it.

He surprised me again by stopping cold in the hallway. He did not turn to face me, but did wait, back all stiff, for me to catch him up. When I was even with him, he gave every evidence of acute discomfort.

"Doctor—"

"Mr. Barrett—"

Knowing ahead of time that I would certainly have the last word, I indicated for him to go ahead.

"I'm sorry," he said. "I did not intend to intrude upon your conversation with Deborah."

"You what?"

"I should have said something when I passed by, but I thought it best to . . . well . . ."

That's when I abruptly realized that his reaction was not that of fear, but rather tremendous embarrassment. *Well-a-day*.

"Deborah," he continued, "often forgets that we are your guests. She's not a very clever woman, that is to say . . . I've tried to talk to her, but she's never been one to listen to me."

I started to speak, but he raised one hand.

"No, please, I just wanted to apologize for her behavior. I'm very sorry if she's caused any distress to your family, especially to your dear sister. I also wanted to say that I'm very glad that you did talk to her just now. It's . . . long overdue. My chief regret is that I have not been more firm with her in the past."

"I . . . don't know what to say, sir," I muttered. "If I have been overly brusk with—"

"No, you spoke your mind to her and that was what was needed."

"You're uncommonly kind, sir."

"As you have been to me, sir, many, many times over." I knew that he harbored a genuine affection for my family, but often as not his natural reticence prevented him from expressing it. I also knew that he harbored a particularly deep affection for me, but had never acted upon it. Now he did look square upon me, and I saw what it was costing him to be so direct. He was skimming rather close to issues that we had long since tabled and was perhaps afraid I might misinterpret his gratitude for something else.

I smiled back at him, offering reassurance. " 'Tis my honor to do so, sir," I said, and gave a little bow.

His relief was hardly subtle, his shoulders visibly relaxed, and a tentative smile crept over his own worried features. "Thank you, Mr. Barrett."

"At your service, Dr. Beldon."

"Good night, then."

"And to you." Having apparently forgotten the errand that had taken him out to start with, he returned to his room. With a light step.

*Well-a-day*, I thought again.

Despite his sometime toad-eating manner, I'd come to regard Beldon as a friend, never more so than now. I'd influenced him before, but only to protect the secret of my changed nature. Such intrusions upon so inoffensive a man often plagued my conscience; I was more than happy to forgo another experience. Thank heavens for his parochial mind, that he'd seen no more than what had seemed natural to him and had not attributed anything outre to it.

With an equally light step, I made my way downstairs, so vastly relieved that I forgot the late hour and began to whistle.

Nights came and went swiftly, blurring together so that I sometimes had the illusion of living through one very lengthy night punctuated only by changes of clothes. The conversations all seemed to be the same, since they concerned but one topic: the wedding. The people were certainly the same. It might have been tedious, but my past experiences had taught me a hard lesson on the priceless value of boredom. Better to be inactive and at peace in the world than to be subjected to the frantic racing about brought on by catastrophe.

Father saw to his practice, Elizabeth sewed on her dress, and I kept them company or went down to The Oak to hear the news. As expected, Mrs. Hardinbrook ceased to be quite so hatefully annoying and looked after Mother, who had come to be remarkably restrained in her manner. She worried me, for I thought she might still be suffering from fright. I tried to catch her eye now and then, but hers would slide past as though I were not there. She played cards, or sewed, or gossiped when such friends as she had came calling, but if she were afraid of me, it did not show. Several times I overheard her requesting sleeping draughts from Beldon, but they must have had an indifferent effect on her, for I'd still hear her moving about in her room late at night and on into the early morning hours. She looked a bit haggard from the lack of sleep and was more withdrawn than before, but that was preferable to her fits.

No one else marked it, though, being so busy with their own projects, and I had no plans to draw it to anyone's attention. After a time I came to consider it to be just another in a series of unpleasant incidents no one ever talked about and was content to lct life run on as usual.

There were plenty of genteel distractions in the early hours of the shortening summer evenings. Cousin Anne had persuaded me to join her in reading some Shakespeare to the others by way of entertainment. Her first choice was the first play I'd recommended, *Twelfth Night*, and she turned out to be something of a natural actress—once she understood what she was saying. Of course, most of the base jokes in the text escaped her and the whole room had a moment of bald embarrassment when she stopped the reading once to ask the meaning of the word "eunuch."

Elizabeth, gallantly stifling a laugh, came to my rescue, saying that it was a boy who would never grow to become a man. Anne's comprehension was questionable, for we continued with no further pauses. Afterward, she sought out Elizabeth for a highly intense conversation.

I found myself too curious to resist. When Anne had finished and glided off, I moved in. "What did she ask you this time?"

Elizabeth kept her laughter quiet and kindly. "Goodness, she should be more observant about what's going on around her here in the country. Then she'd know about these things."

"What things?"

"She wanted to know how a boy could not help but grow into a man, what could possibly prevent it. So I tried a comparison employing the gelding of horses—"

"Good God, Elizabeth!"

"It's close enough," she defended, still trying not to laugh. "I said that since a stallion has private parts to be gelded, then so does a man, and if he is deprived of them at a certain age . . ."

I was all but choking. "Then what?"

"Well, she did want to know . . ." Now she stopped and blushed a very violent red.

I leaned forward, looking expectant.

She gave me a mock-severe look in return. "You're being coarse and prurient, Jonathan."

"Absolutely. What did she want to know?"

She gave up in disgust. "Appearance."

I did choke on that one and fought in vain to hold onto a sober face. "And what did you tell her?"

"*Jonathan!*"

Time to retreat, which I did, laughing, but vowing to avoid any solitary interviews with Anne for the time being. She'd been curious about kissing, which I'd been happy to help on, but I wasn't at all ready to provide answers should she decide to question me on this particular topic. Some days later, Elizabeth informed me that a solution had presented itself during a visit to a friend with an infant boy. When the child's natural requirements dictated a change of diaper, Elizabeth volunteered to do the task for the mother and took Anne along to help. The experience proved to be sufficiently educational to satisfy our sweetly innocent cousin, so I was safe once more.

Also after that incident, having learned the value of discretion, Anne made a point to reserve further inquiries about unfamiliar words until the end of an evening.

And then one day the wedding dress was finished and the event itself was upon us. I was unaware of most of it, being confined to my usually quiet bed in the cellar, but the first thing I heard the instant the sun was gone was one of Mrs. Nooth's many helpers clattering around in search of some supply for the kitchen. I was glad not to have to breathe, for the place reeked of cooking and baking. As soon as the helper was gone, I vanished and let myself float up through the very floors of the house, reappearing in my upstairs room.

Jericho was waiting there for me and only jumped a little when I arrived.

We shared chagrined smiles, then I asked, "How have things been today?"

"Fairly easy. We have not yet run out of food and the young son of one of the guests provided some unexpected entertainment by tumbling from the hayloft and breaking his fall in the muck heap outside the stable."

"Oh, lord."

"Precisely what his mother said, plus quite a bit more. Their own servants saw to his cleaning up, I'm glad to say. It could not have been an especially pleasant job."

"Is everyone else all right?"

"Oh, yes. Mr. Barrett is making sure all the gentlemen have sufficient food with their drink, so there have been no incidents even when politics are being discussed. Miss Elizabeth is well enough, considering."

For the last week Elizabeth had been harried by all the last-minute tasks and planning. She had a true talent for organization, though, otherwise she might not have made it this far.

"Everyone has been asking for you throughout the day," he said, letting me know that I should hurry.

My best clothes had been carefully laid out on the bed and he had the shaving things ready, the water still gently steaming. He must have walked in seconds before me. The man had impeccable timing. Without another word, we fell into our long-practiced routine. He had me shaved, powdered, and dressed fit for a royal audience, or even my sister's wedding, without hurry, yct in a very short time. I'd discovered that it went much faster when I did not argue with him on his choice of clothes for me and offered none now.

He had me very well trained.

Once downstairs and giving belated greetings to the vast number of guests, I felt as though I were back in London again, attending one of the Bolyn family's many lavish parties. War notwithstanding, everyone else was also in their best, either made new for the occasion or refurbished to look like new. Molly Audy had had a surfeit of custom for her legitimate business and scarcely time for anything else, even if it did pay better. After one of our necessarily briefer liaisons, I asked why she even bothered with the sewing and was informed that she derived a great deal of satisfaction from it. This inspired a further query from me, asking if the two businesses—or pleasures as was the case—were remotely comparable in terms of enjoyment, and I promptly got a pillow in my face.

Though discreet herself, her workmanship was strongly in evidence tonight. I recognized many of her completed commissions on the backs (and backsides) of a number of gentlemen, having seen the fabrics and garments in various stages of development in her workroom. They had me wondering which of them availed themselves of both of Molly's services, and doubtless they were thinking the same thing as they eyed each other. I was made exempt from this, in that my clothes had been made in London.

Norwood, too, I noticed with approval, wore a familiar-looking coat, though the waistcoat was new. A gift from Elizabeth. His innate thriftiness had probably encouraged him to use what he had rather than invest in any expansion of his wardrobe. Like me, he might also have a preference for London tailors. I didn't care so long as it meant he was keeping clear of Molly.

I greeted my prospective brother-in-law with a light thump on the back and was relieved to see that he wasn't even remotely drunk, though he seemed rather relaxed for a groom.

"What, have you done this before?" I asked with a gesture at the wedding party.

He laughed. "I don't know why everyone expects me to be nervous. I'm not, really. Really I'm not. Really."

Ah, now *there* was a bit of strain to him, after all. Very cheering, to be sure.

Elizabeth, when I found her, was in the center of a virtual garden of gowns. So thickly were her friends gathered 'round her that their wide-reaching dresses scarcely left any space in the room. I was bumped and crowded and made over and teased as I made my way to her, being very careful where I put my feet, especially around the seated ladies, who had spread their skirts out to show them off. None, I thought, were more beautiful than Elizabeth's, and certainly none of the women wearing them were as beautiful, either.

I bowed deeply and kissed her hand and wished her the best of all possible days. My throat was clogging and my eyes stung a bit.

"Thank you, little brother." She smiled back at me, looking utterly radiant, and I was ready to burst with pride in her. "It's been a truly marvelous day, but now . . ."

"Night is here with my arrival, or is it the other way around?"

"You ass!" But she softened her humor. "You wonderful ass."

"Coming soon, is it?"

She gulped. "Yes, very soon."

"I'm glad you arranged things so I could be here to see."

"That's all Father's doing."

"How is he?"

"Being fatherly. When I came downstairs he had to use his handkerchief a lot. Tried to pretend he had dust in his eyes, but I knew better."

"I know how he feels. All I can say is be happy, Elizabeth."

"I will. I know I will."

And within the hour she married Lord James Norwood amid tears and laughter and glorious celebration. Thus did we observe and acknowledge the change that came to all our lives.

# CHAPTER 12

***June 1777***

Though larger campaigns of destruction were being undertaken by the armies in the greater world outside, we were naturally most concerned for our own area, having endured a number of raids, both bold and vicious. Some of the thieves were caught, and those without commission papers were hanged. Hardworking farmers made desperate by the loss of their produce to the British and the rebels turned to thieving themselves as a means of survival and revenge. Some of them joined with the local militia, others preferred to work on their own. One such group included Mr. Curtis, Mr. Davis, and even Noddy Milverton on occasion. Whenever they were absent from The Oak, it was generally accepted they'd "gone fishing" along the Connecticut coast. No one objected to it, least of all Lieutenant Nash.

Some of the Hessian troops had been transferred out, both to the relief and annoyance of the locals. Our barn was empty once more, as was Mrs. Montagu's. They were hated company, but their presence had been a curtailment to the raids. Father worried for her and visited as often as he could. He'd gifted her with several pistols and a good hunting rifle and had gone to no little trouble to teach her and her servants how to shoot well. The lady had also taken to increasing the numbers of geese around her home, being of the same opinion as the old Romans that they were better than dogs for giving the alarm.

But though the times were hard, we knew they were much worse elsewhere, so we thanked God for our lot and prayed for a swift victory over our enemies and the restoration of peace.

The sun rose later each night and arrived sooner each day, but I'd gotten over the feeling of being deprived of my waking hours. When I lay my head down, the dawn brought such complete oblivion that I had no knowledge of the day's passage, hence the continuation of my illusion of living one endless night. I seemed to find plenty of time to do all that I wanted; I had no more complaints.

I did become a frequent visitor to Elizabeth's new house. She'd made it into a very pretty place despite Norwood's objections to the expense.

"I think it's because of his plans to go back to England," she confided to me. "He thinks it's a waste of money to put it into a house we won't be staying in for very long."

"What's he mean by that? Are you to leave so soon?" The idea had been there for some time, but only in the abstract. Now Elizabeth was speaking as though they were already starting to pack for the journey.

"Oh, not for a while, perhaps. Maybe a year or so."

"That's something, then," I said grudgingly. Though my perception of time had been skewed by my change, a year still seemed a very great interval. "I mean, if you really want to leave . . ."

"Actually, I don't, but I should go and meet his family. I'm rather curious about how a duke lives."

"Doesn't he tell you?"

"Not always. I hear more about his dead ancestors than the living relatives. Do you know his people were at Agincourt? It seems that I've married into a very famous family."

I looked on as she sewed away on some humble task, her head bowed over her work. She'd changed, a bit, and would change more as most of her interests came to center upon her new life. "Are you happy about it?"

"It's not very real to me yet. All I know is James. He's what's real."

"Are you happy with him?"

"Yes, certainly I'm happy. How can you ask such a thing?"

"Just playing the protective brother, is all."

"That can't be all. Don't you like him?"

"Well, yes, but you can't expect me to be in favor of his taking you away to England someday. Father and I would miss you terribly."

"And I would miss you both terribly, but I have to go with my husband. That's the way things are."

"Then it's not right. You should have a say in where you want to live."

"I know, but I'm sure things will work out for the best no matter where we are."

She was in love and would follow her husband. I was only her brother and it wasn't my place to object.

Lady Caroline had come over earlier that day for a visit and had stayed longer than expected. My arrival soon after dusk was greeted with surprise. She had been going to spend the night rather than risk traveling after dark, but at the conclusion of my visit she asked me to escort her home.

"But the roads might be dangerous," said Norwood.

"It will be perfectly safe," I replied. I had confidence in my ability to see and hear a potential hazard long before it saw me. "I'll be going by way of Glenbriar to check the post."

"For that letter from England? I hope it comes soon, or you shall wear out your welcome at the inn."

"I shouldn't want to be any trouble," said Lady Caroline.

"No trouble," I told her. "Besides, Anne will miss your company. She had her heart set on reading that scene with you of Portia and Nerissa discussing the suitors in *The Merchant of Venice*."

"So she did. I recall she wanted you to play the Prince of Morocco."

"And the Prince of Arragon—and Bassanio, too, if there's time."

"She's turned into quite the scholar."

"Actress, more like. If she continues like this, Mr. Garrick will have to come out of retirement."

"Who?"

"David Garrick, the actor."

"Oh, goodness, of course. For some reason I thought you meant one of the farmers hereabouts."

"You'll not catch many of them with time for reading Shakespeare."

"Or aught else, I'm sure."

"I'll go see to the horses, then." I went off toward the miserable-looking structure that served as a stable. Elizabeth had once mentioned her desire to repair and improve it before the winter, lightly complaining when Norwood asked to put it off a while longer. I wondered if his tight-fisted nature would soon be a source of discontent for her.

They had no stablemen, not even a lad to see to their own beasts. Norwood claimed that he enjoyed looking after them himself, which was understandable to me, but I thought it odd for a man in his position not to have at least one servant for the task. There wasn't that much work to do, though, with but two horses. He had a hunter and Elizabeth had brought along her favorite from home, Beauty. So far they had not yet acquired a carriage, not that there were many to be had these days. When

Sunday came along, Father would send a man along in ours to pick them up for church.

I'd taken up riding again to give Rolly some much needed exercise and make a change for me. This included my wish to avoid being seen floating about. I'd been spotted twice, but fortunately both times the men had been rather drunk and no one believed their story about a "flying ghost." After that I became more careful.

Taking Rolly's reins and those of Lady Caroline's horse, I walked back to the house in no particular hurry, but unwilling to waste time. Elizabeth had already said good night and gone upstairs, leaving Norwood and his sister in the front entry. They were speaking in low tones and looked to be having some kind of a disagreement. Before I'd quite gotten close enough to hear anything above the noise of the horses, they broke off and acted as though nothing were amiss. Well, if they wished it to be so, then I would act in kind. I helped Lady Caroline up to her sidesaddle, swung onto Rolly, and bade farewell to Norwood. He stood in the doorway and watched us until we were out of sight down the lane.

"Was there anything wrong between you two?" I asked.

"Not really. He's just worried about my being out, but I told him that we'd be fine."

It had looked more interesting than simple concern, but if so, then she was determined to keep it to herself.

"You are armed, I hope?" she asked.

"I'd feel undressed without these." I touched the specially made case hanging from my saddle that held a set of duelers I'd bought on a whim in London. Since my abduction, I took them everywhere, loaded, and ready at hand. "And you?"

Instead of the "muff gun" favored by some ladies, she pulled out a formidable brass-barreled specimen made by Powell of Dublin that was capable of firing six shots, one after another. It was an amazing piece of work, and I had hopes of someday acquiring one myself. Its appeal lay in the fact that after an initial priming, all one had to do was to pull back the trigger guard after each shot, turn the cylinder, and push the guard forward to lock it, then fire again. Six in a row without reloading. An absolutely marvelous invention.

Our safety assured by our arms collection, we kicked the horses up with confidence and cantered toward Glenbriar. It wasn't far, and I found the ride shortened by her pleasing company. Almost before I knew it, we were reining up before The Oak. As this night I was only interested in the post and not buying a round of drinks and time with Molly Audy, I would only be a moment. There was a room on the side reserved for the ladies if

Lady Caroline desired to come in, and I asked her as much, but she professed that she was content to wait without.

I was hailed by a somewhat thinner crowd than usual. It being a calm night, it was easy to conclude that Nassau County's own irregulars were out prowling the Sound for booty. I didn't approve or disapprove of their work, but did hope that they harmed no one and could avoid capture if at all possible. Their treatment as prisoners would doubtless be short and brutal, for the hangings had made many of the Connecticut "militia" very bitter.

"Anything at all, Mr. Farr?" I asked after giving him greeting.

With a flourish as though he'd brought it across the Atlantic himself, he placed a battered packet before me, smiling broadly. I let out a crow and fell upon it like a starving man to a loaf of bread. This gave much amusement to the other patrons, so I made something of an ass of myself, but I didn't care. I cut the thing open then and there with my penknife and unfolded the sheets within.

The date, as nearly as I could make out from Oliver's atrocious handwriting, was late in February, indicating that he'd replied immediately after the arrival of my last missive to him. So it had taken a solid four months to get to me. Old news by now, but much better than nothing. My eyes flew over the crabbed words, searching for Nora's name.

And when I found it . . . well, I'd hoped for more . . . expected more.

He told me that he'd forwarded my letter to Nora to the Warburtons as per my request and hoped that I should get a speedy reply. He'd had no word from them other than a note from Mrs. Warburton saying that her son, Tony, had improved a little in the temperate Italian climate, though he was still far from recovered.

Damned murdering bastard, I thought, my mood turned foul from this lack of news. I didn't care about him, I wanted news of *Nora*.

"Not bad tidings, I hope?" said Mr. Farr.

"More like no tidings at all," I grumbled.

The rest of the letter reflected the one I'd sent him, chatty and full of comments about things long past and near forgotten. I was to the point of folding it to read later when I caught the name "Norbury," and went a bit farther. I'd asked him for an opinion of the family and he had provided one.

I was reading it for the fourth time when Lady Caroline, apparently impatient with waiting, came in. Mr. Farr went to her and asked permission to show her to the ladies' portion of his house, but she put him off and came smiling over to me.

"Mr. Barrett? I've no wish to rush you, but I thought you might have forgotten that your cousin is waiting for us."

Couldn't speak. Could barely hear her. Could only stare at her face, familiar for so many months, pretty, friendly, intelligent, charming, an entirely lovely woman. I stared and felt a terrible illness creeping up from my belly.

Farr noticed something was wrong. "Mr. Barrett? What is it? Mr. Barrett?"

My eyes jerked from her face to his and I struggled to form an answer. Impossible. The whole world was impossible.

She said my name again. Questioning.

Still couldn't answer. Shock, I suppose. Made it hard to think.

". . . some brandy, sir?" Farr was saying.

I shook my head. Put a hand to my eyes, rubbed them. When I blinked them clear, the horror was still before me. Undeniable. It would not go away on its own. It would have to be dealt with, and the damnable job had fallen to me. Once I understood that, a kind of acceptance and resolve took hold. Without another word, I seized her by the arm and guided her toward one of the more private receiving rooms. I grabbed up a candle from one of the tables in passing, much to the startlement of the men there. Ignoring their comments, I pushed her ahead of me into the room and shut the door.

"What is the matter, Mr. Barrett?" she demanded, nonplussed if not angered by my abrupt behavior.

"That is something for you to explain, madam." I put the candle on a heavy oak table and placed Oliver's letter next to it. "Read," I ordered, pointing.

"This is ridiculous," she protested. "What on earth—?"

"Read, damn you!"

She went pale with true anger, but there was a sudden wavering in her eyes.

Doubt, I thought. Most definitely doubt.

She kept anger to the front, though, and showing it in her every move and gesture, sat in one of the chairs and plucked up the pages. It was slow going, she was not used to the handwriting, but I knew how things stood as I watched her grow paler and paler until she was deathly white. Then there was a strange reversal and her color returned until she was flushed and hot, with two crimson spots high on her cheeks.

Oliver had been fairly succinct on the subject:

"I'd not heard of any Duke of Norbury, but thought if Cousin Elizabeth were considering on adding a peer to the family it wouldn't hurt to improve my knowledge, so I started asking around. The news isn't good, I fear, as it turns out there is no such duke and never has been. The only Norbury I can turn up is some nothing of a little hamlet south of London that doesn't even have a church, much less a duke. There *is* a village called Norwood and I understand it has a rather fine inn, but again, no duke lurking about the place. I'd question this fellow and his sister very closely as they're bound to be bounders, don't you know."

She shook her head, putting on a wonderful puzzlement. "Really, Mr. Barrett, there has been a awful mistake, that, or your cousin is playing a miserable joke upon us all. My family is an old and noble line, why, we even had ancestors with Henry at Agincourt."

"I don't give a damn if they were with Richard at Bosworth Field, you will explain yourself."

"But I tell you there's nothing to be explained, 'tis your cousin who needs to . . ." She saw my look and tried another tack. "This is ridiculous. We've lived with your family for months. You *know* us well. How can we be anything except what we are?"

And for a moment I did experience a twinge of doubt. Oliver was often a rather silly fellow, after all. He *might* have gotten things muddled . . .

"This is a mistake," she said firmly. "You must realize that."

*No*. He could be an ass at times, but he was no fool.

Unlike me. Unlike all of us.

I fixed my eyes hard upon her. "You will *listen* to me . . ."

She hissed as though burned and flinched. After that initial reaction she was as still as stone, expression wide open and blank. Soulless.

Certainly heartless.

Sweet God, *how* . . .

I broke away to pace up and down a few times, trying to calm myself. I was sick and angry and ashamed, with a thousand other similar damnable feelings crowding mind and cowing spirit, filling me with their turbulent hum, making it impossible to think clearly or do anything. No good trying to question her while I was so upset, it could kill her . . . or worse.

Sweet God, it *hurt*.

And it was like this for me for many long and silent moments until it finally settled into something I could control. Only then did I dare look at her and form my first question.

"Who are you?"

"Caroline Norwood."

"Where are you from?"

"London."

"Is your oldest brother the Duke of Norbury?"

"I have no brother."

God. "Then who is James Norwood?"

"My husband."

Turned away. Quickly. Had to, to save her, to save myself. The sickness returned tenfold. For a time I just couldn't do anything, the horror of it was too much. I kept my back to her, breathing in huge gulps of air, trying to clear my mind, and, after a time, succeeding. When I was calm again, I resigned myself to the fact that everything to come was probably going to hurt like blazes, but there was no way it could be avoided. All I could do was to get on with it and over with as quickly as possible.

Pulled a chair out opposite her. Sat. Clasped my hands before me on the table.

"All right, Caroline. I want you to tell me everything about yourself."

It was a wretched story, made more so by their utter lack of conscience.

They'd come across from England over a year ago with some fine clothes and finer manners and posed as Lord James and Lady Caroline, complete with a duke as their elder brother along with a distinguished family history. The pair had had much contact with nobility in England, after all; she had been a music teacher, he a dancing master to scions of the peerage. Both were natural actors. Both were highly discontent with their lot and prepared to do anything to improve it. The titles had been predictably irresistible to certain members of Philadelphia society, and it wasn't hard to dupe the lot.

They made shameless use of their new status to acquire goods, services, favors, and stayed as guests of some of the best families in the city. Though they took out many loans they'd no intention of paying back, they were always short of cash and on the lookout for a means of getting more.

But the trouble in that city from the approaching war made it impossible for them to fulfill such plans as they'd made; escape was necessary. Enter my innocent cousin, Anne, not terribly smart, but possessing relatives with a luxuriant sanctuary far from the conflict.

Possessing money . . . at least on one side of the family.

Once they arrived and got their bearings, it was determined that one of them should try to marry into that money. James would come to pay court to my sister, as there was less difficulty for a husband to control his wife's property than the other way 'round. All he had to do was be what he essentially was, handsome, genial, naturally charming, but without a speck of real feeling or guilt for what he was doing.

Caroline was the same way. They were perfectly matched.

Then they'd found out that Elizabeth was my heir. Her money alone would be a fortune, but how much better would it be to double it. That's when they made their first attempt on my life. During the happy confusion of a tea party, it had been easy enough to keep Anne distracted. Caroline had slipped a good dose of laudanum into my tea and watched with approval as my blameless cousin stirred in plenty of sugar, which would mask the taste for me.

The plan was that I should simply fall asleep, never to wake. If anybody at the party noticed me dozing off in a chair, one or the other of them would prevent any attempt to rouse me. The greater likelihood was that once I felt sleepy enough, I'd go upstairs to bed, never to return.

They couldn't know that I would not be drinking it; I'd long planted that provision into their minds as I'd done with everyone else: that they should entirely ignore the fact I never ate or drank anything.

What a shock it had been to them when Rapelji had come in and raised the alarm about Father.

Father . . . my poor father . . . he might have died in my place, all unknowing.

And Mother . . . all these months ignorantly bearing the stigma of a poisoner.

I roughly pushed the stabbing rage aside and made Caroline go on.

Made cautious by this blunder, they held off for a time, until things could fall back into their usual routine. They did not for a moment believe Beldon's story about the flying gout and noticed right away the new lock on his door. After much speculation and observation, later confirmed when Elizabeth decided to confide in Norwood, they knew it was Mother we all suspected, not them. With relief they watched and waited for another opportunity, and James proceeded with his courtship of Elizabeth.

Caroline apparently had little objection to her husband's conquest of another woman and none at all to his going to a prostitute for the easement of such urges as come to a man forced by circumstances to be celibate. After he'd finished with Molly one night, he'd gone to The Oak for a fortifying drink and had overheard the regulars joking amongst themselves about my recent departure to pay my respects to the lady.

He wasn't aware at that time of Molly's reputation for discretion. He knew that one careless word from her to his prospective brother-in-law could endanger his chances with Elizabeth. Besides, there was the additional gain of inheritance to consider. I had to be silenced.

And the men to do it were right there. Ash, Drummond, all the others. For they were Norwood's men.

He'd met them and secured their services on one of his frequent trips away to see to "business." Faster and more certain than marriage, he'd made lucrative arrangements with them, finding likely places for a raid and taking a portion of the profit. They'd been in Glenbriar that night to plan the next one and he ordered them to kill me, saying that I'd found them out and would talk.

There were two problems with that, though: Ash had decided on his own to try for a ransom on the side . . . and I was no longer the ordinary man I appeared to be. No wonder Norwood had been so completely astonished to see me alive on the road the next night. I was supposed to be dead and drifting somewhere at the bottom of the Sound.

Also to his misfortune, Knox had been captured. He'd been close-mouthed, but then I'd promised to make the man talk. Norwood's wife had to see that he did not.

"You? How were you involved with that?" I demanded. My influence upon her had lowered her guard so much that she was readily answering questions as though they were part of a normal conversation, requiring only a word or two from me to keep her going. It was just as well. The initial effort of concentration had been painless, but to sustain it for any length of time made my head ache terribly.

"I left the house carrying some of James's clothes," she said. "I changed into them, then cut across the fields to get to town, before any of you arrived."

Sweet heavens. She must have taken the idea from the play I'd given Anne to read. Certainly she would have greater mobility and be less noticeable in men's clothing.

"What did you do?"

"Watched and waited. When I saw Knox in the room with you, I broke the window and shot him, then ran. James led them in the wrong direction, away from me. I got back, changed again, and went on to the house with no one the wiser."

"Then what?"

"That was all. The whole thing had been so much of a risk and all for nothing because you obviously didn't know anything harmful against us. I then told James to work on the girl. Marriage to her was safer and more profitable. Besides . . . there would be others soon enough."

*Others?* I didn't take her meaning right away. It was too awful to see, I suppose, and when I did, I wished that I hadn't.

Elizabeth was only to be the first in a series of marriages. Now that they'd worked out their ploy, they would eventually venture forth to take full advantage of any number of other women with money. Over the years they would be able to make thousands of pounds with very little effort or expenditure of their own funds.

Of course to do so, they would have to find a way of divesting themselves of Elizabeth's company fairly soon, but in these unsettled times it would be simple enough to arrange something with Ash. They'd already made mention of it to him. It had been what Norwood and Caroline had been discussing while I'd seen to the horses. Their disagreement had been about whether to keep me there or let me leave. Caroline had wanted me well away from things. Her plans had been laid; she did not want me around to risk the least disruption of them. But to get me out, she'd have to go as well, and Norwood hadn't liked it. His dear and loving wife was the more clever of the two, after all; he'd wanted her with him, just in case anything unexpected did arise.

The idea was to make it look like another rebel incursion. Norwood would emerge to tell the sad tale of how he'd been knocked unconscious trying to defend his house, awakening after all was over to discover the body of his bride, foully murdered by the pitiless raiders in their quest for booty. How easy for him afterward to collect his inheritance from her estate and leave, playing the part of a grief-stricken widower.

I had been able to control myself up to this point. Their attacks upon others, their murder of Knox, their murders using Ash as their weapon, their attack upon me, even upon Father, none of it had been pleasant to hear, but I'd just been able to stand it.

But not this. Not hearing her coldly explaining the fine points of how they would be killing my dearly loved sister. It was impossible for me, impossible for any man with a heart to endure. Until the words were out of her mouth, I thought I'd already reached the limit of my rage. Now a raw and roaring blast of it tore through me like a wild nor'easter.

I was lost to it . . . and then so was Caroline.

Blind and deaf to all reason, all restraint, it clawed its way out of my brain—

And right into hers.

When I came to myself, I was on the other side of the room, face to the wall, hands covering my eyes. I was aware that something had happened, but felt as disoriented as a newly wakened sleeper. It was taking me a moment to sort dream from reality.

The dream was a fading memory of a shapeless dark *thing* that had bounded up from some deep place in my soul. Ugly and huge, if my anger could have taken on a such an amorphous form and size, it might have looked like that. It had been full of force and fury, erupting forth, filling the room, filling the world, overflowing it, overwhelming it. It bellowed and raved, smashed and hurled this way and that before finally driving itself into another vessel other than myself. It seemed too large for the other to hold without breaking.

And so it proved.

I became aware of the reality where it sat slumped at the table.

Caroline's eyes told me the tale of what had happened. I'd seen such eyes on Tony Warburton after Nora's temper had exceeded all control and broken free. She'd snapped his mind like a twig, and now I'd done exactly the same thing to Caroline.

She stared at nothing, shivering a little. Each time she blinked, her whole head twitched slightly. Her hands rested easily upon the table, inches from the incriminating letter.

I plucked it from her reach, folded, and tucked it away, hardly aware of the action. I also eased one hand into the pocket of her riding coat and drew out her pistol, placing it into my own coat pocket. It struck me that it would not be a good idea to leave her armed.

But it would not have mattered. She paid no mind to me. With hard certainty, I knew that she had no mind left. It was just the same as before with Nora and Warburton.

Nora had regretted her loss of control, though; I could not. I regarded Caroline with a cold satisfaction. I could not raise the least shame in me for what I'd done to her, nor was there any desire to try. If that made me wicked, then so be it; it could hardly compare with what she and her husband had planned for Elizabeth.

There was a sudden and strange peace within me, as though Caroline had somehow drained away all my doubts about myself, about what I would have to do in the very near future. For I had determined that Elizabeth would not spend one more hour in that bastard's defiling company.

I walked steadily out into the common room and was somewhat surprised to find that all was as right and normal as could be. I'd had some idea that they might have heard a row coming from our private room and be alert to trouble, but though I got some curious looks, no one said anything. All the noise had been in my head, it seemed, part of the dream . . . or rather, the nightmare.

Only Mr. Farr, who had witnessed my initial reaction to the letter, took it upon himself to come over and have his curiosity answered. "Are you all right, Mr. Barrett?"

Some dissembling was required, then. Very well. I knew I could manage. It did not take much to look stunned and put a small tremor into my voice. "A little brandy for Lady Caroline, if you please. I fear she has suffered some sort of a fit."

"A fit?" he questioned, even as he turned away to find the right bottle.

"One moment we were talking and the next she put her hand to her head and seemed to fall asleep. I got her to wake up, but she seems very dazed. I'd like to send one of your lads to fetch Dr. Beldon as quickly as possible."

"Certainly, sir." He came back with the brandy, full of bustling concern, which blossomed into a fearful shock once he saw the woman's blank face. He immediately sent for his wife to look after her, then dispatched two of his stablemen off to my house to get Beldon.

It went very smoothly, better than I'd hoped. I simply mirrored his feelings, then announced that I'd go to fetch her brother, Lord James. This was met with grim approval. Yes, it was far and away the best thing that could be done, by all means her closest relative should be with her during this strange illness.

He and Mrs. Farr were already speaking in hushed tones about apoplexy as I hurried out the door and jumped onto Rolly's back.

No lights were showing when I arrived. Everyone had gone to bed. Theirs was a small household, just Elizabeth and James and the valet, Harridge. There was a cook, maid, and a scullery boy, all part of the same family, but they lived in their own house a quarter mile farther along. So convenient for the Norwoods, so convenient for Ash.

I dismounted and quietly walked to the front door, vanished, and slipped through the narrow space of the threshold, reappearing on the inside. I had no plan, no idea of what I was going to do, only blind faith that the right path would present itself now that I was here.

Going to the front parlor, I busied myself with the tinder box by the fireplace and soon had a number of candles burning throughout the room. I wanted a lot of light. When I was done, I went out to the staircase landing and bellowed out my sister's name. I couldn't bring myself to go up to their bedroom.

After a moment, Norwood called down. "Jonathan? My God, man! What are you doing here? Has something happened to Caroline?"

"Jonathan?" Elizabeth hesitantly called.

"Come down, please," I said, in a softer tone. I was not talking to him. For a tiny instant, I nearly fled. I was about to deliver a hideous hurt to someone I loved dearly. Perhaps I should wait, go get Father to help.

"What the devil are you about, man?" Norwood demanded, sounding highly aggrieved.

*No*. I crushed my doubts. *Not one more hour with him*.

Soon they came, Elizabeth wrapped in some sort of loose gown over her nightclothes, Norwood still dressed except for his coat and waistcoat. They hurried into the parlor and stopped, faces full of worry and curiosity and with a touch of anger at this unorthodox intrusion.

"What is it, Jonathan?" asked Elizabeth, coming over to me.

"Yes," said Norwood. "Is it the war? What's wrong?" He stopped short, staring at the pistol in my hand. It was Caroline's. I had it pointed at the floor, but he was plainly wondering why I was in possession of it.

Elizabeth noticed as well. "What is it? What's wrong? Was there trouble on the road? Is it Father? Is he ill or hurt?"

"No, nothing like that. I've learned something that you need to know."

"Learned what?"

I drew out the letter. "This arrived from Oliver. It's on the top page." A cowardly way to tell her, but if I'd tried to speak the words would have choked me on the spot.

"Really, Jonathan," said Norwood. "What is so important that you had to come by at this hour? Where's Caroline?"

Elizabeth took the letter and held it so the candlelight fell upon the damning page and read. Then she let out with a moaning gasp and sat heavily on one of the chairs. "My God . . ."

"Elizabeth?" Norwood was made uneasy with her failure to reply and turned back to me. "See here, Jonathan, I won't be having you barging in and just standing there without a word of explanation."

"Be quiet."

He flushed. "And I won't be spoken to like that in my own house even if you are my brother-in-law!"

"You're no relation to me and you know it. Be quiet or I will kill you."

His mouth dropped open, but nothing came forth. He saw how I looked and finally, finally the true meaning behind my actions began to dawn upon him.

"Elizabeth?" I went back to her. She had become smaller and was trembling as though chilled to the bone. The letter shook so much in her hand that she had to press the rattling pages against the chair arm to read it again. She'd have to read it several times, even as I had.

She looked to me. "This is true, isn't it?"

"I'm sorry."

"It's not some silly joke of Oliver's . . ."

"No. I showed this to Caroline. I made her talk. She was . . . unable to lie. She and Norwood are married."

She let the letter drop and looked past me, not to her husband, but to the man who had betrayed her. Her eyes blurred and grew blind from the welling tears.

"How could you?" she asked him in a broken voice that pierced me right through the heart.

"How could I what? Elizabeth—" He reached toward her, putting on a most convincing show of hurt and tender concern.

But she ignored him and looked to me once more, pleading for me to make things right again.

"If I could change it, I would. You know that."

And this confirmation made her smaller still. Elizabeth hunched in on herself, unable to hold back the grief any longer. She gave up fighting it and the tears and sobs came on, leaving her helpless for a time as her emotions overwhelmed her. If she had the least doubt about the truth of things, she had only to look at Norwood. He remained quiet and made not the slightest protest of innocence, nor any gesture of compassion toward the people he'd so callously hurt or displayed a jot of shame for any of it. If anything, he appeared to be disgusted at this turning of events.

Soulless and heartless, the *bastard*.

I put my arms around Elizabeth, offering what small comfort I could, but sickening as it was just to look at him, not once did I take my eyes from Norwood.

"What shall we do?" Elizabeth asked.

The first shattering shock had been the worst, but Elizabeth was a strong woman. She'd recovered for the present, blew her nose, dried her eyes, and braced herself to listen to the full story behind the letter. I told her everything, including what Caroline had imparted to me. The fact that I'd gotten so much information from her both puzzled and frightened Norwood. When it was over, Elizabeth voiced the question that had begun to hammer at me as I talked.

"I don't know," I answered. "We'll have to tell Father. He'll help us work out something."

"I don't see how."

Neither did I, but she didn't need to hear that. "He will."

She nodded dully, accepting it, not really thinking about it. Just as well. "What about Caroline?"

Norwood's eyes flickered and sharpened.

"She'll be no trouble to us, I promise," I said. "Go upstairs. Put on some riding clothes. I'm going to take you home. We'll talk to Father."

"What about him?" She glared at Norwood.

"He'll be here when we come back. I'll make sure of it."

"You'll—"

"I'll do that which is necessary. Now go."

Elizabeth stood, stiff as an old woman one moment, then swaying as though about to swoon the next, but she got hold of herself and paced over to where Norwood was standing. He had no real expression on his face, just a trace of watchfulness, nothing more. She looked him up and down, a tall and handsome man, husband for a month, betrayer for a lifetime.

She slapped him, then spit in his face.

He flinched, but didn't otherwise react. I was right behind Elizabeth and Norwood must have seen his own murder in my eye if he dared to make the smallest move against her. He was not even tempted to wipe away the spittle.

Elizabeth turned her back to him and left the room by the parlor's other door, which led to the kitchen. I wondered why she'd gone that way until I heard the soft splash of water. Yes, she'd want to wash her face first, part and parcel of making a new start on things. I listened to her quiet movements until she was done and slowly climbing the servants' stairs to her room. When her steps faded and a door closed, I told him to sit, but Norwood remained standing, the better to offer arguments in his favor.

"Look, now," he said. "I know it's been a blow to you, but there's no need for this to go any further. You've caught me out and we all know it, but do you want all the rest of the county to know it as well? Do you really want Elizabeth to have to face the scandal, the pointing fingers, the whispers?"

"You don't give a damn for her, so don't try using that excuse to save your skin."

"But it will happen if you turn me in, make this public. Let me go and Caroline and I will leave quietly, we won't ever come back, we'll say nothing."

"Leaving Elizabeth to explain why her 'husband' deserted her?"

"You can say I'd been called back to England, say anything you like. We'll be out of your lives, we'll stay away, I promise."

"You've tried to kill me twice, nearly killed my father, and God knows, you were planning to kill Elizabeth as well and you think that I could cheerfully let you go free just to avoid a little gossip?"

"But—"

"You're a murderer already with blood on your hands from the people killed and robbed by your men, you even slaughtered one of your own to keep him quiet, and by God, I'm going to see that Nash knows all about it. I could strangle you where you stand, but I won't. It'll give me far greater pleasure to wait and watch you dancing under the gallows. There'll be no one pulling on your heels to speed you to hell, I'll see to that."

He went whiter than his shirt and backed away, not far, only into a chair into which he sat rather heavily. He embarrassed himself no more with protests. He finally saw their futility. Some new thought came to him, though. "You'd let them hang Caroline, too? If you turn me in, then she'll have to be part of it. You'd let them hang a woman?"

My hard silence was not the answer he wanted. Caroline was beyond the rope, but I saw no reason to inform or explain to him her condition.

"You *must* let me go." Tears were in his eyes, his voice, but I'd seen them first in my sister. I was not about to be persuaded to pity for this creature.

"Aye, let 'im go an' we'll take care o' things," someone advised me. Ash's voice.

He blocked the doorway that led to the kitchen, holding a pistol in each hand, both aimed at me. I knew they were primed to fire, having done it myself since they were the duelers I'd left on my saddle. Behind him were other men I recognized: Tully, Seth, Abel. Drummond wasn't with them.

"Stand clear of 'im," Ash ordered.

I did just that, smoothly, without haste, and holding my own pistol along the line of my leg, keeping it out of his sight for a moment longer. I presented only my side to him, like a fencer.

"That's far enough."

Norwood was on his feet again, pointing at me. "Look out for him, he's armed."

But Ash had me well covered. " 'E won't make no trouble. 'E's too smart by 'alf to even try. Am I right, ye young bastard? Am I right? Thought as much. Now put that on the table. Reach for it 'n' you'll make me a happy man, 'n' that's God's honest truth."

As instructed, I placed my gun on the table, but did not move from my spot.

Relief flowed out from Norwood so strongly I could almost feel it as a physical presence in the room. "Excellent work, Mr. Ash. I'd nearly despaired of your coming tonight."

"That bloody idiot you sent to fetch us put up more of a fight than we'd reckoned on."

"What? Harridge?"

" 'E squealed a bit, but Tully got 'im quiet. 'E won't be makin' no more noise ever ag'in." Ash chuckled, the others joining him as they separated out over the room.

"Where is he?"

"We drug 'im into yer scullery. It'll look like it's supposed to, you've naught to worry about on that."

"You sent your servant off to be murdered?" I asked Norwood.

He smiled. "Couldn't be helped. He was beginning to realize a few too many things, anyway. It's a good night for the work, right lads? Quiet and dark, just as we like best."

Yes, it was a quiet, moonless night, a rare night for mayhem be you rebel or Loyalist. That was why Norwood and Caroline had chosen to take advantage of it.

Tully sniggered, as did the rest. "Not what I like best. Where's that Tory bitch ye been keepin', yer lordship? I've 'eard she 'ad a fair face. I've a mind t' see it."

And so while Caroline and I rode home, where we planned to sit with Anne and read Shakespeare aloud to each other, my sister would be suffering God knows what horrors at their hands until they finally . . .

"*Devil,*" whispered Abel, staring at me. "See the fire in 'is eyes? 'E's a bloodsucking devil, I tell ye!"

They all looked, and things were silent for a moment, but Ash snorted, waving one of the duelers. "Then 'e won't mind us sendin' 'im back to 'ell, will 'e?"

"Not at all," agreed Norwood. But the man looked uneasy, for my gaze was wholly focused upon him. "Send him along now, if you please, Mr. Ash."

"Oh, but 'e'll need a bit of company to go with 'im."

"The sister? Yes, I'll fetch her down. It'll be less fuss if I—"

"We'll take care of yer Tory doxy soon enough, yer lordship. First I want t' know what this bastard meant when 'e said 'slaughtered one o' yer own.' "

Norwood did not take his meaning right away. "What are you on about?"

"We 'eard 'im talkin' with ye afore we showed ourselves. What did 'e mean?" Ash casually let one of the duelers swing in Norwood's direction.

"He wants to know about Knox," I said, my voice very thick, very low.

The meaning now dawned on him, but his acting skills were so ingrained that he was able to shift his thoughts 'round without showing so much as a flicker of change in his face. The others saw nothing, but in that deathly still room *I* was able to hear the abrupt thump as his heart lurched and pounded in reaction.

"What about Knox?" he asked with just the right touch of annoyed puzzlement.

None of it worked on Ash, who was already predisposed to suspect a lie. "You tell us, yer lordship. What did 'e mean?"

"I haven't the faintest idea. Poor Knox was killed trying to escape—"

"Aye, that's one o' the stories. The other is 'e were 'anged by a mob, 'n' 'nother were 'e were shot through the 'ead while 'e sat 'elpless 'n' chained."

"That's the true one," I put in, slowly, deliberately, watching Norwood with an unholy delight burgeoning within me. "His lady wife shot through a broken window and blew out his brains just as you said."

"Be that true?" Ash demanded of him.

"Of course not! How could it? What a ridiculous idea! He's trying to confuse you—to get you to spare him. He knows you'll be killing him—"

"So I've no reason to lie," I said.

"You do if you want to drag me down as well."

"Norwood was afraid Knox might talk," I went on. "Afraid Knox would betray him. That's why he was murdered."

"But that's—"

"*Norwood . . . look at me!*"

He looked. He couldn't *not* look.

I drove into his mind like an axe. "*Tell them the truth.*"

He gave a little gasp and fell back a step.

"Devil," Abel murmured.

"*The truth, Norwood.*"

He all but strangled on the words, but they did at last come forth. And when he was done, I released him, and he dropped to his knees.

I bowed my head, tired and suddenly aware of the sharp pain crashing around inside my skull. I had not lost control as I'd done earlier; this was the price of it, perhaps. When I came back to myself and glanced up, they were staring at one another, at Norwood, at me. Tully and Ash with fearful wonder, Seth and Abel with fear alone as they shifted nervously from foot to foot as though ready to run. I half expected Abel to call me a devil again.

Norwood made a breathy sob and grabbed at his chair to keep from falling completely over.

Ash turned full upon me. "I don' know 'ow ye done it, but 'tis done, 'n' I believe it."

"No, Ash." Norwood made a valiant effort to straighten himself. "It's a terrible mistake."

"Don't see 'ow it can be, since we all 'eard the story from yer own lips."

"It wasn't true, I swear it! I was forced to say those things. You saw what he did. He made me lie, he made me—you saw! He's not natural, he's—"

"Bastard! I don't give a bloody damn what 'e is, devil, angel or whatever's in between, you've a debt to pay for the murder of a good man."

"But it wasn't even me! Caroline was the one, you know that! I didn't want her to, but she—"

"Oh, now, listen to 'im squeal. Ye make me sick."

And with no more prelude than that, Ash aimed one of the duelers at

Norwood and fired. The ball struck him square in the chest and he collapsed forward, his last cry lost in the deafening blast of the shot. Smoke billowed out from the pistol, obscuring things for a moment, long enough—more than long enough—for me to grab Caroline's gun.

Without thinking, without loss of motion, I raised it and fired at Ash where he stood now half turned from me. The gun cracked sharply and more smoke clouded my vision, but he gave out with a surprised shriek, jerking away, one arm flailing. I was distantly conscious of the others tumbling over themselves to get out of the way.

" 'E's a devil!" screamed Abel, ducking from the line of fire. I wasn't paying much attention, being busy with pulling back the gun's trigger guard.

Turn the cylinder. Push the guard forward . . .

*Lock.*

Tully's reactions were better than the others. He charged at me, arms out to bring me down. I got the muzzle up just in time, but he made a grab at my wrist and the shot went wide. He hadn't expected it, though, and the flash and burn made him jump. I dropped the gun, seized Tully by the shoulders, and hauled him sharply around. His feet left the floor. I swung him like a sack of grain and let him go. He all but flew across the room to smash into a wall with such force as to break bone. Hardly wasting a glance at him, I stooped and retrieved the pistol.

Pull back the guard, turn the cylinder, push, lock . . .

*Fire.*

Seth and Abel had seen it coming and had scrambled for the door, both in a panic to get out. I followed them through the kitchen. They stumbled over Harridge's body in their haste to gain the scullery.

Pull back, turn, push, lock . . .

*Fire.*

By then I wasn't even trying to aim. They were routed, and that was enough. I didn't care if they lived or died as long as they were gone. They broke free of the house and fled away into the summer night. I could have followed them, but simply fired over their heads, inducing them to greater speed.

They ran back the way they'd come: up the road to the cook's home, probably where they stayed when they weren't making raids. I'd allowed for the thieves coming over from Suffolk to prey on us, but it had never occurred to me that they could just as easily work their scheme from Nassau County. If they had any brain at all between them, they'd take to a boat and be long gone before Nash could catch them.

I didn't care. To hell with them.

Returning to the others, I found Ash, Tully, and Norwood as I'd left them. The scents of bloodsmell and powder and fear and death filled the room.

I rolled Norwood over. His eyes were just beginning to film and fade. His last expression was of hurt disbelief. Ash had gotten him right where his heart would have been had he possessed one. He was now past any worldly cares.

A pity. I would have *treasured* the chance to watch him swing, to see this dancing master's legs twitching in his final jig. Too late now.

Tully would trouble us no more, either. His neck had been broken. His spine, too, from the look of things. I took in this indirect evidence of my strength with barely a shrug, as though it had nothing to do with me, as though some other person had gone mad and—

I was numb inside and just a little cold. It was impossible to tell whether it had to do with my body or my soul. An iron hard heaviness dragged at me, slowing my movements, my thoughts. I roused myself just enough to go check on Ash.

He lay on his back, a fearful wound just below his heart and the look of death settling a gray shadow upon his face.

"Curse ye fer a bastard," he grunted as I knelt next to him.

"No doubt."

"That were a righteous execution. 'E were a traitor."

"Yes."

"Curse ye . . . oh, God 'a' mercy." His hands clutched at the wound, unable to stem the outflow of blood or push away the pain.

"Let it go," I told him, knowing exactly, *exactly* what he was going through.

"Wha . . ."

My eyes hard on his, I said, "Let it go. The pain will stop."

"Stop?"

"*Yes* . . ."

We stared at one another for a long minute, me silent with concentration, he gasping out his last breaths. Then his breathing eased, the moans lessened. His eyes were growing distant, starting to focus on something else. I recognized the look. Knew what he saw. Had felt that comforting drowsiness stealing up. I'd been there. Briefly. He would stay forever.

"Go to sleep, Mr. Ash," I whispered.

And he did.

I shut his eyes for him.

I shut my own.

But could not shut out the sights and sounds of what had happened. Of what I'd done.

God have mercy on us all.

* * *

"*Jonathan?*"

Only Elizabeth's voice could have possibly roused me from the blackness that had stolen its way so swiftly and completely over my soul. But I hardly recognized her. Could that thin and fear-filled whisper possibly belong to her?

She called to me again, and I somehow found my feet and went out to the hall. She was at the top of the stairs peering fearfully down at me. She clutched a pistol in one hand.

"It's over," I said.

"I heard them . . . I heard everything"

Hurried up to her. Held her. "It's over. They're gone."

"I wanted to help, but I—"

"No, you did the right thing by staying out of it. God bless you for your good sense. If anything had happened to you . . ."

She pushed away from me. "What's happened to James?"

He'd been the lowest kind of scoundrel and though betrayed in every sense of the word, she had, after all, loved him.

*Still* loved him, if I read her rightly. Such feelings don't die in an instant, no matter how great the killing anger may be. They linger on, full of pain and giving pain.

She saw my answer in my face, then tried to break away from me to go to him. But I held her tight and kept her from rushing down into the hell-pit below.

# EPILOGUE

Day by day, Elizabeth fought to regain herself. She spent a lot of time in Father's library, just sitting and reading, or sewing, or doing nothing much at all. He talked to her when she felt like it, or listened, or held her when she cried. On nights when she could not sleep, I took his place and kept her company.

I was unable to attend the funeral, which was thought of as strange by those outside the immediate family. But if Mother worried about what people might think, she kept it to herself for once. I heard all this afterward from Father, as well as an account of how Elizabeth had startled not a few by insisting that they call her by her maiden name again.

"The man I married is dead," she told them. "I am content to bury him with his name and get on with things."

Brave words, though it took a while before she was up to fulfilling them.

But even the worst wounds can heal, given enough time and care. Father and I did our best for her. Her grief was genuine, her healing slow, but she had no want for support and sympathy from all who knew her.

How terrible it was, they thought, wedded but a month and then to have her husband killed by rebels . . . and her poor sister-in-law gone simpleminded, too. It was wicked, outrageous. Something ought to be done. At least her brother had been there to roust the bastards. He'd gotten two of them, by God, that was something. Well done, Jonathan.

That was the story that was put about, anyway.

Nash had gone after the remaining men and the cook and her family. He missed catching them, which was just as well. We certainly had no need for any truth muddling up the facts at hand.

"How could I have been so wrong?" Elizabeth asked us many, many times.

"You weren't wrong, he was," Father and I would tell her.

She wore mourning clothes and went through the motions and rituals expected of widows, and people assumed that her reason for not wanting to talk about Norwood was a measure of the depth of her grief.

Given the times, other events soon crowded the tragedy from peoples' minds as the realization asserted itself that the war was not going to be over within the year as they'd hoped. More raids took place, more raids were staged, crops matured for the commissary to take away. Summer waxed and waned, and little by little my nights began to lengthen.

I wrote to Oliver about the marriage and enjoined him to say aught to the rest of the family about the business of the false title. As far as they were concerned, she'd married "Lord Norwood" and he'd been killed by the war. His sympathetic answer assured me that they knew nothing of their Cousin Elizabeth's true plight and never would from him.

He had no new word on Nora, except to say that the Warburtons had not seen her for some months. They did not know where she had gone. I grew restless with worry, snappish with unexpressed anger, and by the close of September had made a decision.

I would go back to England.

It had been a long year full of too much waiting. The time had come for me to look for Nora myself, to let her know what had happened to me, to ask her such questions as still remained. After much talk with Father about the practicalities of the journey, I won not only his consent, but full support. He and I began making arrangements for the passage.

Elizabeth was anything but overjoyed. "But how will you feed yourself?"

"I'll be taking along some livestock, of course, though Father thinks a sea voyage might be rough on them. But I shan't be doing any flying about, so each meal should last me a few nights."

"I don't see how you can do it. You're utterly helpless during the day. You'll need a guardian."

"That's why Jericho will be with me, but I should really like some more company, just to be safe . . . will you come?"

That surprised her. In fact, it took all the speech away from her for some minutes. "*Me* go to England?"

"You'd love it there. I did, when it wasn't raining. Damnation, I loved it when it was. Please say yes."

"But what should I do?"

"Anything you like. You're independent now."

That won me a sharp look, but I knew what I was saying. Her marriage had been illegal, but the law did not know that, and to save face we were not prepared to say otherwise. She'd come into her inheritance money. I saw no reason why she shouldn't get some enjoyment out of it.

"There'd be parties . . ."

She shuddered. "I'm not sure I'm ready for those."

"Sight-seeing, then. Cousin Oliver can take you 'round. You can skip Bedlam, if you like."

"Oh, thank you very much."

"You know what I mean. Please come."

"Is this as company for you or to get me out of this house?"

"Both and neither."

"I don't *know* . . ." And she didn't. Not really. Not at all.

My heart sank. She'd been like this for far too long, withdrawn, visibly hurting, and in doubt of herself. No matter how much help and love she had, it would never truly be enough. At some point she would have to learn how to help herself. Elizabeth had not yet reached it and I sadly wondered if she ever would.

Then out of nowhere the idea came to me, or perhaps it had been thrown up from some past memory of a time when my sister had been a happy and confident woman.

"Tell me this, then: if you had never met him, would you go?"

She answered without really thinking. "Why, yes." Then she thought about it . . .

And the thought surprised her.

# DEATH MASQUE

*For Mark,*
*Thanks for the best support, ever.*

*Thanks also to*
*Pegasus House,*
*may you always fly high!*

# CHAPTER 1

***Long Island, September 1777***

Molly Audy opened her eyes, smiled, and said, "I'm that sorry to lose you as a caller, Johnny boy, I really am."

"You're very kind, Miss Audy," I replied lightly, looking down at her with my own smile firmly in place. Her little bedroom was a place of smiles for both of us, but soon to end, alas.

"You're the kind one, I'm sure." She brushed a light hand over her bare breasts. "Some gentlemen I've known couldn't care less about how I feel, but you take the trouble to do things right by me—and every single time. It's just as well you call as late as you do. Come 'round any sooner and I'd not have the strength left to deal with the others."

"You mean none of them bother to—"

"I didn't say that. Some are just as nice, but if I let myself be as free with them as I am with you . . . well, I'd be an old woman in a month from all the good feeling."

I laughed softly. "Now you're just flattering me, Molly."

"Not a bit of it. On nights when I know you're coming over, I hold myself back with them and save it for you."

My jaw dropped quite a lot. "Good heavens, I had no idea. I *am* honored."

"And you really mean that, too. Some men don't give two figs for a whore's feelings, but not you." She tucked her lower lip in briefly, then lifted her head enough to kiss my cheek before dropping back onto her pillow. "You're a lovely, lovely man, Mr. Barrett, and I'm going to miss you terribly." Now her smooth face wrinkled up and her arms went hard around me and she abruptly hiccupped into a bout of sincere sobbing.

I held her close and made comforting noises and wasn't quite able to hold back a few tears of my own that unexpectedly spilled out. In a strangled voice I assured her that she was a lovely, lovely woman and I would also miss her, which was entirely true. In the year since we'd begun our pleasurable exchanges, she'd become a very dear friend, and it was a raw blow to realize anew that this was the last night we'd be together for some considerable time to come, if ever again.

"Just look at us," she said, finally straightening. She groped for a handkerchief from the small table next to the bed and used it thoroughly. "Goodness, you'd think someone had died. You'll be coming back, won't you?"

"I . . . don't know."

Her eyes, reflecting her spirits, fell, but she nodded. "We're all in God's hands, Johnny boy. Well, I can at least pray for a safe crossing for you, if there is such a thing these days."

"We've been told that there will be no trouble from the rebel ships."

"Rebels?" She snapped her fingers to dismiss their threat to my well-being. "It's the sea itself that's so dangerous. I lost my poor husband to it years back, so don't you be forgettin' your own prayers as you go."

"I won't," I promised.

"There now, you come here for cheering up and I've gone all serious."

"It's all right."

She made herself smile once more for me, then slipped from the mess we'd made of the bedclothes. She rose on her tiptoes, arms high overhead in a luxuriant stretch. I watched the easy movement of her rounded muscles, of how the candlelight caught and gilded the sheen of sweat clinging to her skin, and suddenly wanted her all over again. The need swept into me, playing over and through my body like a swift red tide.

"La, but I wish it were cooler," she murmured, lifting her thick hair from the back of her neck. "I've half a mind to sneak down to the stream for a quick wash before I sleep. Want to come along?"

The sight of Molly Audy splashing away like some woodland nymph was not something I was going to deny myself. On past occasions when we'd stolen off for such adventures, the outcome had ever proved to be a happy one for both of us. "I should be most delighted to provide you with safe escort, Miss Audy."

She turned and saw how I was looking at her. "Oh, you're a wicked 'un, all right, Johnny boy. Goin' to make an old woman of me before the night's done, is that it?"

She danced out of my reach and pulled on a light wrapper and some shoes; I left my coat, hat, and neck cloth, knowing I'd be back for them, and didn't bother fastening up my shirt. My breeches and boots I'd left on throughout our recent lovemaking. Perhaps it was not really gentlemanly, but Molly had often expressed to me that she sometimes found their retention on my person to be rather stimulating to her when she was in the mood for it. Being no fool, I was only too happy to comply with her preferences.

The street that her house faced was silent at this late hour, but we still left by her back door rather than the front. Besides being the quickest route to the little stream that flowed through this part of Glenbriar, it spared us from any unexpected observers who might also be wakeful from the warmth of the night. Witnesses for what we had in mind would have been an utterly unwelcome inconvenience.

There was enough of a moon showing to allow Molly to pick her way without much effort or noise. I could see perfectly well. As long as some bit of the sky was visible, the night was as day to me, and I kept an eye out for unwanted attention. The locals did not worry me so much as the Hessians. There had been many terrible incidents involving the army sent to protect us and put down the Rebellion, but many of those troops had left our little portion of the island for other places by now, so perhaps I was being overly cautious. Then again, how could one be overly cautious during these turbulent times? Not only Hessians, but packs of booty-seeking rebels from across the Sound might be lurking about. My past experiences had taught me that avoidance was far preferable to encounter when it came to dealing with either of them.

We reached the stream without trouble, though, and walked upon its bank until coming to a spot lending itself to an easy descent. Giggling, Molly stripped off her thin garment and shoes and gingerly stepped into the shallows.

"It's just right!" she gasped. "Oh, do come in!"

I laughed, shaking my head. "You know it doesn't like me much." She was very well aware of my singular problem with free-flowing water, but chose to ignore it as part of her game with me.

"Coward," she called and bent to sweep her hand in the stream to splash me.

"Right you are," I called back. I made no move to dodge, but waved and teased her on, getting a good soaking before she tired from the play. My hair fell dripping and untidy about my face, and my shirt clung like a second skin. Though the heat of summer had even less effect upon me than the cold of winter, I must have had some sense of it for this state of damp dishevelment to feel so pleasant. Or perhaps it was Molly's undemanding company, her acceptance of me, of my shortcomings as well as my gifts.

I dropped upon our favorite grassy spot, where she'd left her clothes. Propped on my elbows, I had a fine view of her bathing. Moonlight filtered through the scattered branches overhead, making irregular patterns in black and silver over her body that shifted and shimmered as she moved. She didn't look quite real; she'd become a creature of mist and shadow. Even her laughter had been turned into something magical by the wide sky and the woods as it merged with the small sounds of hidden life all around us. I could scent it upon the warm wind, the green things, the musk of passing animals, the last of the summer flowers, the vitality of the earth itself where I lay. To my ears came the soft drift of leaves in the wind, the creeping progress of insects seeking to escape my presence, the annoyed call of a nearby bird and answering cries from those more distant.

This unnatural augmentation of my senses was all part of my changed condition, of course, and could not be ignored any more than I could ignore the blinding explosion of a sunrise. But I was well content, something that would have seemed quite impossible for me a year ago when a musket ball had smashed into my chest one sweltering morning, changing everything in a most extraordinary way.

Thinking me dead, my poor family had buried me, but it was not my lot to remain in the ground, for the legacy hidden in my blood soon expelled me from that early and unfair grave.

Sleeping during the day, abroad during the night, and able to command some very alarming talents, I had no name for this change or whether it was a curse or a miracle, though the latter seemed most likely, once the shock of my return had been overcome.

And now a very full and instructive year had passed; I'd learned of and explored my new gifts . . . and limitations, but was yet consumed with questions about my condition. Only one person in all the world could possibly answer them, but I'd exceeded the last of my patience in waiting for a reply to my many letters to her. The emptiness within could no longer be put off. The time had come for me to somehow find her again.

"What a dark look you have, Mr. Barrett," said Molly.

I gave a small start, then laughed at my own foolish lack of attention to her.

"Thinking about your lady, the one you left in England?" she asked, lying down next to me.

"How the devil did you know that?"

"Because you always wear that same long face when she's on your mind. I hope you don't hate her."

Molly was well known for her discretion. I'd long since confided to her about my other lover. About Nora Jones.

"Of course I don't hate her. I'm . . . disappointed. And hurt. I understand why she so ill-used me at our last parting, but that hardly makes it easier to live with."

"As long as you don't hate her."

"I could never do that."

"Then no more long faces, or you could frighten her away." One of her hands stole into the folds of my wet shirt. "You should take this off and let it dry out. Don't want to catch a fever, do you?"

"No, indeed. But are you quite comfortable yourself?"

She was still dripping from her bath, the ends of her loose hair sticking to her shoulders. "I feel just fine, though I should like to feel even better, if you please."

"And how might that be accomplished, Miss Audy?" I asked, falling in with her humor.

"Oh, in any way as seems best to you, Mr. Barrett." She helped me remove the shirt and tossed it out of the way on a convenient bush, then proceeded on to less prosaic pursuits. My arms were quite full of Molly Audy as we wrestled back and forth in the grass until she began panting less from the exertion and more from what I was doing to her.

"Off with them," she murmured, plucking at the buttons of my breeches.

"As you wish," I said, helping her. Soon my last garments were shoved down about my knees and Molly was straddling my most intimate parts, writhing about in a delightful expression of enthusiasm. I lay back and left her to it, reveling in the fever building within me as the central member of those parts began to swell under her ministrations.

We'd learned very early on that I had no need to make use of that portion of my manhood in order to bring us to a satisfying conclusion, but old habits die hard. So to speak. Though no longer able to expel seed, I was yet capable of using it to help pleasure a woman, though it was no more (or less, for that matter) important to my own climax than any other part of my body. My release came in a far different way from that which other men enjoy. It was far more intense, far longer in duration—far superior in every aspect; so much so that to return to the old way would have meant a considerable lessening of my carnal gratification.

And so, though it was active, if not functional, Molly made warm use of it as she pleased, bringing herself up to a fine pitch of desire, then, leaning far forward, gave me that which *I* most desired.

The marks I'd left upon her throat earlier in the evening were long closed, but that was easily remedied. Mouth wide, I brushed my lips over them, tongue churning against her taut skin. She gasped and drew back, then came close for more, playing upon this pattern until she could no longer bear to pull away. My corner teeth were out, digging into her flesh, starting the slow flow of blood from her into myself.

It had to be slow, for her own well-being as for mine. Thus was I able to extend our climax indefinitely without inflicting harm to her. She moaned and her body went still as I shifted to roll on top of her. Her legs twitched as though to wrap around me, to hold herself in place, but it was unnecessary for her to pursue that joining. The heat that lay between them would have spread throughout all her body by now, even as her gift of blood spread throughout mine.

A few drops. A scant mouthful. So *much* from so little.

Molly shuddered, her nails gouging into my back. In turn, I buried myself more deeply into her neck. The blood flow increased somewhat, allowing me a generous swallow of her life. Another, more forceful shudder beneath me, but I hardly noticed for my own sharing of the ecstasy. I was beyond thought, lost in a red dream of sensation that wrapped me from head to toe in fiery fulfillment.

Only Molly's cry brought me back. I became aware of her thrashing arms and extended my own to pin them down. She pushed up against me, urging me to take more, and I might well have done so, had we not already made love that night. Many long minutes later she gave a second, softer cry, this one of disappointment, not triumph, as she understood I was readying to end things, then came many a long sigh while I licked the small wounds clean, kissing away the last of her blood.

I took my weight from her, but we lay close together, limbs still entangled, bodies and minds slowly recovering themselves from that glorious glimpse of paradise. Molly's breathing evened out as she dozed in my arms. It would have been very good to join her in a nap, but my own sleep could only come with the sunrise.

Which wasn't all that long away, to judge by the position of the stars. Damnation, but the nights were *short.*

I let her rest another few minutes, then gave her a gentle shake. "I'm needing to leave soon, Molly."

She mumbled, more than half asleep, but made no other protest as she got up. I helped her with her wrapper and offered a steadying arm as she slipped on her shoes. She woke up enough to laugh a bit as I struggled to pull my breeches back into place. I made more of an effort than was needed for the task, in order to keep her laughing, and played the clown again when I donned my still damp shirt.

"You'll get a fever for sure," she cautioned.

"I'll risk it."

Taking her arm, I guided us back to her house. Quietly. Some of the very earliest risers of Glenbriar might be out and about by now; it wouldn't do to give them anything to gossip about. Or rather anything more to gossip about. Most of the village knew about Molly's nightly activities, but she made a good fiction of supporting herself with her sewing business during the day and otherwise held to the most modest behavior in public. Between that and a reputation for discretion, no one had cause to complain against her, and I wasn't of a mind to change things.

We eased through her back door and on to the bedroom, where I gathered up the rest of my clothes. I resolved to carry, instead of wear, them home and thus give my shirt a chance to dry.

"Don't forget what I said about sayin' your prayers, Johnny boy."

"I'll say one for you, too," I promised, giving her a final embrace.

"God, but I shall miss having you come by. Nights like tonight make me wish I didn't have to bother with the other chaps. None of them can do it as well as you. I'm that spoiled, I am."

"Then that makes two of us."

She began to sniffle. "Oh, now, there I go again."

"It's all right."

"Well, be off with you," she said, trying to sound brusque. "It won't do for you to be late."

"I know. God bless you, Molly." I kissed her hand and turned toward the doorway, then paused. "One more thing. I left a present for you under my pillow."

"La, Mr. Barrett, but you are—"

"And so are you, Molly dear." Then I had to dart outside and rush away because the sky was fractionally lighter than before. I trusted that she would find the ten guineas in coin—my parting gift to her on top of my normal payment for her services—to be most helpful in getting her quite comfortably through even the harshest of the coming winter.

I sped down the road leading home, feet hardly touching the earth.

The sun had become, if not an outright enemy, then an adversary whose movements must be respected. I had to keep close watch of the time or I'd find myself stranded all helpless in the dawn. That had nearly happened on my first night out of the grave. The old barn on our property had provided a safe enough shelter then, and it struck me that I might have to make use of it once more. The Hessians quartered in it over the last year were gone, thank God, so it would be secure, but my absence for the day would worry Father and my sister, Elizabeth.

I passed by that venerable landmark, ultimately deciding that there was just enough night left for me to make it to the house. Our open fields were tempting, clear of obstacles, unless one wished to count the ripening harvest. As it would be for the best to leave no traces of my passage, I willed myself into a state of partial transparency and, with my feet truly not touching the ground, was able to hurl forward, fast as a horse at full gallop.

It was one of my more exhilarating gifts and my favorite—next to the delight of drinking Molly's blood, of course.

Skimming along like a ghostly hawk, I sped across the gray landscape only a few feet above the ground. I might have laughed from the sheer joy of it, but no sound could issue from my mouth while I held to this tenuous form. Any verbal expression of my happiness would have to wait until I was solid again.

I covered the distance in good time, in better than good time, but saw that it would be a close race, after all. Too late to turn back. Our house was well in sight but still rather far away for the brief period I had left. The grays that formed the world as I saw it in this form were rapidly fading, going white with the advent of dawn.

Damnation, if I couldn't do better than this . . .

Faster and faster, until everything blurred except for the house upon which my eyes were focused. It grew larger, filling my vision with its promise of sanctuary, then I was abruptly in its shadow.

And just as abruptly found myself solid again. I couldn't help it. The sun's force was such as to wrench me right back into the world again. My legs weren't quite under me, and I threw my arms out to cushion the inevitable fall. My palms scraped against grass and weed, elbows cracked hard upon the ground, and any breath left in me was knocked out as my body struck and rolled and finally came to a stop.

If I could move as fast as a galloping horse, then by heavens, this was certainly like being thrown from one.

I lay stunned for a moment, trying to sort myself out, to see if I was hurt or not from the tumble. A few bruises at most, probably; I was not as easily given over to injury as before and knew well how to—

*Light.*

Burning, blinding.

Altogether hellish.

Even on this, the shadowed west side of the great structure, I could hardly bear up to its force. Fall forgotten, I dragged my coat over my head and all but crawled 'round to the back of the house and the cellar doors there. They were as I'd left them, thank God, unlocked. I wrenched one up and nearly fell down the stairs in my haste to get to shelter. The door made a great crash closing; if I hadn't already been keeping my head low, it would have given me a nasty knock.

The darkness helped a little, but provided no real comfort. That lay but a few paces ahead, deeper, in the most distant corner. My limbs were growing stiff, and it was with great difficulty that I staggered and stumped like a drunkard toward my waiting bed. I pitched into it, dropping clumsily on my face onto the canvas-covered earth and knew nothing more . . .

For what seemed only an instant.

Unlike other sleepers, I have no sense at all of time's passage when resting. One second I'm on the shrieking edge of bright disaster, and the next I'm awake and calm and all is safe. Adding to the illusion on this new evening was the welcome sight of my manservant, Jericho, standing over me holding a lighted candle. His black face bore an expression that was a familiar combination of both annoyance and relief.

"Hallo," I said. "Anything interesting happen today?"

The candle flame bobbed ever so slightly. "Half the house was roused at dawn by the slamming of a cellar door, sir. These are not easy times. A loud noise can be most alarming when one is unprepared to hear it."

Oh, dear. "Sorry. Couldn't be helped. I was in a dreadful hurry."

"So I had assumed when I came down to look in on you."

That was when I noticed that I was lying on my back, not my face, and bereft of soiled shirt, breeches, and boots. Some bed linen had been carefully draped over my body to spare the sensibilities of any kitchen servants who might have need to fetch something from the cellar stores. My hands had been washed clean of the grass stains they'd picked up, and my tangled hair was smoothly brushed out. Jericho had been busy looking after me, as usual. I'd slept through it, as oblivious as the dead that I so closely imitated during the day.

Further reproach for me to be more mindful of the time and to have more consideration for the others in the household was unnecessary. He'd made his point, and I was now thoroughly chastised and repentant. After putting his candle aside, he assisted as I humbly traded the bed linens for the fresh clothing he'd brought down. He combed my hair back, tying it with a newly ironed black ribbon, and decided that I could go one more night without shaving.

"You'll want a proper toilet before you have to leave, though," he warned.

"You speak as though you weren't coming along."

"I've been given to understand that the facilities aboard the ship may be severely limited, so I shall take what advantage I may in the time left to me."

No doubt, this advantage would be taken during the day. He got no arguments from me then. If ever a man was in thrall to a benevolent despot, that man was yours most truly, Jonathan Barrett.

Candle held high, Jericho led the way out of the cellar. We climbed the stairs, emerging into the stifling heat of the kitchen to be greeted as usual by Mrs. Nooth. She was busy with preparations for tomorrow's departure. Having decided that no ship's cook could possibly match her own skills, she was seeing to it my party would have sufficient provisions for the voyage. The fact I no longer ate food made no impression upon her; my gift for influencing other minds had seen to that. Except for Jericho, all the servants had been told to ignore such oddities in my behavior, like my sleeping the day through in the cellar. It was an intrusion upon them, yes, but quite for the best as far as I was concerned.

Jericho continued forward, taking me into the main part of the house. Now I could clearly hear my sister Elizabeth at her practice on the spinet. She'd borrowed something or other by Mozart from one of her friends and had labored to make a copy of the piece for herself, which I could only marvel over. From very early on it was discovered I had no musical inclinations to speak of; the terms and symbols were just so much gibberish to me, but I tried to make up for it with an appreciation of their translation from notes on paper into heavenly sounds. Elizabeth was a most accomplished translator, I thought.

I parted company from Jericho and quietly opened the door to the music room. Elizabeth was alone. A half dozen candles were lighted; wasteful, but well worth it as she made a very pretty picture in their golden glow. She glanced up but once to see who had come in, then returned her full concentration upon her music. I sprawled in my favorite chair by the open window, throwing one leg over an arm, and gave myself up to listening.

The last of the sun was finally gone, though its influence lingered in the warm air stirring the curtains. I breathed in the scents of the new night, enjoying them while I could. By this time tomorrow Elizabeth, Jericho, and I would be on a ship bound for England.

A little black spark of worry touched the back of my mind. Molly's concern for a safe voyage was not ill placed. The possibilities of autumn storms or a poorly maintained and thus dangerous ship or a discontented crew or—despite all assurances to the contrary—an attack by rebels or privateers in league with them loomed large before me. The night before I was too engrossed seeking the pleasures Molly offered to think much on them. Free of such distractions, I could no longer push them aside. I watched Elizabeth and worried on the future.

My initial invitation for her to come with me had been prompted by a strong wish to offer a diversion from the melancholy that had plagued her for the last few months. She'd been reluctant, but I'd talked her into it. With all the risks involved I was having second thoughts about having her along. And Jericho. But it was different with him. As his owner, I could command him to remain at home; with Elizabeth I could not. She'd been persuaded once and persuaded she would stay. The one time I'd raised the subject with her had convinced me of her commitment to come. We had not precisely argued, but she'd given me to understand in the clearest of terms that whatever perils that might lie ahead were of no concern to her and I would be advised to follow her example.

Too late to change things now. But as I'd told Molly, we were all in God's hands. I needed to listen better to myself. Sufficient unto the day is its own evil and all that. Or night, as the case was with me.

Elizabeth finished her piece. The last notes fled from her instrument and the contentment that always seemed to engulf her when she played faded away. Her face altered from a beatific smoothness to a troubled tightness, especially around her eyes and mouth.

"What did you think?" she asked.

"You did marvelous well, as always."

"Not my playing, but the piece itself."

"It's very pretty, very pleasant."

"And what else?"

No use trying to keep anything from her; we knew each other rather too well for that. "There did seem to be something of a darkness to it, especially that middle bit and toward the end."

That brought out a smile for me. "There's hope for you, then, if you noticed that."

"Really, now!" I protested, putting on a broad exaggeration of offense. Having played the clown for Molly last night, it was just as easy to do so once more for my sister. God knows, she was in sore need of having her spirits lightened. Elizabeth's smile did become more pronounced, but it failed to turn into laughter.

Then it vanished altogether as she looked back to her music. "That 'darkness' is my favorite, you know. It's the best part of the piece, the whole point of it."

"An interesting sentiment, no doubt."

Her eyes flicked over to mine as she caught my wary tone. "Oh, Jonathan, please stop worrying about me."

"It's gotten to be a habit, I fear."

"Yes, you and Father both. I'm all right. It's been awful and I'd never wish what happened to me upon my worst enemy, but I'm sure God had a good reason for it."

"I should hope it to be a very good reason, because for the life of me *I* can't fathom why. You certainly deserve better than what you've been served."

Her lips compressed into a hard line, and I knew I'd said too much.

"Sorry," I muttered. "But I just get so angry on your behalf sometimes."

"More like all the time. I've worked very hard to try and let it go. Can you not do the same?"

I shrugged, not an easy movement, given my position in the chair.

"You and Father have been of great help and comfort to me, but the need is past—I'm all better now."

Was she trying to convince me or herself? Or was I hearing things that weren't there? She certainly *seemed* better, especially with the trip to look forward to, but I wasn't quite over the shock yet, myself, so how could she be so fully recovered?

She wasn't, then. She was lying. But I'd heard that if one lies often and loud enough, the lie eventually becomes the truth. If that was Elizabeth's solution to living with the catastrophe that had engulfed her, then so be it, and she had my blessing.

"Did you enjoy yourself last night?" she asked, standing up and shuffling her sheets of music into order.

"Quite a lot," I said absently.

"I'm glad to hear it, I'm concerned for your . . . happiness." She paused to smile again and in such a way as to give me to understand that she knew exactly what I'd been doing. My vague stories to the rest of the household about going to The Oak to visit and talk were but smoke to her. And probably to Father. Most certainly to Jericho.

"Very kind, but this is hardly a topic I can discuss with you."

"Because I'm a woman?"

"Because I'm a gentleman," I said, with smug finality.

She chose to ignore it. "Meaning you don't discuss your conquests with other gentlemen?"

"Certainly not. Back at Cambridge you could find yourself bang in the middle of a duel for a careless boast."

"Ah, but I'm not a gentleman and have no wish to give challenge, so you're safe with me."

"But really—"

"I was just wondering who she was."

It wasn't much to ask, but damnation, I had my principles. If Molly could keep silent, then so could I. "Sorry, no."

Elizabeth finished putting her music away. By her manner I could tell she was not pleased, nor at all ready to give up.

"Why this curiosity over the company I keep?" I asked before she could frame another inquiry.

She paused and made a face. "Oh, I don't give a fig about who you're with."

"Then why—"

"Damnation, but I'm as bad as Mrs. Hardinbrook."

Now, *that* was an alarming declaration. "In what way?"

Elizabeth dropped onto a settee, her wide skirts billowing up from the force of the movement. She impatiently slapped them down. "The woman worms her way around, asking a dozen questions in order to work her way up to the one she really wants to ask. What a dreadful thing for me to be doing."

"Given the right situation it has its place, usually for questions that might not otherwise be answered, but I've discovered you out, rendering the ploy inappropriate."

She shot me a sour look. "Indeed, yes, little brother."

"Now, then, what is it you really want to ask me?"

The sourness turned into mischievous caution. "I was curious as to whether you dealt with your lady in the same manner that Miss Jones dealt with you."

Whatever I was using for a mind that night suddenly went thick on me for the next few moments. "I'm not sure I rightly understand your meaning," I finally said, straightening in my chair in order to face her.

"When you're with a lady and addressing certain intimate issues, do you conclude them by drinking her blood?"

"Good God, Elizabeth!"

"Oh, dear, now I've shocked you." And she did appear to be sincerely distressed by that prospect.

"That's hardly the . . . I mean . . . what the devil d'ye want to know that for?"

"I'm just curious. I was wondering about that, and that if you did, whether or not you *exchanged* blood with her, and what she thought about it."

My chin must have been sweeping the floor by then.

"Of course, if this is a breach of confidence, I'll withdraw the question," she continued.

"You can hardly do that! It's been said and . . . and . . . oh, good God."

"I'm sorry, Jonathan. I thought you might be a bit upset—"

*A bit?*

"But I thought that since you've already told me how things were between you and Miss Jones that you would not find it so difficult to . . ."

I waved a hand and she fell silent. "I think I have the general idea. I'm just surprised. This isn't the usual sort of thing one discusses with a woman. Especially when she's your sister," I added. "Why have you not raised the question before?"

"When this change first came to you, you were busy . . . and later on, I was busy."

"With your marriage?"

She snorted with disgust. "With my *liaison,* you mean."

"As far as anyone is concerned, it was a marriage."

"Words, words, words, and you're getting off the subject."

"I thought the two to be somehow related."

"In what way?"

Time for less bewilderment and more truth. "Well, you did sleep with the bastard—as his *wife,* so there's no shame in that—and for the short time you were together, we all got the impression that he pleased you."

It was Elizabeth's turn to go scarlet.

"My conclusion is that you're wondering if other women are also pleased with their men, so you ask me what I do and if the lady I'm with enjoys it."

Her gaze bounced all over the room since she could not quite meet my eyes. "You . . . you're . . ."

"Absolutely right?"

She ground her teeth. "Yes, damn it. Oh, for heaven's sake, don't laugh at me."

"But it *is* funny."

And contagious. She fought it, but ultimately succumbed, collapsing back on the settee, hand over her mouth to stifle the sound. God, but it was good to finally see her laughing again, even given these peculiar circumstances.

"All finished?" I asked.

"I think so."

"Curiosity still intact?"

"Yes. No more embarrassment?"

"No more. If you speak plainly with me, then I shall return the favor."

"Done," she said and leaned forward and we shook hands on it.

The issue settled, I twisted around to hook my leg over the chair arm again, affording myself a view out the window. Nothing was stirring past the curtains, which was a comfort. The events of the last year had taught me to place a high value on what others might consider to be dull: inactivity.

"Jonathan?" she prompted.

"Mm? Oh. As for your initial query, yes, I do consummate things in the same manner that Nora did with me. As for the other, no, I have never exchanged blood with the lady I have been seeing."

"Why not? You once said that Miss Jones found it to be exceedingly pleasurable."

"True, but we've also surmised that it led to this change manifesting itself in me."

"But it was a good thing—"

"I'll not deny it, but until I know all there is to know about my condition, I have not the right to inflict it upon another."

"But Miss Jones did so without consulting you."

"Yes, and that is one of the many questions that lie between us. Anyway, just because she did it, doesn't mean that I have to; it smacks of irresponsibility, don't you know."

"I hope you don't hate her." She said it in almost exactly the same tone that Molly Audy had used, giving me quite a sharp turn. "Something wrong?"

"Perhaps there is. That's the second time anyone's voiced that sentiment to me. Makes me wonder about myself."

"You do seem very grim when you speak of her."

"Well, we both know all about betrayal, don't we?"

Elizabeth's mouth thinned. "The nature of mine was rather different from yours."

"But the feelings engendered are the same. Nora hurt me very much by sending me away, by making me forget, by not telling me the consequence of our exchanges. *That's* what this whole miserable voyage is about, so I can find her and ask her *why.*"

"I know. I can only pray that whatever answers you get can give you some peace in your heart. At least I know why I was betrayed."

We were silent for a time. The candles had burned down quite a bit. I rose and went 'round to them, blowing out all but two, which I brought over to place on a side table near us.

"Is that enough light for you?" I asked.

"It's fine." She gave herself a little shake. "I've not had my last question answered. What does your lady—the one you see now—think of what you do?"

"She thinks rather highly of it, if I do say so."

"It gives her pleasure?"

"So I understand from her."

"Does she not think it unusual?"

"I will say that though at first it was rather outside her experience, it was not beyond her amiable tolerance." I was pleased with myself for a few moments, but my smile faded.

"What is it?"

"I was just thinking of how much I'll miss her. Hated to leave her last night. That's why I was so late getting back. Won't happen again, though, Jericho took me to task on the subject of banging doors at dawn and waking the household."

"Father wasn't amused."

I wilted a bit. "I'll apologize to him. Where is he? Not called away?"

"On our last night home? Hardly. He's playing cards with the others."

Father was not an enthusiastic player and only did so to placate his wife. "Is Mother being troublesome again?"

"Enough so that everyone's walking on tiptoes. You know what she thinks of our journeying together—at least when she's having one of her spells. Vile woman. How could she ever come up with such a foul idea?"

I had a thought or two on that, but was not willing to share it with anyone. "She's sick. Sick in mind and in soul."

"I shall not be sorry to leave *her* behind."

"Elizabeth . . ."

"Not to worry; I'll behave myself," she promised.

Both of us had come to heartily dislike our mother, though Elizabeth was more vocal in her complaints than I. My chosen place was usually to listen and nod, but now and then I'd remind her to take more care. Mother would not be pleased if she chanced to overhear such bald honesty.

"I hope it helps you to know that I feel the same," I said, wanting to soften my reproach.

"Helps? If I thought myself alone in this, then I should be as mad as she."

"God forbid." I unhooked my leg from the chair arm and rose. "Will you stay or come?"

"Stay. It might set her off to see us walking in together."

True, sadly true.

I ambled along to the parlor, hearing the quiet talk between the card players long before reaching the room. From the advantage of the center hall, I could hear most of what was going on throughout the whole house. Mrs. Nooth and her people were still busy in the distant kitchen, and other servants, including Jericho and his father, Archimedes, were moving about upstairs readying the bedrooms for the night.

Long ignored as part of life's normal background, the sounds tugged at me like ropes. I'd felt it a dozen times over since the plans to leave for England had been finalized. Though not all that happened here was pleasant, it was home, *my* home, and who of us can depart easily from such familiarity?

And comfort. I hadn't much enjoyed my previous voyages to and fro. The conditions of shipboard life could be appalling—yet another reason for my second thoughts over having Elizabeth along. But I'd seen other women make the crossing with no outstanding hardship. Some of them even enjoyed it, while not a few of the hardiest men were stricken helpless as babes with seasickness.

Well, we'd muddle through somehow, God willing.

I shed those worries for others upon opening the parlor door. Within, a burst of candlelight gilded the furnishings and their occupants. Clustered at the card table were Father, Mother, Dr. Beldon, and his sister, Mrs. Hardinbrook. Beldon and Father looked up and nodded to me, then resumed attention on their play. Mrs. Hardinbrook's back was to the door, so she noticed nothing. Mother sat opposite her and could see, but was either unaware I'd come in, or ignoring me.

The game continued without break, each mindful of his cards and nothing else as I hesitated in the doorway. For an uneasy moment I felt like an invisible wraith whose presence, if sensed, is attributed to the wind or the natural creaks of an aging house. Well, I could certainly make myself invisible if I chose. *That* would stir things a bit . . . but it wouldn't be a very nice thing to do, however tempting.

Mother shifted slightly, eyebrows high as she studied her hand. Her eyes flicked here and there upon the table, upon the others, upon everything except her only son.

Ignoring me. Most definitely ignoring me. One can always tell.

*Home,* I thought grimly and stepped into the parlor.

# CHAPTER 2

Upon entering, I was able to see that my young cousin, Ann Fonteyn, was also present. She'd taken a chair close to a small table and was poring over a book with fond intensity. More Shakespeare, it appeared. She'd developed a great liking for his work since the time I'd tempted her into reading some soon after her arrival to our house. She was the daughter of Grandfather Fonteyn's youngest son and had sought shelter with us, safely away from the conflicts in Philadelphia. Though somewhat stunted in the way of education, she was very beautiful and possessed a sweet and innocent soul. I liked her quite a lot.

I drifted up to bid her a good evening, quietly, out of deference for the others. "What is it tonight? A play or the sonnets?"

"Another play." She lifted the book slightly. *"Pericles, Prince of Tyre,* but it's not what I expected."

"How so?" I took a seat at the table across from her.

"I thought he was supposed to kill a Gorgon named Medusa, but nothing of the sort has thus far occurred in this drama."

"That's the legend of Perseus, not Pericles," I gently explained.

"Oh."

"It's easy enough to mix them up."

"You must think me to be very stupid and tiresome."

"I think nothing of the sort."

"But I'm always getting things wrong," she stated mournfully.

*That* was my mother's work. Her sharp tongue had had its inevitable effect on my good-hearted cousin. Ann had become subject to much unfair and undeserved criticism over the months. Mother had the idiotic idea that by this means Ann could be made to "improve herself," though what those improvements might be were anybody's guess. Elizabeth and I had long ago learned to ignore the jibes aimed at us; Ann had no such defenses, and instead grew shy and hesitant about herself. In turn, this inspired even more criticism.

"Not at all. I think you're very charming and bright. In all my time in England I never once met a girl who was the least interested in reading, period, much less in reading Shakespeare."

"Really?"

"Really." This was true. Nora Jones had been a woman, not a girl, after all. And some of the other young females I'd encountered there had had interests in areas not readily considered by most to be very intellectual. Such pursuits were certainly enjoyable for their own sake; I should be the last person to object to them, having willingly partaken of their pleasures, but they were not the sort of activities my good cousin was quite prepared to indulge in yet.

"What are they like? The English girls?"

"Oh, a dull lot overall," I said, gallantly lying for her sake.

"Did you get to meet any actresses?" she whispered, throwing a wary glance in Mother's direction. Whereas a discussion of a play, or even its reading aloud in the parlor was considered edifying, any mention of stage acting and of actresses in particular was not.

"Hadn't much time for the theater." Another lie, or something close to it. Damnation, why was I . . . but I knew the answer to that; Mother would not have approved. Though I'd applied myself well enough to my studies, Cousin Oliver and I had taken care to keep ourselves entertained with numerous nonacademic diversions. Then there was all the time I'd spent with Nora. . . .

"I should like to go to a play sometime," said Ann. "I've heard that they have a company in New York now. Hard to believe, is it not? I mean, after the horrid fire destroying nearly everything last year."

"Very. Perhaps one day it will be possible for you to attend a performance, though it might not be by your favorite playwright, y'know."

"Then I must somehow find others to read so as to be well prepared, but I've been all through Uncle Samuel's library and have found only works by Shakespeare."

"I'll be sure to send you others as soon as I get to England," I promised.

Her face flowered into a smile. "Oh, but that is most kind of you, Cousin."

"It will be a pleasure. However, I know that there are other plays in Father's library."

"But they were in French and Greek and I don't know those languages."

"You shall have to learn them, then. Mr. Rapelji would be most happy to take you on as a student."

Instead of a protest as I'd half expected, Ann leaned forward, all shining eyes and bright intent. "I should like that very much, but how would I go about arranging things?"

"Just ask your Uncle Samuel," I said, canting my head once in Father's direction. "He'll sort it out for you."

She made a little squeak to indicate her barely suppressed enthusiasm, but unfortunately that drew Mother's irate attention toward us.

"Jonathan Fonteyn, what is all this row?" she demanded, simultaneously shifting the blame of her vexation to me while elevating it to the level of a small riot. That she'd used my middle name, which I loathed, was an additional annoyance, but I was yet in a good humor and able to overlook it.

"My apologies, Madam. I did not mean to disturb you." The words came out smoothly, as I'd had much practice in the art of placation.

"What are you two talking about?"

"The book I'm reading, Aunt Marie," said Ann, visibly anxious to keep the peace.

"Novels," Mother sneered. "I'm entirely opposed to such things. They're corruption incarnate. You ought not to waste your time on them."

"But this is a play by Shakespeare," Ann went on, perhaps hoping that an invocation of an immortal name would turn aside potential wrath.

"I thought you had some needlework to keep you busy."

"But the play is most excellent, all about Perseus—I mean Pericles, and how he solved a riddle, but had to run away because the king that posed the riddle was afraid that his secret might be revealed."

"And what secret would that be?"

Ann's mouth had opened, but no sound issued forth, and just as well.

"The language is rather convoluted," I said, stepping in before things got awkward. "We're still trying to work out the meaning."

"It's your time to waste, I suppose," Mother sniffed. To everyone's relief, she turned back to her cards.

Ann shut her mouth and gave me a grateful look. She'd belatedly realized that a revelation of the ancient king's incest with his daughter was not exactly a fit topic for parlor conversation. Shakespeare spoke much of noble virtues, but, being a wily fellow, knew that base vices were of far greater interest to his varied audience, sweet Cousin Ann being no exception to that rule.

I smiled back and only then realized that Mother's dismissive comment had inspired a white hot resentment in me. My face seemed to go brittle under the skin, and all I wanted was to get out of there before anything shattered. Excusing myself to Ann, I took my leave, hoping it did not appear too hasty.

Sanctuary awaited in the library. It was without light, but I had no need for a candle. The curtains were wide open, after all. I eased the door shut against the rest of the house and, free of observation, gave silent vent to my agitation. How *dare* she deride our little pleasures when her own were so empty? I suppose she'd prefer it if all the world spent its day in idle gossip and whiled away the night playing cards. It would bloody well serve her right if *that* happened. . . .

It was childish, perhaps, to mouth curses, grimace, make fists, and shake them at the indifferent walls, but I felt all the better for it. I could not, at that moment, tell myself that she was a sick and generally ignorant soul, for the anger in me was too strong to respond to reason. Perhaps it was my Fonteyn blood making itself felt, but happily the Barrett side had had enough control to remove me from the source of my pique. To directly express it to Mother would have been most unwise (and a waste of effort), but here I was free to safely indulge my temper.

God, but I would also be glad to leave *her* behind. Even Mrs. Hardinbrook, a dull, toad-eating gossip if ever one was born, was better company than Mother, if only for being infinitely more polite.

My fit had almost subsided when the door was opened and Father looked in.

"Jonathan?" He peered around doubtfully in what to him was a dark chamber.

"Here, sir," I responded, forcefully composing myself and stepping forward so he might see.

"Whatever are you doing here in the . . . oh. Never mind, then." He came in, memory and habit guiding him across the floor toward the long windows where some light seeped through. "There, that's better."

"I'll go fetch a candle."

"No, don't trouble yourself, this is fine. I can more or less see you now. There's enough moon for it."

"Is the card game ended?"

"It has for me. I wanted to speak to you."

"I am sorry about the banging door, sir," I said, anticipating him.

"What?"

"The cellar door this morning when I came home. Jericho gave me to understand how unsettling it was to the household. I do apologize."

"Accepted, laddie. It did rouse us all a bit, but once we'd worked out that it was you, things were all right. Come tomorrow it'll be quiet enough 'round here."

Not as quiet as one might wish, I thought, grinding my teeth.

Father unlocked and opened the window to bring in the night air. We'd all gotten into the habit of locking them before quitting a room. The greater conflict outside of our little part of the world had had its effect upon us. Times had changed . . . for the worse.

"I saw how upset you were when you left," he said, looking directly at me.

Putting my hands in my pockets, I leaned against the wall next to the window frame. "I should not have let myself be overcome by such a trifle."

"Fleabites, laddie. Get enough of them and the best of us can lose control, so you did well by yourself to leave when you did."

"Has something else happened?" I was worried for Ann.

"No. Your mother's quiet enough. She behaves herself more or less when Beldon or Mrs. Hardinbrook are with her."

And around Father. Sometimes. Months back I'd taken it upon myself to influence Mother into a kinder attitude toward him. My admonishment to her to refrain from hurting or harming him in any way had worked well at first, but her natural inclination for inflicting little (and great) cruelties upon others had gradually eroded the suggestion. Of late I'd been debating whether or not to risk a repetition of my action. I say risk, because Father had no knowledge of what I'd done. It was not something of which I was proud.

"I wish she would show as much restraint with Ann," I said. "It's sinful how she berates that girl for nothing. Our little cousin really should come with us to England."

"They had a difficult enough time getting her to take the ferry from New York to Brooklyn. She's no sailor and more's the pity."

Indeed. A trip to England would do her great good, but Ann was sincerely frightened and made ill by sea travel and had firmly declined the invitation to come with me and Elizabeth.

"What about yourself?" asked Father, referring to my own problem with water.

"I shall be all right."

At least I *hoped* so. The streams that flowed through our lands had come to be something of a barrier to me, a fact that I'd discovered the first time I'd tried crossing one on my own after my change. What had once been an easily forded rivulet had become a near impassable torrent as far as I was concerned. My feet dragged like iron weights over the streambed, and the water felt so chill as to burn me to the bone—or so it seemed to my exaggerated senses. Father and I had investigated the phenomenon at length, but could make no sense of this strange limitation I'd acquired. Like my ability to vanish, we connected it to my condition and had as yet found no cure for it.

Yet another question for Nora.

Thankfully, I was able to manage water crossings on horseback or in a wagon, though it was always hard going. I'd reasoned that taking a ship would entail about the same level of difficulty and was prepared to tolerate the inconvenience. It could be no worse than the bout of seasickness I'd suffered during my initial voyage to England four years ago. That had worn off as my body got used to the motion of the ship, and in this coming voyage I was counting on a similar recovery.

Not that I was giving myself much of a choice. If I had to put up with the discomfort for the next two months or more, then so be it. To England I would go.

"Your livestock was sent ahead this morning," said Father. "I hope to God it arrives safely."

"I'm certain it will."

His eyes gleamed with amusement. "You spoke to Lieutenant Nash?"

"At length. He'll provide as safe an escort as any might hope for in these times."

"My thought is that you've gotten a fox to guard your henhouse."

"This fox is very well trained, sir."

Nash, in charge of the profitable work of collecting supplies for the commissary, possessed the soul of a rapacious vulture, but early in our acquaintance I'd been able to successfully curb his greedy nature to something more moderate. On more than one occasion, I'd been able to put the fear of God into him by means of my unnatural influence, and he took care to pay attention to any little requests we might present to him as though they were written orders from the King himself. In turn, we were most careful not to abuse our advantage lest it draw unwelcome notice upon us.

In this instance, the request was to provide a safe escort for the cattle I would be taking on the ship to England. He was to make sure that all of them were put aboard without incident. Such an undertaking was highly unusual, to say the least, but my need was great enough that I had no heavy weight on my conscience in suborning one of the King's officers to play my private agent for such a task. Only he had sufficient authority to protect them from others and see that they and their fodder for the trip were safely delivered.

Also, with the British army and the Hessians on one side and the rebels on the other and all of them hungry as wolves for fresh beef, the idea of taking good cattle *out* of the country bordered on madness. But I would need to feed myself on the voyage, and for that I required a ready supply of animal blood. I hoped a dozen would be more than sufficient for my modest appetite, since I had no plans for indulging in any unnatural exertions like flying or vanishing while aboard. My only real worry was that the animals might not survive an ocean voyage. Well, if they all died, then so be it. I was not adverse to drinking human blood for food if starving necessity forced me to such an extreme.

Father and I had devoted much thought to the framing of just how to ship the beasts and had planned things carefully. Between us, fees (and bribes) were paid, documents were issued, stamped, and made inarguably legal in ways that only an experienced lawyer could devise. In the end we'd obtained permission from His Majesty's servants in charge of hindering honest travelers to ship one dozen heifers to England ostensibly for the purpose of breeding them to superior stock owned by the Fonteyn side of the family. The logical thing to do, as was pointed out to us by the first official we'd encountered, would be to purchase a bull in England and bring it here, thus reducing our expenses on the venture. I'd "persuaded" the fellow and all the others that came after not to argue, but to simply make the arrangements as we desired, without question.

None of it had been very easy, but there is a great satisfaction to be derived from the accomplishment of a difficult endeavor. Perhaps I would feel this particular satisfaction again once we made landfall in England, God willing.

"Trained or not, I shan't feel easy in my heart until I see the results of his work for myself," said Father.

His voice did not sound right to me, having in it an odd note of strain that I did not like one whit. "What is it, sir?"

He thought long before answering, or so it seemed to me as I waited. He gave a half shrug and nearly smiled, an expression remarkably similar to Elizabeth's own subdued efforts of late. "I shall have to tell you, I see that well enough, and hope that you can forgive me for adding another worry to the others you carry."

"Worry?"

His raised hand held back the formation of more specific questions from me. He pushed the window wide. "Come along with me, laddie," he said, and stepped over the low sill quick as a thief.

Too startled to comment at this unorthodox exit, I simply followed, though I did possess enough mind to finally remember to close my gaping mouth. He led the way toward the parlor window and stopped close enough that we might see those within, but yet be concealed from them by the darkness. Father signed for me to look inside, and I obeyed. It was a cozy enough scene to behold: Ann still read her book, and the others still played at their cards. All was peaceful. Familiar. Normal.

I turned back to Father and indicated that I did not understand his reason for showing this to me. He moved back a little distance now, so there would be no chance of anyone overhearing us.

"Is this what you thought might worry me?"

"I'm coming to the worry, laddie." He struck off slowly over the grounds, his eyes hardly leaving the house as we gradually began to pace around it. "It concerns the French," he stated.

Father had a manner about him when he was in a light mood and wanting to be humorous. That manner was lacking in him now, so I understood he was not trying to make some sort of an oblique jest. That was all I understood, though. "Sir?"

"The damned French. You mark me, they'll be coming into this war like wolves to a carcass. You've heard the news, but have you worked out what it means?"

"I've heard rumors that the French are sending ships loaded with holy water and rosaries and are determined to make us all Catholic."

Father paused and laughed at that one, just as I had done when I'd first caught wind of it at The Oak. Presumably, all good members of the English Church would be righteously horrified at the prospect of a forced conversion to an alien faith. Those who were less than firm in their loyalty to the King might then be persuaded to a more wholehearted support of his rule. It was an utterly ridiculous threat, of course, but some of our sovereign's more excitable subjects were taking it seriously.

"France will be sending shiploads of cargo," said Father, "but it will more likely be gunpowder, arms, and money. Some of their young rascals have already come over to lend their support to the rebel cause; it's only a matter of time before their government officially follows. We slapped them hard fourteen years ago, and they're still stinging from it. They want revenge against England."

"But they'll risk another war."

"Possibly. My thought is that they'll play the rebels against the Crown for as much as it's worth. Wars are expensive, but this one won't have a high price for them at all if they work it to their advantage. 'Tis a fine way to weaken both sides with little effort on their part."

"You'd think the Congress over here would see through the ploy."

"Some of the clever ones do, of that I have no doubt, but they're so desperate for help they dare not say a word to the people they claim to represent. I've no trust for them. My God, barely a year before they came out with that damnable declaration against the King they were just as loudly voicing their undying loyalty to him. Bloody liars and rogues, the lot of them."

I made a noise to indicate my agreement with that sentiment. "And fools, if they will risk trusting the French."

"Indeed, yes."

"But this worry you spoke of . . ."

Father paused. We'd climbed a little rise and had the pleasure of viewing the house and much of its surrounding grounds. He glanced at me, then extended his arm to take in all that lay before us. "This," he said, "won't last." This was a flat and inarguable statement.

Inarguable, but needing an explanation. I asked for one.

"We've been safe enough here almost from the start. There have been raids and outrages and theft, but nothing like *real* war, Jonathan. The west end of the island saw that when General Howe's men landed. Stock was killed, crops burned to the roots, houses looted and burned, and the owners turned out to fend for themselves on what was left. 'Tis one thing to hear of it, but another to have the experience, and we were spared only by God's grace and Washington's prudence in running like a rabbit in another direction. I don't think we can count on many more such miracles."

"But the fighting is over. Gone from here, anyway."

"Who's to say it won't return, though? This has become a civil war with Englishman against Englishman, with each side regarding the other as the worst kind of traitor. Those are the most evil and the bitterest of conflicts, and when peace finally comes it won't matter which side you were on, for there will be reprisals for all."

"But the King must win. What else is possible? And I can't believe that he would be so ignorant as to punish those who have remained loyal to him."

"Stranger things have happened. Oh, don't be alarmed, I'm not speaking treason, I just want you to know that I've had some hard thought over how the world has changed for us and that it is likely to continue changing and not necessarily to our favor or liking."

"How can it not be in our favor once the rebels are subdued?"

"Reprisals, laddie. Not just in taxes to pay for the war, but court work and plenty of it. More than enough to keep me busy for the rest of my days . . . but I've no stomach for it."

I couldn't help but stare. Father loved his vocation, or so he'd always told me.

He was nodding at my reaction. "This won't be arguing the ownership of a stray sheep, or who's the rightful master of what parcel of land, or anything like that. This will be the trying of traitors, the confiscation of their property, jailings, floggings, hangings. Some have used the cloak of patriotism to cover their thefts and murders, and they will get all that they deserve, in this world or the next, but what of the others whose only crime may have been to read the wrong newspaper? I will not be a party to that, to punishing a man just because he *thinks* differently from me."

"You won't have to do any such thing, sir."

"Won't I? If I do not fulfill all the duties thrust upon me by the court, then might I not also be a traitor to the Crown?" He waved his hand against my protest and I fell silent, for I knew that he was right.

"What's to be done, then?"

He gave no answer, but sat down on the grass, still facing the house. I sat next to him, plucking up a stray bit of rock to play with. His somber mood had transferred onto me, and I wanted some distraction for my hands.

"What's to be done," he finally said in a heavy voice, "is to move back to England."

Had he picked up a stone himself and lobbed it square between my eyes, I could not have been more stunned.

He continued, "And before you say aught else, remember that I've first put all that hard thought into my decision."

In truth, I could not bring myself to say a damned thing for a considerable period. It seemed too much of an effort even to think, but think I must if I was to understand him.

But he seemed to anticipate the questions beginning to take form in my mind. "You know why we came here all those years ago? Your mother and I?"

"To put some distance between yourself and her father, you told us," I mumbled, too shaken yet to raise my voice. I made a fist around the little piece of rock so the edges dug hard into my palm.

"Exactly. Old Judge Fonteyn was a monster and no mistake. He did all he could to make our lives miserable, using his influence to intimidate your mother into obedience to his will long after she was a settled matron with a home of her own. How that old sinner could howl and rage, but I thought that that would end once I'd put an ocean between us. And it worked—for a time."

Until things had gone wrong between Father and Mother and she'd left him on Long Island to live a separate life for herself in Philadelphia.

He grimaced. "I won't repeat what you already know. What it has come to is this—the Judge is long dead, and his threat upon my marriage fulfilled itself long ago, so my reason for staying on here has quite vanished. Combine that with the fact that you and Elizabeth are grown adults and more than capable of being on your own, an endeavor you're about to undertake, anyway. Combine it again with the fact that the conflicts taking place all around us have made this into a most hazardous place in which to live. Ergo, I've no sane reason to remain here."

"But this is our *home,"* I said, aware of the plaintive whine in my voice, but not caring.

"Only for as long as no one takes it from us. The rebels have confiscated property before, you've read the accounts and heard them. If there should be an unforeseen setback and our army is forced from this island, those bastards from Connecticut will be over here with the next turn of the tide ready to pick us clean in the name of their precious Continental Congress."

It was impossible to conceive of that ever happening, but the raids from across the Sound were real enough. We'd been watchful of our own and had been lucky, but many of our friends had not been so blessed. The story was still fresh in our minds of how two of the DeQuincey daughters had been burned out of their house and forced into the woods, barefoot, with only their nightdresses to protect them from the March cold. They'd managed to reach the safety of their uncle's home some miles away, but not without great suffering and anguish. Their attackers had even chased them for a goodly distance, hooting after them like schoolboys on a lark. The great Sons of Liberty had given up the hunt, fortunately, wanting to return to their booty-laden whaleboat before the coming of dawn.

That could happen to us, I thought. We were not immune. No one could be so long as such men roamed free and were base enough to think that two helpless girls were such a grave threat to their miserable cause. I now understood Father's worry, but that understanding did not make his words any easier to accept.

He plucked a blade of grass and began to shred it, still looking at the house. At *our* house.

"This is different for you, laddie, I know that, for you were bred and born here. For myself, it has been a home, but never really mine. The lands, the house, all that belongs to your mother because of the agreement I'd signed before our marriage. I've done well enough in my life. I've a few pennies scraped together from my practice and that's all I really need for my comfort, but not here, not anymore. I've lived through one war and count myself blessed that Providence saw fit to spare me, but there is no desire within to go through another—nor do I want my children to have any part of what's likely to come. You've had more than your portion of grief already, as we all have." He let the remains of the grass blade slip away unheeded. "Dear Lord, but we don't need any more. Had it not been for your Miss Jones, we'd have lost you last year. For a terrible time I thought we had. . . ."

His voice caught and I put my hand on his shoulder. My own throat had gone tight in reaction. "It's all right, Father."

He sniffed and laughed a little. "Yes, by God it is, laddie. I just want to keep it so."

"Are you saying that you're coming with us?"

He gave a thick cough and impatiently rubbed his nose. "Not on this voyage, there's too much preparation to do first. But soon. That's the worry I was meaning and I'm sorry to thrust it upon you the night before you leave, but it wanted saying while there was still time to say it. Better now than later in a letter sent to England that will be months out of date by the time you get it."

"You've no need to apologize, sir."

"Well, I thought I should try to be polite about it, considering what a shock this must be."

I smiled and eased my grasp upon the rock. How appropriate. "When will you tell Elizabeth?"

"Tomorrow. When we take the carriage to the harbor."

"Why did you not tell us together?"

"I'd hardly planned on saying anything at all, but the time had come. Besides, one of you is formidable enough, but both at once . . ." He shook his head as though my sister and I could have overwhelmed him in some way, as we had done in play as children when trying to wheedle a special favor from him. But then as now, we knew when he could be persuaded and when he could not. Father had made up his mind, and it was not for me to question his judgment, though I yet had questions on other things.

"Sir, you had me look at the others through the parlor window, but I still do not quite have the purpose of it clear in my mind."

"So you could see how things are for us when compared to the rest of the world. There is a kind of peace here, but it's so damnably fragile. Any banditti claiming to be part of Washington's army can come day or night and shatter it forever. This is your home, but would you rather say goodbye to it now of your own volition and remember it as it is or wait, and live with the possibility that someone will come along to *take* it all away? If that were to happen, then nothing would ever be the same. This sanctuary and any others replacing it would ever and always be tainted by such an invasion."

And in that I could hear echoes of what his mistress, Mrs. Montagu, had frequently said to him on the subject. Last December her house had been broken into by rebels and thoroughly looted. Despite the repairs made and support he had given her over the months, she was still subject to vast distress in her own home and, though better prepared than before, was ever in fear of another attack. I asked after her.

"She's well enough."

"What I mean is, if you're planning a return to England, what will happen to her? Have you told her?"

"Laddie," he said, sounding amused, "it was *her* suggestion."

Well-a-day. Mrs. Montagu was a kind woman, for whom I had a great fondness. As I had lacked a mother for the greater part of my life, she had filled that need in me to some goodly degree. "Then she's preparing to leave as well? When?"

"Soon. That's all I can say. There's much that must be done first . . . like dealing with your mother."

Good God. My face fell at the very thought of her. She almost surely promised to be as fell an obstacle as any in Father's path. "What will you do?"

"I . . . haven't quite worked that out," he confessed. "I'm of a divided mind on whether to present it to her as a concluded arrangement, or to find a way for her to come up with the idea herself. The latter is more appealing to me as it is bound to be quieter."

"It would certainly appeal to Mother's nature, especially if she thought you might—" I cut off what was to come next, realizing how it would sound, but Father only smiled.

"Thought I might not like it? I know you meant no disrespect for me, only that you understand how her mind works. Then so be it. That shall be my strategy, though I doubt it will take much to put her onto the business. She has family in England she hasn't seen for decades, like that harpy of a sister who runs things."

*And people.* Aunt Fonteyn, as she chose to call herself. Horrible woman. At least I wouldn't have to be dependent upon her as were so many of her other relatives. I could thank my inheritance from Grandfather Fonteyn for that blessing.

"What about Dr. Beldon?" I asked. If Father intended to take Mother on a long voyage, Beldon and certainly Mrs. Hardinbrook would be necessary to help maintain his treasured peace.

"Gotten fond of him, have you?" His eyes twinkled.

"When he's not playing the toady, he's witty enough company," I conceded.

"First I'll see about persuading your mother, then I'll worry about the others."

I did not ask him if he had not thought of simply leaving on his own, for that would have been an unforgivable insult to his honor. He was a good and decent man, laboring to keep firm to the vow he'd made on his wedding day. No matter that their love had died, his promise to care for and protect his wife was still to be observed. To ignore that promise for his own convenience would violate all that he held sacred. He would sooner hang himself in church during Sunday services than forget it.

Many another man would not have put up with such a wife, but my Father was of a different heart than they. I was glad of him and proud of him and sorry for all the pain he'd endured and hopeful that the future might somehow be easier for him. For us all.

All. Thus was I reminded to speak on another's behalf.

"I must ask one thing of you, sir. Please don't wait until the morrow to tell Elizabeth. It wouldn't be fair to her. She needs . . . the time."

"Time?"

"So she can say good-bye."

He saw my point, nodding. We'd already made our partings with our friends, but not with the land itself. We might never see our beautiful house again, or the fields around it, or the thousand treasured places we'd explored while growing up. Certainly I'd said farewell before when I'd been packed off to Cambridge, but my home had ever been secure in mind and memory, waiting to welcome me back again upon my return.

No more. And that was a heavy sadness to carry along when, after quite a lot more talk and questions, I took my leave from Father and began walking. Aimless at first, I'd intended to wander the estate and simply stroll the night away. It seemed the best manner in which to bid farewell to my favorite haunts, but I found myself going instead to a place I'd been avoiding for far too long. Just over a year had passed since I'd last been there, and throughout that time the mere thought of it had never failed to make me physically ill.

Not without excellent reason.

As children, Elizabeth, Jericho, and I had played here. We were pirates hunting treasure or scouts and Indians; we gamed and quarreled and laughed and sang as our mood dictated; we called it the Captain's Kettle, this deep arena gouged out by an ancient and long-vanished glacier. A special place, a magical place, once protected by the innocence of young memory from all the harsh assaults of living.

At one time I'd regarded it as a refuge. Safe. But that illusion, like many others as my view of the world expanded, was gone.

Now I stood close by one edge, on the very spot where the musket ball had slammed into my chest, where interminable seconds later I'd gasped out the last of the life I'd known to fall helplessly into what would be the first of my daytime sleeps. If dreams had come to me during that period or if I'd been somehow aware of the goings-on about me, it was just as well no memories lingered to sear my mind. Those I did possess were sufficiently wretched, so much so that I had to cling hard to a tree to keep from collapsing beneath their sickening weight.

My knees had begun quaking long before reaching this ground, though I told myself that anticipation was making the endeavor more difficult than the actuality. Only by this inner chiding was I able to goad myself into coming, to attempt to look upon the last place on earth where I'd felt the then welcome blaze of sunlight and had breathed the free air without conscious effort.

Nothing had really changed here, nor had I expected it to, only my perception of it had suffered for the worse. A childhood playground had been corrupted into a vile pit of black dread, and since the possibility that I might never see it again had become a surety, I'd conceived the perverse necessity to come in the hope of ridding myself of the darkness by facing it. But as I held hard to the tree to keep steady, eyes squeezed tight against the view, the need was all but drowned by long-denied reaction. I hadn't anticipated it being this bad; I felt smothered, cold . . . my hands, my whole body, shaking, shivering.

This was a fool's errand. An idiotic mistake. A disaster. A . . .

*No. God give me strength to fight this.* And I started to mutter a prayer, but could not finish it. No matter. The mere intent to pray was a calming influence, reminding me that I was yet in God's hands.

The experience of my death had been hideous, but it was past and done. Fool or no, idiot or no, I would *not* let myself be defeated by a mere *memory.* Back hunched as though bracing for a blow, I forced my eyes open.

Grass, leaves, twigs, and rock sorted themselves into recognizable shapes, no different from those cloaking the rest of our estate, to be walked over or kicked aside as needed. Trees emerged next, then a bit of sky. High above, the branches had laced themselves together. I stared at their canopy and felt my belly twisting in on itself. Not good. To look made me dizzy, not to look made me a coward. But a little illness was preferable now than to suffer lonely recriminations later; so I stared until my guts ceased to churn and the world left off lurching every time I swallowed back bile.

Better. I straightened, discovering my legs were capable of supporting me unassisted. Releasing my grasp of the tree, I stepped unsteadily closer to the edge of the kettle and looked down. Looked across. Looked to the place where the Finch brothers had crouched, hiding from Hessian searchers. Looked to where I'd seen but not comprehended the meaning of a puff of smoke from a musket aimed at my heart.

I looked and waited for the next wave of illness to pass. It did not seem as severe as the others. The shakiness gradually subsided.

Much better. I sat on the once bloodied patch of earth where I'd fallen. Cautiously. It was impossible to rid myself of the notion that some trace of the agony I'd passed through might be lingering here to seize me once more.

An abrupt twinge through my chest did make me wince, but that, as I well knew, originated in my mind. A memory of pain, but not pain itself. No need to fear. No need. Really.

Father had taught us always to face our fears. Talk about them if need be, then look at them and decide if they're worth any further worry. That had ever and always worked in the past, and since my change I'd seen the need to face this one eventually. But I'd never once spoken of it; not even Jericho knew. Telling others meant I'd soon have to take action, and to come here was a labor I'd not yet been ready to assume, or so I told myself each time I put it off. But no longer. That luxury was no longer mine to have.

Drawing my knees up enough that I might rest my arms across them, I waited to see if more illness might overtake me.

Not exactly comfortable, I thought some little time later as a sharp stone ground against my backside. I shifted enough to allow a brief search for the offending rock, prying it free. I half expected it to be stained with old blood, but its rough surface proved to be as unblemished and innocuous as the rest of the area. Eventually I tossed it into the kettle, listening to it rattle through the trees and the faint thump when it struck the ground far below.

I looked and waited, taking in the night sounds as I'd done the previous evening on the banks of the stream, but it wasn't the same. The peace I'd known then had been sweet; was it so far from me now?

Yes, I grumbled, especially if I had to stay here much longer.

The tedium of waiting for another adverse reaction now became my chief adversary, not the illness. I began to drum my fingers, whistle without mind to the tune, and by degrees I came to think that I had more interesting things to do than this. But if I left now, would that be giving in?

Decidedly not.

Instead, I gave in to something resembling a laugh. It was breathy and had more than a small share of unease and subsided too quickly, yet was an indication of barely realized triumph.

It was absurd, of course. *I* was absurd.

My great and horrible fear had turned into boredom.

A second laugh, more certain than the first.

Absurd, and like many absurdities, it craved expression.

I found another stone and tossed it high. It arced through the trees and crashed into the tangle of growth far below. I grabbed another and another until none were left, then got up and searched for more, eager as a child. Circling the kettle, I let fly dozens of similar missiles. As though in a game of chase, I darted through the trees, shouting greetings at them just to hear the echoes.

Foolish, yes, but gloriously foolish. When one is suddenly liberated from a burden, one must celebrate. So I ran and jumped and called out bits of childish verse and song, careless and free.

The last thing I did was to throw myself over the edge of the kettle at a flat run. The world surged for a mad instant as I suddenly hurtled down, then vanished altogether. I'd swiftly willed myself out of all danger, spinning into that state of joyful weightlessness, like a leaf floating upon the wind. I drifted high, leisurely contesting the gentle pressure of the air, invisible as thought, yet in some way just as substantial.

I know not how long I played at this, but finally I tired and resumed solidity on the spot where I'd died. Whatever hurt I'd suffered, whatever anguish for that which I'd lost was no longer a part of this place. I laughed again, and this time the note of triumph was tempered only by a humble gratitude for that which remained: my life, changes and all, and my family.

My misgivings about a permanent parting from these lands was gone. Perhaps the reluctance most people feel when leaving a home has more to do with the inability to resolve any unhappiness that's occurred there, rather than the loss of the happiness they've had. The memories of dying were with me but could no longer instill their fear and pain. They had diminished; I had grown.

With a much lighter heart than before, I hiked back to the house.

# CHAPTER 3

Much to Father's relief the cattle arrived at the ship and had been safely loaded along with the rest of the baggage we were taking to England. There was quite a lot of it, for at the last we'd applied ourselves to additional packing in light of Father's decision to soon follow. Not everything could come; Elizabeth was already mourning the loss of her spinet, but I'd promised to find her another, better one in London. My own major regret was having to leave behind my favorite hunter, Rolly. From the very start of the conflict I'd dreaded losing him to the commissary men, and I hated the idea of his falling into careless and cruel hands. It was one of the many questions I'd posed for Father during our lengthy talk, and one for which he had no ready answer.

I was held fast by my day sleep during the early morning rushing about as our things were piled into the carriage and wagon taking us to the ship. Though utterly oblivious to it all, I could count myself lucky to be well out of the maelstrom of activities attendant on our departure. That was the one positive aspect of my unconscious condition, and it stood alone against a legion of negatives, the chief of them being that I was forced to trust others to take proper care of me.

Not that I held anything in my heart but confidence for those in my family, but I didn't know the captain or crew of the ship, and it was easy enough to imagine the worst. Even the smallest lapse of attention during the process of putting me aboard could end with me plunging disastrously into the cold waters of the Sound. I'd received many assurances from

Father that all would be well, but reluctantly surrendered to the effects of that morning's dawn with a feeling of dread and murmuring a hasty prayer asking for the care and preservation of my helpless body.

Elizabeth, with her talent for organization and the solving of problems, had early on determined the best means for me to travel while in this state. She had ordered the construction of a sturdy chest large enough for me to curl into like a badger in its dark winter burrow. As I was completely immobile while the sun was up, there was little need to consider the thing's lack of comfort. I'd tried out this peculiar bed and approved it, suffering no ill-effects from its confined space.

No pillows or mattress layered the bottom; instead, it was cushioned by several tightly woven canvas bags, each filled with a goodly quantity of earth from our lands. The grave had rejected me—or perhaps I had rejected it—but it was still necessary for me to carry a portion of it with me whenever traveling. Not to do so meant having to spend the entire day in thrall to an endless series of frightful dreams. Why this had to be I did not know. I hoped Nora would enlighten me.

I was later told that there were no mishaps of any kind in transporting my box to the ship. The only time a question was raised was when Elizabeth insisted that it be placed in the small cabin I'd be sharing with Jericho. For a servant to be in the same room as his master was irregular but not unheard of, but the quarters were very limited and it was logically thought that less baggage meant more space. But Elizabeth turned a deaf ear to any recommendations of stowing the box in the hold, and so I was finally, if obliviously, ensconced in my rightful place.

By nightfall the ship was well on its way, a favorable wind and the tide having aided our progress. Too late now to turn back, or so I soon had to remind myself.

Jericho had been hard at work, having thoughtfully freed me from the limits of the box with the intent of transferring me to the cabin's narrow bed. He'd placed my bags of earth over its straw mattress, concealed them with a coverlet, then eased me on top. The story we'd agreed upon to explain my daytime absences was to say that I was a poor sailor and having a bad attack of seasickness. It was a common enough occurrence and entirely reasonable; what we had not reckoned upon was it being so wretchedly true.

At the risk of making a supreme understatement, this was the second most disagreeable awakening of my life. The first, of course, was when I'd come to myself in that damned coffin over a year ago. That had been awful in terms of straightforward shock; this one was nearly as bad in terms of sheer physical torment.

Rather than my usual instantaneous alertness, I floated sluggishly back to consciousness, confused and strangely anxious. I was wholly aware of an unfamiliar discomfort afflicting every square inch of my body, inside and out. Had I felt an illness upon my return to the Captain's Kettle? Would that such a mild case of it would visit me now. Someone had taken my head and belly and tossed them around like dice in a cup, or so I might conclude in regard to their present lack of settlement. They *still* seemed to be rolling about on their own. Every hair on my head and all down my back stood on end, positively bristling with alarm at this unhappy sensation. My limbs seemed to weigh twice as much as normal, and my muscles seemed too spent to move them.

"Mr. Jonathan?" Jericho hovered over me, and if I read the concern in his face and voice rightly, then I was in a rather bad state.

"We're at sea," I whispered decisively. The very air seemed to press hard on me. My skin was crawling from it.

"I have been told that Sag Harbor is well behind us, sir."

"Oh, God."

"Sir?"

*"Mal de mer,"* I gasped, closing my eyes. There was a lighted candle on the lid of the closed trunk and the motion of its flame was not in keeping with that of our surroundings.

"You look feverish." He put a hand to my forehead.

"Cold."

He found another blanket and tucked it around me. It did not help, but he was worried, and it gave him something to do. I was also worried, but unable to act, which made things worse.

"We can turn back, sir. You look ill enough to justify—"

*"No!"* No matter how awful I felt, I'd get through this somehow. But even if some freak of the wind should sweep us to Plymouth in the very next minute, the voyage would still be much too long for me.

"Perhaps you need something to—"

"If you have any care for me, for God's sake don't mention food."

There was solace in the fact that I had no need to breathe, else the odors permeating the very wood of the ship—tar and mildew and tallow and sweat and night soil and old paint and hundreds of others—would have sent me lunging for the chamber pot.

Someone knocked at the door. The room was so small Jericho had but to reach over to open it.

"Is he all right?" asked Elizabeth, peering in. "Good heavens!"

"He is not feeling well," he said, confirming her reaction to me. He moved past her to stand outside that she might come in. With her wide skirts it was not easily done, but she managed.

Unknowingly imitating Jericho, she put a hand to my forehead. "You're very hot."

"On the contrary—"

"I think I should fetch the ship's surgeon."

"No. I won't see him."

"But, Jonathan—"

*"No.* We don't dare. I'm too different now."

She didn't care for that; all her instincts were to do something for me.

"I forbid it," I said. "First he'd listen for my heart, and God knows what he'd do next when he couldn't hear it. Bleed me, probably, and I know that would be an extremely bad idea."

Elizabeth perceived the sense of my words. Even the most incompetent medical man could not be allowed to examine me. Besides being loath to part with a single drop of precious blood, I was incapable of drinking anything else that might be offered as a restorative. No glass of wine, no cup of brandy, no purge or sleeping draught could get past my lips; my changed condition would not allow it.

"But for you to lie there and just suffer . . ."

"It will pass away with time, I've seen as much happen to others. I don't plan to lie here, either." With an effort I made myself sit up, preparatory to standing.

My dear sister immediately objected.

"I will be the better for it, so indulge me," I said. "If I have something for occupation, the time will go more quickly, and I'll be less mindful of this irksome state."

She and Jericho exchanged places again, allowing him to help with my shoes and coat and offer a steadying arm when I was ready to stand.

"You're not at all ill, are you?" I said to him, making it half question, half accusation.

"No, sir, and that's just as well, don't you think?" He got me out the door into a dim and narrow passage.

By their very nature, all crafts that venture upon water are given a life as they move and react to that element. Our ship was very lively, indeed, as might be judged from the motion of the deck as I staggered along. It also had a voice, formed from wood creaking upon wood and the deep and hollow sound of the sea rocking us. These features I could note, but not in any way appreciate in a positive sense.

Elizabeth led us topside, and only then did I fill my lungs with fresh, cleansing air. The wind was cooler and helped somewhat to clear my head. Fixing my eye on the unbroken gray horizon beyond the rail was of no help to my unsettled stomach, but rather a powerful reminder that we had a lengthy and lonely journey ahead. Lonely, that is, if we were lucky enough to avoid contact with rebels or privateers. I remembered what Molly Audy had said about prayer and vowed to spend some time at that occupation later tonight.

I was introduced to the captain, certain of his officers, and a few of the other passengers who were also taking the air. No one had any comment for not having witnessed my ever coming aboard. For that I could thank the natural activity of preparing a ship for sailing, everyone being busy enough with their own concerns, having no time to spare for others.

Many of the people aboard were fleeing the unrest at home, preferring to take the longer sea voyage to England over risking the unknowns of a much closer Halifax. What news that had come to us on the latter locale had given everyone to understand that it was an altogether dismal place as well as dangerous. The winters there were said to be hellishly cold, plagued by too many other refugees, too few supplies, inadequate shelter, and outbreaks of the pox. *Much* better to go to England, where all one had to worry about was the pox and which coffeehouse to patronize.

As I'd expected, keeping myself busy with conversation helped to take my mind off my interior woes. Within an hour of introductions, several of us had found enough commonalties in our lives to form quick and comfortable friendships. An excellent situation, given the fact that we were going to have to share constant company with one another for the next two months or more.

The universal lament was the detestable unfairness that we, the loyal and law-keeping subjects of His Majesty, had to give way to the damned traitors who were running amok.

"It's too perilous to stay while the fighting's on," stated Mr. Thomas Quinton, an apothecary close to my age traveling with his wife and young daughter. The ladies in his life were in their cabin, feeling the adverse effects of sea travel themselves. We two stood by the rail, braced against the wind and rolling of the ship. Somehow Quinton had been able to light his pipe and was quite enjoying a final smoke before retiring.

"Many share that view, sir," I said. "It only makes sense to remove oneself from the conflict." I was far enough upwind of him so as to avoid his smoke, a little recovered, but still uncertain of my belly. It had a disconcerting habit of cramping at irregular intervals.

"Would that the conflict would remove itself from *me.* Surely the generals can find other places to fight their wars. Of course, the rogues that were raising the devil near my house weren't of any army."

"Who were they? More Sons of Liberty?"

"Damned Sons of Perdition is what I call 'em. For all the soldiers about, they still get up to enough mischief to curdle a butcher's blood. We had a fine house not far from Hempstead, and one night they came storming up demanding to see a neighbor of mine. They were so drunk that they'd come to the wrong door, and I was fearful they'd be dragging me out to be tarred and feathered."

"What incensed them? Besides the drink, that is."

"They'd taken it into their heads that my innocent neighbor was spying for General Howe . . . or Lord North. They weren't very clear about that point, but were damning both with equal fervor."

"What did you do?"

"Called at them from the upper window to disperse and go home. I had a pistol in hand, but one shot's not enough for a crowd, and there looked to be a dozen of them. They even had an effigy of my neighbor hanging from a pole, ready for burning. Took the longest time to convince them they were lost, then they wanted to know about me and whether I was a true follower of their cause. Told them that if their cause was to frighten good people out of their rest in the dead of night, then they should take it elsewhere and be damned."

"Given the circumstances, that doesn't strike me as having been a wise thing to say."

"It wasn't, but I was that angered by them. 'If you're not for us, you're against us!' they cried. They won't let an honest man mind his own business, not them. Some of the fools were for breaking in and taking me off for that sauce, but I decided to aim my pistol right at the leader and made sure he noticed. Asked him if he'd rather go back to his tavern and drink the health of General Washington or take a ball between his eyes right then and there. He chose the tavern and spared us all a great deal of trouble. My poor wife was left half-distracted by all that bother, and the next morning we were packing to leave. It's a hard thing to bear, but it won't be forever. Perhaps in a year or two we can return and resume where we left off."

"I hope all goes well for you, then. Have you any friends in London to help you when you arrive?"

"There are one or two people I know from New York who are now living in Chelsea. They left before Howe's landing and a good thing, too, for the fire last year consumed their houses."

No need to ask what fire. For those who lived within even distant sight of New York, there was only the one.

"Have you friends as well?" asked Mr. Quinton.

"Family. My sister and I will be staying with our cousin Oliver. I hope that he'll have received the letter we sent announcing our coming and will put us up until we find a place of our own."

"Has a large family, does he?"

"No, he just prefers his solitude." After a lifetime of having to account for himself every time his mother pinned him with her glare, my good cousin was positively reveling in his freedom. We'd shared rooms at Cambridge, but that's different from having one's own house and servants. Having also come into his inheritance from Grandfather Fonteyn's estate and with the beginnings of a fine medical practice bringing in a steady income, Oliver was more than content with his lot. "I'm very much looking forward to seeing him again; we had some fine times together."

Quinton's eyes lit up. "Ho, raised a bit of the devil yourselves, did you?"

"Our share, though we weren't as wild as some of our friends."

"But wild enough, hey?"

Compared to some of the others at the university, we were positively sedate, but then both of us would have to work for our suppers someday, so we did apply ourselves to study as it became necessary. Oliver wanted to be out and away from the restrictions of Fonteyn House—his mother's house—and I had pledged to Father that I would do my best. Not that our studies seriously interfered with the pursuit of pleasure, though.

"I suppose my wild days are over," said Quinton. His pipe had gone out and he knocked the bowl against the rail to empty it. "Not that I've any regrets. I've a real treasure in my Polly and little Meg. For all the unrest, I count myself a blessed man. We're all together and in good health, well . . . that is to say . . ."

"I'm sure they'll be fine, given time. This malady is a nuisance, but no one's died from it that I've ever heard."

"Thank you for that comfort, sir. Now that I've reminded myself of their troubles, I think I'll see as to how they're getting along." He excused himself and went below.

I leaned on the rail and fervently wished myself well again. Without his company for a diversion, the illness within rose up, once more demanding attention. As the ship heaved and plunged, so did my belly. My poor head was ready to burst from the constant ache between my ears. On each of my previous voyages I'd been sick, briefly, but it had not been anything as horrid as this. Was the difference in the ship, in the roughness of the sea, or in myself?

Myself, I decided unhappily. If I had difficulty crossing a stream, then a whole ocean would certainly prove to be infinitely more laborious. I gulped several times.

"Perhaps you should be in bed, sir." Jericho had appeared out of nowhere, or so it seemed to my befogged brain.

"Perhaps you're right. Where'd Elizabeth get to?" She'd made off with herself soon after I'd fallen into conversation with Quinton.

"In bed as well. It was a very tiring day for her."

Yes. Day. The one I'd missed, like all the others. And she'd been up for most of the night with packing. Having had more than my share of rest, it was damned inconsiderate of me to forget that she might need some, too.

"My insides are too disturbed for me to retire just yet. The air seems to help a bit."

Jericho nodded, put his hands behind his back, and assumed a stance that would allow him to remain sturdily afoot on the pitching deck. "Very good, sir."

And it was doubly damned inconsiderate of me to forget that of all people, Jericho might also be exhausted. Yes, he was; I could see that once I wrenched attention from myself to give him a close look. "None of that 'very good, sir' nonsense with me," I said peevishly. "Get below and go to sleep. I'll be all right sooner or later. If it turns out to be later, you'll need your strength to deal with me."

Along with the fatigue, amusement fluttered behind his dark eyes. "Very good, sir." He bade me a pleasant night and moved off, his walk timed to match the rhythm of the ship's motion. A natural sailor. Would that some of that inborn expertise could transfer to me.

Alone and with the whole night stretching ahead, I had ample time to feel sorry for myself. Hardly a new experience, but never before had it been so . . . concentrated. I couldn't just float off to visit Molly or gossip at The Oak. Any social activities I could enjoy were restricted to those swift hours between sunset and the time everyone had to sleep. No wonder Nora read so much. I'd brought a number of books, more than enough, but the idea of reading held no appeal as long as I was reacting so badly to the ship's rolling progress.

Despite my profession for not wanting to feed just now, it occurred to me that perhaps some fresh blood might be of help against this miserable condition. It was a wonderful remedy for anything that ailed me on land, after all. Jericho and Elizabeth had both made a point to mention that the cattle were secure in their stalls below and to provide directions on how to reach them, but I'd since forgotten what they'd said. Might as well use the time to see things for myself.

I spied one of the officers who had been introduced earlier and staggered over to make inquiries. He was on watch and could not leave his post, but detailed one of the seamen to take me below. The fellow led the way, surefooted as a goat and full of merriment for my own inept efforts at walking. Things improved somewhat below decks. The passages were so narrow that it was impossible not to remain vertical—as long as one fell sideways.

The darkness was so profound that not even my eyes would have been of use if our candle went out. We slipped through a number of confusing areas, occasionally spotting a feeble gleam from other candles as we passed other tiny cabins, and a somewhat larger chamber filled with hammocks, each one swinging heavily with the weight of a sleeping man. Snores filled the close air; the air itself made me more thankful than ever that I had no pressing need to use it.

Our journey ended in another chamber not far from the slumbering sailors, and the lowing sounds coming from it blended well with the deep noise of the ship. I thanked my guide and gave him a penny for his help, for which he volunteered to lend me any future assistance should it be required. He then sped away, leaving the candle behind, apparently having no need of it to make his way back topside.

The heifers appeared to be all right, given their situation, though none could be said to look very happy about it. Most were restless and complaining, which I took as a good sign; better that than with their heads hanging and voices silent with indifference. Father and I had picked the healthiest from our dwindling herd in the hope that they would last the journey, but sometimes one just could not tell. One moment you'd have a strapping, bright-eyed beast and the next it could be flat on its side, having dropped dead in its tracks. Those were the realities of life for a gentleman farmer. Or any farmer, for that matter.

Well, if it happened, so be it; I was nowhere near upon the verge of starvation, nor ever intended to get that far. I felt absolutely no hunger now, but the hope that blood might ease things impelled me to pick one of the animals to sup from.

I was very careful to make sure the thin partition between the cattle and the sleeping men was firmly in place. Only one other time had anyone witnessed my feeding. Two Hessians had chanced upon me just as I'd finished with blood smeared 'round my mouth and my eyes flushed red, presenting an alarming sight to them and a depressing aftermath for me. *Blutsäuger,* one of them had cried in his fear. I hadn't liked the sound of that appellation, but was more or less used to it by now. There were worse things to be than a bloodsucker in the literal sense . . . such as being one of those damned rebels.

Calming an animal was the work of a moment, then I dropped to one knee and felt for the vein in its leg. Conditions weren't exactly clean here, but that could be remedied with a little water. My God, we were surrounded by the stuff. All that was needed was to pay one of the sailors to try his hand at grooming.

Such were my thoughts as my corner teeth lengthened enough to cut through the flesh and reach the red fountain beneath. I hadn't fed from cattle for some time, preferring horses. Shorter hair, you know. The taste of the blood was nearly the same, though my senses were keen to the point that I could tell the difference between the two as easily as a normal man knows ale from beer.

I managed to choke down a few swallows and they stayed down, but only under protest. It was the same as it would be for any other person with the seasickness; food might be necessary, but not especially welcome.

I pinched the vein above the broken skin until the bleeding stopped, then rinsed my stained fingers in the dregs at the bottom of a slimy water bucket hanging in a corner. Well, something would have to be done about *that.* I'd paid plenty of good money for their care, which included keeping them adequately supplied with water. From the condition of the straw on the deck one could tell that they'd long since passed whatever had been in the bucket.

A quick search for more water was futile. Perhaps it was kept under lock and key like the crew's daily tot of rum. A note to Jericho or Elizabeth would sort things out.

I was about to quit the place and hazard the maze back to my cabin when I heard the achingly familiar snort of a horse. None of the other passengers had mentioned bringing stock aboard, though they'd all commented on my endeavor. Reactions varied from humor to curiosity at the eccentricity. Strange that no one had . . . whose horse was it?

Opening the partition between this stable and the next solved the little mystery. Inside, snug in his own stall was Rolly. His ears were pricked toward me, his nostrils quivering to catch my scent.

Now was I flooded with understanding on why Father had said nothing about what was to be done about this, my special pet. He must have put himself to some trouble to arrange this last-minute surprise. God bless him and his accomplices. Elizabeth and Jericho had not given away the least clue.

I went in and lavished a warm greeting upon Rolly, rubbing between his ears and all down his neck; that was when I discovered a scroll of paper tied to his mane with a ribbon. A note?

A note. I cracked open the drop of sealing wax holding the ribbon to the paper and unrolled the brief missive.

*My dear Jonathan,*

*I hope you will forgive me for this liberty with your property, but I deemed the risk to be worth the taking. I know how much Rolly means to you, and it would be a cruel thing to bear for you to have to give him up because of my plan to leave. Bereft as we are now of the influence you have over the commissary, it is not likely that so fine an animal could long escape their future notice.*

*He has sufficient food to keep him for the duration of even a lengthy voyage. Remember that throughout that time he will miss his usual exercise, so take care to bring him back to it gently once you're in England.*
*In prayer for a safe journey with God's blessings for all of you,*
*Your Loving Father.*

The writing swam before my eyes. For the first time since awakening, a warmth stole over me. *God bless you, too, sir,* I thought, wiping my wet cheeks with my sleeve.

I spent an hour or more with Rolly, checking him over, petting and talking to him, letting him know why he was where he was. Whether he understood or not was of no importance, he was a good listener, and sharing his company was a much better distraction than conversation with Mr. Quinton. I discovered Rolly's tack and other things stowed in a box and filled the time by brushing him down and combing his mane and tail out until they were as smooth and shining as the rest of his coat. A groom's chore, yes, but for me it was pleasure, not work.

Having seen to his comfort and taken some for myself, I was ready to return topside and see how the night was faring. With occupation came forgetfulness and I had to keep track of the time, being determined to forevermore avoid further panicked diving into cellars to escape the dawn.

I had naught to fear; upon emerging, one glance at the sky told me that the greater part of the night still remained. It had to be but a glance; the sight of the masts swaying drunkenly against the background of the more stationary stars brought back the dizziness in full force. Shutting my eyes made things worse. Would to God this misery would pass away. I made a meandering path to the rail and held on for dear life, gulping air and cursing my weakness.

There was soon something else to curse when a wayward gust of wind splashed half a bucket of sea spray in my face. Ugh. I swatted at it, clearing my eyes and sputtering. It was colder than iron.

"Wind's freshening," said one of the ship's officers, by way of a comment on my condition as he strolled past. "Best to find some cover or you'll be drenched right through, sir."

Thanking him, I made a last look around, which convinced me that no further distractions were to be found this night—unless I wanted more chill water slapped in my face. Better to be seasick and dry than seasick and wet. I went below.

Jericho had left the cabin's small lamp burning for my return. He was deeply asleep in his cot jammed against the opposite wall. I was glad that he was getting some rest and took care to be quiet while slipping off my damp clothes. Not quite knowing what to do with them, I left them piled on the traveling box, then gratefully climbed into my own bed.

The presence of my home earth delivered an instant comfort so overwhelming that I wondered whatever had possessed me to leave it in the first place. Until this moment I hadn't realized how much I needed it, and lying back, I finally identified the feeling that had been creeping up on me for the last few hours, one that I'd not had since before my death: I was *sleepy*.

I'd known what it was to be tired, known all its forms, from the fatigue of a dark and discouraged spirit, to the weary satisfaction that stems from accomplishing a difficult task. Much had happened in the last year, but not once had my eyes dragged shut of their own accord as they were doing now.

Damned strange, that.

But so wonderfully pleasant.

To escape into sleep . . . I'd thought that luxury forever lost because of the changes I'd been through.

Out of old habit rather than necessity, I made a deep inhalation and sighed it out again, pulling the blankets up to my chin. Oh, but this felt good; my dizziness and bad belly were finally loosening their grip on my beleaguered frame. The earth-filled bags I rested on were lumpy and hard, but at the same time still made the most comfortable bed I'd ever known. I rolled on my side, punched the pillow once to get it just right . . .

And then someone was tugging at my shoulder and calling my name most urgently.

*Damnation,* I thought, then said it aloud. "What is it?"

"Don't you want to get up, Mr. Jonathan?" Jericho asked.

"I just got to bed. Let me finish what I've started."

"But it's long past sunset," he insisted.

Ridiculous. But he was probably right or he wouldn't be bothering me. I pried my eyes open. The cabin looked the same as before, or nearly so. If his cot had not been made up and my clothes neatly laid out on the box, I would have had good cause for continued annoyance.

"Miss Elizabeth's been by to ask after you. She thought you might still be ailing from the seasickness."

"It's not as bad as before."

"Do you wish me to convey that news to her?"

God, but I wanted to stay in bed. "No, I'll talk to her, perhaps take the air."

He seemed about to ask another question, for he was plainly worried, but I got up and requested my coat. That was all that was required to change the subject. In the next few minutes I was summarily stripped, dressed again, combed out, brushed off, and otherwise made ready for presentation to any polite company, though how he was able to accomplish so much in the tiny space we had was a mystery to me.

My hat in place, my stick in hand, I was bowed out into the passage.

"You're trying to get rid of me so you can tidy things, is that it?" I demanded.

His smile was one of perfect innocence. It was also his only reply as he shut the door.

There being little point in additional contest with him, I made my way topside. Long habit dictated I check the sky, which was clear, but I was surprised at the lateness of the hour. How could I have overslept for so long?

"I thought you'd never show yourself," Elizabeth called from a place she'd taken on the port rail. There was a good color in her cheeks and her mood seemed very light. Perhaps it had to do with the three young ship's officers who were standing about her. Apparently she was not in want of company or amusement.

"Must be the sea air," I said, coming over.

"You're feeling better?"

*That* subject again. "I wish you hadn't reminded me." I clutched the rail hastily, nearly losing my stick. Should have left it in the cabin as I'd done last night. Though an elegant affectation for walking in the city or country, it was quite the impediment on a shifting deck.

"Still seasick?"

"Oh, please don't say it. I'd forgotten until now."

"Sorry. You looked well enough a moment ago."

"It's rapidly reasserting itself, unfortunately."

One of the officers, anxious to make a good impression on Elizabeth, suggested that I consult Mr. Quinton. "He brought several cases of medicines with him. I'm sure he'd be only too happy to provide something to ease your difficulty," said the fellow with some eagerness.

"Thank you, Lieutenant George. I shall give that some consideration." About two second's worth, I thought.

"I can have him fetched for you," he offered helpfully.

"Not necessary, sir. I've no wish to disturb him just yet."

"But he's not at all occupied—"

"That's quite all right, sir," I said firmly, hoping he would accept the hint. Happily, Elizabeth smiled at him and told him not to worry so. He bowed and declared himself to be her most faithful servant, which inspired the other two to gainsay him by assuring her that they were better qualified to such a post by reason of their superior rank. One of them informed Elizabeth about the dates of their respective commissions in order to prove his case for being the senior officer. After that, I lost the thread of the discussion until she touched my arm, giving me a start.

"Are you bored?"

"Not at all. Where'd your suitors go?" I was mildly confused to note that they had quite vanished.

"Back to their duties. The captain caught their eye, raised his chin, and they suddenly remembered things they had to see to. It was very funny, didn't you notice?"

I shrugged, indifferent to her obvious concern.

She put a hand to my forehead. "A bit warm. Is the chill yet with you?"

"Not really, just the misery in my stomach and a spinning head. I was all right when I woke up, but it's returned. Maybe that's why I slept an hour later than usual."

"You look as though you could use even more rest."

"No need for concern, I shall seek it out," I promised, working to rouse myself, lest she continue on the matter. The topic of my well-being had worn rather thin with me. "I found Father's surprise," I said and explained how I'd come across Rolly.

She brightened. "Oh, I wished I'd been there to see. I'd promised to let him know everything."

"You can tell him that I was extremely happy. I plan to as well if I can bring myself to write in a steady hand on this vessel. I thought that a large ship like this would make for a smoother passage. The sea's not that rough."

"It's better than when we first set out. The other passengers are coming 'round from its effect. I hope you're next, little brother."

"As do I. Was I much missed from the table today?"

"Since you were never there to start with you could hardly be missed, though the captain and Mr. Quinton both asked after you. Even when you do recover, you won't want to look too healthy or people will wonder why you're not eating with them."

"Excellent point. I suppose I could be busy with some occupation or other. Tell them I'm involved with my law studies and will take meals in my cabin. Jericho can find some way of disposing of . . . the extra food."

"Jonathan?"

I shook my head. "Can't seem to wake up tonight. I don't remember the last time when I've felt so sleepy."

"Then pay mind to it and go to bed if it's rest you want."

"But so early? I mean, for me that's just not natural anymore."

"Perhaps the constant presence of being over water is especially tiring for you. You said as much last night before I left you in Mr. Quinton's company."

"I suppose I could lie down for a while. Jericho should be done by now."

"Done with what?"

"Oh—ah—doing whatever it is he does when I'm out of the room. The workings of one's valet are a mystery, and every good gentleman understands that they should remain so."

"It seems a one-sided thing."

"Such are the ways of the world when it comes to masters and servants. Believe me when I say that I'm very comfortable in my ignorance."

She fixed me with a most solemn look. "Get some sleep, Jonathan."

I gave a little bow, mocking the recent efforts of the absent officers. "Your servant, Miss Barrett."

"*Lots* of sleep," she added, brows high.

That was enough to carry me back to the cabin. It was empty of Jericho's presence, but not of his influence. My recently discarded clothes were gone and the bed was tidy again. What a shame to have to destroy such order.

Before collapsing, I rooted in the traveling box for something to read, but only for a moment. My eyes were already closing. Giving up the struggle, I dropped into bed.

At some point I became aware of another's presence, but it was a dim and easily ignored incident.

Jericho, probably. Shaking my shoulder again.

I muttered an inarguable order to let me sleep and burrowed more deeply into the pillow.

The next disturbance was more annoying. Elizabeth was calling to me. Being absolutely insistent.

Couldn't seem to respond. Not even to her. It hardly mattered.

Now she was all but bellowing right in my ear. My head jerked and I snarled something or other. It must have been forceful enough to put her off further attempts, for no more were made. I was finally left alone, left to enjoy my sweet, restorative oblivion.

The seasickness was quite gone when I next woke. The combination of my home earth, the extra rest, and last night's fresh blood must have done it. Of course, it might not be a permanent thing, for had it not returned when I'd abandoned my bed for a turn around the deck?

I made a kind of grumbling sigh and stretched. God, but I was stiff.

And slow. I'd not been this sluggish since that time I'd been forced to hide from the day buried under a snowbank. At least I wasn't cold now, just moving as though half frozen. I was . . . numb.

My hands. Yes, they were flexing as I wished, but I had no sense of them belonging to me. I made fists and opened them, rubbed them against the blankets. There, that was better, I could almost feel that. Must have slept wrong, had them under me or . . .

Arms were numb, too.

Legs . . . face . . .

But wearing off. Just had to wake up a bit more. No need for alarm.

"Jonathan?" Elizabeth's voice. Thin. Odd mixing of distress and hope.

The room was dark—or my eyes weren't working properly. Rubbed them. Hard to work my fingers.

She said my name again. Closer this time. More pressing.

Had some trouble clearing my throat. Coughed a few times before I could mumble anything like an answer. Blinked my eyes a lot, trying to see better. The room was foggy as well as dark.

Her face hovered over mine. "Do you hear me?"

"Mm."

"Do you know me?"

What was she on about? "Mm-mu . . . niz . . . beh."

*"Oh, God!"* She dropped her head on my chest and began loudly sobbing.

What in heaven's name was going on? Was the ship sinking? Why was she acting like this? I touched her with one hand. She rose up and seized it, holding it against her wet cheek.

"Miss Elizabeth, please have a care for him." Jericho this time.

But she kept weeping.

*"Please,* miss, you're not helping him this way."

I had not been frightened before. His tone and manner were all wrong. Jericho was ever and always playing the role of imperturbable servant, but now he was clearly afraid, and that pierced right through my heart. And as for Elizabeth's reaction—I reached out to him.

"Wha . . . ss . . ."

"It's all right, Mr. Jonathan." His assurance was so hasty and sincere that I knew that something awful must be happening. I tried to sit up, but my apathetic limbs were as much of a hindrance as Elizabeth's close presence. "Lie still, sir. Please."

There was little else I could do as he got Elizabeth's attention at last and persuaded her to better compose herself. She soaked a handkerchief cleaning away her tears and blowing her nose. I looked to him for some clue to her behavior. He smiled at me, trying to make it an encouraging one, but creating a less positive response instead. His face was very drawn and hollow and . . . thinner? As though he'd not eaten well for some time. But he'd been perfectly fine last night. What in God's name . . . ?

With Elizabeth removed I was able to raise up on my elbows. We were not in the tiny cabin anymore. This room, while not palatial, was quite a bit larger. The walls were vertical, the ceiling higher. Why had I been moved?

"Forgive me, I just couldn't help myself," said Elizabeth. "It's been such an awful time."

"Whaz been?" I slurred. Coughed. Damned tongue was so thick. My voice was much deeper than normal, still clogged from sleep. "Whaz maa-er?"

"Nothing's the matter now, you idiot. You're all right. Everything's all right."

I made a sound to inform her that I knew damned well that everything was *not* all right.

"He doesn't understand, Miss Elizabeth. He's been asleep."

And it was past time to shake it off. With heroic effort, I pushed myself upright and tried to drag my legs from the bed.

It was a real bed, too, with fresh linen and thick dry blankets, not at all like the one in the old cabin. Had we taken over the captain's quarters?

I coughed and worked my jaw, rubbing my face. Yes. That was better. Feeling was returning once more, thank goodness. I could actually tell that my bare feet were touching the cold boards of the deck. Bare? Well, of course Jericho would have readied me for sleep. It was very remiss of me to have made extra work for him by falling into bed with all my clothes on.

Another stretch; this time things popped along my spine. God, but that felt good.

Jericho and Elizabeth watched me closely.

"Wha' iz the ma—matter?"

"You've been asleep, sir."

"S' you'f said. Wh'd 'f it?" Worked my jaw more. "What-of-it?" There, *now* I could understand myself.

"You remember nothing of the voyage?" asked Elizabeth.

"What do . . . you mean? What 'f the voyage? Something happened to Rolly?"

"No, he's fine. He's safely stabled. You—"

Stretched my neck, rubbing it. "Not making much sense, Sister." I saw that like Jericho, she was also very drawn and tired-looking. Circles under the eyes, skin all faded and tight over the bones. "Are you well? What the devil is wrong here?"

"For God's sake, Jonathan, you've been *asleep!*"

Was that supposed to mean something? Apparently so. Something most dreadfully important to them both.

"More than asleep, sir," Jericho put in. "You know how you are during the day. It was like that."

"Will you please be more clear? You're saying I slept, yes. Is it that I slept the whole night through as well as the day?"

"More than a night, Jonathan."

I abruptly fathomed that I was not going to like hearing what Elizabeth was about to say. "More?" I squeaked.

"You slept through the whole *crossing.*"

Oh, to laugh at that one. But I could not. Additional noises issued from me, unintelligible as speech, but nonetheless expressive.

"You went down to your cabin to get some rest on our second night out," she said, speaking carefully as though to prompt a poor memory.

"Yes, you told me to."

"You never woke up from it. You just wouldn't, and when you're that way, it's as if you're dead."

"Never woke up? Whatever do you mean?"

"You *slept* for the whole voyage! You were asleep for over two *months!*"

I was shaking my head. "Oh, no-oo . . . that's impossible."

Their expressions were sufficient to gainsay my weak denial.

"Impossible . . ." But I had only to look around to see that we were in a building, not on a ship. My own body had already confirmed as much. Gone were the raised hackles, the illness, the constant pressure inside and out. Nightshirt trailing, I boosted unsteadily from bed toward a small window.

The glass was cold and opaque with condensation. I fumbled with the catch and thrust the thing open. Cold wind slapped my face, bringing the scent of sleet, mud, coal smoke, the stable. I was on an upper story of a building taking in the view of its courtyard. An inn of some kind. Vaguely familiar.

The Three Brewers. The inn I'd stayed at while waiting to meet Cousin Oliver for the first time four years ago.

"This just cannot be." But the proof remained before my eyes, mocking my denial.

"Jonathan . . ." My sister's tone had taken on patient reproach. She could tolerate confusion, but not willful stupidity.

I stared dumbfounded at the prosaic scene below. Beyond the inn, past the lower roof of its opposite wing, were trees, other roofs, and church steeples stretching miles away into a cloudy winter night.

True, true, and true. We were most definitely, most undeniably, yet most impossibly in *London.*

# CHAPTER
# ◄4►

***London, November 1777***

"It was perfectly horrid, that's how it was," Elizabeth said, her voice a little high.

"I'm sorry, I truly am. If I'd any idea that—"

She waved her third sodden handkerchief at me and told me not to be foolish. "Of course you'd have said something. We both know that. But it's been such a wretched ordeal, and now that it's over I hardly know what to think or do."

"Tea," Jericho firmly stated.

"With lots of brandy," I added to his departing back. Would that I could have some for this shock. Two months? How could two *months* of my life have slipped away?

"You have no memory of *any* of it?" she asked.

"My last recollection was talking with you by the rail, going below, and dropping into bed. As far as I'm concerned, it happened last night."

She shook her head and kept shaking it.

"I don't disbelieve you, Elizabeth, it—it's just very hard to take in. Tell me all that happened, maybe that will help."

"Where to start . . . ?" She rolled her eyes to the ceiling, shut them a moment, then rested them on me. "First, I'll say that I am very glad that you are all right. You've no idea what we've been through."

"Then for God's sake enlighten me." I was sitting on the bed again, wrapped in my dressing gown now and wide awake, if still considerably shaken. By now it had thoroughly penetrated my skull that my mysterious lapse had been a singularly unpleasant experience for Jericho and Elizabeth. Better to concentrate on them than myself. It was more comfortable.

She gave a long sigh, then took a deep breath. "On the third night out Jericho tried to wake you, but you just refused to do so. I'd told him that you'd been very tired, and he let you rest a few more hours, then tried again. Nothing, except for a few grumbles, and you kept on lying there, not moving at all."

"I'm sorry."

She fixed me with a look that told me to cease apologizing. "We decided to let you sleep and try again the next night. Again, nothing. Finally Jericho went down to the hold and drew off some blood from one of the cattle and wet your lips with it. Then he tried putting a few drops in your mouth. Not even that worked."

I spread my hands. Apologetically. Couldn't help it.

"We didn't know whether to leave you alone or try something sterner, then Mr. Quinton, the apothocary, came 'round. Lieutenant George sent him to look in on you, the blasted toady." The tone she used with his name indicated that George was the toady, not Quinton. "Jericho tried to put him off, but he got curious and went in when we weren't around. He promptly ran straight to Mr. George to say you were dead."

"Oh, dear lord."

"That brought the captain down to see, and I was flooded with so much sympathy that I could hardly make myself heard. When I finally got them to listen, they thought I was a madwoman."

"What did you say?"

"That Quinton had got it wrong and you were only deeply asleep. No one believed me, and I was getting more and more angry. Oh, but they were very kind, telling me I was distracted by my grief and they were more than willing to spare me from the sad responsibility of seeing you decently taken care of. By that I understood you were to be in for a sea burial."

"How did you stop them?"

"By grabbing you and shaking you like a butter churn and screaming myself hoarse—"

"Wait, I remember that!"

She paused. "You do?"

"Just vaguely. I don't think I was very polite."

"You weren't. You damned my eyes, shrugged me off, and dropped asleep again."

"I'm terribly sorry."

"Don't be, it saved your life. They stopped trying to remove me from the cabin and had Quinton make another examination. He was very surprised and upset by then and anxious to redeem himself, and though I know he couldn't possibly have found a heartbeat any more than before, he said you were indeed alive, but unconscious. What a relief that was to hear. The captain and Mr. George wanted a closer look for themselves, but I'd caught my breath by then and an idea came to me of how to deal with them.

"Since they'd been so sympathetic, it seemed right to make use of it, so I got the lot of them out into the passage and lowered my voice the way Father does when he really wants people to listen. Then I told them in the strictest confidence that you were sadly addicted to laudanum and—"

*"You WHAT?"*

"I *had* to! It was the one thing I could think of that would explain your condition."

I groaned.

"I said you'd brought a supply with you and were taking it to help your seasickness and it was likely you would remain like this for most of the voyage. Afterward, they had quite a different kind of sympathy for me and were perfectly willing to leave you alone, and that was all I really wanted. Perhaps your reputation might suffer a little should there be any gossip—"

"A *little?"*

"But I doubt if anything will come of it; they gave me their word of honor to say nothing, and unlike some people I've known, I'm willing to believe them." She stalked across the room to rummage in a small trunk, drawing from it her fourth handkerchief. She blew her nose several times. "And so passed the first week."

"I'm afraid to ask about the rest."

"Well, happily they weren't as disruptive. Jericho took small meals to your cabin, supposedly for you, then either ate them himself or hid them in the chamber pot to be thrown overboard. He didn't have much of an appetite, nor did I, we were so damned worried. As the days passed and you kept sleeping, we almost got used to it. We reasoned that since you had survived the grave, you were likely to survive this, but it was such a thin hope to cling to with so much time on our hands and nothing to do but wait it out."

"It must have been awful."

"The word, little brother, is *horrid."*

"Ah . . . yes, of course."

She paced up and down and blew her nose again. Jericho was taking his time bringing the tea and brandy.

Two months. There was much about my changed condition that was unnatural, but this one was beyond comprehension. "It must in some way be connected to my difficulty in crossing water. . . ."

She gave me a sour look.

But I continued. "I was so seasick, perhaps it is meant to spare me the constant discomfort."

"Jericho and I had many, many discussions on the subject and came to the same conclusion."

"And you sound as though you're bloody tired of the subject."

"You are most perceptive."

I decided to be quiet.

She stopped pacing. "I do apologize, Jonathan. I shouldn't be so rude to you. You're safe and well and that's what we've been praying for all this time. I'm just so damnably weary."

"With much justification. Is it very late?"

"Not really. You woke up at sunset as usual—or what used to be usual. I'm glad to see your habit is reasserting itself."

"Is this my first night off the ship?"

"Yes."

Right. I was away from water and doubtless the solid ground below had aided my revival. "Uh . . . just how was I debarked?"

"Jericho put you back into your box and locked it up, same as when you were placed aboard. The sailors shifted it to the quay, I hired a cart—"

"Did no one notice I was missing from the other departing passengers?"

"It was too hectic. After those many weeks aboard, all everyone wanted to do was to get away from one another."

"Thank God for that."

I heard steps in the hall, recognized them, and hurried to open the door.

"Thank you, sir," said Jericho. His hands were fully occupied balancing a tray laden with enough tea and edibles for three. With the crisis past, he anticipated a return to a normal appetite. I got out of his way so he could put it down on the room's one table.

"That smells good." Elizabeth came closer. "Are those seedcakes? And eggs? I haven't had one in ages. . . ." She hovered over the table, looking unsure of where to begin.

The smells may have been toothsome to her, but were enough to drive me away. Cooked food of any kind had that effect on me. While she piled the beginnings of a feast on a plate, Jericho poured tea for her, adding a generous drop or two of brandy to the cup.

"All I really want is the tea," she protested, crumbs of seed cake flying from her mouth. "This only spoils the taste."

"You need it, Miss Elizabeth."

"Then so do you. Stop fussing and sit down. I shan't eat another bite until you have some as well."

This was a violation of custom, to be sure, but the three of us had been friends long before growing up had drawn us irretrievably into our respective stations in life. He hesitated a moment, glancing once at the door to be certain it was closed and once at me to be sure it was all right.

"Never argue with a lady," I told him.

He gingerly sat opposite her and suffered her to pour tea for a change.

"I've missed this," she said. "Remember how we used to take away a big parcel of things from the kitchen and eat in the woods, pretending we were pirates hiding from the king's navy?"

I gave a small chuckle. "I remember you insisting on playing Captain Kidd for all your skirts."

"Only because I'd made an eye patch, but I recall giving it to you when I became 'Scarlet Bess, Scourge of the Island' after Mrs. Montagu's gift of those red hair ribbons."

"Yes, and as Captain Kidd you were a much nicer pirate."

She threw a seedcake at me, and I caught it just to annoy her. She laughed instead. "I wish you could join us."

"But he can," said Jericho, garnering questioning looks from us. For an answer, he reached for a second teapot on the tray and held it ready to pour the contents into a waiting cup. He cocked an eye at me.

"What . . . ?" I drew closer.

He tipped the pot. From the spout came forth not tea, but blood.

Elizabeth gasped, eyes wide and frozen.

When the cup was full, he gently replaced the pot. Then he picked up the cup and a saucer and offered them to me.

Hardly aware that I spoke, I whispered a thanks to him. The scent of the blood filled my head. The sight of it . . . the whole room seemed to have vanished; all I saw was the cup and its contents. I reached out, seeing my fingers closing 'round it of their own accord. Then I was drinking.

*My God, it was wonderful.*

Still warm.

I drained it away in one glorious shuddering draught. Not until it was gone did I understand the breadth of my hunger. Muted by my long sleep, it snarled into life and was only slightly appeased by this minute offering.

"Another, sir?"

I could only nod. He poured. I drank.

So very, very wonderful. Eyes shut, I felt the glad heat spreading from my belly out to the tips of my limbs, felt the weight of need melting away, felt the *life* of it infusing every part of me. Each swallow restoring my depleted body with that much more strength.

Jericho cleared his throat. "I'm sorry, miss, I should have said something before . . ." He sounded mortally stricken.

I opened my eyes, abruptly reminded that I was not alone, and looked at Elizabeth. She was positively ashen. Her gaze fixed on the teapot, then Jericho, then me.

"I am most sincerely sorry." Jericho started to get up, but Elizabeth's hand shot out and fastened on his arm.

"No. Don't." For a long moment she did not move. Her breath was short and fast, then she forcibly slowed it.

"Elizabeth?" I hardly knew what to say.

Her head went down, then she gave herself a shake. "It's all right. I was just surprised. You did nothing wrong, Jericho, I'm just being foolish."

"But—"

"Nothing—wrong," she emphasized. She eased her grip on his arm and patted it. "You stay exactly where you are. Give Jonathan some more if he so desires."

"Elizabeth, I think I should—"

"Well, I don't," she snapped. "It's food to you, is it not? Then it's past time that I got used to the idea. For God's sake, some of our field-workers enjoy eating pigs' brains; I suppose I can stand to watch my brother drink some blood, so sit down with us."

Taking my own advice, I chose not to argue with her and obediently joined them.

In silence Jericho gestured inquiringly at the teapot. I cautiously nodded. Elizabeth looked on, saying nothing. She resumed her meal at the same time I did.

"How did you obtain it, Jericho?" she asked in a carefully chosen tone better suited for parlor talk about the weather.

He was understandably reluctant to speak. "Er . . . while the cook was making the tray ready, I excused myself and went down to the stables."

"There's such a quantity, though. I hope the poor beast is all right."

"I drew it off from several horses."

"And just how did you accomplish the task?"

"I—ah—I've had occasion to give aid to Dr. Beldon when he's found it necessary to bleed a patient. It was easy enough to imitate."

"The taste is agreeable to you, is it not?" Her bright attention was now focused on me.

Anything less than an honest answer would insult her intelligence. "Very agreeable," I said, trying not to squirm.

"How fortunate. What a trial your life would be were it not."

"Elizabeth . . ."

"I was only making an observation. You should have seen your face when Jericho gave you that first cup. Like my cat when there's fish in the kitchen."

Jericho choked on his egg. I thumped his back until he waved me away.

We three looked at one another in the ensuing silence. Very heavy it was, too. I wondered just how much of an effect that drop of brandy was having on her.

Then Elizabeth's face twitched, she made a choking sound of her own, and we suddenly burst out laughing.

"If anything, I feel cheated," I said sometime later.

Very much at ease once more, we lounged 'round the table, content to do nothing more than let peaceful digestion take its course.

"Of the time you lost?" asked Elizabeth.

"Yes, certainly. It's like that story Father told us about the calendar change that happened a couple years before we were born. They were trying to correct the reckoning of the days and made it so the second of September was followed by the fourteenth. He said people were in riot, protesting that they'd been robbed of two weeks of their lives."

Jericho, with both his natural and assumed reticence much weakened by the brandy, snickered.

"How absurd of them," she said. "However, that was a change made on paper, not in actual terms of living. Yours has definitely caused you to miss some time from your life."

"So instead of two weeks I may have been robbed of two months. Unfair, I say, most unfair."

"It's just as well that we will be staying in England, since you can expect a similar long sleep whenever you venture out to sea."

I shook my head and shuddered in a comical manner. "No, thank you. Though I might have to make a channel crossing if Nora is still on the Continent. It won't be pleasant, but it's short enough not to put me to sleep."

"Providing you can find a ship to take you across at night."

"I'm sure something can be arranged, but it's all speculation anyway until I can talk to Oliver. Have you sent word to him that we've arrived?"

"Not yet. I wanted to see if you were going to wake up first."

"I'll write him a letter if you'll have it sent tomorrow."

"Why not go over tonight and surprise him?"

"It's been three years and my memory of the city has faded. I may have his new address, but I don't think I could find it alone. You have the innkeeper find a trusty messenger in the morning."

"We could send one tonight—"

"Not without an army to protect him, dear Sister. London is extremely dangerous at night. I don't want either of you ever going out alone after dark. The streets are ruled by thieves, murderers, and worse; even the children here will cut your throat for nothing if it suits their fancy."

Both bore identical expressions of disgust and horror for the realities of life in the world's most civilized city.

"What about yourself, sir?" asked Jericho. "Will you not find your activities restricted as well since you're limited to the hours of night?"

"I suppose so, but I've got that Dublin pistol and the sword cane—and the duelers . . . but remember, I've also got certain physical advantages because of my change. I should be safe enough if I keep my wits on guard and stay away from the worst places. It's not as though we're imprisoned by the scoundrels, y'know. Once we get settled in and introduced we'll have lots of things to do in good company, parties and such. Oliver's a great one for parties."

"So you've often told us," Elizabeth murmured. Her eyes were half-closed.

I rose and pushed my chair under the table, making it clear that our own celebration was concluded. "Bedtime for you, Miss Barrett. You're exhausted."

"But it's much too early yet." She made an effort to straighten herself.

"For me perhaps, but you've had some hard going for a very long time. You deserve to recover from it. Besides, I've more than once boasted to Oliver about your beauty; you don't want to make a liar of me by greeting him with circles under your eyes, do you?"

She looked ready to throw another seedcake at me, but they'd all been eaten.

"Jericho, is there a maid here who can help her get ready for bed?"

"I can get ready myself, thank you very much," she said. "Though I might like to have some hot washing water. And soap. And a drying cloth."

Jericho stood. "I can see to that, miss. There's a likely wench downstairs who's supposed to help the ladies staying here. I'll send her up straightaway."

Faced with two men determined to see to her comfort, Elizabeth offered no more protest and took my arm as I escorted her across the hall to her room. She did not say good night, but did throw her arms around me in a brief, fierce embrace. I returned it, told her that all was well again, and to take as much rest as she needed. She was snuffling a little when she closed the door, but I knew the worst was over for her. Sometimes tears are the best way to ease a sorely tried soul; hers was on the mend. She'd be fine by the time the hot water arrived.

I felt in want of a good wash as well, and Jericho troubled himself to provide for me, unasked. He moved more slowly than usual because of the brandy, but his hand was as steady as ever while scraping my chin clean with the razor.

"Your beard did not grow much during the voyage," he said, wiping soap and bristles on the towel draped over his free arm. "I only had to shave you but once a week. Even then it hardly looked like half a day's growth."

"Good heavens, really?"

"It must have been a very deep sleep to do that."

"Deep, indeed. But never again. Too frightening."

He quietly agreed.

Hardly before I knew it, he'd finished my toilet and assisted my dressing for the evening. More than half the night remained to me, and I'd expressed a desperate need for fresh air despite the perils of the streets. Perhaps in my own mind I'd been at sea for only two nights, but that was still two too many. Though over solid ground at last, I badly wanted to *feel* it under my feet again.

"But this is my heavy cloak," I said as he dropped it over my shoulders.

"It's cold now, Mr. Jonathan, nearly December. The people here say they've had some snow and there's always a chance for more."

"Oh."

He put my hat in place and handed me my cane. It was so like the last time on the ship that I had a mad thought that their whole story was some sort of ugly trick. *Horrid* was indeed the word, this time to describe me for even thinking them capable of such a poor turn. I silently quelled my unworthy doubts and wished him a good evening.

"Please be mindful of the time," he said. "You've an hour more of darkness now, but there's no reason to take risks."

True. If I got caught out at sunrise, a near-stranger again in this huge and hasty city . . . I gave him my solemn promise to take all care, then exacted one from him to get some rest and not wait up.

Then I was downstairs and crossing the muddy courtyard of the inn, my stride long and free after the confines of the ship. The hour was early enough—at least for London—not more than eleven of the clock. Being used to the quiet of the country nearly half a world away, I found the continued noise and bustle of the streets hard to take in. My memories of previous visits had to do with the daytime, though; at night it was as if another, more wretched city emerged from some hidden concavity of the earth to do its business with a luckless world.

That business was of the darker sort, as might be expected. I kept a tight hand on my cane and my head up, alert to everything around me lest some pickpocket try making a profit at my expense. They were bad enough, but almost genteel compared to their wilder cousins, the footpads. Lacking the skill for subtle thievery, such rascals found it easier to simply murder their victims in order to prevent outcry and pursuit.

My pace brisk and eyes wide, I was well aware of the half-human debris skulking in the black shadows between the buildings. I avoided these by walking close to the street, though that put me to the risk of getting spattered by mud and worse from passing carriages and riders. Most of the thoroughfares were marked out by hundreds of white posts that separated the traffic from the pedestrians. No vehicle would dare cross that barrier, so at least I was safe from getting run over.

I could have made myself invisible, soared high, and easily floated over these perils, but that could have meant forsaking this glimpse of the city. Dangers aside, I'd missed London and wanted to get reacquainted with every square inch of it.

With some exceptions, of course. No man who was not drunk or insane would venture into certain streets, but there were myriad others to make up for that questionable lack. As I traveled from one to the next, I marveled anew at the lines of glass-fronted shops with their best wares displayed in an effort to tempt people inside. All were closed now, except for the taverns and coffee shops, but I had no interest in what they had to sell.

Nor was I particularly eager to sample the goods offered by the dozens of whores I encountered along the way. Most were my age or much younger, some of these desperately proclaiming their virginal state was mine to have if I but paid for it. A few were pretty or had put on enough paint and powder to make themselves so, but I had no desire to stop and bargain for their services or by doing so make myself vulnerable to robbery should they be working with a gang of footpads. I brushed past, ignoring them for the more pressing errand I had in mind.

I briskly crossed through one neighborhood after another, some fashionable, some so rank as to be a lost cause, and others so elegant that they seemed to have been birthed in another land altogether. It was to a particular one in this latter category that I eagerly headed.

Though she had moved to Cambridge to live near me while I pursued my studies, Nora Jones often returned to London to enjoy its pleasures. I just as often followed her whenever possible, for those pleasures were doubled, she said, by my company. We'd take her carriage across London Bridge to Vauxhall Gardens and stroll there, listening to the "fairy music" played by an orchestra located underground. Their sweet melodies magically emerged from the foliage by means of an ingenious system of pipes. Sometimes I would take supper in an alcove of the Chinese Pavilion, and later we would content ourselves with a tour of the Grand Walk. She never tired in her admiration of the innumerable glass lamps that made the whole place as bright as day. Other outings might mean taking a box at the theater or opera or going to Vauxhall's more formal rival, Ranelagh, but always would we return to her own beautiful house and in sweet privacy partake of more carnal forms of diversion.

To this house I now sped, holding a faint spark of hope in my heart that she might now be there.

Since my change I'd written Oliver many times asking him to find her, but his last missive to me on his lack of success was months old. There was every chance that she could have returned in the meantime.

Memory and anticipation are a tormenting combination. The familiarity of the streets brought her face and form back to me with the keenness of a new-sharpened knife. I found myself speaking her name under my breath as if it were a prayer, as though she could somehow hear and come to me. Gone was any shred of anger I'd harbored against her for the manner of our parting. It had been a cruel thing to try to make me forget her, crueler still to leave me with no warning or knowledge about the bequest of her blood, but I had no care for that anymore; all I cared about was seeing her again.

My heart sank as soon as I rounded the last corner and clapped eager eyes on the structure.

Nora was very careful to keep her homes in good order, and this one, though not at all fallen to ruin, yet exuded an unmistakable air of nonoccupation. Leaves and mud cluttered the dingy steps to the front door; its paint was in need of renewal. The brass knob and knocker were tarnished. All the windows were fast shuttered and undoubtedly locked from within.

I could hardly have felt worse if the entire building had been a gutted wreckage.

Slowly completing the last few paces to the door, I knocked, knowing it to be a futile gesture, but needing to do something. No one answered, nor did I hear the least sound from within. I looked 'round the street. It was empty for the moment.

Then it melted away to a gray mist and vanished.

I pressed hard against the door, aware of its solidity, but well able to seep past it like fog through a curtain. Grayness again, then shapes and shadows, then muted colors and patterns. I was standing in her foyer and it was very dark.

Only a few glimmers of illumination from the diffuse winter sky got past the shutters, not enough to really see anything. Opening a window would not be an especially good idea; I saw no advantage advertising my presence to her neighbors. They might come over to investigate the intrusion, and then I'd have to answer questions. . . . I could also ask some, perhaps obtaining a clue to her whereabouts, but Oliver had already done that, I remembered.

This much I could see: The furnishings were either gone or draped in dust sheets. No pictures adorned the walls, no books—no candles, either, I discovered. Not until I bumped my way to the kitchen in the very back of the house did I find one, a discarded stump no more than an inch long. Making use of my tinderbox, I got it lighted, but had no stick or dish to place it on. I made do by fixing it to the box with a drop of melted wax.

The kitchen was not as deserted as the rest of the house. Though clean enough, there were probably still crumbs to be had for the rats and mice. I could hear them scuttling unseen inside and along the walls. Leaving them to their foraging, I went back to the central hall and hurried through the door to her bedroom.

Emptiness, both in the room and in my heart. The walls were stripped, the curtains gone, even the bed where I'd so wonderingly lost my virginity was taken. The dust coating the floor was such as to indicate things had been in this deserted state for a very long time.

All the other chambers were echoes of this one. Everything that was important to her—everything that *was* her—was missing, removed to God knows where. Oliver had said she'd left for the Continent, but he'd not mentioned just how thoroughly she had removed herself.

Feeling ten times worse than dejected, I came down again, this time to investigate one last room. Its door was just off the foyer and locked. Untroubled by this barrier, I passed through it; the candle in my hand flickered once, then resumed a steady flame. The tiny light revealed long-unused steps leading down into overwhelming darkness.

Dank air, more scuttlings; filled with the kind of oppression that's born from morbid imaginings, I'd no desire to be here, but also no choice. I had to see one last thing for myself and not give in to childish trepidations about lurking ghosts. It was a dark cellar and nothing more. The place would be no different if I had a company of soldiers along all armed to the teeth. On the other hand, perhaps it would be. Not so quiet. More light.

No key or bolt on this side of the door, so I couldn't open it and provide myself with an easy escape. Considering my ability to disappear at the least provocation, I was only being foolish. I forced myself down to the landing.

Nothing more threatening awaited here than some old boxes and broken furniture. I threaded a path through them, holding the candle high, squinting ineffectually against the gloom, until I found what seemed to be the opposite wall. Seemed. I knew it to be false.

It had been built out from the actual wall as a carefully constructed duplicate, even down to the coloring of the stones and mortar. There was no opening of any kind; she'd not found one to be necessary. To enter, she had but to vanish and pass through as I was now doing.

Within was a silence so complete that I had to fight to retain solidity. My mind had instantly cast itself back to the hideous moments when I'd first awakened to this life and realized I was in a coffin and *buried.* There was even a strong smell of damp earth here the same as there had been then. They'd put me in my best Sunday clothes, drawn the shroud up past my head and tied it off, then nailed me into a box, and lowered it into the weeping ground.

A sudden hard sob rose up, choking me.

I'd missed the service that they'd said, missed the hymns, missed the prayers, the tears, the hollow impact as the first clods were shoveled into the grave. Asleep. I'd been oblivious in the sleep of the dead until the sun was gone and consciousness returned.

There had been nothing to *hear,* nothing but my own screams.

My hand began to shake in remembrance of that damnable terror.

I wanted out, I had to get *out.*

Nothing to *see.* I'd have sold my soul for even this tiny flame.

And then it began to fade, to diminish.

No . . .

Getting smaller . . . dying.

*No* . . . If it went out now I might never return later, not with this fresh fear close atop the old ones.

I made myself watch the little drop of fire in my hand as though I could will it back to strength again.

And most remarkably, it did grow brighter.

Only then did I understand it was not the candle but myself that had faded. Trying to escape from a memory. From a shadow alive only in my mind. A fool's occupation, I impatiently thought.

Not a fool. Only a frightened man, with a perfectly reasonable fear.

*So face it, laddie.* I could almost hear Father's comforting voice in my head, gentle and at the same time so practical and firm.

Would that the laugh I conjured up from within had some of his tone, but I settled for the thin noise that did come out. It struck flat against the close walls of this chamber, but the fear holding me frozen retreated somewhat. Not far, but far enough.

Able to look around now, I was well aware that no one else other than Nora had been here since the workmen had sealed up the cracks. My shoes scraped over dust that had last been disturbed by her passage. There lay the marks of her own slippers and long swirls where her skirts had brushed the floor.

They led to a sizable rectangular shape rising from the floor; like the remaining furnishings above, it was also protected by a dust sheet. I flipped back a portion of it, revealing a plain oaken construction some two feet high and wide and long enough to serve as a bed.

Lifting the lid, I found that the interior of the box was filled right to the top with what appeared to be small pillows made of thick canvas. They were actually bags hauntingly like those I'd had made, and like mine, were heavy with a quantity of earth. *Her* home earth. This was where she rested during the day. Not inside, of course, as there was no room, but above on the closed lid, thus sparing her clothing from the sifting from the bags.

Now I released a sigh, thanking heaven for this happy discovery. As precious and necessary as it was to my daytime rest, I could expect her need for this portion of the grave to be identical to mine. Certainly she would have taken some with her to wherever she now lived, but if she never intended to return to this house, she'd have removed this cache along with the rest of her things.

Unless something had happened to her.

Her goods could have been carried off and sold and this box left behind because no one knew about it. Or if anyone did, they'd placed no value on it, not bothering to knock down the wall to . . .

*Stop* it. Nora was all right. Until and unless I heard anything different, she was all right.

God, but she was the most cautious soul I'd ever met. Had she not been able to safely juggle the attentions of a dozen or more of her courtiers, taking care that none of them should harm her or each other? There had been the one exception with Tony Warburton, but she'd survived his madness well enough. With my own rough experiences as a guide, I knew it would be difficult, if not impossible, for her to come to permanent physical harm. Sunlight was our only real enemy and, of course, fire, but this chamber was ample proof of the measures she'd taken to ensure her safety should such a calamity occur. With its stone walls and a strong roof made of slate, this sanctuary was as fireproof as a . . . a tomb.

*Better not to dwell on that point, Johnny Boy,* I thought with a shiver.

I replaced the lid and pulled the dust sheet back. A note, then, was necessary. I'd prepared one against this possibility and could leave it here where she was sure to find it . . . no . . . perhaps not. Better she directly learn from me the results of our liaison than to infer it by my invasion of this most private place. I'd leave it upstairs, then.

The outside air, for all its stench of coal smoke and night soil, seemed sweet and fresh after my exploration of Nora's empty house. The wind was not too bad, though it whipped my cloak around a bit on some of the street corners. It had a wet bite, promising rain, but not cold enough for sleet. The sky was still clouded over, but very bright to my eyes, for the most part casting a diffuse and shadowless illumination over the city. Those areas still held fast by the darkness I avoided, having already had a glut of it.

Though I'd gotten past my adverse reaction to the sealed room, I was yet a little shaken. The strength of it surprised me, but what else might I have expected? Perhaps this was a fear I needed to face down the same as I'd done at the Captain's Kettle; however, there was absolutely no desire lurking in me to attend to it in the near future, if ever. For the present, I had other things to think about, with finding Nora being the most pressing.

Since most of her near neighbors appeared to have retired for the night, I could not impose myself upon them to ask questions. That would have to wait until early evening tomorrow. Oliver might have the names of some of them or even know them; he had a very wide circle of friends. My chief hope was that none of this would be necessary. If Oliver had located Nora since his last letter, then all would be well. And if not, then I had at least one other person I could consult, though that would be attempted only with the greatest reluctance.

Again, nothing could be done until the morrow. Well, so be it, but what to do until then?

As ever in these early morning hours, I had much time for thought and little choice for anything else. I wanted conversation, but could hardly be so rude as to inflict my restlessness upon Elizabeth or Jericho. The best entertainment I could expect back at the inn was either to pass the time with some sleepy porter or delve into the stack of books I'd brought along for the voyage.

All two months' worth.

I'd have to widen my own circle of acquaintance in this city unless I wanted to spend the greater part of my life reading. Not that the prospect of a good book was so awful—I was quite looking forward to lengthy expeditions at the many booksellers on Paternoster Row and adding to my collection—but the printed word isn't always the best substitute for cheerful companionship.

My current choices for distraction were small. Winter weather would have closed Vauxhall for the season; I wasn't sure about Ranelagh. It did have that magnificent rotunda with the huge fireplace in the center for the comfort of its patrons. But it could only be reached by a ferry ride across the Thames, and I'd had a surfeit of water travel. Other, lesser gardens remained on this side, but they wouldn't be the same without Nora, and it was so very late now.

Perhaps I could go to Covent Garden. No one slept there at night; they had better things to do in their beds. I felt no carnal stirrings right now, but that might change fast enough if the lady was sufficiently alluring. She'd also be much more expensive than sweet Molly Audy. It was only to be expected in so great a city, though I had coin enough and time. To Covent Garden, then, for should pleasing company not be available, then I could at least find amusement observing the antics of others.

Quickening my steps, I headed with certainty in the right direction. Four years may have passed since my last visit, but there are some things one's memory never gives up to time. On many, many occasions Oliver and I had gone there for all manner of entertainments, sometimes trying the theater or more often offering our admiration to any ladies willing to accept it. My particular favorite had been arranging watery trysts at the Turkish baths, though Oliver always maintained that I was running a great risk to my health with such overly frequent bathing. He blamed my recklessness on the rustic influence of the wild lands where I'd been raised. I blamed my own inner preferences.

Before I'd quite gone half a mile toward my goal, I was stopped short by a commotion that literally landed at my feet. About to pass by the windows of a busy tavern, I was forced to jump back on my heels to avoid a large heavy object as it came hurling through one of those windows.

The object proved to be a half-conscious waiter, and the unfortunate man was bleeding from several cuts. The bloodsmell mixed with wine rolled up at me along with his pitiful groans. From inside the tavern came cries of dismay and outrage and drunken laughter, very loud.

A slurred voice bawled out, "Ha, landlord, put him on the reckoning, there's a good chap."

# CHAPTER
# ◄5►

The jest was followed by more laughter. The man at my feet, his forehead and hands gashed, moaned and cursed. Heads appeared in the remains of the window and jeered at him for being a bloody fool. This witticism inspired more drunken hilarity, and one of them threw out the remains in his tankard, splashing both the injured man and myself.

"Damned louts!" I yelled.

"And you're a thrice damned foreigner," came the return, its originator having taken exception to my simpler clothes and lack of a wig.

Two people cautiously emerged from the door of the tavern, hurried toward the fallen waiter, and lifted him up and away. For their trouble, they were pelted with more drink and several tankards, the uproar within growing each time someone struck true. Their targets hastily removed themselves, leaving me in command of the field. Not unexpectedly, I became the next target of abuse. A tankard was launched at me, but I foiled the attack by catching it as easily as I'd caught Elizabeth's seedcake hours before. Unable to resist the temptation, I returned the missile with as much force as was in my power, which was considerable, if I could judge from the resulting crash and yelp.

This only incensed the aggressors, and before I could also remove myself from the area, several men came boiling through the window. Too many, I thought, with vast alarm. I backed away from them, but several more rushed from the tavern door and cut off my escape. But a second passed and they had me encircled, their swords out and leveled.

"Here's a pretty lad who doesn't know his manners. What say you that we give him the favor of a sweat?" Thus spoke their leader, or so I assumed him to be by his size and manner with the others.

His suggestion was met with sniggering approval.

Though I'd never met them before, I knew who they were, having wisely avoided contact with their ilk on my previous visits to the capital. They were called "Mohocks," perhaps after the Indian tribe, and I'd have preferred the company of the latter over these particular savages. They were well dressed as any of the gentry and quite probably were of that class. Their chief form of pleasure came from terrorizing the helpless citizenry with cruel bullying that ranged from passing water in public to throwing acid.

To think I'd been worried about mere footpads. At least they murdered and maimed for a reason; these beauties did it for the sake of the dirty mischief itself.

The assault planned for me identified them as devotees of "the sweat," the purpose being to raise a warm one on their victim. If I was so rude as to present my back to any of them, I would find my rump pierced by that person's sword. Naturally, I'd be forced to jump around, allowing whoever was behind me at any given moment an opportunity to stab in turn, continuing the grim frolic.

I couldn't expect help from the watch; they were often the frightened victims of the Mohocks themselves, nor would the other patrons of the tavern dare interfere. Being skilled in its use, I could draw my own sword for defense, but they were eight to my one. Even the great Cyrano might hesitate at such odds. I'd left my Dublin revolver at the inn, else I might have been able to account for six of the worst.

All this flashed through my brain so quickly I hardly noticed its passage. As the hooting fools closed in to begin their sport, I took the one excellent advantage left to me and vanished.

My sight was nonexistent and my hearing was grossly impaired, but not so much as to deny me the pleasure of eavesdropping on their cries of shock and fear at this startling turn. I sensed their bodies falling back in confusion as they tried to sort out what had happened. They were very drunk, though, which added to my entertainment. One of them suggested in awestruck tones the possibility of a ghost and got only derision for his thought. I attached myself to the one who laughed the loudest.

Elizabeth had long ago informed me that when assuming this state, I produced an area of intense cold in the place where my body had been. By draping an arm—or what should have been an arm—around this fellow in a mock-friendly fashion, I was soon rewarded by his unhappy response, which was a fit of violent shivering. He complained to indifferent ears about the cold, then hurried off. I clung fast until I realized he was returning to the warmth of the tavern, then abandoned him to seek out another to bedevil.

The remaining men were now searching the area, having muzzily concluded that I'd slipped away by means of some conjuring trick. I picked another man at random and followed until he was well separated from the group. Resuming solidity, I tapped him hard upon the shoulder to gain his attention. He spun, roaring out a cry to his friends as soon as he saw me. His sword was up, but I was faster and put the broad handle of my cane to good use by shoving it into his belly. His foul breath washed into my face. He doubled over, then dropped into whatever filth happened to be lying in the street. I hoped it to be of an exceptionally noxious variety.

I also was not there when his friends came stumbling over.

They had much speculation as to how he'd come to be in such a condition, and found it amusing. None seemed to have any sympathy for their comrade's plight, only disgust that he'd let himself be so used. The big leader was for further search, his frustration growing in proportion to the time consumed trying to find me. He became the next one upon whom I lavished my attention.

As with the first, I gave him good cause to start shaking and moaning as though with an ague. Instead of seeking shelter in the tavern, he stubbornly continued to look, filling the street with a string of curses that would give offense to a sailor. I'm no stranger to profane speech, but I had my limits. When I judged him to be well enough separated from the rest, I took solid form again. Though his clothes proclaimed him a gentleman, I had cause to disagree with the possibility and acted accordingly. Without a thought for being fair or unfair, I struck across the backs of his knees with my cane and, while he was down, followed with another sturdy blow to his sword arm.

His bellow of rage was enough to rattle windows in the next street. He dropped his sword, of course. I'd gotten him hard in the thick meat halfway between the shoulder and elbow. He lunged at me with his other arm, but I swatted that away and danced out of his reach, causing him to fall flat on his face. Perhaps I should not have been laughing, as it only increased his fury, but I couldn't help myself. Mud and worse now stained his finery, an excellent return for that splash of beer I'd gotten.

Someone suddenly laid hands upon me from behind, dragging me backward and off balance. I flailed about with my stick, connected sharply once, then had to fight to keep hold of it. The half dozen remaining men were getting in one another's way but still managing to provide me with a difficult time. I vaguely felt some blows landing on my body, and though there was no real pain, it took damned few to send me back to the safety of an incorporeal state.

If my initial disappearance surprised them, this latest act left them first dumbfounded, then panicked. Those who had been holding me now yelled and reeled into others. The effect was like that of the rings spreading out from a stone dropped in a pond; all they wanted was to remove themselves from where I'd been in the center.

Their leader cursed them for cowardly blockheads, but they were having none of it, calling for a return to the tavern with thin, high voices.

That seemed a good scheme to me as well. One more nudge would do it, I thought.

Rising over and behind the leader some three or four yards above the street, I willed myself to become more and more solid. I could just see them as gray figures against a gray world. As they assumed greater clarity, so did I, until I had to halt my progress or drop from my own weight. As it was, I was substantial enough to be firmly affected by the wind and had to fight to hold my place, instinctively waving my arms like a swimmer.

By their aghast expressions, I must have been a truly alarming vision. Two of them shrieked, threw up their hands, and dropped right in their tracks; the rest fell away and fled. As for the leader, just as he began to turn and look up toward the source of the disturbance, I vanished once more to leave behind a mystery that would doubtless confound them for some time to come.

I remained in the area to descend upon the big fellow because I thought he deserved it. Quaking with cold and surly from his thrashing, he demanded an accounting from the two that remained, but did not get much sense from them. They talked of a flying ghost and how I'd swooped upon them breathing fire and screeching like a demon. He called them—correctly—drunken fools and stalked away. Like dogs at heel, they clattered after him, whimpering.

Time to abandon the game. Doubtless they would comfort themselves with more drink and vent their displeasure upon some other person, but I'd had enough of their demeaning company. I surrendered my amorphous form to the wind and drifted away from the asses. When I judged myself well clear, I cautiously came back into the world, the caution derived from a wish to avoid frightening some undeserving soul into hysterics by my sudden appearance from nowhere.

The street was empty of observers, unless I desired to count a pack of mongrel dogs. They were startled, but after a few warning barks, slipped off on their own business. A pity the Mohocks hadn't done the same, though I was feeling strangely cheered about the whole business. I'd bested eight of them, by God; what man wouldn't enjoy the triumph? My sudden boom of laughter echoed off the buildings and set the dogs to barking again. A not too distant voice called for me to keep the peace or face the wrath of the local watchman. An empty enough threat, but I was in a sufficiently genial mood to be forgiving and subside.

I wondered at my good spirits, for except for finding Nora's cache of earth, this had been a singularly fruitless outing. Also, the loss of those two months still disturbed me mightily, though I'd been shy with myself in thinking about it. It seemed to mean a loss of control as well as a loss in time. Of the two, the lack of control over myself was the greater burden, but unpleasant as it had been, my success against these English vandals had altogether lightened it.

Putting my clothes back into order, I made sure my money was intact and the tinderbox and snuff box were still in place. At least my attackers had not been pickpockets, but perhaps that fine talent was well beyond their limited skills. And just as well, for had it been necessary to reclaim my property, I'd no doubt that my return would have been greeted with much adverse excitement.

London life certainly presented its dangers, but this time I was well pleased with the outcome, though my clothes had suffered. I reeked of beer. Jericho would have a few words to say to me, and Elizabeth would probably admonish me against further nocturnal rambles. Excellent thought, that.

The extranormal activity was having its toll, leaving me feeling both shaken and wan. I wondered at this until recalling that I'd been as one dead for the last two months. Father's note concerning Rolly had warned me to gently ease him back into exercise. The practice held true for a horse, then why not for a man? If so, then my venture to Convent Garden might be too much for my health. Tomorrow night, then, if I was up to it.

Feet dragging, I pressed forward, seeking out what streets I'd used earlier, and took myself back to The Three Brewers Inn.

I returned around four of the clock and made a short visit to the stables to look in on Rolly. He was a little worse from his journey, thinner than he should be, but he'd been cared for if I could judge anything from his well-groomed coat. His teeth were fine and there was no sign of thrush on his hooves. He eagerly accepted an extra measure of oats I found for him, finishing it quickly and shoving his nose at me to ask for more. That was a good sign. Tomorrow night I'd see about giving him a stretch for his legs, but only a moderate one. He'd been without saddle or bridle for far too long.

Before leaving I provided myself with a second supper from one of the other animals. Refreshed somewhat, I solved the problem of making a quiet entry to my room by once more employing my talent for walking through doors. Jericho was asleep, but he'd left a candle burning in a bowl of water against my return. On the verge of sputtering itself out, but I rescued it, putting it in a holder on the table.

From my traveling box, I softly removed my cherrywood writing case, opened it, and sorted things. The ink had since dried, but there was plenty of powder to mix more using water from the bowl. For the next hour or more I was busy composing a short letter to Oliver and a much longer one for Father. In it, I detailed my various experiences concerning the crossing—or rather lack thereof—and my joyful gratitude to him for arranging to send Rolly along. As for the cattle, Elizabeth said that five had died and their fresh meat had been gratefully consumed by the passengers and crew. The remaining seven were penned in a field near the inn, awaiting disposition.

I'd been too much occupied with the voyage itself to think on what to do with the beasts upon arrival. Now I speculated it to be an excellent idea to continue the story we'd given the shippers and have the creatures bred to some of the Fonteyn stock. By the time Father arrived in England, I could have a fine herd well started for whatever future he chose to follow. There were plenty of opportunities for his practice of law here in the city, but others might also be made in the country should he want to resume farming again.

My pen flew over quite a number of pages before I'd finished. It would cost more than a few pence to send this letter a-sailing, but no matter. Writing him was almost like talking to him, so I willingly drew out the conversation, closing it with a promise to write again as soon as we were settled with Oliver. I sanded, folded, and sealed it. On a bit of scrap paper I asked Elizabeth if she wanted to include some of her own thoughts before posting swept the packet away to America.

By this time it was very close to dawn and people were well astir below as the inn began to wake. Jericho would probably soon be roused by the disturbance, and I had no desire for a whispered and possibly reproachful inquiry about the state of my clothes. I stripped out of them and into my nightshirt, raised the lid of the traveling box, and whisked inside, quick as a cat. Just as I lowered it, I heard his first waking yawn. Then I was incapable of hearing anything at all.

Not until the day had passed, anyway.

Jericho stood ready as I emerged, armed with my brushed-off coat, clean linen, and polished shoes.

"Good evening," I said, full of cheer for my rest. "Any news from Cousin Oliver?"

"Mr. Marling arrived some time ago. Miss Elizabeth did ask him to come by in an hour more suitable to your habits, but he stated that he couldn't keep himself in check a moment longer. Miss Elizabeth is presently with him in the common room below." There was a note of disapproval in his tone, probably to do with Elizabeth mixing with the rest of the herd. I knew my sister, though; she'd likely insisted on it herself.

"Best not keep them waiting, then. I'm anxious to see him, too. It's been ages."

"There was a strong smell of beer on your coat, Mr. Jonathan," he began.

"Just a stupid accident. I was in the wrong place at the wrong time. Not ruined, I hope?" I looked vaguely at the coat in question, which was draped over a chair.

"I sponged it with vinegar and tried to air it, but the coal dust is so thick in this city, I feared—"

"And quite right. London is a horribly dirty place, but it can't be helped. Have to hurry now, I don't want to keep Oliver waiting more than necessary." On went my stockings, up went my breeches, on went my shoes. Throughout this and without a word, Jericho managed to convey to me his knowledge that I wasn't being entirely forthright and that a reckoning was in store for me at his next opportunity.

Coat in place and ready for the public, I fled downstairs.

Oliver was as I remembered him, but for being a couple years older and even more fashionably dressed than during our Cambridge days. Same wide mouth, same bright blue eyes in a foolish face, and happily retaining a certain genteel boisterousness in his manner. He knew well how to enjoy himself, but not to the point of causing offense to others, allowing the contradiction to exist.

The second he spotted me coming in, he shouted a good, loud view-halloo in greeting and rushed over. There followed a hearty exchange of embraces and considerable slappings on the back with both of us talking at the same time about how pleased we were to see each other again. It took some few minutes before we were able to troop arm in arm back to the table he'd been sharing with Elizabeth, both of us grinning like apes, with the other occupants of the room looking on in amusement.

"Thought you'd never show yourself," he said, resuming his seat across from her. "Which isn't to say that I'm not enjoying Cousin Elizabeth's company, far from it. Every man in the room has been throwing jealous looks my way since we've been here. I can't wait to take her around the town and make all the rest of the lads in our circle envious for my good luck."

Elizabeth, though she lived up to his praise, had the decency to color a bit. "But I've no wish to impose—"

"Oh, rot—that is, never you mind. I'd count it a distinct honor to introduce you. You can't get out of it, anyway. Since that letter your good brother sent arrived I've been able to speak of nothing else but your visit, and now everyone's mad to meet you. Both of you, of course. Jonathan's met most of 'em, but there's a few new faces in the crowd these days—some of 'em are even worth talking to."

"God, but I've missed this," I said with warm sincerity.

"And so have I, Cousin. Remember all those riots at Covent Garden and—er—tha—that is to say we had excellent good fun at the theater there."

Elizabeth understood that he was making an attempt to protect her sensibilities, but took no exception to it. This time. After she got to know him better, he was likely to be in for something of a shock at just how much I'd confided to her about my previous time in England.

"We'll have even more fun now," I promised.

"I should hope so, enjoy everything you can while you're able. How long are you planning to stay, anyway?"

"Elizabeth didn't tell you?"

As an answer, she shook her head and shrugged. "We never got 'round to it."

"Got 'round to what?" he demanded.

"We're coming to live in England," I said. "For good."

His wide mouth dropped fully open. "Well-a-day! But that's splendid news!"

"I'm glad you think so, Cousin. We'll need your help finding a house—"

"Well, you won't get it, my lad. The both of you are most welcome to live with me for as long as you like."

"But you're being much too kind," said Elizabeth.

"But nothing. It will be my pleasure to have the company of my two favorite relatives. It'll be like Cambridge again with us, Jonathan, except for the added delight of your sister's presence to grace the household."

"And Jericho's," I added.

"Yes, I'd heard that you'd brought this paragon of a man with you. Can't wait to meet him. Have you freed him yet?"

"Freed him?"

"We've slaves here, but the business isn't as popular as it is in America. The fashionable thing these days is freeing 'em. Of course, you'll have to pay him a wage, then."

"I think I can afford it." The only reason I'd not done so before was that Mother would have insisted on then and there dismissing Jericho to replace him with an English-bred valet of her choosing. Though she no longer controlled my purse strings, she would have vigorously exercised her right as mistress of her own house, as well as made life a living hell until she'd gotten her way. Far better for everyone if Jericho remained my legal property until circumstances were more in his favor. Then he could himself choose to leave or not. Not that I harbored the least thought that he would ever forsake my service. We got on very well and I knew he enjoyed playing the despot within his sphere of influence, which was not inconsiderable.

My cousin was chattering on about the splendid times we'd soon be having. "It may not make up for being parted from the rest of your family, but we'll do what we can to keep you in good cheer."

"But, Oliver, it won't be just me and Elizabeth; our father is planning to move to England as well."

"The devil you say! Oh, I do beg pardon, Elizabeth. The whole Barrett clan coming back to the homeland? That *is* good news."

"It also means we still need to find a house."

"But I've *lots* of room," he protested.

"Not enough to accommodate your aunt Marie."

At this mention of Mother—for I had written much to him about her over the years—Oliver's unabashed enthusiasm suddenly shriveled. "Oh, dear God."

"More like the wrath of, Coz. You can see why we're eager to find a separate place for us to be than in your home."

"Maybe she could stay at Fonteyn House," he suggested. "My mother will be glad to see her."

Alone against the whole island of England, I thought, but then Aunt Fonteyn and Mother were cut straight from the same cloth. Human nature being what it is, they'd either despise each other or get along like the kindred spirits they were.

"That's fine for Mother," said Elizabeth, "but what about Father? I can't see him living at Fonteyn House. Please forgive me, Oliver, but from some of the things I've heard said about Aunt Fonteyn . . ."

Oliver waved both hands. "No forgiveness is needed, I *do* understand and have no blame for you. God knows I left the place as soon as I was able. She's a terrible woman and no mistake."

"Elizabeth . . ." An idea popped into my head. "We're forgetting what it was like before."

"Before what?"

"Before Mother left Philadelphia to come live with us. She only came because of the danger in the city. There are no damned rebels at Fonteyn House—"

"Only the damned," Oliver muttered darkly.

"—they might go back to that again, with Mother in her own place and Father in his. Certainly they must. I'll lay you fifteen to five she proposes the idea herself once they've landed."

"Good heavens, yes. After two months or more aboard ship, she'd leap at the chance to get away from him."

"I say," said Oliver. "It doesn't exactly sound right, y'know, two children so enthusiastically talking about their parents parting from each other like that. Not that it bothers me, but I just thought I'd raise the point, don't you know."

"But we aren't just anybody's children," she said, with meaning.

"Yes, I see, now. This has to do with the *Fonteyn* blood, which taints us equally. Good thing I've my Marling half and you've the Barrett side to draw sense from, or we'd all be in Bedlam."

That inspired some laughter, but in our hearts we knew he was speaking the grim truth.

"Now what about a bit of food and a lot of drink?" he suggested. "They didn't christen this place in vain, y'know. Let's have a celebration."

Elizabeth confessed that she was in need of supper, then shot a concerned look at me. I winked back, hoping to reassure her. Eyes sharp and lips compressed into a line, she understood my intent all too well. She then removed her gaze entirely. Ah, well, with or without her approval, it couldn't be helped.

"You two may celebrate with my blessing," I said, "but I'm still unsettled from the traveling. Couldn't eat or drink a thing tonight."

"Really?" said Oliver, brows rising high and making lots of furrows. "Perhaps I can prescribe something for you. There's got to be an apothecary nearby and—"

"No, I'm fine in all other respects. I've had this before. It will pass off soon enough."

"But really, you shouldn't let anything go untreated—"

"Oliver . . ." I fixed my eyes on him.

He blinked and went very still.

"You need not concern yourself with my lack of appetite. It doesn't bother you now, and you need not ever notice it in the future. All right?"

"Yes, of course," he answered, but without his usual animation.

I broke my hold. Elizabeth was very still as well, but nodded slightly. She wasn't happy that I could influence people in this manner, but time and again—at least on the topic of my not eating—it prevented a multitude of unanswerable questions.

"What will you have?" I asked Oliver. As I expected, he was absolutely unaware of what had happened.

"Some ham, I think, if that's what smells so good here. Hope they cut it thicker than at Vauxhall. You'll love Vauxhall, Elizabeth, but it won't be open for months and months, but it's worth the wait even if their ham's so thin you can read a paper through it."

He babbled on and she began to smile again. I called a serving lad over and ordered their supper. That task finished, I assumed another, more important one, the whole point of our long journey.

"Oliver, have you any news of Nora Jones?"

By his initial expression I saw that he had none. He glanced once at Elizabeth and shifted as if uncomfortable.

She correctly understood what troubled him. "It's all right, Jonathan's told me everything about his relationship with Miss Jones."

"Oh—uh—has he, now?"

"So you may speak freely before us both."

With that obstacle removed, Oliver squared his shoulders and plunged forward, addressing me with a solemn face. "Sorry, but I've not heard a word on the lady. I've asked all around for you, called on everyone who'd ever known her or had her to a party, but nothing. The Warburtons saw her last and that was just before they left Italy to come home for the summer. She was a frequent visitor with them while they were there; they had quite a high regard for her. Seems she was always very kind to poor Tony, spent time with him and read to him a lot, which went very well with his mother. She said he was often a bit improved afterward."

"But they'd no idea of her whereabouts?"

"Mrs. Warburton had reckoned that Miss Jones would be returning to England as well and was surprised as any when she did not, what with her attachment to Tony and all."

Not the news I'd been hoping for, but not unexpected after my exploration of her empty house. "Have you talked to her neighbors lately?"

"I took supper with the Everitts only last week—they live next door on the left—and they've not had the least sight of her. Even spoke to one of their footmen when I'd learned she'd given him a special vale to keep the lamp in front of her house charged with oil and lighted after dark. He had nothing to say, either."

"Probably because he's been lax in his duty."

"Eh?"

"I went by there last night and found it singularly deserted. I'd have noticed a lighted lamp."

"So that's where you'd got to," said Elizabeth. "Jericho told me that you'd made some sort of expedition, but he couldn't guess as to how your clothes had gotten into such a state."

"Oh, ho," said Oliver. "Having adventures, were you?"

"Misadventures, more like," I answered. "I happened to have gotten splashed with beer by a careless drunkard, that's all. Next time I'll hire a sedan chair if I want to go anywhere. You said Tony was improved?"

Another glance at Elizabeth.

"I'm also acquainted with Mr. Warburton's plight," she assured him.

He gave a self-deprecating shrug and continued. "Yes, much better than before. The Italian holiday must have helped. He still drifts off while you're talking to him, but not as much as before. Sometimes he can even hold a conversation, as long as it's brief and fairly simple. He enjoys a carriage ride when the weather's nice, and going to St. James's Park. His body's healthy enough, but his mind . . . a most curious case. I'm his physician now, you know; I've got a keen interest in nervous disorders, and Tony is my favorite patient."

"I'm happy to know he's in your capable hands," I said. "The poor fellow didn't ask for what happened to him, whatever that was." Though he'd certainly brought it upon himself with his murderous attack on Nora and me. He'd failed only because of Nora's extranatural abilities, but she'd lost control of her temper and that had resulted in his present condition. Nora had regretted her action against him and had no doubt sought to make amends, but where was she now? Why had she ceased to see Tony when he was apparently recovering a little? Was she afraid of that recovery? I couldn't imagine her to be afraid of anything.

"I'm thinking of trying a course of electrics on Tony," Oliver was saying.

"But I thought such things were for parlor games," said Elizabeth.

"There's use and misuse of anything in the scientific arts. Heaven knows the town is full of quacks, but I've seen favorable results on many hopeless cases by the use of electricity. I've almost got his mother talked into it. A few years ago she was eager enough to try earth baths for Tony, but now when I come along with something that may really help, she becomes the soul of caution. I suppose it's because she remembers me during all those times Tony and I dragged ourselves home at dawn drunk as two lords."

Elizabeth wrinkled her nose. "Earth baths?"

"Oh, yes, it's still very popular, supposed to draw out bodily impurities or something like that. I went to one establishment to see for myself, but the moment they found out I was a doctor, they refused me admittance. Claimed that I'd be stealing their secrets. I might well have done so, if they'd been worth the taking. What I did was simply to go to another place offering the service, claim an imposition, and go inside for a treatment."

"Which involves . . . ?"

"They have you in a state of nature and then bury you up to your neck in earth for as long as is necessary for your complaint. It's quite an elaborate operation, I must say. You don't expect to go into an otherwise respectable-looking house to discover several of the rooms looking like a street after the ditch diggers have had their way with it. Imagine whole chambers piled high with ordinary dirt. Thought I'd walked into some kind of a gardener's haven. Wonder what their landlord makes of it, though they probably pay him well. The only evidence I saw of any kind of 'drawing off' was how they drew off money from their patients."

"And you expect your electrics to be superior?"

"Most anything would be, but yes, I have great confidence that a judicious application of electricity in this case would effect a change for the better."

"One can hope and pray so," Elizabeth said. She looked at me.

"Oh, yes, absolutely," I added. I hardly sounded believable in my own ears or to hers since she knew the truth of what had happened to Tony, but Oliver accepted it well enough.

Their food began to arrive and our talk moved on to other subjects.

The evening was highly successful. Elizabeth took to Oliver as if he were a long misplaced brother and not a first cousin she'd never seen before. He had her laughing over his jokes and dozens of amusing stories and gossip of the town, for which I was exceedingly grateful. I hadn't seen her sparkle with such an inner light for so long I'd forgotten what she'd been like before tragedy had crashed into her life.

We kept our revels going as long as we were able, but the wine and excitement had its way with them. The signs of fatigue had set in, and not long after midnight Oliver said he needed a bed more than another bottle of port. Elizabeth also announced her desire to sleep, and we gave her escort upstairs, bidding her good night at her door, then going across to my own room.

Jericho had taken pains to do some cleaning, or to have it done, so despite the intrusion of our baggage into every corner, the chamber was more livable than before. I made introductions and he gravely bowed, assuming the near-royal dignity he wore as easily as his coat. Oliver was highly impressed, which was a relief to me. As we were intending soon to encroach ourselves upon him, it was important that everyone, including the servants, got along with one another. I told Jericho what had been planned, then asked my cousin if there would be a possible problem between his valet and mine.

"Don't see how there can be since I threw the chap out last week," he responded.

"Heavens, what did he do?"

"What didn't he do, you mean. Said he knew how to barber, but he was the ruin of two of my best wigs. Told him to give my favorite yellow velvet coat a brushing, and the fool washed it in vinegar. 'Enough of you,' I said, and out he went. He had a confident manner about him, that's why I took him into service, acted like he knew everything, but he had less brains than a hedgehog."

Jericho nodded sympathetically, his eyes sliding toward mine with one brow rising slightly for but a second.

"Perhaps Jericho can fill his place until you can secure another," I said, obedient to this silent prompting.

"That would be damned kind of you. You don't mind?"

I professed that I did not.

"As matters stand, I could use a bit of help. I've only got the one scullery and a lad who comes in with the coal," he confessed.

"What?"

"Well, it's bloody hard to get good help, though the city's full of servants if you can believe the notices they post. But I'm busy with my calls all day and haven't the time. I was rather hoping your sister would take things in hand and get me set up, if she had no objection."

"I'm sure she won't, but how long have you been without a household?"

"Couldn't really say," he airily evaded. "You know how it is."

No, but I could deduce what had happened. On his own for the first time he'd found it difficult to get fully established and dared not ask for help from his family or any friends. Word would filter back to his mother, and she'd upbraid him for incompetence in addition to all the thousand other things she upbraided him for on a regular basis. In our four years of correspondence, he had also filled quite a lot of paper up on the topic of maternal woes.

"Yes, I know," I said. "But we'll have things sorted out soon enough."

"Excellent!" He dropped into a chair and propped his feet on the table. I followed his example and we grinned at one another for a moment. "God, but I've missed your company, can't wait to go drinking and whoring with you again—that is, if it won't interfere with your search for Miss Jones."

"We'll sort that out, too. Perhaps if you found her bankers . . ."

"Already tried that. She hasn't any."

"No bankers?"

"Went to everyone in this city and Cambridge. No one had ever heard of her. I also tried the agent who had sold her the London house. She'd paid him directly in cash, no bank draft. Then I asked around for her solicitor and finally found him last spring, but he had no knowledge of her whereabouts or how to contact her."

"Good God, but her solicitor must know of all people," I said.

"Apparently not. I did leave a letter with him to forward to her. I also wrote care of the Warburtons, but they said they never got it. The Italian post, if there is such a thing, would likely explain that. I am sorry, I know this must be frightfully important to you."

"You did your best."

"There's good reason to hope that she'll turn up soon enough."

"Indeed?"

"The coming holidays. There's going to be all sorts of fetes going on next month and for the new year, and you know how she enjoyed going to a good party."

I had to laugh. His unabashed optimism was enough to infuse me with a bit of fresh hope as well. "You may be right."

"Now I've a few questions to pose," he said, raising his chin to an imperious height so he might look down his nose.

"Question away, Cousin."

"About Elizabeth, don't you know, and this Norwood business. My mother had gotten a letter from yours saying that Elizabeth had married the fellow and was now Lady Norwood, but she can't be because there is no Lord Norwood, and all I know about it is the chap was killed and in your last letter you told me for God's sake not to ask her about it or refer to it in any way, that it was very complicated and you'd tell me everything once you were here. I am awaiting enlightenment."

"But it's a long tale and you're sleepy."

"I'm only a little drunk; there's a difference."

True. He looked quite awake and expectant. "I hardly know where to begin. . . ." But I eventually determined a place and filled his ears with the whole miserable story. Jericho brought in tea halfway through, but Oliver was so engrossed he never touched it.

"My God," he said when I'd finished. "No wonder you wanted it kept quiet. The scandal would be horrible."

"The facts are horrible enough without worrying about any trivial gossip, but for Elizabeth's sake we decided to be less than truthful about them. What did my mother write to yours?"

"Only that Norwood had died an honorable death fighting the rebels. From her manner I got the impression she wholly believed it."

"Because that's what my mother was told; thank heavens she believed it, too. Only Father, Elizabeth, and of course Jericho know the truth of the matter. And now you."

Sadly, we had found it necessary to maintain the lie before our neighbors at home. Better that Elizabeth be thought of as the widow of a man who had died defending his family and king, than for her to endure the torment of pointing fingers and whispers if the truth came out. As things were, she'd put up with a certain amount of whispered speculation on why she'd discarded her married for her maiden name, but with our relocation to a new home, perhaps the whole thing could be buried and forgotten along with Norwood.

"I shall keep it in the strictest confidence," Oliver vowed.

"She'll appreciate that."

"She won't mind that you've told me?"

"I was instructed to do so by her. She said that since you were the one who discovered the truth of the matter, you were certainly entitled to hear the outcome of the revelation. If not for you, my dear sister would have been hideously murdered by those bastards. We're all very grateful to you."

Oliver flapped his mouth a bit, overwhelmed. "Well," he said. "Well, well. Glad to have been of service." He cleared his throat. "But tell me one more thing . . . about this 'Lady Caroline' . . . you said the shock that she'd been discovered had brought on a fit of apoplexy that left her simpleminded. What has since happened to her?"

What indeed? Just as Nora had shattered Tony Warburton's mind, so had I broken Caroline's. Like Nora, I'd lost control of my anger while influencing another, but unlike her I had no regrets for the frightening results. Father had been hard shaken by this evidence of the darker side of my new abilities, but placed no blame upon me.

"It was more than justified, laddie," he'd said. "Perhaps it's for the best. At least this way we're spared the riot of a hanging." Not too surprisingly, he'd asked me to avoid a repetition of the experience. I'd willingly given him my word on that endeavor.

"She's being cared for by our minister's family," I answered. "His sister runs a house for orphans and foundlings and was persuaded to take Caroline in as well."

Father had been worried that a creature like Caroline might prove a danger to the children, but that had lasted only until he'd seen she was unaware of them. She was unaware of the world, I thought, though she could respond slowly to any direct request. "Stand up, Caroline. . . . Caroline, please sit down. . . . There's your supper, Caroline. Now pick up your fork. . . ."

She passed her days sitting with her hands loose in her lap, her eyes quite empty whether staring out a window, into a fire, or at the ceiling, but I had not a single regret and never would.

"God 'a' mercy," said Oliver, shaking his head. "I suppose it's all just as well. There'd have been the devil to pay otherwise. Is Elizabeth quite recovered? She seemed fine with me, but you never know how deep a wound might run in these matters."

"She's a woman of great strength, though I can tell you that the voyage was hard on her."

"Not a good sailor, is she?"

"Actually, I was the poor sailor. She and Jericho had their hands full with worry about me."

He cocked a suddenly piercing blue eye in my direction. "Usually a person subject to the seasickness comes away looking like a scarecrow. You look fine now, though, better than fine."

"They made me eat for my own good."

He grunted approval. "It'd be a trial to have to get you fattened up first before indulging in the revels to come. What do you say that we ready ourselves for an outing?"

"At this hour?"

"It's not that late. This is London, not the rustic wilds of Long Island."

"I fear I'm still in need of recovery, but you go on if you wish."

He thought about it and shrugged, shaking his head. "Not as much fun when one is by oneself. Also not as safe—but another night?"

"My word on it, Cousin."

With that assurance, he heaved from his chair, suffered to let Jericho relieve him of his coat and shoes, then dropped into bed. His eyelids had been heavy with long-postponed sleep for the last few minutes, and now he finally surrendered to their weight. Soon he was snoring.

"What shall I do about tomorrow?" Jericho asked. "He will be curious that you are not available."

"Tell him I had some business to see to and did not confide the details to you. I'm sure Elizabeth can put him off until sunset."

"Since we are to all live in his house, would it not be fair to let him know about your condition?"

"Entirely fair," I agreed. "I'll sort it out, but not just yet."

Oliver had not been especially fond of or comfortable with Nora. At one time he'd been one of the courtiers who supplied her with the blood she needed to live, but she'd sensed his lack of enthusiasm and had let him go his own way—after first persuading him to forget certain things . . . like the blood drinking. Though she could have influenced him into behavior more to her liking, it would not have been good for him. She preferred her gentlemen to be willing participants, not slaves under duress.

"I'll be taking a walk," I told Jericho.

Without a word, he shook out my heavy cape. It still had a faint smell of the vinegar he'd used to combat the beer stink. "You will be careful tonight, sir." It was more of an order than an inquiry.

"More than careful, as always. Take good care of Oliver, will you? He shouldn't be much trouble, but if he asks for tea, don't waste any time getting it. I think he consumed the landlord's entire supply of port tonight and will be feeling it in the morning."

With any luck, he'd be in such misery as to not notice my absence for many hours. Hard for my poor cousin, but very much easier for me, I thought as Jericho held the door open, allowing me to slip away into another night.

# CHAPTER
# ◄6►

Church steeples rose from the city fogs like ship masts stripped of their crosspieces. Some were tall and thin, others short and thin, and overtopping them all in terms of magnificence was the great dome of St. Paul's. It was this monument in particular that I used as a landmark to guide me toward the one house I sought in the smoky murks below.

Upon leaving the inn, I lost no time in quitting a solid form in order to float high and let the wind carry me over street and rooftop alike. And mansion and hovel did look alike at first, because of the thick air pouring from the city's countless chimneys. The limitation this form put on my vision added to the illusion, and I'd despaired of reaching my goal until spying the dome. With this friendly milepost fixed in my mind, I varied my direction, wafting along at a considerable pace, far faster than I could have accomplished even on horseback. I was free of the confusing turns otherwise necessary to the navigation of London, able to hold a straight line right across the clustered buildings and trees.

Free was I also of the squalor and danger of the streets, though I was not immune to risk. Anyone chancing to look up or peer from his window at the wrong time might see my ghostly form soaring past, but I trusted that the miserable weather would avert such a possibility. What windows I saw were firmly shuttered, and any denizens out at this hour were likely to be in a state of inebriation. Then might the sight of a ghost be explained away as being a bottle-inspired phantasm and easily discounted.

The time and distance passed without incident until I reached a recognizable neighborhood, though I could not be sure from this lofty angle. To be certain, I materialized on the roof of one of the buildings for a good scout around.

The house I wanted was but a hundred yards distant. I felt quite absurdly pleased at this accurate bit of navigation, but did not long indulge myself in congratulation. The coal dust was thick on my perch, and needle sharp sleet had begun to fall in earnest. Fixing my eye on one window from the many overlooking the street, I made myself light and pushed toward it. Upon arrival, the glass panes proved to be only a minor check. Once fully incorporeal I had but to press forward a little more until their cold brittle barrier was behind me, and I floated free in the still air of the room beyond.

By slow degrees I resumed form, alert to the least movement so as to vanish again if necessary. But nothing moved, not even when I was fully solid and listening with all my attention.

Quite a lot came to me—the small shiftings of the structure itself, the hiss and pop of fires in other rooms, tardy servants finishing their final labors for the night—but I discounted all for the sound of soft breathing very close by. Quietly pulling back the window curtains to avail myself of the outside light that allowed me to see so well in an otherwise pitchy night, I discerned a shape huddled beneath the blankets of a large bed. From the size, it was a man, and he was alone. As I softly came closer, I recognized the wan and wasted features of Tony Warburton.

He was older, of course, but I hadn't expected him to have aged quite so much in the last four years. I hoped that it was but a trick of the pale light that grayed his hair and put so many lines on his slack face.

But no matter. I could not allow myself to feel sorry for him, any more than I could have compassion for Caroline. But for the chances of fate both of them would have murdered me and others in their madness. Another kind of madness had visited them, overwhelmed them, left them in the care of others with more kindness of heart than I could summon. Though I sponsored Caroline's care with quarterly bequests of money, I did so only because it was expected of me. I'd have sooner provided for a starving dog in the gutter than succor one of the monsters who had tried to murder Elizabeth.

Enough of that, old lad, I thought. Put away your anger or you'll get nothing done here.

I gently shook Warburton's shoulder, calling his name.

His sleep must have been very light. His eyes opened right away and looked without curiosity at this post-midnight intruder. He gave not the least start or any hint that he might shout for help. That was no small relief. I'd been prepared for a violent reaction and was most grateful that he'd chosen to be quiescent.

"Do you remember me, Tony?" I kept my voice low, putting on the manner I used when calming a restive horse.

He nodded after a moment.

"I have to talk to you."

Without a word he slowly sat up, slipped from his bed, and reached toward the bell cord hanging next to it.

I threw my hand out to catch his. "No, no. Don't do that."

"No tea?" he asked. The expression he wore had a kind of infantile innocence, and on a face as aged as his, it was a terrible thing to see.

"No, thank you," I managed to get out. "Let's just sit down a moment."

He removed himself to a chair before the fireplace and settled in as though nothing at all were amiss. The room must have been cold after the warmth of the bed; I noticed gooseflesh on the bare legs emerging from his nightshirt, but he gave no complaint or sign of discomfort. The fire had been banked for the night; I stirred it up again and added more coal.

"Is that better?" I asked as the heat began to build.

No answer. He wasn't even looking at me. His eyes had wandered elsewhere, as though he were alone.

"Tony?"

"What?" Same flat voice. I recalled how animated he'd once been.

"Do you remember Nora Jones?"

He blinked once. Twice. Nodded.

"Where is she?"

He drew his right hand up to his chest, cradling and rubbing the crooked wrist with his left. It had never healed properly since that awful night of his attack on myself and Nora.

"Nora has come to visit you, has she not?"

His eyes wandered first to the door, then to the window. He had to turn slightly in his chair to see.

"She's visited you in the late hours? Coming through the window?"

A slow nod. He continued to stare at the window and something like hope flickered over his face. "Nora?"

"When was she last here?" I had to repeat this question several times, after first getting his attention.

"Don't know," he said. "A long time."

A subjective judgment, that. God knows what he meant by it. "Was it this week? This month?"

"A long time," he said mournfully. Then his face sharpened and he sat up a little straighter. A spark of his old manner and mind flared in his eyes. "She doesn't love you. She loves me. I'm the one she cares for. No one else."

"Where is she?"

"Only me."

"Where, Tony? Where is she?"

"Me."

I gave up for the moment and paced the room. Should I attempt to influence him? Might it not upset whatever progress Nora had made for his recovery? Would it even work?

One way to find out.

I knelt before him, got his attention, and tried to force my will upon him. We were silent for a time, then he turned away to look at the fire. I might as well have tried to grasp its smoke as influence Tony.

"Is she even in England?" I demanded, not bothering to keep my voice low.

He shrugged.

"But she's been here. Has she been here since your return from Italy?"

Nothing.

"Tony, have you seen her since Italy?"

He blinked several times. "She . . . was ill."

"What do you mean? How was she ill?"

A shrug.

"Tell me!" I held his shoulders and shook him. *"What* illness?"

His head wobbled, but he would or could not answer.

I broke away, flooded with rage and the futile, icy emptiness of worry. Warburton was focused full upon me, his mouth set and hard as though with anger, but none of it reached his eyes. He reached forth with his left hand, and his fingers dragged at my neckcloth. I started to push him away, but he was swift and had the knot open in an instant. Then he pulled the cloth down to reveal my neck. Unresisting now, I let him have a close look. It was the first sign of interest he'd shown in me.

He smiled, twice tapping a spot under my right ear. "There. Told you. She doesn't love you. Only me. Now look you upon the marks of her love." He craned his head from one side to another to show his own bared throat. "See? There and there. You see how she loves. I'm the only one."

His skin was wholly innocent of any mark or scar.

He continued smiling. "The only one. Me."

The smile of a contented and happy man.

A man in love.

* * *

Elizabeth looked up from the household records book she'd been grimacing over to regard me with an equal sobriety. "Is it our new surroundings or is something else plaguing your spirits?"

"You know it's the same trouble as before."

"I was hoping for a change, little brother."

"Sorry I can't accommodate you," I snapped, launching from my chair to stalk from Oliver's parlor.

"Jonathan!"

I stopped just at the door, back to her. *"What?"*

"You are—"

Anticipating her, I snarled, "What? A rude and testy ass?"

"If that's what you think of yourself, then yes. You're going through this torture for nothing, and by that you're putting the rest of us through it as well, which is hardly considerate."

She was entirely right; since my frustrating interview with Warburton last night, I'd been in the foulest of moods. Not even the move from the inn to the comforts of Oliver's big house had lifted my black spirits to any degree. Oliver had noticed my distraction, but had received only a cool rebuff from me when he made inquiry about it. I had spoken to Elizabeth about what I'd done—briefly—so she knew something of the reason for my boorishness. She also wasn't about to excuse it. Unfortunately, I was still held fast in its grip and was perversely loath to escape.

"Then what am I supposed to do? Act as though nothing was wrong?"

"Use the mind God gave you to understand that you can't do anything about it right now. Oliver and all his friends are doing their best. If Miss Jones is in England, they'll find her for you."

And if she was not in England or lying ill and dying or even dead? I turned to thrust these bitter questions at her, but never got that far. One look at Elizabeth's face and the words withered on my tongue. She sat braced in her chair as though for a storm, her expression as grim and guarded as it had ever been in the days following Norwood's death. By that I saw the extent of my selfishness. The hot anger I'd harbored in my heart now seemed to cool and drain away. My fists relaxed into mere hands and I tentatively raised, then dropped them.

"Forgive me. I've been a perfect fool. A block. A clot. A toad."

Her mouth twitched. With amusement perhaps? "I'll not disagree with you. Are you finished?"

"With my penance?"

"With the behavior that led you to it."

"I hope so. But what am I to do?" I repeated, wincing at the childish tone invading my voice. "To wait and wait and wait like this will soon make me as mad as Warburton."

She patiently listened as I poured out my distress for the situation, only occasionally putting forth a question to clarify a point. Most of my mind had focused upon the one truly worrisome aspect of the whole business: that Nora had fallen ill.

"What could it be?" I asked, full knowing that Elizabeth had no more answer than I'd been able to provide for myself.

"Anything," she said unhelpfully. "But when was the last time you were sick?"

"On the crossing, of course."

"And since your change, nothing. Not even a chill after that time you were buried all day in the snow. And remember how everyone in the house was abed with that catarrh last spring? You were the only one who did not suffer from it. Not natural was what poor Dr. Beldon said, so I am inclined to connect your healthful escape to your condition. Perhaps it's because you don't breathe all the time that you are less likely to succumb to the noxious vapors of illness."

"Meaning that Nora could be just as hardy?"

"Yes, and you might also consider that Mr. Warburton may have last seen Nora when they were crossing the Channel. To him she might appear to be very poorly, if her reaction to sea travel is anything like yours. She could have even told him she was ill so as to gracefully quit his company for some reason."

"It's possible. But Tony's mother said she hadn't seen Nora since Italy."

"There is that, but Nora could have wished to cross incognito to avoid questions on her whereabouts during the day. However, we are straying much too far into speculation. All I intended was to provide you with some comforting alternatives to the dark thoughts that have kept you company all this time."

"I do appreciate it, Sister. Truly I do." God, why hadn't I talked to her before like this? Like the anger, my worries and fears were draining away, but not all, alas. A goodly sized block still remained impervious to Elizabeth's logic, though it was of a size I could manage. "I've been such an oaf. I'm very sorry for—"

She waved a hand. "Oh, never mind. Just assure me that you're back to being your own self again. And Oliver, too. The dear fellow thinks you're angry at him for some reason."

"I'd better go make amends. Is he home yet? Where is he?"

"Gone to his consulting room with the day's post."

"Right, I'll just—"

Before I could do more than even take a step in the door's direction, it burst open. Oliver strode in, face flushed and jaw set. He had a somewhat crumpled piece of paper in one nervous hand.

"Oliver, I've been uncommonly rude to you lately and I—"

"Oh, bother that," he said dismissively. "You're allowed to be peevish around here, it's certainly my natural state."

"You are not."

"Well, I am now and with good reason. We're in for it, Cousins," he announced. "Prepare yourselves for the worst."

"What is it? The Bolyns haven't canceled their party, have they?"

We had hardly been in town long enough to know what to do with ourselves, when the festive Bolyn tribe had yesterday sent along our invitation to their annual masqued ball. It had been the one bright point for me in my self-imposed darkness, for it was at one of their past events where I'd first met Nora. I had a pale hope that she might be in attendance at this coming revel.

"No, nothing like that," he answered.

"More war news?" I'd thought we'd left behind the conflicts of that wretched disturbance forever.

"Oh, no, it's much worse." He shook the paper in his hand, which I perceived to be a letter. *"Mother* has sent us a formal summons for an audience at Fonteyn House. We dare not ignore it."

Elizabeth's face fell, and I mirrored her reaction.

"It was an inevitability," he pronounced with a morbid air. "She'll want to look the both of you over and pass judgment down like Grandfather Fonteyn used to do."

"I'm sure we can survive it," said Elizabeth.

"God, but I wish I had your optimism, Coz."

"Is she really that bad?"

Oliver's mobile features gave ample evidence of his struggle to provide an accurate answer. "Yes," he finally concluded, nearly choking.

She looked at me. I nodded a quick and unhappy agreement. "When are we expected?" I asked.

"At two o'clock tomorrow. God, she'll want us to stay for dinner." He was groaning, actually groaning, at the prospect. Not without good cause, though.

I frowned, but for a somewhat different cause. "Ridiculous! I've other business to occupy me then and so do you. We'll have to change the time."

Oliver's mouth flapped. "But we couldn't possibly—"

"Of course we can. You are a most busy physician with many important calls to make that day. I have my own errands, and Elizabeth is only just getting the house organized and requires that time as much as we do to accomplish what's needed. Why should we interrupt ourselves and all our important work to accommodate the whims of one disagreeable person? Good heavens, she didn't even have the courtesy to ask first if we were even free to attend the engagement."

Elizabeth's eyes were a little wide, but she continued to listen, obviously interested to see what other nonsense I could spout. Full in the path of this wave, Oliver closed his mouth. His expression might well have belonged to a damned soul who had unexpectedly been offered an open door out of hell and a fast horse. All he needed was an additional push to get him moving in the right direction.

So I pushed. Lightly, though. "Just send 'round a note to tell her it will have to be six o'clock instead. That way we can avoid the torture of eating with her and make our escape well before supper." Desperation to avoid anything to do with daylight had inspired me mightily.

"But . . ." He crushed the paper a little more. "She'll be very angry. Horribly angry."

"She always is," I said with an airy wave. "What of it?"

"I—I—well, that is—"

"Exactly. It's not as though she can send you to Tyburn for it."

"Well, that is . . . when you put it that way . . ." Oliver arched one brow and squared his shoulders. "I mean, well, damnation, I'm my own man now, aren't I? There's no reason to dance a jig every time she snaps her fingers, is there?"

"Not at all."

He nodded vigorously. "Right, then. I'll just dash off a letter and inform her about when to expect us."

"Excellent idea!"

Behind him, Elizabeth tapped her fingertips together in silent applause for me, breaking off when Oliver wheeled around to get her approval. She folded her hands and offered one of her more radiant smiles, which was enough to send him forth to the task like a knight into battle for his lady.

"Be sure to send it," I added to his departing back.

He stopped short and glanced over his shoulder. "Oh. Well, yes, of course."

"Are you ever going to talk to him about your condition?" Elizabeth asked *sotto voce* after he'd gone.

"When the time and circumstances are right. There's not been much chance for it, y'know."

She snorted, but abandoned the subject, trusting me to address it when I was ready.

* * *

We did not ignore Oliver's advice to prepare for the worst, but beyond fetching out and putting on our best clothes the following evening, there wasn't that much to do. At least Oliver and Elizabeth could bolster themselves with brandy; I was denied that luxury. Oliver found it puzzling, but again, I urged him to pay no attention. Elizabeth, having just heard several ghastly tales about our aunt, had too much to think about to provide her usual frown for this liberty I'd taken upon his will.

We piled into the carriage that had been sent over and rode in heavy silence. I was thinking that standing with bound hands in an open cart surrounded by jeering crowds might have been more appropriate to our dour mood. We arrived at our destination, however, without such fanfare and much too quickly.

Fonteyn House had been designed to impress those who viewed it from without rather than to provide much comfort to those living within, certainly an architectural reflection of the family itself. The rooms were very large, but cold rather than airy, for the windows were few and obscured with curtains to cut the drafts. When I'd first come here four years past, I'd commented to Oliver on the general gloominess of the place, thus learning that nothing much had been changed since Grandfather Fonteyn's death years before, and it was likely to remain so for the life of its present guardian, Elizabeth Therese Fonteyn Marling.

Once inside again after so long an absence, I saw this to be true, for nothing at all had been altered. I rather expected the same might be said for Aunt Fonteyn when the time came for our audience.

An ancient footman with a face more suited to grave digging than domestic service ushered us into the main hall and said that Mrs. Marling would send for us shortly.

"What's this foolishness?" Elizabeth whispered when he'd gone.

"It's meant to be a punishment," said Oliver, "because I was so impertinent as to insist on changing the time of this gathering."

"Then let us confound her and entertain ourselves. Jonathan has told me that you have an excellent knowledge of the paintings here. Would you be so kind as to share it with me?"

Oliver gave her to understand he would heartily enjoy that distraction and, pointing out one dark portrait after another, introduced her to some of our long dead ancestors. I followed along more slowly, hands clasped behind, not much interested in the lecture since I'd heard it before. Oliver paused in his recital when the doors leading to the main parlor were opened, but instead of the footman come to fetch us, some other guests emerged. I thought I recognized a few faces, but no one paid us any mind, intent as they were themselves to leave.

"Hm. More cousins," said Oliver, scowling. "There's Edmond and the fetching Clarinda. Remember her, Jonathan? Very lively company, and just as well, since her husband's such a rotten old stick."

Edmond Fonteyn wasn't that old, but his sour and surly disposition always made him seem so.

"Yes, I do remember. Lively company, indeed," I murmured.

"Really?" asked Elizabeth. "Lively in what way?"

"Oh, er, just lively," he said, shrugging. "Knows all the best fashions, all the dances and games, that sort of thing. How she and Edmond get along is a major mystery, for the man never has time for any frivolity. Mother doesn't like her at all, but Clarinda was married to Mother's favorite brother's son and provided him with an heir. The poor boy got sent away to school several years back; I doubt if he's ever seen his little half brother."

"I'm sorry, Oliver, but you've quite lost me. Who is Edmond?"

"Clarinda's *second* husband. He's a distant Fonteyn cousin. When Clarinda became widowed, he put forth whatever charm he possessed and managed to marry her. It pleased Mother, not so much that Clarinda had a protector, but that her grandnephew had no need to change his name. As for her other grandnephew, Mother largely ignores him, and he's probably well off for it."

The people in the hall were donning cloaks against the cold outside. They should have retained them for protection from the chill of Aunt Fonteyn. One of the more graceful figures looked in our direction. Cousin Clarinda, without a doubt. She nodded to Oliver and Elizabeth, who offered a slight bow in return. Then she cocked her head at me. I somberly bowed in my turn. She smiled ever so slightly, and I hoped that the dimness of our surroundings would prevent anyone noticing the color creeping into my cheeks. Her eyes were on me a moment longer than they should have been, then she abruptly turned back to her husband. Edmond paid her no mind, concentrating instead upon me. There was a strange heat in his dark-eyed glare, and I wondered if he knew. I bowed to him, but got none back. A bad sign, that.

He broke off to hustle Clarinda out the door. A very bad sign. It was likely that he did know, or at least strongly suspected. Perhaps his reaction was the same for all the men who could count themselves to be admirers of his beautiful wife. If so, then I need not feel so alone in the face of his ill regard.

Besides, the cause had been well worth it, I thought, turning my own attention inward to the past, allowing sweet memory to carry me back to a most unforgettable celebration of the winter holidays, specifically, my first Christmas in England.

I was to spend it at Fonteyn House, and despite Oliver's mitigating presence, had come to regard the idea with the same enthusiasm one might reserve for acquiring a blister. I hoped this experience would heal into a simple callous on the memory, but leave no lingering scars. And so I joined with a hundred or more Fonteyns, Marlings, and God knows what other relations as they merged to cluck over the deaths, coo at the births, shake their heads at the marriages, and gape at me, their colonial cousin. It was Aunt Fonteyn's idea to call this annual gathering, it being her opportunity to inflict the torture of her presence equally throughout all the families.

I was promptly cornered by the men and subjected to an interrogation not unlike my last round of university exams. They were most interested in politics and wanted my opinion of the turmoil going on between the Colonies and the Crown. I told them that it was all a damned nuisance and the pack of troublemakers calling themselves the Continental Congress should be arrested for sedition and treason and hanged. Since my heart was in my words, this resulted in much backslapping and a call for drink to toast my very good health.

They also wanted to know all about my home, asking, like my new friends at Cambridge, the same dozen or so questions over and over. A pattern emerged that had first been set by Oliver as they expressed exaggerated concern over Indian attacks and displayed a serious underestimation of the level of civilized comfort we enjoyed. (They were quite astonished to learn of the existence of a theater house in New York and other cities.) Some colonists lived in isolated forts in constant fear of the local natives, or hand-to-mouth in crude huts, but I was not one of them. The only hardship I'd ever suffered up to that point in my life had been Mother's return from Philadelphia.

Unlike Oliver, they weren't very interested in the truth of things when I tried to correct them on a few of their strange misconceptions. Dispelling the romantic illusions of a reluctant audience turned out to be a frustrating and exhausting exercise. It also made me feel miserably homesick for Father, Elizabeth, Jericho, Rapelji, and oh, God, so many others. This stab of loneliness led to another as I wistfully thought of Nora. She was very much elsewhere, having remained behind in Cambridge. Her aunt, Mrs. Poole, had developed a cough and needed close care lest it become worse.

It just wasn't *fair,* I grumbled to myself, then halfheartedly looked for some distraction from my mood.

I made friends with the cousins of my own age easily enough, though several of the girls had been eagerly pushed in my direction by their ambitious mothers. Apparently they'd developed some hopeful ideas of getting closer to my pending share of Grandfather Fonteyn's money by way of an advantageous marriage. I suppose I could have gathered them all together and told them to cease wasting their time, but something as logical and straightforward as that would have offended them, and I knew better than to give offense to such a crowd. Some acting was required, so I was ingratiating, painfully polite, conservative in talk, and careful to comport myself in a dignified manner, for every eye was upon me. Anything out of the ordinary would certainly be passed on to Oliver's mother, and I was very keen to avoid her displeasure at all times.

Actually, I was just keen to avoid her, period.

In pursuit of this aim I finally quit the crowded rooms to seek out some peaceful sanctuary, trying to remember how to get around in her huge house again. My recollection of the initial tour Oliver had given me earlier that year was pretty fogged, no doubt due to the brandy I'd consumed then.

Brandy. What an excellent idea. Just the thing to get me through the rest of the evening. Surely I could bribe one of the servants to produce a full bottle and guide me to some spot well away from the rest of the family and the threat of Aunt Fonteyn in particular. The problem was choosing the right fellow. An error in character judgment on my part and all would be lost before it could ever begin.

There was one man that Oliver trusted; now if I could just come up with his name . . . so many names had been thrust at me today. Given time, and I'd get it. I had a picture in my mind of a rat on a shelf or something like that. Long ago Rapelji had taught me to associate one thing with another as a spur to memory. Rat on a shelf . . . no, rat on a cliff. Radcliff—that was the fellow. Excellent. Relief was at hand.

While busy thinking this through, I found I'd wandered from the busiest rooms into one of the remoter halls and by accident had gained at least half of what I desired. I wasn't exactly alone, though, not if one wished to count the dozen or so family portraits hanging from the walls. I snarled back at some of the poxy faces glowering down at me and gave thanks to God that I took after Father for my looks rather than the Fonteyn men.

At the far end of this hall a door opened. The light here was very poor; the windows were narrow and the day outside dark and dull. I made out the form of a woman as she entered. She paused, spied me, then pulled the door closed behind her. Heavens. Yet another female relative with a daughter, I thought. She floated toward me, her wide skirts rustling and shoes tapping loud upon the length of floor between us.

"Dear Cousin Jonathan," she said with a joy-filled and decidedly predatory smile.

How many daughters did this one have? I struggled to come up with her name. That I was her cousin was no clue—the whole house was positively crawling with cousins of all sorts. It had something to do with wine . . . claret . . . ah . . .

"Cousin Clarinda," I said smoothly and bowed over her hand. Deep in my mind I once again blessed old Rapelji for that very useful little trick. But I was out of practice, since her last name eluded me. She could be a Fonteyn or a Marling. Probably a Fonteyn from that eager hunter's look she wore. She was in her thirties, but graceful as a girl, with a slim figure and a striking face.

She slipped her arm through mine. "The other rooms are so crowded and noisy, don't you think? I had to get away for a breath of air. How nice we should end up in the same place," she concluded brightly, inviting me to agree with her.

"Indeed, ma'am, but I have no desire to intrude upon your meditations. . . ." Before I could begin a gentle disengagement from her, her other hand came around to reinforce her grip. We—or rather she—started to slowly stroll down the hall. I had to walk with her to be polite.

"Nonsense. It is a positive treat that I should have you all to myself for a few minutes. I wanted to tell you how much I enjoyed hearing you speak about your home so far away."

"Oh. Well. Thank you." I'd been unaware that she'd even been present.

"I'm unclear on one thing: Do you call it Long Island or Nassau Island?"

"Both. Many people use both names."

"Is it not confusing?"

"No, we all know what island it is."

"I meant to strangers."

"Hadn't really thought of it, ma'am."

"Please, you must call me Clarinda. As cousins, we need not be so formal, you know." She squeezed my arm. If affection might be measured by such pressure, then she seemed to be *very* fond of me.

"Certainly, Clarinda."

"Oh, I do like the way you say my name. It must be the oratory training you get at the university."

Even when the flattery was all too obvious, I was not immune to it, and her smile was both charming and encouraging. I stood up a little straighter and volunteered an amusing story about an incident at Cambridge having to do with a debate I'd successfully argued. I hadn't quite gotten to the end of it when we ran out of hall. It terminated with a sitting room that had been stripped of seats; the chairs had been moved elsewhere in the house where they were more needed. All that remained was a broad settee too heavy to lift and a few small tables.

"What a pleasant place this is!" Clarinda exclaimed, breaking away from me to look around.

I didn't share her opinion, but nodded to be amiable. The draperies were partly drawn, and the gray light seeping past them was hardly worth mentioning. The fireplace was bare, leaving the chamber chill and damp. A bust of Aristotle—or maybe it was one of the Caesars—smiled warily from the mantel. So far his was the most friendly expression I'd yet seen represented in the art treasures of the house.

"It is just the kind of restful room one needs now and then when things become too pressing," she continued.

"Indeed." Since she was evidently so distracted by the—ah—allure of the place, I concluded she had no interest in hearing the rest of my story. This would be the best time to make my bows and go hunt up Radcliff, but before I could get away she seized my arm again.

"You know, you are not at all what Therese led us to expect."

Good God, what had Aunt Fonteyn been telling them? Despite my good record at Cambridge, she'd not relinquished the preconceptions set up by my mother's letters, so what . . . ?

"I thought you'd be some horrid, hulking rustic, and instead I meet a very handsome and polished young gentleman with the most perfect manners and a dignified bearing."

"Er . . . ah, thank you. You're very kind." She'd maneuvered herself directly in front of me, and I could not help but glance right into her brilliant eyes. It is amazing how much may be read from a single, piercing look. She held me fixed in place until, like the sun breaking through an especially thick cloud, I suddenly divined her intent.

I was at first unbelieving, then doubtful, then shocked, then strangely interested. The interest was abruptly dampened by a worried thought for Nora. What would she think? I wavered and wondered, then considered that she had time and again expressed her repugnance for any kind of jealousy. She seemed to harbor no ill feelings toward those of her courtiers who saw other women. Taking that as an example that the principles she asked of us also applied to herself, then I was certainly free to do as I liked. On the other hand, I—we—were special to each other. In our time together she'd not slept with another man, nor I with another woman, though I had, admittedly, a singular lack of opportunity for encountering women within the sheltering walls of the university.

And here was a definite opportunity. And I was interested. Perhaps I should at least hear the lady out before refusing.

Then it struck me that such a liaison, if discovered by Aunt Fonteyn—

especially if discovered while being consummated in her own house—might have the most disastrous of consequences. The details of such a scene eluded me, but they would be awful, of that I was sure. My blood went cold remembering the disgusting accusation Mother had made against myself and Elizabeth, of which we were entirely innocent. How much worse would it be with Aunt Fonteyn—particularly with a decided lack of innocence in this case? No. No amount of transitory pleasure could possibly offset *that* storm.

All this and more passed through my mind in less time than it took me to blink. I steeled myself to graciously turn down the lady's generous offer.

Truly, I *did.*

Clarinda, however, was not ready to hear my decision, much less accept it. As I stumbled to find the right words to say, she placed herself closer to me. I had an unimpeded and unsettling view of just how low the bodice of her gown went and just how much filled it.

"Oh, dear," I gulped. My blood ceased to be so cold. Just the opposite, in fact.

"Oh, yes, my dear," she murmured. Without looking down to guide it, her other hand unerringly pounced upon a very vulnerable and now most sensitive portion of my person. I jumped and stifled an involuntary yelp at this action. As if to gainsay me, the hand's quarry began to traitorously rise and swell to full life in my breeches.

"I . . . ah . . . think, that is . . ." *Oh, dear. Again.*

"What *do* you think, dear Cousin Jonathan?" She was all but purring.

"I think . . . it would be best to shut the door. Don't you?"

As a romantic dalliance it was brief in duration, but compensatingly intense in terms of mutual satisfaction. The fact that Clarinda was already more than halfway to her climax before I'd even lifted her skirts had much to do with it. When a woman is that eager it doesn't take long for a lively man to catch up; something I was only too happy to do for this enchanting lady once the door was securely shut. Though the danger of being caught was a contributing factor to our speed, it added a strange enhancement to the intensity of our pleasure.

I was puffing like a runner when we'd finished and, after planting a last grateful kiss on her mouth, gently let myself drop away to the floor to catch my breath. Clarinda was content to recline back on the settee with her legs still invitingly extended over its edge. From my present angle it was all I could see of her, as the upper portion of her body was hidden by what seemed to be an infinite number of petticoats and the fortunately flexible pannier that supported them. It was an absorbing view: white flesh, flushed pink by activity and friction and embellished with silk ruffles all around like a frivolous frame on a painting. I found the study of her upper thighs as they emerged from her stockings to be very fascinating, the fascination growing the farther north I went.

Now that I had the leisure for study, I could not help but make comparisons between Clarinda and Nora. Of their most intimate place, I noticed that Clarinda had more hair and that it was of a lighter color, nearly blond, causing me to speculate on the real color that lay under her wig. Her skin was equally soft, but with a slightly different texture under my hand.

The view—and my exploring hand—was suddenly engulfed by a tumble of underclothes as she straightened up.

"Goodness, but you are a restive young man," she said with a glowing smile.

My hand was still up her dress and I gave her leg a tender squeeze by way of reply.

"I'm not your first, am I?" She had a trace of disappointment in her expression.

It seemed wise to be honest with this woman. "No, dear lady. But if you had been, no man could have asked for or received a better initiation."

"Oh, I *do* like your manners." She leaned forward to brush her lips lightly on my temple. "Whoever your teacher was, she has my admiration. She must be a remarkable woman. You are doubtless one of the most considerate lads to have ridden me in many a year."

I writhed happily under her praise. A pity I would not be passing her compliments on to Nora, but I instinctively knew she might not appreciate them. "Would I be too impertinent if I asked you if . . ."

"If I always go around seducing young men? Yes, that is impertinent, but no more so than I have been with you just now. I hope you will give me pardon."

"With all my heart, dear lady. But as for my question—"

"Not always. Only when I see a handsome fellow who stirs up my . . . my curiosity, then I can't resist the temptation of finding out what he's like. In all things," she added, to clarify her meaning.

"I trust the answer you found was fulfilling?"

She made a catlike growl in her throat that I interpreted as contentment. "May I know the name of this lady to whom I also owe my thanks?"

"I gave her my word I would always be discreet. I am honor-bound to that pledge."

"You gentlemen and your honor." She sighed, mocking me a little.

"But I do see that it is a wise practice. May I ask your pledge to apply to ourselves as well?"

Whatever other differences lay between Nora and Clarinda, their desire for discretion was identical. I wondered if the trait was true for all women. It seemed likely. I readily gave my promise, easing the lady's mind and at the same time providing me with a very legitimate reason to refrain from confiding this episode to Nora.

Clarinda produced a handkerchief and dabbed at my face where some of her powder and paint had rubbed off, then offered it to me for any other cleaning I required. In a flash of interested insight, I noticed that it was a plain bit of linen with no initials. I felt a surge of amused admiration for her forethought as I pocketed her favor.

"May I see you again, soon, dear Cousin?" I asked hopefully. I'd regained my feet and was buttoning my breeches.

She smoothed out the fall of her skirts. "Not soon, perhaps. We live here in London, you see, such a long way from Cambridge."

"How disappointing, but should I get a holiday . . ."

"Then we must certainly arrange for a visit. Of course we can't meet at my home. My husband's there and the servants will gossip."

"Husband?" I squeaked.

"I would rather he not know. I'm sure we can work something out when the time comes."

"Yes, I'm sure we can," I said vaguely, swatting away any dust lingering on my knees and seat.

*Husband,* I thought with a flash of panic. *I've just committed adultery.*

It had happened so easily, so quickly. Surely the breaking of one of the Ten Commandments should have been accompanied by some kind of thunderclap in one's soul. There had been no hint. Nothing. I felt betrayed. Would God hold it against me that I'd done it in ignorance? Possibly not. My knowledge of biblical laws on that point was hazy, but He certainly would if, with this in mind, I repeated the sin.

Clarinda remained serenely unaware of my wave of guilt. I was one of many to her, a happy memory. We parted company on friendly terms, albeit separately. I remained in that cold sitting room for a long time, walking in slow circles, the pacing an outer reflection of inner musings.

Why was I so bothered? Father had his mistress. I'd heard the other lads talking freely about their women, and some of them had mistresses who were married. It was such a common practice as to seem normal and right. But what was right for them was wrong for me in a way I could not yet define. Being with Nora was one thing; neither of us was married. But being with Clarinda—or with any other woman who belonged to another man—was quite something else. It troubled me. Deeply.

As well as betrayed, I also felt rather stupid that I could initially assume her to have children, but fail to consider they might also have a father.

There and then I made a private vow that no matter how pleasurably provoked by a woman, I would first determine whether she was free or not before engaging in any activity that might cause . . . problems later. For either of us. For any of us, I thought, including the husbands. I had no wish to encounter this odd, creeping emptiness again. Clarinda and others might be able to live with it; I could not.

My God, but life was full of surprises.

I'd been very young then and, in matters of the heart and body as well as the mysterious ways of women, still somewhat inexperienced. But after the passage of four very full years, the negative memories of that day had long faded, though I had kept my promise about not bedding married women. Even dear Clarinda. At subsequent gatherings, I avoided being alone with her, but made an effort to be exceedingly polite about it so as not to hurt her feelings. I now could look back upon the interlude and smile with a surge of genuine affection for my sweet, passionate cousin.

Cousin by marriage only, I reminded myself. All the better that she was free of the taint of Fonteyn blood, if not the companionship. I wondered what had ever possessed her to marry again into the same family. Money, perhaps. There was a vague recollection in me that Cousin Edmond had a good income from somewhere. Clarinda might want a share of it to add to her deceased husband's bequest, thus maintaining her preference for the finer comforts of living and assuring a good future for her small brood.

"What amuses you, little brother?" Elizabeth seemed to have suddenly appeared before me, unknowingly interposing herself between me and the past. I did my best not to jump.

"The long face on that one there," I said smoothly, pointing to a handy portrait behind her. "It may surprise you to hear that once when a hunt was called, his grooms put a bit in his mouth and saddled him for the chase."

"Few things would surprise me about this family," she said, narrowing her eyes against my jest. "I suppose once the bit was in, he could not protest further indignities, the poor fellow."

"Far from it," put in Oliver, joining the game. "He was always the first one away over the fences. Might have even done a bit of racing in his time except he'd had the bad luck to break a leg and was shot. Cousin Bucephalaus they all called him."

This was delivered with a perfectly sober demeanor, and for an instant

Elizabeth gaped at him in near-belief before her own good sense prevailed, and she began to laugh. Oliver pretended to ignore her reaction and was drawing her attention to another painting, doubtless with a similar eccentric history attached, when the gravedigger footman approached and bowed.

"Mrs. Marling is ready to receive you, sir," he announced. I couldn't help but think of a judge intoning a death sentence upon the guilty.

"Well," Oliver growled, his cheerful manner quite vanished. "Let's get it over with."

# CHAPTER 7

We entered and marched slowly down the length of a room that was really much too large for the purpose of an intimate reception. Aunt Fonteyn must have found the great distance between herself and the door to be a useful means of studying her prey as it approached.

The room itself had but one window away to the left. Candles were needed in the daytime to illuminate the more isolated corners. Many candles had been lighted, but these were concentrated at the far end. The only other light came from a massive fireplace large enough to burn a tree trunk. Indeed, a great pile of wood was flaming away there, filling the room with suffocating heat.

Above the mantel, bracketed by candelabra, was the full-length life-size portrait of Grandfather Fonteyn, the wicked old devil who started it all as far as my view of the world went. If not for his influence on Mother, then Mother's influence on me, I mightn't be standing here now, braced against whatever onslaught his eldest daughter had readied. On the other hand, without it I might never have met Nora Jones or survived past perils had I been spared so strange a progenitor. Still, it was no small amount of hardy resolution on my part that kept me from thumbing my nose at his fearsome, frowning image on the wall.

The stories that had come to me about him varied. According to Mother and Aunt Fonteyn, he was a stern but fair saint possessing a bottomless wisdom, who was never wrong in his judgments. According to Father, he was an autocrat of the worst sort, subject to impassioned fits bordering on madness whenever anyone crossed him. Having much respect for my father's opinion, I was wholly inclined to believe his version. Certainly the evidence was there to see, since Grandfather's bad temperament had been passed down to his daughters as surely as one passed on hair and eye color.

Enthroned in a big chair below and to one side of the portrait was Aunt Fonteyn, and seeing her again after such a lengthy absence was anything but a pleasure. For a wild second I thought that it was Mother, for the woman scowling at us as we came in had the same posture and even wore a dress in a material identical to one of Mother's favorite gowns. The fashioning was different, though, leading me to recall that about a year ago Aunt Fonteyn had sent her younger sister a bolt of such fabric as a gift.

Her hair was also different, being in a much higher and more elaborate style, but like Mother, she grasped a carved ivory scratching stick in one hand to use as needed, whether to poke at irritations on her long-buried scalp or to emphasize a point when speaking.

She had not aged noticeably, though it was hard to tell under the many layers of bone-white powder caking her face. The frown lines around her mouth were a bit deeper; the laugh lines around her eyes were nonexistent. We each received a cold blast from those frosty orbs before they settled expectantly on Oliver and he formally greeted her with a deep bow. I copied him, and Elizabeth curtsied. Such gestures were better suited for a royal audience, but Aunt Fonteyn was, for all purposes, our royalty. By means of her father's will she controlled the family money, the great house, and in turn the rest of the clan. She never let anyone forget it.

"And it's about time you got here," she berated him, her voice matching her cold eyes. "When I invite you to this house, boy, you are to come at the time specified and without excuses. Do you understand me?"

"Yes, Mother," he said meekly. His own gaze was fixed in its usual spot, a place just beyond her left ear.

"You may think you're well occupied wasting time getting drunk and worse with your so-called friends, but I'll not be mocked in this way ever again."

*And what way would you care to be mocked, madam?* I thought irreverently. Awful as she was, I'd met worse people than Aunt Fonteyn. The realization both surprised and gratified me.

"What are you finding so amusing, Jonathan Fonteyn?" she demanded.

"Nothing, ma'am. My nose tickles." To demonstrate the truth of this, I rubbed it with the knuckle of one finger. Not the best substitute for thumbing, but better than nothing. I stole a glance at Elizabeth, who raised one warning eyebrow. She'd somehow divined the irreverence lurking in me and, being prudent, wanted it curbed.

Aunt Fonteyn noticed the interplay. "You. Elizabeth Antoinette."

Elizabeth, though she despised her middle name as much as I did my own, remained calm and offered another cautious curtsy. "Madam. It is a pleasure and honor to meet you at long last."

Had we been alone, how I might have teased my sister for lying through her teeth with such ease.

Aunt Fonteyn looked Elizabeth up and down for a long moment, obviously disapproving of what she saw. "Why aren't you in mourning, girl?"

The question struck Elizabeth hard enough to rock her. She blinked and her color deepened. "Because I choose not to wear it."

"You *choose?* I've never heard such nonsense. Who put that idea into your head?"

"I did myself. My husband is dead, his name and his body are buried, and with them my marriage. It is a painful memory and I am doing my best to forget it." True enough.

"Ridiculous. Custom demands that you be in mourning for at least a year. You are in a civilized country now, and you will maintain civilized manners. I'll not have it said that my niece denied respect to the memory of her husband. It is especially important that you set an example to others because of your raised status."

"Status?" This one thoroughly puzzled Elizabeth.

"Your being Lady Norwood of course."

"I have forsaken that name for the one I was born with."

"Which is of no value whatever in genteel society. You are Lady Norwood until such time as you might be allowed to remarry."

I felt the mute rage rolling off Elizabeth like a wave of heat from an oven. "I am Miss Barrett again until such time as *I* say otherwise," she stated, carefully grinding out the words.

Aunt Fonteyn was obviously not used to such face to face rebellion. Her jaw tightened to the point of setting her whole body aquiver. Her grip on the scratching stick was so tight it looked ready to break in her hand.

Elizabeth read the signs correctly and added, "My mother was in complete agreement with me on this, Aunt Fonteyn. She knows the depth of pain I have suffered and deemed it best for me to put it all behind me. So it is with her full approval and blessing that I have returned to the use of my maiden name."

And very true that was, too. It was one of the few times Elizabeth had applauded my talent for influencing others.

Now it was Aunt Fonteyn's turn to look as if she'd been slapped. A mighty struggle must have been going on behind all that face paint, to judge by the twitchings beneath its surface. We did our best to remain unmoved ourselves, waiting with keen interest for her reply.

"Very well," she finally puffed out. "If Marie thinks it is for the best, then I shall respect her wishes."

"Thank you, Aunt."

"But it's not a good thing for a female to display any stubbornness in her nature. I expect you to cease such blunt behavior, for you are only hurting yourself. You are forgiven on this occasion. I'm keeping in mind that you are probably still unsettled from your sea voyage."

Oliver and I held our breath, but Elizabeth simply murmured a quiet thank you. She had, after all, won the round and could afford to be generous.

"It took you long enough to get here," Aunt Fonteyn added, addressing me again. I hardly need mention that she made it into an accusation.

"We came as soon as we could, ma'am," I said. "The captain of the ship assured us that we had a very swift crossing." Actually, Elizabeth and Jericho had gotten the assurance, but it was easy enough to repeat what they'd told me.

"I was referring to the fact that you wasted time stopping over at that disreputable inn when you should have sent for my coach to bring you straight from the docks to Fonteyn House."

As there seemed no advantage for any of us to offer comment to her on the subject, we remained silent.

"It was a sinful waste of money and time, and there will be no more of it, y'hear?"

"Yes, ma'am."

"And as for your present arrangements—I suppose Oliver talked you into staying at his house?"

"We accepted his invitation, yes, ma'am. And very comfortable it is, too. Your son is a most generous and gracious host."

"Well, that's fine for you two, but Elizabeth Antoinette will be moving into Fonteyn House. She will remain here tonight. When the coach takes you both back, you will see to it that her things are loaded in and—"

"I will not!" Elizabeth cried.

Aunt Fonteyn turned a calculating eye upon her niece. "Did you say something, girl?"

"I prefer to remain where I am," she stated, lifting her chin.

"Do you, now? Well, I do not, and you can't tell me that you have your mother's support on this one, because I know you don't."

"Nevertheless—"

"You will not argue with me on this, Elizabeth Antoinette. It isn't seemly for an unmarried girl to be living with two unmarried men, any idiot knows that."

"There is nothing unseemly about it," Elizabeth protested.

"You have no chaperon, girl, that's what's—"

"Oliver is my first cousin and Jonathan my own brother—what better chaperons and protectors could I want?"

Aunt Fonteyn abruptly fell into a silence so cold and so hard that Elizabeth instantly halted any further comment she might have put in. Aunt Fonteyn was exuding a near-palpable air of triumph.

Oh, dear God, not *that* again, I thought, groaning inside.

"And so it comes out at last, does it?" she said, and there was a truly evil glint in her small, hate-filled eyes.

Elizabeth must have also seen what was coming. Her whole body stiffened, and she glanced once at me.

Our aunt leaped on it. "I see that it does. See how she blushes for her shame!"

Blushing with anger would have been the correct interpretation of Elizabeth's high color.

Aunt Fonteyn went on, clearly enjoying herself. "You dirty, shameless slut! Did you think I would tolerate such blatant sin under my own nose?"

Shaken beyond words, Elizabeth could do nothing more than tremble. I feared her temper might overtake her as it had once done with Mother and that a physical attack was in the offing. An interruption was desperately needed.

"Tolerate what, Aunt Fonteyn?" I asked in a lazy voice, all bland innocence.

Her stare whipped over to me, but I stared back, quite impervious to any threat this one dungheaded woman might hold. I could feel Oliver's eyes hard on me as well. No doubt he was trying to fathom what had happened to set her off.

"How *dare* you raise such an impertinent face to me, you filthy fornicator!" she screeched. "You know very well what I'm talking about. Your mother has long written to me about your unnatural liaison, and since she cannot get your blind father to end what's been going on, she's begged me to put a stop to it."

Oliver choked with shock as the dawn started to break. "What—what are you saying?"

I readily answered. "It seems that my mother, who suffers from a singularly unstable mind, has the disgusting delusion that Elizabeth and I are engaged in incestuous relation with one another, and that your mother is imbecile enough to believe her lunatic ravings."

"Oh, my God!" That was as much as he could get out before Aunt Fonteyn's shriek of outrage burst forth.

It was more than sufficient to rattle the windows in the next room; it certainly brought the footman running. The parlor door was thrown open, and he and some other servants crowded through. Their swift appearance gave me to understand that they'd been listening all along. Excellent. I'd hand them something worth the hearing.

If I got the chance. Aunt Fonteyn was doing some considerable raving herself, calling me a number of names that a lady in her position should not have even known, much less spoken. She'd risen from her chair and was pointing at me with her ivory stick in such a way as to make me thankful it was only a stick and not a dagger. I held up against this tide of ill-feeling well enough, but Oliver had gone quite pasty. It was difficult to tell whether he was more upset by my revelation or by seeing his mother in such an extreme choleric state. Elizabeth had backed far out of the way and watched me with openmouthed astonishment, but by God I'd had enough of this sly and festering falsehood. It was past time to put an end to it.

When Aunt Fonteyn ran out of breath, I seized the opening and continued, doing a fair imitation of a man bored with the topic. "Of course you're aware that my poor mother has been under a doctor's direct care for several years now. She's often deluded by the heavy influence of the laudanum she takes, and so is hardly responsible for herself or anything she says."

*"Be quiet!"* roared my aunt.

"I only speak the truth," I said, full of offended dignity.

"You! All of you out of here!" she bellowed at the servants. It was quite amusing to watch their scrambling escape into the hall. The door slammed shut, but I had every confidence that their ears were glued fast to the cracks and keyhole.

"You know, Oliver," I went on in a carrying tone, "this display convinces me that your poor mother may also suffer from the same complaint as mine. She seems quite out of control."

Oliver could not yet speak, but Aunt Fonteyn did. Her voice was low and murderous.

"You vicious young *bastard!* Lie all you wish, slander how you like, but I know the truth of things. You and your sister are an unnatural pair and will rot in hell for what you've done—"

"Which is exactly nothing, woman!" I shouted, patience finally broken.

"I know not where Mother got such a ludicrous idea, but surely you're too intelligent to believe her nonsense."

She wasn't listening. "I opened my hearth to you, and here is my repayment. I'll have the both of you arrested and put in the stocks for—"

"Oh, yes, by all means do that. I'm sure the scandal will make a most favorable impression on all your many friends."

And there it was, my killing thrust right into the great weakness she shared with Mother. I had the supreme satisfaction of seeing Aunt Fonteyn snap that foul mouth of hers shut, tighter than any clam. Though it was impossible to judge her color under the paint, it must have been very dark indeed. Had I pushed her too far? Her eyes looked quite mad.

Then, even as I watched, the madness changed to icy hatred with an alacrity that eerily reminded me of Mother's alarming changes of mood.

"You," she whispered in a voice that raised my hackles, "are no longer a part of this family. You are *dead,* the two of you. And like the dead you forfeit all right to your inheritance. You can pander in the street for your bread and your whore-sister with you. I'll see you both cast out."

"No." If she was merely icy, then I was glacial. "You. Will. Not."

From some faraway place I heard Elizabeth calling my name.

I had no mind for her, only for the hideous woman before me. I dared not spare the attention. All was in balance within me between anger and sense. Lean too far in the wrong direction . . .

Aunt Fonteyn blinked rapidly several times. She seemed short of breath or had somehow forgotten to breathe.

"You will not," I carefully repeated. "You will do nothing. The matter ends here and now. No more will be said of it. No changes of any kind will be made. No more accusations will be raised. Do you understand?"

She said nothing, but I saw the answer I wanted. I also saw, once I released her from my influence, a flat look in her eyes that I should have expected, but gave me a wrenching turn all the same.

She was afraid. Of me.

But a moment passed and she'd recovered herself and concealed it. Too late. It had been revealed. She could never take it back again. Not that I was proud of having engendered the feeling in her, but I couldn't help but think that she was more than deserving, the hateful old crow.

"Jonathan." Elizabeth was at my side, touching my arm. She'd seen and known exactly what I'd just done.

"It's all right. It's all over. We're leaving."

Aunt Fonteyn managed one last rally. "Never to return as long as I live."

As a threat it was pathetically wanting in power. If I ever saw the inside of this dungeon and its guardian dragon again, it would be too soon.

"Oliver," she snarled. "Take these two creatures out of this house. Immediately. They are no longer a part of this family."

Oliver made no move to obey. He was pale as fog and looked about as substantial, but he did not so much as shift one shoe.

"Do it, boy! Are you deaf?"

"No," he said, and there was enough force in his reply to suffice as an answer for both questions.

She turned full upon him and in an instant absorbed the fact that the mutiny had spread. "Do you know what you say?"

"Yes, and it's past time that I said it. So far past time that there's too much inside for me to get it all out. You horrify me and make me ashamed I'm your son, but no more. I'm going with them and I won't be back."

He started for the door.

"Oliver!"

And kept going.

*"Oliver!"* But there was no hint of anguish or regret in her, only fury.

Elizabeth and I hurried to follow him. I closed the door behind us, shutting Aunt Fonteyn off in mid-bellow.

The servants who had been listening were now in the process of vanishing, except for the footman who had let us in. I told him to fetch our things, which he did, moving with gratifying speed.

"Well, that's torn it," Oliver gasped. He was shivering from head to toe.

"You can apologize when she's in a cooler mind," I said. "There's no reason for you to cut yourself off just because I—"

"Apologize? I'll be damned before I apologize to that night hag. My God, the years and years I've put up with . . . Well, it's beyond further endurance and no more of it for me." He shrugged into his cloak, arms jerking every which way.

"Then I'm glad for you," said Elizabeth, pulling the hood of her wrap over her head. "Let's get away from this cursed pile of old bones."

"Yes!" he agreed, his voice rather too high and strained.

The footman rushed ahead and threw wide the big double doors of the main entrance. Elizabeth moved past me into the winter night, then Oliver, both of them in a great hurry, for which I could not blame them. Glancing back at the parlor door, I almost expected Aunt Fonteyn to emerge and renew her attack, but happily she did not.

The footman trotted off to one side to fetch the coach, for which action he was probably placing himself at risk. I would not put it past my aunt to dismiss him and the driver for assisting us, sell the horses to the knackers, then burn the coach.

I began to tremble. Reaction, of course.

"Are you all right?" Elizabeth.

"What have I done?"

"Exactly what was needed and in exactly the right way."

"But if I was wrong—"

"That's impossible or I would not feel so well off."

"Nor I," Oliver put in. "By God, I should have done this years ago. By God, by God . . ."

And then it caught up with him. His mouth shut and lines appeared all over his twisting face. He bowed forward twice, his skin gone all green.

"Oh, *hell,"* he wheezed. Then he sightlessly staggered a few yards away and threw up.

The ride back was notable for its atmosphere of barely restrained hysteria. We were each pleased with the outcome of our harrowing audience, each laughing as we recalled who said what, and repeating the better points to one another, but all with an air of doom hanging overhead. This was no petty family breach, but a catastrophic rift, and we were well aware of it despite the shrill giddiness presently buoying up our hearts.

By the time we'd left the coach and mounted the steps into Oliver's house, a certain amount of sobriety had begun to manifest itself. My cousin wasted no time in dealing with it and made straight for the parlor cupboard where he kept his wine and spirits. He fumbled badly with his keys, though.

"Let me," I said, stepping in.

He relinquished them; I found the right one and used it. Wine was for celebrations, but brandy for reflection. I grabbed its decanter and two glasses. Knowing their respective capacities, I poured out four times as much for Oliver as for Elizabeth. Neither said a word until both had finished their portions. Elizabeth, not having much of a head for the stuff at the best of times, succumbed and sat down in the nearest chair, complaining that her legs felt too weak to hold her.

Jericho walked in just then. With a lifetime of finely honed perception behind him, he instantly saw that we had survived a mighty conflict and withdrew again. Not for long, I thought, and was proved right when the scullery girl appeared and began to stoke up the fire and light more candles, acting the part of the maid we did not yet have. Apparently Jericho had been instructing her in the finer points of dealing with the gentry, for she said not a word, though her expression was eloquent enough, filled as it was with excited curiosity.

Taking them away to dry in the kitchen, she stumbled out under the combined weight of our cloaks and hats, nearly running into Jericho, who was just returning. He'd known we'd not be staying for supper at Fonteyn House and had prepared accordingly. Fresh bread, a cold fowl, several kinds of cheese, and two teapots crowded the tray he carried. He put it down on a table, filled a teacup for Elizabeth, and took it straight to her.

She sipped at the steaming brew and sighed gratefully. "Jonathan, you will triple Jericho's wage as of this very moment."

"Done," I said.

Jericho paused, seeing that I was entirely serious. "But, sir . . ." he began, taken aback. I'd made legal arrangements to wrest him from the bonds of slavery soon after we'd moved from the inn, and he was still in the throes of adjusting to his newly bestowed freedom.

After this night, the same might be said for the rest of us.

"But nothing. My sister requests it and so it is done. 'Tis paltry pay for such imperial service."

He gaped and nearly let the pot slip from his fingers before his customary dignity reasserted itself.

Oliver noticed our byplay, but added no remarks, as he might have done if things had been more normal. Instead, he paced in a distracted manner, pausing in each pass before the fire to warm himself.

"Tea, Mr. Oliver?" Jericho asked, reaching for another cup.

"Oh—ah—no, thank you. Need to settle my belly first." Oliver helped himself to another brandy. The glass clinked and rattled from the tremors running through his hands.

Jericho put the first pot down and picked up the second, raising a questioning eyebrow at me. Elizabeth had apparently guessed its contents, but this time offered only a wry smile as her reaction. After a glance at Oliver, I nodded. In his present state my cousin wouldn't have noticed anything short of the roof falling on his head, but just to be safe Jericho obscured the pouring out of my own beverage by interposing his body.

"Bit of a risk, this," I murmured as he presented the cup to me. The warm bloodsmell rising from it was sweet to my senses. I felt my upper corner teeth begin to lengthen in response.

"When you left tonight, you gave me to understand that the circumstances of your visit might be exceptionally difficult. With that in mind, I thought you might be in need of reviving afterward."

"And I am grateful, but don't make a habit of it."

"Of course, sir."

I downed it in one glowing draught and had another. Drinking from a cup did have its advantage over sucking directly from a vein, being much cleaner and more comfortable, but I had some very reasonable fears against making frequent use of it. Though I could readily deal with discovery, it might not go so well for Jericho should someone notice him regularly drawing off blood from our horses.

Elizabeth ate what she'd been given, assuring me that she at least was recovering from the business, but Oliver refused an offered plate and continued pacing nervously around, rubbing his hands together as though to warm them. Elizabeth's eyes followed him for a time, then she looked at me. I raised one finger to my lips and winked to let her know all would be well.

"Oliver," I said gently. "You're making me dizzy with all this walking about to no purpose. Let's get out of here and take a little air."

"But it's freezing," he said, not meeting my eye.

"Just the tonic we want to clear our heads."

"What about Elizabeth? Can't leave her alone with all that's happened. Not right, that."

"I am going up to bed, so don't worry about me," she said. "Jericho, can you trust Lottie to ready my room? Excellent. I'll just finish this and be right up."

"Well, if you're sure . . ." Oliver said doubtfully.

"Wrap up against the chill," she advised him with a careless wave.

Jericho quickly produced dry cloaks for us to don, and with hats in place and sticks in hand, I got us out the door before Oliver could change his mind.

"There's such a thing as too much when it comes to tonics," he remarked as the first blast of wind struck him. "Are you sure you want a walk on a night like this?"

"As long as it ends at a tavern," I said.

"But I've plenty of drink inside."

"It's not the same. Much too quiet for one thing. Elizabeth enjoys it, but I need to see that there are other people in the world right now."

He grunted a reluctant agreement to that and let me lead him away.

The cold air woke him up a bit, and he offered directions as needed to get us to The Red Swan, which he said was one of the more superior establishments of its kind in the neighborhood. It was quite different from The Oak back in Glenbriar, being much louder, smokier, and noisier. Oliver was evidently a favored patron, to judge from the boisterous greeting that was raised when we came in. Several garishly made up women squealed their hellos, but did not forsake their perches on various male customers. That was another difference. The landlord of The Oak never allowed such women into his house . . . more's the pity.

Oliver asked for a private room and got it, and though we were separate from the others, we were not completely isolated. The sounds of their current revel came right through the walls, letting us know we were most certainly not alone in the wide, lonely world.

Drinks were brought, as well as food, and an inquiry on whether additional companionship might be desired. Oliver said later perhaps, and they shut the door on us.

"You and Elizabeth worked this out, didn't you?" he asked, glowering at me, but not in a serious manner.

"It seemed for the best," I said, pouring more brandy for him. By the smell of it, it wasn't of the same quality as his own, but doubtless it would do him some good.

"Without saying a single word?"

"We understand each other very well. It's sometimes easier to talk to one friend at a time, rather than to two at once. Elizabeth knows that, so here we are."

"And if I prefer to drink instead of talk?"

"Then I make sure you come home in one piece so you don't disappoint your patients tomorrow."

"Ugh. Tomorrow. How am I going to face it after this?"

"You have regrets?"

"No, but be assured the story of what happened tonight will run through the town like an outbreak of the pox."

"Idle gossip," I murmured dismissively.

"Not with Mother doing the gossiping. She'll present herself favorably, of course, and I shall be the villain, and what she'll say about you and Elizabeth doesn't bear thinking about."

"Your mother will say nothing."

"Can you really be so sure?"

"I know it for a fact. Granted, there might be some talk of you two having a falling out, but there will be no ill rumors spread about myself and Elizabeth. Like it or not, we are still half Fonteyn and your mother would rather set fire to herself than endanger the good name of her precious father."

He finished his drink, coughed on it, then got another from the bottle. "It's horrible. Absolutely horrible what she said. Absolutely horrible."

I put my hand out, touching his arm. "Oliver."

Reluctantly he looked at me.

"It's not true."

His mouth trembled. "How can you think that I'd believe—"

"I *know* you don't believe, but you are troubled, perhaps by a doubt no larger than a pinprick. There's no reason to be ashamed of it. God knows we all have a thousand doubts bubbling up in our minds about this and that every living moment we're on this earth. It's perfectly normal. All I want is to put this one to rest forever. You have my sacred word of honor as a Barrett to you as a Marling, that Elizabeth and I are brother and sister and nothing more. We'll leave the Fonteyns and their vile delusions right out of it." I gave his arm a quick, solid press and let go.

Oliver let his jaw hang open, then emitted a short, mirthless laugh. "Well, when you put it like that . . . I feel a fool for ever listening to the old witch."

"More fool she for listening to my mother. I'm sorry for letting my temper take hold tonight, but to hear that disgusting lie again was too much for me. I just couldn't help myself."

"Yes, probably in the same way I can't help myself when there's a boil to be lanced. The patient may howl at the time, but it's better done than ignored until it poisons his blood and kills him. No regrets, Cousin," he said, raising his glass to toast me.

"None," I responded and felt badly for not being able to return the honor, but Oliver seemed not to notice. I wondered if this might be the right time to confide to him about my changed condition.

Perhaps not. Later would suffice. He'd been through enough for one evening.

Putting his glass aside, he leaned forward across the table. "Those things you said about your mother, about the doctor and the laudanum . . ."

"All true. She goes into these fits, and Dr. Beldon and his sister are the only ones who can deal with her. The laudanum helps, but Beldon has to be sparing with it."

"Sounds like he knows his business, then."

"He's a decent fellow, all told."

"What's your mother like when she's in one of her fits?"

"About the way your mother was tonight."

"God."

"The difference being that your mother knows what she's doing when it comes to inflicting pain and mine does not."

"Grandfather Fonteyn was the same way," he said, hunching his shoulders as he leaned upon the table. "Certainly in observations I've made outside of my own family, I've seen how a nervous condition can be inherited. Let us pray to heaven that it spares us and our own children."

"Amen to that," I genially agreed.

Oliver's face went all pinched. "I . . . I don't remember much about Grandfather, but he quite terrified me. I used to hide from him, then Mother would make my nurse whip me for being disrespectful, but better that than having to see him."

"Understandable. I've heard that he was a perfectly dreadful man."

"But you don't have all the story. Mother was always a trial, but Grandfather . . . he always treated me like—like a special pet. He'd laugh and try to play with me, gave me sweets and toys. I remember that much."

I found that difficult to believe from the tales told about him and said as much.

"I know. It makes no sense. It made no sense. But you see, children have sharp instincts, like animals sometimes when it comes to surviving a harsh life. Whenever I was with him I felt like a rabbit in a lion's den and the lion was only playing with his supper. Me. I never could fathom why until . . . until tonight."

Something cold was trying to insinuate itself in my stomach. It oozed through my guts, sending a frigid hand up to squeeze my heart.

"You think . . . ?" I had trouble recognizing my own voice, it sounded so faded and lost.

"I think that *something* must have prompted your mother's accusation in the first place—not you and Elizabeth—but something in *her* life. In her past."

My heart seemed empty itself. Making room for the welling coldness. It spread along my limbs, numbing everything, yet bringing pain.

"And in my mother's life as well," he added in a whisper.

"Oh, dear God."

"Sick making, isn't it?"

It was one thing to have the horror of incest as an abstract and untrue accusation, but quite another to be forced to face it as a ghastly probability. Oliver and I stared at each other across the table. I had no need of a mirror; I saw my own abject dismay reflecting back from his haggard face.

"But they *revere* him," I said, making a last futile protest.

"Too much, wouldn't you think?"

"But *why* should they?"

He shrugged. "Couldn't say, but I've seen dogs crawl on their bellies to lick their masters' boots after being kicked. Perhaps the same principle applies here in some way."

"It's abominable."

"I could be wrong, but growing up I heard—overheard—things from the servants. Listened to some of the adults when they thought they were alone. Didn't understand it then, but to look back on it, after this night's work, it makes a deal of sense to me now."

And to me. That time I'd sneaked into Mother's room to influence her into never hurting Father again. What she'd mumbled before she'd fully wakened . . . no wonder Oliver had thrown up. I felt like doing so myself.

"Makes you look at things differently, doesn't it?" he asked in a bitter tone.

That was true enough. It seemed to cast a disfiguring shadow upon all my past. Did Father know or suspect any of this? I couldn't recall anything that might provide an answer, but thought he did not. We had the kind of accord between us that would not allow for such secrets, no matter how ugly.

Oliver tentatively reached for the bottle again, then changed his mind, bringing his hands together. One grasping the other. Wringing away. He became conscious of it, then lay them palms flat upon the table to stop.

"It's not as though any of it were our fault, y'know," I said. "It's something that happened a long time ago. That doesn't make it less of a tragedy, but it's not *our* tragedy."

He frowned at the backs of his hands for a time, then tapped his fingers against the stained wood. "I was hoping . . ." He took in a great breath and released it as an equally great sigh. "I was hoping that you would talk sensibly to me about this. It's so hard being an ass all the time."

"You're not an ass, for God's sake."

"Yes, *I* know that, but few other people know it as well. I count myself very blessed that you're one of 'em."

"Oliver—"

"Oh, just let me say thank you."

"All right." I was a bit surprised and abashed.

He steadily met my eye. *"Thank you."*

"You're welcome."

That achieved, his hunched posture eased, and a ghost of his more cheerful old manner showed itself. "And now, my dear Coz, I should very much like to get as drunk as a lord—if not more so."

It was an excellent idea, as far as it went, but when one is an observer rather than a participant in a drinking bout, one quickly loses a direct interest in the proceedings. It had been the same at The Oak when I'd buy drinks for all just to be sociable, then have to either pretend to drink or politely refuse to join them. The men there had eventually gotten used to my eccentricity and never failed to frequently toast my health. The difficult part was watching them gradually get louder and happier as the evening progressed, while I remained stone sober. I missed that lack of control, the guilty euphoria of doing something that was unquestionably bad for me, of surrendering myself to the heavy-limbed comfort of the bottle.

I'd done a lot of drinking at Cambridge with my cousin and our cronies. It was a wonder we got any studying done at all. Some did not. I recalled one fellow who came up for his exams in medicine full flushed with brandy. The instructors questioning him well knew it, but they'd passed him when his clever reply to a difficult inquiry set them on their heads with laughter. Ever afterward I kept his name in mind as a fellow not to go to for any doctoring no matter how dire the need.

But putting that aside, when it came down to the present, I had nothing to occupy me except to watch Oliver gradually slip into a wobbling good mood, his jokes becoming less coherent, his gestures wider and more clumsy.

"You should have some," he said for the third time over. "Do y' a world of good."

"Another time, thank you."

"Bother that, you're just thinking about the need to get me home again, but there is no need, don't y'know. Mr. Gully takes care of that, y'see. Lots of room for us."

"The landlord here?"

"The very one, only he's a bit more 'n that, 'f y'noticed anything comin' in." Oliver gave a wink, a ponderous one employing his whole face.

"I noticed quite a bit coming in, but they all seemed to be busy."

"Hmph, should be someone free by now. Wha'd'y' say to a bit 'f fun?"

"I'd say that you were beyond such pursuits for the time being."

*"Me?* I beg to differ on that point, Coz. 'N' be more 'n' pleased to prove it t' you."

He staggered to the door and was out before I could quite make up my mind on the wisdom of his course. Just as I was to the point of getting up to follow, he returned, arms around two of the women from downstairs.

"Cousin Jonathan, you have the honor of meeting Miss Frances and Miss Jemma, who are very excellent good friends of mine, aren't you, girls?" With that he pinched or tickled each, causing them to scream and giggle. They were painted and powdered and dressed as gorgeously as peacocks, as fine a pair of London trollops as any man could wish for when he has the time and money. Neither of them looked too drunk for fun, I judged. Perhaps Oliver was on to something here. This was borne out when I found Jemma suddenly squirming on my lap.

"I think she likes you," Oliver said unnecessarily.

"Doctor Owly 'ere sez yer new 'n town, 'zat true?" Jemma asked, looking me over.

"This isn't my first visit, but I have just come from America," I politely responded.

"That means he's been on board ship for *months,* girls," Oliver put in, "so watch yourselves."

They cooed mightily over that one, and from then on the joking got much more suggestive. Jemma made it her business to ask about American men and if they were any measure against the English and so on, and I tried my best to answer, but there comes a point when talk falls and one must fall back upon demonstration.

Again, this might have been easier for me had I been drunk, for Jemma was definitely too far past the first blush of youth to be instantly thought attractive. On the other hand, she knew her business well enough and seemed pleased to find that I was in no headlong hurry to conclude things. At some point in the proceedings, Oliver and Frances disappeared, which was just as well, since Jemma and I were growing increasingly more intimate in our activity.

She had a solid figure under her gown, a little thick in the thighs, but smooth skinned and warm to the touch. I found my interest, among other things, quickening at the sight of the treasure concealed beneath her clothes and was more than happy to oblige her when it came to loosening my own. As ever, there was no real need to drop my breeches, but I found my coat to be somewhat restrictive and then my waistcoat. One was on the floor and the other unbuttoned when I came to see that though active, she was not exactly caught up in the fever of the event.

I thought of Molly Audy and her habit of saving herself up lest she be too exhausted for the work of the evening and divined that Jemma was doing the same thing. Well and good for her, but I became determined to provide this English *houri* with an equal share of delights to come. I had my pride, after all.

She noted the change in me as I began to concentrate more on her than myself, even protesting that she was fine as she was. I said I was glad to hear it and went on regardless, hands and mouth working together over her lush body. Then it was my turn to notice the change in her as she began to succumb, which only made me more eager.

When it was obvious that she was fast approaching her peak, and I found myself in a likewise state, I buried my corner teeth hard into her throat, hurtling us both over the edge. She was so far gone that pleasure, rather than pain, was her reward for this unorthodox invasion of her person. She could not have been prepared for the intensity of rapture it would engender, nor the length of it; for having finally worked things up to this point I wasn't about to abandon them after but a few seconds of fulfillment as would be the case for a normal man reaching a climax. I continued on, drawing a few drops at a time from her, relishing her writhings against me almost as much as the taste of her blood.

Here indeed was a surrender for me, to a different kind of heavy-limbed comfort, and here I intended to stay for as long as it pleased us both. I had no worries for Jemma; she seemed to be well and truly lost to it. As for myself, I knew I could continue for hours, if I was careful enough with her.

However, I had not reckoned on Cousin Oliver walking in on us.

He'd hardly been quite about it, but I was so enmeshed in what I was doing that I paid no mind when he knocked, and none at all when he pushed the door open a crack. What he found was likely a familiar sight to him if he came to this house with any regularity—a half dressed man and woman each well occupied, this time it being myself holding Jemma tight, passionately kissing her neck.

"I say, Coz, I forgot m' brandy 'n'—"

I gave quite a start and glared up at this unwelcome intrusion. Jemma moaned at the interruption and half swooning, reached to pull me back.

Nothing unexpected for him, but that's not what made him stop cold to stare.

There was *blood* oozing from her throat. Unmistakable. Alarming.

Blood also stained my lips. Perturbing. Repellent.

And my eyes . . . by now they would be wholly suffused with blood, crimson orbs showing no trace of white, the pupils lost in the wash of what I'd just fed upon.

All highly visible to Oliver standing not two paces from us. A fearful sight to anyone, however forewarned they might be for it. My good cousin, alas, was not.

Oliver was as one petrified, frozen in mid-word and mid-movement. Only his eyes shifted, from me to Jemma and back again, his face gradually going from shock to gaping horror as he understood exactly what he was seeing.

I was frozen as well, not knowing what to do or say, and so we remained for an unguessable time, until Jemma moaned another gentle complaint.

"Why'd y' stop, luv?" she said groggily, trying to sit up.

Instinct told me that it would be best to keep her ignorant of what was to come. Tearing my eyes from Oliver, I focused entirely on hers. "Hush, Jemma, hush. Go to sleep, there's a good girl." As my emotions rose in pitch, so did the strength of my influence. She promptly lay back in instantaneous slumber.

Oliver, still openmouthed, gave out with a frightened little gasp at this. "God's mercy man, wh-what are you doing to her?"

I didn't quite look at him. "She's all right, I promise you. Now come in here and close the door. Please."

He hesitated, then surprised me and did as requested.

Like it or not, the time of explanations was upon us, but for the life of me I just didn't know where to begin. Not after this infelicitous start.

Slowly he came closer. I continued to avoid his eyes. He leaned over and extended one hand toward Jemma, probing the skin close to the small wounds I'd made, studying them.

"She's all right," I repeated, a little desperately. I tasted her blood on my lips again and, turning from him, quickly wiped it away on my handkerchief. He came 'round to face me. With no small caution, he reached down and touched my chin, lifting it.

"I need to see," he said, in a strange, dark voice.

And so I looked up, and if he was afraid of what he'd find, then I was also for how he might react to it.

He pulled back, fingers to his mouth, breath rushing in and out twice as either a sob or a laugh before he got hold of himself.

"Please, Oliver, I'm not—"

What, I thought, a *Blutsäuger?* What could I tell him? What could I possibly say to ease his fear? There was a way around this awkwardness, of course. I could readily force him to acceptance. Nora had done the same for me at first. But what was right for her was not right for me, especially in this case. To even try would be enormously unfair to Oliver. Dishonorable. Cruel.

"You're like *her,*" he whispered, breaking the impossible silence.

I resisted the urge to glance at Jemma. No, he was speaking not of her but—

*"She would do that . . . to me.* Nora *would . . ."*

Yes, he had been one of her courtiers, but she'd said he'd not been comfortable about it and she'd let him go, making sure to influence him into forgetting certain things. The influence had held firm. Until now.

His hand went to his throat, and he made a terrible mewling sound as he stumbled backward. He got as far as a chair and fell into it and stayed there. He was shivering again, not from fear of me, but from the onrush of restored memory.

"Oh, my God, my God," he groaned over and over, holding his head, giving a voice to his misery.

I swallowed my own anxieties. How unimportant they seemed. Standing, I buttoned my waistcoat, donned my coat, and put myself in order. This done, I went to Jemma and saw to her wounds. The flow from them had ceased, but the drying blood was a nuisance. Slopping some brandy on my handkerchief, I dabbed away until she was clean, then gently woke her.

"You're a lovely darling," I told her, pressing some coins into her hand. "But I need to speak with my cousin, so if you don't mind . . ."

She had no chance for argument as I smoothly bundled her and her trailing clothes out the door, shutting it. I trusted that the money would be more than sufficient compensation for my rudeness.

Oliver watched us, saying nothing. I pulled a chair from the other side of the table and sat across from him.

"Y-you've done that before," he murmured, making a vague gesture to mean Jemma.

"Not quite in the same way, but yes."

"But you . . . take from them."

"I drink their blood," I said, deciding to be as plain as possible. "Just as Nora once drank from you. And me."

He shuddered, then mastered himself. "I remember what she did to me."

"And she stopped. She knew you did not enjoy it."

"But you did?"

"I was—I am—in love with her. It makes a difference."

"So this is just some form of pleasure you've taken to like—like old Dexter and his need for birch rods?"

"No, it's not like that."

*"Then what is it?"* He waited for me to go on. When the pause became too lengthy, he asked, "Does it have to do with why your eyes are like that?"

At this reminder I briefly averted them. "It's everything to do with . . . this is damned difficult for me, Oliver. I'm afraid of—of losing your friendship because of what's happened to me."

He shook his head, puffing out some air in a kind of bitter laugh. "One may lose friends, but never relatives. We both know that all too well. Rely on it, if nothing else."

He'd surprised me again, God bless him. I softly matched his laugh, but with relief, not bitterness inspiring it. "Thank you."

"Right." He sat up, squaring his shoulders. "Now, *talk* to me."

And so I did. For a very long, long time.

# CHAPTER 8

*London, December 1777*

"What's happened today, Jericho? Any new staff taken on?" I asked.

"No, sir. Miss Elizabeth was too busy receiving visitors and had no time for interviewing anyone."

"What visitors, then?"

"Miss Charlotte Bolyn called. She wanted to confirm again for herself that you, Miss Elizabeth, and Dr. Oliver were going to attend the Masque tonight, then she flew off elsewhere, but was rapidly succeeded by a horde of other young ladies and their mothers."

"Oh, dear."

"A number of them were most disappointed that you were not available."

"Which? The young ladies or their mothers?"

"Both, sir."

"Oh, dear, oh, dear."

"Indeed, sir. Some of them had a rather . . . predatory air about them."

"And I was hoping to be spared. Damnation, you'd think they'd realize that not every bachelor is looking for a wife. Can't think where they get the idea. I shall have to acquire a horrible reputation to put them off my scent. Perhaps I can tell the truth about my drinking habits. *That* would send them away screaming."

"I have serious doubts that such a ploy would be particularly effective as a means of avoiding matrimony, sir."

"You're right. There are some perfect rotters out there drinking far worse stuff than blood who've . . . well, I'll think of something. What else for the day? Anything?"

"Several boxes addressed to Dr. Oliver arrived in the early afternoon from Fonteyn House."

"Sounds ominous. Any idea what's in 'em?"

"None, sir. Everything was taken to his consulting room. He shut himself in with the items some time ago and has not yet emerged."

"Most mysterious. Are we done here?"

He gave me a critical look to determine whether or not I was presentable. Since no glass would ever throw back my image, I'd come to rely soley upon Jericho's fine judgment in the matter of my personal toilet. He had excellent taste, though often tending to be too much the perfectionist for my patience.

"You will do, sir," he said grudgingly. "But you really want some new shirts."

"I've already ordered some from the fellow who's done my costume for the Masque."

"Oh, sir, do you really think—"

"Not to worry, it's Oliver's tailor, a most careful and experienced man."

That mollified him. Oliver's own taste was sometimes eccentric, but he was always sensible when it came to shirts.

Released from the evening's ritual, I unhurriedly went downstairs to join the others, giving a polite nod to the new housemaid as she ducked out of my way. Her eyes were somewhat crossed, but she seemed energetic enough for the work, sober, was a devoted churchgoer, and had already had the pox. Elizabeth had only engaged her yesterday morning; that same night I'd conducted my own interview with the girl, influencing her into not being at all curious about my sleeping or eating habits. Or lack thereof. For the last week it seemed that each time I woke up there was a new servant on the premises requiring my attention. Thus far, not one of them had taken the least notice of my differences, not within Jericho's hearing, anyway. It was his job to look for any chinks in my work and give warning when reinforcement seemed required.

But for now, all was safe. My traveling trunk with its bags of earth was secreted in a remote section of Oliver's cellar, allowing me to rest undisturbed through the day. At sunset it was easy enough to make my invisible way up through the floors of the house to re-form in my bedroom and there submit to Jericho's ministrations. It wasn't quite the same as it had been back home, but the inconvenience of curling myself into the trunk each night rather than stretching out on a cot was negligible. Such totality of rest did have its advantages.

As for my excellent good cousin, well, our talk at The Red Swan had been mutually harrowing, but the experience created a more solid bond between us—something I'd badly needed and was humbly grateful to have—and all without having to impose my influence upon him. Though without doubt it was the most difficult conversation I'd been through since my first night out of the grave when I'd encountered Elizabeth. The topic was essentially the same: an explanation of myself, of the changes I'd gone through, and the desperate, unspoken plea for acceptance of the impossible.

But Oliver, my friend as well as my relative, had a large enough heart to hear that which was not said and then provide it.

Not that any of what he heard was particularly easy for *him.* It took a goodly time to persuade him that I really was not like old Dexter, one of the Cambridge administrators whose nature with women was such that he could not achieve satisfaction unless his partner birched his backside raw. We students found out about it from one of the town whores, who was not as discreet as Molly Audy when it came to gossiping about her clients. Most of us thought him a strange fellow though still very likable.

But once I'd convinced Oliver that my need to drink blood was a physical necessity equivalent in importance to his eating every day, things went a bit more smoothly. His medical training (and curiosity) won out over his initial fear and astonishment, and he fairly hammered me with questions. Unfortunately, I could not answer them all, those being the very ones I had in store for Nora.

He had much to speak of himself, mostly of his own feelings toward her, which might best be defined as ambivalent. Certainly he'd found her to be beautiful, even bewitching, the same as many of the other men in our circle, but he'd been highly disturbed by her habits, then and now.

"She was using us—every one of us—to feed on like a wolf upon sheep," he'd said with something close to anger.

"One may look at it like that, but on the other hand, she willingly gave of herself to pleasure others."

"But that makes her a—" He cut off, realizing that I might take exception to his conclusion.

"I know what it makes her, and I'll not deny the similarities between herself and the two ladies we've enjoyed tonight. But God's death, man, I shan't begrudge her the right to make a living in whatever way that she's able. Look at the limitations our condition imposes. She can no more open a dress shop and make a profit than I can go to court to practice the law. Both require that we be up and about during the day, y'know."

He thought it over and saw the sense of it. "But I still feel . . . well, violated in some way. First by her use of me, then again by making me forget it. I'm not sure that I'd care ever to see her again after all that."

"Of course I'll not force you, but I've an idea that if I made mention of it to her, she would doubtless wish to offer an apology."

"And then there's poor Tony Warburton to think about. I can still hardly imagine him doing such a horrible thing except that that's the same time you began acting all peculiar. For three years you had this grand passion for the lady, and then you behaved as if she were no more important than any of the other women we've known."

"Only because she made me think so. She made me forget everything that was truly important between us."

"And you can do the same sort of . . . ? If you don't mind my saying so, I find that to be rather frightening."

"As do I, be assured."

"But you have . . . influenced me?"

"Yes," I admitted. "And I do humbly apologize and promise never to do so again. That's what this talk is all about, so I may be honest with you from now on."

"I can appreciate that, Coz. Apology accepted, though damn it, I've no memory of what *you've* done, either. Insidious stuff, ain't it? And Nora's used it on God knows how many of us." He gave a brief shudder.

"You must understand that she has to be secretive when it comes to certain things. As do I, now. You've only to recall your own reaction when you walked in awhile ago to see why."

"Yes, that quite woke me up. Are you sure Jemma is unharmed?"

"Quite sure. In truth, I went to some effort to see that she enjoyed herself."

"Hmph. If I'd troubled to do the same for Frances, I suppose I'd have come in much later and then we'd have not even had this talk."

"Perhaps so, but only in part. I have always intended to tell you all this, but . . . well . . ."

"Yes," he said, hooking one corner of his mouth up in a smile full tainted with irony. "Well."

And so the nights passed between that one and the present, with Oliver becoming more and more accustomed to my change—now that he'd been made aware of it. Certainly, things were much improved for my own peace of mind, for I'd taken no enjoyment whatever from the previous necessity of having to influence him. It's one thing to be compelled to use it on a paid servant, but quite another to inflict it upon so good and close a friend as he.

Never again, I promised us both.

"Oh, there you are," said Elizabeth, emerging from the kitchen to meet me as I reached the lower landing. "Thought you'd never be coming down."

"Jericho was playing the taskmaster tonight. Wanted to make sure I was properly groomed for the party."

"Did he tell you about Oliver's mysterious treasure?"

"Yes, all the boxes. Where is he? Still in his consulting room?"

She nodded. "He came home an hour ago, went in, and hasn't been out since. I decided to wait until you were up before checking on him. Wonder what they could be?"

"Probably stuffed and mounted specimens from Bedlam, knowing the bent of his studies," I said, strolling in the correct direction.

"Ugh. That's disgusting."

"I've seen worse. If you ask him, he'll arrange to take you on a tour, y'know."

"I think not."

We paused before the consulting room door, and Elizabeth knocked, calling Oliver's name. There was no immediate reply, so she repeated herself.

"Did you hear anything?" she asked, her brow puckering.

"Barely." The noise had been so low as to be impossible for even me to understand what was said, though it sounded vaguely like an invitation. I pushed the door open and peered in, making room for Elizabeth.

"Good heavens," she said, staring in astonishment at a perfect glut of disorder littering the floor. Books, papers, clothing, and toys were spread into every corner, leaving no doubt as to what had once been in the boxes, which were now gaping and empty. Cross-legged, Oliver sat in the middle of it all, a carved wooden horse in one hand, a chapbook in the other. He looked up at us, his eyes rather bleary and lost.

"Hallo, all. Pardon the mess," he said in a faint, tired voice.

"What is all this?" Elizabeth lifted her skirts and picked her way into the room.

"Mo—" He swallowed with difficulty. "Mother sent it. Her way of saying good-bye, I think."

"These are your things?"

"Every one of them. All of it. Clothes I outgrew that weren't passed on to others, letters, even some of the prizes I won at school. Here it is. My whole life. She's sent the lot of it away for good." He spoke unevenly and his eyes were red. He'd been crying, I was sure.

"Dear God," I said. The cruelty of it went right to my heart. "How could she do such a thing?"

"Actually, this was my old nurse's doing. She's working for Cousin Clarinda now, but Mother sent for her and told her to pack everything of mine up, then either burn it or give it away. Nanny couldn't bear to do either, so she sent it over to me with a note of explanation. I suppose I should be glad not to have lost it all. I hadn't even thought of the stuff for ages—I might not have even missed it—but to have it all back again in this way . . . something of a shock, that."

"Oh, poor Oliver," said Elizabeth. She gamely—and carefully—made the hazardous trek across the floor and knelt down next to him, putting an arm around his shoulder. Elizabeth knew all about the speculations Oliver and I had made to each other at The Red Swan by now and so had an understanding of the depth of the pain he was going through.

"Yes, poor me. She's a wretched mother, but the only one I've got. It's—it's so damnable to think she hates me this much."

"She hates herself, that's why she acts as she does. Like a wounded animal lashing out."

"And wounding others in turn. Well, this is it, I should think. She's got nothing else to fling at me after this, not unless she changes her mind about the inheritance money. I wouldn't put it past her."

"But you went by the solicitors, didn't you?" she asked.

"All they would tell me was that she'd not sent for them. She could, though, at any time."

"It's very difficult to alter a will," I said. "Especially one that's been in effect for so long without contest. It's also rather public, and we know she'd be extremely reluctant to carry things that far. Too much like a scandal, y'know. Besides, I can always go back, if necessary, and—"

Elizabeth shot me a warning look.

"And—well, she just won't do anything. We'll get our money every quarter, as usual. We've no need to worry."

"I suppose not." He sighed. "You know, if it hadn't been for the note Nanny put in, I'd have thought Mother had sent it today on purpose just to spoil the party for me."

"I hope she hasn't. Has she?"

"I don't think so, but I am terribly unsettled."

"What you need is your tea." Elizabeth stood and put her hand out to help him up. He accomplished this with considerable groaning, for his legs had gone to sleep. With her to lean on, he limped out of the room's chaos and into the hall.

"I'll have the new maid sort things out for you," she said, holding his arm as she led him into the parlor. "That is, if you don't mind?"

"Not a bit of it. Odd thing is, that it was rather fun seeing my old stuff again. That little wood horse was my favorite toy once upon a time. I played and played with it until the paint was worn off, but by then I was learning to ride real ones, so it was all right."

Elizabeth rang the bell for tea and encouraged him to talk about himself. Being as vulnerable as any to another's interest in the subject, he readily complied, not knowing that it was her way of cheering him. By the time they'd finished their light meal, talk had turned to the upcoming party.

"I shall have to begin dressing soon if we are to be fashionably late," she said, with a glance at the mantel clock.

"I must say that I'm looking forward to helping escort a pirate queen once again," I put in. "You're in for a treat, Oliver. She was quite the spitfire when she was 'Scarlet Bess, Scourge of the Island."

"I think the whole gathering at the Bolyn house is in for a treat," he said. "Think we'll frighten anyone as her 'Cutthroat Captains of the Coast'?"

"We shall certainly try."

The problem of what to costume ourselves in had been much debated until Elizabeth suggested a re-creation of our favorite childhood game. Oliver had enthusiastically fallen in with it, asserting that the three of us together would make a wonderful and memorable entrance to the Masque. Elizabeth, having since become fast friends with our future hostess, promptly took herself off to Charlotte Bolyn's highly recommended dressmaker, while Oliver and I sought help from his tailor. Colors had been agreed upon, fabrics and laces chosen, and a hasty construction was begun. I'd asked Jericho if he wanted to join us, reenacting his role as the "Ebon Shark of Tortuga," but he'd begged to be excused from the honor. No doubt his much valued dignity would have suffered in some way.

"Are you sure you don't wish to come?" I asked him one last time as he helped me to dress. "Other people are bringing their servants. We could yet improvise something for you. I heard that Lady Musgrave was going as an Arab princess and was bringing her maid as her—uh—maid, done up in gold ropes, feathers, and a long silk scarf."

"Thank you, no, sir. I should prefer a quiet evening to organize the new staff. There are also the scattered contents of Mr. Oliver's consulting room to put in order. The new girl is in something of a state about the task and will need help sorting everything. No, sir, I am really quite sure. Now hold still that I may apply your eye patch . . ."

Obediently I held still.

"Now the mask . . ." He tied it firmly in place, concealing me from forehead to nose.

"How do I look?" I asked anxiously.

"Most formidable, sir."

"Trouble is I can't see a damned thing. This patch throws off the eyeholes on the mask."

"Do you wish the patch removed or the mask?"

"The patch. I've been anticipating this gathering too much to end up missing half of it by keeping one eye shut."

He worked for a moment to adjust things. Sans patch, with the mask properly in place, I was able to see excellently and said so. A pity I could not provide myself with the satisfaction of admiring the final results in the mirror, for it seemed a very superior costume. Though the tailor's idea of pirate clothing was probably lacking in accuracy, I did feel that I cut a fine figure in my bloodred coat, gold satin cloak, and sinister black velvet mask. Once the wide baldric had been secured over one shoulder and my cutlass sheathed, Jericho finished it off by presenting me with a hat matching the coat's color, lavishly trimmed with gold lace.

"Have a very good time, Mr. Jonathan. You won't forget to keep track of the hour?"

The Bolyn's Masque would likely not conclude itself until well into the next morning. "I shall be home before dawn, I do promise you. If nothing else, Elizabeth will see to it."

Assured, he finally gave me leave to go.

Oliver's estimation of our reception had been conservative. The three of us sweeping into the entry caused a happy stirring in the crowd that had already arrived, and we were even honored with applause. Though we were indeed resplendent in our black, red, and gold colors, Elizabeth was the best of the lot. She'd found some crimson powder from an unknown source and had used it for dressing her hair, making a fiery difference between herself and the other ladies who were present. Woven into her coiffure were a number of red and black ribbons long enough to trail down to her shoulders. Her gown—and I was thinking as her protective brother in this—was short enough to reveal her legs to a shocking extent, had they not been modestly encased in high boots. The rest of her costume was a wonder in gold lace and rustling red satin. Even her mask was trimmed with lace, the gold showing off well against the black velvet.

Oliver's costume was identical to mine, but the colors were reversed, giving him a gold coat and a red cloak, and he looked very fine in them. A few people recognized him, though; his long chin, left visible below the half-mask, was unmistakable. With his identity discovered, our own was also given away, but only to those who had already met us and could guess that we would be with our cousin.

Charlotte Bolyn immediately came over to give welcome and proclaim her pleasure at the success of our apparel. She was very fetching herself as the Queen of Hearts, and dragged her brother Brinsley over, who was dressed as the Knave of Spades. Someone in the crowd called out that all the reds and blacks together were too much for his bewildered eyes, and Brinsley waved his sword at him in mock threat.

"He may have an idea in that," said Oliver. "Think we should break things up a bit?"

"Refreshments are over there," Brinsley laconically informed him, pointing to a large, well-supplied table.

"Heavens, man, are you a playing card or a reader of minds?"

Oliver excused himself, Brinsley asked Elizabeth if she would honor him with the next dance, and Charlotte had to see to the next group of guests coming in. This suited me, for I was well occupied with study of the mob, trying to guess who this one or that one was under the rainbow of disguises. I wandered from room to room and out into the garden, my eye running over each and every woman of a certain specific height and figure.

I was looking for Nora, of course.

My hope was that she might, just might be here at this, the party of the season. She had been most fond of the Bolyns, never failing to come to any of their gatherings. Brinsley had once been one of her courtiers. I had already asked the Bolyns, particularly Brinsley, if they had any idea of Nora's whereabouts, but got only the speculation that she'd gone to Italy, or so their friends the Warburtons had told them.

Several times during my search my dormant heart gave a sharp upward leap as I spied a woman who matched my memory of Nora. But each closer investigation proved me to be mistaken. As the evening passed, I became frustrated and morose with the constant failure. The worst part was going through the garden when I braved the twistings of its shrubbery maze, for it was here that we'd shared our first kisses. It was here that I had once and for all time fallen in love. Now this magical place with its paper lanterns shedding their fairy lights over other couples seemed a bleak and blasted vanity to my disappointed soul.

I doggedly found the center of the thing, which was a large courtyard decorated by marble statues set 'round a large marble fountain. Its water had been drained from the supply pipes, lest the winter weather freeze and crack them. Without the splashing from the fountain, this was now a strangely desolate spot. No one was here at the moment, probably because of the wind. Outside the shelter of the maze's living walls, it was very bad, a feature that would certainly drive any sightseers to more temperate areas. The cold air was tolerable, but not when combined with so fresh a breeze. The ends of my light satin cloak snapped like flags, and a gust threatened to send my hat flying. I gladly quit the place and hurried back to the house.

The noise, costumes, and lights dazzled me, but there was really no quiet retreat to hide in. Not that I wanted to conceal myself, but I did long for a few moments of solitude. None were to be had, though. A group of the younger men, friends from my previous visit, recognized and hailed me. It proved to be something of a blessing since they took my mind off my inner sorrows for a time.

As ever, the talk was on politics, and I was closely questioned about the war. There was dismay amongst them about General Burgoyne's unfortunate surrender at Saratoga. The first dispatches of the disaster had arrived that week, and though the news was supposed to remain secret, it had escaped, causing no end of speculation on how England might recover her honor from such a setback.

"Mind you, the Frenchies will start pouring themselves across the sea after this," said a short Harlequin. "Once they're in we'll be set for a real war right here and now. We won't have to go to America to fight, just hop across the Channel."

"They wouldn't dare," opined another, taller Harlequin.

"They would, sir. We gave them a thrashing the last time about Canada and they want revenge. You mark me."

This reminded me of all the things Father had said on my last night at home. It had been only a couple of weeks since I'd seen him—at least how I reckoned the time in light of my singular hibernation—but I missed him terribly just then and had to leave or make a fool of myself.

"But you're a fool already, Johnny Boy," I muttered. To be at so fabulous a celebration and in such a dark mood was ridiculous. I was here for distraction from my woes, to sample and enjoy the myriad delights whirling and laughing about me, not to impersonate a waker at a funeral.

As if to help draw me out of the depths, some sprightly music started up nearby, drowning out the nearby conversations. I followed the sounds to the great ballroom, where all the dancers had gathered to indulge themselves in festive exercise. The combinations of partners were astonishing and amusing as I spied a lion dancing with Columbine and a Roman soldier bowing over the hand of an Indian maiden. One lady's costume, what there was of it, caught my eye for some goodly time, for the short skirt was so transparent one could see the supporting panniers, not to mention her very shapely legs and the flash of the silver garters holding up her stockings. Her silver mask covered too much of her face for me to readily identify her, but she was not Nora and that was all that really mattered in the end.

The only thing to distract me from her was a fellow in deep black stalking past holding a skull. His Hamlet might have been more striking had he not been drunk and trying to get the skull to share a sip from his glass. Still, he seemed to be having a fine time providing entertainment for others. He also reminded me that I had not yet bought any plays to send to Cousin Ann as I'd promised. Tomorrow I'd see about making an expedition to Paternoster Row and explore its book stalls. Surely *some* of them would still be open after dark.

Familiar laughter, slightly breathless, came to me over the music, and I saw Elizabeth dancing past, partnered by a big fellow in a Russian coat and tall fur hat. He grinned back at her from behind a vast false beard. For all that covering, he seemed familiar. Probably one of my old schoolmates. If so, then I'd better stay handy to make sure he behaved himself with her.

"Enjoying yourself, Coz?" asked Oliver, who suddenly bumped into me from pushing his way through the press at the edge of the dancing.

"I am. I can see that you are, too."

He had a wineglass in hand. Not his first, to judge by his flushed face and wandering eyes. "Indeed, indeed. Having a marvelous good time in spite of the old hag."

"What do you mean?"

He jerked his head back the way he'd come. "Mother's here, don't you know. Saw her in one of the rooms with some of her cronies, the lot of 'em passing sentence against every pretty girl who happened to walk through. She's not in costume, just has a mask on a stick to hide behind, like the others. Ask me and I tell you I think they need 'em. Nothing like a bit of papier-mâché and paint to improve their sour old faces, the harpies. Hic! 'Scuse me, I'm sure."

"It doesn't seem to have soured you, though."

"Not a bit of it. I'm too drunk to care. In fact, I made a point to stagger right through the room so she could see that her cast-off son is alive, well, and having a devil of a good time."

"You think that was wise?"

" 'Course not, but then I'm too drunk for wisdom. Besides, all her friends saw me, too. Probably embarrassed her to no end, especially when I gave such a loud hail to Cousins Clarinda and Edmond."

"My God, they're here, too?"

"I just said so, din' I? Amazing, ain't it, that Clarinda got Edmond-the-stick out of the house for this. He was even in costume, a Harlequin, no less. Should say more, rather. There must be a dozen of 'em drifting around here tonight. Just shows he hasn't much imagination. Cheap, too. Looked as if it'd been made for someone else and he inherited it. Clarinda is very jaunty, though. Came as a Gypsy. You should see her. Very lively!"

No doubt, I thought, looking around but noticing no Gypsies, lively or otherwise, and feeling absurdly thankful about it. Though my one encounter with her was enchanting, I had no desire to try for a second, particularly in a strange house with her husband lurking about. He'd seemed the jealous type, or so I'd convinced myself from the single look I'd had of him across the dim hallway of Fonteyn House.

The dance ended and the couples bowed to one another. A different fellow came up to claim Elizabeth's attention, smaller than the Russian, but not lacking in verve.

"Hallo," I said, giving Oliver a nudge. "Is that Lord Harvey trying to partner Elizabeth for the next one?"

He gave a wobbly stare, "I think so. No one else has such spindles for legs that I know of."

"Did he ever take care of his creditors?"

"No, had to fly the country to avoid 'em. Heard he got into a card game in France, won a fortune, and returned in triumph to pay off everything. Still, I understand he's not given up looking for a rich wife. Bad luck for Elizabeth if he—no . . . she's too smart for him, and after that bad business she's been through, she won't be much impressed by a title."

"Maybe I should go out and interrupt him before—"

"Too late, the music's already started. Don't worry, old lad, it's just one dance. She can take care of herself."

On that I could only tentatively agree; but once they're stirred up, it's hard to put one's protective instincts aside.

The dancers fell into the patterns required of them and the stragglers cleared themselves from the floor. The Russian, who was heading in another direction, changed course when he spotted Oliver and apparently recognized him. He sauntered over to us.

"Is that you, Marling? Thought so. Grand party, what?"

"Very grand. Ridley, isn't it? Can't mistake you, two yards tall and then some, you great giant. You need to meet my cousin from America, Jonathan Barrett. Jonathan, this is Thomas Ridley."

We bowed to each other. Ridley, red from the dance and sweating, untied his beard and stuffed it into a pocket.

"He was a couple of years ahead of us at Cambridge, weren't you?"

"At Oxford, Marling," he said in a near patronizing drawl.

"Yes, of course. Haven't seen you in ages. Back from the Tour?" Oliver asked, referring to the popular fashion the gentry followed of exploring the Continent.

"Something like that. London gets too small for me, y'see." He grandly stretched his arms wide as if to illustrate.

That was when the now nagging familiarity I felt about him changed instantly to utter certainty. Ridley was the leader of the Mohocks that I'd bedeviled on my first night in London.

Good God.

"And how is America, these days?" he asked me, again with that almost, but not quite, patronizing tone. It was finely balanced, just enough so that he was unpleasant, but not to the point where anyone could take exception to it.

"Fine, very fine," I answered, not really thinking.

"Fine? You're not one of those damned rebels, are you?"

"Absolutely not!" cried Oliver. "My God, but Jonathan's done his share of the fighting for our king. How many have you killed, Coz? Half a dozen?"

"You exaggerate, Oliver." I had no wish to dwell on that part of my past.

"Blazed away at a roomful of 'em, at least, only this summer."

"How interesting," said Ridley, giving me a narrow stare.

Damnation. Had he recognized me as the victim he and his gang had tried to sweat? Hard to tell if it was that or his reaction to Oliver's tipsy boasting.

"Not very," I countered. "Just defending my family. Any man would do the same. Are you enjoying the Masque? That coat must be very warm." God, but I was babbling, too. Really, now, there was nothing to fear. It was unlikely that he'd remember me; it had been dark and he very drunk. Besides, half my face was obscured by my mask. The music and the great press of people were simply making me nervous.

"Rather," he said, a lazy amusement creeping over his heavy features. Neither handsome nor ugly, but possessing distinct enough looks to make him stand out, he seemed to know how to use them to his best advantage. But moments ago he'd almost seemed dashing as he squired Elizabeth 'round the dance floor. Now he was decidedly base as he spoke more loudly than necessary to be heard over the music and other speakers. "There's plenty of other things here to make a man warm, though."

"Yes, all the dancing. I may try a turn or two myself, later."

"It'd be well worth the trying, I can guarantee you, Barrett. The ladies here tonight are of superior stock. Very lively."

"I have noticed."

"Now," he said, pointing out at the couples on the floor. "See that pirate wench with the red hair? There's a pretty slut who knows what's best for a man. It's the way she walks and moves is how you can tell. I'll give you seven to five that I'll be pounding her backside into the floor within the hour. What do you say?" He grinned down at me.

Oliver, for all the wine he'd taken, was just quick enough to get between us. I heard him shouting my name, trying to get through the blast of white-hot rage roaring between my ears. I fought to push him to one side to strike at Ridley, but our violent activity seized the instant attention of some of the other men present who had overheard, and they all leaped in to hold me back.

"Have a care, sir!"

"Calm yourself, sir!"

"For God's sake, Jonathan, don't!"

Through it all, Ridley stood with his hands on his hips, grinning. I wanted to smash his face to a pulp and knew perfectly well that I could do it with ease if only these fools would just let go my arms.

"You heard the bastard!" I shouted. "You heard him!"

"Aye, we did, an' there're ways for gentlemen to settle such things," said an older man with an Irish accent.

"Let them be settled, then. I'm issuing challenge here and now."

"First cool yourself, young sir."

I stopped fighting them, falling back on my heels, but still searing inside and ready to tear Ridley in two at his next word. But he said nothing and just walked away with that ass's grin fixed in place.

"That was a rare harsh insult to you, sir," said the older man with dark sympathy.

"To my sister, sir," I corrected. "And thus making it a greater offense."

"Then you're familiar with the Clonmel Summer Assizes?"

"I am." Oliver had acquired a copy of the Irish Code Duello that autumn, and I'd studied it with interest, hardly dreaming I'd find so quick a use for its rules.

"Are you cooled enough to properly deal with it?"

I could not take my eyes from Ridley's retreating back.

"Jonathan?" Oliver, looking sober, yet held my arm.

"Yes," I snarled. "You heard him? You all heard?"

Some three or four of them said they had. All looked grim.

"I need a second," I heard myself saying. "Oliver, would you—?"

"Need you ask? Of course I will."

"Hold now," said the Irishman. " 'Tis contrary to the rules to deliver a challenge at night. No need for being a hothead. It can wait till the morrow."

"I must beg your pardon, sir, and disagree. If anything I shall be even more angry tomorrow. His insult was too great. We will settle things tonight."

And with those words, a change went over the men around us, a kind of drawing together, as though they'd erected an invisible wall between us and the rest of the crowd. Those outside the wall seemed to sense it. Other men nodded; women whispered behind their fans to each other. Something Had Happened. And even better, Something Was About To Happen. I felt their eyes burning through me as our group left the ballroom.

The older man, whose name was Dennehy, took charge of things, having appointed himself to the position of seeing that all was done according to the strict rules of the Code. He'd heard everything that Ridley had said and been shocked by it, but was no less determined to stick to the rules of gentlemanly behavior, though Ridley had already proved himself to be no gentleman.

I was swept along by the others to a more secluded room. Brinsley Bolyn was sent for, rather than his father, for it was thought the elder Bolyn might have tried to postpone things. Once arrived, he was told what had happened and asked if there was a place nearby where a meeting might be arranged. This put him rather in the middle, being host to both myself and Ridley, but he promptly named an orchard just west of the house as a likely site. He promised to have lanterns brought to shed adequate light for the proceedings and said we could choose whatever was needed from his own collection of arms.

With those important points covered, Oliver was dispatched to speak with Ridley's second. He was back quickly enough. Ridley had decided on the smallsword as his weapon, which was not surprising considering the use he'd tried to make of it at our first meeting. In premeditated encounters like this, pistols were usually more favored than blades, since they tended to level any physical inequalities between opponents, but it made no difference to me. I knew how to use either one.

Though at the center of all their attention, I was also strangely apart from them. Even Oliver, who trudged close by my side on our way to the orchard, was silent, as if afraid to speak with me, yet wanting to very badly. A quarter hour from now, for all he knew, I might be dead.

For all I knew as well.

I'd survived pistol bullets, musket balls, and even a cudgeling hard enough to kill an ordinary man; perhaps because of my change I would survive the sword, but I did not know, nor did it matter one way or another to me. Words had been said, ephemeral words, yet they could not be forgiven or forgotten. That foul-mouthed bastard had grossly insulted my sister, and I was going to kill him for it or die in the trying.

"Oliver, you'll be sure to tell Elizabeth all that happens, should things . . . not go well? She'll not appreciate it if you try to spare her feelings."

"You've the right on your side. Everything will be fine," he said, trying to sound hearty for my sake.

I let him hold on to that. He needed it.

We arrived at the orchard. Apple trees they were, and under Brinsley's direction servants began hanging paper lanterns from the bare limbs. The wind was a nuisance; some of the lanterns went out and could not be relit. Ridley and I were questioned on whether we wanted to proceed under such conditions. We each said yes.

Ridley shed his gaudy coat and fur hat, handing them to someone, then stretched himself this way and that to loosen his muscles. He had a very long reach and obvious strength. Perhaps he thought that might give him the advantage over me, yet another reason for blades over pistols.

Following his example, I did a few stretches after getting rid of my now ludicrous pirate disguise. Stripping away the mask, I took care to study his reaction, but he gave none that could be construed as recognition . . . not right away, that is.

He was inspecting the sets of blades that Brinsley had brought, plucked one up, and swung it around to get the feel of it. Then he briefly leveled it in my direction, looking down its length. Satisfied, he handed it back, but continued favoring me with that same annoying smile.

" 'Fore God, I'll need some beer in me soon for the thirst that's coming. Have you any with you, Barrett?"

No one else understood what he was talking about, only I. Mr. Dennehy told Ridley's second to ask him to refrain from speaking to me unless he was ready to offer apology for his insult.

Ridley laughed, but did not pursue the issue. His point had been made.

"What's behind that?" asked Oliver, leaning close to speak quietly in my ear.

"He's letting me know that we've met before."

"Indeed? When?"

"I'll tell you later, God willing. Let it suffice that his insult to Elizabeth was on purpose in order to provoke me. He knew we all of us were together because of our costumes. He wanted this duel."

"My God."

"I must ask a promise of you should anything adverse happen."

"Whatever I can," he said, too caught up to gainsay my doubts.

"First, to take care of Elizabeth, and second, not to challenge Ridley. If he should better me, the matter ends here, to go no further. Understand?"

He was very white in the lantern light. "But—"

"No further. I won't have your blood shed to disturb my rest."

It ground at him, that was plain, but he finally nodded. "I promise, but for God's sake, be careful. The way he keeps smiling at you like that, he doesn't look right in the head."

"The fool's only trying to unman me."

Then the time was upon us. Swords were presented, the distance marked, and I found myself but a few paces from Ridley preparing to go *en garde.* Again, Ridley was asked if he was prepared to apologize. He said he was not.

"Gentlemen, *en garde* . . ."

Dropping slightly with legs bent in the prescribed manner, I got my blade up and at an angle across my body, its point even with Ridley's head. He mirrored me exactly, but from a higher level because of his height. I found myself noticing small things: how he placed his feet, the pattern of embroidery on his waistcoat, the strange way his sand-colored brows hooked down on the outsides.

*"Allez!"*

I let him make the first pass. As I'd expected, he was relying on his reach and strength. He swatted my blade aside with a powerful slap and lunged, but I backed off in plenty of time, and countered with a feint to the right. He was smart, backing in his turn, and was fast enough to block my true attack to the left. I drove in again on the same side, hoping he'd take it for another feint, but he seemed to know my mind and was ready for it. Damnation, but he was fast. I didn't see his blade so much as his movements.

Some say to watch the other's eyes or his blade or his arm, but the best fencing masters advise their students to watch everything at once. This had seemed an impossibility until my training had advanced to such a degree that I abruptly understood their meaning. To fix upon any single point put you in danger of missing another, more vital one. By focusing only on the blade, I could overlook some telltale shift of an adversary's body as he prepared a fresh attack. Instead, I found myself moving into a strange area of non-thought, where I could see all of my opponent as a single coordinated threat, rather than a haphazard collection of parts, each requiring a separate reaction.

Ridley had apparently followed the same school of training, to judge by his look of serene concentration. I took this in and left it at the door, so to speak. It was important, but only as part of the whole. My mind was empty of thought and emotion; having either cluttering up my actions could be fatal. As great as my anger was toward this man, I could not allow its intrusion, for it would only give him the advantage.

We danced and lunged and parried, playing now, taking each other's measure and comparing it to our own best skills. He was surprisingly fast for so large a man, but I knew myself to be considerably faster. I was also much stronger than he, though this was mitigated by the swords. Had we been grappling in the mud like common street brawlers, I'd have had the better of him without question.

Fencing is like a physical form of chess, requiring similar strategies, but executing them with one's body rather than the board pieces. Ridley knew his business and twice tried a gambit of beating my blade, feinting once, twice, thrice, retreating a step, then simply extending his arm to catch me on my advance. It worked the first time, but all he did was snag and rip my sleeve. No blooding, therefore no pause. The second time I was wise to it, but on the third attempt, he retreated an extra step, leading me to think he'd given up the ploy.

Not so. He grinned, caught my blade, and flicked his wrist 'round in such a way as to disarm me. Even as he began the move, I divined his intent and backed off at the last instant. If I hadn't frozen my hand to the grip, my sword would have gone flying out into the darkness.

He must have fully expected it to work; there was a flash of frustration on his face. He was sweating. It must have felt like a coat of ice on his skin what with the wind. I'd grown warm enough; it would be awhile before any cold could get through to me, and by then we would be long finished.

He had an excellent defense; time and again I'd tried to break past it and failed, but he was starting to breathe hard. My mouth was open, but more for the sake of appearance than any need of air. If nothing else, I could wear him down to the point of exhaustion. As he began to show early signs of it, I played with him more, subtly trying to provoke him into a mistake. Not that I was resorting to anything dishonorable; all I had to do was prevent him from wounding me. For him that was quite sufficient as an annoyance. He was probably very used to winning, and as each moment went by without making progress, his initial frustration looked to be getting the better of him. When that happened, he'd defeat himself.

But in turn, my own great weakness must have been overconfidence. Or underestimation.

The wind tore the plume of his breath right from his lips, and he looked hard-pressed to recover it. The pause between attacks grew perceptively longer; he was slowing down. In another few minutes I'd have him.

I beat him back to tire him that much more. He retreated five or six steps, rapidly, with me following. Then he abruptly halted, beat my blade once, very hard, and as my arm shot wide, he used his long reach and drove in.

Catching me flat.

The first I noticed of it was a damned odd push and tug on my body. I looked down and gaped stupidly. His blade was firmly thrust into my chest, just left of my breast bone. Sickening sight. I also could not move, and so we stood as if frozen for a few seconds, long enough for the shocked groans of the witnesses to reach me. Then he whipped the thing out and stood back, waiting for my fall.

I stumbled drunkenly to both knees. Couldn't help it. The crashing impact of pain was overwhelming. It felt like he'd struck me with a tree trunk, not a slim V-shaped blade of no larger width than my finger. I let go my sword and clutched at my chest, coughed, gagged on what came up, then coughed once more.

Bloodsmell on the winter air.

Taste of blood in my mouth.

*My* blood.

# CHAPTER 9

Oliver was suddenly there, his arm supporting me.

"It's all right," he was saying over and over in a terribly thin, choking voice. Lying to himself. He'd seen. He knew that it was most certainly not all right. He called for Brinsley and for more light to be brought. The others crowded close to see.

The agony was stunning; I wanted only for him to let me alone. I gasped, feebly pushing him off. He would not budge. Instead, he tried to hold me down, just as Beldon had done before him when I'd fallen into that soft sleep one stifling summer day, my last day. Not again. Never again.

Panic tore through me. *"No!* Let me up!"

But he was not listening and told me not to move, to let him help. To get at the wound, he pulled at my hand. It came away covered with blood. The stuff was all over my shirt and waistcoat.

"You must hold still, Jonathan," he pleaded. I heard the tears in his words. Tears for me, for my death.

*"No!"* I couldn't say if I was shouting at him or myself. It wasn't even much of a shout. I had little enough air left to spare for it. To breathe in meant more pain. I doubled over—Oliver kept me from falling altogether—and coughed.

More blood in my mouth. I spat, making a dark stain upon the dead grass, then the grass began to fade away before my fluttering vision.

Good God, *no.* I couldn't . . . not here . . .

I clung to Oliver, *willing* myself to stay solid in spite of every instinct wanting to release me from the fire tearing at my chest. It would have been so easy to surrender to the sanctuary of a noncorporeal state, to its soothing silence, its sweet healing. So easy . . .

I struggled to right myself, ignoring Oliver's protests.

"We'll take him back to the house," Brinsley was saying. "I'll have them fetch a cart."

"No," I said, raising a hand. The bloodied one. "A moment. Wait."

A pause. God knows what they expected of me. Momentous last words? They'd have a hard time of it, for my mind was quite bereft of anything like that. Still, they hovered close in hope.

The seconds passed in disappointing silence . . . and I became aware that my devastating hurt was not as bad as before.

Movement was easier now. Pain. Ebbing. I was able to suck in a draught of air and not forcibly cough it out again.

All I'd wanted was the time to recover myself.

*Recover?*

God's death, what was I on about?

Then as swift as Ridley's attack the comprehension came to me that I was not going to die. Too occupied by the present, I'd forgotten the past. Flashing through my mind was the memory of another dreadful night. I saw Nora once more, heard again her gasp of surprise when a similar blade had pierced her heart. I'd watched in helpless despair as she slid to the floor, thinking her dead—and so she was with neither breath or heartbeat to say otherwise.

But she had come back.

Somehow she had survived that mortal injury.

And by that, I knew I would as well.

With the very thought's occurrence, the raw burning in my chest eased considerably. I even heard myself laugh, though it threatened to become a cough. At least I was in no danger of vanishing in front of—

There they stood about me. Dozens of them. All to bear witness that I'd been run through and had bled like a pig at the butcher's.

And there was poor Oliver, tears on his face as he held me.

What in God's name was I to say to them?

*If one lies often enough and loud enough, the lie eventually becomes the truth.*

But for something like this? It seemed a bit much to expect of them.

On the other hand, there were few other options. I could play the wounded duelist and let them carry me back for a suitably long convalescence, or I could brazen it out right here and hope for the best.

The latter, then, and get it over with.

"Some brandy?" I called, summoning a strong voice from heaven knows where.

Brandy was offered from several different sources, all of them extremely sympathetic. Oliver grabbed at the nearest flask and held it to my lips. So caught up was he in the crisis that he'd forgotten my inability to swallow anything other than blood, but it was of no matter. I'd only asked for brandy for the show of it.

"I can manage, thank you," I told him and reached up to take the flask.

This caused some startled murmuring. Oliver nearly dropped me, but I straightened myself in time. It was difficult not to sneak a look at him, but I had to act as though nothing were seriously amiss. With my clean left hand, I raised the thing to my lips and pretended to drink.

"Much better," I said. "I am most obliged to you, sir."

"Jonathan?" A hundred questions were all over Oliver's strained face, and not one of them could get out.

"I'm fine, Cousin. No need to fear."

"But—you . . . your wound . . ."

"It's nothing. Hurts like blazes. Sweet God, man, I pray I did not worry you over a scratch."

*"A scratch!"* he yelped.

I might have laughed, but for knowing the true depth of what he was going through. "You thought me hurt? But I'm fine or will be. It just scraped the bone, looks worse than it is. Fair knocked the wind from me, though."

This was said loudly enough for the others to hear and pass it along. Those who had not seen the incident clearly took it as the happy truth, but the ones who had been closer were doubtful. Perhaps even fearful.

I noticed this, apparently, for the first time. "Gentlemen, thank you for your concern, but I am much improved." There, that at least was the absolute truth. Not giving anyone time to think and thus dispute the statement, I slowly stood.

Oliver came up with me, mouth hanging, eyes wide with shock. They dropped to my chest and the stains there, but I could do nothing about that for now. The effect on the witnesses was gratifying. The near ones fell back, the far ones leaned closer, but none of them could say that I was even remotely near death.

"Jonathan, in God's name what—?" came my cousin's fierce whisper.

I lowered my head and matched his tone. "It's to do with my changed state. Trust me on this, I am all right."

His mouth opened and shut several times, and his eyes took on the flat cast of fear. "Dear God, you mean—"

"Just play along and I'll explain later. Please!"

The poor fellow looked as if he'd been the one to take the wound, but he bit his lip and nodded. He understood my urgency, if little else.

That settled for the moment, I gave back the flask, then asked to have my sword.

Dennehy came forward, holding it. "Mr. Barrett, are you sure you—"

"I've business to finish, sir. If Mr. Ridley is up to the task, then so am I."

The man in question was not ten paces from me and, if one could tell anything by his expression, was the most dumbfounded of the lot. He had every right to be since he'd certainly *felt* the blade go in and had had to pull it out again. From the twinges still echoing through me, I got the idea the bastard had turned his wrist at the time, just to increase the damage.

He said nothing at first, his gaze going from me to his sword. The end of it was smeared with red for the length of a handspan. He murmured something to the white-faced dandy who was his second. The young man came over to speak to Dennehy and Oliver. I couldn't help but overhear.

"Mr. Ridley has no wish to take the advantage over a wounded man," he said.

"Does Mr. Ridley offer a full and contrite apology for his insult?" I asked.

He glanced back to his friend. Ridley shook his head.

"Then let things proceed as before. He has no advantage over me."

He hesitantly returned, backing all the way.

"Are you sure?" asked Oliver. He was regaining some of his composure, I was glad to see.

"Exceedingly so." Though I'd been very shaken, my unnatural state was such that I was feeling near-normal again.

Or rather extranormal. It was true that Ridley had no advantage on me, but I had a hellish one over him. Unpleasant as it was, he could stab me as much as he liked, but sooner or later I would shrug it off and return to the fray. Not that I planned to give him the chance. I'd learned my lesson and would be more careful than before.

As had he, it seemed. Our next bout was slower, more measured, more cautious, each seeking to find an opening or to make one. I beat him back twice but did not fall for his favorite stratagem, instead pulling away well before he could strike again with his reach. When he saw that was not going to work, he tried to use his strength and speed, and found himself surprisingly outmatched.

I made a rapid high cut, was blocked, got under it, flicked left, right, left, caught his blade, beat it hard to my right, and lunged. It seemed fast enough to me, to him it must have been bewildering. He barely made his defense in time for the first attack; the last one—and it was the last—

took him out of the reckoning. He gave a guttural roar of rage and pain and dropped his sword to clutch at his right arm.

Bloodsmell on the air.

His second rushed forward. Dennehy joined them. Then Oliver. I dropped back and silently looked on.

"Mr. Ridley is sore wounded, sir," reported his second to mine.

"Well blooded and disabled," added Dennehy.

But not dead, I thought. I stalked forward to see for myself. Ridley wasn't going to fight any more this night or any other in the near future. With luck he'd be laid up for weeks.

I raised my blade and touched it to Ridley's shoulder. "I spare your life," I declared loud enough for all to hear. By ancient custom I could have killed him then and there, but the Code had stated once and for all that that was not strictly necessary. With my supreme advantage over him it hardly seemed fair to hold to such a tradition, and besides, to a man like Ridley, this was much more humiliating.

The dandy scrambled to present me with Ridley's dropped sword, and by rights I was entitled to break it. However, since it belonged to Brinsley, I was reluctant to do so. Instead, I handed both blades to him as he came up. "Thank you for the loan of 'em, sir. Uncommonly kind of you."

He began stammering something, but I had no ear for it, feeling suddenly awash with fatigue. My own blood loss was catching me up. There was no rest for me, though, for I found myself abruptly in the center of a cheering, backslapping mob determined to whisk me away and drink to my very good health.

"Best damned fight I've ever seen!"

"A real fire-eater!"

"By God, no one will believe it, but they'll have to or face my challenge!"

"Gentlemen! If you please!"

This last half-strangled cry was from Oliver, who had fought his way to me and seized my arm. I groaned—in gratitude this time—and leaned on him. With the immediate needs of the duel no more, my legs were going all weak.

"Back to the house, if you don't mind?" I asked him.

"Damned right, sir," he promised, an ominous tone in his voice. He threw my cloak over me, and I pulled it tight to conceal the alarming state of my shirtfront. We made a slow parade, but others ran ahead with the news, and as we neared the house, more came out to greet us and hear the story. Unfortunately, it grew in the telling, and nothing I said could stop it. As it was fantastic to begin with, it hardly seemed worth the trouble to try.

Enlisting Brinsley's aid to speed things along, we were soon in the relative peace of a small chamber. I allowed myself to be stretched upon a comfortable settee and disdained all offers of help as being too much fuss. What I wanted was solitude, but my earnest admirers took it as evidence of modest bravery. They held true to their promise and began toasting my health then and there, creating another problem for me since I could not join in their celebration.

Just as things were starting to become unbearable, Elizabeth appeared, pushing her way through the others to get to me.

"Jonathan, someone just told me that you—" She interrupted herself by giving forth a heartfelt shriek. My cloak had slipped open a little, revealing the alarming bloodstains.

"He's in no danger," Oliver hastened to assure her. "He just needs a bit of quiet. Gentlemen, would you please allow me to attend my patient?"

Easier said than done, what with all the crowd. I asked for them to leave, though it was a sore disappointment to my well-wishers. Brinsley, with his authority as host, stepped forward and persuaded them to be herded outside.

Throughout all this, Elizabeth pounded us both with angry questions.

"A duel? How in God's name did you get into a duel?" she demanded.

"That blasted fellow in the Russian costume insulted you," said Oliver. "If Jonathan hadn't challenged him, I certainly would have, the filthy bounder."

"Insulted—what on earth did he say? Jonathan, are you all right? Oh, why did you *do* such a thing?"

And so on. She said quite a lot in a very short time, torn as she was between rage and relief. I had to tell her over and over that I was fine, while keeping one eye on Oliver . . . who was keeping one eye on me.

Once the door was closed and we were blessedly alone, Oliver pulled a chair up next to me, and I did not relish the sick worry that so obviously troubled him. He reached toward me, saying he needed to see my wound.

I tried to wave him off. "This is not necessary. I'm fine. I just need a little rest."

Blinking and swallowing hard, he looked as if I'd slapped him. "I—I know what I saw, Jonathan. Please don't make light of me."

"What does he mean?" asked Elizabeth. "Just how bad is that scratch?"

"Bad enough," I muttered.

Oliver bowed his head, raised it, then quickly moved, and opened my shirt. He gave a kind of gasping sob, full of fear. Just to the right of my breastbone was a fierce-looking red welt, like a fresh scar, about as large around as my thumb. There was drying blood all around it, but the wound itself was cleanly closed. The rest of the area was tender like a bruise and about as troubling.

"It's not possible," he said, as miserable as any man can be on this side of hell. "Not . . . possible."

Elizabeth leaned close. "My God, Jonathan, what happened? What *really* happened?"

"I was careless. Ridley got through. A palpable hit, it was."

"You—"

"Should have killed me, but didn't. Thought I had been killed . . . then I was better. It hurt, though." My voice sounded rather hollow—little wonder when death comes so close. Even a mocking touch from the Reaper is enough to melt one's bones.

"How can this be?" Oliver pleaded. Fear again. Fear sufficient for all of us to have a share.

No more for me. I was weary of that dismal load. I straightened as though to shake it from my back. "Remember what I told you about Nora?"

Elizabeth knew the full story on that and understood of what I was speaking. It took poor Oliver a little longer. To be fair, he'd been rather drunk when we'd had our talk; he might not have possessed a clear recollection of everything. Besides, being told something and actually witnessing it are two very different things.

"You were run right through the heart," he insisted. "I saw it. So did the others, then you—"

"Others?" Elizabeth froze me with a look. "How many others?"

"Most of the lot that Brinsley chased out for us."

"And they saw everything?"

"It was very fast and dark. They've already convinced themselves that they didn't see what they thought they saw."

While she sorted that out, I turned back to Oliver.

"There's no need to be upset about this. It's all part of my changed nature, and I can no more explain why it is than you can tell me what causes the flying gout."

"But for you to survive such a—for you to heal so quickly . . ."

"I know. It's one of the things that puzzles me as well. It's why I have to see Nora and talk to her."

"But it's just not *natural!*" he insisted.

The little room went very silent, with none of us moving. Finally I asked, "What do you want me to do about it?"

"I didn't know you could do anything about it."

"I can't."

"Oh." He sat back, a dull red blush creeping up his long face as the point came home. "Um—well, that is."

"Agreed," I said.

"Guess I'm being an ass again," he mumbled.

"No more than myself for forgetting all about what happened to Nora until after the fact. I was so damned angry at Ridley I couldn't think of anything except smashing his face in."

Elizabeth scowled. "Just what *did* he say about me?"

My turn to blush.

"It was that terrible?"

"Let it suffice that I doubt he will ever be invited to one of the Bolyns' gatherings ever again. He's a genuine rotter—and a Mohock."

"No!" said Oliver, aghast.

"Saw him myself on my first night here. He was leading a pack of 'em, drunk as Davy's sow—"

"And you said nothing of it?" Elizabeth's eyes were fairly blazing.

"Well . . ."

Oliver leaned close once more. "I think you should very quickly tell us about this business."

"There's not that much to tell."

"Nevertheless . . ." He glanced at Elizabeth's eloquent face.

"Nevertheless," I faintly echoed, needing no more prompting, but I was tired and in want of refreshment, so my recounting of my initial meeting with Ridley was straightforward and as brief as I could make it. I thought longingly of Jericho and his clever juggling with teapots, but that was not a luxury I could enjoy just now.

Just as I finished, someone knocked at the door, and Brinsley hesitantly put his head in.

"I say, won't you be wanting some bandaging or water or something?" he asked of Oliver.

It took a moment for my cousin to adjust his attention from my past exploit to his present dilemma. He gave me a wide-eyed look, a mute inquiry of what to do. I answered with a short nod, and he told Brinsley that he had use for those very items, if it would not be too much trouble.

"None at all, old chap. How are you doing, Barrett?"

"Very well. I'll be up and about soon."

"What a relief! Can I get you anything?"

"Perhaps you can spare an old shirt for me? Mine's a bit—"

"Heavens, man, I can do better than that!" He bobbed out again, eager to get things moving.

"It seems to be working," said Oliver. "Brinsley was right next to me and saw the blade go in, and look how he is now. He *believes* you."

I sighed. "Thank heavens for that."

God have mercy, if I'd had to influence the lot of them into denying the evidence of their own eyes, I'd have burst my own head from the effort. As things stood, the witnesses were apparently doing a much better job of it on their own.

"Incredible." Oliver was shaking his head. "And all this because you curtailed Ridley's drunken sport. If he was that far gone in drink, I'm surprised he was able to remember you."

"No more than I was to find how he moves so easily from the gutter to polite company. He's a very dangerous fellow, and you must do all you can to avoid him."

"He's got no quarrel with me, but we two are blood kin—I'll do my best, Coz, but I doubt that he'll be much of a problem for now. You skewered him properly, though killing him would have been better."

"I've had enough of killing, thank you very much." Yes, now. Now that I was cooled enough to think again.

"Still, he's a spiteful type, you can see that. It might be over for tonight, but he's just the sort to come after you later, though. According to the Code, he cannot reopen the argument, but that won't stop him from beginning a new one."

"I'll keep my eyes open, not to fear," I promised.

"I wonder how he's doing, anyway?"

"If you really want to go find out . . ." I began doubtfully.

"Not a bit of it! Just wondered is all. I suppose they've turned up another doctor to attend him or I'd have been called in by now. Just as well, I suppose."

Some of the Bolyn servants appeared, bearing the promised washing water, bandaging, and a clean shirt of very fine silk. Brinsley—it seemed—was in the midst of a very severe bout of hero worship with myself being the object of adulation. I was rather nonplussed to be in such a position, feeling neither worthy of the honor nor comfortable, but it could not be helped.

The room was cleared again, and this time Elizabeth went out to deliver a report to the waiting throng about my condition and to order Oliver's carriage to be brought 'round. It would have been too much to expect us to remain and participate in the rest of the evening's festivities after all this.

I cleaned the dried blood away, donned Brinsley's shirt, and bundled up my torn and stained costume shirt and waistcoat for Jericho to deal with. Perhaps he could work a miracle and salvage them in some way. Oliver, seeing that the bandages were unnecessary, stuffed them away in one of his pockets.

For the sake of appearance and to discourage questions, I leaned heavily on his arm on our way out, keeping my head down. Not all of my weakness was a pose; I was very enervated by the blood loss and would soon need to replace it. My energy came in fits and spurts; I'd have some lively moments, then sink into an abrupt lethargy as if my body was trying to conserve strength.

Though our concerned hosts were disappointed that I would not remain with them for my mending, they got us all to the carriage without too much delay and we piled gratefully in.

"I'm sorry to have spoiled the party for you," I said to Elizabeth as we settled ourselves.

She snorted. "After this kind of excitement a masqued ball, no matter how elaborate, is but a tame occupation by comparison. I shall be in need of rest, anyway, for there will be a hundred callers coming 'round to the house tomorrow to see how things are with you. I hope Jericho and the staff will be up to the invasion. I'll wager that most of them will be young ladies with their mothers, all hoping for a glimpse of you."

My heart plummeted. "You can't mean it?"

"I saw it in their faces before we left. There's nothing so stirring to the feminine heart as watching a wounded duelist stoically dragging himself away from the field of battle."

"That's ridiculous."

"Indeed, many of the girls expressed disdain for any man unless he's blazed away at another in the name of honor—or in your case taken up the sword to—"

"Enough, for heaven's sake!" I moaned.

"No, little brother, I think this is but the beginning. Like it or not, you've become a hero. . . ."

"Oh, my God."

Oliver's eyes had flicked back and forth between us and now came to rest on me. His mobile face twitched and heaved mightily with suppressed emotion for all of two seconds, then he burst forth with a roar of laughter.

Had Oliver not been in sore need of the distraction, I'd have objected to his finding humor in my situation, but I held my peace and endured until he'd quite worked through it. By then we were home and trudging up to our respective rooms to prepare for bed, myself excepted, of course. I went to the parlor to rest a little while, until Jericho came in. Elizabeth had apparently told him about tonight's adventure, for he raised no question concerning the bloodied bundle of clothes I handed him.

"Don't know if you can salvage 'em, but it might be a good idea not to let the others see this lot. Might alarm them or something, and I've no wish to add to the gossip about this incident."

"I shall be discreet, Mr. Jonathan. You're certain that you are all right?"

"I think so, but for being wretchedly weak, and that will soon be remedied. Has the coachman finished with the horses?"

"He just came back from the stables and is having tea in the kitchen. The way is quite clear for you . . . unless you wish me to see to things?" he asked, referring obliquely to fetching the blood himself.

Tempting, but that would involve an additional wait. No, I was tired, but not that far gone. I told him as much and thanked him for the offer.

After he'd gone away to the kitchen, I traded the inadequate pirate cloak for my own heavy woolen one and slipped out the front door to walk unhurriedly around the house. The grounds of Oliver's property were limited, with barely room for a small vegetable garden, now dormant, and the stables, but at least he had no need to board his carriage animals and hunter elsewhere. With Rolly added to this little herd, I had a more than adequate supply of nourishment for my needs, though other sources were available. London was positively bursting with horses, and should it become necessary, I'd be able to feed from them easily enough.

It was Rolly's turn tonight. He'd filled out somewhat now that he was done with ocean voyaging. I'd been generous with his oats and had him groomed every day, and the extra care showed in his bright eyes and shining coat. We'd lately been out for a turn or two around the town when the weather wasn't too wet, so he wasn't snappish for lack of exercise.

I offered him a lump of sugar as a bribe, soothed him down, and got on with my business. He held perfectly still even after I'd finished and was wiping my lips clean. For that he got more sugar. Intelligent beast.

The blood did its usual miracle of restoration on my battered body. I felt its heat spreading from the inside out, though it seemed particularly concentrated on my chest this night. The skin over my heart was starting to itch. Opening Brinsley's shirt, I found the angry red patch around the fresh scar had faded somewhat. Very reassuring, that.

Since I was finally alone, though, I was free to take a shortcut to speed up my healing. I vanished.

Rolly didn't like it much. Perhaps he could sense my presence in some way; perhaps it had to do with the cold I generated in this form. He stirred in his box, shying away in protest. To ease things for him, I quit the stables and floated through the doors into the yard, using memory to find the path leading to the house. Despite the buffeting of the wind, I was able to make my way back again to materialize in the parlor right before the fireplace.

Jericho, being extremely familiar with my habits, had built the fire up into a fine big blaze during my absence and set out my slippers and dressing gown. I listened intently for a moment to the sounds of the house. Jericho was in the kitchen exchanging light conversation with the coachman and the cook. I couldn't quite make out the words, but the voices were calm, ordinary in tone, indicating that all was peaceful below-stairs. Just as well.

The itch in my chest was no more. A second look at the place of my wounding both assured and astonished me. All trace of red was gone, and the scar appeared to be weeks old. In time, most probably after my next vanishing, it would disappear altogether.

Suddenly shivering, I pulled a chair closer to the fire and sat miserably huddled in my cloak.

I thought of Father, missing him and his sensible, comforting manner with me whenever life became troubling.

"You should be glad that you still have a life to be troubled about," I muttered aloud. God knows with the times being what they were, had I not been cut down by that fool at the Captain's Kettle over a year ago, I'd have met a bad fate soon after.

And recovered from it. Because of my change.

A nasty sort of unease oozed through my belly as I pondered on how things might have been had I not met Nora. Without her, I'd have certainly stayed in my early grave; Elizabeth would be dead as well, foully and horribly murdered. That would have shattered Father, to lose us both.

I shivered again and told myself to stop being so morbid. It was all because of that damned duel and that damned Thomas Ridley. The thought of him filled me with fury and disgust, the former for his picking the fight, the latter for his stupidity in continuing it. Blooding aside, I'd not enjoyed my revenge against him. My hand could still feel how my blade had stabbed into the tough resistance of his fleshy arm until it grated upon and was stopped by the bone beneath. A singularly unpleasant sensation, that. He'd be weeks healing, unless it became fevered, and then he'd either lose the arm or die.

Well, as with everything else, it was in God's hands. No need for me to wallow in guilt for something not my fault. Yes, I had wanted to kill him for his insult to Elizabeth, but that desire had gone out of me after the first shock of my own wound had worn off. It was as if I'd seen just how foolish he was, like a child trying to threaten an adult. To be sure, he was a very dangerous child, but he'd no earthly idea of just how overmatched he'd been with me. And I . . . I'd forgotten the extent of my own capabilities, which made me a fool as well.

No more of that, Johnny Boy, I thought, shaking my head.

Warmer, I threw off the cloak, exchanging it for the dressing gown, and struggled to remove my boots. I'd just gotten my left heel lifted free, ready to slip the rest of the way out, when someone began knocking at the front door.

Damnation, what now? Slamming my foot back into the boot, I made my frustrated way to the central hall and peered through one of the windows flanking the entrance.

A man wrapped in a dark cloak stood outside. For a mad second I thought he might be Ridley because of his size, but the set of his shoulders was more squared and there was nothing amiss with his right arm. He turned and raised it now to knock again and I caught his profile.

Cousin Edmond Fonteyn? What on earth did he want?

Probably come to berate me about the duel. He was something of a dogsbody to Aunt Fonteyn—and to her only—and if she wasn't of a mind to vent her doubtless acid opinion of the matter herself, she'd have sent him in her stead. Not that I had a care for the substitution or even his presence. So much had happened tonight that I was simply unable to raise my usual twinge of guilt from having hung the cuckold's horns on him that Christmas years past.

"I'll get it, sir," said Jericho, emerging from the back.

"I'm already here, no need." Obligingly, I unbolted and opened the door, and Edmond swept in, seeming to fill the hall. It was not his size alone that did it, so much as his manner. Stick-in-the-mud he might be, according to Oliver, but when he entered a room, people noticed.

"Hallo, Edmond," I began. "If it's about the duel, I can tell you—"

"Bother that," he said, his brown eyes taking in the hall, noting Jericho's presence, then fastening on me. "Where's Oliver?"

"In bed by now."

"Have him fetched without delay."

Edmond always looked serious, but there was a dark urgency to him now that made my flesh creep with alarm. I signed to Jericho. He'd already started up the stairs.

"There's a fire going in the parlor," I said, gesturing him in the right direction.

He frowned at me briefly, then accepted the invitation, striding ahead without hurry. Under the cloak he still wore his Harlequin guise, though he'd traded the white skullcap for a normal hat. He wore no wig, revealing his close-cropped, graying hair. It should have made him seem vulnerable, half-dressed in some way, but did not.

"What's all this about?" I asked.

His eyes raked me up and down, caught mine, then turned toward the fire. "Duel," he said. There was derision in his tone, like that of a schoolmaster for an especially backward student.

"What about it?"

"Never mind, it's of no importance."

"Then tell me what's going on."

"You'll know soon enough," he growled.

Very well, then, I'd not press things. It seemed forever, though, waiting for Oliver to come down. Edmond was throwing off tension like a fire throws off heat; I could almost feel myself starting to scorch from it. Relief flooded me when Oliver finally appeared, clad also in a dressing gown, but wearing slippers, not boots.

Sleepily he glanced past Edmond to me, as if asking for an explanation. I could only shrug.

"Oliver—" Edmond paused to brace himself. "Look, I'm very sorry, but something terrible has happened, and I don't quite know how to tell you."

All vestige of sleep fell away from Oliver's face at these alarming words. "What's happened?" he demanded.

"What?" I said at the same time.

"Your mother . . . there's been an accident."

"An acci—what sort of—where is she?"

"At the Bolyns'. She had a fall. We think she slipped on some ice."

"Is she all right?" Oliver stepped forward, his voice rising.

"She struck her head in the fall. I'm very sorry, Oliver, but she's dead."

# CHAPTER
# ◄10►

In England, for those in high enough and wealthy enough circles, funerals were customarily held at night, which was just as well for me as it would have raised some comment had I not attended, but then I only wanted to be there for Oliver's sake and not my own.

The weather was atrocious, all bitterly cold wind and cutting sleet—most appropriate, considering Aunt Fonteyn's temperament. Her final chance to inflict one last blast of misery upon her family, I thought, cowering with the rest of the family as we followed the coffin to its final destination. I walked on one side of Oliver, Elizabeth on the other, offering what support we could with the bleak knowledge that it was not enough. For days since the delivery of the bad news, the color had drained right out of his face and had yet to return. He was as gray and fragile as an old man; his eyes were disturbingly empty, as if he'd gone to sleep but forgotten to close them.

I hoped that once the horror of the interment was over, he might begin to recover himself. The ties are strong between a mother and child, whether they love each other or not; when those ties are irreparably severed, the survivor is going to have a strong reaction of some kind. For all his years of abuse from her, for all his mutterings against her, she was, as he'd said, the only mother he'd got. Even if he'd come to hate her, she'd still been a major influence in his life, unpleasant, but at least familiar. Her sudden absence would bring change, and changes are frightening when one is utterly unprepared for them. Certainly I could attest to the absolute truth of that in light of my past experience with death and the profound change it had delivered to my family.

The memory of my demise came forcibly back as we shivered here in the family mausoleum a quarter mile from Fonteyn House. No mixing with other folk in the churchyard for this family; the Fonteyns would share eternity with their own kind, thank you very much; and no muddy graves, either, but a spacious and magnificent sepulcher fit for royalty, large enough to hold many future generations of their ilk.

The huge structure had been built by Grandfather Fonteyn, who was presently moldering in a carved marble sarcophagus a few yards from where I stood. His eldest daughter's coffin was even now being pushed into its nearby niche by the pallbearers. Tomorrow its stone cover with a brass plate bearing her name would be mortared into place on the wall.

As depressing as it was to stand here surrounded by the Fonteyn dead, it was preferable to standing 'round a gaping hole in the ground with the sleet stinging the backs of our necks. The cloying scent of freshly turned earth might have been too much for me, though being at a funeral, period, was bad enough. The same went for Elizabeth, for she not only had memories of my burial to wrestle with, but those of James Norwood's, too.

I glanced over to see how she was holding up, and she gave me a thin but confident smile meant to reassure. Much of her attention was concentrated on Oliver, which was probably why she was able to get through this at all.

Sheet white and shaking miserably with the cold, he looked ready to fall over. He wasn't drunk, and he should have been; he was in sore need of some muzzy-headed insulation from what was happening. He stared unfocused at his mother's coffin as they pushed it into place, and I had no doubt that every detail was searing itself forever into his battered mind.

*He must have help,* I thought, and wondered what I could possibly do for him. No shred of an idea presented itself, though. Perhaps later, after we were out of this damned death house, I could come up with something.

The service finally concluded. Since I'd not listened to one word of it, I knew only by the last *amens* and general stir about me. No mourners lingered in this torch-lit tomb. As one, we left Elizabeth Therese Fonteyn Marling to God's mercy and all but galloped back through the crusty mud and snow to the lights and warmth of Fonteyn House.

The servants had set up a proper feast for the occasion, and the family set to it with an unseemly gusto. Soon the gigantic collection of cold joints, pies, sweets, hams, and lord knows what else began to steadily disappear from the serving trays. The drink also suffered a similar swift depletion, but no one became unduly loud or merry from all the flowing Madeira. Oliver, I noted, never went near the groaning tables.

*Very bad, that,* I thought.

There had been an inquiry about Aunt Fonteyn's death, but only a brief one, since it was obvious to all that it had been an accident. She'd been found in the center of the Bolyns' shrubbery maze, having had the bad luck of somehow slipping on a patch of ice and striking her head on the edge of the marble fountain there. Some servant had found her and raised the alarm. A doctor was sent for, but her skull had been well and truly broken; nothing could be done. At least it had been quick and relatively painless, people had said; that should be something of a comfort to her family. After all, there were worse ways to die.

Of the talk I overheard or participated in, it was universally agreed how unfair and awful it was, but then God's will was bound to be a mystery to those who still lived. Thankfully, Cousin Edmond assumed the duties of making arrangements for the funeral. A lawyer himself, he moved things quickly along out of deference for Oliver's condition, and three nights later most of the family had gathered at Fonteyn House to pay their last respects.

If everyone had not been garbed in black, it might have been another Fonteyn Christmas. All the usual crowd was present, and one by one they expressed their sympathy to Oliver. Some of them, being sensitive to his downcast countenance, were even sincere.

One or two latecomers were ushered in by the sad-faced mute hired for the task. Gloves and rings had been distributed to the closest relatives; I'd gotten a silk hat hand and chamois gloves, all black. God knows what I'd do with them, being unable to truly hold any grief in my heart for the foul-minded old hag, but I was expected to put on a show of it, nonetheless. Hypocritical to be sure, but I took comfort from the fact that I could hardly be the only member in this gathering with such feelings. Aunt Fonteyn had not been the sort of person to inspire deep and sincere mourning from anyone in their right senses . . . then I suddenly thought of Mother and just in time whipped out a handkerchief to cover my painfully twitching mouth before betraying a highly improper grin to the room.

The only thing that settled me was the knowledge that I'd have to write home with the news. Father wouldn't have an easy time of it—not that he ever did—once Mother learned about the demise of the sister she doted upon. With that in mind I was just able to play my part, nodding at the right times and murmuring the right things and trying to keep my eye on Oliver as much as possible.

He was still hemmed in by a pack of relatives and not too responsive to whatever they were saying. Elizabeth was with him, doing her best to make up for his lack. Oh, well, no one would think badly of him for it and only put it off to grief.

My lovely cousin Clarinda moved in and out through the crowds, having assumed the duties of hostess for him. I could not honestly say that black suited her; tonight she looked almost as drawn as Oliver. Though far more animated than he, her natural liveliness was well dampened owing to the circumstances. We'd exchanged formal greetings earlier, neither of us giving any sign of having a shared secret. I suspected, given Clarinda's obvious appetite for willing young men, that our particular encounter had faded quite a bit in her memory. Not that I felt slighted in any way; relief would best describe my reaction if this proved to be so.

I moved among the various relatives as well, shaking a hand here, bowing to a lady there, but inevitably ending up with a group of the men as they spoke in low tones about the tragedy. As there was actually very little one could say about it, and since it was considered bad taste to speak ill of the departed, no matter how deserving, the topics of talk soon shifted from things funereal to things political. The dispiriting details of General Burgoyne's surrender were now in the papers, and the men here had formed the idea that I could somehow tell them more than what had appeared in print. But with my mind on Oliver's problems, I had no interest in discussing the situation in the Colonies tonight.

"Forgive me, gentlemen, but I know only as much as you do from your reading," I said, trying to put them off.

"But you're from the area, from New York," insisted one of my many Fonteyn cousins.

"I'm from Long Island, and it's as far away from Saratoga as London is from Plymouth—and with far worse roads in between."

This garnered some discreet laughter.

"But you weren't so very far from the general fighting yourself if Oliver is to be believed."

"I've been close enough, sir. There have been some incidents near our village concerning the rebels, but the King's army has things well in hand now." *I hope,* I silently added, feeling the usual stab of worry for Father whenever I thought of home.

"You're being too modest, Mr. Barrett," said another young man, one of the many in the crowd. I had a strong idea he was here more for the feasting than to pay his respects. He was a handsome fellow and familiar, since I'd seen him before at other gatherings, but nameless like dozens of others. "I believe by now all of you know that your cousin here is a rare fire-eater when it comes to battle," he added. "Perhaps some of you were there at the Bolyns' party and saw him in action."

I didn't like his manner much or the fact he'd brought up the subject of the duel. Unfortunately, the other men were highly interested and wanted a full recountal of the event.

"Gentlemen, this is hardly an appropriate time or place," I said, being as firmly discouraging as possible.

"Oh, but we may never have another opportunity," the young man drawled with expansive insistence. "I think we'd all like to hear how you defeated Mr. Thomas Ridley after he'd so grievously wounded you."

"Hardly so grievous or I'd not be here, sir."

More suppressed expressions of good humor.

"Do you call me a liar, sir?" he said slowly, deliberately, and worst of all, with no alteration in his pleasant expression.

Great heavens, I'd dreaded that some idiot might turn up and make a nuisance of himself by wanting to provoke a duel with me, but I hadn't expected it to happen so soon and leastwise not at Aunt Fonteyn's funeral. Those around us went very still waiting for my answer.

I could have found a graceful way of getting out of it, but the man's obvious insult was too annoying to disregard. "Your name, sir?" I asked, keeping my own voice and expression as bland as possible.

"Arthur Tyne, sir. Thomas Ridley's cousin."

If he expected me to blanch in terror at this revelation, he was in for a vast disappointment. "Indeed? I trust and pray that the man is recovering from his own wound."

"You have not answered me, Mr. Barrett," he said, putting an edge into his tone that was meant to be menacing.

"Only because I thought you were making a jest, sir. It seemed polite that I should overlook it, since we are all here to pay our solemn respects to the memory of my aunt."

"That was no jest, sir, but a most earnest inquiry. Are you prepared to answer?"

"You astound me, Mr. Tyne. Of course I did not call you a liar."

"I find you to be most insolent, sir."

"Which is not too surprising; poor Aunt Fonteyn often made the same complaint against me." If some of those around us were shocked by my honesty, then more were struggling not to show their amusement.

"Are you deaf? I said you are most insolent, Mr. Barrett."

"Not deaf, only agreeing with you, dear fellow." I fixed my eyes and full concentration upon him. "Certainly you can find no exception to that."

In actuality, Arthur Tyne found himself unable to say anything at all.

"This is a most sad occasion for me," I went on. "I should be sadder still if I've caused you any distress. Come along with me, sir. I am very interested in hearing how things are with your cousin."

So saying, I linked my arm with his and led him out of earshot of the rest. Tyne was just starting to blink himself awake when I fixed him again with my gaze.

"Now, you listen to me, you little toad," I whispered. "I don't care if the idea to have a fight with me was yours or your cousin's, but you can put it right out of your head. You're to leave me and mine alone. Understand? Now get out of my sight and stay out of my way."

And so I had the pleasure of seeing Arthur Tyne's back as he made a hasty retreat. He was visibly shaken, and the other men noticed, but I kept my pretense of a smile and easily ignored them. What I could not ignore was Edmond Fonteyn's sudden presence next to me. Unlike his wife, black suited him well, made him look larger, more powerful, more intimidating.

"What the devil are you up to?" he demanded.

"Just trying to avoid an embarrassing scene, Cousin," I said tiredly, hoping he would go away.

He gave me a stony glare. "More dueling?"

"Just the opposite, as a matter of fact."

He pushed past me and went in pursuit of Arthur. I could trust that Edmond would find things in order. If Arthur was typical of the others I'd influenced, he'd not remember much of it; if not, and Edmond returned with questions . . . well, I could deal with him if necessary. It might even be amusing to see *his* grim face going all blank and vulnerable for a change.

But there were more pressing things for me to deal with tonight than fools and irate cousins, and it was past time I got on with them. Putting Edmond and Arthur firmly from mind, I searched the ranks of the servants, at last spotted the one I wanted, and drifted over.

"Radcliff?"

"Yes, sir?" He was busy supervising the sherry and Madeira, making sure most of it went into the guests, not the servers.

"I should like two bottles of good brandy sent along to the blue drawing room, please. Put some food with it, breads and sweets, some ham if there's any left."

He raised one eyebrow, but offered no more comment, and went to order things for me. I now drifted over to Oliver and Elizabeth. As she looked pale and strained from the effort she was putting forth, her gaze fell on me and she grasped my arm convulsively.

"Here now, you're not planning to faint, are you?" I asked, concerned that this was becoming all too much for her.

"Don't be an ass," she whispered back. "I'm just tired. All these people . . ." There were quite a lot of them, and dealing with each and every one while looking after Oliver had put her teeth dangerously on edge.

"Well, I'm taking over for you and no arguing. See that fellow by the wine table? Go ask him for anything you like and have him send it to some quiet room. Make sure you eat. You look ready to drop in your tracks."

She needed no more persuasion, and I took her place at Oliver's side. I made sure the person who was presently trying to speak with him understood that my interruption had some urgent purpose behind it. He gracefully excused himself and I slipped a hand 'round Oliver's arm.

"Come along with me, old man, something's come up that wants your attention."

He passively allowed himself to be led away. We reached the blue drawing room just as one of Radcliff's efficient minions was leaving. I got Oliver inside, firmly closed the door, then steered him toward the warmth of the fireplace.

"Beastly night for a burying, what?" I asked, pouring brandy for him. There were two glasses; I slopped a few drops into the second one for the sake of appearance.

Oliver shrugged and decorously sat in the chair, rather than resorting to his usual careless fall. One of his hands was closed into a fist. He wore a mourning ring on that one, a ring made from his mother's hair.

I picked up the brandy glass and offered it to him. He listlessly took it, but did not drink.

"Go on, then, do yourself some good," I said encouragingly.

He gave no sign that he'd heard.

"You'll have to sometime, you know damned well I can't touch the stuff. Come on, then."

Casting an indifferent glance at me, he finally raised it to his lips and sipped, then put it aside on a table. "I'd really like to be alone," he mumbled.

He wasn't the only one who could ape deafness. "Radcliff seems to have provided the choicer bits of food for you, so it's pity on me for missing out on the feast." In actuality, the cooked meats smelled nauseating, but I stoutly ignored the sensation.

"Not hungry," he said, still mumbling.

"I can hardly believe that."

"Believe what you like, but please let me alone."

"All right, whatever you say." I started to turn. "Half a minute, there's something on your hand. . . ."

I caught the mourning ring and suddenly pulled it free from his finger, pretending to examine it. “Now, here’s a grisly relic. Wonder if it’s her own hair or from one of her wigs?”

“What the devil are you—give that to me!” He started to lurch from his chair.

“Not just yet.” I shoved him back into place.

He knocked my arm away. “How dare you!”

“It’s easy enough.”

“Have you gone mad? Give that—” He started up again, and I backed away, holding the ring high. He lunged for it, and I let him catch my arm, but wouldn’t allow him to take the ring. I dragged us toward the middle of the room where there was no furniture to trip over, and we wrestled around like boys having a schoolyard scuffle.

“I’m sure your mother . . . would be delighted . . . to know,” I said between all the activity, “the depth of . . . your regard for her.”

Oliver had grown red-faced with anger. “You bastard . . . why are you . . . I hated her!”

Now I showed some of my real strength, getting behind him and pinning his arms back as if he were a small child. Half-lifted from the floor, he struggled futilely, trying to kick my shins and sometimes succeeding; not that it bothered me much, I was too busy taking care not to hurt him.

“You hated her?” I said in his ear, sounding astonished.

“Damn you—let me go!” He wriggled with all his might but was quickly wearing out. His self-imposed fasting for the last few days had done him little good.

“You’re sure you hated her?” I taunted.

*“Damn you!”* he bellowed and landed a properly vicious one on my kneecap with the edge of his heel. I felt it, grunted, and released him. He staggered a step to get his balance and whirled around. His face was so twisted with rage, I hardly knew him. Had I pushed too far?

Apparently so, for he charged at me, fists ready, and made use of them willy-nilly on any portion of me that I was foolish enough to leave within range. I blundered into tables and other furnishings trying to keep away from him. Ornaments fell and shattered, and we managed to knock a portrait from the wall; the worst was when a chair went right over and I went with it—backward. My head struck the wooden floor with a thud, and the candlelight flared and flashed dizzyingly for me.

This is really too wretchedly stupid, I thought as my arms bonelessly flopped at my sides. I was too stunned for the moment to offer further defense and expected Oliver to take advantage of it to really pummel me . . . but nothing happened.

After a minute I cracked an eyelid open in his direction and saw his legs. Traveling upward, I made out his hands—fists no longer, thank God—then his heaving chest, then his mottled face. He hiccupped twice, and that's when I noticed his streaming tears.

"You are. A bastard." He swiped at the tears with the back of one arm.

I felt like one, too. I also felt pretty badly from the fall and took my time getting untangled from the chair and standing. Jericho would be appalled when he saw my clothes; I'd have to assure him that the damage—buttons torn from the waistcoat, a coat sleeve partly ripped from its shoulder, shredded lace, and dirtied stockings with gaping holes over the shins—had all been in a good cause.

"Here," I said shakily, holding the ring out.

He grabbed it away and tried to thrust it back on again, but was trembling and half blinded by tears; he just couldn't do it.

"Damn you, damn you, damn you," he said throughout his efforts.

"And damn you for an idiot, dear Cousin," I growled back.

"You dare? How can you—"

"You hated her, so why do you even bother with that?" I gestured at the ring.

He took another swing at me. A halfhearted attempt. I successfully dodged it.

"You think anyone here cares whether you're in mourning or not? Or are you worried about what they might think?"

"I don't give a bloody damn what they think!" The next time he swung, I caught his arm and, after more scuffling, dragged him to the chair and more or less got him to sit.

"I'll kill you for this!" he roared.

"I don't think so. Now shut up or—"

"Or what? You'll use your unholy influence on me?"

"If I'd planned that, I'd have done it sooner and spared myself a beating. You'll behave now or I'll slap your poxy face until you're silly."

He must have decided that I was serious, for he slumped a bit. "My face isn't poxy," he muttered.

This was said with such pouting sincerity that I stopped short to stare at him. He returned with a stubborn look of his own for a full ten seconds, then both our faces began crumbling, first with a sharp pulling at the mouth corners, then suppressed snickers, then full-blown laughter. His was short-lived, though, quickly devolving back to tears. Once started, he kept going, head bowed as he sobbed away his inner agony. Putting an arm around his shoulders, I wept myself, not for any grief of my own, but out of sympathy for his.

Then some oaf knocked at the door.

I wearily moved toward it, wiping my nose and eyes, and when I'd put myself in order, opened it an inch. "Yes?"

Radcliff was there, along with a few other servants, all seeming very worried. "Sir, we heard something break . . . is there a problem?"

They'd heard more than that from the looks I was getting. I gave them an easy and innocent smile. "No, just had a bit of a mishap. Nothing to worry about. Mr. Marling and I are having a private talk and would appreciate it if we could be left undisturbed for the time being."

"If you're sure, sir . . ."

"Quite sure, thank you. You may all return to your duties."

With considerable reluctance and much doubt, they dispersed, and I shut the door, putting my back to it and leaning against it with a heartfelt sigh. My head ached where it had struck the floor, and I half debated on vanishing for a moment to heal, then dismissed the idea for now. Though Oliver knew about that particular talent of mine, an unexpected exhibition would likely alarm and upset him; he had more than sufficient things to worry about.

He was presently sniffing and yawning and showing evidence of pulling himself together. His eyes were very red, and the white skin above and below them was all puffed, but a spark of life seemed to be returning to them.

He held up the mourning ring. "Did that on purpose, did you?"

"I plead guilty, m'lord."

"Humph."

In deference to my head and bruised shins, I crept slowly from the door, taking a chair opposite him. The table with the food and brandy bottles was between us, and he gestured at it.

"I suppose the next step is to make me eat or get me stinking drunk or both."

"That's exactly right, dear Coz."

"Humph." He turned the mourning ring over and over. "Y'know, this is the closest I ever got to touching her. She wouldn't allow it. Messed up her dress or hair, I suppose, though now when I think about how Grandfather Fonteyn might have treated her . . ."

"There's no need to do so."

"I have, anyway. Because of him I really had no mother, just a woman who filled the position in name only. My God, the only woman who was a real mother to me was my old nanny. Even if she didn't exactly spoil me, she didn't mind getting or giving a hug now and then. I'll weep at *her* funeral—and for the right reason. I wept tonight because . . . because . . . I don't know." He rubbed his face, fingers digging at his inflamed eyes.

I waited until he'd finished and was able to listen. "My father says that guilt is a useless and wasteful thing to carry in one's heart, and it's even worse to feel sorry for oneself for having it."

"I'm guilty?"

"No, but you *have* guilt, which is something else again. It's not your fault you came to hate your mother. What is, is your feeling badly about it."

"Sorry, but I can't seem to help that," he said dryly.

I shrugged. "It'll go away if you let it."

"Oh? And just how might this miracle be accomplished?"

"I'm not really sure, but sooner or later you wake up and it doesn't bother you so much."

"How do you know?"

"It has to do with forgiveness. All this heartache I've felt for Nora . . . she hurt me terribly by making me forget everything. Even when I came to understand that she must have had a good reason for it, I was still hurting. But over the last few weeks . . . well, it's faded. All I want now is to see her again. I suppose I've forgiven her."

"Very fine for you, but then you've said you love her. Besides, Mother had no good reason for how she treated me."

"True, but the similarity is that you were hurt—"

"And the difference is that I can't forgive her," he finished. "I still hate her for what she did to me."

"Which is the source of your guilt. You want to live with that pain the rest of your life?"

"Of course not, but I know of no way past it, do you?"

He had me there . . . until a mad thought popped into my mind. "Maybe if you talked to her."

Incredulity mixed with disdain washed over his face. "I think it's just a bit late for that."

"Not really. Not for you. Have some of that brandy, I'll be back shortly." I limped from the room, pausing once in the thankfully deserted hall to vanish for a few moments. My head was wrenchingly tender, making the process more difficult, but when I returned, my body was much restored. The headache was fading, and I could walk unimpeded by bruises.

I took myself quickly off to find a suitable lackey and sent him to fetch dry cloaks and hats and a couple of thick woolen mufflers. Despite my disheveled appearance, he hurried to obey and got a penny vale for his effort, which impressed him to the point that he wanted to continue his service by carrying the things to my destination. I pleasantly damned his eyes and told him to see to the other guests. When he was gone, I went back to the blue drawing room.

Oliver had drained away a good portion of the brandy I'd poured earlier and had wolfed down some bread and ham. I hated to interrupt the feasting and particularly the drinking, and so slipped one of the brandy bottles into the pocket of my coat.

"Put this lot on and no questions," I said, tossing him half of my woolly burden.

"But—"

I held up a warning hand. "No questions."

Exasperated, but intrigued, he garbed himself and followed me. I took us out one of the back entries, managing to avoid any of the other family members as we quit the house and slogged over the grounds.

Our sudden isolation made the sleet seem worse than before. It cruelly gouged our skin and clung heavily to our clothes, soaking through in spots. The unrelenting wind magnified the glacial chill, clawing at our cloaks. The scarves, which we'd used to tie our hats in place, were scant protection against its frigid force. Someone had opened the door to hell tonight and forgotten to close it again.

"This is bloody cold," Oliver commented, with high disapproval.

I gave him the brandy. "Then warm yourself."

He accepted and drank. Good. The stuff would hit his near-empty stomach like a pistol ball.

Ugh. My hand went to my chest. Wish I hadn't thought of that.

"What's the matter with you?" he demanded, unknowingly pulling me out of my thoughts about black smothering graves.

"No questions," I said, plowing forward through the wind with him in my wake.

It was a devilish thick night, but Oliver's eyes had adjusted to the point where he could see where we were headed.

He balked. "We can't go there!"

"We have to."

"But it's . . . it's . . ."

"What, a little scary?"

"Yes. And I feel like we're being watched."

"So do I, but it's just the wind in the trees."

"You're sure?"

I cast a quick look around. "This is like daylight to me, right? Well, I can't see anyone. We're quite alone."

*"That's* hardly a comfort," he wailed.

"Come *on,* Oliver."

I took his arm and we continued forward until once more we stood in the mausoleum before his mother's coffin. Two lighted torches had been left behind in this house of stone to burn themselves out.

"Now what?" He sounded tremulous and lost, for which I could not blame him. Out here in the dark menace of the cemetery with the wind roaring around the tomb as if to give an icy voice to those departed, I felt my own bravado preparing to pack up and decamp like a vagrant.

I cleared my throat rather more loudly than was needed. "Now you're going to talk to her."

His mouth sagged. "You *have* gone mad."

"True enough, but there's a purpose to it. Talk to her. Tell her exactly how you feel on her treatment of you. I guarantee that she won't object this time."

"I couldn't do that! It's foolish."

"Is it? Hallo there! Aunt Fonteyn! Are you home?" I shouted at the end of the coffin that was visible to us. I thumped at it with a fist. "Are you in there, you horrible old woman? We've come to call on you and we're drunk—Oliver is anyway—"

"I'm *not* drunk!" he protested, looking around fearfully.

"Yes, you are." I addressed the coffin again. "See? Your son's drunk and your least favorite nephew's gone mad and we're here to disturb your eternal rest. How do you like *that,* you bloody harpy?"

Oliver gaped, horrified. I grinned back, then shocked him further by bounding up on Grandfather Fonteyn's sarcophagus and jumping down the other side. "How about that, Grandfather? Did that wake you up? Come on, Oliver, have a bit of exercise."

He took a deep draught of brandy, coughing a bit. "I couldn't," he gasped. It was but a faint protest, though.

"You most certainly can. What's it to him? He can't feel it. But you will." I hopped up, capered on the carved marble, and dropped lightly next to him. "Right, if you don't want to dance, it's all one with me, but you are going to talk to *her.* Scream at her if you like, no one's going to hear a word."

He shot me a dark look. "You will."

"Hardly. I'm going back to the house." So saying, I turned and started away. "Best get on with it. The sooner you begin, the sooner you can enjoy the fire and food waiting there."

He returned about half an hour later, teeth chattering, and skin gone both red and white with the cold, but with a sharp gleam of triumph in his eyes. Not all of it had been inspired by the brandy.

He'd talked to his mother.

He'd also shouted, bellowed, and cursed her in a most splendid and inspired manner. I knew, because I'd hung back out of sight, just close enough to hear his voice but not understand the words. Once I was sure he was truly into the business, I hared off to have some hot broth waiting for him in the drawing room. Radcliff brought it himself, clucking unhappily over the breakage there, but hurriedly leaving at my impatient gesture when Oliver walked in. The talk in the servants' hall would doubtless be quite entertaining tonight.

Oliver flopped into the chair with his familiar abandon and declared that he was ready to perish from the cold.

"Feels like the devil's grabbed my ears and won't let go," he cheerfully complained. He held his hands out to the fire to warm them, then gingerly cupped his palms over his ears. "Ouch! Well, if I lose them, I lose them. I'll just have a wig made to cover my unadorned ear holes and no one'll be the wiser. What's this? Broth? Just the thing, but I'd like more brandy if you don't mind. And some ham, no, that thick slice over there. Gone cold, has it? Just let me catch it with the fire tongs and toast it a bit. . . . there, that'll hot it up nicely. Y'know she would *never* have allowed this. Dining's to be done in the dining room and nowhere else, but to hell with the old ways. This is my house now and there will be changes made, just you wait and see! And see this, too!"

He held up the mourning ring in his long white fingers.

"Are you watching, Coz? Are you? There!" He tossed the ring into the fire. It landed softly and Oliver was silent as the flames crept up and quickly consumed it.

"There," he repeated more softly. "No more hypocrisy. No more damned guilt. Dear me, but the ham's scorching. Hand that plate over, will you? Mind the brandy, precious stuff, that."

I stayed with him, listening with a glad heart to his chatter as he made inroads on the food. He was drunk and getting drunker. Tomorrow he would have a very bad head, but that would give him something else to think about than his guilt—if any remained. I rather thought there might be, for the stuff has a tenacious grip on certain souls and Oliver had already shown his vulnerability to it. But I was also thinking that the next time he felt its talons digging in, he'd go out to shout in the mausoleum again, now that he knew to do so.

Soon Oliver, replete and bone tired, asked if I could take him upstairs and put him to bed.

"Don' think I cou' manage on m' own 'n' tha's God's own truth, Coz." He confessed this woeful tiding with a wobbling head.

I told him that I'd be pleased to assist him. After getting him to his nerveless feet, we staggered into the hall and found a stairway to stumble up. He was not exactly quiet, giggling and declaring that I was the best damned cousin in the world and he'd give challenge to any man who said otherwise. This brought out some servants to investigate the row, one of whom was an older woman that Oliver greeted with tipsy joy.

"Nanny! You won'erful ol' darling! How 'bout a nice hug for your bad lad?" He flailed out with one arm, but I kept him from toppling over and falling on the poor woman.

"Mr. Oliver, you need to be in bed," she said in a scolding tone, putting her hands on her hips. She was tiny, but I got the impression her authority in the nursery was never questioned.

Oliver smiled, beatific. " 'Xactly where 'm goin', Nanny. May I please have a good night choc'late, like ol' times?"

"Have you a room we can put him in?" I asked her.

"His old one's just here—no, that might not be a good choice, being bare as a dog's bone. This way, sir."

She took us along to one that had been made up for the use of guests who would stay overnight. A small chamber for the new master of the house, but the fire was laid and the bed turned down and ready. I eased him onto it and let her fuss over him, taking his shoes off and stripping away his outer clothes as though he were still four years old. Oliver, for what little he was aware of it, seemed to be enjoying every minute. As soon as his head struck the pillow, he was asleep, snoring mightily.

The nanny dutifully tucked him in, then paused to make a curtsy to me on her way out. We got a good look at each other. I saw a cautious but kindly face, not pretty, but certainly intelligent. What she saw I wasn't sure of, but her expression was strangely reminiscent of Oliver's own version of pop-eyed surprise. Then I remembered that my clothes were still in need of repair. No doubt torn sleeves and missing buttons were a rare sight in this house. I made a polite nod to her and sailed from the room as if utterly unaware of my dishevelment.

Unfortunately, I sailed smack into Cousin Edmond, colliding heavily with his sturdy frame. He snarled a justifiable objection to my clumsiness.

"I do beg your pardon," I said, having all but bounced off him. He was about as solid and forgiving as any brick wall.

"What? Are you drunk as well?"

"No, but poor Oliver needed some help finding his way up."

"I'm sure he did. Half the house heard his disgraceful carrying on." Edmond pushed past me for a look into the room to grunt at Oliver's sleeping form and growl at the nanny. "Mrs. Howard, what the devil are you doing here? Get yourself along and see to the other brats. The one in here is long past your help."

Apparently well used to his rough ways, Mrs. Howard plucked her skirts up with underplayed dignity and left. She quickly covered a fair amount of the hall without seeming to hurry and turned a corner without looking back.

Edmond glared after her, then focused the force of it on me for an instant. His lips curled as if he wanted to speak. I waited, but nothing came forth. He thinned the set of his mouth into a tough line of contempt, but after all that had happened, I was utterly immune to intimidation from him. When one has gone to a cemetery in the dark of a winter night to dance with the dead, it takes more than a bad-tempered cousin to shake one's inner esteem. Perhaps he sensed that. Without another word, he pushed past me to go below.

"Edmond?"

He stopped halfway down and did not quite turn to look. "What?"

"Just wanted to let you know that your work making the arrangements was excellent and much appreciated. Oliver is very grateful, y'know."

He said nothing for a moment, then grunted. Then he moved on.

Even as he descended, my sister ascended, glancing after him pensively.

"You look much improved," I commented, happy to see her again.

She reached the landing, her eyes wide as they raked me up and down. "What on earth have you been *doing?*"

"Oh, nothing much. Just had a nice little chat with Oliver. He feels all the better for it."

"You must have been chatting in a cockfighting pit. What's happened to you?"

I gave her a brief explanation for my condition.

"And Oliver's all right?" she asked with justifiable disbelief.

"Right as rain—at least until he wakes up."

Now she took her own opportunity to look in on him. "God, what a row," she said, in reaction to his snores. "I suppose he must be better if he can make that much noise. So what was troubling Cousin Edmond? He seemed more broody than normal."

"He had some objection to Oliver's carrying on is all." Poor old stick-in-the-mud Edmond, I thought. "Maybe his temper will improve with Aunt Fonteyn's absence."

"Jonathan!"

"Or is that too much to hope for?"

"If I didn't know better, I'd say you were drunk. So will anyone else."

"Bother them. They're probably thinking the same as I about her, but they'd just never admit it. Oliver is now the new head of the family, and he's bound to be more congenial in his duties than she, so everyone ought to be celebrating tonight. Things are looking up for the Fonteyns."

"Unless Mother decides to take things over when she comes to England," Elizabeth pointed out.

"She can't. It may have been Aunt Fonteyn's will, but hers was mostly a continuation of Grandfather Fonteyn's testament. Except for a few special bequests and such it stays the same, and his eldest daughter's eldest son inherits the lot."

"What? Nothing for his own sons?"

"That's already covered, as in the case of our incomes. The old man had his favorites—and they were his daughters."

Elizabeth briefly shut her eyes and shook her head. "In light of your speculations about—about how things were with them . . . well . . ." She spread her hands, unhappy with the ugly idea.

"It explains much about Mother and why she is the way she is," I said in a small voice, starting to feel a cold emptiness stealing over me. It was a kind of black helplessness that settled on my heart whenever this subject was mentioned. Perhaps if we had *known,* if any of us had had the least inkling of what her young life might have been like, then things might have been different for our mother. I wondered if we had a similar night like this awaiting us in the nebulous future, requiring that we shout at her coffin to exorcise our guilt.

"God forbid," I whispered.

"What?" Elizabeth gave a little start, having perhaps also been in the thrall of dismal thoughts. "Forbid what?"

"Just thinking aloud. It's nothing. Well-a-day, I wish I could get drunk, but I expect if I mixed brandy with my usual beverage it would just send me to sleep."

She straightened her shoulders. "Yes, and we all know how alarming *that* is."

"Nothing for it, then, I shall have to brave the family sans defenses."

"You've plenty of better ones to make up for that lack, little brother. What was the problem you had with the young man who left you so fast? I saw how you were speaking to him. Who was he?"

"Thomas Ridley's loving cousin Arthur Tyne, and he was either hoping for revenge or to make a name for himself as a duelist. He tried to provoke me tonight."

"Good God! You're not—"

"I've had enough of fire-eating, dear sister. I sent him off for good."

"But if he insulted you and you allowed him to get away with it—"

"He didn't, my honor is unsullied. Not that I give hang for him, but I'm just not in a hurry to send the dolt to hell for just being a dolt. Now, if he'd said anything against *you,* funeral or not, he'd be wishing he hadn't."

"You'd kill him?"

"No, but I'd serve him as well as I served his poxy-faced cousin."

"But Thomas wasn't poxy," she said thoughtfully. "In fact he's . . . Jonathan, what *are* you laughing about?"

# CHAPTER 11

Even the most entertaining funeral must end sometime.

Those mourners who were not staying the night began to take themselves home, causing much bustling for the servants as they prepared things. New torches were lighted, carriages were brought around, farewells were exchanged, and one by one the relatives departed, leaving Fonteyn House a bit roomier than before. Those who remained behind, either because of their reluctance to face the weather or the fact that they lived too far away, were lodged in every likely and unlikely corner of the house.

Clarinda and Elizabeth oversaw things, each bringing her own expertise in organization to the problems that arose, from a shortage of blankets to what would be served to break the morning fast. My talents for such matters were sadly undeveloped, but I made myself useful directing people to this room or that, according to the list I'd been given.

After all were settled, I planned to return to Oliver's house as usual, since my bed of earth was there. Thus would I be spared the task of having to influence a veritable army of servants into ignoring my peculiar sleeping arrangements. Elizabeth had been staying at Fonteyn House since the day after Aunt Fonteyn's death and would yet be lodging here, this time with a roomful of other young women.

"How enviable," I said lightly.

"You may think so, but they're bound to talk until dawn, wanting to know all about you."

"Well, try to be as discouraging as you can. The ones I've met always seem to think that any stray unmarried male is only interested in finding a wife."

"I know, that's been made abundantly clear to me since we moved into Oliver's and started getting callers. The ladies coming by to see you outnumber the gentlemen paying respects to me by nine to four. Perhaps I should be jealous of you."

"Rather blame it on the shortsightedness of the London men. There's also the possibility that they may feel the same about marriage as I."

"I think not, little brother, I've already gotten three proposals."

"What?"

She laughed at my stricken expression. "One was from a mature lad of ten who was pleased with my face."

"And the others?"

"Fortune-hunting cousins on the Fonteyn side of the family."

Now didn't that sound familiar? "What did you say?"

"I told them that my aunt's funeral was hardly the place to be making marriage proposals."

"But that's not a proper refusal," I said, worried. "They might be back."

"Indeed they might," she agreed. "One of them was rather handsome in a horsy sort of way. I wonder if he is descended from Cousin Bucephalus?"

"Good God, Elizabeth, you're not seriously—"

"Certainly not, but I want to have some enjoyment of life while it's still mine to enjoy. When I think of what a cheerless, bitter existence Aunt Fonteyn made for herself, I could just weep at the waste and sadness of it."

"After the awful things she's said and done you can feel sorry for her?"

"Wounded animals, Jonathan," she reminded me. "It's not their fault that someone's been cruel to them. With that in mind, it's easy to understand how they might lash out at those who stray too close."

"Does this mean you'll form a more lenient attitude toward Mother?"

She made a wry face. "You do ask a lot, don't you? I suppose I must then say yes, but then again, it's easy for one to be tolerant when one's source of irritation is several thousand miles away."

"Very well, I'll ask you again when she's closer."

"I'm sure you will." Humor lurked in her dry tone, but I sensed that it was meant to cover some well-concealed low spirits.

"Are you going to be all right here?" I lifted a hand to indicate the vast house. "I mean after the funeral and all. I can take you home, y'know."

She shook her head decisively. "I'm fine. It's not what I'm used to, but

I don't mind a little change now and then. Besides, I'm needed here. Poor Oliver's going to be feeling the torments of hell when he wakes tomorrow, and I thought I'd try one of Dr. Beldon's remedies on him."

"And what would that be?"

"Tea with honey and mint. Better than moss snuff for his head, I'm sure." She wilted a little. "I hope that they're all right, too. Father and the others, I mean."

"As do I, but I'm sure they are, so please don't worry. You've had more than your share of it already. Getting on well with Clarinda?"

"Very well, thank you. She's quite different from Edmond. I wonder how they ever got together."

"Who knows?" I said with a shrug, not really caring.

We said good night, and I promised to be back soon after sunset tomorrow. Oliver's new status as master of Fonteyn House required that he remain in it for some time longer before returning to his own home. As I put on my cloak and wrapped up against the wind, I speculated on whether he would forsake his other household and move back. For all the gloomy corners, it was still a fine big place, and he had promised changes. Heavens, he might even open the shutters and put in some more windows. That would make Grandfather Fonteyn spin in his coffin, and I could think of no one more deserving of the disturbance, unless it might be his eldest daughter. Unlike Elizabeth, I found it difficult to summon compassion for the wretched woman even if she was dead.

On my way out I saw Edmond and the unpleasant Arthur Tyne with their heads together by the main door. I hung back, wanting to avoid both of them. They were garbed for the weather, ready to leave; Edmond was probably headed home, the same as I. Perhaps he didn't mind abandoning Clarinda to her own devices for now, not that anyone remained in the house to tempt her to an indiscretion. The guests were either too young or old, too married or the wrong gender for her—unless one wished to count Oliver. She might find him attractive, I knew, but on the other hand he was dead drunk and not likely to be of much use to her.

I fidgeted, wishing Edmond and Arthur would get on with themselves so I could go. Perhaps I could just vanish and float past them. I'd planned to exercise myself in that manner on the trip home, anyway, providing the wind wasn't too much of a nuisance.

"Jonathan?" A woman whispered from the darkness of the hall behind me, giving me a start.

I squinted against the shadows and made out her figure, then her face. "Clarinda?"

She remained in place, partially hidden, so I went to her. Reluctantly.

Edmond had only to look over and see me, and if he somehow recognized his wife's form in the—

"What is it?" I whispered back, my neck hairs rising.

"I must talk with you."

Oh, dear. Was this the prelude to another seduction to be consummated in some deserted room? "Well, I was just leaving, y'see—"

"This is important. I want only a minute. Please come away."

Her tense tone hardly seemed appropriate for so delicate a thing as a carnal interlude. Perhaps the nearby threat of Edmond was providing a cooling mitigation for her normally ardent nature.

With him discouragingly in mind—not to mention uncomfortably close—I cast a fearful look 'round, then followed her into the deeper darkness of the hall.

She made her way with frequent glances behind to make sure I was there. She tiptoed, swiftly, with her skirts barely making a whisper over the floor. Reluctant to draw any attention as well—especially Cousin Edmond's—I imitated her example of being quiet.

We passed a number of rooms, heading for the far reaches of the house, ultimately ending up in what for me was a most familiar chamber. There was the same settee; the same bust of Aristotle (or one of the Caesars) rested on the mantel as before. The draperies were drawn owing to mourning, and this time the fireplace warmly blazed, but otherwise all was the same as it had been that Christmas when we'd shared a most happy and vigorous encounter here.

*Johnny Boy, whatever are you letting yourself in for?* I thought, but it took no real effort on my part to guess what she had in mind. Heavens, but this would be a serious exercise in diplomacy to make an escape without causing her offense.

She shut the door, turning to face me. Her manner was very nervous, quite different from the randy, confident woman I'd known before. Something was wrong.

"What is it?" I asked.

Her eyes were fixed on mine. "I must ask if Edmond has said anything to you."

"About what?"

She gestured at the room. "What do you think? You do know why he hates you so, don't you?"

"I assumed it was because he was aware of our—ah—past liaison."

"Has he spoken to you about it?"

"No. Not one word."

She seemed extremely relieved to hear it, slumping a bit. "That's good. I saw him glaring so at you earlier, and then when he went upstairs to find out why Oliver was making such a row . . . well, I wasn't sure what to think."

"I've gotten nothing more than some hard looks from him. It's obvious he doesn't care for my company. Not that it really matters."

"But it does," she hissed. "He can be very dangerous, Jonathan."

"I don't doubt it, but he doesn't worry me. Is that what troubles you? You think he might try to harm me?"

"Yes. He's a difficult man and has a particular hatred for you over the other—the other young men I've known." She watched my reaction. "Good. I'm glad you're not going to go all gallant and pretend you weren't aware of them."

She'd made mention of them herself once upon a time, but it seemed more politic to say nothing. "I can only think that they are most fortunate that you should choose to grace them with your company."

The flattery that worked so well on Molly Audy had a similar effect on Clarinda; she broke into a most charming smile. "You have a pleasant memory of me, then?"

"It is one of my treasures. I recall every moment of your most generous gift to me."

"And to myself," she added. "God, but you make me remember it all afresh even now. You've grown even more handsome since. More muscle, too." She gave herself a shake, rolling her eyes. "Back to business, Clarinda."

"What business?" I asked. "A warning to stay out of Edmond's way? I'm already keen to do just that, so you needn't be troubled. But why does he hate me more than the others?"

She looked long at me, studying my face before finally giving an answer. "He hates you because I took a fancy to you that Christmas right here in this house, right under his nose. But I couldn't help myself. He'd been perfectly beastly to me that day, and you were so sweet and kind and *different.* Oh, damn, this must sound like I was with you just to spite him, but that's not true. I wanted to be with someone I *liked,* who liked me in return, as you seemed to."

"Believe me, my affection was quite genuine. It's not something a man can falsify."

She arched a brow. "You'd be surprised, my dear, but bless you for saying so. As for your affection for me now . . . well, I sense that you're somewhat more cautious these days."

"It's because of your being married."

"Married to Edmond?"

"No, just married, period. It's not in my nature to . . ."

"Ah, I see. Fornication's one thing, but adultery's quite another?"

I had to laugh a little, she said it so prettily. "That's it, exactly."

"You are such a sweet fellow. I see no real distinction between the two, myself, but can respect that you do." She pushed from the door, going to the settee, sitting wearily. "Such a ghastly day it's been. This is the first time I've had a bit of quiet for myself and enjoyable conversation with another. I hope I wasn't too alarming when I lured you back here."

"A bit mysterious, nothing more."

"I had to be, what with Edmond in plain sight, but you were about to leave, and I wanted a word with you on this before you got away."

"It couldn't wait until a better time?"

"When might that be with this houseful? I had to act while the chance existed, while you were alone and no one else about to see and tell tales. Please say that you will be careful around him."

"Very careful. He's not likely to give challenge, is he?"

"No. Not that he's a coward to dueling, but the scandal involved would be abhorrent to him. He's very proper, y'know."

That sparked a question in me. "Clarinda, if you would not mind my asking you something personal . . ."

"After what we've shared here? What have I to hide? Ask away."

"I was only wondering why you did . . . why you . . . that is, does Edmond not fulfill his duty toward you?"

She stared blankly a moment, then softly laughed. "Goodness, that is personal—but easily answered. The fact is that Edmond cares for me in his own fashion and I care for him in mine, but we are two extremely different people with different tastes and appetites. To be perfectly honest, the main reason we married was that he wanted a stronger connection within the family by fostering Aunt Fonteyn's pet nephew, and I very much wanted security and a father for my boy. Boys," she corrected, flashing me a rueful look. "We've had a child since, y'know."

"Yes, Oliver mentioned something of it, congratulations. But I thought your children were taken care of by Grandfather's estate."

"To a degree, but Edmond has friends throughout London that will help them when they're older. It's not enough to have money, one must have influence as well, but being in law yourself, you understand that."

"Yes, I do have an idea on the importance of influence," I said, smiling at my unnatural talent in that area.

"As for the interest I have in handsome young men, well, I just can't seem to help myself. Edmond knew about it before our marriage, and we talked about how we would conduct things afterward. He said he wouldn't mind as long as I was discreet, but that didn't last long. He tries not to be jealous, but sometimes he . . ."

"He what? He doesn't mistreat you, I hope?"

Her eyes suddenly dropped and she primly laced her fingers together. "No more than many other husbands with their wives."

"What do you mean by that?"

"Now, Jonathan, I must insist you stop there, as what goes on between us is really not your business. He can be churlish, but I know how to handle him." She still wasn't looking at me.

After her warnings, I could only assume them to have been inspired by her direct experience with his temper. The idea of him harming her in any way was sickening. Perhaps I could arrange an interview with Edmond on the subject. A private little talk to spare Clarinda from future harm . . . Yes, that was very appealing to me. On the other hand, if an alternative presented itself, it should also be explored. My influence, unless regularly reinforced, had its limitations.

"Can you not leave him? I mean, that is, if you don't love him—"

She sighed and shook her head. "God have mercy, but you are so young and dear. You have no idea how complicated life can be for a woman."

"I'm not entirely ignorant. If you need a place to go, Oliver will gladly put you up here and protect you."

She was shaking her head again. "No, no, no, it's impossible or I'd have done that ages ago with Aunt Fonteyn. I have to live the life I've got, but that's all right, I'm happy enough. Besides, it's not as bad as you seem to be imagining. He's very decent most of the time, but the funeral has upset him greatly. I was thinking that with you here he might be tempted to do something rash."

I again reassured her of my intent to avoid all trouble with Edmond.

"Then I shall be relieved on your account. I should feel awful if anything happened to you because of him."

"You flatter me with your concern."

"Flatter? It's more than flattery on my part. My dear, you have no idea of the depth of pleasure you've given me."

"It was so brief, though."

"But treasured, as you've said. Of course, we can always make another happy memory for ourselves . . . if you like."

Oh, but did she not have a bewitching smile? I couldn't help but feel that delightful stirring through all my body as I looked at her. She'd not altered much, a little fuller of figure, but that just made more of her to explore. I wondered if her thighs were as white and silken as I remembered. . . .

*Don't be a fool, Johnny Boy.*

It wasn't just that she was married, though that was a major detraction; it was my change that made me hesitate over her invitation.

I could surge upon her here and now like a tide and bring her to a point where she wouldn't notice my biting in and drinking from her until it was all over. But then she'd want an explanation, and I wasn't about to sit down and tell her my life's story concerning Nora. Enough people knew already. No more.

Or I could make her forget about the blood-drinking part, but Clarinda deserved better treatment than that. It was different when I was with women like Jemma at The Red Swan; their favors were for sale and well paid for, but to treat Clarinda in the same cavalier manner smacked of theft in a way. Or rape. Certainly *I* was not comfortable with either idea.

Perhaps if there was a possibility of having a lengthy liaison with her as I'd had with Molly, I might then . . .

No, that wouldn't be right, either. Not with Edmond lurking around any given corner as we arranged trysts for ourselves. I liked Clarinda, but not that much.

Then there was Elizabeth to consider.

And Oliver.

One look at Clarinda's throat and they'd know what was going on.

No, it was simply too embarrassing. I couldn't possibly . . .

Still, I could go in, leaving my mark on an area not readily visible to others. Her soft belly or the inside of one of those wondrous thighs suggested themselves readily to my hot imagination. The very thought made my mouth dry and my corner teeth begin to extend. I put a hasty hand to my upper lip, trying to push them back.

But even with that caution taken I'd have the same problem as before, having to explain everything about myself to her.

Then again, I *could* just pleasure Clarinda in the more acceptable fashion. I was yet capable of that, but how frustrating since it denied me any kind of a consummation. And if, in the throes of the event, I lost control and took from her anyway . . . I knew myself well enough. Once started it was hard for me to stop, for once the passions are aroused, it's all too easy to forget solemn promises made when the mind is cool and capable of sensible thought.

No. Not this time, sweet Cousin.

*Damnation.*

"Is something wrong, Jonathan?"

My debate was much like the other I'd held with myself in this room, running through my head in the blink of an eye. Only this time I would have to steel myself and hold to my decision. "I wish things—circumstances—could be other than what they are."

"Such as my being married?"

I nodded, grateful to have her taking that as the most obvious excuse for my refusal. "You are a most beautiful, desirable lady, and it is with the greatest reluctance that I must decline your gift."

Another rueful smile. "Then I shall have to be satisfied with a memory?"

"I fear you must, as I must. I do apologize."

"Oh, nonsense. You've not lost your manners, anyway. Yours is the most polite refusal I've ever gotten. Besides, I can hardly force you to bed me—not that I wouldn't like to *try*—but I've no wish to impose upon your honor."

I thanked her for her consideration, then begged to take my leave. "It's a bit of a walk home for me—"

"Walking? You're going to *walk* in this weather?"

"The sleet's stopped and the wind is down. The cold air should be most reviving after the press of tonight's gathering."

"You are perfectly mad," she said, with something between admiration and alarm.

I waved a careless hand. "You are not the first who has made that observation, madam. Nor, I think, the last, but I enjoy a good walk and—"

"No doubt," she interrupted, standing. "Well, my dear cousin, if you are sure of your decision—you are?—then I shall have to wish you Godspeed home. It is very late, after all. . . ."

With that broad a hint placed before me, it would have been rude not to take it. I bowed over her hand, wished her a very good evening, and let myself out.

Apparently that was her room for the night, for she did not follow as I made my way back to the entry hall. I wondered if she'd arranged to have it for her use with a mind to sharing it with me. Now, there was an interesting thought. Instead of a hasty and surreptitious coupling, we could have had hours and hours to—

*None of that, Johnny Boy. You've made your bed, and you* will *sleep in it—even if it is empty.*

Damnation.

Again.

Out the front doors and down along the long drive I went, moving briskly.

The sleet had indeed stopped and the wind had lessened, but that which remained was still knife-sharp and unforgiving. Though I possessed a degree of immunity to the cold, I was not going to unduly strain it. Halfway between Fonteyn House and Oliver's home lay The Red Swan, and there I planned to stop for a time and warm myself by taking full advantage of its hospitality. Clarinda had gotten me quite thoroughly stirred up, and I had a mind to settle those stirrings in the company of the lovely Jemma or one of her sisters in the trade.

Dour Cousin Edmond was also in my mind. If he was treating Clarinda roughly, I wanted to do something about it. We'd likely be running into each other again soon, and it would be the work of a moment to take him to one side to deliver a firm speech on the subject of treating his wife gently from now on. I'd done similar work with Lieutenant Nash often enough to curb his greed; why not again with Edmond for his temper?

Then the thought of Nash reminded me of home and of Father and all the others. I hoped that he was all right, as I'd so quickly assured Elizabeth. We had no letters from him yet, but it was getting on into winter, and the crossing was bound to be more difficult for the ships that followed ours. The war would cause additional delays . . . wretched business, that. As if there weren't enough troubles in the world, those fools and their congress were wanting to add to them. Nothing like a bit of war, famine, and death to provide entertainment for those who would not be directly involved with such horrors.

Death . . .

I'd have to write something tonight on it, or at least begin writing. It had been several days since the accident and past time that I sent off the bad news about Aunt Fonteyn, though it could hardly be called bad from Oliver's point of view now. (I'd not mention *that* in my missive.) I'd enclose a mourning ring for Mother in the packet and hope she wouldn't make life too hellish for Father. God, she might even find a way to blame him for the business. I wouldn't put it past her.

Worry, worry, worry.

So sounded my footsteps as I paced carefully down the drive, avoiding patches of ice. The ground was hard, probably frozen. The tip of my cane made no impression in it. Just as well Aunt Fonteyn went into her niche in the mausoleum instead of a grave; it'd be much too much work for the sexton and his fellows to chop their way down through this stuff. It was probably one of the only times in her existence that she'd done anything for the convenience of another person.

*Wicked thought, Jonathan.*

I grinned. Not all that capering in the mausoleum had been for Oliver's benefit. I'd thoroughly enjoyed myself—once I'd gotten over the unease of being there in the first place. Nasty spot, all cold stone and so far from everything and probably just as cold in the summer. A pity it wasn't summer; then she wouldn't have had any ice to slip on. What had the old crow been doing out in the middle of the maze for, anyway?

An assignation with some man? Not likely with her supremely bad temperament and acidic nature. She'd ever been very clear in her views on carnal exchanges, being so strongly opposed to the act that I wondered just how Oliver had ever come to be conceived.

It was also unlikely that she'd been enjoying the innocent folly of the maze for its own sake. Again, her temperament forbade it.

Also, the wind that night had been almost as keen and cutting as it was now. She would have needed some strong reason to give up the comfort of a fire to be out there.

To meet someone for a private talk? But why go to the maze when there were any number of warm rooms in the Bolyns' house to accommodate a discreet conversation? And what had she to talk about? Whom would she talk with?

My speculations were nothing new; many others both before and after the funeral had asked as much from one another, but without forming any satisfactory answer. The gossips in Fonteyn House could only conclude that It Was Very Mysterious.

But it had all been investigated. No one at the Masque had particularly noticed her leaving the house for the garden that night. They'd been too involved with their own pleasures to pay attention to one disagreeable old woman. Those friends as she'd been with at the ball had likewise nothing to contribute; besides, if she'd been meeting anyone, they'd have come forward by now, wouldn't they? But if not, then why not?

Heavens, I was getting as bad as the gossips.

It was easy for them to speculate, easy to wonder and whisper, but so hard to—

*Now who the devil was that?*

Well ahead of me were the gates to the property, wide open with torches on either side to mark the entry. Their flames were nearly burned out by now. Had my eyes not been so well suited to the dark, I'd have missed seeing the figure entirely. A man it was, made anonymous by the masking shroud of his cape. He stood in the shadows—or what should have been shadows to anyone else—and his posture suggested that he was waiting for someone.

A footpad? They usually operated within the warrens of the city, where the harvest was more abundant, not away here on the West End, where the grand houses stood on their own spacious grounds.

Then it jumped into my head that he might be a medical student come to steal a body for study. Oliver had filled me with plenty of grisly tales on the difficulties of mastering anatomy. So desperate were some for specimens that if they couldn't get a corpse from Tyburn, then they resorted to theft for their needs. Good God, but that would be the worst, for Aunt

Fonteyn to end up as a subject on a dissection table somewhere. I hadn't liked her, but she deserved better than that.

Having come to this conclusion—and it seemed likely, given the late hour and the fact the funeral had hardly been a secret—I debated how best to deal with the situation. Only one man was visible to me, and though one alone could easily bear away her corpse, I could not discount the possibility of his having allies present. The macabre nature of such a dark errand as grave robbing must dictate that the thief bring along at least one friend to bolster his courage.

I held to the same pace, pretending not to see the fellow. He must have been aware of me by now, but made no move to further conceal himself. I'd fully expected him to do so as I got closer, and that's when I'd planned to spring upon him for a reckoning on his intrusion here.

He continued to wait, though. Perhaps he was a footpad, after all, or some highwayman sheltering behind the gates, hoping for a late traveler on the road outside to prey upon. I worked the catch on my cane, readying to draw forth its hidden blade. There's nothing like a yard of Spanish steel for discouraging a man from breaking the law—unless it's a six-shot flintlock revolver by Powell of Dublin. Unfortunately, I'd left that most useful weapon at Oliver's house in the mistaken belief I would not need it while attending a funeral.

He'd not moved yet. I was nearly to the gate, close enough so that even ordinary eyes could see him. As it seemed pointless to extend the fraud of being ignorant of his presence, I slowed and stopped, looking right at him.

"Who are you, sir, and what business have you to be here?" I demanded, half expecting him to run like a startled cat at my hail.

He made no reply.

His lower face was covered by the wide scarf wrapped 'round his head and hat; the brim of the hat was pushed well forward to further obscure things.

"I'm addressing you, sir. I expect an answer." I stepped toward him and pulled the blade free of the cane.

*That* got a reaction. He slipped away suddenly from the gate, moving to my right, where some trees offered a greater darkness to hide in. Because of the wind battering my ears, I couldn't hear his progress, so he seemed to glide along very fast in preternatural silence. Well, he wasn't the only one who could show a bit of heel. I hurried after, almost catching him up until he reached a particularly fat tree and darted sideways. It was a feint, though. Instead of waiting to ambush me from there, he sprinted ahead, perhaps thinking its intervening trunk would conceal his progress. All it did was speed me up. I lengthened my stride, blurring past the tree—

And on the edge of vision glimpsed something scything down in a fearful rush. Instinct made me throw my right arm high to shield my head. The thing, whatever it was, crashed solidly into my forearm, sending a stunning shock through my whole body. My headlong pursuit immediately ceased as I dropped straight onto the frozen earth like a block of stone.

I was aware of a terrible pain along my arm, as if a giant had seized me there and was pinching it between finger and thumb. The agonizing pressure changed to an agonizing burning so great that the force of it left me immobile for several terrible moments. I could see and hear nothing, taste and smell nothing; the only sense I had was for the grinding torment that had fastened itself to my flesh.

What had they done to me?

They. On the dim borders of the mind between sense and nonsense, I was aware of at least two of them. Footpads or grave robbers, it mattered not. Whoever had struck me might do so again. The panicked thought whipped through my mind.

Helpless. I was utterly *helpless.*

I must get *away* . . . vanish . . .

But the pain continued, and I lay there wholly susceptible to its reality, quite horribly solid.

Couldn't move. Whatever the damage, it must be very bad to paralyze me like this. As bad as I'd ever known before. Worse.

I tried again to take myself out of the world. This effort made the burning hotter than it already was, as if someone had stabbed a fiery brand into my arm. I instantly ceased trying and cursed instead.

"He's alive," a man above me said.

"Good," said another a little breathlessly. The one I'd been chasing apparently.

Bloodsmell. My own.

It was all over me.

Ice mixed with the fire as the wind struck the red flow of my life, chilling it. The simple knowledge that I must have been bleeding freely was enough to raise another panic-inspired attempt to vanish.

Another flare of pain. I stopped and cursed again.

"How does it *feel,* Mr. Barrett?" the breathless man taunted. "That's more than a scratch from the look of it. You'll not jump up so fast this time, I'm sure."

I knew his voice now. Thomas Ridley.

"He'll bleed to death," his companion pointed out. Arthur Tyne.

"He's going to die one way or another, but I'd rather it be me that dispatches him."

*Sweet God.*

I was on my left side, exactly as I'd fallen. I saw their boots and little else. Couldn't really move. Not at all. Just softly curse.

"Listen to him whine," said Ridley, enjoying himself.

"You would, too, with something like that in you."

"Then pull it free and see what other noise he can make."

"We don't want to wake anyone, Tom."

"Who's to hear? Come on and do it."

Arthur bent and worked at something, and I madly thought he was tearing my arm from its socket. The fire plaguing me before seemed like cold ashes compared to this. I couldn't help but cry out. The sound itself was frightening, as if it had come from someone else. I did not know my own voice.

Ridley was laughing, giggling like a young child.

No breath left in me to curse. Could only lie there and feel as if my arm had been thrust into a furnace.

"I think I've killed him," said Arthur. He did not seem unduly worried over the possibility.

Ridley crouched next to me, turning me over. He was still swathed in his scarf and cloak; the latter had slipped open enough to reveal his right arm in a sling. He moved carefully so as not to jar it. He put his left hand on my chest, but withdrew it when he saw me glaring at him, very much alive.

"Not yet," he said, grinning. "He'll last a bit longer, I think. Though I'll lay good odds he'll wish otherwise. Here's a pretty souvenir." He reached over to pick up my blade and scabbard.

"You won't want to keep that. Someone'll know it."

"I'm not planning to keep it, but I will put it to good use." He rose slowly. "Stand him up and let's get on from here."

*Stand?* He must have been mad.

"Right, take this, then." Arthur gave Ridley a sword he'd been holding. Blood was all along its blade. My blood. My God, he'd hit me with *that?* It should have taken my arm right off. Maybe it would have, too, had I been an ordinary man.

Arthur was a strong lad. He had no trouble shifting me around like a sack of grain to hook my left arm 'round his shoulders. It didn't matter to him whether I could walk or not, he'd drag me along regardless. It didn't matter to me, either. As soon as he'd hauled me upright, the agony blasted through my body again. I bit out a grunt of protest, which was ignored.

With a heave, he boosted himself straight, taking me with him. The sudden shift from lying down to fully upright had its effect. My vision flickered, then was lost altogether. Myself, the world, everything . . . simply ceased to be.

# CHAPTER 12

The god-awful pain in my arm drew me out of the comfort of nothingness.

I woke aware only of the hurt, lying on something hard and brutally cold. With no understanding of what had happened, I moved not a muscle. It seemed . . . safer.

Some battered portion of sense that was not wholly consumed by the distraction of pain whimpered, feebly protesting something I was unable to comprehend.

It was afraid.

Things had gotten bad.

They could get worse.

*They* will *get worse. That's why you're afraid.*

The thought seemed to take weight and size in my skull. I didn't want it there, but hadn't the strength to get rid of it. No other thoughts could raise themselves against it.

*You have to get up. You have to get away.*

But I was hurt. I could not move. To move meant more pain.

*To not move means death.*

Very well, but something small first. Like opening my eyes.

High overhead, thick with shadows, stretched a broad slice of marble ceiling. Walls of the same pale stone seemed to rush straight toward me. The hard and cold thing I lay upon . . . also marble, but not part of the floor; I was somewhat higher, as if floating above it. Where . . . ?

Down and away to one side was a rectangle of stone leaning against the wall, and propped near it a brass plate with engraved lettering spelling out Aunt Fonteyn's name. Above them was an open niche and just visible within was one end of her coffin.

The *mausoleum?* How had I come to be here?

They'd taken me . . . one of them had . . .

First I'd been hurt, then helped—no, that wasn't right. One of them had struck me . . .

Had struck my *arm.*

Struck to kill.

*Yes.*

The whimpering increased, became a full throated howl of terror, its echoes battering upon my ears from within.

Ridley and Arthur.

There, I'd put names to the shapes that had attacked, had taken me to this house of death.

They weren't here. That was good.

I was quite alone.

And lying on Grandfather Fonteyn's sarcophagus.

Already frightened and not thinking straight, I lurched up—and instantly regretted the action. The fire in my arm blazed high, and at the same time the top of my head felt as if it was coming off. I fell back the way I'd been, breathless, though I had no need of breath.

Lying quietly did not aggravate the hurts, so I lay quietly and tried to reason away the superstitious dread that had seized me. After all, the silent residents here were long past doing harm to anyone. It had just been a shock to realize I was on the old devil's last resting place. It's one thing to dance on it when one is in full control, and very much another to waken on so harsh a bed, injured and frightened and too confused to understand what was going on.

I listened and watched, wanting very much to find some understanding. Ridley and Arthur, if they were still nearby, were out of sight of the mausoleum door and either keeping quiet or too far away to be heard. Nothing outside the structure moved, except the wind shivering against the trees. I hated the sound they made, the loneliness of it, as if God had abandoned us and the dead together forever in this bleak spot.

*Steady, Johnny Boy. No need for that, you're scared enough.*

Right. Back to the problem at hand.

That Ridley was determined to avenge himself for the humiliation of losing the duel was obvious. He'd recruited a cousin to be his ally; for all I knew Arthur might even have been one of the Mohocks who had plagued me on my first night in London. I hadn't seen all their faces, since I'd been incorporeal part of the . . .

Refuge. Healing. Mine, if I could but *vanish.*

Cursing myself for a dolt for not thinking of it sooner, I tried to summon the nothingness back again, this time on my terms.

This was not my usual swift, effortless leaving, though, but an imperfect and prolonged striving. My vision clouded, very slowly, and did not quite depart, which meant that I did not quite depart.

Raising my left hand to judge my progress, I saw that it was only partially transparent and, no matter how hard I tried, stubbornly remained in that halfway state. Disturbed, I ceased and became solid again.

Much too solid. My poor body seemed to weigh a thousand pounds. I was as weak as an infant. My guts felt as if they'd been scraped out, jumbled, and dropped carelessly back, not quite into place. For several bad moments I thought I might faint once more.

*Lie still, still, still. Let it pass.*

Thus did I obey the soft dictate of instinct, not that I was remotely able to ignore it.

Bit by bit, my strength returned, a ghost of it, anyway. At least I was able to move a little and not lie flaccid as a corpse.

Ugh.

Must have been my surroundings.

For all this, my arm . . . was improved. The furnace still raged, still seared my flesh, but its heat was focused on a single area rather than the whole limb. Healing had begun.

Very cautiously I lifted up on my left elbow to take a look at myself. The right sleeve of my coat had been cut through; it and much of the rest of my clothing on that side was soaked with blood. I'd lost a terrifying amount of it. No wonder I was so wretchedly enervated.

And with that knowledge came the *hunger.*

Now it awakened and surged, washing over me, colder than sea spray. My mouth sagged with need. My corner teeth budded, lengthened, fixing themselves hard into place. I absolutely had to feed. Feed immediately.

But how? I barely had the strength to sit, much less walk, much less seek out food. But to lie here starving like a sick dog in the gutter . . .

No. Not for me. I had to get up and would. The hunger would not let me do otherwise.

Stiffly I pushed myself away from the freezing stone slab, twisting at the hips to drag my legs around. They dangled off the edge of the sarcophagus. I shifted again and dropped, jolting as my feet struck the floor.

Swaying. God, but I was *dizzy.*

I slapped a hand on the stone, desperately trying to steady myself.

Falling would only complicate things further, and I had more than enough difficult tasks to occupy me.

Like getting to the doorway.

One step, another, teetering like a drunk. Two more steps and I was at the door, left hand flailing to grab for its iron gate. I caught it just in time, saving myself from dropping on my face.

None of this activity made me feel better. I paused to get a look at the agony in my arm. The coat sleeve gaped wide over a fearful wound. Arthur's blade had cut through the thick part of my forearm right down to the bone. The flesh was well parted here, revealing details about the layers of skin and muscle that I would much rather not have known. I looked away, belly churning, ready to turn itself out.

At least I wasn't bleeding. My body probably had nothing more to spare.

Cold. Colder than before. Cloak useless against it.

Then *move.*

It was a quarter mile to the house. A quarter mile to the stables. All the blood I'd ever need waited there. I had only to walk to get it.

Walk.

Or crawl.

*Shut up and move.*

I pushed on the gate, following its outward swing. The hinges squawked.

"Here! What's this?"

God have mercy. Arthur was standing hardly five paces away. I'd given him a start. Fair enough, for he'd done the same and more for me. I couldn't budge. What would be the point?

"Thought you'd gone and died on us," he said, hurrying toward me. "Not that it matters, but Tom'll be more than pleased. Come along with you."

From this I got the impression that we were alone. Well and good, though if we'd been in the middle of Covent Garden on a theater night, I'd not have been able to stop myself. With a last burst of hunger-inspired strength I lunged at him, reaching.

Instinct is a strange thing. Much of the time we ignore it, but in certain select and extreme moments, it can completely take us over, causing us to do extraordinary things in the name of survival that we would never otherwise attempt. Had I been in my right mind I'd have known it to be impossible to tackle Arthur the way I did. Nor would I have been able to knock him senseless, rip away his neckcloth, and tear into his throat as I did.

But then . . . I was not in my right mind.

I was hurt and hungry and terrified and desperate and this was my enemy

And his body flowed with life. My life.

The stuff crashed into my mouth, the first swallow gone before I was aware of the act. This was not a leisurely feeding for refreshment, but a frantic gorging for existence itself. I drank deeply, not tasting, aware of little else other than the overwhelming necessity to keep on drinking until the hurt ended and the vast hollow within was filled.

I woke out of it as quickly as I'd succumbed. One second I was a mindless thing of raw need and appetite, the next, a man again, suddenly realizing what I was doing.

Dear God, I was *killing* him.

I broke away. Blood on my lips. Blood seeping from the wounds in his throat.

He was deathly white and very still, but I put an ear to his chest and detected the fluttering of his heart. Its beating was too fast, I thought, for all to be well, but as long as he was yet alive . . . In truth, I was less concerned with the prospect of his death than the possibility of my being blamed for it. Callous? Perhaps, but I placed a higher value on my skin than his, and it would have been a damned shame to hang at Tyburn for the likes of him.

I found my feet and stood, the horrible dizziness fading. The burning in my arm was less pronounced than it'd been only moments ago. I'd have looked to see how far the healing had progressed, but decided to spare myself. Instead, I shut my eyes, concentrated, and felt the glad lightness slipping 'round me like a soft blanket as I vanished.

No burning. No pain at all. I felt the tug of wind, nothing more. How tempting it would be to let it carry me away through the woods and far from this place and its problems. So wonderfully, sweetly tempting.

But not the best thing to do, especially for Arthur. Like it or not, I would have to take care of him, which meant resuming form again and deciding how best to go about it.

The next time I felt the wind, it seemed as solid as myself, catching my cloak as if to sweep it from my shoulders. I grabbed the ends and pulled them close. Using both hands. Now I braved a glance at my wound and found it to be no more than a thick red welt of a scar halfway circling my arm, which was sore to the touch, but workable. Overall, I was yet extremely shaky. The blood had saved me, but much of its good had gone toward my healing. I'd want more before the night was out, and this time from a source that could spare it in abundance. A trip to the Fonteyn stables was in order, but before that I had to decide what to do about Arthur Tyne.

He'd freeze to death out here. He'd need warmth and care, though God knows what Oliver could do for him. I winced at the thought of Oliver, of having to try to explain this. Elizabeth would understand, but then she'd had a lot longer to get used to certain facts about my condition.

Later. I'd worry on it later.

Had I been at my full strength I could have carried him back to the house, but I was not, being hard pressed even to get him into the mausoleum. As he'd done before with me, now did I lay him out on the sarcophagus. I noticed I'd left some bloodstains on the marble from my occupation of the same spot and wondered if they might prove permanent, then concluded I didn't really care to know.

I further noticed my hat, lost when Arthur had attacked me, was at the foot of the thing, along with someone's sword and my own swordstick. The former's presence puzzled me, the latter I gladly repossessed. It was still in two pieces, which I remedied, slipping the blade into the stick and engaging the catch. I'd find a good use for it as a simple cane again, until I could bolster myself with more blood.

The wounds I'd made on Arthur's neck had stopped bleeding, but his skin had taken on a bluish cast. Whether from the cold or the damage I'd inflicted by draining him mattered not; with a grimace, I stripped off my cloak and drew it over him. It would be only a five-minute walk to the house, and I could stand up to the chill better than he for that long. As an afterthought, I pulled his neckcloth back and more or less knotted it into place, thus ensuring a bit more protection as well as covering the evidence of my madness.

"I'll be seeing you shortly," I muttered to him and turned to leave.

And alas, did not get far. Only to the gate. In time to see Ridley hurrying down the path from Fonteyn House with another figure behind him. A woman. What the—?

I would have liked to quit the business then and there, to vanish and pass them by and let them find Arthur and do as they pleased, but tired as I was, I was also damned curious.

And angry. I'd paid Arthur back for my injury, but not Ridley.

He and the woman were closer, heading purposefully toward the mausoleum. Melting into the shadows beyond the gate, I slipped behind the far side of the huge sarcophagus, and lay flat on the floor between it and the wall. If it looked as if one of them might come 'round, then would I vanish, but not before. I was of a mind to hear their talk.

"Arthur!" Ridley called impatiently for his cousin. He pushed the gate open and came in.

"*Arthur!*" called the woman in turn.

I recognized her voice, and the sheer surprise of it nearly made me raise up. As it was, all my skin seemed to leap from the shock. What in God's name was Clarinda doing out here with Thomas Ridley?

"Where is he?" she demanded of him.

"How the devil should I know?"

"Then find him. I'm freezing here."

Well-a-day. Wrapped in my cloak and in the darkness, it seemed that they'd mistaken Arthur's body for mine. I wondered how long that would last.

"You could have stayed in the house," Ridley pointed out.

"No. I want to see it done."

He snorted. "You've already missed the best part."

She moved closer to the sarcophagus, but not too close, thank heaven. "You're sure he's—"

"Arthur took care of him, you needn't worry."

"But he was supposed to be shot," she said peevishly.

*What?*

"Too late now. I'll just put swords in their hands and leave it at that."

"But if it doesn't look right . . ."

"It will, and even if anyone should raise a question, you and your precious Oliver can easily hush it up."

Oliver? My God, how was he involved in this? It was hard enough to believe that Clarinda was here and up to heaven knows what, but *Oliver?* I felt a sickening shift in the depths of my belly, ten times worse than any illness I'd ever known. Betrayal. Pale, ugly, unforgivable betrayal. I'd faced it before from Caroline Norwood, but for it to come from my good cousin, my dearest friend . . .

"Have you a candle and tinderbox?" Ridley asked her. "Good, then be useful and make some light. It's black as Hades in here."

"Afraid of the dark, are you?" she countered good-naturedly.

"No, but I can't work in it—not unless it's the right kind of work."

"Time for that afterward. Now get you along and find Arthur."

With a grunt of disappointment, Ridley went out, calling Arthur's name.

I waited with a patience I'd not been aware of possessing as she played with the tinderbox and coaxed sufficient flame from it to transfer to the candle. Its light was unsteady because of the air flowing in from the entry, but it served.

She placed the candle on one corner of the sarcophagus, then paced up and down to keep warm. When the sound of her steps indicated that she was walking away from me, I put a hand on the stone lid and boosted myself up. Damnation, but I was so insidiously weak, shaking from the exertion, but the look on Clarinda's face when she turned and saw me made the effort worth it.

An instant's surprise, an instinctive falling back, and then unhappy recognition.

"Good evening, Cousin," I said calmly.

Oh, but she was clever. Her eyes swept from me to Arthur Tyne and returned. She divined who was really wrapped in the cloak just that fast. Her gaze next fastened on my cut sleeve. In the dim light she'd not be able to see the blood against the black cloth, but the stains had crept as far as my waistcoat and shirt.

She made a step forward, one hand out as though to help. "You're hurt," she observed, putting a convincing tone of concern into her voice.

"But not dead." My own tone was such as to let her understand I was impervious to further attempts at deception.

She let her hand drop to rest on her skirts and suppressed a shiver. She was wrapped well for the weather, but I fancied any chill she felt now was not connected to the cold. "What went wrong?" she asked evenly, abandoning her playacting for a more sober demeanor. She pointed at Arthur.

"Does it matter?"

She made no reply.

"Why, Clarinda?" I whispered. "Tell me *why.*"

More silence.

"Ridley I can understand, he wants revenge for the duel, but why are you involved in this? How?"

I waited in vain.

"Is he one of your lovers, then? Is he doing it for you because of that? Did he force a fight on me because of what happened with us four years past?" It sounded ludicrous even as I spoke it, but I couldn't imagine any other reason.

A smile twitched at the corners of her mouth. A singularly unpleasant smile. "You're remarkably close to the truth, Jonathan, but are too flattering to yourself."

"Then why? Why are you a part of this? What have you against me?" I moved closer, fully intending to force an answer from her, but in the blink of an eye she drew a dueling pistol from the pocket of her skirt and aimed it right at my chest. I stopped hardly two paces from its muzzle. Even an inexperienced shooter could not miss at that distance, and Clarinda appeared to be well acquainted with the workings of her gun.

"I've nothing against you, dear lad," she said, "but it's better for all concerned that you not be around Fonteyn House any longer."

"But *why?* And how is Oliver involved? Where is he?"

"Drunk in his room where you left him, I'm sure."

"How is he a part of this?"

She seemed startled. "He's not. Not yet."

*Yet?* "What do you mean? Answer me!"

But she held her peace and edged toward the entrance. *"Thomas!"*

There wasn't enough light, but I had to try. "Listen to me, Clarinda. I want you to hear me and—"

Perhaps she sensed the danger, somehow. She could not have known what I was trying to do, only that it was a threat. She sighted along the muzzle and fired, just like that.

My only warning was the tiny pause as she aimed. Without hesitation, I made myself fade away—and just barely in time. I glimpsed the explosion and roar, but thank God did not feel the ball scorching through the space where I stood. Floated. For but an instant. A half second later and I was solid again.

Weak. I was so *weak.* Drained. Hollow. Swaying.

Clarinda watched me avidly. The powder flash in this dim chamber must have blinded her to my brief disappearance. She couldn't see that I was untouched. She was waiting for me to fall.

And fall I might. I'd used myself up, pushed myself too far, more of this and I might not—

Ridley appeared at the entrance. The mate to Clarinda's dueler was in his hand.

Damnation. Another vanishing would finish me. And if he fired, the shot might also finish me. I hadn't the strength to handle either.

*I should have gone on to the stables,* I thought, crumpling forward and letting myself gradually slip to the floor. Shutting my eyes, I held very still. Waiting. Hoping.

"What the devil's happened?" Ridley snarled. "Where did he come from?"

Clarinda's voice was high with the strain. "See if he's dead. Go on!"

"You—"

*"Go on!"*

Cautiously Ridley stepped past her and knelt by me, putting a hand on my heart. "Done for," he pronounced.

Thank God for that. Now if they'd only *leave.*

"You're sure?" My, but wasn't she anxious.

"He's gone, I say. What happened?"

Excited as she was, she managed to explain everything to him in a few short rushing words. He seemed caught between admiration for her nerve at being able to kill a man and anger that he'd been cheated of the task.

The winter cold was seeping up from the marble floor and into my very bones. I'd be shivering soon, giving myself away. *No, Johnny Boy, that would be a very bad idea. Let them get on with their work, get out, and then you can stagger to the stables and fill yourself.*

"Why'd you have to shoot him?" Ridley complained. "Now how will it look? A sword cut *and* a pistol ball in one—"

"It will seem as if they'd fired, wounding each other, then finished themselves off with swords."

"But it won't lo—"

"I can't help that! We use what we have and make the best of it. Now see to Arthur. Quickly."

Ridley abandoned me to look at his cousin. Arthur was still with the living, which I found to be something of a relief.

"Wake him," said Clarinda.

But alas for them, Arthur was quite unconscious. "What'd the bastard do to him?" Ridley wanted to know, but I was not planning to answer, having cares of my own.

"Never mind him, then," she said. "We'll manage without."

"The slab's too heavy. It was all we could do to move it earlier. I need Arthur to—"

"Who's not going to wake until spring. I'll help you. Just put your back into it."

With ill-grace, and grumbling, he acquiesced. I cracked an eye open to see what they were about.

Using his good arm and with Clarinda's assistance, Ridley dragged Arthur's body from the lid of the sarcophagus and away to one side. He groaned and complained and favored his wound, but Clarinda had little sympathy for him.

"You should have killed Jonathan outright at that bloody Masque, not played with him," she reproved, catching her breath.

"I thought I had. I *know* I—"

"Yes, you ran him through, so you've told me."

"Right through—and dropped him."

"Except that he got back up again to return the favor."

"Then perhaps you should have fought him yourself."

"I was busy elsewhere."

He gave a mirthless laugh.

"Come along," she said. "I can't be out here all night."

He sighed. "Very well, take that end and push, and I'll pull on the corner."

She did as directed, placing her hands against the edge of the slab covering the sarcophagus. After a bit of Herculean effort on their part, the thing budged. I saw then that the lid was divided into two great squares and that they were trying to move one of them. What devilry was this? Were they planning to hide me away in *there?*

They paused, panting awhile, then tried again, shifting it even more. Perhaps while they were busy with it, I could creep out, lose myself in the woods . . .

Someone *inside* the sarcophagus cursed. Clarinda and Ridley dodged back as a hand shot up from the opening they'd made. Ridley clawed hastily for his dueler and held it ready.

"Awake are you?" he said. "Out, then, and save us some trouble."

My hackles went up. A man began to emerge, a large man, moving slowly as though injured. He sucked air in and all but sobbed it out again. His mourning clothes were much disarrayed, and there was blood on his hands where he'd beaten them against the confines of his ghastly prison.

Edmond Fonteyn.

"Damn you to hell," he grated at them. His eyes were blazing. I could feel the hate, the sheer *fury* rolling from him, filling the room.

"We'll see you there first," said Ridley, showing his teeth. "All the way, now, there's a good fellow."

Edmond painfully struggled to haul his big frame free of the small opening. Clarinda watched from a safe distance behind Ridley. Both were between me and the door.

Finally out, Edmond leaned exhaustedly on the great stone box. He first saw Arthur, then me. I made my eyes fix sightless on nothing at all.

"My God. How many more, Clarinda?" he asked.

"Just you, husband," she softly answered.

"And you think you'll not swing for it?"

"I know I won't. It will seem as though you and Jonathan had your own private duel and killed each other." She smiled. "Over me, of course."

"No one will believe that."

"I'll make certain they do, never you worry. You've already helped things along. All that glaring at Jonathan—anyone with eyes could see how you despised him."

"And then what? You'll marry that fool?" He nodded at Ridley, whose eyes narrowed at the name-calling.

"No . . . not yet, anyway. But dear Cousin Oliver, now—"

*"Oliver?"* Edmond laughed.

"He likes me well enough, and I'll see to it that he has every chance to comfort this grieving widow."

"Oh, yes, you're good at that, aren't you?"

"Excellent good, Edmond." She smirked. "Well do you know yourself."

He started toward her, but Ridley told him to be still, using the gun to enforce his direction. "Let's finish this, Clarinda," he said. "I thought you were in such a hurry."

"All right, but I want to put things properly in order. Where are the swords?"

"There." Ridley indicated the end of the sarcophagus where I lay. She glided over, picking up the sword I'd found earlier.

"Where's the other?"

"In Barrett's cane. There's a trick catch—"

She bent and got it. "Oh, one of those things. How do I . . . yes, there it is." She drew the blade free, discarding the stick. She placed the blade on the floor near my hand, then put her empty pistol next to it. I watched through cracked lids.

"Come on," Ridley urged.

"Never you mind me, just make sure you hit Edmond properly."

"Do you want to do it?" he asked, exasperated.

She gasped a little. It sounded like a laugh. "Yes, I do."

"You've the devil in you, woman, and no mistake."

"Sure you want to marry her later?" Edmond queried. "I assume that's the final plan to all of this. First she marries Oliver, then she inherits his money. How do you plan to kill him, hey?"

I opened my eyes a bit more. None were paying attention to me. The hilt of my sword was only inches from my hand. I moved enough to close my fingers around it.

*Now what, Johnny Boy? Charge Ridley, waving and yelling, and hope he misses?*

Possibly. If I could just stand up.

Edmond continued. "Will you arrange another duel? That is, if she doesn't kill you to keep you quiet."

Ridley laughed in his turn.

"Just look at her. Go ahead. Trust her. She'll soon serve you as you're serving me. See if she doesn't."

"She already *has,* Edmond. And what a marvelous fine piece she is to be sure."

"Joke if you like, but after tonight she won't need your help, you know. She'll soon have what she wants, the Fonteyn money and a protector she can twist round her finger. She won't need you at all."

"It's not working, husband," Clarinda put in. "Thomas and I understand each other too well for you to put doubts between us."

That seemed true enough, though it had been a good argument.

"Give me the pistol," she said.

"Not so close to him," Ridley cautioned. "Don't want him to grab it away from you, do you?"

They stepped back. Clarinda's skirts brushed against me.

Ridley handed over the dueler, swiftly, smoothly. The barrel wavered but a quarter inch, then she fixed it on Edmond. "Don't hit him to kill," he advised. "Remember he's supposed to last long enough for some sword play afterward."

"I know, I know. Where, then? His leg, shoulder—?"

"The stomach, my dear. Will you want to put the sword in yourself, too? To finish him?"

Edmond was dead white, but held his ground. Brave man.

"Yes," she answered. "I think I want to do that, as well."

There were Clarinda's feet peeking from under the hem of her gown. Not quite within reach, but if I let go my sword and . . .

"What will it feel like?" she wondered.

I twisted and dug my knees against the floor, reaching with both hands. Suddenly engulfed in a drift of black fabric and petticoats, I blundered heavily into her. She screeched in surprise as I tried to take hold of her legs. She kicked once and began to fall, overbalanced.

Ridley cursed and I had an impression of him starting for me until something large slammed into him. Edmond, probably. I left them to it, being busy myself.

Clarinda kicked again, viciously, catching me on the forehead with the sharp edge of her heel. I yelped and held fast to the one leg I had. Her vast skirts hampered us both, she for movement and me for sight as I tried to see what was going on. She screamed Ridley's name, fighting to break free. Her heel next caught me on the shoulder. This time I got hold of it while breathlessly damning her to perdition.

I could hear some commotion going on between Edmond and Ridley. Clarinda also seemed aware of them and abruptly ceased trying to get away from me.

Oh, my God.

Letting go of her legs, I surged up and glimpsed her taking aim at Edmond's broad back with the pistol.

*"No!"* I cried, throwing myself bodily forward.

The explosion deafened me. Too late. Too late. In panic as much as anger, I cracked a hand against her jaw. She slumped instantly. Behind and above me I heard more commotion, grunts and thumps ending with a soft but sickening thud. Someone made a gagging sound, then a body fell on the floor next to me.

I pushed and turned away from Clarinda, fearful of an attack from Ridley; I need not have worried. It had been his body that had fallen. Edmond towered over us, chest heaving as he struggled to regain his breath, his eyes dark pinpoints in a white sea, not quite sane. For a second I thought his mad stare was for me, then realized it was Clarinda that held his attention. I was glad she was unconscious. What he might have done had she been awake did not bear imagining.

Neither of us moved. I was too tired, and he, well, his mind was in the grip of the shadows. Having been in their thrall myself more than once, I knew it would take a bit of time for him to break loose. I remained quiet for his sake.

Bloodsmell in the air. Edmond's. Fresh.

There was a long tear on the outside of his left arm. The ball from Clarinda's pistol had come that close. It might have been closer, had I not—

My teeth were out again.

*Ignore it, Johnny Boy. Now's not the time or place.*

God, but I was hungry. Thankfully not to the point of losing control. I wasn't on the edge of starving survival this time. I could wait a little longer.

*But not too long.*

Edmond stalked around us to sit on the defiled sarcophagus. He pressed one hand to his wound, bowing his head. There were lots of new lines on his face, but the old ones had settled back into something resembling their previous order.

"Let's get some help for that, shall we?" I suggested, my voice so thin and shaken I hardly knew it.

Edmond raised his eyes to stare at me. His expression rippled as the muscles beneath the skin convulsed. Not a pleasant sight, that. Even worse when I realized he was starting to laugh. Was laughing. With only the slightest of changes it might also be weeping. I fell quiet again. To offer a comforting arm as I'd done for Oliver would not have been welcome in this case. Edmond shook with laughter, was racked by it, sobbed with it, the sounds reverberating against the shocked walls of the mausoleum until the last of it dribbled away and he was utterly emptied.

In the thick silence that followed, I strove to remove myself from the floor and, after a bit of struggle, succeeded. Like Edmond, I half sat, half leaned on the sarcophagus. Unlike him, I had no laughter in me, only a vast fatigue that would have to be answered for very soon.

Ridley was alive, I noticed, and I was somewhat surprised by the fact. Edmond had thoroughly pulped him from what I could see of the fellow. His face was well bloodied, and there was more blood on the wall that may have come from a nasty-looking patch on one side of his shaved scalp. He'd lost his wig sometime during the battle, else it might have provided a bit of protection. Then again, perhaps not. Edmond had been terrifically incensed.

Now he appeared to have regained a measure of self-possession. He was looking at his unconscious wife.

"I . . . I really thought she loved me, once upon a time," he said softly. "Didn't last long. But it was nice for a while."

"I'm sorry."

He puffed some air out. Almost a laugh. "You've no idea."

I thought I had, but said nothing. I shut my eyes and thanked God that Oliver had not been involved, after all. I let myself feel ashamed for having believed it even for a moment. Ridley's talk had been too vague on the point, and I'd suspected the worst. *Bad, Johnny Boy, very bad of you.*

Yes. Very bad, indeed.

Then there was one other thing that had been said . . .

"Edmond?"

He grunted.

"Did Clarinda kill Aunt Fonteyn?"

His great head swung in my direction. "Why do you think that?"

"Because she reminded Ridley that she'd been busy elsewhere during the duel. It's bothered everyone on why Aunt Fonteyn had gone to the center of the maze that night, but Clarinda might have managed to get her there."

He was quiet for a very long time, head bowed, shoulders down. He took in a draught of air and let it out slowly, shuddering. "I think you're right," he whispered. "Clarinda was somewhat . . . nervous that night. Very bright, she was. I thought it was because of the party, because she may have been going to meet someone. Another man. Always another man in the past. We'd long passed the point where I didn't give a damn what she did anymore and separated at the party soon after arrival. She must have—"

"She killed Aunt Fonteyn so Oliver would inherit everything. Then we were to die tonight so she could be free to marry again. To marry the money."

"With enough scandal involved so that the family would hush the worst of it up."

"But why kill me?" I asked.

"Eh?"

"They wanted me to die at the Masque. Both of them." Yes, I had a separate quarrel with Ridley over that street brawl with him and his Mohocks, but why had Clarinda wanted me dead?

"You really don't know?" He seemed bitterly amused at my ignorance.

"Do you? What is it, then?"

"I'll have to show you. At the house. These three can keep themselves until we can send someone for them. Come along, boy."

He ponderously moved toward the door. I got my cloak back from Arthur, and put my swordstick together to use as a cane. Tired as I was, I needed its support just to hobble. Edmond was in better fettle and walked up the path toward the house more easily. He paused to wait for me, but I waved at him to go on ahead. As soon as he was out of sight, I veered away on a course that would take me directly to the Fonteyn stables and their red promise of swift revival.

Afterward, of course, I took care not to show myself to be too lively when I made it back to the house. The cloak covered the alarming state of my blood-soaked clothing, and while Edmond was busy rousing certain members of the staff and household and giving them orders, I managed to avoid drawing undue attention to myself.

Elizabeth was the one exception to this ploy. The instant she saw me, she knew something was wrong. The next instant she was whisking me away to a room where we could have the privacy necessary to talk.

That talk was both lengthy and brutally truthful. I told her all.

All that I *knew,* that is.

It was just an hour short of dawn when Edmond had sorted things to his satisfaction and Fonteyn House settled a bit.

*Won't last,* I thought, dreading the gossip to come. Not for my sake, but for Oliver's.

He had been awakened early on but had proved too befuddled to make much sense of the business. Elizabeth stayed behind trying to coax some *café noir* into him in the hope that it would help.

Clarinda had recovered very fast from the blow I'd dealt her. At first she'd tried to run, then endeavored to convince Edmond she'd been under duress from Ridley, then attempted to bribe the servants guarding her. Under orders from her husband she was locked into a small upper room usually reserved for storage. He kept the only key. After a time she gave up shouting her outrage to the walls and fell into sullen silence.

Ridley and Arthur, both still unconscious, were being cared for by a closemouthed doctor from the Fonteyn side of the family. He pronounced both to be concussed and not likely to wake anytime soon. He totally missed the wounds on Arthur's neck. Just as well.

"What will you do with them?" I asked Edmond, who was glaring at the two as if to burn them to cinders.

"Nothing," he rumbled.

*"Nothing?"*

"What would be accomplished in a court of law? They'd be let off with a five-shilling fine and advised to behave themselves in the future. Their fathers are too important in the Town for them to get what they really deserve. They didn't actually kill us, y'know."

"It wasn't for lack of trying."

"Yes, but since they failed, what they've done can be put down to the high spirits of youth. They knocked you about and shut me in that damned pit, nothing more. Pranks."

He was right about that. For my own sake I'd had to conceal the true extent of my injury, which was now considerably better. Without such visible evidence of their intent to kill it would be nearly impossible to see any justice done—at least through the courts. However, I had some very firm ideas of my own and planned to act upon them at the earliest opportunity. In the near future both men would have to endure a late night visit from me that neither would remember, but which would have a profound effect on their lives. By God, I might even make churchgoers of them.

"And Clarinda?" I asked.

"Oh, she's mad, Cousin," he informed me matter-of-factly.

"What?"

"Quite, quite mad. I fear she will have to be confined for the rest of her life because of it." He fastened me with a dangerous look. "Any objections?"

I pursed my lips and shook my head.

"She did do murder," he went on softly, "of that I'm now certain. And she planned to do murder, of that we both know, but there's no way in which it might be proven."

"Unless she confesses," I mused.

"Not bloody likely, and even if she should, what then? Better this than watching her dance a jig at Tyburn."

Probably.

"No good would come of it to the family. We have to think of them," he added.

"Oh, yes, certainly the family must be considered first."

I half expected a sharp reproach for my sarcasm, but he only lifted his chin a bit. "Come along with me," he said, starting off without waiting to see if I'd follow.

I caught up. "Why?"

"You wanted to know why she was going to kill you. Still interested?"

I was. He went upstairs and down one of the halls. I worried how long this might take. Brought back to strength again by means of the horse blood I'd lately fed upon, I could float home if pressed for time, but preferred to ride safe in a coach if possible. Before pushing myself further, I wanted a solid day's rest on my earth first.

Edmond stopped before a closed door and gently opened it. The room beyond was lighted by several candles standing in bowls of water. Many cots had been set out, each bearing a small sleeping occupant. When I saw Nanny Howard, I came to the reasonable conclusion that we were in the nursery.

"All's quiet, Mr. Fonteyn," she said in a low voice. I think she meant it as a warning for him not to disturb the children. She gave me a piercing stare, but I'd since borrowed some of Oliver's clothing and was secure that I was more respectable appearing than at our last meeting.

Edmond brushed past her, picking up a candle along the way, and headed for one of the cots, pausing before it. The child lying in it was young, not more than three or four. He was very pretty, with pale clear skin and a headful of thick black hair.

"Clarinda's boy," Edmond told me. "His name is Richard."

Yes, I could see that he'd want to protect his son from the stigma of Clarinda's crimes, but what had this to do with . . .

A cold fist seemed to close upon my belly, tighten its grip, and twist.

"Oh, my God," I breathed.

"Oh, yes, by God," Edmond growled.

"It can't be."

"It *is.* When he opens his eyes, you'll find them to be as blue as your own."

The next few minutes were a dreadful haze as my poor brain tried to keep up with things and failed. I eventually found myself drooping on a settee out in the hall with Edmond looming over me, telling me to pull myself together and not be such a damned fool.

"Too late for that," I muttered, still in the throes of shock.

The Christmas party. My God, my God, my God . . .

"I knew he wasn't mine," Edmond was saying. "And she wouldn't name the father, but when I saw you that night, I understood whose whelp he was right enough. You can be sure that Aunt Fonteyn would have seen as well had she been given the chance. Clarinda was always careful to keep the boy out of her sight. Easy to do when they're young. Must have given her quite a turn for you to come back to England."

"But—"

"She couldn't afford to have you around, y'know. Anyone seeing you and Richard would make the connection, but with you dead and buried, memories would soon fade, and she'd lie her head off, as always, to cover herself. Not with Aunt Fonteyn, though. The old woman was too sharp for such tricks. She'd have cut Clarinda out of the family money quick as thought. Another reason to kill."

"Wh-what's to be done?" I felt as if a giant had stepped on me. I couldn't think, couldn't move. Was this what all men feel when fatherhood is suddenly thrust upon them?

"Done? What do you mean?"

"You can't introduce me to the child and expect me just to walk away. I'd like to get to know him . . . if it's all right with you." That was the problem. Would Edmond allow even that much?

Edmond studied me, and for the first time there seemed to be a kind of sympathetic pity mixed into his normally grim expression. "You—what about the gossip?"

"I don't give a damn about gossip. Nor do you, I think. After all this, people are going to know or guess anyway. Let them do so and be damned for all I care."

A long silence. Then, "You're all in, boy. Time enough to think about such things tomorrow."

"But I—"

"Tomorrow," he said firmly, taking my arm and helping me up. "Now get out of here, before I forget myself and pound your face into porridge for being a better man than I."

# EPILOGUE

But I could not bring myself to leave Fonteyn House. Not after this. The rapid approach of dawn was as nothing to me. When the time came I'd find some dark and distant corner in one of the ancient cellars and shelter there for the duration of the short winter day. There would be bad dreams awaiting me since I'd be separated from my home soil, but I'd survived them before and would do so again. Compared to what I'd just learned, the prospect of facing a week's worth of them hardly seemed worth my notice.

After Edmond had left and under Nanny Howard's eye, I crept back into the nursery to look again at the sleeping child. *My* sleeping child. Richard.

My God, but he was beautiful. Had my heart been beating, surely it would now be pounding fit to burst. As it was, my hands were shaking so much from a heady mixture of excitement, uncertainty, joy, and sheer terror that I didn't dare touch him for fear of waking him.

Questions and speculations stabbed and flickered through my brain like heat lightning, offering only brief flashes of light, but no real illumination about the future. Edmond had not wanted to discuss it, and I could see that he was right to postpone things until the idea had fully been absorbed into my still mostly stunned mind. Certain subjects between us would have to be addressed, though, and soon.

I'd said I didn't give a damn about the gossip, but that wasn't entirely true. It meant little enough to me, but might prove to be a problem for this little innocent. It wasn't his fault that his mother was a murderous—

*Not now, Johnny Boy.*

Or ever. I'd hardly endear myself to the child by expressing an honest opinion to him about Clarinda.

Would he even *like* me?

I chewed my lower lip on that one for several long minutes.

And how in the world would I ever tell Father?

I fidgeted from one foot to the other for even longer.

Good God, what would Mother—no, that didn't even bear thinking about.

I shook myself, nearly shivering from that thought.

Well, we'd all get through it somehow, though for the moment I hadn't the vaguest inkling of what to do besides stare at the little face that so closely mirrored my own and hope for the best.

"He's a very good boy, sir," whispered Nanny Howard from close behind me.

I gave quite a jump, but at least forbore from yelling in surprise.

She couldn't completely hide her amusement at startling me, but diplomatically pretended not to notice my discomfiture.

"A good boy, you say?" I asked, my voice a little cracked.

"Yes, sir. Very smart he is, too, if a bit headstrong."

"Headstrong? I like that."

"Indeed, sir. It complements him, when it's not misplaced."

"I . . . I want to know all about him. Everything."

"Of course, I'll be glad to tell you whatever you like. We should talk elsewhere, though."

At this gentle hint from her we moved out into the hall, leaving the door open so she could keep an eye on her charges. I was eager to hear any scrap of information on the boy, but alas, just as she was settling herself to speak we were interrupted.

*"Jonathan?"* Elizabeth came hurrying toward us, brows high with alarm. "What on earth are you still doing here? You know you—" She stopped when she saw Nanny Howard.

"It's all right," I said, keeping my voice low and making hushing motions with my hands.

"But it's very late for you," Elizabeth insisted, speaking through her teeth. God knows what Mrs. Howard thought of her behavior.

"It doesn't matter, I'm staying here for the day." Now I had shocked her, a portent of things to come, no doubt.

*"You're what?* But you—"

Before her surprise overcame her discretion, I took Elizabeth's elbow and steered her back down the hall out of earshot of Mrs. Howard. My good sister was just starting to sputter with indignation at my action when I reined us up short and turned to face her.

The look on my face must have helped trigger that innate sympathy that sometimes occurs between siblings, where much is said when nothing is spoken.

"What is it?" she asked, suddenly dropping any protest she might have had. "Is something wrong? Has Edmond—"

"No, nothing like that. Nothing's wrong—at least I don't think so, but you'll have to decide for yourself, and I hope to God that you think it's all right, because I really need all the help I can get, especially yours, because this is—is—"

"Jonathan, you're babbling," she stated, giving me a severe look. "For heaven's sake collect yourself and tell me *what* is going on."

And so I did.

# DANCE OF DEATH

*For Mark*
*and exhausting times.*

*A very special thanks to*
*Teresa Patterson,*
*for all your support on and off the field;*
*The Fort Worth Writer's Group,*
*for the help at the start;*
*Nigel Bennett, Deborah Duchêne,*
*and the great gang at Dead of Winter II*
*for the dose of totally wonderful fun;*
*and to Hershey's Chocolate U.S.A.,*
*for without certain of their products*
*portions of this book would not have been possible.*

# CHAPTER 1

*London, December 1777*

"You're certain that he's all right?" asked my cousin Oliver, shifting closer in an anxious effort to see better. "He looks like a dead fish."

Which was a perfectly accurate observation; however, I had no need to be reminded about the effect of my special influence on another person. I really had no need for Oliver's interruption, either, but he'd asked to watch and at the time there seemed no reason to deny his request. Now I was having second thoughts.

"Please," I said in a rather tight voice. "I must concentrate."

"Oh." His hushed tone was contrite, and he instantly subsided into silence and went very still, enabling me to put forth my full attention on the man sitting before us. Focusing my gaze hard upon his slack face, I softly spoke into his all too vulnerable mind.

*You must listen very carefully to what I say. . . .*

In this moment I truly felt myself balanced on the edge of a knife. With Oliver along to witness things, I was steadier than if I'd been alone, and yet I was very much aware of the lamentable consequences should I make a mistake with this fellow. A single word on my part or a brief surge of uncontrolled rage let loose, and the man would most likely be plunged into a madness from which he might never recover. I'd done that once before—unintentionally—and would be a liar not to admit this present circumstance offered me a great temptation to repeat the action. God knows, I'd more than sufficient cause to justify such a malfeasance.

His name was Thomas Ridley, and last night he and his cousin Arthur Tyne had done their damnedest to try to murder me. For this and other crimes they'd committed or participated in, I had been informed it would be too much to expect a just retribution by means of the law; therefore I'd taken upon myself the responsibility to guarantee that they would commit no further mischiefs. Arthur had already been dealt with and would soon be sent away home when he was fit enough to travel. I'd drained quite a lot of blood from him last night—purely for the purpose of survival, not revenge—and he'd been but half awake and easy to influence.

Ridley was another matter.

We'd confined him to one of the more remote cellar storage rooms far beneath Fonteyn House, well away from any ears with no business hearing his bellowed curses. When I'd awakened that evening, had finished with the befuddled Arthur, and was ready to deal with Ridley, he'd worked himself into a truly foul temper, if one might judge anything by the coarsely direct quality of his language. Much of his invective involved both general and specific profanities against myself and my many relatives for his treatment at our collective hands.

Coming down to the cellar together, Oliver and I had dismissed the five footmen detailed to stand watch, and announced our presence to Ridley through the stout oak timbers of the door to his makeshift prison. He responded with a statement to the effect that it would be his greatest pleasure to kill us both with his bare hands. He saw no humor in Oliver's comment that he'd just given us an excellent reason for keeping him incarcerated until he was starved into a better disposition. Ridley's reaction was another tirade against us, accompanied by a solid crashing and thumping to indicate that he'd found something in his cell with which to make an assault on the door.

"I think we should have the footmen back," Oliver advised, casting a nervous eye at me. "We won't be able to handle him alone, he's far too angry for reason."

"He'll not be difficult for me once I'm inside."

"That's a proper lion's den in there and I must remind you that your name's Jonathan, not Daniel."

"And I must remind you that I have a bit more than just my faith to protect me in this instance."

"From the sound of things, you'll need it."

Ridley roared and smashed whatever weapon he'd found upon the door, causing it to rattle alarmingly. I hoped that his improvised club was not made of wood. For reasons unknown to me, wood presents a rare difficulty to my person when brought to bear with violence, and to it was I as susceptible to bodily harm as any ordinary man; I'd have to take care not to allow Ridley the least opening against me.

*Easier said than done, Johnny Boy*, I thought, steeling myself to enter. More out of trepidation of what was to come and to put it off just a bit longer than out of concern for Oliver, I paused to make an inquiry of him.

"You know what to expect, don't you?"

Ridley's commotion must have distracted him. "I expect he'll pulverize you, then come after me."

"He won't be able to. I was asking if you remembered what I was going to do to get inside."

"Oh, that," he said with wan enthusiasm. "Yes, you've mentioned it, but I'm not so sure that I've quite taken it in."

"I've never had cause before to demonstrate it for you. You're not going to swoon or do anything silly, are you?"

"For God's sake, how bad can it be?"

"It's not bad, just something of a surprise if one is unprepared for it."

"I should be able to manage well enough. Once one's witnessed a few amputations there's little enough the world can do to shake one's calm. Nothing like seeing a man getting his leg sawed off for putting you in a proper mood to count your blessings and to ignore most troubles life has to fling at you." As if to give lie to his statement, Oliver jumped somewhat at Ridley's next fit of hammering.

"Steady on, Coz." I found myself near to smiling at his discomfiture and wondered if he was playing the ass on purpose just to lighten things.

He scowled, jerking his head in the direction of the clamor. "Well, get on with it before he has the whole house down. Do what you must—just promise you'll try to come out in one piece."

"I promise." And with those words, I picked up one of the lighted candles left behind by the footmen and vanished.

Oliver emitted a sort of suppressed yelp, but held his ground as far as I could determine without benefit of sight. My hearing was somewhat impaired while in this bodiless state, but I could clearly sense his presence just in front of me—or what had been my front but a moment before. Now I floated, held in place by thought alone, and by that means did I propel myself to one side, find the crack between the cellar bricks and the wooden door, and sweep down and through to become solid once more in the little room beyond.

I say little, for Ridley seemed to fill the whole of its space. I was a tall man, but Ridley was just that much taller, possessing a large and fit body heavy with muscles and all of them full charged with his anger. The remains of some bandaging circled his head; he'd suffered injury last night and taken a shallow but colorful wound. It had probably opened again because of his exertions; the blood had soaked through, and I instantly picked up the scent of it. His right arm had been in a sling the last time I'd seen him. The sling was gone now and his arm hung slack at his side. He still had much energy in him, for he slammed at the door again using his good arm and called us cowards and damned us thrice over. His back was to me when I caused myself to reappear.

The candle I held yet burned, and its sudden radiance drew his instant attention upon me. He whirled, one hand raised holding what had once been a table leg and the other shading his eyes from the brightness of the flame. We'd left him in the dark for the whole of the day lest he work some damage by having fire, and so my tiny light must have been utterly blinding to him. Despite this, he was very game for a fight, and without warning threw his improvised club right at me with a guttural snarl. I wasted no time vanishing again, an action that plunged his room into full darkness once more since I still clutched the candle.

He must have been so lost to his emotions that it had made little or no impression on him that I'd appeared from nowhere and departed in the same manner. I'd held some hope that the surprise alone might slow him enough for me to soothe him to quiescence, but was forced to abandon it as he charged over to the spot where I'd been standing and tried to grab hold of me. I felt his arms passing this way and that through my invisible and incorporeal body. He, I knew, would feel nothing but an unnatural coldness.

Now he blundered about trying to find me, cursing like a dozen sailors.

"Jonathan?" Oliver called out in a worried voice.

I could not answer him in this form, nor could I count on him to be especially patient. We were as close as brothers, and his concern for me would soon cause him to fetch the footmen and come to my rescue. Even with the odds at seven to one Ridley would probably break some heads before being subdued.

I didn't care for that prospect one whit. When Ridley had crossed again to the door in his blind search, I allowed myself to assume a degree of visibility, but not solidity. He saw the candlelight immediately as before, but this time it was pale and watery, the brass holder in the hand of a ghost, not a man. This was so startling that he finally paused long enough to take in a good view of me. I was fairly transparent yet; doubtless he could see right through me to the damp brick wall at my back, an alarming effect that more than served. In the space of a moment Ridley went from a man who looked just short of bursting a blood vessel from his fury, to a man frozen with a profound astonishment beginning to edge into fear.

It was as close as I'd likely be able to come to a favorable condition for what needed to be accomplished. Quick as thought, I assumed full solidity, fastened my gaze unbreakably on to his, and told him to be *still*. Perhaps fed by my own heightened emotions, my order to him must have had more force to it than was necessary for he seemed to turn to cold marble right then and there. An abrupt twinge of dismay shot through me, and for an instant I thought I might have killed him, but this eased almost as quickly as it had come when my sharp ears detected the steady thunder of his heartbeat. I sagged from the relief.

*"Jonathan?"*

"I'm fine," I said loudly so Oliver could hear through the slab of oak between us. "It's safe now. You may unlock the door."

I heard the clink and rattle of brass, and the barrier between us swung hesitantly open. Oliver, his lanky frame blocking the lighted candles behind him, stood braced for trouble with a charged dueler in his hand.

"Where on earth did you get that?" I asked, staring.

"F-from my coat pocket, where d'ye think?"

"You won't need it; Ridley's asleep on his feet, as you can see."

Oliver narrowly examined my charge, then reluctantly put the pistol away. "He's under your influence, then?"

"For the moment."

His gaze alternated between my face and Ridley's. "First you're there and then you're not, and now this. You should have a conjuring show. It's just too uncanny."

"I quite agree," I said dryly.

"Something wrong?"

"I'm tired and I want to have done with this."

And more than that I wanted to feed again. Though outwardly I'd fully recovered from the attack Ridley and Arthur had made upon me the previous evening, I was still mending within. My vanishings just now had depleted my strength more than I cared to think about; my very bones felt hollow.

Perhaps Oliver realized something of this. He stood well aside allowing me to lead Ridley to sit at the table the footmen had recently used for their supper. I sat opposite him, checked on the number of lighted candles, and decided there was enough illumination for me to work by. The single one I'd used in the cell would have been insufficient for the sort of detailed project I was about to attempt.

Finally settled—as well as unable to put it off any longer—I began the dangerous process of rearranging another man's thoughts.

Oliver, after his initial question, was content to leave me undisturbed as I cautiously worked. Whenever I had to pause and think on what to say next, I'd steal a glance at my cousin and find him watching with rapt attention. Since first learning of them he'd been highly curious about my unnatural abilities; I hoped this demonstration would content him, since I wanted it to be the last one for the time being. I had no liking for forcing my influence upon another and took such a liberty with people only when dictated by dire necessity. At the worst it was a terrible and sometimes hazardous intrusion upon another and at the least any lengthy encounter like this one always gave me a god-awful headache.

But for all our sakes and his, Ridley very much needed to forget certain past events, as well as remember to abide by a new pattern of behavior in the future. Though presently under my control, he was as hearty in mind as in body, and I found it a difficult and exhausting task. I not only had to constantly maintain my hold against his strength of will, but labored hard to keep my own perilous emotions in check lest I cause him a permanent injury of mind.

*You're not to pick any more duels, Ridley, do you understand that? It's past time that you assume more peaceful pursuits than harassing honest citizens. No more violence for you, my lad.*

Light enough words, but it was the force I put behind them that counted. He blinked and winced a few times, a warning to me to ease off. I did, but damnation, I'd come so close to dying again . . .

*You know well enough how to cause trouble, so you must certainly know how to avoid it, and that's exactly what you'll be doing from now on. If I hear about you being in any more rows . . . well, you just behave yourself or I'll know the reason why.*

When I'd run out of things to tell Ridley, which were mostly instructions I'd already given to Arthur but requiring much less of an exertion, I leaned back in my own chair to pinch the bridge of my nose and release a small groan of sincere relief that it was finally finished.

"Now you're the one who looks like a dead fish," said my good cousin.

"Then serve me up with some sauce, I'm ready to be carried out on a platter after all this."

Oliver pressed the back of his hand to my forehead. "No fever, but it's clammy down here, so I can't be sure."

"I'm not feverish, only a bit worn down. A little rest and some additional refreshment and I'll be my own self again."

"Which is something more than amazing from what you've told me about your adventure."

"Less adventure than ordeal," I grumbled, rubbing my arm. Arthur had nearly severed it with his sword last night, and though muscle and sinew were knitted up again with hardly a scar to show for the injury, it still wanted to ache. Another visit to the Fonteyn stables might help ease things.

"And I want to hear the full story of it, if you would be so kind. Elizabeth's only been able to repeat the high points you'd given her."

But I'd told my sister all that there was to tell and said as much now to Oliver.

"That's not the same as hearing from the source. Besides, I'm full of questions that she was unable to answer."

"Such as?"

"I'll ask 'em as they occur to me, so expect to be interrupted. For the moment, all I want to know is what do we do with Mr. Ridley here?"

Our guest was still blank-eyed and slack-jawed. Perhaps the experience was tiring to him as well. One could but hope. "Take him upstairs and put him with his cousin, then pack the two of 'em off as soon as Arthur's ready to travel."

"Tomorrow, whether he's ready or not."

That suited me very well. Wearily I stood and instructed Ridley to do the same and follow us out of the cellar and upstairs. He did so, as docile as a sheep. Oliver, leading the way with the one candle we'd not extinguished and left behind, cast a worried look back at our charge.

"We'll not have any more trouble with him? You're sure?"

"Quite sure." At least for the present. Ridley and Arthur would behave themselves for a time, but past experience told me that even the most firm suggestions would eventually erode away and be forgotten. I'd have to make a point of visiting them from time to time to strengthen what had been constructed in their minds tonight. My hope was they would eventually embrace my compelled guidance as their own desire, and no longer have need of my influence to keep out of trouble.

"Seems unnatural, that," Oliver muttered.

"I can readily agree."

"It also doesn't seem . . . well, enough, somehow."

"In what way?"

"After all that he's done and tried to do, just to tell him to run along and sin no more hardly seems fitting. He should be hanged."

"Did Edmond not explain to you how unlikely an occurrence that would be?"

"In rare detail if nothing else about this business. He also said the scandal would be bad for the family, though I'm getting to the point where I think a scandal would do the lot of 'em a world of good."

"I could almost agree with you, except for how it would involve and affect us. I am content to put it all behind me and get on to more rewarding pursuits."

"Damn, but you almost sound like him."

"I suppose I must. After all, think how much we have in common." I meant it as a light jest, but it didn't come out right. Oliver looked back again, eyebrows high with shock. "I'm sorry, Coz. That was very rude of me."

"Think nothing of it. You've had a hard time of things."

Wasn't that the grand understatement? And not just for last night but for the last year or so of my life. Oliver's sympathy coupled with his kind dismissal of my poor manners crushed me down as much as the weight of recent events seemed to be doing. My death, my return to life, my search for the woman who had made such a miracle possible, all pressed close, crowding out any other thoughts in my brain for the next few moments. So thoroughly did they occupy me that I was genuinely surprised to come to myself in the central hall of Fonteyn House with no recollection of how I'd gotten there.

"Now what?" asked Oliver, setting his candle on a table.

As an answer, I looked hard at Ridley until I was certain I had his full attention. "You are a guest of Fonteyn House and will conduct yourself in a gentle and honorable manner. The servants will see to your needs, and don't forget to give them a decent vale when you leave tomorrow morning."

Ridley responded with a slight nod of acknowledgment, and I cocked an eyebrow at Oliver. He regarded each of us with no small amount of wonder.

"He can stay the night in Arthur's room," I said.

Taking the suggestion, Oliver called for a servant. One of the household's larger footmen appeared, stopping short in his tracks to give Ridley first a surprised, then highly wary look. He'd apparently heard tales from the men who had been on duty in the cellar. Of course, Ridley's appearance might have had something to do with it, what with all the bandaging, blood, and damage his clothes had taken from last night's fight and this day's incarceration. Add to that his abnormal *calmness* of manner and you had the makings of what promised to be some very speculative and animated belowstairs gossip.

"Show Mr. Ridley here to his cousin's room," Oliver instructed the man as though nothing at all was or had ever been amiss. "He'll take his supper there, and see that he's cleaned up and has all he needs to stay the night. And be sure to have someone fetch along a very large brandy for me to the blue drawing room."

The fellow looked ready to offer a few dozen questions, but was too well trained to make the attempt. Oliver's mother, the previous mistress of Fonteyn House, had not been one to encourage any kind of familiarity between servants and their betters, and her influence still lingered. The footman bowed and cautiously invited Ridley to follow him upstairs. Our prisoner, now our guest, went along as nice as you please without a backward glance at us. Oliver breathed out a pent-up sigh and let his shoulders sag a trifle. He exchanged a quick look with me; I gave him a short nod meant to reassure him that all was well and would remain so.

We watched until they reached the upper hall and turned into one of the rooms off the stairs where Arthur Tyne had been placed. More heavily concussed than Ridley and missing a goodly quantity of blood, he was slower to recover from his injuries. Bedrest and broth flavored with laudanum had been prescribed and administered, and he'd slept the day away under the watchful eye of one of the maids. The girl, her duties no longer required, soon emerged in the company of the footman and both quickly crossed our line of view to take the back way down to the kitchens. They were doubtless in a great hurry to carry the latest startling developments to the rest of the servants.

"Wonder what they'll make of all this?" I mused.

"Who knows, but we may be certain it will in no wise even remotely approach the truth."

"Mmm, then shall I thank God for such a mighty favor."

We moved along toward the blue drawing room, Oliver's favorite lair, to await the arrival of his brandy. By now I was in very sore need of a restorative as well. That hollow feeling in my bones had progressed to my muscles, and the pain in my head from all the influence I'd exercised against Ridley seemed worse than before. I wanted a deep draught of blood in me and fairly soon; the dull pounding that had taken up residence behind my eyes was threatening to become a permanent lodger.

"Please excuse me for a few minutes," I said as we approached the room. "I'd like to get some air to clear my brain."

"Go out to the stables for a drink, you mean," he corrected. "Of course, you've more than earned it. Would you object if I watched?"

"Good God, why on earth would you want to?"

"I am impelled by scientific curiosity," he stated, full of dignity.

"The same curiosity that allows you to sit through amputations?"

"Something the same as that, yes."

I shrugged, not up to trying to talk him out of it, and, as before when he wanted to see how I was to influence Ridley, there was no reason to deny his request. "Come along, then, let's get it over with."

"Such eagerness," he remarked. "You weren't like this that time with Miss Jemma at the Red Swan."

"That was for pleasure, this is for nourishment. There's a difference."

"So you've said, but don't you look forward to a nice bit of supper as much as any other man?"

"I do, but how would you feel having someone closely watching while you eat?"

"If you really mind that much—"

"I don't, I'm just reluctant lest the process disgust you. But then if you can witness an amputation without so much as batting an eye . . ."

Oliver went somewhat pink along his cheeks and ears. I'd caught him out, but decided against pressing him for embarrassing details. We found a maid to fetch our cloaks and wrapped ourselves against the outside chill, then ventured forth into the night.

The air was cold and clean as only a newly born winter can make it. My lungs normally worked just when I had need of breath to speak; now I made a real bellows of them, flushing out the stale humors lingering from the cellars. Oliver must have felt the same rejuvenating effect, for like schoolboys we contested to see who could make the greatest dragon plume as we crunched our way over the frozen earth to the stables.

Last night's sleet had transformed the world into a silver-trimmed garden that turned the most mundane things magical. My sensitive eyes found delight wherever I looked, a happiness that was somewhat dampened when I realized Oliver was unable to share in it. After my second attempt to point out an arresting view was accompanied by his complaint that he couldn't see a damned thing except that which was in the circle of his lantern light, I gave up and kept my appreciation for nature's joys to myself.

My cousin's presence was not unwelcome to me, though, particularly concerning this errand. In the London house that my sister Elizabeth and I shared with him, the servants had all been carefully influenced by me into ignoring some of my more singular customs, especially any after-dark excursions to visit the stable. The retainers at Fonteyn House were not so well prepared, making me glad of Oliver's company as an insurance against discovery. He was master here now, following the sudden death of his mother, and should anyone interrupt my feeding, he'd be the best man to deal with the problem.

He then demonstrated his own keen understanding about my need for privacy, for when we encountered some of the stable lads, he invented a minor household duty to take them elsewhere.

"Will you be long at this?" he murmured, watching them go.

I shook my head. "Having second thoughts?"

"No. Not trying to discourage me are you?"

"Hardly, since you're doing a fine enough job of it on your own."

"Am not," he stoutly protested, eyes all wide with mock outrage.

Laughing a little, I led the way in, picking out an occupied stall. Within stood one of the estate's huge plow horses. Placid to the point of being half asleep, the beast would hardly notice what would be done to him, and his vast body would provide far more sustenance than I could possibly take in.

Oliver fussed a bit to make sure he was in a position to have a clear line of observation and that his lantern was well placed for the best light. I spoke to the horse in my own way until I was utterly certain of its tranquillity. The inner anticipation I felt building within had swiftly prepared me to sup. My corner teeth, sharp enough to pierce the toughest of hides, had budded to a proper length for the work they were to do. I knelt, closing my eyes, the better to hear the heavy beat of the animal's great heart, the better to shut away my awareness of Oliver's presence. His own heart was thumping madly away, but the sound quickly became a distant triviality as my immediate bodily need was at last free to assert its supremacy over all outside distractions.

Now did I cut hard and fast with my teeth into the thick skin of the animal's leg to tap the vein that lay beneath. I was dimly aware of Oliver's strangled gasp somewhere to one side, and then I heard nothing else for a brief and blessed time as I sucked in all I needed and more of the fiery red vitality that had become my sole nourishment for life.

The night before I'd drunk deeply from another of the animals here, but then I'd been weary beyond thought, hurting, and in need of haste. There'd been no time to savor, no enjoyment to be had beyond the basic sating of appetite. Now could I hold the rich taste in my mouth and revel in it and give wordless thanks for its roaring heat as it rapidly suffused throughout my chilled flesh. The injuries, the worries, the cold failings of a harsh world thawed from my soul and melted into nothing.

Would that all the problems of life could be dealt with so easily.

I drank for as long as necessity dictated and beyond. No imbibing only enough to sustain myself for an evening or two, tonight I felt like playing the glutton. Perhaps I could take in enough blood to hold me for a whole week—an interesting, but questionable accomplishment. To achieve it might mean that my present enjoyment would be less frequent in occurrence. There had ever been a touch of the Hedonist in my nature, and, knowing that quality would not suffer, but quantity would, it seemed most reasonable to bring things to a stop.

But not until many, many delicious minutes passed by.

Reluctantly drawing away, despite the fact that I was full near to bursting, I pressed the vein above the point where I'd gone in and waited until the seeping blood slowed and finally clotted. My handkerchief took care of the few stains on my face and fingers. Practice had made me very tidy in habit.

The pain in my head was quite abated, and the strength had returned to all my limbs. Satisfaction, in every sense of the word, was mine.

Then I looked over at Oliver.

The golden glow of the lantern light lent no illusion of well-being to his face, which had gone very pasty, nor did his cloak seem to be of any use keeping him warm. He shivered from head to toe, exhibiting a misery so palpable that I felt its onrush like a buffet of wind.

Contrite that I'd caused him such distress, I raised one hand, but did not quite touch him for fear he might flinch away. I'd expected him to be affected in some adverse manner, for it is one thing to hear how a thing is done and quite another to watch, but I'd not expected his reaction to be this adverse.

"It's all right," he said quickly, his staring eyes not leaving mine. "Give me a moment."

"I'm sorry," I whispered.

"Sorry for what?" he demanded after taking in a few deep draughts of air. "You do what you must to live. If that involves drinking a bit of blood now and then, what of it?"

*What, indeed?* I thought. *What am I?* I had no name for my condition except for one fastened on me by a terrified Hessian soldier. *Blutsäuger.* Never liked the word. It made me think of spiders and how they sucked the life from their living prey. Ugh. No wonder poor Oliver was having a hard time of it.

He went on. "Pay no mind to me, I'm just cursed with a vivid imagination."

"What's *that* to do with anything?"

He gave a ghastly imitation of a smile. "Most of the time it's well in check, but tonight what with one thing and another . . ."

"What are you on about?"

"The bane of my life as a doctor, but only if I let it get away from me. Have to keep a tight hold on it when I'm dealing with a patient, else I'd be no good at all."

"Oliver—"

He waved a hand to quell my mild exasperation. "While you did your work just now, the physician in me was doing his. I was fine at first, observing, noting everything there was to note. Then I began to wonder what it might be like to be in your boots, downing all that blood like it was so much ale night after night, like it or not. Once my mind fixed on *that,* on all that blood drinking, and on the smell and taste of it . . . well,

I couldn't seem to shake it off, so this foolish reaction is my own damned fault."

"I should not have allowed this."

"God's death, man, you think this is bad? Then you should have been there to see me at that first amputation. Five of the students fainted, and I was one of the dozen others who lost his last meal. Sometimes I can still hear the poor wretch's screams and the rasp of the bone saw. By comparison, this was nothing. Well-a-day, but I'd say I'm doing rather splendidly this time around."

"Oliver, you're—"

"A complete ass? And babbling his head off? Oh, yes, I'm sure of it, but even an ass needs to learn things now and then to get on in the world. Sometimes the lesson is easy and pleasant, and sometimes not, but it doesn't matter, knowledge is the goal."

"And you've gained knowledge from this?"

"Indeed I have, and from now on I'll not take it so lightly when you try to present a warning about any given aspect of your condition. That disappearance you did in the cellar fair gave me a turn, y'know. Thought my poor heart would stop then and there."

"Why didn't you say anything?"

"I thought if I did you'd get the wind up and not let me watch. I'm quite ashamed of myself. To be like this after all the bleedings I've done . . ." He trailed off, shaking his head. "But enough on me, tell me what happened to your teeth. One minute they're normal and the next . . . and I want to know how your eyes feel right now."

"My eyes?"

"They're redder than a sunset—does it hurt? Does it affect your sight?"

"No, not at all, and I can see perfectly well."

"Why do they get like that?"

"Damned if I know. I once asked Nora about it, for hers did the same when she fed, but she said she didn't know, either." Or she chose not to tell me about it as she'd done with a thousand other details.

His mouth twitched at the mention of Nora's name. "And damned funny that she never told you what to expect after . . . well, we've talked that one over often enough. Let me see your teeth."

I obliged and opened my mouth. He muttered that the light wasn't good for a proper examination, and I suggested that we remove ourselves back to the warmth of the house where there were plenty of candles. I also reminded him that a large brandy still awaited him there. Either enticement was enough to inspire him to action; together both inspired him to haste.

Once back in the house, and ensconced before the blazing hearth in the blue drawing room, I found myself to be better disposed to undergo a doctor's examination. Though Oliver had known about my changed condition and the story behind it for some little time, this had been the first opportunity he'd had to really look into things. I harbored a small hope that his training in medicine might yield up some explanation for my unusual physical state.

Since Nora Jones, the woman I had loved—still loved—the woman who had gifted me with this strange condition, had seen fit not to provide me with anything in the way of preparation on how to deal with it, I'd had to learn about my advantages and limitations by many trials and much error. Certainly I'd used what knowledge I recalled about her own habits as a guide, but after more than a year of it, I was still full of many important questions and singularly lacking in answers. The urgency to see her again and to obtain those answers had drawn me from my lifelong home on Long Island and back to England again in an effort to find her.

Unhappily, she was not to be found. Oliver had done his best, moving through his wide circle of friends and acquaintances in London, writing to others on the Continent trying to locate her, or at least a hint of her presence. The only clue I'd had of her passing had come from a madman named Tony Warburton, and it had been less informative than frustrating and the cause of a profound unease on my soul. He'd said she'd been ill. So impervious was I to sickness and injury I could not imagine what she might be suffering from. I also tried very hard not to imagine that she might have succumbed to it. My success at this endeavor was indifferent at best. If not for the support of Oliver and my sister, Elizabeth, I might have turned madman myself. They distracted me from my melancholy fits and helped me to maintain hope, but it was hard going for all of us.

When he'd initially learned about my change, the shock had put Oliver's innate curiosity off for a time, and after that family events and troubles had supplanted all other matters. Only last night we'd interred his mother in the Fonteyn mausoleum, a miserable occupation for everyone concerned, but particularly so for my poor cousin since he'd hated the old harridan.

Because of this hate, he'd had a difficult time dealing with her death. The world expected one kind of response from him and his heart poured forth quite another. He'd retreated into a shell filled with nebulous self-censure for several days, until I'd had enough and took a firm hand, giving him a good talking to about it.

I'd managed to coax him away from his guilt in this very room. The servants had done a remarkable job of cleaning up the mess. Only a bit of scraped wood on the floor, a few dents in the frame of a painting knocked from the wall, and a missing vase broken during our "conversation" gave the least evidence that anything had happened. My injuries from the encounter were all healed, and so, I hoped, were his, particularly the old ones his mother had inflicted, the ones that had threatened to swell and fester upon Oliver's soul.

His reawakened curiosity seemed to be a good sign of his spiritual health, and had been one of the points I'd considered before giving my consent to let him watch me feeding. Whatever adverse reaction he might draw from it could hardly be worse than anything he'd had to deal with while growing up in the dark halls of Fonteyn House.

"Now just you open wide," he told me, looming in close with a candle.

I opened wide, baring my teeth, then squawked when he brought the flame uncomfortably near. "You'll singe my eyebrows off!"

"No, I won't," he insisted. "Oh, very well, hold still and I'll try something else." He pulled a small mirror from a pocket and employed it in such a way as to reflect the candlelight where he wanted. Unfortunately for the purposes of his science, both his hands were occupied and he could not conduct a proper examination. "Damn, but if I could only get a good look in proper daylight," he complained.

"Impossible," I said, hoping he wouldn't insist on trying. The sun and I were no longer friends, but if Oliver's zealousness overtook his sense, he might forget that vital detail and take action.

"Don't talk." He put the candleholder on a small table and asked me to lean in its direction. I did so. Holding the mirror steady in one hand, he used the fingers of the other to grasp one of my corner teeth and tug. I felt it slide down. Surprised, he released it and gaped as it slowly retracted into place.

"Like a deuced cat's claw, only straighter," he said, full of wonder and repeating the action. "Does that hurt?"

"No."

"What does it feel like?"

"Damned strange," I lisped.

"You should see how it looks," remarked a new voice that gave us a start. "The servants will think the both of you have gone mad."

My good sister Elizabeth stood in the open doorway regarding us with a calm eye and a curl of high amusement twisting one side of her mouth.

"Hallo, sweet Cousin," Oliver said, a grin breaking forth upon his mobile features. Elizabeth's presence always had a hugely cheering effect on him. "You couldn't come at a better time. I need you to hold this mirror so I can give your brother's teeth a good looking over."

"Whatever are you doing?" she asked, not moving from her place by the door, God bless her.

"Scientific inquiry, my dear girl. I want to thoroughly examine the workings of Jonathan's condition, and since the good God did not provide me with three hands, I should like to borrow one of yours for a moment."

"Scientific inquiry? How fascinating." With a wicked smile, she determinedly moved in on poor helpless me.

"Now just one moment . . ."

But I had no chance to further object. In a twinkling she was next to Oliver, holding the mirror and watching with avid interest as he poked and tapped and tugged my teeth with happy abandon. I endured it for as long as I could, then made a garbled protest loud enough to inform them that the examination was, for the time being, over.

"Before heaven, I think you've dislocated my jaw," I complained, rubbing the offended area.

"I just wanted to see if the lower teeth were also capable of extension," he explained.

"Next time ask. I could have told you that they don't."

"Sorry, I'm sure, but there's so much that you don't know about yourself that I've gotten used to your negative answers every time I do ask about anything. It seemed simpler just to go ahead and experiment."

"There's no harm done," Elizabeth told him. "But I think we've tried Jonathan's patience sufficiently for this night. Besides, he's needed elsewhere now. That is, if you have concluded your business with those two Mohocks."

"Messieurs Ridley and Tyne have been dealt with, dear sister. I doubt they shall ever resume their destructive activities with their old crowd again."

"Thank God for that. Now straighten your neckcloth, dust off your knees, and let's get along. Nanny Howard's been waiting for more than an hour on you."

"Nanny Howard?" said Oliver, then his expression abruptly altered. "Oh, I'd quite forgotten about that. Really, Jonathan, you should have reminded me. Or did you forget as well?"

"No, that is to say . . ."

"Don't tell me you've been putting it off."

"Not precisely, but there's just been so much to think about that I—"

"You have been putting it off."

"I have not, I've just . . . well . . ."

Elizabeth stepped in. "Don't badger him, Oliver. Can't you see he's terrified?"

"Terrified? Him? After all he's gone through?"

"Do please make allowances, Cousin. He's never been through this beforc."

Oliver frowned and shrugged. "I see what you mean. Come to think of it and given the choice, I'd probably be hiding in the cellar about now, or be halfway to France. It's a hard road you've picked for yourself and no mistake."

"Surely not that hard," I said.

"Consider how much of the way of it you'll be walking with Cousin Edmond, then tell me that again."

He'd made a good point there, but I'd deal with Edmond later.

"Edmond can keep," said Elizabeth. "Our concern is with young Richard. Come along, little brother, put your best foot forward. It's not every day a man gets to meet his son for the first timc."

# CHAPTER ◄2►

This was not strictly true. I had met the child last night, though he'd not been awake for the occasion. It was probably for the best, since the knowledge of his existence had been a frightful surprise for me. Coming as it did some four years after his birth, I was hardly prepared to deal with it in an intelligent manner. For the most part, I'd simply stared in wonder at the little boy asleep on his cot—the little boy bearing my features—that his mother had been so careful to keep insulated from the rest of the family lest they discover his true paternity.

Even now, with Elizabeth and Oliver there to take me in hand, I hardly felt ready to deal with the mere prospect of meeting my natural son, much less a face-to-face encounter. It was enough to make the bravest man's resolve tremble and collapse upon itself. Who was I if not a child myself, surely unable to assume the responsibility involved.

But Elizabeth adjusted my neckcloth, I saw to the dusting of my knees, then out we marched with Oliver to the upstairs rooms that served as the house nursery. My feet threatened to transmute into leaden weights along the way; if left to myself, this few minutes' walk might have turned into an hour's journey. Their company forced me to keep to a normal pace. Before them I had to pretend to an enthusiasm I did not possess as I had no desire to draw additional attention to myself.

*Why so reluctant, Johnny Boy? It's not as though you haven't met him already.*

True, but until then I'd no knowledge of the child's existence and therefore no time to think about things. Besides, he'd been safely asleep. Now that the initial surprise and shock had worn off somewhat I was just beginning to comprehend the enormity of what I was about to face.

I could give the child a looking over, then leave him to Edmond and have done with it, but my heart, quailing as it was at an unknown future, firmly told me that that was not the honorable course to follow. I'd already given Edmond to understand that I was interested in the boy's welfare, something that had surprised him at the time. After thinking about it, my reaction was something of a surprise to me as well, but the words had been said, and I'd have to stand by them. For it was my duty . . . obligation . . . burden . . .

Good God, but Elizabeth and Oliver were positively alight with anticipation for what was to come. I was hard pressed to keep my own shameful cowardice well-hidden—an achievement made particularly difficult because of a craven voice within urging me to bolt and run from the house while I could.

Then I seemed to hear my father's voice as sometimes happened when I most needed his counsel.

*Always move forward, laddie. We're all in God's hands and that's as safe enough place as any in this world.*

It helped steady me, helped to drown out my disgraceful whining.

Would that he could be here, though. Of course, *then* I'd have to break the news to him. . . .

*Later,* I promised myself.

Most of the family members who had stayed overnight after Aunt Fonteyn's funeral had gone home today, taking their own offspring back to more familiar surroundings. It might have been easier to leave the children at home to begin with, but those parents with long-reaching plans found weddings and funerals to be ideal times to allow the coming generation a chance to meet. Thus were advantageous matches often made a dozen years prior to the actual nuptials.

My son's mother—and Edmond's wife—Clarinda Fonteyn, had gone with custom and brought the boy with her. I could assume that it was done for the sake of form so as not to draw attention to him by his absence. Certainly she would not have shown him off to the other adults. His resemblance to me was unmistakable and the reason why she had incited her lover Ridley into murdering me. She'd not wanted me around as a living reminder of her past indiscretion; it would have spoiled her plans for her future.

Clarinda had had ambitions—dangerous for me and for her husband, and entirely fatal for Aunt Fonteyn. Edmond and I had survived them, but what effect the aftermath would have on young Richard was yet to be determined.

"Here," said Elizabeth, pausing and touching my arm. "I thought you should have a present to give him." She drew a parcel from a hidden pocket in her wide skirts and thrust it at me.

Nonplussed, I accepted it, staring as if I might see through the wrappings and string to what lay within.

"It's a toy horse," she explained before I could ask. "Oliver's idea."

"If that's all right with you, Coz," he added. "I mean, I had one myself. You don't mind, do you?"

I spread my hands, deeply touched by their consideration. "Before God, I think I've got the best family that ever was."

"This small part of 'em, anyhow. I'd not be too certain about the rest of the lot if I were you. They're all mad in one way or another y'know. Hope the boy takes after you and not Clar—well . . . that is to say . . ." He suddenly went very red.

"Oh, let's not be silly about this," Elizabeth said, regarding us both with a severe eye. "All right, so young Richard's mother is what she is. That need not affect him in an adverse manner unless we do it ourselves by behaving strangely every time her name comes up in conversation. Jonathan, do you not recall how Father dealt with the subject whenever we inquired after Mother as children?"

"Vividly."

"How?" asked Oliver.

"He'd tell us that she had to be away from home because she was ill and did not want us to become sick as well," she answered.

*Was that not the stark truth of it?* I thought. Later, when we were much older, Father explained that Mother's illness had to do more with her mind than her body. Now did we understand the extent of damage that might have been done had she remained with her family and not gone off to live far away from us as we matured.

"Since Jonathan wants to make himself a part of Richard's life, then I think it best that we decide here and now how to behave ourselves concerning Clarinda. I had a long talk with Edmond about it today—"

"Edmond?" I yelped, leaving my jaw hanging wide.

"Certainly, little brother. You weren't in a condition to do so, and as the boy's aunt, I think I have a justified interest in his future."

Clarinda's husband. With all my physical advantages over normal men and despite the fact that we were on reasonably amicable terms considering the outrageousness of the situation, even I was subject to a tremor or two when it came to facing Edmond Fonteyn. That Elizabeth had done so and apparently emerged unscathed raised my already high respect for her capabilities to a yet loftier elevation.

"We had a very constructive conversation about the whole business," she said, "and he promises to be quite reasonable about how to deal with Richard concerning Clarinda. In fact, he thought that Father's example would work perfectly for him in every way as well."

"You told him about Mother?"

"Certainly, since he knew all about Aunt Fonteyn and her ways. He expressed great curiosity to me over how we managed to turn out to be so sensible, so I thought it the polite thing to inform him."

Unspoken was my thought that Edmond might have been comparing us to Oliver and found my cousin somewhat lacking. Not that Oliver was a fool; it just suited him to assume the role when the need arose. The need, unfortunately, seemed to occur most often whenever Edmond was around.

"Is it agreeable to you both that we should follow this direction?" she asked, knowing full well we'd have to say yes. We did not dare disappoint her. "That's resolved, then. Are there any other points that we need to discuss?"

"I have one," said Oliver. "What does Edmond plan to do when the rest of the family twigs on who the boy's real father is?"

"We did not precisely address that issue, but I got the impression he'd stare them down and dare 'em to say a word to his face."

"That's fine for him, he can take care of himself, but when people start whispering and the other children start bullying the lad—"

"I think that will be best worked out as it happens," I cautiously put in.

Elizabeth favored me with an approving look and turned again to Oliver. "Anything else?"

"One more thing, I fear. What are we to tell the boy? He'll have to learn about his true parentage, y'know."

For this, Elizabeth made no response. Both of them looked expectantly at me. I raised and dropped my hands, giving in to pure helplessness. "I'll have to talk to Edmond about it, I suppose. But for now, the boy's only four, the knowledge will hardly mean anything to him, nor would it do him much benefit. Such a topic can wait until the time is right for it to be addressed."

"Well said," Oliver commented. "I suppose I worry too much and too far ahead of myself for anyone's good."

"I believe that it has become your lot to have to do so. You're head of the family now, aren't you?"

He snorted, rolling his eyes. "Yes, God help me. They're already coming forward, wanting me to settle disputes—or should I say take sides.

You'd think I was a judge and not a doctor the way they go on about their squabbles."

"You'll do all right."

"Humph. Easy for you to say, Coz, you're well out of it for the day. Wish I could hide in the cellars when they come calling with a new problem."

"No, you *don't,"* I told him with such absolute sincerity that he laughed.

"What? You've no liking for sleeping the day through and avoiding its troubles?"

"I told you that it's not really sleep—"

"Bother it, you know what I mean."

"Indeed I do, but I'd gladly take on a bit of trouble if a bit of real daylight went with it, too."

My wistful tone turned him instantly contrite. "I'm sorry, I should have thought first before—"

"No, you shouldn't. You're fine just as you are." Best to curtail *that* kind of thinking, or my poor cousin would end up apologizing every time he opened his mouth for a jest. "I'm the one who's too serious around here. My point was that it is a wise thing to have a care on what you wish for. Now if you *really* want to spend the day skulking in a damp cellar and never ever taste brandy again—"

He raised both hands in a horrified shudder. "Enough, enough already! You make my skin crawl. Ugh!"

Good humor was with us once more. "Right then. You've reminded me of something. I've a question for you, Elizabeth."

She tilted her head expectantly.

"Tell me, dear sister, was it you who went home and fetched some of my earth today?"

Because of all the many distractions the night before I'd had no time to return to my usual sanctuary under Oliver's house in town and had to seek shelter from the dawn in the cellars of Fonteyn House. Safe enough from the hazards of daylight it was, but when denied the comfort of my native soil I was always subject to an endless series of bad dreams and powerless to escape them until the setting of the sun. This time, though, the infernal dreams had mysteriously curtailed themselves, and against all expectations I'd achieved a decent day's rest. Upon awakening this evening I discovered that someone had placed a sackful of earth next to me where I'd made a bed on the floor of an unused wine cupboard.

"I could not go myself—with so much work to do it was just impossible to get away," she said, "but I did dispatch a note along to Jericho to send over a quantity. What a blessing it was that you taught him to read and write. To have given such strange instructions to the footman verbally—well—there's enough gossip belowstairs as it is. No need to add to it."

"Indeed not, and for your trouble you have my thanks. You spared me no end of torment today."

"I'd like to study that aspect of your condition, too," Oliver put in. "There must be some reason behind it."

"Perhaps later," I said, hoping he'd notice my singular lack of eagerness.

Fortunately, he did. "I see. There's better things afoot than having your doctor plague you with questions for hours on end. Come along, then, let's go meet this brat of yours."

"He's not a brat," I objected.

"How do you know? Weren't you a brat at that age? I was, when I could get away with it, and what fun I had, too." Eyes aglow, he tucked Elizabeth's hand over his arm and continued down the hall, leaving me to catch up as best I could.

The nursery looked quite deserted now. The cots and bedding were folded and put away, and all their occupants long gone home except for one. Nanny Howard, the tiny woman in charge of this most important post, sat by a sturdy table with some sewing in her lap, working by the light of several candles. She glanced up as we entered and without saying a word managed to communicate to us that we were very tardy and no excuses would be accepted for the transgression.

Hers was a kind face, though. She'd been Oliver's nanny once upon a time, and his regard and respect for her ran very broad and deep. Certainly she alone had provided him with his only real source of love and protection when he was growing up under the cold eye and critical tongue of his mother. His expression softened and warmed as he looked at her. He silently excused himself from Elizabeth and went over to take the other woman's hand, bending to kiss her cheek.

"Hallo, Nanny. I was a bad lad last evening, or so they tell me."

"Indeed you were. No chocolate for you tonight."

He ducked his head in mock shame, then she tapped his wrist twice with her free hand in an equally mock slap. "There now, all's forgiven. Stand up straight and tell me what you've been about today."

"Oh, just seeing to business. What with all that's happened there's quite a lot of it going around—like an outbreak of the pox."

She nodded. "I've not been able to tell you how sorry I am about your mother's death."

His mouth worked. Her expression of sympathy for him was genuine, probably making it that much harder to accept. He did, though, murmuring his thanks to her.

"Are you also here to see Richard?" she asked him, her eyes glancing over toward me and Elizabeth.

"I should say so. Past time it was done, don't you think?"

"Well past time. I was about to put him to bed. He gets cross when he's kept up too late."

"Oh, but I meant—oh, never mind. Bring him out and let's have a good look at him."

She stood and rustled into an adjoining room.

If my heart was still capable of beating, now would be the time for it to recommence that duty; perhaps then my chest would not feel so appallingly tight. A great lump was trying to rise and lodge in my throat, and I found myself swallowing hard and repeatedly in a vain effort to push it down.

Elizabeth slipped her hand into mine. "It's all right. He's only a little boy."

"I know, but—"

"It's all *right,*" she said, squeezing my fingers.

Another unsuccessful swallow. What would he think of me? *Would* he even think anything? Would he like me? What would he call me?

Nanny Howard provided an answer at least for the last of the many panic-inspired questions bombarding my overactive brain. Herding her charge into the room, she said, "Come along now and meet your cousins, there's a good lad."

He tottered hesitantly in ahead of her, and such a little creature he seemed to me with his diminutive limbs and overly solemn expression. Thick black hair, fine pale skin, huge blue eyes, and rosy lips, he hung back by Nanny Howard, frowning a bit at this formidable gathering of adults. He came in nonetheless.

"He's your living image," Oliver said under his breath.

"In miniature," said Elizabeth in the same hushed tone. "Oh, he's beautiful, Jonathan."

As if I could take much credit for the boy. All I'd done was provide seed for his mother to conceive him. Despite the hasty and imprudent circumstances of that illicit joining, I had to admit that the results were astonishing.

Mrs. Howard urged him forward. "Richard, this is your Cousin Oliver. Remember how you were taught to greet people?"

Mouth pursed in concentration, Richard nodded and made a deep bow, hand to the waist of his petticoats. "At your service, sir," he said, the seriousness of his manner making an appealing contrast to his light, piping voice.

"And yours, young master," Oliver gravely responded.

"Oliver's the head of the family now, did you know that?" Mrs. Howard asked of the boy.

Whatever it might mean to Richard, he decided that another bow was in order and so executed one in good form. This time Oliver returned it with a dignified nod of his head, but he was struggling hard not to smile.

Mrs. Howard turned the boy slightly to face his second visitor. "And this is your pretty Cousin Elizabeth."

"How do you do, Cousin Richard?" Elizabeth asked. She was positively quivering from inner excitement. Above all the others I could hear her heart pattering away as she extended her hand toward him. He bowed deeply over it.

"Very well, thank you." There seemed to be a hint of guarded interest in his eyes for her.

"How old are you?"

"I am four, and next year I shall be five. How old are you?"

This brought forth an admonishment from Mrs. Howard that that was not a proper question for a gentleman to ask a lady. He then inquired why it was so.

"We'll discuss it later. Now you must greet Miss Elizabeth's brother. This is your Cousin Jonathan, and he's come all the way from America to meet you."

Reminded of his social duty, Richard bowed and I returned it. Doubtless our respective dancing masters would have been well pleased.

"What's 'Merica?" he demanded, looking me right in the eye.

"It's a land very far from here," I told him.

"Is it farther than Lon'on?"

"Oh, yes. Very much farther. Right across the ocean."

"What ocean? I can tell them all to you, the 'Lantic, the Pacific, the Ind'n . . ."

"Stop showing off, Richard." said Mrs. Howard.

He subsided, pouting at the interruption of his recitation.

"You're very well up on your geography, aren't you?" I asked.

He nodded.

"Do you know your letters and numbers, too?"

Another nod.

"Mr. Fonteyn is most particular that the boys have their lessons early and regular." Mrs. Howard had not referred to Edmond Fonteyn as Richard's father. I wondered if that was a conscious effort on her part.

"Boys? Oh, yes. Richard's older brother." I recalled Clarinda mentioning him, but not his name.

"Away at school, bless his heart. And then this one will be off himself in a few short years. They grow up much too fast for me."

I vaguely agreed with her and found myself first staring at Richard, then trying hard not to stare. Shifting from one foot to the other, I experienced the uncomfortable realization that I'd run out of things to say to him.

Elizabeth came to my rescue with a gentle tap on the package I held in one arm and had quite forgotten. I shot her a look of gratitude and knelt to be at a better level with Richard.

"Do you like presents?" I asked him. "If you do, then this one is yours."

From his reaction as he took the package, I gathered that he very much liked presents. The string baffled him a moment, but Mrs. Howard's sewing scissors removed it as an obstacle. A few seconds of frenzied action accomplished the release of his prize from the wrappings, and he crowed and held up a truly magnificent horse for all to see. Shiny black with a brightly painted saddle and bridle, it was very lifelike, carved in a noble pose with an arched neck and tail.

"By George," said Oliver, "if it doesn't look like that great beast you brought over with you."

Elizabeth beamed. "The very reason why I picked that one over the others in the shop. It reminded me so much of Rolly."

"You're brilliant," I told her.

"Aren't I just?"

"Who's Rolly?" asked Richard, his bright gaze momentarily shifting toward us.

"Rolly's my own horse," I said. "He's a big black one with some white on his face just like the one you have there. I'll . . . I'll give you a ride on him some day, if you like."

"Yes, please!"

"Not so loud," Mrs. Howard cautioned. "A gentleman never raises his voice to another, you know."

"Yes, please," he repeated in a much lower pitch.

"And what do we say when we get a gift?"

"Thank you very much."

"You're very welcome, I'm sure," I said, feeling all shaky inside. *'Fore God, what was I getting myself into?*

Oblivious to my inner turmoil, Richard darted away and began playing with his new toy, strutting back and forth through the room as if practicing the art of dressage. He provided a variety of horse noises to go with his imagined exhibition, from whinnies to the clip-clop of hooves.

"A success," Elizabeth observed, leaning toward my ear.

"To you goes the credit, if not the thanks."

"I got my thanks when I saw the look on your face."

"Don't you mean his?"

"I mean yours while he opened it up. You looked ready to burst."

"I'm sure I don't know what you mean."

"Do you not?"

Oliver, not to be excluded, got Richard to pause long enough in his parade to ask if he liked chocolate.

"Yes, please!" he bellowed, drawing Mrs. Howard's mild reproof again.

"Well, let's see what I have in my pocket," Oliver said, digging deep. "Here we are—I think. Yes, there it is." He produced a fat twist of paper, collecting a thanks from Richard, who carried off this second prize to enjoy on his own in a far corner of the room.

"You're not to be spoiling him, Mr. Oliver," Mrs. Howard said, hands on her hips.

"Just this once won't hurt."

"Only this once. More than that and I don't care how big you are, I'll put you over my knee just like I used to years ago."

"No doubt. Then I shall consider myself warned off. Does that rule against spoiling infants apply to Jonathan and Elizabeth, too?"

He had her there, and knew it, though she continued to favor him with an arch gaze.

"Of course, we won't presume to infringe on what you deem to be best for the boy, Mrs. Howard," Elizabeth promised. But I knew my sister and had seen that particular look on her face many times before. Richard was going to reap a bountiful crop of gifts from his aunt in the future.

"Thank you, Miss Elizabeth." By her tone, I gathered that Nanny Howard was not for one moment fooled, either. "Well, custom says that first meetings should be brief and polite, and it's past his bedtime . . ."

"I don't want to go to bed," Richard announced. Chocolate smeared the lower part of his face and coated his fingers. Mrs. Howard moved in on him, pulling a handkerchief from her apron pocket. There followed a short struggle as she tried to clean away the worst of it before the stains wandered to his pinafore. She must have dressed him in his best for the occasion, and so her anxiety to spare his garment from damage was most understandable. It reminded me of my own tribulations in the nursery and how glad I'd been to forsake my child's petticoats for my first suit of boy's clothing. He was at least two years away from that glorious rite of passage. I wondered if he'd lie awake nearly all night as I'd done, too excited with anticipation to sleep.

"You seem pensive, little brother."

"Oh, not a bit of it. I was just watching."

Duty done, Mrs. Howard invited Richard to bid us good night. He did so with notable hesitation, but I thought it had less to do with parting from our company than with a natural reluctance to give up the day and go to sleep. Mrs. Howard took him in hand and led him off to the next room. They'd just reached the door when with a cry he broke away from her and darted over to where he'd left his toy horse. He seized it strongly in both hands, hugging it to his body, and marched back.

Then he paused, turned, and looked me right in the eye as before, and flashed me the devil's own grin.

Then he was gone.

My mouth had popped open. What breath I had within simply left, as if it had other business to attend. I stood as dumbfounded as one can be and still have consciousness, though there was little enough evidence of that in my frozen brain. I was dimly aware of Elizabeth exclaiming some words of approval to Oliver and his own reply, but blast me if I was able to discern anything more of their speech.

I felt all light and heavy at the same time, and if my heart no longer beat, then surely it had given a mighty lurch when that exquisite child had smiled at me so. My sight misted over for a second or two. I blinked to clear it, wondering, wondering what on earth was the matter with me.

And then I knew, as clearly and as brightly as if lighted up by a thousand candles. I knew in that moment that I *loved* the boy. The boy. My child. My *son*.

Just like that.

"Jonathan?" Elizabeth pressed a hand on my arm. "What's wrong?"

I shook my head at her foolishness. And at my own foolishness. "Nothing. Absolutely nothing at all."

"Come on, Elizabeth, you must have something to celebrate meeting your nephew," said Oliver. "Since Jonathan can't join in, you'll have to make up for his place in a toast."

"I should be delighted to try, but if you give me anything stronger than barley water or better yet, some tea, I shall fall asleep here and now."

"Asleep! After all that?"

"Especially after all that."

We'd returned to Oliver's drawing room to find the fire was in need of revival. Eschewing the employment of a servant, Oliver set himself to the task, being full of considerable energy and needing to work it off. He did ring for someone to bring in some form of refreshment, though. He chose port for himself and dutifully ordered a pot of tea for Elizabeth.

"You'll be awash with this later when dinner's done," he warned her after a maid had come and gone leaving behind a loaded tray.

"I'm tempted to avoid dinner altogether and have something sent to my room," she said, pouncing on the teapot like a she-cat on a mouse.

"What? Leaving me to face the remaining crowd on my own?"

"Hardly a crowd, Oliver. There's just a few elderly aunts and uncles left, after all."

"And the lot of 'em starin' at me the whole time like a flock of gouty crows. Don't you think they aren't interested in the goings-on last night, because they are. I managed to keep out of their way so far, but there'll be no escaping them at dinner." He shuddered, pouring himself a generous glass of the port, then downing the greater part of it.

Elizabeth was not without pity. "Very well, for your sake I'll play hostess and talk about the weather should anyone ask you an embarrassing question."

"Thank you, dear Coz. The weather! Excellent topic! There's nothing they like better than to discuss how bad it's been and how much better it was when they were younger. We'll give 'em a real debate on it. Well, that's all solved. Now, about young Richard . . ."

"What about him?"

"I was only going to say what a fine lad he seems to be. What about you, Jonathan? We've not heard a peep from you since we came down."

Both looked at me, but I really had nothing to say. I was so full of feeling that words seemed pointless.

"I think my brother is still in the thrall of shock," Elizabeth observed.

Smiling, I shrugged in a way to indicate that she was more than a little correct.

Oliver's face blossomed with sudden anxiety. "You don't dislike him, do you?"

My sister answered for me. "Of course he doesn't, that's why he's in such shock. Give him some time to get used to the idea, then you'll hear him talking about nothing else."

I shrugged again, adding a sheepish smile.

Oliver raised his glass, saw that it was nearly empty, and took the opportunity to fill it again. "Then here's to the very good health of my cousin Jonathan and his son Richard."

Elizabeth raised her teacup and joined him in the toast. I spread my hands and bobbed my head once, modestly accepting the honor. I was yet unable to offer coherent conversation and quietly eased into a comfortable chair near the fire. They occupied themselves with their own talk about Richard, not excluding me so much as allowing me time for my own reflections and speculations. I folded my hands and watched the flames, content with all the world and my lot of it in particular.

"Heavens!" Elizabeth hastily set down her cup and gestured sharply at the mantel clock. "See the time—I'll be late for dinner if I don't go up now and dress for it. You, too, Oliver, unless you want to pique family curiosity even more about what you've been doing today."

"No," he said, sighing deeply. "Can't have that, though it's bound to be a rotten tribulation. Jonathan's the lucky one, he can do whatever he likes while we sit chained to the table for the next few hours."

"Or at least until the ladies take their leave," she reminded him. "Then you and the other men can get as drunk as you please while I drown in tea." Custom held that all ladies had to eventually retire from the table for their tea or coffee until it was time for the gentlemen to rejoin them for the serving of dessert.

"Well, I did warn you. Tell you what, I'll see if Radcliff will sneak some brandy into the teapots for you. That should help you pass the time more merrily."

"Dearest Oliver, it's a wonderful idea, but we ladies have already long made a practice of it."

"Have you, by God! First time I've heard of it. Perhaps I should forsake keeping company with the gentlemen and fall in with your troop."

"Cleave to your duty," she advised him. "Except for me there's not a woman left in the house that's under sixty. You'd be bored to death in five minutes for that's ever been my fate. Now I really *must* go." So saying, she swept out, skirts swinging wide and bumping against the doorframe, and we heard her quick progress down the hall.

"A damn fine girl, your sister," said Oliver. "A pity she didn't find a man worthy of her."

"She probably will, given time and inclination," I murmured. "But whoever she may settle on will have to behave himself with the two of us as her guardians."

He laughed. "Now, isn't that heaven's honest truth, especially with your talents. Tell me, though, if it's not too impertinent, why did you not question that Norwood fellow first before she married him—just to be sure about him?"

What a sore wound it was he'd struck. I actually winced. Oliver started to withdraw the question, but I waved him down. "No, it's all right. All I can say is that it seemed an ungodly intrusion at the time. She was so in love with him that I hesitated to tamper with her happiness. As it turned out, my hesitation damned near got her killed. Be assured, I will not make the same mistake again. Should she seriously take up with another suitor I'll be able to tell soon enough if he's a right one or a rogue."

"Now there's a good idea for an occupation."

"Hmm?"

"It just occurred to me that since you can't practice law because of your condition, you could busy yourself as some sort of inspector of marriage proposals. The ladies could come to you to have you ferret out the truth about their gentlemen prior to committing marriage. That way they can find out the worst about them before it's too late."

"The gentlemen might also be interested in such a service," I pointed out.

"True . . . then it's an idea best forgotten. If engaged couples knew all there was to know awaiting them, then none would marry, and humanity would die out for want of progeny. Unless they do what you've done and father a child by—er—ah—that is to say—well, no offense."

"None taken. Get on with you, Cousin, and ready yourself for dinner. You wouldn't want to leave Elizabeth all alone with the crows, would you?"

"No. But given a choice I'd prefer to leave the crows all alone with themselves, then they could feed on each other and soon disappear altogether."

"Dreamer," I called to his back as he left to prepare himself for the endeavor to come.

Alone and comfortably settled before the revived fire, I let forth a satisfied sigh. Now could I finally give in to my own dreams for a little time. Not the bad ones I'd endured for a brief interval early that morning, but the light and fanciful ones that possess a man so filled with good feeling that it overflows his heart and makes the very air about him seem to hum from it.

I'd met my son, and all was well.

The trepidation and apprehensions had fled. I was so encompassed with warmth for the boy that it seemed impossible I'd ever been worried at all. Whatever problems the future might hold would solve themselves, of that I had no doubt.

There was much work ahead, of course, but it would be easy enough labor. Facing down the disapproval of the family, dealing with the scandal of the boy's conception, dealing with Edmond, even dealing with Clarinda, tribulations all, to be sure, but not terribly important so long as I could spend time with Richard. I could hardly wait to see his face again, to see it glow with another smile like—

*If* Edmond would even allow it. Before God, he could tell me to go to hell and be well within his rights and then I'd never see . . .

My moment of panic came and instantly passed. He *would* allow it. I'd make certain of that no matter what. If I could turn the likes of Ridley into a lamb, then I could just as easily convince Edmond to cheerfully welcome me into his home. Elizabeth would probably disapprove—she usually did when it came to forcing my influence upon another person, but this was a special circumstance. Surely she'd not object to my making life a bit smoother for all concerned by the use of this strange talent.

Then the only limitation I'd have against being with Richard would be my inability to see him during the day. Damnation, but there was one obstacle I could not influence my way around. Half a loaf was better than none, but it irked me all the same. Ah, well, I'd just have to live with it until he got older and could stay up later. By then he'd be away at school, though . . . but he'd be home for visits between terms . . .

So much to think about, so much to dream and plan. I stared at the fire until my eyes watered, blinked to clear them, but they only watered all the more. To my astonishment, first one tear then another spilled forth.

"You're being ridiculous, Johnny Boy," I said aloud, wiping at them with my sleeve before remembering my handkerchief. It was the one I'd used in the stable, the one bearing evidence of my last feeding in the form of some small bloodstains. *No matter,* I thought, scrubbing away at my wet cheeks.

Though in a way it did matter, for now did I realize why I wept. Mixed with my happiness was the certain knowledge that Richard was the only child I would ever father, thus making him immeasurably precious to me.

Because of my changed condition the male member of my body, though still capable of providing enjoyment to any lady so desiring to make use of it, was now incapable of producing seed. Though it could come to glad attention, allowing me to roger away as happily as any other man, it was no longer at all necessary for the achievement of a climax to my pleasures. That sweet accomplishment was only to be found when partaking of the lady's blood, a process we could both enjoy to its fullest for as long as we could stand the ecstasy. Wonderful as it was and superior as it was to the more common way of making love, it had a wretched price. The joys of having a wife and a hearth might yet be mine in the future, but my present state tragically precluded any possibility of ever having a family of my own to cherish.

*Why was it so?* I wondered. The question had long occured to me prior this night, but never before had the lack of an answer seemed so hard to endure.

If I could only find *Nora.*

Seeing her again had ever been the focus of all things for me since that summer night when I'd awakened in a coffin deep beneath the church graveyard. For all its limitations, though, the condition she'd bequeathed upon me had its favorable side. I was grateful for the advantages, but needed to know more about the drawbacks. Ignorance had caused me grief in the past, so I harbored a very reasonable desire to learn all there was to learn before committing additional blunders. If I could just speak with her, even once, and put to rest all my questions, then might I find a bit of peace for my troubled heart.

I'd have to tell her about Richard, of course. There was no way around it. I hoped she would not be too awfully upset.

*If* I found her.

Oliver and I would just have to take on the task with renewed vigor. I could have another look through her London house on the slender chance that I'd missed something earlier, and Oliver could track down the agents who had sold it to her. Perhaps they had records on where she'd lived before. . . .

I quelled the speculations. Firmly. They'd had their race around inside my head far too often before to offer any new approach to this particular hunt. Time to let them rest and cast my mind back to better, more productive thoughts. Like Richard.

Alas, it was not to be. Just as I was summoning the energy to forsake my comfortable chair to build up the dwindling fire, one of the footmen came in with a message for me. Damnation, if it wasn't one thing it was another.

He handed over a small fold of paper, then stepped back a pace to await my reply. I more than half expected it to be from my valet Jericho, who was probably wondering if I planned to return home tonight. An excellent question, that. I opened the thing, but did not recognize the bold, flowing writing within.

*For God's sake, will you come speak with me? I beg only a moment.*

The signature was a large, florid *C* placed in the exact center at the bottom of the sheet.

*Clarinda,* I thought, my spirits sinking. What the devil did she want? And did I really wish to find out?

Edmond Fonteyn had taken full charge of his wife to make sure she was securely confined for the remainder of their stay at Fonteyn House. Had he not been forced by his injuries to rest, he would have swept her away to their own home by now.

A temporary prison for her had been improvised from one of the more distant upstairs rooms. I understood it to be cold, bare of all furnishings except dust, and horrifically dark and stuffy since it had no window. Oliver's description of it, given earlier when he filled me in on the day's events, was vivid, as the chamber had served well enough as a place of punishment for him when he was a child. His mother had a great fondness for shutting him away there for hours at a time whenever she deemed any given transgression of correct behavior to be serious enough to merit it. That meant most of them, he'd added with heartfelt disgust. Nanny Howard hadn't approved, but was forced to comply with orders or risk a dismissal with no reference. To mitigate the worst of it for poor Oliver, she'd sit just outside the door and keep him company, talking and cheering him while pretending for his parent to play the stern and watchful guard.

Clarinda had no such companionable warden. Edmond had instructed two of the footmen to keep a close eye on her locked door, and see to it she didn't make too much noise. He had been up twice today to see she got her meals, but no one else had come since he'd put the story about that she'd fallen ill from the strain of the funeral and needed complete quiet to recover. That and the long climb up the stairs had been sufficient to discourage the remaining elderly relatives from paying any calls, though Oliver reported that speculation on the real nature of her illness was rife. Some took Edmond at his word, but others maintained that he'd gotten tired of her infidelities and had finally decided to lock her away. Though close enough to the truth, the chief mystery for them was why Edmond had chosen this particular time and place to take action.

They would most certainly connect it with the row last night: Edmond and Arthur Tyne's injuries, Ridley being held prisoner in the cellar, Oliver getting roaring drunk, and all the other odd goings-on that had taken place in the wee hours after Aunt Fonteyn's funeral. I grimly wondered how Oliver and Elizabeth would ever manage to hold fast to a topic like the weather throughout the ordeal of supper. The gouty crows would likely be disinclined to ask a direct question, but there was always a chance one of them might pluck up the nerve to try. Just as well for me that I was missing it all, for I'd find myself hard-pressed to keep a neutral and sober face.

I dismissed the footman, thanking him with a penny vale. He had most surely gotten the note directly from Clarinda, and even if he could not read might have some clear idea of what it was about. The fellow would likely go just far enough along the hall to acertain the direction of my own movements. Though the servants of Fonteyn House were fairly trustworthy, they were not above taking an avid interest in the antics of their betters. Would I go to see her or stay? I had intended to have a talk with her, but not really planned out when. It was rather like having a tooth drawn, sooner or later it would have to be done, but neither haste nor delay would make the process the least bit pleasant to endure.

*Well,* I thought, heaving out of my chair with a groan, *mustn't disappoint the belowstairs gossips.*

# CHAPTER 3

Edmond had told the footmen on guard to ignore anything Clarinda said or promised on penalty of a prompt discharge from service and the pain of a sound thrashing that he would administer personally. Either threat was enough to ensure a close observance of his orders; together they had the effect of inspiring a formidable dedication to duty. When I first approached and made known my intention to visit the lady, the fellows were thrown into a painful dilemma. Passing on Clarinda's correspondence—that is to say, the note to me slipped under the door along with a penny bribe—was one thing, but they had no idea on what to do about visitors. Another bribe to grant me admission was out of the question because Edmond possessed the only key to the room. It would seem my one choice would be to confront him and ask if he might grant his consent to this call.

Well, that was one course of action I wasn't too keen to follow. Clarinda was asking much if she expected me to go that far for her. She probably wasn't aware of the business of the solitary key—that or she anticipated conducting a conversation through the locked door. Hardly wise, considering the footmen would hear all and be only too glad to share a detailed recountal with the other servants. Perhaps she would think I'd simply order them out of earshot. Indeed, I could do so, but possessed no enthusiasm for crossing Edmond's instructions.

With a grimace for my own weakness, I chose the lesser of several evil options and quietly persuaded the men on guard to avail themselves of a short nap they would not remember taking. I borrowed one of their candles and stalked up to the storage room door, pausing before it to reflect that this was also a not very wise action. However, it would be easy enough to cause Clarinda to forget anything inconvenient. I vanished, candle and all, and resumed solidity on the other side.

Oliver's description was accurate; it was a depressing little closet right enough: cold, dark, and with a chamber pot smell to it, but not totally bare. A narrow bed with several blankets had been crammed in, along with a small chair and table. The latter held the leavings of her latest meal, paper, pen, and ink, and several candles, though only one was currently lighted. Unlike Ridley, Clarinda could be relied upon not to try burning the house down, though I wasn't sure I would have given her the benefit of the doubt. Perhaps Edmond based his trust on her acute sense of self-regard, and he knew she'd not attempt anything that might miscarry and endanger her own skin.

She faced the door, apparently having heard me outside with the footmen and had composed herself to receive, standing in the small space between the bed and the desk, hands folded demurely at her waist. Still wearing yesterday's black mourning clothes, her dress was the worse for wear with some tears and dried smears of mud, so the suffering dignity she strove to affect was somewhat spoiled.

Of course, she could not have possibly expected me to make the entrance that I did, but before she could do more than widen her eyes in reaction, I bored into their depths with my full concentration.

*Forget what you've just seen, Clarinda.*

Her mouth popped open and she swayed backward one unsteady step as though she'd been physically struck. Had I been too forceful? Bad business for us all if that proved true. Fear of the dire consequences made me turn away from her until my composure was quite restored.

When I had nerve enough to look again, I saw her shake her head and blink as she regained her balance and her senses. Until this moment I'd taken care not to examine my feelings about her; now came the realization of just how strong they were and how dangerous they could prove. If I held mere anger in my heart for Ridley's actions, then Clarinda's had inspired white hot fury. With all this night's preoccupations I'd managed to thoroughly bury it, like heaping earth upon a fire. But instead of smothering the flames, the burial had only served to preserve, if not increase, their heat. I couldn't trust myself to keep my temper under strict control with her. No more influencing for me; that state brought the true wishes of my deeper mind too close to implementation for comfort.

"Jonathan?" Her voice was none too firm, but I found it distinctly reassuring. It would seem that no permanent damage had been done to her mind if not her body. The fight last night had left its mark on her. Her jaw was bruised and swollen where I'd struck her unconscious.

"I got your note," I said in as flat and as discouraging a tone as I could summon. It wasn't at all difficult.

"Thank you for coming."

"What do you want?"

"I—I want nothing. That is to say—"

"Clarinda, you didn't ask me up here without a reason," I said wearily, putting my candle on the table.

She snapped her mouth shut.

"Just speak and have done with it."

She lifted her chin, her eyes steady. "Edmond said that you were well, that when I shot at you I'd missed."

She had not missed, not at two paces, but I'd been able to vanish for a crucial instant, and the darkness and flash of the powder had served well to cover things.

"I thought he might have lied to me. I am glad to see he did not."

"Are you?"

"You can believe what you like, Jonathan, but I never wished you any harm."

"Oh, indeed?"

"What was done was done only to protect my child."

"And what rare pleasure you took from it, madam, trying to murder his father."

"That was only a sham for Thomas Ridley's benefit. All of it. If I hadn't pretended such for him he would have killed me on the spot."

"You were most convincing."

"I *had* to be!"

"Of course."

Her hands formed into fists and dropped to her sides. "I can't expect you to understand, but I did want you to at least know why I was forced—"

"Clarinda," I said in a clear cold voice. "If you want to waste the effort telling me this rot, that's your business, but I have better diversions to occupy my time. I am not a fool and neither are you. I recall exactly everything you tried to do last night and how close you came to success, and nothing, no distortion of truth, half-truth, or outright lie from you will change that memory."

That stung her good and square. Were we in another place, she'd have probably slapped me soundly and marched out. Here all she could do was stand and stare and fume. Not that it lasted long. She recovered beautifully, smooth as a cat. Her fists relaxed and she assumed a rueful expression.

"Very well, no more pretense. Is it possible that with you I may be able to speak the whole truth?"

A cutting reply concerning my sincere doubt that she would know how hovered on the tip of my tongue, but I held it back and gave a brusque nod, instead.

She may have seen or sensed my skepticism, but chose to ignore it. "Edmond doesn't know you're here, does he?"

There. She'd just correctly read one of the other reasons behind my abrupt manner. I should have to take extreme care dealing with her. "It seemed the tactful thing to do for the moment."

"No doubt. He's a formidable man."

I offered no comment, though I could easily agree with her on that point.

"He said that you'd seen Richard."

"Took me by last night."

"Did you like him?"

"What does it matter to you?"

Another sting for her, which was something of a surprise. By now I'd thought her beyond all tender feeling.

"It does matter. I'm afraid for my child. Our child."

"In what way?"

"I'm afraid that because of what's happened Edmond might do him harm. He could punish Richard for the things I've done."

Clarinda was shut away in a most disagreeable spot with only her own dark soul for company, so hers was a reasonable fear, but not one I seriously harbored. Edmond could be unpleasant, but I sensed he would not purposely harm the boy. Even so, I had an excellent means of dealing with him to guarantee Richard's well-being.

"I'll see that the child is safeguarded from any harm." Instinct told me to preserve a cool and indifferent front before her, but she was perceptive enough to see through it.

"You really do care for him, don't you?" she asked with more than a hint of rising hope.

It seemed better not to answer, though my silence was answer enough.

"I'm glad of that. What I say now, what I ask now, is not for my sake, but for the sake of that innocent child. You're a part of this family, but you haven't lived long with them, you don't know them as I do. Richard will need a friend. Will you look out for him?"

A fair request, and certainly for something I'd be doing regardless of her intercession in the matter. "I shall do what I can. What about your other son?"

She looked away briefly. "He's already lost to me. He's away at school, his life has been ordered and set out for him. Edmond saw to that. Edmond and Aunt Fonteyn."

"Whom you murdered." Edmond and I had worked as much out between us, that Clarinda had killed Oliver's mother, but I wanted to know for certain.

Clarinda's lips twitched in a near smile. "If you think I regret helping that evil old harridan along to her place in hell, then please do reconsider. You—any of you—could get away from her. I could not. It was an ill day for me when I married her favorite brother and worse still when I gave him a son. She was always there, interfering, sharp as a thorn, and never once letting me forget who controlled the money."

The Fonteyn money. The inspiration and goal behind all of Clarinda's trespasses. "How did your first husband die?"

"What?" The apparent change of subject first puzzled her, then she divined the reason behind it. "For God's sake, do you think—"

"I don't know what to think, so it seemed best to make a direct inquiry."

"He dropped dead from a bad heart," she answered with no small disgust. "I had nothing to do with it. A pity his sister did not follow his example, else life would have been easier for all of us."

"Then you married Edmond?"

"I needed his protection and he needed my son's money, but what a farce that turned out to be with the lot of us still subject to Aunt Fonteyn's whims. When Richard was born sooner or later she'd know Edmond was not his father, all of them would know, and then what would happen to us? She'd have put me out on the street quick enough or packed me off to Bedlam and done God knows what to my baby."

I didn't see Edmond or even Aunt Fonteyn for that matter allowing things to go so far. The offensive prospect of a scandal would have likely mitigated any judgment she made once her initial outrage had passed. Clarinda had the intelligence to know and play upon that weakness. No, she'd ever been after the family money; it was just that simple.

"So you got the likes of Ridley to be your protector, to be subject to *your* whims."

Various thoughts were clearly flickering back and forth behind her eyes, too fast to interpret. She paused a goodly time to search my face and finally shook her head. "You don't understand," she said with genuine incredulity, then softly laughed.

There was a sound to make my skin crawl. The room seemed to shrink around us. "I think it's best that I don't."

"Or you might have some sympathy for me? For what my life has been like? Don't bother yourself."

"As you wish."

A baleful silence grew between us, filling this dank and chill closet right to the ceiling like smoke. There was no room in it for me. My questions were all satisfied; therefore I had no need to remain. I made to pick up my candle.

"No, wait!" Her hand shot out to seize mine. Because of the restricted space we'd been close enough to easily touch, but had managed to avoid it.

Five years past I'd been more than eager to touch her. Just last night I'd fought off the temptation to do so again only with the greatest difficulty. I saw her still as a very beautiful, desirable woman, but any craving I'd ever fostered for her was now stone dead.

I shook her off. "I'll leave the candle if you like."

"It's not that. I have one more thing to ask of you."

Tempting as it was to point out that I owed her no favors, I waited for her to go on.

"Jonathan, do you know what Edmond has planned for me? What he will do once we're home?"

"He has not communicated that information to me, nor is it really my business."

"He'll have me shut away in a room that will make this seem like a palace."

"There are worse spots, madam. Would you prefer Bedlam or Bridewell?"

"You speak that way because you're angry, but please, try to see things through my eyes, just for a moment, I beg you."

Again, I waited.

Outwardly, she calmed herself, but her heartbeat was very loud to my acute hearing.

I sensed that the earlier talk and questions about Richard had never been a real concern for her. It had been but a useful means to sound me out; was she finally coming to the real reason why she'd asked me here?

"There may be worse places, but I can't think of a single one," she whispered. "I am to be shut away forever and ever. I will be completely alone. After tomorrow, I will never see the sun or even the warmth of a candle flame again. It will be always dark and always cold. He's promised as much. Those are his very words."

I thought that she was lying again, for it would be easy to verify the truth with Edmond, but her fear was genuine enough. I could smell it. I could almost *taste* it.

"He full well knows that it will drive me mad, giving substance to the story he'll tell others. No person with an ounce of compassion in them would treat a mongrel dog with such cruelty, but that's what he's sworn is in store for me."

No sunlight, not even a candle. God, but could I not thoroughly appreciate what kind of darkness *that* was? "Very well, I'll speak to him," I said heavily.

"No! I want you to help me get away from him!"

My turn for a bout of incredulity. "By heaven, I think you're mad already."

"Not yet. Not *yet!* I don't ask you to help me escape, but just to get me away from him. Devise whatever prison you like for me, let me be totally alone, but if I can have but an hour of daylight I'll ask nothing more of you."

*An hour of daylight.* What would I not give to have as little for myself? Most of the time the lack did not grieve me. Not much. But then I had diversions aplenty to fill the hours. I had some choices left. Clarinda had none.

"If . . . if that's impossible," she continued, faltering as her gaze dropped away, "then I would ask you to give me the means of making another kind of escape."

"What means?"

She raised her eyes to search mine and licked her lips. "I've heard it said that if one takes enough opium—"

"Good God, Clarinda!"

"Otherwise I can tear up the bedclothes and find a way to hang myself. It would please Edmond very well, I'm sure."

"There's no need—"

"Is there not? I mean this, Jonathan. You still seem to have a heart left, that's why I thought to talk to you. I can trust no one else. I'm not asking a great deal. You'd put a mad dog out of its misery, would you not?"

"I would, but—"

"But what? It's that or take care of me yourself—or help me escape altogether."

She waited and waited, and for all her skill at deception could not completely keep a sharp little spark of hope from showing in her eyes, but I did not deign to remark on that last absurd suggestion. Any or all of her talk of another prison with me as keeper or of taking her own life might have been meant to soften my resolve so perhaps I would agree to help her escape. Well, I'd already told her I was not a fool. I shook my head. "There's another way of handling this. I'll see to it tonight."

The spark flashed once, then dimmed. "What is that?"

"I'll talk to Edmond—"

*"But that won't—"*

"He'll listen to me, I assure you."

She made a choking sound.

"You may think otherwise, but I will make him. That's really the best I can do for you, and I believe you're well aware of it."

Obviously this was not what she'd hoped to achieve for herself; on the other hand, it was better than an outright refusal. But however much disappointment she showed, I still had a strong impression that she had accomplished *something* with me and was calculating its eventual effect on her. Mildly worrisome, that, but nothing more.

She abruptly lowered her gaze, shoulders slumped as if in defeat or acceptance. "Yes, I am aware of it. For what it's worth, I'm grateful to you."

*For what it's worth, I thought.* Very damned little, but as she'd said, I'd do as much for a mad dog.

Being more unsettled than angry, it was less perilous now to influence her into taking a restful sleep; thus would she have no memory of my egress from the room. I suggested nothing more than that, though, preferring caution over calamity in the event that I'd misjudged my present state of mind and gave in to error. Leaving her reclining peacefully on the narrow bed, I seived past the door and back out into the hall, turning solid again before thinking to remove myself from the immediate view of her guards.

Thankfully, I found the footmen were still lost in their doze, sparing me additional exertion. It struck me that I should wake them and tell them to forget they'd even seen me, but that was too much of an effort for so small a detail. They could tell Edmond what they liked, if they dared. I didn't care one way or another. Whatever they said would be little enough. I quietly made my way down the stairs, for I had much to think about and wanted to be as far away as possible from Clarinda. All the relatives and servants would be busy with supper, so privacy was no problem; I had the pick of Fonteyn House's many rooms.

Only one appealed to me, though.

The nursery.

Not only would I have another look in on Richard, which in itself was sufficient enticement to go there, but the superb idea of plying a few questions to Nanny Howard had popped into my mind.

Clarinda was as full of lies as hive has honey. Some I'd picked out without trouble, others were more elusive, and by God, but didn't the woman have more than her share of brass? Wanting me to take Edmond's place as her warden or to go so far as to help her escape . . . ugh. That was right out. It was also something of an insult since she'd so badly underestimated me. She was not without considerable wit; why had she even proposed such a ludicrous action? Likely it had to do with the theory of venture nothing, gain nothing. I hoped as much, for then it would seem less offensive to endure.

She was unquestionably afraid, but was her fear for the threat of a dark imprisonment or for imprisonment alone? Either one would be more than alarming, and certainly Edmond would make a stern and alert keeper, but I found it difficult to believe he would be as extreme as she'd claimed. Perhaps he'd been giving vent to his own anger with her, making threats he'd probably not fulfill. More likely she'd simply lied to me. Again.

Still and all, I'd have to sort fact from fancy just to be sure, and could think of no better person to consult than Nanny Howard. If she was as intelligent as she looked, then she'd know all the happenings of this particular branch of the Fonteyn family tree and be able to provide any number of necessary details.

She might be reluctant to talk with an outsider, though, for I was just that despite my relationship to Richard. I made a face, not liking the idea of having to influence her. I didn't like it, but would do so if nothing else would move her.

"What a sneaking rogue you're turning into, Johnny Boy," I said aloud, but not too very aloud. Echoes tended to carry far along these dark corridors, and I had no wish to announce my self-reproach to any stray upstairs maid who might be lurking about. Best to remove my mind from the subject until the time was right to approach it.

So I cheerfully speculated on the prospect of slipping in for another peep at Richard. If nothing else, Nanny Howard would gladly tell me all about *him.* What did he like to do? What were his favorite games? Did he have other children to play with at Edmond's estate? Did he have a pony yet? Probably not, considering his reaction to the painted one now in his possession. My heart seemed to quicken with a kind of life again at the splendid thought of eventually giving him a real one. I recalled clearly the delicious excitement that had possessed me on one of my early birthdays with Father's gift of a fine white pony. No more sharing rides with others on the front of the saddle, I'd had a brave charger of my own to play out my daydreams. More than that, I'd learned much on the care and coddling of equines, and had taken to my lessons in dressage like butter to hot bread. Richard looked to have some of that enthusiasm in him, and what a pleasure it would be to nurture it and . . .

Father.

Dear me, but I'd *have* to sit down to write and *somehow* tell him what had happened.

But later, I thought, bounding lightly down the last of the stairs and taking the final turn needed to reach the nursery.

Unfortunately, just outside the nursery door, I encountered my son's *other* father, Edmond Fonteyn.

He was a big man, nearly Ridley's size, and usually as robust, but last night's activities had left him with a gaunt white face, one arm in a sling, bandaging 'round both hands, and an unnatural slowness to his movements. Fire still lurked in his dark eyes, though, and he favored me with some of its heat.

I hauled up short, rocking back on my heels in a most undignified way, at the same time cursing myself for such absurd behavior. After all, what had I to fear from him?

"Where have you been keeping yourself all day?" he growled, not bothering with the courtesy of a greeting beyond a slight raising of his chin. Had he always had that mannerism or taken it from Clarinda? Or had she gotten it from him?

"My doctor recommended rest."

"That fool Oliver."

"He's not a fool," I said mildly.

Edmond chose not to argue the point. "What are you here for? Mrs. Howard said you'd already come and gone."

"And I've come again. What else did Mrs. Howard have to say about my visit?"

His lips parted as though to answer, then snapped shut. I'd caught him out and he was well aware of it. "Come along then. We need to talk." When I hesitated to jump at this command, he added, "The boy's sound asleep and will look just the same later on."

When first we'd met, his brusque manner had intimidated me, for I'd attributed it to the fact that he was aware of my past intimacy with his wife. True enough, but now I was able to understand that such was his manner with everyone and counseled myself to tolerance. I followed as he led off up the hall to again take the stairs to the ground floor.

As he slowly paced along, an uncomfortable foreboding began to assert itself on my spirit, and I soon found my somber expectations fulfilled when he turned into the one room in this whole dismal house I least wanted to visit.

Its fireplace held a hearty blaze; that was the chief difference between my present intrusion and the very first time I'd come here with Clarinda. Then it had been rather cold and cheerless—until she made it her business to warm things up for me. We'd consummated our fit of mutual passion on that settee under the eye of that same bust of Aristotle—or perhaps it was one of the Caesars—sitting on the mantel. Good God, what did Edmond think he was about in bringing me here?

But as he eased his heavy body down on the settee with an audible sigh, I comprehended (and not without considerable relief) that he did not know what had happened here those few short years ago. His present occupancy must be because of its privacy and because this had been Clarinda's room during the funeral. Some of her things still lay scattered about—small things: a handkerchief discarded on the floor, a comb forgotten on a table, a pair of slippers peering shyly out from under a chair. Of her other belongings there was no sign; perhaps they'd been packed and taken away to their home already.

"Sit," he ordered, gesturing to one of the chairs.

I did so.

He had a brandy bottle close at hand and some glasses. Without asking my pleasure, he poured out two portions and nodded for me to take one. I did this without hesitation, for if need be I could alter his memory about my lack of thirst.

He did not trouble to make a toast, but partook himself of a draught that would have done credit to Oliver's reputation for swilling down spirits. That gone, he filled his glass again and emptied it just as swiftly, then availed himself of a third libation. I thought he might deal with it as with the first two, but he contented himself with only half before putting the glass to one side.

"Something disturbs you?" I ventured, indicating the brandy.

He grunted. "Life disturbs me, Barrett. I've been harshly served."

"If you want an apology from me, I should be happy to give—"

He waved me down, shaking his head. "There's no need, what's done is done. I had quite a talk with Clarinda today and got the truth out of her concerning her liaison with you. I think it's the truth, anyway. At long last she has no more reason to lie to me."

"Sir, if you wish the truth, then by my honor, it's yours for the asking."

"That won't be necessary. You need not tell the husband how enjoyable you found his wife's favors."

I winced, recovered myself, and spoke through my teeth. "But I did not *know* she was anyone's wife."

He looked long and hard at me, not moving a muscle. By very slow and small degrees the lines of his face relaxed. "That makes a difference to you?"

"It does."

"Then by God, you're probably the only man in England who can say so."

"Like Clarinda, I have no reason to lie to you, nor would I if I did." I let him think on it a moment, then said, "You wanted to talk. Was this the subject you had in mind?"

"Not quite, but it is directly related to my wife. And you."

"Richard."

"Our mutual son," he rumbled.

"What about him?"

"You surprised me last night. Most fathers want nothing to do with their bastards."

Like a runaway fire, hot anger rushed through my body. One bare instant later and I was on my feet and looming over him. It was only by the greatest effort of forbearance that I didn't haul him up and toss him across the room as he deserved. He flinched, eyes widening, taking in my red face and trembling fists. Apparently my reaction surprised him once more, almost as much as it startled me. "You will *not* refer to him in that way ever again," I whispered, voice shaking with rage.

"Or what?" His eyes had narrowed; his tone was dangerous.

"Or . . ." A number of obvious, violence-oriented threats occurred to me, but I was starting to think once more and knew that none of them would be taken seriously by this man, not without an immediate demonstration, anyway. "Or I'll make it my duty to instruct you on the subject of good manners."

We locked gazes for a goodly period, but there was no need to rely on my unnatural influence this time. Edmond could see just how earnest was the intent behind the temperate words.

Then he smiled.

It was a mere tightening of the straight line of his mouth and very brief, but a smile nonetheless, and enough to give me pause. Had this thrice-cursed villain been *testing* me?

He leaned back upon the settee. "Thank you, but I've had sufficient instruction to last me a fortnight. Thought you had as well, but you seem to have recovered. Sit down, Cousin, there's been enough blood spilled in this family already."

I backed away, not to sit, but to pace about the room and work off the sudden energy that had set my limbs to quivering. Had he always been like this to Clarinda? If so, then though I could not excuse her crimes, I could easily understand one of the reasons why she'd committed them. Certainly continual contact with his abrasive manner could not have done her much good. Or had it been Clarinda's endless infidelities that made him like this? Had they driven him to live in what was apparently a constant state of bitter exasperation? Perhaps by now he knew of no other way to express himself to the world.

"Why am I here, Edmond?" I asked, when I'd gotten my temper under control.

"Because I wanted to have a good look at you. Your sister and I had quite a talk earlier today . . ."

"Yes, she said something of it to me."

"She was most informative about your high sense of honor and good character, but I needed to see for myself what you're made of. A man usually shows one face to women and another to other men, just as they do for us. It would seem that for you there's little difference between the two."

"You have an annoying way of fashioning and bestowing a compliment, sir, if that was your intent."

"The shortcoming has been mentioned to me by others, but for the sake of accuracy think of it as less of a compliment and more of an observation."

I paused by the fireplace. "So you've observed that I seem to be a man of honor and good character. What of it? I thought you wanted to talk about Richard. I am more than willing, provided that you refrain from insulting him."

He snorted. "The truth is not an insult, and you'd best get used to hearing such once news of this gets out. There are others ever willing to make a cruel cut when the fancy strikes 'em. Then what means will you take to improve their manners? More duels?"

"Only when it's impossible to avoid. That business with Ridley—"

"Was all part of Clarinda's scheming, I know. You're damned lucky he didn't kill you. Now that you've raised the subject, how the devil are you to be rid of him without another fight? However right and pleasing it may be, we can't keep him locked in the cellar forever."

"Put your mind at rest on that. I've already dealt with him. He's presently upstairs in Arthur Tyne's room, and they'll both be leaving in the morning."

Before he could master himself I had the great satisfaction of seeing a look of boundless astonishment seize control of Edmond's features. "*What* are you saying?"

"It's all cleared up and put away, so to speak. He and his cousin will trouble us no more. I have his word on it."

"His word!"

"It was all quite easy, once I got him to settle down and listen to reason."

In light of the quarrelsome nature of his character, and not forgetting the implausibility of what I was telling him, I was convinced that my very best assurance would not be enough for Edmond. Even as the words tumbled easily from my mouth, the corners of his own turned markedly down, and he looked ready to offer a considerable debate and a number of bothersome questions I was not prepared to answer. Consequently, I made sure to come close and lock eyes with him again, guaranteeing a successful imposition of my will over his own.

*"You don't have to worry about him at all. . . ."* I whispered into his mind.

He was not easy to influence; for that difficulty I could blame the brandy. It was very like talking to a wall—a rather stoutly made one composed of brick. Several moments passed without my noticing any visible effect beyond a slight deadening of his countenance, but I'd seen that face on him before, usually prior to the delivery of some trenchant remark. Just as I thought my efforts would come to nothing, I observed that he had ceased to blink his eyes quite so much. For that good blessing I allowed myself a small sigh of relief, but continued to concentrate the greater part of my thought and will upon him. There was a kind of instinctual feeling within me that if I let my focus wander for even a second, I'd lose him.

*"It's all been sorted out. . . ."*

When finally finished, I'd acquired a nasty, droning ache behind my eyes, but at least there would be no more discussion of Ridley for now and probably for good. It was well with me; I was altogether sick of the subject. Returning to my post by the fireplace, I pinched the bridge of my nose trying to diminish the pain. Though fading, it was an annoyance. I hoped I could get through the rest of the night without having to resort to that handy talent again.

"Now what about young Richard?" I asked upon seeing Edmond very much needed the prompting.

"Yes. Well . . ." He rubbed his face and neck like a waking sleeper. I was happy enough to wait him out for it had been hard going for us both. "You've seen him. According to Mrs. Howard you seem to like him. So what do you want to do?"

A vague enough question, requiring a general sort of answer, though in my heart I'd already made a thousand plans for the boy. "What's best for him, of course. You're his father as well; what do you recommend?"

"Father? Father in name only," he rumbled, coming fully awake. "I knew he wasn't mine the moment I clapped eyes on him. She used to delight in pretending—oh, never mind. It's all over." He made a throwing-away motion with one hand.

I frowned at him. "Did that child ever suffer because of his mother's betrayal of you?"

His snapped-out answer told me he spoke the truth. "I've never laid a hand on him. God's death, I only saw the boy when it was necessary. He never took to me."

That I could understand.

His gaze canted sharply over to meet mine, and he correctly interpreted my expression. "What would you have? For me to play the saint and clasp him to my bosom as my own? Then wish on, for such sham is beyond my ability."

"My wish . . ." I began with a return of hot anger, but trailed off and made myself cool down. There was no point to it now. There was no point in wishing the child had had even a vestige of kindness from the man he perceived as his father. Whether or not ignoring the boy was better than pretended affection I could not judge. It was just so unutterably *sad.*

"What is your wish?" he finally asked.

"Nothing. As you say, it's all over."

For several more minutes neither of us spoke. I was now abrim with dark perturbation, and Edmond seemed in no better shape. I could almost feel the restless shift of our combined emotions churning through the room like some sort of fog composed of feeling instead of mist. Very much did I want to remove myself from its ill effect, but there was no help for it; I'd have to see this through.

"Edmond."

He didn't move; only his eyes shifted.

"You've asked me what I want. Tell me what it is that *you* want."

He laughed once, softly. "Another life might serve me well, or fewer mistakes in this one."

"I meant concerning Richard."

"I know what you meant. You said you want what's best for him. On that we are in full accord; we should certainly try to do what's best for him. It's not his fault that his mother's a murdering sow."

The brandy must be having its way with him, else he might not be so free with his speech, but after looking up the muzzle of a pistol aimed at him by his own dear wife, he was more than entitled to call her names. Indeed, I could respect him for his extreme restraint in the matter.

He glowered at the fire. "For as long as she lives I'll have to be her keeper. It's my just punishment for marrying the wrong woman and hers for marrying the wrong man. We're stuck with each other, she the prisoner, me the turnkey, not unlike most marriages, I suppose."

Just the subject I'd have to question him about, but it would have to hold for a bit longer, for this one was far more important to me. "What has this to do with Richard?"

"I'm attempting to give you an idea of what sort of growing up awaits him once we're all home again."

He allowed me time to think on it. I didn't much like the images my mind was busily bringing forth for consideration.

"What's best for the boy," Edmond said, reaching for his unfinished glass, "is to not be in a house where his mother must be locked away like the lost soul that she is. What's best is for him to be with his real father."

"Wh-what?"

He caught hold of the glass and downed the last half of his drink. "Would you consider taking him away?"

"To where?" I asked stupidly.

"To any place you damned well please."

I shook my head, not as an answer to his question but from sheer disbelief. The longer I stared, though, the more certain I became that he was utterly serious. "You'd be willing to make such a sacrifice?"

Now it was his turn to favor me with his disbelief. "Sacrifice? Haven't you yet gotten it through your head that I care nothing for the boy? Did someone stuff cloth in your ears when I wasn't looking? God help me, but knowing the things I know I can hardly endure the sight of him anymore. D'ye think I'm making a sacrifice? Don't flatter me."

"But—"

"If it's true that we both want what's best for him, then that's for him to be well away from my house."

"But for you to give him up just like that?"

"Damnation, I'm giving him to a man who might be able to provide better for him than I ever could. I know my limit, Barrett, and I've long since reached the end of mine."

"This is the brandy talking—"

"Brandy be damned, I'm trying to do something right for once. If you don't want him, then I'll find someone else who does and bless him for the favor. I'm trying to give the misbegotten brat a chance to know some kindness and love. I've none of it left in my heart; that bitch I married burned it out of me." He hurled the empty glass across the room. Though aimed nowhere near me, I still instinctively ducked as it flew past, so savage was the force behind his action. Next he picked up the brandy bottle and seemed for a moment ready to send it crashing after the glass, but the moment passed. He collected himself and fell back on the settee.

"D'ye want 'im or not?" he asked, his voice drained of everything except weariness.

There was no need to think on my answer. "Yes, of course I do. I should be more than delighted to take care of him."

"Good." He took a long drink right from the bottle. "You can sort out the details with Mrs. Howard. Take her along as well if you like. I can give her an excellent reference if you need it."

"That won't be necessary. I'm sure she will do admirably with us." God, the man must truly be distracted if he thought I'd separate Richard from the one person who had been his chief source of affection and guidance from the cradle. "What about Clarinda? What if Richard should want to see her?"

"No." There was a finality in his tone reminiscent of the gallows. "Your sister and I discussed that already. Until he's old enough to understand better, his mother is ill and that's the end of it."

"It's a hard business never to see his mother again."

"I cannot perceive that it would be of much advantage to him in the future, since he saw little enough of her in the past."

"Hard for Clarinda, too."

"Indeed it would be if she cared a fig for him. For either of them," he added, reminding me of the other child who was away at school. I wondered if that boy was a true son of Aunt Fonteyn's brother or the first of Clarinda's changelings. Now was not the time to make an inquiry, though. Besides, this was in direct opposition to the impression Clarinda had given me on her feelings for either of them and wanted sorting.

"How can a mother not care for her children?" I mused in a way meant to draw him out. Even my own mother, twisted in mind and heart as she was, cared after a fashion for her two children. She'd removed her damaging presence from us all those years ago, after all. Not unlike what Edmond was trying to do now for Richard.

His answer was curt and lacking in interest. "Ask her sometime, you'll find out soon enough that she hasn't a jot of regard for anyone but herself. But if it were otherwise with her, it still wouldn't matter. She forfeited all rights to them when she did her murder."

I looked at the stone bust on the mantel. On impulse I picked it up and turned it over to see if anything might be marked on the base to indicate who it represented. Neither Aristotle nor a Caesar, the neatly carved inscription identified it to be Homer. That little mystery explained, I put it back in place.

Since Edmond had ascertained for himself the fact of my honor, now would be the time for me to return the favor, to make sure that all would be reasonably well for Clarinda, if not for her sake, then for Richard's. "With you as the turnkey how will she be treated?" I asked very quietly.

"A damned sight better than she deserves. Don't worry yourself. It won't be a Bridewell, she'll not want for creature comforts, but I'm going to make damned sure she has no opportunity to kill ever again."

I believed him. He was as he presented himself. Perhaps Clarinda's constant lies had created in him a need to cleave to the absolute truth. So said all my instinct as I studied his hard face. It was no small reassurance to me that my growing respect for him was not misplaced.

He took another long drink, then glared at me.

"What is it? You want to toast her health or something?" He nodded toward my untouched brandy.

Damnation, but I was tired. "No. Nothing like that." Just the prospect of trying to pierce through his brick wall again was enough to renew the ache behind my eyes. He could think what he liked about my not drinking his brandy, to hell with it.

"What, then?"

For all his roughness, his willingness to do well for Richard spoke of an innate decency in his heart. This told me that Clarinda would be all right for the time being. Complete confirmation of it could wait for another night.

"I just wanted to say that should you ever feel differently about the boy, then you're welcome to come visit him any time."

He seemed on the verge of tossing the invitation back in my face, if I could judge anything by the sneer that briefly crossed his own. Then he visibly reigned himself in. "I'll consider it," he muttered. "Now get along with you. I need my rest."

I took this servant's dismissal in good grace. The man was in pain and only wanted the privacy to get thoroughly drunk. God knows, I'd do the same were I to find myself in his shoes. I wished him a good night, getting no reply beyond an indifferent grunt, and shut the door on him.

Halfway along the hall I had to stop for a moment, staring at nothing in particular while my thoughts finally caught up with events.

Good God in heaven . . . *Richard was going to come home with me.*

Then I clamped my hand over my mouth to keep from shouting the house down.

# CHAPTER 4

"Faster! Faster! Faster!" Richard screamed into my right ear. "Yah-yah-yah!"

I did what I could to oblige him, though things nearly came apart when I made a sharpish turn into the parlour. Our progress was nearly defeated by the high polish on the floor causing my shoes to lose a bit of their grip on the turf so to speak. I just managed to gain the safety of the parlour rug in time to keep us from taking a slide into an inconveniently placed chair. We flashed by Elizabeth and Oliver, who were sensibly sitting and having their tea before the fire, whooped a hallo at them, then shot out the other door and into one of the narrow back halls where the servants usually lurked. It was a straight path on this part of the course, so I stepped up the speed and galloped hard and with lots of needless bounce, much to the delight of my rider. Richard giggled and gasped, tightened his stranglehold around my neck, and dug his heels more firmly into my flanks.

"Have a care," I told him, making sure of my own hold on his legs. "We're coming to a hill."

He shrieked encouragement to his steed and I carried us up the back stairs three at a time, wound my way through the upper back hall to the upper front hall, then jounced roughly down to the front stairs landing, startling the one maid in the house who hadn't heard our noisy progress. She let forth a satisfying screech, throwing up her hands, an action that amused Richard mightily. He yelled out a view-halloo, told her she was the fox, and we gave roaring chase as far as the entry leading to the kitchen. Showing an unexpectedly fleet turn of foot, she ducked through to safety, smartly shutting the door in our faces just in time.

"Outfoxed!" I cried in mock despair to my laughing rider. "She's gone to ground and the dogs can't find her. What shall we do now? Another steeplechase?"

"Yes, please!" he bellowed, freshening his hold 'round my neck. I took us through the house twice more as we pretended each corner was a church steeple we had to make in time to stay ahead of a pack of pretend horsemen who were hot on our heels. We naturally won each race, for I was a steed of superior stock, a point I'd confided to him when I initially proposed our horseback riding game.

This was his first night in London, and it was proving to be a memorable one—for us both. I could not have been happier, and never before in my life had I felt this particular kind of happiness. No plans, no speculations, nothing I'd ever imagined had remotely prepared me for the actuality of his constant and immediate presence. He filled the house, he filled the whole world for me. At times I could scarce take in that he was real, and at others, it seemed that he had been with me always from the very moment of my own birth.

Once he'd learned that Edmond had given Richard over to my care, Oliver generously opened his house to the lad and welcomed him in. Elizabeth was just as keen about having the boy in as well and managed within the space of a few days to turn a couple of the upstairs rooms into a very fine bedroom and nursery for Mrs. Howard and her charge.

That lady was not herself adverse to moving out of Edmond Fonteyn's no doubt gloomy household and into ours, but with all the row going on, I was certain she'd be having second thoughts soon enough. Past personal experience with nannies had taught me that they prefer routines of the quiet, restful sort, something that would likely be lacking during those hours when I was up and around.

My time with Richard was short owing to the limits of my condition, but happily for the present, the winter nights started early and lasted long. Even so, on this first evening the instant I was awake I anxiously bolted from my cellar sanctuary to rush upstairs and see him, taxing the patience of Jericho, my valet. His inviolable custom was to lie in wait in my room, then seize upon and subject my person to an interval of grooming and dressing so I wouldn't shame him before polite company. As Richard and I galloped past, we surprised him emerging from my doorway, razor in one hand and cloth in the other, indication that I was in for a shaving tonight. Jericho's mouth popped open in startled disappointment before he hurriedly retreated out of the way.

The rest of the servants had simply been told that Richard was our cousin and committed to our care. If anyone chose to make anything of his uncanny resemblance to me, Jericho was to report such murmurings, and I'd have a little "talk" with the person to discourage idle gossip. Like Nanny Howard, Jericho knew all about the boy's true paternity, and both could be trusted to keep it to themselves. We'd all planned that Richard would also be informed but only when he was old enough and when the time was right. It seemed best to curtail any possibility of him overhearing something he wasn't ready for by making sure all the other servants were just as discreet.

Richard and I made another circuit of the upper rear hall and emerged into the front again but were forced to abruptly rein in. Nanny Howard stood square in our path, hands on her hips, and a stern cast to the look on her face.

"Mr. Barrett!" she said in a tone to match the look.

"Oy-oy-oy!" Richard yodeled, thumping the top of my head with one fist while the other twisted the remnants of my neckcloth around. "See me, Nanny! We're having a race!"

"You'll race yourself into an upset stomach with all that shouting," she told him, fulfilling my expectations about nannies and their preference for a quiet routine. Her eye fell upon me like the hand of doom. "Mr. Barrett, it will be his bedtime soon and now he'll be hours settling for it."

Not at all contrite, I nonetheless came up with a pretty speech of apology and volunteered to help in that task. "What's your best settling remedy, then? We'll get him fixed right up. How about a tot of hot milk with a little honey for taste? That always worked for me."

This mollified her somewhat, but she still showed some reluctance to let go her chagrin. "You needn't trouble yourself over such trifles, sir. I can see to things."

"Hardly a trifle. Besides, I got him stirred up; it's only fair I stir him down again."

"But, sir—"

"This isn't what you're used to, I'm sure, but we run things differently in this house. I'm very interested in the lad's well-being, so you might as well get used to the fact that I'm going to be underfoot quite a lot. You've got him to yourself all through the day, but for an hour or so at night it's my turn."

She pursed her lips in swift thought and being every bit as intelligent as I'd estimated, decided cooperation was preferable to argument. "Very well, Mr. Barrett. But I must remind you that Richard is not yet used to such excitements. Perhaps it's best to ease him into things a little at a time."

It sounded reasonable to me, and I wasn't one to cross her on anything as important as a growing lad's bedtime. Not yet, anyway. Richard groaned a protest as we ducked into the nursery and pulled on my neck-cloth again in an effort to turn his steed back to the beckoning fields of the rest of the house. The fabric came all undone and slipped free, and not wasting the opportunity, he waved it like a banner, then whipped it around my eyes.

"What's happened?" I gruffly asked, blundering about with one arm extended to feel my way. "Who blew out the candles?"

This game went over enormously well with him. I played it to the limit, pretending to smash face first against a wall resulting in a crash to the floor—a slow and gentle one—with much loud moaning, despair, and calls for caution. We ended up rolling and tussling like puppies until he was breathless. One advantage I had over any other adults he'd ever play with was that I didn't get tired.

"I think you need a carpet in here, Nanny," I said, still lying on the floor because Richard had decided to hold my legs down by sprawling over them. "A nice thick one. Don't want the boy to get any more bruises than necessary."

"It's sure to get very dirty, sir."

"Then let it get dirty, we can always get another. I'll put my sister onto it tomorrow. London's full of shops; the three of you can go pick one out. Does he need anything else—clothes, furniture, that sort of thing?"

"Toys!" Richard shouted, taking off one of my shoes and measuring it against the other, sole to sole.

"He is well supplied with all that he needs, sir, with more than enough, I think."

The furnishings from the nursery at Edmond's home had been carted over and put into place in these rooms. Moving from my childhood home to London had proved to be a bad wrench for me, and I was full grown and well prepared for it. I'd hoped that the sudden change for Richard would be lessened with the presence of having his own familiar things around him. It must have worked, for he seemed carefree enough.

"Well, you be sure to tell us of your least little need, y'hear? The big needs, too. You have any problems, you come straightway to any of us so we can fix 'em."

"Yes, sir."

"One's bigger than the other," Richard observed of the shoes. He looked at me for some sort of reaction. "One's *bigger* than the other."

"So it is," I agreed, propping up on my elbows to see. "By a fraction of an inch. I'll have a word with my shoemaker."

"What's a fraction?"

"A portion of something, usually very small."

"A portion of what?"

"Anything you like."

He now measured my shoe against one of his own. "It's bigger by a fraction of an inch," he pronounced.

"So it is, by lots of fractions of inches. I'll teach you properly about them if you like."

"Yes, please."

"Nanny, have we got a measuring stick about the place?"

"I'm not sure, sir."

"Then perhaps you'd be so kind as to ask Jericho to find one. He usually knows where everything is."

"But, sir, about Richard's bedtime—"

"Oh, bother, I suppose if we must. Tell you what, have Jericho bring a measuring stick, and you go turn up that hot milk and honey. I'll give Richard a lesson in fractions. With any luck, the combination will put him to sleep. It always worked for me."

She tucked in her lower lip in an effort not to smile and whisked out. A moment later Jericho appeared in the doorway bearing the required stick and a pained expression when he saw the state of my clothes.

"Good evening, Jericho. Have to hold off on the nightly wash and brush up for the moment."

"I think it is just as well, Mr. Jonathan. Had you taken the time earlier, it would have all been for nothing."

Richard giggled. "Jericho."

"And what about it?" I asked. "That's his name."

I got another giggle for a reply.

"I believe Master Richard is referring to the unfortunate habit Londoners have of calling the back garden privy a 'jericho,' sir," my excellent friend said with unsuppressed distaste.

Another giggle from below.

Well, I had to put a stop to that. "Richard," I said, fully sitting up and addressing the boy in a serious tone. It took a repetition or two before he calmed down sufficiently to give me the solemn sort of attention the occasion required. "Making fun of a person's name, no matter what it is, is very rude and not at all becoming of a gentleman. You understand that?"

He pouted and nodded.

"Very good. Now I want you to promise not to make fun of anyone's name ever again, particularly Jericho's."

I'd had to deal with this subject before with the servants. Jericho was the true head of this household when it came to all practical matters, and it wouldn't do to have anyone finding amusement in his name and thus undermining his authority. His was an excellent name, after all, and certainly not his fault that it had been corrupted by the locals into something that might be thought basely amusing.

"I promise."

"What an excellent lad you are! Now can you tell us where Nanny keeps your little nightgown? If you're all dressed and ready for bed when she comes back, then she might not be cross with me for keeping you up so late."

Put this way, he had no objection to helping me avoid Nanny's wrath and readily pointed out a chest with drawers. We searched through its contents and discovered a suitable garment.

"I can take over from here, sir," said Jericho. "Perhaps if you would use this time to put yourself into order as well . . ."

I obediently set to work on myself as he turned to take care of Richard.

"Won't that come off?" Richard said, pointing to Jericho's dark skin.

"I assure you it will not, Master Richard. See for yourself." He held his hand out for the child's close inspection. Said hand was peered at, rubbed, and pinched. "See, just like yours but with more color—and a good deal cleaner. A trip to the washbasin is in order, I think. Come along."

He gently guided Richard away, and from that so subtle action smoothly assumed the same position of command he held over me when it came to proper grooming. Jericho could be quite formidable when he chose, but in this instance he was careful not to bowl the lad over by overdoing his grand manner. A soft word here, a delicate recommendation there and he had Richard painlessly scrubbed and dressed for bed before the boy knew what had happened.

"I'll take my turn as soon as I'm done here," I told Jericho.

"One would hope so, sir," he replied, raising an eyebrow at my lackluster turnout. Since all I'd done was replace the shoe on my foot and straighten my waistcoat, he was entitled to all the eyebrow raising he wanted. He plucked my discarded neckcloth from the floor and stalked out just as Nanny Howard returned with a small cup of hot milk in hand.

"All ready," Richard announced to her, showing off his clean hands, face, and change of clothing. "Don't be cross with Cousin Jon'th'n."

The woman was becoming adept at adjusting to changing circumstances, and her look went from questioning to acceptance. "Very well, I won't. Have you had your lesson in fractions yet?"

"We were just about to get down to it," I answered for him.

"Very well," she said, and put the cup of milk on a low table next to a miniature stool. Richard plopped himself onto the latter and gave the cup and its contents a suspicious eye.

"It's too hot," he said decisively.

"No doubt, but it will cool off in a moment. Now where's that measuring stick?" I quickly found it and sat cross-legged on the floor next to him to more easily explain the basic principals of fractions.

For all the fatherly pride that was fast burgeoning in my swelled bosom over his many talents, I couldn't say that he took well to this first lesson. To be fair, he was still very lively from all his hard riding and full of questions for everything except the subject at hand. It didn't take me long to twig to this, so I obligingly did not force him around. Instead, I did my best to answer why I preferred not to wear a wig, where I'd come from, the general location of America in relation to England, and conjectured just how wide and deep the " 'Lantic Ocean" might be. By then his milk was of a suitable drinking temperature, and I managed to coax most of it into him.

"Doesn't taste like real milk," he said.

"That must be the honey in it."

"He's used to fresh cow's milk, sir," Nanny Howard put in. "All the kitchen had was ass's milk."

"Yes, Oliver is particularly fond of it, says it's more wholesome than what comes from a cow."

"Indeed it is, sir, for I shouldn't care to trust any cow's milk bought in the city. Too many things can make it go bad."

"Perhaps if we got our own cow—"

"Oh, no, sir, for it would still be in the city. Better to have ass's milk or none at all."

"You don't care much for the city, then?"

"It's not my place to say, sir."

"Certainly it is if I ask you."

"Well, then, it's fine enough for me, but in all truth, I don't think raising a child in the city is at all wise."

"What have you against it, then?"

"The bad air for one thing, the bad water for another."

I could offer no argument on those points and motioned for her to continue.

"That's more than enough to stunt growth and turn them sickly. There's also soot everywhere you step, rotten food sold by people you don't know, disease, low women, wicked men, and too much noise. How can a child get any sleep with all the constant row?"

"There's low women and wicked men in the country—or so I've heard," I said, dodging the question.

"Perhaps that is so, Mr. Barrett, but I've yet to see any and I've lived in the country considerably longer than you've been alive. But all that aside, I've seen more country children reach their majority than city ones. Raising children is not unlike farming, sir. You need a bit of room to grow, sunshine, and sweet water. Take any one of those away and you'll end up with a failed crop."

Damnation, but she was making perfect sense. "Then you see nothing favorable about the city at all?"

"I'll allow that it has some passable distractions and entertainments, but the nature of such things holds little interest to a boy of four years." Her observations were entirely sensible, but I didn't know what to do about them. The first idea that came to me—and the first one to be discarded—was for Richard to return to Edmond's country home. As for the second idea . . .

"I could possibly look around for a place of my own," I said, without much enthusiasm.

She picked up on that and offered an alternative. "What about Fonteyn House? It's not too far away and has more than enough room."

That was my third idea, and I wasn't too keen on it. "I don't think it would prove very practical. You see, my father and mother may be on their way to England at any time, and I rather expect Mother will want to live in Fonteyn House."

"That's only natural, it being her late sister's home."

"Natural, yes, but to have her sharing it with a young and rowdy child would not be the best for either of 'em."

"But there's more than room enough—"

"Room is not the point, Mrs. Howard. It's best that you know about my mother."

"Indeed?" She assumed a carefully neutral face, having also picked up on a darkening in my tone of voice.

"She's just as horrible in her way as Aunt Fonteyn was." I paused to allow her to take in that bit of blatant honesty, giving her a suitably somber look. "I think we all know what might have happened had Aunt Fonteyn lived to learn about, let us say, certain irregular circumstances in the family progeny. Now multiply that by a factor of ten and you'll have an idea of how my mother might react should she learn of it."

"Oh, dear."

"In truth, her hold on reason is altogether infirm, and when her grasp slips she is capable of the most violent fits imaginable. I would be loath to expose an unprepared innocent to such an irregular temper."

Mrs. Howard nodded. "Yes, old Judge Fonteyn suffered the same sort of malady. Many's the time I had to keep Oliver out of his way when the spell was on him."

Oliver and I had had a lengthy talk about what the old judge suffered from, an entirely horrifying topic. Though she gave me the impression she knew something about it, I wasn't going to pursue it with Mrs. Howard at the present and certainly not while the boy was listening.

"Having my own home might be the best for all concerned, then," I said instead. "But I shouldn't like to be too far from London."

"I'm sure there are any number of suitable places, sir."

I had my doubts, but only because I was reluctant to move from Oliver's comfortable house and assume the responsibility of looking after my own. On the other hand, there was a decided appeal to being one's own master. "You know, if Oliver hadn't invited me and Elizabeth to live with him, I'd have had to find one for us, anyway. It probably would have been in the city, though, and I'd still have the same problem to face now."

Then perhaps it was past time I gave serious thought to finding a separate accommodation for myself, or rather for the Barrett branch of the Fonteyn kindred. And I hadn't exactly come to England empty-handed, being still in the possession of a half dozen cattle that had survived the ocean crossing. They'd originally been put aboard ship to provide me with a fresh source of blood for the long journey, but my condition had changed that plan by causing me to fall into an unnatural sleep for the whole trip. My unnerving hibernation had provided no end of worry for Elizabeth and Jericho at the time. The only favorable thing that might be said of the phenomenon was that it spared me from two months of constant and exhausting *mal de mer.*

Soon after our arrival in England, the Barrett cows had been turned out to mix with Fonteyn stock. My property would soon be in need of a permanent home if they bred as planned. It was my fond hope that when Father arrived he'd have the start of a fine herd to keep him busy if he wanted to retire from his law practice.

Now there was something *else* to think about. "Another thing you need to know about this coming household," I continued, "is that my father and mother are estranged, and I rather think both would be more comfortable if there's some goodly distance between 'em. If I find something suitable, then my father will likely be sharing it with me."

"How will he feel about the—ah—irregularities? That is, if I may be so bold as to ask." She nodded her head very, very slightly in Richard's direction, not looking at him.

"Ask away, dear lady. As for your answer, once he gets over the shock, I think he will be utterly delighted." I hoped for as much. Elizabeth and I had come to that happy and comfortable conclusion after much lengthy discussion. During moments of weakness, I was subject to the occasional doubt or two, but that was from my own inner discomfiture, not because Father would fall short of our expectations. We knew him to be a very wise and compassionate man. Certainly he would welcome a grandson, even one from the wrong side of the blanket.

"There's a comfort," said Mrs. Howard. "I remember him as being a most sensible young fellow."

"You do? You knew him before he left England?"

"Not to speak to, I should say. It wasn't my place, of course. But there was many in the servant's hall who were glad he stood up to the old judge and won Miss Marie away from Fonteyn House. Best thing that ever happened to her. I'm so sorry to know that—that things worked out as they did."

"What was she like then?" I asked, feeling a sudden tightness around my throat at this chance to look into another's past. Part of me wanted nothing to do with Mother, but a different part wanted to know everything. It was like picking a scab to see if it would fall away clean from a healed wound or peel painfully off only to start it bleeding again.

"Oh, she was a very beautiful girl. Sometimes quiet and sometimes very headstrong. Not what I would call too knowledgeable about the world, but then the judge didn't have much use for women learning any more than they needed to run a household. She used to do very clever needlework."

"Mother? Quiet?"

"Silent, then. There's a difference," she said with a sad face.

"I'm done with my milk," Richard announced. His eyes had grown wide and his expression pensive with concern. Even if he didn't understand much of our talk, he was keen enough to perceive the dark emotions running beneath it and be worried.

"What a good lad you are!" she exclaimed approvingly, with a swift brightening in her manner. "Are you ready to go to bed, now?"

"No, please. I want to play with Cousin Jon'th'n."

Nanny Howard shot me a dangerous look, one that I took to heart. "We'll play again tomorrow night, my lad, or we'll both be in trouble. We have to do what Nanny says, y'see. She knows best."

Reluctantly he allowed himself to be led to his bed, and she tucked him in.

"A story, please?" he asked, as appealing as only a four-year-old can manage. I found my throat tightening again, but for a far different reason than before. Mrs. Howard correctly read my face and upon selecting a chapbook from a pile on a shelf, thrust it into my waiting hands.

The book's subject had to do with the alphabet, being full of instructive rhymes of the "A is for Apple" sort. Richard and I went through it together, with him pointing out the letters and naming them and muttering along as I read the rest of the text. He seemed to know the book by heart, but that didn't matter. I'd been told I'd had my favorite stories, too, never tiring of their repetition. He was asleep by the time I'd gotten to the "M is for Mouse" rhyme.

"Thank you, Mrs. Howard," I whispered to her as I prepared to tiptoe out.

"Bless you, sir, but you're the one to be thanked. I think you're the best thing that could ever have happened to the child."

"I can hope as much. I'm new to this and don't mind saying that I should highly value your guidance if you would be so kind."

"Certainly, sir."

"And about the food, I'll have Oliver arrange it so the pick of Fonteyn House's country larder is at your disposal. Will that be satisfactory until such time as I can find my own home outside the city?"

"More than satisfactory, sir."

I fairly bounded down the hall to my room where Jericho waited to repair the damages of my recent romp. Our conversation was a bit one-sided at first, with me rattling on about Richard with hardly a stop except when it was time for my shaving. Jericho had a light touch with a razor, but years back we'd both agreed that any unnecessary talk from me might prove to be a dangerous distraction to his concentration on the task. I was close-mouthed as a clam for the duration.

He took the respite as an opportunity to catch me up on the day's events within his own sphere, reporting about who had paid calls and what their business had been. An invitation had arrived for Elizabeth and me to dine with the Bolyn family. It was worded in a flexible enough manner so as to include Oliver if he chose to come. He was still officially in mourning for his mother and not expected to participate in social gatherings, though an exception could be made for a private informal supper. Considering the restrictions of my diet, it was just as well for me. At least then Elizabeth would not be without an escort if she accepted.

Once Jericho had my chin scraped clean and clothed me in something presentable, I was released from the nightly ritual and free to go about other civilized pursuits. I had to promise not to indulge in additional boisterous play before he let slip the leash, though. Since Richard was safely asleep, it was an easy enough pledge to make.

I found Elizabeth to be alone in the parlour, very much at her ease on the settee staring at some book. All the tea things were cleared away. It was that space of time where most people enjoyed the quiet comfort of their home and family while awaiting the arrival of the supper hour.

"Hallo, where's Oliver got to?" I asked, idly glancing about.

"Off to his consulting room for a bit of work he missed during the day." She put the book to one side on top of a pile of well-thumbed copies of *The Gentleman's Magazine.*

"Is he going to be busy for the whole evening?" Our cousin could disappear for hours on end into his medical studies when the inspiration was upon him.

"I don't think so. He wanted only to read up on a treatment for a complaint he thought too delicate for mixed company."

That sounded interesting. "Delicate?"

"Apparently even reading about it with a female in the room was of considerable discomfort to him, so he excused himself. I can't see what his problem might be, since it was only something in a past issue of a magazine about a new method of cutting into the bladder to remedy the suppression of urine."

"Ugh! Really, Elizabeth!"

"Oh, now don't you object to what is or is not proper for a lady. The article was right there plain and open on the page for anyone to examine." She tapped the stack of publications next to her with her fingertips.

"And bladder operations are the sort of thing you enjoy reading up on?"

"Hardly, but it caught my eye. I was really looking for news about the war and was distracted away by the account."

"So how is the war going?" I asked, eager for a change of subject, any change at all. I vaguely recalled reading the bladder article myself and had no desire to have my memory refreshed.

"It was a September issue, so their news was very dated. All they had was what we already knew when we left, that, and some account of the rebels indulging in a paroxysm of prayer and fasting last July fourth to aid their ill-considered cause. But the December issue is no better. There's not one word in it about General Burgoyne's defeat."

I threw myself into a chair, hooking one leg over its arm. "They're probably afraid it will prove to be too disheartening to the public. Too late for that, though. I'll wager the King and his cronies know all there is to know, and they hope by keeping quiet the whole nasty business will be forgotten."

"Then they are bound to be disappointed, especially if all the rumors in the papers are true."

"Oh, I'm sure they are. I overheard quite a lot during the funeral." A few of the men in the Fonteyn and Marling clans possessed an inside ear to the private workings of the government and when closely questioned, became rather free with their information, most notably after the Madeira started flowing.

"So did I," she said, one corner of her mouth curling down. "If it's true, then we may be here for good."

"I thought we were, anyway. That's what Father—or did he tell you differently?"

She made a sour face at me. "Father's moving here for good, but it doesn't necessarily mean that I have."

This was more than startling news to me. My belly gave a twist as I sat up straight to face her. "What? You want to go back? Into the middle of a war?"

"Certainly not, but the war can't last forever."

"And then you'd go back?"

"I don't know. London's just wonderful from what I've seen of it, but I do get so homesick sometimes."

"But you might return to Long Island after the war finishes?" This came out as less of a question and more like a woebegone whine.

"I've thought of it. But please don't excite yourself yet, little brother. All I've done is think about it."

"Then thank God for that." But I was still very much unnerved.

"Your concern is most flattering."

"I had no idea you felt this way."

"Normally I don't, but it caught up with me today after reading this rubbish. I came suddenly all over homesick. Mostly I miss Father and worry for him. Perhaps once he's here in England, things will brighten up for me."

"I'm sure they will." I sincerely hoped as much, being very attached to my sister. Though ever considerate for her happiness and comfort, the thought of her moving back, perhaps forever, to Long Island made a cold and heavy knot in my heart. I should not like that to happen at all. "I miss Father, too," I added lamely. "Once he's here everything will be all right for you."

"Have you written to him yet?"

"Well . . ." I hedged. "I've started a letter, but there's been so much to do with Richard—"

"Bother that." Some of her dark mood appeared to drop away, and she favored me with a severe eye. "I've heard you complain time and again how heavy the early morning hours are before your bedtime when you've gotten tired of reading and there's no one to talk to except the night watch."

I favored her with a sour face in return. "Be fair, Elizabeth, how do you think I can put all that's happened into a letter? 'Dear Father, Cousin

Clarinda murdered Mother's sister, and damned-near got her husband and myself as well. By the way, I've taken in Clarinda's boy, who's turned out to be my son, so congratulations, you're now a grandfather. How are things faring with you?' He'd burst a blood vessel."

Elizabeth found a cushion on the settee and threw it with a great deal of force, catching me square on the nose. "If you send him such a letter *I'll* burst a blood vessel—one of yours."

The cushion dropped to my lap, and I punched it a few times, feeling quite cheered by her show of temper. "All right, all right, I know better, but it's still anything but an easy task. If you're so keen to let him know what's happened, why don't *you* write him?"

"Because it's all concerned with your business; therefore it's your responsibility."

"But you're the eldest, as you so frequently remind me. Besides, yours is the more legible handwriting."

"Jonathan, if I were a man I'd call you a coward and issue a challenge here and now."

"And you'd never get satisfaction, because I'd here and now freely admit that I'm as craven as a rabbit."

"And properly ashamed of it, I hope."

"Dreadfully ashamed. In fact, I'm quite paralyzed from it, so much so that I don't think I could *possibly* lift pen to—"

Elizabeth reached for another cushion.

"That is to say . . . . never mind."

She put her potential missile back, smiling a cat's smile. Now *that* was a very good sign.

Teasing done and peace preserved, I continued. "It would be easier for me if we heard from him first. Surely he's written us by now."

"I'm sure he must have, but with the war going on, his letters might be delayed or stopped altogether. Those damned rebels have ships and guns, too."

"Oh, I'm sure he'd find a way to get something through. He's got enough well-placed friends to help him. What I'm thinking is that he might have sold the house by now and already be on his way here."

"I hope not—a winter crossing . . ." She shivered, expressing a very real concern for the dangers. "But all that aside, you still have to do something about this yourself. Oliver and I will help all we can, but in the end, it is your task."

"I know. But making a proper job of it requires a lot of thought and I'm not sure I'm up to it."

She made no effort in the least to stifle her laughter. I threw the cushion back, but missed. It landed harmlessly on the magazines next to her.

"Very well," I grumbled when she had control of herself again. "I'll make a real start on it tonight, though what I'll say to him will be anyone's guess."

"I'm sure the simple truth in the order it happened will be fine."

"But there's such a deuced lot of it and—oh, heavens—what if Mother should see it?" We both knew Mother was not beyond opening and reading her husband's letters when the chance presented itself.

Elizabeth's mouth crimped into an unflattering frown. "If she's determined to commit such a trespass, then she should be prepared to accept the consequences."

"I'm all for it, but my worry is what the consequences will be for Father."

"I expect that should the worst happen, he'll just call Dr. Beldon to give her a draught of laudanum, then Mrs. Hardinbrook will pat her hand and offer shrill sympathy as usual."

"If he manages to keep the letter from Mother, I hope Father won't tell her about Richard." My description to Mrs. Howard of Mother's likely reaction was no exaggeration. Far better for all concerned that she never learned of the child's existence.

"He probably won't, but all you need do is ask for his discretion."

"Be assured of my utter determination to do so. But I'm tired of all this, let's talk about Richard instead."

"I wondered how long it would take for you to get 'round to him. Sooner than this, I would have thought."

"Don't fret, I'll make up for the delay. We had a wonderful time tonight."

"So Oliver and I observed whenever you came hurtling through. Did you win your race?"

"Oh, dozens of 'em." Taking this as an invitation, I told her every detail of what we'd done. "He's very smart, y'know." I concluded, sometime later, after letting her know all about the attempted lesson in fractions and the chapbook.

"I know."

"I think he really was reading along with me. He knows all his letters, at least up to M, anyway. I'll take him through the rest of the alphabet tomorrow night."

"That should be nice."

"Something wrong?"

"I hope not." But her face was all serious again. I feared a return of her earlier melancholy.

"Then what is it that you hope is not wrong?"

"Perhaps I'm too much the worrier, but I need some assurance from you."

"On what?"

Her ears went pink. "This is entirely foolish of me. I know you, but I can't seem to quell the worry."

"What worry? Come now and tell me."

"It's just that Richard is tremendous fun for you right now. Everything's all new and exciting. But I have to know that you'll be there for him when he needs more than a playmate. That you'll look after him when things are serious as well, the way Father's always done for us." Her words came out all in a rush, clear evidence of her embarrassment.

In my own heart I'd already thought along those very same paths. I'd worried over the fear that once the novelty of Richard's presence wore off, I'd find other pursuits to occupy me. After a lengthy heart search, I'd concluded the fear to not be worth further examination. "Of course I will," I answered quietly. "Elizabeth . . . know this: That boy is part of my very soul and always will be. That's as certain as the sunrise."

Her face cleared somewhat. Then she smiled, a small one, and gave an equally small sigh. "Thank you for not being angry with me."

I shrugged. "If you care for Richard half as much as I do, then hearing your concerns for him is my duty and pleasure. You've nothing to fault yourself with. I won't pretend to assume I'll make as good a job of it with him as Father did for us, but certainly I'll try my best."

"I don't understand why I thought you might do anything less. I just needed to hear you say it, I suppose."

"It's because you're my sister. You've seen *me* as a child howling away over scraped knees and a bloody nose, and it's hard to accept that the boy you hold in your memory can handle a man's business when he's grown. Good heavens, there's many that can't no matter how old they get."

"Too true." We regarded each other, peace restored—I hoped—to her heart and mine. For all the fun and frolic I had with Richard, I held a keen and clear awareness of the attendant responsibility. In odd moments I sometimes gave in to fear and quailed at the enormous weight of it, of raising a child, but then I'd had a more than decent raising and could draw upon memories of my father's example when necessary. With this and guidance from others I had a more than reasonable expectation of not making a mess of things. Still and all, I would be very, *very* glad when Father arrived in England.

Perhaps I should wait a bit before seeking out a house, on the chance that he would want to help in the choosing. Much of his law practice had been occupied with the details on the buying and selling of property and boundary disputes. I'd very much welcome his vast experience. Damnation, but there would be a thousand decisions to make. The place might even require extensive furnishing. Elizabeth would be of excellent help there. Furnishings . . .

"I was just thinking, dear sister . . ."

Her glance up at me was sharpish. I only used that particular form of address when I wanted something from her and well did she know it.

"Do you think you could teach Richard to play the spinet?"

"I could try, if I had a spinet upon which to teach."

"I was planning to get you one."

"I'm pleased to hear it. But isn't he a bit young, yet?"

"Oh, it's never too early to learn. They say that fellow Mozart started just as young, and he ended up playing before all the royal courts."

"Mozart was born with musical talent—what if Richard takes after you?"

"Then I'll teach him to ride horses instead, and you'll have a fine instrument left over as a souvenir of the attempt. Tomorrow I want you to run out and find the best spinet in London and have them cart it over right away. But all that aside, I miss hearing you play."

Her expression softened. "Why, thank you!"

"And get a carpet, too."

Now did her expression abruptly pinch into blank perplexity. "A carpet?"

"Yes, a nice big thick one, the thickest you can find. I promised Mrs. Howard one for the nursery and said the three of you could go shopping for it tomorrow. Richard should have a say in the choosing, too, I thought."

"How kind of you to find so many enjoyable things for me to do," she said dryly.

"Not at all. I suppose you'll need to take measurements or something so it will fit. You'll find a measuring stick up there, unless Mrs. Howard has given it back to Jericho. I was teaching him about fractions—Richard, that is, not Jericho—with it, if you'll recall. Perhaps you can find a carpet for Mrs. Howard's room, too. An excellent woman, we're so lucky to have her, and I want her made as comfortable as may be."

"Heavens, Jonathan, I don't even have a carpet for *my* room!"

I waved a careless hand. "Then indulge yourself at my expense."

"Don't worry, I will," she muttered darkly.

Dear me, but I knew *that* look. Time for a bit of placation or I'd have another pillow in my face. "Well, I've gone on quite long enough, why don't you tell me everything you did today?"

Elizabeth sighed, apparently exasperated by this latest sudden change in subject, then composed herself to give a summation of the day's events. As with Jericho, it had become a regular custom between us for her to tell me all the news I'd missed while lying oblivious in the cellar.

"Well, to start with, Charlotte Bolyn has invited us to—"

"No, no, no, I don't mean that rot! Tell me all that happened with you and *Richard.*"

She picked up the cushion and once more—and with considerable force—managed to strike my nose dead on.

In an effort to preserve my battered countenance from additional damage, I decided to intrude upon Oliver's ruminations, hoping he wouldn't be too far gone in study for a bit of company. Upon hearing my knock he grunted something that might loosely be interpreted as an invitation to enter. I took it as such and pushed the door open.

His own sanctuary was part study, part consulting room, to be used on those occasions to interview patients when he was not out making calls on them. His practice wasn't a busy one, but he kept himself very active with it. Most of his patients were from within his broad circle of friends, and being a gregarious sort, he often as not paid visits as much to socialize as to render aid. Unless his services as a physician were actually required, he never charged for those visits, claiming he was content enough with the distraction of agreeable company. This made him popular, but it was just as well for him that he had income inherited from Grandfather Fonteyn or he'd not be living in his present comfortable circumstances.

At the moment he was very comfortable, indeed, having pulled his favorite chair close to the fire and treated himself to some port while reading. Like Elizabeth, he had a respectable stack of *The Gentleman's Magazine* nearby and held one in his hand.

"Hallo," he said, looking up. "Is the house still standing?"

"Was it too much row for you?"

"Not at all. You should have heard us earlier when Richard and I were playing hide-and-seek. I was just wondering whether the walls were still intact after the races."

"Intact and likely to stay solid," I said, easing into another chair. "But we'll be more stately tomorrow night if you like."

"Please say you won't. I grew up being forced into stateliness and can't recommend it. Let the boy laugh and shout his head off; I like that kind of noise. The reason I came here was to keep from getting trampled."

"Sorry."

He dismissed my contrition with a wave. "And because I feared you'd invite me to join in and I might not have the will to refuse. The little brat already tired me to the point of fainting once today. Once is more than sufficient."

"He did?"

"Well, perhaps not quite so far, but I was pretty blown. Don't know how Nanny can keep up with him. Paces herself, I suppose."

"She and I had a nice little talk about this and that," I said. "She managed, during that talk, to throw a sizable rock into my tranquil pond."

He squinted. "Sorry, but I don't quite follow."

"Because I've not yet explained."

"Then please do so, Coz."

I did so, recounting to him Mrs. Howard's objections to raising a child in the city.

"Then you also think young Richard would be better off in a rustic setting?" he asked.

"It didn't seem to hurt either of us or Elizabeth."

"True enough. It may have been hard going for me with Mother, but Nanny saw to it I got my share of fresh air and exercise. You'd also be limiting his chances of getting the pox, too."

My dormant heart gave a sudden and sickening lurch. "Pox? Good God, I hadn't thought of that."

His normally jocund expression was now as gloomy as that of a judge. "And well you should. I've seen far too many young souls carried off before their sixth year from that curse, and pox aside, there's any number of a hundred other things that . . ."

Another lurch in my chest. It felt like a great ball of ice was rolling around inside.

I wanted Oliver to stop talking, to stop filling me with fears I didn't want, but as hard as the facts were to hear, they were inescapable.

"He'll have to be inoculated," I whispered.

"Oh, yes, certainly that. I know a good man for it, grinds 'em through a dozen at once."

"What?"

"He's got a big house he's turned into a sort of inoculation mill. Has in a dozen children at a time. They stay for about a week for a bit of purging and bleeding to purify their systems, then he makes the inoculation. They're down sick from it, of course, but he keeps them all bedded up and cared for until they're ready to go home, say after about two weeks. He's very good, very successful."

I recalled my own ordeal had not been quite so involved and said as much.

Oliver frowned mightily, then his face cleared. "Oh, well, that's because it was a few years back and on the other side of the world. There's been a lot of advances made since, y'know. You won't find 'em practicing any wild colonial experimentation here in England! But there's no hurry. The lad needs a little time to grow. Elizabeth made a point of hiring servants who'd already had it, so things should be safe for now. Just make sure it's done before you send him off to school."

*If I send him off,* I thought. At the moment, the idea of hiring a private tutor looked much more appealing to me. Many other boys, myself included, had not suffered from such schooling in the safety of one's home.

So many plans. So many responsibilities. That ball of ice would turn into a leaden weight and take up permanent residence if I let it.

*Always move forward, laddie. We're all in God's hands and that's as safe enough place as any in this world..*

"Jonathan?"

I'd been staring at the fire and now gave a start.

"Don't come all over melancholy on me. Everything's going to be fine."

"Yes, I'm sure you're right. It was just a bit of a jolt, don't you know."

"I know, and I'm glad to hear it. Means you'll be doing something when the time comes."

"Upon my honor and before God, you may be sure of it."

"Excellent. There's nothing that breaks my heart more than hearing the parents wailing away because they'd forgotten or had put it it off until it was too late."

"You won't have that with me."

"Excellent." He tapped his fingers along the spine of the magazine in his hand. The silence that now settled between us thickened like a sudden patch of fog. I didn't care much for it and he seemed not to, either. He cleared his throat. "About this idea of moving to a country home?"

I gratefully seized his opening for a change of subject. "Mrs. Howard recommended Fonteyn House, but I'll have to find some other place." I clarified this statement by mentioning the probable situation ahead once Father and Mother arrived in England.

When I'd finished, he was in full agreement with me, adding, "But whether or not your mother takes up residence there, you still wouldn't want Richard shut away in Fonteyn House. It's much too dark and drafty, but there will soon be changes. I'll be making a deal of those when things settle a bit. Changes, that is. Dress up the insides, knock a few holes in the walls and put in more windows and damnation on the window tax. Once I'm done you won't know the old pile. But as for your having a place of your own—"

"There's no hurry yet. I'm thinking I'll wait until Father's here."

He shrugged. "As you wish, but I was going to say I know of a perfectly nice house standing empty that might suit. The land's been fallow for years, but that can be fixed. There's room for your cattle and what not, and it's just a few miles north of the city. The house will need a bit of work; it's been empty a long time."

"Why is that?"

"Oh, one of Mother's grand imperial orders, y'know. The estate belonged to my late father. Seems when he died, she closed it down hard and fast, wouldn't even rent it out."

"Strange to do that."

"Consider her nature, old lad. Y'see the whole lot was my father's, free and clear, and in accordance with his will it was to come to me when I came of age. But she shut the house up and let the property go, thereby making sure it would eventually become pretty worthless. I remember her sending Edmond around with an offer to buy it from me a day or two after I turned one and twenty."

"Which you turned down?"

"Not exactly. Edmond didn't say it in so many words, but he gave me to understand that her offer was much too low and that I should hang on to the deed for a bit longer. I didn't at first know what he was up to, but twigged to things after she sent him on a second visit and he managed to discourage me again. Mother had been going on about how she was doing me a favor by trying to take the place off my hands since it was essentially a ruin, so I went out to see things for myself. It seems that Edmond had been less than honest with her."

"In what way?"

"Oh, whenever a storm came through, he'd tell her another shutter had dropped off or there was a new hole in the roof. The truth was he'd made it his business to keep the place in tolerable repair. The doors and windows all hang straight and close snug, and it's dry as a drum inside. The land's all overgrown and that gives it a forlorn, ruinous look, but otherwise everything's sound."

"And Edmond did that for you?"

Oliver nodded. "He took a dreadful risk over the years. I mean, he'd have been out in the street quick enough if Mother had ever taken it into her head to pay a visit to the old Marling hold. He must have hidden the expense of repairs and the taxes from her in some clever way. Edmond's as intimidating as a bear with the gout, but deep down quite a decent chap at heart. We should all have such a fellow handling our business, don't you think?"

"Great heavens, yes. Makes you wonder what other little secrets he's got hidden away."

"I'll be finding out soon enough, I'm sure. Before he packed himself and Clarinda off home the other day, he said he'd have to soon sit down with me to go over the accounts. Seems there's a lot of legal nonsense that needs my attention now, and I can't put it off much longer. Anyway, if you want to look the place over some night—"

"Certainly, I'd be most happy to do so." What a painless way to find a home. By keeping all the business within the family I wouldn't have to wait for Father's arrival to avoid any purchasing pitfalls. "If it takes my fancy, then we can work out some sort of rent—or were you thinking of selling?"

"I was thinking of neither." He sat well back in his chair, lifting his chin slightly to peer down his nose. "If you want it—well, then . . . for the price of the yearly taxes you may *have* it!"

For a yawningly long moment I was in complete distrust of my ears. "*What?*"

He repeated it, grinning away like an ass and most certainly because I must have looked exactly like one myself.

# CHAPTER ◄5►

He'd utterly stunned me. That was the only word to describe my feelings when the whole import of his proposal finally sank in. For some considerable period I could do nothing but gape, inspiring a good deal of amusement in him.

"But I couldn't," I objected in a faint voice when partial recovery asserted itself sufficiently for me to speak.

"And why ever not?" He was still grinning.

"It's too magnificent a kindness."

"Don't be sure of that until you see the place—it might not suit, y'know. But all that aside, it's my property and I can do whatever I please with it. Besides, I know damned well such an arrangement would have sent Mother into an apoplectic fit, so that's yet another good reason for me to do it."

I argued a little more, but not too terribly hard. A firm and outright rejection of his generosity in the name of good sense would have been very rude and hurtful, of course, but aside from that I found myself partially willing to let him have his way. It was a magnificent gift, but if it proved to be too much so, then perhaps Edmond and I could argue him into something more equitable for all concerned. I had no wish to cheat my excellent cousin out of any of his rightful incomes. For now, deeply moved, I warmly and sincerely thanked him; he clapped his hands, practically crowing, then sat forward and told me all he could remember about the house and lands.

It was a sizable place not all that far to the north and east of Fonteyn House, but not all that close, either. There were fields and woods in the generous acreage, all overgrown and running wild by now, at least one clear running stream, and several buildings. Edmond had seen to the care of the house, but Oliver wasn't as certain about the condition of the barns and stabling. The house itself had been erected not long after the Great Fire of the previous century.

"Was it involved in that in some way?" I asked, fascinated.

"What, you mean burned up and then put something in on top of the ruins? No, nothing like that. The property's not even close to where all the destruction happened. The story is that one of my Marling ancestors liked the look of all the new buildings going up in London at the time and decided to have one of 'em for himself. Found himself a fashionable architect for the job and . . ."

The more he talked the greater waxed my interest and the more eager I became to see the place. Though it promised to involve a lot of work to make the house livable and get the land producing again, the prospect of undertaking such a project was enormously appealing. Now could I understand some of my father's youthful wish to cross a wild and dangerous ocean to a new land in order to create a place of his own.

In my case it would be going to an old land, but still virtually a foreign country from the one where I'd been raised. That had a very compelling appeal as well, for I'd ever been intrigued by the history of my English ancestry. Who knows but that some famous battle or great event might have taken place on the Marling lands in ages past. Oliver expressed a degree of doubt over this speculation, but that did not dampen my enthusiasm. Even if nothing more exciting than a bit of sheepherding had ever occupied the property over the centuries, what is commonplace to the local is exotic to the visitor.

When Oliver's store of description ran out, we resolved to visit and give the place a thorough inspection within a week if the weather cooperated.

"I'll probably go earlier to have a look 'round in the daylight," he said. "Shan't get much out of it at night I'm afraid, no matter how many lanterns I carry. Are you sure you'll be able to do as well?"

"As well if not better, especially if the sky is clear."

He shook his head. "Amazing business, your condition. That reminds me, I was meaning to ask if I might draw off a bit of your blood."

Again, I found myself gaping at my cousin. "Good God, whatever for?"

"For the purposes of scientific research, of course. A friend of mine has one of those microscope things, and I thought it might be interesting to use it to peep at a sample of your blood and compare it to that of another's, see if there's anything different between the two."

"A microscope?"

"You know, like a telescope, but for much smaller work. I may get one myself now, it's a marvelous toy. You wouldn't believe the things you can find in a humble drop of pond water with one of 'em. Most of my colleagues don't think much of the things, but my friend is always peering through his and making drawings of what he finds. Has an enormous collection of the most fascinating sketches. I don't think he quite knows what to do with any of it, but as a curiosity it'll hold your attention far better than a flea circus."

"And if you find a difference between my blood and another's, what then?"

He gave a great shrug. "It's knowledge and so it must be important. Come to think of it, perhaps I might take a sample from young Richard, then compare it to yours and see what's different and what's the same. I'll wager that might be very interesting, indeed."

"Really, now, Oliver, I don't want you poking at the poor child with one of your fleams unless it's absolutely necessary."

"I doubt that I'll need to; he's bound to get a scrape or two while playing—children are so good at that. I had my share of skinned knees and elbows and know it's only a matter of time for him to turn up with one. All I have to do is wait until he takes a tumble, then sneak a quick sample off him before binding up the wound. He'll never know a thing."

"Oh, you've reassured me to no end," I grumbled, with more than a trace of annoyance. "Now I'll not only be worrying about the pox—which is worry enough—but about skinned knees, broken arms, and who knows what else."

"Yes, the joys of fatherhood. You'll do all right, Jonathan. I've been in many a house where the parents are more concerned about the lapdog than the child, so be glad that you have such a heart in you that cares so. Anyway, God wouldn't have brought the two of you together unless he meant for it to last a bit. Just enjoy Richard one day—I mean, one night at a time, and let the future take care of itself."

"You sound like Elizabeth."

"Well! Thank you! I'll tell her you said that. She's a damn fine girl. Damn fine. I don't mind telling you that if she wasn't my first cousin I'd be sorely tempted to pay her court. With your permission, that is," he quickly added.

This wasn't precisely news to me, for I knew Oliver had been quite taken with her from their first meeting. Certainly I wouldn't have minded having him for a brother-in-law. "Cousins have married before, y'know," I ventured with an optimistic air.

"I know," he said, rolling his eyes. "For the last century or so the Fonteyns have been famous for it and look where it got 'em. Any rustic huddled in his cottage will tell you about the dangers of inbreeding their stock. No, I don't think the Marlings and Barretts would benefit from such a course. Suppose Elizabeth would even have me, our children might turn out like Mother, and then where would we be? Ugh. No, thank you, I shall content myself with admiring your dear sister from afar only."

"Such an inheritance of temper might not happen. Elizabeth and I aren't in the least way like our mother, after all, and I'm going to do my best to see that Richard doesn't turn out to be like Clarinda."

"If anyone can do it, Coz, then it is you. I say, you mean you wouldn't have objected to me and Elizabeth . . . that is, if she'd . . . that is?"

"Not at all. You're an excellent fellow. Not a bit like your mother, either."

This pleased him to no end, and he told me as much, saying it gave him great hope for Richard's prospects. "It was Nanny Howard that trained me up right," he pronounced. "If it hadn't been for her, Lord knows how I might have ended up. Between the two of you, well, maybe the three or four of us—what with Elizabeth and me hanging about the lad—there won't be so much as a trace of Clarinda left in the boy."

"And that's just as well," I muttered.

"Yes, wretched business. I'd never have suspected it of her, but then I'm likely not to suspect it of anyone. It's just not in me to do so."

"Then you are a very blessed man, Coz."

"Not so blessed that I don't have a dark moment here and there. Sometimes I don't know if I should condemn Clarinda or thank her for what she did," he mused. "Murder's a horrible, awful thing, but I don't know of anyone in the family who was truly sorry to see Mother gone, myself included, once you woke me up to it. Do you think I'll be damned for even considering such stuff?"

"I think rather that you might need to go dancing on her grave again and purge any lingering remnant of guilt out of your soul."

"Perhaps you're right on that. What really bothers me about the business is that Clarinda's idea to marry me would have probably worked because, damn it all, I *liked* her. Suppose I still do in a way, though it's all mixed up with a sort of revulsion, like Eve and that serpent, y'know. A pretty animal, but so bloody dangerous. I don't envy Edmond's job of keeping her caged for good and all."

"Neither do I."

"What about Ridley? In a way you've become his keeper, too. You're sure that the influencing you did will hold him and Arthur in check?"

His reminder of this unpleasant task waiting in the near future was hardly a welcome one. I found myself rubbing my arm again. The bone ached yet where Arthur Tyne had nearly severed it. That, or it only seemed to ache in my mind whenever I recalled the incident. "They'll be fine for the time being. I'll visit them within a week or so and bolster things up so they'll behave themselves."

"Pity you can't do the same thing for Clarinda."

"Oh, but I probably could. But I don't think it would—"

His eyes widened. "Really? Well, that would take the load off poor Edmond."

"Indeed, but then I'd have to explain myself to him. I'm not quite prepared to do so just now. It's a damned heavy confidence."

"Yes, that's the stark truth right enough. Edmond might think you'd gone mad and toss you out if you ever told him about your little secret. It's so extraordinary. He'd have to have proof, y'see."

"And then I'd have to give it to him, and I'm not too terribly confident in the benevolence of his reaction." *Which is a mild way of putting it,* I thought, with a nasty cold twisting in my belly. For Edmond to find out that the father of his son was some sort of extra-natural blood drinker didn't bear lengthy consideration. My own immediate family accepted my condition well enough, but then we were held close together by the ties of our deep, mutual affection for one another. Not so with Edmond. "He'd be within his rights to take Richard away from me," I said, thinking aloud.

"Then you could just influence him into leaving well enough alone," Oliver said, with some little heat. He seemed ready to enlarge upon the subject, but the look on my face stopped him. "Whatever is wrong?"

I'd come all over glum at his idea of influencing Edmond, for the very same one had occurred to me as well and made my vitals twist in another direction. "I . . . well . . . damnation, that wouldn't be right."

"In what way?"

"Father and I have talked the length and breadth of this business about enforcing my will upon other people, the good points and the bad. It all comes down to a question of honor."

"Honor? How so?"

"Your suggestion of my influencing Edmond—it's all very well to talk about it, but to actually carry it out would be an unconscionable intrusion upon him. To be telling him what to do just so it's convenient to my needs . . ."

"But you're doing it all the time to keep the servants from being curious about your eccentric habits," he objected.

"Yes, but I'm not telling them how to arrange their very *lives.* That's the difference. I don't think you're fully aware of just how frightening a power this is for me, Oliver. If I wanted to I could make my way right to the bedchamber of the king himself and play him or any of his ministers for a puppet on matters of state."

"Good God." His color flagged. "I never thought of that."

"Then think hard on it now. I have, and in weak moments it makes me tremble."

"I don't fault you for it," he whispered, then recovered somewhat. "Mind you, it would be a way of settling things out with France. You could take a little trip to Paris, talk here and there with some of old Louis's ministers, and remove the threat of them jumping into the war to help those damned rebels."

"God help us, but I could if I had a mind to try."

"Without the French sticking their noses into that which doesn't concern 'em, the rebellion would die down fast enough." He was fast warming to the idea of my becoming some kind of invisible agent for the crown, quietly managing the direction of foreign powers to suit the policies of the king and country.

"Hold and cease, Oliver," I said, raising both hands palm out in a show of not so very mock terror. "I want no part of any of that."

His eyebrows went up. "But you could be of no end of service to the king. By God, you could even make peace with Ireland if you put your mind to it."

I shook my head and continued to shake it, until Oliver finally saw I was not to be moved by any argument.

"Why not?" he demanded.

"Politics is better left to politicians. I am, or would have been a humble lawyer, fit for arguing the law, but not for recreating it to fit my idea of perfection. Besides, even if I had the guidance of the whole of Parliament for my actions I would still have to listen to the reproach of my conscience should things go wrong."

"You're just being the pessimist."

"I'm being an abject coward," I said truthfully. "Suppose I bungled things and started a war? I'm not prepared to have all those deaths haunting me. Other men are able to stand it, but not me. I'll gladly choose my own path, but will not presume to tell others where to walk themselves."

He scowled. "Well, put that way, I can't really blame you, though one might argue that you would also have an equal chance of preventing a war, thus sparing untold lives."

I shifted, uncomfortable, scowling back at him. "There's that," I admitted. "But I'm not wise enough for such work and know it. Please, Oliver, let's not pursue this subject, it's making me liverish."

He acquiesced, much to my relief. "Very well, can't have you coming down sick on me because there's no tonic you can take but the one, is there?"

"Right enough," I agreed, but I was not feeling especially hungry at the moment. Quite the opposite.

"Then politics aside, what about Edmond? You've no plans for him one way or another if he decided to take Richard away?"

"But he's not going to, I only mentioned that as a remote possibility, born out of my own fears. It's true that I could influence Edmond, or most anyone else to suit to my needs, but where does one stop once one has started? No, sir. That takes it back to the political once more and my liver won't stand for it."

He gestured to indicate his dismissal of that topic. "But then what about Ridley and Arthur? You're doing your best to completely change their lives."

"And don't I wish to high heaven to be free of the responsibility. I've come to take no pleasure in any of it, even if it is to change them for the better. I'm hoping that the need for my influence will eventually cease for—believe me—I've a tremendous dislike of playing the god in men's affairs. I am absolutely stuck having to do this to them for the present, because for the life of me I can't think of any way around it. If there is a way out, I shall take it, and if you've any better ideas I should gladly hear them."

"None at the moment. But the changes you are making within them are for the better. Surely that mitigates some of your strong feeling against using your talent for influence?"

"Oliver, how many times have you writhed inside when someone told you that they were doing something awful to you simply because it was for your own good?"

He thought that one over, then said, "Oh."

"And recall your feelings when you remembered how Nora had dealt with you back at Cambridge. It was for your good as well as hers that you should forget your liaisons with her and what she did with you, but still . . ." I spread the fingers of one hand, using a gesture to complete the thought.

"Oh." He gulped, the corners of his mouth turning earthward in a bleak frown.

"Indeed. And again, where does one stop? Who am I to decide whose soul is in need of improvement and whose is not? Who am I to decide what's best for me is also best for another? Remember how you felt when you found out I was influencing you into not noticing my 'eccentricities,' as you call them? It wasn't so intrusive as to make a major change in your life, but I still hated doing it, especially to you of all people. Before God, as hard as it was to go through at the time, I am most thankful that you walked in on me and Miss Jemma that night in the Red Swan or else I might yet be having to gull you of the truth."

He went very pink around the ears and nose and made a business of clearing his throat before speaking again. "No need to be so harsh on yourself, Coz. You did what you thought was necessary and explained things to me quick enough. I don't think badly of you, y'know, for I do understand why you had to do it. All's forgiven and forgot, I hope."

A little wave of relief washed through me and I nodded.

"Well, then, that's that." He gave a shake and shrug of his shoulders. "But just to end my curiosity on the topic for good and all . . ."

In a comical manner I groaned, raising my eyes to heaven, making us both laugh. We needed it, the relief of it, it seemed. "What is it?" I asked after we'd settled ourselves.

"I was just wondering that since you're already influencing Ridley and Arthur, you might think of it in terms of in for a penny, in for a pound."

"Think of what?"

"Of influencing Clarinda, of course. You mentioned it as a possibility earlier."

"A possibility I'm not ready to undertake for all those reasons I've just set before you. Besides, before you took the bit and ran with it, I'd been about to add that I'm also very doubtful it would work on her."

"Why so?"

I hesitated, making a face. "If she's mad—and it is my admittedly unqualified opinion that she is—then it won't work very well—if at all."

"How do you know that? Oh, do stop glowering and tell me."

I stopped glowering and sighed instead. "All right. The first night I was in London I paid a midnight call on Tony Warburton—"

"You *what?*"

"—and tried to find out if he knew anything about Nora's whereabouts." Before being struck down by sudden insanity, Tony had been an especially close friend of Oliver's at Cambridge. He was now one of Oliver's patients.

"The Warburtons never mentioned this to me," he said.

"Because they didn't know about it. I let myself in through a window and left in the same manner."

"What, like the way you passed through Ridley's door that time, and how you get from the cellar to your room here?"

"Exactly the same way."

"And you then influenced him?"

"Tried to. It didn't work. I just couldn't catch hold of his mind—like trying to pick up a drop of mercury with your fingers."

"But what has this to do with Clarinda? She may be as she is, but she's not mad that I can see."

"Are there not kinds of madness that are less obvious to the eye?"

"Of course there are."

"Then my feeling is that Clarinda might be in that number. My mother's like that."

"But I thought your mother yells a lot, then goes into fits."

"She does, but most of the time she's merely disagreeable. When she's with people other than her family, she gets on quite well. One might think of her as being somewhat highly strung, but otherwise unremarkable. I've seen her being very cordial, even charming when she puts some effort into it. She's all right as long as she can keep hold of her temper. Only when her grasp slips does she go flying off into one of her fits and shows all that she's kept hidden about herself."

"I saw no sign of that sort of temper with Clarinda, but then, as you say, her madness must surely be of a different kind. She hides it well enough."

"It's the madness of being so single-minded that she will overcome all obstacles by any means possible in order to obtain what she wants."

"But lots of people are like that," he protested. "Just look at the House of Commons."

"True, but for the most part I don't think they normally run about arranging duels, committing murder, and shutting their spouses into tombs preparatory to shooting them dead to achieve their goals."

"Granted, but doesn't all that just make her clever rather than mad?"

"Good God, Oliver, listen to yourself!"

Apparently he did, and went flame red in reaction. "Yes, I see what you mean. I believe I've been hanging about with you too much, I'm starting to sound like a lawyer, trying to offer a defense when there is none. Very well then, you're telling me that because Clarinda has a touch of hidden—for the most part—madness, you don't think your influence will work on her?"

"Perhaps for a time, but I'd not want to trust my life or another's on it. I couldn't do anything with poor Tony because his mind just isn't there to be touched; Clarinda's is—but it's much too focused and strong to hold for any length of time."

I'd been able to make her forget my unorthodox entry to her temporary prison at Fonteyn House; that was one thing, but to change the very pattern of her will was quite something else again. Add to that my own still very caustic feelings toward her and the likelihood of successfully turning her about became a very remote, if not impossible expectation.

"But how can you be sure without trying it?"

"My mother," I said, not looking at him.

"You mean you tried to influence her?"

I felt myself color a bit in my turn. "Yes. Once. I tried to get her to stop being so cruel to Father. It didn't last long, not long at all. I'm not proud of what I did, either, so promise me on your word of honor that you'll say nothing to him about it."

My tone was so forceful he immediately gave me his solemn pledge of silence.

"From what I've heard from you about Nora and the Warburtons," I continued, "I'm sure that she's been trying to help Tony in the same way, to influence him out of his madness."

"She did spend a goodly time with him when they were all in Italy—or so his mother told me."

"With indifferent results, sad to say." For the present it seemed best I not inform Oliver about Nora causing Tony's madness in the first place. No, that wasn't precisely true. Not at all true, in fact.

Tony had been mad to start with; Nora's influence merely sent him more deeply into its embrace. Perhaps later I might tell Oliver the whole story of that dreadful night when Tony tried to murder Nora and me, but not just now.

"I wonder why she stopped visiting him?" he asked, leaning well back in his chair to gaze at the ceiling.

A long moment passed as I tried to dredge up the words to answer. It was proving unexpectedly difficult to cast them into speech. They felt sticky, hardly able to release themselves from my throat. "Tony said . . . said that she was ill."

"Ill?" He looked hard at me, brows drawing together. "What from, I wonder?"

I spread my hands. "I just don't . . ."

He perceived the sudden rawness of my feelings well enough and, sitting forward once more, raised a hand to make a hushing gesture. "There now, don't come apart on me just yet, you'll make the most awful mess on the floor if you do."

An abrupt choking seized me. Laughter. Brief, but it seemed to clear things inside. Trust my good cousin to know exactly when and how best to play the fool. "Sorry," I mumbled, feeling somewhat sheepish. "It's just that whenever I think about it, that she might be lying sick and helpless somewhere, I come all over—"

"Yes, I know, it's as plain as day—or as night, in your case. No need to feel badly about feeling bad, y'know. Did Tony say anything at all about the nature of her illness?"

"Couldn't get anything else out of him. Maybe he didn't know."

"But his mother might. She's very fond of Nora, very touched by her kindness to Tony, y'see. I'll call 'round first thing tomorrow and have a nice talk with her."

"But you've already questioned Mrs. Warburton ages ago."

"And time and again since, lest we forget. She made no mention of Nora being ill, either. On the other hand, that's the one question I managed not to ask her. Can't make promises, though. It's been so long and her main concern is ever for Tony. The lady might not remember anything useful."

I heaved from my chair, needing to pace the room. My belly was twisting around again from an idea I did not care for one whit. "Oh, God."

My manner puzzled Oliver. " 'Oh, God' what?"

"Oh, God in heaven, why am I in such a cleft stick?"

"What cleft stick?"

"The one where I spend all this time telling you the worthy reasons why I should abstain from influencing people, and now I see an equally worthy reason to use it again."

"On Mrs. Warburton?" His brows shot upward, his eyes going very wide. "You mean you could influence her into a better memory for a past event?"

"Saying one thing and then wanting to do another," I snarled, but to myself, not to him.

Oliver watched open mouthed as I made a few fast turns about the room. "What are you on about? You *are* thinking of influencing Mrs. Warburton, are you not?"

"I'm a damned hypocrite, that's what I am."

He shook his head at me. "A damned fool, you mean."

"Yes, I'm sure of it. To inflict it upon some innocent woman is—"

"It's positively brilliant! I see where you got the idea, if you and Nora are capable of making people forget certain things, then you're just as capable of helping them to remember others. This is marvelous."

"It's deceitful . . . dishonorable . . ."

"Oh, rubbish! It's not as though you were changing the woman's life—and if not precisely honorable, then it's certainly nothing harmful. Heavens, man, you could even ask her permission to do so."

That stopped me exactly in my tracks. "*What?*"

"Ask her permission," he said clearly and slowly.

"How the devil could I do that? I'd have to tell her all about myself and—"

"No, you wouldn't. You think you have to explain yourself to everyone you meet? Vanity, Coz, beware of vanity. If her memory isn't up to the work, then all you have to do is tell her you have a way of refreshing it and ask if she's willing to try. She doesn't have to know *how* you do it, only that you can and that it is perfectly harmless. I'll be there to back you up. Now what do you say?"

*Asking permission.* It was so obvious I felt like one of nature's great blockheads. Perhaps I should put myself on display at Vauxhall or Ranleigh for the entertainment of the crowds.

"If she tells you it's all right, then your conscience is clear, ain't it?" he asked in the manner of a person for whom only one answer will suffice.

"I . . . that is . . ."

"Excellent! I knew you'd be sensible. I'll just tell her that it's something you learned how to do in America. People will believe *anything* you tell them about that land, no matter how outré, y'know."

Oliver went off to supper, leaving me alone in his study to find my own amusement. I did not ordinarily join in on any of the evening meals as the odor of all that cooked food in a confined space was overwhelming to my heightened sense of smell. Here, though, I found a degree of relief from its unseen presence, and if things got too much for me I could always open a window. So far, there was no need to let in the winter cold, and when he returned Oliver would find his room as warm and comfortable as he'd left it.

With weary resignation I seated myself at his desk, found paper, a pen with a good clean nib, and opened the ink bottle.

Time to write to Father.

As I began the salutation and paused to gather my wits, the fervent hope stabbed through me that he was already on his way to England, making this missive unnecessary. *Selfish, Johnny Boy,* I thought.

Extremely selfish it was of me to want to place him on a freezing cold ship crossing a dangerous winter sea just to spare me a bit of letter writing. Yes, that was the light explanation for it. The heavy truth was that I very much wanted to see him again, to have his dear face before me, and to hear his voice. Try as I might, I could find no fault in that wish, for I knew it would be his as well.

Like any other chore, the hardest part was in the mere starting, and once this was achieved I was more of a mind to keep at it until it was finished. I began writing steadily, filling page after page with a recountal of events since Elizabeth, Jericho, and I had first made landfall in England. So much had happened, so many details, events, and speculations rushed at me, that I had to make notes to myself on a bit of used paper to be sure they were all included.

I scratched and scribbled away, hoping Father would be able to read my handwriting without too much difficulty, taking pains to go slower over the more involved bits of narrative so it would be clear to the eye as well as to the mind. One memory jogged another as I set it all down, and I was only occasionally aware of my surroundings, now and then noticing a footstep in the hall without, the snap of the coal in the fireplace, or the wind outside trying to pierce its way through the window. Twice I got up to throw coal on the fire, more to give myself a respite to stretch and think what to write next than for any need of warmth on my part.

The candles on the desk burned down to the point where fresh ones were needed. Rather than halt my work by calling for them, or even opening the curtains to the general glow of the night sky, I simply thieved more from the sconces on either side of the mantel, shoving them into the desk holders.

Some portions of the letter were easier to write than others. Surprising to myself, my past liaison with Clarinda proved to be the easiest of all to get through. I'd resolved to tell it plainly and make no apologies for my actions or hers. Father was a man of the world in his own right, having a dearly loved mistress as well as an estranged wife, so I had no doubt he would clearly understand the needs of passion when they so firmly seized hold of me. I did, however, make it clear to him my surprise and regret at finding Clarinda to be married and of my sober intention to avoid a repetition of the circumstance with other ladies. I then told him that there was a very good reason why I had written at all about my encounter with her, and so word by word and page by page, as I told all there was to tell about Clarinda's now broken plans, I led up to the subject of Richard.

Again I surprised myself, for now the ease of writing deserted me. I could not seem to put pen to paper about him for very long. Each time I tried, my mind wandered off in a dreamy speculation of a happy future, rather than framing a solid report of the happy present. How that child could lay hold of my mind and keep hold of it—had my father felt this way about me at my birth? Perhaps, though, he'd have had several months to anticipate the event, thus getting used to the prospect of having another baby in the house. Richard had been—to grossly understate it—a complete surprise.

At least I could and did say with all truth that there was no question in my mind whatsoever about the child's paternity, adding that I considered myself to be one of the most fortunate of all men. I added also that unless upon finding Nora and she told me otherwise, Richard was like to be my only child because of my changed condition. With that in mind I expressed the profound wish that Father would receive the news he was a grandparent as joyfully as I gave it.

After that, I couldn't think of anything else to say. His acceptance of Richard meant much to me. He would or he would not, but I had every confidence in his love for me and felt he would have no trouble welcoming my son into his own heart as well as I had myself.

I blotted the last page and shuffled them into order like a huge pack of flimsy playing cards. They'd make a sizable parcel and would cost a fortune to post. Well, it wasn't as though I didn't have the money for it. I rolled the letter into a cylinder and tied it up with a bit of string filched from a drawer. Then I wrote a short note to Elizabeth, asking her to wrap it up and post it for me.

The thought came to me on the wisdom of making a copy of the thing. That might not be a bad idea, especially should something adverse happen to this pile of paper while en route to Long Island. But to do all that work over again? Ugh. Though I could easily *have* the whole thing copied for a modest fee. . . .

Oh.

Good heavens, no. I snorted at myself for being such a fool.

To hire someone, to allow some stranger a look at the intimate doings of the Fonteyns and their relations? That was impossible—not to mention ridiculous. The schemes, lying, adultery, assaults, and murder? No, no, no, far better and safer to keep all that within the family where it belonged. I'd do the copying myself.

Then all I had to do was hope neither letter fell into the wrong hands.

Well-a-day, maybe I should have used *that* as an argument with Elizabeth against writing the whole lot down to start with and saved myself an evening's toil. Too late now. For that matter, how late was it, anyway?

When I finally glanced up at the mantel clock, the hour shocked me. Listening closely for a minute or so, I determined the whole house was fast asleep and had likely been so for a long time. If I wanted company to help me pass the meager remains of the night it would have to be chatting with the watch again or reading another book.

Or copy work.

I shuddered and pushed away from the desk. It could keep until tomorrow night; I'd devoted quite enough time on the project.

Quite enough and quite a lot, since I'd been left alone for nearly the whole of the night. In this mild form of abandonment, I sensed Elizabeth's hand. Guessing that I might be writing to Father, she'd probably told Oliver all about it and had cautioned him against a return to his study lest he interrupt the task. If I grew tired of the work, I'd be out to visit them in the parlor. Since I hadn't once emerged, she was likely to be quite pleased with me. I thought of confronting her about it tomorrow and teasing her a bit by saying I'd spent the whole time reading old magazines. It would serve her right for knowing me so well as to predict my behavior with such accuracy.

But my inclination for mischief passed; it occurred to me that Jericho might also have had something to do with it. He possessed an uncanny ability for understanding and predicting the actions not only of me but of others if given enough time to come to acquaint himself with them, and he knew me better than I did myself. He would be aware of Elizabeth's wish for me to write—he knew all the goings-on of the house—and would have arranged for me to work on undisturbed. A keen observer of life was my good friend and valet.

I found evidence of this in the central hall. On a narrow settee he'd laid out my heavy cloak, hat, walking shoes, gloves, and stick, anticipating that I'd want to take a turn about the early morning streets before diving into my cellar sanctuary for the day. Not wanting to disappoint him, I donned the things and quietly let myself out without bothering to open the entry door.

It was a fine clear night, if windy. I had to keep a tight hold on my hat lest it go flying. The ends of my cloak whipped about as though alive and trying to make good an escape from my shoulders. Finally giving up on the hat, I held it close to my chest with one hand and bravely walked into the wind with my cloak streaming behind like a great woolen flag. Not an arrangement to protect one from the elements, but I wasn't one to feel the cold as sharply as other people do. My chief annoyance was the way its collar tie tugged like a hangman's rope at my throat. I thought it might be better after all to turn back to the house and fill the time with a book, but I'd been physically idle for hours and my body craved exercise. Though the wind was a nuisance, it freshened the air marvelously, a rare thing in London, inviting me to partake of it while it lasted. Coming hard out of the north, it reminded me of the wholesome landscape of the country and my desire to eventually move there.

The street was empty, though the tumbling of a stray newspaper and the constant dance on either hand of tree branches in the breeze made it seem less so. The creaks and whispers they made unnerved me at first until I grew used to the sound. Not so for a dog I heard occasionally giving vent to his unease by barking.

Most of the houses had lamps burning outside to aid in the lighting and thus the safety of the street. Oliver's was one of their number because of his profession. Once or twice since moving in, I'd witnessed him being called forth on a late medical errand, and it was best for all concerned that his door be easily found by those in need.

Within the houses all must have been peaceful with sleep, though now and then I'd see candlelight showing through the curtains or shutters. When I did, it was always my hope that it was simply an early riser or another wakeful soul passing the night in study, rather than sickness.

I found the watch, in the person of an elderly man named Dunnett, uneasily dozing on his feet in his narrow box. He wore two cloaks wrapped close about his sturdy frame and a long muffler wound around his hat and head against the bitterness of the night, but the way he huddled in them gave me to understand they were somewhat inadequate to the task. So light was his sleep that he jerked awake at my soft approach, his startled gaze meeting mine in an instant of fearful suspicion until he recognized me.

"Good e'nin', Mr. Barrett," he said, rubbing his red nose with the back of his gloved hand. "Up early or out late ag'in? That is, 'f y' don't mind my askin'."

"Good morning to you, Mr. Dunnett. I'm out late, as always."

"Mus' be rare 'ard for a youngun like you to 'ave such trouble findin' sleep."

"Oh, it comes to me eventually. All quiet tonight?"

"Aye, too cold for the bully boys, I'm thinkin'. Saw 'alf a dozen o' them Mohocks earlier tonight. Gave me a turn. I was afeared they'd be makin' some grief, but they left me alone, thanks be to God."

"I'm glad to hear that." The night watch, mainly composed of unarmed old men, was ever a favorite target for the malice of the city's rowdy element.

"A foolish lot they are, but mebe too cold fer their pranks. 'Tis fine with me."

"Any other visitors aside from them?"

"None as I could see. 'S been rare quiet tonight. 'S I said, 'tis fine with me."

"What, not even footpads?" I asked, pretending surprise.

" 'Tain't no one out fer 'em to rob," he said with a cackle. " 'Ceptin' me, 'n' I don't 'ave nothin'. There's you, but I 'eard as 'ow you c'n take care o' yerself."

"You have? Where?—if you don't mind my asking."

" 'Eard it 'round o'r by the Red Swan. I done a favor f' the landlord 'n' he sees I get a tot o' rum once a night 'f it's to me fancy." From the look of the many veins decorating his nose, one could deduce it suited Dunnett's fancy very well indeed.

I knew about his favor. The Red Swan's chief business was not the sort to have the approval of the law. According to Oliver—himself a regular customer there—Mr. Dunnett had warned the landlord of an impending raid from the forces of justice and decency in time to save the establishment from serious damage. The story went that the raiding party burst into the place ready to face the worst kind of resistance this side of a battlefield, only to find it occupied by a large group of Quakers having some sort of a meeting.

There was vast disappointment on all sides once they worked out their business—the raiders had no one to arrest, and the Quakers failed to interest any of the newcomers in joining them on the closing prayer. Both sides eventually retired unbloodied from the field to go their separate ways. The next day the Swan was open for normal custom, free now of the harassment from the forces of morality because of a well-placed bribe from the landlord.

Dunnett said, "I was in 'avin' me tot not long back, 'n 'eard some gentlemen drinkin' to yer very good 'ealth."

I smiled, feeling absurdly pleased. "Some friends of mine, I suppose, or my cousin Oliver."

"Friends," he confirmed with a nod. "I know Dr. Marlin' well enough. Many's the time I've seen 'im staggerin' from 'is coach to 'is front door when 'e's had a bit o' fun. Always 'as a friendly word for me no matter 'ow much 'e's swilled."

"That's Oliver and no mistake. But you didn't know these men to name? If someone's toasting my health it's only right I should return the courtesy."

"Not to name, nosir, but I've seen one or two of 'em visitin' the doctor now 'n' then. One was a 'andsome perky chap with a mole right 'ere," Mr. Dunnett pointed to a spot on his nose. "I noticed 'im special for it, 'n' for 'im bein' the one t' name you 'n 'is toast. Talked all 'bout that duel you was in, called you a real fire-eater, sir. Those were 'is very words. So that's 'ow I 'eard 'bout you takin' care o' yerself so well."

I felt my face going red, and not from the wind. "I know the fellow," I admitted. The mole on the nose was the clue; he could only have been Brinsley Bolyn. Since the night of my duel with Ridley, young Mr. Bolyn had become my most devoted admirer and supporter. Good lord, but I'd have to find a polite way of asking him not to be so free with his enthusiasm or I'd have no end of challenges from men wanting to test themselves against me. I could fight, but had an unfair advantage over them in terms of strength, speed, and an unnatural ability to heal from even a mortal wound. Besides, unlike most of them, I had killed before and found no pleasure in it.

Dunnett noticed the change in my expression. "Not a friend o' yers, sir?"

I quickly sorted myself and laughed a little. "He's a friend, but he's doing me no favors with such praise, however well intentioned."

"I see 'ow it is, sir," he said with a quick wink. "Too much talk like that makes it 'ard to live up to the 'onor."

"Exactly. You're a most perceptive man, Mr. Dunnett."

"I do wot I can, sir."

"And very well indeed."

"Thank you kindly, sir, 'n' bless you," he said in response to the shilling I slipped him. I bade him a good morning and began to walk away, but he hailed for me to stop a moment more. "There's one thing botherin' me 'bout them Mohocks, sir."

He had my full attention. "What would that be?"

"They walked right past me without hardly a look—which as I've said, 's fine with me. But 's been my experience that they always 'ave at least a curse or two to throw at me. Nothin' like that tonight. They just walked past, lookin' at all the houses like a pack o' damned foreigners. It was dark 'n' they was a ways down so I couldn't see too good, but I think they was payin' some extra mind to yer 'ouse—Dr. Marlin's 'ouse, that is."

I certainly didn't like the sound of this. "Staring at it, you mean?"

"That's what I'm not too sure of, sir. 'F it'd been plain I'd 'ave come 'round to let you know about it, but it wasn't, so I didn't. The 'pression I got was they might 'a' looked at it a bit longer than the other 'ouses, 'n' for that I can't rightly swear to on a Bible. Just thought I should mention it now since yer 'ere 'n' all. I don't mean t' be troubling 'r worryin' ye'."

"Not at all, Mr. Dunnett, as I see it, you're only doing your duty. I'm very grateful you told me. Do you recall what time they came by?"

"Not long after midnight, 'f the church bells rang true."

By then I'd have been deeply occupied with my letter writing and the rest of the house asleep. It may have been nothing, but recent events gave me many excellent reasons to be cautious. Also, though I was endeavoring to bring a change for the better to Ridley and Arthur, it did not mean their friends would also be favorably affected by such reformation.

This time I pressed a handful of shillings into Dunnett's hand, and he was sufficiently overwhelmed to start protesting that it was too much. "Not nearly enough," I said. "If ever you see anything of a similar nature in the future, I want you to come straight to the house as soon as you're able and let me know about it. You need have no fear of waking me no matter how late the hour—that is to say, if I'm home. If I'm not, then you be sure to tell Dr. Marling or Miss Barrett or Jericho, understand? I'll see to it they hear what you've just told me."

"You 'specting' trouble?"

"Not expecting, but it suits me to know all I can about anything to do with Mohocks. That duel I fought may not be quite finished yet. Friends of the man who lost might want to reopen the contest, but not on the field of honor, if you take my meaning."

"God bless you, sir, I understand clear as day. Y' can count on me."

I bade him a good morning and continued along the street, wanting to stretch my legs and needing to think. Neither activity took very long. I walked fast and thought faster.

Tomorrow night, before anything else, I'd pay a call upon Ridley and see to it he kept his friends in check. Arthur Tyne would also briefly receive me as his guest, like it or not. I didn't believe either man to be much, if any sort, of a threat to me or my family now, but had learned to value caution over carelessness.

Of course, the Mohocks Mr. Dunnett had observed might have had nothing to do with Ridley. There were dozens, if not hundreds of their ilk roaming the city at all hours of the night. Word of the duel might have reached some kindred group and they'd only come to look at the house out of a sense of curiosity and nothing more.

And, of course, I was not prepared to believe *that.*

Even knowing it was much too late by now to look for any sign of their band, I surrendered to the desire to take in a broader view of the area. Tucking the ends of my cloak close around my body, I gave the street a quick glance up and down to make sure it was deserted. Only then did I vanish. The world faded to a gray nothingness, though I soon had ample evidence of its continued existence despite my apparent leaving of it.

Well-a-day, but I'd underestimated the *wind.*

The beastly stuff must have blown me a good hundred yards before I knew what was happening. It tumbled me about as easily as that discarded newspaper, and I had to fight it with more than the usual effort of will required for this mode of movement. The wind felt every bit as solid to me without a visible body as with one. After a stint of hard work I managed to force my way back and upward until I reckoned myself to be well above the tops of the immediate houses. Then did I take on the barest amount of solidity to see exactly where I'd gotten myself.

I was just within sight of Mr. Dunnett's box and silently crowed with an inward congratulation I certainly didn't deserve, for it had all been luck. I hovered over this one place a moment, decided it was possible for me to continue with this folly despite the weather, then went higher. The wind slacked off a bit, easing my work. Doubtless its strength was worse closer to the ground, being whipped up by its passage between all the city's many buildings, like that of a river being forced to flow between the pylons of a bridge. The more narrow their placement, the greater the speed of the water.

When I was well over the tops of the tallest chimneys and holding in one spot like a kite on a string, I gave all the streets within range of my cloudy vision a thorough examination. All was as I'd expected, quiet and unremarkable—if one could describe so unorthodox a view as such. I chided myself for taking this aspect of my miraculous condition for granted.

Below stretched the walkways and cobbled streets, some empty, others showing scatterings of people either starting to wake for the coming day or trudging wearily off to bed from the closing night. None of their number looked to be Mohocks; on that point I was torn between annoyance and relief.

Relief, I finally decided. If I'd spotted any of them from my high prospect I might have been tempted to investigate their business, and that might have led to all sorts of unpleasant and time-consuming complications. The morning would be here soon to send me into another day's oblivion. I'd have my fun tomorrow night. For now, I would have to put away my worry since there was nothing I could do about it and try to enjoy my remaining moments of consciousness.

Not a difficult task, that.

Except for a rare balloonist, no others would ever share this sight; I was one of a tiny number and needed to be more aware of and thankful for the privilege. A cartographer drawing at his map might also have so fascinating a view, though all would have to take place in his imagination. He could measure out the streets and write their names, even add tiny squares to his work to mark individual houses, but could never put in all the details as I saw them. Could he see the shadows of the people coming and going from those houses and wonder how their lives and fortunes fared? Could he fill his flat paper streets with the movement of life that I observed like a god from on high? Perhaps he did to some extent, but he could never actually see and know it as I did. It was glorious and at the same time sadly dispiriting. My dismay came from the knowledge I could not share this with anyone. I was doing the impossible and though exhilarating beyond imagining, it was also unutterably lonely.

I thought of Nora. Of all the people of the earth, she was the *only* one who could possibly understand my feeling, could possibly share it, cherish it.

Though she must certainly possess this ability, I'd never heard her speak of doing it. She was ever careful to keep the differences of her changed nature well hidden, using her own talent for influencing others to maintain the illusion she was no different from any other normal woman.

But she was different. Different because I *loved* her.

The remembrance of her face, her voice swept over me more strongly than the wind. I twisted like a leaf and began to descend. Swiftly.

The need to keep that illusion was important to her. I'd seen how it had been when, with the cruel thrust of a blade, Tony Warburton had torn it away from her.

I spiraled down, down, down, skimming close to the harsh brick of the buildings.

*Where are you, Nora? Why did you let me go? Why did you not tell me what would happen?*

I took on solidity. Weight.

Perhaps she'd been unwilling to share her knowledge with me because of that need to pretend. God knows she was reticent enough with all else.

I dropped faster.

Perhaps she thought her silence had all been for my own good.

Faster.

Perhaps she'd been unsure of my love for her, or worse, unsure of her own for me.

With a jolt that shot right through my spine I landed hard on the cobbles. The violence of the impact was too great for my legs to bear. A bone snapped. I heard the sickening crack quite clearly. I fell and rolled. The pain followed but a second later, wrenching from me a strangled cry. I sprawled on the freezing cold street trying to writhe away from the torment.

Perhaps . . . she'd never really loved me at all.

# CHAPTER 6

"Melancholia," Oliver pronounced, glaring at me from his chair by the parlour fire.

I said nothing, only shrugged, though I tended toward full agreement with him.

"It must be from all this black stuff hanging from the windows and mirrors," Elizabeth put in, also favoring me with a dour look as she stirred her tea. "And having the curtains being drawn all the time so as not to offend the neighbors."

"Oh, that will soon change," Oliver said, reaching for a biscuit. "And I'll not care who's offended. God knows Mother never worried about offending people—but back to your good brother's complaint—put those things together with it being winter and all, and without a doubt you have a rampant case of melancholia."

"What will you do about it?" she asked him.

"An outing is in order, I think. Nothing like a change of scenery to change one's outlook. Didn't he say he wanted to go to the bookstalls and hunt for plays?"

"Yes. He promised our cousin Ann . . ."

And so they went on, drinking their tea and talking about me as though I wasn't there. All intentional, of course, sounding almost rehearsed. I stood it patiently.

Melancholia was a fairly close description for my state after all.

Earlier this evening my hour with Richard had helped, but only for that hour. Once he was tucked away and well asleep I tiredly trudged off to my own room for Jericho to repair the damage wrought by playing with a lively four-year-old. He caught me up on the day's events and, as he brushed out my coat, cautiously asked if I'd enjoyed my walk the night before. I told him I had, offering no explanation for the condition of my clothes, made filthy from my fall to the street.

The broken bone in my leg from that abrupt landing had mended with my next vanishing, which had taken place soon after the pain jarred me into a brief period of common sense. Brief, I say, for it fled from me quickly enough. Despondency about Nora seized my spirit once more, slowing my steps toward home even as the vanguard of dawn began to creep over the eastern sky. The watery light was nothing to the early risers I passed, but blinding to me. For all that I held to a perverse need to risk myself—that, or I simply did not care what happened.

Despite my deliberately laggard progress, I managed to reach my bed in the cellar with time to spare. With time to think.

And I did not want to think.

I'd cast off my cloak and shoes and stretched out on the bags of earth that served as my grave for the day and tried very, very hard not to use my mind. And failed. Miserably. Nora's face was the last image I saw before oblivion finally came and the first there at its departure. I could still almost see her, in the corner of my eye, in the flame of a candle, in the shadows of an unlighted corner—almost, for invariably when I looked more closely, she disappeared.

Trying to escape the phantasms, I'd eventually come downstairs to join my sister and cousin, mumbling only the most minimal acknowledgments to their greetings. Oliver immediately remarked that I looked like a dejected gravedigger and inquired why, since last night I'd been fairly cheerful. My vague reply was anything but satisfactory to either of them, and that must have set things in motion.

Their rapport with each other had now grown to the point that with the exchange of a single look they were able to conduct quite a detailed discussion without uttering a word. The conclusion they reached on the best course of action to take soon manifested itself in this rather artificial conversation about me. I took no offense from it since the overall bent was to eventually put me into a good mood. I wasn't adverse to the idea of a change to a more pleasant state of heart, but my spirits were so low that I couldn't see how they'd ever succeed.

However, their obvious concern touched me enough that I at last roused myself to speak in an effort to at least meet them part of the way.

"I'd prefer not to go to Paternoster Row," I said, interrupting them. Both looked at me expectantly. "Not yet, anyhow. Perhaps a little later."

"Where, then?" asked Elizabeth.

"The Everitts house."

She raised her brows slightly, knowing the Everitts to be one-time neighbors to Nora Jones.

"I just thought I could look in, find out if they've heard any news about Nora since Oliver's last visit."

She promptly expressed her full approval of my errand. Being familiar with all my moods, she was fully aware of the usual reason behind my past despondencies, and saw the proposal as a means to lift this one.

"Would you like some company?" Oliver asked, trying to hold to a neutral tone, but still managing to express hopefulness.

"Very much so, Coz. What about you, good sister?"

"I've had more than my share of London for now, thank you very much." She'd spent nearly the whole day out with Mrs. Howard and Richard, shopping for carpets. Their choices were to arrive sometime tomorrow along with Elizabeth's new spinet.

"Probably just as well," I said. "I'll feel easier knowing you're here to look after things." It was then I told them about my conversation with Mr. Dunnett and the men he'd seen looking at the house last night.

"Damned Mohocks," Oliver growled, for once forgetting to apologize to Elizabeth about his language. "Something should be done about 'em."

"Not to worry. If I see them, I most certainly will do something about them," I promised.

"Well, it can't be safe leaving Elizabeth on her own with those louts lurking about."

Elizabeth snorted. "I'll be safe enough if Jonathan loans me his Dublin revolver. Besides, the staff here has nearly doubled in the last week. I'll just warn them to keep their eyes open, the doors bolted, and have a club handy."

"It's a disgrace," he complained. "Decent people having to go about in terror of a lot of worthless bullies with no more manners than a pack of wild dogs—it's just not right."

"No, but I'll be fine, nonetheless."

"One of us should stay here with you."

"Leaving the other to wander the city all unprotected? I think not, Coz. Now you both go along before it gets too late to visit and find out what you may about Miss Jones, and I wish you the best of luck at it."

With this combined blessing and firm dismissal upon our heads, Oliver rang for someone to tell the driver to ready his horses and carriage, then shot off to his room to ready himself. He didn't get past the lower hall; Jericho was coming down the stairs with our cloaks, hats, and canes. He must have heard my proposal for an expedition out and made suitable preparation.

"You're even more uncanny than your master," Oliver remarked, staring at the things.

Jericho's eyelids dipped to half-mast and his lips thinned into a near-smile. I understood that look; he was insufferably pleased with himself. He helped us don the cloaks—he'd long since retrieved mine from the cellar and brushed it thoroughly clean—and handed over our canes. Oliver's was topped by a fine knob of gold, marking him as a medical man; mine was less ostentatious, but still identified me as a gentleman of means. Hidden within its length was a yard of good Spanish steel that would also identify me as a gentleman of sense to any footpad or Mohock. I thought of carrying along one of my duelers as well, but decided it was unnecessary. The two of us, along with the driver and two footmen, would likely be safe enough even on London's dark streets.

Of course, they were not at all dark for me. Another advantage in our favor.

The carriage was brought along to the front, and I took this time to excuse myself, passing quickly through the house as a shortcut to the stables. They would be empty of activity for a short time while the men and lads were busy. I slipped inside, patting Rolly and by way of a greeting slipped him a stolen carrot from the kitchen. Forbidden fruit—or in this case vegetables—must taste best, for he crunched it down with obvious relish. Moving on to Oliver's riding horse, I offered him the same treat. The bribe was greedily accepted. In return, I just as greedily supped on a quantity of his blood and felt the better for it. Last night's efforts and injury had used me up, leaving my body in sore need of refreshment.

This admirable provender, on top of the prospect of our outing, was beginning to have a favorable effect on me already. I didn't really expect the Everitts to have any fresh news, but it felt good just to be able to make the effort to find out for certain. Besides, whatever the outcome, the trip we'd planned afterward to Paternoster Row held more attractions for me than mere shopping for plays. This was London, a city all but bursting with women and opportunities to share their company. If I could not immediately find Nora and settle my questions with her, then I might, for a while at least, find distraction with someone else. Not the same, of course—of that I was very well aware—but passing time with a pretty lady had ever been the best way I'd found for gladdening a sorrowful heart.

Yet another excellent reason to refresh myself. Should things work out as I hoped, I'd not want my prospective liaison spoiled by the needs of my body confusing lust with hunger. I could and had fed on human blood before when forced to by dire need, but when partaking the pleasures of a woman, it was best for us both that I kept control over my appetite. Thus could I prolong our mutual enjoyment without worrying about causing harm to my partner by taking too much from her. Such was the way of it for most men, food first, then love, and so I was unchanged from my fellows in that respect, at least.

Necessity seen to and finished, I hurried 'round the house and climbed into the carriage with Oliver.

"What kept y—oh!" he said, when he caught a glimpse of my reddened eyes in the lantern light.

"They'll be all cleared up by the time we get to the Everitts," I assured him.

"I'm glad to hear it. Most alarming when one doesn't expect it. You sure it doesn't hurt?"

"Can't feel a thing."

He grunted, then called directions to the driver, who in turn called them to the two footmen. They ran with their torches just ahead of the horses, lighting our way. The lot of them had come from the staff of Fonteyn House. Rather than dismissal, since for the time being there was little work for them there, Oliver had moved them to his house in town and kept them busy. He was still getting used to the idea of having to deal with his vast inheritance, and taking the weight of it in this manner, a little at a time.

I didn't talk much during the ride, content to let Oliver rattle on about his day. He'd paid a call on Tony Warburton and chatted with Mrs. Warburton about her son. Eventually he'd led the conversation around to Nora.

"I made out that Tony had muttered something to me about Nora being ill," he said. "Then I asked his mother if she knew what he was talking about. She didn't."

"You're certain about that—I mean—she's certain?"

"Very certain. There's no need for you to jog her memory with your influence, so your conscience may rest easy now. Her recollections of Nora's time with them in Italy are most vivid. What with the girl's kindness for Tony, Mrs. Warburton was quite taken with her. Hung on her every word, if you know what I mean. Anyway, the last she recalled, Nora was fair blooming with health, though perhaps a bit troubled over something."

"Over what?"

"That I could not say, for the lady herself could not say. She asked if all was well with Nora, and was told that things were fine. Still and all, she was a bit surprised when Nora didn't turn up in London that summer as she'd practically promised to do so in order to look in on Tony. I know it's all the same as I'd written before, but at least you know Nora isn't ill."

"It could have been something sudden," I said, unwilling to relinquish the worry so easily. "Something to keep her on the Continent."

"It could," he admitted. "But you must try to be optimistic, old lad. Your constitution's as tough as a country bull's. Who's to say that Miss Jones is any different?"

Who, indeed?

We arrived at the Everitts, where I came up with a suggestion. "What about you going in and paying your respects while I give Nora's house another quiet looking over? It'll save some time."

"Save time for what?"

"As long as we're out, I've a mind to visit Ridley and Arthur tonight. Maybe we can catch them while they're at supper. If those Mohocks that came by have anything to do with them—"

"Say no more, Coz. I'll hurry things through. I'll say I have other calls to make, else old Everitt will have me up to his study to look at his beetle collection again."

We left the carriage and went our separate ways. As it was still somewhat early and the streets busy with evening traffic, I quietly slipped into the shadowed space between the Everitt's house and Nora's. Free from observation and hidden in the darkness, I vanished and sieved my way into her former home through a shuttered window, returning to solidity in what had once been a music room. Nora hadn't been much for playing herself, but delighted in letting her guests indulge themselves. In one corner crouched the rectangular shape of a spinet and close to it stood a tall harp, both protected by musty shrouds. Similar sheets covered the remaining bits of furniture.

I held still and listened, but already knew that I'd hear nothing but the scurry of rats and mice. She was not here.

My last visit had left me very downhearted. Things were only a little improved now, the chief difference being that my hopes were almost nonexistent; therefore any disappointment awaiting me would not be such a crushing blow.

With the shutters all closed fast the house was almost too dark for even my eyes to see. This time I'd thought to bring a candle and, after a bit of work with my tinderbox, soon had it lighted. As before, I moved ghostlike through all the rooms, and as before I found no sign of recent occupation. There were only my own footprints in the dust.

I'd been wrong about the disappointment. Any blow, even one that's expected, hurts just as much as another.

Dragging from one room to the next and up the stairs, I checked the whole place over. I knew I would find nothing, but went through the motions regardless, just to be thorough. The overall gloom of the house gathered heavily on my soul as I seeped into her own bricked-up sanctuary in the cellar. There she had slept during the day on a large chest that held a store of her home earth. Everything was the same as before. The bags of earth were undisturbed, the air around me still and stuffy and wholly silent. I eased the chest lid down, but my fingers slipped, and the sound boomed off the hard walls of the chamber like a cannon shot.

Damnation.

Noise of any kind was all wrong here. It was like laughing in church. A strict one.

The hair on my neck was all on end. I knew there was nothing and no one else in here with me, but my imagination provided the fancy that this place was occupied by some disapproving guardian who had just been awakened by my clumsiness.

I fled by the fastest means, reappearing again just outside the cellar door, candle still alight, but unsteady because of the tremors in my hand. And I thought I'd conquered my fear of dark, closed-in spaces. It would seem I needed to conduct more work in that area, but not tonight. I scuttled away from the door, firmly denying the frightened child in me from giving in to the strong inclination to glance behind. Nothing had followed me up, because nothing was there in the first place. I wasn't so sure about Oliver, but if Elizabeth had been with me, by now she'd likely be doubled over with laughter at my cowardly flight, I was sure of it.

The last stop was the downstairs parlour to look at the note I'd written and left for Nora on my previous visit. I pushed open the door and my gaze went straight to the mantel . . . but the folded and sealed square of paper I'd placed so carefully there was missing. My heart, suddenly coming to a kind of life again, gave a painful leap against my ribs. It was all I could do to hold on to the candle, and then the flame nearly guttered out in my rush to cross the room for a closer look.

The note was gone, truly, truly gone.

"You're sure a rat didn't eat it?" Oliver asked once he'd come back to the carriage. I'd impatiently given him the news of my discovery twice over, having babbled it out too fast the first time. "I don't mean to throw a blanket on your fire, but one must be certain about these things."

"I understand, and believe me, I did consider it, but if it had been a rat I'd have seen signs in the dust. No, I checked the mantel very carefully, and it was untouched except for a thin line where the paper had rested. I also found footprints in the floor dust. A man's shoes by their size and shape." Possibly one of her servants, I thought, sent to see that all was well with her house.

"Might have been a passing thief, y'know."

"I doubt it could be a thief, the house is still locked up tight—I made sure of that. The only person who could get in would have to have a key. That means it must have been a servant or a house agent."

"Or Miss Jones, slipping in the way you did. But then it was a man's shoe. . . ."

I nodded, my mouth too dry for words.

"Or someone *like* Miss Jones. Have you ever considered there might be more chaps about like you, others to whom she's passed this condition?"

I nodded again, trying to clear my throat. "I have. If there are, then I don't know of them; she never mentioned them to me."

"If you don't mind my saying it, your Miss Jones never mentioned a very great number of things. I should be very severe with her about that when you see her again."

The possibility of seeing her . . . it *was* a possibility once more. My poor heart gave another leap, or seemed to, making me gasp with a half-realized laugh.

Oliver grinned and thumped my back. "Well, then, congratulations, Cousin. This must be the best news you've heard all year."

"Just about," I said, with a flicker of warm thought for Richard. "I'd all but lost hope. But . . . but what if she doesn't want to see me?"

"Why the devil shouldn't she? You know in your heart what a great regard she held for you, and probably still does. Even—and mind you it's not likely—if that regard has faded, at the very least she'll be curious about why you're back in London. Of course she'll see you!"

"But she could have had that note a week or more by now. Why hasn't she come by or even written?"

"She might only have gotten it today, it might be en route even, especially if she's still somewhere on the Continent. Patience, Coz, patience. Give the lady some time to pack. You know yourself how difficult it is to travel—especially with your sort of limitations."

"I have to leave her another note. Just in case the first one did go awry. I have to be *sure*."

"Of course you do, but did you bring along any writing paper?"

I made a face. "You know I didn't." Nor pen, nor ink, nor . . .

"Well, then!"

"Well, then, what?" I demanded, growing annoyed.

"It'll have to wait a bit, don't you think? You still have to look in on Ridley tonight, after all."

I let out a thunderous, exasperated sigh. "Damn Ridley and all his cousins—"

"Especially Arthur," he put in brightly.

"—especially Arthur," I echoed. Then I couldn't bring myself to finish. The laughter bubbling up inside prevented it. We hooted at one another like lunatics.

"You can leave another note anytime," Oliver said when he'd recovered some of his breath. "You'll like as not come back later while all the world sleeps, or am I wrong?"

"You are perfectly right." But my good spirits sagged, dragged down by my ever present doubt.

"What is it?" he inquired, seeing the change.

"Well, just look at things. The note I left is gone, and so I make all these assumptions that she has it and will reply as soon as she can."

He sat back, sobering. "You're right, it's not much, but if the worst happens and nothing comes of this, we can still continue on as we'd planned. I was going to go 'round to more house agents tomorrow. Everitt gave me the name of one I've not tried yet—oh, in your mad rush to tell me of your discovery, I've not had the chance to say what I've learned. No, no, don't excite yourself, because I didn't learn a damned thing that's new. No one in that household has the least idea of Miss Jones's whereabouts, sad to say."

"But there's obviously been a visitor or the note would still be there."

He waved one hand. "Then they just didn't notice his coming or going."

"How could they not?" I was outraged.

"I'm sure it wasn't intentional, but certainly they've better things to do with themselves than stare at an empty house all the time. Anyway, be of good cheer and keep thinking she's got your note and is on her way to see you. The world's not that big; she'll get here eventually. Or we'll find her first."

I wanted to believe that, and Oliver's manner was such as to half convince me of the truth of it. Some of my doubt sloughed away.

"Now, then," he said cocking his head, "what about you taking care of the vile Mr. Ridley and his Mohock hordes?"

Not much time passed before our driver, following Oliver's directions, guided the carriage to the right street. While Ridley had still been a "guest" at Fonteyn House, my cousin had taken pains to get his exact address.

"There, I think." He pointed out one in a line of doors as we slowly passed. "He told me it was the fourth over on the west side of the square. Not a very fashionable neighborhood, I'm sure."

His disdain was well founded as he looked down his long nose at the row of narrow, dingy houses. Most buildings in London were dingy regardless of their quality because of the soot-tainted air, but these specimens seemed to be a bit more so than most.

"I thought he had money," I said.

"He does, but only if he doesn't live with his family. The gossips at one of my clubs say they give him a quarterly payment to be elsewhere as much as possible."

"Can't be much of a payment."

"I'm thinking he spends most of it on his pleasures and this is all he can afford on what's left."

We drove by and had the driver stop a hundred yards down, then I got out to walk back. I might not have otherwise troubled myself with such caution, but Mr. Dunnett's observations inspired me to take greater care than usual. If any of Ridley's friends were lurking about, I wanted the chance to spot them first.

The building housed several flats, all occupied, if I correctly discerned the varied noises coming through the many walls. Ridley's was on the first floor. I hurried lightly up the stairs and gave a jaunty double knock on his door as though I were expected. No one answered. After a moment I found my own way in, slowly reforming on the other side of the threshold with my eyes wide for any sign of him.

He had two small chambers, this one serving as a sitting room, and I guessed the one beyond the half open door across from me to hold his bed. From the untidy condition of things, he had no servant. I listened hard, but heard nothing, not even the soft breath of a sleeper. The place was dark, cold, and empty. Well, that's what comes of it when one doesn't make an appointment. I would have to return later.

On my way down I reflected that though I was interfering in the very direction of Ridley's life, it might not be such a bad thing after all. If I got him to improve himself, he might even be able to do the Prodigal Son business with his family and at least end up in a better place than this to live. The trick was to catch him at home.

But later.

My spirits had lifted—because of this failure, not in spite of it. I'd been spared getting a headache from the work, if only for the moment; there was still a call to make on Arthur Tyne. Perhaps he wouldn't be at home, either. Pleasant thought, that.

I walked up the street toward Oliver's carriage, not in a hurry, but not especially slow. Pacing me on the opposite side were three other strollers in gentlemen's dress. None of them seemed to pay me much, if any, attention, but my guard went up nevertheless. I had the strong impression they were very well aware of me, though none looked in my direction beyond a glance or two. They seemed very comfortable with themselves. That's when I understood why I felt the need for caution; their ease of manner did not fit. Only a gang of bullies confident in their numbers would have such bravado. That meant they were likely to be Mohocks.

A quick look behind confirmed that three more of them followed me on this side of the street. Well-a-day, but I must have walked into a veritable nest of rowdies. I quickened my stride to a trot. Taking this as a signal to drop all pretense, they set after me like a pack of hounds on a fox. I broke into a dead run and started yelling at the driver to whip up the horses. The man turned in his seat, divined my intent, and called something to the footmen. Those worthy lads, well used to the rigors of their work, started smartly away with their torches. I wasn't too very worried about coming to harm, but felt a distinct a wash of relief when I tore open the door and jumped onto the carriage. It rocked from my sudden weight, but kept moving forward as I bellowed for the driver to go as fast as he dared.

"What is it?" Oliver demanded, and though astonished at this development, he helped haul me in. I sprawled upon the opposite seat, righted myself, and pulled the door shut.

For an answer I told him to look out one of the windows. He saw all six of the men running after us, waving their sticks and shouting abuse. Fortunately, none was as fit as they might want to be for such exertions and had to give up the chase after a very short distance. They were soon left behind, breathlessly cursing and shaking their fists.

"Good God," he said, drawing his head back inside again. "What on earth was that about?"

"Friends of Ridley, I suppose. He wasn't home, by the way."

"Just as well. If they'd charged in like that while you were trying to influence him—"

"I'd have vanished in a blink, dear Coz. Left 'em with a proper mystery."

He laughed at that idea, but uneasily. After another look back to make sure no one still followed, he told the driver to slow to a safer, more civilized speed. "Was Ridley in that lot?"

"I didn't see him, and he's too large to miss. Of course they might not be connected to him and only be up to general mischief."

He shook his head. "I can hardly believe that. If they're the ones that came by last night, then they must know you both."

"True, and if so, then I'll have a lot of work on my hands finding them one by one and warning them off. I can get their names from Ridley."

"This is positively beastly. There's no reason for such unpleasantness, y'know. Not one that I can see."

"It's bound to be just pure meanness, or revenge. Maybe they've noticed their leader isn't behaving—or misbehaving that is—as usual and have determined I'm somehow responsible."

"I hope to God Elizabeth's all right."

"She's fine."

"How are you so certain of it?"

"If all of Ridley's friends are here then they won't be anywhere near your house."

"Oh."

"Well, shall we pay a call on Mr. Tyne?"

"You are a one for taking chances, aren't you?"

"Hardly, but perhaps Ridley's with him and I can catch them both in one go."

He acquiesced with a short laugh and called fresh directions to the driver. This time our destination was to a long crescent of identical houses in a very fashionable area of town.

"I'd hate to have to find my way home without a guide," Oliver commented. "Look at 'em—like a row of peas in the pod. Too much to drink and you could end up in your neighbor's bed instead of your own."

"I expect one gets used to it—oh, stop braying, you great fool, or you'll have the watch down on us. I meant it in terms of finding one's own door and you know it."

For all their similarity, the overall effect of the houses was very grand. Made of white stone with large windows, the wooden trims still looked freshly painted despite London's soots. The people who lived in these palaces took pains to keep them as perfect as possible. They probably even had vicious rivalries going on amongst themselves over the fine points of how to keep everything clean.

"Is this Mr. Tyne's place or his parents?" I asked.

"His own. Arthur must be rather better than Ridley at keeping his carousing within his means, that or he's confoundedly lucky at the gaming table."

"Where are his parents, then?"

"They live in the country and generally take themselves away to Italy at the first sign of winter. Not a very sociable lot, except for Arthur."

As before, Oliver pointed out the right door and we stopped the carriage a distance down the way so I could walk back. And, as before, the object of my quest was not at home according to the servant who answered my knock. He informed me that the master was staying over with one of his friends, but could not say who it might be. The master had a wide circle of friends. I thanked the fellow with a small vale and retracted my steps. This time the street was clear of bullies.

"There it is, then," said Oliver as I passed the news on in turn. "Nothing for it but to enjoy the ride back home—unless you have a mind to go along to Paternoster Row? It's not that far away."

"If you think the bookstalls will still be open."

"Some of 'em are bound to be. Don't you recall there are parts of this city that never close?"

"It has been a while. . . ." The other sort of stop I had in mind I knew would most definitely be open for custom.

"Then you need to become reacquainted with things."

My thoughts exactly.

Navigation through the sometimes cramped and nearly always crowded streets was quite a demanding art. Happily our coachman was a master at it. The two footmen were also skilled, shouting for people to clear the way, their calls getting more frequent the closer we came to our destination. As they labored, Oliver and I discussed the chances of hunting down some decent plays to send to Long Island for our cousin Ann to read. She'd come to have a fondness for Shakespeare, but wanted to read others. Oliver understood that despite her exposure to such writing she was still not especially worldly, which meant that numbers of the more easily understood modern works would be most inappropriate for her delicate character.

"A pity, really, for some of 'em are quite amusing," he said.

"You mean quite obscene."

"That's what's so amusing about 'em. Here, this place should do, I know the proprietor." He had the driver stop and led the way to a spot that was half shop, half open stall, lighted now by several lanterns. Every horizontal surface was covered with books and manuscripts of all size and description. It was just the sort of place to appeal to my own sense of the hunt, though in terms of knowledge, not for trophies or food. The time fled and so did a goodly quantity of coin from my purse. In a very short hour I had not only a stack of books containing plays suitable for a young lady to enjoy, but several volumes for my own amusement. The weather for the coming year promised to be vile, so I'd probably not be as inclined to fill the early morning hours with outdoor exercise as was my habit. Better to settle before a warm fire with a book when the time came than to brave the fury of the elements.

"I think you bought the store out," Oliver commented, eyeing my purchases.

"Not yet, but next time for sure. Good thing we have the carriage. All this would be a bit much for a sedan chair."

"It may be a bit much anyway. Where are we to sit?"

"I thought we could send the carriage home without us."

"Did you now? To what purpose, other than leaving us stranded?"

I gestured slightly with my head in the direction of a nearby gaggle of trollops who where presently trying to attract business. Some of them were very fine looking, indeed. "Remember at the Three Brewers you suggested we treat ourselves to a real celebratory outing?"

"No, but it certainly sounds like something I'd suggest."

"I was still recovering from the ocean trip at the time, but I gave you my word that—"

He raised a hand. "Say no more, Coz, I take your meaning exactly. Now that you've brought the subject to my attention, it seems to me that we've been denying ourselves a real sampling of the pleasures of life for far too long."

"Have you also a mind to do something about it?"

"More than a mind, though I think we can do a bit better than those ladies, excellent though they may be."

"The Red Swan?"

"Oh, better than that. Since we've been forced to delay celebrating your arrival, I propose we avail ourselves of a place with more sophisticated forms of diversion. What do you say to a few hours at Mandy Winkle's house?"

That surprised me. "I thought you didn't care for Turkish bathing."

"Indeed not. As a doctor I know that frequent indulgence in full bodily immersion in water can be very dangerous to one's health—however, this is in your honor, so we shall yield to your preferences this time. Besides, Mandy has added some dry rooms for her more sensible customers." He jutted his long chin out to clearly indicate himself to be a part of that select group.

"Say no more and lead on, then," I said, laughing. A night at Mandy Winkle's had ever been a favorite diversion during my student days. Not only did I share company with a delightful lady, but had soaked to my heart's content in hot scented water up to my chin. Though free running water had become a nuisance to me since my change, I had no trouble with the contained sort—especially if contained in a large tin tub with a near-naked woman standing close by to scrub my back before proceeding on to other delights.

My heart did provide me a slight twinge of guilt for thinking of having sport with other women when the possibility of seeing Nora again loomed so near. However, she was not near at the moment, and they were.

Having a positive horror of any form of jealousy amongst her gallants, she applied the same rules of conduct to herself, so when apart from her I'd ever been free to nourish my carnal appetites without incurring her disapproval. But I was sensible and sensitive enough not to speak of such little encounters as I had to her. That would have been extremely boorish.

Oliver instructed the driver to go home without us, that we'd find our own way back later. If the man held an opinion on the business he kept it to himself, but the footmen exchanged knowing grins with each other, indicating they were well aware of the nature of our plans.

"Rogues," Oliver commented to their backs as they trotted off with the carriage in their wake. "Heavens, but we should have given some message for Elizabeth so she wouldn't worry."

"She won't. She understands these things."

"Indeed? Doesn't that make her a rare jewel? Well, come along, then." He started off in what I first took to be the wrong direction.

"I thought Mandy's was back that way."

"Not anymore. One of her neighbors was a magistrate and getting too demanding for his bribe money. Mandy found it cheaper to move to new digs. Wait till you see the place."

He threaded his way across the square, down one street and up another, finally stopping before an unpretentious door. He knocked twice and was admitted by a half-grown black child. The boy was such as you might find serving in any genteel home, except for his clothes; he wore sweeping silk robes, had a curved sword thrust through his belt, and perched on his head was a purple and green striped turban trimmed with glass jewels.

Oliver greeted him. "Hallo, Kaseem. Very busy tonight?"

"Busy, but not too busy, sir," came the reply in a very London accent, giving lie to his having any possible eastern origin despite his exotic name. "We have room for you and your friend."

"More than a friend, my lad. This is my cousin from the American colonies, Mr. Barrett. If Mrs. Winkle does her job right tonight, you'll be seeing a lot more of him in the future. He's fond of bathing, y'see."

A flash of white teeth appeared in the boy's dark face, and he bowed, indicating the way with one hand while holding his turban in place with the other. Oliver led me down a short hall, and pushing aside a dark red brocaded curtain, ushered me into a most surprising room.

The war between the Turks and the Greeks had created a vogue for all things eastern in certain quarters, but I'd never seen so much of it gathered into one place before. My eye was so diverted by the mass of colors revealed by the light of dozens of candles that I honestly did not notice the girls at first. The floor was awash with layers of patterned rugs, low tables of intricately carved wood, and mountains of pillows, and it took a bit of concentration to finally pick out the lovely houris reclining over them like so many flower petals. Once partially accustomed to the confusion, I spotted one beauty after another, each a sultan's dream, wrapped in bright wisps of scarves, some of the fabrics so light you could see right through to the charms of the lush flesh beneath.

The only prosaic element in the whole fantastic chamber was Mandy Winkle herself, who was dressed in the normal fashion, and a rather sober version of it. In the past, I'd learned that such conservative garb often served her well when dealing with the forces of morality. On those rare occasions when the law was compelled to take notice of her business, her habit of looking and behaving like any respectable, well-to-do matron was very advantageous. She swore that such affectation had ever kept her out of the stocks.

"Dr. Marling, isn't it?" she said, coming forward, all warm smiles.

"It is, Mandy dear," Oliver replied with a slight bow. "You remember my cousin, Mr. Barrett?"

"Of course I do. The girls still talk about 'the 'andsome infidel from 'Merica.' " She turned her warmth on me. "Where have you been keeping yourself, sir? It's been much too long since we've enjoyed your company."

"He's here to make up for it, I'm sure, so mind you to put forward someone with a hardy constitution."

"My little pets are very sturdy, else they'd not handle all the traveling they've done," she said with a perfectly straight face. Mandy Winkle maintained the illusion for her customers that all her girls had been liberated from the seraglios of various unnamed sultans. Since they knew no other skills than those required for the arts of lovemaking, they were more than happy to exercise that knowledge in order to earn honest living. Some of her customers believed the story, and for the rest of us it was an innocent enough fancy to carry forth.

Mandy did have a fine eye for the exotic, and though none of her girls could have come from farther east than Dover, they yet looked as foreign as one could ask for. Instead of wigs powdered the usual white by rice powder, theirs were made by Mandy's orders to be black as jet. It was at first a shock to the eye, and then a compelling lure to all the rest of the senses, for the dark color made a striking contrast against their pale skin.

"They certainly look to be in excellent form," Oliver said, casting about him with an admiring gaze.

"I'm sure any one of them will be happy to prove themselves to you.

Would you gentlemen prefer some refreshment for starters? We have tea or stronger if you like."

With this gentle prompting, Oliver tore his attention from the girls and settled the business side of things with Mandy. It was expensive compared to the Red Swan—guineas instead of shillings and lots of them. I protested, but he insisted.

"Think of it as a present to welcome you back to England, Coz."

"A Turkish *hareem?* Not terribly English, y'know."

He shrugged. "No matter, just so long as you feel welcome."

"No fear of that."

Several of the girls were eyeing me speculatively. Playacting, perhaps, but ably done and thus quite tempting. My previous experiences at Mandy's old location had ever been satisfactory, and it had not been nearly so well trimmed. This event promised to be even more memorable.

"You may recall that Mr. Barrett is fond of the full treatment," he said to Mandy. "I hope you have room for him."

"Him and all his cousins."

"Ah, no, not this time. I should prefer something a bit less aquatic for my own entertainment tonight, if you don't mind."

"Lord bless you, sir, if I minded anything you gentlemen did, I'd lose all my custom before you could turn 'round."

Mandy got things started with a quick double clap of her hands, and the girls came to their feet for inspection. Unfortunately for me, they all appeared to be equally tempting.

Perplexed for a choice, I appealed to Mandy. "I recall you had someone named Fatima the last time I was here. Might she still be around?"

Mandy was all sympathy. "She's busy with another gentleman, sir, but if you'd like to wait . . . ?"

*Hardly,* I thought to myself, shaking my head.

"If I might make a suggestion?"

"Suggest away, dear lady."

"Yasmin over there is enough like Fatima to be her sister."

To be truthful, I wouldn't know Fatima from Yasmin or vice versa, the former having been but a name dredged up from memory to help make a choice, but I promptly expressed my pleasure to become better acquainted with the celestial Yasmin. Mandy clapped her hands again and one of the girls swayed over to take my arm, smiling—as far as I could tell—through the folds of the nearly transparent veil she wore over the lower half of her face.

"Charming," I said, bowing slightly and patting her hand. "Yes, I think we shall get along just fine."

"If I might be so bold . . ." said Mandy.

I reluctantly paused. "Yes?"

"The specialty of the house has been paid for, sir, so if you would care to—"

Shocked, I rounded on Oliver. "You didn't!"

He grinned and nodded. "Welcome back to England, Coz."

Mandy, reading this as a sign to proceed, called for another girl named Samar to come forward. Like Yasmin, the lower part of her face was concealed by a veil, and neither of them wore very much else, only a few scarves with some beads and bangles. Their eyes were thickly outlined in black paint; their eyelids dusted in a soft gold. The effect on me was not altogether different from the influence I used on others, the difference being that I was yet able to rule my actions somewhat. One of the things I could not rule was putting up any and all resistance to being led away by Yasmin and Samar to the inner areas of the house. The last thing I heard as we departed from the receiving room was Oliver calling after us, wishing me to have an excellent good time.

Given the circumstances I didn't see how I could possibly have anything else.

Giggling, the girls took me step by step down a wide hall. I had an impression of more eastern decor, but didn't pay all that much mind to it, not with these two squirming against me. Well-a-day, but I was already primed to make a conquest of them here and now. My body felt very alert and flushed with desire, and my corner teeth were out. I smiled with my lips sealed shut, not wanting to alarm my companions.

I eventually noticed the air becoming warmer and more moist as we progressed, a reminder of the other unique offerings of this particular house. That helped me shake off some of the combined spell these beauties had cast. I was here to loll about and enjoy myself for as long as it suited; it would be ridiculous to hurry things. From the sounds coming from behind some of the doors we passed I could tell some of the other customers might disagree with me. Their loss, I suppose.

I was ushered into a charming room, and Samar cautioned me against falling into the bath. No fear of that, I had to stop in my tracks and gape a bit. Mandy had gone to considerable effort to enforce her illusion of foreign elegance; I felt as though I'd been whisked halfway 'round the world in a blink.

No tin tub for the sultans in this palace—the bath was a great square pool set right in the floor. I'd read descriptions of those used by the Romans, and this seemed to be an accurate recreation of one. Small tiles, carefully placed in intricate patterns, lined the thing, spilling over the edge to cover the floor. Away to one side was a sort of couch, having a very broad sitting area and armrests, but no back. It was covered with shawls and cushions and looked just as inviting as the bath.

"Does the master wish some help undressing?" asked Yasmin.

Oh, but this girl knew her business. I answered that their help would be very welcome, and she and Samar set to work, leisurely removing my clothes. Each piece was carefully placed on a delicate-looking chair that was far enough from the bath to avoid being splashed. They worked their way down through my coat, waistcoat, neckcloth, and so forth, and, once stripped of everything but my growing feeling of well-being, took my arms to lead me into the bath.

Without removing her own insubstantial garments, Yasmin eased into the water first, drawing me after her. The pool was nearly a yard deep and provided with foot-wide steps along one side so that one might have a choice of depth in which to sit. Samar followed, descending into the pool like a swan. The loose scarves she wore spread out on the water, and once soaked through, flowed around her body like feathery seaweed. I thought of mermaids, and if such creatures bothered with clothing, then this would likely be the kind they'd bother about.

As the hot, scented water crept up my bare chest, I knew without a doubt that this bath was to be the second best thing I was going to feel tonight.

Yasmin continued to hold my arm, and Samar backed away to give her room.

"No need to be shy," I told her, drawing her close again.

"Does the wise master desire both of us at once?" Yasmin asked.

"Yes, but I doubt that would prove me to be very wise. But what do you think of making the attempt for a while and seeing what happens?"

"As the master wishes," they whispered in unison, closing in on me.

It was a difficult thing, but I just managed not to cry out for mercy.

# CHAPTER

# ◄ 7 ►

After an initial frenzied bout of shared kissing and fondling that overwhelmed my senses to the point where I hardly knew which girl was doing what, we paused more or less at the same time to collect ourselves.

"Does the master desire refreshment?" asked Samar, whispering in my left ear. Yasmin was busy putting her tongue into my right.

Oh, how did I desire just that, but not in the form they might be expecting. Still, I was polite and told them to refresh away. Samar clapped her hands twice, and immediately another young lady appeared from behind a brocaded curtain. Instead of a black wig, she wore a turban with a veil attached to conceal her lower face. She also affected a short satin coat with no sleeves or buttons that ended just above her trim waist, and draped around her hips was a length of thin silk that revealed far more than it hid. She carried a huge silver tray loaded with wine, goblets, fruits, and other edibles.

"Have you got any more like her hidden about the place?" I asked as she set the tray near the edge of the pool.

"We are your two most obedient servants tonight, but if the master should desire to have more companions . . ."

I knew my limits—at least for the present. "Very kind of you, I'm sure, but I think you'll both prove just fine for me to be starting with."

The serving maid giggled and bounced her way out.

Yasmin glided over to the tray and poured wine for all of us. I excused myself from joining in by saying that I wanted to have all my wits about me the better to appreciate their favors, which seemed to please them. However, I insisted they indulge themselves all they wanted. Very soon, both girls had tucked away a goodly portion of several bottles and were feeling very lively, indeed.

They now set to work on me in earnest, first one resting a bit and looking on, then the other, all of which had me stirred up to an uncommon fever. I'd not felt it this strongly in far too long a time, and knew I would very shortly have to do something about it or suffer mightily.

Taking Yasmin by the hips I turned her back to me and guided her onto my lap. The buoyant effect of the water was both a nuisance and a titillation for it was hard to keep her anchored in one spot. She had to clamp her legs around mine and brace her arms against the pool's edge and one of the steps to hold on. By this time both girls were highly interested in what they were doing, a very important element to my pleasure-taking, for my own satisfaction was ever the greater when the lady was pleased as well. Yasmin, leisurely moving up and down on me, was happily occupied, so I felt free in leaning back along the steps to make room enough between us to draw Samar close across my chest, facing me.

I kissed her through her wet veil, then slowly peeled it to one side to work my way past her jaw and down her throat. Running my tongue over her taut skin, I felt the blood pounding just beneath, tempting me to release it from the vein. Yasmin was just starting to moan as I buried my corner teeth into Samar, who gasped and made a short soft cry. Both women writhed with the rapture of the moment, but because of the nature of our joining, Samar's ecstasy, like mine, continued on and on long after Yasmin's was exhausted. I held Samar close and sipped from her like taking nectar from a flower. Though her breath was heavy and fast, she held herself as still as possible in my arms, then every few seconds a gentle shuddering wave overswept her body from head to toe. Each time she did this, my own flesh responded, gifting me with a fresh surge of rapture that rushed like flames throughout my whole being.

Time ceased to be. The world ceased. I ceased. I was not a man, but a non-thinking creature of pure flesh and carnal appetite. I was joined to another like to myself, and all that mattered was our shared exultation for as long as we could endure the fiery joy of it.

At some point I became dimly aware of Yasmin gently easing away from me, then drifting around to come close to my side. She ran one of her hands through my hair, down my shoulder and back, and with the other caressed Samar. She would not have done this had she divined what I was really doing to her companion and so must have mistaken it for an especially long kiss. As my awareness of her presence increased I first resented it as an intrusion on what I was doing, but as she began kissing us both, I welcomed it as a new path to try. I blindly reached out for her. . . .

Then Samar arched against me, falling into yet another long shuddering climax; as it rolled through us both, she suddenly went limp in my arms. I felt the change take her, but was so deeply enthralled in sensation that I could do nothing right away. It was a heavy waking, a reluctant waking, for me to go from a state of luxuriant gratification to . . . to almost nothing at all. I was still drawing blood from her, but her response to it had utterly ceased. Finally rousing, I put my back to Yasmin to block her view and pulled away in sudden fear. Had I hurt Samar? The wounds I'd made were very small; for all the needs and drives of my passion, I'd taken care to be gentle.

I shook her a little, saying her name, but her eyes remained shut. She breathed normally through her slightly open mouth, and though her heart was not thundering as it had been a moment before, its beat was yet steady and strong.

Then was I flooded with quick relief. She'd only fainted. I heaved a thankful sigh. This had happened once or twice before when I'd shared company with Molly Audy back in Glenbriar. The cause was not loss of blood, but too much good feeling.

I guided Samar's lax form over to one side, lifting her up enough so her head and upper body were well out of the water. She'd waken when she was ready.

"Is something wrong, sir?" asked Yasmin.

"Your friend's just having a little rest, nothing more."

Eyes nearly closed so their red color would not cause alarm, I turned my full attention upon her, hands and mouth moving lower and lower on her body until she expressed the worry that I might drown myself. At my suggestion we quit the pool to make use of the backless settee, throwing ourselves upon its silk pillows with no mind to the water still streaming from our bodies.

Yasmin had already taken her pleasure of me, but I was determined to offer her yet another, and resumed my work on her with this in mind. She moved more slowly than before, probably because of her recent climax and the wine she'd consumed. Oddly enough, I felt myself slowing, too, as though my bones were gradually turning to lead. Puzzling for a moment, until I recognized the symptoms and realized the wine in Samar's blood was responsible. Of all things—I was becoming tipsy. I hadn't been drunk since . . . lord, I couldn't remember. It had been more than a year, at least since my last visit to England. I laughed aloud as I roamed freely over Yasmin's breasts and belly.

"The wise master is enjoying himself," Yasmin said, in a manner to make it half-question, half-observation.

"The wise master is . . . " but I couldn't think how to finish it, so I fastened my mouth on a place just below Yasmin's navel. It must have tickled her, for she gave a slight jump and squealed. I went on kissing her just there, using my hand on her most intimate area in a way that soon had her squirming.

My corner teeth were well extended and it was a sore temptation to use them to gouge into this soft plain of flesh, but recalling my interest—need—to see to Yasmin's happiness, I progressively worked my way up her body. The quickening of her breath and heartbeat were proof that my efforts were all to the good. Hip to hip, I finally burrowed into her in the normal fashion, then sought out her throat. The sharp gasp that came from her at this double invasion of her person was such as to assure me that her gratification was equal to, if not better than, my own. She pressed her hands first upon my backside to push me in more, then my head to drive me harder against her throat. We thrashed and groaned together like animals in a fever of rut.

She twisted under me, shaking her head side to side; giving in to the heat of the moment, I bit down a little harder, releasing a greater flow of blood. Some of it trickled past my mouth. I raised away from her, but judged that the bleeding wasn't heavy enough to be harmful. With my fingers, I smeared the blood around her throat, first staining her pale skin like paint on a canvas, then licking it clean again. She cried out and demanded more of the same.

Tumbling through my mind and but partially formed was an urge to go beyond this, to somehow carry us just a little distance farther along this path to something even better.

Now I drew my reddened fingers across my own neck and lifted her head that she might kiss it clean as well. She was so caught in the frenzy of the moment she did so without the least demur, licking and biting in imitation of my actions. She could not pierce me in the same manner, but her touch was maddening. Fingers once more at my throat, I now tore hard at my skin, trying to break it.

My nails raked in and I felt the razor-edged sting of success. My blood pattered down on her breasts. The sight and smell of it sent me hungrily back to the wounds I'd made on her. She bucked and moaned as I drank from them, sending her into another peak of pleasure. I tasted the wine she'd had earlier, felt its drowsy strength taking a firmer hold on my body.

I pushed away with an effort. The wine's effect was all the more potent since I'd not had drink in so long a time. Sleep would overcome me if I continued like this, and I wanted no sleep, not now. I wanted, needed, desired better and knew its achievement was very close. Staring at my blood bright upon her fair skin, I understood its import, understood why I'd made myself bleed. She could drink from me, allowing me to ascend to an even greater level of feeling. I wanted her to take my blood, I wanted her to take and then return it again. Nora had done as much for herself, had she not?

The slashes I'd given myself burned. But if I put Yasmin's cool mouth to them . . .

That would not be right, though.

My movements were slowing, turning sluggish. I had to hurry or the moment would pass; it would be too late for either of us. Her arms came up, trying to pull me close again, to guide my mouth back where she wanted it. She had no idea yet how much better it could be for us. I did.

But . . . it would not be *right.*

Doubt made me falter, made me think despite the wine's influence. Never before had I been taken to the physical point of wanting so badly to share my blood with another; I'd never allowed myself to go that far because . . . because . . .

. . . *it would not be right.*

A few more fat drops struck her flesh. A thin stream of it ran from my neck, leaving a hot red trail into the hair of my chest. It would be so easy to cradle her against me, to press her lips against my throat, to let her touch be the means to sweep me out of myself for a time.

I wanted . . . and could not have. Not this way.

Eyes burning from the frustration I thrust myself fully away from her, sinking straight to the floor. She mumbled something that sounded like a protest. I ignored her. If only she'd just fainted like Samar.

The room dipped once and righted itself. *The wine,* I thought with a stab of anger, scrubbing my face roughly with the back of one hand. I was light-headed yet sleepy, and the leaden feeling yet possessed the rest of my body. Most definitely the wine.

And the bloodsmell.

It teased and tugged at me. Yasmin's hand fell upon my shoulder, fingers weakly pulling as she asked me to return to her. Sweet heavens, but I wanted to; the girl would have me drain her to death so long as the draining pleasured her. It would do that all right. Well did I remember what it was like to be kissed in that manner, and how I'd hated for Nora to stop.

Removing myself from the immediate temptation of Yasmin's blood, I literally crawled back to the pool and slipped into the water. Remarkably, it was still hot. Some way must have been found to maintain the heat other than constantly pouring in fresh steaming buckets. I wondered if Mandy would part with the name of the one who had designed this miracle so I could have such a bath for my own.

Gladly did I concentrate on such mundane distraction, forcing myself to make use of it until my body calmed, and I could rely on my mind to start thinking again. Not that the thoughts awaiting would be especially comforting.

As my hair was already fairly soaked, I pulled off the ribbon that kept it tied back and completely immersed myself. Instinct made me take a deep breath before going under, but it was hardly necessary. Without the need to regularly breathe, I was able to stay down as long as I wished. It wasn't all that long, though, the water getting into my ears bothered me. I rose to the surface and tried shaking the stuff out again, with indifferent success.

My movements caused Samar to stir. She lay where I'd left her, half in and out of the pool. There was some blood on her throat, but the wounds had closed. Cupping water in my hands, I cleaned her off, which made her wake up a bit. I didn't want to deal with her at this time, though; in answer to a whispered entreaty from me, she swiftly fell asleep again.

I lightly touched the marks I'd left on her. They were small and would give her no trouble. She'd likely had worse from other patrons, or so I told myself. For all the delight that ever passed between myself and my mistresses, I could not help but feel a pang of remorse for having to bring this necessary injury to them. No more than a pang, though. I'd borne such marks as well during my times with Nora and knew they did not hurt; it was only shameful to have to mar such otherwise unblemished skin.

Faint as it was, I could yet smell the blood hanging in the air, but its effect on me was not as it was before. Though pleasant to the nose, the scent of food is less potent to a man once he has a full stomach—unless he's in the thrall of gluttony. My own fit seemed to have passed, thank God.

Yasmin was also starting to recover as well. She moved as though to sit up and murmured a sleepy question concerning my whereabouts. I heaved from the pool to see to her.

God, but she looked like she'd been murdered. Her throat and breasts were a horrific mess, but most of the blood was mine, so I wasn't worried. She only wanted cleaning up right away lest someone else see her or there'd be no end of trouble and alarm. Again, I whispered soothing words to make her forget and sleep, then carried her to the pool. There was water aplenty to completely wash away the evidence of my passion.

Near-madness, more like.

My head was quickly clearing, making it difficult to see how I could have forgotten myself so thoroughly. I wanted to blame the wine. That could easily excuse my actions, but my conscience wouldn't allow it. The wine had had its influence, but the fact was that I'd come too close to losing control. By God's grace or the devil's own luck, I'd found enough strength to stop things before it was too late. Who was I to impart this condition without warning, without consent, to another? I had not the right to pass it on no matter how glorious the physical fulfillment might prove.

As for Nora . . . well, Nora hadn't been as careful or considerate with me.

No, not fair, for I clearly recalled all that happened between us that night when we'd first exchanged blood. It had been a very deliberate act on her part. She'd asked if I trusted her and I had. If only she'd trusted me in return and given over the knowledge of the change that lay ahead, she'd have saved me much fear and sorrow.

Perhaps she thought her condition to be unique to herself, that it could not be passed on. But if such were so, then why not exchange blood with her other courtiers and afford herself the fullness of carnal pleasure all the time? No, there was some other reason involved. I'd been special to her, or so she said. She might not have wanted to share it with the others, only me. She might not have known I'd become like her and had thought there would be no need to explain things. Perhaps her ignorance about this unnatural state was equal to my own.

Horrible thought, that. I shook it right out of my head.

I carried first Yasmin back to the settee, then Samar, laying them close together and pulling over them some sheets I'd found to spare them from becoming chilled. They made a sweet picture, like two black-haired angels. I went to the chair where they'd put my clothes and found my money purse. They were honest girls, I noted, neither had filched so much as a penny when they'd undressed me earlier, but then Mandy had ever been very strict about that at her other place of business. I placed a guinea each in their hands as they slept. Aware of it or not, they'd performed above and beyond their usual duties for the house and deserved a special vale for their trouble.

The wound I'd made on my neck reminded me of its existence by a prickling itch. I started to scratch and halted just as my fingertips made contact with the flesh. *Close, Johnny Boy, close.* I might have opened it up again. To eliminate the problem, I vanished for a moment so it could heal. The vanishing was strangely difficult, taking much longer than usual to accomplish; I blamed it on the lingering effect of the wine.

The fire had burned low. I saw to its replenishment for the sake of my drowsing houris, then sought the solace of the bath once more. There was time enough and then some for me to loll and soak in its welcome heat and clean off the last of the blood. The water had turned a bit pink. I tried to think of some way to explain it, should anyone ask, then thought better of it. Say nothing and let them come up with their own reasons, but chances were no one would even notice.

Resting my head on the most shallow of the steps so my face was out of the water, I let my body relax and float. The pool was just large enough for it. I had nothing remotely like it at home—though that might change—and would enjoy the luxury while it was yet mine to have. Already I was forming plans to return to this earthly paradise next week. I might indulge myself with the company of but one lady, though, and see to it that she not partake of any wine or spirits until afterward. Much safer for both of us that way.

Notwithstanding the turmoil of soul my lapse of control had thrown upon me, I was well content with Oliver's munificent gift. I felt tired, refreshed, weak, and strong all at once. Not an easy combination to attain, but wonderfully satisfying. I'd have to think of a suitable thank you to give him in return.

As I mused on possibilities, my quick ears caught the distant beginnings of a commotion taking place elsewhere in the house. Raised voices, from both men and women, but nothing really alarming. One of the men was drunk and singing a bawdy song, sometimes even in key. A little row was only to be expected in a brothel, even in those as well run as this one. Mandy had vast experience in dealing with them, and like any sensible procuress, would have several bully boys in her employ to enforce the peace.

The song soon died away to drunken laughter, then loud talk that progressed up toward my end of the hall. The men had imbibed just enough to make them randy, but not so much to prevent them from doing anything about it, I judged. I hoped their ladies for tonight were as hardy as Mandy claimed, for these noise makers would likely give them a strenuous time of it.

I relaxed again, glad that they were someone else's problem and not mine.

*Wrong you are entirely, Johnny Boy,* I thought with disgust as the door to my chamber abruptly opened. Water sloshing about me, I sat up and turned to face the intrusion.

There were three of them, all masked, but that caused no alarm in me. Titled men often wanted anonymity while cavorting outside of their class, and I assumed this lot were no different. They were cloaked, gloved, and muffled to the ears, and their hats obscured the rest. All I could see was a bit of mouth and nose and little enough of those.

The men spilled unsteadily into the room, still laughing at whatever obscure jest had just been made. I debated whether it was worth the trouble to call for assistance or deal with them myself.

"We're in the wrong room," one of them observed, stopping to stare at me. "Not unless they've got uncommonly ugly wenches here."

"That's a man, not a wench," said another with heavy humor. "Though it might not make any difference to you."

The third member of the party whooped in appreciation. For the joke, I hoped. I tried to look past them to see any sign of help, but the view was blocked by their bodies.

"Gentlemen," I said, "as you can see, this room is already occupied—"

"Right you are—by us," declared the wit. "So you can just remove yourself."

I ignored his ridiculous command. "Perhaps your room is just next to this one. If you but look, I'm sure you'll find some very impatient ladies waiting for you there." Quite an assumption to make on my part, but I wanted to be rid of them. There was a draft coming through the open door.

"Don't I know you, sir?" he asked peevishly, stumbling forward.

"I doubt it, sir." Two more steps and he'd be in the bath with me.

"Yes, I do, you're Percy Mott, aren't you?"

"My name is Barrett, and I'd very much appreciate it if you—"

"His name's Barrett, lads."

And with those words, spoken in an unexpectedly stone cold sober voice, the comedy forthwith and bereft of no other warning changed to calamity.

Like an idiot, I still tried to finish my sentence, but the words died on my lips when from the folds of his cloak he smoothly drew forth a primed dueler and aimed the muzzle right at me. Though not faster than thought, he was certainly faster than *my* thought. I had less than an instant to react, but the pure shock was sufficient for me to waste it. Few others would have had the presence of mind to do aught else but stare as I did for that blink in time between seeing his pistol and the tardy arrival of comprehension of his purpose.

But there it was: a blink and nothing more.

Then, at the distance of two short paces, he fired right into my chest.

The roar of discharge did not impress itself upon my senses so much as the powder smoke. The acrid stuff seemed to fill the whole room more thoroughly than the deafening noise. I saw, rather than felt, the ball reaming through me, leaving behind a great blood-spurting hole. My body gave a violent jerk, then collapsed, pitching heavily forward into the water. I had no time to even bring my arms up; I could not feel, much less control them. With all my inert weight I struck the shallow step with my forehead, feeling and hearing the shattering crack of the impact with my whole being. Paralyzed, I lay as one dead for an unutterably long period during which I lived lifetimes of undiluted agony.

Voices and shouts and alarms went unheeded somewhere above him. In the confusion the pistol shooter and his companions would find easy escape.

But he didn't care about them.

It was impossible for him to care about anything.

He simply was not able.

All inner awareness had been brutally compressed down to nothing, and what had once been Jonathan Barrett was replaced by a blazing sphere of misery. He didn't exist anymore, only his pain. Perhaps in a hundred years or so when the pain went away he might think about returning, but no sooner.

His body floated facedown, bobbing and bumping against the sides of the bath, arms and legs dangling and useless in the bloodied water. People swarmed into the room, raising more noise. Somewhere a frightened woman wept, another tried to calm her. A large man seized one of Barrett's arms and turned him over, then dragged his motionless body from the pool. Others stooped to help or backed out of the way. Water streamed from Barrett's nose and open mouth. His open eyes were fixed in place like those painted on a doll.

He could not move, only lie where they left him. The humiliating helplessness should have brought him great distress, but nothing, no thought or action from within—for both were beyond him—no pleas, no prayers, no tears of anguish from without could break past the bloated wall of pain that had fixed itself between him and the rest of the world.

The large man pressed an ear to Barrett's immobile chest, then pronounced him dead. Comments were made about the blood in the pool and the singular lack of any kind of wound showing on the body. Other people joined the press to see for themselves and ask what had happened. They questioned the two girls who had been with Barrett, but could learn nothing useful since both had been fast asleep. Then all talk stopped when an unanticipated tremor ran through Barrett's body, and it gave a powerful cough, dislodging some water clogging its throat. This inspired a fresh bout of commotion as they concluded, with reasonable doubts attached, that he might be alive after all.

The wall of pain was marginally shrinking, but Mr. Barrett was too prudent a man to rush right back into things again. He waited, in no hurry to try answering the frantic questions being flung at him by these absurd strangers. They weren't inside his body; they had no hint as to what it was going through, and until the ordeal was finished, they could damned well wait themselves.

Then his cousin Oliver was there next to him, and care and concern for this one man's fear prompted Barrett to attempt a response. The wall of pain between them was thinner, perhaps enough now to allow him to speak past it and be heard.

" 'M all ri—" he mumbled, lying.

That held things together for a little, kept them busy. Coverings were thrown upon his nakedness, a pillow was slipped under his head. The jarring involved in the latter nearly sent him farther away, but hovering just within him there existed a vague but compelling need to remain where he was. Exactly why was out of his ken for the moment.

"God, he's cold as a corpse," Oliver urgently observed to no one in particular.

"This will help," said a woman.

"No, don't do—"

But the deed was already done. Someone—probably the woman—poured what seemed like a gallon of brandy past the lips of Mr. Barrett.

"Told you," she said with more than a small degree of smugness in her tone as Mr. Barrett's otherwise numbed and lax body twitched and rolled over into a fit of forceful and messy coughing.

That burning, vile, *hideous* excuse for drink accomplished what all the coddling and sympathy could not— brought me straightway back into the thick of things, groaning and cursing and holding my exploding head. This caused some relieved murmuring among the crowd. A man who could still curse his pain had a good chance of surviving it.

Exhausted by the business, I eased onto my back again. Whatever good feeling had been mine while in the company of Yasmin and Samar had vanished completely. I was shaken to the core and trembling despite the coverings heaped over me.

Between weakening spasms as my body sought to rid itself of the poisonous brandy, I managed a feeble scowl for my benefactress, Mandy Winkle, who knelt on one side of me with a flask in her hand. She scowled right back, but with much more ferocity. Couldn't blame her for it, this sort of row could not only get her closed down, but land her in Bridewell.

Oliver regarded me with much more compassion (mixed with barely controlled terror) and strove to find out if I really was all right and if I might give an account of what happened to me. I assured him of the partial truth of the one, but had to be circumspect about the other.

"One of the bastards shot at me." My voice was so faint I hardly knew it.

"Shot *at* you?" he echoed.

"Missed. Hit my head when I ducked." Dear God, but hadn't I just? I wasn't able to decide which had suffered the worst of it, my head or my chest. They pounded and ached for all they were worth, though in different ways. One at a time I might have managed with considerably less hardship to myself and others, but both at once had been too much.

"Who was it?" demanded Mrs. Winkle, bristling with anger. Whether it was for me or for my attacker was hard to judge.

"Don't know. Masked. They were all together. You must have seen. Did you not know them?"

Some of her anger faded. "They were new ones or pretended to be so. I've an eye for faces, but that doesn't work when the face is covered. Why in God's name did they shoot you?"

I could not give a good reply, only adding again that I'd not been shot. A blatant lie, for I'd been caught square in the chest, but it was important—I remembered why, now—that I maintain the fiction that the shootist had missed.

"You must be wrong, sir," she said, glancing at the pool. "There's blood aplenty in that bath or my name is Queen Charlotte."

I followed her gaze and saw the water was not a faint pink as before, but a decidedly nasty and unmistakable red. The pistol ball had inflicted a substantial portion of damage to my flesh, but that same flesh had quickly healed itself, a miraculous but painful process made worse when my head struck the tile steps. Either injury should have caused me to vanish, thus sparing me from much discomfort, but I had a lurking suspicion the wine had yet again mucked things up.

Oliver stared at me all wide of eye and open of jaw. I'd told him in full about my past experiences with pistols and rifles, and he'd apparently just worked out what had really happened. Afraid he might blurt something, I fastened him with my gaze and shook my head once. He gulped and cleared his throat.

"Nosebleed," he pronounced in good imitation of the pedantic tones used by all physicians when they were absolutely certain about something, particularly about something beneath their notice.

"Nosebleed?" asked Mandy.

He nodded emphatically and with a delicate touch pried one of my eyelids up with his thumb as though he were giving a normal examination to any of his other patients. "Oh, yes. My poor cousin is frequently subject to them. Alarming, but harmless. This one must have been brought on by this unconscionable attack."

Mandy snorted, either in acceptance of or derision for his diagnosis; it was hard to say. She then noticed all the people who had crowded in and barked an order for them to remove themselves. While she was occupied, Oliver caught my eye and mouthed the word *Mohocks,* drawing up his eyebrows to make it into a question. I nodded once. We frowned at each other.

"I very much would like to go home," I whispered.

"Are you able to?" he asked, astonished.

"I should be. And if not, I will be anyway."

Mandy had overheard. "Lord bless you, sir, but you can stay until you're more recovered." I could see in her face that this invitation was anything but what she really wanted to say. Hers was a reluctant hospitality, her desire for us to immediately leave coming hard against common Christian charity and the natural wish not to lose a client with such deep pockets as my cousin.

"You're very kind, but it's best that we go so you can put your house in order as soon as may be."

"Perhaps," Oliver added, "you might have one of your men hire a carriage from somewhere to take us home."

Not quite successful at hiding her relief at this proposal, Mandy promised to see what she could do and left to do it. On her way out she cleared the room of remaining stragglers.

Oliver continued to kneel by me, playing the part of attending physician, but as soon as the door closed his shoulders drooped and he released a great sigh. He favored me with a very close look.

"Are you sure you're all right?"

"Yes, though I've been better. I just need a little time."

"What *really* happened?"

"I was shot. Dueling pistol. You'll likely find the ball still in the bath."

He went back on his heels, biting his lip. "Dear God. And there's no mark on you. How can that be?"

"I'll ask Nora, should I get the chance."

"And I shall thank her, should I get one as well. If not for her you'd be—" His gaze flicked to the pool, then he suddenly rose up to pace the room. He'd passed the point of being able to hold in his emotions any longer and was in sore need of expressing them. "Of all the vicious, cowardly . . ."

I rested and let him rant against my would-be killer. I'd have indulged in some myself, but was yet feeling a bit frail. Strength would soon return to me in full measure, if only peace of mind could come as well. The horror I'd been through had made that impossible, nor would I know peace again until I'd dealt with the instigators of this outrage.

When Oliver had divested himself of the worst of his anger, I asked for his assistance to stand, which he instantly provided. The pain in my head was more of an unpleasant hindrance than the one in my chest, for it affected my ability to balance. I excused myself to him and sought relief by briefly vanishing. Again, though difficult to achieve, it worked a charm on both complaints, but upon returning, I found I'd traded two specifically located hurts for an overall weariness.

"You look perfectly awful," he said. He didn't look too well himself, but at least he was dressed or nearly so with only a partially tied neckcloth and some buttons left undone. He must have finished early with his evening's entertainment.

"Which is exactly how I feel, but I think a little refreshment from any stable in the city should fix me up again." Something unpolluted by wine, I silently added.

He looked at the pool again. "But I thought . . . that is . . . didn't you . . . with the girls?"

"As it happens I did. That's my blood, not theirs."

"Oh, that's all ri—I mean . . . but I thought when you were with them you . . ." He turned a fierce pink about the ears.

Good lord, no wonder he'd looked so odd when Mandy had pointed out the state of the water."I'm not so wasteful as that, Oliver. Now stop being so miserable. What's in the pool happened when I was shot. I need to replace it soon, then I'll be fine. Are the girls all right?"

"I don't know. I suppose they must be."

"Look into it, will you? They were asleep, but may have seen something after the shooting."

He was reluctant to leave me, but though tired to the bone, I was able to fend for myself. I was dressed, feeling the better for it, and ready to leave at his return.

"They're right as rain, though quite frightened," he said. "They didn't have anything to tell me, sad to say. The wine they drank left 'em fairly befuddled so they're only just now understanding what's happened, and even they can hardly believe it."

"Then including you that makes four of us."

He grunted. "You must have made an impression on them, Coz, for they were most concerned about your well-being. I tried my best to assure them of it. I think they'll have a warm welcome for you the next time."

"Much good it will do either of us. Mandy Winkle won't let us within a mile of the place after this."

"Oh, she'll settle down. She's not happy over what's happened, but knows none of this is your fault. We had a short talk, and I fell in with her idea that the men were thieves after your purse."

"That's some good luck."

"Don't crow too soon about it. She understands more than she's letting on to the others. If the bastards were real thieves they'd have been busy stealing from everyone, not roaring through the place with their playacting, then blazing away once they'd identified you. Mandy knows this, knows they were trying to kill you, but she's not keen to let it get out. It's bad for business. You're not planning to report this to any magistrate, are you?"

"Much as I'd like to, it wouldn't be practical. I've nothing to tell them that wouldn't eventually do injury to our family if the whole story got out. Besides, the courts generally keep daylight hours."

"Then that's a relief for all of us, as Mandy's not keen having the law in, either. We'll also not have to worry about her carrying tales. She's as closed as a clam when it suits her."

That was good to know. "What did you see of any of this?"

"Damned little. I was in one of the dry rooms toasting the health of the wench I'd been with when I first heard them." From that point his account was similar to my own experience, of hearing the progress of joking and laughter up the hall that ended with a pistol shot. "Then it was women screaming and people getting in the way of each other. I saw the last of the bastards tear past me—he was in a mask so it must have been one of 'em. Didn't think to stop him or give chase, just stood there like a sheep." He scowled, going pink again with shame.

"Thank God for that," I told him, causing him to look up for an explanation. "They might all have been armed. If they've got the kind of cowardly brass to walk in and shoot a man in his bath, then they won't think twice about cutting down another trying to stop their escape. You did well by doing nothing and I'm glad of it."

That seemed to ease any hard feelings he'd taken on himself for his lack of action. He shrugged. "It wasn't just any man in his bath, y'know. It was *you.* They made a special point of getting your name first. Why would strangers try to murder you?"

"Because they might be friends of my enemies?"

"Ridley and Tyne? I know, stupid question. Of course it has to be them."

"I can think of no others bearing me a grudge, but for my influence to have worn off so fast . . ." Granted, I hadn't all that much experience in changing the dispositions of others, but I couldn't fathom how either man could have shaken free so quickly.

"Maybe their friends had some influence of their own. Nothing like falling back in with ill company to make bad habits easier to resume."

I nodded, having no better suggestion to make.

"But how could these fellows know where you'd be? All that lot who chased us from Ridley's place were afoot. Then again, it may not have been all of them. Just one man on a horse could have followed us this far and we'd not have noticed him."

"Then it's best we get home to Elizabeth in case—"

"Good God, yes!" The mention of her name and the hint that she might be in peril got him moving almost too fast for me to keep up. I wasn't too worried for Elizabeth's safety, though; the men had been specifically after me. My present concern was the possibility of there being some immediate endangerment to Oliver since he was in my company.

But I learned Mandy had ensured the street outside her door was clear of everyone except her own lads. A fearsome-looking lot, they saw to it that we were safely loaded into a very smartly turned out carriage and sent well on our way without additional incident.

"Well-a-day, but I think this is Mandy's own conveyance," Oliver said admiringly as he took in the silk and velvet trimmings within. "Certainly gives one an idea of the sort of profit she turns. Did you see the horses? They looked like racers, we'll be home soon enough if not sooner in this wonder."

As the hour was getting late the streets were fairly clear of the worst of the crowds. I might have been able to make better time on horseback, but not by much. I could have certainly arrived faster by floating home on the wind, except for being much too tired for now to try. And cold. I made some sort of a reply of agreement and wrapped my cloak more tightly around my shivering body. It didn't seem to help.

"Uncommonly kind of her to lend it to us, don't you think?" he asked. "I'll have to find a way to thank her—aside from going back after a decent interval and dropping another purseful of guineas on her. What do you say?"

He was only trying to cheer me again. That had been the whole reason behind our going out, after all. It had succeeded very well up to a point. I shrugged, unwilling to speak through my chattering teeth.

"Here now, it's cold, but not that cold. You must have gotten too used to the heat and now this outside air is hurting twice as hard as it might. I told you that bathing was dangerous to your health—in more ways than one it seems. Your hair's still wet, too. If you'd just shave your head and get a wig like the rest of us you wouldn't have to worry about catching a chill."

An ugly gasping sound came from me, suspending his prattle. The gasp came again; I choked, trying to force it back into the icy depths of my belly. Desperate, I sucked in air and tried to hold it; it hiccuped out again.

"Here now," Oliver repeated, but in a tone very different from the mock scolding he'd just used. "There's a good chap, you'll be all right."

I felt a fool and was bitterly embarrassed, but there was no helping it.

"You've had a dreadful shock is all," he told me. "Nothing to worry about. There's a good chap."

The hiccups wrenched away from my futile effort at control and turned into true sobs. I doubled over, unable to stop, and wept into my folded arms. Oliver put a steadying hand on my shoulder and kept it there the whole time, occasionally giving me a reassuring pat and telling me in a low voice that I'd be fine, just fine. After a long, difficult bout of it, the sobs came less frequently, then not at all. Sitting up slowly with all the grace of an old man, I leaned well back into the seat, feeling absolutely wretched.

"Sorry," I mumbled. It hardly seemed, nor was it in truth, an adequate apology.

"For what? Finally having a reaction?"

"It's so bloody stupid of me to be like this." My vision was so thick with tears I couldn't see a damned thing. I fumbled out a handkerchief and roughly scoured my face as if to wipe away my mortification.

"You give me the name of any man who could do better given your circumstances and I'll adopt him for a favorite cousin. You've been through a terrible ordeal; why shouldn't you be upset?"

"It's not as though I'd never been through others."

"Those others don't matter as much as the one you've just had, and don't tell me you can get used to someone trying to murder you, because that has to be impossible."

"But I just *sat* there and let it happen. How could I allow it?"

"Allow it? Listen to yourself, you great ninny. You act as if it was your own fault the man did what he did. Do you really think that?"

After a minute I was able to answer. "No, I don't really think that, but I *feel* it. There's a difference."

"Yes, I understand the difference. None better. You recall how I was the night of Mother's funeral? I was in a pretty state then, was I not?"

He'd not said much about that night, of how he'd been in much the same condition I presently found myself, and the incident that erupted between us, but his mention brought it vividly back to mind. I'd seen him at his worst, just as he saw me now.

"You knocked some sense into me then," he went on. "Am I going to have to return the favor?" He looked as grim as a tax collector.

I felt another hiccuping gasp coming from me, but this time it was the precursor to a laugh, not a sob. As with the weeping, I could not stop it, but unlike the weeping, Oliver was able to join in. When at last it died away, I found I was no longer shivering.

Thanks be to the Almighty, all was safe and secure when we got home. Elizabeth had gone upstairs, but was not yet asleep, and the commotion of our return brought her down again. She had but to glance once at us to know something was seriously amiss. Orders were flung at servants who were still astir, and as they scurried off my good sister swept us into the parlor and saw to the building up of the fire herself. Just as one of the maids brought in a tray loaded with a hastily thrown together tea, Jericho magically appeared, stripped us of our outdoor things, and replaced them with dressing gowns and slippers. Without being asked, he unlocked the cupboard where the household spirits were kept and placed the brandy bottle on the table next to Oliver's chair. By the merest raising of one eyebrow and cant of his gaze he silently inquired if I should like a serving of my own special drink as well. I shut my eyes briefly and shook my head once. I'd see to it myself later. He nodded and stood to one side so as to listen in. Not one of us had any thought of dismissing him.

"You look worse than ghosts," said Elizabeth, rounding on us. "What on earth happened?"

Oliver made the first attempt to deliver an answer and initially tried to shield our reputations by passing Mandy Winkle's place off as being a public bath house—a fiction that lasted all of two seconds with Elizabeth.

"I understand your wish to protect my sensibilities from being shocked," she said. "But I'd appreciate it more if you just be as plain in your speech with me as you would be with Jonathan. Things will go a lot faster if I don't have to interpret what you're really talking about."

While Oliver went red and blinked a lot, I took over the task of relating the incident to her. Of course I left off a large part of it, for my business with Yasmin and Samar had nothing to do with the actual shooting. Elizabeth went very ghostlike herself upon hearing of the attack and my consequent injuries and had to be well assured that though shaken, I was mostly recovered in the physical sense. Her own reaction matched Oliver's, being composed of equal parts of fear, relief, and fury. Once she'd expressed a portion of each to the world at large, she then plied the same questions already plaguing us: Who were the men, how had they found me, and why should they want to murder me?

The who and possible why of it were fairly obvious, but the how was more elusive. Jericho quietly excused himself at that point. Just as we'd concluded that we must have been followed from Ridley's flat, he returned accompanied by our two footmen, both looking exceedingly uncomfortable and crestfallen.

"Didn't mean no 'arm, I'm sure, sir," blurted Jamie, the younger of them. " 'Ow uz we t' know 'e weren't a proper gennl'm'n?"

"If I might clarify things, sir," said Jericho, stepping in before the boy could go further.

"Clarify away," I said, with a wave of my hand.

In a few succinct words Jericho related his formation of the idea to check and see if the other servants had noticed any strangers lurking about the house that evening. None had, except for the footmen, who, in light of Elizabeth's instructions to be watchful, had made a quick circle of the house and grounds before turning in for the night. Coming around to the front they met, as by chance, a very well dressed, well-spoken gentleman who said he was in need of a physician, and asked if Dr. Marling was at home. Having become used to such inquiries, they saw no harm in telling the man the doctor was away that evening, adding that he might be found at Mandy Winkle's. The gentleman seemed to know of the place, gave them each a penny vale for their trouble, and walked off into the darkness.

"We din' think twicet 'bout it, sir, as there's alus someun comin' 'round to fetch the doctor at all 'ours." Poor Jamie looked to be close to tears. "Then when Mr. Jericho 'ere told us that someun 'ad tried shootin' you, sir—"

"What did he look like?" I asked.

Jamie and his companion offered a flood of information on the man; unfortunately none of it was very specific or useful. He'd been muffled to the ears against the weather like most of the upper-class male population of London. He could have been any one of our many friends, but between us, we decided he was most likely from Ridley's crowd. Only a Mohock from the upper class could have combined easy manners with such ruthless action.

Oliver sourly admonished them to be more careful and to report any additional incidents to Jericho. "I could dismiss the both of you on the spot without a character and no one would blame me for it, but you'd only inflict your ignorance all over some other luckless master and then he'd come after *me* with a pistol. Off with you, and if you've any wits left, use them sharp the next time a stranger talks with you or your next billet might be in the King's navy."

They fled without another word.

My good cousin diluted his brandy with a little tea and drained his cup away, making a fearsome face. "Damnation, but if I didn't sound exactly like Mother just then."

"You weren't anywhere as severe with them as she might have been, so take heart," I said.

"It's myself I should be severe with, standing by and talking about taking you to Mandy Winkle's with the two of 'em hanging about with their ears flapping. Those damned Mohocks came straight back here when we slipped 'em and waited. Good God, we'll be murdered in our beds next."

"I think not," said Elizabeth. "At least not right away."

"Come again?"

"They're probably off having a celebration of their own. After all, they think they were successful. Until they learn better, they're under the clear impression that Jonathan is dead."

That shut us all up for a time as we thought it over. Then Oliver began to laugh.

"Well-a-day, but won't they be in for the shock of a lifetime when they find out differently?"

"Until they get over it and try again," I put in, sobering us all. "And who's to say they might not try for you as well? Or Elizabeth?"

"By heavens, if they do—"

"They won't. I'll see to that before another hour's past."

"What?"

"There's plenty of night left; I've time enough to track down Ridley and his crew and sort them out for good." That was putting it in the most mild of terms. When I found them I'd probably wring their necks. And enjoy it.

Elizabeth must have sensed the anger churning inside me and gently touched her hand on my arm. "Stay home, little brother. Please. You've been through too much already for one evening."

"Yes, and it's to prevent my going through any more of it that I must go out again as soon as possible. As you said, they'll all be congratulating themselves over my demise. What better time to deal with them?" My every instinct was against waiting. If I left things until tomorrow evening, who knows what mischief Ridley's friends might plan and accomplish while I slept through the day? There was no reason to think they'd limit their activities only to the hours of darkness.

"He won't go alone, Elizabeth," Oliver said, standing up.

"Oh, yes, he will," I countered.

"But, Jonathan—"

"Believe me, Coz, there's no better man I'd want along to help, but I'd be distracted worrying for your safety. Mine I need not be so concerned about. Besides, you know perfectly well I can travel alone a lot faster and with much less notice."

"You'll still need help once you find them, or do you propose thrashing the whole lot all on your own?"

"I'm not thrashing anyone unless they force it on me. First I find Ridley and make sure he is indeed the one behind this attack."

"Surely there's no doubt over that."

"Not in my mind, but I also have to see why my influence didn't last on him."

"How will you find him, though? If you wait till the morrow I can—"

"Not one minute more. I'll go to his flat again. He may have returned by now, and if not then to Arthur Tyne's. I was too polite with the butler earlier, this time I'll get some names out of him." Perhaps I'd wring his neck, too.

"What will you do when you find them?" Elizabeth asked, wearing a troubled expression. "Not that I give a fig for their welfare, but I wouldn't want your conscience troubling you later with regrets."

*My conscience is my own business,* I thought.

"It makes you too difficult to live with," she added with a crooked smile.

I looked at her. She was trying to be light, but her eyes told me the lie of it.

"What will you do?" she asked again.

I patted her hand. "Not to worry, I'll stay within the law." *Or try to,* I added to myself, shrugging off my dressing gown. Jericho was already holding my cloak ready in the entry hall.

"That did *not* answer my question!" she bellowed after me as I hurried from the room.

# CHAPTER 8

I'd not noticed the wind before quitting the ground. Insubstantial as I appeared to be, skimming across the sky like a wisp of cloud, there was yet enough of me left to feel its effect and have to fight it. But my strength had returned, so the struggle was more of an annoyance than a trial. A clandestine stop in a nearby stable had provided me a swift and much needed physical recuperation. Normally I'd not bother courting the risk of discovery by supping on a neighbor's stock, but our driver and lads were wide awake and like to remain so for longer than I'd wanted to wait. Rather than influencing them all to sleep I simply went elsewhere for my meal. With its red fire still fresh on my tongue and glowing hot in all my limbs, I found a recuperation had taken place in my heart as well as my body, inspiring me to an even greater determination to sort things out for good and all with Ridley and his ilk.

Rooftop and tree, park and street, all rushed beneath my shadowless form as I sped in a nearly straight line from Oliver's house toward the dingy square where Ridley lived. Even though my memory of how to get there was from a much lower perspective than the one I presently enjoyed, I had no trouble finding the way. Unwilling to give up the advantage of so fine an outlook, I solidified on the roof of his building to have a good look at things before going in.

The square below was as quiet as could be expected in London, even at this small an hour on a winter night. A few figures paced along on their own obscure errands, some wearing rags and their walk unsteady, probably from gin, others more respectably garbed, but no less tottery in their gait. I dismissed them from notice, peering closely into the darkest corners within my view. All were empty except for a narrow gap between buildings where a tart was busy earning some money. If her expression held any clue to her true thoughts, then her patron had no gift of talent for his purpose whatsoever. After ascertaining by his humble clothing that he wasn't likely to be part of Ridley's circle, I left them to it and partially vanished.

Moving down the front of the building I found what I guessed to be the window to Ridley's sitting room, it being hard to see anything through the glass while in this state. But it was the work of a moment to vanish altogether, seep through the cracks, and reform again just on the other side of the closed curtain.

I'd found the right flat. All was dark, all was silent. Apparently he was not yet home. Probably out getting drunk or plotting new crimes, the bastard. I drew breath for a soft curse to express my disgust and stopped cold.

*Bloodsmell*—so thick on the air I could taste it. The hair on my head quivered to attention, and my knees wanted to give out as a shudder of recognition tore through me. I knew it to be human blood.

So strong was the urge to leave, I nearly faded away and shot back through the window again. When my nerves settled to the point where I could think, I held as still as possible and listened. I sensed many other people in the building, but none in this room or the next. I was very much alone. Moving cautiously and with leaden feet toward the bedroom door, I paused at the sight of a bold red smear marking the threshold. It was like a line drawn by a bully daring me to cross.

But the bully was dead, I found, when I worked up the courage to look.

The curtain for the window in here was pulled aside, allowing me ample outside light to see every horrid detail. Ridley was sprawled on his back across the bed and very much the source of the bloodsmell. His throat was cut. The blood from that fearful wound saturated the bed linens and his clothing, for he was fully dressed, and a puddle of it stained the floor. His white face was turned to one side, toward me. His were eyes partly open, sending the hackles up along my nape, for he seemed to be aware of my presence. It was fancy only, as I discovered when I stepped farther into the room, and his gaze remained fixed in one spot. Not that that brought any comfort to me; my teeth were chattering again.

It required a great effort to master myself and closely examine the room for any sign of who might have killed him and why. Ridley must have had many enemies, considering the life he'd led; I was almost certain one of them had had his fill of the man and committed the deed.

Almost, for this death coming on the heels as it were of Clarinda's failed scheme struck me as being too highly coincidental for belief.

The room was bare of anything that might be helpful. It was strewn with his clothing and other personal items in such a way as to confirm he had no servant to see to his daily upkeep. Thrown into one corner was the discarded costume he'd worn to the Bolyns' masqued ball where so much mischief had sprouted. I turned this and other things over with a gingerly hand, for I was reluctant to touch any of his property, as though what had happened to him might somehow taint me in turn.

Ridiculous thought, but there it was, joining hard and close with the leaden suspicion that I had somehow caused his death.

I searched through every cranny but found nothing that shouldn't be there. Hidden in one of his boots was a small purse with some guineas and a few smaller coins. I guessed it to have been a sort of emergency fund and put it back. Beyond that there were no papers—no letters of any sort, not even a discarded bill, which was rather odd, though I didn't exactly know what to make of it.

Going to the next room I had to find a candle. There wasn't enough light coming past its window's closed curtain to serve, and I wasn't going to change it lest the rattling of the rings on the rod be noticed and remembered later by his neighbors once word of this matter got out. Though it seemed very unlikely, someone might hear me moving around and be curious enough to investigate, and I had absolutely no desire to draw attention to myself or these rooms until I'd finished with them. With shaking fingers I coaxed a spark from my tinderbox, begrudging even that small noise.

The single small flame was all I needed to resume my search, but if anyone had asked what I might be looking for, I'd not be able to provide a good answer.

The sitting room was not the same as I'd left it, at least to the best of my recollection. If only I'd paid closer attention earlier I might have been able to notice more. Two things did leap forward: A chair was no longer pushed against its table, and an empty brandy bottle and glasses now on the table had previously occupied the mantel. Had the murderer shared a drink with his victim to work up the courage to kill? Or, the deed done, had he come out here to revive himself for an escape? There were four glasses, all the ones in his possession, all with traces of brandy at the bottom. Four murderers? Five, if yet another drank right from the bottle. Even six or more if they shared. Six Mohocks had chased me earlier, but why would Ridley's own men kill him? Or had those six been part of some rival group of troublemakers?

I could carry this no further without more information.

It would be instructive to speak with the other tenants to learn if they'd heard or seen anything, but any inquiry on my part would place me in a most serious position. I could influence people into completely forgetting my existence, but only for a time, and then might they not talk amongst themselves of the gentleman asking questions about a murder prior to the discovery of the body? Might that gentleman be the murderer himself? London was not so large a city that I could hide in it forever.

Ridley's acquaintances would afford another and probably better outlet for my questions, but with them lay the same danger—unless from them I might learn the name of the killer. Then could I influence the fellow into turning himself in and confessing, keeping my own vulnerable self safely removed from necessity of appearing before a judge.

All these thoughts rushed through my mind as I searched, each examined and put to one side like the items I sorted through, none of them being too terribly helpful to the present situation.

Except for the chair, table, and brandy being out of place from my earlier visit, and the fact there were again no papers to be found, nothing else seemed amiss in the sitting room. There was no more reason to delay a closer look at the most important source of information remaining to me.

I returned to the bedroom with the candlestick in hand, making sure to keep it well below the level of the window. There was close work ahead, this little light was wanted to scour away any and all shadows. There was a risk someone might see from the street, but I was willing to take it so long as I missed nothing of import.

Careful to step well over the smear of blood at the entry, I squatted and held the candle near and determined the stain had been caused when someone had stepped into the pool by the bed and then tracked it to this point. Easy enough to follow the trail he'd left, he must have realized it, then tried to wipe the blood from his shoe by scraping its sole across the wood planks of the floor.

I looked closely at the puddle next to the bed and could make out the scuffing indicative of someone having had at least one of his shoes in the mess. Why would he find it necessary to stand in that spot? In my mind I put myself forward to stand in the same place to try determining the answer. It came quickly. Ridley must have been sitting on the other side of the bed with his back to whoever else was in the room. That unknown man must have certainly leaned forward across the bed, perhaps with one knee on it, and one foot anchored on the floor for balance. With a knife in his hand, he could drag its sharp edge hard through Ridley's throat, then retreat, letting the body fall toward him. Thus would he be spared of the initial spray of blood; it would instead strike the wall Ridley faced.

Indeed, to confirm this there was a fearful splashing all over its otherwise plain surface. Anyone who had ever seen a hog hauled up by its hind legs for butchering would understand how the blood would spurt from a man in much the same manner and take care to avoid it.

Then might the killer have stood a moment over his victim, looking down at the final struggles to hold on to life, waiting until it had all run out. Ridley's hands and arms were all covered in dark, dried gore. He'd put them to his throat in a futile effort to stay the flow. His last sight must have been of his murderer backing toward the doorway.

Going around the narrow bed, I now began a reluctant search of Ridley's pockets. It was impossible to avoid contact with his blood. Though my appetite was so completely altered that blood had become the single support of my existence, in this case I felt the same kind of pitiful repugnance any other man might feel. So distracting was it that I could barely control the tremor in my hands; I nearly missed the thin fold of paper secreted deep in one pocket of his waistcoat. Surprised, I carefully drew it forth, turning it over once.

The outside surface was very damp, but it had been closely folded so the inside part had been fairly well protected from damage. Given the fact no other paper was in the whole of the place, I hoped that this one piece would provide some important insight to his death.

It did, but not in a form I could have ever expected.

I took it into the other room to spread it flat on the table. The staining had ruined a portion of what was evidently a letter. The upper half of the page was gone, the ink and blood blending and obscuring everything. The lower part was yet readable:

*. . . an unsettling, dangerous fellow. I do not believe it will reflect badly upon my manhood to admit I harbor a certain cold fear of this Mr. Barrett and of what he might do. He is very handy with his blade, as he proved to my chagrin at the Bolyns', though I was very intoxicated at the time. Certainly upon reflection I realize now how my drunken remarks coming from so befuddled a brain insensed him to the point of giving challenge that night. But I doubt his defeating me then has ended the matter, for he and his cousin, Dr. Marling, have made it obvious they bear me much ill will.*

*I hope that by inviting Barrett to meet with me he will hear my sober apology and we might then calmly settle the differences between us, but if not, then I expect we shall have to have another trial of honor. As I am not yet fully recovered from the cut I got at the previous encounter, I cannot be certain the outcome will prove favorable to me, unless he relents and gives me leave to delay things until I am better able to defend myself. If at the conclusion of my conversation with him I must cross with him again, then I should be very desirous that you act as my second as you did before. I don't reckon him to be quite so ill-bred as to force a conflict between us without going through the proper forms, but in the event that I am wrong, I hope this letter will find its way to you so you will let others know the truth of things.*

The letter had the usual closing compliments and was signed by Ridley.

If I had been cold enough before for my teeth to chatter, now was flesh and soul chilled so solidly that I could hardly bring myself to move or think.

The monstrous unfairness of it was the first thought to blossom to mind. The missive contained just the right amount of truth mixed with lie to be perfectly plausible, especially to anyone not in possession of all the facts.

The second bud to sprout was the absolute certitude that anyone finding the letter on Ridley's corpse would come to the reasonable conclusion the meeting had not gone well, and Mr. Barrett had foully murdered his host, taking a cowardly and dishonorable revenge for past grievances.

And the last bloom to burst forth was the urgent need to quit the premises and take myself directly home as quick as may be. Recognizing my own panic, I forced myself to stop and consider the even greater need for caution. Had I left the moment upon finding the body, I'd have missed this damning letter—what if another such item yet remained?

Pushing the cold, choking fear back down until it was an icy knot twisting deep in my belly, I made another, much more thorough, search of the flat and Ridley's corpse, this time looking for *anything* that might somehow connect me to the crime. I went so far as to turn him over and check through the bedclothes and felt a wave of relief mixed with revulsion when I found nothing more. Only then did I dare put out the candle and leave, never once stopping until I reached the sanctuary of home.

"Goodness, that didn't take long," said Elizabeth, looking up from her book with no small surprise. "We thought you'd be away for hours yet. Did you not find him?" Then she took a second, longer look at me and rose from her chair by the parlor fire. "Jonathan? My God, what's happened?"

Oliver, who had been much at his ease dozing in his own chair, also stood. I must have been in a very poor state indeed for them to wear such expressions, and neither improved when I stumbled out with the bad news. Their initial stunned disbelief followed by a lengthy period of shock and horror as I told them of my discovery was in every way a match for my own reaction. None of us wanted this burden, but stuck with it we were, and none was more anxious than I to be rid of it as quick as may be.

Over the course of the next hour I was questioned, requestioned, and the letter I'd taken from Ridley's pocket was read over and over again, inspected and discussed down to the most minute detail. None of it changed the fact that Ridley had been murdered, and the letter was meant to blame me for the crime.

"It explains why there were no other papers in the flat," said Elizabeth. "Anyone with half a brain would notice the lack and thus be doubly sharp to pay attention to this one. It might be thought you'd cleaned everything out yourself with the idea of disposing of just such a threat."

"But why should Ridley write a letter and then not send it?" asked Oliver. "Just so it could be found on his corpse?"

"If Ridley did write it. His killer may have penned it instead."

"That's hardly likely. Anyone familiar with Ridley's fist would spot it for a forgery, wouldn't they? Perhaps he was tricked into writing it. He might have been told to do it as a devilry against Jonathan, then once finished, his throat's cut and . . . well, there you are."

"Yes," I said. "There I am, dancing a jig at Tyburn or leaving the country forever as fast as sail can take me."

"And you think Clarinda might be connected to this?"

"Who else would have a reason? She hates me enough for how I ruined her plans."

"But she's locked up at Edmond's."

"And probably has friends outside who could still help. Ridley might not have been her only lover, y'know."

"Oh. But if they're so cozy together, why then would she want to kill him?"

My gaze dropped and dragged over the floor. "Perhaps because I was trying to change him. And that could be true whether or not Clarinda's involved. Suppose some of his friends came by to invite him out to a night of prowling and making trouble, and he turns them down?"

Elizabeth shook her head. "That's no reason to kill a man. Besides, such an action would have been a sudden and reckless thing, but the clearing out of the flat and this letter indicates a great deal of planning. Also, if Ridley could be induced to write such a letter in the first place to make mischief, then it's likely he wasn't as heavily influenced into good behavior as you thought. He may have possessed the sort of mind and will to be able to resist better than any of the others you've dealt with before."

Oliver cleared his throat. "You're not planning to take any of this to the authorities, are you?"

"God's death, man, and get myself arrested on the spot?"

"I just wanted to be sure," he said, unoffended by my reaction. "Well, then, what are we to do?"

"Try to find out who did kill him, while avoiding all connection to the crime."

"That may be a bit difficult."

"I'm well aware of it."

A glum silence settled upon us until Elizabeth finally threw it off. "You're forgetting the attack made upon you at Mandy Winkle's and those men who chased you from Ridley's earlier."

"I've not forgotten; I just haven't wanted to think about it," I muttered.

"It's time you did. Certainly the two are linked together."

"Then please enlighten me," said Oliver.

"Let us suppose they saw Jonathan going in and out of Ridley's flat on that first visit this evening, and gave chase just for the sport of it. Then when they went up to see Ridley themselves, they may have had a falling out, forced him to write the letter to put the blame on Jonathan and killed—no, that doesn't work at all, or why should they try to murder Jonathan in his bath later? They need only wait for the body and the letter to be found and laugh themselves sick while the law took its course."

My gaze lifted from the floor. "You almost have it."

"What, then?"

"All right, assume they saw me go in and come out, gave chase and went back to see their friend—then discover Ridley's *already* dead."

"Oh, *hell,*" Oliver whispered.

"They wouldn't need to search the body for any letter, but naturally conclude I'd just cut his throat. They have a quick talk among themselves, cleaning out Ridley's brandy, and decide to come after me in a fit of revenge. One of 'em sets himself to watch our house, finds out we're at Mandy's, and the next thing you know I'm being hauled from the bath like a dead rat. None of that could have been planned by the real killer; he couldn't have known I'd come calling that evening. He'd meant for the body to be found and me to get the blame, which is as it turned out, but not in the way he'd expected."

"But if Ridley was already dead when you called, how could you go into the flat and not notice a dead body? You found him quick enough the second time."

"The second time I stayed long enough to draw a single breath of air.

The scent of blood is what led me to the body. I must not have breathed at all the first time. I was in there and gone in but a matter of seconds."

He sat back to digest this.

Elizabeth, more used to the eccentricities of my condition, found it easier to take in. "Good God, if that's true . . . to think Ridley was lying there dead all that time . . . ugh. I wonder when he was killed, anyway?"

"Perhaps just before dark and a little after," I said.

"Why do you think that?"

"The curtain in the bedroom was open and the only candle I found was out in the sitting room. The killer would have had light enough to do his work until the sun went down. He cleans the place of other paper, shoves the letter into Ridley's pocket, and when it's dark enough to hide his face and form he goes off to wait for Ridley's friends to come over for a visit so they will find the body, not knowing how things would really turn out. They see me leaving the place and assume without reading the accusation in the letter that I'd done it."

"But he gets what he wants; Ridley's dead and you're blamed."

"Only by the Mohocks, and for the moment they think *I'm* dead."

"Until they learn better and make a second try," said Oliver. "Thank heaven you found that letter or the magistrate's men would be hammering on our door any minute now to take us away."

"Ridley knew his killer," Elizabeth said, again breaking into the short silence that followed as we counted our blessings. "Who of his friends could do such a thing?"

"Any one of 'em, as far as I'm concerned," Oliver grumbled. "The letter was to go to that pasty-faced gull who was his second at the duel. His name's Litton, if I got it right. He's not too smart, but loyal as a lapdog to Ridley. If you want the names of any of Ridley's other friends—such as they are—you need only go to Litton to get them."

"I have to," I said. "You know where he lives?"

"No, but I can find out—unless he's been murdered in his bed as well."

"Not likely, or why write a letter to him? He's needed to raise a hue and cry against me."

"What about Arthur Tyne?" asked Elizabeth, looking at each of us and getting an answer from neither. "He was Ridley's cousin and closest friend, close enough to him to be willing to help murder Edmond and Jonathan. Where's he gotten to in all this?"

I spread my hands and shrugged. "For all I know he might have been the one who shot me."

"For all you know he may have cut Ridley's throat himself."

"I doubt that, though stranger things have happened," said Oliver, shaking his head. He turned his gaze on me. "Weren't you going to talk with him as well?"

"It will wait until tomorrow night. I'm much too shaken for further rambles."

"Then perhaps I should have a turn."

"No, you should not!"

"The very idea!" exclaimed Elizabeth.

"I just want to help. Why should Jonathan do all the work?"

"You'll have work aplenty tomorrow finding where Litton is without getting caught at it."

"Without getting caught?"

"You'll have to pretend not to know anything about Ridley's death."

"Yes, I suppose that would be rather odd if I—"

"Odd? It could be fatal, dear Cousin. Promise me you won't risk yourself in any way."

Well, Oliver was as soft as a down pillow when it came to Elizabeth, so he readily gave his word to use the utmost caution in his inquiry. "Tell you what, I can call on Brinsley Bolyn. He knows everyone and can keep his mouth shut when he has to. All I need do is get him started about that duel and let him run with it. He'll probably blurt out the address of Litton and all his relatives without my even asking."

That satisfied Elizabeth, but I saw another problem arising. "That letter was meant to bring harm to both of us, Coz. I may be out of the way of injury for now, but you could be next."

"Or any one of us, for that matter," he added with a glance to Elizabeth.

"Therefore, I propose you move your household to someplace safer until we understand exactly what—"

"*Move?* You think the danger is that great?"

"Certainly I do, and until I learn better, it's wise to expect the worst, is it not?"

"But we're in the heart of London."

"So were Ridley's lodgings."

"Well, his was hardly a decent neighborhood—"

"And you think his killer or killers incapable of traveling to this one?" I tapped the spot on my chest where the pistol ball went in. "Here was I delivered ample proof that they know exactly how to get around the city."

He sucked in his lower lip and nodded.

"We have to think in terms of safety and are in need of a fortress. I can think of none more suitable than Fonteyn House."

"Surely not!"

"It's removed from the city, has lots more servants to keep an eye on things, and a good high wall with a gate."

"May I remind you that none of those things prevented Ridley and Arthur from invading the place earlier."

"But that was during the funeral when the gate was open and no one was expecting trouble. Things will be different this time. It won't be forever, just a night or two until I can sort this business out."

"You're really serious that we should go?"

"So much so that I'll send Richard and Mrs. Howard off there alone to keep him safe."

That was enough to stir Elizabeth to a decision. "Then my mind's made up. That child will have my company, if no one else's."

Thus did she decide for Oliver, who immediately fell in with the idea. "We can start packing a few things tonight."

"Not too much," I advised. "I think we should be as deceptive as possible so this place looks like we're all still at home and nothing is amiss. Load any cases you might want to take into the coach while it's still in the coach house. When you leave, it should be separately and by different routes. Elizabeth, Richard, and Mrs. Howard can take themselves away in the coach at some time in the morning as if going on another shopping expedition. You can take your horse, pretending to go on your usual round of calls. The servants can leave by ones and twos throughout the day—"

"But what about you?" he asked. "You'll be helpless in the cellar all that time."

"I'm well hidden, and it's not likely for anyone to look there, anyway. I should be safe—the Mohocks think I'm dead, so why should they look for me? Besides, they're not likely to put themselves in jeopardy by breaking into the house in broad daylight."

"How do you know?" he muttered.

"I don't, but it's an acceptable risk. More than acceptable."

"I'm not easy in my mind for you to be completely unguarded," said Elizabeth. "What if we ask Jericho to stay until you wake? That way he can answer the door and put off any callers. It will make the house appear more occupied."

I was reluctant to put Jericho in the way of any peril. "Only if he is made fully aware of the danger and has one of the larger footmen for company. Jamie will do. He's as big as a house and can redeem himself for talking to strangers. Once I'm up for the night, then off they go."

Oliver was sucking his lip again. "But could you not just leave for Fonteyn House tonight and save them the trouble?"

"I could, but I plan to be here tomorrow evening to keep watch."

"*Alone?*" Oliver looked ready to offer me some serious argument on that point.

I gently waved him down. "Yes, alone, and I've an excellent reason for it, if you but hear me out."

He worked his mouth. "If I do that, then you're sure to talk me into something I won't like."

"Only if you let me."

"I won't, then."

But in the end, he did just that.

When I awoke the next night it was to a disturbing near-silence, the sort that would have otherwise given me alarm had I not expected it. I was aware of mice going about their business, the scratch of a tree limb brushing against the walls outside, and the tiny creak of my own bones in their sockets, but nothing else. Rising from my pallet on the bags of earth, I traveled invisibly up through the empty floors as usual to my room, reforming just in front of Jericho, who had been waiting for me. He was long used to these appearances from thin air, and without batting an eye in my direction finished shaking out the clean linen he'd picked for me to wear.

"Evening, Jericho, how went the day?"

"Tolerably well, sir," he answered. "Everyone left for Fonteyn House without incident, except for some loud objections from Master Richard when he understood where he was being taken."

"What? He didn't want to go back there?"

"He was simply reluctant to leave without the carpet."

"Carpet?"

"The one you bought for his playroom. It seems he's rather fond of playing rough and tumble over it and insisted his recreation would be seriously limited if he had to leave it behind."

"Well-a-day! Think of that!" I was absurdly pleased with myself.

"He insisted it accompany him for his stay."

"Tell me everything he said, every single word." Since I would be bereft of our regular hour of play tonight, this second-hand accounting of my son's activities would have to do for now. Jericho was well used to this, too, for I always asked him to provide me with all the details of Richard's day, at least for those times when their paths intersected. Jericho didn't mind any of it, for while he spoke at length of domestic things, I would then sit still long enough for him to give me a proper shave.

"Miss Elizabeth's new spinet finally arrived," he said. "It was just as well young Jamie and I were here to take charge of the delivery. The makers sent along a man to see that it was in perfect tune, a rather abrupt Frenchman, but he knew his business."

"You mean it's not likely he might have been a spy for the Mohocks?"

"No, sir. All he had mind for was the spinet. He played it very well. I complimented him on it in his own language, which surprised him, and after that he was somewhat less abrupt in manner. He let it be known that he was a teacher of music for diverse instruments, as well as dance and deportment and should anyone here be desirous of lessons he was available for hire."

"A French musician hanging about the place? That's just the sort of diversion Elizabeth needs, I'm sure. Handsome fellow, was he?"

He knew I was joking and raised both eyebrows in agreeable response. "Passable, I'm sure, though I cannot pretend to be an accurate judge of male comeliness. However, I was thinking you would wish rather to hire him as an instructor for Master Richard."

"I'd have to meet him first. Isn't it a bit early for that? No, I suppose not. Elizabeth's offered to teach Richard the spinet, but suppose he wants to play a fiddle instead? He could learn French at the same time. Well-a-day, but look at me, I'm talking myself into hiring the man already. I'll have to look into it all later; this other business at hand wants clearing up first. What else happened today? Any news on Ridley?"

Jericho had been apprised in full of my wretched discovery the night before, though if we three had said nothing to him, I'm sure he'd have heard about it anyway. Oliver was right about the man's uncanny ability to know all that was going on.

"There was a notice in one of the papers of the incident, sir. You may read for yourself." He gave me the germane sheet, and I squinted at the tiny print.

"Doesn't say much. After all the hue and cry, it only identifies him as Thomas Ridley, Esquire, and says his throat was horribly cut under mysterious circumstances. You'd think they'd have more details. There's not even a speculation on who might be responsible."

"Upon consideration, that lack is in our favor."

"You're right of course, but still . . ."

"I would venture to guess that the murderer may be experiencing the same sort of frustration as yourself."

"Really? How so?"

"Looking at this article, he might expect to read that you'd been taken into custody because of an implicating letter found in Mr. Ridley's clothing."

"Yes, I see it. He's probably grinding his teeth wondering what's gone wrong."

"Unless he's learned from Mr. Ridley's Mohock friends that you were killed by them. Or so they believe. The papers had no mention of your misfortune."

"I should say not. A scion of Fonteyn House shot in a brothel? Unthinkable! They'll assume the family closed ranks with Mandy Winkle to hush it up for the time being. I daresay this Mohock tribe will all be frightfully confounded when I start showing my face around."

"One might hope as much, sir, but please go carefully. Miss Elizabeth and Dr. Oliver were most concerned for your safety."

"No more concerned than I am myself. You can tell 'em I'll be extremely careful. Anything else on this?" I gestured with the paper.

"Only that his death is the talk of London society. There were several callers today. Some of Miss Elizabeth's new friends were disappointed that she was not in, and very disappointed to know you were unavailable as well."

"Marriage-minded females with their mothers?"

"Yes, sir."

"It's all from that damned duel. I should have let Ridley kill me."

"Yes, sir."

"Anyone else?"

"A few gentlemen to see Dr. Oliver came by before he left, and I had opportunity to entertain their servants and learn all the news from them."

"Which was?"

"Little more than what was in the paper. The general opinion they held, which for the most part was the same as their masters, is that Mr. Ridley, in light of the double life he led, had it coming to him. Speculation on the culprit ranged from it being one of his Mohock cronies to a jealous husband to a cheated procurer."

"Doesn't want for variety. Wonder which, if any, is the correct choice? Did Oliver offer an opinion as well?"

"The doctor thought it best to pretend total ignorance of the issue and let his visitors do the talking; thus did he learn all there was to know. He was very pleased about the ploy and asked me to mention it to you."

"Then you can pass my admiration for his wit on to him in turn."

"I will, sir."

"Did he find out where Mr. Litton keeps himself when he's not playing the second at duels?"

Jericho drew a scrap of paper from his pocket and gave it over. "Here are the directions as they were given to him by Mr. Bolyn."

"That's hardly a half-mile from here. You can tell Oliver this will be my second stop on my evening rounds, I'm calling on Arthur Tyne first—and yes, I will be careful."

"Very good, sir. Any other messages?"

"If I think of any I'll deliver 'em myself, though he and Elizabeth are not to wait up for me as I'm not likely to be by unless something extraordinary happens. Otherwise I'll just leave a note on his writing desk and you can give it to them tomorrow. Are you finished with me? I'm ready to set sail from port? Excellent. Time you got away yourself. Have you the means?"

"Jamie and I were going to walk to Fonteyn House."

"Walk? I won't hear of it. Take this and hire yourselves a cart or some sedan chairs."

"I don't think that would be very proper, sir. Jamie might think himself above his station if he—"

"Oh, hang that. These are exceptional times. If he shows any signs of snobbery you deal with it as you please, but I won't have you walking all the way out there on your own after dark. Mohocks aside, it's just too dangerous. Be sure to take one of my sticks, and see to it Jamie has his cudgel."

I saw the both of them off out the scullery door. From there they were to make their way past the stables, down a back lane, and then emerge onto a street some distance from the house. It was the same route the other servants had taken; I hoped that it was still safe. Just to be sure of things, I followed them the whole time, albeit from a height. Neither they nor—presumably—anyone else was aware of my presence, as it's most unheard of for a gentleman to take the evening air by taking *to* the air. Once they were aboard a hired cart and lurching in the right direction for Fonteyn House, I left them behind and returned, making a high circle of the neighborhood to see that all was well.

No loitering dandies, no unfamiliar carriages, chairs, or coaches lurked in the area. I wasn't sure if I should be relieved or annoyed when I slipped back inside the house.

My plan called for me to wait about the place a bit, making sure lights showed in the windows and moving them from room to room to give the impression all was normal. Then would I make another near-invisible circuit of the street, looking for spies. After a reasonable period—or until my impatience got the better of me—I would venture forth as though to take a walk and see if that drew anyone's notice. Going to see Litton might do it for me, but if need be I'd try attracting attention by walking all the way to Arthur Tyne's home, ostensibly to offer condolences, but primarily to interview him. Should he prove ignorant of all these doings, I would at the very least get from him and Litton the names of others who might be more helpful.

After a quarter hour of pacing and peeking past curtains every few minutes, I decided the house was entirely too quiet for me. Lighting more candles did not seem to help, though they gave the place a very occupied look to any watchers—much good it would do me if there was no one out there watching. Perhaps I'd counted too much on the villain's abilities. That or I was just too eager for trouble to start.

*Not wise, Johnny Boy. Not wise at all.*

Another few minutes crawled by while I examined the new spinet. Elizabeth had done herself proud, for it looked to be a very superior instrument. I was sorry to have to deny her the pleasure of playing it now that it was here. My own clumsy fingers picked out a simple tune remembered from long-abandoned childhood lessons. The sound coming from it was beautiful enough to my untrained ears; how might it be once she sat down and called forth its full potential?

My speculations were cut short by a fearful pounding on the front door that made me near jump from my skin. Now, that was unexpected. Were the Mohocks going to try for a bold attack after all? I peered through a window to see who it might be and rocked back on my heels in surprise. What on earth was *he* doing here?

I hurried around to the entry and opened the door to the full force of Edmond Fonteyn's baleful glare.

"Thought you had a butler," he growled, not deigning to cross the threshold. "Never mind that. Throw on something and come with me. I want to talk with you, but not here. Come along with you."

Too bewildered to question him before he turned and walked off, I had the choice of doing what he said or calling after him and insisting he return. Well, he looked to be in a pretty foul mood already, so there was little point in adding to it. If nothing else this might draw the eye of any watchers. I caught up my heavy cloak from where Jericho had laid it out, jammed on a hat, and grabbed my sword cane. Slipping into the cloak was made more difficult when I realized something heavy was in its inner pocket. The thing banged against my side and caused me some puzzlement until a quick look confirmed the weight to be my Dublin revolver. Jericho had, indeed, thought of everything.

Edmond had traveled in his coach, but he'd left it standing before the house and was stumping off down the street even as I twisted my key in the lock. I came even with him and asked him a reasonable question concerning his business with me.

"Someplace less public than this first," he said, and kept walking. We went by Mr. Dunnett's little watch house. I passed a quick greeting with him, noting with pleasure the man had treated himself not only to a new cloak, but a thick muffler and gloves. He bade me a cheerful good evening in return, but was allowed no more than that because of the quick pace Edmond had set. Apparently he was fully recovered from his misadventures at the funeral.

I thought he was heading for the Red Swan—yet another surprise—but instead he proceeded on to Hadringham's Coffee House. Happily, the smells associated with this place of refreshment were somewhat less objectionable to my sensitive nose than most, and I followed Edmond inside with hardly a qualm. Within all was warm and smoky, the very timbers permeated through with the exhalation of countless pipes of tobacco over the years. Quite a few patrons lingered at the many tables even this late, for the establishment was a favorite meeting place for the local illuminati. It provided a place to enjoy the exchange of good conversation with one's fellows, the same as a tavern, but without the resulting drunkenness and debauchery. There were other places to pursue those when the mood struck.

The gentlemen scattered about the main room looked up to see who had come in; one or two were familiar faces since I occasionally came here to pass the time when it pressed heavily upon me. I acknowledged each with a polite bow while Edmond dealt with a waiter. He ordered and got a small private room and two dishes of coffee, then told the waiter not to disturb us further. The man had barely set down his tray before money was thrown at him and he was practically booted out.

"This sounds serious," I ventured to say as Edmond closed the door rather hard.

"It damned well is serious," he snapped back. "I want to know what the devil is going on."

"Could you be more specific?"

From his coat pocket he drew out a folded newspaper and slapped it on the table before me. Though different from the one I'd seen earlier, it was open to a story about Ridley's murder.

I did my best to emulate the proper reaction of one who, though the news be bad, has already heard and discussed it at length with others. Not a difficult ruse to maintain, since it was true. "This is a terrible thing, but I know no more about it than anyone else."

"That account mentions the duel you had with him, 'Mr. Barrett of Fonteyn House.' "

I looked at the print and saw that was exactly how I'd been identified. Oh, dear. More notoriety. Father would hardly be pleased when he heard, Mother might leap into one of her fits, and Edmond was positively furious. "The duel is a matter of fact. I can't help if some fool put it in print. All I can say is that I'm as shocked as anyone about the murder."

"Are you now?" He all but loomed over me. "And who do you think is responsible?"

" 'Fore God, man, are you implying—"

"You told me this whole business with Ridley had been taken care of and a few days later he turns up with his throat cut."

"So you assumed *I* had something to do with it?" I felt my face going all hot and red as the anger flared inside.

"I haven't assumed anything yet. That's why I'm here—to find out what you know. I don't care if the bastard's dead or not or even who killed him, but when the family name is dragged about in public in connection to such a scandal—"

"Oh, yes, certainly, the last thing this family needs is another scandal." I couldn't keep the sarcasm from welling up and spilling over into my voice.

Edmond pushed his face closer to mine, freezing his gaze to mine with the same sort of intensity I'd used often enough to force my will upon another. "Stop to think a minute and you'll see the sense of it." His tone was low but not at all benign. He looked as if he wanted to break me in two. "If the law somehow connects Ridley's death to the goings-on after the funeral, then checks into my household and finds out about Clarinda, she'd cheerfully talk her head off to get back at us all even if she goes to the gallows for it."

Now did I realize why he was so angry. It was his way of expressing a very real fear. "There's that," I said, easing back into a calmer voice and posture. "But you know very well Clarinda is too fond of her own skin to put it at risk."

He grumbled something that might have been an unwilling concurrence for my logic and finally backed away. Despite my lack of need to breathe, I wanted to indulge in a sigh of relief as he put more distance between us by pacing the room. Resisting the impulse, I glanced at the forgotten coffees, which were cooling. Soon they'd be too cold to drink. Just as well, given my limits.

"Have you questioned her?" I asked.

"Of course I have. She claims to be ignorant of the incident and put on a pretty show of tears at the news."

"You think she lied, then?"

"The woman doesn't know how to do anything else, except lift her skirts to anyone in breeches."

I gave him a sour face, but might as well have frowned at a wall for all the effect it had on him. "Perhaps I can talk to her and learn a bit more than you did."

"What makes you think she'll tell you aught?"

I wasn't ready to confide to him about my talent for influence just yet, if ever, and so came up with what I thought to be a plausible excuse. "If I let her think I'm worried, afraid of this business, she might be tempted to gloat a little."

He snorted with scorn. "Yes, I'm sure she'll jump at the chance to do that and thus tell all."

"It's worth a try. Look, I've some errands to do tonight, but I could come by tomorrow evening. Perhaps the magistrates will have Ridley's killer in custody by then and all this will be unnecessary."

He grumbled and growled, but finally gave his assent that I could see her. "But you've still not answered me. What do you know about this?" He tapped the paper with his fingers.

"Enough to think the law should seek out his friends for his killer, not his enemies."

"Who? Arthur Tyne?"

"Possibly."

"Then I hope to God you're wrong. He'd be worse than Clarinda if he ever started talking."

"If he's guilty of this murder, he's not likely to bring it up in conversation."

"He is if he's a fool, and he did not impress me much with his wit at the funeral. Just to be sure, I believe I should go see him."

"*That* would be a very bad idea." He favored me with another scowl, but I was growing used to them. "You want to avoid a scandal, so the best course is to stay as far away from Mr. Tyne and his ilk as you can for as long as you can. He's not in your usual circle of friends, is he?"

"Of course not."

"Nor mine. We'll just go on as though nothing's amiss and this business will simply pass us—and the family—by. But if you go barging in and stirring things up, that could change faster than the weather."

Edmond had no liking for the suggestion, if only because it came from me, but in this case he reluctantly saw the sense of it. The magical word *family* had worked well to persuade him to caution. I'd have to remember to invoke it more often.

"I shall take myself along now," I said, rising. "The evening is wearing."

"What sort of business can you have then?"

He'd probably think it anyway, no matter what I told him. "Just a bit of wenching, dear cousin, nothing more. There's a very fine lady not far from here. I'm sure she can get you an equally fine companion should you wish to come along. Or we can share, if you like."

By means of a most contemptuous and forbidding sneer he gave me a perfect understanding that going with me to such an assignation was the very last thing he desired to do.

"Another time, then," I said with a bright, guileless smile, picking up my cane. At the door, though, I felt a twinge of guilt for my impudence and turned. "Edmond, I know you're upset over all this, but there's nothing to worry about. There's even a chance the murder has nothing to do with Clarinda."

"I don't believe that," he said flatly.

"Neither do I, but there is a remote chance. Hope for it, but keep yourself prepared for the worst."

"And just how do I do that?"

I pulled out enough of the Dublin revolver for him to see what it was. "Get yourself one of these if you haven't already, and watch your back. If Clarinda's involved in some way, remember she holds no love for either of us. Make sure your servants are trusty and fully understand the virtue of bolting the doors and windows, and though I hope to God it's unnecessary, give them instructions to notify me or Oliver immediately should anything inimical happen to you. Left without, she might persuade one of them that she's mistress of her own house again and thus gain her freedom."

He pursed his lips and frowned, but he was listening.

"Otherwise, put an ordinary face to the world and carry on as usual."

Brave words, I thought during a quick walk back with him to his coach. To ensure our mutual safety, we agreed to go together. On the way I gave the street a thorough inspection, finding nothing of note, and made a casual inquiry with Mr. Dunnett when we passed him again. He said all was quiet, and considering the vale I'd given him, I knew his report was to be trusted. Edmond grunted approval at this evidence of my own caution.

I saw him into his conveyance and felt significant relief after the driver had clucked to the horses and driven them all away out of sight. My worry had been Edmond would find a reason to go banging on Oliver's door and discover the house empty. Then I'd either have to explain it or influence him into not caring, and both would delay me for longer than I'd planned.

Rushing into the house, I went from room to room, putting out the candles I'd left alight. Normally I'd not be so foolish, but Edmond's arrival had surprised me, and I was too used to there being servants around—neither being much of an excuse to give to Oliver for burning down his home. There was no harm done, thank God, and the place had looked occupied for Edmond's benefit, but the time for such shamming was past.

Locking the door again, I found my conscience yet smarted over him. I should have told him at least some of what had happened so he might be even more prepared for trouble. But before I did that, I hoped to make it altogether unnecessary. Far better it would be for all concerned if I could clear everything up tonight, and I would, God willing. If the Mohocks or the killer or both would not come to me, then I was surely going to come to them.

It was getting near to the dark of the moon, but the sky had cleared, and what few stars were visible between the city smokes served well to light my way. I felt rather exposed walking along like a normal man, and would have much preferred to rise up and take to the sky. I'd become quite spoiled. Though not so vulnerable to the world's hurts, I was yet as subject to a certain amount of anxiety as anyone. With all that had happened, my nerves were unsettled to the point that I wanted to start at every unexpected sound, and in this precarious state of mind, all sounds seemed unexpected.

I told myself not to be a blockhead and forged onward, determined to cleave to the plan I'd placed before Oliver and Elizabeth. All I had to do was follow it through. I had only to visit Arthur Tyne and hear his story, then, depending on what I heard, call on Mr. Litton or one of the Mohocks and finally sort things out.

But it had made so much *more* sense when argued before a cozy fire in a well-lighted room.

Close upon my approach to the crescent-shaped row of houses where Arthur resided, I half expected to garner some sort of notice. By this time my unease had become so much of a familiarity that it had surprisingly transformed itself to aggravation. If a round dozen Mohocks had leaped out to confront me, I'd have certainly yelled my head off, but would have also perversely welcomed the attack as a sign of progress. However, I proceeded unscathed and somewhat disappointed straight to Arthur's door.

I delivered a brisk knock and waited. Though the hour was rather late for a call, I knew the rigid rules for genteel society were likely to be very bent where someone like Arthur was concerned. I knocked again, but no butler answered.

Damnation, if I'd come all this way for nothing . . . I stepped well back from the door to see the upper windows. One of the curtains twitched. Quick as lightning, it passed through my mind that Arthur, far from being the perpetrator of Ridley's murder, might likewise be a target for harm himself. If so, then he'd have good cause to skulk in his own house, and have especially good cause to avoid me should the rumor have reached him that I had done the deed. I could knock all night and get no reply.

The lamp by the door was unlighted. A favorable thing. I glanced once up and down the street. Not completely empty, but no one seemed to be paying much mind to me, and it was very dark. To the devil with it. I vanished and ghosted through.

The entry was very dim even for my eyes. All the curtains were drawn, and very little outside light seeped inside. I sniffed the air. No blood-smell, thank God. I listened, hearing nothing on this floor. Some stairs leading up were on my right. Rather than announce my presence by the scrape of a shoe or finding a squeaky tread, I made myself transparent and floated to the next landing, solidified, and listened again.

There it was. The intervening floor had muffled the sound of his breathing.

Beyond *that* door. Soundlessly I glided toward it, taking form only when I was on the threshold. I peered in.

It was a bedroom. A single candle burned on a table by the bed. By the window, his back to me, stood my man. He had one eye pressed close to a very slim opening in the curtain and his posture was such as to indicate his whole attention was upon the street below. Had he seen me vanish? Not that it mattered; I could make him forget, and now was a good time as any to begin.

"Hallo, Arthur." The devil was in me, else I'd have had mercy and given him some gentler warning of my intrusion.

He fairly screamed as he whipped around. I gave an involuntary jump at the sound and hoped it wouldn't disturb his neighbors to the point of investigating.

And then . . . I didn't give a tinker's damn for any of them. The dunce who was pressed against the far wall panting with fear was Arthur's butler.

"*Damnation!*" I snarled. "Where is your master?"

Under the circumstances I was much too optimistic about getting an immediate response from him, and too impatient to wait for him to calm down and collect himself. While his knees were still vigorously knocking one against the other, I stepped close and forced my influence upon him, once more demanding an answer.

"N-not home," he finally choked out.

"So I gathered. Where has he gone?"

The combination of his fear and my control was a bad one. His heart hammered away fit to burst. I relaxed my hold on his mind and told him to be easy. It worked, after a fashion, and I was almost able to hold an ordinary conversation with him.

"I don't know," he said in a faded voice after I'd repeated my last question.

"When did he leave?"

"Earlier today."

"Did he know about his cousin's death?"

"Cousin?"

"Thomas Ridley."

"I don't know."

Well-a-day. And I thought it was impossible to keep anything hidden from one's butler. "Where are the other servants?"

"Dismissed."

"What? All of them?"

"Yes."

"Why did he dismiss them?"

"I don't know."

"Did he dismiss you?"

"Yes."

"Why are you still here?"

The answer was not instantly forthcoming, having stopped somewhere halfway up his throat. And little wonder, I thought, once I'd looked around the room; the man had been so terrified not just from my sudden appearance in the house, but because I'd interrupted his thieving. Two bundles lay on the bed, one tied up and ready to carry, the other open to reveal a pile of clothing, some trinkets, and a couple of silver candlesticks. I also noticed why I'd mistook him for Arthur, for he'd donned some of his former master's clothing, a silk shirt and a dark green coat with gold buttons.

"You'll not get a good character doing that, my lad. A noose more like."

He didn't disagree with me.

I spent the next quarter hour in a weary bout of questioning, and though plagued with headache for my efforts, learned a few very interesting things.

Arthur had been somewhat mysterious in his behavior for the few last days, being rather quiet and subdued. Nothing odd in that, considering the injuries he'd suffered along with the effect of my influence, I thought. He'd kept to his room, resting for the most part and refusing to see a doctor for his condition, which was rapidly improving. Today he'd recovered enough to walk to his favorite coffee house to read the papers there as was his usual habit. Hours later he'd returned a changed man, being very nerved up and restless. Pale and abrupt, he ordered the packing of a traveling case, had his horse brought around, and mounted up. He then summarily discharged the entire household and rode off without another word.

This had astonished the lot of them, to say the least. Some departed immediately after packing up their own belongings. The kitchen staff saw no reason why the food, wine, and spirits should go to waste and walked off with all they could carry in lieu of their unpaid wages. The butler, left ostensibly in charge, made no objection and let them plunder at will. Once gone, though, he had his own plan to enrich himself by lifting whatever choice objects Arthur in his haste had left behind.

The pickings were lean. No money, not even a stray silver snuffbox was to be found. If it was small and valuable, Arthur had already taken it. However, he'd left behind some very fine clothes and some other, less portable things, enough to keep the butler in comfort for the next year, longer if he decided to strip and sell the household linens, too.

And though I pressed him until the sweat ran down his face, he could not tell me or offer the least clue on where Arthur had gone.

Disgusted at this turn, I asked where Arthur kept his papers and was directed to a downstairs room that served as a sort of library. I told the man to continue his business, and pay no mind to me, and in fact he could forget he'd even seen me at all. I had no care for his thievery; he could do what he liked so long as it did not interfere with my own searching.

The library had few books, certainly not in the numbers I was used to having about. Some of them had to do with law, indicating what Arthur had read for when he'd been at university. I'd heard nothing about him to indicate he'd taken up practice, and thought it likely he was merely biding his time on a quarterly allowance until coming into his parental inheritance like so many other young men of our generation—that or hoping for a rich marriage.

The writing table he used as a desk held an untidy pile of paper, mostly old invitations, bills, and household accounting. It was very haphazard; some of the stuff was months out of date. I found a few letters from his family, who were presently enjoying the Italian climate, but no other correspondence. A note from one of his Mohock friends with a name and address would have been useful, but none were to be found. I pocketed a letter from his mother on the small chance its address might be of use later, then checked the fireplace. He'd burned paper there recently. The stuff missing from Ridley's flat, perhaps? The ash was very thoroughly stirred and broken up so there was no way to tell what it had been. I couldn't think why he'd want to kill his own cousin, though; their fellowship of murder had struck me as being thicker than cold porridge. Perhaps Clarinda could clear things up.

Or Litton.

I'd wasted too much of the night on this project. I'd best get along to see Ridley's lapdog before he got frightened and disappeared as well.

This time I took to the sky—after first ascertaining the event went unobserved. The wind was not so bad tonight. My progress was swift and exhilarating, but I had little mind for enjoyment of it as a diversion. Perhaps later, after all this business was past, I'd be free to explore and appreciate, but not now.

As Litton's place was so close to Oliver's I decided to delay going there just long enough to look in on our house and street. All was quiet and normal for the latter, not so for the former. Immediately upon my touching to earth and growing solid I saw the lights showing past the edges of the drawn curtains. Of all the infernal cheek—had the bastards invaded our home and were even now plundering it like Tyne's butler?

Of course, Edmond might have come back . . . but no, his coach wasn't waiting for him. More likely Oliver had gotten tired of waiting at Fonteyn House and returned to see how I'd progressed. Blast the man. I'd tell him a thing or two about putting himself at risk—if it was Oliver.

Just to be safe, I let myself inside without using the key and listened hard. Someone was in the sitting room. The door was open and the golden glow from many lighted candles spilled out into the hall. I heard the crackle of flames in the fireplace, and a faint step or two, then came a few experimental notes from the new spinet. Good God, Elizabeth? Fingers ran up and down the scale, faltered, missed a note, then stubbornly resumed.

I drew my pistol—in case I was wrong—and hurried forward, intending to surprise the player. But when I rounded the doorway and saw who stood within, the surprise doubled and redoubled back upon me. I stopped, turned to stone with disbelief.

The woman standing before the spinet was not my sister, but Nora Jones.

She looked up, blank-faced at first with startlement, then her features relaxed into warm recognition. That slow smile, that bewitching smile, the one she gave to me alone emerged to light her expression.

I'd forgotten, forgotten, forgotten how beautiful she was; my heart gave such a tremendous leap that my chest hurt. I staggered forward a step. I tried to speak, but the words wouldn't come out. Through a blur of tears I saw her coming toward me, arms outstretched. She whispered my name. I wanted to shout hers, but it was hopeless. Giving up, I simply held her hard and close as we wept and laughed at the same time.

# CHAPTER 9

Eventually we had to part, if only to look at each other. She touched my face with one hand, even as I touched hers, and probably for the same reason: to reassure herself of my reality.

"I got your letter," she finally said. "The one you left in my house. I didn't know you were in England or I'd have come sooner. I'm so sorry."

"It doesn't matter."

"Can you forgive me for what I did at Cambridge?"

I could forgive her anything now that she was here and told her as much, swiping at my eyes with my sleeve.

"I had to do it. You needed to go home, and I had to take care of Tony Warburton and—"

"Never mind. It's past. Other things . . . there are other things to speak of. Oh, God, there's so much to tell you!"

She smiled up to me, a little one, wavering between joy and tears. I'd missed how her lips curled in just *that* way. I kissed them, softly. The hunger for her was very much with me, but there would be time for that soon enough, I hoped. For now I was content to hold her close.

"Where have you been? I've had Oliver searching for you for more than a year. Are you all right?"

"Of course I am."

I pulled away to look at her. "But Tony Warburton said that you'd been ill. *Are* you all right?"

"I'm fine, as you see." She covered her hands tightly over one of mine. "You spoke to him, then?"

"Almost as soon as we landed in England—I thought he might tell me where you were. You've been trying to help him all this time, haven't you? Oliver said that you'd been in Italy with the Warburtons, and—"

"Then you remember *all* that happened that night?"

"Every minute of it."

Lifting my hand, she kissed it. "And I'd hoped to spare you from—"

"It's nothing, now. It doesn't matter. You're here and well, and that's all that's important to me. Why did he say you were ill? I was so worried for you. Is it to do with his madness?"

"No, no, he must have been speaking of my aunt. Mrs. Poole took sick just before we left Italy. We've been living quietly in Bath since then."

"Very quietly indeed. Why, then? No one in our circle had any word of you. I was coming to think you'd dropped off the face of the earth—or something awful had happened to you or you were purposely hiding for some reason."

"For one such as myself privacy is very necessary. I have to maintain a certain distance from people, as you well know."

"But so much distance? And for so long?"

"I'd had my fill of society. It was empty without your company."

For this I embraced her again, laughing. It promised well for us both to know she'd missed me. I was sorry about Mrs. Poole's sufferings, but within was a selfish gratitude that it had not been Nora. My arms wrapped around her, I gave heartfelt thanks to the heavens for her present and continued well-being.

"How fares your aunt?" I asked, at last recalling my manners.

"The waters there have been a help to her, thank God," she answered. "She's recovered enough that I thought of coming back to London. I sent one of my men to check on the house, and he found your note telling me to see Oliver. I came as soon as I could. No one's here, though. What's going on? Where's Oliver? Why are all the servants gone?"

Suddenly remembering the Dublin revolver I'd been holding all this time and why I was holding it, I leaned over and put it on a table. There was no chance that I would complete my dark errand tonight. Compared to Nora, the importance of finding and dealing with Ridley's murderer lost all impetus. Tomorrow would do just as well for that unpalatable task.

Her eyes went large at the sight of the weapon, bemusement drawing up the corners of her mouth. "What on earth? Jonathan?"

"This may take awhile. You've walked into the middle of a very bothersome situation. I'll explain everything, I do promise." I gently led her over to the settee. We seated ourselves, each turned slightly so as to better regard the other. I wanted to look at her all night—that, and other things. "So much has happened I hardly know where to begin. I've so many questions for you now."

"And I for you."

I gave a short laugh. "I've the feeling yours will be easier to answer. You go first."

She fell in with my humor. "Well, is your family all right? The war news—that letter you got from your father . . ."

God, that was ages ago. "They're all fine or were when I left last September. Father's decided to move the family back to England. That's why I'm here now, or part of the reason. I'd have come back to you no matter what—you have to know that, but—"

"I know."

"—but I was afraid you didn't want to see me again. You made me forget, and I didn't know *why*. And I couldn't underst—" I caught myself. This wasn't the best way to go about it, plunging into the middle with questions sounding too much like accusations. One thing at a time. "My—my sister Elizabeth came over with me, I can't wait for you to meet her. She very much wants to meet you."

She stiffened. "You *told* her about me? About us?"

"Of course I did. I had to—in order to try to explain what had happened to me."

"What ha—I don't understand."

"I didn't either at first. And I was so frightened then." I was frightened now. The words were trying to stick in my mouth again. Rather than fight them, I took her hand and pressed its palm flat against my chest. I knew she would sense the utter silence there even as I perceived the stillness of her own heart. "*This* is what's happened."

She went absolutely quiet, and her color drained away. She shook her head, first in doubt, then in denial. "No . . . it cannot be."

"I'm like you, Nora."

"No, you ca—no, oh, *no*." She pulled her hand away, stood, and backed quickly from me, shaking her head the whole time.

I reached out, but she drew farther and farther off until she bumped against one wall. She stared at me as one stricken and said nothing. "What is it? What's the matter?"

She would only shake her head and stare.

"What is wrong? For God's sake, settle yourself and *talk* to me!" All I wanted was to go to her, but some wise instinct told me to stay as I was and not make the slightest move. She was like a terrified bird ready to take flight. Why was she like this? Why was she afraid of me? I softened my tone. "Nora, please . . . I need you. I love you. For all that's happened I have never stopped loving you."

Trembling now, she made an effort to steady herself. At least she was listening.

"Whe-when?"

"A year ago last August," I answered, divining her meaning.

"How?"

I touched my chest. "I was shot . . . here. When I woke up, I came to realize I was like you. Those times when we exchanged blood . . . that's how it was passed on, wasn't it?"

She nodded once.

"Since then I've been living as you live—"

"Feeding as I feed?" she demanded sharply, voice rising.

"No, not exactly."

There was no breath left in her. Her next whispered question was inaudible. I only saw the words forming on her white lips.

"I'm sorry, what did you say?"

She swallowed hard and breathed in through her mouth. "Have you . . ." another swallow, another breath. "Have you killed anyone?"

I gave back a blank stare. "*Killed?*"

"You heard me."

Certainly I had killed, at Mrs. Montagu's when I had to save Father and Dr. Beldon from those damned rebels, at Elizabeth's house when I'd shot Ash and thrown Tully like a doll across—but how could any of that matter to Nora? Could she somehow know what was going on here in London? Have heard some garbled story about Ridley?

"In my own defense, in defense of others," I began, but stopped, seeing the dismay taking hold of her features. "Nora, what is it?"

She closed her eyes, refusing to meet mine.

Comprehension, ponderous, slow, and appalling, finally dawned for me. "Dear God—I obtain what I need to live from horses or cattle. You don't think I'd kill someone for their blood?"

Oh, but that's exactly what she was thinking if I read her aright. Had I not come close to it with Arthur Tyne? I'd been injured, starving, and mad for revenge of my hurts, but still . . .

"I'd not do that. I'd *never* do that! You must believe me, Nora."

"Never?" Her voice was high with doubt.

I nearly groaned, but nothing less than the truth would serve either of us well. "I almost did. Once. He'd nearly killed me, and I had to take from him to save myself . . . but I didn't kill him. I let him go."

"Who?"

"No one important, no one unimportant. Just a man."

"And what of women?" she murmured.

Here did I begin to blush. "Well, I I've not been celibate, but no woman I've been with has ever suffered for my appetite. Do you know so little of me to think I would hurt anyone for the sake of my own pleasure?" I'd had the hard lesson of that only last night. Never again.

"That's the whole point, Jonathan. You've *changed.* The abilities you have now put you above all other men, beyond their laws, beyond their punishments—"

I responded with a snort of disbelief. "I think not, dear lady."

"Then you just haven't fully grasped it yet."

"Ah, but I have, with both hands, and just as quickly ungrasped it."

"You're still young."

"So my sister tells me, but I'm no fool. Is that what's upset you? You thought I'd turned into some sort of murdering bully?"

"It's not that simple."

"I think it is, but for pity's sake, be assured I am the man you knew before. Perhaps a little wiser, even. Believe me, I've been all over this subject of bullying with my father and sister—"

Another stricken look took her. "Your family *knows?*"

"Only Father, Elizabeth, Oliver, and, of course, my valet Jericho . . ."

She continued to stare.

Impatience got the better of me. "How could I *not* tell them?"

"And they . . . accept you?"

"Of course they did, once they got over the surprise."

"They must be marvelously understanding."

"I'm not saying it was easy for any of us, but between the choice of having me like this or buried and rotting in the churchyard, they had no trouble making their decision. In fact, they want to thank you for what you did."

"*Thank* me?"

"For all the trials we've been through, this change brought me *back* to them, and for that we are all grateful to you. My condition has given me a greater appreciation for life, theirs and mine together. I know how precious and fragile it all is, how quickly and easily it may be destroyed by a careless hand. I think the whole point now is not so much that I've become like you, but whether or not *you* can accept it yourself. I pray that you will."

"I have no choice," she said unhappily.

This low temper of hers baffled me. "Don't you?" I snapped. "Did you not make a choice that time? You took me to your bed and we made love and you gave your blood to me. Did you not choose then to make me as you are? Or was I just a convenient means to increase your own pleasure?"

"*No!*" She raised her fists, all frustration. "Oh, but you don't understand anything."

"Then *help* me to do so!"

But she said nothing. My anger had accomplished that much.

I suddenly wilted in my seat, and turned from her, overcome for the moment by the black pall of fading hope. She was afraid, and I could not fathom why. "Forgive me, Nora. It's that I've waited so long to see you. I have so many questions, and you're the only one who can possibly answer them. But if you can't or won't, I shan't press you. I'll respect whatever reason you have, even if you don't share it with me."

A long time—a long silence—later, she asked, "Do you really mean that?"

"I've made it a habit to only say what I mean. It's no guarantee against my making a fool of myself, though. Perhaps I'm being a fool now, but better that than for me to distress you in any way. Obviously this has been a shock to you, and an unpleasant one; I don't want to make it worse."

"A shock only," she said. "More than you could ever know or guess."

I hardly dared to look at her, but did. She'd relaxed her tense posture and was no longer trembling. That was some little progress. "Will you talk with me, Nora? Please?"

Another long silence as she looked hard into my face. Then she nodded.

I closed my eyes with relief. "Thank you." I remained where I was so she might make the first move. That wise instinct told me she was still quite capable of taking flight, and it was best she advance at her own pace without any push to hurry on my part.

Very guarded and pulled into herself, she perched on Oliver's chair by the fire. I would have to be careful and slow. Difficult, for the strong urge rose in me to enfold her in my arms and try to give comfort. Later, perhaps, if and when she was ready for it. Now was not the time.

"Where shall we start?" she asked, clasping her hands together. She reminded me of a schoolboy about to be tested on a disagreeable topic.

Though the question wanted to leap out as a bellowed demand, I made my voice mild. "Why did you not prepare me, tell me this would happen?"

Her gaze dropped to the floor. "Because I didn't think it ever would."

"What do you mean?"

"You're not the only man I've loved in that way, Jonathan."

"There was another?"

"Several others, long before you."

This was hardly news considering how much she enjoyed the company of her gallants. As skilled as she was in making love, she'd have had to practice with and learn from someone, or many someones. All past and done with to be sure; there was no reason for me to be jealous, but all the same I couldn't help feeling a familiar barbed thorn trying to sprout in a dark place in my mind. I firmly ignored it.

"Others with whom you exchanged blood?" I prompted.

"Yes."

"So they could be like you?"

"Yes. But when they died . . . they stayed in their graves. It *never* worked."

"One must die for the change to occur?"

She nodded. "Over the years I came to think I would ever be lonely, that I could never share this existence with anyone else. That being true, then it wouldn't matter sharing my blood with those I truly loved. It was done for my pleasure—for our pleasure—but also I always hoped that *one* of you just might cheat death as I had. Jonathan, of them all, you're the only one who's ever come back."

Silence between us. Thick, viscid, and perturbing. "Wh-why? What makes me different?"

"I don't know."

"You have to know!"

"I don't! I don't even know why *I* came back!"

My mouth was like sand. "Nora, how did you die?"

She shook her head. "I'm not ready to speak of that yet."

Her voice was so hushed and suffused with pain, I gave up for the time being any thought of pressing her on the subject. A disappointment, and now came to roost the distressing notion that she did not possess the answers to all my questions. I'd feared that possibility. Since it was apparently becoming a reality, I would have to make the best of it. I nodded acceptance and squared up my shoulders. "Well, then. You didn't think any of your lovers would return, and yet you still hoped on? That's why you'd exchange blood, in that hope. Shouldn't you have given any of us some sort of a warning, though?"

She shook her head decisively. "I did once, and when I lost him forever I could not do it again for any other. It would have been too hard to bear."

"How so?"

She grimaced, then looked at me. "Pretend it's that night again, that night I shared all with you, only instead of taking you to my bed and letting it happen as it did, I first explain what I want to do and what might happen to you after you die. Would you not have second thoughts?"

"Possibly, but I'm sure I'd have done it anyway."

"But since none of the others had ever come back, I'd only be filling you with false hopes, the kind so brittle and sharp that when broken cut you right to the bone."

"None of that would matter to me, though, since I'd be dead and uncaring of the business."

"Not so for *me,* dear Jonathan. I told all of this to the first one, the first man I truly fell in love with. I explained everything to him, the consequences, the possibilities, everything there was to know about this—this condition. He had no objections, quite the contrary, and we lived and loved until the year the plague came. Right on his deathbed he was making plans for both of us for his return—only he never returned."

Tears. I'd seen her weep with sorrow but once before. Now did they stream down her cheeks.

"I miss and mourn him to this day. Losing him was made worse for me because of the hopes we'd had. He was so certain that he made me certain, and when I lost that . . . it was too much. Ever after I thought it best to live for the present and not the future. It made the partings when they came . . . easier."

"For you."

"For me. I was ever the one left behind."

"Until now."

She gave me a look such as would crack my heart.

"If this is what you've hoped for for so long, then why be afraid of me?"

"B-because of the one who made me like this. I was not born this way. He was my lover and shared his blood with me."

"Who?"

"You don't know him and likely never will." She brushed impatiently at her wet face. "He fed on people, on women. Said he loved them, said he loved me, but that he couldn't control his hunger. He killed to feed his hunger."

Understanding flooded me. "Dear God, no wonder you—oh, Nora, I'm *not* like him, and may God strike me dead before I ever become like him."

"But he said he couldn't help himself, that he *had* to—"

"Then he was either mad or a liar."

"Perhaps so. When I came back from death, I feared I'd soon be killing, too."

I felt a sharp chill stab through me, but made no sign of it. "And did you?"

"No. It wasn't in my heart to do so. I came to believe it was because

I'm a woman and made of softer feelings. I ran away before he knew of my return."

"To England?"

"France. I knew the language. There I came to see I need not live in fear of what I'd become, that this life could be very pleasant for myself and others, and there I first tried to make another like me."

"But all the while fearing he'd kill for blood like the first man?"

"I'd grown so desperate, was so wretchedly *lonely,* I was willing to sacrifice the lives of others to ease that loneliness."

I tried to imagine such solitude. My own experience with it was limited. I knew what it was to be alone, recalled certain miserable patches while passing from boyhood to manhood, but I'd never endured the kind of isolation Nora described. Even in my worst moments of missing her I knew I'd not have remotely considered taking or even risking the life of some unknown person in order to see her again.

"It must have been wretched, indeed," I whispered.

"It still is."

"Was," I hazarded, adding a note of hope to my tone.

"I don't know."

An honest response. "Then time alone will prove to you I'm no monster killing to feed an uncontrolled appetite."

A smile, so brief it hardly touched her lips. "He was mad or a liar or both. You are not like him. If you were you'd not be so kind to me."

"'Tis love, not kindness."

"People change. We've been apart for a very long while."

"I've not changed where my feelings for you are concerned. You've been in my thoughts constantly, and not just because of the questions I want to ask you. The years we were together here—you've touched me as no other woman could, Nora. Can you tell me they meant and mean nothing? Or have you changed? Or have you . . . have you found another?"

A sharp look. "No, I've not."

"Well, then. Do you love me?"

Eyes shut, then open. "Yes. Always."

I closed my own eyes, grateful, humbly grateful for that blessing. The heaviest burden of all had just lifted from my heart. But when I looked at her again, I saw she was yet watchful. "Then tell me what troubles you. Why are you still this way with me?"

"You'll learn of it sooner or later."

I gestured, silently urging her to go on.

She looked at the floor. "You know how I live. How I take a little from my cavaliers, and in return they gift me with the means to maintain my household. You know how I must keep them under the control of my will so there is no chance of rivalry amongst them, for each other or for me, else they'd be fighting or worse."

"Such as what happened with Tony."

"Yes. Have you done the same kind of thing yourself, bringing people around to your will?"

"Necessity forced me to learn to use that talent."

"Talent or curse."

"Both, then. What of it?"

"I cannot use it on you. It only works on those who are not like us."

I shrugged. "Again, what of it?"

"Don't you see how it is for me?"

I tried, but gave up, shaking my head.

"Because of that . . . talent, I am able to control others exactly the way I want to suit my interests, never mind their own."

"But you've never abused it to my knowledge."

"Have I not? With you? Jonathan, I can *control* them, and at the very last I was forced to control you so you would forget certain things, but now that you've changed—"

"You can't control me. Yes, I do see your meaning, but why would you want to?"

"It's not a question of want but of need. That's why I'm uneasy, fearful. With the others, with the way you were then, I always had that ultimate advantage. I could always be safe from any and all harm, always guide and determine things for my convenience, always avoid being hurt. Now that you've changed, I'm as vulnerable to harm from you as any normal woman is with a normal man."

"You can't think I'd ever want to hurt you," I protested.

She shifted ever so slightly in her chair, not meeting my gaze. It was answer enough.

This was a grievous blow. I bit back the pain as best I could. Nora had ever been the strongest, most confident of women. Now did I see the foundation of that strength and with that came an insight on why she was behaving this way. "You were bitterly injured in the past, were you not? By the one who changed you, perhaps? You must have, to think so badly of me."

Her expression grew dark. From what memory? "You see the face God gave me, because of it I'd ever been property in the eyes of others, a thing to be bargained and haggled over like a piece of cloth in a market and never more so than with him. In the end, when I'd changed, his control over me ceased to be. It was the one thing that saved me so I could leave him. But ever afterward there were always men wanting to possess me, tell me what to do, kill or die for me. I wanted only to be loved, not owned, and using my will on them was the one surety I had for achieving something close to that love."

"You risked this with your first love, did you not?"

"*Because* he was my first. I didn't know as much then as I did later. Things are different for me now."

"Things are different because your life is your own—"

"Then are women no longer property, bought and sold into marriage by custom or law or betrayed into the same by their own feelings? Am I not now betraying myself to you because of my feelings?"

"Or entrusting yourself, knowing that I would never willingly harm you."

"You say that now, but later, when you become jealous . . . I can't abide it. It's ever been the cause of all my sorrows."

"Then I shall have to give it up," I said lightly. "I only want to make you happy."

"I cannot live with you, Jonathan, if that's what you want."

"But can you live without me? How long have you waited to share this life with someone? Will you let past fears and hurts control you now that you've a chance to give up the loneliness? Or have you grown so used to having things your own way, having things so perfectly safe and orderly that you don't dare love for real? I'm taking the *same* risk, Nora. Think of that."

She did, and blushed.

"I'm not the man who hurt you. I am *this* man. He loves you more than life, and will do anything to preserve your happiness. You trusted me once before, did you not? And asked me if I trusted you. You once said you did not want a puppet. Well, here I am!"

Her eyes had grown wide, her mouth pursed; she was silent for so long a time I worried I'd said too much. "You're not afraid," she finally murmured.

"Only of losing you. But if that is what you wish—"

"No!" Very quick, very soft. She tucked in her lower lip and looked away. Betrayed by her feelings, no doubt, as was I.

"Nora?"

"You'll not try to keep me." From the hard, deliberate gaze she now fixed on me this was a statement, not a question.

"Only in my heart."

"And not judge or be jealous of me and what I do."

"If you'll do the same for me."

"I will not marry you."

"Your love is all the marriage we need. Should you cease to love me, then we'll part if you wish . . . but I hope to heaven you won't."

"Your word on this?"

"On my honor as a gentleman. And yours?"

"If my word alone before God will serve. I lost my honor ages ago, and I'm hardly a lady."

"You are and ever will be in my eyes."

That made her smile, bringing one to my lips in turn. Tentatively I extended one hand to her, palm up. As placation, as offering, as a plea, as all or none, for her to take or refuse as she chose.

She slipped her hand into mine.

Thank God.

*Now* was the time. I stood and drew her up to me, holding her close as I'd wanted to for so long, able to finally give her the comfort she very much needed but had been afraid to accept. Perhaps she thought my change had altered things between us, and though I didn't see it myself, I'd respect her experience. It was that or lose her. Never again.

Unlike our first night in her bed, I was now the experienced seducer, not she. Many beginnings suggested themselves, but only one was the best of all choices for this moment. A few kisses and caresses, then I unbuttoned my waistcoat, loosened my neckcloth, opened my shirt. I waited, looking at her.

She laughed, softly. "Like old times?"

"Yes," I whispered. "If you would."

Putting forth her hand, she let her spread fingers trace slowly up my bared chest. "I should like to do more than that . . . if you would."

Nothing could have better pleased me. As for pleasing Nora . . . well, I was determined to do my finest or die trying.

In a few short minutes we'd freed ourselves of most of our encumbering clothing. Being much taller than she, I made things more equal by stretching out on the hearth rug, dragging her down on top of me. There was more voice in her laughter now, I was very glad to hear.

The body remembers what may fade in the mind, and mine fell unresisting into the patterns of the past, recalling her likes and needs without a word being said. To be sure, our time apart did add exceedingly to our mutual desire. We kissed and touched, hands everywhere, limbs entwining as the warmth kindled and grew between us. Soon the fever of it seized me with greater heat than I'd ever known before, and Nora was tearing at me like a wild creature.

Even in the extremes of passion with other women, I had to always be mindful of my unnatural strength so as not to bring harm. Now I was suddenly aware of the hard muscles of Nora's own body and the realization I could venture more with her and do no injury . . . and she with me. I'd often suffered a bruise or two from her in an excellent cause; now were we both free to exercise ourselves fully, and did so with abandon.

I nipped at the velvet skin of her breasts and throat with my lips only, though my corner teeth were out as were hers. The sight of them in such a state had ever brought on arousal for me just as strongly as the sight of her body; I wondered if she had a similar reaction. Apparently so, I soon concluded, for her responses to my actions increased in aggressiveness and demand. We rolled and groaned and bucked against one another like animals. One second I was on her, the next she was on me. Neither of us hesitated, but hurtled forward without pause or waver.

Then was she truly on me, hips grinding away as though independent from the rest of her, pushing me up into her body. This suited well for her initial climax, and as it overtook her she fell forward, moaning, digging her teeth hard into my throat that she might prolong it. My blood surged forth, engendering for me a consummation more sharp, joyful, and delirious than those times past when I'd once merely pumped seed into her. She drew on me, her mouth hot, demanding all and taking more. Gasping from it, I felt my very life rushing out, but made not the least stirring to hinder its flow, so caught was I in the ecstasy of the act. If she wanted to drain me to a husk, then so be it; I was hers to have.

Her frenzied movements eventually slowed, but she continued to drink, pulling strongly on the vein she'd opened. It was wonderful; I'd never known anything to match it. It was keen and blinding, harsh and blazing. Brain and body, mind and spirit, all my being turned itself over to the pleasure. If it went on like this forever, then I'd have no need of heaven.

My sight clouded over. The glow from the candles merged with the shadows; the room seemed filled with a golden fog. It lay warm upon my skin like sunlight.

I held still except for stroking a lazy hand up along her bare back. As more and more of my blood went into her, even that easy motion became too much of an effort. My arm went lax and dropped away. I could not lift it again.

*She's killing me,* I thought. But that inner revelation did not alarm me in the slightest. I'd already died, and not nearly so marvelously as this; I had nothing to fear.

I fell into a kind of sleep close to that which came upon me during the day when I was not on my earth. This was without the bad dreams, though, and much more sensual. I was soaked through, submerged in a sea of absolute bliss. Waves of it overwhelmed me each time she swallowed. I sank far beneath its crystal surface, not caring if I ever come up again.

"Jonathan?"

I hated to respond, to have any interruption, but when she whispered my name a second, then a third time, I finally looked at her.

Her lips were red from my blood. Her eyes burned like living rubies. She ran one hand along my face, fingers brushing into my mouth, against my teeth. Some part of my lethargy tumbled away, and though weak as a kitten from what I'd given, with her help I slowly sat up. She yet crouched over my hips and now wrapped her legs around behind me, locking us together.

"Your turn," she murmured, letting her head fall back.

I could just see the swollen vein waiting under the pale velvet. The scent rising from it, the bloodsmell, pierced through my somnolence. My mouth sagged wide. Hunger and lust became one. Impossibly, for I'd thought myself past it, the fever rose up and seized me once more.

She made a shrill cry when, for the first time, I gouged into the virgin skin of her throat. Her whole body arced into it, pressing, holding, pulling me tighter as I swallowed a great draught of her blood, eagerly reclaiming that which she'd taken from me. My member flooded with new strength. Hips rocking back and forth, she sighed, her breath warm in my ear.

Another draught—no tiny drop carefully teased out and slowly savored, but a flaming mouthful of life's own purest nectar. I drank, deep and long as I could not do with anyone else. She clung to me, shuddering in time to it, one hand on the back of my head to push me harder, more deeply against her throat. I drank until her moans dwindled, hushed, and finally ceased, and she lay limp and unresisting against me like a sleeping child. Then did I stop, holding fast to the last quivers of pleasure as they echoed through me.

Some considerable time later we summoned sufficient will to sort ourselves a bit. Nora rested next to me on her back, serene and smiling; I lay on my side, head propped on one hand that I might gaze down at her. The candles were low, the fire nearly gone. A faint glimmer from the embers remained. Not enough to give warmth, but we had no worry for any chill.

She'd not changed except to become more beautiful in my eyes, and after this night she was above and beyond all other women for me. Though she saw it differently, our shared condition had altered nothing about my feelings toward her. If she felt the need to set limitations—such as they were—on me, on whatever future awaited us, to feel safe, then so be it. Ultimately, I knew only with the passage of time could I show myself worthy of the fragile trust she'd just placed in me. That trust would be tested sooner or later; she'd said as much already. When the test came I prayed I would be wise enough to recognize it and put to rest all her fears of jealousy and betrayal.

The testing would likely have to do with her cavaliers. She might expect me to come to resent them, for I did not see her giving them and their gifts up. Not so much because of the loss of money and blood they provided, but because of their importance to her sense of freedom and confidence. If I made offer to fully support her—as I could well afford to do—she'd not welcome it. I could and would never ask her to cease seeing them. That would violate our pact and drive her from me in one witless move. I'd given my word; I would hold myself to it no matter what.

As for the pleasure they gave her and got in return . . . well, I'd ever had the decided advantage since my days at Cambridge. She may have dallied with them, fed from them, enjoyed their company, affection, attention, and money, but she loved and went to bed with me. So things would be now, I expected, but even better. Without her imposed influence in my mind, I might be subject to a pang or two of jealousy, but I'd just have to live with it or lose her. I could no more resent her diversions with others than she could my sporting with the ladies at Mandy Winkle's—though that sort of pastime might be less frequent for me now that Nora had returned. Compared to her, the other women were little more than a charming temporary distraction.

But the future I contemplated would be with us soon enough and take care of itself. The present had just been and continued to be very agreeable. As to the past . . . there was too much of it that was yet dark to me.

I wondered about this man who had rendered her change. What sort of tyrant was he, and why had he been so cruel to such a woman as Nora? Or to any woman for that matter? To kill others to sustain one's own life . . . ugh. Through no fault of my own and in the most extreme of circumstances I'd come close to doing it myself and could *understand* such hunger, but thankfully, heaven had spared me from committing that particular sin. Apparently this monster wantonly murdered, excusing his abominations by claiming it was beyond his control. What rot—and Nora and I were the solid proof of it. It sickened me that she'd known so evil a man, had endured his touch. Certainly it was a tribute to her inner strength that she was as recovered as she was from what must have been a terrible ordeal.

Where was he now, and was he yet a threat to her? If so, then he was in for a great surprise for here in me was her own special champion. When she was ready I'd question her more closely on the fellow. I'd question her on quite a lot of things. God knows, I'd barely started yet, but there was time for it. Now that we were together again, there would be plenty of time for talk.

"Shall we dress?" she asked, cracking her eyelids a fraction to see me.

"So soon? But it's been such a long time, my dearest." I leaned over to kiss her forehead, my free hand making very free with one of her breasts.

"That it has, but I'm ill-prepared tonight."

"Not that I could tell."

"I can. I'm so feeble I shall have to find refreshment—no, don't you dare tempt me, Jonathan."

"But it's your turn to take from me, is it not?" My hand had wandered down to an even more intimate area of her person. She writhed about, but did not retreat or make me stop. "It will refresh us both, I'm thinking."

"Perhaps so, but I couldn't—oh! Well, perhaps I could. But only to make things even between us. We can't tolerate much blood loss, you know."

I'd tolerate her draining me to the dregs as long as it was this gratifying.

This time were we slower, more gentle with one another. Nora's kiss was soft and lingered long, taking my blood away gradually, and giving back a joyful quickening to my senses so intense that I hovered perilously on the edge of a swoon from the elation.

It had not been like this for me since our time at Cambridge. I'd missed it, craved it. Small wonder I'd been so tempted to want Yasmin to do this to me; I was glad now to have pushed away from her. It had been for the girl's own good, but aside from that responsibility, I realized her efforts, enchanting and exquisite as they might have proved, would have been but a poor substitute. Only Nora could give me such perfect fulfillment.

As always, it was over too soon, alas. She could go on for the rest of the night and it would have still been over too soon, but this would have to suffice until our next meeting. She ceased taking from me, licked one last time at my wounds, and with a sigh settled into the crook of my arm. I was in no hurry to move, both for the opportunity to hold her and because I'd grown weak again; not nearly as bad as before, but it seemed best to indulge in moderation until I'd restored myself at some neighbor's stable.

"I'm glad you shaved," she said, lightly touching her lips. They were a bit puffed and reddened, not from blood this time, but from the constant friction against my skin.

"So am I." I was also careful about touching my neck. She'd exercised great delicacy on me for the last hour or more, but for all that the area was rather tender. Nothing a quick vanishing wouldn't take care of, though. Later, perhaps, when I was more recuperated. "When next we do this, I should like to lay in a good supply of beef or horse blood. Then we won't have to stop."

"An excellent idea, my dear. I shall look forward to it."

"Then let it be soon." If I could have moved I'd have tried loving her again. Sweet heavens, but it had been so damnably long. But she was with me again, and things promised to be better than ever between us.

"Was your death painful?" Her question, breaking into my thoughts out of nowhere, startled me. "If you don't wish to speak of it—"

"No, it's all right. I've just never talked about it before. I didn't want to cause Father or Elizabeth any discomfort, and it's not one of my favorite memories. But to answer, yes, it was, but it was very quick. I've had worse since then."

"What could be worse?"

"If I told you we should be here all night."

"Have you anything else to do?"

"Yes, but I fear it would be too physically taxing for both of us."

"Rogue. You've yet to explain why you were stalking around your cousin's empty house with a pistol."

"Dear me, yes. Are you awake enough for a long listen?"

"You must know by now we don't sleep like other people."

"Indeed I do, and what a trial it was to learn that."

She put her hand on my cheek. "I *am* sorry."

I kissed her palm. "It's all right. I understand now. Past and done. Time to move forward." I paused a moment to think and compose . . . where to begin? At the beginning? And where and when might *that* be? I supposed on the hot August morning when Beldon and I had our unfortunate encounter with Lieutenant Nash and those Hessians. I'd never asked Nash why he'd been blundering about the island with a pack of German soldiers. They should have been with their own officers. I suppose he'd been forced to use whoever had been at hand to hunt down the Finch brothers. Would things have gone differently for me had Beldon and I left a few minutes earlier or later? Or if I'd worn another color coat?

*Past and done,* I thought. Thankfully, because of Nora, I still had a future. One with Nora in it. That was all I ever wanted or needed. Turning on my side again, I put an arm around her and commenced telling her everything.

* * *

Interruptions upon such a lengthy recital are inevitable, but Nora kept hers to a minimum. Still, it seemed a remarkably long while before I thought to pause, and the fancy was becoming fact the next time I noticed the mantel clock. The dawn was too close for me. Now that Nora was here, the dawn would ever be too close for me.

We'd quit the hearth rug and dressed ourselves. This time she sat next to me on the settee, as close as she could get.

"I hope you don't mind about the others," I said, after a diplomatically brief mention of how I'd dealt with my carnal needs with other women.

"You were careful with them?" she asked. She did not seem in the least bothered by the subject. A relief, that.

"Always. Perhaps more so than necessary."

"I'm glad to hear it. You seem to have fared well in your change just by following your own best judgment."

"And what I recalled of your example . . . though I never once saw you vanish."

"I don't do it often. It tires me."

"Why is it we can do it?"

She shook her head. "I don't know the why, only that we can. Perhaps it's to allow us an easy escape from our graves at night and a quick return to them in the morning."

"It was very useful to me that first time, but I've not been back to my grave since. I can't abide closed-in places even now."

"For which I cannot fault you."

"Why do we have such awful dreams without our earth to rest on?"

A shrug this time. "I could not say."

"Elizabeth thinks our return to life requires some sort of a compromise, that we must carry a bit of the grave along with us in exchange for leaving it."

"That sounds as good a reason as any I've ever considered."

"Why are we not permanently harmed by weapons?"

"I'm not sure. We heal so fast, and we vanish to heal. The two might be connected in some way."

"Why do we not reflect in mirrors?"

"I don't know. Perhaps we're invisible to them the way we're sometimes invisible to people, only it's beyond our conscious control. In some parts of the world it is thought it's because we've lost our souls, but I don't believe that."

It did sound foolish. "Why is crossing water such a hardship?"

"Because it separates us from the earth?"

"Not fair, a question for a question."

"Better than my saying 'I don't know' to you all the time."

"What *do* you know, then?"

"To always have a goodly supply of earth with me, to always and ever be prepared for calamities like fire, flood, and gossips, to make sure my servants are loyal, discreet, and well paid, to always be home an hour before dawn . . ." She had quite a list of things, most I already knew, all of them exceedingly practical. "Will that suffice for you?" she asked when finished. "There's more."

"It seems more than enough."

"Not nearly enough, I fear. I cannot reduce all my experience down to but an hour of talk."

"Nor can I give all my questions to you in one evening." Of course there would be many more evenings ahead for us, but I was of a mind to fill them with other activities than lessons. This brought an idea to mind, though. "Dearest, you asked me earlier to pretend it was our first night to exchange blood. I'll ask the same of you. If you had explained all to me at that time, what would you have said?"

She thought for a while. "Well, I would have first asked if you had ever heard of *nosferatu.*" Quite the foreign word it was to judge by her intonation and accent.

Under her intent gaze I cudgeled my brain a moment. "A Baltic seaport, isn't it?"

# CHAPTER

# ◄10►

She looked at me, perplexed and gaping for an instant, then suddenly exploded with laughter, fairly rocking with it. While glad to provide her so much amusement, I was also annoyed at not understanding the reason behind it.

"Nora . . ."

With an effort she managed to restore her poise again, but each time she glanced at me, she seemed ready to burst out again. "I'm sorry. So much has happened tonight I must be giddy."

"Think nothing of it," I said dryly. "Just tell me where *Nosferatu* is and what it has to do with things."

"It is a what, not a where, and it's the name we are called in some parts of the world."

I scowled, pronouncing the unfamiliar syllables in my mind. "Can't say I like it much, then. Sounds like a badly done sneeze."

More sudden mirth. This time I was able to join in to some extent. When the latest fit passed, she said, "There are others you just might know: *upier, murony, strigon, vrykolakas, Blutsäuger—*"

"Wait—I heard that one from some Hessian soldiers . . . don't like it much, either—especially the way they spoke it."

"There's more. I've studied. The common name you might know in English is 'vampire.' "

I mouthed the word experimentally. It was just as strange as the others she'd named. "Can't say that I do."

"Oliver Goldsmith mentioned it in his *Citizen of the World.* Have you read of it?"

"I fear not."

"Well, it was more than a decade and a half ago. I'm as eager to add to my knowledge of this condition as you are and have assembled a nice little collection of all the books I've found with allusions to and reports about vampires. I'll let you browse through it if you like."

"Indeed I would."

"However, what you will read and what we are have ever been two very different things. Many of the accounts of vampires are mixed in with hauntings, grave robbing, devil worship, demonic possession, and some goings-on so ghastly or nonsensical it makes you wonder if people have any wits at all. I'm sure we're linked to it because our drinking blood disgusts and frightens them so much. That's why I have to be so careful about keeping my needs a secret. In the past I'd have been burned for it or had my head cut off and my heart torn out. It could still happen in certain places."

"That's utterly horrible. Who would do such a thing?"

"Any number of otherwise upright God-fearing people. We're different from them, we drink blood to live, therefore we must be evil. I've often thought of writing up my own account of who and what we really are, setting things down correctly for good and all, but for the deep roots of the superstitions and the fact that I've so little real information. The man who changed me was not too forthcoming with his knowledge—"

*Either,* I silently added.

"—and I have no wish for him to know I'd returned."

"He thinks you're dead?"

"I certainly pray so. I've not seen or heard of him for many years. It would be a good thing for the world if he were dead, but considering how the change toughens us, I would not expect it. It grieves me, for it means he's still probably killing others, but there's nothing I can do to stop him."

"Perhaps the two of us together might do something about him."

She pursed her lips and glanced away. "*That* is an undertaking I should have to think over very carefully. He's dangerous."

"So am I. So are we both."

"I wouldn't know where to start looking for him, though I suppose I could learn how. Let me think on it, Jonathan. There's so much more for you to learn first, anyway."

"Such as?"

She stood, as smooth and as supple as a cat, to stretch as much as her corseting would allow. I stayed where I was, watching appreciatively.

There was a portrait of Oliver's late father over the mantel; Nora went for a closer look, then gestured at it. "Do you recall the painting of me in the antique costume?"

"The one in your bedroom? The one that makes it obvious the artist was in love with you?"

My reward was a smile. "That one, yes. What you need to know is that was not a costume, but real clothing. *My* clothing."

Now was I smiling. "What are you saying?"

"The painting was done over a hundred years ago. Just as you see me here, so was I alive a hundred years ago to pose for it."

I shook my head. Was she joking? But her manner was entirely serious.

"It's a lot to take in, I know, but I've not gone mad. This is a very hard truth, the hardest I shall ever impart to you. Please trust that I hardly believed it for myself when I learned of it, so I'll not take it amiss if you don't believe it, either."

"You're telling me you're over one hundred years old?"

"Yes. Our condition makes it possible. I've not aged since my death years and years ago."

"And . . . when was that?"

She tucked in her lower lip. "No, I'll tell you later. You're still trying to accept it. Best if you think it over first. You may take as much time as you like. In a decade or two your friends will finally convince you."

Her plain-spoken bearing alone was starting to convince me. "This is no jest?"

"No."

"We do not age?"

"I think it has to do with how the vanishings heal us. It keeps us young."

"But that's impossible."

"Our very existence should be impossible, Jonathan, yet here we are."

Sitting in one spot, staring at nothing, and no doubt looking like a stunned sheep occupied me for a goodly period. On top of everything else, this particular revelation was just too much to take in, but the certitude that she spoke the truth began to trickle into my overworked brain.

She went on. "We do not age, we do not sicken—I don't know if we can even die."

"But all things die."

"Then perhaps we will, eventually; that knowledge is presently beyond my ken. In the meantime, please don't burden yourself thinking on it too much. I told you this because you need to know it; it's not meant to distress you."

"How could it distress me?"

"You'll discover that soon enough."

"Tell me now," I said, straightening myself to fix her with a direct look.

She turned away, placing her hands on the mantel. "The sad fact is we outlive our loves. That was another reason why I wanted you to forget me. Had you remained in England, we might have lived on together. The years might have passed, with me staying as I am, and you growing older and older . . . then dying. I've been through it before. At times it has almost driven me mad.

"When you got that letter from your father, I hated the thought of losing you, but it seemed better to let you go on with your life. Then would you always be alive in my memory, young and vital as I'd known you best. It was a hard parting for me, but easier than watching the years eating at you. Because of this unnatural lengthening of life and youth, I've had to learn to live one night at a time, to enjoy and cherish whatever time God grants me to be with anyone I love; otherwise I should have truly gone mad years ago from all the losses."

Simple words, simply said, and the appalling possibilities began to yawn before me. That I, too, would live on, that those I loved would age and die while I remained young and strong . . .

She looked back and saw the anguish creeping over me. Coming to sit by me again, she took my hands in her own. "This is the heartbreaking burden we carry that outweighs all the advantages we possess."

"But can—can we not exchange our blood with others? Make them like us?"

"Yes, it need not be done in a carnal manner. I've tried. But except for you and myself, it's never worked."

"Then we must discover what has made us different from them. We must."

"But—"

"Look, Oliver's taken it upon himself to study all he can of my condition. He might be able to help."

She appeared to be dubious over that idea, but made no immediate objection.

I listened to the tick of the clock as a silence settled between us. Would time have a different meaning now that I knew it had no effect on me? Yes. Decidedly yes. Knowing I had so much of it and those I loved had so little, time with them was now more precious than my soul's rest.

How old was Nora? Was she more than one hundred? Possibly. Probably. Sometimes she'd say things, odd things . . . I'd never paid them much mind before. There was a bad habit that wanted correcting. She spoke of the plague, but there hadn't been anything like that in London since the Great Fire. Her portrait, the clothes she'd worn, even the artist's manner of painting, those should have given me ample warning. Perhaps she'd worked her influence on me yet again, keeping me from becoming too curious at the time. Well, I was immune from her influencing, so that was all over and done. The temptation to press her for more information was there, but perhaps not wise to attempt just now. She was right that I was still taking it all in. When she was ready—or rather when she judged me ready—she would tell me more of herself.

"You do understand that we are not fertile?" she asked.

I stirred, dragging my thoughts over to this new subject. "I came to think as much when I failed to expel seed the first time I bedded a lady after my change."

"Does it trouble you?"

"In honesty I can't say I've really missed it—in regards to my achievement of satisfaction, that is; what I take pleasure from now is so much superior than what I experienced before my change that I might be troubled by a return to my previous state."

"A fortunate blessing, that."

"Most fortunate. Though I may no longer procreate, the desire to do so is apparently unimpaired. Quite to the contrary, since the enjoyment is so increased, the desire to have the enjoyment is also . . . increased. Or so I have found it." God, but with that thought invading my mind—and particularly—my body, I abruptly wanted her all over again. Tempting, but dangerous. She'd have to leave soon, far too soon for what I wanted to do. Kissing each of her hands would have to do for now, and a poor substitute it was to be sure.

She favored me with an affectionate smile, for she could certainly read the thoughts that had just flickered over my face. "Yes, I know all about the desire. We are at least allowed fleshly pleasures, if not the usual outcome of them, though this exchanging of blood we do is our own way—our one way of propagating."

"But for its success to also be such a rare occurrence would seem to make it a pointless pursuit—except in terms of expressing affection or giving and gaining pleasure."

"Are you going to ask me why it is so?"

I gave her a wry glance. "Not unless you have an answer."

"Sadly, I do not."

"Then I shall not bother to try."

Soft laughter from her. She seemed very easy in her manner. Now would be the time to introduce a difficult subject of my own.

"Nora, are you sure you don't mind the other women I've known?"

"If I did, then I should be a great hypocrite."

"There were other women before I left England, as well."

"I was ever well aware of them, my dear. Though discreet with me, you and Oliver made quite a name for yourselves around Covent Garden back then. The gossips had a fine time discussing your adventures with the ladies there."

Her tone was light, so I pushed ahead. "You need to know about one lady in particular, though."

"Do I?"

"It has to do with why I was carrying the pistol."

"She has a jealous husband? There are other, less forceful ways of dealing with such problems."

"It's more complicated than that."

I then told her about the family Christmas gathering.

And about Clarinda.

And Aunt Fonteyn's death.

And Ridley and Arthur's attack.

And finally, about Richard.

All in all, she took it rather well.

*"Cousin Jon'th'n!"*

For such a little boy, Richard had quite a bellow. My attention was immediately swept to the top of the stairs where Mrs. Howard firmly held him, else he'd have launched himself down their length to give greeting. As one footman closed the entry doors of Fonteyn House behind me, I threw my discarded cloak to another, then shot forward and up to the landing.

"Hallo, laddie! Hallo, Mrs. Howard," I said, grabbing him away from her and raising him overhead. He squealed and giggled fit to burst, kicking his legs. "I've missed you. How have you been?"

"Very well, thank you. Will we go back to Cousin Ol'ver's now?"

I glanced at Mrs. Howard, who appeared interested to know as well. "Not this evening, I fear."

"When?"

"I don't know."

Nora's arrival had seriously diverted me from necessary business, and would likely delay things again tonight when I talked to Elizabeth and Oliver. I felt badly for all the trouble I'd put them to, for they'd vacated the house and waited all this time for nothing since I'd not accomplished all my errands. But faced with a similar circumstance I doubt anyone else would have chosen differently. Nora had returned at long last; no matter that she'd come at an inconvenient time so long as she *had* come.

I'd been reluctant to part with her this morning, and very unwilling to let her go home unescorted, but she'd insisted, saying she above all people in the city was safest from its dangers. In that I knew her to be wholly correct, but it was still a wrench to say good-bye and just let her walk away. Perhaps this was a test of my promise not to infringe upon her freedom.

If so, then I failed miserably, for tired as I was, I took to the air and spied on her progress.

It was brisk, for she had ever enjoyed a good walk in the past. She was stopped not once, but several times by men. Obviously an unescorted woman was fair and easy game for such predators as roamed about during the darkest hours of the night. But each time she encountered one of these miserable brutes, she spoke fearlessly to him. He would then step out of her way, allowing her to continue on without so much as a backward glance for him. Obviously she was most adept at influencing them, else she'd have come to grief long ago.

I did nearly go solid again when three drunken villains spied her and lurched across the street to cut her off. She'd never be able to influence that many at once, or so I assumed, and prepared myself to dive to her rescue and explain things later. But by the time they got to her, she was, quite literally, no longer in sight.

From my high vantage I tried to find her again, but my vision was limited in this form. I'd only taken my eyes from her for an instant when I'd seen the trio first take notice of her. By the time I'd looked back, she was gone. This confused them as much as it did me, until I understood that she must have vanished to avoid them.

*Well and good for you, Nora,* I thought, headily relieved I did not have to play the hero after all, and feeling foolish that I'd dared even this much. The lady could take care of herself and had done so for better than a century without any help from me. I went home.

Just before retiring to the cellar for the day, I'd left a note in the consulting room addressed to Jericho instructing him not to come by in the evening, that I'd be over directly upon my awakening. A second note for Elizabeth and Oliver promised them I had news, but it was still not safe to return. Someone apparently found and delivered my missives, for Oliver's home was again a silent place when consciousness returned to me at sunset. I quickly dressed and had a thorough look 'round the street for unsavory loiterers. None were to be seen, but whether that was good or ill remained to be discovered. A short walk convinced me I was not being followed, and taking a quick turn in between some buildings where I would not be observed, I vanished and floated high. The wind was fresh and in the right direction; I rode it like an eagle to Fonteyn House.

"You like it there at Oliver's?" I asked my son.

"Yes, sir."

"What about this place?"

"It's all right, but you weren't here."

I hugged him tight, dangerously close to choking on a lump in my throat. "Well, thank you very much. Tell me what you did today."

"We went rabbit hunting, but didn't catch any, and then I played steeplechase."

"You want to play it again?"

"Yes, please!"

"All right, time to mount up." After a number of complicated moves, involving turning him upside down and sideways—much to his delight—I finally got him on my back. He clamped his arms hard around my neck, and I took solid hold of his legs, then we were off.

Fonteyn House, being much larger than Oliver's, afforded us a longer, more interesting course to follow. At his whim we galloped through the lengthy halls, chased a few of the more nimble maids and some of the younger footmen, and otherwise won our combination race and foxhunt. We ended up in the nursery. Mrs. Howard's supervision of that area was as competent as ever, for the room was in good order, warm, and—remarkably for this house—cheerful. Several candles were alight; certainly they were the most helpful in chasing off the shadows. In the middle of the floor lay the square of carpet Richard had insisted on bringing along. Some toys were scattered over it; I noted with a glad heart the painted wooden horse among them.

Richard was anxious to show me something, else we'd have had a second circuit of the house. As soon as I'd put him down, he pushed the toys out of the way and told me several times to watch him. I put on an attentive face and obeyed.

Crouching on all fours at one edge of the carpet, he tucked his head down and rolled forward, heels over head, making a complete turn. He looked at me expectantly. I applauded and told him he was very clever, and if he would be so kind as to give a second demonstration that I might admire his performance once more. He immediately obliged.

After many additional exhibitions of this new skill, he started to look somewhat red in the face and dizzy, so I asked if he would teach me how to do it as well. This struck him most favorably, and he was soon issuing orders like an army sergeant. I had to position myself just this way, put my head down just that way—he was quite the expert. Finally I was allowed to roll forward. My long limbs being an impediment to such games, I tumbled over with a less than graceful form and crashed flat on my back with a thud. The noise impressed Richard, so I added to it, wailing that I'd near broken my spine, and I'd never achieve his expertise at this game. He said I only wanted more practice, so with many a groan I tried again, finishing with even more noise.

"Jonathan?"

Still on my back with my head toward the door, I had a topsy-turvy view of Elizabeth looking down at me. Oliver stood behind her, craning his head over her shoulder to see.

"Hallo, sweet sister and most excellent cousin! Oof!" Richard had thrown himself on my stomach.

"He's gone mad," Elizabeth pronounced in solemn tones. "Not stark staring, but God have pity on us all the same."

"Not mad, just somewhat delirious. Oh, you'll tickle me, will you?"

Richard giggled, again digging his fists into my ribs, responding with more laughter when I threatened to pinch his nose off. Fearlessly, he thrust his face forward, daring me to do my worst. I told him it was no sport that way, stood up—with him clinging to one of my legs—and stumped about the room complaining about my astonishingly bad limp. When I was on the carpet once more, he slipped free, laughing, and started to bolt off, but I caught him 'round the waist and lifted him high, which was very well received.

"You'll upset his stomach with all that larking about," Elizabeth cautioned.

"I'm fine!" Richard yelled, rather muffled as his petticoats engulfed his face. By now I held him by his heels, and his arms dangled loose toward the floor.

"Can you walk on your hands?" I asked.

In answer, he put his palms to the fioor, and letting him have just enough of his weight to feel it, I paraded once around the room.

"Excellent, laddie! I've never seen better." Reaching the carpet, I eased him down until he lay flat, red-faced, and puffing. He'd catch his breath in a minute, then we'd start all over again.

"What about the Mohocks?" Oliver demanded during the respite. "What happened last night? Did you see Arthur?"

"I saw—well, this isn't the time or place to tell you what happened."

Oliver, interpreting this in the worst possible sense, went pale and grim. "Good God."

"No, I don't mean—that is—I've much to tell you but not about what you think. I just can't say anything until—"

"Quite right," agreed Elizabeth. "You'll get no sense from him until he's had his nightly dose of Richard."

"I'll come to the blue drawing room as soon as I can," I promised.

"Soonest, if you please," she told me with an arch look.

Of course they'd be eaten through with curiosity having waited all night and all day for some word from me. The note would have only stirred them up rather than satisfied. Damnation. I hated having this matter encroaching on my time with Richard.

Time . . .

No. That was yet too dark a topic to think about. Nora was right to live within the short increments of a single night. Considerations of future sorrows could wait until their arrival; best to cherish the present while it was here.

Unfortunately, the present was all too brief. Having little else to do that day, Elizabeth and Oliver had spent most of it keeping Richard fully occupied, or so he informed me when he recounted some of his adventures at rabbit hunting. He'd summoned quite a burst of dash at my coming, but was fast losing hold of it, particularly after a second bout of tumbling over the rug. As an alternative to all the exercise, I offered to read aloud from his collection of chapbooks. One of the maids turned up with a cup of ass's milk with honey for him. Mrs. Howard, who had made herself scarce so we could play unimpeded, must have ordered it. The girl stared at us closely, nearly upsetting her tray while putting it on a table.

"Have a care," I said, schooling myself to patience. She'd likely noticed Richard's resemblance to me and my own to him and was having trouble dealing with it. Well, Edmond had warned me about this sort of thing. I wearily wondered if I'd end up influencing every servant on the estate just to spare us the complications of gossip. The maid finally scuttled out, with many a backward look. Silly creature.

"Tastes different," Richard said, looking dubiously into his cup.

"That's because it's from the country. The asses here eat better fodder than their city cousins, so their milk is bound to be different. It's not sour, is it?"

"No. Sweet."

"The cook must like you then and put in extra honey in your honor."

I found a chair, settled him on my lap, and read as he drank. Both worked a charm; by the time I was a quarter through the reading, he'd nodded off.

Though I should have rung for Mrs. Howard and popped him into bed, I lingered a bit, holding him.

He was so precious. In every sense of the word and beyond, until words failed, he was the dearest of all the treasures a generous God had ever bestowed upon me. Precious, for his own sake alone, but also for being my son, the only true legacy of my life as a normal man, if not also the most heartbreaking; for if my acquired agelessness proved true, then in all likelihood I would long outlive him. Ahead of me lay the awful prospect I would outlive everyone I loved. Nora's gift was not a mere mixed blessing, but could also rightly be called a curse.

She tried hard to make that clear to me last night.

Once Nora was over the happy surprise of the boy's existence, she went all sober again, finally divulging afresh the grim inevitability of pending heartache.

"Why are you so anxious to sadden me?" I asked.

"I'm not, but I've lived through this without knowing any of it and have ever regretted my ignorance. Now that I know better, I do all I can to treasure the time I have with those I love and strongly urge you to do the same. Life is so damnably *fleeting,* and not everyone is able to see how carelessly they squander their little portion of it. Empty mundanities crowd their days, their thoughts, their actions, and before they're aware of it their lives are spent and gone forever. I never waste time in futile argument over trifles, but rather cling to the joys I can share and give however great or small they may be. Never, *never* forget how long your time is compared to the brevity of others."

So I held my son and there and then said a humble prayer of gratitude for Richard's life, a plea for his continued health and happiness, and asked to be given the wisdom to provide both to him to the best of my ability. My eyes had misted over by the time I got to the *amen.* Sniffing, I rose and gently lay him on his bed, then just watched him sleep for a while. The rise and fall of his breast, the soft patter of his heart, the pure translucence of his skin, all held me in thrall until Mrs. Howard came back from wherever she'd gotten to and asked if all was well.

"Exceedingly well," I answered. "Fell right to sleep on me."

"He had a very busy day what with the rabbit hunting with Mr. Oliver and Miss Elizabeth. They didn't find any, but I think it was more for the exercise and to pass the time than to put anything on the supper table."

"I shall have to thank them for looking after him. I should like to hear about the rest of his day, but it will have to wait 'til later."

"Yes, sir. Will we be returning to Mr. Oliver's house soon?"

"As soon as may be. I thought you liked it in the country, though."

"Indeed I do, sir. If we could stay on here until your father and mother arrived from the colonies it would suit me well enough."

But it would hardly suit the rest of us to be deprived of Richard's immediate company. On the other hand, if the Marling estate could be made livable, Mrs. Howard would have her country home within a few months. I kept this news to myself for the moment. Mentioning it would lead to more conversation, and I very much needed to be elsewhere. I wished her a good evening, pressed a light good-night kiss on Richard's brow, and hurried downstairs.

* * *

The next hour was an interesting one for Elizabeth and Oliver as I broke the news to them of Nora's return. Elizabeth jumped up to embrace me, for she saw I was in a mood to rejoice, and Oliver grinned and pounded my back in congratulation. Then did they sit again to ply me with a thousand rapid questions, and I did my best to give good replies.

"In Bath all this time?" Oliver shook his head, bemused. "She must have been living quietly indeed. A number of our circle goes there for the waters. Strange none of 'em saw her."

"Not so strange when you consider she's only up and about at night. It was Mrs. Poole who took the waters, and she's not as noticeable as Nora."

"What was the lady suffering from?"

"Nora didn't say. There was so much else to talk about. . . ."

And I talked about it to them—leaving out, of course, the spritely dances Nora and I had enjoyed on the hearth rug. I also left out the business of not aging, thinking it better to introduce that subject at another time. Having barely taken it in myself, I was not prepared to rationally reveal the details to others. Perhaps Nora could be persuaded to tell them, since she knew more of it.

"What did Nora think about Richard?" Elizabeth asked after I got to that point in my tale.

"Oh, she's very pleased about the whole business. Thinks it's just wonderful, seeing how things are for me now." Thus did I delicately allude to my infertile state.

Elizabeth understood, briefly tucking in her lower lip. "Is—is she unable to bear children?"

"Sadly, yes."

"*Sad* is an inadequate word for it, little brother. That poor woman."

"Unless one considers that I'm something of an offspring of hers," I added.

They did, to which Oliver said: "Very 'something of,' Coz, if the achievement of this condition is as rare as she says."

"We're hoping your medical knowledge might be helpful in explaining why this is so."

His eyebrows jumped. "You do expect a lot from me . . . but I'll do all I can, of course. What did she think of Clarinda, though? I mean about the boy's conception taking place while you and Nora were still . . . well . . . *you* know."

"She was not jealous if that's what you're worried about. At most she only questioned my taste. But I told her I was after all very young at the time." Unspoken was her reply that I was *still* very young.

"That's a relief. You've enough complications in your life already. Did you tell her anything about our recent troubles?"

"Seeing how closely they're connected with Richard, I had to tell her everything about them."

"What does she think of it?"

"That it's perfectly horrible, and she's all for my clearing the mess up as quickly as possible. She's offered to help if she can, but at this moment I don't see how."

"She knows plenty of gentlemen in the city. Some of them could secretly be Mohocks, y'know, and have useful information for us."

"We discussed that very possibility, but she hasn't seen any of 'em since she left for Italy all that time back. Her offer to help is more in the line of lending any and all aid from her household if we need it. Fonteyn House is ably defended, but it would harm nothing to have some extra eyes and ears about the place until this business is done."

"Excellent idea. When shall we see 'em?"

"I hadn't really settled that with her, but I can go by and talk with her later." Indeed, I was most anxious to see her again. Last night had been a true wonder, but we had much lost time to make up.

"When will she be coming for a visit?" asked Elizabeth. "Did you tell her how much I wanted to meet her?"

"Yes, I did, and she was a bit taken aback by it, too."

"Whatever for?"

"This condition of being a 'vampire,' as she calls it, has made her very shy about revealing it to people. Times were when one could be burned at the stake for taking such peculiar nourishment, so you can understand why she's a bit wary. To hear that you not only know of it, but fully accept it is quite much more than a novelty to her. It may take her awhile to get used to the idea, but she expressed a stong interest in meeting Richard, so it shouldn't be very difficult to persuade her to a visit."

"We'll have a late tea with her or something," she said, "with the two of you having your own preferred drink in a separate pot." Oliver made a slight choking sound, but she ignored him. "Where is she staying?"

"At her London house."

"But I thought it was deserted."

"Not anymore. As soon as she got my note, she came up from Bath in her coach with a few of her people. They'll have the place opened and aired out by now, perhaps not to the point of receiving guests, but they should have the worst of the cobwebs swept away."

"Admirable, very admirable," said Oliver, who was starting to squirm in his chair. "But while I don't wish to belittle the importance of Miss

Jones turning up, I shall burst a blood vessel if you don't give us any news about the business at hand. *Did* you talk to Arthur?"

Lest his growing agitation do him harm, I quickly imparted what I'd learned, namely about Arthur Tyne's hasty dissappearance. "He must have got the wind up once he saw the story of Ridley's murder in the papers," I added. "He's probably halfway to France by now."

"If he has any sense," said Elizabeth. "What about the Mohocks? Did you see Mr. Litton?"

"Not a sign of them, and I was interrupted by Nora before I could visit the chap. Oh, yes, Edmond came by just before I left to see Arthur."

"Did he? You have had a busy time of it. What did he want?"

I told them of my conversation with our justifiably ill-tempered cousin at the coffee house. "He said I could talk to Clarinda to see if she knew more than she was telling. I promised to come by tonight."

"Will you be influencing her?"

"Only if necessary," I hedged.

Elizabeth did not approve of this talent, handy as it was to us all, and she knew what I was trying to avoid discussing with her. "I rather think it will be very necessary, so do be careful, Jonathan."

"Do you want company?" asked Oliver.

"Not unless you plan to keep Edmond entertained while I'm interviewing his wife."

"Ulp. Hadn't thought of that, but I'll do it if you—"

I waved him down. "No need to make such a noble sacrifice just yet, Coz. I'd be glad to have you along, but he was reluctant enough to let me in, and for the both of us to turn up might be more than his temper will bear. Besides, Edmond could heap you with questions neither of us is prepared to answer just yet, if ever. I should be much easier in my heart not to have that possibility as a distraction while I'm talking with Clarinda, and very much easier knowing you were on watch here, keeping everyone safe."

Happily, additional persuasion was not needed. He was more than pleased to play the guardian and endure another long wait at Fonteyn House rather than spend even a minute with the grim Edmond. At my request, Oliver called for someone to ready a horse for me. Though I could travel easily enough to Edmond's by the same means I'd used to get to Fonteyn House, it seemed wiser to use a more mundane form of conveyance. My recent travel combined with last night's endeavors with Nora had left their physical impression, and I was yet a bit weary despite a full feeding I'd made after coming back from following her. Later, I'd have to make up for it. Neither of us would benefit tonight if I appeared on her doorstep in less than perfect vigor. To fill in the wait, I asked Elizabeth how the day had gone.

"Most agreeably," she said, and I was treated to an engaging summation of the rabbit hunt. It cheered me mightily, until I realized it was yet another activity I could never share with the boy. Deeply frustrating, but I swallowed it back along with the dark feelings of regret and disappointment. At least I was here and able to share some things with him and not long dead and moldering in the churchyard at Glenbriar.

Blessing and curse. As there was no escape from either, I'd have to accept both.

All the horses in Oliver's stable in town had been taken away to the safety of the one at Fonteyn House, including my beloved Rolly. He was very full of himself tonight, prancing about, hardly able to hold still enough for me to mount. Once in the saddle, reins firmly in hand, I had better control over him, but was not adverse to allowing him to have his head for a short canter to the gates. The two footmen posted on watch there obligingly opened them, allowing us to pass through. If they had any wonder for how I'd gotten inside in the first place, I heard nothing of it. I waved once to them, clucked at Rolly, and let him stretch his neck.

Floating high over the land is one thing, but it's no substitute for the shivering exhilaration of riding a horse at full gallop. Your life is in your hands, completely dependent on your skill, sense of balance, and sheer luck. A misplaced hoof, an unexpected concavity in your path, a startled bird flying up in your face, these and a hundred other lurking dangers can make for an easy disaster. Rolly and I ignored the lot and sped recklessly down the road, my laughter hanging in the air behind as we cut through the cold night. He was a splendid animal and not for the first time I blessed Father for putting him aboard the ship that had taken me to England.

Eventually, though, even Rolly had enough giddy exercise for the time being and slowed to a cooling walk. I felt the untroubled movement of his breathing with my legs; there was no sweat on his neck. He had miles more travel left in him yet, I judged. He'd recovered beautifully from the sea voyage. He was fit and ready for . . . well, now, there was an interesting speculation to dwell on.

My mind swiftly turned to the prospect of having my own estate courtesy of Oliver's generosity. An estate meant land enough for farming—or husbandry. Certainly the idea of breeding Rolly to some fine English fillies was far more tempting than tilling soil. Profitable, too. The gentry's fondness for horse racing was never better what with the royal enthusiasm for the sport. I had but to raise a single favorite to win one race to make a name for myself and better my fortune.

And there was Richard to consider. He was already showing an early love for horses that could be cultivated into an effortless expertise. What better gift could I bestow upon him than a stableful of assets in a business he might enjoy as a lifelong vocation?

*But you're getting ahead of yourself, Johnny Boy. Let the lad make up his own mind.*

True. He was only four. Anything could seize his fancy between now and the time he reached four and twenty—if it was God's will he should live that long.

*Live for the present,* I firmly reminded myself, lest I grow melancholy again.

Very well. But aside from Richard's possible interest, I'd not hinder my own indulgence for such a pursuit. And if my son wanted to join in on the game, then he'd be more than welcome to do so.

Thus did I occupy myself with pleasant considerations, for their own sake and for the distraction they offered.

I needed it. Every mile closer to Edmond's home brought me back to the dreadful business of Ridley's murder and my own attempted murder. The sweet interlude Nora had given with her presence began to fade from mind and heart, to be replaced by the brutal memory of a masked coward raising a dueler on me with intent to kill.

Of course he was a coward, for only such a man would shoot another in the manner that I'd been shot. If and when I found him, I'd teach him a few hard lessons about the value of honor—if he had wit enough to learn. Doubtless he and his friends would be very much surprised to discover I was yet among the living.

Then there was Ridley's murderer to think about. It couldn't have been Arthur; his actions were those of a frightened man. The Mohocks were unlikely to be involved as well, since they'd been so bent on avenging their fallen leader's death. Someone had killed him and wanted me blamed, and as improbable as it seemed, I wondered if Clarinda had somehow arranged it. If she'd had a falling out with Ridley . . . though how any of it could have been managed with her locked up fast by Edmond I could not imagine.

Unless Edmond was behind it all. If so, then he was a finer actor than even the great Garrick; he'd not been the least startled to see me last night. Besides, what would be his purpose?

No, not Edmond. For lack of solid information I was growing too distrustful, not to mention absurd. A short talk with Clarinda would clear this part of things up, or so I fervently hoped. If nothing else I'd get the names of Ridley's companions from her; between her and Litton, whom I would call on later, I expected to obtain solid information to examine, explore, and put to good use.

I'd never been to Edmond's home, but Oliver had given me precise directions, and I found the gate without trouble just where he said it would be. I looked for and spied two small towers made of white stone with an iron arch connecting them overhead. Had I any lingering hesitancy that I'd come to the wrong place, it was abolished by the name 'Fonteyn' spelled out in the design of the arch.

The gate stood open, something I found to be rather disturbing since I'd been very clear to Edmond about the need to protect himself from attack. I thought he'd taken me seriously, but perhaps with the passage of a day with nothing happening, he'd relaxed his guard.

No. Edmond would not be so foolish. His nature wouldn't allow it. There was something wrong here.

Rolly had cooled enough from the walk so as to not take harm if I tied him up for a while. Dismounting, I led him through the gate and some yards into the property. The trees were thick here, which suited me well. I wrapped his reins around a low branch and, keeping to their cover, furtively moved parallel to the lane leading toward the house.

That structure was not far from the main road. Parts of it had been new when Queen Elizabeth's privateers plied their trade against the Spanish. One of the stories firmly discouraged by Aunt Fonteyn was that prize money from such raids had built it and founded much of the family fortune.

Changing fashion and the passage of time called for improvements to be made by each succeeding generation until one of them had given up altogether and moved elsewhere to build Fonteyn House. Edmond's branch of the family inherited what came to be called Fonteyn Old Hall, and if it lacked a certain freshness of design, it made up for it in history. There was a strong tradition one of the great Elizabeth's ministers had spent the night here, possibly with the lady of the hall while her husband was away fighting the Armada. Aunt Fonteyn had, not unexpectedly, discouraged that story as well, preferring to state it was but a rumor and far more likely Elizabeth herself had been the guest. But as the other legend was more amusing, no one really believed her.

As I came closer I picked out the different architectural styles, one atop the other, each an attempt to obliterate the one below. Sometimes such combinations work; this was not one of those times. No wonder Edmond was such a stick if he had to live in this place. One could only hope the interior was more attractive.

All seemed quiet, but then I wasn't sure what sort of trouble I expected, people running around, waving their arms and shouting perhaps? Not here that I could see. The grounds about the place were serene; lights showed through some of the lower windows as normal as can be. I found one with open curtains and peered into some sort of parlour. No occupants, just an ordinary chamber with too much old furniture. I was tempted to ghost my way inside, but did not relish the prospect of explaining my sudden presence to Edmond or, failing that, influencing him to forgetfulness. If something was seriously wrong, the best way to discover it was to ring the front bell and see what happened.

Except the house had none. Instead, I made use of a massive brass door knocker in the shape of a ship's anchor. With its obvious link to ships and ships to privateering, I'd have wagered that device had given Aunt Fonteyn much annoyance whenever she saw it. The thing clanked like the chains of hell, loud enough to be heard through the whole rambling house.

No one came forth to answer, though. I looked about for a carriage or a horse, for some reason why the gate had been left open. None was present. Perhaps they'd been taken around behind the house. The graveled drive carried the impress of wheels, of course, but I could not tell much more than that. It could have been from Edmond's own carriage for all I knew.

I knocked again, the sharp sound hurting my ears. The house was big, but surely there was some servant lurking close by to answer. I could not imagine Edmond keeping any laggards in his employ. Perhaps I should check around the back. The kitchens and stables would be . . .

The door swung open, cutting short my invasive plans.

The man who answered was not a servant, or so his garb instantly told me. He scrutinized me up and down with a bland eye and invited me in. Stepping past the threshold, I studied him just as closely. Dark clothes of good cut, a well-fitted, well-dressed wig, and a calm, commanding eye marked him as some sort of professional man. Ruddy skinned and a few years older than I, he wore enough Flanders lace to brand him for a dandy, but the frivolous effect was offset by the gravity of his demeanor. He was likely to be a lawyer, then, probably one of Edmond's cronies. He looked to be lately arrived himself, for he still wore his cloak and hat and carried his stick.

"Where is Mr. Fonteyn?" I asked guardedly.

"I was just determining that myself," he replied with an air of puzzled amusement. "We'd had plans to take supper together, but he wasn't available when I arrived. I sent the butler off to find him. My name is Summerhill, by the way," he added with a bow.

"Mr. Barrett," I said, returning the courtesy. His easy manner did much to reassure me. Edmond must have had the gate open in expectation of his visitor. Not a wise thing to do, I thought, planning to mention it to him at the first chance. I'd worked myself into a great worry over nothing.

"Barrett?" Summerhill appeared surprised. "But you're—"

"Yes, Mr. Fonteyn's cousin from America." Thus had I come to introduce myself to those people who had heard my name but were unable to place where they'd heard it. Usually, though, I connected myself with Oliver, not Edmond.

Summerhill took this in with more interest than I thought the subject warranted. I suppose I was growing tired of it. "Well, well, I've not met many Americans," he finally said.

"You're not meeting one now, sir, for I have ever been an Englishman."

"Then you are yet loyal to the King?"

"And like to remain so, sir. My family has no desire to involve themselves with a mob of radical lunatics determined to send themselves to the gallows."

He managed a small laugh. "Then you disagree with this notorious declaration that all men are created equal?"

"There are some points in that document worthy of note, but overall it doesn't even make for a good legal argument. Too many broad and impossible to prove assumptions. Besides, the conflict they started isn't about equality, but their reluctance to pay their lawful taxes. By heavens, if it hadn't been for Pitt's intervention in the war twenty years ago with the French, I might this moment be babbling to you in that language, so I for one don't mind rendering to Caesar his due."

Summerhill laughed again.

I'd given the entry hall a careful look 'round while I spoke, but nothing at all seemed amiss. Part of the original Elizabethan core of the house, its ceiling was a good two stories overhead; this and the walls were heavy with black-stained oak trim and white painted plaster work. Off to the right leading up to a gallery was a steep staircase with a thick balustrade made of the same dark wood. Ponderous furnishings and dim portraits of the long departed lent the room an air of determined respectability. Some walls had obviously been cut into to allow access for later additions, and though all very well kept and polished, it had the same unfortunate cobbled together effect as the exterior. Still, if one was of an optimistic turn of mind, one could say that, in terms of variety, it lacked for nothing.

"Wonder what's keeping that dratted butler?" asked Summerhill.

"I wonder what's keeping Edmond." He'd said nothing last night about having a supper guest, but then why should he?

"Will you be joining us?"

"I think not. I've just some brief things to sort out with him, then I must be away to another appointment."

He grunted. "A pity, I should have enjoyed hearing more of your views on the American situation. It's strange, but I've met many an English gentleman with great sympathy for their cause, yet the ones from America are entirely against it."

I detected a trace of an accent in his speech. "You speak as one who is not from England, sir."

He gave a deprecatory chuckle. "Oh, dear, but my foreign roots betray me again. I was raised by English parents in Brittany, sir, and I fear the mix of heritage and place has left an indelible imprint upon my speech."

Blood rushed to my face. "My apologies, sir. I meant no offence when I spoke to you about the French language a moment ago."

"Not at all, sir. I am not in the least offended, but found it most refreshingly honest and amusing."

That was a relief. "You are too kind, sir. May I inquire how you are acquainted with my cousin?"

"Again, you take me back to my roots. My family has ever had a connection with shipping. Mr. Fonteyn sees to the legal necessities of my firm."

Shipping . . . that would explain Summerhill's ruddy complexion. The stray idea entered my head that he was a smuggler and seeing personally to the delivery of a cask or two of duty-free French brandy to a valued customer. Thousands of otherwise law-abiding English subjects readily shunned the practice of paying the King's tax on certain goods, but though I could see Oliver doing it without a second thought, Edmond would choke himself first. I tucked the ridiculous notion away with a smile.

"Well, perhaps I should ring for another butler to go find the first," said Summerhill with a rueful curl to his mouth. "Not that you are unwelcome company, sir, but I was looking forward to my meal."

Reflexively I sniffed the air, but detected no sign of cooking. Of course, the kitchens were likely to be very much elsewhere along with their myriad smells, which suited me well enough. The miasma of cooked food was not one of my favorites these nights.

"And I should like to get on with my own business," I added agreeably. "I hope my cousin is not ill." But except for the healing wounds lingering on his hands, he'd seemed sufficiently fit last night to take on a bear.

"As do I, but to make sure—"

"Did you hear that?"

Summerhill struck a listening pose in response to my interruption, then shook his head. "The butler returning, I should think, and about time."

Whatever small noise it was that caught my attention repeated itself. It was very distant, but clear to my acute hearing. A woman's voice, I finally determined. I looked expectantly at Summerhill, but he seemed not to have heard. He shook his head again.

The sound came again and I thought it contained a note of distress, or anger. Clarinda? God's death, but I thought Edmond would have the sense to keep her well away from the chance of discovery. Thank goodness Summerhill did not have my sharp ears or some awkward questions might be raised.

Unfortunately, the intrusion of the faint noise left us in a temporary state in which we had nothing to say to each other. So it was that in the pause the sounds insistantly repeated, and this time Summerhill heard them, too.

"I say, that's rather odd. There's something happening up there—" He broke off, his gaze drawn to the top of the stairs.

Now did I hear my mistake, for it was not one woman's voice, but two, both raised to the point of shrillness by some desperate excitement. Though the words were muffled, they were undoubtedly calls for help. Neither voice belonged to Clarinda. I glanced once at Summerhill, then hastened up the stairs with him at my heels. On the landing I paused to listen and determined the calls came from the right-hand branching, but before I could take a step in that direction, something went *crack* and the left side of my head abruptly went numb.

As did my legs, for they ceased to hold me.

As did my arms, for they were unable to break my drop to the floor.

The fall knocked the air from my lungs. I lay still, so wretchedly disoriented I could not for the moment understand what had happened.

Much to my grief, the numbness did not last. It retreated all too quickly before the onslaught of a miserably sharp agony that swelled in my head to the bursting point. The first shock of it left me immobilized, allowing an army of drums to march in and take possession. Their deafening thunder left me on the far side of merely addled. I was helpless to do anything for myself except to sprawl on the polished wood floor and start to groan.

Wood . . . Nora had said we were strangely vulnerable to it.

Summerhill. He'd used his cane on me. Why in God's name had he struck me down?

The booming of the army began to fade, and I made out the thin sound of the women again, their cries frantic, like hungry kittens. Over them I heard a door open, followed by footsteps coming toward me. I felt the vibration of their approach through the floor: a man's heavy boots, moving slowly, and the lighter clatter of a woman's shoes. Both paused not two paces from my inert body.

"All taken care of, as I promised," said Summerhill, as calm as you please.

"Of all the damned inconvenient times for Edmond to have visitors," one of the newcomers snarled.

A singularly unpleasant thrill of alarm rushed through me as I recognized the man's voice. Arthur Tyne?

The woman uttered a soft curse in agreement. Clarinda.

God Almighty. What *had* I walked into?

# CHAPTER
# ◄11►

Clarinda spoke again. "That's not any visitor—that's Jonathan Barrett!"

"Impossible," said Arthur.

"But it is. See the hair—he never wears a wig."

"It cannot be," he insisted.

"Then turn him over and prove me wrong."

Hands seized one of my shoulders and I was roughly flipped around. This mistreatment was nearly too much for me. Unpleasant as it was, I fought to stay conscious and won . . . barely. Groggily and past half-closed lids I made out their looming forms: Clarinda on the left, Arthur on the right. Arthur's expression was a study in bald-faced astonishment.

"But Litton told me he was dead! He saw Royce shoot him. Got him square in the chest."

"Then he killed another man or simply missed."

"But he was absolutely certain, boasted about there being blood everywhere."

"Perhaps you'd care to bring your friend 'round here for a nice debate," suggested Summerhill dryly, catching Arthur's reluctant attention. "I got him for you. What do you want done with him?"

This induced a lively discussion. Of all the people who might have paid a call on Edmond, I was certainly the last one they expected. Arthur continued to gnaw on about how I'd escaped getting murdered at Mandy Winkle's; Clarinda cared nothing for such details, however, being more concerned with present problems over past failures.

"What in God's name is he doing here?" she wanted to know.

"Come to visit Edmond about your brat, I expect," said Arthur, having provisionally accepted the undeniable. He continued to stare unhappily at me as though I might vanish and pop up again elsewhere to plague him. Oh, would that I could.

"Unless it's about Thomas."

"How could that be?"

"You were closest to him," she reminded. "They're neither of them fools. They'd expect you to know best who would have—"

"Never mind that," he said sharply, his face going dark as he glanced at Summerhill. "The good captain has asked what's to be done about Barrett and time is passing."

Clarinda looked me right in the eye, as appraising as a butcher considering the best way to chop up a carcass. "Can't leave him alive," she concluded. "He knows who tried to kill him now."

Arthur nodded. "Very well. I'll see to it, and this time it'll be done right. Have you found that chest yet? Then get on with it. Captain, would you be so kind as to assist her?"

This last was addressed to Summerhill. My fancy must have been right. He probably was a smuggler, but come up from his ship not with illicit cargo, but to convey two important passengers off to a safe port. He'd calmly stood to one side, listening, but not interfering with their talk. He offered no comment one way or another at Clarinda's suggestion to kill me and bowed slightly in polite acquiescence to Arthur's request.

Husbanding my strength, I continued to remain quiet until Clarinda and Summerhill were gone. They hurried off up the right-hand hall where I could yet discern faint cries for help.

"And tell those wenches to stop that row!" Arthur called after them. A moment later I heard Summerhill gruffly rumble something in a threatening tone, and the cries abruptly ceased.

"Where's Edmond?" I croaked, having summoned enough of myself together to do so.

He hadn't expected me to speak. His gaze fixed on me, half-contemptuous, half-incredulous, and wholly cold. He looked very pale yet from our previous encounter and used his walking stick as though he needed it for balance, not affectation. "He's none of your concern."

"Where is he?"

His answer was a jolting dig to my ribs with one toe. His riding boots, I discovered, were made of a very sturdy type of leather. I grunted unhappily. The sudden jar reminded me all too clearly of my bursting head. Overcome for the moment, I could do nothing for myself. I'd just have to wait until the worst of it passed away; then might I be able to settle things between us more to my satisfaction.

Arthur eased down on one knee next to me. His expression was wary, but with curiosity rapidly overwhelming his caution. "Who was it that Royce killed in the brothel?" he demanded.

"He killed no one. He missed," I said through my teeth. It would do no harm to repeat the story and might just undermine any confidence Arthur may have had for his tools.

"But Litton had been so *sure.*"

How good to know for certain the names of two of my attackers. Litton and Royce. Shouldn't be hard to find the third one once I spoke to either of the others. *If* I got out of this. "Probably lied to you or was drunk. Does Clarinda know you killed Ridley?"

His face went all stony, but he might as well have grinned and nodded in affirmation.

"It was her idea."

I had wondered if she'd arranged it and should not have been surprised, but was; I should not have been sickened, but felt a twist in my vitals nonetheless. "How could you murder your own cousin?"

He snorted. "Oh, he was a useful ox, very good for some kinds of work, but in the way for others."

"But Clarinda was going to marry him."

He laughed. "He thought so, too. Had himself well convinced that a woman like her would settle for a brainless brute like himself. When pigs fly—perhaps."

"But she was locked up . . . how . . . ?"

"Edmond's servants aren't all that loyal or rich. It's amazing how much a few shillings can buy from the right person. Why did you come here?"

"Your cousin was murdered, your friends try to kill me, then you run away—or appear to—Clarinda was the handiest one to question."

"You'd have got nothing from her. How did you know I'd run away?"

"Went by your house last night. Your butler told me everything."

"Couldn't have been all that much or you wouldn't have walked in here as you did."

*Indeed,* I thought with vast self-disgust for having turned my back on the ingenuous-seeming Summerhill. My head fairly burned along one side where he'd struck. I wanted to vanish and heal, but knew it was too soon for that. A little more rest, or even better, some fresh blood would ease me. It wasn't as bad as the last time this had happened; I was sure the bone hadn't been cracked open again, but it was quite bad enough. I had to keep Arthur talking, postponing whatever it was he planned to do to me until I was ready to deal with him and the others. "Your own loyal retainers are all gone," I said. "They picked your place clean."

He made a throwing-away gesture. "I expected as much, but it suits me. Because of it they'll not be volunteering to talk with the magistrates for fear of hanging as thieves. I took what I needed and left them to it. Now I can quietly disappear."

"With Clarinda?"

"And Edmond's money."

"Tired of living on a quarterly allowance from your parents?" I hazarded, getting a sneer for a reply. "Or perhaps you'd hoped to take the whole Fonteyn fortune if Clarinda had gotten her way with things the first time."

"I'll settle for Edmond's money chest, if the damned vixen can find it." He peered down the hall where she'd gone with Summerhill.

"Why not ask Edmond about it? Where is he?" I demanded.

But Arthur made no answer.

What in God's name had they done with Edmond? My heart sank rapidly, weighed down by the most wretched of conclusions. "What about Ridley?" I asked, hoping a change of subject might draw him out. "There was no need to kill him."

"That depends on your need. Poor Thomas was no good to us anymore; he lost all belly for the task at hand and became completely useless as well as an inconvenient witness. He'd have raised a stink about Clarinda running off with me, too. But to have him dead and you getting the blame for it was sweet. Why should you care for him? He tried his best to kill you."

He waited in vain for a reply. If he couldn't understand my horror, then I'd never be able to explain it to him.

After a moment he shrugged slightly. "Thought you'd have been taken into custody by now, anyway. Who did you bribe?"

"No one. I found the letter about me in his pocket."

His eyes flashed wide. "Did you, now? Very mettlesome of you, I'm sure, pawing through a dead man's clothes."

"Better than cutting throats. You tricked him into writing it, didn't you?"

"It wasn't too hard. When Litton and the others found him first and bolted after you, I thought it wouldn't be necessary. Pity that you've more lives than a cat. Where is the letter?"

"Burned," I said truthfully.

"No matter. It was still a clever bit of business to put you out of the way and disgrace Edmond's precious family. Too bad for you that you did find it, else you'd be safe in a cell right now instead of here."

That sounded ominous, for I was still in a poor state for winning a physical contest.

After a moment's hard staring, he grabbed my right arm. I could offer no resistance. He pushed back my coat and shirtsleeve, exposing the skin, eyeing it closely. "I *know* I caught you there with my blade," he muttered through his teeth. "I *felt* it. You bled like a pig. Where is the wound?"

"You dreamed it," I said, hardly putting breath to the words.

*"Dreamed?* No, not that. You were half dead when . . . thought you were dead, then you came out of the mausoleum and . . . and . . ." His face crimped as he tried to remember, but he'd been safely unconscious when necessity had forced me to take his blood that night. The temptation to do it again rose in me, but I wasn't quite able to act upon it.

"Dream," I murmured.

"Dream indeed, and one of your making. You tried to make it seem so in my mind, to change things." Arthur leaned close, his voice dropping to a whisper. *"What did you do to Thomas?"*

I'd have shaken my head pretending not to take his meaning, but knew better than to try. He'd not have believed me, and it would have hurt too much to move. Instead, I stared hard at him, trying to summon enough will to influence. Our gazes locked for a little time. I felt him wavering as I pushed, but the struggle went awry. Even as his eyes began to go flat and blank, an appalling pain knifed through my head. The harder I tried to exert my will, the more deeply it carved until I could stand it no longer. On the edge of passing out, I broke off with a sob of frustration and agony.

Released so abruptly, Arthur wrenched away, then clumsily scrambled to his feet. He was much paler than before, sweating and panting like an animal.

"Trying to do it again? You damned bastard!" He raised his cane and gave me a vicious stab in the stomach with the base end. My breath hissed out, and I twisted onto my side, curling nearly double. I waited in dreadful apprehension and hurt for another blow to fall, but he held back. Not out of mercy, I thought when I next dared to look, but from weariness. He'd gone gray faced and labored hard for his breath. I likely shared his appearance, but without the desperate need for air. Even so, I wasn't able to move much, not yet.

"What *is* that?" he snarled. "You must have done it to Thomas, and I know you used it on me after the funeral."

Indeed. And *why* hadn't it worked on him?

"Is that what you did to turn him on us? Is it?"

Arthur's blood loss keeping him muddled, the laudanum they'd given him, either might account for my failure to successfully influence him.

That or he was mad. I should have foreseen this; I should have attended to him sooner and not let myself get distracted.

"What are you?" he demanded, voice rising.

*A vampire,* I thought. *And a damned tired one.* I wished Nora here. She could take care of this lout without much effort.

*"What are you?"*

He looked ready to kill me right there and then. The mix of terror and malevolence on his drawn face was an awful sight, the force of his emotions striking me almost as solidly as his cane. All I could hope for now was one good chance to somehow seize him and drag him down to a more primitive level of conflict. Even in this injured state, I was still stronger than most men. Out of pure desperation I might be able to manage, but he'd backed well out of my reach, cursing me.

Footsteps. Summerhill's long stride, Clarinda's quick pace. Damn, damn, *damnation* to them all.

Clarinda paused in the hall doorway. "What's the matter?" she asked of Arthur.

"Nothing," he snapped, straightening with a visible effort. "Where's the chest?"

"I found it, but it's empty. My bastard of a husband hid his money elsewhere."

"*What!*" This was a grievous blow for Arthur, worse than any I might have given him. He fairly fell against one wall, needing its support.

"It could be anywhere in this house," she went on. "We could look all night and not find it or my jewels. He might have taken it to his bankers or even hidden it at Fonteyn House or with that dunce Oliver—"

Arthur started to rant to the best of his limited ability, but Clarinda forcefully interrupted.

"Don't break a blood vessel, you fool! I've thought of a way around it!"

"Have you now? And what will you do, raise your damned husband from the dead and ask him nicely if you please?"

"That's no fault of mine. If you hadn't been so impatient to be rid of him—"

"If he hadn't tried to shoot me—"

*Edmond . . . oh, God.*

"A moment, if you please," said Summerhill calmly with a tilt of his head. Such was his air of command that the two of them stopped bickering long enough to glare at him. "Very good. Now, sir, Mrs. Fonteyn anticipated something like this might happen and prepared for it. I would recommend you hear her out."

"What is it, then?" Arthur barked at her.

His temper did not sit well with sweet Clarinda. She closed her mouth tight.

Summerhill intervened once more. "I believe there was a cabinet full of spirits in one of the downstairs rooms. Mr. Tyne looks in need of a restorative, and it may put him in a better mood to listen, dear lady."

The practicality of the suggestion won their grudging agreement to act upon it. Arthur, leaning heavily on the banister, began his descent. Clarinda followed a moment later, picking up her skirts as she delicately stepped around me.

"Where's Edmond?" I asked Summerhill when they'd gone. Damnation, but I sounded hatefully weak. My effort to influence Arthur had drained me to the dregs.

He glanced down. "Away behind the house. Not to worry, someone's bound to sniff him out after the spring thaw. We'd put you in the same spot, but that would look just a little too suspicious. Once just might be thought an accident, but twice . . ." He lifted a hand, palm out.

"Killing me will only put you all into more trouble," I whispered.

"Really?"

"I've no solid proof against Arthur about Ridley, so I'm no danger to any of you."

"I'm in no danger anyway, not with a dozen of my lads willing to swear themselves blue in the face on a Bible on my behalf."

His crew? I'd speculate later. "Leaving me here won't harm you. Tyne's just running off with another man's wife; no one will pay much mind to that. But kill me and people will blame it on him or Clarinda or both with you as an accomplice. You can't afford the hue and cry of murder to be following you everywhere."

"No one will blame any of us for your death, because it will really be just a tragic accident. Two in one night might cause some comment, but I think we can take that chance—or rather they will, since I'm not officially here."

"Smuggler?"

"Merely a gentleman who advocates the practice of free trade between nations."

"Especially if it profits you."

"Particularly when it profits me."

"I'll double whatever they're paying you."

His eyebrows went up. "That would be a princely sum, but I'm a man of my word and I have given it to—"

"Triple."

He blinked, then shook his head. "Tempting, Mr. Barrett, but if all goes well, even that ransom will seem but a trifle to the bounty we'll be collecting from the whole of your family."

"What are you planning?"

"Not I, but the redoubtable Mrs. Fonteyn."

"What is—"

"Soothe yourself, sir. It's nothing you ever need worry about. Now say a prayer for your soul like a good chap while you yet have the time." He quickly stooped and caught hold of my ankles, dragging me toward the edge of the stairs. "Mrs. Fonteyn thought Mr. Tyne might not be up to the labor of it yet—he's still feeling pretty thin—so she asked me to see to things. I've no personal grudge against you, this is just business, y'know."

Realizing what he had in mind, panic took over. I started to kick and struggle, putting up enough of a fight to inconvenience him. He let go, and with a deft move, gave me another bitter tap on the side of my head with his cane. Lights flashed between my eyes and the rest of the world. I heard myself pant out a last breath. My body went utterly limp.

He got a strong grip under my arms and with a great heave hauled me upright. I was maddeningly helpless. The room lurched. Sickness clawed at my belly, threatening to turn it inside out. I couldn't even gulp to hold back the rising vomit.

My legs were useless; my arms dangled loose. I had a hideous, dizzying view of the steep stairs and the entry hall miles below.

"There now," said Summerhill comfortingly into my ear as he swung me into place. "At least it'll be quick, and that's more than most of us get." He planted a firm hand in the small of my back and pushed for all he was worth.

I was flying in open space for an instant. Almost like those times when I floated.

The room tumbled madly. Almost like my game with Richard.

Then something struck me lethally hard all over my shoulders and back, like a hundred Summerhills attacking me not with mere canes but with clubs. I heard thuds and thumps, a pain-filled cry, cut short . . . then nothing at all.

Mr. Barrett lay still as stone at the foot of the stairs, his body as beyond movement as his mind was beyond thought.

His head was at an unnatural angle in regard to his neck; one of his arms was also bent in an abnormal manner under him. Some distant and restive portion of his brain was very aware of these and other, lesser injuries, but unable to do more than simply recognize their existence.

His enemies were gone.

The house around him was deadly quiet.

A lifetime crawled by before his eyelids briefly fluttered. He got a vague glimpse of black-stained wood steps stretching upward into cold darkness. Try as he might, he could not open his eyes again. It seemed an important thing to do, though he could not recall why.

After another lifetime the fingers of his unbroken arm shivered once. He'd not consciously initiated the faint movement, but felt its occurrence. When he attempted to repeat it, a white hot spike of lightning shot through his neck, forcing an unwelcome wakening upon his battered flesh. He tried to retreat back to the kind sanctuary of unconsciousness, but the pain followed, tenacious as a shadow, not permitting him any such mercy. He'd have whimpered a protest had there been air in his lungs. His fingers twitched again instead.

With them he felt the cold hard surface of the floor he sprawled over and slowly came to understand his circumstance.

He was in serious trouble.

And being quite alone now, he could expect no help.

That terrified him, the aloneness.

But he had family, friends, even a stranger on the road would be moved by pity to lend him aid. None of them was present, though, or likely to come.

Internal protests against this unfairness rose, fell, and died, but not the self-reproach. That whipped at him with a sting like sleet, unrelenting.

The aloneness worsened every ache and agony afflicting him. It made the prospect of escaping them doubtful. It drained away what little strength remained in him. Even silently praying for simple comfort seemed too great a labor to dare.

But not weeping. That he could not control. The hurts of his body demanded tears, and they flowed over his face, burning like acid.

Then he heard his own drawn-out moan of despair and thought what an altogether wretched fellow he'd become. He was less a mass of pain from all the injuries than a mass of self-pity from the misery of his own heart, certainly not the sort of son his father could take pride in and not the sort of father his own son could admire.

And unless he sorted himself out, he wouldn't see either of them or anyone else ever again.

I came fully and unhappily alert. The half dreams, half nightmares fled, leaving nothing of themselves behind except an earnest need to overcome the hopelessness they'd engendered. If the people I loved were not here, then by God I'd just have to go to them.

Somehow.

*Any* movement was a torment, especially movement associated with my head and neck. There was something appallingly wrong in that area, and I was fearful of making it worse. By comparison, my broken arm and assorted bruises were nothing. That damned Summerhill had thrown me around like a sack of grain and with about as much consideration. When I got my hands on him . . .

Anger helped. I drew it to me, held it fast, fed on the strength of it until it filled me, became *my* strength. There was an astonishing amount of it . . . for *them.*

Arthur Tyne. Ruthless cutthroat. Not for long. He'd wish himself dead before I was finished with him.

Clarinda. Unrepentant murderer. Instigator of all that had happened to me. Guilty mother of my innocent son. I'd bring her back and take poor Edmond's place as her jailer and be glad of the privilege.

The anger flared to fury, warming me, quickening bone, muscle, and nerve.

And for a very brief moment, it displaced the devastating agony.

I seized the chance while it lasted.

Inside, I felt a shuddering swoop, as though falling again. Something harsh blasted through my vitals like a frost-charged wind. It scoured me from end to end. The sharp edges of the world swiftly twisted, suddenly faded. I'd have cried out, but suddenly had no voice for my fear and pain.

Then it was over.

I was sightless, weightless, formless.

Without a solid body to cling to, to torture, the pain lifted and floated away, even as I floated above the floor.

I was free.

And tired. The effort to let go of the physical world had cost me and would surely cost more when I came back to it, but for now I reveled in the blessed liberty of this discarnate form. Whatever bones had been broken, whatever flesh had been torn, it didn't matter now. All would be whole again when it was time to return.

Sweet it was, and great was my desire to stay like this, but I had things to do or at least to attempt. Giving the alarm about Clarinda's escape was the most important—but only after I'd fed myself. Even in this state every portion of my being cried out for the nourishment of fresh blood and plenty of it. I'd have to find the stables.

Tentatively I made myself stretch forth.

Using the stairs as a landmark, I pushed away from them in the general direction of the front door. Soon I bumped against the opposite wall and felt for openings with whatever it was that now served me as hands. I could have tried materializing just enough to allow me some vision, but was uncertain of my ability to maintain the careful balance needed to hold to that partial condition. Instinct told me not to take that chance, lest I grow abruptly solid and be too feeble to vanish again. Bad luck for me if I did and found the door locked.

An opening, long and very thin, presented itself to my questing senses—the slender crack between the door and the threshold. I dived for it, pouring through like a river mist. It seemed to take forever.

Outside.

I felt the familiar gentle tug of the wind and rode it, letting it carry me along the front of the house. Keeping the building's fixed contours on my left, I turned one corner, then another, trying to remember what I'd seen of the place when I'd initially approached it. One wing, two? The track of carriage wheels in the gravel drive had been to the left, but how far? Easy as this form of travel was, I'd have to give it up before getting lost.

I found a clear space and tried a partial reformation, but alas, my instinct had been right. Once begun, the process continued unstoppable until I was standing fully solid again.

Standing, but that changed quickly and with no warning; I dropped to my hands and knees, weak as a babe. Normally I hardly noticed the cold; now its talons gouged deep and held fast. I was hatless and with no cloak, having lost both in the house. The wind wasn't high, but more than enough to inspire me to movement again.

I'd come fully around to the back of the house and was not far from the drive. Its gravel path broadened until it covered most of the yard, but some places were thin, allowing muddy patches churned up by wheels and hooves to show through. The tracks could have come from whatever conveyance they'd used. My guess was—since the doors to an empty carriage house gaped wide—they'd taken Edmond's for their escape.

Where was he?

No one was immediately in sight; I saw only the various outbuildings and yard clutter one would expect to find for such a household. Summerhill had said the body was hidden in some way and that the death might look like an accident. Perhaps in the barn or the stables . . . but I had no time or desire to look. With the return to solidity came also the unimpaired resumption of physical need.

My corner teeth were well out and ready. I was ravenous.

Driven by the hunger, I got to my feet and reeled toward the stables. I could hear and smell the horses remaining there, then I was at the nearest door and saw a half dozen of them in their stalls. A few were curious, heads turned, ears twitched; others dozed on their feet. I went to the closest, a bay gelding with a drowsy eye. He hardly reacted when I slipped into his stall, and barely noticed when I knelt and cut into the vein of his near leg.

The stuff fair streamed into my mouth. I gulped and guzzled, swilling it down like a drunkard with his day's first bottle of gin. Its glad warmth, its taste, its strength *flooded* through my hollow form, easing the last aches, healing the lingering bruises. The chill air around me retreated before this pulsing onslaught of hot, red life.

I drank deeply, vanished, and drank again until I was quite filled to the brim.

Then I had to lean on the horse, fold my arms over his back, and bury my head in them. The heavy beat of his heart coming up through his solid frame was a welcome comfort to my battered senses and soul. After all the abuse, I needed to touch something that bore no ill will against me, something to remind me that not all the world was evil. The big animal snuffled once and shoved his nose into the hay manger, supremely indifferent to my little concerns. I liked him for that.

It could not and did not last long, but I needed only a moment or two. Encroaching upon my respite was the need for haste.

Even as I reluctantly straightened, I felt the fresh blood had revived more than just my body. Plans for what to do were popping into my head, demanding attention. I'd have to find Rolly—heavens, I'd have to find the servants here, if any were left. Surely not all of them had been bribed into betrayal. . . .

Dear God, I'd have to find Edmond. What had they done to him?

The anger for Clarinda and the others that had saved me before flared up once again. It burned bright and hot, closer than my own skin. In time, I'd hunt down and deal with the lot of them, this I promised myself.

I'd start with a search of the house and gather allies and information.

Those cries I'd heard must have been from two of the maids. Locked up somewhere, and no doubt quite miserable over it by now. There had to be others as well, but before looking for them I'd have to clean myself, having not been particularly neat in my feeding this time. Appearance would have to take precedence over all else for the moment. The drying crusts of blood around my mouth might alarm the servants here far more than their imprisonment.

I quit the stables and went straight to the low rectangular structure in the yard that marked the well. The shape of the thing was disturbingly like a grave, being two yards long and over a yard wide. Its brick sides rose about a foot past the ground, the opening neatly covered by six-inch-thick oak timbers. A square cut into their middle was covered by a stout plank lid fitted with a lifting knob and simple latch lock. Fixed above was a sturdy winch and rope mechanism and the cranking handle, all polished by frequent use.

The lid was pushed up and open, with the bucket already at the bottom, which struck me as odd, not to mention dangerous, but that would save me from having to do the work. I put a hand to the crank and tried to give it a turn. It moved only a little way, then mysteriously stopped. The crank was free of obstructions; perhaps the rope or bucket had gotten entangled on something. I caught at the rope and tugged. It gave but a little. I pulled hard, and it reluctantly came up a few inches then sank again when the weight at the other end became too much. Far below I heard a soft splash . . . and a voice . . . a faint, faint voice?

*Someone's bound to sniff him out after the spring thaw. We'd put you in the same spot, but that would look just a little too suspicious. Once is an accident, but twice . . .*

Unbidden, Summerhill's words ripped through my brain; gooseflesh erupted over all my body. Oh, my God, *what* had those monsters done?

Bending dangerously over the edge of the opening I bawled Edmond's name into the blackness. I could see nothing inside. The natural light from the sky was blocked by my own form and hindered by the depth of the shaft. I *thought* I heard a reply to my calls, but it could have been my own echoes. Hope and horror seized me. I stood and stared wildly about the yard and toward the house. Help might be there, but I couldn't take the time to go looking for it. Could I do something myself? Possibly. But—and I shrank from the thought—could I even bring myself to *try?*

The inky square of the opening looked like a gaping mouth, seeming to eat all the ambient light. My acquired fear of little dark places came roaring up in my mind like a storm, paralyzing me with its thunderous force. Waking in a buried coffin seemed but a triviality compared to descent into this hellhole. Here was a place where darkness was conceived, born, lived, and thrived, devouring everything that came near it. Though fully aware that very little could ever really hurt me, imagination was the great enemy here, striking hard at my weakness. The reproachful awareness of my own vast abilities made the weakness even worse. I was a hopeless coward, dooming my poor cousin to a hideous death because I was too white-livered to—*Enough, Johnny Boy. Stop whining and just get on with it.*

I allowed myself one uncurbed sob of pure shuddering terror, then brutally pushed it away. It rolled up into a ball of ice somewhere between my throat and belly and held in place, trembling, but out of the way.

My mind was clear. Now, what to do?

The winch mechanism presented an obvious solution. Quickly I made some slack by letting out the rope to the end of its length, praying this would work. Making myself go nearly transparent, I floated up over the short wall, and drifted inside the black mouth.

The wind ceased after a few feet. My sight, ever limited in this form, perceived nothing but darkness unless I looked up. The square opening above grew uncomfortably small. Every foot I went down was worse than the last, but I forced myself on. If Edmond was here and alive, his need far outweighed my childish dreads.

I moved blindly now. My ghostly hands could just sense the impression of the bricks lining the walls and the rope in front of me. Then I was aware of the water immediately below. I reached down toward it, trying to find him. Heart in my mouth, I had the sudden hope that he wasn't here at all, that I'd made a hasty conclusion based on an error, that I could leave this awful place and . . .

An object. Large. Bobbing heavily in the water.

And, unmistakably now, someone's faint moan.

I caught at the rope without thinking. My hand passed through it. Damnation. There was no way around it; I'd have to go in, too, to get to him. Making myself more solid, I sank ever lower. First my feet touched the water, then did it creep up my legs and waist like grim death. Free-flowing streams were always a problem for me, but this tamer stuff was still perversely malignant. With cold. With excruciating, mind-numbing, body-killing *cold.*

Completely solid, my weight bore me right into it—and briefly under. Black on black, freezing, smothering, it closed right over me, shutting out everything. Disoriented, I lashed out wildly to find the surface, cracking a hand against a slimed wall. It hurt, but the pain jarred me out of the impending hysteria. I *forced* myself to hold still until natural buoyancy made me sure of my direction. A push, then my head broke free of the water. I spat and blew the stuff from my nose and mouth, sucking in cold, dank air I did not need, but instinct was trying to drive me here, not intellect. Indeed, I was very hard-pressed to maintain a solid form under these adverse conditions and had to fight an impulsive reaction to vanish again and escape.

Kicking to keep afloat, I cast frantically about for the rope, blessed link to the world above. My hands slapped instead against sodden material. My fingers closed on I know not what.

"Edmond?"

No reply.

If I could only *see.* I felt around, then unexpectedly touched flesh. It was his hand, and it was holding hard to the only other thing floating in this pit, the wooden bucket. There was no warmth to him, but that meant little enough in a place like this. Tracing up his arm, I found his face. It was above water, but only just. With all the splashing and distorting echoes I couldn't discern anything as subtle as his heartbeat or breathing. The moan I'd heard was proof enough of lingering life, though.

Trying not to disturb his grip on the bucket, I found its handle, then the chain on the handle, then the rope tied to the chain. The slack was all around me I was sure, but drifting and dangerous if it should twist about us in the wrong way.

I drew rope through my grasp like a fat thread through a needle until I came down to the knots that tied it to the bucket's chain. Fumbling badly from the cold and fright, I got my folding penknife from its usual pocket, clutching it hard lest I drop it. Carefully, with rapidly deadening fingers, I opened it. I made a loop in the rope and began sawing desperately away at it with the blade. The soaked fibers were thick, tough, and I was uncertain about the sharpness of my tool. But just as frustration set in and I began to think my teeth would do a better job, the thing finally parted.

Cramming the open knife back into a pocket, I crowded close to Edmond. Another loop, larger, this time threading the rope under his arms and around his back. Not easy, he kept trying to drift away from me, and all the time I was trying to keep both our heads above water. Though in no danger for lack of air, I'd be damned before I let that utter blackness close over me again.

I made several knots centered over his chest, talking to him, babbling out waterlogged assurances that everything would be all right and not to worry and God knows what other nonsense. Perhaps it was more for my benefit than his. He made no sound or response; I still couldn't see a damned thing, and was rapidly losing my sense of touch.

One last knot. Time and past time to leave. With a singular lack of control I disappeared completely and shot up from the well like a ball from a pistol barrel. The little protective roof was in my way, and though it slowed me somewhat I'd sieved right through it before regaining command of myself. In too much of a hurry to be vexed, I touched upon the earth and went solid again.

Water running from my clothes, I put both hands on the well crank and began turning. Easy at first as it took up all the slack, it halted as Edmond's weight became part of the load. I prayed the thing would support him and put my back into the work. Round and round, with the wood creaking, the rope coiling about the dowel, and my heart in my mouth, I pulled him slowly up, trying not to think of all the things that could go wrong.

Then from the square of darkness his head emerged. It lolled backward, jaw sagging; there was a nasty-looking graze seeping red along one side of his scalp. I looked away and gave another turn on the crank until his shoulders were visible. He swung to and fro ponderously, a man on a gibbet. Not trusting the ratchet pawl to hold, I reached across with one hand while bracing the crank with the other as he swung toward me again. I snaked my arm under his and around his chest, then let go of the crank. He abruptly slumped away, threatening to drop back in. I got my other arm around him just in time and *pulled.*

It was a hard hauling. He was a big bear of a man, wet right through, and utterly motionless. His clothes snagged on the sides of the opening. I heaved him as high as I could and finally lugged him past the edge. He'd have scrapes and bruises—if he lived. I lay him flat on the cold ground and pressed an ear against his chest. For a terrible moment I heard nothing, then nearly crowed with relief when a near indistinct *thump* announced he was still on this side of the veil.

Determined to keep him here, I slapped his white face, shouting at him to wake up. He was past responding, though, and not like to do so soon unless I got him out of this winter air and inside near a fire. More lifting and dragging, this time toward what I hoped was the scullery door. Cursing like a heathen, I had to stop once to find the knife again and cut him free of the rope. It had played out like a leash and we'd reached its limit.

The door did turn out to be the scullery entry and had been left unlocked. Clarinda and the others must have come this way to get to the carriage house. That simplified things. I pulled Edmond up the step and inside, bulling through to the kitchen. My hope was that like other kitchens this would be the warmest room in the house owing to the need for a constant fire. Hope was fulfilled, I saw, when I blundered inside with my burden. For once I was glad to have the stink of cooked food assaulting my senses.

The fire here was little more than a mass of glowing coals, but easily remedied. I lay Edmond on the still warm stones of the hearth and threw on fresh dry kindling, knocking over the fire tongs and other things in my shivering haste.

The noise attracted notice. I heard a sudden loud banging and a chorus of calls for help coming from behind a solid-looking bolted door.

Edmond's missing servants.

It's amazing how much calamity can be turned about in a quarter hour's time. And what a wonderful, luxuriously wonderful relief it is to turn one's cares over to others and let them deal with the work.

Most of Edmond's people had been closed up in one of the pantries, except for two women who were soon found shut away in an upstairs cupboard. Fortunately, the pantry door had been bolted, not locked with a key, so I soon had everyone else out, blinking in the growing firelight after being in the dark and asking a hundred questions at once. All were agitated in one form or another from red-faced anger to teary-eyed fear, but were otherwise no worse for wear. I determined a middle-aged woman named Kellway was in charge of them, told her who I was, and after one glimpse at her master's desperate condition she forgot all about her own difficulties. She instantly set things in motion, shouting out orders for brandy, bandaging, blankets, and hot water, sending people scurrying off in every direction.

Evicting all female members of her staff but herself from the kitchen, she commanded two of the footmen to strip off Edmond's wet clothes. By the time things reached the point where she would be forced to leave as well the blankets arrived, preserving decorum. She made me strip down, also, which I did not mind, and questioned me closely over what had happened, which I did mind. It worried me at how easily I was given to lying and improvisation when forced to by the demands of an uncomfortable situation. Hardly honorable, but certainly necessary.

Wrapped in dry blankets and with a perfectly smooth face I told of my appointment with Edmond and of being surprised by Summerhill and knocked unconscious.

"I woke up lying on the ground next to the well. In want of water to ease my injury, I tried to draw some, then discovered Mr. Fonteyn was inside."

A general murmur of dismay went around.

"He'd tied the rope about himself to stay afloat, so I managed to haul him up. The poor man collapsed just as I got him out."

This inspired a general murmur of approval. Considering my cowardly delay in getting started, I did not allow myself to bask in their admiration.

"But how did you get so wet, sir?" one of them asked, having observed my own drenched and half frozen condition. I'd been far too thoroughly saturated for them to think I'd gotten in such a state merely from dragging Edmond around. At least the immersion had cleaned all the blood from my face.

"The bucket came up with him and was full of water. When I cut him free of the rope the damned thing tipped and slopped it all over me, then fell back into the well." I left it to their imaginations to work out just how that kind of clumsiness could have possibly happened. "You'll want a replacement."

"God bless you, sir, as if we cared about an old bucket," said Mrs. Kellway, wiping tears from her eyes before bellowing at a distracted scullery boy to keep heaping wood on the fire.

Indeed, but I wanted to account for everything. They might well have suspected me of being in on the foul deed, after all.

While Mrs. Kellway gently dabbed salve on Edmond's head wound and bandaged it, I learned from them that Summerhill, Tyne, and two men dressed like sailors had suddenly appeared in the house, brandishing pistols, then smartly locked everyone up. Not long afterward the coachman and a groom were also forced into the pantry, bearing the news their master had arrived home, but not knowing what had happened to him after their own capture. All waited in vain for him to either rescue them or join them, taking turns to listen, but hearing nothing until my noisy entrance.

No one knew how the men had gotten in, but after a quick head count by the butler, a missing footman was promptly declared to be the traitor who had likely given entry to the intruders. An enthusiastic round of invective aimed at the fellow started up, with each declaring him to have ever been an untrustworthy rogue and listing all his bad points, slights they'd suffered from him, and various other character flaws. So many piled up in such a short time I wryly wondered how the man had ever been employed here in the first place.

Under Kellway's ministrations, Edmond looked a bit less blue than before, but still unconscious. Having myself been through a similar experience of nearly freezing, I told them to start massaging his limbs and cover him with hot wet linens, replacing them as they cooled. People were sent off to fetch more water for heating and to find the household's bathtub. I meant to have him fully immersed in steaming hot water, but that good intention was dashed when a boy hefted the unwieldy thing in. It was not much more than a wildly overgrown tin punch bowl a half-foot deep. The bather was to sit or stand in the thing and have water poured over him, I supposed. Oh, for the soothing delights of Mandy Winkle's house.

"But hasn't he had enough water already, sir?" asked a dubious Mrs. Kellway, when I explained my disappointment over the limits of their "tub."

"As long as the stuff was good and hot this time. It would have warmed him all over." Then I recalled what Oliver said of people believing anything about my birthplace. "It's something I learned in America. We know all there is to know on this sort of thing there."

It worked a charm on her, and thus enlightened, she gave a sage nod of agreement.

Oliver. I'd have to go back to Fonteyn house and tell him and Elizabeth about this latest disaster. Clarinda's mischief was not over yet, I judged. From what I'd heard, she had something else planned, and we'd have to be doubly on our guard now. Edmond needed a doctor anyway, and Oliver was nearest.

I raked my bedraggled hair back with my fingers, untidily retying it with a damp ribbon. Now that work had calmed them, some of Edmond's people found time to stare at my revealed features. My sharp ears plucked Richard's name out of a medley of whispered comments. So, Edmond had not seen fit to confide family secrets to them. I didn't think that was even possible, but he'd apparently managed. Would this weaken my position of assumed authority with them? Might they not think I was somehow allied with Clarinda since I'd so obviously once been her lover? Better to leave quickly before I found out.

Then Edmond stirred and gave a thick, water-choked cough, distracting us all. I pushed in close just in time to see his eyes open.

"Thank God!" cried Mrs. Kellway, saying it for everyone.

He had a stark staring cast to his expression. Understandable, then I had a swift flash of perception and told them to gather as many candles as they could find.

"Sir?" questioned a hesitating butler.

"He's been in the very heart of hell, man, give him some light for pity's sake."

My urgency and insight got through, and soon the kitchen was brighter than a ballroom. Whether it was a help to Edmond or not was hard to tell, but certainly it could do him no harm. When his eyes looked a bit less feral, I pressed a cup of brandy to his lips. He took that down easily enough, which was most encouraging.

"Do you remember what happened to you?" I asked him. "Just nod, there's no need to speak yet."

He did nod, but ignored the rest. "That bastard Tyne. Where?"

"He got away—for now."

"Clarinda?"

"She went with him. I think they're going to try getting away by ship." And would do so unless I got moving myself and arranged to cut them and Summerhill off.

"Riddance," he sighed out. "Good . . . riddance."

By that I could assume Edmond wanted no more to do with her, but it was out of his hands. I had my own special plans for his wife and her charming friends. Half-formed, to be sure, but doubtless when I caught up with them the other half would be fully matured.

"Tyne shot at me," Edmond said, responding to Kellway's question of how he got in the well. "Dismissed the coach. Alone at the front. He and some others came up. Tried to shoot him. Saw his pistol go off. Couldn't hear either of 'em. Strange. Thought someone hit me from the side." He gingerly touched his head and encountered the bandages.

"Just a graze by God's good will," I said, pulling his hand away. "Leave it for now until a doctor can see it. Do you recall anything else?"

His eyes shut a moment, then snapped open, focusing on the nearest of the candles. "Blackness. Cold. So cold. Water. Thought I'd been killed. Tried hard to breathe. Woke me a bit. Heard you next to me, jabbering on. Wanted to box you sharp and shut you up, but I couldn't move."

"That was after you were out of the well," I said carefully, hoping he'd accept it. "You got things jumbled."

"The *well?*" He tried to sit up, but for once the feeble state of his body won out over his disposition. "I was in the well?"

"It's a miracle, sir," pronounced Mrs. Kellway. "The good God and all his angels took your part tonight and saved you, and that's a fact. If Mr. Barrett hadn't been there to pull you out we'd be praying for your soul's rest now instead of for your recovery."

He fastened his dark eyes on me, still trying to take it all in, I suppose. "How?" he demanded.

I shrugged. "You did the real work tying the rope around yourself."

"But I didn't—*you* were there . . . I know you—"

"And you damned near broke the winch with your weight," I pressed on, not giving him a chance to continue. "I'd have had an easier task of it if you were built less like Hercules and more like Mercury. Next time you fall in a well I'll leave you there and spare myself a strained back."

I'd hoped a brusque manner would put him off and counted upon raising a snarl from him at least. Instead, he gave me a long hard look. I'd have been worried, but his eyes were going cloudy. He put a hand on my arm and squeezed once with a bare ghost of his usual strength.

"Thank you," he whispered, then fell back into a doze.

I expected to be hanged there and then by the staff, but Mrs. Kellway only dabbed at her face again and gazed at me with the sort of unaccountable fondness usually reserved for favorite children and small dogs. "Bless you, sir, for saying *just* the right thing to him."

"But I—oh, never mind." I stood up, nearly tripping on my blanket. "Blast it. I need to borrow some proper clothes. I'm sure my cousin won't mind if I raided his cupboard."

"But, sir, you're in no fit state to be—"

"I'm quite recuperated, thank you, and someone has to go for a doctor. My horse is out front and all saddled, so if you please . . ." I'd put on a firm unarguable manner, asserting my place again after the previous near-familiarity, and it worked, at least in this household. Jericho would have offered considerably more resistance—and would have probably won.

Dry garments from Edmond's wardrobe were found, all rather large, of course, and I had to wear my own damp riding boots, but none of it was of any real concern for me. My cousin still needed help, and Oliver was but a few miles down the road.

I sent one of the stablemen to find Rolly, absentmindedly omitting to explain why I'd left my horse that far from the house. Donning my reclaimed cloak and hat (both found on the stair landing) I was ready to rush outside before anyone else decided to ply me with questions best left unanswered, when a commotion at the front door halted my progress. To my surprise, Oliver strode forcefully in past a protesting maid, looked quickly around, and spied me. Had Elizabeth gotten impatient for news and sent him along? No, that couldn't have been it.

"What in heaven's name are you doing here?" I asked, not bothering to check my utter bewilderment. But even as the words came out I knew something was dreadfully wrong. My otherwise cheerful cousin wore an awful expression and visibly trembled from head to toe. "What is it? Is Elizabeth—?"

Oliver bit his lip and gave a violent shake of his head. His hands were clenched into quivering fists, and he looked ready to burst from the extreme inner agitation he was trying hard to keep under control. "Th-they got into the house," he finally said in a voice, a terrible broken voice I'd never heard him use before.

My belly turned to water. I did not have to ask who "they" were.

"Held pistols on us all. Took him away. You must come."

"T-took who?" But in my heart of hearts I already *knew.*

"Oh, Jonathan." Tears started from his eyes. "They've kidnapped Richard."

# CHAPTER 12

"They *won't* hurt him," Elizabeth told me. "They wouldn't dare."

"That bitch would dare anything," I whispered, staring past her at nothing but my own rage blasting against the confining walls of the room. I couldn't risk looking at her in this state. Too dangerous.

"But she won't hurt him. She'd never endanger her chance of collecting the money for him. You have to believe that of her if nothing else."

Yes, it was onc thing we could trust about Clarinda, her avarice. But if she was capable of holding her own son for ransom, might she also get rid of him the moment he became useless to her? Or if oncc she had her money would she even give him up? Not because she held any maternal affection for him, but to make him a continual source of spoils from the family coffers. How would she treat him? How was he being treated? Like my anger, my anguished uncertainty was bottomless.

Oliver came into the blue parlour from his latest trip down to the front gates. I didn't quite look at him either as he paused just inside the door, only swung my head part way in his direction, keeping my gaze from touching his. "No news yet," he said in a subdued voice.

"We should have heard something by now," I rumbled, glaring at the mantel clock. Useless thing. Last night Clarinda had promised to communicate with us, but she'd not said *when.* Forced into hateful rest by the rising sun, I'd lain oblivious in the cellar through the whole helpless day and upon awakening was incensed near to madness to learn no word from her had come to us.

"It's only to make us more anxious," Oliver added.

And it was working all too well on me. I paced to the fireplace and back, too restless to sit. That wasn't enough, though. Hardly aware of the act, I curled my hand into a fist and smashed it into the wall above the wainscoting. I pounded right through the paper and plaster and whatever lay beyond. Something wood, no doubt, to tell from the pain shooting up from my knuckles. I pulled free, spreading plaster dust all over, mixed with the smell of my own blood. A quick vanishing and I was whole again, ready to do more damage.

"I say," said Oliver, sounding shaken. "I say—for God's sake, Jonathan . . ."

I understood now why Clarinda hadn't been overly distressed at not finding Edmond's money. With or without it, she'd planned all along to take Richard away; he was her surety of a clean and profitable escape. She'd made careful arrangements, indeed, and had smoothly carried them out with Summerhill's help. Last night Clarinda and her friends had forced themselves into Fonteyn House in much the same way Edmond's home had been invaded, with help from a turncoat inside.

In our case it had been one of the maids. The same one who had brought Richard's milk. He'd fallen asleep so quickly because of the laudanum she'd put in it. A half full phial of the stuff was later discovered hidden away in her bed. Thank God she'd not given him the lot, though what she'd done was harsh enough. I'd been right there *holding* him while it had done its work. I should have sensed something was wrong. I should have *known.*

At about seven of the clock, apparently in accordance with instructions from Clarinda, the traitorous maid then snuck out to the front gate to distract the guards there from their duties. So successful was she in her mock flirtations that Summerhill and two of his sailors had the easy advantage of them, knocking them senseless, then the whole party came rolling onto the grounds in Edmond's carriage. They halted far enough from the house so its noise would not be marked, and went in through a door the maid had left unlocked for them.

Summerhill and his men kept everyone in place at pistol point while Clarinda rushed upstairs to fetch the sleeping Richard out of his nursery bed. Mrs. Howard had pleaded and finally screamed at her to desist. Clarinda knocked the tiny woman to the floor with one swipe of her hand. With Richard's unconscious form wrapped in a blanket, she carried him down to face Elizabeth and Oliver.

"We're going on a little trip," she told them with a smile. "Not a long one, for children can be so tiresome when traveling. You may have him back again if you likc."

"What do you want?" Elizabeth asked, her voice thin with fury. Oliver, though infuriated himself, had the presence of mind to hold tight to one of her arms to prevent her from charging into their midst and possibly getting shot for her trouble.

Clarinda continued to smile unnervingly. "I judge this little man to be worth much more than ten thousand guineas to you, but that's all I want for him. You have all tomorrow to collect it together. When you've got it, tie a white rag to the front gate. Don't do anything foolish like trying to follow us or calling in the magistrates or I promise you'll not see your dear nephew again. This is a family matter. Just keep it quiet and within these walls and all will be well for him."

When asked if she understood, Elizabeth nodded, giving Clarinda a look that should have burned a hole right through the woman's skull. A pity for us all that it had not.

The invaders, along with the maid, then backed their way from the house. Arthur Tyne had driven the coach right up to the entry doors by then, and from his high perch covered the watching household with a pistol until Clarinda and the others were aboard. Summerhill climbed up with him to take the reins, and off they cantered.

Jericho, driven by his own anger and outrage into taking a chance, broke away from the house to follow the coach, avoiding the curving drive and making a straight line shortcut through the grounds to reach the gates. Alas, he did not get there in time to close them and delay the party, but was at least able to report they'd turned south. Since Edmond's house lay to the north and east, a rider could go there and fetch me back without putting Richard into additional danger. Oliver was mad to do it anyway, to find out how she'd escaped and if anyone had been hurt in the process. Thus when he arrived, he had his traveling medicine box with him, which was fortunate for poor Edmond.

Since then, Oliver had been kept busy running back and forth between Fonteyn Old Hall, Fonteyn House, and his bankers in London. The latter had been understandably curious about why he had need for such a tremendous amount of money, but had turned it over to him all the same. Clarinda had calculated well; it was more than enough to set her up in royal style wherever she wanted, but not so much that it could not be readily collected together. As soon as he had it, Oliver sped home, pausing at the gates to rip away his own neckcloth and tie it to the bars for the signal. Since then, Jericho and others of the household—including the now recovered and quite angry Mrs. Howard—had spent the time in futile watch for any sign from Clarinda.

"I . . . I brought along some help," said Oliver, dragging me from the wretched past to the wretched present.

"Who? Edmond? I thought he was still confined to bed."

"And so he is." Oliver now came in the room and stood aside. "This way, dear lady," he said.

Nora swept in, arms stretching out to me, and my whole world turned right over.

We clung to each other without speaking, she giving comfort, me shamelessly taking it, and for a few moments all was well. I choked on some long held back tears, but she said everything would be all right, and that gentle reassurance was sufficient to keep me from completely breaking down. When I next looked up, I discovered Oliver and Elizabeth had tactfully departed, allowing us some privacy.

"Oliver told me all that's happened," she said. "I'll do anything I can to help."

"It's a godsend just to have you here."

"He's worried about you. Said you were in quite a bad state last night." She glanced at the hand I'd put through the wall. "It seems you still are."

"The day's rest took care of my body, but not the torments in my mind."

"That's how it's ever been for me. I've seen wickedness, Jonathan, but nothing to measure to this. All that I have is at your service."

"Bless you for it. Just looking at you gives me new hope. Between the two of us we have an army." But an army held in abeyance, forced to near-unbearable waiting until word came from Clarinda. Damn the woman.

Seeming to sense my thoughts, Nora embraced me again, then asked if I was up to introducing her to Elizabeth.

"What?"

"Oliver just rushed me right in. I don't want to be rude."

There was more here than simple etiquette, I knew. She wanted to help and would begin by trying to distract me out of myself. A change of subject, a resumption of innocuous social obligations, perhaps then I wouldn't feel the brutal, raging emptiness of guilt tearing my heart to bits.

I glanced at my knuckles with their smears of drying blood and dusting of plaster. *It's better than beating at the walls, Johnny Boy.*

Swallowing back the cloying self-pity, I said, "God bless you, Nora," then went to fetch my sister and cousin.

We all assumed a kind of defiant desperation, resolutely carrying on in a nearly normal manner against the strain of the situation. I say nearly, for we were drawn tighter than a fiddle string and like to snap at the least noise, real or imagined.

Because of this shared adversity, Nora forgot about any trepidations she'd confided to me earlier over meeting Elizabeth. Both ladies took to each other, but I'd expected as much, knowing them so well; still, it was heartening to see them getting on together.

Of all things, Oliver was the one who proved to be the most shy around Nora.

"Because of what she did, don't you know," he said, when I went aside to ask why he was holding his distance from the group. He touched his throat with nervous fingers. "I mean, *you* know. All this while a chap's not even aware of it. Doesn't seem quite right."

"That's why she stopped with you. Stopped a long time ago."

"And made me forget it. Couldn't have me carrying that sort of stuff around in my head and not expect me to mention it to someone sooner or later. She didn't have much choice, did she, though? Notwithstanding, I feel rather peculiar about it."

"You should talk to her, then."

"Well—ah—well, I'm not so sure about trying *that.* Besides, she already apologized to me about it, y'see, when I went to fetch her over here. Bringing it up again might seem ill-mannered."

"True. Then perhaps what you need is some ordinary converse with her to help you see there's more to her than what you've experienced in the past. I will tell you it means a great deal to Nora that, knowing what you know, you've still extended a welcoming friendship to her."

"Does it?"

"This condition isolates her dreadfully. I've been given to understand that she's only ever rarely found people who freely accept it. She was quite thunderstruck when I told her how many knew about my change. For her to be drawn into a circle of friends where she is free to be herself and not have to lie or influence to avoid a fear-filled reaction is a great comfort to her soul."

"Is it, by God?" He looked at her with new eyes. "But she seems so confident with herself."

"That's from years of practice." I dared not guess how many years, nor did I share this thought with him. "Just be easy with her, Oliver, as you are with me, and be her friend. She'll ask nothing more of you, I promise." My gaze darted significantly to his neck and he went beet red.

"Uh—ah—well, of course. Be glad to do it, Coz. If you're sure."

"My word on it."

Then I jerked my head around, as did Nora, being the first to hear. Elizabeth and Oliver froze to listen and perceived it for themselves: the sound of quick footsteps in the hall without.

Jericho had stationed himself by the front gate for much of the day, keeping watch with others for Clarinda's promised message. Sweating and breathless from his run, he burst in holding a thin oilcloth packet in one hand. No need for him to say what it was; tied to it was a scrap of white cloth. We rushed him like thieves falling upon a treasure. This time I recognized Clarinda's bold handwriting; it was addressed to Elizabeth, which seemed odd until I remembered that they thought me to be dead. With a great effort of will I gave it to her to open. I couldn't have done it anyway, my hands shook too much.

She tore at it and unfolded the oilcloth. Inside was a single sheet of paper bearing but a few lines, which she read aloud:

> *"Come to the town of Brighthelmstone by this time tomorrow night. You'll find The Bell to be a most agreeable place to lodge. Don't forget to bring along your special gift for R."*

"No signature," said Elizabeth. "And it's vague enough to be no more than an innocent invitation. She's not risking herself here."

"That's fine for her," grumbled Oliver. "Where the devil is Brighthelmstone?"

"A little seaside town about fifty miles south of London," Nora told us. "I stopped there once years ago after a storm on a channel crossing drove our ship off course. Afraid I don't remember much about it, though."

"I'll wager *they* know all about it, especially that Summerhill rogue. Our going there will make it very easy for them to make their own crossing once they get the money, unless they have us running off to some other place. Clarinda will lead us a merry dance before this is done."

"Not to worry, she doesn't yet know the tune is about to change."

"Jericho," said Elizabeth, "did you see who left this?"

He'd recovered somewhat from his run. "Only a glimpse of him, Miss. We heard a horse galloping up from the southern branch of the road and presently saw it. His rider was all cloaked and muffled. As he came even with our gate, he threw down the packet, turned the horse, and went back south again. He'll be halfway to the Thames by now."

"Damn," I said. "I should have been there. I could have followed him, caught and questioned him."

"And have possibly put Richard in more danger," said my sister. "You'll have your chance at them, little brother, when they turn up to collect their ransom. Until then we'll do what we're told and give them no suspicion or excuse to hurt Richard."

I nodded, seeing the sense of it, but wanting to pound more holes in the wall. Then my heart sank as another difficulty raised itself to mind. Though I could gallop all the way to this seaside town in one night given the proper changes of horses, no delays, and a guide who knew the road, I'd still have to find some kind of safe shelter before the next sunrise. The limits of my condition chafed at me as they never had before. I imparted these thoughts to the others.

"Now that *is* dangerous," Oliver said. "You talk like you're going to run off on your own. I won't hear of it. We've more than time enough to get there by coach if we leave right away. Elizabeth and I can look out for you during the day, and by the time you wake tomorrow night we'll be there."

"Besides," Elizabeth added, "they might have people watching the roads and inn, and if you arrived so openly that would put the wind up them."

My impatience to go forth and do something was such that I was ready to offer argument against all this sense. But even as I drew breath to do it, Nora touched her hand to mine.

"My coach," she said in a gentle tone, "is completely enclosed."

We all stared at her.

"Quite sheltered from the light, very comfortable to sleep in for the day, and all ready to go," she continued. "Will it do?"

Oliver's face lighted up with unchecked admiration. "Well-a-day, I should say it's just the thing. Miss Jones, you are truly a wonder."

"Thank you, Dr. Marling," she said with a gracious smile.

The five of us—for Jericho insisted on coming as well—were ready to leave within half an hour. Along with Nora's coach and driver, we saddled four extra riding horses, provisions for the road, and, of course, the ransom money. Mrs. Howard wanted to come, too, being quite tearful about it, but after a short discussion, I convinced her she would be the best help to us by staying behind. I would not have objected to her presence, but for the fact of Nora's and my condition. All the rest of the party were in on the secret, so there was no need to guard our speech or actions with them, but with Mrs. Howard in tow, the poor woman would certainly hear or see something she shouldn't. I had no wish to further influence her into forgetting things.

Nor was it necessary to influence her to stay, for she accepted the inevitable with snuffling grace, and pressed into my hands a little bundle of Richard's things: extra clothing, some chocolates wrapped in twists of paper, and his toy horse. The sight of the last item near brought me to tears, too.

As for Cousin Edmond, we'd not yet said anything to him about the dark business, and didn't plan to until it was done. He was still weak from his awful experience, and Oliver thought it better for him to learn about it after the fact, lest he lurch from his sickbed and try to interfere. He'd probably burst a blood vessel when he did find out, but we'd deal with it then, having enough problems to occupy us for the present.

We gathered together a goodly number of firearms and a store of powder and lead for the journey. England was as civilized as any country in the world, meaning we had plenty of justification to defend ourselves against the many thieves prowling outside the family circle. Oliver packed his duelers and small sword; Elizabeth and Nora each carried their muff pistols; I had my Dublin revolver and sword stick, and lent my own duelers and small sword to Jericho. Nora's driver had his own weaponry ready to hand. Any highwayman foolish enough to stop us would be in for a very disagreeable surprise.

It occurred to us that Clarinda might have arranged to waylay our party at some point along the road and simply take the money. Against such a chance, I would ride up with the driver to play the lookout, and Jericho planned to take my place come morning.

The journey was not an easy one for any of us, but I found it particularly difficult to endure. Once the whirl of preparation was done and we'd set out, I had nothing to occupy my mind except the constant worry for Richard. I was not disposed to pass the time with Nora's driver. That dour-faced individual sat silent the whole while I was with him, speaking only to the horses. He seemed to know his business, though, never once stopping or slowing to ask direction and never expressing even a hint of an opinion about our irregular expedition. An excellent man, I thought.

He took the southern road, for all we know following the exact route of the messenger who'd brought the packet to our gates. Even at this time of night London's streets were something of a snarl. He kept to the westernmost roads to avoid the bulk of the city and skirted 'round the west and south sides of St. James's Park. He then made his way through a number of turns before finally coming onto Bridge Street and thus Westminster Bridge. The water crossing was hard, as usual; I found myself pressed back into the solid barrier of the coach as it took us forward over the Thames. With a tight grip on the bench, I shut my eyes and concentrated on not vanishing and not being sick as we passed over the wide, stinking swirl of gray water.

Then we were free of it and on Bridge Street again, but only briefly, for it soon became the New Road, and we now rumbled through empty farm land. An astonishing change, that, being in a crowded noisy city one minute and in silent countryside the next. The very air was different, no smokes or night soil fumes to assault the senses, but clean and cold and heavy with moisture. It did not feel like rain, though, and so it proved as the hours passed and the heavens spared us further problems. Not that it was an easy road, being as rutted and muddy as any I'd known on Long

Island. It took some practice to balance against the irregular swaying as the coach rolled over the ruts, but I soon got used to it and was better able to keep my attention on the way ahead rather than on my seating.

The miles crawled ever so slowly under us. My impatience was such that more than once I had to fight down the near irresistible urge to float up and soar ahead. Not that it would have done any of us much good. Clarinda's note had been clear enough on the time. Even if I got to the town before dawn, nothing would be like to happen until tomorrow evening. So I ground my teeth until my jaw ached, and kept my eyes open for highwaymen. None showed themselves; perhaps it was too cold for them.

I think the others managed to sleep a little, for after a few hours the sound of voices within the coach finally ceased. It must have been lonely for Nora, being unable to escape into slumber for herself, but she made no complaint or comment on it when we stopped to make our first change of horses at a large inn. Elizabeth, Oliver, and Jericho all climbed out to stretch themselves and take refreshment while Nora made special arrangements with the chief hostler for the care of her four matched bays.

"We should be back in a day or two," she said, pressing enough money on him for a week's worth of stabling. "See well to their care and you'll have this much again on our return." Her promise, reinforced by a piercing look that I recognized, left me in no doubt her animals would be the pets of the stable.

"How are things with you and the others?" I asked her.

"Most agreeable. Oliver's been even more thorough in his questions about me than you were that night. Quite the inquisitor, your cousin."

"He's not annoyed you, I hope?"

"Not at all. I forgot how amusing he can be. There are some questions I'm sure he wants to ask, but his sense of delicacy in Elizabeth's presence is holding him back from too much frankness. He hardly need trouble himself, though, Elizabeth's well on to him."

"Then you're still getting on easily with her?"

"Very easily. We won't be exchanging recipes or lace patterns or that sort of rot, but I think it likely we'll be friends long after this crisis is past, however its outcome. She's a very dear, sweet girl, brave and smart. I don't wonder that you love her so much."

"Yes, after Father, she's quite the best, most sensible one in the family."

"You do yourself a disservice, dear Jonathan."

"I think not," I said, holding up my hand. There was still some dried blood and plaster dust clinging to my skin, evidence of my loss of restraint.

She had only a wry smile for it. "That's only natural frustration. I don't know how you've held yourself together even this long, but hold on just a little longer. We *will* get your boy back."

Such was her conviction and so strongly did she pass it to me that I almost thought myself under the spell of her influence again. It was enough to bolster me for miles on end, until the dawn came creeping over the vast stretch of sky on our left, and we had to stop the coach so I could take shelter within.

Nora had spared herself no available convenience in its special construction. Each bench opened up like a kind of long chest and might otherwise have been employed for the storage of travel cases. Nora had one of them lightly padded for her use, the pads containing quantities of her earth. Thus might she comfortably rest during the day. The other bench, though not so softly appointed, was cleared of the few stores we'd thrown in that I might also have room to recline. It was a bit of a press because I could not really stretch out, but no more so than in my own traveling box. It was of no matter to me; with my head pillowed on a sack full of my own earth, I passed quickly into uncaring insensibility the moment the sun was up.

The coach was quite still when I woke, though I was sharply aware of sundry noises about me: the voices of men and women, the clop of hooves, the honking of disturbed geese, and dogs barking. I cautiously raised the bench seat and peered out, giving a jump when I realized with horror someone was inside the coach. One glimpse of a dark figure crouching between the seats and I ducked, the lid slamming down with a thump, giving away my own presence.

"We're in Brighthelmstone, Mr. Jonathan," Jericho informed me in a calm, patient tone.

My hair eased back into place on my scalp. I belatedly grasped the notion that he and the menacing figure were one and the same, and the man had only been waiting for me to waken as usual. " 'Fore God, what a start you gave me."

"Sorry, sir."

Lifting the lid again, I staggered to my feet, stepped out, and let it drop back into place.

"What a row you make," said Nora, sounding rather muffled from her own hiding place.

To give her room, Jericho backed out of the coach. She emerged from her haven, looking less crushed than might be expected, though she fussed a bit about her skirts. "Much more of this and I'll take to wearing breeches," she said, swatting at some wrinkles. She gave up trying to flatten them and bade us a good evening. Jericho replied in kind; all I wanted to do was kiss her, which I did when the first chance presented itself. That pleasantry accomplished, I had a look through the open door, but could see little enough past Jericho. Part of a muddy yard and what looked to be the windowless side of a large brick building made up the totality of our view. The coach's closed and latched windows hid the rest. Nora sat on her bench and signed for me to take the other. Until we knew better, we dared not show ourselves yet.

"What's the news?" I asked Jericho. "Are we at the Bell?"

He'd brought a lantern with him and set it on the floor between us. "We are, sir, and have been for quite some time. We found a sitting room had been reserved for Dr. Marling or Miss Barrett and party by a well-dressed gentleman calling himself Mr. Richard."

I stiffened at the name. Was Clarinda indulging in some tangled attempt at humor or simply tormenting us? Probably both.

"We've been resting there, waiting to hear something from Mrs. Fonteyn. Dr. Marling thinks the man might have been Captain Summerhill from your description of him."

"Perhaps Arthur Tyne is still too feeble yet for such errands, that or they prefer having Summerhill taking the risks."

Jericho lifted one hand to indicate his lack of knowledge on that point. "What matters most is for you and Miss Jones to remain unseen here in the coach for the moment; the whole of this inn must certainly be under watch."

"We have a way of leaving without anyone knowing about it," I reminded him.

He nodded. "True, sir, but it will not be necessary, we'll be departing shortly. This was left with the innkeeper not a quarter hour ago." He presented me with a sheet of paper. I held it so Nora could read as well.

*At your earliest convenience, do come and take the view at the Seven Sisters. The way is sure to be dark, so bring lots of lanterns and keep them lighted. Don't go too near the edge between the fifth and sixth Sister, for the chalk crumbles easily. Be sure to bring R's gift.*

On the reverse side of the paper was a map and directions with a small circle to indicate our destination.

"The Seven Sisters?" I asked after a moment's study. "What's that, another inn?" The markings and place names meant nothing to me.

"They're a series of chalk cliffs on this side of Eastbourne," said Nora. "A long way for us, I fear."

"At least a dozen miles, according to the landlord, sir," added Jericho.

"Then what?" I said with no small amount of bitterness. "A note telling us to turn around and go to Land's End?"

"Dr. Marling expressed a similar sentiment; however, Miss Elizabeth thinks their purpose in bringing us here may be to see how obedient we are to their orders. So far we've done nothing to merit reproach."

"Let us hope they think so, too," I grumbled.

Another cold night, another cold, jolting ride. Despite my complaining, I also thought—fervently hoped—this would be the end of it at last. Surely Clarinda would be as anxious to collect the money as I was to rescue Richard. Besides, she might not want to press us too far lest we finally rebel and seek outside help.

After we quit the Bell and finally Brighthelmstone altogether, we paused long enough for me to climb up to sit with the driver again. He had to go north a few miles to find and follow a thready east-west road through the downs. The softly rolling countryside held no beauty for me, but rather I imagined spies lurking in every fold of the land or modest clumping of hedges. They could well be there, too, either Summerhill or some of his men, watching from a distance. The night was moonless and overcast, but by observing the driver I determined there was just enough light for ordinary men to see by. The noise and movement of our coach and all the horses were visible against the pale chalky soil and dead grass; the lanterns were but an extra insurance for them. I kept my face well covered against any chance of recognition.

"Almost there, sir," the driver announced, and I asked him to slow and stop the horses.

The land ahead rose on either side into two great rounded hills with a well-defined valley between. In the near distance I spied more such formations, a large one to my right and several more of varying sizes undulating away to the left.

"The Seven Sisters," I said, making it half question, half statement.

"If the map is right, sir. Can't really count 'em from here."

The wind was high, carried a strong sea smell, and was, as ever, cold. It pounded at my ears and would have torn my hat away if I hadn't already tied it fast with my woolen scarf.

*Not a place I care to linger,* I thought as I clambered down from my perch. The others came one by one out from the coach and stood with me.

"Do you see anything?" Elizabeth asked, directing her query equally between Nora and myself.

We stepped away from the lanterns on the coach and carefully looked all about us.

"Nothing and no one," Nora answered after a moment.

I pointed at the lowest part of the little valley ahead. "There's something white."

"White?" asked Oliver, stepping forward. "Like a rag?"

"I can't quite make it out. Who's for having a better look?"

They all were, it seemed. Oliver and Jericho carried lanterns while Nora and I led the way, with the coach slowly following our little party. We trudged as best we could over the uneven ground, until the white object became more clear to us. Someone had gone to considerable trouble building up a substantial cairn using chalk shards gleaned from the immediate area. Just over a foot high at its peak and several feet across, a length of white cloth had been placed in its midst, well anchored so as not to blow away.

The sea sound came to me now, strong and unexpectedly loud. The land, even in this depressed point, slanted up and away from us, cutting off the view beyond. I walked past the cairn and abruptly halted, realizing I was getting close to the brink of a fearful drop. Far past the ragged edge of eroded chalk was the vast restless shadow of the sea, dark gray under a gray sky.

"I'd say this was the place," said Oliver, catching up with me.

"Have a care," I told him, stepping back several yards and holding out one hand as a warning. "The earth is badly crumbled here. Clarinda mentioned it in the note."

"So she did," he said, frowning. "And very decent of her, I'm sure. Now what?"

I looked left and right up at the crests of the hills, half expecting armed men to appear and come bearing down on us like a barbarian hoard.

"Jonathan, we've found something," Nora called, drawing us back.

Oliver's circle of light joined theirs where Elizabeth and Jericho stared at the cairn. I followed the line of their gaze to the white rag, which was not held in place by the weight of the chalk, but from having one end tied to a partly buried leather pouch.

"It must be theirs," said Nora. "That hasn't been left in the weather."

Jericho started to drag it out, grunting when it caught on something. He freshened his grip and pulled hard. It came free, at the same time revealing the impediment. The pouch had a long carrying strap, and the strap was wrapped around a man's arm.

Thus did we discover Arthur Tyne's body.

The grim disinterment did not take long; we all worked at it. Shaken as we were after the first terrible shock, the activity was necessary to keep from thinking too much, or so it was for me. My worry of the moment was mostly for Elizabeth and Nora, on how this might affect them—until I came to understand they were far more concerned over my well-being than their own.

"Shot," said Oliver after a brief examination. "Clean through the heart."

"Why would they kill him?" asked Jericho, brushing dust from his hands.

They looked to me. As if I had any answers. "Perhaps he slowed them down."

"Or Clarinda didn't need him anymore," said Elizabeth. "Or this Captain Summerhill was more to her liking."

"Whatever the reason, they wanted us to find him, to know how easily . . . how easily and how willing they are to kill."

Oliver stood. "Clarinda's *not* going to let them touch Richard." He said it firmly, as though he believed it.

Any reply from me would have either been a lie of agreement or throwing the hope he meant to impart back in his face. Instead, I gestured at the leather pouch. "Anything in it?" I asked.

Jericho plucked it up and pushed back the thing's flap. "Yes! Some paper . . . here!" He hurriedly unfolded it, holding it flat against the wind so we could read.

*Put the gift in the bag, then throw it over the cliff. R will be waiting below if you want him. There's a village about a mile east of this point with a path down to the beach. Go there, then come west again. Use great care and caution lest harm befall you.*

I left my lantern and tore back to the cliff. The closer I got to the edge, the more perilous the footing. I didn't care. Oliver called out to me, but I chose not to listen. The last few feet I fell to my hands and knees and crept up to the fragile brink.

Oh, but it was a well-considered spot for them. From this more immediate vantage I saw how the Sisters, a series of hills overlooking the sea, seemed to have been sliced down the middle by a giant's knife to reveal their chalky vitals. The knife had been a jagged thing, for the cliff sides rose high in long irregular vertical slashes, marred with many cracks and few if any ledges, impossible to climb up or down. At their base far below ran a wide strip of beach, covered with fallen debris from the cliffs, broken stones, seaweed, and other tidal flotsam.

On that beach I now spied several figures, a boat, and waiting out in deeper water, a small ship.

"What is it?" Oliver demanded. He also dropped to his hands and knees, crawling the remaining distance to join me. "What do you see?"

"They're down there," I said. "The lot of 'em, I think. There's their ship. Do you see it?" I pointed.

He squinted. "I think so. Where are they?" A pause as I pointed again. "No, sorry, can't make out a thing in this murk. Damn good luck for us that you can. Is Richard—?"

"I'm looking."

The figures huddled near the boat, which had been dragged up onto the beach. I saw several men, then a woman sitting on one of the larger rocks—Clarinda. My heart jumped right into my throat, for close against her breast she held a child-sized bundle.

"God, he's down there! She has him!"

His hand fell hard on my shoulder, keeping me from going right over. "Steady on, Coz. Look at this carefully first before you go charging in."

"Your light—hold it up so they know you've come."

"All right, but I'll remind you they might want to blow my head off."

"I don't think so . . . yes, that's it! That's stirred them, they're moving about, pointing up at us."

"They'll recognize you."

"Hardly—all they can really see is your light and perhaps some silhouettes, y'know. That's why she wanted us to carry lanterns. Hah! One of 'em has a dark lantern, he's opening it—"

"Yes, I see it swinging, a signal for me I suppose. Hope to God it *is* them and not a pack of smugglers going at cross purposes with us."

The others came up with Elizabeth in the lead. "Is it Richard? Is it?"

Oliver looked over his shoulder to her. "I can't see him, but Jonathan can. Stay back now."

"Is he all right?"

"He's too far away to tell," I answered. "It's all very clever. You throw them the money, then by the time you find a way down the cliff to get to Richard they're on their ship and heading for France."

"If they even leave him behind," she said, putting into words one of my countless fears.

"They will, whether they've planned it or not."

"What are you thinking?"

"That they'll be feeling very safe from attack thinking none of us can get down this cliff. The very last thing they'll expect is for someone to turn up in their midst and take him away. I'll be on them and out before they know what's happened."

"You'll be . . . but it's too danger—oh! Never mind. None safer here than you and Nora."

"True, but I will be careful, dear sister, if you'll do the same for me."

"Gladly, but for God's sake tell us what you're planning."

My brain fairly hummed with ideas now that I had a definite and visible goal to go after. "Oliver, I'll want you to shout at them and get them to come closer to the foot of the cliff. Say that you've got the money and for them to be ready when you throw it down, but instead of the money, I want you to fill the pouch with the rocks from the cairn."

He grinned. "They won't like that."

"Indeed. I want all their attention on you. Distract them as much as you can, get their hopes up—it will be that much more of a frustration to them when they find their treasure is a false one."

"But won't it further endanger Richard?"

"No, because by then I'll have him. You have to keep them busy for as long as you can and give me the time to slip in close and get to him."

"But Clarinda will have them on you first thing."

"No doubt, but after ten paces they won't know me from the rest of the shadows. This darkness will be in my favor, I'll be able to run where they can only stumble. The lot of you need to have your pistols ready, too. A few shots and—"

Oliver shook his head, outraged. "And chance shooting you or the boy? I think not! We can't see a bloody thing from up here and could hit one of you by accident."

"I can help on that," said Nora. "I'll be able to direct your fire." She looked at me. "I assume you just want them busy ducking while you get away, because it's not likely we'll any of us be able to hit someone on purpose under these circumstances."

"Exactly, a few shots straight down the cliff should be enough to send them scurrying for their boat, though I'd be well pleased if you should happen to drop one or two of 'em by accident. Once you see me get Richard you open up and distract them from pursuing us. If they were fools enough to give us the high ground, then we'd be fools not to use it. If they do shoot back, with the distance and the dark you should all be fairly safe, but keep your heads low, and be sure to put out the lanterns. Right, then."

My sudden energy to do something was contagious. Jericho and Oliver hurried to the coach to get the pistols and powder. Elizabeth began putting rocks into the pouch.

With a hand on my arm, Nora stayed me from helping. "Remember he won't vanish with you. You won't be able to bring him up the cliff in the same manner of travel you'll use to descend."

Damnation, but I wouldn't. "Then I'll make for that village in the note.

Leave the riding horses here and send your driver ahead with the coach. You can catch up with us later."

"Very well—but Jonathan, the shooting. If one of the pistol balls should hit you while you're holding the boy . . . it will go right through you to him. You're taking an appalling risk with his life."

And did I not clearly know it? "F-for all I know he might already be dead." I pointed to Tyne's partially uncovered corpse. "But if alive I'm ready to do anything to get him away from those monsters. I'll take that chance rather than leave him with them."

Her hand tightened, then fell away, and she said nothing more.

When all was made ready, I gave my sword stick and Dublin revolver into Elizabeth's keeping, knowing they would only be a hindrance.

"You should at least have the pistol," she protested.

"It takes two hands to bring a new chamber to bear on the thing, and I'll need both to carry Richard."

"Then God go with you, little brother."

I saw her prayer echoed in the faces of the others and suddenly felt a wash of fear. Not for myself but for my helpless son. What if my actions brought him harm instead of deliverance? What if, God forbid, I got him killed? If I truly wished for his safety would it not be better to let him go? My brave words to Nora seemed but a hollow pretension. Clarinda could not possibly be so heartless as to hurt her own child. Surely some of the worry for him she'd expressed to me had had some tiny seed of sincerity within. The sensible thing would be to give her the money and hope for the best. It was entirely reasonable, much more preferable than the wild, perilous, half-thought-through plan I'd just improvised.

Much more preferable, but for the voice within telling me—all but screaming at me—to ignore sense and let my heart lead in this matter. Against all reason it cried alone. Undeniable, my instinct told me this was the right thing to do, the one thing I *had* to do.

But that did not make me any less afraid.

Confidence is an intensely ephemeral quality, flooding you fit to burst one instant and miles away the next leaving you dry and gasping in the emptiness. I was wretchedly parched by the time I'd eased my way down the cliff face to crouch immobile in a jumble of water-smoothed rock.

Oliver was already calling down from his now distant perch. He couldn't keep them occupied forever while I wavered between sense and folly. Perhaps in some distant corner of my mind I'd anticipated this hesitation, and that's why the pouch was filled with rock, not money. For then against its discovery would I be forced to take swift action.

But no matter the reasons—the time had finally come. Working or not, my heart had taken up lodging high in my throat, and I wasted several precious moments trying to swallow it back into place.

I'd drifted down and lighted just to the east of the men on the beach. The whole area seemed horribly bright, and I quailed each time a head swung in my direction. None of them saw me, though. None. What was like day to me was pitchy midnight to them.

"I don't think the pouch is big enough," Oliver bawled from on high. "It's sure to be too heavy to throw very far."

"Do the best you can, Dr. Marling," Summerhill bawled back, sounding unflappable and thoroughly in control. He was turned away from me, but I recognized his voice and bearing. He stood a prudent distance from the base of the cliff, cane in one hand and dark lantern in the other. He'd covered its light over; Oliver wouldn't be able to see him at all.

"Silly ass," grumbled one of two men hovering close by.

"Long as 'e's a rich ass," put in the other, identifying the object of comment as my cousin and not their captain.

I slipped off my cloak, hat, and scarf, forsaking their protection for ease of movement. Then did I also forsake solidity and float low over the ground, skirting Summerhill and his men, as substantial as a ghost and just as silent. My vision limited, but still better than theirs, I made a straight line toward the boat and Clarinda.

Changes had taken place. She was no longer seated on a pile of rock, easy to get to, but was in the boat itself, with six more men standing around it. Richard was in her arms. My instinct had been true. She'd had no intention of leaving him after getting the money. No surprise was left in me concerning this woman, only fury, which carried me forward—just in time, it seemed.

No sooner was I started than Summerhill shouted something to the men, and they turned upon the boat and began shoving it into the water. I heard curses for its coldness and rebukes to hurry as "the Captain 'uz comin'." I hurtled toward them.

And was stopped.

It wasn't quite as severe as falling off a horse at full gallop, since my body was not solid enough for bruising, but the shock was just as brutal.

The sea. The damned sea.

I was hard pressed to cross free-flowing water normally; in this near-nebulous state I'd *never* do it. The limits of my condition utterly prevented me from pushing so much as an inch farther.

No time for thought about the consequences—I reformed and plunged up to my waist into the surf. By comparison, the freezing immersion in Edmond's well had been a summer lark. This winter sea was so icy that the cold burned my skin, seeming to eat right through to the bone like acid. I must have cried out from it, for two of the sailors so diligently pushing the boat turned to look.

In no frame of mind to be polite or careful, I was on them like a storm, knocking them out of the way and devil take the hindmost. My hands found the gunwale, grasped hard, and I heaved up and into the boat, sprawling over the ribbed bottom, water streaming from my clothes.

Clarinda half stood, but the craft bobbed crazily, forcing her to sit again. She gave out with an abortive screech, whether from the sight of me or from the danger of falling in, I could not tell. I had a single image of her staring at me, wide of eye and with a sagging mouth, of her trying to back away while holding tight to her precious bundle, of Richard's dark head poking out from the illusory protection of the blanket she'd wrapped around him. His eyes were shut fast. Asleep or made insensible by more laudanum?

And then the narrow boat was full of men, cursing, shouting, all their anger and fight centered upon me, the unexpected intruder. I had no thought for anything but to get to Richard, though. They were merely obstacles in the way, inconvenient, but surmountable. Even as a man raised a pistol level with my face I kicked out with one leg and knocked him right over into the water. Two more had slid aboard, one of them falling upon me more by accident than design because of the boat's now very erratic rocking. They got in one another's way in the confining space, and I took advantage of it by striking the nearest senseless, then pushing him back against his friend.

The way clear for a moment, I found my feet and surged forward again. Now Clarinda let go with a fully realized shriek. I heard Summerhill distantly barking commands, trying to instill order upon the chaos, and succeeding. There was one man left with the wit and speed to act; he bent and picked up one of the oars, bringing it hard around with intent to clout me flat with the thing. Fast as he was, the movement seemed slow to my perception. I caught the stave of wood before it could do me harm and wrenched it from him with a strong sideways twist that sent him overboard.

The last man had recovered somewhat from being pushed, tried to drag me down, and promptly discovered himself to be on the wrong end of the oar for his trouble.

The boat had drifted far enough from shore that Summerhill and his ruffians were no immediate threat. The rest of the men were unconscious or floundering. None stood between me and Clarinda now. Unsteady from the boat's motion I moved closer to her.

"Give him to me," I said, reaching out with one hand.

She half rose, but could not back any farther away. Thrice now I'd returned from the dead, from the fight in the mausoleum, from the attempt in the bath, from the push down the stairs in her own home, the last being the most impossible to deny. What thoughts were in her mind I could not guess, but the emotions were obvious, being equal parts of rage and terror. Her white face contorting into something inhuman, she lifted Richard's limp form high, and hurled him into the sea.

Of all the horrors that had run through my mind since she'd taken him, this had never once shown itself. It was too abominable. My reaction was without thought, instantaneous. I swung the end of the oar wide and hard toward her. I had an impression of it striking her head, the impact traveling up the wood to bruise my hand, of her swift and abrupt drop; impression only, for by then I was diving into the corrosive water after my child.

No time to register the pain, all my effort was concentrated on maintaining a solid form against the overwhelming urge to vanish. He was not far, little more than five yards, but they might well have been miles for my slow progress. I lived lifetimes until my hand thrashed against the edge of his blanket, eternities until I found his small body in the mass of soaked fabric. I got his head clear of the smothering water. After all this his eyes were yet shut. Dear God, no . . .

The shore. Where? That way. Close and too far. Hurry.

More eternities until my toes brushed and caught on the rocky bottom. Staggering, holding him tight, I lurched from the sea's caustic grasp, then fell to my knees. Sobbing with dread, I tore away his wet clothes, searching his pinched blue face for sign of life. Pressing my ear to his chest I forced myself to silence, listening with all my soul.

*There,* I thought I heard it . . . a faint flutter like a bird's wing. His heart. His *living* heart . . .

"You murdering bastard," said Summerhill, almost conversationally.

I looked up at him, up into the barrel of his pistol.

"You—" he broke off, recognizing me. His aim wavered as amazement finally penetrated his imperturbable armor. I'd seen such uncertainty before, such hesitation; it would not last long. With Richard close in my arms, I rose and bolted like a deer.

Ten paces, I'd said. Ten paces and they'd lose me in the dark. I'd been wildly, fatally optimistic, and Richard would be the one to suffer for my misjudgment.

Shots. A veritable hail of fire.

I ran faster.

A second volley.

I flinched and sought shelter behind the low mass of stones where I'd left my cloak.

"Run!" someone called in a thin, faraway voice.

Nora.

I glanced up the cliff. Yes. They were firing down at Summerhill and his men, scattering them, giving me the chance to get clear.

"*Run!*" Elizabeth now, strident with urgency.

I swept up the dry cloak for Richard and fled east, threading madly between the stones, skidding, nearly tripping, but always rushing forward, and never more looking back.

# EPILOGUE

It was a fine, clear Christmas Eve, not too cold, not too windy. Tomorrow promised a continuation of the good weather, though I'd be sleeping right through it, as always. No church for me, alas, but we'd made a merry party of it tonight having trooped out for evening services. I had innumerable blessings to be grateful for—though some weren't fit for the peace of the sanctuary, like my grim thankfulness for Clarinda's death.

But others, like Richard's recovery, brought me to kneel before God with sincere and humble gratitude.

Thus far the boy had shown no ill reaction from his kidnapping. Clarinda had apparently kept him drugged for nearly the whole time, as he had nothing to tell us of the experience, not even a stray nightmare. I know, for since then I'd lately taken to watching him in his sleep when the mood struck, sitting close by with a book and alert to any change in him that might indicate distress. Mrs. Howard complimented my zealous concern and at the same time reproved me for being overly protective. I smiled and told her she was right, but begged her to indulge me until I felt more secure about his safety.

Richard continued healthy despite his plunge in the freezing sea water. I'd run nearly the whole way along the beach to the tiny village mentioned in Clarinda's note and had all but broken into its one tavern seeking help. One look at us and our bedraggled condition and the owner's anger changed to instant compassion as he took us for shipwreck survivors and roused the rest of his house to beneficent action.

As fires were built up, broth was heated, and our clothes were set out to dry, I improvised a poor tale of an overturned boat for their many questions. This inspired even more queries as they wanted to know where the boat was like to be found, why I'd been out at sea at night, how I'd upset the boat, and other annoying details. I was spared from additional bad lying by the timely arrival of Nora's coach driver, soon followed by Nora herself and the others. Oliver, taking charge as the one doctor on the premises, pronounced that I was too addled for talk and told me to rest while he tended Richard, something I was more than glad to carry out. What with the number of our party and all obviously being well to-do, the interrogators retired to watch and draw their own conclusions about the strangeness of the situation.

We stopped long enough on the return trip for Oliver and Jericho to re-bury Arthur Tyne. His improvised grave went undiscovered for more than a week and was quite a mystery to the Brighthelmstone magistrates as was stated in the one paper we found that reported the incident. The man's murder was popularly blamed on smugglers or pirates, and in a way the conclusion was perfectly right. Certainly no one of us ever stepped forward with further information for the inquiry.

Oliver stayed on in Brighthelmstone and kept an ear open to all the news. When talk came of a woman's body found on the beach near the Seven Sisters, he went along with the rest of the curious for a look and, putting on a convincing show of surprised sorrow, proclaimed her to be his long missing cousin, feared lost at sea. Thus was he able to bring Clarinda back for interment in the family mausoleum. Her terrible head wound was dismissed as having been caused by a rough encounter with the rocks when she'd washed ashore. So far no one had connected her in any way to Arthur Tyne.

I was thankful also for Edmond's full recovery from his own dance with the Reaper.

He eventually got the full story of all that had happened from me—or most of it. There were certain aspects I chose not to include, like my extra-natural abilities and the exact manner of Clarinda's demise. I baldly perjured myself, saying she'd fallen and hit her head in the boat during the fight. He grunted, and asked no other questions. The official story given to the rest of the family was that Clarinda had run away from him and drowned at sea by misadventure—something just scandalous enough to put off deeper inquiry. Edmond, already in mourning for Aunt Fonteyn, didn't have to change much of his outward show of grief, only to extend its duration. I think he did grieve in his heart for his wayward wife. Apparently he had been happy with her, once.

I was also thankful for the end of all persecution from Ridley's Mohocks.

It was but small work to find Royce and Litton, his would-be avengers, as well as a few others who had been connected to him. Though the task of reforming the lot of them into good citizens seemed rather too overwhelming, I was willing to take it on, but upon discussing the prospect with Nora, I gladly adopted her suggestion. Rather than trying to convert them, I simply instilled in each an irresistible desire to take a grand tour of the Continent. Some were bound for France, others for Italy, and none was like to return anytime soon. They could have Europe and all the rest of the world if they'd but leave me and mine in the peace of England.

The only dark spot was Summerhill's escape.

Oliver was yet busy making diligent inquiries about him. It seemed the captain was from Brittany as he'd said, and had in the past engaged Edmond's services for certain legal matters, none of it connected with smuggling, though. Edmond had little to add about the man, except to say that Clarinda had taken to him. As Clarinda had taken to quite a number of men, Edmond had paid no more attention to this particular indiscretion than the others. Since she had been adept at using, then discarding a man when another more useful one appeared, I wondered whom she might have had waiting when she'd finished with Summerhill or if he had indeed been her final aspiration.

It mattered not now, but I would keep my eyes open for the captain. He'd bear watching against future mischief, I thought.

But for now, all was peace. We'd moved back into Oliver's home in town, once more leaving Fonteyn House to the care of some trusted servants. The parlour fire roared with warm comfort for the body, while the excellent sermon we'd recently heard did the same for our souls.

Nora and Oliver were seated near the fire showing Richard how best to toast bread. Elizabeth was at her spinet, engaged in learning a new piece of music, an occupation that held her attention only until Jericho came in with a tray laden for tea. According to the others, supper was too long a wait for refreshment. Elizabeth played the hostess and served all but Nora and me. We thought it best not to indulge our own specific appetite in front of an actively curious four-year-old.

"I hear Jericho gives a good report of a certain French dancing master," Oliver said. "What do you say to sending for the fellow after the New Year, see if he suits?"

"Indeed?" I arched an eyebrow at Elizabeth, the obvious source of my cousin's information, since I'd imparted it to her only last night as but a distant possibility.

She shrugged prettily. "One can't start too soon in teaching a boy the finer points of gentlemanly behavior."

"He's very much the little gentleman now," I said in mild protest. "Though I might consider employing someone. In the not so near future, mind you."

"Brother, you just don't want to share him with anyone else."

"A palpable hit," said Nora, correctly reading my expression. "Keep pressing, Elizabeth, he'll call for quarter in another minute."

"Let's play fox hunt," said Richard, his bright face covered with toast crumbs and butter.

"There's a perfect example of the need for someone to teach him proper manners." Elizabeth wiped at the boy's face with her handkerchief.

"Example? He just wants a game." I winked at him, a silent promise to steal him away at the first opportunity.

"Yes, but he must learn to say 'excuse me,' and 'may I please' when breaking into a conversation."

"Excuse-me-may-I-please play fox hunt," said her resolute nephew, his voice somewhat muffled by her efforts at cleaning.

"A quick learner, is he not?" I asked, and no one offered to disagree. "Come here, Richard, time to ride to the hounds."

He broke away from Elizabeth, leaping onto me like a monkey.

"Gently, Jonathan, not so much bouncing, he's just eaten."

I promised to be sedate, keeping my word for almost one whole circuit of the house. Richard's enthusiasm carried over to me, and I forgot about caution in the face of fun. We galloped as madly, as noisily, as joyfully as ever before, so much so that I paid scant mind to the outcry that followed when Jericho answered a knock at the front door.

Just as I cantered into the parlor by way of the servant's entrance, I saw Elizabeth and the others suddenly rushing out the main door into the entry hall. I stopped, hearing more exclamations and outcry, the happy kind. I felt myself kindling to a unique, near forgotten warmth at the sound of a voice, low and clear and very much loved.

*Father. Father has come at last.*

"Left your Mother at Fonteyn House with all the mourning," he was saying. "It's true then? She still wasn't believing it when I had the head groom take me here. This will be hard. At least Beldon's there to help. Yes, Beldon and his sister came along, quite the mixed blessing on the crossing. . . ."

"What's wrong, Cousin Jon'th'n?" Richard tugged at one of my ears.

"Nothing, laddie. You're about to meet someone very special."

"Who?"

I swung him around so as to seat him on one arm, and with a flock of birds flapping around in my belly, walked toward the entry hall.

They were all gathered about Father, Elizabeth still holding tight to him as he shook hands for the first time with Oliver. Nora stood close by awaiting introduction; Jericho also hovered near, his face alight with genuine pleasure. The lot of them looked up and fell silent as Richard and I came in.

Father broke into a great smile at the sight of me and stepped forward, arms open to embrace . . . then he faltered. A most amazing expression possessed his face as he stared first at me, then at Richard, and perceived the *exact* resemblance between us. His mouth dropped open.

"Welcome back to England, Father." I lifted Richard up to get a better hold on him. "I—ah—I have a bit of news for you. . . ."